新制 NEW TOEIC 聽力超高分

最新多益改版黃金試題1000題

作者 • Ki Taek Lee
審訂 • Helen Yeh

新制多益超級熱銷！

最多人推薦多益用書！

實戰NEW TOEIC聽力1000題
訓練直覺答題，聽出多益超高分

MP3

寂天雲 APP

或登入官網下載音檔
www.icosmos.com.tw

新制 NEW TOEIC 聽力超高分

最新多益改版黃金試題1000題

作者 • Ki Taek Lee
審訂 • Helen Yeh

MP3
寂天雲 APP

如何下載 MP3 音檔

❶ **寂天雲** APP **聆聽**：掃描書上 QR Code 下載「寂天雲 - 英日語學習隨身聽」APP。加入會員後，用 APP 內建掃描器再次掃描書上 QR Code，即可使用 APP 聆聽音檔。

❷ **官網下載音檔**：請上「寂天閱讀網」（www.icosmos.com.tw），註冊會員／登入後，搜尋本書，進入本書頁面，點選「MP3 下載」下載音檔，存於電腦等其他播放器聆聽使用。

目錄 Contents

多益測驗改制介紹
&
高分戰略

多益測驗的出現

TOEIC 多益測驗（Test of English for International Communication）是針對非英語人士所設計的英語能力測驗。多益測驗的內容主要與職場環境的英語使用有關，能測驗一個人在工作場合上使用英語與人溝通的能力，故有「商業托福」之稱。多益測驗在許多國家施行多年，如今已經成為「職場英語能力檢定」的國際標準。

多益英語測驗是由「美國教育測驗服務社」（Educational Testing Service, ETS）所研發出來。ETS 於 1947 年成立，總部位於美國紐澤西州，是全球最大的私立教育考試機構。ETS 提供標準化的考試和測評服務，除了多益測驗，還包括托福（TOEFL）、GRE 和 GMAT 等等。ETS 在 1979 年時，應日本企業領袖的要求，制定出一套可以用來評估員工英語能力的測驗，以了解員工在貿易、工業和商業領域上所具備的英語程度，以利人力規劃與發展。

如今，多益測驗是全球最通行的職場英語能力測驗，共有超過 165 個國家在施行多益測驗，每年的測試人口超過五百萬。此外，許多校園也要求畢業生須接受多益測驗，而且成績須達一定的分數，以幫助學生在畢業後能更加順利地進入職場。

多益測驗考哪些內容？

多益測驗的研發者強調「國際英語」，而不以「美式英語」和「英式英語」來區分，並重著於測驗非英語人士對母語人士的英語溝通能力。多益的測驗內容不會考專業知識或詞彙，而是測試在日常生活中使用英文的能力。2006 年改版的新多益測驗，還特別加入了四種不同的英語口音，包括：

1. 美式英語
2. 英式英語
3. 澳洲英語
4. 加拿大英語

多益題目的設計，以「職場需求」為主，測驗題目的內容則是從全球各地職場的英文資料中蒐集而來，題材多元（但考生毋需具備專業的商業與技術辭彙），包含各種地點與狀況：一般商務、製造業、金融／預算、人事、企業發展、辦公室、採購、技術層面、房屋／公司地產、旅遊、外食、娛樂、保健等主題大類。

多益測驗的方式

1	考試方式	「紙筆測驗」
2	出題方式	所有試題皆為「選擇題」
3	題目類型	聽力測驗（又細分成 4 大題） 閱讀測驗（又細分成 3 大題）
4	考試題數	總共有 200 題（聽力 100 題，閱讀 100 題）
5	作答	考生選好答案後，要在與題目卷分開的「答案卷」上劃卡
6	考試時間	總計 2 小時（聽力考 45 分鐘，閱讀考 75 分鐘，兩者分開計時）

＊但在考試時，考生尚須在答案卷上填寫個人資料，並簡短的回答求學與工作經歷的問卷，因此真正待在考場內的時間會比較長。

多益計分方式

多益測驗沒有「通過」與「不通過」之區別──考生用鉛筆在電腦答案卷上作答，考試分數由答對題數決定，將聽力測驗與閱讀測驗答對之題數換算成分數，聽力與閱讀得分相加即為總分；答錯並不倒扣。聽力得分介於 5-495 分、閱讀得分介於 5-495 分，兩者加起來即為總分，範圍在 10 到 990 分之間。

答對題數	聽力分數	閱讀分數	答對題數	聽力分數	閱讀分數	答對題數	聽力分數	閱讀分數	答對題數	聽力分數	閱讀分數
100	495	495	**85**	465	420	**70**	365	320	**55**	295	230
99	495	495	**84**	455	415	**69**	360	315	**54**	290	225
98	495	495	**83**	450	410	**68**	355	310	**53**	280	220
97	495	490	**82**	445	400	**67**	350	300	**52**	275	215
96	495	485	**81**	440	395	**66**	350	295	**51**	265	210
95	495	480	**80**	435	385	**65**	345	290	**50**	260	205
94	495	475	**79**	430	380	**64**	340	285	**49**	255	200
93	490	470	**78**	425	375	**63**	335	280	**48**	250	195
92	490	465	**77**	420	370	**62**	330	270	**47**	245	190
91	490	460	**76**	410	365	**61**	325	265	**46**	240	185
90	485	455	**75**	400	360	**60**	320	260	**45**	230	180
89	485	450	**74**	390	350	**59**	315	255	**44**	225	175
88	480	440	**73**	385	345	**58**	310	250	**43**	220	170
87	475	430	**72**	380	335	**57**	305	245	**42**	210	165
86	470	425	**71**	375	330	**56**	300	240	**41**	205	160

＊此表格僅供參考，實際計分以官方分數為準 。
＊分數計算方式，例如：聽力答對 70 題，閱讀答對 78 題，總分為 365+375=740 分 。

2018年新制多益變革表

多益英語測驗有什麼改變？為什麼？

為確保測驗符合考生及成績使用單位之需求，ETS 會定期重新檢驗所有測驗試題。本次多益英語測驗題型更新，反映了全球現有日常生活中社交及職場之英語使用情況。測驗本身將維持其在評量日常生活或職場情境英語的公平性及可信度。其中一些測驗形式會改變，然而，**測驗的難易度**、**測驗時間**或**測驗分數所代表的意義不會有所更動**。

新舊制多益測驗結構比較

聽力測驗 Listening Comprehension　45 分鐘　100 題　495 分

測驗總題數、整體難易程度及測驗時間不變

Part	題型	舊制題數	新制題數	題型題數變更說明
1	**Photographs** 照片描述	10 題	6 題	題型不變，題數減少 4 題。
	說明：從四個選項當中，選出一個和照片最相近的描述，問題與選項均不會印在試卷上。			
2	**Question-Response** 應答問題	30 題	25 題	題型不變，題數減少 5 題。
	說明：從三個選項當中，選出與問題最為符合的回答，問題與選項均不會印在試卷上。			
3	**Conversations** 簡短對話	30 題 3 題 x 10 組	39 題 3 題 x 13 組	加入三人對話、加入圖表，題數增加 9 題。
	說明：從四個選項中，選出與問題最為符合的回答，對話內容不會印在試卷上。 對話中將會有較少轉折，但來回交談較為頻繁。 部分對話題型將出現兩名以上的對談者。			
4	**Talks** 獨白	30 題 3 題 x 10 組	30 題 3 題 x 10 組	新增圖表作答題型，題數不變。
	說明：從四個選項中，選出與問題最為符合的回答，獨白內容不會印在試卷上。			

- 聽力測驗將包含母音省略（elision，如：going to → gonna）和不完整的句子（fragment，如：Yes, in a minute. / Down the hall. / Could you? 等省去主詞或動詞的句子）。
- 配合圖表，測驗考生是否聽懂對話，並測驗考生能否理解談話背景與對話中隱含的意思。

閱讀測驗 Reading Comprehension　75 分鐘　100 題　495 分

測驗總題數、整體難易程度及測驗時間不變

Part	題型	舊制題數	新制題數	題型題數變更說明
5	Incomplete Sentences 句子填空	40 題	30 題	題型不變，題數減少 10 題。
	說明：從四個選項中，選出最為恰當的答案，以完成不完整的句子。			
6	Text Completion 段落填空	12 題 4 題 X 3 篇	16 題 4 題 X 4 組	加入將適當的句子填入空格的題型，題數增加 4 題。
	說明：從四個選項中，選出最為恰當的答案，以完成文章中不完整的句子。 選項類別除原有之片語、單字、子句之外，另新增完整句子的選項。			
7	Reading Comprehension–Single Passage 單篇文章理解	28 題 共 9 篇 每篇 2 到 5 題	29 題 共 10 篇 每篇 2 到 4 題	題型不變，題數增加 1 題。
	Reading Comprehension–Multiple Passage 多篇文章理解	20 題 雙篇閱讀共 4 篇 每篇 5 題	25 題 雙篇閱讀 2 篇 三篇閱讀 3 篇 每篇 5 題	少 2 篇雙篇閱讀文章，加入 3 篇三篇閱讀文章。
	說明：閱讀單篇或兩或三篇內容相關的文章，從四個選項中，選出最為恰當的答案以回答問題。 加入篇章結構題型，測驗考生能否理解整體文章結構，並將一個句子歸置於正確的段落。			

◆ 閱讀測驗將包含文字簡訊、即時通訊，或多人互動的線上聊天訊息內容。
◆ 新增引述文章部分內容，測驗考生是否理解作者希望表達之意思。

◆ 為新制題型說明

資料來源：ETS 官方網站
http://www.toeic.com.tw/2018update/info.html

各大題答題技巧戰略

聽力部分答題技巧

第一大題	照片描述 （6 題）	這個部分是要考你看圖片、選答案的能力。你可以用以下的方法來練習：自己找一些照片來看，並思索根據照片的內容，有哪些問題可以提問。
第二大題	應答問題 （25 題）	這個部分是提出各種問題，問題的開頭—— What、How、Why、When、Where、Who 六大問句——可以提示我們需要什麼樣的答案。
第三大題	簡短對話 （39 題）	這個部分會先播放簡短的對話，再考你對對話的理解程度。回答技巧是你可以**先看問題、答案選項和圖表**，然後再聽對話內容，這樣你在聽的時候會比較知道要專注答案的線索。
第四大題	獨白 （30 題）	這個大題可以說是聽力測驗中最難的部分，平時就需要多聽英文對話和廣播等來加強聽力能力。

聽力題目前的英文指示 & 高分戰略

In the Listening test, you will be asked to demonstrate how well you understand spoken English. The entire Listening test will last approximately 45 minutes. There are four parts, and directions are given for each part. You must mark your answers on the separate answer sheet. Do not write your answers in your test book.

聽力測驗在測驗考生聽懂英語的能力。整個聽力測驗的進行時間約 45 分鐘，共分四大題，每一大題皆有做答指示。請把答案寫在另一張答案卡上，而不要把答案寫在測驗本上。

I. Photographs 第一大題：照片描述

Part 1

Directions: For each question in this part, you will hear four statements about a picture in your test book. When you hear the statements, you must select the one statement that best describes what you see in the picture. Then find the number of the question on your answer sheet and mark your answer. The statements will not be printed in your test book and will be spoken only one time.

Look at the example item below. Now listen to the four statements.

(A) They're pointing at the monitor.
(B) They're looking at the document.
(C) They're talking on the phone.
(D) They're sitting by the table.

Statement (B), "They're looking at the document," is the best description of the picture, so you should select answer (B) and mark it on your answer sheet.

第一大題

指示：本大題的每一小題，在測驗本上都會印有一張圖片，考生會聽到針對照片所做的四段描述，然後選出最符合照片內容的適當描述，接著在答案卡上找到題目編號，將對應的答案選項圓圈塗黑。描述的內容不會印在測驗本上，而且只會播放一次。

（A）他們正指著螢幕。
（B）他們正在看文件。
（C）他們正在講電話。
（D）他們正坐在桌子旁。

描述 (B)「他們正在看文件」是最符合本圖的描述，因此你應該選擇選項 (B)，並在答案卡上劃記。

高分戰略

❶ 以人物為主的照片，要注意該人物的動作特徵。

照片題中有 70 ～ 80％的題目是以人物為照片主角，這些照片時常會考人的動作特徵，因此要先整理好相關的動作用語。舉例來說，一看到人在走路的照片，就立刻想到 walking、strolling 這些和走路有關的動詞，聽題目的時候會更有幫助。

❷ 以事物為中心的照片，要注意事物的狀態或位置。

以事物為中心的照片，其事物的狀態或位置是出題的要點。所以，表示「位置」時經常會用到的介系詞，還有表現「狀態」的片語，要先整理好。舉例來說，在表示位置「在……旁邊」時，要整理出 next to、by、beside、near 等用語，最好整個背下來。另外，多益時常出現的事物名稱，也要事先準備好。

❸ 要小心出人意料之外的問題。

不同於過往題型，題目的正確答案可能會出現描寫事物，這已成為一種出題趨勢。舉例來說，照片是一個男人用手指著掛在牆上的畫，按照常理，會想到是要考這個人的動作，要回答 pointing 這樣的動詞。但意外地，本題以掛在牆上的畫當作正確答案（The picture has been hung on the wall.）。所以出現人的照片時，不僅要注意人的動作，連周邊事物也必須要注意一下。只有提到照片中出現的內容，才會是正確答案；想像的內容絕對不會是正確答案。

II. Question-Response 第二大題：應答問題

Part 2

Directions: You will hear a question or statement and three responses spoken in English. They will be spoken only one time and will not be printed in your test book. Select the best response to the question or statement and mark the letter (A), (B), or (C) on your answer sheet.

第二大題

指示：考生會聽到一個問題句或敘述句，以及三句回應的英語。題目只會撥放一次，而且不會印在測驗本上。請選出最符合擺放內容的答案，在答案卡上將 (A)、(B)、(C) 或 (D) 的答案選項塗黑。

高分戰略

❶ 新制有言外之意的考題增加

PART 2 少了五題，但命題方式變得更巧妙、難度也隨之提升。有言外之意的考題增加，考生必須要聽出背後的含意才能找出答案。碰到此類題型時，在聽完題目後，需要思考一番，才能挑出正確的答案。只要稍不留神，很容易就錯失下一題的解題機會。請務必勤加練習，熟悉此類題型的模式。

❷ 沒聽清楚題目最前面的疑問詞，很可惜。

大部分 Part 2 出現的疑問句都會在最前面提示核心要點，尤其是以疑問詞（Who、What、Where、When、Why、How）開頭的疑問句題目，會出約 9 ～ 10 題。這些題目只要聽到句首的疑問詞，幾乎就能找到正確答案，所以平常要常做區分疑問詞的聽力練習。

❸ 利用錯誤答案消去法。

Part 2 是最多陷阱的部分，所以事先把常見的陷阱題整理起來，是很重要的。舉例來說，以疑問詞開頭的疑問句題目，用 yes 或 no 回答的選項，幾乎都是錯誤答案，可以先將其刪除。另外，重複出現題目中的單字，或出現與題目中字彙發音類似的單字，如 copy 與 coffee，也是常出的錯誤答案模式。平常一邊做題目，一邊將具代表性的陷阱題整理好是必要的。

❹ 常考的片語要整個背起來。

多益中常出現的用語或片語，最好當作一個單字一樣地整個背起來。舉例來說，疑問句「Why don't you . . . ?」的用法並非要詢問原因，而是「做……好嗎？」的代表句型。像這樣的用語，時常會快速唸過，所以事先整個背起來，考聽力時會很有幫助。

因此平常花功夫多做聽力訓練，並跟著一起唸，把重要的用語整段背下來，征服 Part 2 之路就不遠了。

III. Conversations 第三大題：簡短對話

Part 3

Directions: You will hear some conversations between two or more people. You will be asked to answer three questions about what the speakers say in each conversation. Select the best response to each question and mark the letter (A), (B), (C), or (D) on your answer sheet. The conversations will not be printed in your test book and will be spoken only one time.

第三大題

指示：考生會聽到一些兩個人或多人的對話，並根據對話所聽到的內容，回答三個問題。請選出最符合播放內容的答案，在答案卡上將 (A)、(B)、(C) 或 (D) 的答案選項塗黑。這些對話只會播放一次，而且不會印在測驗本上。

高分戰略

❶ 一定要先瞄題目，以找出要聆聽的重點。

Part 3 是兩到三人的對話，每組對話要回答三道題，所以**事先把題目快速掃描過**，找出重點，是很重要的。若不事先看題目，就不知道要把注意力集中在哪裡，而必須理解並記下整個對話，十分吃力。所以事先看一下題目問什麼，會對接下來的對話有概念，並知道要注意聽哪些地方。

有關圖表的試題，要**先看一下圖表訊息**，再綜合試題和選項後，仔細聽對話的內容。有策略地去聽是很重要的。

❷ 一面聽一面找答案！

即使先掃描過了題目，卻沒有練習邊聽邊找答案，容易會出現漏掉正確答案的情況。因為即使之前非常注意聽的對話，但有些細微的訊息，之後可能會記不起來，尤其是新制多益中，出現三個人的對話，所以談話者的性別，及彼此間的關係會更加複雜。所以一聽到答案出現，立刻作答，是最有利的。這麼做剛開始可能有點困難，但只要勤奮地練習，以後瞄過題目就大概就能猜出答案

❸ 千萬不要錯失對話開頭！

在 Part 3 中，時常出現問**職業**、**場所或主題**的問題，這些問題的答案時常會出現在對話開頭。要快速掌握對話一開始揭示的主題，才能判斷出接下來會出現什麼內容，對解其他的題目很有幫助。所以要勤加練習，把對話開頭確實聽清楚。

IV. Talks 第四大題：簡短獨白

Part 4

Directions: You will hear some talks given by a single speaker. You will be asked to answer three questions about what the speaker says in each talk. Select the best response to each question and mark the letter (A), (B), (C), or (D) on your answer sheet. The talks will not be printed in your test book and will be spoken only one time.

第四大題

指示：考生會聽到好幾段單人獨白，並根據每一段話的內容，回答三個問題。請選出最符合播放內容的答案，在答案卡上將 (A)、(B)、(C) 或 (D) 的答案選項塗黑。每一段話只會播放一次，而且不會印在測驗本上。

高分戰略

❶ 要事先整理好常考的詢問內容！

和 Part 3 不同，Part 4 的談話種類是有一定類型的。也就是說，會重複聽到有關**交通廣播、天氣預報、旅行導覽、電話留言**等的談話，內容大同小異。所以只需要按這些談話種類，整理出常考的問題類型即可。舉例來說，跟電話溝通相關的主題，時常都在談話一開始出現「I'm calling to . . .」，聽到這個敘述後，要找出正確答案就容易多了。

❷ 具備背景知識的話，答題會更加容易上手。

Part 4 的談話種類是有固定框架的，會感覺好像談話的內容及題目都很類似。所以即使不聽談話，光看題目，就能推測出答案是什麼。舉例來說，若是機場的情境談話，也許會出有關飛機誤點或取消的問題。這時誤點或取消的原因，最常出現的可能是天候不佳。這就是多益的背景知識，即使沒聽清楚，光看題目，也能選出最接近正確答案的選項。所以平常要努力累積多益常考題型的背景知識，不能懶惰。

❸ 要花功夫訓練自己找出問題的要點。

和 Part 3 一樣，Part 4 也是每段談話出三道題，所以要養成先掃描過題目和表格並整理出重點的習慣。由於 Part 4 的談話內容更長，不太可能把全部內容聽完後再答題。因此可以先找出題目的要點，利用背景知識，在試題本上推敲正確答案。不像 Part 3，Part 4 的答案通常會按照題目的順序，一一出現在對話中，答案逐題出現的機率很高。

閱讀部分答題技巧

第五大題	句子填空 （30 題）	在第五大題中，字彙和文法能力最重要。其所考的字彙大都跟職場或商業有關，平時就要多背誦單字。
第六大題	段落填空 （16 題）	除了單字，也需要將比較長的片語或子句，甚至是一整個句子填入空格中，要掌握整篇文章來龍去脈才能找出最合適的答案。
第七大題	單篇文章理解 （29 題） 多篇文章理解 （25 題）	第七大題比較困難，你需要知道有哪幾類的商業文章，像是公告或備忘錄等。平時就要訓練自己能夠快速閱讀文章和圖表，並且能夠找出主要的內容。當然，在這個部分字彙能力也是很重要的。

閱讀題目前的英文指示 & 高分戰略

In the Reading test, you will read a variety of texts and answer several different types of reading comprehension questions. The entire Reading test will last 75 minutes. There are three parts, and directions are given for each part. You are encouraged to answer as many questions as possible within the time allowed.

You must mark your answers on the separate answer sheet. Do not write your answers in your test book.

在閱讀測驗中，考生會讀到各種文章，並回答各種型式的閱讀測驗題目。整個閱讀測驗的進行時間為 75 分鐘 。本測驗共分三大題，每一大題皆有做答指示。請在規定的時間內，盡可能地作答。

請把答案寫在另一張答案卡上，而不要把答案寫在測驗本上。

V. Incomplete Sentences 第五大題：單句填空

Part 5

Directions: A word or phrase is missing in each of the sentences below. Four answer choices are given below each sentence. Select the best answer to complete the sentence. Then mark the letter (A), (B), (C), or (D) on your answer sheet.

第五大題

指示：本測驗中的每一個句子皆缺少一個單字或詞組，在句子下方會列出四個答案選項，請選出最適合的答案來完成句子，並在做答卡上將 (A)、(B)、(C) 或 (D) 的答案選項塗黑。

高分戰略

❶ 要先看選項。

試題大致可分為**句型、字彙、文法以及慣用語**四種試題。要先看選項，掌握是上述四種題型中的哪一種，便能更快速解題。所以，要練習判斷題型，並正確掌握各題型的解題技巧。

❷ 找出意思最接近的單字。

Part 5 是填空選擇題，若能找出和空格關係最密切的關鍵字彙，便能快速又正確地解題。所以，要練習**分析句子的結構**，並找出和空格關係最密切的字彙作為答題線索。一般來說，**空格前後的單字，就是線索**。舉例來說，如果空格後有名詞，此名詞就是空格的線索單字，以此名詞可以猜想出空格可能是個形容詞。

❸ 要盡力廣泛地蒐羅字彙。

多益會拿來出題的字彙，通常以**片語**形式出現。最具代表的是：動詞和受詞、形容詞和名詞、介系詞和名詞、動詞和副詞等。有些詞組中每個單字都懂，但合起來就很難猜出它的中文意思，所以不要直接用中文而要用英文去理解。因此，平日要養成將這些片語詞組視為整體一起背下來的習慣。

舉例來說，中文說「打電話」，但英文是「make a phone call」；而付錢打電話不能用「pay a phone call」，要用「pay for the phone call」。但是多益中 Part 5 考「pay for the phone call」的 可能性很低，因為多益大多出常見用語，而這句不是。所以，要用英文去理解常見用語，要整個背起來，不要直接用中文理解，因為這是得高分最大的障礙。

VI. Text Completion 第六大題：短文填空

Part 6

Directions: Read the texts that follow. A word, phrase, or sentence is missing in parts of each text. Four answer choices for each question are given below the text. Select the best answer to complete the text. Then mark the letter (A), (B), (C), or (D) on your answer sheet.

第六大題

指示：閱讀本大題的文章，文章中的某些句子缺少單字、片語或句子，這些句子都會有四個答案選項，請選出最適合的答案來完成文章中的空格，並在做答卡上將 (A)、(B)、(C) 或 (D) 的答案選項塗黑。

高分戰略

❶ 要研究空格前後句子連結關係，掌握上下文。

Part 5 和 Part 6 不同的地方是，Part 5 只探究一個句子的結構，而 Part 6 要探究句子和句子間的關係，因此要練習觀察空格前後句子彼此的連結關係。如果有空格的句子是第一句，要看後一句來解題；如果有空格的句子是第二句，就要看前一句來解題。偶爾，也有要看整篇文章才能作答的題目。

PART 6 最難處在於要從選項的四個句子中，選出適當的句子填入空格中。此為新制增加的題型，不僅要多費時解題，平時也得多花功夫如何掌握上下文意上。

❷ Part 6 的動詞時態問題

Part 5 的動詞時態問題，只要看該句子內的動詞是否符合時態即可，但 Part 6 的動詞時態，要看其他句子才能決定該句空格中的時態。大部分的時態題目都區分為：已發生的事或尚未發生的事。從上下文來看，已發生的事，要用現在完成式或過去式；尚未發生的事，就選包含 will 等與未來式相關的助動詞（will、shall、may 等）選項，或用「be going to . . .」。針對 Part 6 的時態問題，多練習區分已發生的事和尚未發生的事便能順利答題。

❸ Part 6 的連接副詞

所謂的連接副詞，是指翻譯時要和前面的內容一起翻譯的副詞。一般來說，這不會出現在只考一句話的 Part 5，而會出現在考句間的關係的 Part 6。舉例來說，副詞 therefore 是「因此」的意思，所以若前後句的內容有因果關係，用它就對了。若是轉折語氣的話，用有「然而」含意的 however 準沒錯。此外，連接副詞還有 otherwise（否則）、consequently（因而導致）、additionally（此外）、instead（反而）等。另外，連接詞用於連接句子，而介系詞是連接名詞，連接副詞是單獨使用的，這是區分它們最便捷的方法。

VII. Single Passage / Multiple Passage 第七大題：單篇／多篇文章理解

Part 7

Directions: In this part you will read a selection of texts, such as magazine and newspaper articles, emails, and instant messages. Each text or set of texts is followed by several questions. Select the best answer for each question and mark the letter (A), (B), (C), or (D) on your answer sheet.

第七大題

指示：這大題中會閱讀到不同題材的文章，如雜誌和新聞文章、電子郵件或通訊軟體的訊息等。每篇或每組文章之後會有數個題目，請選出最適合的答案，並在做答卡上將 (A)、(B)、(C) 或 (D) 的答案選項塗黑。

高分戰略

❶ 要熟記類似的字彙及用語。

做 Part 7 的題目，字彙能力最為重要，它能幫助你正確且快速地找出與題目或文章用語最接近的選項。一邊研究 Part 7 的題目，一邊整理並熟記意思相似的字彙或用語，能快速增加字彙。

❷ Part 7 的問題也是有類型的。

Part 7 的題目乍看好像很多元，事實上可以分作幾種類型，如：

① **具體訊息類型**：詢問文章的一些訊息。
② **主題類型**：要找出文章主題。
③ **NOT 類型**：提供的選項中有三項是對的，而要找出錯誤項目。
④ **邏輯推演類型**：從一些線索中推知內容。
⑤ **文意填空類型**：閱讀段落，將題目中的句子填入文中適當的地方。

解題時先將題目分類，再來研究該如何解題，速度會快很多。

❸ 要注意複合式文章題目。

從 176 題開始，是由兩篇到三文章組成的複合式文章類型，有許多問題出自多篇文章內容的相關性。所以在這部分，相關或相同的地方要連貫起來作答。出這種相關連帶問題時，要注意文章的共通點是以何種方式連接。

❹ 培養耐力。

Part 7 是最後一個單元，解題實力雖然重要，但長時間解題能否集中注意力也是勝負的關鍵。平常要訓練自己，至少要持續一個小時不休息地解題，時常以這種方式來訓練閱讀十分重要。多做解題耐力練習，是考高分的必要條件。

ACTUAL TEST

ACTUAL TEST 01

LISTENING TEST 01

In the Listening test, you will be asked to demonstrate how well you understand spoken English. The entire Listening test will last approximately 45 minutes. There are four parts, and directions are given for each part. You must mark your answers on the separate answer sheet. Do not write your answers in your test book.

PART 1

Directions: For each question in this part, you will hear four statements about a picture in your test book. When you hear the statements, you must select the one statement that best describes what you see in the picture. Then find the number of the question on your answer sheet and mark your answer. The statements will not be printed in your test book and will be spoken only one time.

Example

Sample Answer

Ⓐ ● Ⓒ Ⓓ

Statement (B), "They're looking at the document," is the best description of the picture, so you should select answer (B) and mark it on your answer sheet.

1.

2.

GO ON TO THE NEXT PAGE

3.

4.

5.

6.

GO ON TO THE NEXT PAGE

PART 2 02

Directions: You will hear a question or statement and three responses spoken in English. They will not be printed in your test book and will be spoken only one time. Select the best response to the question or statement and mark the letter (A), (B), or (C) on your answer sheet.

7. Mark your answer on your answer sheet.

8. Mark your answer on your answer sheet.

9. Mark your answer on your answer sheet.

10. Mark your answer on your answer sheet.

11. Mark your answer on your answer sheet.

12. Mark your answer on your answer sheet.

13. Mark your answer on your answer sheet.

14. Mark your answer on your answer sheet.

15. Mark your answer on your answer sheet.

16. Mark your answer on your answer sheet.

17. Mark your answer on your answer sheet.

18. Mark your answer on your answer sheet.

19. Mark your answer on your answer sheet.

20. Mark your answer on your answer sheet.

21. Mark your answer on your answer sheet.

22. Mark your answer on your answer sheet.

23. Mark your answer on your answer sheet.

24. Mark your answer on your answer sheet.

25. Mark your answer on your answer sheet.

26. Mark your answer on your answer sheet.

27. Mark your answer on your answer sheet.

28. Mark your answer on your answer sheet.

29. Mark your answer on your answer sheet.

30. Mark your answer on your answer sheet.

31. Mark your answer on your answer sheet.

PART 3 (03)

Directions: You will hear some conversations between two or more people. You will be asked to answer three questions about what the speakers say in each conversation. Select the best response to each question and mark the letter (A), (B), (C), or (D) on your answer sheet. The conversations will not be printed in your test book and will be spoken only one time.

32. What are the speakers mainly discussing?

(A) A training seminar
(B) The installation of a television
(C) The date of a presentation
(D) A software upgrade

33. What is the problem?

(A) The necessary tools are unavailable.
(B) The office is closed.
(C) The wall is too weak.
(D) The phone number was wrong.

34. What most likely will the man do first tomorrow?

(A) Order a replacement part
(B) Consult an instruction manual
(C) Contact the woman
(D) Fill out a work order

35. What position is the man applying for?

(A) Lecturer
(B) Editor
(C) Journalist
(D) Superintendent

36. What makes the man qualified for the position?

(A) His academic background
(B) His work experience
(C) His popularity
(D) His eloquence

37. What extra benefit does the woman mention?

(A) Health insurance
(B) Flexible hours
(C) A lot of free time
(D) Regular incentives

GO ON TO THE NEXT PAGE

38. What are the speakers mainly discussing?
(A) An interior renovation
(B) A product launch
(C) A luncheon reservation
(D) A budget proposal

39. What does the man say about the dining room?
(A) It needs more lighting.
(B) It is quite cold.
(C) It is spacious.
(D) It is too loud.

40. What does the man suggest the woman do?
(A) Repaint the walls a brighter color
(B) Compensate guests who have reservations
(C) Draft a budget proposal
(D) Open a bank account

---

41. What is the man concerned about?
(A) Getting his camera fixed
(B) Receiving sick leave from work
(C) Preparing for a party
(D) Introducing a client

42. According to the man, why does Greg like his new job?
(A) It offers better vacation time.
(B) It pays a higher salary.
(C) It matches his abilities.
(D) It provides health benefits.

43. What most likely will the woman do next?
(A) Take a group photo
(B) Attend a Christmas party
(C) Contact Greg
(D) Send an email attachment

---

44. What is the man concerned about?
(A) Finishing a project on time
(B) Paying for his new mobile phone
(C) Repairing a piece of equipment
(D) Learning a new skill

45. Where do the speakers work?
(A) At a repair shop
(B) At an electronics store
(C) At a marketing firm
(D) At a design company

46. What does the woman offer to do?
(A) Provide assistance
(B) Pay in cash
(C) Fill in for the man
(D) Email a user manual

---

47. Who most likely is the man?
(A) A shop owner
(B) A construction worker
(C) A local resident
(D) A market researcher

48. What does the woman mention about the mall?
(A) It was recently renovated.
(B) It has sufficient parking space.
(C) It is attracting many tourists.
(D) It is located outside of town.

49. Why does the woman usually visit the mall?
(A) To purchase groceries
(B) To meet with her clients
(C) To buy clothing
(D) To deliver products

---

50. What are the speakers discussing?
(A) Orders for office supplies
(B) Equipment for a conference
(C) The budget reports
(D) Their colleague

51. Why does the man mention to the woman when the supply company closes?
(A) To inform her of the business hours
(B) To let her know she can't order anything
(C) To explain that the second order would be late
(D) To imply that new equipment can't be ordered tomorrow

52. What does the woman offer to do?
(A) Pay for the new order
(B) Order the supplies herself
(C) Cancel a meeting
(D) Speak to their colleague

---

53. What is the problem?
(A) The plane tickets were not booked
(B) A meeting had to be rescheduled
(C) The meeting was a failure
(D) A deadline has been changed

54. Which part of the business trip will be postponed?
(A) The meeting in New York
(B) The meeting in Wisconsin
(C) The meeting in Washington
(D) The meeting in Westboro

NEW
55. What does the man mean when he says, "that's not a bad idea"?
(A) He thinks it is a bad idea.
(B) He agrees with the proposed solution.
(C) He wants to hear other ideas.
(D) He disagrees with the solution.

---

56. What was the woman doing in Australia?
(A) Conducting business
(B) Studying abroad
(C) Taking a vacation
(D) Searching for employees

NEW
57. What does the woman imply when she says, "is this Robert Wilder's application"?
(A) She is surprised to see the application.
(B) She will reject the application.
(C) She doesn't understand something.
(D) She agrees with the application.

58. How does the woman know Robert Wilder?
(A) They went to college together.
(B) They work in the same department.
(C) They play baseball together.
(D) They play tennis together.

---

59. What is the woman concerned about?
(A) Getting extra vacation
(B) Doing too much work
(C) Not having time for her children
(D) Preparing a report

60. What does the man suggest?
(A) Fire the manager
(B) Wait until their vacation
(C) Hire a new employee
(D) Have some extra vacation days

61. What does the woman say she will have to do?
(A) Hire a babysitter
(B) Go to another company
(C) Ask her husband
(D) Finish her sales reports

GO ON TO THE NEXT PAGE

Conference Table Price List	
Pine	$165
Maple	$195
Walnut	$225
Cherry	$307

62. What does the woman have on Friday?

(A) A dinner
(B) A seminar
(C) A meeting
(D) An office party

NEW

63. Look at the graphic. How much will the woman pay for the furniture?

(A) $165
(B) $195
(C) $307
(D) $614

64. What does the man say he will do?

(A) Arrange free delivery
(B) Deliver the furniture in the evening
(C) Send a confirmation
(D) Deliver the table himself

Airline Mileage Redemption Points	
To East Asia	50,000
To Southeast Asia	60,000
To the Middle East	70,000
To Europe	80,000

65. Why does the woman call?

(A) To get an upgrade
(B) To book a flight to Korea and Japan
(C) To cancel her flight to Singapore
(D) To sign up for a mileage card

NEW

66. Look at the graphic. How many points will the woman use?

(A) 50,000
(B) 60,000
(C) 70,000
(D) 80,000

67. What suggestion does the man give the woman?

(A) Upgrade her flight to Korea
(B) Make the request after her trip to Korea and Japan
(C) Book a different flight
(D) Cancel her reservation

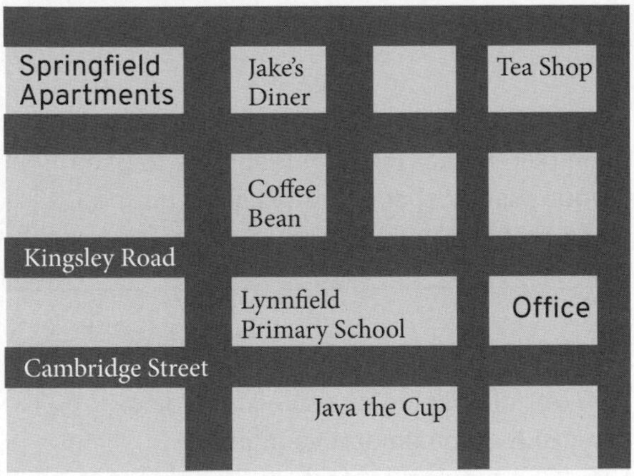

68. What are the speakers discussing?

(A) Their GPS systems
(B) Which coffee shop to visit
(C) How far Cambridge is from their apartments
(D) The fastest route to work

69. What does the woman want to do?

(A) Keep losing the game
(B) Make more money than the man does
(C) Get to work faster than the man does
(D) Participate in a car race

NEW
70. Look at the list. Which shop does the man most likely stop at?

(A) Coffee Bean
(B) Tea Shop
(C) Java the Cup
(D) Jake's Diner

GO ON TO THE NEXT PAGE

PART 4 04

Directions: You will hear some talks given by a single speaker. You will be asked to answer three questions about what the speaker says in each talk. Select the best response to each question and mark the letter (A), (B), (C), or (D) on your answer sheet. The talks will not be printed in your test book and will be spoken only one time.

71. Where most likely does the speaker work?
(A) At a theater
(B) At a car dealership
(C) At a retail store
(D) At a library

72. What is the listener asked to double-check?
(A) Accurate pricing
(B) Sales figures
(C) Business hours
(D) Name tags

73. When should the listener contact the speaker?
(A) If an employee is late for work
(B) If a technical problem occurs
(C) If an item is out of stock
(D) If a customer is dissatisfied

74. What is the announcement about?
(A) An opening of a public building
(B) A commemorative statue
(C) A singing contest
(D) A survey result

75. Who is Jim Neilson?
(A) A mayor
(B) An instructor
(C) A musician
(D) An architect

76. What are attendees asked to do?
(A) Reserve seats in advance
(B) Complete a survey
(C) Subscribe to a newsletter
(D) Contribute to a fundraiser

77. Who most likely is the speaker?
(A) A scholar
(B) A producer
(C) A pilot
(D) A programmer

78. Who most likely are the listeners?
(A) Potential investors
(B) Actors
(C) Homemakers
(D) University students

79. What will the listeners do in the meeting room?
(A) Participate in a raffle
(B) Watch a video
(C) Enroll in a class
(D) Attend an interview

---

80. What is the purpose of the broadcast?
(A) To announce the results of a soccer match
(B) To promote a store's grand opening
(C) To advertise a new product
(D) To inform the listeners of a special event

81. What does the speaker suggest doing?
(A) Wearing comfortable clothing
(B) Exercising on a regular basis
(C) Bringing personal belongings
(D) Booking a ticket in advance

82. What does the speaker say about the summer camp?
(A) It is free of charge.
(B) It will last three months.
(C) It has a restricted number of participants.
(D) It will be sponsored by Dave's Sport Shop.

---

83. What does the speaker mention about her company?
(A) They have merged with another company.
(B) They are manufacturing a new product.
(C) They are creating new policies.
(D) They had record profits.

NEW
84. Why does the woman say, "my schedule is too tight to do that"?
(A) Because the email is secure
(B) To sign a new contract
(C) She needs some help.
(D) She doesn't have time.

85. What will they be sending a lot of?
(A) Portfolios
(B) Contract forms
(C) Vital data
(D) Building plans

---

86. What is *The Tempest* about?
(A) The evolution of man
(B) A love affair between a man and a woman
(C) A ghost ship
(D) Magic and illusion

NEW
87. Why does the speaker say, "remember, last year the Bromley Actors Guild won first place at this event"?
(A) To suggest that they are impressive
(B) To recommend that you join them
(C) To explain why they are here
(D) To excuse a poor performance

88. What will most likely happen after the performance?
(A) Dinner and drinks
(B) Question time with the actors
(C) DVDs will be sold.
(D) The actors will sign autographs.

GO ON TO THE NEXT PAGE →

89. What types of products are being discussed?

(A) Cell phone cases and selfie sticks
(B) Cell phones and MP3 Players
(C) Selfie sticks and headphones
(D) Software programs

NEW

90. Why does the speaker say, "I wonder if the cost is too high compared to the other products on the market"?

(A) To ask for assistance
(B) To offer help
(C) To suggest a change
(D) To create some new products

91. What will the listeners most likely do after lunch?

(A) Review a safety policy
(B) Attend a seminar
(C) Go back to work
(D) Have a conference call

ORDER FORM

Item	Quantity in stock	Quantity to order
Office Table	13	0
Whiteboard	0	12
Office Chair	0	20
Drafting Table	6	0

NEW

92. Look at the graphic. Which items need to be ordered?

(A) Office tables and chairs
(B) Chairs and drafting tables
(C) Whiteboards and office chairs
(D) Whiteboards and drafting tables

93. What does the speaker anticipate about the company?

(A) It won't need any more furniture.
(B) It will have more staff in their building.
(C) The boardrooms will be renovated.
(D) Their staff are moving offices.

94. What is the listener asked to do before making any orders?

(A) Sign them herself
(B) Make sure the manager signs them
(C) Bring some extra paper
(D) Prepare a delivery receipt

MARKET SHARE

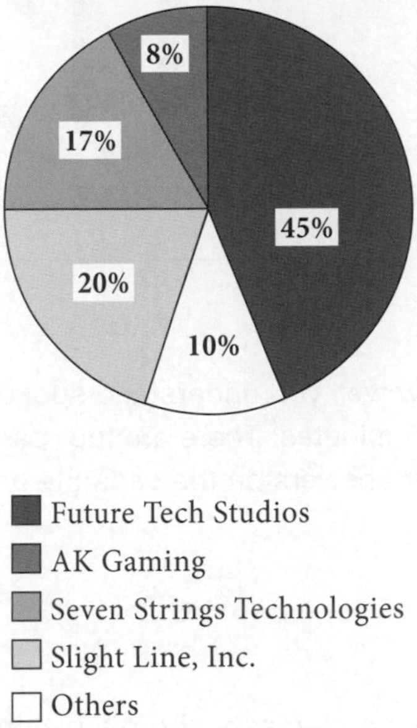

95. Which industry does the speaker work in?

(A) Computer hardware
(B) Computer games
(C) Computer software
(D) Computer microchips

NEW

96. Look at the graphic. What company does the speaker work for?

(A) Future Tech Studios
(B) Slight Line Inc.
(C) Seven Strings Technologies
(D) AK Gaming

97. According to the speaker, what will the company do in the next quarter?

(A) Give away gifts
(B) Give away expansion packs
(C) Offer free software with new products
(D) Install a new security system

Training Schedule

Tuesday	Wednesday	Thursday	Friday
Basic knife skills and food preparation	Health and safety in the kitchen	Food safety and hygiene	Time management
	Team lunch		Evaluation

98. What are the listeners training to be?

(A) Factory workers
(B) Store owners
(C) Restaurant chefs
(D) Medical workers

99. According to the speaker, what will the listeners enjoy doing?

(A) Working with the celebrity chefs
(B) Becoming a celebrity chef
(C) Using the kitchen tools
(D) Working with each other

NEW

100. Look at the graphic. On which day will the listeners learn food safety and hygiene?

(A) Tuesday
(B) Wednesday
(C) Thursday
(D) Friday

This is the end of the Listening test.

ACTUAL TEST 02

LISTENING TEST 05

In the Listening test, you will be asked to demonstrate how well you understand spoken English. The entire Listening test will last approximately 45 minutes. There are four parts, and directions are given for each part. You must mark your answers on the separate answer sheet. Do not write your answers in your test book.

PART 1

Directions: For each question in this part, you will hear four statements about a picture in your test book. When you hear the statements, you must select the one statement that best describes what you see in the picture. Then find the number of the question on your answer sheet and mark your answer. The statements will not be printed in your test book and will be spoken only one time.

Example

Sample Answer

Ⓐ ● Ⓒ Ⓓ

Statement (B), "They're looking at the document," is the best description of the picture, so you should select answer (B) and mark it on your answer sheet.

1.

2.

GO ON TO THE NEXT PAGE

3.

4.

5.

6.

GO ON TO THE NEXT PAGE

PART 2 (06)

Directions: You will hear a question or statement and three responses spoken in English. They will not be printed in your test book and will be spoken only one time. Select the best response to the question or statement and mark the letter (A), (B), or (C) on your answer sheet.

7. Mark your answer on your answer sheet.

8. Mark your answer on your answer sheet.

9. Mark your answer on your answer sheet.

10. Mark your answer on your answer sheet.

11. Mark your answer on your answer sheet.

12. Mark your answer on your answer sheet.

13. Mark your answer on your answer sheet.

14. Mark your answer on your answer sheet.

15. Mark your answer on your answer sheet.

16. Mark your answer on your answer sheet.

17. Mark your answer on your answer sheet.

18. Mark your answer on your answer sheet.

19. Mark your answer on your answer sheet.

20. Mark your answer on your answer sheet.

21. Mark your answer on your answer sheet.

22. Mark your answer on your answer sheet.

23. Mark your answer on your answer sheet.

24. Mark your answer on your answer sheet.

25. Mark your answer on your answer sheet.

26. Mark your answer on your answer sheet.

27. Mark your answer on your answer sheet.

28. Mark your answer on your answer sheet.

29. Mark your answer on your answer sheet.

30. Mark your answer on your answer sheet.

31. Mark your answer on your answer sheet.

PART 3 (07)

Directions: You will hear some conversations between two or more people. You will be asked to answer three questions about what the speakers say in each conversation. Select the best response to each question and mark the letter (A), (B), (C), or (D) on your answer sheet. The conversations will not be printed in your test book and will be spoken only one time.

32. What are the speakers discussing?
(A) A business trip
(B) A budget proposal
(C) An upcoming conference
(D) A package delivery

33. What problem does the woman mention?
(A) The address is no longer relevant.
(B) A company has gone bankrupt.
(C) A budget must be revised.
(D) A flight has been canceled.

34. What does the woman say she will do?
(A) Review a contract
(B) Go to Tokyo
(C) Visit the post office
(D) Ask for compensation

35. Who most likely is the woman?
(A) A radio host
(B) A professor
(C) A business owner
(D) An athlete

36. What did the woman want to do?
(A) Make use of her education
(B) Open a fitness center
(C) Appear on radio
(D) Teach food and nutrition

37. According to the woman, what is the main reason for her success?
(A) Effective advertisements
(B) Considerable interest in nutrition
(C) Long-term investments
(D) Government policies

GO ON TO THE NEXT PAGE

38. Where most likely are the speakers?

(A) At a children's hospital
(B) At a university
(C) At a music store
(D) At a concert hall

39. What does the woman suggest doing?

(A) Purchasing a piano
(B) Writing a birthday card
(C) Playing string instruments
(D) Attending advanced classes

40. What does the woman give the man?

(A) A receipt
(B) A business card
(C) A map
(D) A pamphlet

41. Who most likely are the speakers?

(A) Show hosts
(B) Advertisers
(C) Television producers
(D) Viewers

42. According to the woman, what is the reason for the problem?

(A) A new product was recalled.
(B) An actor was injured.
(C) A television show was canceled.
(D) A new host is not well-liked.

43. What solution does the man suggest?

(A) Rewriting the script
(B) Replacing the host
(C) Conducting a survey
(D) Placing an advertisement

44. What does the man ask about?

(A) The reason the woman arrived early
(B) The date of the woman's wedding
(C) The name of a client
(D) Directions to the office

45. What will the woman do after work?

(A) Organize a party
(B) Try on a dress
(C) Attend a wedding
(D) Purchase office supplies

46. What will the man probably do next?

(A) Reply to an invitation
(B) Write an email
(C) Order a supply closet
(D) Go to the second floor

47. Where do the speakers work?

(A) At an electronics store
(B) At a software company
(C) At a clothing store
(D) At a photography studio

48. What does the man want to do with the website?

(A) Make the interface easier to use
(B) Enlarge the font
(C) Change the colors
(D) Increase the number of menus

49. What does the woman suggest doing?

(A) Hiring a professional
(B) Lowering the prices
(C) Changing the color scheme
(D) Including more images

50. What does the man talk about?

(A) His upcoming business trip
(B) His co-worker's wedding
(C) Where the conference should be
(D) His unfinished reports

51. What does the woman mention about the venue?

(A) They provide excellent services.
(B) She had her wedding at the venue.
(C) The venue may be booked quickly.
(D) They don't have enough rooms.

52. What does the woman offer to do?

(A) Send out emails.
(B) Work on newsletters.
(C) Contact co-workers.
(D) Help with organizing an event.

---

53. What are the speakers mainly discussing?

(A) An issue with the new contract
(B) The new contract states a longer vacation period
(C) A vacation in America
(D) Flights and accommodation

NEW

54. What does the woman mean when she says, "I'm on my way to an appointment"?

(A) She has a lunch meeting.
(B) She doesn't have much time to talk.
(C) She wants the man to sign the contract.
(D) She has a lot of time to talk.

55. What does the woman want to know?

(A) If he will sign the new contract
(B) If he can come to her office at 3 p.m.
(C) If he is going to Europe for vacation
(D) If he has paid for his trip already

NEW

56. What does the man imply when he says, "Some of us from the accounting department are going to Dreamworld on Saturday for a team bonding day"?

(A) He is recommending the theme park.
(B) He needs some documents signed.
(C) He wants the sales figures for this month.
(D) He is inviting her to join them.

57. What does the woman say about her plans?

(A) She can't change them.
(B) She can change them.
(C) They've been cancelled.
(D) They've been postponed.

58. What does the woman offer to do?

(A) Pick everyone up in her car
(B) Meet them at the amusement park
(C) Book the tickets online
(D) Pay for the tickets with cash

---

59. Where are the speakers planning to go?

(A) To the cinema
(B) To a restaurant
(C) To a friend's house
(D) To a Broadway show

60. What does the woman offer to do?

(A) Buy the tickets
(B) Call John and tell him something
(C) Pick John up in her car
(D) Send John a text message

61. What does the man offer to give to the woman?

(A) Money for parking
(B) A text message
(C) A bottle of champagne
(D) A ride to the show

GO ON TO THE NEXT PAGE

Maxx Cosmetics
Gift Card

10% off any purchase over $50

Expires March 1

62. What does the woman ask the man?
   (A) If the body wash is on sale
   (B) If he has a loyalty card
   (C) If he wants to use a credit card
   (D) If the body wash is good

NEW

63. Look at the graphic. Why is the gift card rejected?
   (A) Because he is in the wrong store
   (B) It has already been used too many times.
   (C) He doesn't have items over $50.
   (D) It has expired.

64. What does the woman offer to do?
   (A) Find some other products
   (B) Give him a new card
   (C) Get her manager
   (D) Hold his products at the counter

Network Closures December 1st	
Accounting	10:00 p.m.—11:00 a.m.
Customer Service Call Center	1:00 p.m.— 2:00 p.m.
Human Resources	2:00 p.m.— 3:00 p.m.
Research and Development	3:00 p.m.— 4:00 p.m.

65. What is happening next month?
   (A) An annual software convention
   (B) Their software is being upgraded.
   (C) The software will be sold early.
   (D) The monthly hardware update

NEW

66. Look at the graphic. Which department is on the 2nd floor?
   (A) Accounting
   (B) Human Resources Department
   (C) Research and Development
   (D) Customer Service Call Center

67. What does the man suggest the woman do?
   (A) Call Human Resources
   (B) Call her manager
   (C) Call the sales department
   (D) Call the software company

Airline Mileage Redemption Points

To East Asia	60,000
To North America	80,000
To South America	90,000
To Europe	70,000

68. Why does the woman call?
(A) To cancel a flight
(B) To register a membership
(C) To use her mileage points
(D) To confirm an appointment

NEW
69. Look at the graphic. How many points does the woman currently have?
(A) 20,000 points
(B) 40,000 points
(C) 50,000 points
(D) 70,000 points

70. What does the man ask the woman to tell him?
(A) Her plane ticket
(B) Her membership number
(C) Her cell phone number
(D) Her flight itinerary

GO ON TO THE NEXT PAGE

PART 4 08

Directions: You will hear some talks given by a single speaker. You will be asked to answer three questions about what the speaker says in each talk. Select the best response to each question and mark the letter (A), (B), (C), or (D) on your answer sheet. The talks will not be printed in your test book and will be spoken only one time.

71. Who is the message probably for?

(A) A carpenter
(B) A store manager
(C) A furniture designer
(D) A bank teller

72. According to the speaker, when does he think he lost his wallet?

(A) When he used a dressing room
(B) When he visited a bookstore
(C) When he presented his ID card
(D) When he tried some furniture

73. What does the speaker plan to do?

(A) Replace an item
(B) Call the police
(C) Go to the store again
(D) Stop by the listener's home

74. Who most likely is the speaker?

(A) A historian
(B) An artist
(C) An antiques dealer
(D) A museum guide

75. What is mentioned about the exhibit?

(A) It is sponsored by the Egyptian government.
(B) Most of its artifacts had not been seen by the public.
(C) It will run until the end of the month.
(D) It includes works from modern Egyptian artists.

76. According to the speaker, how can listeners receive more information?

(A) By reading a sign
(B) By searching online
(C) By purchasing a publication
(D) By listening to a presentation

77. What has caused the problem?

(A) A traffic accident
(B) A heavy workload
(C) Bad weather
(D) A vehicle malfunction

78. According to the speaker, around what time will the bus arrive at the destination?

(A) 4:00 p.m.
(B) 5:00 p.m.
(C) 6:00 p.m.
(D) 7:00 p.m.

79. What does the bus provide to passengers?

(A) Free Internet access
(B) A discounted ticket
(C) A complimentary meal
(D) A comfortable connecting bus service

---

80. Who is being introduced?

(A) A chef
(B) A backpacker
(C) A critic
(D) A producer

81. What is the documentary about?

(A) World-famous restaurants
(B) Traditional Chinese cuisine
(C) A celebrity's life
(D) Popular recipe books

82. According to the speaker, what can listeners find on the website?

(A) A review
(B) A menu
(C) A preview
(D) An interview

---

83. What type of products are being discussed?

(A) Computer parts
(B) Hair products
(C) Beauty products
(D) Cell phones

84. According to the speaker, what happened last month?

(A) Sales went down.
(B) A product launch went better than expected.
(C) Their products were featured in a magazine.
(D) Another company took over their contract.

NEW

85. What does the woman mean when she says, "How about that?"

(A) She doesn't understand the situation.
(B) She expected a customer return policy.
(C) She wants to purchase some products.
(D) She is happy with the company's progress.

GO ON TO THE NEXT PAGE

86. According to the speaker, why are changes being made?

(A) Because of poor working condition
(B) To save the company money
(C) So that they can afford a Christmas party
(D) He expected a better contract.

NEW

87. What does the speaker imply when he says, "when the software is installed I don't think you will need any training"?

(A) The new system is easy to learn.
(B) He doesn't want to train people.
(C) There is no budget for training.
(D) Everyone must attend a meeting.

88. What does the speaker tell the listeners they will have to start bringing to work?

(A) Extra uniforms
(B) Other people's lunch
(C) Their own lunch
(D) A new contract

---

89. What position is being advertised?

(A) Legal assistant
(B) Dental assistant
(C) Foreign coordinator
(D) Bank manager

NEW

90. What does the man imply when he asks, "Have you seen the criteria for the dental assistant position?"

(A) He is looking at some forms.
(B) He is asking if Julia is familiar with the requirements.
(C) He needs some extra work done.
(D) He wants to apply for the job.

91. Why does the man want to meet the woman?

(A) To show him the criteria
(B) To make some changes to his office
(C) To sign the contract
(D) To change the criteria

IN-HOUSE DIRECTORY

Extension	Name
10	John Trizz
11	Don Trenton
12	Shubert Mendez
13	Sally Howle

92. Who most likely is the speaker?

(A) A content developer
(B) A secretary
(C) A company manager
(D) A police officer

93. Why most likely is the speaker calling?

(A) To confirm the size of an order
(B) To request some delivery information
(C) To send an extra gift
(D) To purchase a new set of cards

NEW

94. Look at the graphic. What is the planner's extension number?

(A) 10
(B) 11
(C) 12
(D) 13

BEST-SELLING ALBUMS

Rank	Name
1	Talk Down
2	Valleys of Fire
3	Tunnel Vision
4	Step It Up

NEW

95. Look at the graphic. What is the name of the guest's new album?

(A) Valleys of Fire
(B) Step It Up
(C) Tunnel Vision
(D) Talk Down

96. What does the speaker say has influenced the guest's music?

(A) Getting married
(B) Moving to America
(C) Moving to London
(D) Meeting Joey Denton

97. What will the guest most likely do next?

(A) Move back to his hometown
(B) Get engaged to his girlfriend
(C) Release a new album
(D) Get married to his girlfriend

GRANGE RIVER TOWER DIRECTORY

Floor	Name
3rd Floor	Corporate Suites
4th Floor	Rosella Ballroom
5th Floor	Gloria Westwood Ballroom
6th Floor	Main Office

NEW

98. Look at the graphic. Where is the celebration taking place?

(A) 3rd floor
(B) 4th floor
(C) 5th floor
(D) 6th floor

99. What is the reason for the celebration?

(A) To introduce a new employee
(B) Mr. Jang's birthday
(C) The retirement of Mr. Jang
(D) A wedding anniversary

100. Who is Mr. Hopkins?

(A) Mr. Jang's nephew
(B) An employee of Mr. Jang
(C) The owner of the company
(D) A waiter

This is the end of the Listening test.

ACTUAL TEST 03

LISTENING TEST 09

In the Listening test, you will be asked to demonstrate how well you understand spoken English. The entire Listening test will last approximately 45 minutes. There are four parts, and directions are given for each part. You must mark your answers on the separate answer sheet. Do not write your answers in your test book.

PART 1

Directions: For each question in this part, you will hear four statements about a picture in your test book. When you hear the statements, you must select the one statement that best describes what you see in the picture. Then find the number of the question on your answer sheet and mark your answer. The statements will not be printed in your test book and will be spoken only one time.

Example

Sample Answer

Ⓐ ● Ⓒ Ⓓ

Statement (B), "They're looking at the document," is the best description of the picture, so you should select answer (B) and mark it on your answer sheet.

1.

2.

GO ON TO THE NEXT PAGE

3.

4.

5.

6.

GO ON TO THE NEXT PAGE

PART 2 10

Directions: You will hear a question or statement and three responses spoken in English. They will not be printed in your test book and will be spoken only one time. Select the best response to the question or statement and mark the letter (A), (B), or (C) on your answer sheet.

7. Mark your answer on your answer sheet.

8. Mark your answer on your answer sheet.

9. Mark your answer on your answer sheet.

10. Mark your answer on your answer sheet.

11. Mark your answer on your answer sheet.

12. Mark your answer on your answer sheet.

13. Mark your answer on your answer sheet.

14. Mark your answer on your answer sheet.

15. Mark your answer on your answer sheet.

16. Mark your answer on your answer sheet.

17. Mark your answer on your answer sheet.

18. Mark your answer on your answer sheet.

19. Mark your answer on your answer sheet.

20. Mark your answer on your answer sheet.

21. Mark your answer on your answer sheet.

22. Mark your answer on your answer sheet.

23. Mark your answer on your answer sheet.

24. Mark your answer on your answer sheet.

25. Mark your answer on your answer sheet.

26. Mark your answer on your answer sheet.

27. Mark your answer on your answer sheet.

28. Mark your answer on your answer sheet.

29. Mark your answer on your answer sheet.

30. Mark your answer on your answer sheet.

31. Mark your answer on your answer sheet.

PART 3

Directions: You will hear some conversations between two or more people. You will be asked to answer three questions about what the speakers say in each conversation. Select the best response to each question and mark the letter (A), (B), (C), or (D) on your answer sheet. The conversations will not be printed in your test book and will be spoken only one time.

32. Which department does the man most likely work in?
(A) Human Resources
(B) Accounting
(C) Marketing
(D) Technical Support

33. What is the woman unable to do?
(A) Contact a client
(B) Write an email
(C) Access a file
(D) Purchase a laptop computer

34. What does the man suggest doing?
(A) Stopping by his office
(B) Enrolling in a class
(C) Replacing a part
(D) Reading a manual

35. Why is the man calling?
(A) To request a payment
(B) To confirm an order
(C) To offer a room upgrade
(D) To advertise a product

36. What does the woman inquire about?
(A) Difference in price
(B) Valet parking
(C) Local entities
(D) A warranty period

37. What does the woman say she will do?
(A) Pay by credit card
(B) Compare options
(C) Take pictures
(D) Rearrange her schedule

GO ON TO THE NEXT PAGE

38. Why is the man calling?

(A) To cancel an order
(B) To ask for advice
(C) To purchase an air conditioner
(D) To schedule an appointment

39. How long has the man most likely used the air conditioner?

(A) About a day
(B) About a week
(C) About a month
(D) About a year

40. What information does the woman request?

(A) The year of production
(B) Contact information
(C) A model number
(D) The date of purchase

41. What type of event are the speakers discussing?

(A) A fundraiser
(B) A workshop
(C) An anniversary
(D) A music festival

42. What is the woman concerned about?

(A) Reserving tickets
(B) Finding a parking space
(C) Arriving on time
(D) Accommodating more attendees

43. How is the event different from the one held last year?

(A) There will be a family ticket option.
(B) A shuttle bus will be available.
(C) No cameras will be allowed.
(D) A different place will be used.

44. How did the man find out about the yoga class?

(A) From a public posting
(B) From a coworker
(C) From the woman
(D) From a company's website

45. Why can't the woman attend the yoga class?

(A) She hurt her back.
(B) She can't afford the fee.
(C) She has to take care of her children.
(D) She must attend a different class.

46. What will the woman do next month?

(A) Apply for a new job
(B) Watch the man's jazz dance
(C) Appear in a performance
(D) Register for a class

47. Who most likely is the woman?

(A) A customer service representative
(B) A travel agent
(C) A fashion designer
(D) An event coordinator

48. According to the woman, why can't the item be refunded immediately?

(A) A computer system is not working.
(B) A manager is absent.
(C) It has already been sent.
(D) The man is not eligible for a refund.

49. What does the woman say she will do?

(A) Offer a discount
(B) Send an email
(C) Provide a product catalog
(D) Contact a manager

50. Why is it hot inside the office?
(A) The air conditioner was on.
(B) The air conditioner was broken.
(C) There is no air conditioning.
(D) The air conditioner had been off.

51. What is the man's problem with the office?
(A) There is no public transport close by.
(B) The carpet is not clean.
(C) The contract is not signed.
(D) The office is too small.

52. How does the woman respond to the man's problem?
(A) She tells him they are putting in new carpets.
(B) She tells him that the carpets aren't dirty.
(C) She prepares the contract for tomorrow.
(D) She shows him another office.

---

53. What are the speakers discussing?
(A) A real estate deal
(B) The condition of the property
(C) The terms of a contract
(D) Renovating the property

NEW
54. Why does the woman say, "I've had several other offers that are higher than that from other real estate agents"?
(A) To offer a contract
(B) To negotiate a higher price
(C) To settle a deal
(D) To recommend a realtor

55. Why is the woman pleased?
(A) Because she completed her work.
(B) The renovations will go ahead.
(C) She found a new realtor.
(D) The buyer will pay more money.

---

56. Where do the speakers most likely work?
(A) A research facility
(B) A legal firm
(C) A construction company
(D) A pharmacy

NEW
57. What does the man mean when he says, "I've been meaning to visit him"?
(A) He has already visited him.
(B) He knows that he should have visited him.
(C) He will visit him tonight.
(D) He forgot about it.

58. What will the woman include in her email?
(A) When to visit Joseph
(B) The contract details
(C) Joseph's phone number
(D) The lawyer's documents

---

59. What kind of work are the men doing?
(A) Remodeling the foyer
(B) Renovating the bathrooms
(C) Repainting the foyer
(D) Renovating the kitchen

60. What does the man explain to the woman?
(A) Why she has a low budget
(B) Why the price is above her budget
(C) Why the foyer isn't ready to be painted
(D) Why the paint in the foyer is peeling

61. When does the woman want the men to begin work?
(A) The second week of September
(B) Anytime during August
(C) After August
(D) The first Saturday of August

GO ON TO THE NEXT PAGE

Nutrition Information Serving Size: 150 g	
Calories	**200**
Fat	5 grs
Protein	10 grs
Sugar	28 grs

62. What is the woman trying to do?

(A) Gain some weight
(B) Eat foods with more sugar
(C) Skip breakfast
(D) Lose some weight

NEW

63. Look at the graphic. Which content is the woman concerned about?

(A) Fat
(B) Sugar
(C) Protein
(D) Eggs

64. What does the man recommend the woman do?

(A) Have some bacon and eggs
(B) Just drink coffee in the morning
(C) Don't eat breakfast
(D) Have coffee and eggs

Frankie's Dry Cleaning	
Fabric	Price
Polyester	$10
Cotton	$12
Wool	$20
Silk	$30

65. What does the man say he will do on the weekend?

(A) Go on a vacation
(B) Host a business lunch
(C) Go on a business trip
(D) Get some new suits

NEW

66. Look at the graphic. What is the suit made of?

(A) Polyester
(B) Silk
(C) Cotton
(D) Wool

67. What does the woman say she will do?

(A) She won't do it for twenty dollars.
(B) She will charge the man the original price.
(C) She will do it for more than twenty dollars.
(D) She will do it by next week.

Franklin Towers

First floor:	Trinity Construction
Second Floor:	Mullberry & Co.
Third Floor:	Olive Cosmetics
Fourth Floor:	Torrenz Inc.

68. Who most likely are the speakers?

(A) Plumbers
(B) Office workers
(C) Electricians
(D) Carpet cleaners

NEW

69. Look at the graphic. Where is the woman currently working?

(A) Trinity Construction
(B) Mullberry & Co.
(C) Olive Cosmetics
(D) Torrenz Inc.

70. What does the woman ask the man to do?

(A) Install some piping in the wall
(B) Install some cables in the ground
(C) Install some cables in the roof
(D) Install some new software on the computers

GO ON TO THE NEXT PAGE

PART 4 (12)

Directions: You will hear some talks given by a single speaker. You will be asked to answer three questions about what the speaker says in each talk. Select the best response to each question and mark the letter (A), (B), (C), or (D) on your answer sheet. The talks will not be printed in your test book and will be spoken only one time.

71. Why is the speaker calling?

(A) To order food delivery
(B) To advertise a cooking class
(C) To report a problem
(D) To make a reservation

72. What will the speaker celebrate next week?

(A) A birthday
(B) A promotion
(C) A retirement
(D) A wedding

73. What does the speaker want the listener to do?

(A) Contact some guests
(B) Decorate a space
(C) Meet special dietary needs
(D) Prepare an estimate

74. What does the factory produce?

(A) Appliances
(B) Clothes
(C) Toys
(D) Shoes

75. What is special about the factory?

(A) Its size
(B) Its production method
(C) Its automated machines
(D) Its location

76. What will listeners do at the end of the tour?

(A) Participate in a hands-on experience
(B) Receive a free product
(C) Have refreshments
(D) Return to the tour bus

77. What will happen next week?

(A) A budget proposal
(B) A business event
(C) A performance evaluation
(D) A shareholders' meeting

78. What benefit does the speaker mention?

(A) Fewer complaints
(B) Reduced travel time
(C) Access to clients
(D) Strengthened security

79. What are the listeners asked to do?

(A) Delete unnecessary data
(B) Submit a report
(C) Contact clients directly
(D) Email an order confirmation

---

80. Who most likely are the listeners?

(A) Professional novelists
(B) University professors
(C) Potential writers
(D) Prospective clients

81. What are the listeners asked to do?

(A) Fill out a questionnaire
(B) Attach a name tag
(C) Introduce themselves
(D) Read a book

82. Who is Natasha Marsh?

(A) An athlete
(B) A children's author
(C) An event organizer
(D) A guest speaker

---

83. According to the speaker, what is happening?

(A) A new product is being released.
(B) The store is closing down.
(C) Their staff are all quitting.
(D) The company is shooting a commercial.

NEW

84. What does the speaker mean when she says, "you'd think they were giving the shoes away"?

(A) The store is giving the shoes away.
(B) There are a lot of people waiting to buy the product.
(C) They ran out of stock.
(D) A few people were upset about the product.

85. According to the speaker, what is WingTip offering the first 100 customers?

(A) 10% discount
(B) A new pair of headphones
(C) Free shoes
(D) Special edition shoes

GO ON TO THE NEXT PAGE

86. According to the speaker, how can we see the value of Mr. Hardwell's work?

(A) By looking at all the paintings on his walls
(B) By looking at all the pictures on his walls
(C) By looking at all the fan mail in his office
(D) By looking at all the special awards on his desk

NEW
87. Why does the speaker say, "I think it's safe to say Mr. Hardwell should leave some room on his walls"?

(A) To discuss another issue
(B) To suggest he is going to continue doing more work
(C) To recommend a friend to him
(D) To make sure the audience is familiar with him

88. What will Mr. Hardwell do today?

(A) Share some of his business knowledge
(B) Preview the book and show some video
(C) Read some excerpts from his book
(D) Read a chapter from his book

---

89. Where does the speaker most likely work?

(A) In a law office
(B) In a fashion company
(C) In an airline company
(D) In an accounting firm

NEW
90. Why does the speaker say, "I was out of town on a business trip"?

(A) To explain why she hadn't called
(B) To arrange an appointment
(C) To sign the contract
(D) To discuss the building plan

91. What does the speaker offer to the woman?

(A) A free plane ticket
(B) Another portfolio
(C) A deposit for rent
(D) A possible contract

Order Form 5521673 Customer: Winbox Computers	
Item	**Quantity**
Cold meat tray	3
Mixed salad plates	5
12 pack bread rolls	2
Cutlery sets	10

92. What type of event is being catered?

(A) A business dinner
(B) A business luncheon
(C) A corporate breakfast
(D) An annual picnic

NEW
93. Look at the graphic. Which items were not changed?

(A) Cold meat trays and mixed salad plates
(B) 12 pack bread rolls
(C) Cutlery sets
(D) Cutlery sets and bread rolls

94. What is the listener asked to do?

(A) Send an email confirmation
(B) Call the man to confirm the changes
(C) Not to change the order
(D) Cancel the whole order

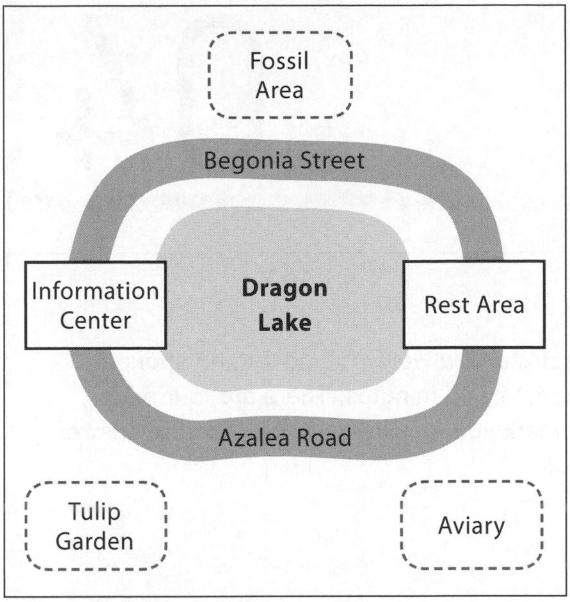

95. Who most likely is the speaker?
(A) President of the Maryland Florist Association
(B) President of the annual florist convention
(C) President of Tulip Garden
(D) President of the rest area

NEW
96. Look at the graphic. Where will the listeners go first?
(A) The Aviary
(B) Begonia Street
(C) Dragon Lake
(D) Azalea Road

97. What does the speaker encourage listeners to do before they leave?
(A) Visit the Tulip Garden
(B) Buy some flowers
(C) Pick some roses
(D) Visit the Aviary

HEIRLOOM TOMATOES!
Prices are per pound~

Black Cherry	$1.09
Brandywine	$1.39
Black Krim	$2.64
Amana Orange	$1.30

98. When will the special sale be over?
(A) Monday
(B) Saturday
(C) Sunday
(D) It is weekly.

99. What is indicated about Granville Produce?
(A) They have a wide variety of potatoes.
(B) They highlight their heirloom tomatoes.
(C) They are an inexpensive grocer.
(D) They have been in business for several years.

NEW
100. Look at the graphic. Why is the Brandywine such a good deal?
(A) It is cheaper than the Black Krim.
(B) It is a delicious tomato.
(C) It is normally over a dollar more expensive per pound.
(D) It is normally not in season.

This is the end of the Listening test.

ACTUAL TEST 04

LISTENING TEST 13

In the Listening test, you will be asked to demonstrate how well you understand spoken English. The entire Listening test will last approximately 45 minutes. There are four parts, and directions are given for each part. You must mark your answers on the separate answer sheet. Do not write your answers in your test book.

PART 1

Directions: For each question in this part, you will hear four statements about a picture in your test book. When you hear the statements, you must select the one statement that best describes what you see in the picture. Then find the number of the question on your answer sheet and mark your answer. The statements will not be printed in your test book and will be spoken only one time.

Example

Sample Answer

Ⓐ ● Ⓒ Ⓓ

Statement (B), "They're looking at the document," is the best description of the picture, so you should select answer (B) and mark it on your answer sheet.

1.

2.

ACTUAL TEST 04

GO ON TO THE NEXT PAGE

3.

4.

5.

6.

GO ON TO THE NEXT PAGE

PART 2 14

Directions: You will hear a question or statement and three responses spoken in English. They will not be printed in your test book and will be spoken only one time. Select the best response to the question or statement and mark the letter (A), (B), or (C) on your answer sheet.

7. Mark your answer on your answer sheet.

8. Mark your answer on your answer sheet.

9. Mark your answer on your answer sheet.

10. Mark your answer on your answer sheet.

11. Mark your answer on your answer sheet.

12. Mark your answer on your answer sheet.

13. Mark your answer on your answer sheet.

14. Mark your answer on your answer sheet.

15. Mark your answer on your answer sheet.

16. Mark your answer on your answer sheet.

17. Mark your answer on your answer sheet.

18. Mark your answer on your answer sheet.

19. Mark your answer on your answer sheet.

20. Mark your answer on your answer sheet.

21. Mark your answer on your answer sheet.

22. Mark your answer on your answer sheet.

23. Mark your answer on your answer sheet.

24. Mark your answer on your answer sheet.

25. Mark your answer on your answer sheet.

26. Mark your answer on your answer sheet.

27. Mark your answer on your answer sheet.

28. Mark your answer on your answer sheet.

29. Mark your answer on your answer sheet.

30. Mark your answer on your answer sheet.

31. Mark your answer on your answer sheet.

PART 3 15

Directions: You will hear some conversations between two or more people. You will be asked to answer three questions about what the speakers say in each conversation. Select the best response to each question and mark the letter (A), (B), (C), or (D) on your answer sheet. The conversations will not be printed in your test book and will be spoken only one time.

32. What did the man recently do?

(A) Purchased a house
(B) Went on a business trip
(C) Signed up for a service
(D) Installed a television

33. Why must the man pay a fee?

(A) He wants to change his schedule.
(B) He returned an item late.
(C) He lost his membership card.
(D) He needs an additional service.

34. What will the woman include in an email?

(A) A receipt
(B) Log-in information
(C) A membership contract
(D) Driving directions

35. What does the woman say caused the problem?

(A) A repair cost has increased.
(B) A reservation has been canceled.
(C) A client arrived too late.
(D) A tire needed to be replaced.

36. Why is the man concerned?

(A) He lost an important receipt.
(B) He needs a car to greet a client.
(C) He has to reschedule a meeting.
(D) He was unable to contact a client.

37. What does the woman suggest?

(A) Preparing an alternative plan
(B) Ordering a replacement part
(C) Attending a conference
(D) Reserving a less expensive ticket

GO ON TO THE NEXT PAGE

38. What problem is the woman reporting?
(A) An accounting error has been made.
(B) A printer is out of order.
(C) Some office supplies have run out.
(D) A document has been lost.

39. What does the man ask the woman to do?
(A) Check some product information
(B) Install new equipment
(C) Update customer information
(D) Stop by his office

40. What is mentioned about Mr. Hills?
(A) He is in charge of a new project.
(B) He is in the same department as the woman.
(C) He has recently ordered a new item.
(D) He wrote a hardware list.

41. How did the man learn about the store?
(A) By watching television
(B) By talking to a friend
(C) By reading a brochure
(D) By listening to the radio

42. According to the woman, what is being offered this month?
(A) A discount coupon
(B) A reduced membership fee
(C) Free delivery
(D) A lifetime warranty

43. What does the woman suggest doing?
(A) Paying in advance
(B) Getting measurements taken
(C) Submitting a proposal
(D) Hiring an assistant

44. What kind of services are the speakers discussing?
(A) Catering for company events
(B) Business consultation
(C) Workforce training
(D) Delivery services

45. Why has the man NOT used Rose and Lily Co.'s services before?
(A) He was unaware of them.
(B) He was reluctant to pay a membership fee.
(C) He was on bad terms with the owner.
(D) He did not realize their availability.

46. What does the man ask the woman to do?
(A) Try some food and beverages
(B) Send a catalog
(C) Provide a sample
(D) Expedite an order

47. What does the woman say she has heard about?
(A) The joining of two businesses
(B) The construction of a factory
(C) An international conference
(D) A highway expansion project

48. What benefit does the man mention?
(A) Lower insurance costs
(B) Increased vacation days
(C) International competitiveness
(D) Updated equipment

49. What does the man suggest the woman do?
(A) Visit his office
(B) Post an advertisement
(C) Submit a proposal
(D) Check job listings

50. What is the reason for Joseph's call?

(A) To relate a problem concerning the apartment
(B) To sign the contract for the apartment
(C) To discuss another apartment
(D) To discuss the price of rent

51. What does Joseph say about the Kahlua Apartment?

(A) It's ready to be occupied anytime.
(B) There are renovations occurring.
(C) It is near a new fitness center.
(D) There is a major pest problem.

52. What does Joseph offer to do?

(A) Find a new apartment at Graceville Towers
(B) Arrange all of the moving
(C) Move her furniture personally
(D) Move into the Kahlua Apartment building

---

53. Why is the woman calling the man?

(A) To ask a favor of him
(B) To order some flowers
(C) To find a rental property
(D) To rent a house

54. What does the woman say she has done recently?

(A) Been promoted at her company
(B) Closed down her business
(C) Got a new job
(D) Opened her own business

NEW

55. Why does the man say, "What's your afternoon like"?

(A) To figure out when they can meet
(B) To ask her to dinner
(C) To explain rental conditions
(D) To get some keys for the office

---

56. What did the company do recently?

(A) Renovated the lobby
(B) Built new research facilities
(C) Hired new staff
(D) Built new offices

NEW

57. What does the woman mean when she says, "it's about time"?

(A) She thinks the company deserves to have new offices.
(B) She thinks construction has taken too long.
(C) She doesn't like the new offices.
(D) She wants a raise in her salary.

58. What does the woman imply about the company?

(A) They have been very lucky to grow so fast.
(B) Some of the staff is not working hard.
(C) The company worked hard to grow fast.
(D) The new offices aren't very nice.

---

59. What are the speakers mainly discussing?

(A) Getting ready for a work party
(B) Getting the sales report ready
(C) Getting ready for a promotion
(D) Getting ready to finish the quarter

60. What does the man say about Andrew?

(A) That he left work early the night before
(B) That he thinks Andrew isn't a hard worker
(C) That he worked late the night before
(D) That he had a good quarter

61. What does Roger tell Andrew to do?

(A) Send a letter to Roger when he is finished
(B) Bring the email to the meeting
(C) Not to come to the meeting
(D) Send an email when he is finished

GO ON TO THE NEXT PAGE →

Part A — 90 mm Bolts

Part B — 25 mm Wood Screws

Part C — Barrel Nuts x 6

Part D — Long Allen Key x 1

62. Where does the man most likely work?

(A) At a university
(B) At a furniture store
(C) At a bedding store
(D) At a technical college

63. Look at the graphic. What is the woman missing?

(A) 90 mm Bolts
(B) Wood Screws
(C) Barrel Nuts
(D) Allen Key

64. What does the man offer to do?

(A) Deliver the parts to her house by post
(B) Deliver the parts to her house in person
(C) Have the parts delivered by his staff
(D) Leave the parts at the front counter

Bridge closed until
Jan. 12 due to upgrade of
infrastructure

65. According to the woman, what is causing people to arrive late to work?

(A) A meeting was postponed.
(B) The bridge was very busy.
(C) The bridge was closed.
(D) They had car problems.

66. Look at the graphic. Where is the sign most likely located?

(A) The Brooklyn Bridge
(B) The Tower Bridge
(C) The East Bay Tunnel
(D) The Express Tunnel

67. What does the woman recommend to the man?

(A) Take the bus to work
(B) Share a taxi to work
(C) Take the subway to work
(D) Take the Express Tunnel

Fisherman's Wharf
Discount Coupon

10% off any order above $100

Expires November 1st

68. Where most likely are the speakers?

(A) In a hospital
(B) In a restaurant
(C) In a bar
(D) In a hotel

NEW

69. Look at the graphic. Why is the coupon rejected?

(A) The order was above $100.
(B) It is expired.
(C) Their order was below $100.
(D) The coupon didn't have credit on it.

70. What does the woman offer to do?

(A) Give them a new card
(B) Put the coupon in the computer system
(C) Hold the card for them
(D) Provide a refund

GO ON TO THE NEXT PAGE

PART 4 16

Directions: You will hear some talks given by a single speaker. You will be asked to answer three questions about what the speaker says in each talk. Select the best response to each question and mark the letter (A), (B), (C), or (D) on your answer sheet. The talks will not be printed in your test book and will be spoken only one time.

71. What is causing the delay?

(A) Bad weather
(B) A canceled flight
(C) A scheduling error
(D) A technical difficulty

72. According to the speaker, after how long will the presentation begin?

(A) 5 minutes
(B) 30 minutes
(C) 45 minutes
(D) 60 minutes

73. What will happen when it's time for the presentation to begin?

(A) An announcement will be made.
(B) Lighting will be adjusted.
(C) A keynote speaker will appear on the stage.
(D) Refreshments will be served.

74. What is the radio broadcast about?

(A) The opening of a pet store
(B) A newly introduced law
(C) A new council hall
(D) An upcoming election

75. According to the speaker, what did Tim Kellerman do recently?

(A) He ran for office.
(B) He won an award.
(C) He selected a pet.
(D) He paid a fine.

76. What will listeners most likely hear next?

(A) A weather forecast
(B) Some breaking news
(C) Community members' opinions
(D) A telephone interview

77. Where should listeners get carts?
(A) In the parking lot
(B) At the entrance
(C) Near the lobby
(D) From a cashier

78. According to the speaker, who is wearing green vests?
(A) Cashiers
(B) Store managers
(C) Additional staff
(D) Parking lot attendants

79. What will the speaker most likely do at the end of the day?
(A) Announce winners
(B) Collect donations
(C) Give a demonstration
(D) Purchase an item

---

80. What business is being advertised?
(A) A computer retailer
(B) An electronics repair shop
(C) An office supply store
(D) A cosmetics store

81. What service is available in April?
(A) Installment payments
(B) Express shipping
(C) Online assistance
(D) Free installation

82. How can listeners get a discount?
(A) By bringing a coupon
(B) By buying in bulk
(C) By becoming a regular customer
(D) By signing up for a newsletter

---

83. According to the speaker, why are changes being made?
(A) The government took the company to court
(B) To conform to government regulations
(C) To enact a new labor law
(D) To arrange lower-paying contracts

NEW
84. What does the speaker imply when she says, "it's a very simple device; you just attach it to your work belt and it will do the rest, so you won't need any training with that"?
(A) The new system requires no training.
(B) She doesn't like the new system.
(C) There is no budget for staff uniforms.
(D) Everyone needs training.

85. What does the speaker tell the listeners they will have to start bringing to work?
(A) Extra pairs of work pants
(B) Other people's helmets
(C) Their own boots and helmets
(D) A new financial plan

GO ON TO THE NEXT PAGE

86. According to the man, what did the company recently do?

(A) Began operating out of Beijing
(B) Began operating in India
(C) Hired some new designers
(D) Created some special dishes

87. What most likely will the Xinhua Fashion magazine do next Thursday?

(A) Interview the models
(B) Make a video of the street outside
(C) Photograph clothing
(D) Sign a new contract

NEW

88. What does the man mean when he says, "our success is going to skyrocket"?

(A) Their business is going to grow quickly
(B) They will discuss the future plan
(C) They will prevent the photo shoot
(D) They will transfer some documents via mail

---

89. According to the speaker, who is introducing the new regulations?

(A) The Board of Directors
(B) Head Office
(C) Management
(D) The secretary

NEW

90. What does the speaker imply when she says, "we really need to stay on top of this, or some people might get fired"?

(A) There is a lot of work to do.
(B) It isn't that important.
(C) They can wait a week to start.
(D) The project will begin soon.

91. What does the speaker tell the listeners to do?

(A) Bring their lunch to work
(B) Occasionally work on Saturdays
(C) Work every Sunday
(D) Have some time off on Saturday

This Weekend's Events in Columbia

Afternoon Theater
Columbia's own theater troupe stages short versions of classic plays for free in Central Park every Thursday at noon.

Friday Night Concert in the Park Series
The show begins at 8:30 P.M. and lasts until 10:30 P.M.!

Midnight Wine Tasting
Regional wines sampled under the stars at the Black Cat, every Friday and Saturday night!

Appropriate for all ages!

92. What kind of transportation company is Continental Lines?

(A) Bus
(B) Train
(C) Limousine
(D) Taxi

93. What is the last stop for Continental Lines this trip?

(A) Charleston
(B) Columbia
(C) Eastport
(D) Chesterville

NEW

94. Look at the graphic. What activity will still be available for the passengers to participate in when they arrive in Columbia?

(A) None
(B) Friday Night Concert in the Park
(C) Afternoon Theater
(D) Midnight Wine Tasting

Customer Service FAQ Analysis

Disputed Long Distance/Overcharges	37%
Disputed Data Charges	36%
Service Plan Change	11%
Dropped Calls	9%
Replacement Phones	5%
Miscellaneous	2%

95. What is indicated about Monster Telecom?

(A) They are having customer service problems.
(B) There are too many calls for the number of employees.
(C) Customer service is not important to them.
(D) They need to hire more people.

NEW

96. Look at the graphic. What areas should the leaders focus their training on?

(A) How to deal with upset customers by overcharges
(B) Knowledge of all of the service plans
(C) Helping customers replace phones
(D) Knowledge of Monster Telecom's cellular coverage area

97. What is the goal for Monster Telecom?

(A) Reduce the number of dropped calls
(B) Expand their coverage area
(C) Add new cellular phone options
(D) Reduce the number of customer calls they receive by 50%

LAP POOL SIGN-UP SHEET

LANE	9:00 a.m.	10:00 a.m.	11:00 a.m.	12:00 p.m.	1:00 p.m.	2:00 p.m.	3:00 p.m.	4:00 p.m.	5:00 p.m.
1									
2									
3									

98. What is indicated about Springdale Fitness Club?

(A) They have a tennis court.
(B) They take pride in their customer service.
(C) They specialize in children's pool parties.
(D) They have a variety of swimming facilities.

NEW

99. Look at the graphic. What are the hours of the lap pool?

(A) 8 a.m. to 5 p.m.
(B) 9 a.m. to 5 p.m.
(C) 9 a.m. to 6 p.m.
(D) 8 a.m. to 6 p.m.

100. What does Springdale Fitness Club say about the new lap pool?

(A) It is Olympic size.
(B) It has four lanes.
(C) It's for serious swimmers.
(D) It will host weekly races.

This is the end of the Listening test.

ACTUAL TEST 05

LISTENING TEST 17

In the Listening test, you will be asked to demonstrate how well you understand spoken English. The entire Listening test will last approximately 45 minutes. There are four parts, and directions are given for each part. You must mark your answers on the separate answer sheet. Do not write your answers in your test book.

PART 1

Directions: For each question in this part, you will hear four statements about a picture in your test book. When you hear the statements, you must select the one statement that best describes what you see in the picture. Then find the number of the question on your answer sheet and mark your answer. The statements will not be printed in your test book and will be spoken only one time.

Example

Sample Answer

Ⓐ ● Ⓒ Ⓓ

Statement (B), "They're looking at the document," is the best description of the picture, so you should select answer (B) and mark it on your answer sheet.

1.

2.

GO ON TO THE NEXT PAGE

3.

4.

5.

6.

PART 2 18

Directions: You will hear a question or statement and three responses spoken in English. They will not be printed in your test book and will be spoken only one time. Select the best response to the question or statement and mark the letter (A), (B), or (C) on your answer sheet.

7. Mark your answer on your answer sheet.

8. Mark your answer on your answer sheet.

9. Mark your answer on your answer sheet.

10. Mark your answer on your answer sheet.

11. Mark your answer on your answer sheet.

12. Mark your answer on your answer sheet.

13. Mark your answer on your answer sheet.

14. Mark your answer on your answer sheet.

15. Mark your answer on your answer sheet.

16. Mark your answer on your answer sheet.

17. Mark your answer on your answer sheet.

18. Mark your answer on your answer sheet.

19. Mark your answer on your answer sheet.

20. Mark your answer on your answer sheet.

21. Mark your answer on your answer sheet.

22. Mark your answer on your answer sheet.

23. Mark your answer on your answer sheet.

24. Mark your answer on your answer sheet.

25. Mark your answer on your answer sheet.

26. Mark your answer on your answer sheet.

27. Mark your answer on your answer sheet.

28. Mark your answer on your answer sheet.

29. Mark your answer on your answer sheet.

30. Mark your answer on your answer sheet.

31. Mark your answer on your answer sheet.

PART 3 (19)

Directions: You will hear some conversations between two or more people. You will be asked to answer three questions about what the speakers say in each conversation. Select the best response to each question and mark the letter (A), (B), (C), or (D) on your answer sheet. The conversations will not be printed in your test book and will be spoken only one time.

32. What is the woman's problem?

(A) A meeting room is occupied.
(B) A piece of equipment is out of stock.
(C) An appointment has been canceled.
(D) Some software is not installed.

33. Why does the man mention a system malfunction?

(A) To apologize for an incorrect charge
(B) To explain a scheduling error
(C) To warn of security threats
(D) To change a company policy

34. What does the man say he will do?

(A) Fix a computer
(B) Provide an alternative
(C) Attend a meeting
(D) Check the employee manual

35. What does the woman ask the man about?

(A) How to write a report
(B) Whether a document is finished
(C) How to reserve a meeting room
(D) Whether a client has been contacted

36. What does the man say he will do?

(A) Prioritize the woman's request
(B) Extend a deadline
(C) Draft a budget
(D) Visit the woman's office

37. What does the woman need?

(A) A list of clients
(B) A sample product
(C) Meeting materials
(D) A revised itinerary

GO ON TO THE NEXT PAGE

38. What career is the woman interested in?

(A) College professor
(B) Web programmer
(C) Dental assistant
(D) Financial adviser

39. What does the woman say she will do?

(A) Submit an application
(B) Inquire about a loan
(C) Consult a doctor
(D) Apply for a scholarship

40. According to the man, what advantage does the college offer?

(A) Convenient class times
(B) Small class sizes
(C) Advanced level courses
(D) Reduced tuition

---

41. Where most likely do the speakers work?

(A) At a software company
(B) At a marketing firm
(C) At a travel agency
(D) At a graphic design company

42. What is the woman's complaint about the training session?

(A) There were not enough seats.
(B) The registration fee was too high.
(C) There was no time for inquiries.
(D) The instructor's presentation was lengthy.

43. What does the man suggest?

(A) Attending another training session
(B) Transferring to a new department
(C) Reviewing a training manual
(D) Contacting the instructor

---

44. What is the topic of the conversation?

(A) A pay raise
(B) An upcoming deadline
(C) A prescription for the flu
(D) A new work procedure

45. What does the woman ask about?

(A) Pay compensation
(B) Promotion opportunities
(C) Sick leave availability
(D) Official forms

46. What will the man most likely do next?

(A) Send an email
(B) Revise a budget
(C) Deliver a document
(D) Call a doctor

---

47. Where most likely does the man work?

(A) At a real estate agency
(B) At a bank
(C) At an art gallery
(D) At a landscaping agency

48. How long does the man say the woman will have to wait?

(A) For a day
(B) For a week
(C) For a month
(D) For two months

49. What information will the man send the woman?

(A) A job opening
(B) An itinerary
(C) A price quote
(D) A meeting agenda

---

50. What does the man ask about?

(A) A lunch meeting location
(B) The schedule for the week
(C) The budget reports
(D) A client list

51. What does the woman remind the man about?

(A) A dinner meeting
(B) A restaurant reservation
(C) A presentation
(D) A client's demands

52. What does the woman offer to do?

(A) Meet with a colleague
(B) Talk to a client
(C) Call some coworkers
(D) Organize the reports

---

53. What is the problem?

(A) The man forgot to book his plane ticket.
(B) The flight is delayed.
(C) The flight is canceled.
(D) The man lost his ticket.

54. What solution does the woman propose?

(A) To book a bus for the man
(B) To pay for his hotel room
(C) To send him documents
(D) To call his client in Vancouver

NEW

55. What does the man mean when he says, "that's not a bad idea"?

(A) He wants a better solution.
(B) He agrees with the proposed solution.
(C) He would like to hear more options.
(D) He wants to keep the plane ticket.

---

56. What was the woman doing in New York?

(A) Taking a vacation
(B) Visiting family
(C) Looking for new staff
(D) Meeting clients

NEW

57. What does the woman imply when she says, "are they real"?

(A) The flowers look really bad.
(B) The flowers look fake.
(C) She is surprised to see them.
(D) She thinks they are real.

58. What does the man offer to do?

(A) Give her a promotion
(B) Send her a gift card
(C) Have flowers delivered to her office
(D) Send her to New York

---

59. Why is the man calling Jennifer?

(A) To ask about her vacation
(B) To transfer her to another department
(C) To ask about a money transfer
(D) To talk to Mr. Woods

60. What does Grace say about the bank?

(A) They were closed when she got there.
(B) They are having problems with their computers.
(C) She emailed the receipt.
(D) She couldn't find the location.

61. What does the man say he needs?

(A) The transfer receipt
(B) The bank check
(C) The company credit card
(D) The transfer system

GO ON TO THE NEXT PAGE

Subway Closures September 24th	
Line 2	6:00 a.m.—10:00 a.m.
Line 4	10:00 a.m.—11:00 a.m.
Line 6	11:00 a.m.—12:00 p.m.
Line 7	1:00 p.m.—2:00 p.m.

62. Why is the subway being closed on September 24th?

(A) To upgrade the audio system
(B) Because the drivers are striking
(C) There is a safety issue
(D) Problems with the air conditioner

NEW
63. Look at the graphic. Which subway line do the speakers need to take?

(A) Line 6
(B) Line 7
(C) Line 2
(D) Line 4

64. What does the man suggest doing?

(A) Taking the subway
(B) Using the taxi service
(C) Taking the bus
(D) Driving his car

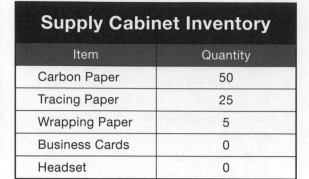

Supply Cabinet Inventory

Item	Quantity
Carbon Paper	50
Tracing Paper	25
Wrapping Paper	5
Business Cards	0
Headset	0

65. Why do they need to send the order today?

(A) Because the company is closing for Christmas
(B) Because the company is closing for New Years
(C) The company doesn't have the item.
(D) They have delayed the order.

NEW
66. Look at the graphic. What will the man NOT order for the woman?

(A) Wrapping paper
(B) A headset
(C) Business cards
(D) Carbon paper

67. What does the woman ask the man to do?

(A) Send her the order form
(B) Send her a headset
(C) Revise the memo
(D) Send a receipt

Nutrition Information Serving Size: 150 g	
Calories	**173**
Fat	5 g
Protein	10 g
Sugar	22 g
Sodium	60 mg
Caffeine	80 mg

68. Why is the man looking for a certain product?

(A) He is on a diet.
(B) He doesn't like sugar.
(C) He will compete in a race.
(D) He has a test soon.

NEW

69. Look at the graphic. Which of the ingredients is the man interested in?

(A) Fat
(B) Sugar
(C) Caffeine
(D) Protein

70. What does the woman suggest the man do?

(A) Drink a lot of caffeine before taking the gel
(B) Don't drink a lot of caffeine before taking the gel
(C) Drink some caffeine before bed
(D) Drink some caffeine in the morning

GO ON TO THE NEXT PAGE

PART 4 (20)

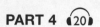

Directions: You will hear some talks given by a single speaker. You will be asked to answer three questions about what the speaker says in each talk. Select the best response to each question and mark the letter (A), (B), (C), or (D) on your answer sheet. The talks will not be printed in your test book and will be spoken only one time.

71. Where does the speaker work?

(A) At a retail store
(B) At a bank
(C) At a gift shop
(D) At a shipping company

72. What does the speaker apologize for?

(A) A delivery mistake
(B) An incorrect charge
(C) A scheduling error
(D) A defective product

73. What does the speaker ask the listener to do?

(A) Return a call
(B) Renew his credit card
(C) Get rid of the recently delivered card
(D) Sign an application form

74. Where is the announcement being made?

(A) In a subway station
(B) In a conference hall
(C) In a shopping mall
(D) In a baggage claim area

75. What are the listeners asked to do?

(A) Proceed to the checkout immediately
(B) Register for a workshop
(C) Search for a missing item
(D) Visit a different location

76. Why should Ms. Goya go to the front desk?

(A) To pay a membership fee
(B) To recover a lost item
(C) To receive a voucher
(D) To return an item

77. What business created the message?

(A) A glassware factory
(B) A pharmacy
(C) An eyeglasses store
(D) An insurance company

78. According to the speaker, what service does the business offer?

(A) Free eye examinations
(B) Online purchases
(C) Special discounts for regular customers
(D) Free delivery on large orders

79. Why would listeners press 2?

(A) To cancel an order
(B) To change delivery information
(C) To schedule an appointment
(D) To leave a message

---

80. What special feature of the new laptop does the speaker mention?

(A) It is the lightest in the market.
(B) It has a built-in high-definition camera.
(C) It is water resistant.
(D) It is convenient to carry.

81. How can customers purchase the new laptop?

(A) By accessing a website
(B) By stopping by the speaker's office
(C) By visiting a local store
(D) By calling a customer service hotline

82. What can customers receive this week?

(A) An additional battery
(B) A carrying case
(C) A portable speaker
(D) A small printer

---

83. What is the reason for the meeting?

(A) To announce a new partnership
(B) To introduce a new manager
(C) To propose a budget plan
(D) To announce her retirement

NEW

84. What does the woman imply when she says, "and why wouldn't we"?

(A) To suggest the partnership is good
(B) To review some materials
(C) To recommend a new method
(D) To offer a training program

85. What does the woman suggest the studio staff do?

(A) Go on vacation
(B) Continue using the old equipment
(C) Produce a movie
(D) Study the new equipment

---

86. What problem does the speaker mention?

(A) A shipment was missed.
(B) The order was wrong.
(C) The center will have no hot water.
(D) There will be no water.

NEW

87. What does the speaker imply when he says, "you might want to hold off until later"?

(A) Members of the center should come in the afternoon.
(B) Members of the center shouldn't come.
(C) There will be a meeting in the morning.
(D) The center is closed in the afternoon.

88. What does the speaker say he will do?

(A) Send a text message
(B) Send an email
(C) Make a phone call
(D) Post a letter

GO ON TO THE NEXT PAGE

89. Where does the speaker work?

(A) At a market
(B) At a clinic
(C) At a restaurant
(D) At a factory

90. What problem does the speaker describe?

(A) Extra items were delivered.
(B) The delivery is late.
(C) The business was closed.
(D) There is a special event planned.

NEW

91. What does the woman mean when she says, "I have to finish the kitchen inventory by 11 a.m."?

(A) She would like a response soon.
(B) She doesn't need to know soon.
(C) She needs some help with the new menu.
(D) They have the right ingredients.

Training Schedule

Monday	Tuesday	Wednesday	Thursday
Meet and greet	Machine training	Machine training	Machine training
Factory tour			Lunch meeting with president

92. What are the listeners training to be?

(A) Airline attendants
(B) Military soldiers
(C) Assembly line workers
(D) Computer programmers

93. According to the speaker, what will the listeners enjoy doing?

(A) Learning their job
(B) Assembling products
(C) Producing quality materials
(D) Going to company events

NEW

94. Look at the graphic. On what day will the listeners meet with the company president?

(A) Monday
(B) Tuesday
(C) Wednesday
(D) Thursday

FOCUS GROUP QUESTIONAIRE RESULTS:
Majority respondents selected the following

Alright Ales New Styles	Do you like the label?	Do you like the flavor?	Would you choose this again?	Would you recommend this beer?
Dark Ale	Yes	No	Maybe	Maybe
Red Ale	No	Yes	Yes	Yes
Belgium Style	Yes	No	No	No
Wheat Ale	Yes	Yes	Yes	Yes

Zone 1 — Board Games and Video Games
Zone 2 — Action Figures and Dolls
Zone 3 — Sports Equipment
Zone 4 — Learning and Education Games

Toy List
Z1 Laughing Logs, **Z2** Macho Man, **Z2** Lovely Lady, **Z3** Soccer Ball, **Z3** Golf Clubs, **Z4** Animal ID, **Z1** Business Tycoon, **Z1** Fighting Forces.

95. Why is Alright Ales worried?
(A) They have a new competitor.
(B) They are nervous about their new beers.
(C) They are not in the top 5 of the market share in Northcut.
(D) They will have to cut staff.

96. What will the company likely do with the results of the survey?
(A) Change the label of the Red Ale
(B) Work on the Belgium Style
(C) Begin marketing the chosen beers
(D) Start working on a new style of beer

NEW
97. Look at the graphic. What beer is least likely to be part of Alright Ales' new product line?
(A) Wheat Ale
(B) Dark Ale
(C) Red Ale
(D) Belgium Style

98. What is indicated at the orientation?
(A) Big Toys will be a boring job.
(B) Big Toys has a large selection of products.
(C) Their inventory system is confusing.
(D) The managers will be very critical of mistakes.

NEW
99. Look at the graphic. Where will the trainees spend most of their time during the training exercise?
(A) Zone 1
(B) Zone 2
(C) Zone 3
(D) Zone 4

100. How quickly should the trainees complete their exercise?
(A) 2 hours
(B) 45 minutes or less
(C) 1.5 hours
(D) 1 hour or less

This is the end of the Listening test.

ACTUAL TEST 06

LISTENING TEST 21

In the Listening test, you will be asked to demonstrate how well you understand spoken English. The entire Listening test will last approximately 45 minutes. There are four parts, and directions are given for each part. You must mark your answers on the separate answer sheet. Do not write your answers in your test book.

PART 1

Directions: For each question in this part, you will hear four statements about a picture in your test book. When you hear the statements, you must select the one statement that best describes what you see in the picture. Then find the number of the question on your answer sheet and mark your answer. The statements will not be printed in your test book and will be spoken only one time.

Sample Answer

Example

Ⓐ ● Ⓒ Ⓓ

Statement (B), "They're looking at the document," is the best description of the picture, so you should select answer (B) and mark it on your answer sheet.

1.

2.

GO ON TO THE NEXT PAGE

3.

4.

5.

6.

GO ON TO THE NEXT PAGE

PART 2 22

Directions: You will hear a question or statement and three responses spoken in English. They will not be printed in your test book and will be spoken only one time. Select the best response to the question or statement and mark the letter (A), (B), or (C) on your answer sheet.

7. Mark your answer on your answer sheet.

8. Mark your answer on your answer sheet.

9. Mark your answer on your answer sheet.

10. Mark your answer on your answer sheet.

11. Mark your answer on your answer sheet.

12. Mark your answer on your answer sheet.

13. Mark your answer on your answer sheet.

14. Mark your answer on your answer sheet.

15. Mark your answer on your answer sheet.

16. Mark your answer on your answer sheet.

17. Mark your answer on your answer sheet.

18. Mark your answer on your answer sheet.

19. Mark your answer on your answer sheet.

20. Mark your answer on your answer sheet.

21. Mark your answer on your answer sheet.

22. Mark your answer on your answer sheet.

23. Mark your answer on your answer sheet.

24. Mark your answer on your answer sheet.

25. Mark your answer on your answer sheet.

26. Mark your answer on your answer sheet.

27. Mark your answer on your answer sheet.

28. Mark your answer on your answer sheet.

29. Mark your answer on your answer sheet.

30. Mark your answer on your answer sheet.

31. Mark your answer on your answer sheet.

PART 3 23

Directions: You will hear some conversations between two or more people. You will be asked to answer three questions about what the speakers say in each conversation. Select the best response to each question and mark the letter (A), (B), (C), or (D) on your answer sheet. The conversations will not be printed in your test book and will be spoken only one time.

32. Why is the woman calling?

(A) To extend a rental period
(B) To confirm an appointment
(C) To offer an assignment
(D) To accept a proposal

33. What does the man ask the woman to do?

(A) Interpret for her supervisor
(B) Send an advance payment
(C) Submit an official request
(D) Provide a work space

34. What will the woman inform the man about?

(A) A requirement
(B) A deadline
(C) A meeting time
(D) A company policy

35. What did the woman make a copy of?

(A) A receipt
(B) A meeting schedule
(C) An expense report
(D) A prescription

36. What does the man ask the woman to do?

(A) Sign a contract
(B) Write a message
(C) Contact a receptionist
(D) Go on a business trip to Tokyo

37. What does the man plan to do?

(A) Visit his co-worker
(B) Submit a report
(C) Make a new reservation
(D) Work overtime

GO ON TO THE NEXT PAGE

38. What field do the speakers work in?

(A) Education
(B) Manufacturing
(C) Product development
(D) Interior design

39. What does the man plan to do?

(A) Choose different furniture
(B) Share a building plan
(C) Change a color scheme
(D) Place an order for wallpaper

40. According to the woman, why will the speakers have to wait?

(A) A shipment has been delayed.
(B) A contract has not been signed yet.
(C) Authorization must first be obtained.
(D) Some equipment is out of order.

41. Where most likely are the speakers?

(A) At a pet shop
(B) At a catering company
(C) At a fire station
(D) At an animal shelter

42. What aspect of the woman's needs is mentioned?

(A) The price
(B) The size
(C) The age
(D) The color

43. According to the man, what does the woman have to do?

(A) Make an advance payment
(B) Bring her identification
(C) Fill out some documents
(D) Submit a letter of reference

44. Who most likely is the man?

(A) A photographer
(B) A talent agent
(C) A performer
(D) A receptionist

45. Why is the man calling?

(A) To buy a ticket in advance
(B) To confirm a reservation
(C) To provide a reminder
(D) To inquire about an advertisement

46. What does the woman offer to do?

(A) Restrict backstage access
(B) Take pictures of Mr. Jackson
(C) Show the man a list of guests
(D) Make an official announcement

47. What is mentioned about the product?

(A) It is affordable.
(B) It is superior to competitors'.
(C) It is safe for children to use.
(D) It is simple to install.

48. According to the man, what will the advertisement help to do?

(A) Promote new products
(B) Increase stock value
(C) Encourage innovations
(D) Reduce customer complaints

49. What will the man do next?

(A) Create a website
(B) Buy a magazine
(C) Revise an article
(D) Contact an agency

50. Why is the woman calling?
(A) She hasn't received her product.
(B) She was overcharged for the item.
(C) She wants a product exchanged.
(D) She wants to return a product.

51. Why does Michael transfer the call?
(A) He is busy with another customer.
(B) The woman requested another representative.
(C) The woman called the wrong department.
(D) The manager is unavailable.

52. What does Brian ask the woman for?
(A) The tracking number
(B) Her receipt
(C) Her full name
(D) The product name

53. What are the speakers mainly discussing?
(A) Merging with another company
(B) Last month's sales reports
(C) The woman's anniversary party
(D) When the band will arrive

NEW
54. What does the man mean when he says, "But it's your fifth anniversary party"?
(A) He wants her to change her schedule.
(B) He thinks it's not important.
(C) He will tell the band not to come.
(D) He wants her to go to the meetings.

55. What solution does the woman provide?
(A) She will cancel the band.
(B) She will cancel the dinner service.
(C) She will cancel her meeting.
(D) She will fire the man.

56. Why is the man calling the woman?
(A) To check the sales figures
(B) To check if she received the flowers
(C) To check if she wanted to go to dinner
(D) To check if the documents were ready

57. What does the woman say he should do?
(A) Take her to the hospital
(B) Pay her hospital bills
(C) Take her out for dinner
(D) Buy her more flowers

NEW
58. Why does the man say, "I thought you would like them"?
(A) To express disappointment
(B) To show appreciation
(C) To show respect
(D) To show he thinks it's funny

59. What is the main problem the speakers are discussing?
(A) What they should eat for lunch
(B) Going out for dinner
(C) High entertainment expenses
(D) Getting more customers

60. What does the woman suggest they do?
(A) Stop going out for dinner
(B) Reduce client numbers
(C) Stop having lunches
(D) Pay for their own lunches

61. What does the woman say she will send the man?
(A) A monthly budget plan
(B) This month's sales report
(C) The old budget plan
(D) Last month's marketing materials

GO ON TO THE NEXT PAGE

Lifts will be out of order	
North Wing	8:00 a.m.—9:00 a.m.
East Wing	11:00 a.m.—12:00 p.m.
South Wing	1:30 p.m.—2:30 p.m.
West Wing	3:00 p.m.—4:00 p.m.

62. What did Harriet see last week?

(A) Technicians in the building next door
(B) Technicians posting about lift repairs
(C) Some technicians installing lighting
(D) Her boss having a meeting with some technicians

NEW
63. Look at the graphic. Which is the busiest wing in the hospital?

(A) West
(B) East
(C) North
(D) South

64. What does the man suggest the woman do?

(A) Cancel the repairs immediately
(B) Talk to Dr. Franklin
(C) Ask Dr. Franklin to lunch
(D) Close the North Wing

Camping Pack

4 Rectangular Sleeping Bags
4 Camping Mats
Carry Bag
Portable Gas Stove

65. Where does the woman likely work?

(A) A camping store
(B) A hardware store
(C) A medical clinic
(D) A shipping company

NEW
66. Look at the graphic. What is the man missing?

(A) Carry bag
(B) Portable gas stove
(C) Camping mats
(D) Sleeping bags

67. What does the woman offer to do?

(A) Give him a full refund
(B) Give him a 15% discount voucher
(C) Give him a 15% refund
(D) Give him a free tent

Henson's Corporate Cleaners Carpet Cleaning	
Frieze	$100 per room
Shag Pile	$150 per room
Velvet	$250 per room
Woven Carpet	$400 per room

68. What does the man say he is planning on doing with his office?

(A) Renovate it
(B) Sell it
(C) Clean it
(D) Repaint it

NEW

69. Look at the graphic. What is the carpet made of?

(A) Frieze
(B) Shag Pile
(C) Velvet
(D) Woven Carpet

70. What does the man say he will do?

(A) Buy the carpet today
(B) Ask his wife about it
(C) Tell his manager
(D) Think about it and come back

GO ON TO THE NEXT PAGE

PART 4 (24)

Directions: You will hear some talks given by a single speaker. You will be asked to answer three questions about what the speaker says in each talk. Select the best response to each question and mark the letter (A), (B), (C), or (D) on your answer sheet. The talks will not be printed in your test book and will be spoken only one time.

71. What is the announcement about?
(A) An opinion survey
(B) An upcoming election
(C) An election outcome
(D) A website update

72. What can listeners do on the website?
(A) Register as a candidate
(B) Cast their vote
(C) Find some information
(D) Enter a contest

73. What are listeners encouraged to do?
(A) Participate in an official occasion
(B) Reserve a ticket in advance
(C) Exercise on a daily basis
(D) Listen to an upcoming announcement

74. What is the outlet store celebrating?
(A) An anniversary
(B) A festival
(C) An opening
(D) A holiday

75. What must customers do to receive the promotional offer?
(A) Become a member
(B) Purchase a certain amount
(C) Recommend some brands
(D) Trade in a television

76. When does the promotion end?
(A) At the beginning of next month
(B) At the end of the year
(C) On the second Sunday of the month
(D) At the end of the month

77. Who most likely are the listeners?
(A) Environmentalists
(B) Instructors
(C) Factory workers
(D) Factory consultants

78. What document has the speaker reviewed?
(A) An employee roster
(B) An annual budget
(C) A project overview
(D) Accident reports

79. What does the speaker suggest listeners do?
(A) Get enough rest
(B) Work a day shift
(C) Receive more training
(D) Read a handout

---

80. What is the purpose of the trip to Moscow?
(A) To finalize a contract
(B) To visit a factory
(C) To give a product demonstration
(D) To renovate a building

81. What is the reason for the postponed departure?
(A) A necessary document is not ready.
(B) Some construction is underway.
(C) A company has gone out of business.
(D) Building materials have not arrived yet.

82. What does the speaker say she will send to the listener?
(A) A copy of her passport
(B) A plane ticket
(C) An itinerary
(D) A blueprint

---

83. What is the purpose of the speech?
(A) To announce a discovery
(B) To announce a retirement
(C) To accept a promotion
(D) To accept an award

NEW
84. Why does the speaker say: "I could not have done this without highly skilled crew"?
(A) She wants to thank her team.
(B) She hasn't worked on a team before.
(C) She dislikes her coworkers.
(D) She wants to accept the award.

85. Where most likely does the speaker work?
(A) At a hotel
(B) At a travel agency
(C) At a restaurant
(D) At a warehouse

---

86. Why is the woman calling?
(A) To express her gratitude
(B) To discuss a recipe
(C) To report some news
(D) To make a complaint

NEW
87. What does the woman imply when she says, "you have to show me the recipe"?
(A) She didn't enjoy it.
(B) She wants to recommend a different ingredient.
(C) She wants to cook the dish herself.
(D) She wants her friend to try it.

88. Why is the woman looking forward to next week?
(A) She is going to the movies.
(B) She is taking her son to school.
(C) Some new project will be completed.
(D) They will work together again.

GO ON TO THE NEXT PAGE

89. Who most likely is the speaker?

(A) A news editor
(B) A filmmaker
(C) A news reporter
(D) A movie star

90. What is Bernberg Studios looking for?

(A) An actress
(B) A filming location
(C) A new script
(D) More ideas for movies

NEW

91. What does the speaker imply when she says, "After all, this is Robert Holloway we are talking about"?

(A) Robert Holloway is very famous.
(B) Robert Holloway owns the house.
(C) She will interview him next.
(D) She doesn't know who Robert Holloway is.

MAMA SAN premium pillows

Beauty Sleep	£ 30.00
Soft Night	£ 35.00
Dreamtime	£ 42.00
Lovely Rest	£ 50.00

NEW

92. Look at the graphic. How much can a shopper purchase the Dreamtime Pillow for before Friday?

(A) £15.00
(B) £11.50
(C) £21.00
(D) £50.00

93. What is indicated about Happy Day?

(A) They have a wide variety of toys.
(B) They are bringing in more merchandise.
(C) They specialize in low-end furniture.
(D) They are going out of business this Friday.

94. What service does Happy Day offer?

(A) Personalized interior design advice
(B) Free shipping
(C) Home installation
(D) Wall papering services

ORDER FORM OF BLANDERS & CO. 14 March	
Product	**Quantity**
Case binders	30
Envelopes	20
Flags & Tabs	40
Legal pads	10

NEW

95. Look at the graphic. How many items were not delivered in total?

(A) 40
(B) 30
(C) 20
(D) 10

96. According to the speaker, why are the case binders important?

(A) To look professional in the office
(B) To look professional in court
(C) To organize their financial record
(D) To maintain the deadline

97. Where does Trent Herrington most likely work?

(A) At an accounting firm
(B) At a law firm
(C) At a patenting firm
(D) At a catering business

MIDNIGHT CRUISE ITINERARY

5 p.m.	Captain's address
6 p.m.	Cocktails and dinner
7 p.m.	Constellation orientation
8 p.m. — 10 p.m.	Social mixer
10 p.m.	Port Lewis for champagne toast
11 p.m.	Cast off and back to Billing's Bay
12 a.m.	Midnight constellation lesson and meteor shower on Top Deck

98. Where will the cruise spend most of its time?

(A) Eagle Island
(B) Port Lewis
(C) Billing's Bay
(D) Socializing

99. Who is Star Master Jenkins?

(A) Host
(B) Captain
(C) Bartender
(D) Security guard

NEW

100. Look at the graphic. How long will the cruise stop at Port Lewis?

(A) All evening
(B) 3 hours
(C) 2 hours
(D) 1 hour

This is the end of the Listening test.

ACTUAL TEST 07

LISTENING TEST 25

In the Listening test, you will be asked to demonstrate how well you understand spoken English. The entire Listening test will last approximately 45 minutes. There are four parts, and directions are given for each part. You must mark your answers on the separate answer sheet. Do not write your answers in your test book.

PART 1

Directions: For each question in this part, you will hear four statements about a picture in your test book. When you hear the statements, you must select the one statement that best describes what you see in the picture. Then find the number of the question on your answer sheet and mark your answer. The statements will not be printed in your test book and will be spoken only one time.

Example

Sample Answer

Ⓐ ● Ⓒ Ⓓ

Statement (B), "They're looking at the document," is the best description of the picture, so you should select answer (B) and mark it on your answer sheet.

1.

2.

GO ON TO THE NEXT PAGE

3.

4.

5.

6.

GO ON TO THE NEXT PAGE

PART 2 (26)

Directions: You will hear a question or statement and three responses spoken in English. They will not be printed in your test book and will be spoken only one time. Select the best response to the question or statement and mark the letter (A), (B), or (C) on your answer sheet.

7. Mark your answer on your answer sheet.

8. Mark your answer on your answer sheet.

9. Mark your answer on your answer sheet.

10. Mark your answer on your answer sheet.

11. Mark your answer on your answer sheet.

12. Mark your answer on your answer sheet.

13. Mark your answer on your answer sheet.

14. Mark your answer on your answer sheet.

15. Mark your answer on your answer sheet.

16. Mark your answer on your answer sheet.

17. Mark your answer on your answer sheet.

18. Mark your answer on your answer sheet.

19. Mark your answer on your answer sheet.

20. Mark your answer on your answer sheet.

21. Mark your answer on your answer sheet.

22. Mark your answer on your answer sheet.

23. Mark your answer on your answer sheet.

24. Mark your answer on your answer sheet.

25. Mark your answer on your answer sheet.

26. Mark your answer on your answer sheet.

27. Mark your answer on your answer sheet.

28. Mark your answer on your answer sheet.

29. Mark your answer on your answer sheet.

30. Mark your answer on your answer sheet.

31. Mark your answer on your answer sheet.

PART 3 (27)

Directions: You will hear some conversations between two or more people. You will be asked to answer three questions about what the speakers say in each conversation. Select the best response to each question and mark the letter (A), (B), (C), or (D) on your answer sheet. The conversations will not be printed in your test book and will be spoken only one time.

32. What does the woman ask the man to do?

(A) Introduce a new client
(B) Help to prepare a presentation
(C) Repair malfunctioning equipment
(D) Look for an instruction manual

33. Why is the man unable to help?

(A) He has to meet a major client soon.
(B) He finds the problem too complicated.
(C) He isn't nearby at the moment.
(D) He doesn't have the necessary tools.

34. What will the woman do next?

(A) Attempt to solve the problem herself
(B) Cancel an appointment
(C) Print out a document
(D) Have a meeting with a client

35. What problem does the woman mention?

(A) The advertisements are not widely circulated.
(B) The store inventory is inadequate.
(C) The discounted price is not competitive.
(D) The product is not selling well.

36. What does the woman say about this month's sales figures?

(A) They are beginning to decrease.
(B) They are similar to last month's figures.
(C) They are unusually high.
(D) They are impossible to predict.

37. What does the man ask the woman to do?

(A) Extend the length of the promotion
(B) Direct customers to the online store
(C) Secure more advertising space
(D) Offer customers a bigger discount

GO ON TO THE NEXT PAGE

38. Where most likely does the man work?

(A) At a hospital
(B) At a factory
(C) At a clothing store
(D) At a restaurant

39. Why does the woman think she is qualified for the job?

(A) She completed a training course.
(B) She has worked similar jobs before.
(C) She likes interacting with people.
(D) She majored in a related field.

40. What will the speakers discuss next?

(A) Work hours
(B) An annual salary
(C) Job qualifications
(D) Previous jobs

---

41. Where most likely does the woman work?

(A) At a wedding hall
(B) At a bakery
(C) At a clothing store
(D) At a shipping company

42. Why is the man unable to visit the woman's workplace?

(A) He has urgent arrangements to make.
(B) He must attend a wedding today.
(C) He is not feeling well.
(D) He has to prepare an order.

43. What information will the man probably provide?

(A) Directions to a location
(B) An individual's name
(C) His home address
(D) His phone number

---

44. Where most likely do the speakers work?

(A) At a souvenir shop
(B) At a language school
(C) At a restaurant
(D) At a travel agency

45. What does the man recommend doing?

(A) Hiring bilingual staff
(B) Opening a second location
(C) Taking language classes
(D) Planning a vacation

46. What has the woman done?

(A) Contacted a translation agency
(B) Scheduled job interviews
(C) Extended operating hours
(D) Hired new employees

---

47. Why did Jessica leave work early?

(A) She had a prior engagement.
(B) She wasn't feeling well.
(C) Her doctor called.
(D) She had to attend a wedding.

48. What does the man ask the woman to do?

(A) Work another person's shift
(B) Clean the store tomorrow morning
(C) Deliver a presentation at a meeting
(D) Calculate sales figures

49. What will the woman do next?

(A) Fill out a form
(B) Distribute paychecks
(C) Go to the hospital
(D) Call her coworkers

---

50. What problem does the man mention?
(A) The fridge is not working.
(B) The temperature is too low.
(C) The freezer temperature is too high.
(D) Water is leaking from the fridge.

51. What does the woman mention about the fridge?
(A) It is a very old model.
(B) It is no longer manufactured.
(C) It is not from their company.
(D) It is a popular model.

52. What does the woman offer to do?
(A) Give him a new manual
(B) Give him a link to a website
(C) Let him get a replacement
(D) Send a technician over to him

53. Where do the speakers most likely work?
(A) At a plumbing company
(B) At an electrical company
(C) At a construction company
(D) In an office

NEW
54. What does the woman mean when she says, "I intended to call them today"?
(A) She wasn't going to call them.
(B) They were going to call her back.
(C) She was going to call them that day.
(D) She was going to send them an email.

55. What is the problem?
(A) They can't install the electrical system.
(B) The plumbing is already installed.
(C) There is some problem with the payment.
(D) They may need to dig deeper to install the plumbing.

NEW
56. What does the man mean when he says, "Are you serious"?
(A) He believes the woman is correct.
(B) He thinks the woman made a mistake.
(C) He is going to pay by card.
(D) He will pay with cash.

57. What does the woman want to know?
(A) How much room service he ordered
(B) Which room he is staying in
(C) His credit card number
(D) Whether he ordered room service

58. What does the woman offer to do?
(A) Give him his room for free
(B) Give him a discount on his next visit
(C) Give him free room service
(D) Give him a gift certificate

59. What is Robert Porter's position?
(A) Lead repairer
(B) Head engineer
(C) Main engineer
(D) Main repairer

60. What problem does Susan Sherman describe?
(A) Some of the measurements weren't done.
(B) Some of their receipts are missing.
(C) Some of their equipment is missing.
(D) A piece of equipment is still in the office.

61. Why did Robert take the equipment away?
(A) To review it further
(B) For special repairs
(C) For replacement
(D) To evaluate its condition

GO ON TO THE NEXT PAGE

Discount Voucher
10% off any order over $100
Valid until December 31st

62. Where most likely are the speakers?

(A) At a stand
(B) At a café
(C) At a restaurant
(D) At the airport

63. Look at the graphic. Why is the voucher invalid?

(A) Their bill is under $100.
(B) The food was not good.
(C) Their bill was over $100.
(D) The voucher is expired.

64. What does the man ask the woman?

(A) If they can have more food
(B) If they can have more drinks
(C) If they can have a refund
(D) If they can come back another time

No Parking
After 9 A.M.

65. According to the man, why are people arriving late to work?

(A) The parking lot on Swan Street was closed.
(B) The Franklin Avenue parking lot was closed.
(C) Everyone was feeling sick.
(D) The traffic was bad.

66. Look at the graphic. Where is the sign most likely located?

(A) On Franklin Avenue
(B) On Swan Street
(C) In front of the building
(D) On Swanson Avenue

67. What does the woman recommend to the man?

(A) Take the subway
(B) Take a bus
(C) Take a taxi
(D) Drive his car

Laptop Package

1 laptop computer
Wireless mouse
Wireless keyboard
Office software
Detachable webcam
Free 8 gigabyte USB stick

68. Where does the woman most likely work?

(A) At a hardware store
(B) At an online store
(C) At a home appliance store
(D) At an electronics store

NEW

69. Look at the graphic. What is missing from the man's laptop package?

(A) Office software
(B) An 8 gigabyte USB stick
(C) A wireless keyboard
(D) A wireless mouse

70. What does the woman offer to do?

(A) Send a delivery driver the next day
(B) Give him a coupon
(C) Have him come and pick the gift up
(D) Deliver the gift in person

GO ON TO THE NEXT PAGE

PART 4 (28)

Directions: You will hear some talks given by a single speaker. You will be asked to answer three questions about what the speaker says in each talk. Select the best response to each question and mark the letter (A), (B), (C), or (D) on your answer sheet. The talks will not be printed in your test book and will be spoken only one time.

71. What is the advertisement about?
(A) A martial arts class
(B) An athletic contest
(C) A city tour bus
(D) A downtown festival

72. Who is the special offer directed at?
(A) Senior citizens
(B) Beginners
(C) Children
(D) Local residents

73. What does the speaker say about the advertised location?
(A) It is accessible by public transportation.
(B) It has no parking space available.
(C) It is near a train station.
(D) It is in the same building as Geller Bank.

74. Where is the introduction taking place?
(A) At a school
(B) At a museum
(C) At a radio station
(D) At a community center

75. Who is George Butler?
(A) A computer technician
(B) A mechanical engineer
(C) An electrician
(D) A technology expert

76. What is offered to teenage students?
(A) Hands-on experience
(B) A weekly after-school class
(C) A complimentary souvenir
(D) A discounted ticket price

77. What has caused the change in plans?
(A) Broken kitchen equipment
(B) The absence of some clients
(C) A late delivery
(D) Traffic congestion

78. What will listeners receive?
(A) A conference schedule
(B) A meal voucher
(C) A lunch menu
(D) A name tag

79. What will begin at 1:00 p.m.?
(A) A software demonstration
(B) A leadership workshop
(C) A luncheon
(D) A client meeting

---

80. What is the purpose of the planning committee?
(A) To tighten some regulations
(B) To supervise a construction project
(C) To review employee performance
(D) To develop a new curriculum

81. What does the volunteer need to do?
(A) Pick up a client
(B) Introduce a guest
(C) Write down an agenda
(D) Give a presentation

82. What will listeners do next?
(A) Go on a business trip
(B) Participate in a workshop
(C) Introduce themselves
(D) Select a group leader

---

83. Who most likely are the listeners?
(A) Factory workers
(B) Lawyers
(C) Accountants
(D) Web developers

NEW
84. What does the woman mean when she says, "I know that you have all been overworked"?
(A) She recognizes the listeners concerns.
(B) She doesn't really mind what they think.
(C) She wants them to work less.
(D) She is inviting them to a meeting.

85. What task does the speaker assign to the listeners?
(A) Prepare some instructions
(B) Prepare a new budget
(C) Revise some training materials
(D) Hire new staff

---

86. What is *Beyond the Blue* about?
(A) Online bullying
(B) The ocean
(C) Whales and sharks
(D) Sea water

NEW
87. Why does the speaker say, "Remember, this is the first film Mr. Harris has made"?
(A) To suggest that he is an impressive director
(B) To suggest the film will be poor
(C) To recommend him as a good worker
(D) To suggest they shouldn't watch the film

88. What is going to happen after the film?
(A) They will give away free DVDs.
(B) They will watch it again.
(C) The director will have a short Q&A.
(D) An actor will sign autographs.

GO ON TO THE NEXT PAGE

89. According to the speaker, what has happened to the company in the last year?

(A) Their products have gained global success.
(B) Their sales have gone down.
(C) The quality of the products has changed.
(D) Their CEO has changed many times.

90. What most likely are the CNU reporters doing on Wednesday?

(A) Interviewing some office workers
(B) Interviewing the president
(C) Making a music video
(D) Promoting their new web series

NEW

91. Why does the man say, "you realize what this means"?

(A) To discuss future renovations
(B) To make a point clear
(C) To highlight that the company will grow
(D) To give staff some bonuses

SAM'S SALON PRICING FOR THE HOMELESS BENEFIT

Men's trim	$10
Men's full cut and shave	$25
Women's trim	$20
Women's styling	$45
Sorry! No coloring or perms for this Saturday's benefit!	

92. What is indicated in the article?

(A) Sam's Salon is just starting to interact with the homeless.
(B) Sam's Salon has been involved with improving the lives of homeless people.
(C) Sam's Salon employs a high quality manicurist.
(D) Sam's Salon is trying to make extra money from coloring and perms.

NEW

93. Look at the graphic. What is true about the benefit?

(A) People should get their hair colored another time.
(B) Women's trim is expensive.
(C) Most men will choose a trim.
(D) Homeless people need to shave.

94. How much does Sam's Salon charge the homeless for a shampoo, shave, and a haircut?

(A) $25
(B) $45
(C) $10
(D) Nothing; its free

	Option 1	Option 2	Option 3	Option 4
Price	$1,000	$1,200	$1,300	$2,000
Back-up System	yes	no	no	no
Data Archive	1 week	10 weeks	30 weeks	52 weeks

95. Where does the talk most likely take place?

(A) The cafeteria
(B) The conference room
(C) The new break room
(D) The new foyer

NEW
96. Look at the graphic. Which option does the speaker recommend?

(A) Option 1
(B) Option 2
(C) Option 3
(D) Option 4

97. Why is Option 4 more expensive than the others?

(A) It has state-of-the-art surveillance.
(B) It has video cameras.
(C) It includes a one-year data archive.
(D) It offers a back-up system.

A LETTER TO MILTON'S DINER

Dear Milton's Staff,

My name is Jerome and I am a long haul trucker. I saw the sign from the highway, "Milton's Diner, home of classic pies," and thought, you know what, I am going to treat myself. I was exhausted, but as soon as I walked into the diner and smelled the pies, saw all the decorations, and was greeted by the hostess, I just felt so good. You really made my weekend special, and I wanted to thank you with all sincerity.
Happy Holidays,

Jerome Simmons

98. Who is speaking to the staff?

(A) Milton
(B) The manager
(C) The chef
(D) Jerome Simmons

NEW
99. Look at the letter. What do you think Milton's Diner prides itself on?

(A) Cakes
(B) Pies
(C) Drinks
(D) Steaks

100. What effect did Jerome's letter have?

(A) The staff will get a day off.
(B) Everyone will get to take home a pie.
(C) Everyone will get holiday gift cards.
(D) The staff will receive an extra holiday bonus.

This is the end of the Listening test.

ACTUAL TEST 08

LISTENING TEST 29

In the Listening test, you will be asked to demonstrate how well you understand spoken English. The entire Listening test will last approximately 45 minutes. There are four parts, and directions are given for each part. You must mark your answers on the separate answer sheet. Do not write your answers in your test book.

PART 1

Directions: For each question in this part, you will hear four statements about a picture in your test book. When you hear the statements, you must select the one statement that best describes what you see in the picture. Then find the number of the question on your answer sheet and mark your answer. The statements will not be printed in your test book and will be spoken only one time.

Example

Sample Answer

Ⓐ ● Ⓒ Ⓓ

Statement (B), "They're looking at the document," is the best description of the picture, so you should select answer (B) and mark it on your answer sheet.

1.

2.

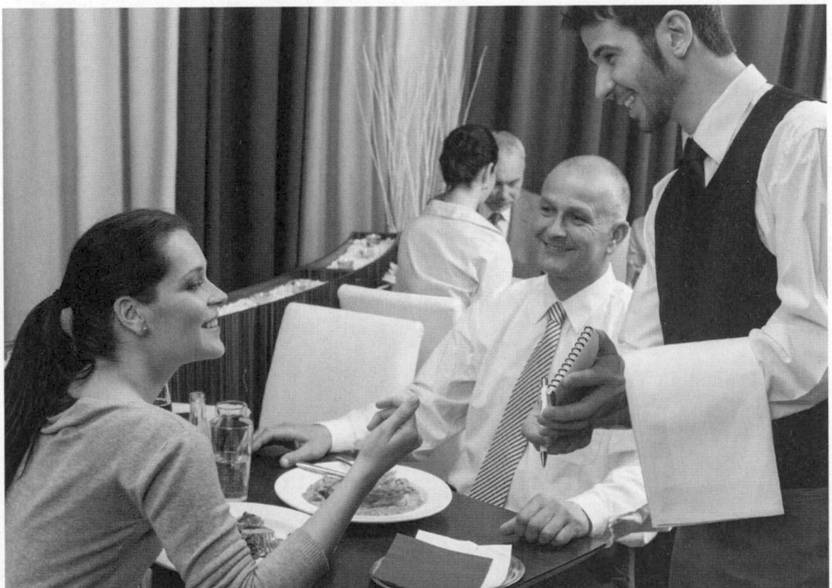

GO ON TO THE NEXT PAGE

3.

4.

5.

6.

GO ON TO THE NEXT PAGE

PART 2 30

Directions: You will hear a question or statement and three responses spoken in English. They will not be printed in your test book and will be spoken only one time. Select the best response to the question or statement and mark the letter (A), (B), or (C) on your answer sheet.

7. Mark your answer on your answer sheet.

8. Mark your answer on your answer sheet.

9. Mark your answer on your answer sheet.

10. Mark your answer on your answer sheet.

11. Mark your answer on your answer sheet.

12. Mark your answer on your answer sheet.

13. Mark your answer on your answer sheet.

14. Mark your answer on your answer sheet.

15. Mark your answer on your answer sheet.

16. Mark your answer on your answer sheet.

17. Mark your answer on your answer sheet.

18. Mark your answer on your answer sheet.

19. Mark your answer on your answer sheet.

20. Mark your answer on your answer sheet.

21. Mark your answer on your answer sheet.

22. Mark your answer on your answer sheet.

23. Mark your answer on your answer sheet.

24. Mark your answer on your answer sheet.

25. Mark your answer on your answer sheet.

26. Mark your answer on your answer sheet.

27. Mark your answer on your answer sheet.

28. Mark your answer on your answer sheet.

29. Mark your answer on your answer sheet.

30. Mark your answer on your answer sheet.

31. Mark your answer on your answer sheet.

PART 3 (31)

Directions: You will hear some conversations between two or more people. You will be asked to answer three questions about what the speakers say in each conversation. Select the best response to each question and mark the letter (A), (B), (C), or (D) on your answer sheet. The conversations will not be printed in your test book and will be spoken only one time.

32. Who is the man?

(A) A hotel guest
(B) A janitor
(C) A night manager
(D) A receptionist

33. Why is Mr. Carter unavailable?

(A) He is meeting a client.
(B) He is on vacation.
(C) He has not arrived at work yet.
(D) He is giving a presentation.

34. What will the man do next?

(A) Watch training videos
(B) Conduct an interview
(C) Contact Mr. Carter
(D) Fill out paperwork

35. What are the speakers discussing?

(A) Preparations for a meeting
(B) A keynote speech
(C) A seminar agenda
(D) Meeting locations

36. What does the man say he is relieved about?

(A) A product is selling well.
(B) A trip was not delayed.
(C) A new employee was hired.
(D) A meeting room is available.

37. What does the woman offer to do?

(A) Act as an interpreter during a meeting
(B) Call before she arrives
(C) Call Mr. Takahashi's secretary
(D) Listen to a weather report

GO ON TO THE NEXT PAGE

38. What does the woman ask the man about?

(A) The status of a project
(B) The location of a store
(C) The list of clients
(D) The cause of a problem

39. Why was the man unable to complete his work?

(A) He didn't have enough time.
(B) His car wouldn't start.
(C) He was busy with other projects.
(D) His computer malfunctioned.

40. What is the woman planning to do?

(A) Terminate a contract
(B) Ask for a deadline extension
(C) Meet with a company executive
(D) Hire a new designer

---

41. What problem does the man report?

(A) Internet access has been disconnected.
(B) A delivery has not arrived yet.
(C) A power outage occurred.
(D) Some equipment has malfunctioned.

42. Where most likely does the woman work?

(A) At an electronics store
(B) At a power company
(C) At a toy factory
(D) At a communications provider

43. What does the woman suggest the man do?

(A) Take shelter elsewhere
(B) Report the incident to the police
(C) Restart his computer
(D) Arrive ahead of schedule

---

44. Where does the man work?

(A) At an immigration office
(B) At a public school
(C) At a post office
(D) At a travel agency

45. Why is the woman in a hurry?

(A) She is late to work.
(B) She forgot an important event.
(C) She must meet a deadline.
(D) She has another appointment.

46. What does the man recommend?

(A) Making a phone call
(B) Visiting a different business
(C) Sending an email
(D) Canceling a subscription

---

47. What type of business does the man work for?

(A) An auto repair shop
(B) An insurance company
(C) An automobile dealership
(D) A construction contractor

48. What does the woman say is her top priority when she makes a purchase?

(A) Affordability
(B) Popularity
(C) Design
(D) Safety

49. What does the man suggest doing?

(A) Replacing a broken part
(B) Evaluating a different model
(C) Visiting a new branch
(D) Paying a deposit

---

50. What are the speakers mainly discussing?
(A) High sales figures
(B) A staff conflict
(C) Low sales figures
(D) A new training manual

NEW
51. What does the woman mean when she says, "I'm actually on my way to a meeting"?
(A) She doesn't have a lot of time to talk.
(B) She can stay and chat for a long time.
(C) She is asking the man out to lunch.
(D) She will send him an email later on.

52. What possible solution does the man suggest?
(A) To employ more staff members
(B) That the woman should be fired
(C) They should have lunch together.
(D) The woman might have to fire someone.

---

53. What is the problem?
(A) The person who was supposed to give the speech is sick.
(B) The person who was supposed to give the speech doesn't want to do it now.
(C) There is no keynote speech anymore.
(D) The keynote speaker is late.

54. What does the woman say to the man?
(A) To find someone to do the speech.
(B) She will deliver the speech.
(C) To deliver the keynote speech.
(D) The board is not happy.

NEW
55. What does the man imply when he says, "thanks, but I'll have to pass on it"?
(A) He will deliver the speech.
(B) He doesn't want to deliver the speech.
(C) He will talk to the board of directors.
(D) He needs some more information.

---

56. Why is the man calling Tristar Logistics?
(A) To reschedule a delivery
(B) To cancel his order
(C) To change his address
(D) To update his details

NEW
57. What does he imply when he says, "that won't work for me"?
(A) The package contains important documents.
(B) He will pay with a money order.
(C) He doesn't want them to leave the package with someone else.
(D) He wants it left at the office.

58. What does the woman say she wants?
(A) The office address
(B) His cell phone number
(C) The order number
(D) His building number

---

59. What are the speakers mainly discussing?
(A) The delivery of some furniture
(B) The signing of a rental contract
(C) The drafting of a document
(D) The delivery of computer equipment

60. What problem do Ruth and Greg have?
(A) They don't need the equipment.
(B) They could miss some important deadlines.
(C) They need to train their new staff.
(D) They haven't found the documents.

61. What does the woman suggest she'll do?
(A) Accept the late order
(B) Cancel the order
(C) Call another supplier
(D) Rent some equipment

GO ON TO THE NEXT PAGE →

Office Directory

1st FL	Harlington Accounting
2nd FL	Jersey Construction
3rd FL	Swanson and Sons
4th FL	Grounds Ltd

62. Who most likely are the speakers?

(A) Store clerks
(B) Artists
(C) Painters
(D) Electricians

NEW

63. Look at the graphic. Where is the man currently working?

(A) Swanson and Sons
(B) Harlington Accounting
(C) Jersey Construction
(D) Grounds Ltd

64. What does the woman recommend to the man?

(A) To bring more paint
(B) To bring one ladder
(C) To bring at least three ladders
(D) To paint the roof first

Harron Dry Cleaning

Fabric	Price
Cotton	$10
Denim	$15
Wool	$20
Silk	$12

65. What does the woman say she will do tomorrow?

(A) Go out for dinner
(B) Visit her family
(C) Host an award show
(D) Attend an award ceremony

NEW

66. Look at the graphic. What is the gown made of?

(A) Cotton
(B) Wool
(C) Denim
(D) Silk

67. What does the woman say she will do?

(A) Pick it up at 9 p.m.
(B) Send her husband to pick it up
(C) Send her daughter to pick it up
(D) Cancel the order

68. According to the man, what is causing people to arrive late to work?

(A) An electrical storm
(B) A closed parking lot
(C) A protest
(D) Some new traffic rules

NEW
69. Look at the graphic. Where is the sign most likely located?

(A) On Swinton Road
(B) At the Cranson Lot
(C) On Menzies Street
(D) On Prunkel Street

70. What does the man suggest they do?

(A) Go home
(B) Buy some parking tickets
(C) Have an early dinner
(D) Walk to work

ACTUAL TEST 08

GO ON TO THE NEXT PAGE

PART 4 (32)

Directions: You will hear some talks given by a single speaker. You will be asked to answer three questions about what the speaker says in each talk. Select the best response to each question and mark the letter (A), (B), (C), or (D) on your answer sheet. The talks will not be printed in your test book and will be spoken only one time.

71. Where does the announcement most likely take place?

(A) On a train
(B) On a bus
(C) On a plane
(D) On a ship

72. What is the speaker waiting for?

(A) An itinerary
(B) Authorization to depart
(C) Some passengers to board
(D) A parking permit

73. What does the speaker suggest listeners do?

(A) Have their tickets reissued
(B) Transfer to another line
(C) Stay near a departure gate
(D) Modify their plans

74. What type of business does the speaker work for?

(A) An electronics store
(B) A furniture outlet
(C) A clothing store
(D) A theater company

75. What improvement is mentioned?

(A) Product selection will be increased.
(B) More staff will be able to help.
(C) Free parking will be offered.
(D) Store hours will be extended.

76. When can customers receive a discount?

(A) On Tuesday
(B) On Wednesday
(C) On Thursday
(D) On Friday

77. What is being advertised?
(A) A security system
(B) A rented house
(C) A gardening tool
(D) An insulating product

78. What is mentioned about the product?
(A) It is domestically produced.
(B) It reduces the cost of living.
(C) It won several awards.
(D) It received positive reviews.

79. What must listeners do to receive a discount?
(A) Buy a certain amount of products
(B) Apply for a membership card
(C) Talk about the advertisement
(D) Make a payment in cash

---

80. What event is ending?
(A) A grand opening
(B) A consumer electronics expo
(C) A product demonstration
(D) A museum tour

81. What is required of volunteers?
(A) Relevant experience
(B) A degree in engineering
(C) Availability to work on weekends
(D) Fluency in two languages

82. What are potential volunteers cautioned about?
(A) Missing a deadline
(B) Leaking confidential information
(C) Damaging a device
(D) Interrupting a presenter

---

83. What is the company recruiting?
(A) Programmers
(B) Chefs
(C) Interns
(D) Factory workers

NEW
84. What does the man imply when he says, "Have you seen the interview questions we use"?
(A) He is postponing an appointment.
(B) He needs a record of the report.
(C) He wants her to help him with the questions.
(D) He will recruit some accountants.

85. Why does the man want to meet with the woman?
(A) To get some assistance from her
(B) To ask her for some records
(C) To get a new letterhead
(D) To plan an orientation

---

86. What is the purpose of the announcement?
(A) To announce an achievement
(B) To announce a rise in sales
(C) To announce a new team member
(D) To complete a project

NEW
87. What does the woman imply when she says, "so let's keep moving up"?
(A) They need to continue working hard.
(B) They are moving buildings.
(C) She is renovating the office.
(D) They are going on a business trip.

88. What does the woman ask the staff to do?
(A) Study the new handbook
(B) Prepare a report
(C) Study material on corporate law
(D) Write a memo

GO ON TO THE NEXT PAGE

89. Why is the woman calling?

(A) To say thank you
(B) To ask a favor
(C) To discuss travel plans
(D) To request a form

90. What does the woman imply when she says, "you have to show me the design sometime"?

(A) She wants to learn how to make it.
(B) She wasn't sure about the details.
(C) She needs a dentist recommendation.
(D) She is writing a design manual.

91. What will the women do next week?

(A) Plan for the Grayson wedding
(B) Plan for the Christmas party
(C) Design a new invitation
(D) Meet for coffee

SPRINGDALE MUSIC CLUB'S
SATURDAY CONCERT LINE UP

5 p.m.—8 p.m.	Barbeque Cookout, bring your own meat!
8 p.m.—9 p.m.	Djubai Djinn, all the way from East Timor
9 p.m.—10 p.m.	Swinging Devils touring from Memphis
10 p.m.—11 p.m.	Rock or Die! Local Heroes
11 p.m.—12 a.m.	Ferocious Four all the way from New York City

92. What is indicated about Springdale Music Club?

(A) They love all music equally.
(B) They take pride in their location.
(C) They specialize in country music.
(D) They didn't carry world music before.

NEW
93. Look at the graphic. What can you infer about the bands?

(A) They will be great.
(B) They are jazz musicians.
(C) The acts following Djubai Djinn play rock and roll.
(D) They will be loud.

94. Why does Springdale Music Club ask you to bring your money?

(A) The concert will be expensive.
(B) There is a bar.
(C) To help support Djubai Djinn's US tour
(D) To pay for your meats

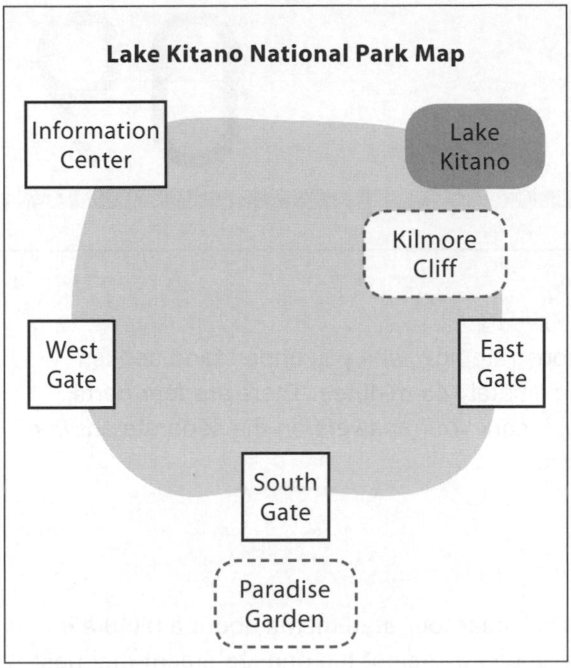

Order form	
Item	**Quantity**
Desks	1
Chairs	8
File Binders	3

95. Who most likely are the listeners?
(A) Residents
(B) Tourists
(C) Park employees
(D) Forest rangers

NEW
96. Look at the map. What place are the listeners unable to go to?
(A) Lake Kitano
(B) East Gate
(C) Kilmore Cliff
(D) Paradise Garden

97. What does the woman mention about Kilmore Cliff?
(A) It is dangerous.
(B) The views are spectacular.
(C) People who fear heights may not enjoy it.
(D) It is 50 meters from the final destination.

NEW
98. Look at the graphic. Which department filled out the order form?
(A) Finance
(B) IT
(C) Public Relations
(D) Human Resources

99. What does the speaker anticipate may happen?
(A) Some departments may go over budget.
(B) The warehouse may not have enough supplies.
(C) The orders may not arrive on time.
(D) The departments may forget some items.

100. What does the speaker request of Lima?
(A) To fax over the orders
(B) To file the papers
(C) To arrange a meeting
(D) To contact him

This is the end of the Listening test.

ACTUAL TEST 09

LISTENING TEST 33

In the Listening test, you will be asked to demonstrate how well you understand spoken English. The entire Listening test will last approximately 45 minutes. There are four parts, and directions are given for each part. You must mark your answers on the separate answer sheet. Do not write your answers in your test book.

PART 1

Directions: For each question in this part, you will hear four statements about a picture in your test book. When you hear the statements, you must select the one statement that best describes what you see in the picture. Then find the number of the question on your answer sheet and mark your answer. The statements will not be printed in your test book and will be spoken only one time.

Example

Sample Answer

Ⓐ ● Ⓒ Ⓓ

Statement (B), "They're looking at the document," is the best description of the picture, so you should select answer (B) and mark it on your answer sheet.

1.

2.

GO ON TO THE NEXT PAGE

3.

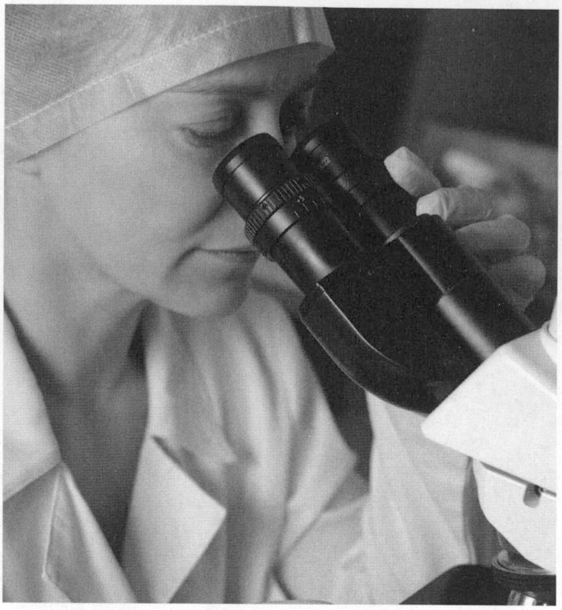

4.

5.

6.

GO ON TO THE NEXT PAGE

PART 2 (34)

Directions: You will hear a question or statement and three responses spoken in English. They will not be printed in your test book and will be spoken only one time. Select the best response to the question or statement and mark the letter (A), (B), or (C) on your answer sheet.

7. Mark your answer on your answer sheet.

8. Mark your answer on your answer sheet.

9. Mark your answer on your answer sheet.

10. Mark your answer on your answer sheet.

11. Mark your answer on your answer sheet.

12. Mark your answer on your answer sheet.

13. Mark your answer on your answer sheet.

14. Mark your answer on your answer sheet.

15. Mark your answer on your answer sheet.

16. Mark your answer on your answer sheet.

17. Mark your answer on your answer sheet.

18. Mark your answer on your answer sheet.

19. Mark your answer on your answer sheet.

20. Mark your answer on your answer sheet.

21. Mark your answer on your answer sheet.

22. Mark your answer on your answer sheet.

23. Mark your answer on your answer sheet.

24. Mark your answer on your answer sheet.

25. Mark your answer on your answer sheet.

26. Mark your answer on your answer sheet.

27. Mark your answer on your answer sheet.

28. Mark your answer on your answer sheet.

29. Mark your answer on your answer sheet.

30. Mark your answer on your answer sheet.

31. Mark your answer on your answer sheet.

PART 3 (35)

Directions: You will hear some conversations between two or more people. You will be asked to answer three questions about what the speakers say in each conversation. Select the best response to each question and mark the letter (A), (B), (C), or (D) on your answer sheet. The conversations will not be printed in your test book and will be spoken only one time.

32. What is the woman requesting?
(A) Time off from work
(B) A recommendation letter
(C) A schedule change
(D) A pay raise

33. Why is the woman unsure about the man's question?
(A) She wants to quit her job.
(B) She is waiting for her exam results.
(C) She got a job offer from another restaurant.
(D) She has not registered for classes.

34. What does the man ask the woman to do?
(A) Work overtime this week
(B) Inform him about her availability
(C) Recommend her acquaintance
(D) Create a new menu design

35. Why is the man calling?
(A) To order a product
(B) To postpone an appointment
(C) To book a wedding hall
(D) To hire a photographer

36. What does the man inquire about?
(A) A price quote
(B) A product sample
(C) A list of employees
(D) An event schedule

37. Why does the woman say the service might be quite expensive?
(A) Her services are in high demand.
(B) She will need additional staff.
(C) She uses high-end equipment.
(D) She has to meet a tight deadline.

ACTUAL TEST 09

GO ON TO THE NEXT PAGE

38. Who is Nathan Gates?

(A) A sales clerk
(B) A customer
(C) A private detective
(D) A product inspector

39. What does the man ask the woman to do?

(A) Run a training session
(B) Enforce safety measures
(C) Introduce a new employee
(D) Inspect a construction site

40. What will the woman give Mr. Gates?

(A) A training manual
(B) Safety gear
(C) A work schedule
(D) An identification card

---

41. What problem are the speakers discussing?

(A) Unsatisfied customers
(B) An unexpected drop in sales
(C) Damaged inventory
(D) A delayed shipment

42. What caused the problem?

(A) An electrical fire
(B) A burst water pipe
(C) A sudden flood
(D) A gas leak

43. What will happen on Friday?

(A) Construction will be completed.
(B) Stock prices will increase.
(C) A shipment will arrive.
(D) A supplier will be changed.

---

44. What are the speakers discussing?

(A) A public lecture
(B) An upcoming exam
(C) A graduation requirement
(D) A recent publishing trend

45. Who is Charlie Klein?

(A) A scientist
(B) An inventor
(C) A professor
(D) A writer

46. Why is the woman planning to visit the man tomorrow?

(A) To return an item
(B) To borrow a book
(C) To meet Mr. Klein
(D) To sign up for a course

---

47. Who is Dr. Moran?

(A) A university professor
(B) A patient
(C) A pharmacist
(D) A medical practitioner

48. What problem does the woman mention?

(A) An incorrect diagnosis
(B) A family problem
(C) Persistent pain
(D) An outstanding balance

49. What does the man offer to do?

(A) Provide contact information
(B) Drive the woman to the hospital
(C) Set up an appointment
(D) Offer a free consultation

---

50. What is the man concerned about?

(A) The messaging system
(B) Cell phone reception
(C) Phone transfer software
(D) A new computer system

51. What does the woman suggest?

(A) Deleting all his software
(B) Getting a new computer
(C) Downloading a movie
(D) Upgrading his software

52. What does the woman say she will do?

(A) Send him a link for a free upgrade
(B) Upgrade his phone model
(C) Revise the schedule
(D) Check with management

---

53. What is the man worried about?

(A) Buying new software
(B) The production rate of the machine
(C) Finding a repair shop
(D) An increase in production

NEW
54. What does the man imply when he says, "It doesn't make sense to keep going like this"?

(A) He wants to take action immediately.
(B) He wants to continue business as usual.
(C) He wants to repair the software.
(D) He doesn't agree with the woman.

55. What does the woman say she will do?

(A) Call the software engineer
(B) Contact the IT department
(C) Call the machine repair shop
(D) Buy new software

---

56. What did the man do last weekend?

(A) He went to a conference.
(B) He finished his sales reports.
(C) He gave a presentation.
(D) He visited his family.

NEW
57. What does the woman imply when she says, "wow, sounds like you've really made it"?

(A) He failed.
(B) He was successful with his presentation.
(C) His presentation wasn't well received
(D) His book didn't sell well.

58. What does the man plan on doing next year?

(A) Retire from writing
(B) Move to another country
(C) Have a child with his wife
(D) Release another book

---

59. Why most likely is the man calling?

(A) To discuss an issue with the apartment
(B) To offer a lower rental price
(C) To negotiate a contract
(D) To make an appointment

60. What does the man say about the Swiss Tower building?

(A) It is too far away from her office.
(B) It is being renovated at the moment.
(C) It is being closed down.
(D) It is located close to a dry cleaner.

61. What does the man offer the woman?

(A) Give her a lower rental price
(B) Extend the lease
(C) Pay for her hotel costs
(D) Arrange to move her furniture

GO ON TO THE NEXT PAGE

Bernard & Son's Tailors
Gift Certificate

10% off any purchase of $500 or more

Expires March 10

Nutrition Information Serving Size: 1 Rounded Scoop (29.4g)	
Calories	**120**
Fat	10 grams
Carbohydrate	3 grams
Protein	24 grams
Calcium	10%
Contains milk and soy products	

62. What is the woman doing?
(A) Giving away free suits
(B) Helping a customer
(C) Updating software
(D) Celebrating with friends

63. Look at the graphic. Why is the gift certificate rejected?
(A) It is expired.
(B) Because he is in the wrong store
(C) Because he didn't purchase enough
(D) The certificate is damaged.

64. What does the woman offer to do?
(A) Give him another certificate
(B) Help him try on a suit
(C) Show him some pants
(D) Give him a refund

65. Why is the man looking for a certain product?
(A) He stopped working out.
(B) His trainer told him to.
(C) Because he is a trainer.
(D) He had a favorite brand.

66. Look at the graphic. Which content is the man worried about?
(A) Carbohydrate
(B) Fat
(C) Milk
(D) Protein

67. What does the woman suggest?
(A) Purchasing a milk-based product
(B) Getting a full refund
(C) Using soy beans
(D) Buying a soy-based powder

Park Tower
Office Directory

1st	Floor	Farnod Computing
2nd	Floor	Chaims & Son
3rd	Floor	Raptas
4th	Floor	Hecadi Constructing

68. Who most likely are the speakers?

(A) office cleaners
(B) computer repair technicians
(C) telephone operators
(D) athletes

69. Look at the graphic. Where is the woman going next?

(A) Raptas
(B) Farnod Computing
(C) Chaims & Son
(D) Hecadi Constructing

70. What are the speakers going to do when they're finished with the windows?

(A) go home
(B) eat lunch
(C) clean the carpets
(D) leave the building

GO ON TO THE NEXT PAGE

PART 4 36

Directions: You will hear some talks given by a single speaker. You will be asked to answer three questions about what the speaker says in each talk. Select the best response to each question and mark the letter (A), (B), (C), or (D) on your answer sheet. The talks will not be printed in your test book and will be spoken only one time.

71. Who most likely is the speaker?

(A) A potential buyer
(B) A bank teller
(C) A real estate agent
(D) An architect

72. Why would the speaker like to arrange a meeting?

(A) To discuss a sale
(B) To renew a contract
(C) To draw up a budget
(D) To introduce his coworker

73. What does the speaker suggest doing?

(A) Updating a website
(B) Accepting an offer
(C) Making the house neat
(D) Lowering a price

74. What is the news report mainly about?

(A) A weather forecast
(B) A road construction project
(C) A traffic accident
(D) A cooking contest

75. What event has been delayed?

(A) A sports game
(B) A live concert
(C) An opening ceremony
(D) An orientation

76. What will the winner of the eating contest receive?

(A) A concert ticket
(B) A gift certificate
(C) A cash prize
(D) A plane ticket

77. Where is the announcement being made?

(A) At a campground
(B) At a movie theater
(C) At a concert hall
(D) At a sports stadium

78. What is being announced?

(A) A new restriction
(B) Operating hours
(C) Price changes
(D) A discount policy

79. What is said about some of the proceeds?

(A) They will be used for a worthy cause.
(B) They will be put toward updating facilities.
(C) They will be saved for a special event.
(D) They will be awarded to some spectators.

---

80. What is the speaker discussing?

(A) A new curriculum
(B) A weather warning
(C) A quarterly report
(D) A travel advisory

81. What has been canceled?

(A) Television programs
(B) Graduation ceremonies
(C) Educational programs
(D) Fundraising events

82. What are local residents advised to do?

(A) Update their anti-virus software
(B) Wear protective gear
(C) Go into a safe place
(D) Take an alternative route

---

83. What is the purpose of the speech?

(A) To accept a nomination
(B) To announce a retirement
(C) To announce a merger
(D) To request funding

NEW

84. Why does the speaker say: "I couldn't have done this without my talented team"?

(A) She dislikes her team.
(B) She is asking for some extra awards.
(C) She wants to thank her colleagues.
(D) She wants to offer her services.

85. Where most likely does the speaker work?

(A) At a cell phone shop
(B) At a computer shop
(C) At a shoe store
(D) At a flower shop

---

86. What problem does the speaker mention?

(A) No breakfast service
(B) No dinner service
(C) Missing items on the menu
(D) Rats in the kitchen

NEW

87. What does the speaker imply when he says, "you might want to come in the evening"?

(A) He will offer free breakfast.
(B) The dinner menu is better.
(C) Don't come during the day.
(D) They are installing air conditioners.

88. What does the speaker say he will do?

(A) Serve breakfast at night
(B) Charge more
(C) Offer free breakfast
(D) Offer a discount

GO ON TO THE NEXT PAGE

89. Where does the speaker work?

(A) A fashion company
(B) A restaurant
(C) A factory
(D) A clinic

90. What problem does the speaker describe?

(A) The delivery driver is lost.
(B) The delivery is late.
(C) The order is not perfect.
(D) The order has extra items.

NEW

91. What does the woman imply when she says, "I need to let head office know what to do by 1 p.m., and it's already midday"?

(A) She would like a response after midday.
(B) She would like a response as soon as possible.
(C) She would like extra time off.
(D) She will call head office now.

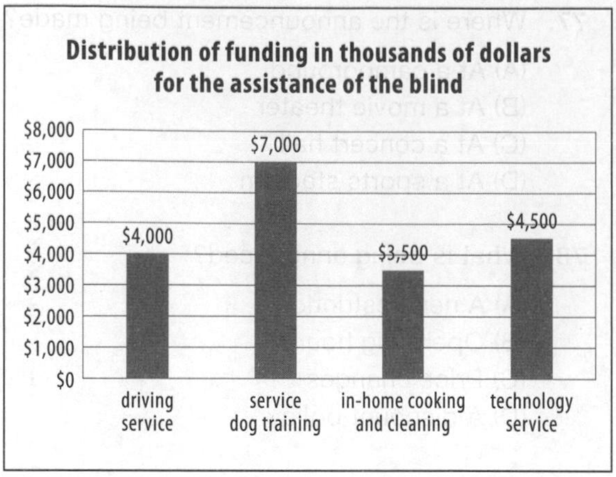

NEW

92. Look at the graphic. What is the largest expense?

(A) Dog training
(B) Technology
(C) Meal preparation
(D) Driving assistance

93. What is the listener asked to do?

(A) Give more money than last year
(B) Listen to some information
(C) Become a volunteer
(D) Become a member of the National Center for the Blind

94. Where does the speaker most likely work?

(A) A hospital
(B) The National Center for the Blind
(C) A church
(D) The local government

FFFS Seminar Schedule and Price Guide

Orlando	"3 Weeks to Riches!"	3 weeks	$1,500
New York	"The Big Apple is Yours"	5 days	$750
Boston	"Revolutionary Wealth"	13 days	$1,200
Seattle	"Prepare for Your Rainy Day"	20 days	$3,000

NEW

95. Look at the graphic. Where will the longest course take place?

(A) Orlando
(B) Boston
(C) New York
(D) Seattle

96. Who most likely are the people attending the seminar?

(A) Wealthy people
(B) People who want to get rich
(C) Those who are bored
(D) Those invited by friends

97. What is the speaker trying to do?

(A) Sell real estate
(B) Sell seminar packages
(C) Sell vacations
(D) Sell small businesses

Common Area Cleanliness Checklist

Area	Monday	Tuesday	Wednesday	Thursday	Friday
Kitchen	Scott W	Scott W	Scott W	Bill T	Bill T
Foyer	Bill T	Bill T	Hillary P	Hillary P	Hillary P
Rec. A	Lawrence P.	Lawrence P.	Lawrence P.	Hillary P	Scott W
Lounge C	Hillary P	Hillary P	Bill T	Scott W	Lawrence P.

98. Who is speaking to the staff?

(A) Human Resources
(B) The regional manager
(C) The CEO
(D) The sales manager

NEW

99. Look at the graphic. Which employee was given responsibility for two common areas on the same day?

(A) Lawrence P.
(B) Hillary P.
(C) Scott W.
(D) Bill T.

100. What is indicated in the meeting?

(A) The staff will get reprimanded.
(B) The staff will need to work weekends.
(C) Everyone will get a holiday bonus.
(D) There have been a lot of complaints.

This is the end of the Listening test.

ACTUAL TEST 10

LISTENING TEST 37

In the Listening test, you will be asked to demonstrate how well you understand spoken English. The entire Listening test will last approximately 45 minutes. There are four parts, and directions are given for each part. You must mark your answers on the separate answer sheet. Do not write your answers in your test book.

PART 1

Directions: For each question in this part, you will hear four statements about a picture in your test book. When you hear the statements, you must select the one statement that best describes what you see in the picture. Then find the number of the question on your answer sheet and mark your answer. The statements will not be printed in your test book and will be spoken only one time.

Example

Sample Answer

Ⓐ ● Ⓒ Ⓓ

Statement (B), "They're looking at the document," is the best description of the picture, so you should select answer (B) and mark it on your answer sheet.

1.

2.

ACTUAL TEST 10

GO ON TO THE NEXT PAGE

3.

4.

5.

6.

ACTUAL TEST 10

GO ON TO THE NEXT PAGE

PART 2 (38)

Directions: You will hear a question or statement and three responses spoken in English. They will not be printed in your test book and will be spoken only one time. Select the best response to the question or statement and mark the letter (A), (B), or (C) on your answer sheet.

7. Mark your answer on your answer sheet.

8. Mark your answer on your answer sheet.

9. Mark your answer on your answer sheet.

10. Mark your answer on your answer sheet.

11. Mark your answer on your answer sheet.

12. Mark your answer on your answer sheet.

13. Mark your answer on your answer sheet.

14. Mark your answer on your answer sheet.

15. Mark your answer on your answer sheet.

16. Mark your answer on your answer sheet.

17. Mark your answer on your answer sheet.

18. Mark your answer on your answer sheet.

19. Mark your answer on your answer sheet.

20. Mark your answer on your answer sheet.

21. Mark your answer on your answer sheet.

22. Mark your answer on your answer sheet.

23. Mark your answer on your answer sheet.

24. Mark your answer on your answer sheet.

25. Mark your answer on your answer sheet.

26. Mark your answer on your answer sheet.

27. Mark your answer on your answer sheet.

28. Mark your answer on your answer sheet.

29. Mark your answer on your answer sheet.

30. Mark your answer on your answer sheet.

31. Mark your answer on your answer sheet.

PART 3 (39)

Directions: You will hear some conversations between two or more people. You will be asked to answer three questions about what the speakers say in each conversation. Select the best response to each question and mark the letter (A), (B), (C), or (D) on your answer sheet. The conversations will not be printed in your test book and will be spoken only one time.

32. How do the speakers know each other?
(A) They met through a friend.
(B) They take a class together.
(C) They live in the same apartment complex.
(D) They work at the same company.

33. What does the woman suggest that the man do?
(A) Introduce himself to his coworkers
(B) Wear a work uniform
(C) Learn how to make a list of goods
(D) Have a house-warming party

34. What does the man need to do first?
(A) Change his clothes
(B) Attach a name tag
(C) Contact a warehouse supervisor
(D) Read an employee handbook

35. Why is the man calling?
(A) He forgot a document password.
(B) He needs an important document.
(C) He wants to apply for a job.
(D) His computer is not working.

36. When will the woman leave work?
(A) 4:00 p.m.
(B) 5:00 p.m.
(C) 6:00 p.m.
(D) 7:00 p.m.

37. What does the woman suggest the man do?
(A) Extend a warranty
(B) Come to work early tomorrow
(C) Participate in a survey
(D) Check his email

GO ON TO THE NEXT PAGE

38. Where does the woman work?

(A) At a restaurant
(B) At a hostel
(C) At a movie theater
(D) At a hotel

39. Why are the tables and chairs currently unavailable?

(A) A shipment has not arrived.
(B) The woman didn't permit their use.
(C) Other people are using them.
(D) The storage room is locked.

40. What does the man clarify?

(A) The expected number of guests
(B) The location of stored supplies
(C) The starting time of an event
(D) The necessary documents

---

41. What are the speakers mainly discussing?

(A) A new recipe
(B) A grand opening
(C) An interview
(D) A detailed itinerary

42. What change does the woman mention about the restaurant?

(A) A menu was expanded.
(B) An address was changed.
(C) A document was revised.
(D) An opening date was delayed.

43. What does the man suggest doing?

(A) Redecorating the space
(B) Hiring a Mexican chef
(C) Meeting at a different time
(D) Making a reservation

---

44. Where is the conversation taking place?

(A) At a hardware store
(B) At a fish market
(C) At a pet store
(D) At an animal shelter

45. What problem does the man mention?

(A) A piece of equipment is out of order.
(B) Some fish was not cooked properly.
(C) A personal item has been lost.
(D) An extra charge was added.

46. What does the woman say she will do?

(A) Deliver an item
(B) Fix a computer error
(C) Replace a purchase
(D) Offer a discount

---

47. Who most likely is the man?

(A) A recording technician
(B) A tour guide
(C) A musician
(D) A radio host

48. What kind of music does the woman currently play?

(A) Pop
(B) Rock
(C) Folk
(D) Blues

49. According to the woman, what will be different about her upcoming performance?

(A) It will begin at midnight.
(B) It is free to the public.
(C) It will be broadcast live.
(D) It will include more performers.

50. Who is Mr. Hyatt?

(A) Building Manager
(B) Funds Manager
(C) Accountant
(D) Construction worker

51. What problem does Mrs. Jasmin mention?

(A) The main branch is closed.
(B) Construction is continuing.
(C) She didn't receive some funds.
(D) The timing was incorrect.

52. What does Mr. Hyatt ask Mrs. Jasmin to do?

(A) Not to message him back
(B) Send him a message back
(C) Review the receipt
(D) Cancel the transfer

---

53. What does the woman say about the restaurant space?

(A) She thinks it's too big.
(B) It has a good location.
(C) The location is not good.
(D) It's a bit far from her office.

NEW

54. Why does the woman say, "I've looked at another location up the street that is about 10% cheaper"?

(A) To get a lower rental price
(B) To buy the property
(C) To prepare a new contract
(D) To deny the request

55. What does the man say about the price?

(A) He agrees to reduce it.
(B) He has to ask his co-worker.
(C) He has to ask his manager.
(D) He refuses to reduce it.

---

56. What are the speakers discussing?

(A) Sales results of last quarter
(B) Sales results of last month
(C) Sales of the new range
(D) Sales for the coming month

NEW

57. What does the woman imply when she says, "that's interesting"?

(A) She wants to work at the Collingwood store.
(B) She knows their sales are down.
(C) She wasn't listening to the man.
(D) She wants to know why sales are down.

58. What does the man suggest they do?

(A) Visit Head Office
(B) Visit the Woodsdale store
(C) Visit the Collingwood store
(D) Visit their manager

---

59. Where most likely are the speakers?

(A) At an office
(B) At a lawyer's office
(C) At a hardware store
(D) At a restaurant

60. What does the man mention about the delivery?

(A) He isn't getting any equipment delivered to the office.
(B) He is getting the small equipment delivered to the office.
(C) He is getting a drill delivered to the office.
(D) He is getting some documents delivered to the office.

61. What does the man say he needs?

(A) A saw
(B) Some tapes
(C) A shovel
(D) Some nails

GO ON TO THE NEXT PAGE

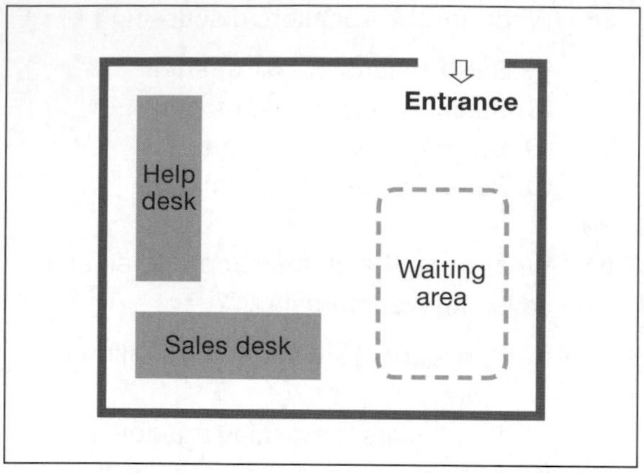

62. What did the man recently do?

(A) He met with a photographer.
(B) He met with a sales associate.
(C) He met with an interior decorator.
(D) He met with his supervisor.

63. Why does the man want to move the sales desk?

(A) To increase the company's sales
(B) To make it look nicer
(C) To make more room for the woman to work
(D) To give waiting customers more space

64. Look at the graphic. Where will the sales desk be moved to?

(A) Where the help desk is now
(B) So it is to the right of the entrance
(C) Where the waiting area is
(D) They will move the help desk instead

Fire Drill Procedures January 21st		
Level 1	8 a.m. - 9 a.m.	Human Resources Department
Level 2	9 a.m. - 10 a.m.	Accounting Department
Level 3	11 a.m. - 12 p.m.	Customer Service Department
Level 4	12 p.m. - 1 p.m.	Legal Department

65. What did the man say about next week?

(A) There will be an inspection.
(B) Some new computers will arrive.
(C) They will have fire drills.
(D) Someone called in sick.

NEW

66. Look at the graphic. What department do the speakers work in?

(A) Human Resources
(B) Accounting
(C) Customer Service
(D) Legal

67. What does the woman suggest they do?

(A) Don't say anything
(B) Print out some extra copies
(C) Speak to their supervisor
(D) Put up a sign

1980 Mazda Mikado Plastic Model

Part A - 1:25 scale plastic model kit
Part B - Snap fit tool
Part C - Rubber tires
Part D - Rub-on decals

68. Where does the man most likely work?
(A) At a stationery shop
(B) At a hardware store
(C) At a model shop
(D) At a medical clinic

NEW
69. Look at the graphic. Which part is the woman missing?
(A) Decals
(B) Model kit
(C) Snap fit tool
(D) Rubber tires

70. What does the man offer to do?
(A) Deliver it to her
(B) Give her a refund
(C) Cancel the order
(D) Express-post it to her

GO ON TO THE NEXT PAGE

PART 4 (40)

Directions: You will hear some talks given by a single speaker. You will be asked to answer three questions about what the speaker says in each talk. Select the best response to each question and mark the letter (A), (B), (C), or (D) on your answer sheet. The talks will not be printed in your test book and will be spoken only one time.

71. What did Ms. Jansen offer to do?

(A) Attend a meeting
(B) Go to New York
(C) Take care of the speaker's child
(D) Lend a personal item

72. What will happen in April?

(A) An annual conference
(B) A business merger
(C) A budget review
(D) A town meeting

73. What will the listener most likely inform the speaker about?

(A) The time of arrival
(B) The payment
(C) An event location
(D) A weekend schedule

74. Where most likely is this announcement being made?

(A) In a factory
(B) On an airplane
(C) At a bus terminal
(D) At an airport

75. What can listeners receive at the counter?

(A) A name tag
(B) A receipt
(C) A meal ticket
(D) Some refreshments

76. What are listeners asked to do?

(A) Form a line
(B) Stay nearby
(C) Sign a document
(D) Present a ticket

77. Where most likely is the speaker?
(A) In a museum
(B) In a library
(C) In a lecture hall
(D) In a gift shop

78. According to the speaker, what is Dr. Simmons famous for?
(A) Writing best-selling books
(B) Making important discoveries
(C) Finding ancient buildings
(D) Conducting groundbreaking experiments

79. What does the speaker request that listeners do?
(A) Purchase a day pass
(B) Turn off a camera
(C) Refrain from using a flash
(D) Stay with the group

---

80. What is the speaker mainly discussing?
(A) A company picnic
(B) A job opportunity
(C) A new benefit
(D) Overseas expansion

81. According to the speaker, what can listeners do online?
(A) Find out a new payment
(B) Register for a workshop
(C) Remit a monthly payment
(D) Review a proposal

82. Why should some listeners contact Suzie Summers?
(A) To request a schedule change
(B) To obtain personal information
(C) To cancel a subscription
(D) To congratulate a co-worker

---

83. Who most likely are the listeners?
(A) Lawyers
(B) Accountants
(C) Bankers
(D) Cashiers

NEW
84. What does the woman mean when she says, "I know that you are all very busy"?
(A) She wants to organize a meeting.
(B) She needs more printers.
(C) She is recognizing their concerns.
(D) She isn't sure what to do.

85. What task does the speaker assign to the listeners?
(A) Spend a week with the interns
(B) Not to speak to the interns
(C) Write a training manual
(D) Report on sales figures

---

86. What product does the speaker's company sell?
(A) Electronics
(B) Software
(C) Wearable technology
(D) Automobile

87. According to the speaker, what happened last month?
(A) Someone was fired.
(B) Some products sold well.
(C) The company went bankrupt.
(D) There was a merger.

NEW
88. What does the woman mean when she says, "sit in on the meeting"?
(A) She will send employees an email.
(B) She wants employees to prepare a report.
(C) She wants employees to come to the meeting.
(D) She will have a conference call.

GO ON TO THE NEXT PAGE →

89. What product does the speaker's company sell?

(A) Heating products
(B) Air conditioners
(C) Vacuum cleaners
(D) Magazines

90. According to the speaker, what happened last month?

(A) They signed a special contract.
(B) They bought out another company.
(C) They traded stocks.
(D) Their sales went down.

NEW
91. What does the man mean when he says, "How about that?"

(A) He is confused about the situation.
(B) He is pleased with the results.
(C) He isn't happy.
(D) He wants to try to upgrade their computers.

SPRINGFIELD DANCE TROUPE CLASS SCHEDULE

Class	Mon	Tue	Wed	Thu	Fri	Sat	Sun
Hip Hop	X	X	X	Tiffany 11-2	Tiffany 11-2	Owen 11-2	Owen 11-2
Swing	Beth 11-2	Beth 11-2	Beth 11-2	Beth 11-2	Beth 11-2	X	X
Jazz	Gwen 5-8	X	Gwen 5-8	X	X	Gwen 5-8	X
Ballet	Sally 1-4	Sally 1-4	X	X	X	X	X

92. What is indicated about Springfield Dance Troupe?

(A) They are changing the music they like.
(B) They are moving to a new location.
(C) They want to find a new swing class instructor.
(D) They are changing the courses they will offer.

NEW
93. Look at the graphic. What can you infer about the dance classes?

(A) They will be difficult.
(B) They are for beginners.
(C) Dance classes last for three hours.
(D) They are coed.

94. What does Springfield Dance Troupe invite the public to do?

(A) Come to their picnic
(B) See them in the concert hall downtown
(C) Watch them perform a hip-hop dance routine
(D) Say goodbye to Sally Jones

Presidential Tailoring Pricing Structure

FIRST MEASUREMENTS ARE FREE

Men's trousers	$35*
Men's jackets	$150*
Women's ensembles	$130*
Women's gowns	$200*

*Prices may vary by choice and volume of fabric chosen or required.

95. What is indicated in the advertisement?

(A) Presidential Tailoring is just getting started in their business.
(B) Jeffrey Frye is an experienced American tailor trained overseas.
(C) Presidential Tailoring is having a big sale.
(D) They only have one tailor on staff.

NEW

96. Look at the graphic. What is true about the pricing?

(A) It can change based on the material chosen.
(B) Women's gowns are cheaper than women's ensembles.
(C) Women's ensembles cost more than men's jackets.
(D) All of the clothes are 10% off.

97. What can you infer about Presidential Tailoring?

(A) They are a discount clothier.
(B) They work with leather.
(C) Their target market is children.
(D) They take a lot of pride in their work.

INVOICE

Item	Quantity	Volume discount
Foot Stools	36	3%
Chairs	12	0%
Small End tables	117	5%
Large End tables	24	5%

NEW

98. Look at the graphic. Which item was incorrectly discounted?

(A) Foot stools 3%
(B) Chairs 0%
(C) Small end tables 5%
(D) Large end tables 5%

99. What is Mr. Johnson asked to do with the invoice?

(A) Change the large end table orders to two dozen
(B) Make the invoice match the order
(C) Send the invoice to the factory for completion
(D) Send the invoice to accounting

100. What does the speaker anticipate will happen next?

(A) He will receive his order.
(B) He will receive a new invoice.
(C) He will have to place the order a third time.
(D) He will need to use a different supplier.

ACTUAL TEST 10

GO ON TO THE NEXT PAGE

This is the end of the Listening test.

AUDIO SCRIPT
&
TRANSLATION

ACTUAL TEST ①

PART 1 P. 18–21

01

1. **A The woman is talking on the phone.**
B The woman is using her cell phone.
C The woman is typing on the laptop.
D The woman is writing in her notebook.

2. **A The woman is cooking some bacon.**
B The woman is baking a cake.
C The woman is preparing for dinner.
D The woman is frying some fish.

3. **A The man is holding some seafood.**
B The woman is baking a crab.
C They are scared of the crab.
D The family is shopping for breakfast.

4. A The man is using a screwdriver to screw a nail into the building frame.
B The man is hammering something into a building frame.
C The man is making the frame with his hand.
D The man is wearing protective glasses.

5. **A There are some tables and chairs outdoors.**
B There are some people sitting at the tables.
C There are plastic umbrellas on the tables.
D There are many flowers in the garden.

6. A They are looking at each other.
B The woman is typing on her computer.
C The man is using the calculator.
D The man is writing something onto the notepad.

1. **A 女子正在講電話。**
B 女子正在使用手機。
C 女子正在用筆記型電腦打字。
D 女子正在筆記本裡寫字。

2. **A 女子正在烹煮培根。**
B 女子正在烘焙蛋糕。
C 女子正在準備晚餐。
D 女子正在煎某種魚。

3. **A 男子正拿著海鮮。**
B 女子正在烘焙螃蟹。
C 他們都害怕這隻螃蟹。
D 這家人正在購買早餐。

4. A 男子正在使用螺絲起子將釘子鎖進建築物的框架。
B 男子正在用鐵鎚將某個物件敲進建築物的框架。
C 男子正在用手製作框架。
D 男子戴著護目鏡。

5. **A 戶外有一些桌椅。**
B 有些人坐在桌子旁。
C 桌子上有塑膠傘。
D 花園裡有許多花朵。

6. A 他們正看著彼此。
B 女子正在用電腦打字。
C 男子正在使用計算機。
D 男子正在記事本上寫字。

PART 2 P. 22

02

7. Where was the company picnic held?
A In April.
B Refreshments will be provided.
C At a park next to a lake.

7. 公司的野餐在哪裡舉行？
A 在四月。
B 將會供應茶點。
C 在湖邊的公園。

8. Who's working at the front desk today?
A That's a difficult request.
B It's Katie Miller.
C Make room on your desk.

8. 今天是誰站櫃檯？
A 那是個困難的請求。
B 是凱蒂・米勒。
C 把你的書桌騰出空間。

9. Would you like to work together or separately?
A Actually, I prefer working alone.
B Let's gather the company's data.
C Before next Friday.

9. 你想要一起或是個別工作？
A 其實，我偏好單獨工作。
B 我們來匯集電腦資料吧。
C 在下個週五前。

10. Have you introduced yourself to the new employee?
A A new reward system will be introduced soon.
B No, I've been too busy today.
C Nice to meet you.

10. 你向新進員工自我介紹了嗎？
A 很快會推行一個新的獎勵機制。
B 還沒有，我今天太忙了。
C 很高興見到你。

11. Where does this bus go to?
A You need a transit card.
B The bus stop is over there.
C It is headed downtown.

11. 這班公車開往哪裡？
A 你需要一張轉乘卡。
B 公車站就在那裡。
C 它開往市區。

12. The elevator has been repaired, right?
A She works on the third floor.
B Yes, it is working again.
C That's not what I saw.

12. 電梯已經修好了，對吧？
A 她在三樓上班。
B 是的，它又正常運轉了。
C 我看到的並非如此。

13. What was the cost of replacing the window?
A I think it was less than 60 dollars.
B In a department store.
C It wasn't difficult at all.

13. 更換窗戶要多少錢？
A 我想還不到 60 元。
B 在百貨公司裡。
C 一點都不困難。

14. Will you be checking your email tomorrow?
A Look at the attachment.
B Actually, I'll be on vacation.
C We accept cash or check.

14. 你明天會查看電子郵件嗎？
A 看附件。
B 事實上，我將要去度假。
C 我們接受現金或支票。

15. Have you considered building a fence?
A The house is for sale.
B Yes, we're doing that next.
C His remarks caused offense.

15. 你考慮過要圍個籬笆嗎？
A 房子在出售中。
B 是的，我們接下來將會那麼做。
C 他的話語冒犯了人。

16. Why did the subway stop running early tonight?
A Because it's a holiday.
B Let's get off at the next station.
C No, I won't be running tomorrow.

16. 地鐵為何今晚提早收班？
A 因為今天是假日。
B 我們在下一站下車吧。
C 不，我明天不會跑步。

17. How was the museum tour?
A The window faces the street.
B Between Williams Street and Keller Avenue.
C It was very informative.

17. 博物館之旅怎麼樣？
A 這扇窗面向街道。
B 在威廉斯街和凱勒大道之間。
C 很有教育意義。

18. Why weren't the flyers ready in time for the event?
Ⓐ They're not frequent flyers.
Ⓑ The copier malfunctioned.
Ⓒ It was the company's 40th anniversary.

19. Who's speaking at tonight's opening ceremony?
Ⓐ Front row seats.
Ⓑ Mr. Gibson will close the door.
Ⓒ A famous novelist.

20. When should I turn on the air conditioner?
Ⓐ When it reaches 25 degrees.
Ⓑ I agree with you.
Ⓒ They'll be on air in about an hour.

21. Which seat is mine?
Ⓐ It's a comfortable chair.
Ⓑ Please sit anywhere.
Ⓒ Keep that in mind.

22. I couldn't get a hold of George.
Ⓐ Hold the line, please.
Ⓑ Some empty boxes.
Ⓒ Try calling back later.

23. Shouldn't our food have been served by now?
Ⓐ It was delicious.
Ⓑ Yes, the service is rather slow tonight.
Ⓒ I'll order the tomato pasta.

24. Why don't we take a group picture?
Ⓐ Sure, let's do it on the steps.
Ⓑ A digital camera.
Ⓒ Yes, she looks attractive in this picture.

25. This new coffee maker was very expensive.
Ⓐ He has extensive management experience.
Ⓑ There's a paper jam in the copy machine.
Ⓒ That's why the coffee tastes great.

26. Are you going out for dinner or staying in?
Ⓐ I'm going to order delivery.
Ⓑ Please bring the bill.
Ⓒ At a convenient time.

27. Would you like to borrow this book when I finish reading it?
Ⓐ Ms. Watson will be leading the team.
Ⓑ I'm going to book a table for dinner.
Ⓒ No, I'll get it from the library.

18. 傳單為何沒及時在這場活動前準備好？
Ⓐ 它們不是飛行常客。
Ⓑ 影印機故障了。
Ⓒ 這是公司 40 週年紀念日。

19. 誰要在今晚的開幕典禮演講？
Ⓐ 前排的座位。
Ⓑ 吉普森先生將會關門。
Ⓒ 一位知名的小說家。

20. 我應該什麼時候開空調？
Ⓐ 氣溫到達 25 度時。
Ⓑ 我同意你的看法。
Ⓒ 它們大約一小時後會播出。

21. 哪一個座位是我的？
Ⓐ 這是一張舒適的椅子。
Ⓑ 請隨意就座。
Ⓒ 請謹記在心。

22. 我無法與喬治取得聯繫。
Ⓐ 請先別掛電話。
Ⓑ 一些空的盒子。
Ⓒ 試著稍後再打電話。

23. 現在不是該上我們的餐點嗎？
Ⓐ 相當美味。
Ⓑ 是的，今晚的服務速度很緩慢。
Ⓒ 我要點番茄義大利麵。

24. 我們何不來拍團體照？
Ⓐ 好啊，我們在階梯上拍吧。
Ⓑ 一台數位相機。
Ⓒ 是的，照片裡的她看起來很迷人。

25. 這台新的咖啡機非常貴。
Ⓐ 他擁有很廣泛的管理經驗。
Ⓑ 影印機卡紙了。
Ⓒ 那就是為什麼這咖啡很好喝。

26. 你要外出吃晚餐還是待在家裡？
Ⓐ 我要點外送。
Ⓑ 請將帳單拿過來。
Ⓒ 在方便的時候。

27. 等我讀完這本書時，你想要借閱嗎？
Ⓐ 華生女士將會帶領這個團隊。
Ⓑ 我將要訂晚餐的桌位。
Ⓒ 不，我要去圖書館借。

28. Didn't you receive a paycheck?
A No, they are distributed next week.
B Sure, I'll send him an email.
C She wants to get the promotion.

29. You set up chairs in the conference room, didn't you?
A I need a reference book.
B Yes, 200 seats in total.
C No, I couldn't find the email address.

30. I was very impressed with Alex's singing.
A I forgot the singer's name.
B Where is the concert?
C Yes, he has a wonderful voice.

31. How about renting a larger space for the party?
A Is that really necessary?
B I returned the equipment.
C I'm not a tenant.

28. 你沒有收到薪資支票嗎？
A 沒有，下星期才會發放。
B 當然，我會寄電子郵件給他。
C 她想要獲得晉升。

29. 你在會議室裡擺放了椅子，對吧？
A 我需要一本參考書籍。
B 是的，總共 200 個座位。
C 不，我找不到那個電子郵件信箱。

30. 我對亞力克斯的歌聲印象深刻。
A 我忘了歌手的名字。
B 音樂會在哪裡？
C 是的，他有很棒的聲音。

31. 為這派對租個較大的場地如何？
A 有這個必要嗎？
B 我歸還了設備。
C 我不是房客。

PART 3 P. 23-27 03

32–34 conversation

M：Hello, I'm Steven from Home Appliance Mart. **(32) I'm here to install the UHD television that you ordered last week.**

W：Yes, come right this way. We would like to mount the television on this wall. We plan to use it for presentations and training seminars.

M：Oh, no. **(33) It looks like I forgot the tools that I need to screw the television to the wall mount.** I'm sorry. I'll have to come back tomorrow morning.

W：Oh, that's all right. **(34) However, please call me before you come tomorrow to make sure that someone is in the office to meet you.**

32–34 對話

男：您好，我是家用寶超市的史帝芬。**(32) 我是來安裝您上星期訂購的超高畫質電視。**

女：好的，請往這裡來。我們想要將電視安裝在牆上，我們打算用它來做簡報和培訓研討會。

男：糟了，**(33) 我似乎忘了帶將電視栓在壁掛上所需要的工具**。很抱歉，我得明天早上再來。

女：喔，沒關係。**(34) 不過，明天你來之前請打電話給我，以確保辦公室有人能接待你。**

32. What are the speakers mainly discussing?
A A training seminar
B The installation of a television
C The date of a presentation
D A software upgrade

32. 對話者主要在討論什麼？
A 培訓研討會
B 安裝電視機
C 簡報日期
D 軟體更新

33. What is the problem?

A The necessary tools are unavailable.

B The office is closed.

C The wall is too weak.

D The phone number was wrong.

34. What most likely will the man do first tomorrow?

A Order a replacement part

B Consult an instruction manual

C Contact the woman

D Fill out a work order

33. 出了什麼問題？

A 缺少必要的工具

B 辦公室關閉了

C 牆壁太薄弱

D 電話號碼有誤

34. 男子明天最有可能先做什麼？

A 訂購更換的零件

B 查詢說明書

C 聯繫女子

D 填寫工作通知單

35–37 conversation

W：Hello, Mr. Weaver. (35) **You are one of the final applicants that we are considering for the teaching position at Belmont University.** How do you think your previous jobs have prepared you to teach at our university?

M：(36) **Well, I used to be editor-in-chief at a literary magazine.** Therefore, I think it has prepared me well to teach in the English literature department at your university. I would be able to help students to become better writers.

W：Well, I think you are right about that. You seem to be qualified for the position. As you may know, we don't pay a lot for this position. (37) **However, if you take the job, you would receive a lot of time off during the summer vacation.**

M：Actually, that's one of the reasons I chose to apply for this job.

35–37 對話

女：您好，威佛先生。(35) **您是我們考慮要錄取擔任貝爾蒙特大學教職的決選人。**您覺得您先前的工作是如何預備您在我們的大學教書呢？

男：(36) **嗯，我以前是文學雜誌的主編。**因此我認為這讓我準備好能在貴大學的英國文學系教書。我能幫助學生更擅長寫作。

女：嗯，我想關於這點您說的是對的，您看起來很適合擔任這項職務。您可能知道，我們這個職務的給薪並不高。(37) **然而，您若接受這份工作，就能在暑假期間享有許多休假。**

男：實際上，這就是我選擇這份工作的原因之一。

35. What position is the man applying for?

A Lecturer

B Editor

C Journalist

D Superintendent

36. What makes the man qualified for the position?

A His academic background

B His work experience

C His popularity

D His eloquence

35. 男子應徵什麼職務？

A 講師

B 編輯

C 記者

D 主管

36. 什麼使男子符合此項職務的資格？

A 他的學術背景

B 他的資歷

C 他的名氣

D 他的口才

37. What extra benefit does the woman mention?

A Health insurance

B Flexible hours

C A lot of free time

D Regular incentives

37. 女子提到什麼額外的福利？

A 健康保險

B 彈性工時

C 許多的空閒時間

D 常態的獎勵

38–40 conversation

W：(38) **Chris, how are the renovations going in the dining room?** Do you think we'll be ready to reopen by this Saturday?

M：No, definitely not. The shipment of floor tiles still hasn't arrived. (39) **Because the floor space is so large, it'll take at least a week to finish the entire project.**

W：Ah, I see. Well, we have a lot of dinner reservations for the weekend. What should I do about that?

M：(40) **Why don't you call everyone who already made a reservation and offer them a 20% discount on their next meal by way of compensation?**

38–40 對話

女：(38) **克里斯，飯廳的翻修進行得如何？**你認為我們在這週六之前能準備好重新開幕嗎？

男：不，一定不行，地磚還沒有送達。(39) **因為地板的面積很大，所以至少要花一個星期才能完成整個工程。**

女：啊，我了解了。週末有很多的晚餐訂位。我該怎麼處理？

男：(40) **你何不打電話給已經訂位的人，並提供他們下次用餐打八折的優惠作為補償？**

38. What are the speakers mainly discussing?

A An interior renovation

B A product launch

C A luncheon reservation

D A budget proposal

38. 對話者主要在討論什麼？

A 室內整修

B 產品發表

C 午餐訂位

D 預算提案

39. What does the man say about the dining room?

A It needs more lighting.

B It is quite cold.

C It is spacious.

D It is too loud.

39. 關於飯廳，男子說了什麼？

A 它需要更多採光

B 它相當寒冷

C 它空間寬敞

D 它太過大聲

40. What does the man suggest the woman do?

A Repaint the walls a brighter color

B Compensate guests who have reservations

C Draft a budget proposal

D Open a bank account

40. 男子提議女子做什麼？

A 將牆壁重新油漆為較亮的顏色

B 補償已經訂位的客人

C 起草預算提案

D 開立銀行帳戶

41–43 conversation

M：Hi, Linda. I'm responsible for putting together a slide show for Greg's going-away party this Friday. (41) **However, I can't find many pictures.** Do you happen to have any photos of Greg that you could send to me?

41—43 對話

男：嗨，琳達。我負責籌辦幻燈片秀，要用在本週五葛雷格的歡送派對。(41) **但是我找到的照片不多。**你是否恰好有葛雷格的一些照片能夠寄給我？

W：What? Greg is leaving the company? I had no idea.

M：Yeah, he is taking a job at a design company. (42) **He said the job is more suited to his skills.**

W：Oh, I'm happy for him. I have a few photos from last year's Christmas party. (43) **I'll find the ones with Greg in them and email them to you.**

女：什麼？葛雷格要離開公司了？我完全不知道。

男：是的，他要去一家設計公司工作。(42) **他說這份工作更符合他的專長。**

女：喔，我很為他感到高興。我有一些去年聖誕派對的照片，(43) **我會把裡面有葛雷格的照片找出來並用電子郵件寄給你。**

41. What is the man concerned about?

A Getting his camera fixed
B Receiving sick leave from work
C Preparing for a party
D Introducing a client

42. According to the man, why does Greg like his new job?

A It offers better vacation time.
B It pays a higher salary.
C It matches his abilities.
D It provides health benefits.

43. What most likely will the woman do next?

A Take a group photo
B Attend a Christmas party
C Contact Greg
D Send an email attachment

41. 男子在擔心什麼事？

A 修理他的相機
B 請病假不去上班
C 為派對做準備
D 介紹一名客戶

42. 根據男子，葛雷格為何喜歡他的新工作？

A 它提供較好的休假時間
B 它付給較高的薪資
C 它符合他的能力
D 它提供了健康福利

43. 女子接下來最有可能做什麼？

A 拍團體照
B 參加聖誕派對
C 聯繫葛雷格
D 寄電子郵件附件

44–46 conversation

M：Joanne, did you hear that all employees will be receiving free tablet computers next week? (44) **I'm excited about it, but actually I don't know how to use one.** Even my mobile phone is not a smartphone.

W：Don't worry about it. I have one at home and they are very user-friendly. You won't have any trouble familiarizing yourself with it.

M：I'm glad to hear that. (45) **As a logo design company, we can definitely use the tablet computers to increase work efficiency.**

W：You're right. (46) **If you have any questions, feel free to ask me for help.**

44–46 對話

男：喬安，你有聽說所有員工下星期都會拿到免費的平板電腦嗎？(44) **我對此感到很興奮，但其實我不知道如何使用平板電腦。**就連我的行動電話都不是智慧型手機。

女：別擔心，我家裡有一台平板電腦，它們非常容易上手。要熟悉平板電腦並不困難。

男：我很高興聽你這麼說。(45) **作為商標設計公司，我們一定可以使用平板電腦來增加工作效率。**

女：你說得對。(46) **如果你有任何問題，請儘管找我幫忙。**

44. What is the man concerned about?
A Finishing a project on time
B Paying for his new mobile phone
C Repairing a piece of equipment
D Learning a new skill

45. Where do the speakers work?
A At a repair shop
B At an electronics store
C At a marketing firm
D At a design company

46. What does the woman offer to do?
A Provide assistance
B Pay in cash
C Fill in for the man
D Email a user manual

44. 男子在擔心什麼事？
A 準時完成專案
B 付款買新的行動電話
C 修理一件器材設備
D 學習新技巧

45. 對話者們在哪裡工作？
A 在維修店
B 在電子產品店
C 在行銷公司
D 在設計公司

46. 女子提議要做什麼？
A 提供協助
B 以現金付款
C 為男子代班
D 用電子郵件寄送使用者手冊

47–49 conversation

M：Excuse me. (47) **I'm conducting research on the effect that the new downtown mall is having on local residents' shopping habits.** Do you have a moment to talk to me?

W：Sure, no problem. I can tell you that since the mall was built, I find myself coming downtown a lot more. (48) **I think what I like most is that I never have to struggle to find a parking spot.**

M：I see. What about the variety of shops? Are you satisfied with that?

W：(49) **Well, I usually come to the mall to shop for clothes.** I think there is a wide selection of women's clothes.

47–49 對話

男：不好意思，(47) **我正在進行研究，想了解新的市區商場對於在地居民的購物習慣有什麼影響。**請問你有空可以與我談一下嗎？

女：當然，沒問題。我可以告訴你，自從商場蓋好以來，我發覺自己更頻繁地來市區。(48) **我想我最喜歡的一點是，我從不用辛苦找停車位。**

男：我了解。你覺得商店的種類多不多？你對此滿意嗎？

女：(49) **我通常去商場買衣服**，我認為那邊女性服飾的選擇很多。

47. Who most likely is the man?
A A shop owner
B A construction worker
C A local resident
D A market researcher

48. What does the woman mention about the mall?
A It was recently renovated.
B It has sufficient parking space.
C It is attracting many tourists.
D It is located outside of town.

47. 男子最有可能是什麼人？
A 商店業主
B 建築工人
C 當地居民
D 市場研究員

48. 關於商場，女子提到什麼？
A 它才剛翻修過
B 它有足夠的停車空間
C 它吸引了許多遊客
D 它座落於城鎮之外

49. Why does the woman usually visit the mall?
A To purchase groceries
B To meet with her clients
C To buy clothing
D To deliver products

49. 女子為何經常逛商場？
A 為了購買雜貨
B 為了與客戶會面
C 為了購買服飾
D 為了運送貨品

NEW

50–52 conversation

W：(50) **Have you placed the order yet? Mr. Johnson just called and said he wants two more laptops, and a 50-inch monitor.**
M：Well, I already placed the previous order, (51) **but the laptops and monitor will have to wait until tomorrow. The supply company closes at 8 p.m.**
W：Oh, will they be able to deliver to us on the same day? Mr. Johnson was hoping to get everything tomorrow.
M：I'm not sure. I'll call them first thing in the morning and find out.
W：Meanwhile, how much was the total for the order?
M：It came to $12,500. Do we have enough in our budget for more laptops and a monitor?
W：(52) **I'll call Mr. Johnson and ask.** It looks like we've gone over our budget.

50–52 對話

女：(50) **你已經下訂單了嗎？強森先生剛打電話來，說他還想要兩台筆記型電腦以及一台 50 吋螢幕。**
男：我已經下了先前的訂單，(51) **但是筆記型電腦和螢幕要等到明天。供貨公司晚上八點鐘就關門了。**
女：喔，他們能在同一天把貨送來嗎？強森先生希望明天就收到所有貨品。
男：我不確定，我明天一早就會打電話確認。
女：還有，我想問這份訂單總共多少錢？
男：總計 12,500 元。我們還有足夠的預算可以加購筆記型電腦和一台螢幕嗎？
女：(52) **我會打電話問強森先生。**看起來我們已經超過預算了。

50. What are the speakers discussing?
A Orders for office supplies
B Equipment for a conference
C The budget reports
D Their colleague

51. Why does the man mention to the woman when the supply company closes?
A To inform her of the business hours
B To let her know she can't order anything
C To explain that the second order would be late
D To imply that new equipment can't be ordered tomorrow

52. What does the woman offer to do?
A Pay for the new order
B Order the supplies herself
C Cancel a meeting
D Speak to their colleague

50. 對話者們在討論什麼？
A 辦公用品的訂單
B 會議使用的設備
C 預算報告
D 他們的同事

51. 男子為何跟女子提到供貨公司何時關門？
A 為了告知她營業時間
B 為了讓她知道她無法訂購任何東西
C 為了解釋第二份訂單將會延遲
D 為了暗示新的設備明天無法訂購

52. 女子提議她要做什麼事？
A 為新的訂單付款
B 親自訂購用品
C 取消會議
D 與他們的同事交談

53–55 conversation

W：Hi, Mr. Jeffries. (53) **Unfortunately our client in New Jersey called and said they have to reschedule the meeting date to the 5th of July.** I went ahead and booked a ticket for the 4th. Is it OK if you go straight to Washington after New Jersey?

M：What about the client in Washington? Were they comfortable with the schedule?

W：Yes. (54) **I explained that we need to postpone the meeting in Washington because of our client in New Jersey.** I think this gives us time to prepare some additional materials for your presentation. I would like to add some more details to your PowerPoint slides about our new products. Let's meet this afternoon and discuss it.

M：(55) **That's not a bad idea. I'll see you this afternoon.**

53–55 對話

女：嗨，傑佛瑞斯先生。(53) **很可惜，我們在紐澤西的客戶打電話來，說他們要將會議的日期改到七月五日。**我直接預訂了七月四日的票，你可以在紐澤西行程後直接前往華盛頓嗎？

男：華盛頓的客戶怎麼辦？他們可以接受行程安排嗎？

女：是的。(54) **我向他們說明，由於紐澤西的客戶改期，所以我們需要將華盛頓的會議延後。**我想這樣我們有就時間為你的簡報多準備額外的資料。我想要在新產品的投影片上多增加一些細節。我們今天下午會面來討論此事。

男：(55) **那是個不錯的點子，我們今天下午見。**

53. What is the problem?

Ⓐ The plane tickets were not booked
Ⓑ A meeting had to be rescheduled
Ⓒ The meeting was a failure
Ⓓ A deadline has been changed

54. Which part of the business trip will be postponed?

Ⓐ The meeting in New York
Ⓑ The meeting in Wisconsin
Ⓒ The meeting in Washington
Ⓓ The meeting in Westboro

NEW
55. What does the man mean when he says, "that's not a bad idea"?

Ⓐ He thinks it is a bad idea.
Ⓑ He agrees with the proposed solution.
Ⓒ He wants to hear other ideas.
Ⓓ He disagrees with the solution.

53. 出了什麼問題？

Ⓐ 未預訂機票
Ⓑ 必須重新安排會議時間
Ⓒ 會議很失敗
Ⓓ 變更最後的期限

54. 這趟出差的哪個部分將會被推遲？

Ⓐ 在紐約的會議
Ⓑ 在威斯康辛的會議
Ⓒ 在華盛頓的會議
Ⓓ 在威斯特布路的會議

55. 男子說「那是個不錯的點子」時，指的是什麼意思？

Ⓐ 他認為那是個壞點子
Ⓑ 他同意所提出的解決方案
Ⓒ 他想要聽其他的想法
Ⓓ 他不同意解決方案

NEW
56–58 conversation

M：(56) **Rachel, how was your vacation in Australia?**

56–58 對話

男：(56) **瑞秋，你在澳洲的假期如何？**

W：It was fantastic! It is a beautiful country, but we did not get to see everything we wanted to see. Maybe we will go back in the future. Have you managed to find a new account manager yet? We are starting to get busy and we need some more staff.

M：Actually, there is someone we are looking to hire. His CV is quite impressive. Here, take a look.

W：(57) **What's this? Is this Robert Wilder's application?** I have known him for years! (58) **We play tennis together on the weekends.** So you are thinking about hiring him?

M：Yeah. The interview went really well and he has all the qualifications. I think he can be a great member of our team.

W：I agree. I have never worked with him, but personally I think he will be an excellent employee. I'm just surprised to see him applying here.

女：假期很棒。澳洲是個美麗的國家，但我們沒看到所有想看的東西。也許我們將來會再去造訪。你找到了新的客戶經理了嗎？我們開始要忙了，需要多一些人手。

男：實際上，我們有個想要僱用的人。他的履歷表相當令人印象深刻。拿去，你看看。

女：(57) **這是什麼？是羅伯．懷德的應徵函嗎？**我認識他好多年了，(58) **我們週末時會一起打網球。**你考慮要僱用他嗎？

男：是的。面試進行得很順利，而且他具備所有的條件。我認為他可以成為我們團隊很棒的一員。

女：我同意。我從未與他共事，但就我個人認為，我想他會是很好的員工，我只是很訝異得知他來求職。

56. What was the woman doing in Australia?

A Conducting business
B Studying abroad
C Taking a vacation
D Searching for employees

NEW

57. What does the woman imply when she says, "is this Robert Wilder's application"?

A She is surprised to see the application.
B She will reject the application.
C She doesn't understand something.
D She agrees with the application.

58. How does the woman know Robert Wilder?

A They went to college together.
B They work in the same department.
C They play baseball together.
D They play tennis together.

56. 女子在澳洲做什麼？

A 出差
B 留學
C 度假
D 找員工

57. 女子說「這是羅伯．懷德的應徵函嗎」，她在暗示什麼？

A 她看到這份應徵函感到很驚訝
B 她將會拒絕這項應徵
C 她不了解某件事
D 她同意這項申請

58. 女子是如何認識羅伯．懷德的？

A 他們一起上大學
B 他們在相同的部門工作
C 他們一起打棒球
D 他們一起打網球

NEW

59–61 conversation

M1：Tom and Julie, I need the sales reports for this month ready a bit early. Next month is really

59–61 對話

男1：湯姆和茱莉，我要你們早一點備妥這個月的銷售報告。下個月對我

important for our company, so we need to prepare a bit earlier than usual.

W：Sure. But we will need to do some overtime. **(59) We are really busy at the moment, so it's going to be a lot of extra hours after work, and I have to take care of my children.**

M2：Yeah, that's a lot of extra work. **(60) I think after next month we should get a few days added to our vacation.**

W：That sounds reasonable. **(61) I will need to hire a babysitter while I'm doing the overtime,** so the extra vacation time seems fair.

M1：I agree. OK, we will discuss the details later, but I definitely agree with you.

們公司非常重要，因此我們需要比平常更早一點做好準備。

女：當然，但我們需要加班。**(59) 我們現在真的很忙，因此在下班後還要多花很多時間，而且我必須要照顧孩子。**

男 2：是的，那會額外增加很多的工作。**(60) 我認為，下個月之後我們應該要多休幾天假。**

女：這聽起來很合理。**(61) 加班的時候，我需要請保母**，因此多給幾天假似乎很合理。

男 1：我同意。好，我們以後再討論細節，但我非常同意你們的看法。

59. What is the woman concerned about?
- A Getting extra vacation
- B Doing too much work
- **C Not having time for her children**
- D Preparing a report

60. What does the man suggest?
- A Fire the manager
- B Wait until their vacation
- C Hire a new employee
- **D Have some extra vacation days**

61. What does the woman say she will have to do?
- **A Hire a babysitter**
- B Go to another company
- C Ask her husband
- D Finish her sales reports

59. 女子在意什麼事？
- A 獲得額外的假期
- B 做太多的工作
- **C 沒有時間陪孩子**
- D 準備一份報告

60. 男子建議什麼？
- A 解聘經理
- B 等到放假再說
- C 僱用一名新員工
- **D 多放幾天假**

61. 女子說她將必須做什麼？
- **A 僱用一名保母**
- B 去另一家公司
- C 詢問她的丈夫
- D 完成她的銷售報告

NEW

62–64 conversation

W：Hi, we are renovating our boardroom and I'd like to purchase some cherry wood tables for our conference room. **(62) I am having a meeting with some very important clients on Friday. So I'd like to have them delivered tomorrow.** What is the cost for an emergency delivery?

M：Hold a moment, please. Next day delivery is an extra seventy-five dollars.

62–64 對話

女：嗨，我們正在翻修會議室，我想要為會議室採買一些櫻桃木桌。**(62) 我星期五要與一些很重要的客戶開會，因此我希望桌子能在明天到貨。急件運費是多少？**

男：請稍等，隔日到貨要多收 75 元。

W：Really? That is expensive. I thought if my order was over three hundred dollars delivery would be free of charge.
M：Well, yes. (63) **Are you planning to order the cherry wood tables?**
W：Yes, I would like two of them.
M：OK then, (64) **I will make sure that your order arrives tomorrow morning before midday, and delivery will be free of charge.**

女：真的嗎？那真是昂貴。我以為如果訂貨超過 300 元就可以免費運送。
男：嗯，是的。(63) **您打算訂購櫻桃木桌嗎？**
女：是的，我想要兩張。
男：好的，那麼，(64) **我會確保您訂的貨品在明天中午之前送達，並且免運費。**

Conference Table Price List 會議桌價目表	
Pine 松木	165 元
Maple 楓木	195 元
Walnut 核桃木	225 元
Cherry 櫻桃木	307 元

62. What does the woman have on Friday?
Ⓐ A dinner
Ⓑ A seminar
Ⓒ A meeting
Ⓓ An office party

62. 女子在星期五有什麼事？
Ⓐ 晚餐
Ⓑ 研討會
Ⓒ 會議
Ⓓ 公司聚會

NEW
63. Look at the graphic. How much will the woman pay for the furniture?
Ⓐ $165
Ⓑ $195
Ⓒ $307
Ⓓ $614

63. 參看圖表，女子要為家具付多少錢？
Ⓐ 165 元
Ⓑ 195 元
Ⓒ 307 元
Ⓓ 614 元

64. What does the man say he will do?
Ⓐ Arrange free delivery
Ⓑ Deliver the furniture in the evening
Ⓒ Send a confirmation
Ⓓ Deliver the table himself

64. 男子說他會做什麼？
Ⓐ 安排免費運送
Ⓑ 在夜晚運送家具
Ⓒ 寄送確認書
Ⓓ 親自運送桌子

NEW
65–67 conversation

W：Hi, this is Rachel. (65) **I'm calling to see if I can upgrade from coach to business for my flight to (66) Thailand this June.**
M：OK, can I have your membership number please?
W：Yes, it's EM3985771.

65–67 對話

女：嗨，我是瑞秋。(65) **我打電話是要了解，我今年六月 (66) 到泰國的班機是否可以從經濟艙升等為商務艙。**
男：好的，可以告訴我您的會員號碼嗎？
女：好的，是 EM3985771。

M：(67) **I'm sorry. You don't have enough points for this trip. However, I see that you're traveling to Korea and Japan next week. That should give you enough points to upgrade in June. Why don't you call again after your trip?**

W：OK, that's a great idea. I'll call again in two weeks.

男：(67) **很抱歉，您沒有足夠的點數供這趟旅程使用。但是我看到您下星期將要前往韓國和日本。這樣應該能讓您有足夠的點數在六月進行升等。您何不在這趟旅程後再打電話來？**

女：好的，這是個好主意。我兩週後會再打來。

Airline Mileage Redemption Points
航空哩程兌換點數

To East Asia 到東亞	50,000
To Southeast Asia 到東南亞	60,000
To the Middle East 到中東	70,000
To Europe 到歐洲	80,000

65. Why does the woman call?

A To get an upgrade
B To book a flight to Korea and Japan
C To cancel her flight to Singapore
D To sign up for a mileage card

65. 女子為何打電話？

A 為了獲得升等
B 為了預訂前往韓國和日本的班機
C 為了取消前往新加坡的班機
D 為了申請哩程卡

NEW

66. Look at the graphic. How many points will the woman use?

A 50,000
B 60,000
C 70,000
D 80,000

66. 參看圖表，女子將會使用多少點數？

A 50,000
B 60,000
C 70,000
D 80,000

67. What suggestion does the man give the woman?

A Upgrade her flight to Korea
B Make the request after her trip to Korea and Japan
C Book a different flight
D Cancel her reservation

67. 男子給女子什麼建議？

A 升等她的韓國班機
B 在韓日之旅後提出申請
C 訂不同的班機
D 取消她的預訂

NEW

68–70 conversation

W：(69) **You beat me again! You always get to work before I do, even though I leave before you.** How do you do that?

M：Which road do you take?

W：(68) **I just follow my GPS and it shows that Kinsley Road is the most direct route to work.**

68–70 對話

女：(69) **你再次贏過我了！你總是比我早來上班，即使我比你早出門。**你是怎麼辦到的？

男：你走哪一條路？

女：(68) **我照 GPS 指示走，它顯示金斯利路是來上班最直接的路線。**

M：No, don't follow your GPS. Your route passes through several residential areas and school zones as well as traffic signs, so it takes much longer to get here.

W：Which route do you take then?

M：(70) **I go to Cambridge Street, which takes a bit of a detour from our apartments, but it's practically a highway. I even have enough time to stop for some coffee before work.**

W：Wow, I always thought Cambridge would take much longer.

M：No, it's really quick. I can show you next time.

男：不，別照你的 GPS 走。你走的路線會經過幾個住宅區和學區，還有交通號誌，因此來到這裡要花更久的時間。

女：那麼你走哪一條路線？

男：(70) **我走到康橋街，從我們的公寓出發會需要稍微繞路，但它其實是一條公路。我甚至有足夠的時間停下來，在上班前喝點咖啡。**

女：哇，我一直以為走康橋街要更久。

男：不，真的很快。我下次可以帶你走看看。

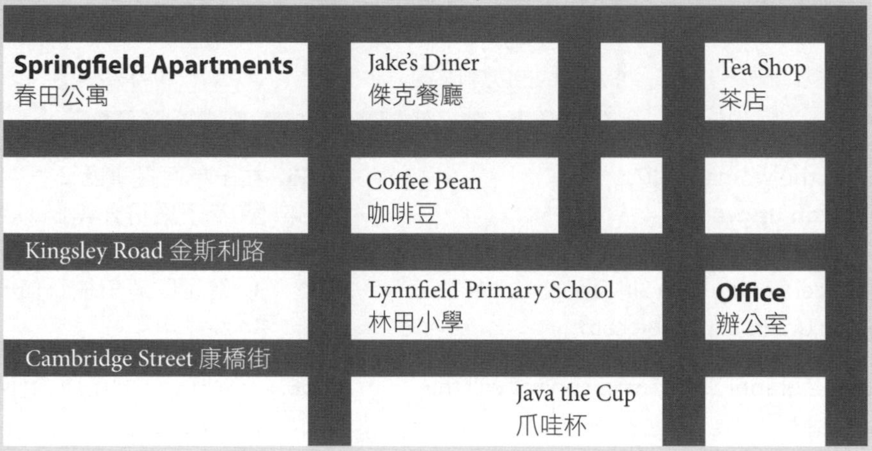

68. What are the speakers discussing?
- A Their GPS systems
- B Which coffee shop to visit
- C How far Cambridge is from their apartments
- **D The fastest route to work**

69. What does the woman want to do?
- A Keep losing the game
- B Make more money than the man does
- **C Get to work faster than the man does**
- D Participate in a car race

NEW

70. Look at the list. Which shop does the man most likely stop at?
- A Coffee Bean
- B Tea Shop
- **C Java the Cup**
- D Jake's Diner

68. 對話者們在討論什麼？
- A 他們的 GPS 系統
- B 要造訪哪家咖啡店
- C 康橋街距離他們的公寓有多遠
- **D 上班最快速的路線**

69. 女子想要做什麼？
- A 持續輸掉比賽
- B 比男子賺更多的錢
- **C 比男子更快到公司**
- D 參加賽車

70. 參看圖表，男子最有可能去哪一家店？
- A 咖啡豆
- B 茶店
- **C 爪哇杯**
- D 傑克餐廳

71–73 instructions

M：(71) **Amy, it is your responsibility to check that the store is clean and well-stocked for customers before we open for the day.** (72) **Most importantly, I would like you to make sure that the proper price tags are displayed in front of their corresponding products.** Customers get really confused and upset when the price of a product is displayed incorrectly. (73) **In the case that a customer ever does get displeased, please let me know right away, so I can come and deal with the problem in person.**

71–73 指示

男：(71) **艾美，你的責任是要在當天營業以前，為顧客確保店內清潔並且貨品充足。**(72) **最重要的是，我希望你能確認正確的價格標籤是放置在它們相對應的商品前面。**產品的標價放錯位置時，顧客會很困惑和不悅。(73) **若是顧客真的感到不高興，請立即告知我，讓我親自過來處理問題。**

71. Where most likely does the speaker work?
- A At a theater
- B At a car dealership
- **C At a retail store**
- D At a library

72. What is the listener asked to double-check?
- **A Accurate pricing**
- B Sales figures
- C Business hours
- D Name tags

73. When should the listener contact the speaker?
- A If an employee is late for work
- B If a technical problem occurs
- C If an item is out of stock
- **D If a customer is dissatisfied**

71. 發話者最有可能在哪裡工作？
- A 在戲院
- B 在汽車經銷商
- **C 在零售店**
- D 在圖書館

72. 聽者被要求要再確認什麼？
- **A 正確的標價**
- B 銷售數字
- C 營業時間
- D 名牌

73. 聽者應該何時聯繫發話者？
- A 若員工遲到時
- B 若發生了技術性的問題時
- C 若產品缺貨時
- **D 若顧客不滿意時**

74–76 announcement

W：(74) **The town of Dayton is excited to announce the opening of a new community center.** The center provides daytime activities for kids and adults of all ages. (75) **For the grand opening, the local band Summer Heat, led by Jim Neilson, will perform a show in half an hour.** (76) **Afterwards, attendees are encouraged to fill out a survey meant to judge the needs of local citizens.** Thank you.

74—76 宣布

女：(74) **德頓鎮很高興宣布，新的社區活動中心開幕了。**中心為各年齡層的孩子和成人提供日間的活動。(75) **為了慶祝盛大開幕，由吉姆・尼爾森領銜演出的本地樂團夏季之熱，將在半小時後演出。**(76) **在那之後，我們希望與會者能填寫問卷，以評估本地人的需求。**謝謝您。

74. What is the announcement about?
A An opening of a public building
B A commemorative statue
C A singing contest
D A survey result

75. Who is Jim Neilson?
A A mayor
B An instructor
C A musician
D An architect

76. What are attendees asked to do?
A Reserve seats in advance
B Complete a survey
C Subscribe to a newsletter
D Contribute to a fundraiser

74. 這個宣布與什麼有關？
A 公共建築物的開幕
B 紀念雕像
C 歌唱比賽
D 調查結果

75. 吉姆．尼爾森是什麼人？
A 市長
B 講師
C 音樂家
D 建築師

76. 出席的人被要求做什麼？
A 提前訂位
B 填寫問卷
C 訂閱電子報
D 捐錢給募款者

77–79 talk

W：Good morning, everyone. (77) **Welcome to the test screening of our pilot for a new daytime sitcom entitled *Once Upon a Romance*.** Your participation in this focus group is essential for assessing audience reception. (78) **This television show is meant to appeal to middle-aged housewives, and that is why you have all been selected.** (79) **After watching the pilot, we will take you to a meeting room, where we will conduct an in-depth interview that will help us gather your feedback and responses.** Thank you again for your cooperation.

77–79 談話

女：各位早安。(77) **歡迎來到日間情境喜劇《昔日浪漫》的首集試映會。**你們來參與此焦點小組的訪談，對於評估觀眾的接受度非常重要。(78) **這個電視節目是要迎合中年家庭主婦，這也是各位被選中的原因。**(79) **觀賞過試播影片後，我們會帶各位到會議室進行深度訪談，以幫助我們收集各位的意見和回應。**再次感謝各位的合作。

77. Who most likely is the speaker?
A A scholar
B A producer
C A pilot
D A programmer

78. Who most likely are the listeners?
A Potential investors
B Actors
C Homemakers
D University students

77. 發話者最有可能是什麼人？
A 學者
B 製作人
C 飛行員
D 程式設計師

78. 聽眾最有可能是什麼人？
A 潛在投資者
B 演員
C 家庭主婦
D 大學生

79. What will the listeners do in the meeting room?
(A) Participate in a raffle
(B) Watch a video
(C) Enroll in a class
(D) Attend an interview

79. 聽眾將會在會議室做什麼？
(A) 參與抽獎
(B) 觀賞影片
(C) 報名參加課程
(D) 參與訪談

80–82 radio broadcast

M：**(80) This is a reminder that legendary soccer player Tommy Durant will be signing autographs at Dave's Sport Shop at 1:00 p.m. tomorrow. (81) You are encouraged to bring your own items, such as clothes or books, for Mr. Durant to autograph.** Also at this time, parents will be able to sign their children up for a summer soccer camp that will be run by Tommy Durant. **(82) The camp is limited to twenty children, so anyone who is interested should sign up early.**

80–82 收音機廣播

男：**(80) 這則廣播是要提醒大家，傳奇足球選手湯米．杜蘭將於明天下午一點在戴夫運動用品店舉辦簽名會。(81) 各位可以帶自己的物品給杜蘭先生簽名，像是衣服和書本等。**父母亦可在此時可為子女們報名由湯米．杜蘭承辦的夏季足球營隊。**(82) 這個營隊人數限制為 20 名孩童，因此有興趣的人應該盡早報名。**

80. What is the purpose of the broadcast?
(A) To announce the results of a soccer match
(B) To promote a store's grand opening
(C) To advertise a new product
(D) To inform the listeners of a special event

80. 這則廣播的目的是什麼？
(A) 為了宣布足球比賽的結果
(B) 為了宣傳商店的盛大開幕
(C) 為了廣告新產品
(D) 為了告知聽眾一項特別活動

81. What does the speaker suggest doing?
(A) Wearing comfortable clothing
(B) Exercising on a regular basis
(C) Bringing personal belongings
(D) Booking a ticket in advance

81. 發話者提議做什麼？
(A) 穿著舒適衣物
(B) 規律運動
(C) 攜帶個人物品
(D) 提前訂票

82. What does the speaker say about the summer camp?
(A) It is free of charge.
(B) It will last three months.
(C) It has a restricted number of participants.
(D) It will be sponsored by Dave's Sport Shop.

82. 關於夏令營，發話者說了什麼？
(A) 它是免費的
(B) 它將為期三個月
(C) 它有限制參與人數
(D) 它將會由戴夫運動用品店贊助

83–85 announcement

W：As I'm sure everyone is aware, **(83) we have recently merged with another company that is located in India.** Now that we have become an international corporation, **(85) we will be sending a lot of our most vital data through unsecure email systems.** According to the I.T.

83–85 宣布

女：我相信各位都知道，**(83) 我們最近與另外一家位於印度的公司合併了。**因為我們已經成為國際企業，**(85) 我們將透過不安全的電子郵件系統，寄送許多重要資料。**根據資訊科技部門的說法，這是無可避免

department this is unavoidable. Unfortunately, this means we have to be very careful with what data we send through email. This afternoon everyone must attend a seminar explaining the new procedures for what data can be sent via email. The rest will be sent using secure air mail. If you don't come to the meeting, then I will have to explain the same thing over and over again and (84) **my schedule is too tight to do that.** So, everyone should come to the 1st floor meeting room at 2:30 p.m.

的。很可惜地，這表示對於要透過電子郵件寄送的資料，我們都必須採取非常謹慎的態度。今天下午所有人都必須出席一場研討會，會中將解釋新程序，是關於哪些資料可以透過電子郵件寄送，而其他的資料將使用安全的航空郵件寄送。如果各位不來開會，那麼我就要反覆解釋相同的東西，但 (84) **我的行程太緊湊而無法這麼做**。因此所有人都應該在下午兩點半來到一樓的會議室。

83. What does the speaker mention about her company?

A They have merged with another company.
B They are manufacturing a new product.
C They are creating new policies.
D They had record profits.

83. 發話者提到關於她公司的什麼事？

A 他們已經與另一家公司合併
B 他們正在生產一項新產品
C 他們正在制定新政策
D 他們先前有破紀錄的獲利

NEW

84. Why does the woman say, "my schedule is too tight to do that"?

A Because the email is secure
B To sign a new contract
C She needs some help.
D She doesn't have time.

84. 女子為何說「我的行程太緊湊而無法這麼做」？

A 因為電子郵件是安全的
B 為了簽署一個新合約
C 她需要一些協助
D 她沒有時間

85. What will they be sending a lot of?

A Portfolios
B Contract forms
C Vital data
D Building plans

85. 他們將會大量寄送什麼？

A 文件夾
B 合約表格
C 重要資料
D 建築計畫

86–88 speech

W： First of all, I'd like to thank everyone for attending the annual Bob Shilling Short Theater festival. I'm sure you have all enjoyed the performances so far. The actors have put in many nights of rehearsal to bring you some excellent performances! Next up is the Bromley Actors Guild, and they will be doing Shakespeare's play *The Tempest*. (86) **This is a play that focuses on the themes of magic and illusion.** (87) **Remember, last year the Bromley Actors Guild won first place at this**

86–88 演說

女： 首先，我想要感謝各位出席年度的「鮑伯．先令短劇節」。我想你們都很喜歡目前為止的演出。演員們花了許多晚排練，為各位帶來很棒的演出。接下來上場的是布朗利演員協會，他們將演出莎士比亞的戲劇《暴風雨》。(86) **這齣戲的主題集中在魔法及幻覺。**(87) **還記得，去年布朗利演員協會在這場活動中奪得冠軍，因此各位應該很期待看他們演出這齣佳劇。**(88) **演出結束**

event, so you should look forward to seeing them perform this wonderful play. (88) **After the play finishes, we will have question-and-answer time**, and you can get to know some of the members of the Guild.

後，我們將會有問答時間，屆時各位就有機會認識協會的一些成員。

86. What is *The Tempest* about?
[A] The evolution of man
[B] A love affair between a man and a woman
[C] A ghost ship
[D] Magic and illusion

86. 《暴風雨》與什麼有關？
[A] 人類進化
[B] 男女愛情故事
[C] 一艘幽靈船
[D] 魔法和幻象

NEW
87. Why does the speaker say, "remember, last year the Bromley Actors Guild won first place at this event"?
[A] To suggest that they are impressive
[B] To recommend that you join them
[C] To explain why they are here
[D] To excuse a poor performance

87. 為何發話者說「請記得，去年布朗利演員協會在這項活動中奪得冠軍」？
[A] 為了表示他們令人印象深刻
[B] 為了推薦你加入他們
[C] 為了解釋他們為何來到這裡
[D] 為了幫差勁的演出找藉口

88. What will most likely happen after the performance?
[A] Dinner and drinks
[B] Question time with the actors
[C] DVDs will be sold.
[D] The actors will sign autographs.

88. 在表演之後最有可能發生什麼事？
[A] 晚餐和飲料
[B] 與演員們的提問時間
[C] 將會販售 DVD
[D] 演員們將會簽名

89–91 announcement

W： I'm sure you are all aware that the (89) **new line of cell phone cases and selfie sticks we released are selling very well.** For some reason though, our range of portable batteries are selling quite poorly. (90) **I wonder if the cost is too high compared to the other products on the market. We need to develop a strategy to start selling more batteries, so I've consulted with a marketing specialist in regard to changing our prices.** (91) **This afternoon we will have a conference call, so please come to my office after lunch and sit in on the discussion.**

89–91 宣布

女： 我相信各位都知道，(89) **我們推出的新系列手機殼和自拍棒銷售極佳。**然而，基於某個理由，我們的可攜式電池賣得相當差。(90) **我在想，其售價與市面上其他產品相比是否太高了。我們需要制定一項新策略，開始增加電池的銷售量。因此我已經向一位行銷專家請教調整售價的事。**(91) **今天下午我們將進行電話會議，因此午餐後請到我的辦公室來參與討論。**

89. What types of products are being discussed?

A Cell phone cases and selfie sticks

B Cell phones and MP3 Players

C Selfie sticks and headphones

D Software programs

NEW

90. Why does the speaker say, "I wonder if the cost is too high compared to the other products on the market"?

A To ask for assistance

B To offer help

C To suggest a change

D To create some new products

91. What will the listeners most likely do after lunch?

A Review a safety policy

B Attend a seminar

C Go back to work

D Have a conference call

89. 是什麼類型的商品正被討論？

A 手機殼和自拍棒

B 手機和 MP3 播放器

C 自拍棒和耳機

D 軟體程式

90. 發話者為何說「我在想，其售價與市面上其他產品相比是否太高」？

A 為了求助

B 為了提供幫助

C 為了提出一項改變

D 為了創造新的產品

91. 聽眾在午餐後最有可能做什麼？

A 檢視安全政策

B 參與研討會

C 返回工作

D 進行電話會議

92–94 telephone message

M：Hi, Susan. I'm calling about the office furniture we delivered to Harmons & Sons recently. They said their first floor looks really good, but they are going to need 20 chairs and 12 whiteboards for their boardrooms upstairs. (93) **They recently merged with another company, so I think they will have a lot more staff in their building soon.** Make sure you check what we have in the warehouse. If we are missing anything, we need to order it today. (94) **Also, before you send the order, please have me sign off on it. As the manager, I need to sign all outgoing orders before they leave the office.** Please let me know when you have the order prepared.

92–94 電話留言

男：嗨，蘇珊。我打電話來，是關於我們最近運送到哈蒙斯家族公司的一批辦公室家具。他們說一樓看起來很不錯，但還需要 20 張椅子和 12 個白板供樓上的會議室使用。(93) **他們最近與另一家公司合併，因此我認為他們的大樓很快就會增加許多員工。**請務必確認我們倉庫裡有哪些品項，如果有任何缺貨，今天就需要訂購。(94) **此外，你送出訂單之前，要給我簽名。身為經理，所有訂單離開辦公室之前，都需要由我簽署。**請告知我你何時能將訂單準備好。

ORDER FORM 存貨訂貨表

Item 項目	Quantity in stock 庫存量	Quantity to order 訂貨量
Office Table 辦公桌	13	0
Whiteboard 白板	0	12
Office Chair 辦公椅	0	20
Drafting Table 繪圖桌	6	0

NEW

92. Look at the graphic. Which items need to be ordered?
(A) Office tables and chairs
(B) Chairs and drafting tables
(C) Whiteboards and office chairs
(D) Whiteboards and drafting tables

92. 參看圖表，需要訂購哪些品項？
(A) 辦公桌椅
(B) 椅子和繪圖桌
(C) 白板和辦公椅
(D) 白板和繪圖桌

93. What does the speaker anticipate about the company?
(A) It won't need any more furniture.
(B) It will have more staff in their building.
(C) The boardrooms will be renovated.
(D) Their staff are moving offices.

93. 發話者該對公司有何預期？
(A) 他們不需要更多家具
(B) 他們大樓會有更多的員工
(C) 會議室將進行翻修
(D) 員工正在搬遷辦公室

94. What is the listener asked to do before making any orders?
(A) Sign them herself
(B) Make sure the manager signs them
(C) Bring some extra paper
(D) Prepare a delivery receipt

94. 聽者被要求在訂貨之前要做什麼？
(A) 親自簽名
(B) 確保經理簽名
(C) 帶來額外的紙張
(D) 備妥送貨收據

95–97 talk

W：OK, everybody, thank you for coming in. (95) **I received the statistics for this year's software market shares.** Although we are still in the top four, we need to work harder. (96) **Slight Line, Inc. has just moved past us by three percent in one year. We were much bigger than them last year.** Analysts are suggesting that Slight Line's success is due to their giving away a lot of free software updates after people buy their games. (97) **In the next quarter, we are going to begin to offer all of our expansion packs for free download.** I think this can give us the edge we need and help us get back on track.

95–97 談話

女：好的，各位。感謝你們過來。(95) **我收到了今年度軟體市佔率的統計資料。**雖然我們仍是排名前四名的公司，我們需要更加努力。(96) **斯萊特線公司今年才剛超越我們三個百分比，而我們去年的市佔率比他們大得多。**分析師指出斯萊特線公司的成功，是因為人們購買他們的遊戲之後，他們還會發送許多免費的軟體更新。(97) **我們在下一季時將開始提供所有的擴充包讓人免費下載。**我認為這能給我們帶來所需的優勢，並且幫我們重振旗鼓。

MARKET SHARE 市場佔有率

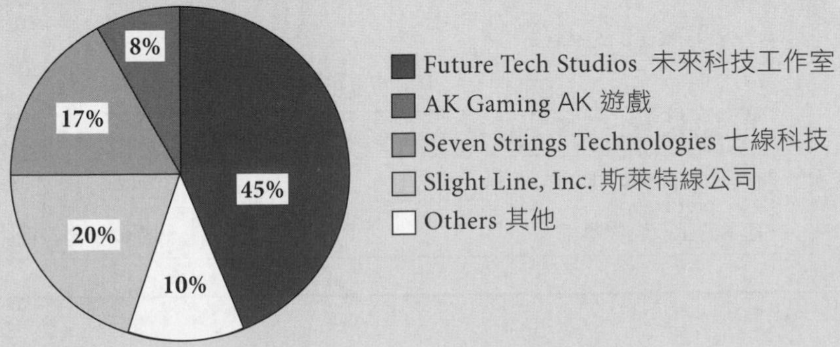

95. Which industry does the speaker work in?
(A) Computer hardware
(B) Computer games
(C) Computer software
(D) Computer microchips

NEW
96. Look at the graphic. What company does the speaker work for?
(A) Future Tech Studios
(B) Slight Line Inc.
(C) Seven Strings Technologies
(D) AK Gaming

97. According to the speaker, what will the company do in the next quarter?
(A) Give away gifts
(B) Give away expansion packs
(C) Offer free software with new products
(D) Install a new security system

95. 發話者從事哪一門行業？
(A) 電腦硬體
(B) 電腦遊戲
(C) 電腦軟體
(D) 電腦微晶片

96. 參看圖表，發話者在哪一家公司工作？
(A) 未來科技工作室
(B) 斯萊特線公司
(C) 七線科技
(D) AK 遊戲

97. 根據發話者，這家公司在下一季將會做什麼？
(A) 送禮物
(B) 送擴充包
(C) 隨新產品提供免費軟體
(D) 安裝新的保全系統

98–100 introduction

M：Hello everyone! (98) **Welcome to your first day at Valencia's Culinary Training Center. Your ability to combine cooking skills with health and safety procedures will be crucial for your future career.** Here's our training schedule for the next four days. Today, we will work on basic knife skills and food preparation. This is an essential first step in becoming a skilled chef. For the rest of the week, each day will have a different theme relating to the most important aspects of working in a kitchen. (99) **We have some celebrity chefs coming in who are highly skilled, and I'm sure you will enjoy working with them.** One more thing to remember is we will have a special team lunch on Wednesday that will be prepared by everyone together.

98–100 介紹

男：哈囉，大家好。(98) **歡迎各位首次來到凡妮莎烹飪訓練中心。將烹飪技巧和健康以及安全程序結合，對於你們未來的職涯相當重要。**這裡是接下來四天的訓練時間表。今天我們會進行基本刀工訓練以及食物準備。如果要成為一名專業大廚師，這是必要的第一步。本週其餘的日子，每天皆有不同的主題，與廚房工作的各種層面相關。(99) **我們請來了一些知名廚師，他們都很技巧純熟，我肯定你們會喜歡與他們共事。**還要記住一件事，就是我們將在星期三將舉辦一場由大家合力準備的特別團隊午餐。

Training Schedule 訓練計劃表

Tuesday 星期二	Wednesday 星期三	Thursday 星期四	Friday 星期五
Basic knife skills and food preparation 基本刀工及食物準備	Health and safety in the kitchen 健康及廚房安全	Food safety and hygiene 食物安全及衛生	Time management 時間管理
	Team lunch 團隊午餐		Evaluation 評量

98. What are the listeners training to be?

A Factory workers

B Store owners

C Restaurant chefs

D Medical workers

99. According to the speaker, what will the listeners enjoy doing?

A Working with the celebrity chefs

B Becoming a celebrity chef

C Using the kitchen tools

D Working with each other

NEW

100. Look at the graphic. On which day will the listeners learn food safety and hygiene?

A Tuesday

B Wednesday

C Thursday

D Friday

98. 聽者正在為了成為什麼而受訓？

A 工廠工人

B 商店業主

C 餐廳廚師

D 醫療工作者

99. 根據發話者，聽者將會喜愛什麼事？

A 與名廚合作

B 成為名廚

C 使用廚房器具

D 與彼此合作

100. 參看圖表，聽者將在哪一天學習食物安全與衛生？

A 星期二

B 星期三

C 星期四

D 星期五

ACTUAL TEST ②

PART 1 P. 32-35

05

1. **A The plane is docked at the airport.**
   B There is luggage being put onto the plane.
   C There are many people boarding the plane.
   D There are maintenance workers fixing the plane.

1. **A 這架飛機停靠在機場。**
   B 有行李正被放上飛機。
   C 有許多人在登機。
   D 有維修工人在修理飛機。

2. **A The woman is drinking a cup of coffee.**
   B The woman is listening to music.
   C The woman is talking on her cell phone.
   D The woman is looking at the newspaper.

2. **A 女子正在喝一杯咖啡。**
   B 女子正在聆聽音樂。
   C 女子正在講手機。
   D 女子正看著報紙。

3. A She is fixing the wheel on her bike.
   B She is changing the tire on her car.
   C She is putting oil into her car.
   D She is standing behind the windmill.

3. A 她正在修理腳踏車的輪子。
   B 她正在換汽車的輪胎。
   C 她正在為汽車加油。
   D 她正站在風車的後方。

4. A They are very close to the chairlift.
   B They are making snow.
   C The people are skiing down the mountain.
   D All of the skiers are wearing helmets.

4. A 他們很靠近滑雪升降椅。
   B 他們正在造雪。
   C 人們正在滑雪下山。
   D 所有的滑雪者都戴著頭盔。

5. A The people are drinking glasses of juice.
   B She is giving a presentation about September's sales figures.
   C All of the women are sitting down.
   D One of the women is giving a business presentation on a whiteboard.

5. A 人們正在喝杯裡的果汁。
   B 她正在做九月分銷售數字的簡報。
   C 所有的女子都坐著。
   D 其中一名女子正在白板上進行商務簡報。

6. A The men are adjusting headsets.
   B The women are wearing headsets.
   C The men are using a mouse with the laptop.
   D The women are talking to each other.

6. A 男子們正在調整頭戴式耳機。
   B 女子們正帶著頭戴式耳機。
   C 男子們在使用連接筆電的滑鼠。
   D 女子們正在與彼此交談。

PART 2 P. 36

06

7. Where should I put the extra extension cords?
   A In the top drawer.
   B The deadline is strict.
   C After today's meeting.

7. 我應該把多的延長線放在哪裡？
   A 在最頂層的抽屜。
   B 截止期限很嚴格。
   C 在今天的會議後。

8. How often should the windows be washed?
   A Please pass me my glasses.
   B At least twice a year.
   C Friday, March 3.

8. 這些窗戶應該多久洗一次？
   A 請幫我把眼鏡傳過來。
   B 至少一年兩次。
   C 三月三日，星期五。

9. I'd be happy to make you dinner.
A Thanks, but let's go out.
B At most 50 dollars.
C It was wonderful.

10. Which shoes fit you the best?
A He's physically fit.
B Make sure to tie them tight.
C The striped ones.

11. Is this the theater box office?
A The head office is in Chicago.
B Yes, you can buy tickets here.
C The play was impressive.

12. Where is the entrance to the parking garage?
A It's $10 per hour.
B Take a right turn up ahead.
C The entrance exam was difficult.

13. Do you have the key to the meeting room or should I ask someone else?
A The meeting will last over an hour.
B I think I have it in my desk.
C It's a key factor.

14. Did Mark submit a proposal yet?
A Yes, he's in charge of waste disposal.
B Print it double-sided.
C No, he is still working on it.

15. Would you please help Janet move that table?
A Where should we put it?
B Yes, she made a great impression.
C On the third floor.

16. What style of dress do you want to buy?
A In the dressing room.
B I'd like to try this on.
C Something appropriate for summer.

17. When is the new department store scheduled to open?
A In time for Christmas.
B I never opened it.
C Yes, you can use a shopping cart.

9. 我會很樂意為你做晚餐。
A 謝謝，但我們出去吃吧。
B 最多 50 元。
C 那很不錯。

10. 哪雙鞋子最適合你？
A 他體格很好。
B 務必要把它們綁緊。
C 有條紋的那雙。

11. 這是戲院的售票處嗎？
A 總部在芝加哥。
B 是的，你可以在這裡買票。
C 這齣戲很令人印象深刻。

12. 停車場的入口處在哪裡？
A 每小時十元。
B 在前面右轉。
C 入學考試很困難。

13. 你有會議室的鑰匙嗎，或者我該問別人？
A 會議將超過一小時。
B 我想我把它放在桌子裡。
C 這是一項關鍵因素。

14. 馬克繳交提案了嗎？
A 是的，他負責處理廢棄物。
B 將它雙面印刷。
C 不，他還在處理。

15. 可以請你們幫珍妮搬那張桌子嗎？
A 我們該把它放在哪裡？
B 是的，她讓人留下好印象。
C 在三樓。

16. 你想要購買哪種風格的洋裝？
A 在更衣室裡。
B 我想試穿這一件。
C 適合夏天穿的。

17. 新的百貨公司預計何時開幕？
A 趕在聖誕節前。
B 我從來沒有將它打開過。
C 是的，你可以使用購物推車。

18. The advertisement has been effective, hasn't it?
[A] No, it was an Internet advertisement.
[B] Yes, sales have increased.
[C] Turn on the television.

19. How can I help out?
[A] I was inside the room.
[B] It was helpful.
[C] You could wash the dishes.

20. Why hasn't the delivery person come all this week?
[A] I heard he was sick.
[B] No, I read it in the newspaper.
[C] I think it's $5.

21. I don't expect to be able to finish this work in time.
[A] A finished product.
[B] Maybe you should ask for help.
[C] We should inspect the equipment.

22. Shall we ship this package at an express or normal rate?
[A] It's not an urgent shipment.
[B] It was a very large ship.
[C] Due to the high unemployment rate.

23. Why don't you buy a new suit for the presentation?
[A] Did you win the award?
[B] Hmm . . . I'll follow your advice.
[C] It'll suit your company's needs.

24. Where can I call a taxi?
[A] At the intersection over there.
[B] Today at 3:00 p.m.
[C] No, there is no tax on this.

25. We had dinner at the new Italian restaurant last night.
[A] You will have a good time.
[B] Yes, he's a chef from Milan.
[C] I still haven't been there.

26. The merger hasn't been finalized yet, has it?
[A] They exceeded the initial sales forecast.
[B] No, but it will be soon.
[C] I'll return it by the end of the day.

18. 這則廣告很有效，不是嗎？
[A] 不，它是網路的廣告。
[B] 是的，銷售量增加了。
[C] 打開電視。

19. 我能幫什麼忙？
[A] 我在房間裡。
[B] 這很有幫助。
[C] 你可以洗餐盤。

20. 為何那名快遞整個星期都沒來？
[A] 我聽說他生病了。
[B] 不，我在報紙裡讀到的。
[C] 我想它要價五元。

21. 我不指望能及時完成這項工作。
[A] 一件完成的商品。
[B] 也許你該尋求協助。
[C] 我們應該檢查這個設備。

22. 我們要將這個包裹用限時快遞或普通郵件寄送？
[A] 這不是急件。
[B] 這是一艘很大的船。
[C] 因為高失業率。

23. 你何不為做簡報買件新的西裝？
[A] 你贏得這個獎了嗎？
[B] 嗯……我會聽從你的建議。
[C] 這會很符合你公司的需求。

24. 我可以在哪裡叫計程車？
[A] 在那裡的十字路口。
[B] 今天下午三點。
[C] 不，這不含稅。

25. 我們昨晚在那家新開的義大利餐廳吃晚餐。
[A] 你們將有愉快的時光。
[B] 是的，他是來自米蘭的廚師。
[C] 我還沒有去過那裡。

26. 這個合併案還沒有定案，不是嗎？
[A] 它們超過原本的銷售預估。
[B] 還沒有，但很快就會了。
[C] 我會在今天結束前歸還。

27. Who reserved the convention center?
A It is located near a subway station.
B She deserved the award.
C An election candidate.

28. Don't you need to get to the airport at least three hours early?
A I need a few hours to read it.
B No, that's unnecessary.
C She lost her boarding pass.

29. Why don't we take a tour of the house?
A No, I already saw this exhibit.
B Sure, I'd like to take a look, too.
C Because the tenant will be moving out soon.

30. How long has this company been in business?
A It was founded in 1958.
B The meeting is at 5 o'clock.
C It's around 5 meters, I guess.

31. Jonathan knows the sales figures.
A Enter the figures in the spreadsheet.
B Is he in the office now?
C I can't figure out what's going on.

27. 誰訂走會議中心？
A 它位於地鐵車站附近。
B 她應得這個獎。
C 一位選舉候選人。

28. 你不是需要提早至少三小時到達機場嗎？
A 我需要幾小時來閱讀它。
B 不，那沒有必要。
C 她遺失了她的登機證。

29. 我們何不參觀這間房子？
A 不，我已經看過這個展覽了。
B 好啊，我也想要看看。
C 因為房客很快就要搬出去了。

30. 這間公司營運多久了？
A 它成立於 1958 年。
B 會議在五點鐘舉行。
C 我猜想，大約五公尺吧。

31. 強納森知道銷售額。
A 在試算表中輸入這些數字。
B 他現在在辦公室嗎？
C 我不知道到底正在發生什麼事。

PART 3 P. 37-41

07

32-34 conversation

M：**(32) Ms. Potter, the package that you sent to the advertising agency in Tokyo was returned today.** It seems that you sent it to the wrong address.

W：**(33) Actually, I received an email from the Tokyo office today informing me that they relocated their office yesterday.** I wish they had told me earlier.

M：Well, that's unfortunate. It seems unfair that you had to pay for the postage. It must have been expensive to send such a large package.

W：Yes, it was. **(34) I'm going to request that the company in Tokyo pay me back.**

32–34 對話

男：**(32) 波特女士，你寄到東京廣告代理商的包裹今天被退回來了。**你似乎寄到錯誤的地址了。

女：**(33) 其實，我今天收到東京辦公室的電子郵件，告知我他們辦公室昨天搬遷。**真希望他們能提早告訴我。

男：那還真倒楣，要你付郵資似乎並不公平，寄那麼大的包裹一定很貴吧。

女：沒錯，的確如此。**(34) 我將會要求那家在東京的公司退我錢。**

32. What are the speakers discussing?
A A business trip
B A budget proposal
C An upcoming conference
D A package delivery

32. 對話者們在討論什麼？
A 出差旅行
B 預算提案
C 即將舉辦的會議
D 包裹寄送

33. What problem does the woman mention?
A The address is no longer relevant.
B A company has gone bankrupt.
C A budget must be revised.
D A flight has been canceled.

34. What does the woman say she will do?
A Review a contract
B Go to Tokyo
C Visit the post office
D Ask for compensation

33. 女子提到什麼問題？
A 地址不再適用
B 公司已經破產
C 必須重新編預算
D 班機被取消了

34. 女子說她將要做什麼？
A 檢視合約
B 去東京
C 去郵局
D 要求賠償

35-37 conversation

M：This is Mike Judge, your host for the morning news here at QQBC 99.5. Today our guest is business leader Karen Chambers. (35) **She recently opened a chain of health food stores across the state.** How did you get the idea, Ms. Chambers?

W：Well, I majored in food and nutrition and I minored in business administration. (36) **So, my goal was to utilize what I learned in college to open a successful company.**

M：Ah, I see. What factor do you think has contributed most to the success of your chain of stores?

W：(37) **I think it's due to the recent trend of people showing enormous interest in health and fitness.**

35–37 對話

男：我是麥克．賈奇，QQBC 99.5 晨間新聞的主持人。今天我們的來賓是企業領導者凱倫．錢伯斯。(35) **她最近在全國各地開了健康食品連鎖店。**您是如何有這個想法的，錢伯斯女士？

女：我以前主修食物和營養，副修企業管理。(36) **因此，我的目標是利用大學所學開一家成功的公司。**

男：啊，原來如此。您認為什麼是讓您連鎖店成功最大的因素？

女：(37) **我認為這是因為近來人們對健康和體適能很有興趣的趨勢。**

35. Who most likely is the woman?
A A radio host
B A professor
C A business owner
D An athlete

36. What did the woman want to do?
A Make use of her education
B Open a fitness center
C Appear on radio
D Teach food and nutrition

37. According to the woman, what is the main reason for her success?
A Effective advertisements
B Considerable interest in nutrition
C Long-term investments
D Government policies

35. 女子最有可能是什麼人？
A 廣播主持人
B 教授
C 企業主
D 運動員

36. 女子想要做什麼？
A 利用她受的教育
B 開設健身中心
C 上廣播節目
D 教授食物和營養

37. 根據女子的說法，她成功的主因為何？
A 有效的廣告
B 對營養有強烈興趣
C 長期投資
D 政府政策

38-40 conversation

M：**(38) Hello, I'm here because I'm interested in buying an instrument.** My son just turned seven years old today and I thought it would be a great birthday present. Could you give me some advice on what to buy?

W：**(39) Well, I usually suggest that children start by learning the piano.** String instruments such as guitars or violins can be difficult for children to hold. On the other hand, a piano is fine for children and they can learn musical principles easily.

M：I see. However, do you think my son is too young to begin learning an instrument?

W：Not at all. Actually, children can learn as young as three years old. **(40) Here is a pamphlet that will give you some information about the lessons for children that we offer.**

38–40 對話

男：**(38) 哈囉，我來這裡是因為我想買樂器。**我的兒子今天剛滿七歲，我覺得樂器會是很好的生日禮物。你可以建議我該買什麼嗎？

女：**(39) 我通常會建議兒童先從學鋼琴開始。**吉他和小提琴這類的弦樂器，兒童很難握住。相對的，鋼琴則很適合兒童，而且他們很容易就能學會樂理。

男：我懂了。但是你會不會覺得我兒子太小，還不適合開始學樂器？

女：一點也不。其實孩子三歲就可以學樂器了。**(40) 這裡有一本手冊，能給您一些我們兒童課程開課的相關資訊。**

38. Where most likely are the speakers?
- (A) At a children's hospital
- (B) At a university
- **(C) At a music store**
- (D) At a concert hall

38. 對話者們最有可能在什麼地方？
- (A) 在兒童醫院
- (B) 在大學
- **(C) 在樂器行**
- (D) 在音樂廳

39. What does the woman suggest doing?
- **(A) Purchasing a piano**
- (B) Writing a birthday card
- (C) Playing string instruments
- (D) Attending advanced classes

39. 女子提議要做什麼？
- **(A) 購買一架鋼琴**
- (B) 寫生日卡片
- (C) 演奏弦樂器
- (D) 參加進階課程

40. What does the woman give the man?
- (A) A receipt
- (B) A business card
- (C) A map
- **(D) A pamphlet**

40. 女子給男子什麼？
- (A) 收據
- (B) 名片
- (C) 地圖
- **(D) 手冊**

41-43 conversation

W：**(41) Steve, did you notice that this month there was a slight decrease in the number of viewers for our show? (42) I'm worried our new host, Jim Cruz, isn't very popular with viewers.**

M：I know. I was expecting a lot more viewers. **(43) I think we need to spend more money on advertising.**

41–43 對話

女：**(41) 史蒂夫，你有注意到這個月我們節目的收視人數有些微下滑嗎？(42) 我擔心我們的新主持人吉姆·克魯茲不太受觀眾歡迎。**

男：我知道，我原本預期會有更多觀眾。**(43) 我認為我們需要多花錢做廣告。**

W：I see. Maybe a lot of people are just unaware of the show. I'll get in touch with an advertising agency right away.

M：Thanks. Tell me if you need any assistance.

女：我知道了。也許很多人只是不知道有這個節目。我會立刻與廣告公司聯絡。

男：謝謝你。若需要協助，請告訴我。

41. Who most likely are the speakers?

[A] Show hosts
[B] Advertisers
[C] Television producers
[D] Viewers

42. According to the woman, what is the reason for the problem?

[A] A new product was recalled.
[B] An actor was injured.
[C] A television show was canceled.
[D] A new host is not well-liked.

43. What solution does the man suggest?

[A] Rewriting the script
[B] Replacing the host
[C] Conducting a survey
[D] Placing an advertisement

41. 對話者最有可能是什麼人？

[A] 節目主持人
[B] 廣告客戶
[C] 電視製作人
[D] 觀眾

42. 根據女子所言，問題的原因是什麼？

[A] 新產品被召回
[B] 演員受傷了
[C] 電視節目被取消了
[D] 新的主持人不受喜愛

43. 男子提出什麼解決方法？

[A] 重寫劇本
[B] 更換主持人
[C] 進行調查
[D] 做廣告

44-46 conversation

M：Good morning, Ms. Spencer. (44) **Why did you come to work particularly early today?** Usually I'm the only one here at this time.

W：(45) **Well, I have to leave work early today in order to attend my sister's wedding, so I came in early.** By the way, do you think you could do me a favor?

M：Sure, I'd be happy to. What seems to be the problem?

W：The stapler ran out of staples. (46) **Do you think you could bring me some more from the supply closet on the second floor?** I have something to do right now.

44–46 對話

男：早安，史本瑟女士。(44) **你今天為何特別早來上班？**通常在這個時候，我是唯一到班的人。

女：(45) **我今天必須提早下班去參加我妹妹的婚禮，因此我提早來上班。**對了，你覺得你可以幫我個忙嗎？

男：當然，我很樂意。有什麼問題？

女：釘書機沒有釘書針了。(46) **你想你可以從二樓的用品櫃幫我多拿一些過來嗎？**我現在得處理一些事情。

44. What does the man ask about?

[A] The reason the woman arrived early
[B] The date of the woman's wedding
[C] The name of a client
[D] Directions to the office

44. 男子詢問什麼事？

[A] 女子提早到班的原因
[B] 女子婚禮的日期
[C] 客戶的姓名
[D] 到辦公室的路

45. What will the woman do after work?
A Organize a party
B Try on a dress
C Attend a wedding
D Purchase office supplies

46. What will the man probably do next?
A Reply to an invitation
B Write an email
C Order a supply closet
D Go to the second floor

47-49 conversation

W：Marcus, have you finished designing the layout for our new online clothing store? (47) **I'm really excited to start selling our clothes online as well as at the offline store.** Can I see the website?

M：Sure, but there are still a few changes I would like to make. I'm worried that some customers might get confused while navigating the website. (48) **I think I need to simplify the interface more.** What do you think?

W：Actually, I like it the way it is. I don't think it's too confusing. (49) **However, I think we need to add more photographs of the products.** If customers can't see exactly how the products look, they might be discouraged from making a purchase online.

47. Where do the speakers work?
A At an electronics store
B At a software company
C At a clothing store
D At a photography studio

48. What does the man want to do with the website?
A Make the interface easier to use
B Enlarge the font
C Change the colors
D Increase the number of menus

49. What does the woman suggest doing?
A Hiring a professional
B Lowering the prices
C Changing the color scheme
D Including more images

45. 女子下班後將要做什麼？
A 籌劃派對
B 試穿洋裝
C 參加婚禮
D 購買辦公用品

46. 男子接下來也許會做什麼？
A 回覆邀請
B 寫電子郵件
C 訂購用品櫃
D 去二樓

47–49 對話

女：馬可斯，你是否已經完成我們新線上服飾店的版型設計？(47) **我很興奮能開始在網路商店和實體店面同時販售我們的衣服。**我可以看看網站嗎？

男：當然，但是我還想要做一些改變。我擔心一些顧客在瀏覽網站時可能會感到困惑，(48) **我認為我需要再簡化介面**，你覺得呢？

女：其實，我喜歡現在的樣子。我不認為這會太令人困惑。(49) **不過，我認為我們需要增加商品的照片。**如果顧客無法確切看見商品的樣子，他們也許會不想在網路上購買。

47. 對話者在哪裡工作？
A 在電子用品店
B 在軟體公司
C 在服飾店
D 在攝影工作室

48. 男子想要如何處理網站？
A 使介面更好用
B 放大字體
C 改變顏色
D 增加選單數量

49. 女子提議要做什麼？
A 僱用專業人士
B 降低售價
C 改變配色設計
D 囊括更多圖片

NEW

50-52 conversation

M：Hi, Sarah. (50) **I'm making plans for the next business conference in the summer. What venues would you recommend?**

W：(51) **I think Highwind Hotel has great conference rooms and all the equipment you might need.** I've planned seminars as well as weddings there, and they always do a great job.

M：All right, I'll give them a call and reserve their spaces today.

W：Did you release a newsletter about it yet?

M：No, I just want to confirm the venues first and then we'll start sending out emails and newsletters.

W：Great, (52) **let me know if you need any help.**

M：Thanks, in fact, can you take a look at a draft I'm working on? I'd like your opinion on it.

50–52 對話

男：嗨，莎拉。(50) **我正在規劃下次的夏季商務會議。你會推薦哪些地點？**

女：(51) **我認為疾風飯店有很好的會議室以及你可能需要的一切設備。**我曾經在那裡籌劃研討會以及婚禮，他們一職辦得不錯。

男：好吧，我今天會打電話給他們並且預訂場地。

女：你已經發出電子報了嗎？

男：還沒有，我想要先確認地點，然後我們就會開始寄出電子郵件以及電子報。

女：很好。(52) **若你需要任何協助，請告知我。**

男：謝謝。實際上，你可以看看我正在處理的草案嗎？我想聽聽你對它的看法。

50. What does the man talk about?
- A His upcoming business trip
- B His co-worker's wedding
- **C Where the conference should be**
- D His unfinished reports

51. What does the woman mention about the venue?
- **A They provide excellent services.**
- B She had her wedding at the venue.
- C The venue may be booked quickly.
- D They don't have enough rooms.

52. What does the woman offer to do?
- A Send out emails.
- B Work on newsletters.
- C Contact co-workers.
- **D Help with organizing an event.**

50. 男子在談論什麼？
- A 他近期的出差
- B 他同事的婚禮
- **C 會議應該要在哪裡舉行**
- D 他未完成的報告

51. 關於地點，女子提到了什麼？
- **A 他們提供很好的服務**
- B 她之前在該地點舉辦婚禮
- C 場地可能很快就被訂走
- D 他們沒有足夠的空房

52. 女子提議要做什麼？
- A 寄電子郵件
- B 處理電子報
- C 聯繫同事
- **D 協助籌辦活動**

NEW

53-55 conversation

M：Excuse me, Mrs. Stevenson. (53) **Do you have a minute to discuss the new contract you offered me?**

53–55 對話

男：不好意思，史蒂文生太太。(53) **你有空可以討論一下你給我的新合約嗎？**

W：(54) **Actually, I'm on my way to an appointment. Is there a problem with the contract?**
M：Actually there is. The vacation time is much shorter on the new contract, and I had planned a trip to Europe this summer.
W：I see. (55) **Have you already paid for your flights and accommodation?**
M：Yes, I have. I had been planning it for months. It is a large amount of money.
W：I see. I'm sure we can work it out. I think I can extend your old contract until after your vacation. I don't want you to lose your money. Come to my office at around 3 p.m. today and we will try to work something out.

女：(54) **其實我正要去赴約，合約有什麼問題嗎？**
男：的確有。新合約的休假時間短很多，而我已經計劃今年夏季要到歐洲旅遊。
女：這樣啊。(55) **你已經支付班機和住宿的費用了嗎？**
男：是的，我付了。我已經計劃好幾個月了，那可是一筆大錢。
女：我了解，我想我們可以想辦法解決。我想我可以把你的舊合約延到你假期結束，我不想讓你虧錢。今天下午三點左右到我辦公室來，我們試著想辦法解決。

53. What are the speakers mainly discussing?
A An issue with the new contract
B The new contract states a longer vacation period
C A vacation in America
D Flights and accommodation

NEW
54. What does the woman mean when she says, "I'm on my way to an appointment"?
A She has a lunch meeting.
B She doesn't have much time to talk.
C She wants the man to sign the contract.
D She has a lot of time to talk.

55. What does the woman want to know?
A If he will sign the new contract
B If he can come to her office at 3 p.m.
C If he is going to Europe for vacation
D If he has paid for his trip already

53. 對話者主要在討論什麼？
A 新合約的問題
B 新合約的休假較長
C 在美國的假期
D 班機及住宿

54. 女子說「我正在去赴約的路上」，她指的是什麼？
A 她有一場午餐會議
B 她沒有太多時間講話
C 她想要男子簽署合約
D 她有很多時間講話

55. 女子想要知道什麼？
A 他是否會簽署新合約
B 他是否可以在下午三點來到她的辦公室
C 他是否要去歐洲度假
D 他是否已經付旅遊費了

NEW
56-58 conversation

M：Hi, Beth. Do you like amusement parks?
W：Yeah! I really like them.
M：(56) **Some of us from the accounting department are going to Dreamworld on Saturday for a team bonding day.**
W：Oh really? I've never been there before. (57) **I had some plans this Saturday but I can easily change them.** What time were you thinking of going?

56–58 對話

男：嗨，貝絲。你喜歡遊樂園嗎？
女：是的！我真的很喜歡。
男：(56) **我們會計部門有些人要在星期六的團隊聯誼日去夢幻世界。**
女：喔，真的嗎？我從來沒有去過那裡。(57) **我這星期六已有安排一些計劃，但我很容易就能改變計劃。**你們想要幾點去？

M：We should meet around 10 a.m. at Central Station. It will be much easier to take the subway because it's hard to find parking at the amusement park.

W：OK. Sounds good. (58) **I will book all of the tickets on my credit card online so we don't have to wait in the line.**

男：我們應該會於上午十點在中央車站會面。搭地鐵會容易得多，因為在遊樂園很難找到停車位。

女：好的，聽起來不錯。(58) **我會用信用卡在網路上訂所有的票，這樣我們就不用排隊。**

NEW

56. What does the man imply when he says, "Some of us from the accounting department are going to Dreamworld on Saturday for a team bonding day"?

A He is recommending the theme park.
B He needs some documents signed.
C He wants the sales figures for this month.
D He is inviting her to join them.

56. 男子說「我們會計部門有些人要在星期六的團隊聯誼日去夢幻世界」時，在暗示什麼？

A 他推薦這個主題樂園
B 他需要有人簽署一些文件
C 他想要本月的銷售數字
D 他在邀請她加入他們

57. What does the woman say about her plans?

A She can't change them.
B She can change them.
C They've been cancelled.
D They've been postponed.

57. 關於她的計劃，女子說了什麼？

A 她無法改變計劃
B 她可以改變計劃
C 計劃被取消了
D 計劃被延後了

58. What does the woman offer to do?

A Pick everyone up in her car
B Meet them at the amusement park
C Book the tickets online
D Pay for the tickets with cash

58. 女子提議做什麼？

A 開她的車去接大家
B 與他們在遊樂園碰面
C 在網路上訂票
D 用現金付款買票

NEW

59-61 conversation

W：Are you guys ready? We need to leave shortly because the show starts in an hour. The traffic will be very heavy.

M1：Yeah, we better go soon. I'm so excited! (59) **I've never seen a Broadway show before.** I'll call John and see if he is ready to go or not.

W：(60) **Tell him I can pick him up with my car on the way there.** Otherwise, he has to take the subway and that will take a long time.

M2：Yeah, you're right. I will text him and let him know we are on our way.

M1：Do not text him. I will just call him now and let him know. (61) **Oh, and Judy, I will give you some money for parking because it is quite expensive in that area.**

59–61 對話

女：你們準備好了嗎？我們馬上就得出發了，因為表演一小時後就要開始。交通很繁忙。

男 1：是的，我們最好快點走。我超興奮的！(59) **我以前從來沒看過百老匯的表演。**我打電話給約翰看看他是否準備好要出發了。

女：(60) **告訴他我可以開車順路去接他。**否則他就得搭地鐵，那樣要很久。

男 2：沒錯，你說的對。我傳簡訊給他讓他知道我們上路了。

男 1：別傳簡訊給他。我現在就打電話並跟他說。(61) **對了，茱蒂，我會給你一些停車的費用，因為在那地區停車相當昂貴。**

59. Where are the speakers planning to go?
- A To the cinema
- B To a restaurant
- C To a friend's house
- **D To a Broadway show**

60. What does the woman offer to do?
- A Buy the tickets
- B Call John and tell him something
- **C Pick John up in her car**
- D Send John a text message

61. What does the man offer to give to the woman?
- **A Money for parking**
- B A text message
- C A bottle of champagne
- D A ride to the show

59. 對話者們正打算要去哪裡？
- A 去電影院去
- B 去餐廳
- C 去朋友的家
- **D 去看百老匯的表演**

60. 女子提議要做什麼？
- A 買票
- B 打電話給約翰並告知他某件事
- **C 開她的車載約翰**
- D 傳簡訊給約翰

61. 男子提議要給女子什麼？
- **A 停車費**
- B 簡訊
- C 一瓶香檳
- D 載她去看表演

NEW

62-64 conversation

W：OK,(62) **the body wash set on special today is $48. Do you have a customer loyalty card?**

M：I have a discount coupon I want to use while it's still valid. It's in my bag . . . here it is.

W：OK. Hmm, it's not registering on the computer. Let me try to figure this out.

M：Wait a minute . . . Oh, I see what the problem is. (63) **I don't have enough items.** Let me get some more things and I will be right back.

W：No problem. (64) **I will hold this stuff at the counter for you while you take a look.**

62–64 對話

女：好的，(62) **今日特價的沐浴組要 48 元。你有會員卡嗎？**

男：我有一張折價券，想趁它還在有效期限內使用。它在我的包包裡……找到了。

女：好的，嗯，電腦無法讀取。我來想辦法處理。

男：等等……喔，我知道問題出在哪了。(63) **我購買的品項不夠多**，讓我再多拿幾樣東西，我很快就會回來。

女：沒問題。(64) **你去逛的時候，我會把這些物品保留在櫃台。**

Maxx Cosmetics 麥克斯化妝品

Gift Card 折價券

10% off any purchase over $50 消費滿 50 元可打九折

Expires March 1 三月一日到期

62. What does the woman ask the man?
A If the body wash is on sale
B If he has a loyalty card
C If he wants to use a credit card
D If the body wash is good

NEW
63. Look at the graphic. Why is the gift card rejected?
A Because he is in the wrong store
B It has already been used too many times.
C He doesn't have items over $50.
D It has expired.

64. What does the woman offer to do?
A Find some other products
B Give him a new card
C Get her manager
D Hold his products at the counter

62. 女子詢問男子什麼？
A 沐浴乳是否在特價
B 他是否有會員卡
C 他是否想要使用信用卡
D 沐浴乳是否好用

63. 參看圖表，這張折價券為何不能用？
A 因為他來錯商店
B 它已經被使用過太多次了
C 他沒有買超過 50 元的商品
D 它已經過期了。

64. 女子提議要做什麼？
A 找一些別的產品
B 給他一張新的卡
C 找她的經理來
D 把他要買的商品留在櫃台

NEW
65-67 conversation

W：Did you hear about the network closures next week?
M：Mr. Bronson got the email about this yesterday. (65) **They need to upgrade our network so we can update our software next month.**
W：Oh, ok. But (66) **why would they put the 2nd floor offline at 1 o'clock?** They are usually so busy during that period. I don't understand why they would schedule it like that. They should do it on their lunch break.
M：Hmm . . . (67) **Good point. You should go talk to the manager. I'm sure he will agree with you, and then he can get the schedule changed.**
W：Yeah, I will. I think I better tell him now so we can arrange it.

65–67 對話

女：你聽說了下個星期網路會斷線的事了嗎？
男：布朗森先生昨天有收到關於此事的電子郵件。(65) **他們需要升級我們的網路，以便我們在下個月更新軟體。**
女：好的，但是 (66) **他們為何要在一點時關閉二樓的網路？**他們在那段時間通常很忙。我不懂為何他們要這樣子安排時間，他們應該要在午休時這麼做。
男：嗯，(67) **說得好。你應該去和經理談談，我相信他會同意你的看法，然後他就可以更改計劃。**
女：好的，我會去談談。我認為我最好現在就告知他，以便我們安排此事。

Network Closures 網路斷線 **December 1st　12 月 1 日**	
Accounting 會計部	10:00 p.m. — 11:00 a.m. 晚上 10 點－早上 11 點
Customer Service Call Center 電話客服中心	1:00 p.m. — 2:00 p.m. 下午 1 點－下午 2 點
Human Resources 人資部	2:00 p.m. — 3:00 p.m. 下午 2 點－下午 3 點
Research and Development 研發部	3:00 p.m. — 4:00 p.m. 下午 3 點－下午 4 點

65. What is happening next month?
A An annual software convention
B Their software is being upgraded.
C The software will be sold early.
D The monthly hardware update

65. 下個月會發生什麼事？
A 年度的軟體會議
B 他們的軟體將被升級
C 他們的軟體將會提早販售
D 每個月的硬體更新

NEW
66. Look at the graphic. Which department is on the 2nd floor?
A Accounting
B Human Resources Department
C Research and Development
D Customer Service Call Center

66. 參看圖表，在二樓的是哪一個部門？
A 會計部
B 人資部
C 研發部
D 電話客服中心

67. What does the man suggest the woman do?
A Call Human Resources
B Call her manager
C Call the sales department
D Call the software company

67. 男子提議女子做什麼？
A 打電話給人資部
B 打電話給她的經理
C 打電話給業務部
D 打電話給軟體公司

NEW
68-70 conversation

W：Hello, I'm travelling to Barcelona, Spain on business next month. (68) **I'd like to use my mileage points to upgrade my seat.**
M：Of course, (70) **can you please tell me your JenAir membership number?**
W：OK, it's JA388739.
M：Give me a minute as I bring up your information. Oh, I'm sorry. You don't have enough points to upgrade for this trip.
W：Oh, that's too bad. How many more points do I need?
M：(69) **About 20,000 more points. You should have enough to upgrade after your trip to Spain, however.**
W：Oh, that's so disappointing. I'll have to come to terms with waiting another few months before that upgrade then.

68–70 對話

女：哈囉，我下個月要到西班牙巴塞隆納出差。(68) **我想要使用我的里程點數來升級座位。**
男：當然，(70) **可以請您告訴我您的珍航會員號碼嗎？**
女：好的，號碼是 JA388739。
男：請稍待，讓我找出你的資訊。很抱歉，你這趟旅行沒有足夠的點數可以升級。
女：太可惜了。我還需要多少點數？
男：(69) **大約還要 20,000 點，不過你去西班牙之後應該就有足夠的點數可以升級了。**
女：喔，真令人失望。我也只好接受再多等幾個月才能升級。

Airline Mileage Redemption Points 航空哩程兌換點數

To East Asia 到東亞	60,000
To North America 到北美	80,000
To South America 到南美	90,000
To Europe 到歐洲	70,000

68. Why does the woman call?
A To cancel a flight
B To register a membership
C To use her mileage points
D To confirm an appointment

NEW
69. Look at the graphic. How many points does the woman currently have?
A 20,000 points
B 40,000 points
C 50,000 points
D 70,000 points

70. What does the man ask the woman to tell him?
A Her plane ticket
B Her membership number
C Her cell phone number
D Her flight itinerary

68. 女子為何打電話？
A 為了取消班機
B 為了註冊會員身份
C 為了使用她的哩程點數
D 為了確認一場會面

69. 參看圖表，女子目前有多少點數？
A 20,000 點
B 40,000 點
C 50,000 點
D 70,000 點

70. 男子要求女子告訴他什麼？
A 她的機票
B 她的會員編號
C 她的手機號碼
D 她的航班行程資訊

PART 4 P. 42-45

08

71-73 telephone message

M：Hello, my name is Rick Dunn. (71) **I was in your store today and I'm worried I may have left my wallet there.** Earlier today I was in the home furniture section looking at some couches. (72) **I think my wallet may have slipped out of my pocket while sitting on one of the couches.** If you could please look for it, I would really appreciate it. (73) **I'd like to stop by your store when you open it at 9:00 a.m. tomorrow.** I hope you have good news for me. My phone number is 023-555-6541. Thank you in advance.

71–73 電話留言

男：哈囉，我的名字是李克・鄧恩。(71) **我今天去了你的店，我擔心我可能把皮夾留在那裡了。**今天稍早我在家具區看一些沙發椅。(72) **我想當我坐在其中一張沙發椅時，皮夾可能滑出口袋了。**可以的話，請你幫我找找，我會很感激的。(73) **我想在你明天早上九點開門時到你店裡。**我希望你能給我好消息。我的電話號碼是 023-555-6541。那就先謝謝你了。

71. Who is the message probably for?
A A carpenter
B A store manager
C A furniture designer
D A bank teller

72. According to the speaker, when does he think he lost his wallet?
A When he used a dressing room
B When he visited a bookstore
C When he presented his ID card
D When he tried some furniture

71. 這則留言可能是要給誰的？
A 木匠
B 商店經理
C 家具設計師
D 銀行櫃員

72. 根據發話者所言，他認為他何時遺失皮夾的？
A 當他使用更衣室時
B 當他去書店時
C 當他拿出證件時
D 當他試用某件家具時

73. What does the speaker plan to do?

A Replace an item

B Call the police

C Go to the store again

D Stop by the listener's home

73. 發話者打算做什麼？

A 換貨

B 報警

C 再去商店

D 去聽者的家

74-76 introduction

W： Welcome to the Gould Museum of Ancient Artifacts. (74) **I'll be your guide today for the Ancient Egypt exhibit.** (75) **The majority of the artifacts you will see today are being put on public display for the first time.** In particular, this exhibit features the everyday objects used by ancient Egyptian people. These items include jewelry, pots, and kitchen utensils. (76) **After this tour, you can purchase a book in our gift shop that includes photographs of the artifacts with more detailed background information explaining their origins.**

74–76 介紹

女： 歡迎來到古爾德古代工藝品博物館。(74) **今天由我擔任各位的古埃及展的導覽。**(75) **各位今天所見的文物大多都是首度參展。**尤其，這個展覽的主題是古埃及人的日常用品。這些物品包含珠寶、盆器以及廚房用品。(76) **導覽過後，各位可以在禮品部買書，書裡有展品的照片，及更詳細的背景資料，解釋這些展品的來源。**

74. Who most likely is the speaker?

A A historian

B An artist

C An antiques dealer

D A museum guide

74. 發話者最有可能是什麼人？

A 歷史學家

B 藝術家

C 古董經銷商

D 博物館導覽人員

75. What is mentioned about the exhibit?

A It is sponsored by the Egyptian government.

B Most of its artifacts had not been seen by the public.

C It will run until the end of the month.

D It includes works from modern Egyptian artists.

75. 關於這個展覽，有提到什麼？

A 展覽是由埃及政府贊助的

B 大部分的展品先前未曾公開展出

C 展覽將持續到月底

D 展品包含現代埃及藝術家的作品

76. According to the speaker, how can listeners receive more information?

A By reading a sign

B By searching online

C By purchasing a publication

D By listening to a presentation

76. 根據發話者所言，聽者要如何獲得更多資訊？

A 藉由閱讀解說告示

B 藉由上網搜尋

C 藉由購買出版品

D 藉由聆聽簡報

77-79 announcement

W: Attention, passengers. Our arrival in Chicago is expected to be somewhat behind schedule. (77) **Due to the heavy snowfall, our bus driver must use appropriate caution and drive at a slower speed.** (78) **Therefore, we will probably be arriving an hour later than our scheduled arrival time, which was 5:00 p.m.** Although these circumstances are out of our control, we do apologize for any inconvenience it may cause you. (79) **We would like to remind passengers that this bus offers free Wi-Fi connection.** This is just one of the amenities that make riding with us more comfortable than with our competitors.

77–79 宣布

女：各位乘客請注意。我們抵達芝加哥的行程預計會有些延後。(77) **因為這場大雪，我們的巴士司機必須謹慎以對，用較慢的速度行駛。**(78) **因此，我們也許會比原定下午五點鐘的抵達時間晚一小時到達。**雖然這些情況並非我們所能控制，我們仍要為造成您的不便致歉。(79) **我們想要提醒乘客，這輛巴士提供免費的無線網路。**這只是其中一項便利設施，讓搭乘本公司的車，比搭乘同業的車更為舒適。

77. What has caused the problem?

A A traffic accident
B A heavy workload
C Bad weather
D A vehicle malfunction

78. According to the speaker, around what time will the bus arrive at the destination?

A 4:00 p.m.
B 5:00 p.m.
C 6:00 p.m.
D 7:00 p.m.

79. What does the bus provide to passengers?

A Free Internet access
B A discounted ticket
C A complimentary meal
D A comfortable connecting bus service

77. 什麼導致了這個問題？

A 交通事故
B 繁重的工作量
C 天候不佳
D 車輛故障

78. 根據發話者所言，巴士將大約在幾點到達目的地？

A 下午四點
B 下午五點
C 下午六點
D 下午七點

79. 巴士為乘客提供了什麼？

A 免費上網
B 打折車票
C 免費餐點
D 舒適的接駁車服務

80-82 radio broadcast

M: Good afternoon, dedicated listeners. You are listening to the weekly broadcast of *World Table*, the program that explores culinary traditions from all around the world. (80) **On today's show, our guest is Cindy Mills, a renowned documentary producer.** Ms. Mills is going to speak about her new documentary,

80–82 收音機廣播

男：午安，各位忠實聽眾。你們收聽的是每週播出的廣播節目《世界餐桌》，本節目探索世界各地的烹飪傳統。(80) **在今天的節目裡，我們的來賓是辛蒂·米爾斯，她是知名的紀錄片製作人。**米爾斯女士將要談論她的新紀錄片《中國的飲食和

Food and Life of China. (81) **She produced the documentary while visiting traditional Chinese restaurants and interviewing chefs and restaurant patrons.** (82) **If you visit the website at www.tmostation.com, you can view a trailer for the documentary.**

生活》。(81) **她製作這部紀錄片的期間，造訪傳統的中國餐館，並採訪廚師和餐廳主顧。**(82) **若你上網站 www.tmostation.com，可以看到這部紀錄片的預告。**

80. Who is being introduced?

Ⓐ A chef
Ⓑ A backpacker
Ⓒ A critic
Ⓓ A producer

81. What is the documentary about?

Ⓐ World-famous restaurants
Ⓑ Traditional Chinese cuisine
Ⓒ A celebrity's life
Ⓓ Popular recipe books

82. According to the speaker, what can listeners find on the website?

Ⓐ A review
Ⓑ A menu
Ⓒ A preview
Ⓓ An interview

80. 正在介紹的是什麼人？

Ⓐ 廚師
Ⓑ 背包客
Ⓒ 評論家
Ⓓ 製作人

81. 這部記錄片與什麼有關？

Ⓐ 世界知名餐廳
Ⓑ 傳統中國菜餚
Ⓒ 名人生活
Ⓓ 受歡迎的食譜書

82. 根據發話者所言，聽眾可以在網站上找到什麼？

Ⓐ 評論
Ⓑ 菜單
Ⓒ 預告片
Ⓓ 訪談

83-85 excerpt from a meeting

W： Great news everybody! Quarterly profits are up 23%. (83) **The introduction of our new range of body washes has exceeded all of our expectations.** Our other products have continued to sell well, particularly our facial creams and hand creams. (84) **Last month our products were featured in *En Vogue* magazine, and they had a three-page story on the quality of our manufacturing process.** This must have helped with our sales increase. We are expecting more media exposure in the following months, and the release of several new products. (85) **How about that? I'm proud of all the work you have put into this quarter.** Let's keep it up!

83–85 會議摘錄

女： 各位，有好消息！季度的獲利增加了 23%。(83) **我們推出的新沐浴乳系列表現超越預期。**我們其他的產品持續暢銷，尤其是面霜和護手乳。(84) **上個月我們的產品受到《風尚》雜誌的報導，他們用了三頁來報導我們生產過程的品質。**這肯定有助於我們銷售量的增加。我們預期在接下來幾個月中有更多的媒體曝光機會，還有幾項新產品的上市。(85) **你們覺得如何？我對於你們這一季的努力感到驕傲。**我們繼續保持下去吧！

83. What type of products are being discussed?

A Computer parts
B Hair products
C Beauty products
D Cell phones

84. According to the speaker, what happened last month?

A Sales went down.
B A product launch went better than expected.
C Their products were featured in a magazine.
D Another company took over their contract.

NEW

85. What does the woman mean when she says, "How about that?"

A She doesn't understand the situation.
B She expected a customer return policy.
C She wants to purchase some products.
D She is happy with the company's progress.

83. 討論的是什麼類型的產品？

A 電腦零件
B 美髮用品
C 美容產品
D 手機

84. 根據發話者所言，上個月發生了什麼事？

A 銷售下滑
B 產品發表會比預期更好
C 他們的產品受到雜誌的報導
D 另一家公司接手了他們的合約

85. 女子說「你們覺得如何」，她指的是什麼？

A 她不了解情況
B 她預期有顧客退貨政策
C 她想要購買一些產品
D 她對於公司的進步感到滿意

86-88 announcement

M：Hello, everyone. (86) **I'd like to announce a few changes in our procedure that are designed to save us money.** Firstly, we will no longer be sending statements to clients through the post. We'll be using email to send monthly statements. (87) **It is a simple procedure, and when the software is installed I don't think you will need any training. The system is very straightforward.** We are also renting out the catering room, and installing some refrigerators in the cafeteria, (88) **so you will have to start bringing your own lunches to work.**

86–88 宣布

男：哈囉，大家好。(86) **我想宣布程序上的幾項改變，其目的是要節省開銷。**首先，我們不再透過郵件寄送報表給客戶，我們將使用電子郵件來寄月報表。(87) **這是很簡單的程序，等軟體安裝完成後，我認為你們不會需要任何訓練，該系統非常簡明易懂。**我們也將出租餐廳，並且在自助餐廳裡安裝幾台冰箱。(88) **因此，你們必須開始帶自己的午餐來上班。**

86. According to the speaker, why are changes being made?

A Because of poor working condition
B To save the company money
C So that they can afford a Christmas party
D He expected a better contract.

86. 根據發話者，為何做出這些改變？

A 因為不良的工作環境
B 為了節省公司的錢
C 這樣他們就能負擔得起聖誕派對
D 他預期會有更好的合約

NEW

87. What does the speaker imply when he says, "when the software is installed I don't think you will need any training"?

A The new system is easy to learn.
B He doesn't want to train people.
C There is no budget for training.
D Everyone must attend a meeting.

88. What does the speaker tell the listeners they will have to start bringing to work?

A Extra uniforms
B Other people's lunch
C Their own lunch
D A new contract

89-91 telephone message

M： Hi, Julia, This is Frank Walton from Human Resources. (89) **We need to post an ad this week for a new dental assistant.** A colleague told me you are really good at making job application ads. (90) **Have you seen the criteria for the dental assistant position?** This is my first time recruiting new staff, so I'm a little unfamiliar with some of the questions. (91) **I would really appreciate it if you could come by my office today and show me the criteria.** Thanks.

89. What position is being advertised?

A Legal assistant
B Dental assistant
C Foreign coordinator
D Bank manager

NEW

90. What does the man imply when he asks, "Have you seen the criteria for the dental assistant position?"

A He is looking at some forms.
B He is asking if Julia is familiar with the requirements.
C He needs some extra work done.
D He wants to apply for the job.

87. 發話者說「等軟體安裝完成後，我認為你們不會需要任何訓練」，他在暗示什麼？

A 新的系統很容易上手
B 他不想訓練員工
C 沒有訓練的預算
D 大家都必須出席會議

88. 發話者告訴聽眾他們必須開始帶什麼來上班？

A 額外的制服
B 其他人的午餐
C 自己的午餐
D 新的合約

89–91 電話留言

男： 嗨，茱莉亞。我是人力資源部的法蘭克．沃頓。(89) **我們這星期需要張貼一則徵才廣告**，要找新的牙醫助理。有個同事告訴我你很擅長製作徵才廣告。(90) 你**是否看過牙醫助理一職的資格條件？**這是我第一次招募新員工，因此我對於當中的一些問題不太熟悉。(91) **若你今天能到我辦公室來並告訴我這些資格條件，我會很感激的。**謝謝。

89. 這是什麼職務的廣告？

A 法律助理
B 牙醫助理
C 國外協調員
D 銀行經理

90. 男子問說「你是否看過牙醫助理一職的資格條件」，他在暗示什麼？

A 他正在看一些表格
B 他在問茱莉亞是否熟悉這些條件
C 他需要有人做一些額外的工作
D 他想要應徵這份工作

91. Why does the man want to meet the woman?
A To show him the criteria
B To make some changes to his office
C To sign the contract
D To change the criteria

91. 為何男子想與女子見面？
A 請女子告訴他這些資格條件
B 要變動他的辦公室
C 要簽署合約
D 要改變資格條件

92-94 telephone message

W：Hi, this message is for Ronald Benson. (92) **My name is Amy Lawson, the manager at Rosewood Printing Company.** We just received an online order from you for 2000 wedding invitations with lace and gold fabric wrappings. (93) **I'm calling just to confirm your order is for 2000 invitations and not 200.** It is unusual to get such a large order so I just want to make sure it is correct. Please call me back to confirm when you have a chance. We will not proceed with the order until you confirm. (94) **Also, if you are planning such a large event, we have an excellent planner in the office named Shubert Mendez. If you want to speak with him, I will make sure he gives you a free consultation.**

92–94 電話留言

女：嗨，這則留言是要給羅納德．班森的。(92) **我的名字是艾咪．洛森，我是羅斯伍德印刷公司的經理。**我們剛收到您寄來的一份線上訂單，要印製 2000 份有蕾絲和金色織品包裝的婚禮邀請函。(93) **我打電話是要確認你的訂單是要 2000 份邀請函而不是 200 份。**那麼大筆的訂單很不尋常，因此我想要確認訂單是正確的，請您有空的時候回電給我進行確認，在您確認之前我們不會開始處理這份訂單。(94) **此外，如果你正在籌劃這麼大型的活動，我們公司有位很優秀的婚禮規劃師，名叫舒伯特．曼德茲。如果您想與他洽談，我會請他提供您免費諮詢。**

IN-HOUSE DIRECTORY 同事通訊錄

Extension 分機	Name 姓名
10	John Trizz 約翰．特利斯
11	Don Trenton 唐．德蘭頓
12	Shubert Mendez 舒伯特．曼德茲
13	Sally Howle 莎莉．荷伊

92. Who most likely is the speaker?
A A content developer
B A secretary
C A company manager
D A police officer

92. 發話者最有可能是什麼人？
A 網頁內容開發者
B 秘書
C 公司經理
D 警官

93. Why most likely is the speaker calling?
A To confirm the size of an order
B To request some delivery information
C To send an extra gift
D To purchase a new set of cards

93. 發話者最有可能是為了什麼打電話？
A 為了確認訂單的數量
B 為了請求某些運送資訊
C 為了寄送附加贈品
D 為了購買一套新卡片

NEW
94. Look at the graphic. What is the planner's extension number?
A 10
B 11
C 12
D 13

94. 參看圖表，籌辦者的分機為何？
A 10
B 11
C 12
D 13

TEST 2
PART 4
08

95-97 radio broadcast

M：Hi everybody, this is the late shift with Joey Denton on Free Net Radio. (95) **Today we have George Farrelli in the studio to talk about his hit new album, which has been number one on the charts for six weeks.** Earlier today, (96) **George was telling me how his album was heavily influenced by his recent move to London**, and the growing rock-and-roll scene there. You can definitely hear the British influence in the title track "Frankly Speaking." (97) **Coming up next, we will discuss George's up and coming marriage to his longtime girlfriend Cindy Pullman.** Thanks for joining us today George.

95–97 廣播節目

男：大家好，這裡是免費網路廣播電台晚班的喬伊・丹頓。(95) **今天我們特別邀請到喬治・法拉利來到錄音室，要談論他新的暢銷專輯，此專輯已蟬聯六週的排行榜冠軍。**今天稍早，(96) **喬治告訴我，他最近搬遷到倫敦及該地日漸盛行的搖滾氛圍，皆對他的專輯產生深遠的影響。**各位在主打歌〈老實說〉當中一定能聽出英倫風格的影響。(97) **接下來，我們會討論喬治與愛情長跑的女友辛蒂・普曼即將舉行的婚禮。**感謝你今天加入我們，喬治。

BEST-SELLING ALBUMS 暢銷專輯

Rank 排名	Name 名稱
1	Talk Down《高聲駁倒》
2	Valleys of Fire《火焰之谷》
3	Tunnel Vision《狹隘之見》
4	Step It Up《向上提升》

NEW
95. Look at the graphic. What is the name of the guest's new album?
A Valleys of Fire
B Step It Up
C Tunnel Vision
D Talk Down

95. 參看圖表。來賓的新專輯名稱為何？
A 《火焰之谷》
B 《向上提升》
C 《狹隘之見》
D 《高聲駁倒》

96. What does the speaker say has influenced the guest's music?
Ⓐ Getting married
Ⓑ Moving to America
Ⓒ Moving to London
Ⓓ Meeting Joey Denton

97. What will the guest most likely do next?
Ⓐ Move back to his hometown
Ⓑ Get engaged to his girlfriend
Ⓒ Release a new album
Ⓓ Get married to his girlfriend

96. 發話者說什麼影響了來賓的音樂？
Ⓐ 結婚
Ⓑ 搬遷到美國
Ⓒ 搬遷到倫敦
Ⓓ 與喬伊・丹頓會面

97. 來賓接下來最有可能做什麼事？
Ⓐ 搬遷回故鄉
Ⓑ 與女友訂婚
Ⓒ 發表新專輯
Ⓓ 與女友結婚

98-100 introduction

M：Hi, everybody. (99) **Welcome to the retirement celebration of our long-time president Mr. Jang.** Mr. Jang has served as president for the last 22 years and has helped build our business from its humble beginnings to a fortune 500 company. (98) **It's a pleasure to host this special event in the famous Gloria Westwood Ballroom.** I consider it an indication of the success we have experienced. (100) **My name is Bob Hopkins, and I've worked for Mr. Jang for over 20 years.** I consider him to be one of the most talented, honest, and hardworking people I know, and I feel privileged to call him my friend. So, with no further ado, please put your hands together for Mr. Jang.

98–100 介紹

男：嗨，大家好。(99) **歡迎來到常任董事長張先生的退休歡送會。**張先生在過去22年以來一直擔任董事長，協助公司從草創初期，發展成如今的全球五百大企業。(98) **我很榮幸能在著名的葛洛莉・威斯伍德宴會廳主持這場特別的活動**，我認為這代表了我們擁有的成功。(100) **我的名字是鮑伯・霍普金斯，我在張先生的旗下超過 20 年了。**我認為他是我所認識最聰明、最誠實和最努力的人，我有幸稱他為我的朋友。那麼，廢話不再多說，請大家鼓掌歡迎張先生。

GRANGE RIVER TOWER DIRECTORY 格蘭治河大樓名錄

Floor 樓層	Name 名稱
3rd Floor 三樓	Corporate Suites 公司套房
4th Floor 四樓	Rosella Ballroom 羅賽拉宴會廳
5th Floor 五樓	Gloria Westwood Ballroom 葛洛莉・威斯伍德宴會廳
6th Floor 六樓	Main Office 主要辦公室

NEW

98. Look at the graphic. Where is the celebration taking place?

A 3rd floor

B 4th floor

C 5th floor

D 6th floor

99. What is the reason for the celebration?

A To introduce a new employee

B Mr. Jang's birthday

C The retirement of Mr. Jang

D A wedding anniversary

100. Who is Mr. Hopkins?

A Mr. Jang's nephew

B An employee of Mr. Jang

C The owner of the company

D A waiter

98. 參看圖表，慶祝會在哪裡舉行？

A 三樓

B 四樓

C 五樓

D 六樓

99. 開慶祝會的原因是什麼？

A 介紹一名新員工

B 張先生的生日

C 張先生的退休

D 婚禮週年紀念

100. 霍普金斯先生是誰？

A 張先生的外甥

B 張先生的員工

C 企業主

D 服務生

ACTUAL TEST ③

PART 1 P. 46-49

09

1. A The woman is looking at some menu.
   B There is a measuring tape around her neck.
   C She is holding a pair of scissors.
   D She is making some curtains with her measuring tape.

2. **A She is looking at the laptop.**
   B The vegetables are behind the laptop.
   C She is writing an email.
   D She is cutting some cucumber and carrot.

3. A All of the men are wearing glasses.
   B All of the people are looking at the laptop.
   C There are glasses of water on the table.
   D All of the men are leaning over the table.

4. A The man is throwing a snowball at the wood.
   B They are making a snowman.
   C The man is breaking the snowball.
   D They are having a snowball fight.

5. **A All of the chairs are the same.**
   B There are a lot of people swimming in the water.
   C The pool is nearby the sea.
   D The umbrellas are closed.

6. A She is at the supermarket.
   B She is selecting a pot of flowers.
   C She is with her best friend.
   D She is paying for a pot of flowers.

1. A 女子正在看菜單。
   B 她的脖子上掛著一條捲尺。
   C 她正拿著一把剪刀。
   D 她正用捲尺製作一些簾幕。

2. **A 她看著筆記型電腦。**
   B 蔬菜在筆記型電腦的後方。
   C 她在寫電子郵件。
   D 她在切一些小黃瓜和紅蘿蔔。

3. A 男子們全都帶著眼鏡。
   B 所有人都看著筆記型電腦。
   C 桌上有數杯水。
   D 男子們全都倚靠著桌子。

4. A 男子正在對著木頭丟雪球。
   B 他們正在堆雪人。
   C 男子正在打破雪球。
   D 他們正在打雪仗。

5. **A 這些椅子全都相同。**
   B 有很多人在水中游泳。
   C 這個水池在海邊。
   D 傘是收起來的。

6. A 她在超級市場。
   B 她正在挑選一盆花。
   C 她和最好的朋友在一起。
   D 她正在付錢購買一盆花。

PART 2 P. 50

10

7. Where are the training materials being distributed?
   A Please pass me the stapler.
   B In Room 403.
   C On-the-job training.

8. Is this the last train?
   A Yes, it's the nature trail I visited a month ago.
   B It'll last two hours.
   C No, there will be another.

7. 訓練教材正在哪裡發放？
   A 請將訂書機傳來給我。
   B 在 403 室。
   C 在職訓練。

8. 這是最後一班火車嗎？
   A 是的，這就是我一個月前走過的天然步道。
   B 它將持續兩小時。
   C 不，還有另一班。

9. Jesse left an envelope for me, didn't he?
A It's at the front desk.
B No, turn right at the corner.
C Yes, he will develop a new product.

10. When will the construction be completed?
A In three months.
B They're building a bridge.
C It was too complicated.

11. Won't you try the dessert?
A Try on this one.
B The area is mostly desert.
C Sorry, but I'm full.

12. Why didn't you call our client today?
A I saw it yesterday.
B I emailed her instead.
C Thank you for calling us.

13. Who still hasn't arrived yet?
A I'll ask Mr. Simpson.
B He arrived an hour ago.
C The train has been delayed.

14. What do you think about our new television advertisement?
A I watched the show yesterday.
B Through the advertising agency.
C It's very eye-catching.

15. Where are the stairs to the basement?
A He stared at the sign.
B At the end of the hall.
C There's no elevator in the building.

16. Can you give me a hand now, or should I ask again later?
A Please hand out these flyers.
B How about after lunch?
C It's my pleasure.

17. Should we hire a new employee to handle this project?
A Yes, we'll need help.
B Turn the handle.
C A little higher, please.

9. 傑西留了一個信封給我，對不對？
A 它在櫃台。
B 不，在街角右轉。
C 是的，他將開發一個新產品。

10. 這項工程何時會完工？
A 三個月內。
B 他們正在建造橋樑。
C 它太複雜了。

11. 你不試試這個甜點嗎？
A 試穿這一件。
B 這個地區大多是沙漠。
C 抱歉，但我飽了。

12. 你今天為何沒有打電話給我們的客戶？
A 我昨天看見它了。
B 我改成寄電子郵件給她。
C 感謝你打電話給我們。

13. 誰還沒到？
A 我來問辛普森先生。
B 他一小時前就到了。
C 這列火車誤點了。

14. 你覺得我們新的電視廣告怎麼樣？
A 我昨天看了這個節目。
B 透過這家廣告代理商。
C 它非常吸睛。

15. 通往地下室的樓梯在哪裡？
A 他盯著這個號誌看。
B 在走廊的盡頭。
C 這棟大樓裡沒有電梯。

16. 你現在可以幫我嗎，或是我晚點再問你？
A 請發這些傳單。
B 午餐之後如何？
C 我很樂意。

17. 我們應該僱用一名新員工來處理這個專案嗎？
A 是的，我們將需要協助。
B 轉動這個把手。
C 請稍微高一點。

18. The concert isn't sold out already, is it?
A The guitarist is Andy Gordon.
B No, tickets just went on sale today.
C I sold my vehicle.

19. I'm here to return some shoes.
A Do you have the receipt?
B They fit perfectly.
C Before the race starts.

20. Have you tested the product?
A Yes, it was an aptitude test.
B I saw it on the news.
C No, should I?

21. Who had lunch delivered to the office today?
A Ms. Adams will.
B I don't know, since I just arrived.
C In the meeting room.

22. What's the address of our buyer in Hong Kong?
A Check the client database.
B From the shipping company.
C Fragile contents.

23. Would you like to go through the quarterly report?
A I already did.
B How about through the consulting firm?
C According to the news report.

24. Did you purchase tickets for the performance?
A No, it's a one-way ticket.
B We could watch it live on television.
C The band is world-famous.

25. Do you remember the name of the presenter?
A No, I didn't present my ID card.
B It's written in the program.
C He was named after his grandfather.

26. How did you find my wallet?
A It was less than $50.
B He paid in cash.
C I asked at the lost and found.

27. Why didn't Sam publish his book yet?
A He is still revising it.
B The library is closed today.
C I'll book a flight.

18. 音樂會的票還沒賣完，對嗎？
A 吉他手是安迪．歌頓。
B 還沒有，票今天才開賣。
C 我賣了我的車。

19. 我是來退還鞋子的。
A 你有收據嗎？
B 它們很合身。
C 在賽跑開始之前。

20. 你測試過這項產品了嗎？
A 是的，這是性向測驗。
B 我在新聞上看到它。
C 還沒有，我該這麼做嗎？

21. 今天是誰叫了午餐外送到辦公室？
A 將會是亞當斯女士。
B 我不知道，因為我才剛來。
C 在會議室。

22. 我們香港買家的地址是什麼？
A 查閱客戶資料庫。
B 從貨運公司。
C 易碎的內容物。

23. 你想要檢視季度報告嗎？
A 我已經這麼做了。
B 透過這家顧問公司怎麼樣？
C 根據新聞報導。

24. 你買了這場表演的門票了嗎？
A 不，這是單程票。
B 我們可以看電視直播。
C 這個樂團世界知名。

25. 你記得簡報者的姓名嗎？
A 不，我沒有拿出證件。
B 它就寫在活動大綱中。
C 他是以他祖父的名字命名的。

26. 你是怎麼找到我的皮夾的？
A 不到 50 元。
B 他用現金付款。
C 我去失物招領處詢問。

27. 為何山姆還沒有出版他的書？
A 他還在修改它。
B 圖書館今日不開放。
C 我將會訂機票。

28. Could you post this announcement on the front door?
A Sure, wait a minute.
B Yes, he applied for the post.
C They made an announcement yesterday.

29. Didn't the courier already come today?
A I replaced the broken part.
B No, he usually arrives after lunch.
C It was an international carrier.

30. We can't accept credit cards at our store for now.
A It was on sale.
B The last four digits of my credit card.
C What about checks?

31. Why don't you bring a camera along?
A In a frame.
B An amateur photographer.
C Actually, I don't have one.

28. 你可以將這個布告張貼在前門嗎？
A 當然可以，請稍等。
B 是的，他應徵了這個職位。
C 他們昨天宣布了。

29. 快遞今天不是來過了嗎？
A 我更換了壞掉的零件。
B 不，他通常在午餐之後來。
C 這是一家國際運輸公司。

30. 本店暫時無法接受信用卡。
A 它在特價中。
B 我信用卡的最後四碼。
C 那用支票可以嗎？

31. 你為何不帶著相機？
A 在相框裡。
B 業餘攝影師。
C 其實我沒有相機。

PART 3 P. 51-55

11

32-34 conversation

W：Hello, this is Julia Kramer calling from Human Resources. (32) **I gave your department a laptop computer to be fixed last week, and I still haven't received an update**. The keyboard needed to be replaced.

M：Ah, yes, Ms. Kramer. We have had a lot of work orders lately, so we are a little behind with repairs. Is the matter urgent?

W：(33) **Well, I just forgot to copy an important file off the hard drive that I need for my work.**

M：I can transfer that file onto a storage device for you. (34) **Come to my office at your convenience.**

32–34 對話

女：哈囉，我是人力資源部門的茱莉亞．克萊門。(32) **我上星期拿了一台筆記型電腦到你的部門修理，而我還沒有被告知目前的進度**。鍵盤需要更換。

男：是的，克萊門女士。我們最近接到許多工單，因此維修進度有點落後。是很緊急的事情嗎？

女：(33) **我只是忘了從硬碟複製工作需要的重要檔案。**

男：我可以幫你將檔案傳輸到儲存裝置。(34) **你方便時請到我的辦公室來。**

32. Which department does the man most likely work in?
A Human Resources
B Accounting
C Marketing
D Technical Support

32. 男子最有可能在哪個部門工作？
A 人力資源部
B 會計部
C 行銷部
D 技術支援部

33. What is the woman unable to do?
- (A) Contact a client
- (B) Write an email
- **(C) Access a file**
- (D) Purchase a laptop computer

34. What does the man suggest doing?
- **(A) Stopping by his office**
- (B) Enrolling in a class
- (C) Replacing a part
- (D) Reading a manual

35-37 conversation

M：Hello, Ms. Turner. This is Michael Schmidt calling from the Yorkshire Seaside Hotel. It says here that you would like to be informed if a seaside room becomes available. (35) **Well, someone has just canceled, so if you would like to upgrade, you may.**

W：Oh, great. Thanks so much for informing me. (36) **How much more is the upgraded room compared to the standard room?**

M：Well, it will cost an extra $50 a night. However, the room comes with a larger bed and a hot tub. I recommend you visit our website to see pictures and information.

W：OK. (37) **I'll look at your website and then call you back with my decision.**

35. Why is the man calling?
- (A) To request a payment
- (B) To confirm an order
- **(C) To offer a room upgrade**
- (D) To advertise a product

36. What does the woman inquire about?
- **(A) Difference in price**
- (B) Valet parking
- (C) Local entities
- (D) A warranty period

37. What does the woman say she will do?
- (A) Pay by credit card
- **(B) Compare options**
- (C) Take pictures
- (D) Rearrange her schedule

33. 女子無法做什麼？
- (A) 聯繫客戶
- (B) 寫電子郵件
- **(C) 取用檔案**
- (D) 購買筆記型電腦

34. 男子提議做什麼？
- **(A) 前往他的辦公室**
- (B) 報名參加課程
- (C) 更換零件
- (D) 閱讀使用手冊

35–37 對話

男：哈囉，透納女士。我是麥克．史密特從約克夏海濱飯店的來電。資料顯示，您希望海濱房間有空房時能收到通知。(35) **嗯，剛剛有人取消訂房，因此如果您想要升級的話，是可以的。**

女：喔，太好了，很感謝你通知我。(36) **與標準房相比，升級的房間要再加少錢？**

男：嗯，一晚要多 50 元。不過，房間的床比較大，還有一個浴缸。我建議您上我們的網站看看照片以及相關資訊。

女：好的。(37) **我會上你們的網站然後回你電話，告知我的決定。**

35. 男子為何打電話？
- (A) 為了要請求付款
- (B) 為了確認訂單
- **(C) 為了提供房間升等**
- (D) 為了宣傳產品

36. 女子詢問什麼？
- **(A) 費用差額**
- (B) 代客泊車
- (C) 當地的公司行號
- (D) 保固期限

37. 女子說她將會做什麼？
- (A) 以信用卡付費
- **(B) 比較選項**
- (C) 拍攝照片
- (D) 重新安排行程

38-40 conversation

M：Hello. Since I bought an air conditioner from your store, I have never changed the air filter. (38) **Should I replace it soon?**

W：When did you buy it? (39) **We recommend changing the filter once a year at a minimum.** If you suffer from allergies, you should change it even more often.

M：(39) **Oh, I guess I'm due for a new filter then.** How can I purchase a replacement? Do you carry it there?

W：Yes, we do. (40) **All you need to tell us is the model number of your air conditioner.** Do you happen to know it?

38–40 對話

男：哈囉，自從我在你的店裡買了一台冷氣機以後，還沒有換過濾網。(38) **我是否得盡快更換？**

女：你是何時購買的？(39) **我們建議至少一年更換濾網一次。**如果你會過敏，應該要更經常更換。

男：(39) **喔，那麼我猜想我該換新的濾網了。**我要怎麼購買替換的濾網呢？你們有賣嗎？

女：是的，我們有。(40) **你只需要跟我們說冷氣機的型號即可。**你會不會剛好知道呢？

TEST 3 PART 3 11

38. Why is the man calling?

A To cancel an order
B To ask for advice
C To purchase an air conditioner
D To schedule an appointment

39. How long has the man most likely used the air conditioner?

A About a day
B About a week
C About a month
D About a year

40. What information does the woman request?

A The year of production
B Contact information
C A model number
D The date of purchase

38. 男子為什麼打電話？

A 為了取消訂單
B 為了尋求建議
C 為了購買冷氣機
D 為了安排會面

39. 男子最有可能已使用這台冷氣機多久？

A 大約一天
B 大約一週
C 大約一個月
D 大約一年

40. 女子要求什麼資訊？

A 製造年分
B 聯繫方式
C 型號
D 購買日期

41-43 conversation

M：(41) **Katrina, I'm going to pick you up at 5 o'clock to go to the rock festival.** I had such a great time last year. I hope it's even better this year.

W：Yeah, I'm excited, too. (42) **However, are you sure if we leave at 5:00 we will still get there on time?** It starts at 5:30 and I think it takes at least an hour to get there.

M：Huh? (43) **Isn't it being held in Harpersville like last year?**

41–43 對話

男：(41) **卡崔娜，我五點鐘會去接你參加搖滾音樂節。**我去年玩得很愉快，希望今年會更棒。

女：沒錯，我也很興奮。(42) **但是你確定我們五點鐘離開還能夠準時到達嗎？**音樂節五點半就開始，我認為到那裡至少需要一小時。

男：什麼？(43) **它不是像去年一樣在哈波斯威爾舉辦嗎？**

W：(43) **No, the festival is being held in Bristol this year.** The festival organizers are expecting more attendees this year. They were concerned that there wouldn't be enough parking spaces, so they moved it to Bristol.

女：(43) **不，今年是在布里斯多舉辦。** 音樂節主辦單位預計今年會有更多人參與。他們擔心停車位不足，因此將地點改到布里斯多。

41. What type of event are the speakers discussing?
A A fundraiser
B A workshop
C An anniversary
D A music festival

41. 對話者們在討論哪一種活動？
A 募款會
B 研習會
C 週年慶
D 音樂節

42. What is the woman concerned about?
A Reserving tickets
B Finding a parking space
C Arriving on time
D Accommodating more attendees

42. 女子擔心什麼？
A 訂門票
B 找停車位
C 準時到達
D 容納更多參與者

43. How is the event different from the one held last year?
A There will be a family ticket option.
B A shuttle bus will be available.
C No cameras will be allowed.
D A different place will be used.

43. 今年的活動與去年辦的有何不同？
A 將會有家庭票的選擇
B 將會有接駁巴士可坐
C 不准使用相機
D 將使用不同的地點

44–46 conversation

M：(44) **Stephanie, did you see the flyer hanging on the bulletin board in the hallway?** It says a yoga class will be available to all employees free of charge. Are you planning on signing up?

W：Yeah, I saw that. (45) **It looks like a great opportunity, but the class is held on Wednesday nights, and that's the same day as my jazz dance class.**

M：Oh, I didn't know you took a dance class. You have so many talents I didn't know about. I would love to see you dance sometime.

W：(46) **Well, actually, we are putting on a performance next month at the Mond Theater.** I would be so happy if you and our team members came.

44–46 對話

男：(44) 史蒂芬妮，你看見貼在走廊布告欄上的傳單了嗎？它說所有員工都可以免費參加一門瑜伽課程，你打算要報名嗎？

女：對啊，我看見了。(45) **看起來是個不錯的機會，但課程是在星期三晚上，與我的爵士舞蹈課同一天。**

男：喔，我不知道你在上舞蹈課。你有很多我不知道的才華，我改天想看你跳舞。

女：(46) **其實，我們下個月將在門德戲院演出。** 如果你和我們的團隊成員能來，我會很開心。

44. How did the man find out about the yoga class?
A From a public posting
B From a coworker
C From the woman
D From a company's website

44. 男子如何得知瑜伽課程的事？
A 從公告
B 從同事
C 從女子
D 從公司網站

45. Why can't the woman attend the yoga class?

A She hurt her back.

B She can't afford the fee.

C She has to take care of her children.

D She must attend a different class.

46. What will the woman do next month?

A Apply for a new job

B Watch the man's jazz dance

C Appear in a performance

D Register for a class

45. 女子為何無法上瑜伽課？

A 她的背受傷

B 她負擔不起費用

C 她必須照顧孩子

D 她必須上另一堂課

46. 女子下個月將會做什麼？

A 應徵新工作

B 觀賞男子的爵士舞蹈表演

C 參與演出

D 報名課程

47–49 conversation

M：Hello, this is Axel Fischer calling. I placed an order last week for a blouse that I was going to give to my wife as a present. However, I think I bought the wrong size. (47) **I'd like to cancel the order.**

W：(48) **I'm sorry, but that item has already been shipped.** You'll have to wait until it arrives and then return it. But don't worry. We can still refund your purchase.

M：Oh, thanks. Wow, I'm surprised it was shipped so soon after the order was placed. By the way, will I have to pay for shipping?

W：Unfortunately, yes. According to our policy, in this case you will have to pay for the return shipping. (49) **I'll send you a return shipping label via email.** What's your email address?

47–49 對話

男：哈囉，我是阿克塞爾．費雪。我上星期下了訂單要買一件女用襯衫，想送給我妻子當禮物。但我覺得我買錯尺寸了，(47) **我想要取消訂單。**

女：(48) **很抱歉，但該商品已經出貨了，**必須要等它送達後再退貨。但別擔心，我們仍可退款。

男：喔，謝謝。哇，我很驚訝下訂單後那麼快就出貨了。對了，我需要付運費嗎？

女：很遺憾，需要。根據我們的規定，在這種情況下，您必須要負擔退貨的運費。(49) **我會透過電子郵件寄給您退貨的托運標籤。**您的電子郵件地址是什麼？

47. Who most likely is the woman?

A A customer service representative

B A travel agent

C A fashion designer

D An event coordinator

48. According to the woman, why can't the item be refunded immediately?

A A computer system is not working.

B A manager is absent.

C It has already been sent.

D The man is not eligible for a refund.

47. 女子最有可能是什麼人？

A 客服人員

B 旅行社代辦人員

C 時裝設計師

D 活動籌辦者

48. 根據女子所言，為何此商品不能立刻退款？

A 電腦系統無法運作

B 經理不在

C 商品已出貨

D 男子不符合退款資格

49. What does the woman say she will do?

Ⓐ Offer a discount

Ⓑ Send an email

Ⓒ Provide a product catalog

Ⓓ Contact a manager

49. 女子說她將會做什麼？

Ⓐ 提供折扣

Ⓑ 寄電子郵件

Ⓒ 提供產品型錄

Ⓓ 聯繫經理

NEW

50-52 conversation

W：Here is the office space you asked me about.(50) **It is hot inside because the air conditioners have been off, but usually the temperature is fine.** What do you think?

M：It's quite nice. There is a lot of natural sunlight, which I really like.

W：Me, too. It's a little small, but we only have five employees, so it would be fine.

M：Is there any public transport close by? Some of our employees take the subway to work.

W：Yes. Actually, the Brighton street stop is about a five-minute walk, so it's pretty close.

M：(51) **The only problem is the carpet.** It's quite dirty. Does the owner plan on changing it anytime soon?

W：(52) **Actually, we are having new carpets put in next week.** So don't worry about that. If you sign the contract, you won't move your stuff in for a month.

M：That's great. I think we will take it. When do we need to sign the contract?

W：I will prepare it when I get back to the office, and we can sign it all tomorrow afternoon.

50–52 對話

女：這就是你先前向我詢問的辦公場所。(50) **裡面很熱，因為沒開空調。但是室溫通常還算適宜**。您覺得如何？

男：這地方很不錯，有很多的自然光，我很喜歡。

女：我也是。這裡有點小，但我們只有五名員工，因此這不成問題。

男：附近有任何大眾運輸嗎？我們有一些員工搭地鐵上班。

女：有，其實，走路去布萊敦街車站大約只要五分鐘，因此很近。

男：(51) **唯一的問題是地毯**，它很髒。屋主打算最近要換地毯嗎？

女：(52) **實際上，我們下星期就會鋪新的地毯**。所以別擔心這件事。如果您簽了合約，您也得等一個月後才能把東西搬進來。

男：太好了，我想這個地方我們要了。我們什麼時候要簽合約？

女：我回到辦公室後會去準備合約，然後我們明天下午就可以簽約。

50. Why is it hot inside the office?

Ⓐ The air conditioner was on.

Ⓑ The air conditioner was broken.

Ⓒ There is no air conditioning.

Ⓓ The air conditioner had been off.

51. What is the man's problem with the office?

Ⓐ There is no public transport close by.

Ⓑ The carpet is not clean.

Ⓒ The contract is not signed.

Ⓓ The office is too small.

50. 為何辦公室裡很熱？

Ⓐ 空調開著

Ⓑ 空調壞了

Ⓒ 沒有裝空調

Ⓓ 空調關了

51. 男子覺得辦公室有什麼問題？

Ⓐ 附近沒有大眾運輸

Ⓑ 地毯不乾淨

Ⓒ 還沒有簽合約

Ⓓ 辦公室太小了

52. How does the woman respond to the man's problem?

A She tells him they are putting in new carpets.
B She tells him that the carpets aren't dirty.
C She prepares the contract for tomorrow.
D She shows him another office.

52. 女子如何回應男子的問題？

A 她跟他說會鋪新的地毯
B 她告訴他地毯並不髒
C 她會備妥明天所需的合約
D 她帶他看另一間辦公室

53-55 conversation

M：(53) **OK, Ms. Florence, I have talked with my colleagues about purchasing your office building.** The total offer, including tax, is three hundred thousand dollars.

W：That's much lower than I had expected. (54) **I've had several other offers that are higher than that from other real estate agents.** One agent offered me three hundred and fifty thousand dollars.

M：Well, there is room for negotiation. We are very interested in the property, so I will pay more if you have other offers. We would like to sign a contract as soon as possible.

W：(55) **I'm pleased you can match their offer.** I will give you a call this afternoon and we can arrange the contract.

53–55 對話

男：(53) **好的，佛羅倫斯女士，我已經與我的同事討論過購買你辦公大樓的事。**含稅的總出價是 30 萬元。

女：那比我先前預期的低很多。(54) **其他幾位房仲報給我的價錢更高，**其中一名房仲出價 35 萬元。

男：嗯，我們還有協商的空間。我們對這個房產很有興趣，因此如果你有其他的出價，我願意付更多錢。我們想要盡快簽署合約。

女：(55) **我很高興你願意比照抬高價碼。**我今天下午會打電話給你，然後我們可以安排合約的事。

TEST 3
PART 3
11

53. What are the speakers discussing?

A A real estate deal
B The condition of the property
C The terms of a contract
D Renovating the property

53. 對話者們在討論什麼？

A 房地產交易
B 該房地產的狀況
C 合約條款
D 翻修房產

NEW

54. Why does the woman say "I've had several other offers that are higher than that from other real estate agents"?

A To offer a contract
B To negotiate a higher price
C To settle a deal
D To recommend a realtor

54. 為何女子說「其他幾位房仲報給我的價錢更高」？

A 為了提供合約
B 為了談到較高的價格
C 為了成交
D 為了推薦房仲

55. Why is the woman pleased?

A Because she completed her work.
B The renovations will go ahead.
C She found a new realtor.
D The buyer will pay more money.

55. 為何女子感到高興？

A 因為她完成了工作
B 翻修會繼續進行
C 她找到了新的房仲
D 買家會付更多的錢

56-58 conversation

W：Hi, Simon. I just got a phone call from Joseph Hardy at Datsio Construction. (56) **He is wondering why we have not started construction on the Marshall Tower yet.** He wants to begin construction as soon as possible because they are losing money while they wait.

M：I see. My lawyers are still going over some of the clauses in the contract that may need changing. (57) **I've been meaning to visit him, but I have been busy with the new mall we are building on West Point. I'll go down this afternoon and have a talk with him.**

W：OK, I understand. It's probably best we make sure that the contract is right before you sign it. (58) **I'll call Joseph and organize a meeting time, and I'll email and tell you what time to go and see him.**

56–58 對話

女：嗨，賽門。我收到了達西歐建設公司約瑟夫・哈地的來電。(56) **他想問我們為什麼還沒開始馬歇爾塔的建設工程。**他想要盡快開工，因為他們等候的同時也在虧錢。

男：我了解了。我的律師們正在審閱合約當中一些可能需要異動的條款。(57) **我一直想要拜訪他，但我忙著處理我們在西點搭建新商場的事。我今天下午會過去並且與他談談。**

女：好的，我知道了。我們或許該在你簽署前確保合約是正確的。(58) **我會打電話給約瑟夫並且安排會議時間，然後我會寄電子郵件給你，告訴你什麼時候去見他。**

56. Where do the speakers most likely work?

Ⓐ A research facility
Ⓑ A legal firm
Ⓒ A construction company
Ⓓ A pharmacy

NEW

57. What does the man mean when he says, "I've been meaning to visit him"?

Ⓐ He has already visited him.
Ⓑ He knows that he should have visited him.
Ⓒ He will visit him tonight.
Ⓓ He forgot about it.

58. What will the woman include in her email?

Ⓐ When to visit Joseph
Ⓑ The contract details
Ⓒ Joseph's phone number
Ⓓ The lawyer's documents

56. 對話者們最有可能在哪裡工作？

Ⓐ 研究機構
Ⓑ 法律事務所
Ⓒ 建設公司
Ⓓ 藥局

57. 男子說「我一直想要拜訪他」，他指的是什麼？

Ⓐ 他已經拜訪過他了
Ⓑ 他知道他早該拜訪他
Ⓒ 他今晚將會拜訪他
Ⓓ 他忘了此事

58. 女子將會在電子郵件中包含什麼？

Ⓐ 何時要拜訪約瑟夫
Ⓑ 合約細節
Ⓒ 約瑟夫的電話號碼
Ⓓ 律師的文件

NEW

59-61 conversation

M1：OK, Ms. Mendez. (59) **The total cost to repaint the foyer will be around $4,000.** That includes after-service for six months if you have any problems with our work.

59–61 對話

男 1：好的，曼德茲女士。(59) **重新油漆門廳的總價大約是 4000 元。**這包含了六個月的售後服務，如果您對於我們的工作有任何問題的話。

W：Hmm . . . That's more expensive than I thought it would be. Our budget was $3,000. Why is the price so high?

M2：[60] **I can explain why the price is over your budget.** It is because the old paint is peeling badly in some areas. We have to remove it all before repainting, which takes a long time. If you had repainted it earlier, it would be less expensive.

M1：In the future I would recommend painting it every seven years.

W：OK. I thought I was being overcharged, but that makes sense. [61] **You can go ahead and begin painting on the first weekend of August.**

女：嗯……這比我先前想的還要貴。我們的預算是 3000 元。為何價格如此高？

男 2：[60] **我可以解釋為何價格會超過你們的預算**。這是因為有幾個地方的老舊油漆嚴重剝落。重新粉刷之前我們必須將它全都清除乾淨，這要花很長的時間。如果你早一點重新油漆，就會比較便宜。

男 1：我會建議以後每七年油漆一次。

女：好的，我以為我被多收了，但你說得有道理。[61] **你們可以從八月的第一個週末開始油漆。**

59. What kind of work are the men doing?
- A Remodeling the foyer
- B Renovating the bathrooms
- **C Repainting the foyer**
- D Renovating the kitchen

60. What does the man explain to the woman?
- A Why she has a low budget
- **B Why the price is above her budget**
- C Why the foyer isn't ready to be painted
- D Why the paint in the foyer is peeling

61. When does the woman want the men to begin work?
- A The second week of September
- B Anytime during August
- C After August
- **D The first Saturday of August**

59. 男子們在做哪一種工作？
- A 改建門廳
- B 翻修浴室
- **C 重新粉刷門廳**
- D 翻修廚房

60. 男子對女子解釋什麼？
- A 為何她的預算很低
- **B 為何價格超過她的預算**
- C 為何門廳還不可以油漆
- D 為何門廳的油漆在剝落

61. 女子想要男子們何時開始工作？
- A 九月的第二週
- B 八月的任何時候
- C 八月之後
- **D 八月的第一個星期六**

62-64 conversation

W：Excuse me? [62] **I'm on a diet at the moment, so I'm looking for some healthier food options.** I like to have cereal in the morning. Can you recommend something to me? My nutritionist said I should eat a lot of protein.

M：There are many different breakfast options. One of my favorites is the new Protein Plus range. It has oats, fruits, and extra protein added. Here, take a look.

62–64 對話

女：不好意思？[62] **我正在節食，因此我在找尋比較健康的食物。**我喜歡早上吃玉米片，你可以幫我推薦嗎？營養師說我應該吃大量的蛋白質。

男：有很多不同的早餐選擇。我最喜歡的其中一項是新的「蛋白質加量」系列產品。它們有燕麥、水果，還添加了額外的蛋白質。拿去看看吧。

W：Hmm, this looks delicious! (63) **But my nutritionist said I should keep my sugar intake below 20 grams a day.** One serving of this cereal contains 28 grams!

M：Yes. In that case (64) **I recommend that you try having eggs in the morning with some coffee.** Then you can eat some sugar later in the day.

女：這看起來很美味，(63) **但營養師說我應該將糖份攝取量保持在每日 20 公克以內。**這個玉米片一份就包含 28 公克！

男：是的。這樣的話，(64) **我建議你試著早餐吃蛋並搭配咖啡**，然後可以在當天稍晚再吃一些糖。

Nutrition Information 營養資訊
Serving Size: 150 g　每份份量：150 公克

Calories 熱量	**200 大卡**
Fat 脂肪	5 g 公克
Protein 蛋白質	10 g 公克
Sugar 糖	28 g 公克

62. What is the woman trying to do?
A Gain some weight
B Eat foods with more sugar
C Skip breakfast
D Lose some weight

NEW
63. Look at the graphic. Which content is the woman concerned about?
A Fat
B Sugar
C Protein
D Eggs

64. What does the man recommend the woman do?
A Have some bacon and eggs
B Just drink coffee in the morning
C Not to eat breakfast
D Have coffee and eggs

62. 女子正嘗試做什麼？
A 增加體重
B 吃含有更多糖份的食物
C 略過早餐
D 減重

63. 參看圖表，女子擔心哪一個成分？
A 脂肪
B 糖
C 蛋白質
D 蛋

64. 男子建議女子做什麼？
A 吃培根和蛋
B 早上只喝咖啡
C 別吃早餐
D 喝咖啡和吃蛋

NEW
65-67 conversation

M：Hi, I need this suit cleaned. (65) **I'm going overseas on a business trip on the weekend, and all my suits are getting a bit old now.** How much would it cost to clean this?

65–67 對話

男：嗨，我需要清洗這件西裝。(65) **我週末要到國外出差，而我所有的西裝都有點舊了。**清潔這個要多少錢？

W：Hmm . . . (66) **Usually twenty dollars.** But this one will cost a bit more.
M：Really? Why is that?
W：Well, you're very tall. This suit is going to take longer to clean and require more products. It will incur a surcharge.
M：Hmm . . . Maybe I will take it somewhere else. That doesn't seem fair.
W：(67) **OK. I will do it for twenty dollars.** And whenever you need a suit cleaned, please come back to me.

女：嗯……(66) **通常是 20 元**，但這件要稍微貴一點。
男：真的嗎？為什麼？
女：嗯，你個頭很高。這件西裝要花比較久的時間清潔，而且要用較多的清潔產品，會導致費用增加。
男：嗯……也許我該將西裝帶去別的地方洗，這價格似乎並不公道。
女：(67) **好吧，我幫你清洗，只收 20 元。** 以後無論你何時需要清潔西裝，請回來找我。

TEST 3
PART 3
11

Frankie's Dry Cleaning 法蘭琪乾洗

Fabric 布料	Price 價格
Polyester 聚酯纖維	$10
Cotton 棉	$12
Wool 羊毛	$20
Silk 蠶絲	$30

65. What does the man say he will do on the weekend?
A Go on a vacation
B Host a business lunch
C Go on a business trip
D Get some new suits

NEW
66. Look at the graphic. What is the suit made of?
A Polyester
B Silk
C Cotton
D Wool

67. What does the woman say she will do?
A She won't do it for twenty dollars.
B She will charge the man the original price.
C She will do it for more than twenty dollars.
D She will do it by next week.

65. 男子說他將在週末做什麼？
A 度假
B 舉辦商業午餐會
C 出差
D 買新西裝

66. 參看圖表，這件西裝是用什麼材質製成的？
A 聚酯纖維
B 蠶絲
C 棉花
D 羊毛

67. 女子說她將會做什麼？
A 她不會收 20 元就做此事
B 她將收男子原價
C 她會收超過 20 元以做此事
D 她會在下星期前做此事

68-70 conversation

W：Hi, Jimmy. Just checking up on you. (68) **Have you finished installing wiring for the lighting in Olive Cosmetics?**

M：I've nearly finished. There were some problems with the electrical box, so I had to fix some old fuses. It took longer than expected.

W：(69) **OK. I'm nearly finished with the lighting on the first floor, but** (70) **I need help installing some cables on the roof.** Can you come downstairs when you are finished?

M：Sure. This will take me another 20 minutes. Then I will come down.

68–70 對話

女：嗨，吉米，你好。我是來看看你的。(68) **你安裝好奧利佛化妝品公司的照明線路了沒？**

男：我快完成了。之前配電箱有些問題，因此我必須修理一些老舊的保險絲，所以花了比預期更久的時間。

女：(69) **好的，我快要完成一樓的照明了**，但是 (70) **我需要協助安裝天花板上的纜線**。你完成後可以到樓下來嗎？

男：當然，這還要再花 20 分鐘，然後我就會下去了。

Franklin Towers 富蘭克林塔樓

First floor 一樓：	Trinity Construction 三元建築
Second Floor 二樓：	Mullberry & Co. 穆貝利公司
Third Floor 三樓：	Olive Cosmetics 奧利佛化妝品
Fourth Floor 四樓：	Torrenz Inc. 托倫茲公司

68. Who most likely are the speakers?
- A Plumbers
- B Office workers
- **C Electricians**
- D Carpet cleaners

NEW

69. Look at the graphic. Where is the woman currently working?
- **A Trinity Construction**
- B Mullberry & Co.
- C Olive Cosmetics
- D Torrenz Inc.

70. What does the woman ask the man to do?
- A Install some piping in the wall
- B Install some cables in the ground
- **C Install some cables in the roof**
- D Install some new software on the computers

68. 對話者最有可能是什麼人？
- A 水管工人
- B 辦公室員工
- **C 電工**
- D 地毯清潔人員

69. 參看圖表，女子目前正在哪裡施工？
- **A 三元建築**
- B 穆貝利公司
- C 奧利佛化妝品
- D 托倫茲公司

70. 女子要求男子做什麼？
- A 在牆壁安裝管線
- B 在地底安裝纜線
- **C 在天花板安裝纜線**
- D 在電腦安裝新軟體

71-73 telephone message

W：Hello, my name is Alice Keller. (71) **I'm calling to reserve some tables for a private party next Thursday.** (72) **I have been a loyal customer of your restaurant for years and trust it will be the perfect place for my wedding after-party.** We are expecting around 50 guests and will pay for food and drinks to be served to all guests. (73) **One of our requests is that vegetarian options be available for some of the guests.**

71–73 電話留言

女：哈囉，我的名字是愛麗絲·凱勒。(71) **我打電話是要為下星期四的一場私人派對訂位。** (72) **我多年來一直是貴餐廳的忠實顧客，我相信貴的餐廳會是我婚宴派對的最佳地點。** 我們預計大約有 50 名賓客。我們會付費購買食物和飲料提供給所有賓客。(73) **我們的要求之一是要為一些賓客提供素食的選擇。**

71. Why is the speaker calling?
- A To order food delivery
- B To advertise a cooking class
- C To report a problem
- **D To make a reservation**

71. 發話者為什麼打電話？
- A 為了訂外送食物
- B 為了宣傳烹飪課
- C 為了提出問題
- **D 為了預訂場地**

72. What will the speaker celebrate next week?
- A A birthday
- B A promotion
- C A retirement
- **D A wedding**

72. 發話者下星期將會慶祝什麼？
- A 生日
- B 升遷
- C 退休
- **D 婚禮**

73. What does the speaker want the listener to do?
- A Contact some guests
- B Decorate a space
- **C Meet special dietary needs**
- D Prepare an estimate

73. 發話者想要聽者做什麼？
- A 聯繫賓客
- B 裝飾會場
- **C 滿足特殊的飲食需求**
- D 準備估價單

74-76 talk

M：Welcome to the Taylor Footwear factory. (74) **On this tour, you will see how shoes are made and packaged before they are shipped to our distributors.** (75) **One aspect that makes our factory special is that everything is done by hand.** Unlike most factories, where automated machines do all the work, at Taylor Footwear factory everything is done by a team of experienced shoemakers. (76) **Before this tour ends, everyone will get a chance to try making soles of leather sandals themselves, with the assistance of some of our staff members.**

74–76 談話

男：歡迎來到泰勒製鞋廠。(74) **在這次導覽中，你們會看到鞋子在運送到經銷商之前的製作和包裝過程。** (75) **我們工廠很特別的一點是，所有一切皆為手工製成。** 有別於大部分工廠都是由自動化的機器進行所有工作，在泰勒製鞋廠，一切都是由經驗豐富的製鞋團隊完成的。(76) **在參觀行程結束之前，大家在我們一些員工的協助下，都有機會體驗親手製作皮製涼鞋的鞋底。**

74. What does the factory produce?
A Appliances
B Clothes
C Toys
D Shoes

75. What is special about the factory?
A Its size
B Its production method
C Its automated machines
D Its location

76. What will listeners do at the end of the tour?
A Participate in a hands-on experience
B Receive a free product
C Have refreshments
D Return to the tour bus

77-79 announcement

W：(77) **The last item on today's meeting agenda is preparations for next week's business conference in Germany.** Linda Wong from marketing and Chris Owen from sales will be representing our company at the conference. (78) **This conference will connect us with more clients and more advantageous business opportunities.** (79) **Therefore, everyone is asked to email a departmental status report for the first quarter to both Ms. Wong and Mr. Owen before the end of the week to help them prepare.** Thank you.

77. What will happen next week?
A A budget proposal
B A business event
C A performance evaluation
D A shareholders' meeting

78. What benefit does the speaker mention?
A Fewer complaints
B Reduced travel time
C Access to clients
D Strengthened security

74. 這家工廠生產什麼？
A 家電用品
B 衣服
C 玩具
D 鞋子

75. 這家工廠有何特別之處？
A 它的規模
B 它的生產方式
C 它的自動化機器
D 它的地點

76. 聽眾在導覽結束時將會做什麼？
A 親自動手做
B 收到免費的產品
C 享用茶點
D 返回遊覽車

77–79 宣布

女：(77) **本日會議議程的最後一項，是為下週在德國商務會議做準備。**行銷部門的琳達．王以及業務部門的克里斯．歐文，將代表公司出席會議。(78) **這場會議能讓我們有更多的客戶以及更有利的商業機會。**(79) **因此，在這個星期結束以前，大家都要將第一季的部門狀況報告，以電子郵件寄給王女士及歐文先生，以協助他們做準備。**謝謝。

77. 下星期將會發生什麼事？
A 預算提案
B 商務活動
C 表現評量
D 股東會議

78. 發話者提到有什麼好處？
A 較少客訴
B 縮短旅遊時間
C 獲得客戶
D 強化保全

79. What are the listeners asked to do?

A Delete unnecessary data

B Submit a report

C Contact clients directly

D Email an order confirmation

79. 聽眾被要求做什麼？

A 刪除不必要的檔案

B 繳交報告

C 直接聯繫客戶

D 以電子郵件寄送訂單確認信

80-82 introduction

M：Welcome to the opening ceremony for this year's Young Novelists Seminar. (80) **This seminar is available to students from high school to university and will help aspiring novelists grow and develop into the masters of tomorrow.** (81) **The first thing we ask everyone to do is to fill out a name tag and attach it to your shirt.** There are over one hundred students here, and it's difficult to keep track of everyone. (82) **Next up, Natasha Marsh, the renowned literary critic, is going to give the opening speech for the ceremony.** Please listen up. She has some inspiring words for everyone today.

80–82 介紹

男：歡迎來到今年「新銳小說家研討會」的開幕典禮。(80) **從高中到大學的學生都可以參加，而且研討會能幫助有志成為小說家的人成長並發展成為明日的大師。**(81) **我們要求大家所做的第一件事，就是填寫名牌並貼在衣服上。**這裡有超過100名學生，要記得每個人是不容易的事。(82) **接下來，著名的文學評論家娜塔莎·馬歇將要發表開幕致詞。**請仔細聆聽，她今天要給大家一些啟發性的話語。

80. Who most likely are the listeners?

A Professional novelists

B University professors

C Potential writers

D Prospective clients

81. What are the listeners asked to do?

A Fill out a questionnaire

B Attach a name tag

C Introduce themselves

D Read a book

82. Who is Natasha Marsh?

A An athlete

B A children's author

C An event organizer

D A guest speaker

80. 聽者最有可能是什麼人？

A 專業小說家

B 大學教授

C 潛力作家

D 潛在客戶

81. 聽者被要求做什麼？

A 填寫問卷

B 黏貼名牌

C 自我介紹

D 閱讀書籍

82. 娜塔莎·馬歇是什麼人？

A 運動員

B 兒童文學作家

C 活動規劃者

D 演講貴賓

83-85 news report

W： This is Sarah Brixton from CCR News. I'm here at the WingTip shoe store next to Hyde Park, where **(83) hundreds of people are waiting to buy the new running shoes the company will release tomorrow. (84) Some people have camped here overnight, while others have taken the day off work to be here. From the look of it, you'd think they were giving the shoes away.** The new shoe design is a huge upgrade from WingTip's last design because of their new Boost technology. The Boost technology is made with three strips of an innovative material the company has developed, which contains thousands of specially formulated foam pellets called "energy capsules". To show appreciation to its most loyal customers, **(85) WingTip is giving away a limited edition shoes to the first 100 customers on the first day of sales, featuring the signature of the Chicago Blue's star forward Jerry Halliwell.**

83–85 新聞報導

女： 我是《CCR 新聞》的莎拉．布萊克斯頓。現在我在海德公園旁的翼尖鞋店，在這裡 **(83) 數以百計的人們已在等候要買這家公司明天上市的新款跑鞋。(84) 有些人已在此紮營過夜，也有些人請假前來。從這個情況看起來，你會以為他們在免費贈送鞋子。**這款新鞋的設計是翼尖鞋店上代鞋款的大幅升級，因為有了新的 Boost 科技。Boost 科技是由三條該公司研發的創新材料製成，包含了數千個專門配製的膠粒，稱為「能量膠囊」。為了對最忠實的顧客表達感激之意，**(85) 翼尖鞋店將在開賣首日送出一款限量版的鞋給前 100 名顧客，上面有芝加哥藍隊明星前鋒傑瑞．哈利維爾的簽名。**

83. According to the speaker, what is happening?

A A new product is being released.

B The store is closing down.

C Their staff are all quitting.

D The company is shooting a commercial.

NEW

84. What does the speaker mean when she says, "you'd think they were giving the shoes away"?

A The store is giving the shoes away.

B There are a lot of people waiting to buy the product.

C They ran out of stock.

D A few people were upset about the product.

85. According to the speaker, what is WingTip offering the first 100 customers?

A 10% discount

B A new pair of headphones

C Free shoes

D Special edition shoes

83. 根據發話者，即將發生什麼事？

A 一項新產品即將上市

B 這家店要歇業了

C 他們的員工要全體辭職

D 這家公司正在拍攝廣告

84. 發話者說「你會以為他們在免費贈送鞋子」，她指的是什麼？

A 這家商店正在送鞋

B 有很多人在等候購買此商品

C 他們用盡庫存了

D 有些人對此產品感到不高興

85. 根據發話者所言，翼尖鞋店會提供前 100 名顧客什麼？

A 10% 的折扣

B 一副新的耳機

C 免費的鞋子

D 特別版的鞋子

86-88 introduction

M：Our next guest speaker is Gary Hardwell, CEO of Broadbank Industries. His company is responsible for funding our latest work, building wells in Africa. (86) **The value of his contributions can be seen on the walls of his office, which are lined with pictures of the villages he has provided with clean drinking water.** In the last year, Broadbank Industries has donated over 12 million dollars and built over 3000 wells across the poorest regions of Africa. This has grown into Mr. Hardwell's greatest passion, and (87) **he now spends about six months of each year in Africa overseeing his workers and ensuring his money is being spent in the right places. I think it's safe to say that Mr. Hardwell should leave some room on his walls.** In the next year he intends to increase well production by 10 percent. He has written a book about his experiences titled *Water Is Life: Giving Back to the World.* (88) **Today he will preview the book and show us some video footage of the work he is doing in Africa.** Please put your hands together for Mr. Hardwell.

86-88 介紹

男：我們的下一位來賓講者是蓋瑞・哈德威爾，他是布洛德班克工業的總裁。他的公司負責資助我們最新的工程，要在非洲建造水井。(86) **在他辦公室的牆上可以看見他的貢獻值，牆上排滿了他提供乾淨飲用水的村落照片。**在過去一年，布洛德班克工業已經捐了超過 1200 萬元，並且建了超過 3000 座水井，遍及非洲最貧窮的地區。這已成為哈德威爾先生最大的愛好，而且 (87) **他現在每年花大約六個月的時間在非洲，監督他的工人並且確保他的錢用得其所。我認為如此說並不為過，哈德威爾先生應該要在他的牆上留下一些空間。**在接下來的一年，他打算要增加 10% 的水井建造量。他已經寫了一本關於他經驗的書，書名是《水即生命：回饋世界》。(88) **今天他將會導讀這本書，並且讓我們觀賞他在非洲工作的影片。**請大家鼓掌歡迎哈德威爾先生。

86. According to the speaker, how can we see the value of Mr. Hardwell's work?

(A) By looking at all the paintings on his walls
(B) By looking at all the pictures on his walls
(C) By looking at all the fan mail in his office
(D) By looking at all the special awards on his desk

NEW

87. Why does the speaker say, "I think it's safe to say Mr. Hardwell should leave some room on his walls"?

(A) To discuss another issue
(B) To suggest he is going to continue doing more work
(C) To recommend a friend to him
(D) To make sure the audience is familiar with him

88. What will Mr. Hardwell do today?

(A) Share some of his business knowledge
(B) Preview the book and show some video
(C) Read some excerpts from his book
(D) Read a chapter from his book

86. 根據發話者，我們如何看見哈德威爾先生做此事的價值？

(A) 看他牆上的所有畫作
(B) 看他牆上的所有照片
(C) 看他辦公室裡所有的粉絲來信
(D) 看他書桌上所有的特別獎項

87. 發話者為何說「我認為如此說並不為過，哈德威爾先生應該要在他的牆上留下一些空間」？

(A) 為了討論另一項議題
(B) 為了暗示他即將繼續做更多事
(C) 為了向他推薦一名朋友
(D) 為了確保觀眾熟悉他

88. 哈德威爾先生今天將會做什麼？

(A) 分享他的商業知識
(B) 導讀這本書並且播放影片
(C) 朗讀他書中的摘錄
(D) 朗讀他書中的一個章節

89-91 telephone message

W：Hello, Ms. Francis. (89) **This is Barry Walls from Calvin Fashion. We received your design portfolio last month.** (90) **I'm sorry I didn't call you sooner, I was out of town on a business trip.** I really liked your designs; it is exactly the kind of look we are going for in our summer collection. I would like to meet you for dinner in the next few days and show you the designs we are interested in. (91) **If you are happy with the arrangement, we can go back to my office and prepare a contract.** Please get back to me as soon as possible, so we can arrange a time. I really look forward to working with you.

89–91 電話留言

女：您好，法蘭西斯女士。(89) **我是喀爾文時尚的巴莉．華爾斯。我們上個月收到你的設計作品集。**(90) **很抱歉我沒有早一點打電話給您，我到城外出差了。**我真的很喜歡您的設計作品，我們夏季商品想要尋找的款式就是這樣。我想要過幾天與你碰面吃晚餐，並且讓您了解我們感興趣的設計。(91) **如果你滿意這樣的安排，我們就可以回到我的辦公室準備合約。**請盡快回我電話，這樣我們就可以安排時間。我很期待與你合作。

89. Where does the speaker most likely work?
(A) In a law office
(B) In a fashion company
(C) In an airline company
(D) In an accounting firm

89. 發話者最有可能在哪裡工作？
(A) 在律師事務所
(B) 在時尚公司
(C) 在航空公司
(D) 在會計事務所

NEW

90. Why does the speaker say, "I was out of town on a business trip"?
(A) To explain why she hadn't called
(B) To arrange an appointment
(C) To sign the contract
(D) To discuss the building plan

90. 發話者為何說「我到城外出差了」？
(A) 為了解釋她為何先前沒有打電話
(B) 為了安排會面
(C) 為了簽署合約
(D) 為了討論建築平面圖

91. What does the speaker offer to the woman?
(A) A free plane ticket
(B) Another portfolio
(C) A deposit for rent
(D) A possible contract

91. 發話者提供什麼給女子？
(A) 免費機票
(B) 另一份作品集
(C) 租賃押金
(D) 可能的合約

92-94 telephone message

M：Hello, this is George Benson from Winbox Computers. We made a catering order two weeks ago but we need to make some changes. (92) **We have added some additional businesses to the luncheon** (93) **so, we are going to need to increase the number of cold meat trays we ordered to 10, and the mixed salad plates to 8.** Everything else can

92–94 電話留言

男：哈囉，我是 Winbox 電腦公司的喬治．班森。我們兩星期前訂了外燴服務，但我們需要做一些更動。(92) **我們的午餐會多增加了幾家企業參與，**(93) **因此，我們需要將原先訂購的肉品冷盤增加為十份、綜合沙拉盤增加為八份。**其他部分可以維持原樣，我們的訂單號碼是

remain the same. Our order number is 5521673. (94) **Please give me a call back to confirm the changes. Thanks.**

5521673。(94) **請回我電話確認這些更動，謝謝你。**

Order Form 訂購單 5521673 Customer 客戶 : Winbox Computers 電腦	
Item 項目	**Quantity 數量**
Cold meat tray 肉品冷盤	3
Mixed salad plates 綜合沙拉盤	5
12 pack bread rolls 麵包捲 12 包裝	2
Cutlery sets 餐具組	10

92. What type of event is being catered?
- A A business dinner
- **B A business luncheon**
- C A corporate breakfast
- D An annual picnic

92. 是什麼類型的活動要提供外燴？
- A 商務晚餐
- **B 商務午餐會**
- C 公司早餐
- D 年度野餐

NEW

93. Look at the graphic. Which items were not changed?
- A Cold meat trays and mixed salad plates
- B 12 pack bread rolls
- C Cutlery sets
- **D Cutlery sets and bread rolls**

93. 參看表格，哪些項目沒有更動？
- A 肉品冷盤和綜合沙拉盤
- B 麵包捲 12 包裝
- C 餐具組
- **D 餐具組和麵包捲**

94. What is the listener asked to do?
- A Send an email confirmation
- **B Call the man to confirm the changes**
- C Not to change the order
- D Cancel the whole order

94. 聽者被要求做什麼？
- A 寄電子郵件確認信
- **B 打電話給男子確認更動**
- C 不更動訂單
- D 取消整份訂單

95-97 tour guide

W： Hi, all. Welcome to the annual Florist Convention. It's a pleasure to see so many people here today. (95) **My name is Juliette White and I am the President of the Maryland Florist Association.** Today will be a great day filled with a lot of informative seminars and practical examples of how to improve your skills in all areas of floristry. (96) **First thing in the morning, everyone should meet**

95–97 旅遊導覽

女： 嗨，各位好。歡迎來到年度的花卉業者大會，今天很高興看到這麼多人出席。(95) **我的名字是茱莉葉・懷特，我是馬里蘭花卉業者協會的主席。**今天將會是個很棒的日子，充滿許多資訊豐富的研討會以及實用案例，說明如何增進花藝各領域的技能。(96) **早上的第一件事，大家上午九點要在鬱金香花園前面的**

at 9 a.m. on the road in front of the tulip garden. In the tulip garden we have the most diverse collection of tulips in England. At the moment, most are blooming, so it's a fantastic opportunity to see how you can make new and exciting arrangements. (97) **One more thing I suggest is that you visit the aviary before you go home. The combination of animal life and flowers is truly a sight to behold.**

那條路會面。在鬱金香花園裡種有英格蘭最多種類的鬱金香。現在大部分的鬱金香正在盛開，因此這是很好的機會，可以看看大家會插出什麼創新又令人興奮的花。(97) **我還想再建議一件事，就是在回家之前要參觀鳥園。動物和花卉的結合真的很值得一看。**

95. Who most likely is the speaker?
- **A President of the Maryland Florist Association**
- B President of the annual florist convention
- C President of Tulip Garden
- D President of the rest area

NEW

96. Look at the graphic. Where will the listeners go first?
- A The Aviary
- B Begonia Street
- C Dragon Lake
- **D Azalea Road**

97. What does the speaker encourage listeners to do before they leave?
- A Visit the Tulip Garden
- B Buy some flowers
- C Pick some roses
- **D Visit the Aviary**

95. 發話者最有可能是什麼人？
- **A 馬里蘭花卉業者協會的主席**
- B 年度花卉業者大會的主席
- C 鬱金香花園的主席
- D 休息區的主席

96. 參看圖表，聽眾首先會去哪裡？
- A 鳥舍
- B 秋海棠街
- C 龍湖
- **D 杜鵑路**

97. 發話者鼓勵聽眾離開之前做什麼？
- A 參觀鬱金香花園
- B 買花
- C 摘採玫瑰
- **D 參觀鳥舍**

98-100 advertisement

M: Hello, Granville Produce shoppers. (98) **It's our first birthday, and we're commemorating it with a special offer this week through Sunday.** You'll be able to take advantage of our great savings. (99) **Make sure you stop by our heirloom tomato corner, where you can find our award-winning selection of heirloom tomatoes of every variety and color.** (100) **By far the best deal is the Brandywine this season. Normally at $2.50 per pound, the Brandywine won't last long.** Don't wait! Come into Granville Produce right away, before all of the fresh, delicious vegetables are gone. Thank you for being our loyal customers over the past year. We hope to make this birthday the first of many!

98–100 廣告

男：哈囉，格蘭威爾農產品的顧客們，(98) **今天是我們開幕週年慶，為了慶祝，我們這週到週日提供特價優惠**，各位可以把握我們的超優價格。(99) **請務必前往祖傳番茄一隅，各位可以在那裡看到我們各式各色的獲獎祖傳番茄。**(100) **目前最划算的是這季的白蘭地番茄，平常要價每磅 2.5 元，白蘭地番茄產期很短。**別再等了！立刻來到格蘭威爾農產品，以免所有新鮮美味的蔬菜都銷售一空。感謝您在過去一年成為我們的忠實顧客，我們希望以後還有許多週年慶！

HEIRLOOM TOMATOES! 祖傳番茄！

Prices are per pound — 價格為每磅——

Black Cherry 黑櫻桃番茄	$1.09 元
Brandywine 白蘭地番茄	$1.39 元
Black Krim 黑克里木番茄	$2.64 元
Amana Orange 阿馬納橙色番茄	$1.30 元

98. When will the special sale be over?

A Monday
B Saturday
C Sunday
D It is weekly.

99. What is indicated about Granville Produce?

A They have a wide variety of potatoes.
B They highlight their heirloom tomatoes.
C They are an inexpensive grocer.
D They have been in business for several years.

NEW

100. Look at the graphic. Why is the Brandywine such a good deal?

A It is cheaper than the Black Krim.
B It is a delicious tomato.
C It is normally over a dollar more expensive per pound.
D It is normally not in season.

98. 特賣會什麼時候結束？

A 星期一
B 星期六
C 星期日
D 每星期舉辦。

99. 關於格蘭威爾農產品有提到哪一點？

A 他們有很多種類的馬鈴薯
B 他們主打祖傳番茄
C 他們是平價雜貨商
D 他們已經營業了好幾年

100. 參看圖表，為何白蘭地番茄很划算？

A 它比黑克里木番茄便宜
B 它是美味的番茄
C 它通常每磅要貴一塊多
D 它通常不是當季

ACTUAL TEST ④

PART 1 P. 60-63

13

1. A There are a lot of other people at the park.
B The boy is riding on his daddy's shoulders.
C They are taking a walk in the park.
D The boy is running on the path.

2. A The men are all wearing glasses.
B One of the men is typing on his laptop.
C The women are looking at each other.
D They are having a business meeting.

3. **A She is putting air into her car tire.**
B Someone is helping her fill the tire with air.
C She is pumping gas into her car.
D She is changing the tire on the car.

4. A She is cooking a steak in a frying pan.
B She is tasting the food while cooking.
C There are many fruits on the counter.
D She is cutting vegetables.

5. **A They are running on the treadmills.**
B They are using exercise bikes.
C All of the treadmills are being used.
D The man is pressing some buttons on the treadmill.

6. **A He is taking the hook out of the fish's mouth.**
B There are several men in the boat.
C He is cooking the fish.
D He has a lot of fish in the boat.

1. A 公園裡有很多其他的人。
B 男孩騎坐在父親的肩膀上。
C 他們在公園裡散步。
D 男孩在路上奔跑。

2. A 男子們全都戴眼鏡。
B 其中一名男子用筆記型電腦打字。
C 女子們看著彼此。
D 他們正在開商務會議。

3. **A 她正在為汽車輪胎打氣。**
B 某人正在協助她為輪胎打氣。
C 她正在為汽車加油。
D 她正在換汽車輪胎。

4. A 她用煎鍋烹飪牛排。
B 她一邊烹飪一邊品嚐食物。
C 料理台上有很多水果。
D 她在切蔬菜。

5. **A 他們正在跑步機上跑步。**
B 他們正在使用健身車。
C 所有的跑步機都有人在使用。
D 男子正在按跑步機上的按鈕。

6. **A 他正從魚嘴裡取出魚鉤。**
B 船上有數名男子。
C 他正在烹煮這條魚。
D 他船上有許多魚。

PART 2 P. 64

14

7. When will the meeting be held?
A After lunch.
B Yes, it will be.
C Next to the conference room.

8. Do you want me to sign this document?
A The recent documentary.
B Yes, right here.
C I can't read them.

7. 會議將在何時舉行？
A 午餐後。
B 是的，它將會。
C 在會議室旁邊。

8. 你要我簽署這份文件嗎？
A 最近的紀錄片。
B 是的，在這裡簽名。
C 我讀不懂。

9. Who will be responsible for interviewing new job applicants?
Ⓐ Before the New Year.
Ⓑ That's Jenny's duty.
Ⓒ Just apply online.

10. How many hotel rooms would you like to reserve?
Ⓐ I think at least five.
Ⓑ He stayed overnight.
Ⓒ At the beginning of March.

11. Was that the last speaker of the conference?
Ⓐ The conference schedule.
Ⓑ At 5:00 p.m.
Ⓒ No, there will be another this afternoon.

12. When will workshop registration happen?
Ⓐ The shop opened last year.
Ⓑ He is the new instructor.
Ⓒ It will begin next week.

13. Where should I store these books?
Ⓐ Yes, they are for sale.
Ⓑ Please put them in the closet.
Ⓒ He came in first place.

14. Could you pick up our client from the airport as soon as possible?
Ⓐ It's a domestic flight.
Ⓑ Check the contract.
Ⓒ Sure, I'll leave now.

15. You locked the front door after you left, didn't you?
Ⓐ No, she left early.
Ⓑ It's in the front.
Ⓒ Yes, don't worry.

16. Why was the quarterly training session canceled?
Ⓐ He's undergoing intensive training.
Ⓑ Actually, it was rescheduled.
Ⓒ Because the pencil was broken.

17. Can you give me the email address for the sales department?
Ⓐ I'll forward it to you.
Ⓑ It's a sale price for a limited time.
Ⓒ What a nice dress!

9. 誰要負責面試新的求職者？
Ⓐ 在新年之前。
Ⓑ 那是珍妮的職責。
Ⓒ 只要上網申請即可。

10. 你想要訂幾間旅館的房間？
Ⓐ 我認為至少要五間。
Ⓑ 他在此過夜。
Ⓒ 在三月初。

11. 那位是會議的最後一位演講人嗎？
Ⓐ 會議時程表。
Ⓑ 下午五點。
Ⓒ 不，今天下午還有另一位。

12. 研討會將在何時開放報名？
Ⓐ 這家店去年開張。
Ⓑ 他是新的講師。
Ⓒ 將會在下週開始。

13. 我應該將這些書收到哪裡？
Ⓐ 是的，它們供販售。
Ⓑ 請將它們放在櫃子裡。
Ⓒ 他得了第一名。

14. 你可以盡快去機場接我們的客戶嗎？
Ⓐ 那是國內航班。
Ⓑ 檢查合約。
Ⓒ 當然，我現在就出發。

15. 你離開的時候有鎖前門，對吧？
Ⓐ 不，她提早離開了。
Ⓑ 它在前面。
Ⓒ 是的，別擔心。

16. 為何季度訓練課程被取消了？
Ⓐ 他正在接受密集訓練。
Ⓑ 事實上，它被改期了。
Ⓒ 因為鉛筆斷了。

17. 你可以給我銷售部門的電子郵件地址嗎？
Ⓐ 我會將它轉寄給你。
Ⓑ 這是限時的拍賣價。
Ⓒ 這件洋裝真不錯！

18. Didn't you get my proposal?
Ⓐ It's not a new garbage disposal.
Ⓑ Yes, and I replied.
Ⓒ I didn't get there in time.

19. Are you interested in a year-long membership or something short-term?
Ⓐ I'll try just a month at first.
Ⓑ It's only available for members.
Ⓒ This loan offers low interest.

20. You can park your car in front of our building.
Ⓐ Oh, that's convenient.
Ⓑ I ran out of gas.
Ⓒ It overlooks an amusement park.

21. Is this laptop very portable?
Ⓐ Yes, it's small and lightweight.
Ⓑ It's comfortable to sit on.
Ⓒ No, it wasn't on my lap.

22. How can I find a roster of all the volunteers?
Ⓐ He volunteered to attend the conference.
Ⓑ Please register your complaint.
Ⓒ Just access the company database.

23. Please take a brochure before the presentation.
Ⓐ Thanks. I'll read it.
Ⓑ At the podium.
Ⓒ I forgot her present.

24. Ms. Schneider didn't call yet.
Ⓐ They did call for help.
Ⓑ Don't worry. She will soon.
Ⓒ Please transfer her call to me right away.

25. Shouldn't we inform our customers of the policy change soon?
Ⓐ Yes, it's custom furniture.
Ⓑ That was my application form.
Ⓒ I'll let them know.

26. You can fix my bicycle, can't you?
Ⓐ I ride the bus to work.
Ⓑ Sure, but it will take some time.
Ⓒ Yes, I can teach a graphics course.

18. 你沒有收到我的提案嗎？
Ⓐ 它不是新的廚餘粉碎機。
Ⓑ 有的，而且我回覆了。
Ⓒ 我沒有及時趕到那裡。

19. 你感興趣的是一年期的會員資格還是較短期的？
Ⓐ 我要先試用一個月。
Ⓑ 這只供會員使用。
Ⓒ 這個借款提供低利率。

20. 你可以將車子停在我們的大樓前面。
Ⓐ 喔，那真是方便。
Ⓑ 我的車沒油了。
Ⓒ 它俯瞰一座遊樂園。

21. 這台筆電易於攜帶嗎？
Ⓐ 是的，它又小又輕。
Ⓑ 坐在上面很舒服。
Ⓒ 不，它沒在我的腿上。

22. 我如何找到所有志工的名單？
Ⓐ 他自願參加這場會議。
Ⓑ 請提出你的投訴。
Ⓒ 只要進到公司的資料庫。

23. 請在簡報前拿一份手冊。
Ⓐ 謝謝，我會閱讀它的。
Ⓑ 在講台。
Ⓒ 我忘了她的禮物。

24. 史奈德女士還沒有打電話來。
Ⓐ 他們的確求救了。
Ⓑ 別擔心，她很快就會。
Ⓒ 請立刻將她的電話轉給我。

25. 我們不是該盡快告訴顧客這項政策的更動嗎？
Ⓐ 是的，這是客製化家具。
Ⓑ 那是我的申請表。
Ⓒ 我會告知他們的。

26. 你可以修好我的腳踏車，對不對？
Ⓐ 我搭公車上班。
Ⓑ 當然，但這要花一些時間。
Ⓒ 是的，我可以教一門影像設計課程。

27. I didn't turn in the assignment punctually.
(A) Take a left turn at the corner.
(B) We appreciate your punctuality.
(C) Maybe you should contact your professor.

27. 我沒有準時繳交作業。
(A) 在街角左轉。
(B) 我們感激你的準時。
(C) 也許你該聯絡你的教授。

28. What kind of ink does the printer use?
(A) He's a world-famous sprinter.
(B) Consult the manual.
(C) It's very kind of you to say so.

28. 這台印表機使用哪一種墨水？
(A) 他是世界知名的短跑選手。
(B) 查詢這本手冊。
(C) 你這麼說真是太客氣了。

29. Would you like to go out for lunch?
(A) It was tasty.
(B) The lights will go out after 7:00 p.m.
(C) When is your break?

29. 你想外出用午餐嗎？
(A) 那很美味。
(B) 晚上七點後就會熄燈。
(C) 你什麼時候休息？

30. Why was the manuscript I submitted rejected by the editor?
(A) Submit the form online.
(B) It doesn't fit the style of writing he was looking for.
(C) It was written on the menu.

30. 為什麼我交出去的稿子被編輯退回了？
(A) 用網路提交表格。
(B) 這不符合他要的寫作風格。
(C) 它就寫在菜單上。

31. I need to confirm your reservation.
(A) I'll send the confirmation number.
(B) No, there is no room.
(C) The seat was fairly firm.

31. 我需要確認你的預訂。
(A) 我會寄送認證號碼。
(B) 不，沒有空間了。
(C) 這個座位相當穩固。

PART 3 P. 65-69

15

32-34 conversation

M：Hello. (32) **Last Thursday, I arranged to have cable television installed at my house this Wednesday.** Unfortunately, I will have to be out of town that day because of some urgent matters and would like to reschedule the appointment for Friday afternoon.

W：OK, that shouldn't be a problem. (33) **However, I would like to warn you that there is a $5 rescheduling fee.** That's our company's policy. Can I have your name, please?

M：Oh, I see. My name is Charlie Kramer. I live in Hainesville. Do you know when I will have to pay this fee?

W：(34) **I'll email you soon about a user name and temporary password that you can use on our website.** Please check the email and pay all your bills through our website.

32–34 對話

男：哈囉。(32) **上週四，我安排了本週三要在我家安裝有線電視。**不巧的是，我當天因為有些急事而必須要出城去，我想要將時間改到星期五下午。

女：好的，那應該不成問題。(33) **但是我想要提醒您，將會有五元的改期費用，**這是我們公司的規定。可以請您告訴我您的名字嗎？

男：喔，我知道了。我的名字是查理．克萊門。我住在漢尼斯維爾。你知道我什麼時候要付這筆費用嗎？

女：(34) **我很快就會將適用於我們網站的使用者名稱和暫用密碼，以電子郵件寄給你。**請檢查電子郵件並透過網站繳付所有的帳款。

32. What did the man recently do?
A Purchased a house
B Went on a business trip
C Signed up for a service
D Installed a television

33. Why must the man pay a fee?
A He wants to change his schedule.
B He returned an item late.
C He lost his membership card.
D He needs an additional service.

34. What will the woman include in an email?
A A receipt
B Log-in information
C A membership contract
D Driving directions

32. 男子最近做了什麼？
A 買房子
B 出差
C 登記一項服務
D 安裝電視

33. 為何男子必須支付一筆費用？
A 他想要更改時間
B 他延遲退還一項物品
C 他遺失會員卡
D 他需要額外的服務

34. 女子將在電子郵件中包含什麼？
A 收據
B 登入資訊
C 會員合約
D 交通指引

35-37 conversation

M：Hi, Tiffany. Do you know what happened to the company car? I tried to reserve it today, but I was told it's being repaired.

W：(35) **When Mark was driving yesterday, he got a flat tire.** I just heard that the car should be out of the repair shop by this evening. I'll let you know when they call me.

M：Oh, that's good news. (36) **I was worried because I need it tomorrow morning to pick up an important client from the airport.**

W：Ah, isn't that Mr. Lee from Beijing? (37) **Just in case, why don't you call a local car rental business and reserve a car for tomorrow?** If the company car is fixed in time, you can cancel.

35–37 對話

男：嗨，蒂芬妮。你知道公司的車發生了什麼事嗎？我今天試著預訂，但卻被告知它正在維修中。

女：(35) **馬克昨天開車的時候爆胎了。**我剛才聽說車子今晚前會出維修廠，他們打電話給我的時候，我會告知你。

男：喔，那真是好消息。(36) **我本來很擔心的，因為我明天早上要用車，去機場接一名重要的客戶。**

女：啊，是來自北京的李先生嗎？(37) **為了預防萬一，你何不打電話給本地的租車行，並且預訂一輛明天要用的車？**如果公司的車及時修好了，你可以取消預訂。

35. What does the woman say caused the problem?
A A repair cost has increased.
B A reservation has been canceled.
C A client arrived too late.
D A tire needed to be replaced.

36. Why is the man concerned?
A He lost an important receipt.
B He needs a car to greet a client.
C He has to reschedule a meeting.
D He was unable to contact a client.

35. 女子說是什麼導致了這個問題？
A 修理費用增加
B 預約被取消
C 客戶太晚到達
D 輪胎需要更換

36. 男子為何擔心？
A 他遺失了重要的收據
B 他需要車輛去迎接客戶
C 他必須重新安排會議時間
D 他無法聯繫到客戶

37. What does the woman suggest?

A Preparing an alternative plan

B Ordering a replacement part

C Attending a conference

D Reserving a less expensive ticket

37. 女子提出什麼建議？

A 備妥備案

B 訂購替換零件

C 出席會議

D 訂較不昂貴的票

38-40 conversation

W： Hello, this is Kelly in the accounting department. (38) **The ink cartridge in the printer on the fourth floor has run out.** Do you think you could come to replace it today?

M： Sure. By the way, can I ask you a favor? (39) **I need you to let me know what model the machine is so I can bring the correct one.** Actually, I'm not in the office right now, so I can't see what it is.

W： OK. But how can I find that information? Do I have to open the printer cover or press some function buttons?

M： No, you don't. (40) **Just ask Mr. Hills in your department.** He should have a complete list of all the hardware on the fourth floor.

38–40 對話

女： 哈囉，我是會計部門的凱莉。(38) **四樓印表機的墨水匣沒墨水了**，你今天能過來更換嗎？

男： 當然。對了，可以請你幫個忙嗎？(39) **我需要你告訴我機器的型號，以便帶正確的墨水匣過去**。我其實現在不在辦公室，因此無法知道是什麼型號。

女： 好的，但我如何能找到這項資訊？我需要打開印表機的外殼或按下某些功能按鍵嗎？

男： 不，你不需要。(40) **只要問你部門的希爾斯先生**。他應該有四樓所有硬體設備的完整清單。

38. What problem is the woman reporting?

A An accounting error has been made.

B A printer is out of order.

C Some office supplies have run out.

D A document has been lost.

39. What does the man ask the woman to do?

A Check some product information

B Install new equipment

C Update customer information

D Stop by his office

40. What is mentioned about Mr. Hills?

A He is in charge of a new project.

B He is in the same department as the woman.

C He has recently ordered a new item.

D He wrote a hardware list.

38. 女子回報什麼問題？

A 犯了會計的錯誤

B 印表機故障

C 某些辦公用品已經用完

D 文件遺失了

39. 男子要求女子做什麼？

A 查看某項產品資訊

B 安裝新設備

C 更新客戶資訊

D 去他的辦公室

40. 關於希爾斯先生有提到什麼？

A 他負責新專案

B 他與女子在相同的部門

C 他最近訂了新物品

D 他寫下硬體設備的清單

41-43 conversation

M： (41) **Hello, I saw your advertisement on TV promoting your grand opening.** Can you tell me about your clothing store?

41–43 對話

男： (41) **哈囉，我在電視上看到宣傳你們盛大開幕的廣告**。你可以跟我介紹你們的服飾店嗎？

W：Welcome to our store. Our store specializes in men's suits and formal wear. (42) **As a grand opening promotion, we are offering free delivery on all purchases this month.**

M：Wow, that's great. I need to buy a suit for my wedding, so I stopped by. Could you show me something I might like?

W：Sure. We have a variety of wedding suits. Please come here. (43) **First, I would like to have my assistant take your measurements so we can find a suit that fits you well.** It won't take much time.

女：歡迎光臨。本店專賣男士西服和正式穿著。(42) **作為盛大開幕促銷，我們將為所有在本月購買的商品提供免運服務。**

男：哇，那真是太好了。我需要為我的婚禮買一套西裝，所以我才來。你可以讓我看看我可能會喜歡的衣服嗎？

女：當然可以。我們有各式婚禮西裝，請來這裡。(43) **首先，我想請我的助理為你測量尺寸，這樣我們就可以為你找到合適的西裝。**這不會花太多時間。

41. How did the man learn about the store?

A By watching television

B By talking to a friend

C By reading a brochure

D By listening to the radio

42. According to the woman, what is being offered this month?

A A discount coupon

B A reduced membership fee

C Free delivery

D A lifetime warranty

43. What does the woman suggest doing?

A Paying in advance

B Getting measurements taken

C Submitting a proposal

D Hiring an assistant

41. 男子如何得知關於這家店的事？

A 看電視

B 與朋友談話

C 閱讀手冊

D 聽收音機

42. 根據女子，本月會提供什麼？

A 折價券

B 減收會員費

C 免費運送

D 終身保固

43. 女子提議要做什麼？

A 事先付款

B 進行尺寸測量

C 繳交提案

D 僱用助手

44-46 conversation

W：Nice to meet you, Mr. Gomez. (44) **I'm sure after you hear about our business, you will want us to provide food and beverages for your company's various events.**

M：Nice to meet you, Ms. Gates. Thank you for coming today. I haven't inquired about your services because your company is located out of town. (45) **I didn't think you could provide services to us.**

W：Rose and Lily Co. is willing to travel anywhere within the state in order to meet our clients' needs. Our prices don't change depending on distance, so you don't need to worry about that.

44–46 對話

女：很高興見到您，戈梅茲先生。(44) **我相信當你了解我們公司的業務之後，會想要由我們來提供貴公司各種活動所需的食物和飲料。**

男：很高興見到你，蓋茲女士。感謝你今天過來。我尚未詢問關於貴公司的服務，因為貴公司位於城外。(45) **我以為你們不能為我們提供服務。**

女：蘿絲和莉莉公司願意前往本州任何地方，以滿足我們客戶的需求。我們的價格不會因為距離而改變，因此您不需擔心這點。

M：Oh, I'm glad to hear that. In that case, we will consider your services. What are your specialties? (46) **Do you think I could sample some of the food and beverages you provide?**

男：我很高興聽你這麼說。這樣的話，我們將會考慮你們的服務。貴公司的特色是什麼？(46) **我可以試吃你們提供的一些食物和飲料嗎？**

44. What kind of services are the speakers discussing?
[A] Catering for company events
[B] Business consultation
[C] Workforce training
[D] Delivery services

44. 對話者在討論何種服務？
[A] 公司活動的外燴
[B] 商業諮詢
[C] 人力訓練
[D] 送貨服務

45. Why has the man not used Rose and Lily Co.'s services before?
[A] He was unaware of them.
[B] He was reluctant to pay a membership fee.
[C] He was on bad terms with the owner.
[D] He did not realize their availability.

45. 男子為何先前並未使用蘿絲和莉莉公司的服務？
[A] 他不知道有這家公司
[B] 他不想付會員費
[C] 他與業主關係不好
[D] 他不知道該公司能提供服務

46. What does the man ask the woman to do?
[A] Try some food and beverages
[B] Send a catalog
[C] Provide a sample
[D] Expedite an order

46. 男子要求女子做什麼？
[A] 試吃食物和飲料
[B] 寄商品型錄
[C] 提供試吃品
[D] 加速訂單處理速度

47-49 conversation

W：Hi, Josh. You work at Sentry Insurance, don't you? (47) **I heard from a friend they are expected to merge with another company.** Is your position secure?

M：Yes, no problem. I will be keeping my position. (48) **In fact, my company plans to expand internationally so that we can compete with other global corporations.** I'm certain it will be beneficial for both me and my company.

W：I'm glad to hear that. Actually, I've recently been thinking about changing my line of employment. Will there be any opportunities for getting hired at your company?

M：(49) **Well, you should visit my company's website because we are posting new job positions that will be available after the merger.**

47–49 對話

女：嗨，喬許。你在崗哨保全工作，對不對？(47) 我聽一個朋友說，他們預計會與另一家公司合併。你的職位有保障嗎？

男：是的，沒問題。我會保有我的職位。(48) **實際上，我們公司計劃要拓展到國際市場，因此我們會與其他全球性的企業競爭。**我相信這對我和公司都會有好處。

女：我很高興聽你這麼說。其實我最近在考慮換工作，我有機會被你公司僱用嗎？

男：(49) **嗯，你可以上我公司的網站，因為我們會在上面公告合併後的新職缺。**

47. What does the woman say she has heard about?

A The joining of two businesses

B The construction of a factory

C An international conference

D A highway expansion project

48. What benefit does the man mention?

A Lower insurance costs

B Increased vacation days

C International competitiveness

D Updated equipment

49. What does the man suggest the woman do?

A Visit his office

B Post an advertisement

C Submit a proposal

D Check job listings

47. 女子說她聽說了什麼？

A 兩家公司的合併

B 工廠的建造

C 國際會議

D 公路擴展計劃

48. 男子提到什麼好處？

A 較低的保險費

B 增加的休假天數

C 國際競爭力

D 更新的設備

49. 男子建議女子做什麼？

A 造訪他的辦公室

B 刊登廣告

C 繳交提案

D 查看工作職缺

NEW

50-52 conversation

M：Hi, Ms. Parker? This is Joseph Sterling, from Green Creek Realtors. (50) **We need to talk about an issue with the apartment you wanted.**

W：Oh, hi Joseph. Did you manage to find me a place in the Kahlua Apartment building?

M：Yes, that's the reason I'm calling. But there is a bit of an issue.

W：Really? What is it?

M：(51) **There is a major pest problem in the building, and they need to clear the whole building and carry out pest control.** It's going to take them at least three months to make sure the building is clean. So you would have to wait three months to get a place there.

W：I see.

M：There is a building just nearby called Graceville Towers. It's very close to the Kahlua building, so you could stay there for three months and then move over to the Kahlua building. (52) **I will arrange all of the moving for you.** Why don't you go online and check out Graceville Towers and get back to me?

W：Sure, that sounds good. Thanks, Joseph.

50–52 對話

男：嗨，帕克女士嗎？我是綠溪房地產的約瑟夫．史特林。(50) **我們來談談關於你想要的那間公寓。**

女：喔，嗨，約瑟夫。你已幫我在卡魯哇公寓大樓找到住處了嗎？

男：是的，這就是我打了這通電話的原因。但出了一些問題。

女：真的嗎？什麼問題？

男：(51) **大樓內有嚴重的蟲害問題，他們要淨空整棟大樓並且進行驅蟲。**至少要三個月才能確保大樓乾淨。因此，你要等三個月才能入住。

女：我知道了。

男：在那裡附近有一棟叫做格瑞思維爾塔大樓。它很接近卡魯哇大樓，因此你可以在那裡住三個月，然後再搬到卡魯哇大樓。(52) **我會為你安排所有的搬遷事宜。**你可以上網看看格瑞思維爾塔，再回電話給我。

女：當然，聽起來不錯。謝謝你，約瑟夫。

50. What is the reason for Joseph's call?
A To relate a problem concerning the apartment
B To sign the contract for the apartment
C To discuss another apartment
D To discuss the price of rent

51. What does Joseph say about the Kahlua Apartment?
A It's ready to be occupied anytime.
B There are renovations occurring.
C It is near a new fitness center.
D There is a major pest problem.

52. What does Joseph offer to do?
A Find a new apartment at Graceville Towers
B Arrange all of the moving
C Move her furniture personally
D Move into the Kahlua Apartment building

50. 約瑟夫打電話的原因為何？
A 為了說公寓的問題
B 為了簽署公寓的租約
C 為了討論另一間公寓
D 為了討論租金價格

51. 關於卡魯哇公寓，約瑟夫說了什麼？
A 它隨時可以入住
B 正在進行翻修
C 在一家新的健身中心附近
D 有嚴重的蟲害問題

52. 約瑟夫提議要做什麼？
A 在格瑞思維爾塔找新公寓
B 安排所有搬遷事宜
C 親自幫她搬家具
D 搬進卡魯哇公寓大樓

15

53-55 conversation

W：Hi, Amos. This is Elizabeth Cox. (53) **Last year you helped find some office space for my company, and I was hoping you could help me find something in the same area.**

M：Hi, Elizabeth. It's good to hear from you. If I remember correctly, your office is in the Barnsbury area, right?

W：Yes. (54) **Actually, I recently left that company and I've opened my own legal firm.** I only have four staff members, so we don't need a big space. As long it is in good condition and the location is fine.

M：No problem. I have a few in the area I think you would like. (55) **What's your afternoon like?**

53–55 對話

女：嗨，阿摩司，你好。我是伊莉莎白．考克斯。(53) **去年你為我的公司找辦公室，我希望你可以在同一地區再幫我找個地方。**

男：嗨，伊莉莎白，您好。很高興接到您的來電。如果我沒記錯，您的辦公室是在巴恩斯伯里地區，對嗎？

女：是的。(54) **其實，我最近才離開那家公司，開了自己的法律事務所。**我只有四名員工，因此不需要很大的空間，只要狀況好、地點佳即可。

男：沒問題。我在該地區有些物件，我認為你會喜歡，(55) **你下午忙嗎？**

53. Why is the woman calling the man?
A To ask a favor of him
B To order some flowers
C To find a rental property
D To rent a house

54. What does the woman say she has done recently?
A Been promoted at her company
B Closed down her business
C Got a new job
D Opened her own business

53. 女子為何打電話給男子？
A 為了請他幫忙
B 為了訂花
C 為了尋找出租的房子
D 為了租屋

54. 女子說她最近做了什麼？
A 獲得公司的升遷
B 結束她的事業
C 找到新的工作
D 開立自己的公司

55. Why does the man say, "What's your afternoon like"?

A To figure out when they can meet

B To ask her to dinner

C To explain rental conditions

D To get some keys for the office

55. 男子為何說「你下午忙嗎」？

A 要知道他們何時可以會面

B 要邀請她吃晚餐

C 要解釋出租的情況

D 要拿辦公室的鑰匙

56-58 conversation

M：Hey Judy, (56) **did you see the new offices the company built?** They look fantastic.

W：(57) **Yeah it's about time!**

M：I know we had some slow years, but the last five years everyone has worked so hard, and now it's finally paying off.

W：(58) **Our company's growth has been fast, but there has been a lot of long nights and hard work.**

M：I agree with you. But it is nice to see it finally paying off. I can't wait to move into my new office!

56–58 對話

男：嗨，茱蒂，(56) 你看過公司蓋的新辦公室了嗎？看起來很棒。

女：(57) **是的，也該是時候了！**

男：我知道我們有幾年成長緩慢，但大家在過去五年都很努力，現在也終有所回報了。

女：(58) **我們公司成長得很快，但都是許多夜晚加班和拚命工作的累積。**

男：我同意。但看到終於有所回報真的很不錯，我等不及要搬進我的新辦公室了！

56. What did the company do recently?

A Renovated the lobby

B Built new research facilities

C Hired new staff

D Built new offices

56. 這家公司最近做了什麼？

A 翻修大廳

B 蓋了新的研究機構

C 僱用新員工

D 蓋了新辦公室

57. What does the woman mean when she says, "it's about time"?

A She thinks the company deserves to have new offices.

B She thinks construction has taken too long.

C She doesn't like the new offices.

D She wants a raise in her salary.

57. 女子說「也該是時候了」，她指的是什麼？

A 她認為公司該有新的辦公室

B 她認為工程花了太久的時間

C 她不喜歡新的辦公室

D 她想要加薪

58. What does the woman imply about the company?

A They have been very lucky to grow so fast.

B Some of the staff is not working hard.

C The company worked hard to grow fast.

D The new offices aren't very nice.

58. 關於這家公司，女子在暗示什麼？

A 他們很幸運能成長得如此快速

B 其中一些員工不努力

C 公司很努力而成長快速

D 新的辦公室不太好

NEW

59-61 conversation

W：Hi, Roger. (59) **Is last month's sales report ready for our meeting today?**

M1：I have finished my section. Andrew, have you finished yours? (60) **I noticed you were at work late last night, so I assume you have finished.**

M2：My part is finished. Give me your part and I will get everything ready for the meeting. Sales are really high this quarter, so management will be very pleased.

W：Oh, that's great. We needed a good quarter after our last one. That was our lowest in history.

M1：(61) **Andrew, when you're finished send us an email and we can prepare for the meeting.**

59–61 對話

女：嗨，羅傑。(59) **你準備好了上個月的銷售報告，供今日會議使用嗎？**

男 1：我的部分已經完成了。安德魯，你的部分完成了嗎？(60) **我注意到你昨晚加班加到很晚，因此我猜你已經完成了。**

男 2：我的部分完成了。把你的部分給我，我就可以備妥開會所需的資料。本季銷售額很高，因此管理階層會很高興。

女：喔，太好了。這一季我們要表現亮眼一點。上一季是我們歷年來銷售最低迷的一季。

男 1：(61) **安德魯，你做好之後寄電子郵件給我們，然後我們就可以為開會做準備。**

59. What are the speakers mainly discussing?

A Getting ready for a work party
B Getting the sales report ready
C Getting ready for a promotion
D Getting ready to finish the quarter

60. What does the man say about Andrew?

A That he left work early the night before
B That he thinks Andrew isn't a hard worker
C That he worked late the night before
D That he had a good quarter

61. What does Roger tell Andrew to do?

A Send a letter to Roger when he is finished
B Bring the email to the meeting
C Not to come to the meeting
D Send an email when he is finished

59. 對話者們主要在討論什麼？

A 準備辦員工派對
B 準備好銷售報告
C 準備做促銷
D 準備結束一季

60. 關於安德魯，男子說了什麼？

A 他前一晚提早下班
B 他認為安德魯工作不努力
C 他前一晚工作得很晚
D 他上季表現良好

61. 羅傑要安德魯做什麼？

A 完成時寄信給羅傑
B 將電子郵件帶去開會
C 別去開會
D 完成時寄電子郵件

NEW

62-64 conversation

M：Hello, this is Warren speaking. How can I help you today?

W：(62) **Hello, Warren. I purchased a work desk from your store.** I'm trying to put it together but there are some important parts missing.

62–64 對話

男：哈囉，我是華倫。今天有什麼需要我協助的嗎？

女：(62) **哈囉，華倫。我從你的店買了一張工作桌。**我正在嘗試組裝，但有一些重要的零件不見了。

M： I'm sorry about that. Sometimes the manufacturer makes mistakes. What are you missing?

W： (63) **Well, the biggest problem is I don't have the tool to put in the bolts.** And I'm missing 3 barrel nuts.

M： OK, I have those parts in the shop. (64) **I have a lunch break at 2 p.m. I can bring them over to your place if you like.**

W： Oh, wow. That would be fantastic. Wait one moment and I will give you my address.

男：很抱歉，製造商有時候會出錯，你缺少了什麼？

女：(63) **最大的問題是，我沒有鎖上螺栓的工具**，還少了三個圓柱帽。

男：好的，我店裡有這些零件。(64) **我下午兩點午休。如果你要的話，我可以把零件帶去給你。**

女：喔，哇，那樣太棒了。請稍等，我給你我的地址。

Part A 部分 — 90 mm Bolts	90 厘米螺栓
Part B 部分 — 25 mm Wood Screws	25 厘米木螺釘
Part C 部分 — Barrel Nuts x 6	圓柱帽 *6
Part D 部分 — Long Allen Key x 1	長的六角扳手 *1

62. Where does the man most likely work?
- A At a university
- **B At a furniture store**
- C At a bedding store
- D At a technical college

NEW

63. Look at the graphic. What is the woman missing?
- A 90 mm Bolts
- B Wood Screws
- **C Barrel Nuts**
- D Allen Key

64. What does the man offer to do?
- A Deliver the parts to her house by post
- **B Deliver the parts to her house in person**
- C Have the parts delivered by his staff
- D Leave the parts at the front counter

62. 男子最有可能在哪裡工作？
- A 在大學
- **B 在家具店**
- C 在寢具店
- D 在技術學院

63. 參看圖表。女子缺少了什麼？
- A 90 厘米螺栓
- B 木螺釘
- **C 圓柱帽**
- D 長的六角扳手

64. 男子提議要做什麼？
- A 將零件郵寄到她家
- **B 親自將零件送到她家**
- C 請員工將零件送過去
- D 將零件留置在櫃台

65-67 conversation

M： Hi, Sandra. I'm so sorry I missed our meeting this morning. **(66) I didn't realize the Tower Bridge was closed for upgrading.** I had to go over the Brooklyn Bridge.

W： Don't worry about it, Rob. **(65) Most of the staff was late because of that. It's going to be annoying to have to go over the Brooklyn Bridge every day.** I might just take the Express Tunnel.

M： Yeah, I know. But the traffic is just so terrible in that tunnel. I can't really handle it.

W： I agree. **(67) I think we should all just take the subway until the Tower Bridge is open again.**

65–67 對話

男：嗨，珊卓。很抱歉我錯過今天早上的會議。**(66) 我不知道高塔橋封閉進行改良工程**，我得繞道走布魯克林橋。

女：別在意，羅伯。**(65) 大部分員工也都因此遲到了，以後每天要走布魯克林橋很令人困擾。**我可能會走快速隧道。

男：是的，我知道。但那條隧道的交通很糟糕，我真的無法忍受。

女：我同意。**(67) 我認為在高塔橋重新開放之前，我們應該都搭地鐵。**

Bridge closed until
Jan. 12 due to upgrade of infrastructure
因進行改善工程
橋梁封閉至 1 月 12 日

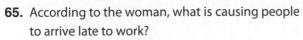

65. According to the woman, what is causing people to arrive late to work?
- (A) A meeting was postponed.
- (B) The bridge was very busy.
- **(C) The bridge was closed.**
- (D) They had car problems.

NEW

66. Look at the graphic. Where is the sign most likely located?
- (A) The Brooklyn Bridge
- **(B) The Tower Bridge**
- (C) The East Bay Tunnel
- (D) The Express Tunnel

67. What does the woman recommend to the man?
- (A) Take the bus to work
- (B) Share a taxi to work
- **(C) Take the subway to work**
- (D) Take the Express Tunnel

65. 根據女子，什麼導致員工上班遲到？
- (A) 會議延後
- (B) 橋梁壅塞
- **(C) 橋梁封閉**
- (D) 汽車故障

66. 參看圖表，這個標誌最有可能在哪裡？
- (A) 布魯克林橋
- **(B) 高塔橋**
- (C) 東海岸隧道
- (D) 快速隧道

67. 女子建議男子做什麼？
- (A) 搭公車上班
- (B) 共乘計程車上班
- **(C) 搭地鐵上班**
- (D) 走快速隧道

68-70 conversation

W：OK, your total bill comes to $75. (68) **I hope you enjoyed your food tonight.** Would you like to split the bill?

M：No, I will pay. I have a coupon for a 10 percent discount. It's in my wallet. Here it is.

W：OK. Hmm, it doesn't seem to work when I try to scan it. Let me get the manager.

M：(69) **Oh, never mind, I can see the problem. I didn't read it properly. I'm so careless sometimes. We should have ordered more drinks!**

W：Well next time you come in, you should bring a bigger group, and you will get a better discount that way anyhow. (70) **If you like I can put the coupon in our computer system so next time you come in you don't need to bring the card.**

68–70 對話

女：好的。您的帳單總計為 75 元。(68) **希望你們喜歡今晚的餐點。**你們要分開結帳嗎？

男：不，由我來付帳。我有九折優惠券。在我皮夾裡，在這裡。

女：好的，嗯，我嘗試刷條碼，但似乎沒辦法刷。讓我去找經理來。

男：(69) **喔，沒關係喔，我知道問題出在哪裡了，我沒看清楚。我有時候很粗心，我們應該多點一些飲料的！**

女：下次你們來，應該多帶點人，這樣會折扣比較多。(70) **如果您要的話，我可以把優惠券存在電腦系統裡。這樣你們下一次來就不用帶這張卡了。**

Fisherman's Wharf 漁人碼頭

Discount Coupon 優惠券

10% off any order above $100　超過 100 元打九折

Expires November 1st　有效期限至 11 月 1 日

68. Where most likely are the speakers?

(A) In a hospital
(B) In a restaurant
(C) In a bar
(D) In a hotel

69. Look at the graphic. Why is the coupon rejected?

(A) The order was above $100.
(B) It is expired.
(C) Their order was below $100.
(D) The coupon didn't have credit on it.

70. What does the woman offer to do?

(A) Give them a new card
(B) Put the coupon in the computer system
(C) Hold the card for them
(D) Provide a refund

68. 對話者最有可能在哪裡？

(A) 在醫院
(B) 在餐廳
(C) 在酒吧
(D) 在旅館

69. 參看圖表，為何優惠券不能使用？

(A) 餐點超過 100 元
(B) 它過期了
(C) 他們的餐點未滿 100 元
(D) 優惠券上頭沒寫折扣額

70. 女子提議要做什麼？

(A) 給他們新的卡片
(B) 將優惠券存在電腦系統
(C) 為他們保留這張卡片
(D) 提供退費

71-73 announcement

W：Attention, conference attendees. Thank you for your patience while you wait for us to solve this delay. (71) **Unfortunately, the computer that is to be used during the keynote speaker's presentation is having problems.** As a result, we are currently transferring the necessary files onto a different computer. (72) **We plan to get underway with the presentation in half an hour.** In the meantime, feel free to enjoy some of the refreshments provided near the entrance. (73) **We will dim the lights in order to indicate that the presentation will be beginning.** Please return to your seats at that time.

71–73 宣布

女：各位與會人士請注意，感謝你們耐心等候我們解決延誤的問題。(71) **很不巧地，主講演講時所需的電腦出了問題。**因此，我們正在把必要的檔案傳輸到另一台電腦。(72) **我們打算在半小時後開始演講。**同時，請儘情享用入口附近提供的茶點。(73) **我們會將燈光調暗以表示演講即將開始。**屆時請各位回到座位。

71. What is causing the delay?
- A Bad weather
- B A canceled flight
- C A scheduling error
- **D A technical difficulty**

71. 什麼導致了延誤？
- A 惡劣的天氣
- B 取消的航班
- C 時間規劃錯誤
- **D 技術性問題**

72. According to the speaker, after how long will the presentation begin?
- A 5 minutes
- **B 30 minutes**
- C 45 minutes
- D 60 minutes

72. 根據發話者，演講將在多久之後開始？
- A 5 分鐘
- **B 30 分鐘**
- C 45 分鐘
- D 60 分鐘

73. What will happen when it's time for the presentation to begin?
- A An announcement will be made.
- **B Lighting will be adjusted.**
- C A keynote speaker will appear on the stage.
- D Refreshments will be served.

73. 當演講要開始時會發生什麼事？
- A 將會進行宣布
- **B 將調整光線**
- C 主講人將上台
- D 將提供茶點

74-76 radio broadcast

M：Welcome back to your local radio station WXFD 93.7 with the morning news update. (74) **Yesterday, the Clinton Town council passed a new law prohibiting pet owners from bringing their pets onto public beaches.** (75) **Tim Kellerman, who was newly elected to the town council last month, justified the decision by arguing that pets can bother other beach-goers.** Those who violate the law will have to pay a fine of $300. (76) **Up next, we will be taking calls from listeners to hear their reaction to this new measure.**

74–76 電台廣播

男：歡迎回到本地廣播電台 WXFD 93.7，給您帶來最新的晨間新聞。(74) **昨天柯林頓鎮議會通過了一項新法律，禁止寵物主人將寵物帶到公有海灘。**(75) **上個月剛當選進入鎮議會的提姆．克勒曼，主張這項決定是由於寵物可能會對其他海灘遊客造成困擾。**違反這項法令的人將要支付 300 元的罰鍰。(76) **接下來我們要接聽眾的來電，聽聽大家對這項新措施的反應。**

74. What is the radio broadcast about?

A The opening of a pet store

B A newly introduced law

C A new council hall

D An upcoming election

75. According to the speaker, what did Tim Kellerman do recently?

A He ran for office.

B He won an award.

C He selected a pet.

D He paid a fine.

76. What will listeners most likely hear next?

A A weather forecast

B Some breaking news

C Community members' opinions

D A telephone interview

74. 這則電台廣播與什麼有關？

A 寵物店開幕

B 新施行的法律

C 新議會廳

D 即將舉行的選舉

75. 根據發話者，提姆·克勒曼最近做了什麼？

A 他競選公職

B 他獲獎

C 他挑選了寵物

D 他繳交罰款

76. 聽眾接下來最有可能聽到什麼？

A 天氣預報

B 突發新聞

C 公眾的意見

D 電話訪談

77-79 advertisement

W：Welcome to our Holiday Sale here at Leeman's Department Store. We are currently running our Red Cart Savings Event. Pay just $100 for all the clothing that you can fit in a single red cart. (77) **You can get a cart immediately inside the main entrance to the store.** Make sure to take advantage of this sale. It only happens once a year! (78) **In order to accommodate the high volume of customers, we have extra staff located throughout the store. You can spot them easily because they are wearing green vests.** Also, you can enter your name into our raffle event by visiting the front desk. (79) **I will announce the results at the end of the day.**

77–79 廣告

女：歡迎來到李曼百貨公司的節慶特賣。我們現在正在進行紅色購物車省錢活動。只要付 100 元，就可以買到你所有塞進一台紅色購物車的衣物。(77) **你現在就可以在百貨公司大門處取得推車。**請務必把握這場特賣會，一年僅有一次！(78) **為了容納大量的顧客，我們在整間百貨公司都有增加員工。你很容易就能找到他們，因為他們穿著綠色的背心。**此外，你也可以到櫃台報名抽獎。(79) **今天結束時我會宣布結果。**

77. Where should listeners get carts?

A In the parking lot

B At the entrance

C Near the lobby

D From a cashier

77. 聽眾應該從哪裡取得推車？

A 停車場

B 入口處

C 大廳附近

D 收銀員

78. According to the speaker, who is wearing green vests?
- A Cashiers
- B Store managers
- **C Additional staff**
- D Parking lot attendants

79. What will the speaker most likely do at the end of the day?
- **A Announce winners**
- B Collect donations
- C Give a demonstration
- D Purchase an item

80-82 advertisement

M : (80) **If you're looking for reasonable prices on ink toner, then stop by Quill Office Supplies in Rochester!** We have replacement ink toner to fit all models of printers and copy machines. (81) **During the month of April, we will send a technician to your location at no charge to help you remove an old ink cartridge and install a new one.** (82) **If you sign up for regular cartridge refills, you can receive a 5 percent discount on all of your purchases.** For more information, please visit our website at www.quillofficesupplies.com.

80. What business is being advertised?
- A A computer retailer
- B An electronics repair shop
- **C An office supply store**
- D A cosmetics store

81. What service is available in April?
- A Installment payments
- B Express shipping
- C Online assistance
- **D Free installation**

82. How can listeners get a discount?
- A By bringing a coupon
- B By buying in bulk
- **C By becoming a regular customer**
- D By signing up for a newsletter

78. 根據發話者，什麼人穿著綠色的背心？
- A 收銀員
- B 店經理
- **C 增設的員工**
- D 停車場服務員

79. 發話者在當天結束時最有可能做什麼？
- **A 宣布得獎者**
- B 收取捐款
- C 進行演示
- D 購買商品

80–82 廣告

男：(80) **如果您正在尋找價格公道的墨水匣，請來位於洛徹斯特的羽毛筆辦公用品店！**我們有適合各種印表機和影印機型號的替換墨水匣。(81) **在四月期間，我們將會免費派遣技術人員到府，協助您拆下舊的墨水匣並安裝新的。**(82) **如果您簽約定期補充墨水匣，就能享有 95 折的購買折扣。**欲知詳情，請上我們的網站 www.quillofficesupplies.com。

80. 這是什麼行業的廣告？
- A 電腦零售商
- B 電子設備維修行
- **C 辦公用品店**
- D 化妝品店

81. 四月時會提供什麼服務？
- A 分期付款
- B 快遞送貨
- C 線上支援
- **D 免費安裝**

82. 聽眾要如何獲得折扣？
- A 攜帶折價券
- B 大量購買
- **C 成為常客**
- D 訂閱電子報

83-85 announcement

W: Hi, everyone, thanks for meeting with me today. (83) **I'd like to announce a few changes in our health and safety policy that are designed to conform to the new government regulations.** Firstly, we can no longer work a shift longer than six hours without taking a one-hour break. We'll be using a clock-in system that is automated to send you a text message once you reach six hours. You will also wear a device that monitors your time on the shift. (84) **It's a very simple device; you just attach it to your work belt and it will do the rest, so you won't need any training with that.** (85) **Sharing helmets and work boots is also now prohibited. You will have to buy your own equipment**, and then later you can claim the money back on your tax return.

83–85 宣布

女：嗨，大家好，感謝大家今天與我會面。(83) **我要宣布在健康及安全政策方面的幾項變革，這是為了要符合政府的新規定。**首先，不得再輪班六小時而沒有休息一小時。我們會使用打卡系統，能自動在工作滿六小時傳送簡訊給你。你們也要在輪班時穿戴監控工時的裝置，(84) **這是個很簡單的裝置，你只需要將它繫在工作腰帶上，剩下的就交給它了，因此你不需要為此做任何訓練。**(85) **現在也禁止共用安全帽和工作靴，你必須購買屬於自己的設備**，之後可以在退稅時領回這筆錢。

83. According to the speaker, why are changes being made?

A The government took the company to court

B To conform to government regulations

C To enact a new labor law

D To arrange lower-paying contracts

NEW

84. What does the speaker imply when she says, "it's a very simple device; you just attach it to your work belt and it will do the rest, so you won't need any training with that"?

A The new system requires no training.

B She doesn't like the new system.

C There is no budget for staff uniforms.

D Everyone needs training.

85. What does the speaker tell the listeners they will have to start bringing to work?

A Extra pairs of work pants

B Other people's helmets

C Their own boots and helmets

D A new financial plan

83. 根據發話者，變革的原因是什麼？

A 政府控告這家公司

B 為了符合政府規定

C 為了施行新的勞動法案

D 為了安排較低薪資的合約

84. 發話者說「這是個很簡單的裝置，你只需要將它繫在工作腰帶上，剩下的就交給它了，因此你不需要為此做任何訓練」，她暗示的是什麼？

A 新的系統不需要訓練

B 她不喜歡新的系統

C 沒有預算可購買員工制服

D 大家都需要受訓

85. 發話者告訴聽眾要開始帶什麼來上班？

A 額外的工作褲

B 其他人的安全帽

C 自己的靴子及安全帽

D 新的財務計劃

86-88 excerpt from a meeting

M：[86] **Well, it's only been a year since we began operating out of Beijing**, but our clothing has become a nationwide success. I got a call from a reporter at Phoenix Television, and they want to do a 30-minute story documenting our rise to success. They want to interview the designers about the clothing we are creating here. Also, *Xinhua Fashion* Magazine wants to come in next Thursday and do a full photo shoot of one our stores, so we need to book models for that day. [87] **They want to take photos of our new range of denim clothing.** The publicity is really going to get our name out. [88] **Our success is going to skyrocket! We should expect to get a lot busier soon.**

86–88 會議摘錄

男：[86] **嗯，自我們走出北京營運只有一年的時間**，但我們的服飾已獲得全國性的成功。我收到鳳凰電視台記者的來電。他們想要進行一個30 分鐘的報導，記錄我們的成功之路。他們想要訪問設計師，談論我們設計的服飾。此外，《新華流行雜誌》想要在下星期四來訪，並詳細拍攝我們其中一家店的照片。因此，我們需要預約當天的模特兒。[87] **他們想要拍攝我們新系列的牛仔服飾**。這樣的宣傳能讓我們出名！ [88] **我們的成功將會一飛衝天！我們預計業務很快會會更加繁忙**。

86. According to the man, what did the company recently do?

(A) Began operating out of Beijing
(B) Began operating in India
(C) Hired some new designers
(D) Created some special dishes

86. 根據男子，這家公司最近做了什麼？

(A) 開始在北京外營運
(B) 開始在印度營運
(C) 僱用新設計師
(D) 創造特別的菜餚

87. What most likely will the *Xinhua Fashion* magazine do next Thursday?

(A) Interview the models
(B) Make a video of the street outside
(C) Photograph clothing
(D) Sign a new contract

87. 《新華流行雜誌》下星期四最有可能做什麼？

(A) 訪問模特兒
(B) 拍攝外面街道的影片
(C) 拍攝服飾
(D) 簽署新的合約

NEW

88. What does the man mean when he says, "our success is going to skyrocket"?

(A) Their business is going to grow quickly
(B) They will discuss the future plan
(C) They will prevent the photo shoot
(D) They will transfer some documents via mail

88. 男子說「我們的成功將會一飛衝天」，他指的是什麼？

(A) 他們的生意將會快速成長
(B) 他們將要討論未來的計劃
(C) 他們將要避免拍攝相片
(D) 他們將要透過郵件傳輸一些文件

89-91 announcement

W：Hi, everyone. (89) **There have been some new regulations sent in from Head Office.** Our productivity assessment was quite poor. They aren't very happy with our performance compared to last year. (90) **So we are going to have to put in some overtime to get ahead of schedule. We really need to stay on top of this**, or some people might get fired. (91) **We are going to need to make a roster and work some weekend overtime shifts.** We will have a rotation list, so each staff member works one Saturday every three weeks. I know this is a burden, but once we get high enough above our targets, things will go back to normal.

89–91 宣布

女：嗨，大家好。(89) **總公司寄來一些新規定。**我們的生產力考核相當差，與去年相比，我們的表現讓他們很不滿意。(90) **因此，我們要加班將進度提前，我們真的必須表現優異，**否則有人會被開除。(91) **我們需要製作一份執勤表，並且在週末進行加班輪值。**我們會有輪值名單，每位員工每三週需在週六上班一次。我知道這會造成負擔，但是我們一旦超越目標夠多，就會回歸正常。

89. According to the speaker, who is introducing the new regulations?

(A) The Board of Directors
(B) Head Office
(C) Management
(D) The secretary

NEW

90. What does the speaker imply when she says, "we really need to stay on top of this, or some people might get fired"?

(A) There is a lot of work to do.
(B) It isn't that important.
(C) They can wait a week to start.
(D) The project will begin soon.

91. What does the speaker tell the listeners to do?

(A) Bring their lunch to work
(B) Occasionally work on Saturdays
(C) Work every Sunday
(D) Have some time off on Saturday

89. 根據發話者，誰推行新規定？

(A) 董事會
(B) 總公司
(C) 管理階層
(D) 秘書

90. 發話者說「我們真的必須表現優異，否則有人會被開除」，她暗示什麼？

(A) 有很多工作要做
(B) 這沒有那麼重要
(C) 他們可以等一週後才開始
(D) 這項計劃將很快開始

91. 發話者告訴聽眾要做什麼？

(A) 帶午餐來上班
(B) 偶爾在週六上班
(C) 每週日上班
(D) 週六休假

92-94 tour guide

M：Attention, passengers. (92) (93) **Welcome aboard Continental Lines, with bus service to Columbia, Charleston, and terminating in Eastport.** We will be spending the majority of our trip on the highways, so please make sure you have your seatbelts buckled. (94) **We will reach our first destination, Columbia, in approximately 2 hours, making our time at arrival 10:30 p.m., Friday the 15th.** We'll be getting on the road shortly, please make sure all of your luggage is secure and out of your neighbor's way. You can learn about attractions in Columbia, and all of our destinations, in the travel brochure located in the seat pocket. Now sit back, relax, and enjoy the scenery!

92–94 導遊

男：各位乘客請注意。(92)(93) **歡迎搭乘大陸幹線，本班巴士行經哥倫比亞市及查爾斯頓市，終點站在東港。**我們的大半旅程會在公路上度過，因此請務必繫好安全帶。(94) **我們大約兩小時後會抵達第一個目的地：哥倫比亞市，到達時間為 15 號星期五晚上十點 30 分。**我們很快將啟程，請確認你的行李都已放好且不會阻礙旁邊乘客的進出。你可以從座椅口袋內的旅行手冊中，了解哥倫比亞市的景點及其他的目的地。現在請坐好、放鬆，並且享受風景吧！

This Weekend's Events in Columbia
哥倫比亞的週末活動

Afternoon Theater 午後劇場
Columbia's own theater troupe stages short versions of classic plays for free in Central Park every Thursday at noon.
哥倫比亞的劇團每週四中午在中央公園免費演出經典戲劇的刪減版

Friday Night Concert in the Park Series
週五夜間公園音樂會
The show begins at 8:30 P.M. and lasts until 10:30 P.M.!
表演從晚上 8 點 30 分開始，持續到晚上 10 點 30 分！

Midnight Wine Tasting 午夜品酒
Regional wines sampled under the stars at the Black Cat, every Friday and Saturday night!
每週五和週六夜晚，在黑貓酒吧的星光下品嚐當地美酒！

Appropriate for all ages!
老少咸宜！

92. What kind of transportation company is Continental Lines?

A Bus
B Train
C Limousine
D Taxi

92. 大陸幹線是哪一種運輸公司？

A 公車
B 火車
C 豪華轎車
D 計程車

93. What is the last stop for Continental Lines this trip?
A Charleston
B Columbia
C Eastport
D Chesterville

93. 大陸幹線的旅途終點是哪裡？
A 查爾斯頓
B 哥倫比亞
C 東港
D 查斯特維爾

NEW

94. Look at the graphic. What activity will still be available for the passengers to participate in when they arrive in Columbia?
A None
B Friday Night Concert in the Park
C Afternoon Theater
D Midnight Wine Tasting

94. 參看圖表，乘客抵達哥倫比亞時，還有什麼活動可以參與？
A 沒有
B 週五夜間公園音樂會
C 午後劇場
D 午夜品酒

95-97 excerpt from a meeting

W：Hello everyone, (95) **I wanted to get you together to go over the recent failures in our customer service department here at Monster Telecom.** As you know, customer service is at the heart of everything we do. We receive on average 3,000 calls per week from customers with a wide range of needs. (96) **In order to prepare you all to handle the most frequently asked questions from our customers, I have distributed the graph in front of you.** Please go over this graph with your team leader and develop a plan to improve our customer service. Next quarter's reviews will be in two months. (97) **We aim to have half as many weekly calls by then.**

95–97 會議摘錄

女：哈囉，大家好，(95) **我想把大家找來，檢視我們最近在怪物電信客服部門一些失敗的例子。**各位都知道，客戶服務是我們所有事務的核心。我們平均每星期接到三千通的顧客來電，需求五花八門。(96) **為了使各位都能準備好處理顧客的常見問題，我已發下各位眼前的圖表。**請與你的小組長一起檢視這張圖表，並且想出計劃來改善我們的客戶服務。下一季的審核將在兩個月後舉行。(97) **我們的目標是減少一半每週的顧客來電數。**

Customer Service FAQ Analysis 客服常見問題分析

Disputed Long Distance/Overcharges 有爭議的長途電話／超額收費	37%
Disputed Data Charges 有爭議的傳輸量費用	36%
Service Plan Change 服務方案異動	11%
Dropped Calls 通話中斷	9%
Replacement Phones 電話更換	5%
Miscellaneous 其他	2%

95. What is indicated about Monster Telecom?

A They are having customer service problems.

B There are too many calls for the number of employees.

C Customer service is not important to them.

D They need to hire more people.

95. 關於怪物電信，有指出哪一點？

A 他們的客服出了問題

B 電話太多，員工人數不足

C 客服對他們的公司並不重要

D 他們需要僱用更多人

NEW

96. Look at the graphic. What areas should the leaders focus their training on?

A How to deal with upset customers by overcharges

B Knowledge of all of the service plans

C Helping customers replace phones

D Knowledge of Monster Telecom's cellular coverage area

96. 參看圖表，小組長應該將訓練重點放在哪些領域？

A 如何處理因超額收費而不悅的顧客

B 對所有服務方案的了解

C 協助顧客更換電話

D 知道怪物電信訊號的涵蓋區域

97. What is the goal for Monster Telecom?

A Reduce the number of dropped calls

B Expand their coverage area

C Add new cellular phone options

D Reduce the number of customer calls they receive by 50%

97. 怪物電信的目標是什麼？

A 減少通話中斷的數量

B 拓展訊號涵蓋地區

C 增加新手機的選擇

D 將客戶來電減少 50%

98-100 advertisement

M：(98) **Springdale Fitness Club has just expanded its swimming facilities to include a lap pool.** We are extremely excited to be able to build on our already impressive offerings of aquatic fitness! We'll be having a ribbon cutting ceremony this Saturday at noon, and to celebrate we will be holding a timed lap race! (99) **Because we created the lap pool for our members who are serious about training, we must enforce a policy that requires members to sign up for times to use the pool.** (100) **Additionally, the pool is not to be used for free style play.** Please come down to Springdale Fitness Club on Saturday and join us in the good time!

98–100 廣告

男：(98) **斯普陵代爾健身俱樂部剛擴建游泳設施，新增一個水道泳池。**能以原本已經很棒的水中體適能設施為基礎進行擴建，我們感到很興奮。我們將在星期六中午舉行剪綵典禮，為了慶祝，我們將舉辦游泳計時賽。(99) **由於我們興建此泳池是為了讓想認真訓練的會員使用，所以我們必須執行一項規定，要求會員登記使用泳池的時間。**(100) **此外，此泳池不得用於戲水。**歡迎於星期六蒞臨斯普陵代爾健身俱樂部，與我們共度美好時光！

TEST 4 PART 4 16

LAP POOL SIGN-UP SHEET 水道泳池登記表									
LANE 水道	9:00 a.m. 上午 9 點	10:00 a.m. 上午 10 點	11:00 a.m. 上午 11 點	12:00 p.m. 中午 12 點	1:00 p.m. 下午 1 點	2:00 p.m. 下午 2 點	3:00 p.m. 下午 3 點	4:00 p.m. 下午 4 點	5:00 p.m. 下午 5 點
1									
2									
3									

98. What is indicated about Springdale Fitness Club?
A They have a tennis court.
B They take pride in their customer service.
C They specialize in children's pool parties.
D They have a variety of swimming facilities.

NEW
99. Look at the graphic. What are the hours of the lap pool?
A 8 a.m. to 5 p.m.
B 9 a.m. to 5 p.m.
C 9 a.m. to 6 p.m.
D 8 a.m. to 6 p.m.

100. What does Springdale Fitness Club say about the new lap pool?
A It is Olympic size.
B It has four lanes.
C It's for serious swimmers.
D It will host weekly races.

98. 關於斯普陵代爾健身俱樂部，有提到哪一點？
A 他們有網球場
B 他們對於客戶服務感到自豪
C 他們專營孩童泳池派對
D 他們有各種游泳設施

99. 參看圖表，水道泳池的開放時間為何？
A 上午八點到下午五點
B 上午九點到下午五點
C 上午九點到下午六點
D 上午八點到下午六點

100. 關於新的水道泳池，斯普陵代爾健身俱樂部提到什麼？
A 它符合奧運尺寸
B 它有四個水道
C 它是設置給想認真游泳的人士用
D 它每週都會舉辦比賽

ACTUAL TEST 5

PART 1 P. 74-77

17

1. **A The man is pointing at the flowers.**
   B She is picking some flowers.
   C The man is holding a flower.
   D They are all looking at the plants.

2. A He is wearing a tool belt.
   B The man is loading a cart.
   C He is changing the tire in the garage.
   D The tire is brand new.

3. A He is driving a car in the snow.
   B He has already shoveled the snow off the roof.
   C His car door is covered in snow.
   D He is playing with friends in the snow.

4. A The lecture theater is full of students.
   B The lecture theater is empty.
   C All of the students are outside the lecture theater.
   D There is a man giving a lecture.

5. **A The woman is looking at the computer.**
   B The woman is eating some fruits.
   C The woman has her hair down.
   D The woman is typing on the computer.

6. **A She is holding a vegetable.**
   B She is looking at some fish.
   C She is checking her shopping list.
   D She is tasting some vegetables.

1. **A 男子正指著花朵。**
   B 她正在採一些花。
   C 男子拿著一朵花。
   D 他們全都看著植物。

2. A 他戴著工具腰帶。
   B 男子正在裝載手推車。
   C 他正在車庫更換輪胎。
   D 輪胎是全新的。

3. A 他正在雪中開車。
   B 他已經剷掉車頂的雪。
   C 他的車門被雪覆蓋。
   D 他正在雪裡與朋友玩耍。

4. A 演講廳擠滿了學生。
   B 演講廳是空的。
   C 所有的學生都在演講廳外頭。
   D 一名男子正在講課。

5. **A 女子正在看著電腦。**
   B 女子正在吃水果。
   C 女子放下了頭髮。
   D 女子正在用電腦打字。

6. **A 她正拿著蔬菜。**
   B 她正在看魚。
   C 她正在查看購物清單。
   D 她正在品嚐蔬菜。

PART 2 P. 78

18

7. Who's presenting the sales report at the next meeting?
   A I think Jason is.
   B It's already been sold.
   C At the nearest port.

8. Would you prefer an appointment today or tomorrow?
   A I arrived yesterday.
   B This afternoon is fine.
   C The office on the second floor.

7. 誰下次開會要由誰進行銷售報告的簡報？
   A 我想是傑森。
   B 它已經被賣掉了。
   C 在最近的港口。

8. 你想要約今天還是明天？
   A 我昨天抵達。
   B 今天下午就可以了。
   C 二樓的辦公室。

9. How can you improve product quality?
A By using better materials.
B I can prove him wrong.
C Production costs.

10. Which road is fastest?
A Why don't I drive?
B Take the highway.
C Slow down.

11. Do you mind if I print a document?
A It's black and white.
B This is not mine.
C No problem. Go ahead.

12. Who's welcoming our guest?
A I think it's April 24.
B Please reserve a room.
C Mary is responsible for that.

13. That piano player played really well, didn't he?
A Yes, I was very impressed.
B It was rather expensive.
C I bought the player online.

14. Why is the copy center closed today?
A 300 copies, please.
B In the storage closet.
C It's Sunday.

15. Where can I apply for a job?
A The application fee.
B On our website.
C Mr. Marshall will conduct an interview.

16. I signed up for the leadership workshop.
A At the local community center.
B I've been assigned the role.
C Oh, so did I.

17. The wellness seminar is this afternoon, isn't it?
A Yes, don't be late.
B No, please register online.
C It was quite informative.

18. Where can I find the client's phone number?
A Before 5:00 P.M.
B The secretary should know.
C No, she never called back.

9. 你可以如何改善產品品質？
A 藉由使用較好的材料。
B 我可以證明他是錯的。
C 生產成本。

10. 哪條路最快？
A 我何不開車？
B 走公路。
C 減速。

11. 你介意我印一份文件嗎？
A 這是黑白的。
B 這不是我的。
C 沒問題，印吧。

12. 誰要歡迎我們的客人？
A 我認為是 4 月 24 日。
B 請訂一間房間。
C 瑪莉負責此事。

13. 那位鋼琴演奏者彈得真好，對吧？
A 是的，我感到印象深刻。
B 它相當昂貴。
C 我從網路上購買那台播放器。

14. 影印中心今天為何關閉？
A 300 份，謝謝。
B 在儲藏櫃裡。
C 今天是星期天。

15. 我可以在哪裡應徵工作？
A 申請費用。
B 在我們的網站上。
C 馬歇爾先生將進行面試。

16. 我報名了領導能力研習會。
A 在當地的社區活動中心。
B 我被指派了這個職務。
C 喔，我也是。

17. 健康研討會是在今天下午，不是嗎？
A 是的，別遲到了。
B 不，請上網登記。
C 它資訊豐富。

18. 我可以在哪裡找到客戶的電話號碼？
A 下午五點以前。
B 秘書應該知道。
C 不，她沒有回電。

19. The network system isn't functioning.
[A] New login information.
[B] For the corporate function.
[C] It's being repaired.

20. Why are you still advertising this position?
[A] The new advertising strategy.
[B] We still haven't hired anyone.
[C] Every other week.

21. When are membership fees due?
[A] No, but you can upgrade.
[B] A bank account number.
[C] The last week of every month.

22. Are you scheduled for a private consultation?
[A] No, I forgot to call ahead.
[B] That was helpful.
[C] She departed on schedule.

23. Weren't you going to purchase a large-screen television?
[A] I bought a projector instead.
[B] How much did it cost?
[C] Turn down the volume.

24. Do you want to work on this task together?
[A] I'll walk on the treadmill for half an hour.
[B] A family get-together.
[C] Sure. When do you want to start?

25. The manager expects everyone to arrive by 7:00 a.m.
[A] I'll set the alarm.
[B] What did you expect?
[C] Leave it at the front desk.

26. Where do we store past years' sales records?
[A] I'll inform a store manager.
[B] Yes, it's an expense report.
[C] They have all been digitized.

27. Would you be willing to organize the conference?
[A] The keynote speaker.
[B] Regarding consumer preferences.
[C] Well, it depends on when it is.

19. 網路系統無法運作。
[A] 新的登入資料。
[B] 為了公司的聚會。
[C] 已在修理中。

20. 你為何仍在徵才？
[A] 新的廣告策略。
[B] 我們還沒僱用任何人。
[C] 每隔一個星期。

21. 什麼時候要交會費？
[A] 還沒有，但是你可以升等。
[B] 銀行帳號。
[C] 每個月的最後一星期。

22. 你安排了私人晤談的時間嗎？
[A] 不，我忘了提早打電話。
[B] 那很有幫助。
[C] 她依照計劃離開了。

23. 你不是要買一台大螢幕電視嗎？
[A] 我改買了投影機。
[B] 那要多少錢？
[C] 將音量調低。

24. 你想要一起處理這件事嗎？
[A] 我會在跑步機上走半小時。
[B] 一場家族聚會。
[C] 當然，你想要什麼時候開始？

25. 經理期望大家上午七點以前到達。
[A] 我會設定鬧鐘。
[B] 不然你以為是怎樣？
[C] 把它放在櫃台。

26. 我們把過去幾年的銷售記錄存放在哪裡？
[A] 我會通知一位商店經理。
[B] 是的，這是一份費用報告。
[C] 它們全都被數位化了。

27. 你願意籌劃這場會議嗎？
[A] 主講者。
[B] 關於消費者喜好。
[C] 嗯，要視時間而定。

28. Have you found a new intern, or are you still searching?
A The new intern starts tomorrow.
B The sales department.
C They will found a new company later this year.

29. Can I talk to Mr. Marquez in the finance department, please?
A Yes, I'll transfer you.
B He lives in a studio apartment.
C No, he's a finance expert.

30. Is it possible to have this repaired today?
A Yes, a pair of scissors.
B Won't the event be held tomorrow?
C No, we have to order new parts.

31. Why don't we send the parcel express?
A It still won't arrive in time.
B Throughout the press conference.
C They deliver supplies to your doorstep.

28. 你已找到新的實習生，還是你仍在找人呢？
A 新的實習生明天就會開始工作。
B 銷售部門。
C 他們今年稍晚將會成立新公司。

29. 我可以與財務部門的馬奎茲先生說話嗎，謝謝。
A 好的，我幫你轉接。
B 他住在套房。
C 不，他是財經專家。

30. 今天有可能把這個修好嗎？
A 是的，一把剪刀。
B 明天不會舉辦這個活動嗎？
C 不行，我們得訂購新的零件。

31. 我們何不用快遞寄這個包裹？
A 這樣仍來不及送達。
B 在整個記者會期間。
C 他們會將貨品送到你家。

PART 3 P. 79-83

19

32-34 conversation

W： Hi, James. This is Candice in the marketing department. (32) **I'm supposed to be leading a weekly meeting in Room 302 soon, but I just discovered that the room is already in use.**

M： I'm sorry, Candice. Actually, I have been getting calls like this all day. (33) **It looks like an error with our computer system is to blame for the mix-up.**

W： Oh, I see. Well, is there a currently vacant room that I could use for the meeting? The room will need to be equipped with a computer and a projector.

M： I'll need to check manually to determine which room will be available. (34) **I'll let you know as soon as I find another suitable room.** Please wait for a moment.

32-34 對話

女： 嗨，詹姆士。我是行銷部門的凱蒂絲。(32) **我本來不久後要在 302 室主持週會，但我剛發現那個會議室已經有人使用了。**

男： 很抱歉，凱蒂絲。事實上，我已經接這樣的電話一整天了。(33) **看起來是我們電腦系統出錯而造成混亂。**

女： 喔，我懂了。那麼，現在有空的會議室讓我開會嗎？裡面將需要有電腦和投影機。

男： 我得以人工方式查看，來確認哪間會議室可用。(34) **我一找到合適的會議室就會通知你**，請稍等。

32. What is the woman's problem?
A A meeting room is occupied.
B A piece of equipment is out of stock.
C An appointment has been canceled.
D Some software is not installed.

32. 女子有什麼問題？
A 會議室被占用
B 設備缺貨
C 預約被取消
D 沒有安裝某些軟體

33. Why does the man mention a system malfunction?
Ⓐ To apologize for an incorrect charge
Ⓑ To explain a scheduling error
Ⓒ To warn of security threats
Ⓓ To change a company policy

34. What does the man say he will do?
Ⓐ Fix a computer
Ⓑ Provide an alternative
Ⓒ Attend a meeting
Ⓓ Check the employee manual

33. 男子為何提到系統故障？
Ⓐ 為了錯誤的收費道歉
Ⓑ 解釋時間安排的錯誤
Ⓒ 警告安全威脅
Ⓓ 改變公司政策

34. 男子說他將會做什麼？
Ⓐ 修理電腦
Ⓑ 提供替代方案
Ⓒ 出席會議
Ⓓ 查看員工手冊

35-37 conversation

W：Hi, Craig. (35) **I was expecting you to submit the market analysis report yesterday, but I still haven't received it.** Do you need more time to work on it?

M：Hi, Ms. Watson. I'm really sorry I didn't send it to you by the determined deadline. I have recently been very busy with another urgent task. (36) **I'll make sure I finish the report before doing anything else.** Is that OK?

W：(37) **Well, I really need that document for a meeting with a potential client tomorrow morning.** I'll stop by later today and help you so that we can finish it in time.

35–37 對話

女：嗨，克雷格。(35) **我原本以為你昨天就會繳交市場分析報告，但我還沒有收到。**你需要更多時間處理它嗎？

男：嗨，華生女士。很抱歉我沒有在預定期限前把它寄給你。我最近在忙另一項緊急的工作。(36) **我一定會在做任何其他事情前先完成那份報告，**這樣可以嗎？

女：(37) **嗯，我明天早上與潛在客戶開會時會很需要那份文件。**我今天稍後會去幫你，這樣我們就可以及時完成它。

35. What does the woman ask the man about?
Ⓐ How to write a report
Ⓑ Whether a document is finished
Ⓒ How to reserve a meeting room
Ⓓ Whether a client has been contacted

36. What does the man say he will do?
Ⓐ Prioritize the woman's request
Ⓑ Extend a deadline
Ⓒ Draft a budget
Ⓓ Visit the woman's office

37. What does the woman need?
Ⓐ A list of clients
Ⓑ A sample product
Ⓒ Meeting materials
Ⓓ A revised itinerary

35. 女子問男子什麼事？
Ⓐ 如何寫報告
Ⓑ 文件是否已完成
Ⓒ 如何預約會議室
Ⓓ 是否連繫了客戶

36. 男子說他將會做什麼？
Ⓐ 優先處理女子的要求
Ⓑ 延長截止期限
Ⓒ 擬定預算
Ⓓ 去女子的辦公室

37. 女子需要什麼？
Ⓐ 客戶名單
Ⓑ 產品樣本
Ⓒ 會議資料
Ⓓ 修改過的行程

38-40 conversation

W： Hello. (38) **I'm interested in enrolling in your school's vocational training program to become a dental assistant, but I couldn't find any information about tuition on your website.**

M： Thank you for your interest. We offer a two-semester training program to become a dental assistant at our community college. Tuition for a single semester is $6,500.

W： Oh, I see. Honestly, that is a little more than I expected. (39) **I will have to ask my bank about the possibility of getting a student loan.** Is there anything else you can tell me?

M： (40) **Well, one thing to keep in mind is that our community college offers night classes for all our programs.** This is very good for students who work during the day. And please remember that we are one of the top-ranked schools in the state, and so far more than 5,000 of our graduates have become dental assistants.

38-40 對話

女：哈囉。(38) **我想報名貴校牙醫助理的職業培訓課程，但我在你們網頁上找不到關於學費的資訊。**

男：感謝您有興趣。我們社區大學提供兩學期的牙醫助理培訓課程，單一學期的學費是 6500 元。

女：喔，這樣啊。老實說，這比我原先預期的高了一點。(39) **我得問銀行讓我申請學生貸款的可能性。**你還有什麼可以告訴我的嗎？

男：(40) **嗯，要記得，我們社區大學的所有課程都提供夜間課程。**這對於白天需要工作的學生很有益。還有請記得，我們是本州的頂尖學校，到目前為止，我們畢業生中超過 5000 人已經成為牙醫助理。

38. What career is the woman interested in?

Ⓐ College professor
Ⓑ Web programmer
Ⓒ Dental assistant
Ⓓ Financial adviser

39. What does the woman say she will do?

Ⓐ Submit an application
Ⓑ Inquire about a loan
Ⓒ Consult a doctor
Ⓓ Apply for a scholarship

40. According to the man, what advantage does the college offer?

Ⓐ Convenient class times
Ⓑ Small class sizes
Ⓒ Advanced level courses
Ⓓ Reduced tuition

38. 女子對於什麼工作有興趣？

Ⓐ 大學教授
Ⓑ 網路程式設計師
Ⓒ 牙醫助理
Ⓓ 財務顧問

39. 女子說她將會做什麼？

Ⓐ 繳交申請書
Ⓑ 詢問貸款
Ⓒ 請教醫師
Ⓓ 申請獎學金

40. 根據男子，這間大學提供什麼好處？

Ⓐ 方便的上課時間
Ⓑ 小班教學
Ⓒ 進階課程
Ⓓ 學費減免

41-43 conversation

M： Did you enjoy this afternoon's training session for the new software? (41) **I think it'll really help us improve the quality of our graphic design work.**

41-43 對話

男：你喜歡今天下午為新軟體舉行的訓練課程嗎？(41) **我認為那對於我們增進平面設計作品的品質很有幫助。**

W：I thought it was very informative, but there are still a lot of details that I'm unsure about. (42) **I wish the instructor had allowed some time for participants to ask questions.**

M：Yeah, I agree with you. However, I heard that the instructor of the training session left his contact information with the human resources department. (43) **Why don't you try contacting him via email?**

女：我認為資訊很豐富，但還有許多我不確定的細節。(42) **要是講師當時有留一些時間讓參與者提問就好了。**

男：是的，我同意你的看法。但是我聽說訓練課程的講師留下聯絡方式給人力資源部門。(43) **你何不試著透過電子郵件與他聯繫？**

41. Where most likely do the speakers work?

(A) At a software company
(B) At a marketing firm
(C) At a travel agency
(D) At a graphic design company

42. What is the woman's complaint about the training session?

(A) There were not enough seats.
(B) The registration fee was too high.
(C) There was no time for inquiries.
(D) The instructor's presentation was lengthy.

43. What does the man suggest?

(A) Attending another training session
(B) Transferring to a new department
(C) Reviewing a training manual
(D) Contacting the instructor

41. 對話者們最有可能在哪裡工作？

(A) 軟體公司
(B) 行銷公司
(C) 旅行社
(D) 平面設計公司

42. 女子對於訓練課程有何怨言？

(A) 座位不足
(B) 報名費太高
(C) 沒有時間提問
(D) 講師的簡報很冗長

43. 男子建議什麼？

(A) 參加另一場訓練課程
(B) 調至新的部門
(C) 檢視訓練手冊
(D) 聯繫講師

44-46 conversation

M：Welcome back, Catherine. I hope you are feeling better after recovering from the flu. (44) **I wanted to make sure you know about the new policy concerning sick leave.**

W：I did hear that now we need to submit a doctor's note along with the sick leave form. (45) **Will I still be paid the same amount for my sick leave as I would a normal workday?**

M：Actually, the terms of compensation have changed as well. (46) **I'll print out a copy of the new policy and leave it on your desk later today.** If you have more questions, you should contact Jennifer in human resources.

44–46 對話

男：歡迎回來，凱薩琳。我希望你從流感康復後身體有比較好了。(44) **我只是想確認你知道病假的新作法。**

女：我的確聽說現在我們需要連同病假單一起附上醫師證明，(45) **病假會跟正常工作日給付同樣的薪資嗎？**

男：實際上，薪資條款也更改了。(46) **我今天會幫你印一份新的規定，稍晚時會放在你桌上。**如果你還有其他的問題，你應該聯繫人力資源部門的珍妮佛。

44. What is the topic of the conversation?
(A) A pay raise
(B) An upcoming deadline
(C) A prescription for the flu
(D) A new work procedure

44. 對話的主題是什麼？
(A) 加薪
(B) 接近的截止期限
(C) 流感的處方箋
(D) 新的工作流程

45. What does the woman ask about?
(A) Pay compensation
(B) Promotion opportunities
(C) Sick leave availability
(D) Official forms

45. 女子詢問關於什麼事？
(A) 薪資給付
(B) 升遷機會
(C) 是否可請病假
(D) 正式表格

46. What will the man most likely do next?
(A) Send an email
(B) Revise a budget
(C) Deliver a document
(D) Call a doctor

46. 男子接下來最有可能做什麼？
(A) 寄電子郵件
(B) 修改預算
(C) 提供文件
(D) 打電話給醫師

47-49 conversation

W：Hello. (47) **I'm calling to ask about the landscaping services you advertised in the newspaper.** I moved into a new house two months ago and would like to have some work done on my front yard.

M：Thanks for calling us. Unfortunately, we are currently swamped with requests from a lot of customers. Summer is our busiest season. (48) **I'm afraid you will have to wait a month until we can help you.**

W：Oh, I understand. I heard your business is professional and reliable, so it's worth the wait. In the meantime, I can provide you with a plan of what I have in mind.

M：OK, that would be great. (49) **After reviewing your plan, I can send you an estimate of potential costs.**

47–49 對話

女：你好。(47) **我打電話是要詢問你們在報紙上刊登的造景服務廣告。**我兩個月前搬進新家，想要打造前院的景觀。

男：感謝您的來電。很可惜我們目前有很多顧客的案子，忙得不可開交。夏天是我們最忙碌的季節。(48) **恐怕你要等一個月，我們才能為你服務。**

女：喔，了解。我聽說你們公司專業又可靠，因此值得等候。在這期間，我可以提供你我心中的平面圖。

男：好的，那樣很好。(49) **等我看過你的平面圖後，會把估價單寄給你。**

47. Where most likely does the man work?
(A) At a real estate agency
(B) At a bank
(C) At an art gallery
(D) At a landscaping agency

47. 男子最有可能在哪裡工作？
(A) 房地產仲介公司
(B) 銀行
(C) 畫廊
(D) 造景公司

48. How long does the man say the woman will have to wait?

A For a day

B For a week

C For a month

D For two months

49. What information will the man send the woman?

A A job opening

B An itinerary

C A price quote

D A meeting agenda

NEW

50-52 conversation

M：Hello, Charlotte. (50) **I'll be meeting a client for lunch next week. Do you know any great restaurants around here?**

W：Yes, Lament's Kitchen in Hildorf Hotel has a quiet atmosphere for meetings and the food is delicious.

M：That's good to know. I'll make a reservation today.

W：(51) **Oh and don't forget that Mr. Willis wants to meet you over dinner today to talk about this month's budget reports.**

M：I completely forgot. I'll need to cancel tonight's meeting then.

W：Don't worry about that. (52) **I'll inform everyone for you.**

M：Thanks!

50. What does the man ask about?

A A lunch meeting location

B The schedule for the week

C The budget reports

D A client list

51. What does the woman remind the man about?

A A dinner meeting

B A restaurant reservation

C A presentation

D A client's demands

48. 男子說女子必須等候多久？

A 一天

B 一星期

C 一個月

D 兩個月

49. 男子將會寄什麼資訊給女子？

A 職缺

B 旅遊行程

C 估價單

D 會議議程

50–52 對話

男：哈囉，夏洛特。(50) **我下星期要與一位客戶吃午餐，你知道附近有什麼好餐廳嗎？**

女：是的，希朵夫飯店的拉曼廚房氣氛很適合開會，而且食物很美味。

男：那真是太好了。我今天就去訂位。

女：(51) **喔，別忘了威利斯先生今天想要與你碰面吃晚餐，討論這個月的預算報告。**

男：我完全忘了，那麼我得要取消今晚的會議。

女：別擔心。(52) **我會幫你通知大家。**

男：謝謝！

50. 男子詢問什麼事？

A 午餐會議的地點

B 這星期的行程表

C 預算報告

D 客戶名單

51. 女子提醒男子什麼事？

A 晚餐會議

B 餐廳訂位

C 簡報

D 客戶要求

52. What does the woman offer to do?

Ⓐ Meet with a colleague

Ⓑ Talk to a client

Ⓒ Call some coworkers

Ⓓ Organize the reports

52. 女子提議做什麼？

Ⓐ 與同事碰面

Ⓑ 與客戶談話

Ⓒ 致電給同事

Ⓓ 整理報告

53-55 conversation

W： Hi, this is Shelly from Bafta Airlines. (53) **Unfortunately your flight to Vancouver tomorrow has been canceled due to weather conditions.** The earliest we can fly you out is tomorrow night at 11 p.m.

M： Oh, I actually have an important meeting tomorrow. It won't be easy to reschedule. Is there any way you can get me on an earlier flight?

W： I'm sorry sir, but we are not allowed to fly under certain weather conditions. We understand the inconvenience and would like to offer your return ticket free of charge. (54) **There is an overnight bus that will get you there by the morning.** I can make the booking for you.

M： Hmm . . . (55) **That's not a bad idea.** Let me phone my client in Vancouver and I will call you back shortly.

53–55 對話

女： 嗨，我是巴夫塔航空的雪莉。(53) **很可惜地，您明天到溫哥華的航班因為天氣的原因而取消了。**我們明天最早能飛的航班是在晚上 11 點。

男： 喔，我明天其實有場重要的會議，不太容易重新安排時間。你有辦法能讓我搭早一點的班機嗎？

女： 很抱歉，先生。但我們不被允許在某些特定的天候條件下飛航。我們了解這造成的不便，願意免費提供您回程機票。(54) **您有夜車可搭，能在明天早上抵達目的地，我可以幫您訂位。**

男： 嗯……(55) **這樣還不錯。**讓我打電話給溫哥華的客戶，我會很快會回你電話。

53. What is the problem?

Ⓐ The man forgot to book his plane ticket.

Ⓑ The flight is delayed.

Ⓒ The flight is canceled.

Ⓓ The man lost his ticket.

54. What solution does the woman propose?

Ⓐ To book a bus for the man

Ⓑ To pay for his hotel room

Ⓒ To send him documents

Ⓓ To call his client in Vancouver

NEW

55. What does the man mean when he says, "that's not a bad idea"?

Ⓐ He wants a better solution.

Ⓑ He agrees with the proposed solution.

Ⓒ He would like to hear more options.

Ⓓ He wants to keep the plane ticket.

53. 有什麼問題？

Ⓐ 男子忘了訂機票

Ⓑ 班機延誤了

Ⓒ 班機取消了

Ⓓ 男子遺失了票券

54. 女子提出什麼解決方法？

Ⓐ 為男子訂車票

Ⓑ 為男子支付旅館費用

Ⓒ 寄送文件給他

Ⓓ 致電給他在溫哥華的客戶

55. 男子說「這樣還不錯」，他指的是什麼？

Ⓐ 他想要更好的解決方法

Ⓑ 他同意提出的解決方法

Ⓒ 他想要聽到更多的選擇

Ⓓ 他想要保有機票

NEW

56-58 conversation

M：Hi, Carol. How was the recruitment fair in New York?

W：It was good. (56) **We recruited two new customer service managers, and I got to look around the city.** New York is a beautiful place! When did you start having flowers in your office?

M：Oh, you noticed them? I had them delivered today to freshen up the place a bit.

W：Um . . . (57) **Are they real?**

M：Of course! Go and smell them, they are beautiful. (58) **I can have some delivered to your office if you like.**

W：No, don't worry about it. That's too much bother, but I appreciate the offer!

56. What was the woman doing in New York?

A Taking a vacation

B Visiting family

C Looking for new staff

D Meeting clients

NEW

57. What does the woman imply when she says, "are they real"?

A The flowers look really bad.

B The flowers look fake.

C She is surprised to see them.

D She thinks they are real.

58. What does the man offer to do?

A Give her a promotion

B Send her a gift card

C Have flowers delivered to her office

D Send her to New York

56–58 對話

男：嗨，卡羅。在紐約的招募展進行得如何？

女：很不錯。(56) **我們招募了兩名新的客服經理，而且我有去城裡四處逛逛。**紐約是個美麗的地方！你什麼時候開始在辦公室裡擺花的？

男：喔，你注意到啦？我今天請人送過來的，讓辦公室變得更宜人一點。

女：呃……(57) **它們是真花嗎？**

男：當然！你可以聞聞看，它們真美。(58) **如果你要的話，我可以請人送一些到你的辦公室。**

女：不，不用了，那樣太麻煩了。但感謝你的提議。

56. 女子之前在紐約做什麼？

A 度假

B 拜訪家人

C 找新員工

D 與客戶會面

57. 女子說「它們是真的嗎」，她暗示的是什麼？

A 花看起來狀況很差

B 花看起來很假

C 她很驚訝看見花

D 她認為花是真的

58. 男子提議做什麼？

A 給她升遷

B 寄禮卡給她

C 送花到她的辦公室

D 派她去紐約

59-61 conversation

M：(59) **Hi Jennifer, this is Scott. Did you transfer some money to Mr. Woods yesterday?** He called me today and said they haven't received the funds yet. They are one of our most important clients and I don't want to upset them.

W1：Grace, did you do it? I asked you to go to the bank yesterday and take care of it.

W2：Yes, I did it at about 4 p.m. (60) **The bank said it might take an extra business day to go through because they are having some problems with their computer system.** Sorry, I should've told you.

M：I see. In the future please let me know. This client is quite strict about time so we need to be careful not to upset them. They bring us a lot of business. (61) **I need you to email me the transfer receipt so I can send them evidence of the payment.**

W2：I'm sorry. I'll email you the transfer receipt right away.

59–61 對話

男：(59) **嗨，珍妮佛，我是史考特。你昨天匯了錢給伍德斯先生了嗎？**他今天打電話給我，說他們還沒有收到款項。他們是我們最重要的客戶之一，我不想讓他們生氣。

女 1：葛蕾絲，你匯錢了嗎？我昨天要你去銀行處理此事。

女 2：是的，我在下午四點左右匯了錢。(60) **銀行說可能需要多一個營業日才能匯過去，因為他們的電腦系統有點問題。**很抱歉，我該早點告訴你的。

男：我知道了，以後請告知我。這名客戶相當注重時間，因此我們需要很小心別惹惱他們。他們為我們帶來許多生意。(61) **我需要你用電子郵件把匯款單寄給我，這樣我就可以把付款證明寄給他們。**

女 2：很抱歉。我立刻就用電子郵件把匯款單寄給你。

59. Why is the man calling Jennifer?

A To ask about her vacation
B To transfer her to another department
C To ask about a money transfer
D To talk to Mr. Woods

60. What does Grace say about the bank?

A They were closed when she got there.
B They are having problems with their computers.
C She emailed the receipt.
D She couldn't find the location.

61. What does the man say he needs?

A The transfer receipt
B The bank check
C The company credit card
D The transfer system

59. 男子為什麼打電話給珍妮佛？

A 詢問她的假期
B 將她調到另一個部門
C 詢問匯款的事情
D 要與伍德斯先生談話

60. 關於銀行，葛蕾絲說了什麼？

A 她抵達時銀行已經關門了
B 他們的電腦有問題
C 她用電子郵件寄了單據
D 她找不到該地點

61. 男子說他需要什麼？

A 匯款單
B 銀行支票
C 公司信用卡
D 匯款系統

NEW

62-64 conversation

W：Did you see this notice? The subways will be out of service during peak time tomorrow morning.

M：I know. (63) **The line that we need to catch is closed during morning peak time.** (62) **They are having some problems with tracks and they need to fix them.** I think it's a safety issue.

W：It's very irritating. That's probably the busiest line at that time of the morning. I don't know why they decided to do that.

M：(64) **I think if we get a few other people together, I can drive my car into work.** Traffic will be bad, but it's much better than taking the bus.

W：Oh, great idea. I'll ask around the office and let you know later.

62–64 對話

女：你看見通知單了嗎？地鐵將在明天晨間高峰時段停止營運。

男：我知道。(63) **我們要搭的路線在晨間高峰時段關閉。**(62) **他們的軌道有問題，需要進行檢修。**我想這是安全問題。

女：這真煩人。那可能是早上該時段最繁忙的路線，我不懂他們為何決定要這麼做。

男：(64) **我想如果我們找幾個人一起，我就可以開我的車上班。**交通狀況會很差，但比搭公車好得多。

女：好主意，我會在辦公室詢問，稍後再告訴你。

Subway Closures 地鐵封閉 September 24th 9 月 24 日	
Line 2 路線 2	6:00 a.m. 上午 6 點—10:00 a.m. 上午 10 點
Line 4 路線 4	10:00 a.m. 上午 10 點—11:00 a.m. 上午 11 點
Line 6 路線 6	11:00 a.m. 上午 11 點—12:00 p.m. 中午 12 點
Line 7 路線 7	1:00 p.m. 下午 1 點—2:00 p.m. 下午 2 點

62. Why is the subway being closed on September 24th?

- A To upgrade the audio system
- B Because the drivers are striking
- **C There is a safety issue**
- D Problems with the air conditioner

NEW

63. Look at the graphic. Which subway line do the speakers need to take?

- A Line 6
- B Line 7
- **C Line 2**
- D Line 4

62. 地鐵為何在 9 月 24 日關閉？

- A 為了升級音響系統
- B 因為駕駛罷工
- **C 有安全上的問題**
- D 冷氣機的問題

63. 參看圖表，對話者們需要搭乘的是哪個地鐵路線？

- A 路線 6
- B 路線 7
- **C 路線 2**
- D 路線 4

64. What does the man suggest doing?

A Taking the subway

B Using the taxi service

C Taking the bus

D Driving his car

64. 男子建議做什麼？

A 搭乘地鐵

B 使用計程車服務

C 搭乘公車

D 開他的車

NEW

65-67 conversation

M：Ms. Franklin, here is the inventory list in case we need to order anything. (65) **Please let me know by today because the supply company is closing for Christmas soon.**

W：I see. Well, Christmas is coming up, so we will need to wrap a lot of gifts for the staff presents. (66) **Also, I'm tired of holding my phone while typing, and we don't have anything for me to use. Can you please order me something?**

M：Yes, no problem. I will order that for you. Also, we are out of business cards, and we have some new employees beginning after Christmas. I suggest we have business cards ready when they arrive. Otherwise, we may look unprofessional.

W：Good idea. Go ahead and order those, too. (67) **Can you please send me the order form so I can double check it before you send it away?**

M：I'll email it to you soon.

65–67 對話

男：富蘭克林女士，這是物品存貨清單，看我們是否需要訂購任何東西。(65) **請在今天以前告知我，因為用品公司很快就要休息過聖誕節了。**

女：了解，聖誕節快到了，因此我們需要包裝很多要送給員工的禮物。(66) **此外，我很討厭打字時還要拿電話，又沒有什麼東西可以讓我用。可以請你幫我訂購嗎？**

男：好的，沒問題。我會幫你訂購。此外，我們的名片用完了，而有些新員工會在聖誕節後開始上班。我建議在他們上班之前把名片準備好，否則我們會看起來很不專業。

女：好主意，也一起訂購那些吧。(67) **可以請你把訂購單寄給我嗎？這樣我可以在你把它寄出去之前再次確認。**

男：我馬上就用電子郵件寄給你。

Supply Cabinet Inventory 用品櫃物件存貨清單

Item 品項	Quantity 數量
Carbon Paper 複寫紙	50
Tracing Paper 描圖紙	25
Wrapping Paper 包裝紙	5
Business Cards 名片	0
Headset 頭戴式耳機	0

65. Why do they need to send the order today?

A Because the company is closing for Christmas

B Because the company is closing for New Years

C The company doesn't have the item.

D They have delayed the order.

65. 他們為何今日就要寄出訂購單？

A 因為公司要休息過聖誕節

B 因為公司要休息過新年

C 公司沒有該用品

D 他們延誤了訂單

NEW

66. Look at the graphic. What will the man NOT order for the woman?
 (A) Wrapping paper
 (B) A headset
 (C) Business cards
 (D) Carbon paper

66. 參看圖表，男子「不會」為女子訂購什麼？
 (A) 包裝紙
 (B) 頭戴式耳機
 (C) 名片
 (D) 複寫紙

67. What does the woman ask the man to do?
 (A) Send her the order form
 (B) Send her a headset
 (C) Revise the memo
 (D) Send a receipt

67. 女子要求男子做什麼？
 (A) 將訂購單寄給她
 (B) 將頭戴式耳機寄給她
 (C) 修改備忘錄
 (D) 寄送收據

68-70 conversation

M：Hi, (68) **I'm competing in a triathlon next week and I need some energy bars or drinks to have during the race.** It's a six-hour race so it will be exhausting. I'd like something that is low in fat and will give me a boost of energy quickly.

W：Wow! That sounds exhausting. We actually have a new range of energy gels. My personal favorite is this one, it's called Hammer Gel.

M：Oh wow! I've never heard of energy gels. That's convenient. (69) **Oh, this looks great. It is basically just sugar.** That's perfect!

W：It also has caffeine, which is really helpful. Our other products don't have that. (70) **But I suggest you don't have too much caffeine before you take this because this has quite a lot.**

68–70 對話

男：嗨，(68) **我下星期要參加鐵人三項比賽，我需要一些能量棒或能量飲料，好在比賽期間補充。**這場比賽耗時六小時，會讓人很疲倦。我想要低脂而且能快速為我提升能量的東西。

女：哇！聽起來真累人。我們其實有新系列的能量凝膠。我個人最喜歡的是這個，叫做「猛槌凝膠」。

男：我從來沒有聽過能量凝膠，真是方便。(69) **這看起來很不錯，基本上只是糖而已。**這太完美了。

女：它還含有咖啡因，會很有幫助。我們其他的產品都沒有咖啡因。(70) **但我建議在你吃之前別攝取太多咖啡因，因為這個咖啡因的含量很高。**

Nutrition Information 營養資訊
Serving Size 每份：150 g（公克）

Calories 熱量	173 大卡
Fat 脂肪	5 g（公克）
Protein 蛋白質	10 g（公克）
Sugar 糖	22 g（公克）
Sodium 鈉	60 mg（毫克）
Caffeine 咖啡因	80 mg（毫克）

68. Why is the man looking for a certain product?
A He is on a diet.
B He doesn't like sugar.
C He will compete in a race.
D He has a test soon.

NEW
69. Look at the graphic. Which of the ingredients is the man interested in?
A Fat
B Sugar
C Caffeine
D Protein

70. What does the woman suggest the man do?
A Drink a lot of caffeine before taking the gel
B Don't drink a lot of caffeine before taking the gel
C Drink some caffeine before bed
D Drink some caffeine in the morning

68. 男子為何在尋找某種產品？
A 他正在節食
B 他不喜歡糖
C 他將會參加比賽
D 他很快就要參加考試

69. 參看圖表，男子在意的是哪一個成分？
A 脂肪
B 糖
C 咖啡因
D 蛋白質

70. 女子建議男子做什麼？
A 食用凝膠之前喝富含咖啡因的飲品
B 食用凝膠之前別喝富含咖啡因的飲品
C 睡覺之前喝一些含咖啡因的飲品
D 早上喝一些含咖啡因的飲品

PART 4 P. 84-87

20

71-73 telephone message

M：Hello, Ms. Grayson. (71) **This is Michael Cook calling from Alliance Financial Bank.** (72) **It has recently come to my attention that some clients who renewed their credit card this month were sent the wrong card.** We have had multiple calls from bank members saying that they were sent a credit card with someone else's name on it. According to our records, you were also sent the wrong credit card. (73) **We ask that you please dispose of the credit card by cutting it with a pair of scissors.** In the meantime, we will issue a new credit card and have it delivered by express mail. We apologize for the inconvenience.

71–73 電話留言

男：哈囉，葛瑞森女士。(71) **我是聯合金融銀行的麥可．庫克。** (72) **我注意到，最近有些本月換新信用卡的客戶被發放錯誤的卡片。**我們收到許多銀行會員的來電，說他們收到的信用卡上寫著別人的名字。根據我們的紀錄，寄給您的卡片也是錯誤的。(73) **請您用剪刀將卡片剪掉，以將它廢止。**同時我們將會簽發新的信用卡，並用快遞寄送給您。我們為此不便向您道歉。

71. Where does the speaker work?
A At a retail store
B At a bank
C At a gift shop
D At a shipping company

72. What does the speaker apologize for?
A A delivery mistake
B An incorrect charge
C A scheduling error
D A defective product

71. 發話者在哪裡工作？
A 零售店
B 銀行
C 禮品店
D 貨運公司

72. 發話者為何道歉？
A 寄送錯誤
B 收費錯誤
C 時間安排錯誤
D 商品瑕疵

73. What does the speaker ask the listener to do?
Ⓐ Return a call
Ⓑ Renew his credit card
Ⓒ Get rid of the recently delivered card
Ⓓ Sign an application form

73. 發話者要求聆聽者做什麼？
Ⓐ 回撥電話
Ⓑ 換新信用卡
Ⓒ 處理掉最近寄來的卡片
Ⓓ 簽署申請表

74-76 announcement

W：(74) **Attention, all shoppers. The West Point Mall will be closing in 10 minutes.** We thank you for shopping with us and greatly appreciate your business. (75) **To purchase items, please bring them to the cashier right now.** Also, we would like to inform you that a wallet that was found inside the store has been sent to the front desk. (76) **If your name is Catherine Goya, please stop by the front desk to claim the wallet.** Once again, we will be closing in 10 minutes. Please finish your shopping immediately.

74–76 廣播

女：(74) **各位顧客請注意，西點購物中心將在十分鐘後打烊。**我們感謝您前來購物，也很感激您的惠顧。(75) **如需購買物品，請現在將商品帶到收銀員處。**此外，我們想要通知各位，我們在店內撿到皮夾並已送到櫃台。(76) **若您的名字是凱薩琳．戈雅，請到櫃台領取皮夾。**再重申一次，我們即將於十分鐘後打烊。請立即結束購物。

74. Where is the announcement being made?
Ⓐ In a subway station
Ⓑ In a conference hall
Ⓒ In a shopping mall
Ⓓ In a baggage claim area

75. What are the listeners asked to do?
Ⓐ Proceed to the checkout immediately
Ⓑ Register for a workshop
Ⓒ Search for a missing item
Ⓓ Visit a different location

76. Why should Ms. Goya go to the front desk?
Ⓐ To pay a membership fee
Ⓑ To recover a lost item
Ⓒ To receive a voucher
Ⓓ To return an item

74. 這則廣播是在哪裡進行的？
Ⓐ 在地鐵車站
Ⓑ 在會議廳
Ⓒ 在購物中心
Ⓓ 在行李提領區

75. 聽眾被要求做什麼？
Ⓐ 立刻前去結帳
Ⓑ 報名研習會
Ⓒ 尋找遺失物品
Ⓓ 去別的地點

76. 戈雅女士為何應該前往櫃台？
Ⓐ 繳交會員費
Ⓑ 取回遺失物品
Ⓒ 收取禮券
Ⓓ 辦理退貨

77-79 recorded message

M：Thank you for calling Joyce Optical. If you are calling to check on the status of an order, press 1. (77) **Remember, we are the only glasses store in town that offers the services of our opticians free of charge.** (78) **That means you can get a complimentary eye examination as your vision changes.** (79) **If you would like to meet with one of our opticians, press 2 now.** We appreciate you choosing Joyce Optical and we hope to see you soon.

77-79 留言錄音

男：感謝您來電喬伊斯光學公司。如果您來電是為了要確認訂單狀況，請按 1。(77) **請記得，我們是鎮上唯一免費提供驗光服務的眼鏡行。**(78) **也就是說，若您的視力改變了，可以到本店進行免費的視力檢查。**(79) **若您想要與我們的驗光師會面，現在請按 2。**我們感謝您選擇喬伊斯光學公司，希望很快能與您見面。

77. What business created the message?

A A glassware factory
B A pharmacy
C An eyeglasses store
D An insurance company

77. 這是哪個行業的留言？

A 玻璃工廠
B 藥局
C 眼鏡行
D 保險公司

78. According to the speaker, what service does the business offer?

A Free eye examinations
B Online purchases
C Special discounts for regular customers
D Free delivery on large orders

78. 根據發話者，該企業提供什麼服務？

A 免費的眼睛檢查
B 線上購物
C 常客的特別折扣
D 大量訂購可免運

79. Why would listeners press 2?

A To cancel an order
B To change delivery information
C To schedule an appointment
D To leave a message

79. 聽者為何要按 2？

A 取消訂單
B 更改運送資訊
C 預約時間
D 留言

80-82 advertisement

M：(80) **Would you like to own a high-powered laptop that is small enough to fit in your suit pocket or purse?** Then the new compact laptop Hypertop from Hyperline is the one you have been waiting for. The laptop also boasts impressive graphics and fast processing times. However, this is not available at our stores for now. (81) **To purchase this laptop, you need to visit our website and place an order.** (82) **If you order this laptop this week, we will provide a portable printer at no extra charge as a special promotion.** Don't hesitate. Take advantage of this amazing opportunity!

80-82 廣告

男：(80) **你想要擁有一台高性能又體積小，能放進你西裝口袋或女用皮包的筆記型電腦嗎？**那麼超線公司的新型迷你筆記型電腦「超頂」，正是您所期待的產品。這台筆記型電腦號稱有很棒的影像處理元件以及高速處理效能，但是目前我們店內沒有貨。(81) **若要買這台筆記型電腦，您需要到我們的網站下訂單。**(82) **如果您本週訂購這台筆記型電腦，我們將會免費贈送可攜式印表機作為促銷優惠。**別猶豫，把握這個大好機會吧！

80. What special feature of the new laptop does the speaker mention?
A It is the lightest in the market.
B It has a built-in high-definition camera.
C It is water resistant.
D It is convenient to carry.

80. 發話者提到新筆記型電腦的哪個特點？
A 它是市面上最輕的
B 它內建高解析度相機
C 它能防水
D 它很便於攜帶

81. How can customers purchase the new laptop?
A By accessing a website
B By stopping by the speaker's office
C By visiting a local store
D By calling a customer service hotline

81. 顧客如何購買這台新的筆記型電腦？
A 使用網站
B 去發話者的辦公室
C 去當地的店家
D 撥打客服熱線

82. What can customers receive this week?
A An additional battery
B A carrying case
C A portable speaker
D A small printer

82. 顧客本週可以收到什麼？
A 額外的電池
B 隨身包
C 可攜帶式喇叭
D 小型印表機

83-85 excerpt from a meeting

W： Hi, thanks for coming to this special meeting today. (83) **The reason I called everyone is to announce our new partnership with Walker Studios.** As the CEO of Metro Studios, I'm pleased to witness this amazing opportunity to work with such a high-caliber company like Walker Studios. They possess a number of studios that are capable of producing cutting edge quality 3-D films. This will allow our company to begin producing 3-D films. (84) **And why wouldn't we?** The majority of our films are science fiction, and I believe a transition into 3-D is an excellent path for us. I have ensured that we will have full access to Walker Studio's equipment, and in return they will become a shareholder in our company. (85) **I suggest that our studio staff should spend the next following weeks studying how this new type of equipment works, so we can begin producing content as soon as possible.**

83–85 會議摘錄

女： 各位好，感謝大家今天參加這場特別的會議。(83) **我找大家來是要宣布我們與渥克電影公司的新合夥關係。**身為都會電影公司的執行長，我很高興能見證這個極佳的機會，與渥克電影公司這麼強的公司合作。他們擁有數間工作室，能夠製作品質最先進的 3-D 電影，這能讓我們公司也開始製作 3-D 電影。(84) **而這又有何不可呢？**我們的電影絕大部分都是科幻片，我相信轉換成 3-D 對我們而言是極佳的做法。我已經確保我們能夠完全取用渥克電影公司的設備，而給他們的回報則是成為我們公司的股東。(85) **我建議我們電影公司的員工，應該在接下來幾個星期學會使用這種新設備，這樣我們就可以盡快開始製作電影內容。**

83. What is the reason for the meeting?
A To announce a new partnership
B To introduce a new manager
C To propose a budget plan
D To announce her retirement

83. 為何召開會議？
A 要宣布新的合夥關係
B 要介紹新經理
C 要提出預算計劃
D 要宣布她的榮退

NEW

84. What does the woman imply when she says, "and why wouldn't we"?

A To suggest the partnership is good

B To review some materials

C To recommend a new method

D To offer a training program

84. 女子說「而這又有何不可呢」，她暗示什麼？

A 要表示合夥關係是好的

B 要檢視一些題材

C 要推薦新的方法

D 要提供訓練課程

85. What does the woman suggest the studio staff do?

A Go on vacation

B Continue using the old equipment

C Produce a movie

D Study the new equipment

85. 女子建議電影公司員工做什麼？

A 去度假

B 持續使用舊設備

C 製作電影

D 研究新設備

86-88 notice

M：Hi, everybody. This Saturday the fitness center will be upgrading our water-heating system in the bathrooms. (86) **Unfortunately, the hot water will be off from 9 a.m. to 12 p.m.** If anyone was planning to come in and exercise, (87) **you might want to hold off until later.** If the work gets delayed (88) **I will send a text message to all club members to notify you of any changes.**

86–88 通知

男：嗨，大家好。本週六健身中心將要改善浴室的熱水系統。(86) **麻煩的是，從上午九點到中午 12 點，熱水將會關閉。**如果有人打算要來運動，(87) **可能要晚點再來。**如果工程延誤了，(88) **我會傳簡訊給所有會員，告知任何異動。**

86. What problem does the speaker mention?

A A shipment was missed.

B The order was wrong.

C The center will have no hot water.

D There will be no water.

86. 發話者提到了什麼問題？

A 錯過了送貨

B 訂單有誤

C 健身中心將沒有熱水可用

D 將會停水

NEW

87. What does the speaker imply when he says, "you might want to hold off until later"?

A Members of the center should come in the afternoon.

B Members of the center shouldn't come.

C There will be a meeting in the morning.

D The center is closed in the afternoon.

87. 發話者說「可能要晚點再來」，他暗示什麼？

A 健身中心的會員應該下午再來

B 健身中心的會員不應該來

C 早上要開會

D 健身中心下午關閉

88. What does the speaker say he will do?

A Send a text message

B Send an email

C Make a phone call

D Post a letter

88. 發話者說他將會做什麼？

A 傳簡訊

B 寄電子郵件

C 打電話

D 郵寄信件

89-91 telephone message

W：[89] **Hi, Chef Garder, this is Lauren Cole phoning from the restaurant kitchen.** The delivery just came in, and [90] **there is a lot more meat and fish delivered that we don't usually have on our list.** I don't recall any special events coming up, and the calendar doesn't have anything on it. Did you make the order? I'm going to call the supplier but I want to check with you first in case you need the products. [91] **Give me a call back, and please bear in mind I have to finish the kitchen inventory by 11 a.m., and it's already 9:30.** Thanks, Chef.

89–91 電話留言

女：[89] **嗨，加德主廚，我是餐廳廚房的蘿倫·科爾。**貨剛送到了，[90] **送來的肉和魚比我們平常訂購的多出很多。**我不記得近期有任何特別的活動，日曆上也沒有任何紀錄。是你訂貨的嗎？我會打電話給供應商，但我想先與你確認，看是否是你需要這些貨品。[91] **請回電給我，請記得，我必須在上午 11 點前完成廚房存貨盤點，而現在已經九點半了。**感謝你，主廚。

89. Where does the speaker work?
- (A) At a market
- (B) At a clinic
- **(C) At a restaurant**
- (D) At a factory

90. What problem does the speaker describe?
- **(A) Extra items were delivered.**
- (B) The delivery is late.
- (C) The business was closed.
- (D) There is a special event planned.

NEW

91. What does the woman mean when she says, "I have to finish the kitchen inventory by 11 a.m."?
- **(A) She would like a response soon.**
- (B) She doesn't need to know soon.
- (C) She needs some help with the new menu.
- (D) They have the right ingredients.

89. 發話者在哪裡工作？
- (A) 市場
- (B) 診所
- **(C) 餐廳**
- (D) 工廠

90. 發話者描述了什麼問題？
- **(A) 送來多餘的物品**
- (B) 運送延遲了
- (C) 商店關門了
- (D) 有規劃特別活動

91. 女子說「我必須在上午 11 點前完成廚房存貨盤點」，她指的什麼？
- **(A) 她想趕快得到回覆**
- (B) 她不需要盡快知道
- (C) 她需要有人幫忙處理新菜單的事
- (D) 他們有正確的食材

92-94 introduction

W: Welcome to your first training session at Jarret's! The next four days will be quite intense, as you will be shown a lot of different equipment you will be required to handle in your daily job. Try not to get too overwhelmed. **(92) Once you get used to the assembly process, your efficiency at working the line will grow rapidly within a year.** At Jarret's we pride ourselves on producing quality materials in a positive environment. We hold weekly team-building exercises and a monthly staff getaway. **(93) I'm sure you will enjoy our company events and become good friends with your colleagues.** Today we will have a tour of the factory and meet the workers. The next three days are spent on machine training. **(94) One of the days we will have a special team lunch and the president will be coming in to meet everybody.**

92–94 介紹

女： 歡迎來到你在傑洛特工廠的第一堂訓練課程。接下來的四天會很辛苦，因為你會看到許多不同的設備，這些都是妳往後日常工作要操作的，試著別被嚇著了。**(92) 一旦你習慣了裝配過程，你在裝配線的工作效率就會在一年內快速提升。** 在傑洛特工廠，我們很自豪能在積極的環境中生產出高品質的材料。我們每星期舉辦團隊凝聚運動，每個月還有員工出遊。**(93) 我相信你們會喜歡公司的活動，而且會與同事成為好朋友。** 今天我們要參訪工廠，並且和工人會面，接下來的三天要做機器操作訓練。**(94) 其中一天，我們會有特別的團隊午餐，董事長會來和大家見面。**

Training Schedule 訓練時間表

Monday 星期一	Tuesday 星期二	Wednesday 星期三	Thursday 星期四
Meet and greet 相見歡	Machine training 機器操作訓練	Machine training 機器操作訓練	Machine training 機器操作訓練
Factory tour 工廠參訪			Lunch meeting with president 與董事長午餐會

92. What are the listeners training to be?
- A Airline attendants
- B Military soldiers
- **C Assembly line workers**
- D Computer programmers

93. According to the speaker, what will the listeners enjoy doing?
- A Learning their job
- B Assembling products
- C Producing quality materials
- **D Going to company events**

92. 聽眾正在受訓成為什麼？
- A 空服員
- B 士兵
- **C 裝配線工人**
- D 電腦程式設計師

93. 根據發話者，聽眾將會喜歡做什麼？
- A 學習他們的工作
- B 裝配產品
- C 生產高品質的材料
- **D 參加公司活動**

NEW

94. Look at the graphic. On what day will the listeners meet with the company president?

(A) Monday
(B) Tuesday
(C) Wednesday
(D) Thursday

94. 參看圖表，聽眾在哪一天將與公司的董事長會面？

(A) 星期一
(B) 星期二
(C) 星期三
(D) 星期四

95-97 excerpt from a meeting

M：Alright everyone, here's the analysis of this year's microbrew market shares. The good news is, Alright Ales is still in the top five small breweries in the Northcut region. (95) **The bad news is, the newest entry into our market, Strange Brew Ales, has a directly competing beer and is making strong gains.** In order to stay competitive we must be able to introduce new styles of craft beer to our consumers. Our analysts agree, if the current trend continues, Strange Brew Ales will bump us out of the top five by this time next year. Our master brewers have come up with four new styles of beer that we will introduce to a focus group at the upcoming Northcut Beer Festival. (96)(97) **Once we get consumer feedback we will select the two most popular offerings and create an aggressive marketing campaign.** Our sales must increase by at least 5% over the next quarter in order to maintain our market share in Northcut.

95–97 會議摘要

男：好的，各位，這裡是今年小型釀酒廠市佔率的分析。好消息是，好呀麥芽啤酒廠仍然是諾斯卡特地區排名前五的小酒廠。(95) **壞消息是，新加入的奇特釀麥芽啤酒廠有直接與我們競爭的啤酒，而且市場增長快速。**為了維持競爭力，我們必須有能力為消費者推出新風味的精釀啤酒。我們的分析師都認為，如果目前的趨勢持續下去，奇特釀麥芽啤酒廠在明年此時會把我們擠出前五名。我們的釀酒師已經想出四種新風味的啤酒，我們會在近期的諾斯卡特啤酒節時介紹給焦點小組。(96)(97) **只要一收到顧客的意見回饋，我們就會挑選最受歡迎的兩種啤酒，並進行積極的行銷活動。**下一季我們的銷售量至少要增加5%，才能維持我們在諾斯卡特的市佔率。

FOCUS GROUP QUESTIONAIRE RESULTS: 焦點團體問卷調查結果：

Majority respondents selected the following 多數受訪者選擇如下

Alright Ales New Styles 好呀麥芽啤酒新風味	Do you like the label? 你是否喜歡此品牌？	Do you like the flavor? 你是否喜歡此口味？	Would you choose this again? 你是否會再次選擇此產品？	Would you recommend this beer? 你是否會推薦這款啤酒？
Dark Ale 黑麥芽啤酒	Yes 是	No 否	Maybe 也許	Maybe 也許
Red Ale 紅麥芽啤酒	No 否	Yes 是	Yes 是	Yes 是
Belgium Style 比利時風味啤酒	Yes 是	No 否	No 否	No 否
Wheat Ale 小麥芽啤酒	Yes 是	Yes 是	Yes 是	Yes 是

95. Why is Alright Ales worried?
A They have a new competitor.
B They are nervous about their new beers.
C They are not in the top 5 of the market share in Northcut.
D They will have to cut staff.

96. What will the company likely do with the results of the survey?
A Change the label of the Red Ale
B Work on the Belgium Style
C Begin marketing the chosen beers
D Start working on a new style of beer

NEW
97. Look at the graphic. What beer is least likely to be part of Alright Ales' new product line?
A Wheat Ale
B Dark Ale
C Red Ale
D Belgium Style

95. 好呀麥芽啤酒廠為何憂心？
A 他們有新的競爭對手
B 他們對於自家的新啤酒感到緊張
C 他們不在諾斯卡特市佔率的前五名
D 他們將要裁員

96. 這份調查的結果很可能會讓這家公司做什麼？
A 改變紅麥芽啤酒的標籤
B 努力改進比利時風味啤酒
C 開始行銷獲選的啤酒
D 開始研發新款的啤酒

97. 參看圖表，哪種啤酒最不可能是好呀麥芽啤酒廠推出的新產品？
A 小麥麥芽啤酒
B 黑麥芽啤酒
C 紅麥芽啤酒
D 比利時風味啤酒

98-100 announcement

W： Welcome to Big Toys' warehouse orientation. As the industry leader in children's toys, (98) **it is essential that you understand the huge volume of merchandise that you will be dealing with as a stock room worker.** The worksheet in front of you is a map of our warehouse. Each section of the warehouse is divided into zones by the type of toy, and then arranged alphabetically by manufacturer. (99) **At the bottom of the map is a list of toys we would like you to collect and place on the designated pallet for shelving.** There will be a "Z" and a number before the name of the toy, to let you know what zone it is in. (100) **This is a timed exercise, and all toys should be collected within 1 hour.** I understand this is a trial by fire, but once you get the hang of our organization, you will be able to complete a task like this with ease.

98–100 介紹

女： 歡迎來到大玩具公司倉儲新進人員訓練。身為兒童玩具業的領導者，(98) **各位有必要知道，身為倉庫員工，你們將會處理大量商品。**你們眼前的作業單是我們倉儲的地圖。倉儲的每個部分都依據玩具的種類劃分成若干區域，然後再依製造商的字母順序排列。(99) **地圖下方列出的玩具清單則是要各位去取來並且放在指定的貨板上，以供上架。**玩具的名稱前面會有個字母 Z 和數字，是要讓你知道它在哪個區域。(100) **這是個計時訓練，所有玩具都要在一小時內蒐集完成。**我了解這是嚴酷的考驗，但是你一旦熟悉我們的安排，就能輕而易舉完成像這樣的任務。

Zone 1 第一區 — Board Games and Video Games 桌遊和電玩
Zone 2 第二區 — Action Figures and Dolls 可動公仔和洋娃娃
Zone 3 第三區 — Sports Equipment 運動器材
Zone 4 第四區 — Learning and Education Games 學習與教育遊戲

Toy List 玩具清單
Z1 Laughing Logs 大笑木頭、**Z2** Macho Man 猛男、**Z2** Lovely Lady 美麗女士、**Z3** Soccer Ball 足球、**Z3** Golf Clubs 高爾夫球桿、**Z4** Animal ID 動物識別證、**Z1** Business Tycoon 企業大亨、**Z1** Fighting Forces 戰鬥兵力。

98. What is indicated at the orientation?
Ⓐ Big Toys will be a boring job.
Ⓑ Big Toys has a large selection of products.
Ⓒ Their inventory system is confusing.
Ⓓ The managers will be very critical of mistakes.

98. 新進人員訓練時提到了什麼？
Ⓐ 大玩具公司是個無聊的工作
Ⓑ 大玩具公司有大量的產品
Ⓒ 他們的存貨目錄系統很難懂
Ⓓ 經理對於錯誤很嚴苛

NEW
99. Look at the graphic. Where will the trainees spend most of their time during the training exercise?
Ⓐ Zone 1
Ⓑ Zone 2
Ⓒ Zone 3
Ⓓ Zone 4

99. 參看圖表，受訓人員大部分的訓練時間都會在哪裡？
Ⓐ 第一區
Ⓑ 第二區
Ⓒ 第三區
Ⓓ 第四區

100. How quickly should the trainees complete their exercise?
Ⓐ 2 hours
Ⓑ 45 minutes or less
Ⓒ 1.5 hours
Ⓓ 1 hour or less

100. 訓練人員應該要多快完成任務？
Ⓐ 兩小時
Ⓑ 45 分鐘以內
Ⓒ 1.5 小時
Ⓓ 1 小時以內

TEST 5
PART 4
20

ACTUAL TEST 6

PART 1 P. 88-91

21

1. A She has some grocery bags.
   B She is holding some flowers.
   C She is reaching out to pick up a vegetable.
   D She is washing the fruits.

2. A The boy is putting bait on the hook.
   B The father has his right arm around the boy.
   C The boy is reeling in a fish.
   D They are fishing on the pier.

3. A He is washing the fruits.
   B He is cutting up some vegetables.
   C There are some glasses of water on the table.
   D She is standing next to him.

4. **A They are looking at some documents on the table.**
   B They are wearing helmets.
   C There are some people working behind them.
   D One of the men is writing on the document.

5. A There are some building designs on the table.
   B The woman is drinking a cup of coffee.
   C The woman is writing a recipe.
   D The woman is talking on the phone.

6. A The man is typing on the computer.
   B They are both looking at the laptop.
   C The men are wearing ties.
   D The men are checking some blueprints.

1. A 她拿著一些雜貨袋。
   B 她拿著一些花朵。
   C 她伸手去拿蔬菜。
   D 她正在洗水果。

2. A 男孩將魚餌放上魚鉤。
   B 父親用右手摟著男孩。
   C 男孩正在捲線拉魚。
   D 他們正在碼頭上釣魚。

3. A 他正在洗水果。
   B 他正在切蔬菜。
   C 桌上有幾杯水。
   D 她正站在他身邊。

4. **A 他們看著桌上的文件。**
   B 他們戴著安全帽。
   C 有些人在他們後面工作。
   D 其中一名男子在文件上寫字。

5. A 桌上有些建築物設計圖。
   B 女子正在喝咖啡。
   C 女子正在寫食譜。
   D 女子正在講電話。

6. A 男子正在用電腦打字。
   B 他們兩人都看著筆記型電腦。
   C 男子們都打領帶。
   D 男子們在檢視一些藍圖。

PART 2 P. 92

22

7. Who's responsible for the report?
   A Sometime in the afternoon.
   B In the news report.
   C It's John Draper.

8. Where can I buy a ticket?
   A A round-trip ticket.
   B On the official website.
   C By 5:00 at the latest.

7. 誰負責這份報告？
   A 下午的時候。
   B 在新聞報導裡。
   C 是約翰・德瑞伯。

8. 我可以在哪裡買票？
   A 來回票一張。
   B 在官方網站。
   C 最晚五點。

9. Did Mr. Stacks show you the new work schedule?
(A) Yes, he was.
(B) It's behind schedule.
(C) Actually, Ms. Dwain did.

10. When should I call the travel agency?
(A) Sometime before Friday.
(B) In my desk drawer.
(C) We don't allow refunds.

11. How many tables should I set up?
(A) It's a table for four.
(B) There isn't enough time.
(C) At least twenty.

12. Let's take a short break.
(A) I'd like that.
(B) It's a short-term contract.
(C) I put the brakes on.

13. Why won't the television turn on?
(A) Because of a scheduling conflict.
(B) Maybe it isn't plugged in.
(C) It was yesterday.

14. Would you rather eat out or pack a lunch?
(A) It was delicious.
(B) We're preparing for a new product launch.
(C) Let's go to a restaurant.

15. Sam is a really great clerk, isn't he?
(A) Yeah, he is very hard-working.
(B) Well, the clock is a few minutes slow.
(C) No, he just moved last week.

16. How often does this bus come?
(A) I will come up with some ideas.
(B) Every twenty minutes.
(C) The train to Hemsville.

17. When is Mary due to give birth?
(A) No, it was a baby toy.
(B) Of course. I'd love to.
(C) Sometime next month, I think.

9. 史達克先生給你看新的工作時間表了嗎？
(A) 是的，他是。
(B) 進度落後了。
(C) 其實，是德溫女士給我看的。

10. 我應該什麼時候打電話給旅行社？
(A) 星期五前。
(B) 在我書桌的抽屜裡。
(C) 我們不退款。

11. 我應該要擺幾張桌子？
(A) 這是四人座的餐桌。
(B) 時間不夠了。
(C) 至少 20 張。

12. 我們短暫休息一下吧。
(A) 我很樂意。
(B) 這是短期合約。
(C) 我踩煞車了。

13. 電視為何無法開啟？
(A) 因為時程安排衝突。
(B) 也許它沒有插電。
(C) 是昨天。

14. 你要在外用餐或帶便當？
(A) 那很美味。
(B) 我們正在準備新產品上市會。
(C) 我們去餐廳吧。

15. 山姆是很棒的店員，不是嗎？
(A) 是的，他非常努力。
(B) 時鐘慢了幾分鐘。
(C) 不，他上星期剛搬家。

16. 公車多久來一班？
(A) 我會想出一些點子。
(B) 每 20 分鐘。
(C) 開往荷姆斯維爾的火車。

17. 瑪莉何時要生小孩？
(A) 不，那是個嬰兒玩具。
(B) 當然，我很樂意。
(C) 我猜想是下個月的時候。

18. Is this food enough, or should I prepare more?
(A) The restaurant is busy.
(B) That will be plenty.
(C) I need a pair of gloves.

19. When will the manager be making the announcement?
(A) At around 3:00 p.m.
(B) Yes, that's what I heard, too.
(C) In the auditorium.

20. Which shirt did you decide to buy for your sister?
(A) I decided to hire more employees.
(B) Actually, I bought a scarf instead.
(C) How much is it?

21. Would you like me to return this book for you?
(A) No, I haven't finished it yet.
(B) I'll book a room for you.
(C) Please help me lift this.

22. I'm having a hard time choosing what to wear.
(A) I bought the clothes last week.
(B) Where is the exit?
(C) I can help you decide.

23. Isn't the museum closed on Mondays?
(A) Sometime this morning.
(B) You're right.
(C) We will open a new branch.

24. Mr. Yamaoka will be dropping by today, won't he?
(A) Can you pick it up for me?
(B) No, he said he's too busy.
(C) Yes, it was his first visit.

25. I think I need to fill the car up with gas.
(A) Take a right turn here, then.
(B) It's a natural gas company.
(C) Don't forget to pack the truck.

26. Could you come to the office early tomorrow?
(A) It's reflected on the surface.
(B) Yes, I met him in the office.
(C) What time?

27. Why hasn't the delivery arrived yet?
(A) Let me call Ms. Anderson.
(B) I've signed the contract.
(C) A cardboard box.

18. 食物足夠嗎？或者我該多準備一些？
(A) 餐廳很忙碌。
(B) 這樣就很足夠了。
(C) 我需要一雙手套。

19. 經理什麼時候會宣布？
(A) 大約下午三點。
(B) 是的，我也是聽說如此。
(C) 在禮堂。

20. 你決定要買哪件襯衫給你的妹妹？
(A) 我決定要僱用更多的員工。
(B) 實際上，我改買圍巾。
(C) 那要多少錢？

21. 你要我幫你還這本書嗎？
(A) 不，我還沒看完。
(B) 我會幫你訂房。
(C) 請幫我抬起這個。

22. 我難以抉擇該穿什麼。
(A) 我上星期買了這些衣服。
(B) 出口在哪裡？
(C) 我可以協助你做決定。

23. 博物館星期一不是休館嗎？
(A) 今天上午某時。
(B) 沒錯。
(C) 我們將開新分店。

24. 山崗先生今天將會來訪，不是嗎？
(A) 你可以幫我把它撿起來嗎？
(B) 不，他說他太忙碌了。
(C) 是的，他那次是第一次來訪。

25. 我想我需要為這輛車加滿油。
(A) 那麼，在這裡右轉。
(B) 這是一家天然氣公司。
(C) 別忘了把東西裝上卡車。

26. 你明天可以提早到辦公室來嗎？
(A) 它反射在表面上。
(B) 是的，我在辦公室遇到他。
(C) 幾點鐘？

27. 為什麼貨物還沒有送達？
(A) 讓我打電話問安德森女士。
(B) 我已經簽了合約。
(C) 一個硬紙箱。

28. Were you at the workshop this weekend?
A I'll visit her next weekend.
B Yes, I attended with Jake and Melissa.
C I was going to shop for groceries.

28. 你這個週末在研習會嗎？
A 我下週末要去拜訪他。
B 是的，我與傑克和瑪麗莎一起參加。
C 我當時正要去購買雜貨。

29. Would you prefer to meet this Wednesday or on Saturday?
A I won't refer to the matter again.
B We can meet the deadline.
C I'm most free on the weekends.

29. 你比較想在這星期三或是星期六見面？
A 我不會再提及此事。
B 我們可以趕上最後期限。
C 我週末最有空。

30. Have you printed a copy of the itinerary for everyone?
A Yes, right here.
B A cup of coffee, please.
C No one knows where she is.

30. 你幫每個人印旅遊行程表了嗎？
A 是的，就在這裡。
B 一杯咖啡，謝謝。
C 沒有人知道她在哪裡。

31. This book is too difficult for me.
A Then I'll pick out a different one.
B The library is close by.
C Try this hat on.

31. 這本書對我而言太難了。
A 那麼我要挑選另一本。
B 圖書館就在附近。
C 試戴這頂帽子。

PART 3 P. 93-97

23

32–34 conversation

W：Hi, Mr. Joyce. This is Sally Walker calling from Frohman Publishing. (32) **My company has a three-page text that we need translated into Chinese. I know you sometimes do these kinds of smaller jobs for our company.**

M：Yeah, I would be happy to. (33) **However, you should know that it is my policy to be paid in advance.** Is that OK?

W：That's no problem. I'll transfer the money into your bank account immediately. (34) **The deadline for this translation hasn't been decided yet. Once I know, I will inform you.**

M：Thank you for your understanding. Please email me the document. I'll do my best.

32–34 對話

女：嗨，喬伊斯先生。我是弗羅曼出版社的莎莉 ‧ 沃克。(32) **我的公司有一份三頁的文件需要翻譯成中文，我知道你有時候會為我們公司做這種短期的工作。**

男：是的，我很樂意。(33) **但是你應該要知道，我的作法是提前收費。**這樣可以嗎？

女：沒問題。我會立刻將錢匯入你的銀行帳戶。(34) **這份翻譯的交件日期還沒有決定，我一知道就會通知你。**

男：感謝你體諒，請用電子郵件把文件寄給我，我會盡力做好。

32. Why is the woman calling?
A To extend a rental period
B To confirm an appointment
C To offer an assignment
D To accept a proposal

32. 女子為什麼打電話？
A 要展延租賃時間
B 要確認預約
C 要提供兼職工作
D 要接受提案

33. What does the man ask the woman to do?

A Interpret for her supervisor

B Send an advance payment

C Submit an official request

D Provide a work space

34. What will the woman inform the man about?

A A requirement

B A deadline

C A meeting time

D A company policy

35–37 conversation

W：Good morning, James. (35) **Here is a copy of your expense report from last month's business trip to Tokyo.**

M：Thanks, Mary. (36) **Oh, while you're here, can you leave a message in this get-well-soon card for Bryce?** He had knee surgery yesterday and I was thinking this card might cheer him up.

W：Oh, did he? I didn't even know he was in the hospital. I was out of town yesterday. Is it serious?

M：Not that I know of. But he said he had to stay in the hospital for a few days. (37) **I'm planning on visiting him this evening after work.**

35. What did the woman make a copy of?

A A receipt

B A meeting schedule

C An expense report

D A prescription

36. What does the man ask the woman to do?

A Sign a contract

B Write a message

C Contact a receptionist

D Go on a business trip to Tokyo

37. What does the man plan to do?

A Visit his coworker

B Submit a report

C Make a new reservation

D Work overtime

33. 男子要求女子做什麼？

A 為她的主管進行口譯

B 付預付款

C 繳交正式的請求

D 提供工作空間

34. 女子會告知男子什麼？

A 要求條件

B 交件日期

C 會面時間

D 公司政策

35–37 對話

女：早安，詹姆士。(35) **這裡是你上個月出差到東京的支出報告。**

男：謝謝你，瑪莉。(36) **喔，既然你來了，你可以在這張慰問卡上留言給布萊斯嗎？**他昨天膝蓋手術，我想這張卡片可能會讓他心情好一點。

女：喔，真的嗎？我甚至不知道他住院了。我昨天出城去了，很嚴重嗎？

男：就我所知並不嚴重。但他說他必須住院幾天，(37) **我打算今晚下班後去探視他。**

35. 女子印了一份什麼？

A 收據

B 會議時程表

C 支出報告

D 處方箋

36. 男子要求女子做什麼？

A 簽合約

B 寫留言

C 聯繫接待員

D 到東京出差

37. 男子打算要做什麼？

A 探視同事

B 繳交報告

C 重新訂位

D 加班工作

38–40 conversation

W：[(38)] **I need to talk to you about the interior decoration we are doing at the Carletons' property.** They are a major client, so we need to make sure that they are completely satisfied. Have you consulted with them about the furniture for the master bedroom?

M：I have. They agreed on all of our plans except for the choice for the master bed. [(39)] **They're worried it is too big and will occupy too much space, so I'm looking for something smaller that still fits the color scheme of the room.**

W：OK. [(40)] **I was planning on ordering all the furniture today, but I think we'll have to wait until we get their permission.**

38–40 對話

女：[(38)] **我需要和你討論我們在卡爾頓房子的室內裝潢。**他們是大客戶，因此我們需要確保他們完全滿意。你是否諮詢過他們關於主臥室的家具？

男：是的。他們同意我們所有的規劃，除了主臥室床舖的選擇。[(39)] **他們擔心床太大，會佔去太多空間。因此我在找比較小又能夠符合房間配色設計的床。**

女：好的。[(40)] **我原本打算今天要訂購所有的家具，但我想我們還是等到他們同意後再買。**

38. What field do the speakers work in?
(A) Education
(B) Manufacturing
(C) Product development
(D) Interior design

39. What does the man plan to do?
(A) Choose different furniture
(B) Share a building plan
(C) Change a color scheme
(D) Place an order for wallpaper

40. According to the woman, why will the speakers have to wait?
(A) A shipment has been delayed.
(B) A contract has not been signed yet.
(C) Authorization must first be obtained.
(D) Some equipment is out of order.

38. 對話者在哪個領域工作？
(A) 教育
(B) 製造業
(C) 產品開發
(D) 室內設計

39. 男子打算要做什麼？
(A) 選擇不同的家具
(B) 分享建築計劃
(C) 改變配色設計
(D) 下訂單購買壁紙

40. 根據女子，對話者們為何必須等候？
(A) 運送耽擱了
(B) 尚未簽署合約
(C) 必須先取得授權
(D) 某些設備故障了

41–43 conversation

W：[(41)] **Hi, I'd like to adopt a pet.** I live alone and feel that a dog would be great company.

M：You came to the right place. [(41)] **We have many cute dogs here who were rescued from the street and don't have a home.** What kind of dog are you looking for specifically?

41–43 對話

女：[(41)] **嗨，我想要領養寵物。**我獨居，覺得狗會是很好的夥伴。

男：你來對地方了。[(41)] **我們這裡有很多可愛的狗，都是從街道上救回來的，還沒有家。**你想找什麼特定的狗呢？

W：(42) **Well, my house is not that big, so I was hoping for a dog small enough to hold in my lap.**

M：All right. (43) **Before we can allow you to adopt a dog, we need you to complete some official paperwork.** If you have a seat in the lobby, I'll bring you the documents immediately.

女：(42) **嗯，我的房子沒那麼大，因此我希望有一隻可以放在腿上的小型犬。**

男：好的。(43) **在我們同意你領養小狗之前，我們有一些正式的文書需要你寫。**請你在大廳就座，我會立刻幫你把文件帶過來。

41. Where most likely are the speakers?

(A) At a pet shop
(B) At a catering company
(C) At a fire station
(D) At an animal shelter

41. 對話者最有可能在哪裡？

(A) 寵物店
(B) 外燴公司
(C) 消防局
(D) 動物收容所

42. What aspect of the woman's needs is mentioned?

(A) The price
(B) The size
(C) The age
(D) The color

42. 對話中提及女子哪方面的需求？

(A) 價格
(B) 大小
(C) 年紀
(D) 顏色

43. According to the man, what does the woman have to do?

(A) Make an advance payment
(B) Bring her identification
(C) Fill out some documents
(D) Submit a letter of reference

43. 根據男子的說法，女子必須做什麼？

(A) 預先付款
(B) 帶來她的身分證明
(C) 填寫一些文件
(D) 繳交介紹信

44–46 conversation

M：Hello, this is David Wright. (44) **I represent the guitar player Joe Jackson, who will be performing at your venue this weekend.** (45) **I wanted to remind you that Mr. Jackson requests that no photography be allowed during the duration of his performance.**

W：Yes, I remember. We have posted flyers at the entrance prohibiting cameras and have asked our staff to remind guests that photography is not allowed.

M：Thank you for your cooperation. As you know, Mr. Jackson is very sensitive when he plays.

W：(46) **I'll make an announcement onstage before the show to inform the audience one more time about this restriction.**

44–46 對話

男：哈囉，我是大衛・萊特。(44) **我代表吉他手喬・傑克森，他將在本週末到你們的場地表演。**(45) **我想要提醒你，傑克森先生要求演出期間不得拍攝。**

女：是的，我記得。我們已經在入口處張貼禁止相機的傳單，並且要求工作人員提醒來賓禁止攝影。

男：感謝你們的合作。你知道的，傑克森先生在演奏時非常敏感。

女：(46) **演出前我會上台宣布，再次告知觀眾這項限制。**

44. Who most likely is the man?
A A photographer
B A talent agent
C A performer
D A receptionist

45. Why is the man calling?
A To buy a ticket in advance
B To confirm a reservation
C To provide a reminder
D To inquire about an advertisement

46. What does the woman offer to do?
A Restrict backstage access
B Take pictures of Mr. Jackson
C Show the man a list of guests
D Make an official announcement

44. 男子最有可能是什麼人？
A 攝影師
B 藝人經紀人
C 表演者
D 接待員

45. 男子為何打電話？
A 要提前購票
B 要確認預約
C 要做出提醒
D 要詢問廣告的事

46. 女子提議做什麼？
A 限制進入後台
B 為傑克森先生拍照
C 給男子看來賓名單
D 公開聲明

47–49 conversation

M：Hi, Kelly. Did you see our advertisement in this month's issue of *Fishing Fanatic*? **(47) The accompanying graphic shows how our fishing rods are stronger than any other product on the market.**

W：Yeah, I saw it this morning. **(48) I'm hoping the advertisement will help convince customers to purchase our newest line of fishing rods.**

M：**(48) I'm sure it will. (49) I'll get in touch with the advertising agency and request that the ad be placed in other magazines as well.**

47–49 對話

男：嗨，凱莉。你有看見我們的廣告，出現在本月出刊的《釣魚狂人》裡嗎？**(47) 附圖顯示出我們的釣竿比市面上的其他產品都更堅固。**

女：有，我今天早上看到了。**(48) 我希望這則廣告能有助於說服顧客購買我們最新系列的釣竿。**

男：**(48) 我相信它會的。(49) 我會與廣告公司聯繫，要求這則廣告也要刊登在其他的雜誌裡。**

47. What is mentioned about the product?
A It is affordable.
B It is superior to competitors'.
C It is safe for children to use.
D It is simple to install.

48. According to the man, what will the advertisement help to do?
A Promote new products
B Increase stock value
C Encourage innovations
D Reduce customer complaints

47. 對話裡提到這項產品的哪一點？
A 它不貴
B 它優於競爭者的產品
C 它可以讓孩童安全使用
D 它很容易安裝

48. 根據男子，這則廣告將將有助於什麼？
A 推廣新產品
B 提高股票價值
C 鼓勵創新
D 減少顧客投訴

49. What will the man do next?
A Create a website
B Buy a magazine
C Revise an article
D Contact an agency

49. 男子接下來要做什麼？
A 建構網站
B 購買雜誌
C 修改文章
D 聯繫代理商

NEW

50–52 conversation

M1：Heights Department Store, Michael speaking, how can I help you?

W：Hi, (50) **this is Sarah. I purchased a Regan cashmere coat from you two weeks ago, but I still haven't received it yet. I was told that I'd get it in 2 to 3 days.**

M1：Hold on a second; (51) **you'll need to speak with a representative from the Regan boutique. I'll transfer your call.**

W：No problem.

M2：Hello, this is Regan Luxury Boutique. Brian speaking. What can I help you with?

W：Yes, Brian, this is Sarah. I bought a coat from you two weeks ago and I'm wondering what happened to the shipment.

M2：Oh, hello Sarah, I'm sorry to hear that you haven't received it yet. Let me check the computer here. (52) **Can you give me your full name?**

W：Sure, it's Sarah Jane Park.

50–52 對話

男 1：高地百貨公司，我是麥克。有什麼可以為您服務的地方嗎？

女：嗨，(50) **我是莎拉。我兩個星期前從你們那裡購買了一件里根喀什米爾羊毛大衣，但我都還沒收到。我被告知兩到三天就會收到。**

男 1：請稍等。(51) **請您與里根精品店的客服談談，我幫您轉接。**

女：沒問題。

男 2：哈囉，這裡是里根高級精品店。我是布萊恩。有什麼可以為您服務的地方嗎？

女：是的，布萊恩。我是莎拉。我兩週前從你們那裡買了一件大衣，我不知道運送出了什麼問題。

男 2：喔，哈囉，莎拉。很抱歉您還沒有收到。讓我查電腦。(52) **可以告訴我您的全名嗎？**

女：當然。全名是莎拉 ‧ 珍 ‧ 帕克。

50. Why is the woman calling?
A She hasn't received her product.
B She was overcharged for the item.
C She wants a product exchanged.
D She wants to return a product.

50. 女子為何打電話？
A 她還沒收到產品
B 她買東西被多收錢
C 她想要更換產品
D 她想要退還產品

51. Why does Michael transfer the call?
A He is busy with another customer.
B The woman requested another representative.
C The woman called the wrong department.
D The manager is unavailable.

51. 麥克為何轉接電話？
A 他忙著處理另一名顧客的事
B 女子要求找另一名客服
C 女子打錯部門了
D 經理不在

52. What does Brian ask the woman for?
A The tracking number
B Her receipt
C Her full name
D The product name

52. 布萊恩向女子要什麼？
A 追蹤號碼
B 她的收據
C 她的全名
D 產品名稱

NEW
53–55 conversation

M：Hi, Mrs. West. (53) **Everything is set up for your anniversary party tonight.** If you can arrive at about 6 p.m. that would be great.

W：6 p.m.? I have meetings until 8 p.m. tonight. You know we are merging with another company at the moment, so it's a very important time for our company.

M：Oh, no! I've scheduled the band to play from six to ten o'clock. And dinner will be served at seven o'clock.

W：Well, I wish you would have told me about this earlier.

M：(54) **But it's your fifth anniversary party.**

W：OK. (55) **I will cancel my last meeting tonight and arrive around 6:30.** So, don't worry; everything will be fine. I will just be a little late.

53–55 對話

男：嗨，威斯特女士。(53) **您今晚週年派對的一切都已經準備就緒。**如果您可以在晚上六點抵達，那就太好了。

女：晚上六點？我今晚要開會到八點。您知道我們正要與另一家公司合併，現在對於我們公司是很重要的時刻。

男：糟了……我已經安排樂團從六點演出到十點，晚餐會在七點上菜。

女：要是你早一點告訴我就好了。

男：(54) **但這是您的五週年派對耶。**

女：好吧。(55) **我會取消今晚最後一場會議，並在大約六點半時抵達。**所以，別擔心，一切都會沒事。我只會稍微晚一點到。

53. What are the speakers mainly discussing?
- A Merging with another company
- B Last month's sales reports
- **C The woman's anniversary party**
- D When the band will arrive

NEW
54. What does the man mean when he says, "But it's your fifth anniversary party"?
- **A He wants her to change her schedule.**
- B He thinks it's not important.
- C He will tell the band not to come.
- D He wants her to go to the meetings.

55. What solution does the woman provide?
- A She will cancel the band.
- B She will cancel the dinner service.
- **C She will cancel her meeting.**
- D She will fire the man.

53. 對話者們主要在討論什麼？
- A 與另一家公司合併
- B 上個月的銷售報告
- **C 女子的週年派對**
- D 樂團何時會抵達

54. 男子說「但這是你的五週年派對耶」，他指的是什麼？
- **A 他希望她改變行程**
- B 他認為這不重要
- C 他會請樂團不要來
- D 他希望她去開會

55. 女子提出什麼解決方法？
- A 她將要取消樂團
- B 她將要取消晚餐服務
- **C 她將要取消會議**
- D 她將要開除男子

NEW
56–58 conversation

M：Hi, Susan. This is Rob. (56) **Did you get the flowers I sent you?**

W：Yes, I did. But unfortunately I'm allergic to sunflowers. I had to go to the hospital because they had been in my office for several hours.

M：(58) **Oh, I thought you would like them.**

W：You know I'm allergic to pollen, Rob. How could you forget? (57) **You should take me to dinner tomorrow night to apologize.**

M：OK. I will! I'll take you somewhere nice. Sorry about the flowers!

56–58 對話

男：嗨，蘇珊，我是羅伯。(56) **你收到我送給你的花了嗎？**

女：有，我收到了。但很可惜，我對向日葵過敏。我得去就醫，因為它們放在我的辦公室裡好幾個小時。

男：(58) **喔，我以為你會喜歡那些花。**

女：你知道我對花粉過敏，羅伯。你怎麼可以忘記？(57) **你明天晚上該請我吃晚餐做為道歉。**

男：好，我會的。我會帶你去個好地方。關於那些花，我很抱歉！

56. Why is the man calling the woman?

Ⓐ To check the sales figures
Ⓑ To check if she received the flowers
Ⓒ To check if she wanted to go to dinner
Ⓓ To check if the documents were ready

57. What does the woman say he should do?

Ⓐ Take her to the hospital
Ⓑ Pay her hospital bills
Ⓒ Take her out for dinner
Ⓓ Buy her more flowers

NEW
58. Why does the man say, "I thought you would like them"?

Ⓐ To express disappointment
Ⓑ To show appreciation
Ⓒ To show respect
Ⓓ To show he thinks it's funny

56. 男子為何打電話給女子？

Ⓐ 確認銷售數字
Ⓑ 確認她是否收到花
Ⓒ 確認她是否想去吃晚餐
Ⓓ 確認文件是否備妥了

57. 女子說他應該做什麼？

Ⓐ 帶她去醫院
Ⓑ 支付她就醫的費用
Ⓒ 請她吃晚餐
Ⓓ 買更多花給她

58. 男子為何說「我以為你會喜歡那些花」？

Ⓐ 為了表達失望
Ⓑ 為了表示感激
Ⓒ 為了表示尊敬
Ⓓ 為了表示他認為這很好笑

NEW
59–61 conversation

M1：Hi Bob. Hi Karen. The reason I called you in is to talk about the budget. (59) **This biggest issue is that our entertainment expenses are way too high.** I think we need to reduce the amount we are spending on company lunches and dinners.

W：(60) **Yes, I agree. I think we need to start paying for our own lunches.**

59–61 對話

男1：嗨，鮑伯。嗨，凱倫。我找你們來的原因是要討論預算的事情。(59) **最大的問題是，我們的交際費太高了。**我認為我們需要減少公司午餐和晚餐的開銷。

女：(60) **是的，我同意。我認為我們需要開始自費買自己的午餐。**

M2： I agree with both of you, but I think we need to keep entertaining clients. I think if we pay for our own lunches, then that will leave money to take clients out for dinner.

M1： That's a pretty good idea, Bob. Karen, does that sound OK with you?

W： I think that's a great compromise, Bob. **(61) I will make a monthly budget plan and email it to you this afternoon.**

男 2：我的看法和你們兩人相同，但我認為需要繼續招待客戶。我想如果我們為自己的午餐付錢，這樣就能把錢省下來請客戶吃晚餐。

男 1：那是個好點子，鮑伯。凱倫，你覺得這聽起來可行嗎？

女：我認為那是個很好的折衷方法，鮑伯。**(61) 我會做出每月的預算計劃，今天下午用電子郵件寄給你們。**

59. What is the main problem the speakers are discussing?
A What they should eat for lunch
B Going out for dinner
C High entertainment expenses
D Getting more customers

59. 對話者在討論的主要問題是什麼？
A 他們午餐該吃什麼
B 外出吃晚餐
C 高額的交際費
D 獲得更多顧客

60. What does the woman suggest they do?
A Stop going out for dinner
B Reduce client numbers
C Stop having lunches
D Pay for their own lunches

60. 女子建議他們做什麼？
A 不再外出吃晚餐
B 減少客戶人數
C 不再吃午餐
D 午餐自費

61. What does the woman say she will send the man?
A A monthly budget plan
B This month's sales report
C The old budget plan
D Last month's marketing materials

61. 女子說他會寄什麼給男子？
A 月度預算計劃
B 本月的銷售報告
C 舊的預算計劃
D 上個月的行銷資料

NEW

62–64 conversation

W： Do you know why the lifts will be out of order next week?

M： **(62) Last week, Harriet saw that there were some inspectors in the building next door.** Our maintenance checks aren't up to date, so if we get inspected, the building manager might be in trouble.

W： Oh, OK. But did you see the work schedule? **(63) The busiest wing in the hospital will be closed from 8 to 9 a.m.** So many people will be arriving to work at that time. I don't understand why they would schedule the repair at that time.

62–64 對話

女：你知道為何下星期電梯不能用嗎？

男：**(62) 上星期哈莉葉在隔壁大樓看見一群檢查員。**我們的維修檢查沒有更新，因此如果我們受檢，大樓經理會有麻煩。

女：喔，好吧。但是你看到工作時間表了嗎？**(63) 上午八點到九點，醫院最忙碌的一側會關閉。**那是很多人的上班時間，我不懂他們為何要在那時間安排維修。

M：Hmm . . . Yes, you're right. (64) **I think we should talk to Dr. Franklin about this.** I'm sure he can get the schedule changed.
W：I'd better do it now so the technicians have time to reschedule.

男：嗯……對，你說的沒錯。(64) **我認為我們應該與富蘭克林醫師討論此事。**我確定他可以更改時程。
女：我最好現在就去。這樣技術人員就有時間重新安排時程。

Lifts will be out of order 電梯將無法使用	
North Wing 北側	8:00 a.m.–9:00 a.m. 上午 8:00–9:00
East Wing 東側	11:00 a.m.–12:00 p.m. 上午 11:00 – 中午 12:00
South Wing 南側	1:30 p.m.–2:30 p.m. 下午 1:30–2:30
West Wing 西側	3:00 p.m.–4:00 p.m. 下午 3:00–4:00

62. What did Harriet see last week?
A Technicians in the building next door
B Technicians posting about lift repairs
C Some technicians installing lighting
D Her boss having a meeting with some technicians

62. 哈莉葉特上星期看見什麼？
A 技術人員在隔壁大樓
B 技術人員在張貼電梯維修的公告
C 技術人員在安裝燈具
D 她的老闆正與技術人員開會

NEW
63. Look at the graphic. Which is the busiest wing in the hospital?
A West
B East
C North
D South

63. 參看圖表，何者是醫院最忙碌的一側？
A 西
B 東
C 北
D 南

64. What does the man suggest the woman do?
A Cancel the repairs immediately
B Talk to Dr. Franklin
C Ask Dr. Franklin to lunch
D Close the North Wing

64. 男子建議女子做什麼？
A 立刻取消維修
B 與富蘭克林醫師談話
C 請富蘭克林醫師吃午餐
D 關閉北側

NEW
65–67 conversation
W：Good morning, this is Hardy's All Purpose. How can I help you?
M：(65) **Hello. I picked up a camping pack this morning, but it's missing some of the items.**
W：Do you know which items aren't there?

65–67 對話
女：早安，這裡是哈地全方位，有什麼需要服務的嗎？
男：(65) **哈囉，我今天早上買了一個露營套裝組，但裡面缺了某些東西。**
女：你知道裡面缺了哪些物品嗎？

M：[66] **I have the mats, sleeping bags, and the carry bag. I thought there was supposed to be one more item in there.**

W：Ah yes, I know what it is. Are you able to drop in the store today? [67] **I will give you a 15% refund because of the mistake.**

M：Oh, really? That's very kind of you. I'll come this afternoon and pick it up.

男：[66] **裡面有墊子、睡袋和手提袋。我認為裡面應該還要有一項物品。**

女：啊，沒錯，我知道是什麼了。你今天可以來到店裡嗎？[67] **因為這項疏失，我會幫你打八五折。**

男：喔，真的嗎？你真好。我今天下午會過去拿。

Camping Pack 露營套裝組

4 Rectangular Sleeping Bags 四個長方形睡袋
4 Camping Mats 四個露營墊
Carry Bag 手提袋
Portable Gas Stove 可攜式瓦斯爐

65. Where does the woman likely work?
A A camping store
B A hardware store
C A medical clinic
D A shipping company

NEW
66. Look at the graphic. What is the man missing?
A Carry bag
B Portable gas stove
C Camping mats
D Sleeping bags

67. What does the woman offer to do?
A Give him a full refund
B Give him a 15% discount voucher
C Give him a 15% refund
D Give him a free tent

65. 女子可能在哪裡工作？
A 露營用品店
B 五金行
C 醫療診所
D 貨運公司

66. 參看圖表，男子少了什麼？
A 手提袋
B 可攜式瓦斯爐
C 露營墊
D 睡袋

67. 女子提出要做什麼？
A 給他全額退款
B 給他八五折優惠券
C 給他八五折
D 給他免費的帳篷

NEW
68–70 conversation

M：Hi, I have a carpet that is identical to this one here. [68] **I need it cleaned as I'm going to be selling my office soon.** There are 3 rooms.

W：[69] **Three rooms of that carpet would cost 750.**

68–70 對話

男：嗨，我有和這邊這個一模一樣的地毯。[68] **我需要找人清理它，因為我很快就要出售我的辦公室了，**辦公室有三個房間。

女：[69] **三房的那種地毯要 750 元。**

M：Oh, really? I thought you were advertising a 15% discount on all your carpets?
W：That discount only covers our frieze and shag pile carpets.
M：Hmm . . . (70) **I see. OK. I will need some time to think about it, and I will come back.**

男：喔，真的嗎？我以為你們廣告說所有地毯都打八五折？
女：那項折扣只適用於起絨粗呢和長絨粗呢地毯。
男：嗯……(70) **我知道了，好吧，我需要一些時間考慮，我會再回來的。**

Henson's Corporate Cleaners
韓森公司清潔人員
Carpet Cleaning 地毯清潔

Frieze 起絨粗呢	$100 per room（每個房間）
Shag Pilet 長絨粗呢	$150 per room（每個房間）
Velvet 絲絨	$250 per room（每個房間）
Woven Carpet 編織地毯	$400 per room（每個房間）

68. What does the man say he is planning on doing with his office?
(A) Renovate it
(B) Sell it
(C) Clean it
(D) Repaint it

NEW
69. Look at the graphic. What is the carpet made of?
(A) Frieze
(B) Shag Pile
(C) Velvet
(D) Woven Carpet

70. What does the man say he will do?
(A) Buy the carpet today
(B) Ask his wife about it
(C) Tell his manager
(D) Think about it and come back

68. 男子說他打算要如何處理辦公室？
(A) 翻修
(B) 出售
(C) 清潔
(D) 重新粉刷

69. 參看圖表，地毯是什麼材質？
(A) 起絨粗呢
(B) 長絨粗呢
(C) 絲絨
(D) 編織地毯

70. 男子說他將會做什麼？
(A) 今天購買地毯
(B) 詢問妻子
(C) 告訴經理
(D) 考慮後再回覆

71–73 radio broadcast

W：You are listening to the news for the town of Clinton on your local CCBN radio station. (71) **School district officials have announced that they will be extending the deadline for new candidates to register for the upcoming school board election this May.** (72) **Remember, you can find the location of your voting district by visiting the official website of the town of Clinton.** (73) **We encourage all of the citizens of Clinton to exercise their right to vote in the May election.**

71–73 電台廣播

女：你正在收聽的是柯林頓鎮本地電台 CCBN 的新聞報導。(71) **教育局官員宣布，他們將延長教育委員會新候選人的登記期限，選舉將在五月舉行。**(72) **請記得，你可以上柯林頓鎮的官方網站，找到你選區的位置。**(73) **我們鼓勵柯林頓鎮的所有市民，在五月這場選舉中行使投票權。**

71. What is the announcement about?
- (A) An opinion survey
- **(B) An upcoming election**
- (C) An election outcome
- (D) A website update

72. What can listeners do on the website?
- (A) Register as a candidate
- (B) Cast their vote
- **(C) Find some information**
- (D) Enter a contest

73. What are listeners encouraged to do?
- **(A) Participate in an official occasion**
- (B) Reserve a ticket in advance
- (C) Exercise on a daily basis
- (D) Listen to an upcoming announcement

71. 這則廣播與什麼有關？
- (A) 意見調查
- **(B) 近期選舉**
- (C) 選舉結果
- (D) 網站更新

72. 聽眾可以在網站上做什麼？
- (A) 登記為候選人
- (B) 投票
- **(C) 找到某些資訊**
- (D) 參加比賽

73. 廣播鼓勵聽眾做什麼？
- **(A) 參加官方活動**
- (B) 提前訂票
- (C) 每天運動
- (D) 聆聽接下來的公告

74–76 radio advertisement

M：Hello, everyone. (74) **Help us celebrate the 10-year anniversary of Salem Furniture Outlet in downtown Marion.** (75) **From now until the end of the month, you can get a free 22-inch flat-screen television with a purchase of $1,500 or more!** So come on down and check out our fine selection of couches, chairs, dining room tables, and much more. (76) **This anniversary offer only lasts until the end of the month.** Don't miss this great opportunity. Come in today!

74–76 電台廣告

男：哈囉，大家好。(74) **來幫我們慶祝馬里蘭市區薩倫家具直營店的 10 週年慶吧。**(75) **從現在起到月底，購物消費滿 1500 元以上，就可以免費獲得 22 吋平面電視！**因此，請來店看看我們精選的沙發、椅子、餐桌，還有許多其他商品。(76) **週年慶優惠只到本月底。**別錯過這個大好機會，今天就過來！

74. What is the outlet store celebrating?

A An anniversary

B A festival

C An opening

D A holiday

74. 這家直營店在慶祝什麼？

A 週年慶

B 節慶

C 開幕

D 國定假日

75. What must customers do to receive the promotional offer?

A Become a member

B Purchase a certain amount

C Recommend some brands

D Trade in a television

75. 顧客必須做什麼才能獲得促銷優惠？

A 成為會員

B 達到消費門檻

C 推薦某些品牌

D 以電視換購

76. When does the promotion end?

A At the beginning of next month

B At the end of the year

C On the second Sunday of the month

D At the end of the month

76. 促銷何時結束？

A 下個月初

B 今年底

C 本月的第二個星期日

D 本月底

77–79 instructions

M： Thank you for attending today's safety workshop. My name is Tim Hines, and I'll be instructing everyone on how to maintain a safe work environment. (77) **As you know, a factory is full of safety hazards.** (78) **I have looked over the history of accidents for this factory, and it appears most accidents happen during the night shift.** (79) **Therefore, my first suggestion for everyone here is to make sure you are getting enough sleep before your night shift.** Sufficient rest is one of the best methods for avoiding work accidents.

77–79 說明

男： 感謝大家參加今天的安全研習，我的名字是提姆・海恩斯，我會教大家如何維持安全的工作環境。(77) **各位都知道，工廠裡充滿了工安危害。**(78) **我看過這家工廠歷年來發生的意外事件，大部分的事故似乎都發生在晚班期間。**(79) **因此，我給大家的第一個建議是，上晚班前務必要有充足的睡眠。**充分休息是避免工作意外的最佳方法。

77. Who most likely are the listeners?

A Environmentalists

B Instructors

C Factory workers

D Factory consultants

77. 聽眾最有可能是什麼人？

A 環保人士

B 講師

C 工廠工人

D 工廠諮詢員

78. What document has the speaker reviewed?

A An employee roster

B An annual budget

C A project overview

D Accident reports

78. 發話者看過了什麼文件？

A 員工名冊

B 年度預算

C 企劃概述

D 意外報告

79. What does the speaker suggest listeners do?
A Get enough rest
B Work a day shift
C Receive more training
D Read a handout

79. 發話者建議聽眾做什麼？
A 有足夠休息
B 上白班
C 接受更多訓練
D 閱讀講義

80–82 telephone message

W：Hello, Roger. This is Jenna speaking. According to an email I received from Tina Miller, our business trip to Moscow has been postponed until next month. (80) **The factory we were scheduled to tour is closed for some renovations.** (81) **We will have to wait until the construction at the factory is finished.** (82) **In the meantime, I'll send you the revised travel itinerary for you to review.** Let me know if you have any questions about this change.

80–82 電話留言

女：哈囉，羅傑，我是珍娜。根據提娜・米勒寄給我的電子郵件，我們到莫斯科的出差已經延後到下個月了。(80) **我們安排好要參訪的工廠已經關閉，要進行翻修。**(81) **我們得要等到工廠的工程結束。**(82) **在此同時，我會把修訂過的旅遊行程表寄給你看。**若你對於這項更動有任何問題，請告訴我。

80. What is the purpose of the trip to Moscow?
A To finalize a contract
B To visit a factory
C To give a product demonstration
D To renovate a building

80. 莫斯科之行的目的是什麼？
A 敲定合約
B 參訪工廠
C 進行產品示範
D 翻修建築物

81. What is the reason for the postponed departure?
A A necessary document is not ready.
B Some construction is underway.
C A company has gone out of business.
D Building materials have not arrived yet.

81. 延遲出發的理由是什麼？
A 必要的文件未備妥
B 工程正在進行中
C 公司停止營運
D 尚未送來建築材料

82. What does the speaker say she will send to the listener?
A A copy of her passport
B A plane ticket
C An itinerary
D A blueprint

82. 發話者說她會寄什麼給聽者？
A 她的護照影本
B 機票
C 旅遊行程表
D 藍圖

83–85 speech

W：Thank you, thank you so much. (83) **I feel truly honored to be promoted to executive chef at such a prestigious establishment such as Gray's on High Street.** I have been here for five years, and during that time we have been able to achieve a two-star Michelin rating. (85) **We have spent hundreds of hours in the kitchen at night perfecting our recipes and working on new and exciting culinary techniques.** (84) **I have to say, this promotion is not just for me. I could not have done this without highly skilled crew.** Their diligence and hard work have led to our success. So, please join me in giving them a warm round of applause. To our future!

83–85 演說

女：謝謝，非常感謝。(83) **我真的覺得非常光榮，能在高街上如此知名的的蓋瑞餐廳裡晉升為行政總廚。**我已經在此工作五年，期間我們獲得了米其林的二星評比。(85) **我們在廚房裡度過了數百小時的夜晚，完善我們的食譜並且精進新穎又令人興奮的廚藝技巧。**(84) **我必須說，這次升遷不只是給我個人，若沒有如此廚藝精湛的團隊，我無法有這樣的成就。**他們的勤奮努力造就了我們的成功，因此，請和我一同為他們熱烈鼓掌。敬我們的未來！

83. What is the purpose of the speech?

- (A) To announce a discovery
- (B) To announce a retirement
- **(C) To accept a promotion**
- (D) To accept an award

NEW

84. Why does the speaker say: "I could not have done this without highly skilled crew"?

- **(A) She wants to thank her team.**
- (B) She hasn't worked on a team before.
- (C) She dislikes her coworkers.
- (D) She wants to accept the award.

85. Where most likely does the speaker work?

- (A) At a hotel
- (B) At a travel agency
- **(C) At a restaurant**
- (D) At a warehouse

83. 演說的目的是什麼？

- (A) 要公布一項發現
- (B) 要宣布退休
- **(C) 要接受升遷**
- (D) 要接受頒獎

84. 發話者為何說「若沒有如此廚藝精湛的團隊，我無法有這樣的成就」？

- **(A) 她想要感謝她的團隊**
- (B) 她先前未曾在團隊工作
- (C) 她不喜歡同事
- (D) 她想要接受頒獎

85. 發話者最有可能在哪裡工作？

- (A) 在旅館
- (B) 在旅行社
- **(C) 在餐廳**
- (D) 在倉庫

86–88 telephone message

W：(86) **I'm just calling because I wanted to say thank you so much for helping with the catering at last week's gallery opening.** I really wouldn't have been able to do it alone, and I'm so grateful that you helped me on such short notice. The green curry you made was absolutely delicious! (87) **You have to show me**

86–88 電話留言

女：(86) **我打電話是想要向你道謝，因為你上星期協助藝術館開幕的外燴。**我真的不可能獨力完成這件事，而我很感謝你能臨危受命來幫我。你做的綠色咖哩真的很美味！(87) **你一定要讓我看看食譜！**我想在場沒有一位嘉賓不喜歡那道菜。

the recipe! I think there was not a single person who didn't love that dish. (88) **Anyway, I'll see you next week for the Charity Ball. I'm really excited to see what dishes you cook for us!**

(88) **總之，我們下週慈善舞會見，我真的很興奮想知道你會為我們烹調什麼菜餚。**

86. Why is the woman calling?
A To express her gratitude
B To discuss a recipe
C To report some news
D To make a complaint

86. 女子為何打電話？
A 要表達謝意
B 要討論食譜
C 要報告消息
D 要客訴

NEW
87. What does the woman imply when she says, "you have to show me the recipe"?
A She didn't enjoy it.
B She wants to recommend a different ingredient.
C She wants to cook the dish herself.
D She wants her friend to try it.

87. 女子說「你一定要讓我看看食譜」，她暗示什麼？
A 她不喜歡那道菜
B 她想要建議不同的食材
C 她想要自己做那道菜
D 她想要讓朋友試做看看

88. Why is the woman looking forward to next week?
A She is going to the movies.
B She is taking her son to school.
C Some new project will be completed.
D They will work together again.

88. 女子為何期待下個星期？
A 她要去看電影
B 她要帶兒子上學
C 某個新案子即將結案
D 他們將再次合作

89–91 news report

W：(89) **In other news . . .** Bernburg Studios, which is the studio responsible for such blockbuster hits as *Rolling Hills*, and *Standing Tall* is looking to film a movie in Westchester. (90) **The CEO has made an announcement requesting someone to allow them to film inside their home.** In the movie, the chosen place will be the home of the Oscar winning actor Robert Holloway. (91) **The CEO admitted that it is awkward to impose upon someone's private life, but he also said he has received hundreds of applications. After all, this is Robert Holloway we are talking about.** The studio has not chosen a location yet, so if you are still interested, visit Bernburg Studios' website.

89–91 新聞報導

女：(89) **其他新聞……**曾拍攝過《綿延山丘》和《屹立不搖》等賣座電影的伯恩堡電影公司要在威徹斯特拍片。(90) **該公司總裁公開宣告，想請求民眾讓他們進屋內拍攝**，被選中的地方將是曾獲奧斯卡獎的影星羅伯特 · 哈洛威在片中的家。(91) **該總裁承認，打擾別人的私生活很令人尷尬，但他也表示，他們已收到數百件的申請。畢竟，我們說的是羅伯特 · 哈洛威。**電影公司還沒有選定地點，因此如果你仍然有興趣，可以上伯恩堡電影公司的網站。

89. Who most likely is the speaker?
(A) A news editor
(B) A filmmaker
(C) A news reporter
(D) A movie star

90. What is Bernberg Studios looking for?
(A) An actress
(B) A filming location
(C) A new script
(D) More ideas for movies

NEW
91. What does the speaker imply when she says, "After all, this is Robert Holloway we are talking about"?
(A) Robert Holloway is very famous.
(B) Robert Holloway owns the house.
(C) She will interview him next.
(D) She doesn't know who Robert Holloway is.

89. 發話者最有可能是什麼人？
(A) 新聞編輯
(B) 製片家
(C) 新聞記者
(D) 電影明星

90. 伯恩堡電影公司在尋找什麼？
(A) 女演員
(B) 拍攝地點
(C) 新的劇本
(D) 更多拍片的想法

91. 發話者說「畢竟我們說的是羅伯特 · 哈洛威」，她暗示什麼？
(A) 羅伯特 · 哈洛威非常有名。
(B) 羅伯特 · 哈洛威擁有那間房子。
(C) 她接下來要訪問他。
(D) 她不知道羅伯特 · 哈洛威是誰。

92–94 advertisement

M: Hello, Happy Day shoppers. (92) **It's our anniversary, and we're offering 50% off the prices advertised on everything until Friday night at midnight!** Save on everything in our store, including our premium selection of pillows. Collect the whole series of Mama San brand pillows for half off! (93) **At the end of our sale, we will be restocking our shelves with a brand-new inventory**, so everything must go! (94) **Be sure to stop by our stylists. Bring a picture of a room you want to redecorate, and we will help you decide what colors to choose. Make every day a Happy Day!** Thank you for being our loyal customers, and we look forward to making you smile!

92–94 廣告

男：哈囉，快樂日子的買家們。(92) **現在正值我們的週年慶，星期五晚上午夜以前，我們會提供所有廣告商品半價優惠！**購買我們店內的各種商品省錢吧，包含我們的精選枕頭，現在只要半價就能收藏全系列「媽媽桑」品牌的枕頭！(93) **特賣會結束時，我們將上架全新商品**，因此要清空全數現有商品！(94) **請務必來找我們的設計師，只要帶著你想要重新裝潢的房間照片，我們就會幫你挑選顏色，讓你的每一天都是「快樂日子」！**感謝你對我們的忠實惠顧，我們期待能讓你開心微笑！

MAMA SAN premium pillows
媽媽桑高級枕頭

Beauty Sleep 美容睡眠	£30.00（英鎊）
Soft Night 輕柔之夜	£35.00（英鎊）
Dreamtime 夢幻時光	£42.00（英鎊）
Lovely Rest 美麗休憩	£50.00（英鎊）

NEW

92. Look at the graphic. How much can a shopper purchase the Dreamtime Pillow for before Friday?

(A) £15.00
(B) £11.50
(C) £21.00
(D) £50.00

92. 參看圖表，買家在星期五之前可以用多少錢買到「夢幻時光」枕頭？

(A) 15.00 英鎊
(B) 11.50 英鎊
(C) 21.00 英鎊
(D) 50.00 英鎊

93. What is indicated about Happy Day?

(A) They have a wide variety of toys.
(B) They are bringing in more merchandise.
(C) They specialize in low-end furniture.
(D) They are going out of business this Friday.

93. 關於快樂日子，廣告中有提到什麼？

(A) 他們有各式各樣的玩具。
(B) 他們要進更多的商品。
(C) 他們專營廉價家具。
(D) 他們本週五要結束營業。

94. What service does Happy Day offer?

(A) Personalized interior design advice
(B) Free shipping
(C) Home installation
(D) Wall papering services

94. 快樂日子提供什麼服務？

(A) 個人化的室內設計建議
(B) 免費運送
(C) 居家安裝
(D) 貼壁紙服務

95–97 telephone message

M： Hello, this is Trent Herrington from Blanders & Co. We recently received an order from you, and there are some missing items. (95) **On the invoice it clearly says we ordered 30 case binders, but we only received 20. We also did not receive any of the legal pads we ordered.** (96) **We have some important cases today, and we need those case binders to organize our client's defense professionally.** (96) (97) **As a law firm it is very important that we arrive to the court organized.** Is it possible for us to pick up the binders and legal pads this morning? Please call me back on 2612-4547 as soon as possible. Thanks.

95–97 電話留言

男： 你好，我是布蘭德斯事務所的特倫特・海靈頓。我們最近收到貴公司寄來的貨品，但有些東西遺漏了。(95) **發票上清楚顯示，我們訂了 30 個盒裝文件夾，但是我們只收到 20 個。我們也沒收到訂購的黃色橫條記事本。**(96) **我們今天有幾個重要的案子，需要用到盒裝文件夾，才能事業地整理好委託人的辯護。**(96)(97) **我們是法律事務所，上法庭時必須要條理分明。** 我們可以早上去拿文件夾和黃色橫條記事本嗎？請盡快回電給我，號碼是 2612-4547。謝謝。

ORDER FORM OF BLANDERS & CO.
布蘭德斯事務所的訂單
14 March 3 月 14 日

Product 產品	Quantity 數量
Case binders 盒裝文件夾	30
Envelopes 信封	20
Flags & Tabs 指示標籤和索引標籤	40
Legal pads 黃色橫條記事本	10

95. Look at the graphic. How many items were not delivered in total?

A 40

B 30

C 20

D 10

96. According to the speaker, why are the case binders important?

A To look professional in the office

B To look professional in court

C To organize their financial record

D To maintain the deadline

97. Where does Trent Herrington most likely work?

A At an accounting firm

B At a law firm

C At a patenting firm

D At a catering business

95. 參看圖表，總共缺了多少件物品？

A 40

B 30

C 20

D 10

96. 根據發話者，盒裝文件夾為何很重要？

A 要在辦公室裡表現得很專業

B 要在法庭上表現得很專業

C 要整理他們的財務紀錄

D 要趕上截止期限

97. 特倫特 · 海靈頓最有可能在哪裡工作？

A 會計事務所

B 法律事務所

C 專利事務所

D 外燴公司

98–100 tour guide

W：Welcome aboard the Midnight Cruise, Loveport's most romantic evening! (98) **We will be spending the majority of our cruise in Billing's Bay,** (100) **but we will also be following the coastline of Eagle Island to Port Lewis for a champagne toast.** During our cruise, our host, (99) **Star Master Jenkins, will be directing you through the constellations that are in view, and with any luck we will be able to witness tonight's meteor shower!** While we are cruising, we ask that you wear your life jackets at all times when on deck for your safety. If you begin to feel sea sick at any time, I encourage you to visit our onboard clinic for some medication. Now I would like to ask everybody to join the captain in the stateroom for a rundown of this evening's services!

98–100 導覽

女：歡迎登上午夜航行號，度過樂芙港最浪漫的夜晚！ (98) **我們航行的大部分時間都會在比琳海灣，** (100) **但是也會循著老鷹島的海岸線航行到路易斯港喝香檳。**航行期間，我們的主持人 (99) **史塔詹金斯會指引您欣賞今晚會出現的星座。運氣好的話，我們將能看到今晚的流星雨！**航行期間，我們要求各位在甲板上時要隨時穿著救生衣，以策安全。若你在任何時候開始暈船，建議您去船上的醫務室取藥。現在我想請各位和船長一起進入船艙裡，聽取今晚各項服務的詳細報告！

MIDNIGHT CRUISE ITINERARY 午夜航行號的行程表

5 p.m. 下午 5 點	Captain's address 船長致詞
6 p.m. 下午 6 點	Cocktails and dinner 雞尾酒和晚餐
7 p.m. 晚上 7 點	Constellation orientation 星座介紹
8 p.m. – 10 p.m. 晚上 8–10 點	Social mixer 社交活動
10 p.m. 晚上 10 點	Port Lewis for champagne toast 路易斯港喝香檳
11 p.m. 晚上 11 點	Cast off and back to Billing's Bay 解纜啟返回到比琳海灣
12 a.m. 午夜 12 點	Midnight constellation lesson and meteor shower on Top Deck 頂層甲板的午夜星座課和流星雨

98. Where will the cruise spend most of its time?
(A) Eagle Island
(B) Port Lewis
(C) Billing's Bay
(D) Socializing

99. Who is Star Master Jenkins?
(A) Host
(B) Captain
(C) Bartender
(D) Security guard

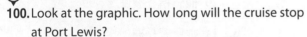

NEW
100. Look at the graphic. How long will the cruise stop at Port Lewis?
(A) All evening
(B) 3 hours
(C) 2 hours
(D) 1 hour

98. 航行的大部分時間會待在哪裡？
(A) 老鷹島
(B) 路易斯港
(C) 比琳海灣
(D) 社交活動

99. 史塔詹金斯是什麼人？
(A) 主持人
(B) 船長
(C) 酒保
(D) 保全人員

100. 參看圖表，船將在路易斯港停留多久？
(A) 整個晚上
(B) 三小時
(C) 二小時
(D) 一小時

ACTUAL TEST ⑦

PART 1 P. 102-105

25

1. A They are drinking cups of coffee.
B He is pointing at some information.
C The man is writing something on the document.
D All of the women are looking at the man.

1. A 他們正在喝咖啡。
B 他指著一些資料。
C 男子正在文件上寫字。
D 女子全都看著男子。

2. A He is mixing the snow.
B He is making snow for skiing.
C He is clearing some snow with a snow blower.
D He is cleaning the road with a broom.

2. A 他正在混合雪。
B 他正在造雪以供滑雪。
C 他正在用除雪機除雪。
D 他正在用掃帚清理道路。

3. **A The cars are being transported in a truck.**
B The cars are being fixed.
C There are many people in the cars.
D There are cars on the top level of the truck.

3. **A 汽車正被卡車運送。**
B 汽車在維修中。
C 很多人在車上。
D 汽車在卡車的上層。

4. **A She is pumping gas into the car.**
B She is paying for the gas.
C She is changing the oil in her car.
D She is putting air into her tires.

4. **A 她正在幫汽車加油。**
B 她正在付油錢。
C 她正在為汽車換油。
D 她正在為輪胎打氣。

5. A They are fixing the computer.
B They are pointing at the computer screen.
C They are both holding documents.
D They are pointing at each other.

5. A 他們在修理電腦。
B 他們指著電腦螢幕。
C 他們兩人都拿著文件。
D 他們指著彼此。

6. A She is wearing long pants.
B She is paying the bill.
C Her reflection is in the mirror.
D She is looking at her reflection.

6. A 她穿著長褲。
B 她在付帳。
C 她的倒影在鏡子裡。
D 她看著她的倒影。

PART 2 P. 106

26

7. Who are you going to send on the business trip?
A I've picked Susan in accounting.
B It was a very rewarding trip.
C At the start of next year.

7. 你要派誰去出差？
A 我已選了會計部門的蘇珊。
B 這是一趟很有收穫的旅程。
C 在明年初。

8. Why don't we go for a bike ride tomorrow?
A I gave Mr. Holland a ride to the airport.
B That sounds like fun.
C It was 3:30.

8. 我們明天何不去騎腳踏車呢？
A 我載哈蘭德先生去機場。
B 聽起來很有趣。
C 當時是下午三點半。

9. Did Monica answer the phone, or was she away from the office?
[A] I'll mark it on the calendar at the office.
[B] Please leave a message.
[C] She was meeting her client at that time.

10. Which theater is the movie showing at?
[A] He's a famous actor.
[B] I'll have to check.
[C] She's over there.

11. Why is there a moving truck parked outside?
[A] We're removing coffee stains.
[B] Into a bigger office.
[C] Because new neighbors are moving in.

12. What should I bring on the camping trip?
[A] You'll need hiking boots.
[B] He's on a business trip with his colleague.
[C] Yes, we should.

13. You will receive five days off next month.
[A] I had a great time at the resort.
[B] I turned the equipment off.
[C] Will it be paid or unpaid?

14. Did Olivia already return the rental car?
[A] Yes, just this morning.
[B] There are several different models.
[C] I'm ready to order now.

15. Isn't this area off limits to motor vehicles?
[A] It's fifty percent off today.
[B] There is a walking path only.
[C] Actually, it's a stolen vehicle.

16. I'd recommend using the stairs today.
[A] Can you tell me why?
[B] No, I didn't stare straight into the camera.
[C] I usually use the copy machine at the corner.

17. When will I receive this month's paycheck?
[A] The conference will be held next month.
[B] Before March 3.
[C] In the bottom drawer.

9. 是莫妮卡接的電話，還是她不在辦公室？
[A] 我會將它標記在辦公室的日曆上。
[B] 請留言。
[C] 她當時正在與客戶會面。

10. 這部電影在哪個戲院播放？
[A] 他是知名演員。
[B] 我得查查看。
[C] 她就在那裡。

11. 搬家公司的卡車為何停在外頭？
[A] 我們正在清除咖啡污漬。
[B] 搬進比較大的辦公室。
[C] 因為新鄰居正要搬入。

12. 我應該帶什麼去露營？
[A] 你會需要健行用的靴子。
[B] 他和同事出差了。
[C] 是的，我們應該要。

13. 你下個月會有五天休假。
[A] 我在度假村玩得很愉快。
[B] 我關掉了設備。
[C] 有薪價還是無薪假？

14. 奧莉維亞已經歸還租賃的車子了嗎？
[A] 是的，就在今天早上。
[B] 有好幾種不同的型號。
[C] 我已經準備好要點餐了。

15. 這個地區不是禁止汽車進入嗎？
[A] 今天打五折。
[B] 這裡只有步道。
[C] 事實上，這是失竊車輛。

16. 我建議今天走樓梯。
[A] 可以告訴我為什麼嗎？
[B] 不，我沒有直視相機鏡頭。
[C] 我通常使用角落的那台影印機。

17. 我何時會收到這個月的薪水？
[A] 會議將在下個月舉行。
[B] 三月三日之前。
[C] 在最底層的抽屜裡。

18. Do we have enough gas to get to the airport?
A Who arrived at the airport yesterday?
B We don't have to worry about it.
C She's the chief flight attendant.

19. Why hasn't the travel itinerary been sent out yet?
A At Terminal 6.
B He was a travel agent.
C We haven't decided on the dates.

20. Who forgot to turn off the lights last night?
A We were waiting at the traffic lights.
B I'm guessing it was John.
C Kelly will take a day off tomorrow.

21. We are offering a promotional deal at the moment.
A Congratulations on your promotion.
B What benefit can I get?
C Jenny will deal with the complaint.

22. I can borrow your book for a few days, can't I?
A A few coworkers.
B Of course. It's no trouble at all.
C They booked tickets in advance.

23. Didn't your team improve your sales figures compared to last month?
A Yes, the budget proposal is due this Friday.
B Actually, they were about the same.
C I couldn't figure out how to use this product.

24. How can I find her contact information?
A We negotiated a contract.
B By Wednesday at the latest.
C Check the client list.

25. Where is the coffee shop you recommended?
A I usually wear a suit.
B It's across from the post office.
C It's 3 o'clock sharp.

26. Would you like to drive instead of me?
A It looks like he missed the bus.
B Yes, I'll call right now.
C Sorry, I can't. I forgot my glasses.

18. 我們的油夠開到機場嗎？
A 昨天是誰抵達機場了？
B 我們不需要擔心這件事。
C 她是座艙長。

19. 旅遊行程表為何還沒寄出？
A 在第六航空站。
B 他以前是旅遊業者。
C 我們尚未決定好日期。

20. 昨晚誰忘了關燈？
A 我們當時在等紅綠燈。
B 我猜想是約翰。
C 凱莉明天會請假一天。

21. 我們目前有提供促銷方案。
A 恭喜升官。
B 我可以得到什麼好處？
C 珍妮會處理這起客訴。

22. 我可以把你的書借走幾天，可以嗎？
A 幾位同事。
B 當然，沒問題。
C 他們提前訂票了。

23. 與上個月相比，你團隊的銷售額沒有提高嗎？
A 是的，預算提案的期限是這星期五。
B 實際上，銷售額大致相同。
C 我不知道要如何使用這個產品。

24. 我要如何找到她的聯絡資訊？
A 我們談了一項合約。
B 最晚在星期三。
C 去查客戶名單。

25. 你推薦的咖啡店在哪裡？
A 我通常穿西裝。
B 在郵局對面。
C 現在三點整。

26. 你想要代替我開車嗎？
A 他似乎錯過了公車。
B 是的，我現在就打電話。
C 抱歉，我不行。我忘了戴眼鏡。

27. Did you say you were stopping by today or tomorrow?
A Actually, I said this weekend.
B A nice day for a walk.
C Yeah, I thought so, too.

27. 你是說你要今天還是明天來訪？
A 實際上，我是說週末。
B 很適合散步的日子。
C 是的，我也這麼認為。

28. Food will be catered for tonight's party, won't it?
A It was my birthday party.
B It's scheduled to arrive at 6 o'clock.
C No, he isn't registered here.

28. 今晚派對會提供餐點，對不對？
A 那是我的生日派對。
B 餐點預計會在晚上六點送達。
C 不，他沒有被登記在這裡。

29. Isn't Mr. Rolland away from the office this week?
A Yes, he comes back next Monday.
B This product will be released next week.
C Don't throw the receipt away.

29. 羅蘭先生這星期不會來上班吧？
A 是的，他下星期一會回來。
B 這項產品下星期會上市。
C 別丟了那份食譜。

30. I fixed the printer in the break room this morning.
A You're welcome.
B Was it out of order?
C I was in the meeting room.

30. 我今天早上在修理休息室的印表機。
A 不客氣。
B 它壞了嗎？
C 我在會議室。

31. What did the tennis instructor say?
A She said to practice more.
B Have you decided on a date?
C I told you so.

31. 網球教練說了什麼？
A 她說要多練習。
B 你決定好日期了嗎？
C 我就說吧。

PART 3 P. 107-111

27

32–34 conversation

W：Hi, Mark. This is Julie in accounting. (32) **Our printer has broken down again, and nobody in our department knows how to fix it. Could you stop by and give us a hand?**

M：(33) **I wish I could help, but I have a meeting with an important client in half an hour.** I have to be fully prepared when he arrives.

W：I understand. (34) **I'll try to find an instruction manual. I hope it will help me figure out what exactly is wrong.**

M：All right. I'll check on you right after the meeting.

32–34 對話

女：嗨，馬克。我是會計部門的茱莉。(32) **我們的印表機又故障了，我們部門沒人知道如何修理。你可以過來幫我們嗎？**

男：(33) **真希望我能幫忙，但我半小時後要與一位重要的客戶開會。**我必須要做好充分準備等他來。

女：我了解。(34) **我會試著找使用手冊，我希望它能幫我找到問題所在。**

男：好的，開完會後我就立刻去找你。

32. What does the woman ask the man to do?
- (A) Introduce a new client
- (B) Help to prepare a presentation
- **(C) Repair malfunctioning equipment**
- (D) Look for an instruction manual

32. 女子要求男子做什麼？
- (A) 介紹新客戶
- (B) 協助準備簡報
- **(C) 修理故障的設備**
- (D) 尋找使用手冊

33. Why is the man unable to help?
- **(A) He has to meet a major client soon.**
- (B) He finds the problem too complicated.
- (C) He isn't nearby at the moment.
- (D) He doesn't have the necessary tools.

33. 男子為何無法幫忙？
- **(A) 他很快要去見大客戶**
- (B) 他覺得這個問題太複雜
- (C) 他現在不在附近
- (D) 他沒有必要的工具

34. What will the woman do next?
- **(A) Attempt to solve the problem herself**
- (B) Cancel an appointment
- (C) Print out a document
- (D) Have a meeting with a client

34. 女子接著會做什麼？
- **(A) 嘗試自己解決問題**
- (B) 取消預約
- (C) 列印一份文件
- (D) 與客戶開會

35–37 conversation

W：(35) **Mr. Hawke, I just looked over our projected sales for this month and it looks like our current inventory of televisions won't be enough to meet demand.**

M：Do you think so? But I thought we increased our stock this month compared to last. How are we already running out?

W：Well, all of the advertisements we placed seem to be having the intended effect. (36) **Thanks to the promotional sale this month, we are selling a lot more televisions than usual.**

M：(37) **OK, if anyone tries to buy a television that is out of stock, tell them that they can still get the same promotional deal next month as well.**

35–37 對話

女：(35) **赫克先生，我剛看過我們這個月的銷售預估，我們目前電視的庫存似乎供不應求。**

男：你這麼認為嗎？但我以為我們這個月的存貨跟上個月比已經增加了，怎麼會快不夠了呢？

女：嗯，我們買的所有廣告似乎達到預期的效果。(36) **因為這個月的促銷活動，我們賣出的電視比平常多很多。**

男：(37) **好的，如果有人要買缺貨的電視，告訴他們，下個月還是能享有相同的折扣價。**

35. What problem does the woman mention?
- (A) The advertisements are not widely circulated.
- **(B) The store inventory is inadequate.**
- (C) The discounted price is not competitive.
- (D) The product is not selling well.

35. 女子提到什麼問題？
- (A) 廣告並未廣泛散佈
- **(B) 商品庫存不足**
- (C) 折扣價沒有競爭力
- (D) 產品賣得不好

36. What does the woman say about this month's sales figures?
- (A) They are beginning to decrease.
- (B) They are similar to last month's figures.
- **(C) They are unusually high.**
- (D) They are impossible to predict.

36. 關於這個月的銷售量，女子說了什麼？
- (A) 開始減少
- (B) 與上個月相似
- **(C) 異常地高**
- (D) 無法預測

37. What does the man ask the woman to do?

A Extend the length of the promotion

B Direct customers to the online store

C Secure more advertising space

D Offer customers a bigger discount

37. 男子要求女子做什麼？

A 延長促銷時間

B 指引顧客到網路商店

C 取得更多廣告空間

D 提供顧客更多的折扣

38–40 conversation

M：Ms. Simpson, can you tell me why you applied to work at our store? (38) **Judging from your résumé, it appears you have no retail experience. What do you think makes you qualified for selling apparel?**

W：You're right. I previously worked as a secretary at a hospital. (39) **At that time I learned that I really enjoy working with people.** So I thought working in retail would be a good fit for me.

M：Yes, that is very important. Here at our store, we expect all employees to be kind and helpful with each and every customer. (40) **Next, I'd like to ask about your availability during the week.**

38–40 對話

男：辛普森女士，你可以告訴我為何你想來我們店裡工作呢？(38) **從你的履歷看起來，你似乎沒有零售的經驗。你認為你具備什麼賣服飾的條件呢？**

女：你說的對。我之前在醫院當秘書，(39) **當時我發現我真的很喜歡和人們往來，因此我認為零售業很適合我。**

男：是的，那很重要。在我們的店裡，我們期待所有員工都能親切並樂於協助彼此以及每位顧客。(40) **接下來，我想問你每週的空檔。**

38. Where most likely does the man work?

A At a hospital

B At a factory

C At a clothing store

D At a restaurant

38. 男子最有可能在哪裡工作？

A 醫院

B 工廠

C 服飾店

D 餐廳

39. Why does the woman think she is qualified for the job?

A She completed a training course.

B She has worked similar jobs before.

C She likes interacting with people.

D She majored in a related field.

39. 女子為何認為她符合這個工作的資格？

A 她完成了訓練課程

B 她先前做過類似的工作

C 她喜歡與人們互動

D 她主修相關領域

40. What will the speakers discuss next?

A Work hours

B An annual salary

C Job qualifications

D Previous jobs

40. 對話者們接著會討論什麼？

A 工作時間

B 年薪

C 工作資格

D 先前的工作

41–43 conversation

W：Hello, this is Suzy Smith calling for Dan Harmon. I work at Danny Sweets. (41) **I'm calling to let you know that the wedding cake you ordered is ready to be picked up at any time.**

M：Oh, thanks for calling. (42) **I'm extremely busy making other preparations for the wedding tomorrow, and won't have time to stop by.** Can you deliver the cake instead?

W：I'm sorry, but we don't offer any delivery service. (43) **However, if you give us a name in advance, you could have someone else pick it up for you.**

M：(43) **OK, I'll try to find someone to do that for me. I'll call back later.**

41–43 對話

女：哈囉，我叫蘇西 · 史密斯，我要找丹 · 哈蒙。我在丹尼甜點店工作，(41) **我打電話是要告訴您，您訂購的結婚蛋糕已經備妥，隨時可以來領取。**

男：感謝你的來電。(42) **我現在正忙著為明天的婚禮作其他準備，沒空過去。**你可以把蛋糕送過來嗎？

女：很抱歉，但我們不提供運送服務。(43) **不過，若您事先提供我們姓名，就可以請別人幫您領取。**

男：(43) **好的，我會試著找人幫我拿。我晚點再回電給你。**

41. Where most likely does the woman work?
(A) At a wedding hall
(B) At a bakery
(C) At a clothing store
(D) At a shipping company

42. Why is the man unable to visit the woman's workplace?
(A) He has urgent arrangements to make.
(B) He must attend a wedding today.
(C) He is not feeling well.
(D) He has to prepare an order.

43. What information will the man probably provide?
(A) Directions to a location
(B) An individual's name
(C) His home address
(D) His phone number

41. 女子最有可能在哪裡工作？
(A) 婚禮會場
(B) 烘焙坊
(C) 服飾店
(D) 貨運公司

42. 男子為何無法去女子的工作處？
(A) 他有緊急的事務要安排
(B) 他今天必須參加婚禮
(C) 他身體不適
(D) 他必須備妥訂單

43. 男子可能會提供什麼資訊？
(A) 到某地點的路線指示
(B) 某人的名字
(C) 他家的地址
(D) 他的電話號碼

44–46 conversation

W：I have noticed that a lot of our customers are from all over the world. (44) **I think it's because we provide exotic and delicious food, and we are near very popular tourist attractions.**

44–46 對話

女：我注意到我們有很多來自於世界各地的顧客。(44) **我認為那是因為我們提供有異國風情且美味的料理，而且我們位於熱門觀光景點附近。**

M：You're right. I have noticed that, too. (45) **I was thinking maybe it would be very helpful if some of our servers could speak other languages fluently.** That would make things much more comfortable for our customers.

W：(46) **Actually, I have already scheduled two interviews next week with potential employees.** I'm going to interview a woman who can speak Japanese and a man who can speak Spanish.

男：你說的對，我也注意到這點。(45) **我認為，我們的服務人員如果能夠流利地說其他語言，會很有幫助，**這樣能讓我們的顧客更舒適。

女：(46) **實際上，我已經在下週安排兩場與應聘者的面試。**我將面試一名會說日文的女子，還有一名會說西班牙文的男子。

44. Where most likely do the speakers work?

(A) At a souvenir shop
(B) At a language school
(C) At a restaurant
(D) At a travel agency

45. What does the man recommend doing?

(A) Hiring bilingual staff
(B) Opening a second location
(C) Taking language classes
(D) Planning a vacation

46. What has the woman done?

(A) Contacted a translation agency
(B) Scheduled job interviews
(C) Extended operating hours
(D) Hired new employees

44. 對話者們最有可能在哪裡工作？

(A) 紀念品店
(B) 語言學校
(C) 餐廳
(D) 旅行社

45. 男子建議做什麼？

(A) 僱用雙語員工
(B) 開第二家店
(C) 修語言課程
(D) 計劃度假

46. 女子已經做了什麼？

(A) 聯繫翻譯社
(B) 安排工作面試
(C) 延長營運時間
(D) 僱用新員工

47–49 conversation

M：Hi, Lindy. (47) **Jessica just left to go home because she had a bad headache.** I told her to take the day off tomorrow as well to go to the hospital. (48) **Do you think you could come in to fill in for her tomorrow morning?**

W：Oh, I'm really sorry, but tomorrow I have to attend a close friend's wedding. (49) **However, I'll call around to see if any other employee is available to work tomorrow in place of Jessica.**

M：OK, thanks. Just let me know immediately if you find somebody.

47–49 對話

男：嗨，琳蒂。(47) **潔西卡剛下班回家，因為她頭很痛。**我要她明天休假一天並且去醫院。(48) **你覺得你明天早上可以來幫她代班嗎？**

女：喔，真的很抱歉，但明天我得參加一位好友的婚禮。(49) **但我會打幾通電話，看看別的員工明天是否可以來代潔西卡的班。**

男：好的，謝謝。如果有找到人，請立刻告訴我。

47. Why did Jessica leave work early?
Ⓐ She had a prior engagement.
Ⓑ She wasn't feeling well.
Ⓒ Her doctor called.
Ⓓ She had to attend a wedding.

48. What does the man ask the woman to do?
Ⓐ Work another person's shift
Ⓑ Clean the store tomorrow morning
Ⓒ Deliver a presentation at a meeting
Ⓓ Calculate sales figures

49. What will the woman do next?
Ⓐ Fill out a form
Ⓑ Distribute paychecks
Ⓒ Go to the hospital
Ⓓ Call her coworkers

47. 潔西卡為何提早下班？
Ⓐ 她已經有約在先
Ⓑ 她身體不適
Ⓒ 她的醫生打電話來
Ⓓ 她必須參加婚禮

48. 男子要求女子做什麼？
Ⓐ 幫別人值班
Ⓑ 明天早上清理商店
Ⓒ 開會時做簡報
Ⓓ 計算銷售額

49. 女子接著會做什麼？
Ⓐ 填寫表格
Ⓑ 發工資
Ⓒ 去醫院
Ⓓ 打電話給同事

NEW

50–52 conversation

W： Wilmore Appliance customer service. How can I help you?
M： Hi, (50) **I'm having problems with the freezer part of my fridge. The temperature never goes below 5 degrees Celsius even when I set it below freezing.**
W： Do you know the model number?
M： Let me check. It's the Azura 783XB model.
W： (51) **Oh, I'm sorry, but we no longer make that model, so I can't help you over the phone.**
M： That's going to be a problem. I purchased several gallons of ice cream for a party tomorrow.
W： I'm so sorry. (52) **I'll send a technician over as soon as possible so that the problem is looked at.** Will anyone be home at around 5 p.m. tonight?
M： Yes, I'll be here.
W： Good. Our technician will be there between 5 and 6 tonight.

50–52 對話

女： 威莫家電客服部，有什麼需要服務的嗎？
男： 嗨，(50) **我冰箱的冷凍庫有問題，即使我將溫度設定為零度以下，溫度仍無法低於攝氏五度。**
女： 你知道產品型號嗎？
男： 讓我看一下。是亞斯拉 783XB 型。
女： (51) **喔，很抱歉，但我們不再生產該型號了，因此我無法透過電話協助你。**
男： 這樣就麻煩了，我為了明天的派對買了好幾加侖的冰淇淋。
女： 很抱歉。(52) **我會派技術人員過去盡快處理問題。**今天大約五點的時候有人在家嗎？
男： 是的，我會在。
女： 很好。我們的技術人員會在五點與六點之間抵達。

50. What problem does the man mention?
A The fridge is not working.
B The temperature is too low.
C The freezer temperature is too high.
D Water is leaking from the fridge.

50. 男子提到什麼問題？
A 冰箱故障
B 溫度太低
C 冷凍庫溫度太高
D 冰箱漏水

51. What does the woman mention about the fridge?
A It is a very old model.
B It is no longer manufactured.
C It is not from their company.
D It is a popular model.

51. 關於冰箱，女子提到什麼？
A 它是很舊的機型
B 它停產了
C 它不是他們公司製造的
D 它是暢銷的機型

52. What does the woman offer to do?
A Give him a new manual
B Give him a link to a website
C Let him get a replacement
D Send a technician over to him

52. 女子建議做什麼？
A 給他新的手冊
B 給他網路連結
C 給他換貨
D 派技術人員過去他那邊

53–55 conversation

M：Hi, Angela. I just got an email from UHP incorporated. (53) **They are asking about installing the plumbing systems in their new offices.** They want to know when we will begin.

W：(54) **I intended to call them today, but I'm waiting for a call from some workers.** They are at the building site now testing the ground. (55) **It seems as though there may be some problems installing the pipes underground. We may need to dig deeper than we expected.** I will let them know by this afternoon.

M：I see. I'll call UHP and let them know the situation. They didn't sound like they were angry; they were just curious to know what was going on. Let me know when you hear back from the workers.

53–55 對話

男：嗨，安琪拉。我剛收到 UHP 公司寄來的電子郵件。(53) **他們在詢問要在新辦公室安裝配管工程的事情**，他們想知道我們何時會動工。

女：(54) **我今天原本打算要打電話給他們，但我在等一些工人的來電。**他們正在工地那裡測試土地。(55) **在地下安裝管線似乎會有些問題，我們可能需要挖得比先前預期還深。**我今天下午之前會告訴他們。

男：了解。我會打電話給 UHP 公司，讓他們知道情況。他們聽起來沒生氣，只是好奇發生了什麼事。工人回覆你之後，請告訴我。

53. Where do the speakers most likely work?
A A plumbing company
B An electrical company
C A construction company
D In an office

53. 對話者們最有可能在哪裡工作？
A 配管工程公司
B 電力公司
C 建築公司
D 辦公室

54. What does the woman mean when she says, "I intended to call them today"?

A She wasn't going to call them back.
B They were going to call her back.
C She was going to call them that day.
D She was going to send them an email.

55. What is the problem?

A They can't install the electrical system.
B The plumbing is already installed.
C There is some problem with the payment.
D They may need to dig deeper to install the plumbing.

54. 女子說「我今天原本打算要打電話給他們」，她指的是什麼？

A 她本來沒有要打電話給他們
B 他們本來要回電話給她
C 她當天本來就要打電話給他們
D 她本來要寄電子郵件給他們

55. 有什麼問題？

A 他們無法安裝電力系統
B 管線已經安裝好了
C 付款有些問題
D 他們可能需要挖得更深，才能安裝配管工程

56–58 conversation

W：OK, sir. Your total bill comes to $1,000. Would you like to pay with cash or card?

M：One thousand dollars? (56) **Are you serious?**

W：Yes, sir. You ordered a lot of room service over the last few days and spent a lot of money at the bar and restaurant downstairs. (57) **You stayed in Room 208, didn't you?**

M：No. I was in Room 207. I think you've made a mistake.

W：Oh, I'm sorry, sir. (58) **I will give you a 10% discount next time you stay with us.** I apologize for the confusion.

56–58 對話

女：好的，先生。您的帳單總計是一千元。您要用現金或是信用卡付款呢？

男：一千元？(56) **你是說真的嗎？**

女：是的，先生。過去這幾天你點了很多次客房服務，而且在樓下的酒吧和餐廳花了很多錢。(57) **您住 208 號房，對吧？**

男：不，我住 207 房。我想你弄錯了。

女：喔，很抱歉，先生。(58) **下次您來住房，我會給您 10% 的折扣。**很抱歉弄錯了。

56. What does the man mean when he says, "Are you serious"?

A He believes the woman is correct.
B He thinks the woman made a mistake.
C He is going to pay by card.
D He will pay with cash.

57. What does the woman want to know?

A How much room service he ordered
B Which room he is staying in
C His credit card number.
D Whether he ordered room service

56. 男子說「你是說真的嗎」，他指的是什麼？

A 他相信女子是對的
B 他認為女子弄錯了
C 他將要用信用卡付費
D 他將要用現金付費

57. 女子想要知道什麼？

A 他點了多少錢的客房服務
B 他住在哪個房間
C 他的信用卡卡號
D 他是否使用客房服務

58. What does the woman offer to do?

A Give him his room for free

B Give him a discount on his next visit

C Give him free room service

D Give him a gift certificate

58. 女子提出要做什麼？

A 免費給他房間

B 他下一次住房時給他折扣

C 給他免費的客房服務

D 給他禮券

TEST 7 PART 3 27

NEW

59–61 conversation

W1：Hi, can I please talk to Robert Porter? It's regarding the repairs to the office equipment at Baker & McKenzie. (59) **He is the head engineer, right?**

W2：Yes. May I ask who is calling?

W1：This is Susan Sherman. I'm the maintenance manager at Baker & McKenzie. (60) **Some of our equipment is missing, and I'd like to know where it is and when we will get it back.**

W2：OK, wait a moment. I will try to put you through to Robert. Please hold the line.

W1：Thank you.

M：Hello? Susan?

W1：Hi, Robert. I'm calling in regards to the missing office equipment you repaired at Baker & McKenzie yesterday. Where is it and when will we get it back?

M：Oh, I left a note with your receptionist. (61) **I told her we needed to take it away to our workshop for special repairs.** We should have it ready by the end of the week.

59–61 對話

女 1：嗨，我找羅伯特 · 波爾特，這是有關貝克和麥肯錫公司的辦公設備維修一事。(59) **他是總工程師，對嗎？**

女 2：是的。請問您是？

女 1：我是蘇珊 · 謝爾曼。我是貝克和麥肯錫公司的維修經理。(60) **我們有些設備不見了，我想要知道它們在哪裡，以及什麼時候可以取回。**

女 2：好的，請稍等。我會嘗試幫您轉接給羅伯特。請別掛斷。

女 1：謝謝。

男：哈囉？是蘇珊嗎？

女 1：嗨，羅伯特。我打電話來問遺失的設備，你昨天在貝克和麥肯錫公司修理的那些。請問現在在哪裡？我們什麼時候可以取回？

男：喔，我留了字條給你們的接待員。(61) **我告訴她我們需要將設備帶回廠房，以進行特別維修。**這個星期結束前應該可以修好。

59. What is Robert Porter's position?

A Lead repairer

B Head engineer

C Main engineer

D Main repairer

59. 羅伯特 · 波爾特的職務是什麼？

A 主任修理員

B 總工程師

C 主工程師

D 主維修員

60. What problem does Susan Sherman describe?

A Some of the measurements weren't done.

B Some of their receipts are missing.

C Some of their equipment is missing.

D A piece of equipment is still in the office.

60. 蘇珊 · 謝爾曼描述什麼問題？

A 部分測量沒有完成

B 他們有些單據不見了

C 他們有些設備不見了

D 一件設備還在辦公室

61. Why did Robert take the equipment away?

A To review it further

B For special repairs

C For replacement

D To evaluate its condition

61. 羅伯特為何把設備帶走了？

A 為了進一步檢視

B 為了特別的維修

C 為了替換

D 為了評估其狀況

NEW

62–64 conversation

W：**(62) Ok, your total bill is $75. Did you enjoy your food tonight?**

M：Yes it was delicious! Oh, I have a voucher here. Let me find it. Here you go.

W：Hmm. I'm not sure if you can use this.

M：**(63) Oh! I see the problem. Never mind. (64) Can we sit back down and have some drinks so I can use the voucher?**

W：Certainly. I will find a table for you now.

62–64 對話

女：**(62) 好的，你的帳單總額是 75 元。你喜歡今晚的食物嗎？**

男：是的，很美味！對了，我有折價券。讓我找找看，在這裡。

女：嗯……我不確定你是否可以使用這個……

男：**(63) 喔，我知道是什麼問題了。沒關係。(64) 我們可以回座位再喝點飲料嗎？這樣我就可以使用折價券了。**

女：當然，我現在就為你們找座位。

Discount Voucher 折價券

10% off any order over $100
點餐超過 100 元折價 10%

Valid until December 31st 12 月 31 日前有效

62. Where most likely are the speakers?

A At a stand

B At a café

C At a restaurant

D At the airport

62. 對話者最有可能在哪裡？

A 攤販

B 咖啡店

C 餐廳

D 機場

NEW

63. Look at the graphic. Why is the voucher invalid?

A Their bill is under $100.

B The food was not good.

C Their bill was over $100.

D The voucher is expired.

63. 參看圖表，為何折價券無效？

A 他們的帳單未滿 100 元

B 食物不好吃

C 他們的帳單超過 100 元

D 折價券已經過期了

64. What does the man ask the woman?

A If they can have more food
B If they can have more drinks
C If they can have a refund
D If they can come back another time

64. 男子問女子什麼問題？

A 他們是否可以吃更多食物
B 他們是否可以喝更多飲料
C 他們是否可以退費
D 他們是否可以改天再來

NEW

65–67 conversation

W：I apologize for being late to work. (65) **The parking lot on Swan Street was closed for some reason.** I think they are moving to another location.

M：I understand. Most of the staff were late because of this issue. Where did you find a parking space? On Franklin Avenue?

W：Yeah. There was some parking on Franklin Avenue. So I parked there. (66) **The sign on Swan Street said I could not park there after nine o'clock in the morning.**

M：That's a good idea. Franklin Avenue has parking until ten o'clock.

W：(67) **I suggest you take the bus tomorrow; it took me 30 minutes to walk to the office from Franklin Avenue.**

65–67 對話

女：很抱歉上班遲到了。(65) **天鵝街的停車場不知為何關閉了。**我猜想他們要搬到另外的地點。

男：我了解。大部分員工都因為這個問題而遲到了。你在哪裡找到停車位的？富蘭克林大道上嗎？

女：是的，富蘭克林大道上有停車位，因此我把車停在那裡。(66) **天鵝街的告示牌說，上午九點之後不得在那裡停車。**

男：那是個好主意，富蘭克林大道的停車位十點前都可停車。

女：(67) **我建議你明天搭公車，從富蘭克林大道走到辦公室花了我 30 分鐘。**

No Parking
After 9 A.M.
上午九點之後
禁止停車

65. According to the man, why are people arriving late to work?

A The parking lot on Swan Street was closed.
B The Franklin Avenue parking lot was closed.
C Everyone was feeling sick.
D The traffic was bad.

65. 根據男子，為何大家上班都遲到了？

A 天鵝街的停車場關閉
B 富蘭克林大道的停車場關閉
C 大家都身體不適
D 交通不好

66. Look at the graphic. Where is the sign most likely located?

(A) On Franklin Avenue
(B) On Swan Street
(C) In front of the building
(D) On Swanson Avenue

67. What does the woman recommend to the man?

(A) Take the subway
(B) Take a bus
(C) Take a taxi
(D) Drive his car

66. 參看圖表，這個告示牌最有可能出現在哪裡？

(A) 富蘭克林大道
(B) 天鵝街
(C) 大樓前面
(D) 史文森大道

67. 女子建議男子做什麼？

(A) 搭地鐵
(B) 搭公車
(C) 搭計程車
(D) 開他的車

68–70 conversation

W：Hello, this is Will's Hi-Fi; Margaret speaking. How can I help you today?

M：**(68) Hi, I bought a laptop package from you today. (69) It was supposed to have a gift, but it wasn't in the bag.**

W：Oh, is this Graham? I served you today. I'm sorry that we left out the gift.

M：Yes, this is Graham. Do I need to come and pick up the gift?

W：No. **(70) We can send it to you by post. I will have the delivery driver drop it off tomorrow. Can you give me your address?**

M：Oh, that's great! My address is 1900 Forest Street, West Hampton.

68–70 對話

女：哈囉，這裡是威利高傳真，我是瑪格麗特。有什麼我可以幫忙的嗎？

男：**(68) 你好。我今天從你們店裡買了一個筆記型電腦套件組。(69) 它應該要有個贈品，但袋子裡頭沒有。**

女：喔，是葛拉罕嗎？今天是我為你服務的。很抱歉我們遺漏了贈品。

男：是的，我是葛拉罕。需要我過去拿贈品嗎？

女：不用。**(70) 我們可以用郵件寄給你。我會請貨運司機明天送過去，可以給我你的地址嗎？**

男：喔，太好了！我的地址是西漢普敦，森林街 1900 號。

Laptop Package 筆記型電腦套件組

1 laptop computer 一台筆記型電腦
Wireless mouse 無線滑鼠
Wireless keyboard 無線鍵盤
Office software 辦公室軟體
Detachable webcam 可拆卸式網路攝影機
Free 8 gigabyte USB stick 免費 8G USB 隨身碟

68. Where does the woman most likely work?
A At a hardware store
B At an online store
C At a home appliance store
D At an electronics store

68. 女子最可能在哪裡工作？
A 在五金行
B 在網路商店
C 在家電行
D 在電子用品店

NEW
69. Look at the graphic. What is missing from the man's laptop package?
A Office software
B An 8 gigabyte USB stick
C A wireless keyboard
D A wireless mouse

69. 參看圖表，男子的筆電組少了什麼？
A 辦公軟體
B 8G USB 隨身碟
C 無線鍵盤
D 無線滑鼠

70. What does the woman offer to do?
A Send a delivery driver the next day
B Give him a coupon
C Have him come and pick the gift up
D Deliver the gift in person

70. 女子提議要做什麼？
A 隔天派貨運司機送過去
B 給他折價券
C 要他過來領取贈品
D 親自送贈品過去

PART 4 P. 112-115

28

71–73 radio advertisement

W：Are you feeling down this fall season? (71) **Then come down to Kim's tae kwon do center and energize yourself with the healthy and exciting sport of tae kwon do.** (72) **We are offering a special discounted membership to those with no prior experience.** So even if it's your first time, don't hesitate. Come sign up today. We are located on Main Street. (73) **You can come by bus and get off at the bus stop near Geller Bank.** Now is the time to refresh yourself with tae kwon do.

71–73 電台廣告

女：今年秋季心情不好嗎？(71) **那就快來金恩跆拳道中心，讓跆拳道這種健康又刺激的運動為自己充電。**(72) **我們提供新手會員特別折扣價。**因此，即使這是你的第一次，也別猶豫，今天就來報名。我們的地址在緬恩街。(73) **你也可以搭公車來，在靠近蓋勒銀行的車站下車**，現在正是用跆拳道振奮自己的好時機。

71. What is the advertisement about?
A A martial arts class
B An athletic contest
C A city tour bus
D A downtown festival

71. 這則廣告與什麼有關？
A 武術課
B 運動競賽
C 市區導覽公車
D 市中心的節慶

72. Who is the special offer directed at?
A Senior citizens
B Beginners
C Children
D Local residents

72. 特殊優惠是提供給什麼人的？
A 老年人
B 初學者
C 孩童
D 當地居民

73. What does the speaker say about the advertised location?
A It is accessible by public transportation.
B It has no parking space available.
C It is near a train station.
D It is in the same building as Geller Bank.

73. 關於廣告的地點，發話者說了什麼？
A 可搭乘大眾運輸到達
B 沒有停車位
C 在火車站附近
D 與蓋勒銀行在同一棟大樓

74–76 introduction

M：(74) **Welcome to the Museum of Electronics.** Here you can see some of the earliest televisions, radios, and telephones ever made. This month we have a special exhibition that focuses on radar and other technologies developed during World War II. (75) **George Butler, an expert in the field, will be giving a short talk describing the history behind this marvelous technology.** (76) **There is also a workshop for students aged 13 to 19, where they can assemble their own radio transmitter.** It will be a good opportunity to learn a few basic principles of electronic engineering.

74–76 介紹

男：(74) **歡迎光臨電子用品博物館。**在這裡，你們可以看到一些最早期的電視機、收音機和電話。本月我們有一項特展，重點是雷達和其他第二次世界大戰期間研發的各種科技。(75) **喬治・巴特勒是這個領域的專家，他會簡短地描述這項神奇科技背後的歷史。**(76) **還有個供 13 到 19 歲的學生所使用的廠房，他們可以在那裡組裝自己的無線電傳輸器，**這會是學習一些電子工程基本原理的大好機會。

74. Where is the introduction taking place?
A At a school
B At a museum
C At a radio station
D At a community center

74. 這則介紹在哪裡進行？
A 學校
B 博物館
C 廣播電台
D 社區活動中心

75. Who is George Butler?
A A computer technician
B A mechanical engineer
C An electrician
D A technology expert

75. 喬治・巴特勒是什麼人？
A 電腦技術人員
B 機械工程師
C 電工
D 科技專家

76. What is offered to teenage students?
A Hands-on experience
B A weekly after-school class
C A complimentary souvenir
D A discounted ticket price

76. 博物館提供什麼給青少年學生？
A 手作體驗
B 每週的課後課程
C 免費紀念品
D 票價折扣

77–79 announcement

W：Attention, all conference attendees. (77) **Due to the late arrival of a shipment of food, the conference center cafeteria will not be able to serve lunch this afternoon**. We apologize for this inconvenience. (78) **We will be issuing meal vouchers that can be used at any restaurant in the surrounding neighborhood.** (79) **Please be back in the conference center by 1:00 p.m. in time for Janet Wallace's presentation on how to use the new client management software.**

77–79 廣播

女：所有與會人員請注意。(77) **因為食物延後送達，所以今天下午會議中心的自助餐廳將無法供應午餐。**我們為此不便道歉。(78) **我們將會發放可用於附近任何一家餐廳的餐券。**(79) **請在下午一點以前回到會議中心，參加珍娜特．華勒斯的簡報，主題是如何使用新的客戶管理軟體。**

TEST 7

PART 4

28

77. What has caused the change in plans?

Ⓐ Broken kitchen equipment
Ⓑ The absence of some clients
Ⓒ A late delivery
Ⓓ Traffic congestion

77. 什麼導致了計劃的異動？

Ⓐ 廚房設備損壞
Ⓑ 某些客戶缺席
Ⓒ 運送延遲
Ⓓ 交通阻塞

78. What will listeners receive?

Ⓐ A conference schedule
Ⓑ A meal voucher
Ⓒ A lunch menu
Ⓓ A name tag

78. 聽眾會收到什麼？

Ⓐ 會議時程表
Ⓑ 餐券
Ⓒ 午餐菜單
Ⓓ 名牌

79. What will begin at 1:00 p.m.?

Ⓐ A software demonstration
Ⓑ A leadership workshop
Ⓒ A luncheon
Ⓓ A client meeting

79. 什麼將於下午一點開始？

Ⓐ 軟體示範
Ⓑ 領導力研討會
Ⓒ 午餐會
Ⓓ 客戶會議

80–82 excerpt from a meeting

M：Hello, everyone. (80) **Welcome to the planning committee, which is in charge of overseeing the construction of a new elementary school here in Eagleton.** (81) **I'm looking for someone to volunteer as the note taker during this meeting. His or her duty will be to keep track of what is debated.** After this meeting, you will need to send a summary of it to all attendees. In order to perform this duty, he or she needs to be a careful listener. (82) **But for now, I would like you to give personal introductions.** That way, we can get to know each other better.

80–82 會議摘錄

男：哈囉，大家好。(80) **歡迎來到籌劃委員會，我們負責監督伊格頓本地一所新小學的建設工程。**(81) **我在徵求自願者在開會期間當會議記錄，任務是記下辯論的內容。**會後要將紀錄的摘要寄給每位與會者，為了要執行這項任務，會議記錄需仔細聆聽細節。(82) **但現在，我要各位自我介紹，**這樣我們就能夠更認識彼此。

80. What is the purpose of the planning committee?
A To tighten some regulations
B To supervise a construction project
C To review employee performance
D To develop a new curriculum

81. What does the volunteer need to do?
A Pick up a client
B Introduce a guest
C Write down an agenda
D Give a presentation

82. What will listeners do next?
A Go on a business trip
B Participate in a workshop
C Introduce themselves
D Select a group leader

83–85 excerpt from a meeting

W： Hi, everyone. Let's start the weekly work meeting. (83) **Firstly, I want you to know that I've hired five more staff for the main factory.** (84) **I know that you have all been overworked**, I'm trying hard to push for funding to get two more people in over the next few months. The new staff will be here on Monday morning, and I want everyone to go out of their way to train them as quickly as possible. To do this efficiently, I'm going to have each of you train the new staff in a particular section of the factory. (85) **Please prepare some instructions and email them to me** so I can double check them.

83. Who most likely are the listeners?
A Factory workers
B Lawyers
C Accountants
D Web developers

NEW

84. What does the woman mean when she says, "I know that you have all been overworked"?
A She recognizes the listeners concerns.
B She doesn't really mind what they think.
C She wants them to work less.
D She is inviting them to a meeting.

80. 籌劃委員會的功能是什麼？
A 使規定更嚴格
B 監督建設案
C 檢視員工表現
D 發展新課程

81. 自願者需要做什麼？
A 接送客戶
B 介紹來賓
C 寫下議程
D 發表簡報

82. 聽眾接著會做什麼？
A 出差
B 參與研討會
C 自我介紹
D 選擇團體領導人

83–85 會議摘錄

女： 嗨，大家好，我們開始每週工作會議吧。(83) **首先，我要告訴你們，我已經為主要廠房多僱用五名員工。**(84) **我知道你們的工作量超過負荷**。我正在努力爭取經費，要在接下來的幾個月多僱用兩個人。新進人員星期一早上會來，因此我要大家格外費心盡快訓練他們。為了有效率地進行此事，我要你們每人在工廠的特定區域訓練新進人員。(85) **請備妥操作說明並以電子郵件寄給我**，以便我再次確認。

83. 聽者最有可能是什麼人？
A 工廠工人
B 律師
C 會計師
D 網路開發者

84. 女子說「我知道你們的工作量超過負荷」，她指的是什麼？
A 她了解聽眾在意的事
B 她不太在意他們的想法
C 她想要他們工作得少一點
D 她邀請他們去開會

85. What task does the speaker assign to the listeners?

A Prepare some instructions
B Prepare a new budget
C Revise some training materials
D Hire new staff

86–88 talk

M：I appreciate the number of people who have attended the Westbridge Film Festival this evening. I hope that all the films have been enjoyable so far. The next film we are going to show is particularly special. The film is called *Beyond the Blue*, and is the debut release from documentary film maker Michael Harris. **(86) The film captures the deepest parts of the ocean, and explores the complex ecosystems that exist in the areas of the ocean that humans cannot survive in. (87) The film has already been nominated for multiple awards, most recently at the BAPTA Film Festival. Remember, this is the first film Mr. Harris has made. (88) After the film Mr. Harris will come to the front for a short Q&A session.** Anyway, please enjoy the show.

86. What is *Beyond the Blue* about?

A Online bullying
B The ocean
C Whales and sharks
D Sea water

NEW

87. Why does the speaker say, "Remember, this is the first film Mr. Harris has made"?

A To suggest that he is an impressive director
B To suggest the film will be poor
C To recommend him as a good worker
D To suggest they shouldn't watch the film

88. What is going to happen after the film?

A They will give away free DVDs.
B They will watch it again.
C The director will have a short Q&A.
D An actor will sign autographs.

85. 發話者指派什麼任務給聽眾？

A 備妥操作說明
B 備妥新的預算
C 修正訓練教材
D 僱用新員工

86–88 談話

男：我感謝那麼多人參加今晚的西橋電影節。我希望目前為止大家都喜歡這些電影。接下來我們要放的影片尤其特別，片名叫做《越過蔚藍大海》」，是紀錄片製片人麥克・哈里斯首部公開放映的電影。**(86) 電影拍攝了海洋的最深處，並在人類無法存活的區域，探索複雜的生態系。(87) 這部電影已經獲得多項獎項提名，最近的是在 BAPTA 電影節。請記得，這是哈里斯先生製作的第一部電影。(81) 電影結束後，哈里斯先生會到前面來進行簡短的問答時間。**總之，請欣賞這部電影。

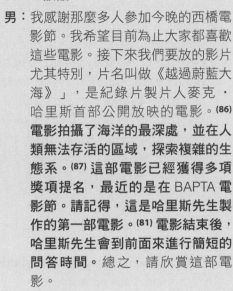

86. 《越過蔚藍大海》與什麼有關？

A 網路霸凌
B 海洋
C 鯨魚和鯊魚
D 海水

87. 發話者為何說「請記得，這是哈里斯先生製作的第一部電影」？

A 要暗示他是令人印象深刻的導演
B 要暗示這部電影會很差
C 要推薦他為優秀員工
D 要暗示他們不該看這部電影

88. 電影放映後會發生什麼事？

A 他們將發送免費的 DVD
B 他們將再次觀賞電影
C 導演將會進行簡短的問答
D 一位演員將會舉辦簽名會

89–91 speech

M：[89] **Well, it's only been one year since I took over the position of company president. Since then our products have become the most sought-after watches in the world.** Our unique designs, excellent price point, and promotional campaigns have proven to be miraculous. This has led to a lot of media attention. The worldwide CNU Business channel wants to run a special story about our company next month. [90] **They are sending some reporters to interview me on Wednesday, and to take some video footage of our manufacturing processes.** [91] **You realize what this means. CNU is broadcasted globally, and this could cause our business to grow even more.**

89–91 演講

男：[89] **我自從開始接掌公司董事長職務也有一年了。從那時起，我們的手錶已經成為全世界最熱門的商品。**我們的獨特設計、極佳價位以及促銷活動，都證實有奇蹟神效。這引起了媒體很大的關注，國際知名的的 CNU 商業頻道想在下個月特別專題報導我們的公司。[90] **他們星期三會派記者來訪問我，並且拍攝我們的生產過程。**[91] **你們都了解此事的意義。CNU 在全球播出，這可能使我們的業績更加成長。**

89. According to the speaker, what has happened to the company in the last year?

A Their products have gained global success.
B Their sales have gone down.
C The quality of the products has changed.
D Their CEO has changed many times.

90. What most likely are the CNU reporters doing on Wednesday?

A Interviewing some office workers
B Interviewing the president
C Making a music video
D Promoting their new web series

NEW

91. Why does the man say, "you realize what this means"?

A To discuss future renovations
B To make a point clear
C To highlight that the company will grow
D To give staff some bonuses

89. 根據發話者，過去一年這家公司發生了什麼事？

A 他們的產品在全球大獲成功
B 他們的業績下滑
C 產品品質改變
D 他們的總裁換了很多人

90. CNU 的記者最有可能在星期三做什麼？

A 訪問一些辦公室員工
B 訪問董事長
C 製作音樂影片
D 宣傳他們新的網路節目

91. 為何男子說「你們都了解此事的意義」？

A 為了討論未來的創新
B 為了使論點清楚
C 為了強調公司將會成長
D 為了給員工紅利

92–94 announcement

M：(92) **Sam's Salon is committed to helping aid the homeless.** If you have been a resident of Freewater over the last year, you have surely noticed the pop up salon on the corner of Cornwall Avenue and Dupont. (92) **This pop up is not for hipsters though. It's for the homeless.** (92) (94) **Sam's Salon has been volunteering to give the homeless in our community shampoos, shaves, and haircuts in order to help them get back on their feet.** To further this effort, Sam's Salon is having a Saturday-only haircut special, where half of all sales will go to help the local homeless shelter. This is a great opportunity to show that you care, support a local business, and to get a darn good haircut.

92–94 宣布

男：(92) **山姆美髮店致力於協助遊民。**若你在過去一年曾經是自由水鄉的居民，那麼你一定曾注意到在康瓦爾大街與杜邦街角的行動美髮店。(92) **但這家行動美髮店並不是為了服務趕時髦的人，而是為了服務遊民。**(92)(94) **山姆美髮店自願為社區的遊民洗髮、刮鬍及剪髮，幫助他們重新振作。**為了更進一步推展這件事，山姆美髮店要舉辦僅限週六的剪髮優惠活動。期間一半的營業額，將用於幫助本地的遊民收容所。這是讓你表示關懷遊民、支持在地企業、又能剪一頭美髮的好時機。

SAM'S SALON PRICING FOR THE HOMELESS BENEFIT
山姆美髮店關懷遊民優惠活動價目表

Men's trim 男士修髮	$10
Men's full cut and shave 男士整頭理髮及刮鬍	$25
Women's trim 女士修髮	$20
Women's styling 女士造型	$45

Sorry! No coloring or perms for this Saturday's benefit!
抱歉！本週六優惠不提供染髮和燙髮！

92. What is indicated in the announcement?
(A) Sam's Salon is just starting to interact with the homeless.
(B) Sam's Salon has been involved with improving the lives of homeless people.
(C) Sam's Salon employs a high quality manicurist.
(D) Sam's Salon is trying to make extra money from coloring and perms.

92. 這則宣布表示什麼？
(A) 山姆美髮店正要開始與遊民互動
(B) 山姆美髮店向來致力於改善遊民的生活
(C) 山姆美髮店僱用優秀的美甲師
(D) 山姆美髮店正試著從染髮和燙髮得到額外收入

93. Look at the graphic. What is true about the benefit?

A People should get their hair colored another time.

B Women's trim is expensive.

C Most men will choose a trim.

D Homeless people need to shave.

94. How much does Sam's Salon charge the homeless for a shampoo, shave, and a haircut?

A $25

B $45

C $10

D Nothing; it's free

93. 參看圖表，關於優惠活動，何者為真？

A 人們應該找別的時間染髮

B 女士修髮很昂貴

C 大部分男士會選擇修髮

D 遊民需要刮鬍

94. 山姆美髮店會向遊民索取多少洗髮、刮鬍和理髮的費用？

A 25 元

B 45 元

C 10 元

D 不收，是免費的

95–97 excerpt from a meeting

W : (95) **Hello everyone, and thank you for inviting me to speak with you all in this beautiful new conference room.** Our newest line of office security systems is really impressive, and I am sure it will meet your needs. We have developed four options to choose from. (96) **Let me just say that Option 1 is by far the best value because of the back-up system that we offer with this package.** It is not as expensive as Option 4, but don't let that fool you. Option 1 still offers all of the security that your business could want. All of our options include state-of-the-art video surveillance. (97) **Option 4 is more expensive because we offer 365 days of archived data.** After taking a tour of your facilities, I feel that this option would not be the best for your company.

95–97 會議摘錄

女：(95) **哈囉，大家好，感謝各位邀請我來這個漂亮的新會議室與大家談話。**我們最新系列的辦公室保全系統真的很令人印象深刻，我確信它能符合各位的需求。我們研發出四種方案。(96) **在我看來，方案一最划算，因為我們在此套件提供了備份系統。**它沒有方案四那麼貴，但別讓這點誤導了你。方案一仍提供貴公司所需的一切保全需求。我們所有選項都包含最先進的錄影監視器。(97) **方案四比較昂貴，因為我們提供了 365 天的檔案儲存。**參訪過你們的設施之後，我認為這個方案對你們公司而言並非最佳選擇。

	Option 1 方案一	Option 2 方案二	Option 3 方案三	Option 4 方案四
Price 價格	$1,000	$1,200	$1,300	$2,000
Back-up System 備份系統	yes 有	no 無	no 無	no 無
Data Archive 資料檔案庫	1 week（週）	10 weeks（週）	30 weeks（週）	52 weeks（週）

95. Where does the talk most likely take place?
(A) The cafeteria
(B) The conference room
(C) The new break room
(D) The new foyer

NEW
96. Look at the graphic. Which option does the speaker recommend?
(A) Option 1
(B) Option 2
(C) Option 3
(D) Option 4

97. Why is Option 4 more expensive than the others?
(A) It has state-of-the-art surveillance.
(B) It has video cameras.
(C) It includes a one-year data archive.
(D) It offers a back-up system.

95. 談話最有可能在哪裡進行？
(A) 自助餐廳
(B) 會議室
(C) 新的員工休息室
(D) 新的門廳

96. 參看圖表，發話者推薦哪個選項？
(A) 方案一
(B) 方案二
(C) 方案三
(D) 方案四

97. 為何選擇四比其他選擇貴？
(A) 它有最先進的監視設備
(B) 它有攝影機
(C) 它包含了一年的資料檔案庫
(D) 它提供了備份系統

98–100 excerpt from a meeting

M：(98) **Hello everyone, I wanted to get you together to go over the recent successes in our customer service here at Milton's Diner.** Milton's Diner is an institution here in Petersburg, and although we have always been complimented on our polite and timely service, the comments and tips we received over this long holiday weekend were extraordinary. I want to tell you all how proud I am of all of your hard work and dedication. (98) **It is my name on the sign, but this is really your business.** I have made a copy of a thank you letter that really touched my heart. We received it from a customer, and I wanted to share it with you so you could all see exactly how our hard work pays off. (100) **It moved me so much that I decided to give everyone who worked over the weekend an extra holiday bonus!** You all are the best!

98–100 會議摘錄

男：(98) **哈囉，大家好，我想要把大家聚在一起，逐一檢視我們最近在米爾頓餐廳客服方面的成功。**米爾頓餐廳是彼得斯堡本地的一家機構，雖然我們向來因為禮貌和有效率的服務而廣受讚美，但在這週末的長假期間，我們收到的好評和小費更超乎平常。我想要告訴各位，我多麼為你們的努力和奉獻感到驕傲。(98) **招牌上面寫的是我的名字，但這實際上這是各位的事業。**我印了一張令我感動的感謝函，它來自於一位顧客。我想要與你們分享，這樣你們就都能確切了解我們的努力是值得的。(100) **我覺得很感動，我決定要給該週末上班的每個人一份額外的假期津貼！**你們全都是最棒的！

A LETTER TO MILTON'S DINER
致米爾頓餐廳的一封信

Dear Milton's Staff,
米爾頓餐廳的員工你們好：

My name is Jerome and I am a long haul trucker. I saw the sign from the highway, "Milton's Diner, home of classic pies," and thought, you know what, I am going to treat myself. I was exhausted, but as soon as I walked into the diner and smelled the pies, saw all the decorations, and was greeted by the hostess, I just felt so good. You really made my weekend special, and I wanted to thank you with all sincerity.
我的名字是傑洛米，我是長途卡車司機。我在公路上看見招牌寫著「米爾頓餐廳：經典派的家鄉」，我就想，對了，我要款待自己。我當時很累，但當我走進餐廳、聞到派的味道、看見所有裝飾品，還有女服務生和我打招呼，我就感覺很愉快。你們真的使我的週末變得特別。我想要誠心的向你們道謝。

Happy Holidays,
祝假期愉快

Jerome Simmons
傑洛米 ・ 西蒙斯

98. Who is speaking to the staff?
A Milton
B The manager
C The chef
D Jerome Simmons

NEW
99. Look at the letter. What do you think Milton's Diner prides itself on?
A Cakes
B Pies
C Drinks
D Steaks

100. What effect did Jerome's letter have?
A The staff will get a day off.
B Everyone will get to take home a pie.
C Everyone will get holiday gift cards.
D The staff will receive an extra holiday bonus.

98. 誰在對員工們說話？
A 米爾頓
B 經理
C 廚師
D 傑洛米 ・ 西蒙斯

99. 參看這封信，你認為米爾頓餐廳對什麼感到自豪？
A 蛋糕
B 派
C 飲料
D 牛排

100. 傑洛米的信有什麼影響？
A 員工們將休假一天
B 每個人都可以帶派回家
C 每個人都會收到節日禮物卡
D 員工會收到一份額外的假期津貼

ACTUAL TEST 8

PART 1 P. 116-119

29

1. **A One of the women is handing some paper to the man.**
   B They are all using laptops.
   C The lady is typing on the laptop.
   D The man is presenting in the office.

2. A The waiter is writing in his notepad.
   B The man is drinking a cup of coffee.
   C The woman is ordering some food.
   D The waiter is talking to the man.

3. A There are cleaners in the lecture hall.
   B The lecture hall is occupied.
   C There are many people in the lecture hall.
   D The lecture hall is unoccupied.

4. **A The man is holding the umbrella with his hand.**
   B The woman is strolling along the path.
   C They are boarding the train.
   D They are lined up against the wall.

5. A The woman is boiling water in the pot.
   B The woman is putting pepper into the pot.
   C The woman is pouring oil into the pan.
   D The woman is wearing a chef's hat.

6. A They are signing a contract.
   B They are shaking hands with each other.
   C They are sitting next to each other.
   D They are exchanging business cards.

1. **A 其中一名女子將紙張拿給男子。**
   B 他們全都在使用筆記型電腦。
   C 女子用筆記型電腦打字。
   D 男子在辦公室做簡報。

2. A 服務生正在記事本上寫字。
   B 男子正在喝一杯咖啡。
   C 女子正在點餐。
   D 服務生正在與男子說話。

3. A 演講廳裡有清潔人員。
   B 有人在使用演講廳。
   C 有許多人在演講廳裡。
   D 演講廳沒有人用。

4. **A 男子用手拿著傘。**
   B 女子沿著小路散步。
   C 他們正在上火車。
   D 他們靠著牆壁排隊。

5. A 女子正用鍋子煮水。
   B 女子正將胡椒粉倒入鍋子裡。
   C 女子正在倒油到平底鍋裡。
   D 女子戴著廚師帽。

6. A 他們正在簽署合約。
   B 他們正與彼此握手。
   C 他們正坐在彼此身旁。
   D 他們正在交換名片。

PART 2 P. 120

30

7. How often should I replace the battery in this device?
   A It is in place.
   B At least once a year.
   C He often goes on business trips.

7. 我應該要多久更換一次這個儀器裡的電池？
   A 已經就定位了。
   B 至少一年一次。
   C 他經常出差。

8. Where do you keep the spare tire?
A In the trunk of the car.
B For an unexpected emergency.
C Yes, I'm a little bit tired.

9. Weren't you going to send an email with corrections to the document?
A Driving directions.
B I'll change the format.
C It's not finished yet.

10. Did you sign up for the special workshop on Monday?
A Yes, I'm looking forward to it.
B No, I didn't see the road sign.
C He rescheduled the appointment.

11. Haven't you backed up your files yet?
A She installed the hardware.
B Actually, it does so automatically.
C She'll be back soon.

12. When did I talk to you last?
A No, not right now.
B Sometime last winter.
C I'll take you there immediately.

13. The reservation is for 8:00 p.m., isn't it?
A The dinner was a vegetarian meal.
B He worked all night.
C Let me check the schedule.

14. We'd appreciate it if you would not park near the entrance.
A The park closes before midnight.
B I won't do that.
C Between the two buildings.

15. Which paint would be best for these walls?
A Probably three or four cans.
B Yes, we ordered it already.
C Light blue would look nice.

16. I can't find our tickets anywhere.
A You should check your backpack.
B She already boarded the airplane.
C It's more expensive than expected.

8. 你把備胎放在哪裡？
A 在汽車的後車箱裡。
B 以備意外緊急之需。
C 是的，我有點疲憊。

9. 你不是要寄一封附有修正文件的電子郵件嗎？
A 行車路線。
B 我要改變格式。
C 還沒有完成。

10. 你報名參加星期一的特別研討會了嗎？
A 是的，我很期待。
B 不，我沒看見路標。
C 他重新安排這項預約。

11. 你還沒有備份檔案嗎？
A 她安裝了硬體。
B 其實，它會自動。
C 她很快就會回來。

12. 我上次什麼時候和你說話的？
A 不，現在不行。
B 去年冬天的時候。
C 我立刻帶你過去。

13. 訂位是在晚上八點，不是嗎？
A 晚餐是素食。
B 他整夜工作。
C 讓我查看行程表。

14. 若你不把車停在入口附近，我們會很感激的。
A 公園在午夜之前關閉。
B 我不會那麼做的。
C 在兩棟建築物之間。

15. 哪種油漆最適合這些牆面？
A 也許三或四罐。
B 是的，我們已經訂購了。
C 淺藍色看起來不錯。

16. 我到處都找不到我們的票。
A 你該查看你的背包。
B 她已經上飛機了。
C 這比預期的還貴。

17. Who will be giving the keynote speech at the conference?
A Mr. Franks wrote a reference letter.
B It was very impressive.
C A famous novelist.

18. How do you get to work each day?
A I have to leave home before 8:00.
B I ride my bike or walk.
C The office on the first floor.

19. Will the contest be held in the courtyard or the auditorium?
A On a stage would be preferable.
B He will announce the winner.
C I'm too tired to go.

20. Could you move the air conditioner to the other room?
A Yes, I've moved into a new apartment.
B What is the temperature?
C I'll need help to do that.

21. Did you clean the meeting room for our clients?
A The hotel is affordable.
B No, but I will shortly.
C They were satisfied with our proposal.

22. Why didn't the train arrive on time today?
A It was delayed because of construction.
B Yes, it's always punctual.
C Actually, the tickets are non-refundable.

23. Should I put the clothes in the dryer or hang them outside?
A No, this shirt is too small.
B It's a brand-new hairdryer.
C Either is fine with me.

24. How do you access the company database?
A He will accompany you.
B You need Mr. Harrison's permission.
C At the annual conference.

25. Let's ask Mr. Miller to increase the budget for the business trip.
A We're going to Atlanta.
B Yes, I will right away.
C I booked the airplane tickets.

17. 誰將在會議發表主要演說？
A 法蘭克斯先生寫了一封介紹信。
B 很令人印象深刻。
C 一位知名的小說家。

18. 你每天如何上班？
A 我必須在八點之前出門。
B 我騎腳踏車或走路。
C 在一樓的辦公室。

19. 比賽會在庭院還是禮堂舉行？
A 在舞台上比較好。
B 他將會宣布獲勝者。
C 我太累了去不了。

20. 你可以將冷氣機搬到另一個房間嗎？
A 是的，我已經搬進了新公寓。
B 溫度是多少？
C 我需要有人幫忙做這件事。

21. 你打掃要接見我們客戶的會議室了嗎？
A 這個旅館不貴。
B 還沒有，但我很快就去。
C 他們對我們的提案很滿意。

22. 火車今天為何沒有準時抵達？
A 它因為施工而延誤了。
B 是的，它總是很準時。
C 實際上，這些票不能退。

23. 我應該把衣服放進烘衣機裡，還是掛在外頭？
A 不，這件襯衫太小了。
B 這是全新的吹風機。
C 我都可以。

24. 你如何進入公司的資料庫？
A 他將會陪伴你。
B 你需要哈里森先生的允許。
C 在年度會議。

25. 我們要求米勒先生提高這次出差的預算吧。
A 我們要去亞特蘭大。
B 好的，我立刻就去。
C 我訂了機票。

26. Can you make a reservation for the company dinner next week?

A Let me know how many people will attend.

B We ordered too much food.

C Because Ms. Dean has recently been promoted.

27. Who did you hire to fix your broken refrigerator?

A I went grocery shopping this morning.

B This is his business card.

C A little bit higher.

28. I've been reviewing several candidates for a vacant position.

A I hope you can find a qualified person.

B The election is next month.

C Congratulations on your new job.

29. Don't you want to see the apartment for rent next week?

A I paid the rental fee.

B It's not close enough to the subway.

C Because of a population increase.

30. This television isn't still under warranty, is it?

A We replaced the item at no cost to the customer.

B A trusted brand for over 30 years.

C I believe it expired just a month ago.

31. I just spoke with Jonathan on the phone.

A A spokesperson for Hines Tours.

B Oh, is he feeling better?

C I'll adjust the microphone.

26. 你可以為下週公司的聚餐訂位嗎？

A 告訴我會有多少人參加。

B 我們點了太多食物。

C 因為迪恩女士最近升遷了。

27. 你僱用誰來修理壞掉的冰箱？

A 我今天早上去買雜貨。

B 這是他的名片。

C 再稍微高一點。

28. 我一直在審查職缺的應徵者。

A 我希望你可以找到符合資格的人。

B 選舉是在下個月。

C 恭喜你找到新工作。

29. 你下個星期不是要去看出租的公寓嗎？

A 我付了租金。

B 它距離地鐵不夠近。

C 因為人口增加。

30. 這台電視已經過了保固期限，對吧？

A 我們為顧客免費更換了此物件。

B 一個超過 30 年的可靠品牌。

C 我想它一個月前就過期了。

31. 我剛與強納森講過電話。

A 海恩斯旅遊的發言人。

B 喔，他有好一點了嗎？

C 我會調整麥克風。

PART 3 P. 121-125

31

32–34 conversation

M：Hi. (32) **I was hired yesterday to work here on the night cleaning staff.** Today is my first day and I'm not sure who I need to talk to.

W：Oh, welcome to the staff of the Hampton Lodge Hotel. (33) **Mr. Carter is in charge of the cleaning staff, but he doesn't come into work for another hour.** I think you're here early.

32–34 對話

男：嗨。(32) **我昨天受僱成為夜班清潔人員。**今天是我第一天上班，我不太確定我需要去找誰。

女：喔，歡迎成為漢普敦旅館的工作人員。(33) **卡特先生負責清潔人員的事宜，但他還要一小時後才會來上班。**我想你太早到了。

M：They told me to report to work at 11 o'clock. Then what should I do in the meantime?

W：I see. (34) **Well, normally new employees watch a series of training videos as part of their orientation.** Please follow me.

男：他們要我在 11 點報到，那麼，現在我該做什麼？

女：我了解。(34) **嗯，一般狀況下，新進員工會看一系列的訓練影片，當作新進人員訓練。**請跟我來。

32. Who is the man?

A A hotel guest

B A janitor

C A night manager

D A receptionist

32. 男子是什麼人？

A 旅館房客

B 清潔工

C 夜班經理

D 接待員

33. Why is Mr. Carter unavailable?

A He is meeting a client.

B He is on vacation.

C He has not arrived at work yet.

D He is giving a presentation.

33. 卡特先生為何不在？

A 他在與客戶開會。

B 他在度假。

C 他還沒來上班。

D 他在發表簡報。

34. What will the man do next?

A Watch training videos

B Conduct an interview

C Contact Mr. Carter

D Fill out paperwork

34. 男子接著會做什麼？

A 看訓練影片

B 進行面試

C 聯繫卡特先生

D 填寫文書

35–37 conversation

W：Hi, Chris. Our client from Japan, Mr. Takahashi, just arrived at the airport. I'm going to leave in a few minutes to pick him up. (35) **Will everything be ready for the meeting once we arrive?**

M：(36) **Oh, that's good to hear. I was worried he wouldn't be able to arrive today because of the bad weather.** I have just about everything prepared. All I need to do is print out a blueprint for the new prototype.

W：OK, great. (37) **I'll call you 30 minutes before we arrive.** See you soon in the meeting room.

35–37 對話

女：嗨，克里斯。我們的日本客戶高橋先生剛抵達機場。我幾分鐘後要去接他。(35) **我們抵達時，會議所需的一切都會準備就緒嗎？**

男：(36) **喔，很高興聽你這麼說。我還擔心他會因為天氣不佳而無法於今日到達。**我幾乎準備好了所有的東西，只需要印出新原型的藍圖即可。

女：好的，很好。(37) **我會在到達前 30 分鐘打電話給你，**待會會議室見。

35. What are the speakers discussing?

A Preparations for a meeting

B A keynote speech

C A seminar agenda

D Meeting locations

35. 對話者們在討論什麼？

A 會議的準備工作

B 主要演說

C 研討會議程

D 會議地點

36. What does the man say that he is relieved about?
Ⓐ A product is selling well.
Ⓑ A trip was not delayed.
Ⓒ A new employee was hired.
Ⓓ A meeting room is available.

37. What does the woman offer to do?
Ⓐ Act as an interpreter during a meeting
Ⓑ Call before she arrives
Ⓒ Call Mr. Takahashi's secretary
Ⓓ Listen to a weather report

36. 男子說他對什麼鬆了一口氣？
Ⓐ 產品賣得很好
Ⓑ 旅程未受延誤
Ⓒ 僱用新員工
Ⓓ 有會議室可以使用

37. 女子提議要做什麼？
Ⓐ 會議期間當口譯員
Ⓑ 在到達前打給男子
Ⓒ 致電給高橋先生的秘書
Ⓓ 聽氣象報導

38–40 conversation

W：(38) **Kevin, did you finish the billboard design for Frank's Tires Plus yet?** They want the advertisement to be up in time for their big sale next week.

M：(39) **I was just about to finish it this morning when my computer crashed suddenly.** Unfortunately, I lost some of my data, including the work I had done on the billboard design.

W：Oh, no. That's a shame. (40) **I'll call Frank's Tires Plus and ask for a few more days to complete the design.** In the meantime, I hope you can find a solution.

38–40 對話

女：(38) **凱文，你完成法蘭克優級輪胎廣告看板的設計了嗎？**他們希望廣告能趕在下星期的特賣會前刊登出來。

男：(39) **我今天早上快要做完的時候，電腦突然當機了。**不幸地，我失去了部分資料，包含我為廣告看版設計所做的部分。

女：糟了，真可惜。(40) **我會致電法蘭克優級輪胎，並要求他們多給幾天來完成設計。**在此同時，我希望你能夠找到解決方法。

38. What does the woman ask the man about?
Ⓐ The status of a project
Ⓑ The location of a store
Ⓒ The list of clients
Ⓓ The cause of a problem

39. Why was the man unable to complete his work?
Ⓐ He didn't have enough time.
Ⓑ His car wouldn't start.
Ⓒ He was busy with other projects.
Ⓓ His computer malfunctioned.

40. What is the woman planning to do?
Ⓐ Terminate a contract
Ⓑ Ask for a deadline extension
Ⓒ Meet with a company executive
Ⓓ Hire a new designer

38. 女子詢問男子什麼事？
Ⓐ 一項企劃的狀況
Ⓑ 商店的位置
Ⓒ 客戶名單
Ⓓ 問題原因

39. 男子為何無法完成工作？
Ⓐ 他時間不夠
Ⓑ 他的車發不動
Ⓒ 他忙著其他的案子
Ⓓ 他的電腦故障了

40. 女子打算做什麼？
Ⓐ 終止合約
Ⓑ 請求延展期限
Ⓒ 與公司行政主管會面
Ⓓ 僱用新設計師

41–43 conversation

M：Hello, this is Tim Mason speaking. I live on Maria Street. [41] **All the electricity at my house has gone out.**

W：I'm very sorry, sir. It looks like a tree fell on a power line and knocked out all the power on your street.

M：Yeah, that's what I expected. Do you know how long it will take to restore the electricity?

W：[42] **Because of all the storm damage, our repair teams are behind schedule.** [43] **In the meantime, I suggest you stay at a family member or friend's house.**

41–43 對話

男：哈囉，我是提姆 · 梅森。我住在瑪麗亞街。[41] **我家完全停電了。**

女：很抱歉，先生。似乎有棵樹倒在電線上，並且切斷了你們街道上的所有電力供應。

男：是的，正如我所料。你知道要多久才能恢復電力嗎？

女：[42] **因為暴風雨造成多起損壞，我們維修團隊的進度落後。**[43] **在此期間，我建議你待在家人或朋友的家裡。**

41. What problem does the man report?

(A) Internet access has been disconnected.
(B) A delivery has not arrived yet.
(C) A power outage occurred.
(D) Some equipment has malfunctioned.

41. 男子提報什麼問題？

(A) 網路連線被切斷
(B) 貨品尚未送到
(C) 發生停電
(D) 某些設備故障了

42. Where most likely does the woman work?

(A) At an electronics store
(B) At a power company
(C) At a toy factory
(D) At a communications provider

42. 女子最有可能在哪裡工作？

(A) 電器行
(B) 電力公司
(C) 玩具工廠
(D) 通訊供應商

43. What does the woman suggest the man do?

(A) Take shelter elsewhere
(B) Report the incident to the police
(C) Restart his computer
(D) Arrive ahead of schedule

43. 女子建議男子做什麼？

(A) 到別處避難
(B) 向警方提報此事件
(C) 重新開啟電腦
(D) 提早抵達

44–46 conversation

W：Hello, I need to send a package to my brother who lives overseas in Germany. What delivery method would be best?

M：Well, it really depends on what you're sending. [44] **Because we are a public post office, we don't offer that many options.**

W：[45] **Actually, it was my brother's birthday last week, but I forgot. So I'm in a hurry to send this package.** Also, what I'm sending is somewhat fragile.

44–46 對話

女：哈囉，我需要寄一個包裹給住在德國的哥哥，什麼運送方式最好？

男：嗯，要視你所寄送的物品而定。[44] **因為我們是公立郵局，所以我們提供的選擇並不多。**

女：[45] **實際上，上星期是我哥哥的生日，但我忘了。因此我急著要寄這個包裹。**此外，我要寄的東西算是易碎品。

M：(46) **In that case, I suggest you use a private delivery service.** Private companies provide a larger variety of services that we don't offer.

男：(46) **那樣的話，我建議你使用私人貨運服務。**私人公司提供我們沒有的多樣化服務。

44. Where does the man work?
- A At an immigration office
- B At a public school
- **C At a post office**
- D At a travel agency

44. 男子在哪裡工作？
- A 移民局
- B 公立學校
- **C 郵局**
- D 旅行社

45. Why is the woman in a hurry?
- A She is late to work.
- **B She forgot an important event.**
- C She must meet a deadline.
- D She has another appointment.

45. 女子為何匆忙？
- A 她上班遲到了
- **B 她忘了一件重要的事**
- C 她必須趕上截止期限
- D 她有另一項約會

46. What does the man recommend?
- A Making a phone call
- **B Visiting a different business**
- C Sending an email
- D Canceling a subscription

46. 男子建議什麼？
- A 打電話
- **B 去另一家公司**
- C 寄電子郵件
- D 取消訂閱

47–49 conversation

W：Hi, Mr. Winston. This is Sharon Smith. (47) **I was the person interested in buying the used Speedster sports car that you showed me last week.** I checked my financial situation, and I've decided to go ahead with the purchase.

M：Hi, Ms. Smith. Well, unfortunately, we already sold that car to somebody yesterday. However, I have a similar model that you could look at. The car is used, but it is in great shape and just had new tires put on it.

W：Oh, that's too bad that you already sold the model. (48) **That car had a really good safety rating, which is what I consider most important when buying a car.**

M：I see. Well, this similar model also has a five-star safety rating. (49) **Why don't you come here this week? You can take a look at it and take it for a test drive.**

47–49 對話

女：你好，溫士頓先生。我是雪倫・史密斯。(47) **我就是上週有意購買你向我展示的勁速二手跑車的那個人。**我查看了我的財務狀況，決定要購買。

男：嗨，史密斯女士。很可惜，我們昨天已經將車賣給別人了。然而，我還有一個相似車款，你可以來看看。它是二手車，但車況很好，而且才剛換新輪胎。

女：喔，真可惜你已經賣了那款車。(48) **那輛車的安全評比很高，我認為這是購車時最重要的考慮因素。**

男：我了解。嗯，這台相似車款也有五顆星的安全評比。(49) **你何不這週過來？你可以來看看這台車並且進行試駕。**

47. What type of business does the man work for?
Ⓐ An auto repair shop
Ⓑ An insurance company
Ⓒ An automobile dealership
Ⓓ A construction contractor

48. What does the woman say is her top priority when she makes a purchase?
Ⓐ Affordability
Ⓑ Popularity
Ⓒ Design
Ⓓ Safety

49. What does the man suggest doing?
Ⓐ Replacing a broken part
Ⓑ Evaluating a different model
Ⓒ Visiting a new branch
Ⓓ Paying a deposit

47. 男子從事什麼行業？
Ⓐ 汽車修理廠
Ⓑ 保險公司
Ⓒ 汽車經銷商
Ⓓ 建築承包商

48. 女子說她購買時的首要考量是什麼？
Ⓐ 價格
Ⓑ 知名度
Ⓒ 設計
Ⓓ 安全

49. 男子建議做什麼？
Ⓐ 更換損壞的零件
Ⓑ 評估另一款車
Ⓒ 造訪新的分店
Ⓓ 付訂金

NEW

50–52 conversation

M：Hello, Judy. (50) **Have you got a moment to discuss last week's sales figures?**

W：(51) **I'm actually on my way to a meeting, but you can ask me something briefly.**

M：The sales figures for your branch are much lower than they have ever been. The board of directors is pretty upset about it. Is everything ok at the office?

W：Well, not really. There are some problems with my staff at the moment, and they aren't working like they used to. There is a conflict between some of the staff. I know it's affecting sales figures and it is a serious problem.

M：Really? (52) **Do you think we need to fire someone?**

W：I think that's the only solution. I'm going to see how they go in the next week and I will make a decision.

50–52 對話

男：哈囉，茱蒂。(50) **你有空討論上星期的銷售業績嗎？**

女：(51) **我其實正要去開會，但你可以簡短詢問。**

男：你分公司的銷售業績遠低於以往，董事會對此很不高興，辦公室一切都還好嗎？

女：嗯，不盡然。我的員工目前有些問題，他們工作狀況不如以往，部分員工之間起了衝突。我知道這影響了銷售業績，而且這是個嚴重的問題。

男：真的嗎？(52) **你認為我們需要開除什麼人嗎？**

女：我認為這是唯一的解決方法，我要看看他們下星期的狀況，然後做出決定。

50. What are the speakers mainly discussing?
Ⓐ High sales figures
Ⓑ A staff conflict
Ⓒ Low sales figures
Ⓓ A new training manual

50. 對話者們主要在討論什麼？
Ⓐ 高的銷售業績
Ⓑ 員工衝突
Ⓒ 低的銷售業績
Ⓓ 新的訓練手冊

51. What does the woman mean when she says, "I'm actually on my way to a meeting"?
A She doesn't have a lot of time to talk.
B She can stay and chat for a long time.
C She is asking the man out to lunch.
D She will send him an email later on.

52. What possible solution does the man suggest?
A To employ more staff members
B That the woman should be fired
C They should have lunch together.
D The woman might have to fire someone.

51. 女子說「我其實正要去開會」，她指的是什麼？
A 她沒有太多可以講話的時間
B 她可以留下來聊很久
C 她約男子去吃午餐
D 她之後會寄電子郵件給他

52. 男子提出什麼可能的解決方法？
A 僱用更多員工
B 應該開除女子
C 他們應該共進午餐
D 女子可能必須開除某人

53–55 conversation

W： Hello, Mr. Morgan. This is Debra. (53) **We have a bit of a problem.** The person that was supposed to give the keynote speech next week is sick. So we need to find a replacement. Would you be able to do it?

M： I'll be out of town for the next four days on business, and when I get back I'll be quite busy.

W： I see. (54) **The board of directors would love to have you do the speech.** They really liked it the last time you delivered it.

M： (55) **Thanks, but I'll have to pass on it.** I just have too much on my plate at the moment. If I had some more time to prepare, I would have considered it.

W： OK, I understand. I'll let the board know. I hope you have a safe trip.

M： Thanks for your understanding, Debra.

53–55 對話

女：哈囉，摩根先生。我是黛布拉。(53) **我們有點問題。**原定下星期要發表主題演講的人生病了。因此我們需要找人替補。您可以嗎？

男：我接下來四天要出城去洽公，回來後會很忙碌。

女：了解。(54) **董事會很想邀您來演講，**他們很喜歡您上次的演講。

男：(55) **謝謝，但我必須放棄這次機會。**我現在事情太多了。如果有多一些時間可以準備，我會考慮的。

女：好的，我懂。我會告訴董事會，祝您旅途平安。

男：感謝你的體諒，黛布拉。

53. What is the problem?
A The person who was supposed to give the speech is sick.
B The person who was supposed to give the speech doesn't want to do it now.
C There is no keynote speech anymore.
D The keynote speaker is late.

53. 問題是什麼？
A 本來要發表演講的人生病了
B 本來要發表演講的人現在不想演講了
C 沒有主題演講了
D 主講人遲到了

54. What does the woman say to the man?
A To find someone to do the speech.
B She will deliver the speech.
C To deliver the keynote speech.
D The board is not happy.

54. 女子對男子説什麼？
A 找人演講
B 她將要發表演講
C 發表主題演講
D 董事會不開心

NEW
55. What does the man imply when he says, "thanks, but I'll have to pass on it"?
A He will deliver the speech.
B He doesn't want to deliver the speech.
C He will talk to the board of directors.
D He needs some more information.

55. 男子説「謝謝，但我必須放棄這次機會」，他暗示什麼？
A 他將會發表演講
B 他不想要發表演講
C 他會與董事會討論
D 他需要更多資訊

NEW
56–58 conversation

W：Tristar Logistics, How can I help you?
M：Hello. (56) **I have a delivery coming today, but I won't be at the office.** Can you reschedule the delivery?
W：No problem. If you prefer, we can leave it with someone at your office?
M：(57) **That won't work for me.** The delivery contains some expensive pieces of art, so I want to personally receive it.
W：That's fine. When would you like it delivered?
M：Before midday would be perfect.
W：(58) **OK, if you could give me your cell phone number, I can have the delivery man call you when he is in your neighborhood.**

56–58 對話

女：三星物流，有什麼需要服務的嗎？
男：你好，(56) **我今天會有貨物送達，但我不在辦公室。**你可以更改送貨時間嗎？
女：沒問題。如果您要的話，我們或許可以將貨品留給你辦公室的人？
男：(57) **這對我而言行不通。**貨品包含幾件昂貴的藝術品，因此我想要親自收貨。
女：沒關係，您想要何時送達呢？
男：最好中午之前。
女：(58) **好的，請你給我您的手機號碼，這樣我可以請貨運人員到您附近時打給你。**

56. Why is the man calling Tristar Logistics?
A To reschedule a delivery
B To cancel his order
C To change his address
D To update his details

56. 男子為何打電話給三星物流？
A 要重新安排送貨時間
B 要取消訂貨
C 要更改住址
D 要更新細節資料

NEW
57. What does he imply when he says, "that won't work for me"?
A The package contains important documents.
B He will pay with a money order.
C He doesn't want them to leave the package with someone else.
D He wants it left at the office.

57. 當他説「這對我而言行不通」時，他暗示什麼？
A 包裹包含了重要的文件
B 他會以匯票付款
C 他不想把包裹留給別人
D 他想要把包裹留在辦公室

58. What does the woman say she wants?

A The office address

B His cell phone number

C The order number

D His building number

NEW

59–61 conversation

M1：Hi Ruth; hi Greg. (59) **Unfortunately, there is going to be a delay on the delivery of your computer equipment.** We won't be able to deliver it until tomorrow.

W：We needed that equipment today. (60) **We are going to miss some important deadlines without that equipment.**

M2：If we miss that deadline, we might lose some very important clients. Is there any possible way you can get it to us today?

M1：I'm sorry it's not possible. We haven't received the equipment at our distribution center yet.

W：OK. I know another supplier who can guarantee same day delivery. (61) **I'm going to call them and ask if they can supply us with the equipment.**

59. What are the speakers mainly discussing?

A The delivery of some furniture

B The signing of a rental contract

C The drafting of a document

D The delivery of computer equipment

60. What problem do Ruth and Greg have?

A They don't need the equipment.

B They could miss some important deadlines.

C They need to train their new staff.

D They haven't found the documents.

61. What does the woman suggest she'll do?

A Accept the late order

B Cancel the order

C Call another supplier

D Rent some equipment

58. 女子說她想要什麼？

A 辦公室地址

B 他的手機號碼

C 訂單編號

D 他的大樓編號

59–61 對話

男 1：嗨，露絲，嗨，格雷。(59) **很不幸地，你們電腦設備的運送將會延誤。**我們要到明天才能送貨。

女：我們今天就需要那項設備。(60) **沒有那項設備，我們會錯過一些重要的截止期限。**

男 2：如果我們錯過截止期限，可能會失去一些很重要的客戶。你是否有可能今天就將設備交給我們？

男 1：很抱歉，這不可能。我們的配送中心尚未收到那項設備。

女：好的，我知道另一家可以保證當天送達的供應商。(61) **我要打電話給他們，詢問是否能供應我們那項設備。**

59. 對話者們主要在討論什麼？

A 運送家具

B 簽署租約

C 草擬文件

D 運送電腦設備

60. 露絲和格雷有什麼問題？

A 他們不需要這項設備

B 他們可能會錯過重要截止期限

C 他們需要訓練新進員工

D 他們尚未找到文件

61. 女子說她會做什麼？

A 接受晚到的訂單

B 取消訂單

C 打電話給另一個供應商

D 租用某些設備

62–64 conversation

W：[62] **Hi, Aaron. How is the painting going?** [63] **Have you finished most of the work on level two?**

M：No, it is taking longer than we thought it would. We had to get some more paint delivered to the site, so we just started working again.

W：OK. When you finish on level two please come up to the fourth floor. We need your help to paint the ceiling. We don't have enough ladders. [64] **I suggest you bring at least three more ladders; there is a lot of work to be done here.**

M：Sure. We just have one more coat to put here, and then I will come up and help you finish.

62–64 對話

女：[62] **嗨，亞倫。粉刷進行的怎麼樣了？** [63] **你已經完成二樓大部分的工作了嗎？**

男：還沒有，這所需的時間比我們原先預期的還長。我們得請人多送一些油漆來這裡，所以才剛重新上工。

女：好的，等你完成二樓後請來四樓。我們需要你幫忙油漆天花板。我們梯子不夠。[64] **我建議你至少再帶三個梯子過來，這裡有很多工作要做。**

男：好的，我們這裡只需要再上一層漆，然後我就上樓幫你完成。

Office Directory
公司行號一覽表

1st FL 一樓	Harlington Accounting 哈林頓會計事務所
2nd FL 二樓	Jersey Construction 澤西建設公司
3rd FL 三樓	Swanson and Sons 史文森氏公司
4th FL 四樓	Grounds Ltd. 地域有限公司

62. Who most likely are the speakers?
- A Store clerks
- B Artists
- **C Painters**
- D Electricians

62. 對話者最有可能是什麼人？
- A 店員
- B 藝術家
- **C 油漆工**
- D 電工

NEW

63. Look at the graphic. Where is the man currently working?
- A Swanson and Sons
- B Harlington Accounting
- **C Jersey Construction**
- D Grounds Ltd.

63. 參看圖表，男子正在哪裡工作？
- A 史文森氏公司
- B 哈林頓會計事務所
- **C 澤西建設公司**
- D 地域有限公司

64. What does the woman recommend to the man?
- A To bring more paint
- B To bring one ladder
- **C To bring at least three ladders**
- D To paint the roof first

64. 女子建議男子什麼？
- A 多帶一些油漆
- B 帶一個梯子
- **C 至少帶三個梯子**
- D 先粉刷屋頂

65–67 conversation

W：Good morning, I need this gown cleaned. (65) **I have to attend an award ceremony tomorrow night,** and I've only just noticed that there is a big stain on the back here. I need it cleaned by today. I know your service usually requires two days, but this is an emergency. Can you help me?

M：Yes, I can have it ready for you by 9 p.m. It will cost $36.

W：Are you serious? (66) **But your price list says $12.**

M：Well, yes, but if you need rush service, we charge three times the price. I have to delay other people's orders to clean yours, so it causes me some problems.

W：OK. I understand. That's fine. (67) **I'm busy this evening so I will send my daughter to pick it up tonight at 9 p.m.** Her name is Julie.

M：That sounds fine. I'll have it cleaned by 9 p.m.

65–67 對話

女：早安，我需要送洗這件禮服。(65) **我明晚要參加頒獎典禮**，而我剛才注意到在背後這裡有一塊很大的污漬。我今天就得把它清乾淨。我知道你們的服務通常需要兩天，但這是緊急情況，你可以幫我嗎？

男：是的，我可以在晚上九點以前為你處理好，這樣是 36 元。

女：你是說真的嗎？ (66) **但是你們價目表上寫的是 12 元。**

男：是的，但是如果你需要緊急服務，我們會收三倍的價格。我必須延後其他人的訂單才能清潔你的衣服，因此這會造成一些問題。

女：好，我了解，沒關係。(67) **我今天晚上很忙，因此我會請我女兒今晚九點過來拿。**她的名字是茱莉。

男：聽起來沒問題，我會在九點之前清洗好。

Harron Dry Cleaning 哈倫乾洗

Fabric 布料	Price 價格
Cotton 棉花	$10
Denim 牛仔布	$15
Wool 羊毛	$20
Silk 蠶絲	$12

65. What does the woman say she will do tomorrow?

(A) Go out for dinner
(B) Visit her family
(C) Host an award show
(D) Attend an award ceremony

66. Look at the graphic. What is the gown made of?

(A) Cotton
(B) Wool
(C) Denim
(D) Silk

65. 女子說她明天要做什麼？

(A) 外出吃晚餐
(B) 拜訪家人
(C) 主持頒獎表演
(D) 參加頒獎典禮

66. 參看圖表，這件禮服是由什麼製成的？

(A) 棉花
(B) 羊毛
(C) 牛仔布
(D) 蠶絲

67. What does the woman say she will do?

A Pick it up at 9 p.m.
B Send her husband to pick it up
C Send her daughter to pick it up
D Cancel the order

67. 女子說她將會做什麼？

A 晚上九點來領取
B 請她先生來領取
C 請她女兒來領取
D 取消訂單

68–70 conversation

W：I apologize for being late, Bruce. (68) **The Cranson Lot on Prunkel Street was shut because of water damage from the recent hurricane, so I couldn't find a parking spot.**

M：That's fine. Most of the staff is late today because of the Cranson Lot closure. Where did you park? Swinton Road?

W：(69) **There was a couple of spaces there but the sign said I couldn't park there past 8 p.m.** I think we will be working late tonight so I just parked on Menzies St.

M：Oh, that's a smart move. I think Menzies St. parking is 24 hours, (70) **so I suggest we have an early dinner** and then get this project finished tonight.

68–70 對話

女：很抱歉我遲到了，布魯斯。(68) **普朗克街的克蘭森停車場因為最近颶風的水災而封閉了，因此我找不到停車位。**

男：沒關係，大部分員工今天都因為克蘭森停車場封閉而遲到。你車停在哪裡？是史文敦路嗎？

女：(68) **那裡還有幾個停車位，但告示牌上寫晚上八點之後就不可以在那裡停車。**我想我們今晚會工作到很晚，因此我就把車停在曼西斯街。

男：喔，這招很聰明。我想曼西斯街停車場 24 小時開放，(70) **因此我建議我們提早吃晚餐**，然後今晚就完成這個案子。

No Parking
After 8 P.M.
晚上八點之後禁止停車

68. According to the man, what is causing people to arrive late to work?

A An electrical storm
B A closed parking lot
C A protest
D Some new traffic rules

68. 根據男子，什麼導致人們上班遲到？

A 雷暴
B 關閉的停車場
C 抗議遊行
D 新的交通規則

69. Look at the graphic. Where is the sign most likely located?

A On Swinton Road

B At the Cranson Lot

C On Menzies Street

D On Prunkel Street

69. 參看圖表，這個告示牌最有可能立在哪裡？

A 在史文敦路

B 在克蘭森停車場

C 在曼西斯街

D 在普朗克街

70. What does the man suggest they do?

A Go home

B Buy some parking tickets

C Have an early dinner

D Walk to work

70. 男子建議他們做什麼？

A 回家

B 買停車票券

C 提早吃晚餐

D 走路上班

PART 4 P. 126-129

32

71–73 announcement

M：Hello, passengers. (71) **This is an announcement from your conductor.** Due to a freight train stalled at the next station, our departure will be delayed. The train ahead of us seems to be suffering a slight malfunction. (72) **Once we receive official permission from the traffic control center, we will proceed as normal.** Unfortunately, we will arrive a little bit later than the scheduled arrival time. We apologize for this inconvenience. (73) **Please adjust your plans accordingly.** Thank you for your patience. We should be on the move shortly.

71–73 宣布

男：哈囉，各位乘客。(71) **這是列車長的廣播**。由於有列貨運火車在下一站拋錨，我們將延後發車。前方的火車似乎有些微故障。(72) **一旦我們從交管中心獲得許可，就會恢復正常運行**。很遺憾，我們會比預定抵達時間稍晚到達。我們為此不便道歉。(73) **請依此調整你的計劃**。感謝您的耐心，我們應該很快就會出發。

71. Where does the announcement most likely take place?

A On a train

B On a bus

C On a plane

D On a ship

71. 廣播最有可能是在哪裡播送？

A 火車上

B 公車上

C 飛機上

D 船上

72. What is the speaker waiting for?

A An itinerary

B Authorization to depart

C Some passengers to board

D A parking permit

72. 發話者在等什麼？

A 旅遊行程表

B 發車授權

C 一些乘客上車

D 停車許可

73. What does the speaker suggest listeners do?

A Have their tickets reissued

B Transfer to another line

C Stay near a departure gate

D Modify their plans

73. 發話者建議聽眾做什麼？

A 改車票

B 轉乘另一路線

C 待在登機口附近

D 修改他們的計劃

74–76 recorded message

W：[74] **Hello, you've reached Susan and Clare's Downtown Shop.** Beginning this Tuesday, we are closed for three days in order to expand the display space. [74] [75] **We will open this Friday with a much wider selection of women's pants and sweaters.** [76] **To celebrate our renovation, we will be offering 10% off all purchases on our first day back in business.** Thank you for your interest.

74. What type of business does the speaker work for?

(A) An electronics store
(B) A furniture outlet
(C) A clothing store
(D) A theater company

75. What improvement is mentioned?

(A) Product selection will be increased.
(B) More staff will be able to help.
(C) Free parking will be offered.
(D) Store hours will be extended.

76. When can customers receive a discount?

(A) On Tuesday
(B) On Wednesday
(C) On Thursday
(D) On Friday

74–76 錄製語音

女：[74] **哈囉，你已來到蘇珊和克萊兒的市區分店。**從本週二開始，我們要歇業三天，以拓寬展示區。[74][75] **我們將於本週五恢復營業，屆時將有更多女性長褲和毛衣的款式。**[76] **為了慶祝翻修，我們將在恢復營業的首日，提供所有商品九折優惠。**感謝您的關注。

74. 發話者從事什麼行業？

(A) 電子產品店
(B) 家具直營店
(C) 服飾店
(D) 劇團

75. 訊息中提到改善了什麼部分？

(A) 將會增加產品選擇性
(B) 將有更多員工能幫忙
(C) 將提供免費停車
(D) 將延長營業時間

76. 顧客何時能享有折扣？

(A) 星期二
(B) 星期三
(C) 星期四
(D) 星期五

77–79 radio advertisement

M：Every winter, families waste hundreds of dollars paying unreasonable prices to heat their homes. [77] [78] **By installing Garcia MX insulated windows in your home, you can add an extra layer of protection against dust and noise as well as lower your monthly heating costs.** [79] **You can get 20% off installation costs this month just by mentioning this radio advertisement when you call.** So why wait? Call today at 555-7263!

77. What is being advertised?

(A) A security system
(B) A rented house
(C) A gardening tool
(D) An insulating product

77–79 電台廣告

男：每年冬天，家家戶戶為了暖氣，浪費數百元支付不合理的價格。[77] [78] **只要在家裡安裝加西亞 MX 隔熱窗，你就可以增加一層保護來隔離灰塵和噪音，並降低每月的暖氣費。**[79] **本月來電時，只要提及這則電台廣告就能享有八折安裝費的優惠。**還在等什麼？今天就打 555-7263 ！

77. 這是什麼的廣告？

(A) 保全系統
(B) 出租房屋
(C) 園藝工具
(D) 隔熱產品

78. What is mentioned about the product?
A It is domestically produced.
B It reduces the cost of living.
C It won several awards.
D It received positive reviews.

79. What must listeners do to receive a discount?
A Buy a certain amount of products
B Apply for a membership card
C Talk about the advertisement
D Make a payment in cash

78. 廣告中提到產品的什麼事？
A 它是國內生產的
B 它減少生活開銷
C 它贏得了數個獎項
D 它獲得好評

79. 聽眾要怎麼做才能獲得折扣？
A 買特定份量的產品
B 申請會員卡
C 提及這則廣告
D 用現金付款

80–82 instructions

W：**(80) This is the end of today's product demonstration for our newest model of cell phone.** If you would like to become a beta tester for this cell phone, please wait and talk to our representative, James Goldman. **(81) Volunteers must have worked in the consumer electronics industry for at least 5 years. (82) Remember, during the beta trial period, volunteers are strictly forbidden to release any details about the product.** Thank you very much for your interest in our brand-new model. I hope you enjoyed the presentation.

80–82 指示

女：**(80) 今日新款手機的產品示範會到此為止**，若您想成為這款手機的試用者，請稍等並與我們的代表詹姆士・戈曼洽談。**(81) 自願者必須在消費者電子產業有至少五年的工作經驗。(82) 請記得，在試用期間，將嚴格禁止自願者洩漏任何產品相關細節。**感謝您對我們全新產品的關注，希望您喜歡今天的簡報。

80. What event is ending?
A A grand opening
B A consumer electronics expo
C A product demonstration
D A museum tour

81. What is required of volunteers?
A Relevant experience
B A degree in engineering
C Availability to work on weekends
D Fluency in two languages

82. What are potential volunteers cautioned about?
A Missing a deadline
B Leaking confidential information
C Damaging a device
D Interrupting a presenter

80. 什麼活動快要結束了？
A 盛大開幕
B 消費者電子產品展
C 產品示範
D 博物館導覽

81. 自願者需要具備什麼？
A 相關經驗
B 工程學的學位
C 可在週末上班
D 能流利說兩種語言

82. 潛在的自願者被告誡什麼？
A 錯過截止期限
B 洩漏機密資訊
C 破壞裝置
D 打斷簡報人員

83–85 telephone message

M：Hi, Josephine, this is Robert Marcus calling from Human Resources. (83) **We're due to recruit some more interns for next year.** I've only been working here for a year, so I don't know the intern screening process. (84) **Have you seen the interview questions we use?** (85) **It would be great if you could just give me a quick rundown on what I need to do.** I can drop by your office anytime this week. Let me know a suitable time for you and I'll mark it in my calendar. Thanks.

83–85 電話留言

男：嗨，約瑟芬，我是人力資源部的羅伯特 ‧ 馬可斯。(83) **我們要再多招募一些明年的實習人員**。我只在這裡工作一年，不知道實習人員的篩選過程。(84) **你看過我們面試時要用的問題了嗎？** (85) **若你能很快概述我需要做的事，那就太好了。**我這週隨時可以去你的辦公室。請告訴我你可以的時間，我會將它標在我的日曆上。謝謝。

TEST 8

PART 4

32

83. What is the company recruiting?

Ⓐ Programmers

Ⓑ Chefs

Ⓒ Interns

Ⓓ Factory workers

83. 這家公司在招募什麼？

Ⓐ 程式設計師

Ⓑ 廚師

Ⓒ 實習生

Ⓓ 工廠工人

NEW

84. What does the man imply when he says, "Have you seen the interview questions we use"?

Ⓐ He is postponing an appointment.

Ⓑ He needs a record of the report.

Ⓒ He wants her to help him with the questions.

Ⓓ He will recruit some accountants.

84. 男子說「你看過我們面試時要用的問題了嗎」，他暗示什麼？

Ⓐ 他要將會面延期

Ⓑ 他需要這份報告的紀錄

Ⓒ 他想要她協助擬定問題

Ⓓ 他將要招募一些會計師

85. Why does the man want to meet with the woman?

Ⓐ To get some assistance from her

Ⓑ To ask her for some records

Ⓒ To get a new letterhead

Ⓓ To plan an orientation

85. 男子為何想與女子會面？

Ⓐ 獲得她的協助

Ⓑ 向她要求一些紀錄

Ⓒ 取得新的信頭

Ⓓ 籌劃新進人員訓練

86–88 talk

W：Welcome to the 2nd Annual Ball for Smith & Bradley. First of all, (86) **I'm pleased to announce that we have won Law Firm of The Year this year!** We had a win rate of 98% this year. We have beaten all the competition, with the second highest at 92%. This means a lot for us, since it will allow us to move into corporate law! Our success is due to the diligence and hard work of our legal team. (87) **So, let's keep**

86–88 談話

女：歡迎來到第二屆史密斯和布萊德公司的年度舞會。首先，(86) **我很高興宣布，我們今年被選為年度法律事務所！**我們今年的贏率是98%。我們打敗了所有的競爭對手，第二高的是 92%。這對我們來說意義重大，因為這能讓我們進展到公司法。我們的成功都是因為法務團隊的辛勞和努力。(87) **因此，**

moving up! Corporate law is very technical, however. So I will be sending out a lot of information through email over the next several weeks. (88) **I'm going to need all of you to study this material, so we can maintain our win rate and continue growing as a firm.**

讓我們繼續努力吧！公司法非常的專業，因此在接下來的幾個星期中，我會透過電子郵件寄出大量資訊。(88) **我要你們全體都研讀這些資料，這樣我們就可以保持贏率，讓事務所持續成長。**

86. What is the purpose of the announcement?

A To announce an achievement

B To announce a rise in sales

C To announce a new team member

D To complete a project

86. 這則宣布的目的是什麼？

A 要宣布一項成就

B 要宣布銷售的增加

C 要宣布一位新的團隊成員

D 要完成一項企劃

NEW

87. What does the woman imply when she says, "so let's keep moving up"?

A They need to continue working hard.

B They are moving buildings.

C She is renovating the office.

D They are going on a business trip.

87. 女子說「因此，讓我們繼續努力吧」，暗示什麼？

A 他們需要持續努力工作

B 他們要搬家

C 她正在翻修辦公室

D 他們要出差

88. What does the woman ask the staff to do?

A Study the new handbook

B Prepare a report

C Study material on corporate law

D Write a memo

88. 女子要求員工做什麼？

A 研讀新的手冊

B 備妥報告

C 研讀公司法的資料

D 寫備忘錄

89–91 phone message

W：Grace! (89) **Thank you so much for helping set up the Simpson wedding last weekend.** The centerpieces and floral arrangements you made were amazing! (90) **You have to show me the design sometime!** The bride and groom absolutely loved your work. (91) **Anyway, I'll see you on Tuesday. We have to go over the centerpieces and flower setups for the Grayson wedding next week.** I'm very excited to work with you again! Talk soon.

89–91 電話留言

女：葛瑞思！(89) **很感謝你協助布置上週末辛普森的婚禮。**你所做的餐桌擺飾和插花真令人驚艷！(90) **你一定要找時間讓我看看設計！**新娘和新郎真的很喜歡你的作品。(91) **總之，我下星期二會見到你。我們要看下星期格瑞森婚禮的餐桌擺飾和花朵布置。**我很興奮能夠再與你合作！再聊囉。

89. Why is the woman calling?

A To say thank you

B To ask a favor

C To discuss travel plans

D To request a form

89. 女子為何打電話？

A 道謝

B 請求幫忙

C 討論旅遊計劃

D 要求表格

90. What does the woman imply when she says, "you have to show me the design sometime"?
A She wants to learn how to make it.
B She wasn't sure about the details.
C She needs a dentist recommendation.
D She is writing a design manual.

91. What will the women do next week?
A Plan for the Grayson wedding
B Plan for the Christmas party
C Design a new invitation
D Meet for coffee

90. 女子說「你一定要找時間讓我看看設計」，她暗示什麼？
A 她想要學習如何製作
B 她不確定細節
C 她需要牙醫的推薦
D 她正在寫設計手冊

91. 女子下星期要做什麼？
A 籌劃格瑞森婚禮
B 籌劃聖誕派對
C 設計新的邀請函
D 約會面喝咖啡

TEST 8
PART 4
32

92–94 announcement

W：(92) **Springdale Music Club has just expanded its music selection to include world music artists.** We are extremely excited to be able to build on our already impressive offering of domestic recording artists! We'll be having a live performance of international sensation, Djubai Djinn this Saturday at 8 p.m. Come early for the cook out, too. Bring your own meats though, since we can't feed everyone! (94) **Djubai Djinn will be signing autographs and selling their own albums and merchandise to help promote their US tour, so be sure you bring your money** and your dancing feet! For those of you worried that we may be changing our focus too much, fear not! Springdale Music Club will still keep a healthy emphasis on rock and roll, and this Saturday's concert is no exception with 3 rockin' acts.

92–94 宣布

女：(92) **春谷音樂俱樂部擴增其精選音樂，納入了世界音樂演奏家。**能從原本就令人印象深刻的國內錄製歌手為基礎進行擴增，使我們很興奮！我們將舉辦一場充滿國際觀的現場演出，邀請到迪拜・狄金於本週六晚上八點開唱。也可以早點來參加野炊，但要自己帶肉來，我們無法餵飽每個人！(94) **迪拜・狄金將簽名並且販售他們的專輯和商品，以協助宣傳他們的美國之行，因此請務必帶錢**，還有舞動的雙腳！擔心我們可能會大幅改變音樂重心的人，請別害怕！春谷音樂俱樂部仍然會持續以健康的方式把搖滾樂當成重點。本週六的音樂會也不例外，會有三場搖滾樂演出。

SPRINGDALE MUSIC CLUB'S SATURDAY CONCERT LINE UP
春谷音樂俱樂部週六音樂會陣容

5 p.m. to 8 p.m. **晚上 5 到 8 點**	Barbeque Cookout, 烤肉野炊， bring your own meat! 帶自己的肉品！
8 p.m. to 9 p.m. **晚上 8 到 9 點**	Djubai Djinn, 迪拜・狄金， all the way from East Timor 遠從東帝汶而來
9 p.m. to 10 p.m. **晚上 9 到 10 點**	Swinging Devils 搖擺惡魔 touring from Memphis 從曼菲斯來此巡迴演出
10 p.m. to 11 p.m. **晚上 10 到 11 點**	Rock or Die! 不搖滾就去死！ Local Heroes 本地英雄
11 p.m. to 12 a.m. **晚上 11 到 12 點**	Ferocious Four 兇猛四人組 all the way from New York City 遠從紐約市而來

92. What is indicated about Springdale Music Club?
- [A] They love all music equally.
- [B] They take pride in their location.
- [C] They specialize in country music.
- **[D] They didn't carry world music before.**

NEW
93. Look at the graphic. What can you infer about the bands?
- [A] They will be great.
- [B] They are jazz musicians.
- **[C] The acts following Djubai Djinn play rock and roll.**
- [D] They will be loud.

94. Why does Springdale Music Club ask you to bring your money?
- [A] The concert will be expensive.
- [B] There is a bar.
- **[C] To help support Djubai Djinn's US tour**
- [D] To pay for your meats

92. 關於春谷音樂俱樂部有提到哪一點？
- [A] 他們同樣喜歡各種類型的音樂
- [B] 他們對於地點很自豪
- [C] 他們擅長鄉村音樂
- **[D] 他們先前從未有世界音樂**

93. 參看圖表，關於這些樂團，你可以得到什麼推論？
- [A] 他們將會很棒
- [B] 他們是爵士音樂家
- **[C] 迪拜・狄金之後的演出是搖滾樂**
- [D] 他們會很大聲

94. 春谷音樂俱樂部為何要求帶錢？
- [A] 音樂會很昂貴
- [B] 有吧台
- **[C] 要協助支持迪拜・狄金的美國之旅**
- [D] 要為自己的肉品付錢

95–97 tour guide

W：Welcome to Lake Kitano National Park. (95) **I'm Jane Black, your guide for today.** If you look at your map, we'll start our tour from the Information Center and head to West Gate. (96) **Now, we usually continue our journey to South Gate after a short break, but that path is closed to the public this season.** Instead, we'll take the path to East Gate and hike up the Kilmore Cliff trail until we reach Lake Kitano. (97) **For those of you who are afraid of heights, Kilmore Cliff is a trail that goes along the 50 meter cliff drop.** If you have any concerns, please voice them now. Otherwise, we'll begin our tour.

95–97 旅遊導覽

女：歡迎來到北野湖國家公園。(95) **我是珍・布萊克，你們今天的導遊。**請參看地圖，我們的行程將由旅遊諮詢中心開始，並前往西側大門。(96) **我們通常在短暫休息後會繼續行程前往南側大門，但本季那條小徑不開放給大眾通行。**我們會改走通往東側大門的路，並且健行基墨峭壁的小徑，直到我們到達北野湖。(97) **對於怕高的人，基墨峭壁是一條挨著50公尺峭壁走的山路。**如果你有任何顧慮，請現在就說出來。否則我們將要開始行程。

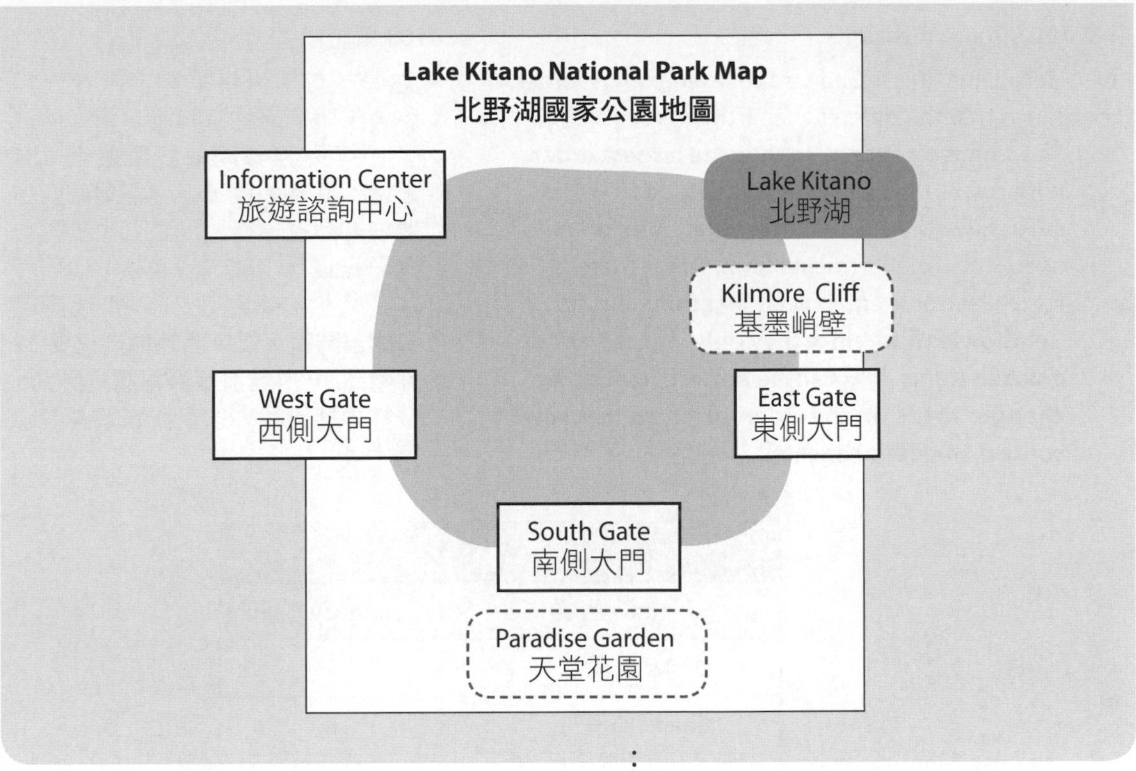

TEST 8
PART 4
32

95. Who most likely are the listeners?
(A) Residents
(B) Tourists
(C) Park employees
(D) Forest rangers

NEW
96. Look at the map. What place are the listeners unable to go to?
(A) Lake Kitano
(B) East Gate
(C) Kilmore Cliff
(D) Paradise Garden

97. What does the woman mention about Kilmore Cliff?
(A) It is dangerous.
(B) The views are spectacular.
(C) People who fear heights may not enjoy it.
(D) It is 50 meters from the final destination.

95. 聽眾最有可能是什麼人？
(A) 居民
(B) 觀光客
(C) 公園員工
(D) 森林管理員

96. 參看地圖，聽者無法去什麼地方？
(A) 北野湖
(B) 東側大門
(C) 基墨峭壁
(D) 天堂花園

97. 關於基墨峭壁，女子提到什麼？
(A) 它很危險
(B) 景色很壯觀
(C) 懼高的人可能不會喜歡
(D) 它距離最終目的地 50 公尺

98–100 phone message

M：Hello Lima, this is George. I've faxed you the order forms that the different departments sent. (99) **The finance department has the largest order with over 100 items, but you'll need to make sure they stay within the budget.** Also, double check the IT department's form. They ordered a lot of electronic equipment. (98) **I think Public Relations is fine, since they only wanted about a dozen items.** (100) **Call me if there need to be changes made on the order forms, so that I can contact the departments.**

98–100 電話留言

男：你好，莉瑪，我是喬治，我已經將各部門寄來的訂購表格傳真給你了。(99) **財務部門的訂單最大，有超過 100 件物品，但你需要確認他們沒有超過預算。**此外，也要再次確認資訊科技部門的表格，他們訂購了大量的電子設備。(98) **我認為公關部門還可以，因為他們只要 12 件物品。**(100) **若訂單表格需要更動，請打電話給我，以便我聯繫各個部門。**

Order form 訂單表格	
Item 品項	Quantity 數量
Desks 書桌	1
Chairs 椅子	8
File Binders 檔案夾	3

NEW

98. Look at the graphic. Which department filled out the order form?
A Finance
B IT
C Public Relations
D Human Resources

99. What does the speaker anticipate may happen?
A Some departments may go over budget.
B The warehouse may not have enough supplies.
C The orders may not arrive on time.
D The departments may forget some items.

100. What does the speaker request of Lima?
A To fax over the orders
B To file the papers
C To arrange a meeting
D To contact him

98. 參看圖表，這張訂購表是哪個部門填寫的？
A 財務
B 資訊科技
C 公關
D 人力資源

99. 發話者預期可能發生什麼事？
A 一些部門可能超過預算
B 倉庫可能沒有足夠的辦公用品
C 訂單可能不會準時送達
D 各個部門可能忘了某些物件

100. 發話者要求莉瑪做什麼？
A 傳真訂單給他
B 將文件歸檔
C 安排會議
D 與他聯繫

ACTUAL TEST 9

PART 1 P. 130-133

1. A There are many people in the store.
   B She is purchasing a garment.
   C She is looking at some clothing.
   D There are clothes on all the coat hangers.

2. **A One woman is raising her hand.**
   B The presenter is looking at the watch.
   C The presenter is using the microphone.
   D The presentation is very boring.

3. A She is wearing safety glasses.
   B She is looking for some bacteria.
   C She is looking through the microscope.
   D She is using the microphone.

4. A They are playing golf.
   B They are carrying their golf clubs over their right shoulder.
   C They are setting up the golf clubs.
   D They are trading used golf clubs.

5. A She is repairing the shoes.
   B There are other people in the store.
   C They are trying on some shoes.
   D She has a sock on her left foot.

6. **A The man is giving a presentation in front of a screen.**
   B The man is typing on his laptop.
   C The woman is writing some notes with her right hand.
   D They all have computers.

1. A 商店裡有許多人。
   B 她正在買衣服。
   C 她看著服飾。
   D 所有的大衣衣架上都有掛衣服。

2. **A 一名女子正在舉手。**
   B 簡報者正在看手錶。
   C 簡報者正在使用麥克風。
   D 簡報非常無聊。

3. A 她戴著護目鏡。
   B 她正在尋找某些細菌。
   C 她正在透過顯微鏡觀察。
   D 她正在使用麥克風。

4. A 他們正在打高爾夫球。
   B 他們的右肩背著高爾夫球桿。
   C 他們正在擺放高爾夫球桿。
   D 他們在買賣二手高爾夫球桿。

5. A 她正在修理鞋子。
   B 商店裡有其他人。
   C 她們正在試穿鞋子。
   D 她的左腳有穿襪子。

6. **A 男子正在螢幕前進行簡報。**
   B 男子正用筆記型電腦打字。
   C 女子正用右手寫筆記。
   D 他們都有電腦。

PART 2 P. 134

7. Is Mr. Johnson joining us for lunch?
   A Yes, I'm hungry, too.
   B No, he's occupied.
   C I brought a sandwich.

7. 強森先生要和我們一起吃午餐嗎？
   A 是的，我也餓了。
   B 不，他有事要忙。
   C 我帶了三明治。

8. When will the company release its newest video game console?
A At midnight tonight.
B He will renew his lease next month.
C It's on the desk.

9. How did you get such great seats for the concert?
A By winning tickets at a raffle.
B At least once a week.
C He's a world-renowned musician.

10. Why are the lights off in the conference room?
A I was sitting there.
B They are watching a video.
C Yes, she's off duty.

11. Do you know where the employee break room is?
A We will take a 10-minute break.
B Have you worked here long?
C On the second floor.

12. Who replaced the ink cartridge?
A Suzy did this morning.
B In the shopping cart.
C It's a brand-new printer.

13. I'm so thankful for all your help in preparing this report.
A You're welcome to stay.
B Don't mention it.
C I need a pair of gloves.

14. Would you like to make a reservation for tonight?
A The dinner was delicious.
B I would, for six people.
C It's an expensive hobby.

15. Why did you open the window?
A To let in some fresh air.
B In the master bedroom.
C Because the store will open next month.

16. Let's stop by the post office on the way.
A A letter to my cousin.
B OK, where is it?
C The delivery arrived yesterday.

8. 這家公司何時會發表最新的電玩遊戲機？
A 今天午夜。
B 他下個月會簽新租約。
C 在書桌上。

9. 你是怎麼得到位子那麼棒的演唱會門票？
A 在抽獎活動中贏得門票。
B 至少一星期一次。
C 他是世界的知名的音樂家。

10. 會議室為什麼要關燈？
A 我當時坐在那裡。
B 他們正在看影片。
C 是的，她下班了。

11. 你知道員工休息室在哪裡嗎？
A 我們休息 10 分鐘。
B 你在這裡工作很久了嗎？
C 在二樓。

12. 誰換了墨水匣？
A 蘇西今天早上換的。
B 在購物推車裡。
C 這是全新的印表機。

13. 我很感謝你幫忙備妥這份報告。
A 很歡迎你留下來。
B 別客氣。
C 我需要一雙手套。

14. 您想要預約今天晚上的位子嗎？
A 晚餐很美味。
B 是的，六個人。
C 這是個昂貴的嗜好。

15. 你為何打開窗戶？
A 要讓新鮮空氣進來。
B 在主臥室裡。
C 因為這家商店下個月將會開幕。

16. 我們順便去郵局吧。
A 一封給我表哥的信。
B 好的，郵局在哪？
C 貨運昨天送到了。

17. There's a name missing from the list of speakers.
A Oh, who is it?
B I'll make 20 copies.
C Yes, he agreed to the contract.

18. What day are we hosting that party?
A Yes, it's ready.
B He requested a chocolate cake.
C Check the calendar in the office.

19. You should sign up for a computer programming workshop.
A Mr. Greene will assign more employees to the project.
B You don't think it would be too difficult for me?
C Please refund this purchase.

20. You've finished interviewing the candidates, haven't you?
A It was in the meeting room.
B Yes, the last person just left.
C Where did you put the applications?

21. Would you like to be in charge of entertainment or catering?
A I'll take care of food and drinks.
B It was a great party.
C The stage is too small.

22. Don't we need to check out soon?
A No, I reserved the room until tomorrow.
B The hotel doesn't provide room service.
C Let's make a reservation for 6 o'clock.

23. I'm excited to start using this new software.
A Yes, it should make work easier.
B It's old, but still usable.
C I was disappointed in him.

24. Why don't we hand out free samples to customers?
A No, it's the customer service department.
B Because we conducted a survey.
C Yeah, that's a good strategy.

17. 講者名單上有個名字漏掉了。
A 喔，是誰？
B 我要印 20 份。
C 是的，他同意這個合約。

18. 我們要在星期幾辦那場派對？
A 是的，已經準備好了。
B 他要求有個巧克力蛋糕。
C 查看辦公室的日曆。

19. 你應該報名參加電腦程式設計研討會。
A 格林先生將指派更多員工參與計劃。
B 你不覺得這對我而言太困難了嗎？
C 請退還這個商品的款項。

20. 你已經結束應徵者的面試了，不是嗎？
A 在會議室裡。
B 是的，最後一人剛離開。
C 你把求職表放在哪裡？

21. 你想要負責娛樂或者是外燴？
A 我來負責食物和飲料。
B 這是場很棒的派對。
C 舞台太小了。

22. 我們不是很快就要退房了嗎？
A 不，房間我訂到明天。
B 這家飯店不提供客房服務。
C 我們訂六點鐘吧。

23. 我很興奮能開始使用這個新軟體。
A 是的，它應該能讓工作更容易。
B 它很舊，但仍可使用。
C 我對他很失望。

24. 我們何不發送免費試用品給顧客？
A 不，這是客服部門。
B 因為我們進行了一項調查。
C 好啊，那是個好策略。

25. The building site hasn't been selected, has it?
A We are still considering multiple options.
B It's a luxury apartment complex.
C He will cite a passage from his book.

26. How did you hear about the meeting on Thursday?
A Mr. Shepard told me at lunch.
B My neighbor gave it to me.
C I can't tell them apart.

27. Should I tell Susan for you, or do you want to tell her yourself?
A She's a bank teller.
B I want to do it directly.
C I forgot the phone number.

28. The annual sales report is finished.
A We should proofread it before printing.
B I watched the weather report, too.
C They raised the price by 10 dollars.

29. Is this used vehicle for sale?
A Yes, and I changed the tires on it.
B The price of gas is reasonable.
C I used it for cooking.

30. What is needed to apply for this job?
A Yes, she starts on Monday.
B A bachelor's degree or higher in engineering.
C The rule doesn't apply to children under 8.

31. Who's in charge of designing promotional handouts?
A Mr. Wilson was promoted to sales manager.
B The man wearing the blue shirt.
C We don't charge for delivery.

25. 建築地點還沒有選定，不是嗎？
A 我們還在考量多種選擇。
B 這是一棟豪華公寓大樓。
C 他將從他的書中引用一段話。

26. 你如何得知星期四的會議？
A 薛帕先生午餐時告訴我的。
B 我鄰居給我的。
C 我無法分辨他們。

27. 我應該幫你跟蘇珊説，還是你想親自跟她説？
A 她是一名銀行櫃員。
B 我想要直接跟她說。
C 我忘了電話號碼。

28. 年度銷售報告完成了。
A 我們應該在付印之前進行校對。
B 我也看了氣象報導。
C 他們把價格調漲十元。

29. 這輛二手車供販售嗎？
A 是的，而且我已經為它換了輪胎。
B 油價很合理。
C 我用它來烹飪。

30. 應徵這份工作需要什麼資格？
A 是的，她星期一開始工作。
B 工程學學士或以上的學位。
C 這項規則不適用於八歲以下的孩童。

31. 誰負責設計促銷的傳單？
A 威爾森先生被晉升為銷售經理。
B 穿藍色襯衫的男子。
C 我們不收運費。

32–34 conversation

W： Hello, Mr. Penn. (32) **I wanted to ask about changing my work hours.** I will be entering university starting next month, and my availability is going to change.

M： Well, Nami, we really value you as a hard-working employee at this restaurant, so I want you to continue working here. What do you think your schedule will be?

W： Thank you for saying so. (33) **I haven't registered for classes yet, so I'm not completely sure.**

M： I see. (34) **Once you find out, please let me know.** I'm sure we can figure something out so that you can attend university and continue working here.

32–34 對話

女： 哈囉，潘恩先生。(32) **我想要詢問改變工時的事。**我下個月要上大學，我的空檔時間將會改變。

男： 這樣啊，娜米，我們這家餐廳很看重你這位努力的員工，因此我希望你繼續在這裡工作，你認為你的時間表會是什麼樣子？

女： 感謝您這麼説。(33) **我還沒選課，所以我還不太確定。**

男： 了解。(34) **你一知道就請告訴我。**我們一定能想出方法，讓你能上大學又能繼續在這裡工作。

32. What is the woman requesting?
(A) Time off from work
(B) A recommendation letter
(C) A schedule change
(D) A pay raise

33. Why is the woman unsure about the man's question?
(A) She wants to quit her job.
(B) She is waiting for her exam results.
(C) She got a job offer from another restaurant.
(D) She has not registered for classes.

34. What does the man ask the woman to do?
(A) Work overtime this week
(B) Inform him about her availability
(C) Recommend her acquaintance
(D) Create a new menu design

32. 女子要求什麼？
(A) 休假
(B) 推薦函
(C) 班表更動
(D) 加薪

33. 關於男子的問題，女子為何不能確定？
(A) 她想要辭職
(B) 她在等候考試結果
(C) 她找到另一家餐廳工作
(D) 她尚未註冊課程

34. 男子要求女子做什麼？
(A) 這週加班
(B) 告訴男子她有空的時間
(C) 推薦她認識的人
(D) 設計新的菜單

35–37 conversation

M：Hello, my name is Jordan Briggs. (35) **I'll be getting married next week and we are looking for someone to photograph our wedding.** A friend of mine showed me photographs you took, and I was really impressed.

W：Thanks for calling me, Mr. Briggs. What type of photographs are you interested in exactly?

M：Well, we would want you to take photographs of everything including the guests, the food, the ceremony, and the after-party. (36) **How much would that cost?**

W：Well, it could be quite expensive. (37) **In order to photograph the event that extensively, I would need to hire two or three assistants.**

35–37 對話

男：哈囉，我的名字是喬丹 ・ 布力格斯。(35) **我下個星期就要結婚了，我們在找人為婚禮攝影。**我的一個朋友讓我看你拍的照片，讓我留下深刻的印象。

女：感謝您打電話給我，布力格斯先生。您對什麼類型的照片特別感興趣呢？

男：我們想要你為所有東西拍照，包含賓客、食物、典禮以及婚禮後的派對。(36) **這樣要多少錢？**

女：這可能會很貴。(37) **若要完整捕捉這場活動，我需要僱用兩或三名助理。**

35. Why is the man calling?
- [A] To order a product
- [B] To postpone an appointment
- [C] To book a wedding hall
- **[D] To hire a photographer**

36. What does the man inquire about?
- **[A] A price quote**
- [B] A product sample
- [C] A list of employees
- [D] An event schedule

37. Why does the woman say the service might be quite expensive?
- [A] Her services are in high demand.
- **[B] She will need additional staff.**
- [C] She uses high-end equipment.
- [D] She has to meet a tight deadline.

35. 男子為何打電話？
- [A] 訂購產品
- [B] 延後預約
- [C] 預訂婚宴廳
- **[D] 僱用攝影師**

36. 男子詢問什麼事？
- **[A] 估價**
- [B] 產品樣本
- [C] 員工名單
- [D] 活動行程表

37. 女子為何說這項服務可能很貴？
- [A] 她的服務很熱門
- **[B] 她需要額外的工作人員**
- [C] 她使用高檔的設備
- [D] 她必須趕很緊迫的截止期限

38–40 conversation

M：We will have a new quality control inspector joining our staff as of tomorrow. (38) **His name is Nathan Gates, and he'll be examining products for any defects before being shipped.**

38–40 對話

男：明天開始將有一位新的品管員加入我們的團隊。(38) **他的名字是納森 ・ 蓋茲，他會在出貨前查看產品以找出瑕疵品。**

W：I'm glad to hear that. We have had a lot of customers returning defective items lately. It's not good for our company's image and reputation.

M：(39) **When he comes to work tomorrow, please introduce him to everyone in the factory.**

W：Sure, I will. (40) **I'll also make sure to give him all the proper safety gear he needs to wear inside the factory.**

女：我很高興聽見這件事。我們最近有很多顧客退回瑕疵品，這有損我們公司的形象和名聲。

男：(39) **他明天上工時，請你把他介紹給工廠裡的所有人。**

女：當然，我會的。(40) **我也一定會提供他在工廠裡面必須穿戴的合適安全裝備。**

38. Who is Nathan Gates?
- A A sales clerk
- B A customer
- C A private detective
- **D A product inspector**

39. What does the man ask the woman to do?
- A Run a training session
- B Enforce safety measures
- **C Introduce a new employee**
- D Inspect a construction site

40. What will the woman give Mr. Gates?
- A A training manual
- **B Safety gear**
- C A work schedule
- D An identification card

38. 納森 · 蓋茲是什麼人？
- A 銷售店員
- B 顧客
- C 私家偵探
- **D 品管員**

39. 男子要求女子做什麼？
- A 辦理訓練課程
- B 加強安全措施
- **C 介紹新員工**
- D 檢查工地

40. 女子會給蓋茲先生什麼？
- A 訓練手冊
- **B 安全裝備**
- C 工作時間表
- D 識別證

TEST 9

PART 3

35

41–43 conversation

M：We finally were able to pump all of the water from the basement today. (41) **Unfortunately, a lot of our inventory was damaged by the water.**

W：(42) **I've never seen a flood occur so fast like that.** Because of the damaged inventory, we won't be able to open for a few days.

M：Well, at least it didn't happen over the weekend when no one was in the office. The damage could have been much worse.

W：That's true. (43) **I heard from our supplier, and they said they can restock our storage room this Friday.** I guess we'll just have to wait patiently until then.

41–43 對話

男：我們今天終於能把地下室的水都抽掉。(41) **不幸的是，我們有很多存貨因水而受損。**

女：(42) **我從來沒看過水淹得這麼快。**因為存貨受損，我們有幾天都不能開店。

男：至少淹水不是發生在週末沒有人在辦公室的時候，不然損失可能更加慘重。

女：沒錯。(43) **我收到供貨商的消息，他們這星期五可以為我們的儲藏室補貨。**我想在那之前，我們只能耐心等候。

41. What problem are the speakers discussing?
A Unsatisfied customers
B An unexpected drop in sales
C Damaged inventory
D A delayed shipment

42. What caused the problem?
A An electrical fire
B A burst water pipe
C A sudden flood
D A gas leak

43. What will happen on Friday?
A Construction will be completed.
B Stock prices will increase.
C A shipment will arrive.
D A supplier will be changed.

41. 對話者們在討論什麼問題？
A 顧客不滿
B 業績意外下跌
C 存貨受損
D 運送延遲

42. 是什麼導致這個問題？
A 電線走火
B 水管爆裂
C 突發水災
D 瓦斯漏氣

43. 星期五會發生什麼事？
A 工程將完工
B 股價將會上漲
C 貨品將會送到
D 供應商將被更換

44–46 conversation

M：(44) **Next week at Harrison University, Charlie Klein will be conducting an introductory lecture on creative writing. It's open to the public and it isn't very expensive.**

W：Charlie Klein? (45) **Doesn't he currently have a book on the bestseller list?** I heard his stories are very moving and powerful. I'd like to attend it.

M：Yes. I recently bought one of his books and was really impressed. That's why I don't want to miss this opportunity to learn from him. Would you like to read it before the lecture?

W：Sure. (46) **I'll stop by your home tomorrow and pick up the book from you.** Thanks for letting me know.

44–46 對話

男：(44) **下星期查理 · 克萊恩將在哈里森大學進行創意寫作介紹演講。演講會對大眾開放，而且並不會很昂貴。**

女：查理 · 克萊恩？(45) **他現在不是有本書在暢銷書排行榜上嗎？**我聽說他的故事很深刻感人，我想要參加。

男：是的，我最近買了一本他的書，而且真的覺得印象深刻。這就是我為什麼不想錯過這次向他學習的機會。你想在演講前閱讀這本書嗎？

女：當然。(46) **我明天會去你家拿那本書。**謝謝你告訴我。

44. What are the speakers discussing?
A A public lecture
B An upcoming exam
C A graduation requirement
D A recent publishing trend

45. Who is Charlie Klein?
A A scientist
B An inventor
C A professor
D A writer

44. 對話者們在討論什麼？
A 公開演講
B 近期的考試
C 畢業要求
D 最近的出版趨勢

45. 查理 · 克萊恩是什麼人？
A 科學家
B 發明家
C 教授
D 作家

46. Why is the woman planning to visit the man tomorrow?
Ⓐ To return an item
Ⓑ To borrow a book
Ⓒ To meet Mr. Klein
Ⓓ To sign up for a course

46. 女子為何打算明天要拜訪男子？
Ⓐ 歸還物件
Ⓑ 借書
Ⓒ 與克萊恩先生會面
Ⓓ 報名參加課程

47–49 conversation

W： I saw an advertisement on the subway today for back pain relief at Frank Logan Hospital. The advertisement offers a free consultation to assess a patient's situation and suggest a course of treatment. I'm thinking of going.

M： (47) **Actually, I was treated by Dr. Moran at the hospital for back pain last year.** After five years of enduring the pain, my pain was drastically reduced under the care of Dr. Moran. In addition to medication, he showed me some useful stretching exercises. I really recommend seeing him.

W： You're right. I shouldn't hesitate anymore. (48) **My work is disrupted by my back pain almost every day.**

M： (49) **If you would like, I can give you the number for Dr. Moran's office.** That way you can set up an appointment with him directly.

47–49 對話

女： 我今天在地鐵看到一則廣告，是法蘭克 · 羅根醫院的背痛緩解。廣告提供免費諮詢來評估病人的病況，並建議療程，我考慮要去。

男： (47) **實際上，我去年就是由該醫院的莫倫醫師治療背痛的。** 忍受疼痛五年之後，在莫倫醫師的照料下，我的疼痛大幅減輕。除了用藥以外，他還教我一些實用的伸展運動，我真心推薦你去看他。

女： 你說的對，我不該再猶豫。(48) **我的工作幾乎每天都會受到背痛的干擾。**

男： (49) **如果你要的話，我可以給你莫倫醫生辦公室的電話號碼。** 這樣你就可以直接跟他預約看診。

TEST 9
PART 3
35

47. Who is Dr. Moran?
Ⓐ A university professor
Ⓑ A patient
Ⓒ A pharmacist
Ⓓ A medical practitioner

47. 莫倫醫生是誰？
Ⓐ 大學教授
Ⓑ 病人
Ⓒ 藥劑師
Ⓓ 執業醫生

48. What problem does the woman mention?
Ⓐ An incorrect diagnosis
Ⓑ A family problem
Ⓒ Persistent pain
Ⓓ An outstanding balance

48. 女子提到什麼問題？
Ⓐ 誤診
Ⓑ 家庭問題
Ⓒ 持續性疼痛
Ⓓ 未清償餘額

49. What does the man offer to do?
Ⓐ Provide contact information
Ⓑ Drive the woman to the hospital
Ⓒ Set up an appointment
Ⓓ Offer a free consultation

49. 男子提議要做什麼？
Ⓐ 提供聯絡資訊
Ⓑ 開車載女子去醫院
Ⓒ 預約掛號
Ⓓ 提供免費諮詢

NEW

50–52 conversation

M：Sarah, I need your help. (50) **There is something wrong with the phone transfer software.**

W：What exactly is the problem?

M：I can't get through to Human Resources and Accounting. When I try to call through to them, I just hear a strange noise and then the phone just goes silent.

W：Oh. They are on a different version now, I think. (51) **You might need to update your software so it's compatible with theirs.**

M：Oh. Yeah, I haven't updated for over a year.

W：That is definitely the problem then. (52) **I will send you the link for a free upgrade, and you shouldn't have any more problems.**

M：Great! Thanks, Sarah!

50–52 對話

男：莎拉，我需要你的幫忙。(50) **電話轉接軟體有問題。**

女：究竟出了什麼問題？

男：我無法接通人資部門和會計部門，我試著與他們通話時，只會聽見奇怪的噪音，然後電話就沒有聲音了。

女：我猜他們現在是用不同的版本。(51) **你可能需要更新軟體，才能跟他們的相容。**

男：喔，對耶，我超過一年沒有更新了。

女：這肯定是問題所在。(52) **我會寄免費升級連結給你，應該就不會再有問題了。**

男：太好了！謝謝你，莎拉！

50. What is the man concerned about?
- A The messaging system
- B Cell phone reception
- **C Phone transfer software**
- D A new computer system

51. What does the woman suggest?
- A Deleting all his software
- B Getting a new computer
- C Downloading a movie
- **D Upgrading his software**

52. What does the woman say she will do?
- **A Send him a link for a free upgrade**
- B Upgrade his phone model
- C Revise the schedule
- D Check with management

50. 男子擔心什麼事？
- A 訊息系統
- B 手機訊號
- **C 電話轉接軟體**
- D 新的電腦系統

51. 女子建議什麼？
- A 刪除所有軟體
- B 取得新的電腦
- C 下載電影
- **D 升級軟體**

52. 女子說她將會做什麼？
- **A 寄給他免費升級的連結**
- B 升級他的電話型號
- C 更正時程表
- D 與管理階層進行確認

NEW

53–55 conversation

M：I'm concerned about the output of some of our machinery. (53) **Production has slowed by 8% since June; I think there must be a problem with the software.** We are losing money over this, and I'm not sure who to ask about it.

53–55 對話

男：我很擔心我們部分機器的產量。(53) **從六月以來，生產量已減緩 8%。我認為軟體一定有問題。**我們因此而虧損，我也不確定該向誰詢問此事。

W：We had it repaired once in the past, but it was so expensive we ended up just buying a new one. Now it is slowing down as well. Do you think we should just replace the machine again?

M：(54) **Yeah, it doesn't make sense to keep going like this.**

W：(55) **I'll call the machine repair shop and get a quote on the repairs, and we can decide what to do.**

M：OK, but let's get it done as quickly as possible, please.

女：我們以前曾經修理過機器，但太貴了，我們最後買了一台新的，現在它也變慢了。你認為我們應該再次更換機器嗎？

男：(54) **是的，繼續這樣下去沒有意義。**

女：(55) **我會打電話給機器維修廠，進行維修估價，然後我們可以決定該怎麼辦。**

男：好的，但請盡快完成此事。

53. What is the man worried about?

Ⓐ Buying new software
Ⓑ The production rate of the machine
Ⓒ Finding a repair shop
Ⓓ An increase in production

53. 男子擔心什麼事？

Ⓐ 購買新軟體
Ⓑ 機器的生產率
Ⓒ 找到維修廠
Ⓓ 生產量增加

NEW

54. What does the man imply when he says, "It doesn't make sense to keep going like this"?

Ⓐ He wants to take action immediately.
Ⓑ He wants to continue business as usual.
Ⓒ He wants to repair the software.
Ⓓ He doesn't agree with the woman.

54. 男子說「繼續這樣下去沒有意義」，他暗示什麼？

Ⓐ 他想要立即採取行動
Ⓑ 他想要如往常般持續營業
Ⓒ 他想要修理軟體
Ⓓ 他不同意女子的話

55. What does the woman say she will do?

Ⓐ Call the software engineer
Ⓑ Contact the IT department
Ⓒ Call the machine repair shop
Ⓓ Buy new software

55. 女子說她將會做什麼？

Ⓐ 打電話給軟體工程師
Ⓑ 聯繫資訊科技部門
Ⓒ 打電話給機器維修廠
Ⓓ 購買新軟體

NEW

56–58 conversation

W：Hey Joe! (56) **How did your presentation go last weekend?**

M：It was great! We sold a lot of books after the seminar.

W：(57) **Wow, sounds like you've really made it!** So what are your plans for the future?

M：(58) **I'm writing another book, which is due for release next year. In the meantime, I will just continue doing seminars and try to get more exposure.**

W：Excellent. If you need any help, let me know. I have a few connections in the publishing industry.

56–58 對話

女：嘿，喬！(56) **你上週末的演講進行得如何？**

男：很好啊！研討會後我們賣了很多書。

女：(57) **哇，聽起來你真的很成功！**那麼你未來有什麼計劃？

男：(58) **我正在寫另一本書，明年就會出版，在此期間，我會持續開研討會，並試著增加曝光率。**

女：太好了。如果你需要任何協助，請告訴我。我在出版業有一些人脈。

56. What did the man do last weekend?
Ⓐ He went to a conference.
Ⓑ He finished his sales reports.
Ⓒ He gave a presentation.
Ⓓ He visited his family.

56. 男子上週末做了什麼？
Ⓐ 他去參加會議
Ⓑ 他完成銷售報告
Ⓒ 他發表一場演說
Ⓓ 他去拜訪家人

NEW
57. What does the woman imply when she says, "wow, sounds like you've really made it"?
Ⓐ He failed.
Ⓑ He was successful with his presentation.
Ⓒ His presentation wasn't well received.
Ⓓ His book didn't sell well.

57. 女子說「哇，聽起來你真的很成功」，她暗示什麼？
Ⓐ 他失敗了
Ⓑ 他的演說很成功
Ⓒ 他的演說不受歡迎
Ⓓ 他的書賣得不好

58. What does the man plan on doing next year?
Ⓐ Retire from writing
Ⓑ Move to another country
Ⓒ Have a child with his wife
Ⓓ Release another book

58. 男子明年打算做什麼？
Ⓐ 退休不再寫作
Ⓑ 搬到別的國家
Ⓒ 與妻子生小孩
Ⓓ 出另一本書

NEW
59–61 conversation

M1： Hi, Mrs. Kraft? This is Logan from Yellow Bank Realtors. (59) **I am calling about some problems with the apartment you will be renting in the Swiss Tower Building.** Let me put you through to our manager and he will tell you.

W： OK, I'll wait.

M2： Hi, Mrs. Kraft. (60) **They are having some renovations done at the Swiss Tower Building, so we need to change your move-in date to the end of October.** Will that be OK with you?

W： Well, not really. I will have nowhere to live, and it's far too expensive to stay in a hotel.

M2： OK. (61) **We will be happy to pay for your hotel expenses until you can move into the apartment.** I'm really sorry for the inconvenience. We only found out about this today.

W： That sounds fine.

59–61 對話

男 1： 嗨，是克拉夫特女士嗎？ 我是黃色河岸房地產的羅根。(59) **我打這通電話，是為了要談您想要租賃瑞士塔大樓公寓的相關問題。** 讓我將電話轉接給我們的經理，他會向您說明。

女： 好的，我會等候。

男 2： 嗨，克拉夫特女士。(60) **瑞士塔大樓正在進行翻修，因此我們需要將您的遷入日期更改到 10 月底。** 您可以接受嗎？

女： 不太行。我會沒有地方住，而住旅館太貴了。

男 2： 好的。(61) **我們會很樂意為您支付旅館的費用，直到您可以搬入公寓為止。** 我為這項不便道歉，我們今天才得知此事。

女： 聽起來沒問題。

59. Why most likely is the man calling?
Ⓐ To discuss an issue with the apartment
Ⓑ To offer a lower rental price
Ⓒ To negotiate a contract
Ⓓ To make an appointment

59. 男子最有可能為何而打這通電話？
Ⓐ 要討論公寓的問題
Ⓑ 要提供較低的租賃價格
Ⓒ 要協商合約
Ⓓ 要約定會面

60. What does the man say about the Swiss Tower building?
Ⓐ It is too far away from her office.
Ⓑ It is being renovated at the moment.
Ⓒ It is being closed down.
Ⓓ It is located close to a dry cleaner.

60. 關於瑞士塔大樓，男子說了什麼？
Ⓐ 距離她的辦公室太遠
Ⓑ 現在正在進行翻修
Ⓒ 正被封閉
Ⓓ 地點在乾洗店附近

61. What does the man offer the woman?
Ⓐ Give her a lower rental price
Ⓑ Extend the lease
Ⓒ Pay for her hotel costs
Ⓓ Arrange to move her furniture

61. 男子提議要為女子做什麼？
Ⓐ 給她較低的租賃價格
Ⓑ 延展租約
Ⓒ 支付她的旅館花費
Ⓓ 安排搬遷她的家具

NEW
62–64 conversation

W：OK, sir. (62) **This suit comes to $385. Would you like to pay cash or by card?**
M：I have a gift certificate here for a 10% discount. Wait, I can't find it. OK, here it is.
W：Thank you, sir. Hmm, unfortunately you won't be able to use this with this suit.
M：(63) **Ah, I see the problem. Well, I need some more dress pants for work; do you mind if I go and pick some items out so I can use my gift certificate?**
W：Of course, sir. Please follow me. (64) **I will help you pick out some pants I think will suit you well.**

62–64 對話

女：好的，先生。(62) **這套西裝要價 385 元，您要付現金或者是用信用卡？**
男：我這裡有九折的禮券。等等，我找不到。好，在這裡。
女：謝謝您，先生。很可惜，您買這套西裝不能使用。
男：(63) **啊，我知道是什麼問題了。我上班需要更多條西裝褲，你介意我再去挑選一些商品，以便使用禮券嗎？**
女：沒問題，先生。請跟我來。(64) **我會幫您挑些我認為很適合的長褲。**

Bernard & Son's Tailors 巴納德父子裁縫店
Gift Certificate 禮券

10% off any purchase of $500 or more
消費滿 500 元可享九折優惠

Expires March 10
3 月 10 日到期

62. What is the woman doing?
Ⓐ Giving away free suits
Ⓑ Helping a customer
Ⓒ Updating software
Ⓓ Celebrating with friends

62. 女子在做什麼？
Ⓐ 贈送免費西裝
Ⓑ 協助顧客
Ⓒ 更新軟體
Ⓓ 與朋友慶祝

NEW

63. Look at the graphic. Why is the gift certificate rejected?

A It is expired.

B Because he is in the wrong store

C Because he didn't purchase enough

D The certificate is damaged.

64. What does the woman offer to do?

A Give him another certificate

B Help him try on a suit

C Show him some pants

D Give him a refund

63. 參看圖表，禮券為何不能使用？

A 過期了

B 因為他走錯商店了

C 因為他買得不夠

D 禮券遭到毀損

64. 女子提議做什麼？

A 給他另一張禮券

B 協助他試穿西裝

C 拿長褲給他看

D 退他錢

65–67 conversation

M：Excuse me? (65) **I've just started a new exercise program, and my trainer told me I should buy some protein powder to have after I work out.** Most importantly, I need something that is high in protein, but doesn't have a lot of carbohydrates. Do you have anything you can recommend?

W：We have a wide variety of protein powders, but there is one I particularly like the taste of. It is a protein drink made from milk and soy.

M：Oh. (66) **Actually, I'm lactose intolerant.** Are there any other options?

W：(67) **I suggest you purchase a powder that is only soy-based.** You won't have any problems with that.

65–67 對話

男：不好意思？(65) **我剛開始進行一項新的運動計劃，而教練告訴我應該購買乳清蛋白，在健身之後服用。**最重要的是，我需要含高蛋白質但碳水化合物成分不高的產品。你有什麼可以推薦的嗎？

女：我們有各種的乳清蛋白，但其中有種口味我特別喜歡，是由奶類和黃豆做成的高蛋白飲。

男：(66) **實際上，我有乳糖不耐症。**有別種選擇嗎？

女：(67) **我建議你購買主要成分只有黃豆的蛋白質粉。**那種的對你就不會有問題。

Nutrition Information 營養資訊
Serving Size: 1 Rounded Scoop (29.4 g)
每份：一圓匙（29.4 公克）

Calories 熱量	120大卡
Fat 脂肪	10 grams（公克）
Carbohydrate 碳水化合物	3 grams（公克）
Protein 蛋白質	24 grams（公克）
Calcium 鈣質	10%
Contains milk and soy products 含奶類和大豆產品	

65. Why is the man looking for a certain product?
A He stopped working out.
B His trainer told him to.
C Because he is a trainer.
D He had a favorite brand.

NEW
66. Look at the graphic. Which content is the man worried about?
A Carbohydrate
B Fat
C Milk
D Protein

67. What does the woman suggest?
A Purchasing a milk-based product
B Getting a full refund
C Using soy beans
D Buying a soy-based powder

65. 男子為何要找某種產品？
A 他停止健身
B 他的教練要他這麼做
C 因為他是教練
D 他有最喜愛的品牌

66. 參看圖表，男子擔心哪種成分？
A 碳水化合物
B 脂肪
C 奶類
D 蛋白質

67. 女子建議什麼？
A 購買以奶類為主要成分的產品
B 全額退費
C 使用黃豆
D 購買以黃豆為主要成分的乳清蛋白

TEST 9 PART 3 35

68–70 conversation

W：Hi, Harold. Just wanted to let you know I'm nearly finished with all of Farnod Computing's windows. (68) **I'm going to move up to the next floor in about 20 minutes.** Are you finished with Raptas' windows?

M：Hi, Batty. Yeah, I have finished Raptas' and I'm going upstairs to the next floor. The windows are already pretty clean up there, so I think we can get the job done pretty soon.

W：Great. Before you start on the 4th floor, can you please bring me some more window cleaner? I have run out.

M：Sure, I'll be up in about 20 minutes. It will be good to see how clean your windows are compared to mine. (70) **When we are finished with the windows we need to start on the carpets.**

68–70 對話

女：嗨，哈洛德。我只是想讓你知道我快完成法納德電腦公司的全部窗戶了。(68) **我大約 20 分鐘後就要往上一樓了**。你完成了鋭普塔公司的窗戶了嗎？

男：嗨，芭蒂，你好。是的，我已經完成了鋭普塔公司的窗戶，即將要往上一樓。上面的窗戶已經很乾淨了，因此我認為我們很快就可以把工作做完。

女：太好了。你開始四樓的工作之前，可否請你為我多帶一些窗戶清潔劑？我的已經用完了。

男：好的，我大約 20 分鐘後就會上去，能看看你的窗戶和我的比有多乾淨很不錯。(70) **清洗完窗戶後，我們要開始清潔地毯。**

Park Tower 帕克塔大樓
Office Directory 公司行號一覽表

1st	Floor 一樓	Farnod Computing 法納德電腦公司
2nd	Floor 二樓	Chaims & Son 查姆斯父子公司
3rd	Floor 三樓	Raptas 鋭普塔公司
4th	Floor 四樓	Hecadi Constructing 西卡蒂建設公司

68. Who most likely are the speakers?
A Office cleaners
B Computer repair technicians
C Telephone operators
D Athletes

NEW
69. Look at the graphic. Where is the woman going next?
A Raptas
B Farnod Computing
C Chaims & Son
D Hecadi Constructing

70. What are the speakers going to do when they're finished with the windows?
A Go home
B Eat lunch
C Clean the carpets
D Leave the building

68. 對話者們最有可能是什麼人？
A 辦公室清潔工
B 電腦維修人員
C 接線生
D 運動員

69. 參看圖表，女子接下來會去哪裡？
A 鋭普塔公司
B 法納德電腦公司
C 查姆斯父子公司
D 西卡蒂建設公司

70. 對話者們在清洗完窗戶後接下來也許會做什麼？
A 回家
B 吃午餐
C 清潔地毯
D 離開大樓

PART 4 P. 140-143 36

71–73 telephone message

M： Hello, this is Sam Booth calling from Crimson Realty. (71) **This message is for Jordan King. I'm happy to say that someone is interested in making an offer on your house.** (72) **I would like to stop by with the potential buyer this Thursday to discuss the sale in more detail.** Please let me know what time on Thursday you're available and I'll arrange a time with the potential buyer. (73) **In the meantime, I suggest you clean up the house so it looks as impressive as possible for Thursday.** Thank you.

71–73 電話留言

男： 哈囉，我是克里門森房地產的山姆．伯斯。(71) **我是要留言給喬登．金。我很高興告訴您，有人有意對您的房子出價。**(72) **我這星期四想帶潛在買家過去，討論出售的詳細事宜。**請告訴我您星期四何時有空，我會與潛在買家安排時間。(73) **同時，我建議您打掃房屋，讓它在星期四時盡量有好賣相。**謝謝您。

71. Who most likely is the speaker?
- (A) A potential buyer
- (B) A bank teller
- **(C) A real estate agent**
- (D) An architect

71. 男子最有可能是什麼人？
- (A) 潛在買家
- (B) 銀行櫃員
- **(C) 房地產仲介**
- (D) 建築師

72. Why would the speaker like to arrange a meeting?
- **(A) To discuss a sale**
- (B) To renew a contract
- (C) To draw up a budget
- (D) To introduce his coworker

72. 發話者為何想要安排會面？
- **(A) 討論買賣事宜**
- (B) 續約
- (C) 規劃預算
- (D) 介紹同事

73. What does the speaker suggest doing?
- (A) Updating a website
- (B) Accepting an offer
- **(C) Making the house neat**
- (D) Lowering a price

73. 發話者建議做什麼？
- (A) 更新網站
- (B) 接受出價
- **(C) 清理乾淨房屋**
- (D) 降低價格

74–76 news report

M：Good morning, radio listeners. This is Tim Lester with your Morning Newsflash. (74) **An hour ago there was a serious collision at the intersection of Smith Avenue and Main Street.** Traffic is extremely congested and it's almost impossible to get anywhere downtown. (75) **As a result, tonight's soccer match has been delayed by two hours to allow spectators time to make it to the stadium.** Oh, also remember, during half time there will be a hot dog eating contest. (76) **The winner will receive an airline ticket to Hawaii.**

74–76 新聞報導

男：早安，廣播聽眾們。我是提姆・雷斯特，為您帶來晨間新聞快報。(74) **一小時前，在史密斯大道和緬恩街的路口發生一場嚴重車禍。**交通嚴重壅塞，在市區幾乎無法動彈。(75) **因此，今晚的足球賽將延後兩小時，讓觀眾有時間到達體育場。**喔，對了，也請記得，中場時間會有熱狗大胃王比賽。(76) **贏家將得到一張飛往夏威夷的機票。**

74. What is the news report mainly about?
- (A) A weather forecast
- (B) A road construction project
- **(C) A traffic accident**
- (D) A cooking contest

74. 新聞報導主要與什麼有關？
- (A) 天氣預報
- (B) 道路修建工程
- **(C) 交通意外**
- (D) 烹飪比賽

75. What event has been delayed?
- **(A) A sports game**
- (B) A live concert
- (C) An opening ceremony
- (D) An orientation

75. 什麼活動受到耽擱？
- **(A) 運動比賽**
- (B) 現場演唱會
- (C) 開幕典禮
- (D) 新進人員訓練

76. What will the winner of the eating contest receive?

A A concert ticket

B A gift certificate

C A cash prize

D A plane ticket

77–79 announcement

W：(77) **Welcome, spectators. Please listen to a short announcement before the match begins.** (78) **As of today, you are no longer allowed to bring food and drinks from outside into the stadium. Please adhere to this new regulation.** However, there are concession stands selling a variety of delicious snacks and beverages at reasonable prices. (79) **In addition, 5% of the proceeds made from concession stands will be donated to a charity that helps children with disabilities.** Thank you.

77. Where is the announcement being made?

A At a campground

B At a movie theater

C At a concert hall

D At a sports stadium

78. What is being announced?

A A new restriction

B Operating hours

C Price changes

D A discount policy

79. What is said about some of the proceeds?

A They will be used for a worthy cause.

B They will be put toward updating facilities.

C They will be saved for a special event.

D They will be awarded to some spectators.

76. 大胃王比賽的獲勝者能得到什麼？

A 一張演唱會門票

B 一張禮券

C 一筆獎金

D 一張機票

77–79 公告

女：(77) **歡迎光臨，各位觀眾。比賽開始之前，請先聽一則簡短的廣播。**(78) **今天起不能再帶外食和飲料進體育場，請遵守這項新規定。**然而，販賣部會用合理價格販售各種美味的零食和飲料。(79) **此外，販賣部收益的 5% 將會捐給幫助殘障孩童的慈善機構。**感謝您。

77. 這則公告是在哪裡發布的？

A 營地

B 電影院

C 音樂廳

D 體育場

78. 公告的內容是什麼？

A 新的限制

B 營運時間

C 價格更動

D 折扣方案

79. 提到什麼關於收益的事？

A 將用在有意義的事上

B 將用於更新設施

C 將留給特別活動使用

D 將頒發給某些觀眾

80–82 weather report

M：(80) The National Weather Service has issued a tornado warning for Allison County beginning at 4:00 p.m. and lasting until 8:00 p.m. (81) Therefore, all after-school activities in Allison County have been canceled. (82) Local residents are urged to take shelter in a basement or windowless room and wait until the tornado has passed. Please stay tuned for more updates.

80–82 氣象報導

男：**(80) 國家氣象局已對愛莉森縣發出下午四點到晚上八點的龍捲風警報，(81) 因此，所有愛莉森縣內的課後活動都已經取消。(82) 呼籲在地居民盡快前往地下室或沒有窗戶的房間避難，等候龍捲風過去。**請持續收聽更多最新報導。

80. What is the speaker discussing?

A A new curriculum
B A weather warning
C A quarterly report
D A travel advisory

81. What has been canceled?

A Television programs
B Graduation ceremonies
C Educational programs
D Fundraising events

82. What are local residents advised to do?

A Update their anti-virus software
B Wear protective gear
C Go into a safe place
D Take an alternative route

80. 發話者主要在談論什麼？

A 新課程
B 天氣警報
C 季度報告
D 旅遊忠告

81. 什麼事被取消？

A 電視節目
B 畢業典禮
C 教育課程
D 募款活動

82. 在地居民應該要做什麼？

A 更新防毒軟體
B 穿戴防護裝置
C 進入安全的地方
D 走替代路線

83–85 speech

W：Thank you, thank you so much. **(83) It's an incredible honor to be nominated as sales manager of the year.** I have enjoyed working at Optimal Telecommunications since my first day and it's a privilege to be acknowledged for doing a job that I really love. **(85) This year our branch broke all the records for cell phone contracts,** and I have to say **(84) I couldn't have done this without my talented team.** Their passion and persistence has been vital to our success. So, I'd like to say I'm going to share my bonus amongst my team members as a sign of my appreciation for their hard work.

83–85 演講

女：謝謝，很感謝各位。**(83) 被提名為年度銷售經理，令我感到非常榮耀。**從我第一天上班以來，我就很享受著在理想電信公司上班，能夠因為從事我真心熱愛的工作而獲得肯定，真是一種殊榮。**(85) 我們分店今年打破了手機合約的各項紀錄。我必須說 (84) 沒有這才華洋溢的團隊，我無法有此成就。**他們的熱情和堅持對於我們的成功至關重要。因此，我想宣布，我要將我的紅利與團隊成員分享，以表達我對他們努力工作的感激之意。

83. What is the purpose of the speech?

A To accept a nomination

B To announce a retirement

C To announce a merger

D To request funding

83. 演說的目的是什麼？

A 接受提名

B 宣布退休

C 宣布合併

D 要求資助

NEW

84. Why does the speaker say: "I couldn't have done this without my talented team"?

A She dislikes her team.

B She is asking for some extra awards.

C She wants to thank her colleagues.

D She wants to offer her services.

84. 發話者為何說「沒有這才華洋溢的團隊，我無法有此成就」？

A 她不喜歡她的團隊

B 她要求一些額外的獎賞

C 她想要感謝她的同事們

D 她想要提供服務

85. Where most likely does the speaker work?

A At a cell phone shop

B At a computer shop

C At a shoe store

D At a flower shop

85. 發話者最有可能在哪裡工作？

A 在手機店

B 在電腦店

C 在鞋店

D 在花店

86–88 talk

M： Hi, everybody. This week we will be renovating the restaurant. The work will be taking place from 8 a.m. to 11:30 a.m. for one week. (86) **Unfortunately, we will not be offering breakfast service during this period.** If anyone was planning to come in and eat, (87) **you might want to come in the evening.** I know a lot of people really love our breakfast menu, so (88) **I will be giving a 10% discount on all dinner meals until renovations are complete.**

86–88 談話

男： 嗨，大家好。本週我們餐廳將進行翻修，工程會從上午八點開始進行到 11 點半，持續一週。(86) **可惜，在此期間我們將不提供早餐。**若有人原本打算來用餐，(87) **可以選在晚上過來。**我知道許多人都很喜歡我們早餐的菜色，因此 (88) **我將會提供所有晚餐餐點九折的折扣，直到翻修工程結束。**

86. What problem does the speaker mention?

A No breakfast service

B No dinner service

C Missing extra items on the menu

D Rats in the kitchen

86. 發話者提到什麼問題？

A 沒有供應早餐

B 沒有供應晚餐

C 菜單上沒有的餐點

D 廚房裡有老鼠

NEW

87. What does the speaker imply when he says, "you might want to come in the evening"?

A He will offer free breakfast.

B The dinner menu is better.

C Don't come during the day.

D They are installing air conditioners.

87. 發話者說「可以選在晚上過來」，他暗示什麼？

A 他將會提供免費早餐

B 晚餐菜色比較好

C 白天別過來

D 他們要安裝冷氣機

88. What does the speaker say he will do?

(A) Serve breakfast at night

(B) Charge more

(C) Offer free breakfast

(D) Offer a discount

88. 發話者說他會做什麼？

(A) 在夜晚供應早餐

(B) 多收費

(C) 提供免費早餐

(D) 提供折扣

89–91 telephone message

W：(89) **Hi, Trent, this is Fiona calling from the warehouse.** The delivery just came in, and (90) **there is a lot of clothing on here we don't usually order.** I don't recall any special fashion sale coming up, and I phoned Head Office and they said there is no reason why we received them. Did you make the order? I'm going to call the supplier, but I want to check with you first in case you ordered the products. (91) **Please call me back. I need to let Head Office know what to do by 1 p.m. and it's already midday.** Thanks, Trent.

89–91 **電話留言**

女：(89) **嗨，特倫，我是倉庫的費歐娜。**貨品剛送到了，然後 (90) **有很多我們平常不會訂的衣服。**我不記得最近有什麼時尚服飾特賣會，我打電話給總公司，他們說我們不應該收到這些衣服。這是你訂的嗎？我會打電話給供貨商，但我想先與你確認，以免這些產品是你訂的。(91) **請回我電話，我需要在下午一點之前讓總公司知道該怎麼辦，而現在已經中午了。**謝謝你，特倫。

TEST 9

PART 4

36

89. Where does the speaker work?

(A) A fashion company

(B) A restaurant

(C) A factory

(D) A clinic

89. 發話者在哪裡工作？

(A) 時裝公司

(B) 餐廳

(C) 工廠

(D) 診所

90. What problem does the speaker describe?

(A) The delivery driver is lost.

(B) The delivery is late.

(C) The order is not perfect.

(D) The order has extra items.

90. 發話者描述什麼問題？

(A) 貨運司機迷路了

(B) 送貨延遲了

(C) 訂貨不完整

(D) 訂貨有多出來的品項

NEW

91. What does the woman imply when she says, "I need to let Head Office know what to do by 1 p.m., and it's already midday"?

(A) She would like a response after midday.

(B) She would like a response as soon as possible.

(C) She would like extra time off.

(D) She will call head office now.

91. 女子說「我需要在下午一點之前讓總公司知道該怎麼辦，而現在已經中午了」，她指的是什麼？

(A) 她想在中午後得到回覆

(B) 她想盡快得到回覆

(C) 她想要額外的休假

(D) 她現在要打電話給總公司

92–94 telephone message

M： Hello, is this Barry White? (94) **This is James Holden calling on behalf of the National Center for the Blind.** We noticed that you did not renew your yearly donation to our center. (93) **If you could give me a few moments of your time, I would like to share some information with you. I would appreciate the opportunity to tell you how we use the donations we receive to help the blind.** You should have received a brochure in the mail. If I could direct your attention to it while we talk, I am sure that you will see how valuable our service is.

92–94 電話留言

男：哈囉，是貝瑞 · 懷特嗎？(94) **我是詹姆斯 · 霍頓，代表國家盲人中心來電。**我們注意到您今年並未繼續捐獻給本中心。(93) **如果您可以給我一些時間，我想跟您分享一些資訊，感謝您讓我有機會訴說我們如何使用捐款以幫助盲人。**您該已經收到郵寄給你的手冊。我們談話時，請您參閱那本手冊，我相信您會了解我們的服務是多麼地有價值。

Distribution of funding in thousands of dollars for the assistance of the blind
以千元為單位，用以幫助盲人的資金分配

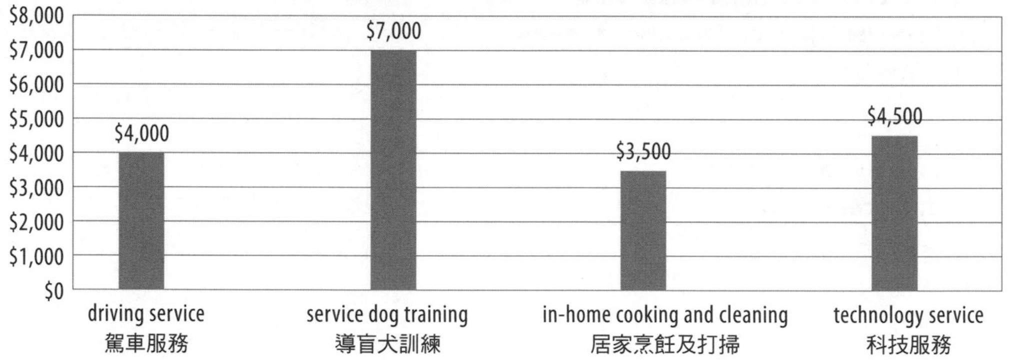

NEW

92. Look at the graphic. What is the largest expense?
A Dog training
B Technology
C Meal preparation
D Driving assistance

93. What is the listener asked to do?
A Give more money than last year
B Listen to some information
C Become a volunteer
D Become a member

94. Where does the speaker most likely work?
A A hospital
B The National Center for the Blind
C A church
D The local government

92. 參看圖表，哪一項的花費最大？
A 導盲犬訓練
B 科技
C 備餐
D 代駕

93. 聆聽者被要求做什麼？
A 比前一年捐更多錢
B 聆聽一些資訊
C 成為志工
D 成為會員

94. 發話者最有可能在哪裡工作？
A 醫院
B 國家盲人中心
C 教會
D 當地政府機構

95–97 speech

W：Hello, everyone. I would like to begin today's seminar by asking you all to consider a few questions. First, how many of you would like to be rich? Everyone? Exactly. Second, how many of you would like to be happy? Everyone? Of course! **(96) I can promise you all that if you follow a few simple steps, you will be able to make your financial and life goals a reality.** The Fast Forward Financial System, or FFFS, that I have developed, is an easy step-by-step guide to living the good life. **(97) Today's seminar is just an introduction of course. In order to fulfill your financial potential you will need to enroll in one of our immersion programs.**

95–97 演說

女：哈囉，大家好。今天研討會一開始，我想先要求大家思考幾個問題。首先，各位當中有多少人想變得富有？大家都是嗎？沒錯。第二，各位當中有多少人想要快樂？大家都是嗎？當然！**(96) 我可以向各位保證，如果你依循幾個簡單的步驟，就能夠實現你的財務和人生目標。**我所開發出來的快轉財務系統，或簡稱 FFFS，是個能使你過美好生活的簡易逐步指南。**(97) 今天的研討會當然只是基本介紹。要實現你的財務潛力，你需要報名參加我們其中一門深入課程。**

FFFS Seminar Schedule and Price Guide
研討會時間表及價格指南

Orlando 奧蘭多	"3 Weeks to Riches!" 三週致富！	3 weeks（週）	$1,500
New York 紐約	"The Big Apple is Yours" 大蘋果屬於你	5 days（天）	$750
Boston 波士頓	"Revolutionary Wealth" 革命性的財富	13 days（天）	$1,200
Seattle 西雅圖	"Prepare for Your Rainy Day" 未雨綢繆	20 days（天）	$3,000

NEW

95. Look at the graphic. Where will the longest course take place?

A Orlando
B Boston
C New York
D Seattle

95. 參看圖表，哪裡的課程時間最長？

A 奧蘭多
B 波士頓
C 紐約
D 西雅圖

96. Who most likely are the people attending the seminar?

A Wealthy people
B People who wants to get rich
C Those who are bored
D Those invited by friends

96. 最有可能是什麼人參加研討會？

A 富有的人
B 想變得富有的人
C 感到無聊的人
D 受朋友邀約的人

97. What is the speaker trying to do?

A Sell real estate
B Sell seminar packages
C Sell vacations
D Sell small businesses

97. 發話者試著要做什麼？

A 賣房地產
B 賣研討會套裝課程
C 賣假期
D 賣小型企業

98–100 excerpt from a meeting

W：Thank you all for coming to this meeting on such short notice. (100) **It has come to my attention that the human resource department has been overwhelmed lately with reports about messes in the common areas.** (98) **As your regional manager**, I feel it is my responsibility to take ownership of this problem before it gets completely out of control. Just so everybody is clear, the common areas include the kitchen, the foyer, recreation room A, and lounge C on the second floor. I don't know who is responsible for this recent run of uncleanliness, but from now on we are going to assign a staff member to monitor the condition of each area and sign off on it at the end of every day. We will do this until I feel everyone has learned to respect the space. Be sure to check the schedule to see which area you will be responsible for.

98–100 會議摘錄

女：感謝大家一接到臨時通知就來參加這場會議。(100) **我注意到人資部門最近收到大量有關公共區域髒亂的報告，**(98) **身為各位的區域經理，**我覺得我有責任在這個問題完全失控之前加以處理。為了讓大家都清楚，我要說明：公共區域包含廚房、門廳、休閒室 A，以及二樓的休息室 C。我不知道誰要為最近的髒亂負責，但從現在起，我們將指派員工來監看每個區域的狀況，並且在每天下班時簽名。我們會持續這麼做，直到我覺得大家都已經學會重視這個空間。請務必確認時程表，以了解你將負責的區域。

Common Area Cleanliness Checklist 公共區域清潔檢核表

Area 區域	Monday 星期一	Tuesday 星期二	Wednesday 星期三	Thursday 星期四	Friday 星期五
Kitchen 廚房	Scott W 史考特 ・W	Scott W 史考特 ・W	Scott W 史考特 ・W	Bill T 比爾 ・T	Bill T 比爾 ・T
Foyer 門廳	Bill T 比爾 ・T	Bill T 比爾 ・T	Hillary P 希拉蕊 ・P	Hillary P 希拉蕊 ・P	Hillary P 希拉蕊 ・P
Rec. A 休閒室 A	Lawrence P. 勞倫斯 ・P	Lawrence P. 勞倫斯 ・P	Lawrence P. 勞倫斯 ・P	Hillary P 希拉蕊 ・P	Scott W 希拉蕊 ・P
Lounge C 休息室 C	Hillary P 希拉蕊 ・P	Hillary P 希拉蕊 ・P	Bill T 比爾 ・T	Scott W 考特 ・W	Lawrence P. 勞倫斯 ・P

98. Who is speaking to the staff?

A Human Resources

B The regional manager

C The CEO

D The sales manager

NEW

99. Look at the graphic. Which employee was given responsibility for two common areas on the same day?

A Lawrence P.

B Hillary P.

C Scott W.

D Bill T.

98. 誰在對員工說話？

A 人資部門

B 區域經理

C 總裁

D 銷售經理

99. 參看圖表，哪位員工在同一天被指派要負責兩個共同區域？

A 勞倫斯 ・P

B 希拉蕊 ・P

C 史考特 ・W

D 比爾 ・T

100. What is indicated in the meeting?

A The staff will get reprimanded.

B The staff will need to work weekends.

C Everyone will get a holiday bonus.

D There have been a lot of complaints.

100. 會議中指出什麼？

A 員工將遭到責罵

B 員工將需要週末上班

C 員工將獲得假日津貼

D 近來有許多投訴

TEST 9

PART 4

36

ACTUAL TEST ⑩

PART 1 P. 144-147

1. A The woman is looking at the computer.
   B The woman is typing on the computer.
   C The woman is taking a phone call.
   D The woman is talking on the cell phone.

2. A He is looking at the laptop computer.
   B They are having a discussion in a meeting room.
   C They are all looking in the same direction.
   D She is writing in her notepad.

3. A He is selling the bread.
   B The bread is in the oven.
   C He is holding bread using a bread paddle.
   D He is wearing safety gloves.

4. **A She is walking her dog at the sea shore.**
   B She is collecting sea shells at the shore.
   C The dog is walking behind the girl.
   D She is swimming in the water.

5. A The man is wearing safety gloves.
   B The man is using the remote control to move the pipe.
   C There are many people in the factory.
   D The man is moving the pipe with his hands.

6. A The lady is looking away from the man.
   B The man is touching the bench with his left hand.
   C They are both holding the flower.
   D The man is sitting with his legs crossed.

1. A 女子正在看著電腦。
   B 女子正在用電腦打字。
   C 女子正在講電話。
   D 女子正在講手機。

2. A 他正看著筆記型電腦。
   B 他們正在會議室進行討論。
   C 他們全都看著相同的方向。
   D 她正在記事本上寫字。

3. A 他正在賣麵包。
   B 麵包在烤箱裡。
   C 他正用麵包木鏟拿麵包。
   D 他戴著安全手套。

4. **A 她正在海邊遛狗。**
   B 她正在海邊收集貝殼。
   C 狗走在女子後面。
   D 她正在水中游泳。

5. A 男子戴著安全手套。
   B 男子使用遙控器來移動水管。
   C 工廠裡有許多人。
   D 男子用手移動水管。

6. A 女子轉頭不看男子。
   B 男子用左手觸碰長椅。
   C 他們兩人都拿著花。
   D 男子雙腿交叉而坐。

PART 2 P. 148

7. You've been to Japan before, haven't you?
   A After 3:30 p.m.
   B I prefer Japanese food.
   C No, never.

8. Where's the light switch?
   A We switched suppliers.
   B On the back wall.
   C It's too heavy.

7. 你以前曾去過日本，是嗎？
   A 下午三點半後。
   B 我偏好日式料理。
   C 不，不曾。

8. 電燈開關在哪裡？
   A 我們換了供應商。
   B 在後面的牆上。
   C 它太重了。

9. Would you like to return this item?
A Yes, it doesn't fit.
B A medium size, I think.
C No, he left already.

10. How late did you work last night?
A Past midnight.
B Three times, I guess.
C Don't be late again.

11. Why isn't the heater on?
A A cold winter day.
B It broke this morning.
C Yes, it's on.

12. What's the name of the company?
A A new CEO has been named.
B Submit an application.
C It's at the top of the page.

13. Are you picking up the client today or tomorrow?
A She works in China.
B A taxi driver.
C This afternoon.

14. Who should I assign this task to?
A Someone in marketing.
B I'll finish it by Tuesday.
C Please sign here.

15. You are planning to attend the concert on Wednesday, aren't you?
A No, something urgent came up.
B He tends to speak indirectly.
C Yes, it was very good.

16. Isn't Mr. Moore married?
A It's after the wedding.
B No, it wasn't.
C Yes, since last year.

17. Can I help you carry that?
A That would be appreciated.
B The box is full of paper.
C I couldn't find an empty seat.

9. 你要退這件商品嗎？
A 是的，它不合身。
B 我猜想尺寸是中號。
C 不，他已經離開了。

10. 你昨晚工作到多晚？
A 午夜之後。
B 我想是三次。
C 別再遲到了。

11. 為何沒開暖氣？
A 冬季寒冷的一天。
B 它今天早上壞掉了。
C 是的，它開著。

12. 這家公司叫什麼名字？
A 已選定新的總裁。
B 繳交一份申請書。
C 名字在頁面的頂端。

13. 你是今天還是明天要去接客戶？
A 她在中國工作。
B 計程車司機。
C 今天下午。

14. 我該把這項工作指派給誰？
A 行銷部門的人。
B 我星期二之前會完成。
C 請在這裡簽名。

15. 你打算參加星期三的音樂會，不是嗎？
A 不，有緊急的事情發生了。
B 他傾向拐彎抹角的說話。
C 是的，演出很精采。

16. 摩爾先生不是已婚了嗎？
A 那是在婚禮之後。
B 不，它不是。
C 是的，去年結婚的。

17. 我可以幫你提嗎？
A 太感謝了。
B 箱子裡裝滿紙張。
C 我找不到空的座位。

18. When is the payment due?
A You may use a credit card.
B Before March 3.
C Yes, I do.

19. Which pattern do you like best?
A Let's choose the best idea.
B I think the striped shirt is nice.
C The store closes soon.

20. Do you want to take the bus or drive to the mall?
A The price of gas.
B Just look at a map.
C I prefer public transportation.

21. How many new computers were purchased?
A One for each employee.
B It's an email attachment.
C For the business conference.

22. I can't find the file on that client.
A That's fine with me.
B Look in this file cabinet.
C Before the end of the day.

23. Why don't we rent bicycles?
A Because Jake wants to.
B Yes, just like the directions said.
C That sounds fun.

24. Don't you live in the same neighborhood as Jim?
A No, I don't leave until 6:00 p.m.
B Yes, very close, in fact.
C It's different from this new product.

25. Where's the nearest gas station?
A It's toxic gas.
B He is at the car show.
C Just around the corner.

26. Why is nobody at the park today?
A I forgot the picnic basket.
B It is expected to rain.
C No, he changed his mind.

27. Has your daughter decided on a wedding date?
A No, that sounds too luxurious.
B Yes, the last weekend in August.
C She likes the white dress.

18. 付款截止日為何？
A 你可以使用信用卡。
B 三月三日之前。
C 是的，我要。

19. 你最喜歡哪個樣式？
A 我們選出最好的點子吧。
B 我覺得這件條紋襯衫不錯。
C 這家店很快就要關門。

20. 你想要搭公車或是開車到購物中心？
A 油價。
B 看地圖。
C 我偏好大眾運輸。

21. 買了幾台新電腦？
A 每位員工一台。
B 它是電子郵件附件。
C 供商務會議使用。

22. 我找不到那名客戶的檔案。
A 我覺得可接受。
B 在這個檔案櫃裡看看。
C 在今天結束前。

23. 我們何不租用腳踏車？
A 因為傑克想要。
B 是的，就像指示所說的。
C 聽起來很有趣。

24. 你不是和吉姆住在同一區嗎？
A 不，我下午六點才會離開。
B 是的，其實很接近。
C 它與這個新產品不同。

25. 最近的加油站在哪裡？
A 這是有毒氣體。
B 他在車展。
C 就在街角處。

26. 今天公園裡為什麼沒有人？
A 我忘了野餐籃。
B 預計會下雨。
C 不，他改變主意了。

27. 你女兒決定好婚禮日期了嗎？
A 不，那聽起來太奢華了。
B 是的，八月的最後一個週末。
C 她喜歡這件白色婚紗。

28. Should I park on the street or in the garage?
A Wherever there is space.
B You left your keys on the counter.
C They started from a garage band.

29. We are going to open a second location next month.
A Your business is going well.
B I often visit my cousins.
C No, it was on the third floor.

30. Why don't you ask for a few days off from work?
A I guess I'll have to do that.
B Yes, I'll turn it on.
C He received a promotion.

31. Who's most qualified for this position?
A Complete the form online.
B Actually, I'll have to review their résumés.
C They filed an official complaint.

28. 我該把車停在街道上還是室內停車場中？
A 有空位的地方都可以。
B 你把鑰匙遺留在櫃台了。
C 他們是從車庫樂團起家的。

29. 我們下個月即將開第二家店。
A 你們的生意很好。
B 我經常拜訪我的表親們。
C 不，它在三樓。

30. 你何不請幾天假？
A 我想我得那麼做。
B 是的，我會開啟它。
C 他獲得升遷。

31. 誰最符合這個職務的資格？
A 上網完成表格。
B 其實，我得檢視他們的履歷表。
C 他們提出正式的客訴。

PART 3 P. 149-153

39

32–34 conversation

M：Hello. Are you Ms. Joyce? (32) **I just started working here today and I was told to shadow you.** Is it OK if I follow you around and watch how you do things?

W：Nice to meet you. Of course you can shadow me today. And if you ever have any questions, don't hesitate to ask. (33) **I was just about to take inventory in the warehouse. Let's do it together.**

M：That sounds great. (34) **But before I do anything, I just need to change into my work uniform.** I'll join you in the warehouse in 10 minutes.

32–34 對話

男：哈囉。你是喬伊絲女士嗎？(32) **我今天開始上班，有人告訴我要跟著你見習。**我可以跟著你四處走動並看你做事嗎？

女：很高興見到你。當然，你今天可以跟著我見習。如果你有任何疑問，請別猶豫，儘管發問。(33) **我正要去倉庫清點存貨，我們一起去吧。**

男：聽起來很不錯。(34) **但我開始工作之前，需要換穿工作服。**我十分鐘後到倉庫與你會合。

39

32. How do the speakers know each other?
A They met through a friend.
B They take a class together.
C They live in the same apartment complex.
D They work at the same company.

32. 對話者們如何認識彼此？
A 他們透過朋友認識
B 他們共同修一門課
C 他們住在同一棟公寓大樓
D 他們在同一家公司上班

33. What does the woman suggest that the man do?
(A) Introduce himself to his coworkers
(B) Wear a work uniform
(C) Learn how to make a list of goods
(D) Have a house-warming party

34. What does the man need to do first?
(A) Change his clothes
(B) Attach a name tag
(C) Contact a warehouse supervisor
(D) Read an employee handbook

33. 女子建議男子做什麼？
(A) 向同事們自我介紹
(B) 穿工作服
(C) 學習如何列商品清單
(D) 舉辦喬遷派對

34. 男子需要先做什麼？
(A) 換衣服
(B) 掛上名牌
(C) 聯繫倉庫管理人
(D) 閱讀員工手冊

35–37 conversation

M： Hello, Tina. This is Michael Hall calling. (35) **I just left the office a minute ago and realized I forgot to email myself an important document.** It's a spreadsheet that I need for my presentation in Tokyo tomorrow. Are you still at the office?

W： Yes, I am. (36) **It's 6:00 p.m. now. I still have an hour left to leave work.** So, how can I help you?

M： Oh, great. If you turn my computer on, the spreadsheet document will be right on the desktop. If you could just email it to me, I would be so grateful.

W： No problem. Wait a moment. I'll look for the document and email it. (37) **Why don't you make sure that you receive it in about five minutes?**

35–37 對話

男： 哈囉，提娜。我是麥可 · 霍爾。(35) **我一分鐘前離開辦公室後，才想起我忘了將一份重要文件用電子郵件寄給自己。**那是我明天要在東京做簡報用的試算表，你還在辦公室嗎？

女： 是的，我在。(36) **現在是下午六點鐘。我還要一個小時才下班。**那麼，我要如何幫你？

男： 喔，太好了。如果你開啟我的電腦，會看到試算表檔案就在電腦桌面上。請你將它用電子郵件寄給我，我會很感激的。

女： 沒問題。請稍等。我會尋找那份文件並且將它用電子郵件寄給你。(37) **你要不要在五分鐘後確認是否收到了？**

35. Why is the man calling?
(A) He forgot a document password.
(B) He needs an important document.
(C) He wants to apply for a job.
(D) His computer is not working.

36. When will the woman leave work?
(A) 4:00 p.m.
(B) 5:00 p.m.
(C) 6:00 p.m.
(D) 7:00 p.m.

35. 男子為何打電話？
(A) 他忘了文件的密碼
(B) 他需要一份重要的文件
(C) 他想要應徵工作
(D) 他的電腦故障了

36. 女子將於何時下班？
(A) 下午四點
(B) 下午五點
(C) 下午六點
(D) 下午七點

37. What does the woman suggest the man do?

A Extend a warranty

B Come to work early tomorrow

C Participate in a survey

D Check his email

37. 女子建議男子做什麼？

A 延長保固期

B 明天早點來上班

C 參與一項調查

D 查看電子郵件

38–40 conversation

M：Hello. This is Chris Holt calling on behalf of the World Science Fiction Convention. (38) **We reserved the conference center at your hotel for our event this weekend.** I visited the space today and noticed that there were no tables and chairs set up.

W：The seating will be ready in time for the event. (39) **Those items are currently needed for another convention in a different section of the hotel.** By the way, exactly how many attendees are you expecting?

M：(40) **We have 248 confirmed guests.** Therefore, we will need around 50 tables with 5 chairs each. Please let me know once these preparations are done.

38–40 對話

男：哈囉。我是克里斯 · 霍爾特，代表世界科幻小說大會來電。(38) **我們為了這週末的活動預訂了貴飯店的會議中心。**我今天去看場地，注意到那裡沒有擺設桌椅。

女：座位會在活動時準備好。(39) **目前飯店別區正在進行另一場會議，需要使用那些桌椅。**對了，你們預期會有多少與會者前來？

男：(40) **我們有 248 名確認會出席的賓客。**因此我們需要大約 50 張桌子，每張桌子搭配五張椅子，請在準備就緒後立即通知我。

38. Where does the woman work?

A At a restaurant

B At a hostel

C At a movie theater

D At a hotel

39. Why are the tables and chairs currently unavailable?

A A shipment has not arrived.

B The woman didn't permit their use.

C Other people are using them.

D The storage room is locked.

40. What does the man clarify?

A The expected number of guests

B The location of stored supplies

C The starting time of an event

D The necessary documents

38. 女子在哪裡上班？

A 餐廳

B 青年旅館

C 電影院

D 飯店

39. 現在為何沒有桌椅可用？

A 貨運尚未抵達

B 女子不允許他們使用桌椅

C 其他人正在使用桌椅

D 儲藏室被鎖上

40. 男子說明什麼事？

A 預計的賓客人數

B 儲存用品的地點

C 活動開始的時間

D 必要的文件

41–43 conversation

M： Hello, Ms. Morris. It's Marvin Gibson from *New York Eats*. (41) **I'm calling because I write a weekly column for the magazine and would like to profile your restaurant this week.**

W： Wow, I'm honored. (42) **We recently added some Mexican dishes to our menu.** Why don't you come by tonight and try some? Afterwards you can interview me and the chefs about the restaurant.

M： That sounds great. (43) **However, I'd like to come during the day so that I can take some nice pictures.**

W： All right, then. How about this Friday?

41–43 對話

男：哈囉，莫莉絲女士。我是《紐約美食》的馬文 ・ 吉普森。(41) **我打這通電話是因為我為這本雜誌寫每週專欄，而這個星期我想介紹貴餐廳。**

女：哇，我很榮幸。(42) **我們的菜單最近新增一些墨西哥菜。**您何不今晚過來並試吃？然後您可以採訪我和廚師關於餐廳的事。

男：聽起來不錯。(43) **然而，我想要在白天時過去，以便拍攝不錯的照片。**

女：好的。這星期五如何？

41. What are the speakers mainly discussing?

A A new recipe
B A grand opening
C An interview
D A detailed itinerary

42. What change does the woman mention about the restaurant?

A A menu was expanded.
B An address was changed.
C A document was revised.
D An opening date was delayed.

43. What does the man suggest doing?

A Redecorating the space
B Hiring a Mexican chef
C Meeting at a different time
D Making a reservation

41. 對話者們主要在討論什麼？

A 新食譜
B 盛大開幕
C 一場訪談
D 詳細的旅遊行程

42. 關於餐廳，女子提到了什麼改變？

A 新增菜色
B 地址更動
C 文件修訂
D 開幕日延後

43. 男子建議做什麼？

A 重新裝飾場地
B 僱用墨西哥廚師
C 在另一時間會面
D 預約訂位

44–46 conversation

M： Excuse me. (44) **I bought a fish tank and some goldfish here yesterday.** (45) **However, the water filter doesn't seem to be working properly.**

W： Ah, yes. I remember you from yesterday. I'm sorry to hear that. Could you tell me more?

44–46 對話

男：不好意思。(44) **我昨天在這裡買了一個魚缸和幾條金魚，**(45) **但是濾水器似乎沒有正常運作。**

女：啊，是的，我記得您昨天有來，很遺憾聽見這件事。您可以說得更詳細嗎？

M：Well, I turned it on, but it doesn't appear to be running. I'm worried the fish won't survive without the filter functioning. I brought it for you to take a look at.

W：Hmm, you're right. It appears to be broken. I'm so sorry about that. (46) **I'll give you a new one immediately.** Wait a moment, please.

男：嗯，我開啟濾水器時，它似乎沒有運轉。我擔心濾水器故障，魚就無法生存。我有把它帶來給你看。

女：嗯，您說的對，它壞掉了，我對此感到抱歉。(46) **我馬上給您一個新的**，請稍等。

44. Where is the conversation taking place?

A At a hardware store
B At a fish market
C At a pet store
D At an animal shelter

45. What problem does the man mention?

A A piece of equipment is out of order.
B Some fish was not cooked properly.
C A personal item has been lost.
D An extra charge was added.

46. What does the woman say she will do?

A Deliver an item
B Fix a computer error
C Replace a purchase
D Offer a discount

44. 這則對話是在哪裡進行的？

A 五金行
B 魚市場
C 寵物店
D 動物收容所

45. 男子提到什麼問題？

A 設備故障
B 部分的魚肉烹調不當
C 私人物品遺失
D 增添了額外的收費

46. 女子說她會做什麼？

A 運送一件物品
B 修改電腦錯誤
C 替換貨品
D 提供折扣

TEST 10
PART 3
39

47–49 conversation

M：(47) **My guest today is Donna Fuller, a famous singer-songwriter currently touring the United States.** Her newest album just came out this week. Thanks for joining us, Donna. First, could you describe your musical style for listeners who may be unfamiliar with you?

W：Well, my style has changed a lot over the years. (48) **Originally, I wrote and performed jazz music, but this new album is in the rock genre.** I think my fans will be a little surprised, but I hope they like it.

M：What can your fans expect if they come to see you live on this new tour?

W：(49) **There will be a lot more musicians on stage than before.** So, the stage will be full of energy and excitement.

47–49 對話

男：(47) **今天的來賓是知名的創作型歌手唐娜・富勒，她現在正在美國進行巡迴演出**，她的最新專輯本週才剛發行。感謝你來上節目，唐娜。首先，你可以向還不熟悉你的聽眾描述你的音樂風格嗎？

女：嗯，我的風格在這幾年改變很多。(48) **我原本創作和演奏的是爵士樂，但這張新專輯是搖滾類型的**。我認為我的粉絲們會有些驚訝，但我希望他們會喜歡。

男：如果你的粉絲們來看你新的現場巡迴演出，他們可預期會看到什麼？

女：(49) **舞台上將會比先前增加許多的樂手**。因此，舞台會充滿活力及興奮感。

47. Who most likely is the man?
A A recording technician
B A performer
C A musician
D A radio host

48. What kind of music does the woman currently play?
A Pop
B Rock
C Folk
D Blues

49. According to the woman, what will be different about her upcoming performance?
A It will begin at midnight.
B It is free to the public.
C It will be broadcast live.
D It will include more performers.

47. 男子最有可能是什麼人？
A 錄音師
B 表演者
C 音樂家
D 廣播主持人

48. 女子現在演奏哪種類型的音樂？
A 流行樂
B 搖滾樂
C 民謠
D 藍調

49. 根據女子，她近期的演出會有何不同？
A 將從午夜開始
B 免費公開演出
C 將現場直播
D 將包含更多演出者

NEW

50–52 conversation

W1：Hi, can I speak with (50) **Thomas Hyatt? It's regarding the construction at Franklin Studios. He's the funds manager, right?**

W2：Yes. Can I ask who's calling?

W1：This is Sharon Jasmin, the studio director at Franklin's Studios. We are upgrading our studios but (51) **we're supposed to receive some funding today that didn't go through.** The builders have stopped construction until I can guarantee payment.

W2：OK, I'll put you through to Mr. Hyatt now. Hold, please.

M：Hello? Mrs. Jasmin?

W1：Good morning, Mr. Hyatt. Are those funds coming through today? I really want to stay on target with our project, so we need to keep construction going.

M：Definitely. I'm actually at the bank now doing all the transfers so the money should be in your account within half an hour. (52) **I'll send you a confirmation receipt via cellphone. Please message me back when you get it.**

50–52 對話

女 1：嗨，我可以找 (50) **湯瑪士 · 海亞嗎？這是關於富蘭克林工作室工程的事。他是財務經理，對嗎？**

女 2：是的，請問您是誰？

女 1：我是夏倫 · 茉莉，富蘭克林工作室的總監。我們要升級工作室，但 (51) **我們今天應該要收到的款項還沒匯入。**營建商已經停止工程，直到我確認付款。

女 2：好的，我現在為您轉接海亞先生。請稍等。

男：哈囉，茉莉女士嗎？

女 1：早安，海亞先生。資金今天會匯過來嗎？我很希望我們的計劃能朝目標前進，因此我們需要讓工程繼續進行。

男：當然。其實我正在銀行匯款，因此款項在半小時內就會進到你的帳戶。(52) **我會透過手機將確認匯款收據寄給你，你收到後請傳訊息給我。**

50. Who is Mr. Hyatt?

A Building Manager

B Funds Manager

C Accountant

D Construction worker

51. What problem does Mrs. Jasmin mention?

A The main branch is closed.

B Construction is continuing.

C She didn't receive some funds.

D The timing was incorrect.

52. What does Mr. Hyatt ask Mrs. Jasmin to do?

A Not to message him back

B Send him a message back

C Review the receipt

D Cancel the transfer

50. 海亞先生是什麼人？

A 建築經理

B 財務經理

C 會計師

D 建築工人

51. 茉莉女士提到什麼問題？

A 主要分公司關閉

B 工程持續進行

C 她沒有收到某些資金

D 時機不對

52. 海亞先生要求茉莉女士做什麼？

A 別回傳訊息給他

B 回傳訊息給他

C 檢視收據

D 取消匯款

NEW

53–55 conversation

M: Here is the restaurant space I told you about last week. I think it's perfect for a small café. There is also a patio area out the back; you can see it from here.

W: (53) **Oh yeah, that look's nice. I think this is a little small, but I like the location.**

M: It is small, but with the patio space you could probably seat 20 people.

W: (54) **I've looked at another location up the street that is about 10% cheaper than this, so it's a tough choice.**

M: I see. (55) **Well, we can negotiate on the price.** I'll just have to talk to my manager first.

W: That would be great. If you can match their rental cost, I would probably take this location because of the patio.

M: OK. Let me talk to my manager and get back to you.

53–55 對話

男： 這就是我上星期和您說過的餐廳場地，我認為這很適合小型咖啡店。後面還有露台區，您從這裡就可以看見。

女： (53) **喔，對耶，那裡看起來很不錯。我認為場地有點小，但我喜歡這個地點。**

男： 的確是小，但加上露台空間，也許可以容納 20 個人的座位。

女： (54) **我看過這條街的另一個地點，比這裡便宜一成左右。因此，很難做抉擇。**

男： 了解。(55) **價格部分可做協商**，但我得先和我們經理商量。

女： 那太好了。如果你的出租價格可以比照他們的，那麼我也許會因為露台而選這個地點。

男： 好的，讓我與經理談過後再回覆您。

53. What does the woman say about the restaurant space?

A She thinks it's too big.

B It has a good location.

C The location is not good.

D It's a bit far from her office.

53. 關於餐廳場地，女子說了什麼？

A 她認為場地太大

B 地點很好

C 地點不好

D 離她辦公室有點遠

NEW

54. Why does the woman say, "I've looked at another location up the street that is about 10% cheaper"?

A To get a lower rental price

B To buy the property

C To prepare a new contract

D To deny the request

54. 女子為何說「我看過這條街的另一個地點，比這裡便宜大約一成」？

A 為了獲得較低的出租價格

B 為了購買房地產

C 為了準備新合約

D 為了拒絕要求

55. What does the man say about the price?

A He agrees to reduce it.

B He has to ask his co-worker.

C He has to ask his manager.

D He refuses to reduce it.

55. 關於價格，男子說了什麼？

A 他同意降低價格

B 他必須詢問同事

C 他必須詢問經理

D 他拒絕降低價格

NEW

56–58 conversation

W：Hi, Matthew. (56) **Any news on our sales results for last month?**

M：I am just finishing the report now. Looks like our sales are booming in our Woodsdale stores, but the Collingwood stores aren't doing well. Usually it's the other way around.

W：Hmm. (57) **That's interesting.**

M：(58) **Maybe we need to take a trip to Collingwood and talk to the management team about why their sales changed so quickly.**

W：Yep. Let's go this afternoon.

56–58 對話

女：嗨，馬修。(56) **有任何關於我們上個月業績結果的新消息嗎？**

男：我正要完成這份報告。看起來伍茲戴爾分店似乎生意興隆，但是科林伍德分店表現不好。通常情況是正好相反的。

女：嗯。(57) **那真是耐人尋味。**

男：(58) **也許我們該去科林伍德一趟，並且與管理團隊討論為何他們業績變化如此迅速。**

女：對。我們下午就去吧。

56. What are the speakers discussing?

A Sales results of last quarter

B Sales results of last month

C Sales of the new range

D Sales for the coming month

56. 對話者們在討論什麼？

A 上一季的業績結果

B 上個月的業績結果

C 新系列產品的業績

D 下個月的業績

NEW

57. What does the woman imply when she says, "that's interesting"?

A She wants to work at the Collingwood store.

B She knows their sales are down.

C She wasn't listening to the man.

D She wants to know why sales are down.

57. 女子說「那真是耐人尋味」，她暗示什麼？

A 她想要在科林伍德分店上班

B 她知道他們的業績下滑

C 她沒在聽男子說話

D 她想要知道為何業績下滑

58. What does the man suggest they do?

A Visit Head Office

B Visit the Woodsdale store

C Visit the Collingwood store

D Visit their manager

58. 男子建議他們做什麼？

A 去總公司

B 去伍茲戴爾分店

C 去科林伍德分店

D 找他們的經理

NEW

59–61 conversation

M1：Harry, Anne, what kind of tools did you say we need?

M2：(59) **Look over there. We need a drill, and two hammers.** We don't need anything else because (60) **I'm getting all the small equipment delivered to the office today.**

W：What about paint?

M2：We don't need paint. We already have it.

M1：OK. (61) **But we do need some nails. I know you didn't order those. I saw the invoice.**

M2：Yes, you're right. Let's get what we need here and then go.

59–61 對話

男 1：哈利、安妮，你們說我們需要什麼工具？

男 2：(59) **去那裡找找，我們需要一個鑽子和兩把鐵鎚。**我們不需要其他別的東西，因為 (60) **小型工具今天會直接送到辦公室來。**

女：油漆呢？

男 2：我們不需要油漆，我們已經有了。

男 1：好的。(61) **但我們確實需要釘子，我知道你沒有訂購釘子，我有看到發票。**

男 2：是的，你說得對。我們在這裡買所需的東西，然後就走吧。

59. Where most likely are the speakers?

(A) At an office
(B) At repair shop
(C) At a hardware store
(D) At an electrical appliance store

60. What does the man mention about the delivery?

(A) He isn't getting any equipment delivered to the office.
(B) He is getting the small equipment delivered to the office.
(C) He is getting a drill delivered to the office.
(D) He is getting some documents delivered to the office.

61. What does the man say he needs?

(A) A saw
(B) Some tapes
(C) A shovel
(D) Some nails

59. 對話者們最有可能在哪裡？

(A) 辦公室
(B) 修繕店
(C) 五金行
(D) 電子用品器材行

60. 關於貨品運送，男子提到什麼？

(A) 他不要宅配任何用具到辦公室
(B) 他要宅配小型用具到辦公室
(C) 他要宅配鑽子到辦公室
(D) 他要宅配一些文件到辦公室

61. 男子說他需要什麼？

(A) 一把鋸子
(B) 一些膠帶
(C) 一把鏟子
(D) 一些釘子

62–64 conversation

M：Hi Sally, how has your day been?

W：Really great, Jim. I have been busy, but productive. (62) **How was your meeting this morning?**

M：It went better than I expected. The interior design specialist just gave us some recommendations for our office layout. We don't need to purchase anything new, just rearrange a few things.

W：Oh really? What did he say?

M：(63) **He suggested that we move the help desk and the sales desk so that they are on opposite sides of the entrance. That way if we have people waiting in line they won't be crowded.** (64) **We will just slide the sales desk to where the waiting area is now.**

W：That is a good idea, and this way when people come into the office, they can see all of our products displayed against the back wall.

M：Exactly, and then after they purchase their items they can just step out the door. Glad we are already on the same page.

W：Well, I think we should start moving the sales desk right away, don't you?

62–64 對話

男：嗨，莎莉，今天過得怎麼樣？

女：很棒，吉姆。我一直很忙但很充實。(62) **你今天早上的會議如何？**

男：比我預期的還好。室內設計專家給我們一些辦公室空間規劃的建議。我們不用購買任何新東西，只要重新安排幾件物品就行了。

女：喔，真的嗎？他說了什麼？

男：(63) **他建議我們挪動服務台及銷售櫃台，讓它們在入口處對面兩側。這樣的話如果有人排隊等候也不會擁擠。**(64) **我們只要將銷售櫃台推到現在等候區的位置。**

女：那是個好主意，這樣人們進到辦公室時，就可以看見後牆展示著我們全部的產品。

男：沒錯，然後在他們購買商品後就可以直接出門。很高興我們的意見一致。

女：我認為我們該立刻移動銷售櫃台，不是嗎？

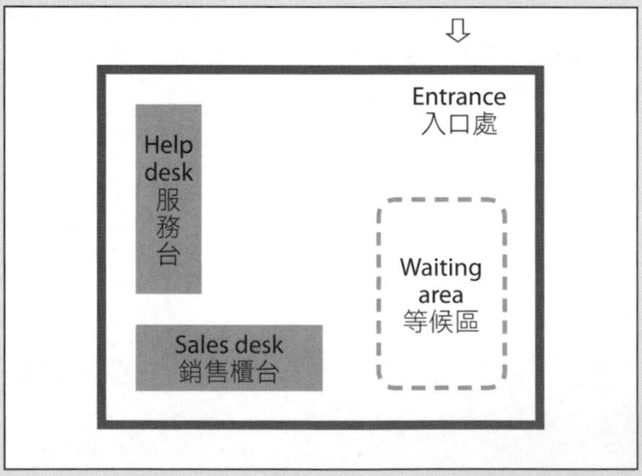

62. What did the man recently do?

(A) He met with a photographer.
(B) He met with a sales associate.
(C) He met with an interior decorator.
(D) He met with his supervisor.

62. 男子最近做了什麼？

(A) 他與攝影師會面
(B) 他與業務同事會面
(C) 他與室內裝潢師會面
(D) 他與主管會面

63. Why does the man want to move the sales desk?

Ⓐ To increase the company's sales

Ⓑ To make it look nicer

Ⓒ To make more room for the woman to work

Ⓓ To give waiting customers more space

64. Look at the graphic. Where will the sales desk be moved to?

Ⓐ Where the help desk is now

Ⓑ So it is to the right of the entrance

Ⓒ Where the waiting area is

Ⓓ They will move the help desk instead.

63. 男子為何想要搬動銷售櫃台？

Ⓐ 為了增加公司業績

Ⓑ 為了使它更為美觀

Ⓒ 為了騰出空間讓女子工作

Ⓓ 為了給等候的顧客較多空間

64. 參看圖表，銷售櫃台將會被搬動到哪裡？

Ⓐ 現在服務台的位置

Ⓑ 在入口處的右邊

Ⓒ 現在等候區的位置

Ⓓ 他們將會改為搬動服務台

NEW

65–67 conversation

M：Hi, Rosalie, did you hear about the fire drills next week?

W：Yeah. **(65) I can't believe they scheduled ours during our lunch break. (66) They need to reschedule our lunch break, or change the fire drill time to 1 to 2 p.m.** They shouldn't expect us to skip lunch and practice the fire drills.

M：I know. I don't think it is very fair. They should have had all the drills in the afternoon. The other departments actually get extra time off work, and we lose our lunch break.

W：**(67) I think we should go and speak to our supervisor.** What do you think?

M：I agree. Should we go now?

W：Yes. Let me quickly send an email and I will come with you.

65–67 對話

男：嗨，羅絲莉。你聽說下星期的消防演習了嗎？

女：是的。**(65) 我真不敢相信他們把我們的演習時段安排在午餐休息時間。(66) 他們需要重新安排我們的午休時間，或者是把消防演習時間改到下午一點到兩點。**他們不該要我們不吃午餐進行消防演習。

男：我知道，我認為這樣並不公平，他們應該要把所有演習都安排在下午。其實其他部門在下班後會有額外時間，而我們卻沒了午餐休息時間。

女：**(67) 我認為我們該去與主管討論。**你覺得呢？

男：我同意。我們要現在去嗎？

女：是的。讓我很快寄出一封電子郵件，然後我和你一起去。

Fire Drill Procedures 火警演習流程
January 21st 1 月 21 日

Level 1 一樓	8 a.m. – 9 a.m. 上午 8 點 – 上午 9 點	Human Resources Department 人力資源部門
Level 2 二樓	9 a.m. – 10 a.m. 上午 9 點 – 上午 10 點	Accounting Department 會計部門
Level 3 三樓	11 a.m.– 12 p.m. 上午 11 點 – 上午 12 點	Customer Service Department 客戶服務部門
Level 4 四樓	12 p.m. – 1 p.m. 中午 12 點 – 下午 1 點	Legal Department 法務部門

65. What did the man say about next week?
A There will be an inspection.
B Some new computers will arrive.
C They will have fire drills.
D Someone called in sick.

NEW
66. Look at the graphic. What department do the speakers work in?
A Human Resources
B Accounting
C Customer Service
D Legal

67. What does the woman suggest they do?
A Don't say anything
B Print out some extra copies
C Speak to their supervisor
D Put up a sign

65. 關於下星期，男子說了什麼？
A 將會進行檢查
B 將會送來一些新電腦
C 他們將進行消防演習
D 某人請病假

66. 參看圖表，對話者們在哪個部門工作？
A 人力資源部門
B 會計部門
C 客戶服務部門
D 法務部門

67. 女子建議他們做什麼？
A 保持沉默
B 再多印幾份
C 與主管商談
D 設立標語

NEW
68–70 conversation

M：(68) **Mark's Models, this is Greg speaking. How can I help you today?**
W：Hi Greg. I bought a snap fit Mazda Mikado plastic model kit yesterday and I'm just starting to put it together now, but some of the pieces are missing.
M：Oh, that's not good. What exactly is missing?
W：(69) **Well, it seems like all the parts are here, but I have nothing to put them together with.**
M：Ah. It must be the snap fit tool. With our older model kits that's a pretty common problem. We have a lot in the store. (70) **I'll express-post one to you today if that's OK?**
W：Oh, that's great. Thanks for your help!

68–70 對話

男：(68) **馬克模型店，我是格雷。您今天需要什麼服務呢？**
女：嗨，格雷。我昨天買了一個馬自達天皇塑膠模型扣合組。我現在正要開始組裝，但有些物件不見了。
男：喔，真糟糕。究竟是什麼不見了？
女：(69) **看起來全部零件都在，但我沒有組裝它們的工具。**
男：一定是扣合工具，我們較舊款的模型組常常出現這個問題。我們店裡還有很多，(70) **我今天用快捷郵件寄給您好嗎？**
女：喔，太好了。感謝你的幫忙！

1980 Mazda Mikado Plastic Model　1980 年馬自達天皇塑膠模型組

Part A 零件 A	- 1:25 scale plastic model kit 1:25 比例的塑膠模型組
Part B 零件 B	- Snap fit tool 扣合工具
Part C 零件 C	- Rubber tires 橡膠輪胎
Part D 零件 D	- Rub-on decals 感壓轉印貼紙

68. Where does the man most likely work?

A At a stationery shop
B At a hardware store
C At a model shop
D At a medical clinic

NEW **69.** Look at the graphic. Which part is the woman missing?

A Decals
B Model kit
C Snap fit tool
D Rubber tires

70. What does the man offer to do?

A Deliver it to her
B Give her a refund
C Cancel the order
D Express-post it to her

68. 男子最有可能在哪裡工作？

A 文具店
B 五金行
C 模型店
D 醫療診所

69. 參看圖表，女子缺少了什麼？

A 感壓轉印貼紙
B 模型組
C 扣合工具
D 橡膠輪胎

70. 男子提議要做什麼？

A 送去給她
B 退款給她
C 取消訂單
D 用快捷郵寄給她

PART 4 P. 154-157

40

71–73 telephone message

W：Hello, Ms. Jansen. It's Kate Douglas. (71) **I'm so grateful that you offered to babysit my son Michael this weekend.** As you know, something urgent came up and I have to be away on business this weekend. (72) **An important merger will take place in April, and I need to be in New York in order to lead a meeting between my company and NX Electronics.** (73) **Oh, and also, please let me know how much you expect to be compensated for babysitting.** Thanks again.

71–73 電話留言

女：哈囉，簡森女士，我是凱特・道格拉斯。(71) **我很感激你願意在這個週末當保母照顧我兒子麥克。**你知道的，由於有緊急事務，我週末必須出差。(72) **四月將有重要的合併案，我需要在紐約主持我公司與 NX 電子的會議。**(73) **喔，對了，還要請你告訴我，你當保母想要的報酬。再次感謝你。**

71. What did Ms. Jansen offer to do?

A Attend a meeting
B Go to New York
C Take care of the speaker's child
D Lend a personal item

72. What will happen in April?

A An annual conference
B A business merger
C A budget review
D A town meeting

71. 簡森女士欲提供什麼幫助？

A 出席會議
B 去紐約
C 照顧發話者的孩子
D 出借一項私人物品

72. 四月將會發生什麼事？

A 年度會議
B 企業合併
C 預算審查
D 小鎮會議

73. What will the listener most likely inform the speaker about?
A The time of arrival
B The payment
C An event location
D A weekend schedule

73. 聆聽者最有可能告知發話者什麼事？
A 抵達時間
B 薪資
C 活動場地
D 週末行程

74–76 announcement

M：Good morning, ladies and gentlemen. (74) **On behalf of the staff, I regretfully announce that Flight 344 will be slightly delayed.** The fueling process is taking longer than expected but should be completed soon. (75) **Passengers who are hungry can receive complimentary snacks and fruit juices here at the counter.** (76) **However, we will be boarding relatively shortly, so we ask that passengers not leave the boarding area.** Thank you for your cooperation.

74–76 公告

男：早安，各位先生、女士。(74) **謹代表全體員工很遺憾地宣布 344 號班機將會稍微延誤。**加油的過程比原先預期的還要久，但應該很快就會完成了。(75) **感到飢餓的乘客可以在櫃台這裡領取免費的零食以及果汁。**(76) **但是我們很快就要登機，因此請乘客不要離開登機區。**感謝各位的配合。

74. Where most likely is this announcement being made?
A In a factory
B On an airplane
C At a bus terminal
D At an airport

74. 這則公告最有可能在哪裡進行？
A 工廠裡
B 飛機上
C 公車總站
D 機場

75. What can listeners receive at the counter?
A A name tag
B A receipt
C A meal ticket
D Some refreshments

75. 聽眾可以在櫃台領取什麼？
A 名牌
B 收據
C 餐券
D 茶點

76. What are listeners asked to do?
A Form a line
B Stay nearby
C Sign a document
D Present a ticket

76. 聽眾被要求做什麼？
A 排隊
B 待在附近
C 簽署文件
D 出示票券

77–79 tour guide

M： Hello, everyone. (77) **Welcome to the guided tour of the Giant Dinosaurs exhibit.** Today you will be able to see dinosaur skeletons that were excavated by Dr. Mark Simmons while on an expedition in South Africa. (78) **Dr. Simmons is one of the most respected scientists in the field and has discovered some of the oldest and most well-known fossils in the field.** These fossils here were found in layers of sedimentary rock dated back over 65 million years ago. (79) **Because these fossils are delicate, I remind everyone that if you want to take pictures, please turn the flash off on your camera.**

77–79 導覽

男： 哈囉，大家好。(77) **歡迎來到大型恐龍展的導覽**，今天各位將能見到馬克・西蒙斯博士在南非探險時挖掘出來的恐龍骨骼。(78) **西蒙斯博士是這個領域最受推崇的科學家之一，他發現了這個領域最古老且最著名的一些化石。**這裡的化石是在超過 6500 萬年前的沉積岩層中發現的。(79) **因為這些化石很脆弱，所以我要提醒大家，如果想要拍照，請關閉相機的閃光燈。**

77. Where most likely is the speaker?

A In a museum
B In a library
C In a lecture hall
D In a gift shop

78. According to the speaker, what is Dr. Simmons famous for?

A Writing best-selling books
B Making important discoveries
C Finding ancient buildings
D Conducting groundbreaking experiments

79. What does the speaker request that listeners do?

A Purchase a day pass
B Turn off a camera
C Refrain from using a flash
D Stay with the group

77. 發話者最有可能身在何方？

A 博物館
B 圖書館
C 演講廳
D 禮品店

78. 根據發話者，西蒙斯博士以何聞名？

A 寫暢銷書
B 提出重大發現
C 找到古代建築物
D 進行開創性的實驗

79. 發話者要求聽眾做什麼？

A 購買一日通行票
B 關閉相機
C 不要使用閃光燈
D 團體行動

80–82 excerpt from a meeting

W：Before this meeting concludes, I would like to mention a new opportunity available to all employees. (80) **As a benefit of our recent merger with TechSoft Solutions, you can now expand your medical insurance to include vision and dental coverage.** (81) **You can visit our company website to calculate exactly how much this change would increase your monthly payment.** (82) **If you have never accessed our website in the past, you will first need to contact Suzie Summers in order to get your login information.** Please make sure to keep your login information private.

80–82 會議摘要

女：會議結束之前，我想要提出一項所有員工都可以利用的新機會。(80) **這是我們最近與科技軟體公司合併所帶來的好處，各位可以增加醫療保險的項目，涵蓋視力和牙齒的保險給付。**(81) **各位可以上公司網站試算這項改變究竟會增加多少你每月的保險費。**(82) **如果你過去從未登入我們的網站，你需要先聯繫蘇西・薩默斯，以獲得你的登入資訊。**請務必將你的登入資訊保密。

80. What is the speaker mainly discussing?

(A) A company picnic
(B) A job opportunity
(C) A new benefit
(D) Overseas expansion

81. According to the speaker, what can listeners do online?

(A) Find out a new payment
(B) Register for a workshop
(C) Remit a monthly payment
(D) Review a proposal

82. Why should some listeners contact Suzie Summers?

(A) To request a schedule change
(B) To obtain personal information
(C) To cancel a subscription
(D) To congratulate a co-worker

80. 發話者主要在討論什麼？

(A) 公司野餐
(B) 工作機會
(C) 新的福利
(D) 海外擴展

81. 根據發話者，聽眾可以上網做什麼？

(A) 了解新支付項目
(B) 報名研討會
(C) 匯寄每月的款項
(D) 檢視提案

82. 聽眾為何需要聯繫蘇西・薩默斯？

(A) 要求改變時程
(B) 獲得個人資訊
(C) 取消訂閱
(D) 祝賀同事

83–85 talk

W： Hi, everyone, we should get started with the monthly meeting. (83) **First of all, we have two knew interns starting next week. They are both accounting majors who specialize in auditing.** (84) **I know that you are all very busy**, but I really need you to help the interns settle in as quickly as possible. I'm going to give each of you a specific job that I want you to personally train the intern. I think it is the most efficient way to get them up to speed. I'm going to prepare a task for each of you and email it to you. When the interns arrive (85) **I want each of you to spend one full week with them and train them.** Thanks for your patience.

83–85 談話

女： 嗨，大家好，我們應該開始進行月會了。(83) **首先，我們下週將有兩位新的實習生。他們兩人都主修會計，專攻審計。**(84) **我知道你們全都很忙**，但我真的需要各位協助實習生盡快適應新環境。我將會指派你們每個人一份特定的工作，我要你們親自訓練實習生，我認為這是使他們跟上進度最有效的方式。我會為你們每個人準備一項任務，並且用電子郵件寄送給你們。實習生到的時候，(85) **我要你們每個人各花整整一週訓練實習生。**感謝你們的耐心。

83. Who most likely are the listeners?

(A) Lawyers
(B) Accountants
(C) Bankers
(D) Cashiers

NEW

84. What does the woman mean when she says, "I know that you are all very busy"?

(A) She wants to organize a meeting.
(B) She needs more printers.
(C) She is recognizing their concerns.
(D) She isn't sure what to do.

85. What task does the speaker assign to the listeners?

(A) Spend a week with the interns
(B) Not to speak to the interns
(C) Write a training manual
(D) Report on sales figures

83. 聽眾最有可能是什麼人？

(A) 律師
(B) 會計師
(C) 銀行家
(D) 收銀員

84. 女子說「我知道你們全都很忙」，她指的是什麼？

(A) 她想要籌辦一場會議
(B) 她需要更多的印表機
(C) 她了解他們的顧慮
(D) 她不確定該做什麼

85. 發話者指派什麼任務給聽者？

(A) 與實習生共度一星期
(B) 別與實習生交談
(C) 寫訓練手冊
(D) 提報銷售數據

86–88 announcement

W： As everyone knows, (86) **the line of keyboards and web cameras we produced this year are selling extremely well.** I'm not sure why, but our LCD monitors are not selling well at all. I suspect the price point might be too high when compared with other brands. Whatever the reason, we need to start selling more, (87) **so I have hired some marketing analysts that can help us try to figure out what the problem is.** (88) **I've arranged a meeting with them this afternoon after lunch, so please come to the boardroom on the 2nd floor and sit in on the meeting.**

86–88 宣布

女： 大家都知道，(86) **我們今年生產的系列鍵盤和網路攝影機賣得非常好。**我不確定為什麼，但我們的 LCD 螢幕賣得不太好。我猜想可能是零售價與其他廠牌相比太高了。不論是什麼原因，我們都需要增加銷量 (87) **因此我已經僱用了幾位能幫助我們試圖了解問題所在的市場分析師。**(88) **我已經安排今天下午午餐過後要與他們開會，因此請各位到二樓的會議室出席這場會議。**

86. What product does the speaker's company sell?

A Electronics

B Software

C Wearable technology

D Automobile

87. According to the speaker, what happened last month?

A Someone was fired.

B Some products sold well.

C The company went bankrupt.

D There was a merger.

NEW

88. What does the woman mean when she says, "sit in on the meeting"?

A She will send employees an email.

B She wants employees to prepare a report.

C She wants employees to come to the meeting.

D She will have a conference call.

86. 發話者的公司販售什麼產品？

A 電子產品

B 軟體

C 穿戴科技

D 汽車

87. 根據發話者，上個月發生了什麼事？

A 有人被解僱

B 有些產品銷售良好

C 公司破產

D 公司併購案

88. 女子說「出席這場會議」，她指的是什麼？

A 她將寄電子郵件給員工

B 她想要員工準備一份報告

C 她想要員工參加會議

D 她將進行電話會議

89–91 speech

M： Great news, everybody. Our sales are up by 12 percent compared to last year. (89) **Our new range of electric blankets and space heaters sold more than we expected. The biggest seller was our new heated pillow inserts.** (90) **Last month we signed a special contract to have our pillows used exclusively in Charleston Hotels, which means a huge boost in sales figures.** We are expecting even more contracts like this in the future. (91) **How about that? Everyone should give themselves a pat on the back. I'm really proud of your efforts.**

89–91 演說

男： 各位，有好消息，我們的業績與去年相比提高了一成。(89) **我們新系列的電毯和暖氣機賣得比預期的更好，銷售最好的是我們的加熱枕芯。**(90) **我們上個月簽署了一份特別的合約，讓查斯頓旅館獨家使用我們的枕頭，這表示業績會大幅增加。**我們預計未來會有更多像這樣的合約。(91) **很棒吧？大家應該給自己一點鼓勵。我對於你們的努力感到非常的驕傲。**

89. What product does the speaker's company sell?

A Heating products

B Air conditioners

C Vacuum cleaners

D Magazines

90. According to the speaker, what happened last month?

A They signed a special contract.

B They bought out another company.

C They traded stocks.

D Their sales went down.

NEW

91. What does the man mean when he says, "How about that?"

A He is confused about the situation.

B He is pleased with the results.

C He isn't happy.

D He wants to try to upgrade their computers.

89. 發話者的公司販售什麼商品？

A 加熱產品

B 冷氣機

C 吸塵器

D 雜誌

90. 根據發話者，上個月發生了什麼事？

A 他們簽署了特別的合約

B 他們收購另一家公司

C 他們交易股票

D 他們的業績下滑

91. 男子說「很棒吧」，他指的是什麼？

A 他對於情況感到困惑。

B 他對於成果感到很滿意

C 他不高興

D 他想要試著升級他們的電腦

92–94 advertisement

M：(92) **Springfield Dance Troupe has just added a new hip-hop workshop to our winter schedule.** We are extremely excited to be able to offer more contemporary dance routines to the members of our community! (94) **We'll be having a live performance of some of the moves that we will be teaching people to master this Saturday at 12 p.m. We would like to invite all members of the community, young and old, boys and girls, to come down to the Recreational Center and enjoy the performance.** Springfield Dance Troupe will of course be continuing to teach the courses that we have always offered, with one exception. Sally Jones, whom many of you know from her fantastic *Nutcracker* performances, will be moving back to Westport. As a result, after this week we will not be offering ballet classes until we can find a teacher to replace her. I hope to see you all at the Recreation Center this Saturday at noon!

92–94 廣告

男：(92) **春田舞團剛為我們冬季的課程表新增了嘻哈工作坊。**我們很興奮能為我們社區的居民提供更多當代舞步。(94) **我們將在本週六中午 12 點舉行現場演出，內容包含一些我們將在課程中教授的舞步。我們想邀請社區的所有居民，不論男女老少，都來休閒中心欣賞表演。**春田舞團當然會持續教授已開設的課程，只有一項除外。在《胡桃鉗》中有精彩演出並一鳴驚人的莎莉・瓊斯，將搬回威斯特波特。因此這星期後，我們就不會開芭蕾課，直到我們能找到代替她的老師。我希望本週六中午能在休閒中心看到各位！–

SPRINGFIELD DANCE TROUPE CLASS SCHEDULE 春田舞團課程表

Class 課程	Mon 星期一	Tue 星期二	Wed 星期三	Thu 星期四	Fri 星期五	Sat 星期六	Sun 星期日
Hip Hop 嘻哈	X	X	X	Tiffany 蒂芬妮 11 – 2	Tiffany 蒂芬妮 11 – 2	Owen 歐文 11 – 2	Owen 歐文 11 – 2
Swing 搖擺	Beth 貝絲 11 – 2	Beth 貝絲 11 – 2	Beth 貝絲 11 – 2	Beth 貝絲 11 – 2	Beth 貝絲 11 – 2	X	X
Jazz 爵士	Gwen 葛溫 5 – 8	X	Gwen 葛溫 5 – 8	X	X	Gwen 葛溫 5 – 8	X
Ballet 芭蕾	Sally 莎莉 1 – 4	Sally 莎莉 1 – 4	X	X	X	X	X

92. What is indicated about Springfield Dance Troupe?

(A) They are changing the music they like.
(B) They are moving to a new location.
(C) They want to find a new swing class instructor.
(D) They are changing the courses they will offer.

92. 關於春田舞團，廣告中有提到哪一點？

(A) 他們改變了音樂喜好
(B) 他們要搬到新地點
(C) 他們想找新的搖擺課老師
(D) 他們要更改提供的課程

93. Look at the graphic. What can you infer about the dance classes?
[A] They will be difficult.
[B] They are for beginners.
[C] Dance classes last for three hours.
[D] They are coed.

93. 參看圖表，關於舞蹈課程，你可以推論出什麼？
[A] 課程會很困難
[B] 課程是要給初學者的
[C] 舞蹈課要三個小時
[D] 課程是男女合班的

94. What does Springfield Dance Troupe invite the public to do?
[A] Come to their picnic
[B] See them in the concert hall downtown
[C] Watch them perform a hip-hop dance routine
[D] Say goodbye to Sally Jones

94. 春田舞團邀請大家做什麼？
[A] 參加他們的野餐
[B] 去市區的音樂廳看他們表演
[C] 觀賞他們表演嘻哈舞蹈
[D] 與莎莉 · 瓊斯道別

95–97 advertisement

W：(97) **Presidential Tailoring is committed to helping you look your best.** If you have been thinking about updating your wardrobe to include custom fit ensembles, we would like to invite you to stop by our shop on the corner of Lexington and Dupont for complimentary measurement. Our tailors have a combined 120 years of experience with men's and women's tailoring. (95) **Our master tailor, Jeffrey Frye, apprenticed in London for 15 years at the prestigious Lorde Homme Tailors before returning home here to the US.** Let us make you look presidential. You deserve it.

95–97 廣告

女：(97) **老董裁縫店致力於為您打造最出色的樣貌。**如果您在想要為衣櫥添加合身套裝，那麼我們想邀請您蒞臨我們位於列星頓和迪朋街角的店面，進行免費的套量。我們的裁縫師在男裝和女裝方面共計有 120 年的經驗，(95) **我們的裁縫大師傑佛瑞 · 弗萊在返回美國家鄉之前，曾在倫敦知名的羅德 · 霍姆裁縫店當過 15 年的學徒。**讓我們幫您看起來如董事長一般；因為您值得。

Presidential Tailoring Pricing Structure 老董裁縫店價目表
FIRST MEASUREMENTS ARE FREE 首次套量免費

Men's trousers 男士長褲	$35*
Men's jackets 男士夾克	$150*
Women's ensembles 女士套裝	$130*
Women's gowns 女士禮服	$200*

*Prices may vary by choice and volume of fabric chosen or required.
* 價格可能因為所選或所需的布料種類或數量而異動。

TEST 10
PART 4
40

95. What is indicated in the advertisement?

(A) Presidential Tailoring is just getting started in their business.

(B) Jeffrey Frye is an experienced American tailor trained overseas.

(C) Presidential Tailoring is having a big sale.

(D) They only have one tailor on staff.

NEW

96. Look at the graphic. What is true about the pricing?

(A) It can change based on the material chosen.

(B) Women's gowns are cheaper than women's ensembles.

(C) Women's ensembles cost more than men's jackets.

(D) All of the clothes are 10% off.

97. What can you infer about Presidential Tailoring?

(A) They are a discount clothier.

(B) They work with leather.

(C) Their target market is children.

(D) They take a lot of pride in their work.

95. 廣告中指出哪一點？

(A) 老董裁縫店的生意剛起步

(B) 傑佛瑞 · 弗萊是一名在海外受訓且經驗豐富的美國裁縫師

(C) 老董裁縫店正要舉辦大拍賣

(D) 他們員工中只有一名裁縫師

96. 參看圖表，關於定價，何者為真？

(A) 定價會依所選擇的質料而變動

(B) 女士禮服比女士套裝便宜

(C) 女士套裝比男士夾克還貴

(D) 所有服飾都打九折

97. 關於老董裁縫店，你可以推論什麼？

(A) 他們是折扣服裝廠商

(B) 他們用皮革製衣

(C) 他們的目標市場是孩童

(D) 他們對自家商品感到自豪

98–100 telephone message

M： Hello, Ms. Johnson, I am calling about the invoice that you sent me last week. (99) **I just have a few questions I need to ask you about the quantities and pricing of some of the supplies that I ordered.** (98) **I thought that you told me that if I ordered more than two dozen of any item that I would receive a discount of 5%.** Is this correct? Additionally, I want to just confirm the numbers with you. I ordered 36 foot stools, 12 chairs, 117 small end tables and NO large end tables. I believe there was some confusion. (100) **Can you change the invoice to reflect my requested items?**

98–100 電話留言

男： 哈囉，強森女士。我打這通電話是要談關於你上週寄給我的發票。(99) **我想請教你幾個問題，是有關部分我所訂購的用品數量和價格。**(98) **我以為你告訴我說，如果我任何品項的訂購數量超過兩打，就會得到5%的折扣**，這是正確的嗎？此外，我想要與你確認這些數字。我訂了36張腳凳、12張椅子、117張小茶几、沒有大茶几。我認為有些地方弄錯了。(100) **你可以更改符合我訂購品項的發票？**

INVOICE 發票

Item 品項	Quantity 數量	Volume discount 批量折扣
Foot Stools 腳凳	36	3%
Chairs 椅子	12	0%
Small End Tables 小茶几	117	5%
Large End Tables 大茶几	24	5%

NEW

98. Look at the graphic. Which item was incorrectly discounted?

- **A Foot stools 3%**
- B Chairs 0%
- C Small end tables 5%
- D Large end tables 5%

99. What is Ms. Johnson asked to do with the invoice?

- A Change the large end table orders to two dozen
- **B Make the invoice match the order**
- C Send the invoice to the factory for completion
- D Send the invoice to accounting

100. What does the speaker anticipate will happen next?

- A He will receive his order.
- **B He will receive a new invoice.**
- C He will have to place the order a third time.
- D He will need to use a different supplier.

98. 參看圖表，哪個數量折扣有誤？

- **A 腳凳 3%**
- B 椅子 0%
- C 小茶几 5%
- D 大茶几 5%

99. 強森女士被要求如何處理發票？

- A 將大茶几的訂單改為兩打
- **B 使發票與訂單相符**
- C 將發票寄到工廠以完成訂購物品
- D 將發票送交給會計部門

100. 發話者預期接下來會發生什麼事？

- A 他會收到訂購的物品
- **B 他會收到新的發票**
- C 他必須下第三次的訂單
- D 他會需要使用不同的供應商

TEST 10

PART 4

40

ANSWER KEY

Actual Test 01

1	(A)	26	(A)	51	(C)	76	(B)
2	(A)	27	(C)	52	(D)	77	(B)
3	(A)	28	(A)	53	(B)	78	(C)
4	(B)	29	(B)	54	(C)	79	(D)
5	(A)	30	(C)	55	(B)	80	(D)
6	(D)	31	(A)	56	(C)	81	(C)
7	(C)	32	(B)	57	(A)	82	(C)
8	(B)	33	(A)	58	(D)	83	(A)
9	(A)	34	(C)	59	(C)	84	(D)
10	(B)	35	(A)	60	(D)	85	(C)
11	(C)	36	(B)	61	(A)	86	(D)
12	(B)	37	(C)	62	(C)	87	(A)
13	(A)	38	(A)	63	(D)	88	(B)
14	(B)	39	(C)	64	(A)	89	(A)
15	(B)	40	(B)	65	(A)	90	(C)
16	(A)	41	(C)	66	(B)	91	(D)
17	(C)	42	(C)	67	(B)	92	(C)
18	(B)	43	(D)	68	(D)	93	(B)
19	(C)	44	(D)	69	(C)	94	(B)
20	(A)	45	(D)	70	(C)	95	(C)
21	(B)	46	(A)	71	(C)	96	(C)
22	(C)	47	(D)	72	(A)	97	(B)
23	(B)	48	(B)	73	(D)	98	(C)
24	(A)	49	(C)	74	(A)	99	(A)
25	(C)	50	(A)	75	(C)	100	(C)

Actual Test 02

1	(A)	26	(B)	51	(A)	76	(C)
2	(A)	27	(C)	52	(D)	77	(C)
3	(B)	28	(B)	53	(A)	78	(C)
4	(C)	29	(B)	54	(B)	79	(A)
5	(D)	30	(A)	55	(D)	80	(D)
6	(B)	31	(B)	56	(D)	81	(B)
7	(A)	32	(D)	57	(B)	82	(C)
8	(B)	33	(A)	58	(C)	83	(C)
9	(A)	34	(D)	59	(D)	84	(C)
10	(C)	35	(C)	60	(C)	85	(D)
11	(B)	36	(A)	61	(A)	86	(B)
12	(B)	37	(B)	62	(B)	87	(A)
13	(B)	38	(C)	63	(C)	88	(C)
14	(C)	39	(A)	64	(D)	89	(B)
15	(A)	40	(D)	65	(B)	90	(B)
16	(C)	41	(C)	66	(D)	91	(A)
17	(A)	42	(D)	67	(B)	92	(C)
18	(B)	43	(D)	68	(C)	93	(A)
19	(C)	44	(A)	69	(C)	94	(C)
20	(A)	45	(C)	70	(B)	95	(D)
21	(B)	46	(D)	71	(B)	96	(C)
22	(A)	47	(C)	72	(D)	97	(D)
23	(B)	48	(A)	73	(C)	98	(C)
24	(A)	49	(D)	74	(D)	99	(C)
25	(C)	50	(C)	75	(B)	100	(B)

Actual Test 03

1	(B)	26	(C)	51	(B)	76	(A)
2	(A)	27	(A)	52	(A)	77	(B)
3	(C)	28	(A)	53	(A)	78	(C)
4	(D)	29	(B)	54	(B)	79	(B)
5	(A)	30	(C)	55	(D)	80	(C)
6	(B)	31	(C)	56	(C)	81	(B)
7	(B)	32	(D)	57	(B)	82	(D)
8	(C)	33	(C)	58	(A)	83	(A)
9	(A)	34	(A)	59	(C)	84	(B)
10	(A)	35	(C)	60	(B)	85	(D)
11	(C)	36	(A)	61	(D)	86	(B)
12	(B)	37	(B)	62	(D)	87	(B)
13	(A)	38	(B)	63	(B)	88	(B)
14	(C)	39	(D)	64	(D)	89	(B)
15	(B)	40	(C)	65	(C)	90	(A)
16	(B)	41	(D)	66	(D)	91	(D)
17	(A)	42	(C)	67	(B)	92	(B)
18	(B)	43	(D)	68	(C)	93	(D)
19	(A)	44	(A)	69	(A)	94	(B)
20	(C)	45	(D)	70	(C)	95	(A)
21	(B)	46	(C)	71	(D)	96	(D)
22	(A)	47	(A)	72	(D)	97	(D)
23	(A)	48	(C)	73	(C)	98	(C)
24	(B)	49	(B)	74	(D)	99	(B)
25	(B)	50	(D)	75	(B)	100	(C)

Actual Test 04

1	(C)	26	(B)	51	(D)	76	(C)
2	(D)	27	(C)	52	(B)	77	(B)
3	(A)	28	(B)	53	(C)	78	(C)
4	(B)	29	(C)	54	(D)	79	(A)
5	(A)	30	(B)	55	(A)	80	(C)
6	(A)	31	(A)	56	(D)	81	(D)
7	(A)	32	(C)	57	(A)	82	(C)
8	(B)	33	(A)	58	(C)	83	(B)
9	(B)	34	(B)	59	(B)	84	(A)
10	(A)	35	(D)	60	(C)	85	(C)
11	(C)	36	(B)	61	(D)	86	(A)
12	(C)	37	(A)	62	(B)	87	(C)
13	(B)	38	(C)	63	(C)	88	(A)
14	(C)	39	(A)	64	(B)	89	(B)
15	(C)	40	(B)	65	(C)	90	(A)
16	(B)	41	(A)	66	(B)	91	(B)
17	(A)	42	(C)	67	(C)	92	(A)
18	(B)	43	(B)	68	(B)	93	(C)
19	(A)	44	(A)	69	(C)	94	(D)
20	(A)	45	(D)	70	(B)	95	(A)
21	(A)	46	(C)	71	(D)	96	(A)
22	(C)	47	(A)	72	(B)	97	(D)
23	(A)	48	(C)	73	(B)	98	(D)
24	(B)	49	(D)	74	(B)	99	(B)
25	(C)	50	(A)	75	(A)	100	(C)

Actual Test 05

1	(A)	26	(C)	51	(A)	76	(B)
2	(C)	27	(C)	52	(C)	77	(C)
3	(C)	28	(A)	53	(C)	78	(A)
4	(B)	29	(A)	54	(A)	79	(C)
5	(A)	30	(C)	55	(B)	80	(D)
6	(A)	31	(A)	56	(C)	81	(A)
7	(A)	32	(A)	57	(B)	82	(D)
8	(B)	33	(B)	58	(C)	83	(A)
9	(A)	34	(B)	59	(C)	84	(A)
10	(B)	35	(B)	60	(B)	85	(D)
11	(C)	36	(A)	61	(A)	86	(C)
12	(C)	37	(C)	62	(C)	87	(A)
13	(A)	38	(C)	63	(C)	88	(A)
14	(C)	39	(B)	64	(D)	89	(C)
15	(B)	40	(A)	65	(A)	90	(A)
16	(C)	41	(D)	66	(D)	91	(A)
17	(A)	42	(C)	67	(A)	92	(C)
18	(B)	43	(D)	68	(C)	93	(D)
19	(C)	44	(D)	69	(B)	94	(D)
20	(B)	45	(A)	70	(B)	95	(A)
21	(C)	46	(C)	71	(B)	96	(C)
22	(A)	47	(D)	72	(A)	97	(D)
23	(A)	48	(C)	73	(C)	98	(B)
24	(C)	49	(C)	74	(C)	99	(A)
25	(A)	50	(A)	75	(A)	100	(D)

Actual Test 06

1	(C)	26	(C)	51	(C)	76	(D)
2	(D)	27	(A)	52	(C)	77	(C)
3	(B)	28	(B)	53	(C)	78	(D)
4	(A)	29	(C)	54	(A)	79	(A)
5	(D)	30	(A)	55	(C)	80	(B)
6	(D)	31	(A)	56	(B)	81	(B)
7	(C)	32	(C)	57	(C)	82	(C)
8	(B)	33	(B)	58	(A)	83	(C)
9	(C)	34	(B)	59	(C)	84	(A)
10	(A)	35	(C)	60	(D)	85	(C)
11	(C)	36	(B)	61	(A)	86	(A)
12	(A)	37	(A)	62	(A)	87	(C)
13	(B)	38	(D)	63	(C)	88	(D)
14	(C)	39	(A)	64	(B)	89	(C)
15	(A)	40	(C)	65	(A)	90	(B)
16	(B)	41	(D)	66	(B)	91	(A)
17	(C)	42	(B)	67	(C)	92	(C)
18	(B)	43	(C)	68	(B)	93	(B)
19	(A)	44	(B)	69	(C)	94	(A)
20	(B)	45	(C)	70	(D)	95	(C)
21	(A)	46	(D)	71	(B)	96	(B)
22	(C)	47	(B)	72	(C)	97	(B)
23	(B)	48	(A)	73	(A)	98	(C)
24	(B)	49	(D)	74	(A)	99	(A)
25	(A)	50	(A)	75	(B)	100	(D)

Actual Test 07

1	(B)	26	(C)	51	(B)	76	(A)
2	(C)	27	(A)	52	(D)	77	(C)
3	(A)	28	(B)	53	(A)	78	(B)
4	(A)	29	(A)	54	(C)	79	(A)
5	(B)	30	(B)	55	(D)	80	(B)
6	(C)	31	(A)	56	(B)	81	(C)
7	(A)	32	(C)	57	(B)	82	(C)
8	(B)	33	(A)	58	(B)	83	(A)
9	(C)	34	(A)	59	(B)	84	(A)
10	(B)	35	(B)	60	(C)	85	(A)
11	(C)	36	(C)	61	(B)	86	(B)
12	(A)	37	(A)	62	(C)	87	(A)
13	(C)	38	(C)	63	(A)	88	(C)
14	(A)	39	(C)	64	(B)	89	(A)
15	(B)	40	(A)	65	(A)	90	(B)
16	(A)	41	(B)	66	(B)	91	(C)
17	(B)	42	(A)	67	(B)	92	(B)
18	(B)	43	(B)	68	(D)	93	(A)
19	(C)	44	(C)	69	(B)	94	(D)
20	(B)	45	(A)	70	(A)	95	(B)
21	(B)	46	(B)	71	(A)	96	(A)
22	(B)	47	(B)	72	(B)	97	(C)
23	(B)	48	(A)	73	(A)	98	(A)
24	(C)	49	(D)	74	(B)	99	(B)
25	(B)	50	(C)	75	(D)	100	(D)

Actual Test 08

1	(A)	26	(A)	51	(A)	76	(D)
2	(C)	27	(B)	52	(D)	77	(D)
3	(D)	28	(A)	53	(A)	78	(B)
4	(A)	29	(B)	54	(C)	79	(C)
5	(C)	30	(C)	55	(B)	80	(C)
6	(B)	31	(B)	56	(A)	81	(A)
7	(B)	32	(B)	57	(C)	82	(B)
8	(A)	33	(C)	58	(B)	83	(C)
9	(C)	34	(A)	59	(D)	84	(C)
10	(A)	35	(A)	60	(B)	85	(A)
11	(B)	36	(B)	61	(C)	86	(A)
12	(B)	37	(B)	62	(C)	87	(A)
13	(C)	38	(A)	63	(C)	88	(C)
14	(B)	39	(D)	64	(C)	89	(A)
15	(C)	40	(B)	65	(D)	90	(A)
16	(A)	41	(C)	66	(D)	91	(A)
17	(C)	42	(B)	67	(C)	92	(D)
18	(B)	43	(A)	68	(B)	93	(C)
19	(A)	44	(C)	69	(A)	94	(C)
20	(C)	45	(B)	70	(C)	95	(B)
21	(B)	46	(B)	71	(A)	96	(D)
22	(A)	47	(C)	72	(B)	97	(C)
23	(C)	48	(D)	73	(D)	98	(C)
24	(B)	49	(B)	74	(C)	99	(A)
25	(B)	50	(C)	75	(A)	100	(D)

Actual Test 09

1	(C)	26	(A)	51	(D)	76	(D)
2	(A)	27	(B)	52	(A)	77	(D)
3	(C)	28	(A)	53	(B)	78	(A)
4	(B)	29	(A)	54	(A)	79	(A)
5	(C)	30	(B)	55	(C)	80	(B)
6	(A)	31	(B)	56	(C)	81	(C)
7	(B)	32	(C)	57	(B)	82	(C)
8	(A)	33	(D)	58	(D)	83	(A)
9	(A)	34	(B)	59	(A)	84	(C)
10	(B)	35	(D)	60	(B)	85	(A)
11	(C)	36	(A)	61	(C)	86	(A)
12	(A)	37	(B)	62	(B)	87	(C)
13	(B)	38	(D)	63	(C)	88	(D)
14	(B)	39	(C)	64	(C)	89	(A)
15	(A)	40	(B)	65	(B)	90	(D)
16	(B)	41	(C)	66	(C)	91	(B)
17	(A)	42	(C)	67	(D)	92	(A)
18	(C)	43	(C)	68	(A)	93	(B)
19	(B)	44	(A)	69	(C)	94	(B)
20	(B)	45	(D)	70	(C)	95	(A)
21	(A)	46	(B)	71	(C)	96	(B)
22	(A)	47	(D)	72	(A)	97	(B)
23	(A)	48	(C)	73	(C)	98	(B)
24	(C)	49	(A)	74	(C)	99	(B)
25	(A)	50	(C)	75	(A)	100	(D)

Actual Test 10

1	(C)	26	(B)	51	(C)	76	(B)
2	(B)	27	(B)	52	(B)	77	(A)
3	(C)	28	(A)	53	(B)	78	(B)
4	(A)	29	(A)	54	(A)	79	(C)
5	(B)	30	(A)	55	(C)	80	(C)
6	(C)	31	(B)	56	(B)	81	(A)
7	(C)	32	(D)	57	(D)	82	(B)
8	(B)	33	(C)	58	(C)	83	(B)
9	(A)	34	(A)	59	(C)	84	(C)
10	(A)	35	(B)	60	(B)	85	(A)
11	(B)	36	(D)	61	(D)	86	(A)
12	(C)	37	(D)	62	(C)	87	(B)
13	(C)	38	(D)	63	(D)	88	(C)
14	(A)	39	(C)	64	(C)	89	(A)
15	(A)	40	(A)	65	(C)	90	(A)
16	(C)	41	(C)	66	(D)	91	(B)
17	(A)	42	(A)	67	(C)	92	(D)
18	(B)	43	(C)	68	(C)	93	(C)
19	(B)	44	(C)	69	(C)	94	(C)
20	(C)	45	(A)	70	(D)	95	(B)
21	(A)	46	(C)	71	(C)	96	(A)
22	(B)	47	(D)	72	(B)	97	(D)
23	(C)	48	(B)	73	(B)	98	(A)
24	(B)	49	(D)	74	(D)	99	(B)
25	(C)	50	(B)	75	(D)	100	(B)

答案紙

ACTUAL TEST 01

LISTENING SECTION	1	Ⓐ Ⓑ Ⓒ Ⓓ	11	Ⓐ Ⓑ Ⓒ Ⓓ	21	Ⓐ Ⓑ Ⓒ Ⓓ	31	Ⓐ Ⓑ Ⓒ Ⓓ	41	Ⓐ Ⓑ Ⓒ Ⓓ	51	Ⓐ Ⓑ Ⓒ Ⓓ	61	Ⓐ Ⓑ Ⓒ Ⓓ	71	Ⓐ Ⓑ Ⓒ Ⓓ	81	Ⓐ Ⓑ Ⓒ Ⓓ	91	Ⓐ Ⓑ Ⓒ Ⓓ
	2	Ⓐ Ⓑ Ⓒ Ⓓ	12	Ⓐ Ⓑ Ⓒ Ⓓ	22	Ⓐ Ⓑ Ⓒ Ⓓ	32	Ⓐ Ⓑ Ⓒ Ⓓ	42	Ⓐ Ⓑ Ⓒ Ⓓ	52	Ⓐ Ⓑ Ⓒ Ⓓ	62	Ⓐ Ⓑ Ⓒ Ⓓ	72	Ⓐ Ⓑ Ⓒ Ⓓ	82	Ⓐ Ⓑ Ⓒ Ⓓ	92	Ⓐ Ⓑ Ⓒ Ⓓ
	3	Ⓐ Ⓑ Ⓒ Ⓓ	13	Ⓐ Ⓑ Ⓒ Ⓓ	23	Ⓐ Ⓑ Ⓒ Ⓓ	33	Ⓐ Ⓑ Ⓒ Ⓓ	43	Ⓐ Ⓑ Ⓒ Ⓓ	53	Ⓐ Ⓑ Ⓒ Ⓓ	63	Ⓐ Ⓑ Ⓒ Ⓓ	73	Ⓐ Ⓑ Ⓒ Ⓓ	83	Ⓐ Ⓑ Ⓒ Ⓓ	93	Ⓐ Ⓑ Ⓒ Ⓓ
	4	Ⓐ Ⓑ Ⓒ Ⓓ	14	Ⓐ Ⓑ Ⓒ Ⓓ	24	Ⓐ Ⓑ Ⓒ Ⓓ	34	Ⓐ Ⓑ Ⓒ Ⓓ	44	Ⓐ Ⓑ Ⓒ Ⓓ	54	Ⓐ Ⓑ Ⓒ Ⓓ	64	Ⓐ Ⓑ Ⓒ Ⓓ	74	Ⓐ Ⓑ Ⓒ Ⓓ	84	Ⓐ Ⓑ Ⓒ Ⓓ	94	Ⓐ Ⓑ Ⓒ Ⓓ
	5	Ⓐ Ⓑ Ⓒ Ⓓ	15	Ⓐ Ⓑ Ⓒ Ⓓ	25	Ⓐ Ⓑ Ⓒ Ⓓ	35	Ⓐ Ⓑ Ⓒ Ⓓ	45	Ⓐ Ⓑ Ⓒ Ⓓ	55	Ⓐ Ⓑ Ⓒ Ⓓ	65	Ⓐ Ⓑ Ⓒ Ⓓ	75	Ⓐ Ⓑ Ⓒ Ⓓ	85	Ⓐ Ⓑ Ⓒ Ⓓ	95	Ⓐ Ⓑ Ⓒ Ⓓ
	6	Ⓐ Ⓑ Ⓒ Ⓓ	16	Ⓐ Ⓑ Ⓒ Ⓓ	26	Ⓐ Ⓑ Ⓒ Ⓓ	36	Ⓐ Ⓑ Ⓒ Ⓓ	46	Ⓐ Ⓑ Ⓒ Ⓓ	56	Ⓐ Ⓑ Ⓒ Ⓓ	66	Ⓐ Ⓑ Ⓒ Ⓓ	76	Ⓐ Ⓑ Ⓒ Ⓓ	86	Ⓐ Ⓑ Ⓒ Ⓓ	96	Ⓐ Ⓑ Ⓒ Ⓓ
	7	Ⓐ Ⓑ Ⓒ Ⓓ	17	Ⓐ Ⓑ Ⓒ Ⓓ	27	Ⓐ Ⓑ Ⓒ Ⓓ	37	Ⓐ Ⓑ Ⓒ Ⓓ	47	Ⓐ Ⓑ Ⓒ Ⓓ	57	Ⓐ Ⓑ Ⓒ Ⓓ	67	Ⓐ Ⓑ Ⓒ Ⓓ	77	Ⓐ Ⓑ Ⓒ Ⓓ	87	Ⓐ Ⓑ Ⓒ Ⓓ	97	Ⓐ Ⓑ Ⓒ Ⓓ
	8	Ⓐ Ⓑ Ⓒ Ⓓ	18	Ⓐ Ⓑ Ⓒ Ⓓ	28	Ⓐ Ⓑ Ⓒ Ⓓ	38	Ⓐ Ⓑ Ⓒ Ⓓ	48	Ⓐ Ⓑ Ⓒ Ⓓ	58	Ⓐ Ⓑ Ⓒ Ⓓ	68	Ⓐ Ⓑ Ⓒ Ⓓ	78	Ⓐ Ⓑ Ⓒ Ⓓ	88	Ⓐ Ⓑ Ⓒ Ⓓ	98	Ⓐ Ⓑ Ⓒ Ⓓ
	9	Ⓐ Ⓑ Ⓒ Ⓓ	19	Ⓐ Ⓑ Ⓒ Ⓓ	29	Ⓐ Ⓑ Ⓒ Ⓓ	39	Ⓐ Ⓑ Ⓒ Ⓓ	49	Ⓐ Ⓑ Ⓒ Ⓓ	59	Ⓐ Ⓑ Ⓒ Ⓓ	69	Ⓐ Ⓑ Ⓒ Ⓓ	79	Ⓐ Ⓑ Ⓒ Ⓓ	89	Ⓐ Ⓑ Ⓒ Ⓓ	99	Ⓐ Ⓑ Ⓒ Ⓓ
	10	Ⓐ Ⓑ Ⓒ Ⓓ	20	Ⓐ Ⓑ Ⓒ Ⓓ	30	Ⓐ Ⓑ Ⓒ Ⓓ	40	Ⓐ Ⓑ Ⓒ Ⓓ	50	Ⓐ Ⓑ Ⓒ Ⓓ	60	Ⓐ Ⓑ Ⓒ Ⓓ	70	Ⓐ Ⓑ Ⓒ Ⓓ	80	Ⓐ Ⓑ Ⓒ Ⓓ	90	Ⓐ Ⓑ Ⓒ Ⓓ	100	Ⓐ Ⓑ Ⓒ Ⓓ

ACTUAL TEST 02

LISTENING SECTION	1	Ⓐ Ⓑ Ⓒ Ⓓ	11	Ⓐ Ⓑ Ⓒ Ⓓ	21	Ⓐ Ⓑ Ⓒ Ⓓ	31	Ⓐ Ⓑ Ⓒ Ⓓ	41	Ⓐ Ⓑ Ⓒ Ⓓ	51	Ⓐ Ⓑ Ⓒ Ⓓ	61	Ⓐ Ⓑ Ⓒ Ⓓ	71	Ⓐ Ⓑ Ⓒ Ⓓ	81	Ⓐ Ⓑ Ⓒ Ⓓ	91	Ⓐ Ⓑ Ⓒ Ⓓ
	2	Ⓐ Ⓑ Ⓒ Ⓓ	12	Ⓐ Ⓑ Ⓒ Ⓓ	22	Ⓐ Ⓑ Ⓒ Ⓓ	32	Ⓐ Ⓑ Ⓒ Ⓓ	42	Ⓐ Ⓑ Ⓒ Ⓓ	52	Ⓐ Ⓑ Ⓒ Ⓓ	62	Ⓐ Ⓑ Ⓒ Ⓓ	72	Ⓐ Ⓑ Ⓒ Ⓓ	82	Ⓐ Ⓑ Ⓒ Ⓓ	92	Ⓐ Ⓑ Ⓒ Ⓓ
	3	Ⓐ Ⓑ Ⓒ Ⓓ	13	Ⓐ Ⓑ Ⓒ Ⓓ	23	Ⓐ Ⓑ Ⓒ Ⓓ	33	Ⓐ Ⓑ Ⓒ Ⓓ	43	Ⓐ Ⓑ Ⓒ Ⓓ	53	Ⓐ Ⓑ Ⓒ Ⓓ	63	Ⓐ Ⓑ Ⓒ Ⓓ	73	Ⓐ Ⓑ Ⓒ Ⓓ	83	Ⓐ Ⓑ Ⓒ Ⓓ	93	Ⓐ Ⓑ Ⓒ Ⓓ
	4	Ⓐ Ⓑ Ⓒ Ⓓ	14	Ⓐ Ⓑ Ⓒ Ⓓ	24	Ⓐ Ⓑ Ⓒ Ⓓ	34	Ⓐ Ⓑ Ⓒ Ⓓ	44	Ⓐ Ⓑ Ⓒ Ⓓ	54	Ⓐ Ⓑ Ⓒ Ⓓ	64	Ⓐ Ⓑ Ⓒ Ⓓ	74	Ⓐ Ⓑ Ⓒ Ⓓ	84	Ⓐ Ⓑ Ⓒ Ⓓ	94	Ⓐ Ⓑ Ⓒ Ⓓ
	5	Ⓐ Ⓑ Ⓒ Ⓓ	15	Ⓐ Ⓑ Ⓒ Ⓓ	25	Ⓐ Ⓑ Ⓒ Ⓓ	35	Ⓐ Ⓑ Ⓒ Ⓓ	45	Ⓐ Ⓑ Ⓒ Ⓓ	55	Ⓐ Ⓑ Ⓒ Ⓓ	65	Ⓐ Ⓑ Ⓒ Ⓓ	75	Ⓐ Ⓑ Ⓒ Ⓓ	85	Ⓐ Ⓑ Ⓒ Ⓓ	95	Ⓐ Ⓑ Ⓒ Ⓓ
	6	Ⓐ Ⓑ Ⓒ Ⓓ	16	Ⓐ Ⓑ Ⓒ Ⓓ	26	Ⓐ Ⓑ Ⓒ Ⓓ	36	Ⓐ Ⓑ Ⓒ Ⓓ	46	Ⓐ Ⓑ Ⓒ Ⓓ	56	Ⓐ Ⓑ Ⓒ Ⓓ	66	Ⓐ Ⓑ Ⓒ Ⓓ	76	Ⓐ Ⓑ Ⓒ Ⓓ	86	Ⓐ Ⓑ Ⓒ Ⓓ	96	Ⓐ Ⓑ Ⓒ Ⓓ
	7	Ⓐ Ⓑ Ⓒ Ⓓ	17	Ⓐ Ⓑ Ⓒ Ⓓ	27	Ⓐ Ⓑ Ⓒ Ⓓ	37	Ⓐ Ⓑ Ⓒ Ⓓ	47	Ⓐ Ⓑ Ⓒ Ⓓ	57	Ⓐ Ⓑ Ⓒ Ⓓ	67	Ⓐ Ⓑ Ⓒ Ⓓ	77	Ⓐ Ⓑ Ⓒ Ⓓ	87	Ⓐ Ⓑ Ⓒ Ⓓ	97	Ⓐ Ⓑ Ⓒ Ⓓ
	8	Ⓐ Ⓑ Ⓒ Ⓓ	18	Ⓐ Ⓑ Ⓒ Ⓓ	28	Ⓐ Ⓑ Ⓒ Ⓓ	38	Ⓐ Ⓑ Ⓒ Ⓓ	48	Ⓐ Ⓑ Ⓒ Ⓓ	58	Ⓐ Ⓑ Ⓒ Ⓓ	68	Ⓐ Ⓑ Ⓒ Ⓓ	78	Ⓐ Ⓑ Ⓒ Ⓓ	88	Ⓐ Ⓑ Ⓒ Ⓓ	98	Ⓐ Ⓑ Ⓒ Ⓓ
	9	Ⓐ Ⓑ Ⓒ Ⓓ	19	Ⓐ Ⓑ Ⓒ Ⓓ	29	Ⓐ Ⓑ Ⓒ Ⓓ	39	Ⓐ Ⓑ Ⓒ Ⓓ	49	Ⓐ Ⓑ Ⓒ Ⓓ	59	Ⓐ Ⓑ Ⓒ Ⓓ	69	Ⓐ Ⓑ Ⓒ Ⓓ	79	Ⓐ Ⓑ Ⓒ Ⓓ	89	Ⓐ Ⓑ Ⓒ Ⓓ	99	Ⓐ Ⓑ Ⓒ Ⓓ
	10	Ⓐ Ⓑ Ⓒ Ⓓ	20	Ⓐ Ⓑ Ⓒ Ⓓ	30	Ⓐ Ⓑ Ⓒ Ⓓ	40	Ⓐ Ⓑ Ⓒ Ⓓ	50	Ⓐ Ⓑ Ⓒ Ⓓ	60	Ⓐ Ⓑ Ⓒ Ⓓ	70	Ⓐ Ⓑ Ⓒ Ⓓ	80	Ⓐ Ⓑ Ⓒ Ⓓ	90	Ⓐ Ⓑ Ⓒ Ⓓ	100	Ⓐ Ⓑ Ⓒ Ⓓ

答案紙

ACTUAL TEST 03

LISTENING SECTION	1	Ⓐ Ⓑ Ⓒ Ⓓ	11	Ⓐ Ⓑ Ⓒ Ⓓ	21	Ⓐ Ⓑ Ⓒ Ⓓ	31	Ⓐ Ⓑ Ⓒ Ⓓ	41	Ⓐ Ⓑ Ⓒ Ⓓ	51	Ⓐ Ⓑ Ⓒ Ⓓ	61	Ⓐ Ⓑ Ⓒ Ⓓ	71	Ⓐ Ⓑ Ⓒ Ⓓ	81	Ⓐ Ⓑ Ⓒ Ⓓ	91	Ⓐ Ⓑ Ⓒ Ⓓ
	2	Ⓐ Ⓑ Ⓒ Ⓓ	12	Ⓐ Ⓑ Ⓒ Ⓓ	22	Ⓐ Ⓑ Ⓒ Ⓓ	32	Ⓐ Ⓑ Ⓒ Ⓓ	42	Ⓐ Ⓑ Ⓒ Ⓓ	52	Ⓐ Ⓑ Ⓒ Ⓓ	62	Ⓐ Ⓑ Ⓒ Ⓓ	72	Ⓐ Ⓑ Ⓒ Ⓓ	82	Ⓐ Ⓑ Ⓒ Ⓓ	92	Ⓐ Ⓑ Ⓒ Ⓓ
	3	Ⓐ Ⓑ Ⓒ Ⓓ	13	Ⓐ Ⓑ Ⓒ Ⓓ	23	Ⓐ Ⓑ Ⓒ Ⓓ	33	Ⓐ Ⓑ Ⓒ Ⓓ	43	Ⓐ Ⓑ Ⓒ Ⓓ	53	Ⓐ Ⓑ Ⓒ Ⓓ	63	Ⓐ Ⓑ Ⓒ Ⓓ	73	Ⓐ Ⓑ Ⓒ Ⓓ	83	Ⓐ Ⓑ Ⓒ Ⓓ	93	Ⓐ Ⓑ Ⓒ Ⓓ
	4	Ⓐ Ⓑ Ⓒ Ⓓ	14	Ⓐ Ⓑ Ⓒ Ⓓ	24	Ⓐ Ⓑ Ⓒ Ⓓ	34	Ⓐ Ⓑ Ⓒ Ⓓ	44	Ⓐ Ⓑ Ⓒ Ⓓ	54	Ⓐ Ⓑ Ⓒ Ⓓ	64	Ⓐ Ⓑ Ⓒ Ⓓ	74	Ⓐ Ⓑ Ⓒ Ⓓ	84	Ⓐ Ⓑ Ⓒ Ⓓ	94	Ⓐ Ⓑ Ⓒ Ⓓ
	5	Ⓐ Ⓑ Ⓒ Ⓓ	15	Ⓐ Ⓑ Ⓒ Ⓓ	25	Ⓐ Ⓑ Ⓒ Ⓓ	35	Ⓐ Ⓑ Ⓒ Ⓓ	45	Ⓐ Ⓑ Ⓒ Ⓓ	55	Ⓐ Ⓑ Ⓒ Ⓓ	65	Ⓐ Ⓑ Ⓒ Ⓓ	75	Ⓐ Ⓑ Ⓒ Ⓓ	85	Ⓐ Ⓑ Ⓒ Ⓓ	95	Ⓐ Ⓑ Ⓒ Ⓓ
	6	Ⓐ Ⓑ Ⓒ Ⓓ	16	Ⓐ Ⓑ Ⓒ Ⓓ	26	Ⓐ Ⓑ Ⓒ Ⓓ	36	Ⓐ Ⓑ Ⓒ Ⓓ	46	Ⓐ Ⓑ Ⓒ Ⓓ	56	Ⓐ Ⓑ Ⓒ Ⓓ	66	Ⓐ Ⓑ Ⓒ Ⓓ	76	Ⓐ Ⓑ Ⓒ Ⓓ	86	Ⓐ Ⓑ Ⓒ Ⓓ	96	Ⓐ Ⓑ Ⓒ Ⓓ
	7	Ⓐ Ⓑ Ⓒ Ⓓ	17	Ⓐ Ⓑ Ⓒ Ⓓ	27	Ⓐ Ⓑ Ⓒ Ⓓ	37	Ⓐ Ⓑ Ⓒ Ⓓ	47	Ⓐ Ⓑ Ⓒ Ⓓ	57	Ⓐ Ⓑ Ⓒ Ⓓ	67	Ⓐ Ⓑ Ⓒ Ⓓ	77	Ⓐ Ⓑ Ⓒ Ⓓ	87	Ⓐ Ⓑ Ⓒ Ⓓ	97	Ⓐ Ⓑ Ⓒ Ⓓ
	8	Ⓐ Ⓑ Ⓒ Ⓓ	18	Ⓐ Ⓑ Ⓒ Ⓓ	28	Ⓐ Ⓑ Ⓒ Ⓓ	38	Ⓐ Ⓑ Ⓒ Ⓓ	48	Ⓐ Ⓑ Ⓒ Ⓓ	58	Ⓐ Ⓑ Ⓒ Ⓓ	68	Ⓐ Ⓑ Ⓒ Ⓓ	78	Ⓐ Ⓑ Ⓒ Ⓓ	88	Ⓐ Ⓑ Ⓒ Ⓓ	98	Ⓐ Ⓑ Ⓒ Ⓓ
	9	Ⓐ Ⓑ Ⓒ Ⓓ	19	Ⓐ Ⓑ Ⓒ Ⓓ	29	Ⓐ Ⓑ Ⓒ Ⓓ	39	Ⓐ Ⓑ Ⓒ Ⓓ	49	Ⓐ Ⓑ Ⓒ Ⓓ	59	Ⓐ Ⓑ Ⓒ Ⓓ	69	Ⓐ Ⓑ Ⓒ Ⓓ	79	Ⓐ Ⓑ Ⓒ Ⓓ	89	Ⓐ Ⓑ Ⓒ Ⓓ	99	Ⓐ Ⓑ Ⓒ Ⓓ
	10	Ⓐ Ⓑ Ⓒ Ⓓ	20	Ⓐ Ⓑ Ⓒ Ⓓ	30	Ⓐ Ⓑ Ⓒ Ⓓ	40	Ⓐ Ⓑ Ⓒ Ⓓ	50	Ⓐ Ⓑ Ⓒ Ⓓ	60	Ⓐ Ⓑ Ⓒ Ⓓ	70	Ⓐ Ⓑ Ⓒ Ⓓ	80	Ⓐ Ⓑ Ⓒ Ⓓ	90	Ⓐ Ⓑ Ⓒ Ⓓ	100	Ⓐ Ⓑ Ⓒ Ⓓ

ACTUAL TEST 04

LISTENING SECTION	1	Ⓐ Ⓑ Ⓒ Ⓓ	11	Ⓐ Ⓑ Ⓒ Ⓓ	21	Ⓐ Ⓑ Ⓒ Ⓓ	31	Ⓐ Ⓑ Ⓒ Ⓓ	41	Ⓐ Ⓑ Ⓒ Ⓓ	51	Ⓐ Ⓑ Ⓒ Ⓓ	61	Ⓐ Ⓑ Ⓒ Ⓓ	71	Ⓐ Ⓑ Ⓒ Ⓓ	81	Ⓐ Ⓑ Ⓒ Ⓓ	91	Ⓐ Ⓑ Ⓒ Ⓓ
	2	Ⓐ Ⓑ Ⓒ Ⓓ	12	Ⓐ Ⓑ Ⓒ Ⓓ	22	Ⓐ Ⓑ Ⓒ Ⓓ	32	Ⓐ Ⓑ Ⓒ Ⓓ	42	Ⓐ Ⓑ Ⓒ Ⓓ	52	Ⓐ Ⓑ Ⓒ Ⓓ	62	Ⓐ Ⓑ Ⓒ Ⓓ	72	Ⓐ Ⓑ Ⓒ Ⓓ	82	Ⓐ Ⓑ Ⓒ Ⓓ	92	Ⓐ Ⓑ Ⓒ Ⓓ
	3	Ⓐ Ⓑ Ⓒ Ⓓ	13	Ⓐ Ⓑ Ⓒ Ⓓ	23	Ⓐ Ⓑ Ⓒ Ⓓ	33	Ⓐ Ⓑ Ⓒ Ⓓ	43	Ⓐ Ⓑ Ⓒ Ⓓ	53	Ⓐ Ⓑ Ⓒ Ⓓ	63	Ⓐ Ⓑ Ⓒ Ⓓ	73	Ⓐ Ⓑ Ⓒ Ⓓ	83	Ⓐ Ⓑ Ⓒ Ⓓ	93	Ⓐ Ⓑ Ⓒ Ⓓ
	4	Ⓐ Ⓑ Ⓒ Ⓓ	14	Ⓐ Ⓑ Ⓒ Ⓓ	24	Ⓐ Ⓑ Ⓒ Ⓓ	34	Ⓐ Ⓑ Ⓒ Ⓓ	44	Ⓐ Ⓑ Ⓒ Ⓓ	54	Ⓐ Ⓑ Ⓒ Ⓓ	64	Ⓐ Ⓑ Ⓒ Ⓓ	74	Ⓐ Ⓑ Ⓒ Ⓓ	84	Ⓐ Ⓑ Ⓒ Ⓓ	94	Ⓐ Ⓑ Ⓒ Ⓓ
	5	Ⓐ Ⓑ Ⓒ Ⓓ	15	Ⓐ Ⓑ Ⓒ Ⓓ	25	Ⓐ Ⓑ Ⓒ Ⓓ	35	Ⓐ Ⓑ Ⓒ Ⓓ	45	Ⓐ Ⓑ Ⓒ Ⓓ	55	Ⓐ Ⓑ Ⓒ Ⓓ	65	Ⓐ Ⓑ Ⓒ Ⓓ	75	Ⓐ Ⓑ Ⓒ Ⓓ	85	Ⓐ Ⓑ Ⓒ Ⓓ	95	Ⓐ Ⓑ Ⓒ Ⓓ
	6	Ⓐ Ⓑ Ⓒ Ⓓ	16	Ⓐ Ⓑ Ⓒ Ⓓ	26	Ⓐ Ⓑ Ⓒ Ⓓ	36	Ⓐ Ⓑ Ⓒ Ⓓ	46	Ⓐ Ⓑ Ⓒ Ⓓ	56	Ⓐ Ⓑ Ⓒ Ⓓ	66	Ⓐ Ⓑ Ⓒ Ⓓ	76	Ⓐ Ⓑ Ⓒ Ⓓ	86	Ⓐ Ⓑ Ⓒ Ⓓ	96	Ⓐ Ⓑ Ⓒ Ⓓ
	7	Ⓐ Ⓑ Ⓒ Ⓓ	17	Ⓐ Ⓑ Ⓒ Ⓓ	27	Ⓐ Ⓑ Ⓒ Ⓓ	37	Ⓐ Ⓑ Ⓒ Ⓓ	47	Ⓐ Ⓑ Ⓒ Ⓓ	57	Ⓐ Ⓑ Ⓒ Ⓓ	67	Ⓐ Ⓑ Ⓒ Ⓓ	77	Ⓐ Ⓑ Ⓒ Ⓓ	87	Ⓐ Ⓑ Ⓒ Ⓓ	97	Ⓐ Ⓑ Ⓒ Ⓓ
	8	Ⓐ Ⓑ Ⓒ Ⓓ	18	Ⓐ Ⓑ Ⓒ Ⓓ	28	Ⓐ Ⓑ Ⓒ Ⓓ	38	Ⓐ Ⓑ Ⓒ Ⓓ	48	Ⓐ Ⓑ Ⓒ Ⓓ	58	Ⓐ Ⓑ Ⓒ Ⓓ	68	Ⓐ Ⓑ Ⓒ Ⓓ	78	Ⓐ Ⓑ Ⓒ Ⓓ	88	Ⓐ Ⓑ Ⓒ Ⓓ	98	Ⓐ Ⓑ Ⓒ Ⓓ
	9	Ⓐ Ⓑ Ⓒ Ⓓ	19	Ⓐ Ⓑ Ⓒ Ⓓ	29	Ⓐ Ⓑ Ⓒ Ⓓ	39	Ⓐ Ⓑ Ⓒ Ⓓ	49	Ⓐ Ⓑ Ⓒ Ⓓ	59	Ⓐ Ⓑ Ⓒ Ⓓ	69	Ⓐ Ⓑ Ⓒ Ⓓ	79	Ⓐ Ⓑ Ⓒ Ⓓ	89	Ⓐ Ⓑ Ⓒ Ⓓ	99	Ⓐ Ⓑ Ⓒ Ⓓ
	10	Ⓐ Ⓑ Ⓒ Ⓓ	20	Ⓐ Ⓑ Ⓒ Ⓓ	30	Ⓐ Ⓑ Ⓒ Ⓓ	40	Ⓐ Ⓑ Ⓒ Ⓓ	50	Ⓐ Ⓑ Ⓒ Ⓓ	60	Ⓐ Ⓑ Ⓒ Ⓓ	70	Ⓐ Ⓑ Ⓒ Ⓓ	80	Ⓐ Ⓑ Ⓒ Ⓓ	90	Ⓐ Ⓑ Ⓒ Ⓓ	100	Ⓐ Ⓑ Ⓒ Ⓓ

答案紙

ACTUAL TEST 05

LISTENING SECTION	1	Ⓐ Ⓑ Ⓒ Ⓓ	11	Ⓐ Ⓑ Ⓒ Ⓓ	21	Ⓐ Ⓑ Ⓒ Ⓓ	31	Ⓐ Ⓑ Ⓒ Ⓓ	41	Ⓐ Ⓑ Ⓒ Ⓓ	51	Ⓐ Ⓑ Ⓒ Ⓓ	61	Ⓐ Ⓑ Ⓒ Ⓓ	71	Ⓐ Ⓑ Ⓒ Ⓓ	81	Ⓐ Ⓑ Ⓒ Ⓓ	91	Ⓐ Ⓑ Ⓒ Ⓓ
	2	Ⓐ Ⓑ Ⓒ Ⓓ	12	Ⓐ Ⓑ Ⓒ Ⓓ	22	Ⓐ Ⓑ Ⓒ Ⓓ	32	Ⓐ Ⓑ Ⓒ Ⓓ	42	Ⓐ Ⓑ Ⓒ Ⓓ	52	Ⓐ Ⓑ Ⓒ Ⓓ	62	Ⓐ Ⓑ Ⓒ Ⓓ	72	Ⓐ Ⓑ Ⓒ Ⓓ	82	Ⓐ Ⓑ Ⓒ Ⓓ	92	Ⓐ Ⓑ Ⓒ Ⓓ
	3	Ⓐ Ⓑ Ⓒ Ⓓ	13	Ⓐ Ⓑ Ⓒ Ⓓ	23	Ⓐ Ⓑ Ⓒ Ⓓ	33	Ⓐ Ⓑ Ⓒ Ⓓ	43	Ⓐ Ⓑ Ⓒ Ⓓ	53	Ⓐ Ⓑ Ⓒ Ⓓ	63	Ⓐ Ⓑ Ⓒ Ⓓ	73	Ⓐ Ⓑ Ⓒ Ⓓ	83	Ⓐ Ⓑ Ⓒ Ⓓ	93	Ⓐ Ⓑ Ⓒ Ⓓ
	4	Ⓐ Ⓑ Ⓒ Ⓓ	14	Ⓐ Ⓑ Ⓒ Ⓓ	24	Ⓐ Ⓑ Ⓒ Ⓓ	34	Ⓐ Ⓑ Ⓒ Ⓓ	44	Ⓐ Ⓑ Ⓒ Ⓓ	54	Ⓐ Ⓑ Ⓒ Ⓓ	64	Ⓐ Ⓑ Ⓒ Ⓓ	74	Ⓐ Ⓑ Ⓒ Ⓓ	84	Ⓐ Ⓑ Ⓒ Ⓓ	94	Ⓐ Ⓑ Ⓒ Ⓓ
	5	Ⓐ Ⓑ Ⓒ Ⓓ	15	Ⓐ Ⓑ Ⓒ Ⓓ	25	Ⓐ Ⓑ Ⓒ Ⓓ	35	Ⓐ Ⓑ Ⓒ Ⓓ	45	Ⓐ Ⓑ Ⓒ Ⓓ	55	Ⓐ Ⓑ Ⓒ Ⓓ	65	Ⓐ Ⓑ Ⓒ Ⓓ	75	Ⓐ Ⓑ Ⓒ Ⓓ	85	Ⓐ Ⓑ Ⓒ Ⓓ	95	Ⓐ Ⓑ Ⓒ Ⓓ
	6	Ⓐ Ⓑ Ⓒ Ⓓ	16	Ⓐ Ⓑ Ⓒ Ⓓ	26	Ⓐ Ⓑ Ⓒ Ⓓ	36	Ⓐ Ⓑ Ⓒ Ⓓ	46	Ⓐ Ⓑ Ⓒ Ⓓ	56	Ⓐ Ⓑ Ⓒ Ⓓ	66	Ⓐ Ⓑ Ⓒ Ⓓ	76	Ⓐ Ⓑ Ⓒ Ⓓ	86	Ⓐ Ⓑ Ⓒ Ⓓ	96	Ⓐ Ⓑ Ⓒ Ⓓ
	7	Ⓐ Ⓑ Ⓒ Ⓓ	17	Ⓐ Ⓑ Ⓒ Ⓓ	27	Ⓐ Ⓑ Ⓒ Ⓓ	37	Ⓐ Ⓑ Ⓒ Ⓓ	47	Ⓐ Ⓑ Ⓒ Ⓓ	57	Ⓐ Ⓑ Ⓒ Ⓓ	67	Ⓐ Ⓑ Ⓒ Ⓓ	77	Ⓐ Ⓑ Ⓒ Ⓓ	87	Ⓐ Ⓑ Ⓒ Ⓓ	97	Ⓐ Ⓑ Ⓒ Ⓓ
	8	Ⓐ Ⓑ Ⓒ Ⓓ	18	Ⓐ Ⓑ Ⓒ Ⓓ	28	Ⓐ Ⓑ Ⓒ Ⓓ	38	Ⓐ Ⓑ Ⓒ Ⓓ	48	Ⓐ Ⓑ Ⓒ Ⓓ	58	Ⓐ Ⓑ Ⓒ Ⓓ	68	Ⓐ Ⓑ Ⓒ Ⓓ	78	Ⓐ Ⓑ Ⓒ Ⓓ	88	Ⓐ Ⓑ Ⓒ Ⓓ	98	Ⓐ Ⓑ Ⓒ Ⓓ
	9	Ⓐ Ⓑ Ⓒ Ⓓ	19	Ⓐ Ⓑ Ⓒ Ⓓ	29	Ⓐ Ⓑ Ⓒ Ⓓ	39	Ⓐ Ⓑ Ⓒ Ⓓ	49	Ⓐ Ⓑ Ⓒ Ⓓ	59	Ⓐ Ⓑ Ⓒ Ⓓ	69	Ⓐ Ⓑ Ⓒ Ⓓ	79	Ⓐ Ⓑ Ⓒ Ⓓ	89	Ⓐ Ⓑ Ⓒ Ⓓ	99	Ⓐ Ⓑ Ⓒ Ⓓ
	10	Ⓐ Ⓑ Ⓒ Ⓓ	20	Ⓐ Ⓑ Ⓒ Ⓓ	30	Ⓐ Ⓑ Ⓒ Ⓓ	40	Ⓐ Ⓑ Ⓒ Ⓓ	50	Ⓐ Ⓑ Ⓒ Ⓓ	60	Ⓐ Ⓑ Ⓒ Ⓓ	70	Ⓐ Ⓑ Ⓒ Ⓓ	80	Ⓐ Ⓑ Ⓒ Ⓓ	90	Ⓐ Ⓑ Ⓒ Ⓓ	100	Ⓐ Ⓑ Ⓒ Ⓓ

ACTUAL TEST 06

LISTENING SECTION	1	Ⓐ Ⓑ Ⓒ Ⓓ	11	Ⓐ Ⓑ Ⓒ Ⓓ	21	Ⓐ Ⓑ Ⓒ Ⓓ	31	Ⓐ Ⓑ Ⓒ Ⓓ	41	Ⓐ Ⓑ Ⓒ Ⓓ	51	Ⓐ Ⓑ Ⓒ Ⓓ	61	Ⓐ Ⓑ Ⓒ Ⓓ	71	Ⓐ Ⓑ Ⓒ Ⓓ	81	Ⓐ Ⓑ Ⓒ Ⓓ	91	Ⓐ Ⓑ Ⓒ Ⓓ
	2	Ⓐ Ⓑ Ⓒ Ⓓ	12	Ⓐ Ⓑ Ⓒ Ⓓ	22	Ⓐ Ⓑ Ⓒ Ⓓ	32	Ⓐ Ⓑ Ⓒ Ⓓ	42	Ⓐ Ⓑ Ⓒ Ⓓ	52	Ⓐ Ⓑ Ⓒ Ⓓ	62	Ⓐ Ⓑ Ⓒ Ⓓ	72	Ⓐ Ⓑ Ⓒ Ⓓ	82	Ⓐ Ⓑ Ⓒ Ⓓ	92	Ⓐ Ⓑ Ⓒ Ⓓ
	3	Ⓐ Ⓑ Ⓒ Ⓓ	13	Ⓐ Ⓑ Ⓒ Ⓓ	23	Ⓐ Ⓑ Ⓒ Ⓓ	33	Ⓐ Ⓑ Ⓒ Ⓓ	43	Ⓐ Ⓑ Ⓒ Ⓓ	53	Ⓐ Ⓑ Ⓒ Ⓓ	63	Ⓐ Ⓑ Ⓒ Ⓓ	73	Ⓐ Ⓑ Ⓒ Ⓓ	83	Ⓐ Ⓑ Ⓒ Ⓓ	93	Ⓐ Ⓑ Ⓒ Ⓓ
	4	Ⓐ Ⓑ Ⓒ Ⓓ	14	Ⓐ Ⓑ Ⓒ Ⓓ	24	Ⓐ Ⓑ Ⓒ Ⓓ	34	Ⓐ Ⓑ Ⓒ Ⓓ	44	Ⓐ Ⓑ Ⓒ Ⓓ	54	Ⓐ Ⓑ Ⓒ Ⓓ	64	Ⓐ Ⓑ Ⓒ Ⓓ	74	Ⓐ Ⓑ Ⓒ Ⓓ	84	Ⓐ Ⓑ Ⓒ Ⓓ	94	Ⓐ Ⓑ Ⓒ Ⓓ
	5	Ⓐ Ⓑ Ⓒ Ⓓ	15	Ⓐ Ⓑ Ⓒ Ⓓ	25	Ⓐ Ⓑ Ⓒ Ⓓ	35	Ⓐ Ⓑ Ⓒ Ⓓ	45	Ⓐ Ⓑ Ⓒ Ⓓ	55	Ⓐ Ⓑ Ⓒ Ⓓ	65	Ⓐ Ⓑ Ⓒ Ⓓ	75	Ⓐ Ⓑ Ⓒ Ⓓ	85	Ⓐ Ⓑ Ⓒ Ⓓ	95	Ⓐ Ⓑ Ⓒ Ⓓ
	6	Ⓐ Ⓑ Ⓒ Ⓓ	16	Ⓐ Ⓑ Ⓒ Ⓓ	26	Ⓐ Ⓑ Ⓒ Ⓓ	36	Ⓐ Ⓑ Ⓒ Ⓓ	46	Ⓐ Ⓑ Ⓒ Ⓓ	56	Ⓐ Ⓑ Ⓒ Ⓓ	66	Ⓐ Ⓑ Ⓒ Ⓓ	76	Ⓐ Ⓑ Ⓒ Ⓓ	86	Ⓐ Ⓑ Ⓒ Ⓓ	96	Ⓐ Ⓑ Ⓒ Ⓓ
	7	Ⓐ Ⓑ Ⓒ Ⓓ	17	Ⓐ Ⓑ Ⓒ Ⓓ	27	Ⓐ Ⓑ Ⓒ Ⓓ	37	Ⓐ Ⓑ Ⓒ Ⓓ	47	Ⓐ Ⓑ Ⓒ Ⓓ	57	Ⓐ Ⓑ Ⓒ Ⓓ	67	Ⓐ Ⓑ Ⓒ Ⓓ	77	Ⓐ Ⓑ Ⓒ Ⓓ	87	Ⓐ Ⓑ Ⓒ Ⓓ	97	Ⓐ Ⓑ Ⓒ Ⓓ
	8	Ⓐ Ⓑ Ⓒ Ⓓ	18	Ⓐ Ⓑ Ⓒ Ⓓ	28	Ⓐ Ⓑ Ⓒ Ⓓ	38	Ⓐ Ⓑ Ⓒ Ⓓ	48	Ⓐ Ⓑ Ⓒ Ⓓ	58	Ⓐ Ⓑ Ⓒ Ⓓ	68	Ⓐ Ⓑ Ⓒ Ⓓ	78	Ⓐ Ⓑ Ⓒ Ⓓ	88	Ⓐ Ⓑ Ⓒ Ⓓ	98	Ⓐ Ⓑ Ⓒ Ⓓ
	9	Ⓐ Ⓑ Ⓒ Ⓓ	19	Ⓐ Ⓑ Ⓒ Ⓓ	29	Ⓐ Ⓑ Ⓒ Ⓓ	39	Ⓐ Ⓑ Ⓒ Ⓓ	49	Ⓐ Ⓑ Ⓒ Ⓓ	59	Ⓐ Ⓑ Ⓒ Ⓓ	69	Ⓐ Ⓑ Ⓒ Ⓓ	79	Ⓐ Ⓑ Ⓒ Ⓓ	89	Ⓐ Ⓑ Ⓒ Ⓓ	99	Ⓐ Ⓑ Ⓒ Ⓓ
	10	Ⓐ Ⓑ Ⓒ Ⓓ	20	Ⓐ Ⓑ Ⓒ Ⓓ	30	Ⓐ Ⓑ Ⓒ Ⓓ	40	Ⓐ Ⓑ Ⓒ Ⓓ	50	Ⓐ Ⓑ Ⓒ Ⓓ	60	Ⓐ Ⓑ Ⓒ Ⓓ	70	Ⓐ Ⓑ Ⓒ Ⓓ	80	Ⓐ Ⓑ Ⓒ Ⓓ	90	Ⓐ Ⓑ Ⓒ Ⓓ	100	Ⓐ Ⓑ Ⓒ Ⓓ

答案紙

ACTUAL TEST 07

LISTENING SECTION	1	Ⓐ Ⓑ Ⓒ Ⓓ	11	Ⓐ Ⓑ Ⓒ Ⓓ	21	Ⓐ Ⓑ Ⓒ Ⓓ	31	Ⓐ Ⓑ Ⓒ Ⓓ	41	Ⓐ Ⓑ Ⓒ Ⓓ	51	Ⓐ Ⓑ Ⓒ Ⓓ	61	Ⓐ Ⓑ Ⓒ Ⓓ	71	Ⓐ Ⓑ Ⓒ Ⓓ	81	Ⓐ Ⓑ Ⓒ Ⓓ	91	Ⓐ Ⓑ Ⓒ Ⓓ
	2	Ⓐ Ⓑ Ⓒ Ⓓ	12	Ⓐ Ⓑ Ⓒ Ⓓ	22	Ⓐ Ⓑ Ⓒ Ⓓ	32	Ⓐ Ⓑ Ⓒ Ⓓ	42	Ⓐ Ⓑ Ⓒ Ⓓ	52	Ⓐ Ⓑ Ⓒ Ⓓ	62	Ⓐ Ⓑ Ⓒ Ⓓ	72	Ⓐ Ⓑ Ⓒ Ⓓ	82	Ⓐ Ⓑ Ⓒ Ⓓ	92	Ⓐ Ⓑ Ⓒ Ⓓ
	3	Ⓐ Ⓑ Ⓒ Ⓓ	13	Ⓐ Ⓑ Ⓒ Ⓓ	23	Ⓐ Ⓑ Ⓒ Ⓓ	33	Ⓐ Ⓑ Ⓒ Ⓓ	43	Ⓐ Ⓑ Ⓒ Ⓓ	53	Ⓐ Ⓑ Ⓒ Ⓓ	63	Ⓐ Ⓑ Ⓒ Ⓓ	73	Ⓐ Ⓑ Ⓒ Ⓓ	83	Ⓐ Ⓑ Ⓒ Ⓓ	93	Ⓐ Ⓑ Ⓒ Ⓓ
	4	Ⓐ Ⓑ Ⓒ Ⓓ	14	Ⓐ Ⓑ Ⓒ Ⓓ	24	Ⓐ Ⓑ Ⓒ Ⓓ	34	Ⓐ Ⓑ Ⓒ Ⓓ	44	Ⓐ Ⓑ Ⓒ Ⓓ	54	Ⓐ Ⓑ Ⓒ Ⓓ	64	Ⓐ Ⓑ Ⓒ Ⓓ	74	Ⓐ Ⓑ Ⓒ Ⓓ	84	Ⓐ Ⓑ Ⓒ Ⓓ	94	Ⓐ Ⓑ Ⓒ Ⓓ
	5	Ⓐ Ⓑ Ⓒ Ⓓ	15	Ⓐ Ⓑ Ⓒ Ⓓ	25	Ⓐ Ⓑ Ⓒ Ⓓ	35	Ⓐ Ⓑ Ⓒ Ⓓ	45	Ⓐ Ⓑ Ⓒ Ⓓ	55	Ⓐ Ⓑ Ⓒ Ⓓ	65	Ⓐ Ⓑ Ⓒ Ⓓ	75	Ⓐ Ⓑ Ⓒ Ⓓ	85	Ⓐ Ⓑ Ⓒ Ⓓ	95	Ⓐ Ⓑ Ⓒ Ⓓ
	6	Ⓐ Ⓑ Ⓒ Ⓓ	16	Ⓐ Ⓑ Ⓒ Ⓓ	26	Ⓐ Ⓑ Ⓒ Ⓓ	36	Ⓐ Ⓑ Ⓒ Ⓓ	46	Ⓐ Ⓑ Ⓒ Ⓓ	56	Ⓐ Ⓑ Ⓒ Ⓓ	66	Ⓐ Ⓑ Ⓒ Ⓓ	76	Ⓐ Ⓑ Ⓒ Ⓓ	86	Ⓐ Ⓑ Ⓒ Ⓓ	96	Ⓐ Ⓑ Ⓒ Ⓓ
	7	Ⓐ Ⓑ Ⓒ Ⓓ	17	Ⓐ Ⓑ Ⓒ Ⓓ	27	Ⓐ Ⓑ Ⓒ Ⓓ	37	Ⓐ Ⓑ Ⓒ Ⓓ	47	Ⓐ Ⓑ Ⓒ Ⓓ	57	Ⓐ Ⓑ Ⓒ Ⓓ	67	Ⓐ Ⓑ Ⓒ Ⓓ	77	Ⓐ Ⓑ Ⓒ Ⓓ	87	Ⓐ Ⓑ Ⓒ Ⓓ	97	Ⓐ Ⓑ Ⓒ Ⓓ
	8	Ⓐ Ⓑ Ⓒ Ⓓ	18	Ⓐ Ⓑ Ⓒ Ⓓ	28	Ⓐ Ⓑ Ⓒ Ⓓ	38	Ⓐ Ⓑ Ⓒ Ⓓ	48	Ⓐ Ⓑ Ⓒ Ⓓ	58	Ⓐ Ⓑ Ⓒ Ⓓ	68	Ⓐ Ⓑ Ⓒ Ⓓ	78	Ⓐ Ⓑ Ⓒ Ⓓ	88	Ⓐ Ⓑ Ⓒ Ⓓ	98	Ⓐ Ⓑ Ⓒ Ⓓ
	9	Ⓐ Ⓑ Ⓒ Ⓓ	19	Ⓐ Ⓑ Ⓒ Ⓓ	29	Ⓐ Ⓑ Ⓒ Ⓓ	39	Ⓐ Ⓑ Ⓒ Ⓓ	49	Ⓐ Ⓑ Ⓒ Ⓓ	59	Ⓐ Ⓑ Ⓒ Ⓓ	69	Ⓐ Ⓑ Ⓒ Ⓓ	79	Ⓐ Ⓑ Ⓒ Ⓓ	89	Ⓐ Ⓑ Ⓒ Ⓓ	99	Ⓐ Ⓑ Ⓒ Ⓓ
	10	Ⓐ Ⓑ Ⓒ Ⓓ	20	Ⓐ Ⓑ Ⓒ Ⓓ	30	Ⓐ Ⓑ Ⓒ Ⓓ	40	Ⓐ Ⓑ Ⓒ Ⓓ	50	Ⓐ Ⓑ Ⓒ Ⓓ	60	Ⓐ Ⓑ Ⓒ Ⓓ	70	Ⓐ Ⓑ Ⓒ Ⓓ	80	Ⓐ Ⓑ Ⓒ Ⓓ	90	Ⓐ Ⓑ Ⓒ Ⓓ	100	Ⓐ Ⓑ Ⓒ Ⓓ

ACTUAL TEST 08

LISTENING SECTION	1	Ⓐ Ⓑ Ⓒ Ⓓ	11	Ⓐ Ⓑ Ⓒ Ⓓ	21	Ⓐ Ⓑ Ⓒ Ⓓ	31	Ⓐ Ⓑ Ⓒ Ⓓ	41	Ⓐ Ⓑ Ⓒ Ⓓ	51	Ⓐ Ⓑ Ⓒ Ⓓ	61	Ⓐ Ⓑ Ⓒ Ⓓ	71	Ⓐ Ⓑ Ⓒ Ⓓ	81	Ⓐ Ⓑ Ⓒ Ⓓ	91	Ⓐ Ⓑ Ⓒ Ⓓ
	2	Ⓐ Ⓑ Ⓒ Ⓓ	12	Ⓐ Ⓑ Ⓒ Ⓓ	22	Ⓐ Ⓑ Ⓒ Ⓓ	32	Ⓐ Ⓑ Ⓒ Ⓓ	42	Ⓐ Ⓑ Ⓒ Ⓓ	52	Ⓐ Ⓑ Ⓒ Ⓓ	62	Ⓐ Ⓑ Ⓒ Ⓓ	72	Ⓐ Ⓑ Ⓒ Ⓓ	82	Ⓐ Ⓑ Ⓒ Ⓓ	92	Ⓐ Ⓑ Ⓒ Ⓓ
	3	Ⓐ Ⓑ Ⓒ Ⓓ	13	Ⓐ Ⓑ Ⓒ Ⓓ	23	Ⓐ Ⓑ Ⓒ Ⓓ	33	Ⓐ Ⓑ Ⓒ Ⓓ	43	Ⓐ Ⓑ Ⓒ Ⓓ	53	Ⓐ Ⓑ Ⓒ Ⓓ	63	Ⓐ Ⓑ Ⓒ Ⓓ	73	Ⓐ Ⓑ Ⓒ Ⓓ	83	Ⓐ Ⓑ Ⓒ Ⓓ	93	Ⓐ Ⓑ Ⓒ Ⓓ
	4	Ⓐ Ⓑ Ⓒ Ⓓ	14	Ⓐ Ⓑ Ⓒ Ⓓ	24	Ⓐ Ⓑ Ⓒ Ⓓ	34	Ⓐ Ⓑ Ⓒ Ⓓ	44	Ⓐ Ⓑ Ⓒ Ⓓ	54	Ⓐ Ⓑ Ⓒ Ⓓ	64	Ⓐ Ⓑ Ⓒ Ⓓ	74	Ⓐ Ⓑ Ⓒ Ⓓ	84	Ⓐ Ⓑ Ⓒ Ⓓ	94	Ⓐ Ⓑ Ⓒ Ⓓ
	5	Ⓐ Ⓑ Ⓒ Ⓓ	15	Ⓐ Ⓑ Ⓒ Ⓓ	25	Ⓐ Ⓑ Ⓒ Ⓓ	35	Ⓐ Ⓑ Ⓒ Ⓓ	45	Ⓐ Ⓑ Ⓒ Ⓓ	55	Ⓐ Ⓑ Ⓒ Ⓓ	65	Ⓐ Ⓑ Ⓒ Ⓓ	75	Ⓐ Ⓑ Ⓒ Ⓓ	85	Ⓐ Ⓑ Ⓒ Ⓓ	95	Ⓐ Ⓑ Ⓒ Ⓓ
	6	Ⓐ Ⓑ Ⓒ Ⓓ	16	Ⓐ Ⓑ Ⓒ Ⓓ	26	Ⓐ Ⓑ Ⓒ Ⓓ	36	Ⓐ Ⓑ Ⓒ Ⓓ	46	Ⓐ Ⓑ Ⓒ Ⓓ	56	Ⓐ Ⓑ Ⓒ Ⓓ	66	Ⓐ Ⓑ Ⓒ Ⓓ	76	Ⓐ Ⓑ Ⓒ Ⓓ	86	Ⓐ Ⓑ Ⓒ Ⓓ	96	Ⓐ Ⓑ Ⓒ Ⓓ
	7	Ⓐ Ⓑ Ⓒ Ⓓ	17	Ⓐ Ⓑ Ⓒ Ⓓ	27	Ⓐ Ⓑ Ⓒ Ⓓ	37	Ⓐ Ⓑ Ⓒ Ⓓ	47	Ⓐ Ⓑ Ⓒ Ⓓ	57	Ⓐ Ⓑ Ⓒ Ⓓ	67	Ⓐ Ⓑ Ⓒ Ⓓ	77	Ⓐ Ⓑ Ⓒ Ⓓ	87	Ⓐ Ⓑ Ⓒ Ⓓ	97	Ⓐ Ⓑ Ⓒ Ⓓ
	8	Ⓐ Ⓑ Ⓒ Ⓓ	18	Ⓐ Ⓑ Ⓒ Ⓓ	28	Ⓐ Ⓑ Ⓒ Ⓓ	38	Ⓐ Ⓑ Ⓒ Ⓓ	48	Ⓐ Ⓑ Ⓒ Ⓓ	58	Ⓐ Ⓑ Ⓒ Ⓓ	68	Ⓐ Ⓑ Ⓒ Ⓓ	78	Ⓐ Ⓑ Ⓒ Ⓓ	88	Ⓐ Ⓑ Ⓒ Ⓓ	98	Ⓐ Ⓑ Ⓒ Ⓓ
	9	Ⓐ Ⓑ Ⓒ Ⓓ	19	Ⓐ Ⓑ Ⓒ Ⓓ	29	Ⓐ Ⓑ Ⓒ Ⓓ	39	Ⓐ Ⓑ Ⓒ Ⓓ	49	Ⓐ Ⓑ Ⓒ Ⓓ	59	Ⓐ Ⓑ Ⓒ Ⓓ	69	Ⓐ Ⓑ Ⓒ Ⓓ	79	Ⓐ Ⓑ Ⓒ Ⓓ	89	Ⓐ Ⓑ Ⓒ Ⓓ	99	Ⓐ Ⓑ Ⓒ Ⓓ
	10	Ⓐ Ⓑ Ⓒ Ⓓ	20	Ⓐ Ⓑ Ⓒ Ⓓ	30	Ⓐ Ⓑ Ⓒ Ⓓ	40	Ⓐ Ⓑ Ⓒ Ⓓ	50	Ⓐ Ⓑ Ⓒ Ⓓ	60	Ⓐ Ⓑ Ⓒ Ⓓ	70	Ⓐ Ⓑ Ⓒ Ⓓ	80	Ⓐ Ⓑ Ⓒ Ⓓ	90	Ⓐ Ⓑ Ⓒ Ⓓ	100	Ⓐ Ⓑ Ⓒ Ⓓ

答案紙

ACTUAL TEST 09

LISTENING SECTION																				
	1	Ⓐ Ⓑ Ⓒ Ⓓ	11	Ⓐ Ⓑ Ⓒ Ⓓ	21	Ⓐ Ⓑ Ⓒ Ⓓ	31	Ⓐ Ⓑ Ⓒ Ⓓ	41	Ⓐ Ⓑ Ⓒ Ⓓ	51	Ⓐ Ⓑ Ⓒ Ⓓ	61	Ⓐ Ⓑ Ⓒ Ⓓ	71	Ⓐ Ⓑ Ⓒ Ⓓ	81	Ⓐ Ⓑ Ⓒ Ⓓ	91	Ⓐ Ⓑ Ⓒ Ⓓ
	2	Ⓐ Ⓑ Ⓒ Ⓓ	12	Ⓐ Ⓑ Ⓒ Ⓓ	22	Ⓐ Ⓑ Ⓒ Ⓓ	32	Ⓐ Ⓑ Ⓒ Ⓓ	42	Ⓐ Ⓑ Ⓒ Ⓓ	52	Ⓐ Ⓑ Ⓒ Ⓓ	62	Ⓐ Ⓑ Ⓒ Ⓓ	72	Ⓐ Ⓑ Ⓒ Ⓓ	82	Ⓐ Ⓑ Ⓒ Ⓓ	92	Ⓐ Ⓑ Ⓒ Ⓓ
	3	Ⓐ Ⓑ Ⓒ Ⓓ	13	Ⓐ Ⓑ Ⓒ Ⓓ	23	Ⓐ Ⓑ Ⓒ Ⓓ	33	Ⓐ Ⓑ Ⓒ Ⓓ	43	Ⓐ Ⓑ Ⓒ Ⓓ	53	Ⓐ Ⓑ Ⓒ Ⓓ	63	Ⓐ Ⓑ Ⓒ Ⓓ	73	Ⓐ Ⓑ Ⓒ Ⓓ	83	Ⓐ Ⓑ Ⓒ Ⓓ	93	Ⓐ Ⓑ Ⓒ Ⓓ
	4	Ⓐ Ⓑ Ⓒ Ⓓ	14	Ⓐ Ⓑ Ⓒ Ⓓ	24	Ⓐ Ⓑ Ⓒ Ⓓ	34	Ⓐ Ⓑ Ⓒ Ⓓ	44	Ⓐ Ⓑ Ⓒ Ⓓ	54	Ⓐ Ⓑ Ⓒ Ⓓ	64	Ⓐ Ⓑ Ⓒ Ⓓ	74	Ⓐ Ⓑ Ⓒ Ⓓ	84	Ⓐ Ⓑ Ⓒ Ⓓ	94	Ⓐ Ⓑ Ⓒ Ⓓ
	5	Ⓐ Ⓑ Ⓒ Ⓓ	15	Ⓐ Ⓑ Ⓒ Ⓓ	25	Ⓐ Ⓑ Ⓒ Ⓓ	35	Ⓐ Ⓑ Ⓒ Ⓓ	45	Ⓐ Ⓑ Ⓒ Ⓓ	55	Ⓐ Ⓑ Ⓒ Ⓓ	65	Ⓐ Ⓑ Ⓒ Ⓓ	75	Ⓐ Ⓑ Ⓒ Ⓓ	85	Ⓐ Ⓑ Ⓒ Ⓓ	95	Ⓐ Ⓑ Ⓒ Ⓓ
	6	Ⓐ Ⓑ Ⓒ Ⓓ	16	Ⓐ Ⓑ Ⓒ Ⓓ	26	Ⓐ Ⓑ Ⓒ Ⓓ	36	Ⓐ Ⓑ Ⓒ Ⓓ	46	Ⓐ Ⓑ Ⓒ Ⓓ	56	Ⓐ Ⓑ Ⓒ Ⓓ	66	Ⓐ Ⓑ Ⓒ Ⓓ	76	Ⓐ Ⓑ Ⓒ Ⓓ	86	Ⓐ Ⓑ Ⓒ Ⓓ	96	Ⓐ Ⓑ Ⓒ Ⓓ
	7	Ⓐ Ⓑ Ⓒ Ⓓ	17	Ⓐ Ⓑ Ⓒ Ⓓ	27	Ⓐ Ⓑ Ⓒ Ⓓ	37	Ⓐ Ⓑ Ⓒ Ⓓ	47	Ⓐ Ⓑ Ⓒ Ⓓ	57	Ⓐ Ⓑ Ⓒ Ⓓ	67	Ⓐ Ⓑ Ⓒ Ⓓ	77	Ⓐ Ⓑ Ⓒ Ⓓ	87	Ⓐ Ⓑ Ⓒ Ⓓ	97	Ⓐ Ⓑ Ⓒ Ⓓ
	8	Ⓐ Ⓑ Ⓒ Ⓓ	18	Ⓐ Ⓑ Ⓒ Ⓓ	28	Ⓐ Ⓑ Ⓒ Ⓓ	38	Ⓐ Ⓑ Ⓒ Ⓓ	48	Ⓐ Ⓑ Ⓒ Ⓓ	58	Ⓐ Ⓑ Ⓒ Ⓓ	68	Ⓐ Ⓑ Ⓒ Ⓓ	78	Ⓐ Ⓑ Ⓒ Ⓓ	88	Ⓐ Ⓑ Ⓒ Ⓓ	98	Ⓐ Ⓑ Ⓒ Ⓓ
	9	Ⓐ Ⓑ Ⓒ Ⓓ	19	Ⓐ Ⓑ Ⓒ Ⓓ	29	Ⓐ Ⓑ Ⓒ Ⓓ	39	Ⓐ Ⓑ Ⓒ Ⓓ	49	Ⓐ Ⓑ Ⓒ Ⓓ	59	Ⓐ Ⓑ Ⓒ Ⓓ	69	Ⓐ Ⓑ Ⓒ Ⓓ	79	Ⓐ Ⓑ Ⓒ Ⓓ	89	Ⓐ Ⓑ Ⓒ Ⓓ	99	Ⓐ Ⓑ Ⓒ Ⓓ
	10	Ⓐ Ⓑ Ⓒ Ⓓ	20	Ⓐ Ⓑ Ⓒ Ⓓ	30	Ⓐ Ⓑ Ⓒ Ⓓ	40	Ⓐ Ⓑ Ⓒ Ⓓ	50	Ⓐ Ⓑ Ⓒ Ⓓ	60	Ⓐ Ⓑ Ⓒ Ⓓ	70	Ⓐ Ⓑ Ⓒ Ⓓ	80	Ⓐ Ⓑ Ⓒ Ⓓ	90	Ⓐ Ⓑ Ⓒ Ⓓ	100	Ⓐ Ⓑ Ⓒ Ⓓ

ACTUAL TEST 10

LISTENING SECTION																				
	1	Ⓐ Ⓑ Ⓒ Ⓓ	11	Ⓐ Ⓑ Ⓒ Ⓓ	21	Ⓐ Ⓑ Ⓒ Ⓓ	31	Ⓐ Ⓑ Ⓒ Ⓓ	41	Ⓐ Ⓑ Ⓒ Ⓓ	51	Ⓐ Ⓑ Ⓒ Ⓓ	61	Ⓐ Ⓑ Ⓒ Ⓓ	71	Ⓐ Ⓑ Ⓒ Ⓓ	81	Ⓐ Ⓑ Ⓒ Ⓓ	91	Ⓐ Ⓑ Ⓒ Ⓓ
	2	Ⓐ Ⓑ Ⓒ Ⓓ	12	Ⓐ Ⓑ Ⓒ Ⓓ	22	Ⓐ Ⓑ Ⓒ Ⓓ	32	Ⓐ Ⓑ Ⓒ Ⓓ	42	Ⓐ Ⓑ Ⓒ Ⓓ	52	Ⓐ Ⓑ Ⓒ Ⓓ	62	Ⓐ Ⓑ Ⓒ Ⓓ	72	Ⓐ Ⓑ Ⓒ Ⓓ	82	Ⓐ Ⓑ Ⓒ Ⓓ	92	Ⓐ Ⓑ Ⓒ Ⓓ
	3	Ⓐ Ⓑ Ⓒ Ⓓ	13	Ⓐ Ⓑ Ⓒ Ⓓ	23	Ⓐ Ⓑ Ⓒ Ⓓ	33	Ⓐ Ⓑ Ⓒ Ⓓ	43	Ⓐ Ⓑ Ⓒ Ⓓ	53	Ⓐ Ⓑ Ⓒ Ⓓ	63	Ⓐ Ⓑ Ⓒ Ⓓ	73	Ⓐ Ⓑ Ⓒ Ⓓ	83	Ⓐ Ⓑ Ⓒ Ⓓ	93	Ⓐ Ⓑ Ⓒ Ⓓ
	4	Ⓐ Ⓑ Ⓒ Ⓓ	14	Ⓐ Ⓑ Ⓒ Ⓓ	24	Ⓐ Ⓑ Ⓒ Ⓓ	34	Ⓐ Ⓑ Ⓒ Ⓓ	44	Ⓐ Ⓑ Ⓒ Ⓓ	54	Ⓐ Ⓑ Ⓒ Ⓓ	64	Ⓐ Ⓑ Ⓒ Ⓓ	74	Ⓐ Ⓑ Ⓒ Ⓓ	84	Ⓐ Ⓑ Ⓒ Ⓓ	94	Ⓐ Ⓑ Ⓒ Ⓓ
	5	Ⓐ Ⓑ Ⓒ Ⓓ	15	Ⓐ Ⓑ Ⓒ Ⓓ	25	Ⓐ Ⓑ Ⓒ Ⓓ	35	Ⓐ Ⓑ Ⓒ Ⓓ	45	Ⓐ Ⓑ Ⓒ Ⓓ	55	Ⓐ Ⓑ Ⓒ Ⓓ	65	Ⓐ Ⓑ Ⓒ Ⓓ	75	Ⓐ Ⓑ Ⓒ Ⓓ	85	Ⓐ Ⓑ Ⓒ Ⓓ	95	Ⓐ Ⓑ Ⓒ Ⓓ
	6	Ⓐ Ⓑ Ⓒ Ⓓ	16	Ⓐ Ⓑ Ⓒ Ⓓ	26	Ⓐ Ⓑ Ⓒ Ⓓ	36	Ⓐ Ⓑ Ⓒ Ⓓ	46	Ⓐ Ⓑ Ⓒ Ⓓ	56	Ⓐ Ⓑ Ⓒ Ⓓ	66	Ⓐ Ⓑ Ⓒ Ⓓ	76	Ⓐ Ⓑ Ⓒ Ⓓ	86	Ⓐ Ⓑ Ⓒ Ⓓ	96	Ⓐ Ⓑ Ⓒ Ⓓ
	7	Ⓐ Ⓑ Ⓒ Ⓓ	17	Ⓐ Ⓑ Ⓒ Ⓓ	27	Ⓐ Ⓑ Ⓒ Ⓓ	37	Ⓐ Ⓑ Ⓒ Ⓓ	47	Ⓐ Ⓑ Ⓒ Ⓓ	57	Ⓐ Ⓑ Ⓒ Ⓓ	67	Ⓐ Ⓑ Ⓒ Ⓓ	77	Ⓐ Ⓑ Ⓒ Ⓓ	87	Ⓐ Ⓑ Ⓒ Ⓓ	97	Ⓐ Ⓑ Ⓒ Ⓓ
	8	Ⓐ Ⓑ Ⓒ Ⓓ	18	Ⓐ Ⓑ Ⓒ Ⓓ	28	Ⓐ Ⓑ Ⓒ Ⓓ	38	Ⓐ Ⓑ Ⓒ Ⓓ	48	Ⓐ Ⓑ Ⓒ Ⓓ	58	Ⓐ Ⓑ Ⓒ Ⓓ	68	Ⓐ Ⓑ Ⓒ Ⓓ	78	Ⓐ Ⓑ Ⓒ Ⓓ	88	Ⓐ Ⓑ Ⓒ Ⓓ	98	Ⓐ Ⓑ Ⓒ Ⓓ
	9	Ⓐ Ⓑ Ⓒ Ⓓ	19	Ⓐ Ⓑ Ⓒ Ⓓ	29	Ⓐ Ⓑ Ⓒ Ⓓ	39	Ⓐ Ⓑ Ⓒ Ⓓ	49	Ⓐ Ⓑ Ⓒ Ⓓ	59	Ⓐ Ⓑ Ⓒ Ⓓ	69	Ⓐ Ⓑ Ⓒ Ⓓ	79	Ⓐ Ⓑ Ⓒ Ⓓ	89	Ⓐ Ⓑ Ⓒ Ⓓ	99	Ⓐ Ⓑ Ⓒ Ⓓ
	10	Ⓐ Ⓑ Ⓒ Ⓓ	20	Ⓐ Ⓑ Ⓒ Ⓓ	30	Ⓐ Ⓑ Ⓒ Ⓓ	40	Ⓐ Ⓑ Ⓒ Ⓓ	50	Ⓐ Ⓑ Ⓒ Ⓓ	60	Ⓐ Ⓑ Ⓒ Ⓓ	70	Ⓐ Ⓑ Ⓒ Ⓓ	80	Ⓐ Ⓑ Ⓒ Ⓓ	90	Ⓐ Ⓑ Ⓒ Ⓓ	100	Ⓐ Ⓑ Ⓒ Ⓓ

新制 New TOEIC
聽力閱讀超高分
最新多益改版黃金試題 2000 題【聽力＋閱讀雙書裝】

作　　者	Ki Taek Lee
譯　　者	王傳明
編　　輯	Gina Wang
審　　訂	Helen Yeh
校　　對	黃詩韻
內文排版	林書玉（題目）／葳豐企業有限公司（聽力對白和翻譯）
封面設計	林書玉
製程管理	洪巧玲
出 版 者	寂天文化事業股份有限公司
發 行 人	黃朝萍
電　　話	+886-(0)2-2365-9739
傳　　真	+886-(0)2-2365-9835
網　　址	www.icosmos.com.tw
讀者服務	onlineservice@icosmos.com.tw
出版日期	2024 年 8 月 初版再刷 (寂天雲隨身聽 APP 版) (0106)

郵撥帳號 1998620-0 寂天文化事業股份有限公司
訂書金額未滿 1000 元，請外加運費 100 元。
〔若有破損，請寄回更換，謝謝〕

國家圖書館出版品預行編目 (CIP) 資料

新制 New TOEIC 聽力閱讀超高分 : 最新多益改版黃金試題 2000 題 (聽力 + 閱讀雙書版)(寂天雲隨身聽 APP 版) / Ki Taek Lee, The Mozilge Language Research Institute 著 ; 王傳明 , 林育珊譯 .
-- 初版 . -- [臺北市] : 寂天文化 , 2022.05
面；　公分

ISBN 978-626-300-126-8 (16K 平裝)

1. 多益測驗
805.1895　　　111005748

新制 NEW TOEIC 閱讀超高分

最新多益改版黃金試題1000題

作者 • Ki Taek Lee
審訂 • Maddie Smith/
Richard Luhrs

目錄 Contents

多益測驗改制介紹
&
高分戰略

多益測驗的出現

TOEIC 多益測驗（Test of English for International Communication）是針對非英語人士所設計的英語能力測驗。多益測驗的內容主要與職場環境的英語使用有關，能測驗一個人在工作場合上使用英語與人溝通的能力，故有「商業托福」之稱。多益測驗在許多國家施行多年，如今已經成為「職場英語能力檢定」的國際標準。

多益英語測驗是由「美國教育測驗服務社」（Educational Testing Service, ETS）所研發出來。ETS 於 1947 年成立，總部位於美國紐澤西州，是全球最大的私立教育考試機構。ETS 提供標準化的考試和測評服務，除了多益測驗，還包括托福（TOEFL）、GRE 和 GMAT 等等。ETS 在 1979 年時，應日本企業領袖的要求，制定出一套可以用來評估員工英語能力的測驗，以了解員工在貿易、工業和商業領域上所具備的英語程度，以利人力規劃與發展。

如今，多益測驗是全球最通行的職場英語能力測驗，共有超過 165 個國家在施行多益測驗，每年的測試人口超過五百萬。此外，許多校園也要求畢業生須接受多益測驗，而且成績須達一定的分數，以幫助學生在畢業後能更加順利地進入職場。

多益測驗考哪些內容？

多益測驗的研發者強調「國際英語」，而不以「美式英語」和「英式英語」來區分，並著重於測驗非英語人士對母語人士的英語溝通能力。多益的測驗內容不會考專業知識或詞彙，而是測試在日常生活中使用英文的能力。2006 年改版的新多益測驗，還特別加入了四種不同的英語口音，包括：

1. 美式英語
2. 英式英語
3. 澳洲英語
4. 加拿大英語

多益題目的設計，以「職場需求」為主，測驗題目的內容則是從全球各地職場的英文資料中蒐集而來，題材多元（但考生毋需具備專業的商業與技術辭彙），包含各種地點與狀況：一般商務、製造業、金融／預算、人事、企業發展、辦公室、採購、技術層面、房屋／公司地產、旅遊、外食、娛樂、保健等主題大類。

多益測驗的方式

1	考試方式	「紙筆測驗」
2	出題方式	所有試題皆為「選擇題」
3	題目類型	聽力測驗（又細分成 4 大題） 閱讀測驗（又細分成 3 大題）
4	考試題數	總共有 200 題（聽力 100 題，閱讀 100 題）
5	作答	考生選好答案後，要在與題目卷分開的「答案卷」上劃卡
6	考試時間	總計 2 小時（聽力考 45 分鐘，閱讀考 75 分鐘，兩者分開計時）

＊但在考試時，考生尚須在答案卷上填寫個人資料，並簡短的回答求學與工作經歷的問卷，因此真正待在考場內的時間會比較長。

多益計分方式

多益測驗沒有「通過」與「不通過」之區別——考生用鉛筆在電腦答案卷上作答，考試分數由答對題數決定，將聽力測驗與閱讀測驗答對之題數換算成分數，聽力與閱讀得分相加即為總分；答錯並不倒扣。聽力得分介於 5-495 分、閱讀得分介於 5-495 分，兩者加起來即為總分，範圍在 10 到 990 分之間。

答對題數	聽力分數	閱讀分數	答對題數	聽力分數	閱讀分數	答對題數	聽力分數	閱讀分數	答對題數	聽力分數	閱讀分數
100	495	495	85	465	420	70	365	320	55	295	230
99	495	495	84	455	415	69	360	315	54	290	225
98	495	495	83	450	410	68	355	310	53	280	220
97	495	490	82	445	400	67	350	300	52	275	215
96	495	485	81	440	395	66	350	295	51	265	210
95	495	480	80	435	385	65	345	290	50	260	205
94	495	475	79	430	380	64	340	285	49	255	200
93	490	470	78	425	375	63	335	280	48	250	195
92	490	465	77	420	370	62	330	270	47	245	190
91	490	460	76	410	365	61	325	265	46	240	185
90	485	455	75	400	360	60	320	260	45	230	180
89	485	450	74	390	350	59	315	255	44	225	175
88	480	440	73	385	345	58	310	250	43	220	170
87	475	430	72	380	335	57	305	245	42	210	165
86	470	425	71	375	330	56	300	240	41	205	160

＊此表格僅供參考，實際計分以官方分數為準 。
＊分數計算方式，例如：聽力答對 70 題，閱讀答對 78 題，總分為 365+375=740 分 。

2018年新制多益變革表

多益英語測驗有什麼改變？為什麼？

為確保測驗符合考生及成績使用單位之需求，ETS 會定期重新檢驗所有測驗試題。本次多益英語測驗題型更新，反映了全球現有日常生活中社交及職場之英語使用情況。測驗本身將維持其在評量日常生活或職場情境英語的公平性及可信度。其中一些測驗形式會改變，然而，**測驗的難易度**、**測驗時間**或**測驗分數所代表的意義不會有所更動**。

新舊制多益測驗結構比較

聽力測驗 Listening Comprehension　45 分鐘　100 題　495 分
測驗總題數、整體難易程度及測驗時間不變

Part	題型	舊制題數	新制題數	題型題數變更說明
1	**Photographs** **照片描述**	10 題	6 題	題型不變，題數減少 4 題。
	説明：從四個選項當中，選出一個和照片最相近的描述，問題與選項均不會印在試卷上。			
2	**Question-Response** **應答問題**	30 題	25 題	題型不變，題數減少 5 題。
	説明：從三個選項當中，選出與問題最為符合的回答，問題與選項均不會印在試卷上。			
3	**Conversations** **簡短對話**	30 題 3 題 x 10 組	39 題 3 題 x 13 組	加入三人對話、加入圖表，題數增加 9 題。
	説明：從四個選項中，選出與問題最為符合的回答，對話內容不會印在試卷上。 對話中將會有較少轉折，但來回交談較為頻繁。 部分對話題型將出現兩名以上的對談者。			
4	**Talks** **獨白**	30 題 3 題 x 10 組	30 題 3 題 x 10 組	新增圖表作答題型，題數不變。
	説明：從四個選項中，選出與問題最為符合的回答，獨白內容不會印在試卷上。			

- 聽力測驗將包含母音省略（elision，如：going to → gonna）和不完整的句子（fragment，如：Yes, in a minute. / Down the hall. / Could you? 等省去主詞或動詞的句子）。
- 配合圖表，測驗考生是否聽懂對話，並測驗考生能否理解談話背景與對話中隱含的意思。

閱讀測驗 Reading Comprehension 75 分鐘 100 題 495 分

測驗總題數、整體難易程度及測驗時間不變

Part	題型	舊制題數	新制題數	題型題數變更說明
5	Incomplete Sentences 句子填空	40 題	30 題	題型不變，題數減少 10 題。
	說明：從四個選項中，選出最為恰當的答案，以完成不完整的句子。			
6	Text Completion 段落填空	12 題 4 題 X 3 篇	16 題 4 題 X 4 組	加入將適當的句子填入空格的題型，題數增加 4 題。
	說明：從四個選項中，選出最為恰當的答案，以完成文章中不完整的句子。 選項類別除原有之片語、單字、子句之外，另新增完整句子的選項。			
7	Reading Comprehension–Single Passage 單篇文章理解	28 題 共 9 篇 每篇 2 到 5 題	29 題 共 10 篇 每篇 2 到 4 題	題型不變，題數增加 1 題。
7	Reading Comprehension–Multiple Passage 多篇文章理解	20 題 雙篇閱讀共 4 篇 每篇 5 題	25 題 雙篇閱讀 2 篇 三篇閱讀 3 篇 每篇 5 題	少 2 篇雙篇閱讀文章，加入 3 篇三篇閱讀文章。
	說明：閱讀單篇或兩或三篇內容相關的文章，從四個選項中，選出最為恰當的答案以回答問題。 加入篇章結構題型，測驗考生能否理解整體文章結構，並將一個句子歸置於正確的段落。			

◆ 閱讀測驗將包含文字簡訊、即時通訊，或多人互動的線上聊天訊息內容。
◆ 新增引述文章部分內容，測驗考生是否理解作者希望表達之意思。

◆ 為新制題型說明
資料來源：ETS 官方網站
http://www.toeic.com.tw/2018update/info.html

各大題答題技巧戰略

聽力部分答題技巧

第一大題	照片描述（6 題）	這個部分是要考你看圖片、選答案的能力。你可以用以下的方法來練習：自己找一些照片來看，並思索根據照片的內容，有哪些問題可以提問。
第二大題	應答問題（25 題）	這個部分是提出各種問題，問題的開頭—— What、How、Why、When、Where、Who 六大問句——可以提示我們需要什麼樣的答案。
第三大題	簡短對話（39 題）	這個部分會先播放簡短的對話，再考你對對話的理解程度。回答技巧是你可以**先看問題、答案選項和圖表**，然後再聽對話內容，這樣你在聽的時候會比較知道要專注答案的線索。
第四大題	獨白（30 題）	這個大題可以說是聽力測驗中最難的部分，平時就需要多聽英文對話和廣播等來加強聽力能力。

聽力題目前的英文指示 & 高分戰略

In the Listening test, you will be asked to demonstrate how well you understand spoken English. The entire Listening test will last approximately 45 minutes. There are four parts, and directions are given for each part. You must mark your answers on the separate answer sheet. Do not write your answers in your test book.

聽力測驗在測驗考生聽懂英語的能力。整個聽力測驗的進行時間約 45 分鐘，共分四大題，每一大題皆有做答指示。請把答案寫在另一張答案卡上，而不要把答案寫在測驗本上。

I. Photographs 第一大題：照片描述

Part 1

Directions: For each question in this part, you will hear four statements about a picture in your test book. When you hear the statements, you must select the one statement that best describes what you see in the picture. Then find the number of the question on your answer sheet and mark your answer. The statements will not be printed in your test book and will be spoken only one time.

Look at the example item below. Now listen to the four statements.

(A) They're pointing at the monitor.
(B) They're looking at the document.
(C) They're talking on the phone.
(D) They're sitting by the table.

Statement (B), "They're looking at the document," is the best description of the picture, so you should select answer (B) and mark it on your answer sheet.

第一大題

指示：本大題的每一小題，在測驗本上都會印有一張圖片，考生會聽到針對照片所做的四段描述，然後選出最符合照片內容的適當描述，接著在答案卡上找到題目編號，將對應的答案選項圓圈塗黑。描述的內容部會印在測驗本上，而且只會播放一次。

（A）他們正指著螢幕。
（B）他們正在看文件。
（C）他們正在講電話。
（D）他們正坐在桌子旁。

描述 (B)「他們正在看文件」是最符合本圖的描述，因此你應該選擇選項 (B)，並在答案卡上劃記。

高分戰略

❶ 以人物為主的照片，要注意該人物的動作特徵。

照片題中有 70 ～ 80％的題目是以人物為照片主角，這些照片時常會考人的動作特徵，因此要先整理好相關的動作用語。舉例來說，一看到人在走路的照片，就立刻想到 walking、strolling 這些和走路有關的動詞，聽題目的時候會更有幫助。

❷ 以事物為中心的照片，要注意事物的狀態或位置。

以事物為中心的照片，其事物的狀態或位置是出題的要點。所以，表示「位置」時經常會用到的介系詞，還有表現「狀態」的片語，要先整理好。舉例來說，在表示位置「在……旁邊」時，要整理出 next to、by、beside、near 等用語，最好整個背下來。另外，多益時常出現的事物名稱，也要事先準備好。

❸ 要小心出人意料之外的問題。

不同於過往題型，題目的正確答案可能會出現描寫事物，這已成為一種出題趨勢。舉例來說，照片是一個男人用手指著掛在牆上的畫，按照常理，會想到是要考這個人的動作，要回答 pointing 這樣的動詞。但意外地，本題以掛在牆上的畫當作正確答案（The picture has been hung on the wall.）。所以出現人的照片時，不僅要注意人的動作，連周邊事物也必須要注意一下。只有提到照片中出現的內容，才會是正確答案；想像的內容絕對不會是正確答案。

II. Question-Response 第二大題：應答問題

Part 2

Directions: You will hear a question or statement and three responses spoken in English. They will be spoken only one time and will not be printed in your test book. Select the best response to the question or statement and mark the letter (A), (B), or (C) on your answer sheet.

第二大題

指示：考生會聽到一個問題句或敘述句，以及三句回應的英語。題目只會撥放一次，而且不會印在測驗本上。請選出最符合擺放內容的答案，在答案卡上將 (A)、(B)、(C) 或 (D) 的答案選項塗黑。

高分戰略

❶ 新制有言外之意的考題增加

PART 2 少了五題，但命題方式變得更巧妙、難度也隨之提升。有言外之意的考題增加，考生必須要聽出背後的含意才能找出答案。碰到此類題型時，在聽完題目後，需要思考一番，才能挑出正確的答案。只要稍不留神，很容易就錯失下一題的解題機會。請務必勤加練習，熟悉此類題型的模式。

❷ 沒聽清楚題目最前面的疑問詞，很可惜。

大部分 Part 2 出現的疑問句都會在最前面提示核心要點，尤其是以疑問詞（Who、What、Where、When、Why、How）開頭的疑問句題目，會出約 9 ～ 10 題。這些題目只要聽到句首的疑問詞，幾乎就能找到正確答案，所以平常要常做區分疑問詞的聽力練習。

❸ 利用錯誤答案消去法。

Part 2 是最多陷阱的部分，所以事先把常見的陷阱題整理起來，是很重要的。舉例來說，以疑問詞開頭的疑問句題目，用 yes 或 no 回答的選項，幾乎都是錯誤答案，可以先將其刪除。另外，重複出現題目中的單字，或出現與題目中字彙發音類似的單字，如 copy 與 coffee，也是常出的錯誤答案模式。平常一邊做題目，一邊將具代表性的陷阱題整理好是必要的。

❹ 常考的片語要整個背起來。

多益中常出現的用語或片語，最好當作一個單字一樣地整個背起來。舉例來說，疑問句「Why don't you . . . ?」的用法並非要詢問原因，而是「做……好嗎？」的代表句型。像這樣的用語，時常會快速唸過，所以事先整個背起來，考聽力時會很有幫助。

因此平常花功夫多做聽力訓練，並跟著一起唸，把重要的用語整段背下來，征服 Part 2 之路就不遠了。

III. Conversations 第三大題：簡短對話

Part 3

Directions: You will hear some conversations between two or more people. You will be asked to answer three questions about what the speakers say in each conversation. Select the best response to each question and mark the letter (A), (B), (C), or (D) on your answer sheet. The conversations will not be printed in your test book and will be spoken only one time.

第三大題

指示：考生會聽到一些兩個人或多人的對話，並根據對話所聽到的內容，回答三個問題。請選出最符合播放內容的答案，在答案卡上將 (A)、(B)、(C) 或 (D) 的答案選項塗黑。這些對話只會播放一次，而且不會印在測驗本上。

高分戰略

❶ 一定要先瞄題目，以找出要聆聽的重點。

Part 3 是兩到三人的對話，每組對話要回答三道題，所以**事先把題目快速掃描過**，找出重點，是很重要的。若不事先看題目，就不知道要把注意力集中在哪裡，而必須理解並記下整個對話，十分吃力。所以事先看一下題目問什麼，會對接下來的對話有概念，並知道要注意聽哪些地方。

有關圖表的試題，要**先看一下圖表訊息**，再綜合試題和選項後，仔細聽對話的內容。有策略地去聽是很重要的。

❷ 一面聽一面找答案！

即使先掃描過了題目，卻沒有練習邊聽邊找答案，容易會出現漏掉正確答案的情況。因為即使之前非常注意聽的對話，但有些細微的訊息，之後可能會記不起來，尤其是新制多益中，出現三個人的對話，所以談話者的性別，及彼此間的關係會更加複雜。所以一聽到答案出現，立刻作答，是最有利的。這麼做剛開始可能有點困難，但只要勤奮地練習，以後瞄過題目就大概就能猜出答案

❸ 千萬不要錯失對話開頭！

在 Part 3 中，時常出現問**職業、場所或主題**的問題，這些問題的答案時常會出現在對話開頭。要快速掌握對話一開始揭示的主題，才能判斷出接下來會出現什麼內容，對解其他的題目很有幫助。所以要勤加練習，把對話開頭確實聽清楚。

IV. Talks 第四大題：簡短獨白

Part 4

Directions: You will hear some talks given by a single speaker. You will be asked to answer three questions about what the speaker says in each talk. Select the best response to each question and mark the letter (A), (B), (C), or (D) on your answer sheet. The talks will not be printed in your test book and will be spoken only one time.

第四大題

指示：考生會聽到好幾段單人獨白，並根據每一段話的內容，回答三個問題。請選出最符合播放內容的答案，在答案卡上將 (A)、(B)、(C) 或 (D) 的答案選項塗黑。每一段話只會播放一次，而且不會印在測驗本上。

高分戰略

❶ 要事先整理好常考的詢問內容！

和 Part 3 不同，Part 4 的談話種類是有一定類型的。也就是說，會重複聽到有關**交通廣播**、**天氣預報**、**旅行導覽**、**電話留言**等的談話，內容大同小異。所以只需要按這些談話種類，整理出常考的問題類型即可。舉例來說，跟電話溝通相關的主題，時常都在談話一開始出現「I'm calling to . . .」，聽到這個敘述後，要找出正確答案就容易多了。

❷ 具備背景知識的話，答題會更加容易上手。

Part 4 的談話種類是有固定框架的，會感覺好像談話的內容及題目都很類似。所以即使不聽談話，光看題目，就能推測出答案是什麼。舉例來說，若是機場的情境談話，也許會出有關飛機誤點或取消的問題。這時誤點或取消的原因，最常出現的可能是天候不佳。這就是多益的背景知識，即使沒聽清楚，光看題目，也能選出最接近正確答案的選項。所以平常要努力累積多益常考題型的背景知識，不能懶惰。

❸ 要花功夫訓練自己找出問題的要點。

和 Part 3 一樣，Part 4 也是每段談話出三道題，所以要養成先掃描過題目和表格並整理出重點的習慣。由於 Part 4 的談話內容更長，不太可能把全部內容聽完後再答題。因此可以先找出題目的要點，利用背景知識，在試題本上推敲正確答案。不像 Part 3，Part 4 的答案通常會按照題目的順序，一一出現在對話中，答案逐題出現的機率很高。

閱讀部分答題技巧

第五大題	句子填空（30 題）	在第五大題中，字彙和文法能力最重要。其所考的字彙大都跟職場或商業有關，平時就要多背誦單字。
第六大題	段落填空（16 題）	除了單字，也需要將比較長的片語或子句，甚至是一整個句子填入空格中，要掌握整篇文章來龍去脈才能找出最合適的答案。
第七大題	單篇文章理解（29 題） 多篇文章理解（25 題）	第七大題比較困難，你需要知道有哪幾類的商業文章，像是公告或備忘錄等。平時就要訓練自己能夠快速閱讀文章和圖表，並且能夠找出主要的內容。當然，在這個部分字彙能力也是很重要的。

閱讀題目前的英文指示 & 高分戰略

In the Reading test, you will read a variety of texts and answer several different types of reading comprehension questions. The entire Reading test will last 75 minutes. There are three parts, and directions are given for each part. You are encouraged to answer as many questions as possible within the time allowed.

You must mark your answers on the separate answer sheet. Do not write your answers in your test book.

在閱讀測驗中，考生會讀到各種文章，並回答各種型式的閱讀測驗題目。整個閱讀測驗的進行時間為 75 分鐘 。本測驗共分三大題，每一大題皆有做答指示。請在規定的時間內，盡可能地作答。

請把答案寫在另一張答案卡上，而不要把答案寫在測驗本上。

V. Incomplete Sentences 第五大題：單句填空

Part 5

Directions: A word or phrase is missing in each of the sentences below. Four answer choices are given below each sentence. Select the best answer to complete the sentence. Then mark the letter (A), (B), (C), or (D) on your answer sheet.

第五大題

指示：本測驗中的每一個句子皆缺少一個單字或詞組，在句子下方會列出四個答案選項，請選出最適合的答案來完成句子，並在做答卡上將 (A)、(B)、(C) 或 (D) 的答案選項塗黑。

高分戰略

❶ 要先看選項。

試題大致可分為**句型**、**字彙**、**文法以及慣用語**四種試題。要先看選項，掌握是上述四種題型中的哪一種，便能更快速解題。所以，要練習判斷題型，並正確掌握各題型的解題技巧。

❷ 找出意思最接近的單字。

Part 5 是填空選擇題，若能找出和空格關係最密切的關鍵字彙，便能快速又正確地解題。所以，要練習**分析句子的結構**，並找出和空格關係最密切的字彙作為答題線索。一般來說，**空格前後的單字，就是線索**。舉例來說，如果空格後有名詞，此名詞就是空格的線索單字，以此名詞可以猜想出空格可能是個形容詞。

❸ 要盡力廣泛地蒐羅字彙。

多益會拿來出題的字彙，通常以**片語**形式出現。最具代表的是：動詞和受詞、形容詞和名詞、介系詞和名詞、動詞和副詞等。有些詞組中每個單字都懂，但合起來就很難猜出它的中文意思，所以不要直接用中文而要用英文去理解。因此，平日要養成將這些片語詞組視為整體一起背下來的習慣。

舉例來說，中文說「打電話」，但英文是「make a phone call」；而付錢打電話不能用「pay a phone call」，要用「pay for the phone call」。但是多益中 Part 5 考「pay for the phone call」的可能性很低，因為多益大多出常見用語，而這句不是。所以，要用英文去理解常見用語，要整個背起來，不要直接用中文理解，因為這是得高分最大的障礙。

VI. Text Completion 第六大題：短文填空

Part 6

Directions: Read the texts that follow. A word, phrase, or sentence is missing in parts of each text. Four answer choices for each question are given below the text. Select the best answer to complete the text. Then mark the letter (A), (B), (C), or (D) on your answer sheet.

第六大題

指示：閱讀本大題的文章，文章中的某些句子缺少單字、片語或句子，這些句子都會有四個答案選項，請選出最適合的答案來完成文章中的空格，並在做答卡上將 (A)、(B)、(C) 或 (D) 的答案選項塗黑。

高分戰略

❶ 要研究空格前後句子連結關係，掌握上下文。

Part 5 和 Part 6 不同的地方是，Part 5 只探究一個句子的結構，而 Part 6 要探究句子和句子間的關係，因此要練習觀察空格前後句子彼此的連結關係。如果有空格的句子是第一句，要看後一句來解題；如果有空格的句子是第二句，就要看前一句來解題。偶爾，也有要看整篇文章才能作答的題目。

PART 6 最難處在於要從選項的四個句子中，選出適當的句子填入空格中。此為新制增加的題型，不僅要多費時解題，平時也得多花功夫如何掌握上下文意上。

❷ Part 6 的動詞時態問題

Part 5 的動詞時態問題，只要看該句子內的動詞是否符合時態即可，但 Part 6 的動詞時態，要看其他句子才能決定該句空格中的時態。大部分的時態題目都區分為：已發生的事或尚未發生的事。從上下文來看，已發生的事，要用現在完成式或過去式；尚未發生的事，就選包含 will 等與未來式相關的助動詞（will、shall、may 等）選項，或用「be going to . . .」。針對 Part 6 的時態問題，多練習區分已發生的事和尚未發生的事便能順利答題。

❸ Part 6 的連接副詞

所謂的連接副詞，是指翻譯時要和前面的內容一起翻譯的副詞。一般來說，這不會出現在只考一句話的 Part 5，而會出現在考句間的關係的 Part 6。舉例來說，副詞 therefore 是「因此」的意思，所以若前後句的內容有因果關係，用它就對了。若是轉折語氣的話，用有「然而」含意的 however 準沒錯。此外，連接副詞還有 otherwise（否則）、consequently（因而導致）、additionally（此外）、instead（反而）等。另外，連接詞用於連接句子，而介系詞是連接名詞，連接副詞是單獨使用的，這是區分它們最便捷的方法。

VII. Single Passage / Multiple Passage 第七大題：單篇／多篇文章理解

Part 7

Directions: In this part you will read a selection of texts, such as magazine and newspaper articles, emails, and instant messages. Each text or set of texts is followed by several questions. Select the best answer for each question and mark the letter (A), (B), (C), or (D) on your answer sheet.

第七大題

指示：這大題中會閱讀到不同題材的文章，如雜誌和新聞文章、電子郵件或通訊軟體的訊息等。每篇或每組文章之後會有數個題目，請選出最適合的答案，並在做答卡上將 (A)、(B)、(C) 或 (D) 的答案選項塗黑。

高分戰略

❶ 要熟記類似的字彙及用語。

做 Part 7 的題目，字彙能力最為重要，它能幫助你正確且快速地找出與題目或文章用語最接近的選項。一邊研究 Part 7 的題目，一邊整理並熟記意思相似的字彙或用語，能快速增加字彙。

❷ Part 7 的問題也是有類型的。

Part 7 的題目乍看好像很多元，事實上可以分作幾種類型，如：

① **具體訊息類型**：詢問文章的一些訊息。
② **主題類型**：要找出文章主題。
③ **NOT 類型**：提供的選項中有三項是對的，而要找出錯誤項目。
④ **邏輯推演類型**：從一些線索中推知內容。
⑤ **文意填空類型**：閱讀段落，將題目中的句子填入文中適當的地方。

解題時先將題目分類，再來研究該如何解題，速度會快很多。

❸ 要注意複合式文章題目。

從 176 題開始，是由兩篇到三文章組成的複合式文章類型，有許多問題出自多篇文章內容的相關性。所以在這部分，相關或相同的地方要連貫起來作答。出這種相關連帶問題時，要注意文章的共通點是以何種方式連接。

❹ 培養耐力。

Part 7 是最後一個單元，解題實力雖然重要，但長時間解題能否集中注意力也是勝負的關鍵。平常要訓練自己，至少要持續一個小時不休息地解題，時常以這種方式來訓練閱讀十分重要。多做解題耐力練習，是考高分的必要條件。

ACTUAL TEST

ACTUAL TEST 01

READING TEST

In the Reading test, you will read a variety of texts and answer several different types of reading comprehension questions. The entire Reading test will last 75 minutes. There are three parts, and directions are given for each part. You are encouraged to answer as many questions as possible within the time allowed.

You must mark your answers on the separate answer sheet. Do not write your answers in your test book.

PART 5

Directions: A word or phrase is missing in each of the sentences below. Four answer choices are given below each sentence. Select the best answer to complete the sentence. Then mark the letter (A), (B), (C), or (D) on your answer sheet.

101. When filling out the order form, please ------- your address clearly to prevent delays.

(A) fix
(B) write
(C) send
(D) direct

102. Ms. Morgan recruited the individuals whom the company ------- for the next three months.

(A) will employ
(B) to employ
(C) has been employed
(D) employ

103. The contractor had a fifteen percent ------- in his business after advertising in the local newspaper.

(A) experience
(B) growth
(C) formula
(D) incentive

104. The free clinic was founded by a group of doctors to give ------- for various medical conditions.

(A) treatment
(B) treat
(C) treated
(D) treating

105. Participants in the walking tour should gather ------- 533 Bates Road on Saturday morning.

(A) with
(B) at
(C) like
(D) among

106. The artist sent ------- best pieces to the gallery to be reviewed by the owner.

(A) him
(B) himself
(C) his
(D) he

107. The figures that accompany the financial statement should be ------- to the spending category.

(A) relevance
(B) relevantly
(C) more relevantly
(D) relevant

108. The building owner purchased the property ------- three months ago, but she has already spent a great deal of money on renovations.

(A) yet
(B) just
(C) few
(D) still

109. We would like to discuss this problem honestly and ------- at the next staff meeting.

(A) rarely
(B) tiredly
(C) openly
(D) highly

110. The store's manager plans to put the new merchandise on display ------- to promote the line of fall fashions.

(A) soon
(B) very
(C) that
(D) still

111. During the peak season, it is ------- to hire additional workers for the weekend shifts.

(A) necessitate
(B) necessarily
(C) necessary
(D) necessity

112. ------- that the insulation has been replaced, the building is much more energy-efficient.

(A) Now
(B) For
(C) As
(D) Though

113. Mr. Sims needs a more ------- vehicle for commuting from his suburban home to his office downtown.

(A) expressive
(B) reliable
(C) partial
(D) extreme

114. The company ------- lowered its prices to outsell its competitors and attract more customers.

(A) strategy
(B) strategically
(C) strategies
(D) strategic

115. ------- Mr. Williams addressed the audience, he showed a brief video about the engine he had designed.

(A) Then
(B) So that
(C) Before
(D) Whereas

116. For optimal safety on the road, avoid ------- the view of the rear window and side-view mirrors.

(A) obstructs
(B) obstructed
(C) obstruction
(D) obstructing

GO ON TO THE NEXT PAGE

117. Having proper ventilation throughout the building is ------- for protecting the health and well-being of the workers.

(A) cooperative
(B) visible
(C) essential
(D) alternative

118. ------- sales of junk food have been steadily declining indicates that consumers are becoming more health-conscious.

(A) In addition to
(B) The fact that
(C) As long as
(D) In keeping with

119. The sprinklers for the lawn's irrigation system are ------- controlled.

(A) mechanically
(B) mechanic
(C) mechanism
(D) mechanical

120. The library staff posted signs to ------- patrons of the upcoming closure for renovations.

(A) notify
(B) agree
(C) generate
(D) perform

121. Mr. Ross, ------- is repainting the interior of the lobby, was recommended by a friend of the building manager.

(A) himself
(B) he
(C) who
(D) which

122. The guidelines for the monthly publication are ------- revised to adapt to the changing readers.

(A) curiously
(B) initially
(C) periodically
(D) physically

123. ------- an ankle injury, the baseball player participated in the last game of the season.

(A) In spite of
(B) Even if
(C) Whether
(D) Given that

124. The governmental department used to provide financial aid, but now it offers ------- services only.

(A) legal
(B) legalize
(C) legally
(D) legalizes

125. At the guest's -------, an extra set of towels and complimentary soaps were brought to the room.

(A) quote
(B) graduation
(C) request
(D) dispute

126. The upscale boutique Jane's Closet is known for selling the most stylish ------- for young professionals.

(A) accessorized
(B) accessorize
(C) accessorizes
(D) accessories

127. The company started to recognize the increasing ------- of using resources responsibly.

(A) more important
(B) importantly
(C) importance
(D) important

128. ------- restructuring several departments within the company, the majority of the problems with miscommunication have disappeared.

(A) After
(B) Until
(C) Below
(D) Like

129. The riskiest ------- of the development of new medications are the trials with human subjects.

(A) proceeds
(B) perspectives
(C) installments
(D) stages

130. ------- seeking a position at Tulare Designs must submit a portfolio of previous work.

(A) Anyone
(B) Whenever
(C) Other
(D) Fewer

GO ON TO THE NEXT PAGE

PART 6

Directions: Read the texts that follow. A word, phrase, or sentence is missing in parts of each text. Four answer choices for each question are given below the text. Select the best answer to complete the text. Then mark the letter (A), (B), (C), or (D) on your answer sheet.

Questions 131-134 refer to the following email.

To: samsmith@digitalIT.com
From: sharronb@bmail.com
Date: September 24
Subject: Business Contract

Dear Mr. Smith,

I am Sharron Biggs, CEO and founder of BiggsGraphics. I recently came across your advertisement ------- **131.** the partnership of a graphic design company for a number of your projects. BiggsGraphics has ------- **132.** experience working with various small businesses and companies in designing advertising campaigns, logos, and websites. ------- **133.** Our website, www.biggs-graphics.com, also has more information about our company.

I'm interested in working with your company on your projects and hope we can build a beneficial partnership. I look forward ------- **134.** your reply.

Sincerely,

Sharron Biggs

CEO, Biggs Graphics

131. (A) seek
(B) to seek
(C) seeking
(D) are seeking

132. (A) extensive
(B) restricted
(C) generous
(D) limitless

NEW

133. (A) I would really appreciate the opportunity to work with you.
(B) I heard that DigitalIT is a great company.
(C) In fact, our designs are often copied by other companies.
(D) I have attached a number of our past designs to illustrate what we specialize in.

134. (A) at
(B) to
(C) with
(D) from

Questions 135-138 refer to the following announcement.

Thank you for shopping at Larson's China. Our products are known for their modern and unique patterns and color combinations, as well as ------- (**135.**) and strength. ------- (**136.**) Please note, however, that repeated drops and rough handling will ------- (**137.**) eventual breakage. We suggest that you store them carefully and that you don't use harsh chemicals, steel sponges, or ------- (**138.**) scrubbing when cleaning them. Please visit our website at www.larsonchina.com for information about handling and care, or call us at 555-1234 if you have any questions or concerns.

135. (A) durable
(B) durability
(C) durableness
(D) duration

NEW

136. (A) Larson's utensils and silverware go great with the dinnerware.
(B) Our most popular line, the Spring Flower China, is sold out at most locations.
(C) Visit our store to check out our other beautiful products.
(D) They are dishwasher and microwave safe, and we're confident that you'll be using them for years to come.

137. (A) result in
(B) occur to
(C) ending at
(D) stop with

138. (A) ambitious
(B) combative
(C) aggressive
(D) complacent

GO ON TO THE NEXT PAGE

Questions 139-142 refer to the following notice.

Entry Position: Gold & Slide Accounting Firm

We are looking for enthusiastic candidates with an educational background in finance or ------- (**139.**). All candidates should have some computer experience. Job experience is not ------- (**140.**), but preferred. Candidates with bilingual language ability ------- (**141.**) favored. Positions include jobs in accounting, statistics, and general office assistant. If you are interested, please visit our website at www.G&Saccountingfirm.com/employment for more information. You can send your cover letters and résumés to Karen Hill at khill@G&S.com. We will begin interviewing candidates on Monday, November 5th. ------- (**142.**)

139. (A) account
(B) accountant
(C) accounting
(D) accounted

140. (A) basic
(B) decisive
(C) additional
(D) necessary

141. (A) is being
(B) will be
(C) has been
(D) were being

NEW

142. (A) We sincerely thank you for your kindness.
(B) The position will begin work the following month.
(C) Please call us for more information.
(D) We apologize for any inconvenience.

Questions 143-146 refer to the following email.

To: Kitchen Staff, Office Employees

From: Manager, Larry Park

Date: March 23

Subject: Renovations

To all kitchen staff and Harmon employees,

From Sunday, March 23rd to Thursday, March 27th, the employee cafeteria kitchens will undergo renovations as new appliances and equipment ------- **143.** in to replace the old ones. ------- **144.** Instead, the convenience shops will carry more sandwiches, prepared lunch boxes, and snacks for the employees during this time.

The renovations will increase the number of sinks, ovens, and stove tops, so that a larger volume of meals can be provided ------- **145.** the lunch and dinner rushes. We apologize for the inconvenience, but we hope that the changes will ------- **146.** the services in the cafeteria.

143. (A) are bringing
(B) have brought
(C) bring
(D) are brought

NEW

144. (A) This will take a lot of work.
(B) As a result, the convenience shops will be closed.
(C) Because of this, hot meals will not be available for the patrons.
(D) There will be noise and chaos as a result.

145. (A) before
(B) after
(C) during
(D) outside

146. (A) develop
(B) improve
(C) rectify
(D) recover

GO ON TO THE NEXT PAGE

PART 7

Directions: In this part you will read a selection of texts, such as magazine and newspaper articles, emails, and instant messages. Each text or set of texts is followed by several questions. Select the best answer for each question and mark the letter (A), (B), (C), or (D) on your answer sheet.

Questions 147-148 refer to the following email.

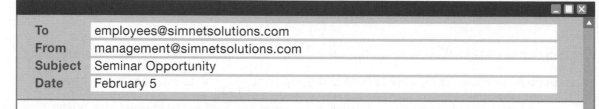

To	employees@simnetsolutions.com
From	management@simnetsolutions.com
Subject	Seminar Opportunity
Date	February 5

Dear female employees,

Only one week remains until registration will be closed for the Women's Leadership Seminar. This seminar is offered free of charge to all of our female employees at Simnet Solutions. To accommodate our female employees' busy schedules, identical seminars will be held on two different dates—February 21 and February 23.

In order to register for this specially designed seminar, you must email James Taylor in human resources by 5:00 P.M. on February 12. This seminar will teach our female employees how to communicate with confidence and credibility in the workplace.

The Simnet Solutions Management Team

147. What is indicated about the seminar?

(A) It will feature speaker James Taylor.
(B) It is held annually.
(C) Its fee is more expensive than the last one.
(D) It is designed for women.

148. When will the free registration offer end?

(A) On February 5
(B) On February 12
(C) On February 21
(D) On February 23

Questions 149-150 refer to the following text message chain.

Kyle **2:42**
Nancy, it's Kyle. I'm in Conference Room B setting up for the meeting at 5. The projector doesn't work. Can you search for another in the supply room?

Nancy **2:45**
Hey. No problem, I'm heading there now.

Kyle **2:46**
Thanks, I really appreciate it.

Nancy **2:57**
Kyle, there are no projectors here. I've called the IT Department and asked if they have any spare ones. I'll get back to you when I get a reply.

Kyle **3:00**
Thanks again. Oh, and can you check for extra microphones?

Nancy **3:08**
There are two here. I'll take them both. Meanwhile, the IT department says they don't have extra projectors, but they'll send a guy down now to check what's wrong. They say it worked fine at yesterday's presentation.

Kyle **3:09**
Great! I'll see you soon then.

149. Where is Nancy most likely located?

(A) In a conference room
(B) At the IT Department
(C) In the supply room
(D) In her office

NEW

150. What did Nancy mean when she said, "I'm heading there now"?

(A) She was going to the location.
(B) She would lead the presentation.
(C) She knew where the room was.
(D) She was going straight to meet him.

GO ON TO THE NEXT PAGE

Questions 151-152 refer to the following ticket.

Purchased By: Tim Bailey

Tate Theater

The Kelly Cooper Concert

Time: 7:00 P.M.
Date: Friday, May 20
Section: General Admission
Row: F
Seat: 26

– Guests seated in general admission should arrive at least 30 minutes before the concert begins.
– For those coming by car, the location of the theater can be found on our website at www.tatetheater.com.
– All ticket sales are non-refundable.

151. What is Mr. Bailey advised to do?

(A) Contact the theater for a refund
(B) Select his preferred seat on a website
(C) Arrive at the venue in advance
(D) Post a review later

152. According to the ticket, what can be viewed on the theater's website?

(A) A list of past performances
(B) Driving directions
(C) Concert reviews
(D) Pictures of the theater

Questions 153-154 refer to the following information.

Gilmore Good Buy

Order Confirmation

Name: Jenny Collins
Customer ID: F833J
Address: 808 Columbus Avenue, New York, NY 10025
Order date: August 22

Item(s)	Price
Springform pans (5 @ $5.00 each)	$25.00
4 oz. cocoa butter	$10.99
Confectioner's glaze (3 @ $5.90 each)*	$17.70
Cupcake pans (2 @ $4.00 each)	$8.00
Merchandise Total	$61.69
Delivery	$8.99
Total	$70.68
Payment: Credit Card XXXX XXXX XXXX 4026	

* Notes: Will be delivered at a quicker speed to prevent melting or damage

153. What kind of business are the items most likely intended for?

(A) A shopping mall
(B) A bakery
(C) An appliance store
(D) A convenience store

154. What is indicated about the order?

(A) It will be paid in installments.
(B) It will be sent separately.
(C) It has been discounted.
(D) It will be delivered at no charge.

GO ON TO THE NEXT PAGE

Questions 155-157 refer to the following article.

Community Victory

After a months-long battle to stop the development of a new shopping mall on the location of the former Rivervalley Courthouse, residents, local businesses, and civic groups are cheering the decision to keep the 150-year-old building intact. – [1] – "We're disappointed," added Branford Construction's CEO. "We felt that the community would benefit and grow, but obviously, residents want to preserve their history, and I respect that."

Instead, efforts are being made to restore the old, deserted courthouse to its former glory. – [2] – "The community is getting together for this, and we are collecting donations to have the building renovated," said local resident Enid Tran. "We hope to make a public library or school out of the building."

– [3] – "It's been here for as long as I can remember. In fact, my grandfather worked as a clerk there," added a local business owner, Kevin Lamb. "It's an iconic symbol of our community, and we don't want it destroyed." The community has already raised over $100,000 through an online petition, and donations keep pouring in. – [4] – The community hopes that restoration of the building will begin within the next couple of months.

155. What is indicated about the old courthouse?

(A) Branford Construction wants to renovate the building.
(B) The residents want to turn the building into a shopping mall.
(C) It may become a public library or school.
(D) It may be destroyed.

NEW

156. In which of the positions marked [1], [2], [3], and [4] does the following sentence best belong?

"Branford Construction, the development company that originally planned to build the shopping mall, is looking to build the mall outside of the Rivervalley Community."

(A) [1]
(B) [2]
(C) [3]
(D) [4]

157. What is suggested about the fundraising efforts?

(A) The community made a lot of money from the land.
(B) It has been occurring online.
(C) The city government has been helping.
(D) They haven't raised enough money.

Questions 158-160 refer to the following email.

To	Stacey Johnson <sjohnson@toplineelec.com>
From	Josh Fleck <jfleck@toplineelec.com>
Date	October 22
Subject	Strategic Planning

Dear Ms. Johnson,

District management at Topline Electronics would like to inform you about a new development that will be affecting your store. Another competing consumer electronics store will be opening in the Crayville area on November 12.

In order to ensure that Topline Electronics does not lose business to this new store, district management is advising you to run a special sale on our new line of curved UHD televisions. These televisions provide state-of-the-art features at moderate prices. By showing your customers that Topline Electronics offers the best deals in the area, you will be able to maintain customer loyalty. We will be shipping the new televisions to your store within the next week. We suggest you prepare a prominent display space in your store to feature them. You should also update your website to advertise the sale.

Smooth communication between you and us is vital to effective operational practices. If you have any questions concerning the new televisions or the marketing campaign in general, please don't hesitate to contact district management.

Sincerely,

Josh Fleck, District Manager
Topline Electronics

158. Who most likely is Ms. Johnson?

(A) A store manager
(B) A customer
(C) A product developer
(D) A marketing specialist

159. What is indicated about Topline Electronics?

(A) It recently opened a new store location.
(B) It will be relocated to the Crayville area.
(C) It is concerned about market competition.
(D) It was nominated for an annual award.

160. What is Ms. Johnson NOT instructed to do?

(A) Add new information to a website
(B) Hire additional staff
(C) Contact management if necessary
(D) Arrange a sale display area

GO ON TO THE NEXT PAGE

Questions 161-164 refer to the following text message chain.

Nickson, Harry **10:10**
Any word yet from the distributers about the desks and office chairs we were supposed to get on Tuesday?

Jordan, Johnny **10:11**
Monica is waiting to hear from them. Last I heard, there has been a bit of a delay due to problems at the manufacturing site. Apparently, one of the conveyor belts is down.

Nickson, Harry **10:12**
Have you told this to our clients at P&R Industries?

Jordan, Johnny **10:13**
No, because I want to get a definitive answer from our manufacturers first before I relay any sort of a message about a delay. Hey Monica, have you gotten a response yet?

Stein, Monica **10:14**
Yes, I just spoke with them. Great news; it looks like we can get the job done on Friday as originally scheduled. The desks and chairs will arrive directly at P&R Industries from the assembly lines on Thursday.

Nickson, Harry **10:15**
That's great to hear. Please inform Mr. Kline about this. We can get started on the 5th floor offices and work our way down once the furniture arrives.

Stein, Monica **10:15**
I'm on it.

Jordan, Johnny **10:16**
Alright, and I'll get a large crew there, so that the work can be finished by Friday as planned.

Nickson, Harry **10:17**
Yes, please make sure that the job is done not only efficiently but also well. They have a couple of other buildings that they may want our services for.

Jordan, Johnny **10:18**
I'll keep that in mind.

161. What kind of business do the online speakers work at?

(A) A law firm
(B) An office supply company
(C) A furniture shop
(D) A moving company

162. When will the crew begin work?

(A) Tuesday
(B) Wednesday
(C) Thursday
(D) Friday

163. What will Johnny Jordan probably do next?

(A) Contact the distributors
(B) Organize a meeting
(C) Gather a large crew
(D) Call the client

NEW

164. What does Monica Stein mean by "I'm on it"?

(A) She'll organize the movers.
(B) She'll wait until she gets more information.
(C) She'll visit the manufacturers.
(D) She'll contact the client.

GO ON TO THE NEXT PAGE

Questions 165-167 refer to the following business profile.

Fulton Stainless Steel Products

Fulton Stainless Steel Products is a large-scale manufacturer making stainless steel industrial kitchen appliances in factories in Germany and France. The company's products are trusted by chefs and bakers around the world to be durable, long-lasting, and of superb quality. The company produces kitchen stoves, ovens, microwaves, refrigerators, food processors, electric kettles, coffee makers, and other products.

After acquiring the Visor Home Products Company in a deal last month, the company expects its overall profits to increase 20% compared to the last fiscal year. As a result, to meet increased demand, the company will employ more than 300 full-time workers in its six factories and offer good pay with an excellent benefits package. The company considers all of its employees valuable members of the Fulton family. Additionally, the company continues to research and develop new products to satisfy its customers and compete with other companies.

165. Who is most likely to be a customer of Fulton Stainless Steel Products?

(A) A car manufacturer
(B) A restaurant
(C) A real estate agency
(D) A clothing store

166. What did Fulton Stainless Steel Products do last month?

(A) It held a press conference.
(B) It opened a new factory.
(C) It obtained a company.
(D) It laid off some workers.

167. What is mentioned about Fulton Stainless Steel Products?

(A) It recently provided extra funding for research and development.
(B) It has released a budget proposal for next year.
(C) It offers a benefits package to its part-time employees.
(D) It plans to hire additional employees to work in factories.

Questions 168-171 refer to the following article from a company newsletter.

Employee Winner of National Contest

One of our employees here at Arrow Design Laboratory, Jennifer Holt, has won first place in a Web design contest hosted by the Association of Web Designers (AWD). Entrants were judged according to clarity of idea, quality of execution, and aesthetics. Ms. Holt was selected among over 300 different applicants. We applaud her achievement and are so happy to have her as an employee at Arrow Design Laboratory.

The Association of Web Designers is an organization founded in 2002 with the goal of emphasizing the importance of Web design and protecting the rights of Web designers. The AWD has members all over the world and is constantly gaining new members. The AWD hosts a variety of contests in order to promote Web design as a professional field. The AWD believes that good design can enhance people's lives and build better communities.

As a recipient of the first place for the Web design contest, Ms. Holt will receive a cash prize as well as free membership in the Association of Web Designers. In addition, she has been invited to give a speech at the Annual Web Designers' Conference to be held next month in Los Angeles, California. The AWD will be holding more contests in the future, and those interested should visit the website at www.awd.com/contests to find out more information.

168. Why most likely was the article written?
(A) To introduce a new employee
(B) To report on an award winner
(C) To announce an annual competition
(D) To describe a change in company policy

169. The word "founded" in paragraph 2, line 1, is closest in meaning to
(A) discovered
(B) learned
(C) established
(D) equipped

170. What is suggested about the Association of Web Designers?
(A) It holds a conference every year.
(B) It is based in Los Angeles.
(C) It currently offers free membership.
(D) It donates to community projects.

171. According to the article, what can be found on the website?
(A) A transcript of a speech
(B) An application for an open position
(C) Details about upcoming contests
(D) A list of Ms. Holt's accomplishments

GO ON TO THE NEXT PAGE

Questions 172-175 refer to the following article.

16 July, Newtown—Health Shack is downtown Newtown's hottest new hangout for fitness buffs and corporate employees alike. – [1] – Owners Jill and Barry Baker opened the shop last month to rave reviews and long lines. Getting a seat or table at Health Shack can take as long as 30 minutes on a good day, and the place is always crowded no matter the time of day. Health Shack offers only six items on its menu—all protein shakes including the best sellers, Apple Pie, Peanut Butter Cup, and Tuity Fruity. – [2] –

"We were overwhelmed by the response," says Jill Baker. "In fact, everything spread by word of mouth so we didn't even need to advertise." Fitness Instructor Julian Miles said, "I love coming here for a quick lunch that won't wreck my fitness goals. I even recommend this place to all my patrons." – [3] – "I come here to get a healthy but satisfying meal during my short break with my co-workers," added business man Tim Hammer. "Without Health Shack, we'd be eating junk food." – [4] – Health Shack is open from 7 A.M. to 8 P.M. on Monday through Friday, and from 9 A.M. to 7 P.M. on Saturday. It closes on Sunday. The owners hope to add new flavors to the menu in the coming months.

172. What is suggested about the shop?

(A) It is very successful.
(B) It only offers takeout.
(C) It has been open for a long time.
(D) Only fitness experts patron the shop.

173. What is suggested about Health Shack products?

(A) They are very delicious.
(B) They are healthy.
(C) They are cheap.
(D) They are easy to get.

174. Why don't the owners advertise?

(A) They don't have enough money.
(B) They are too busy.
(C) Their customers recommend the place to others.
(D) They don't want to.

NEW

175. In which of the positions marked [1], [2], [3], and [4] does the following sentence best belong?

"Despite the limited number of items on the menu, customers can't get enough of the tasty but healthy shakes that are on offer."

(A) [1]
(B) [2]
(C) [3]
(D) [4]

Questions 176-180 refer to the following brochure and email.

Summer Lecture Series

Sponsored by the Department of City Planning at Wurnster University

The Department of City Planning is excited to announce a summer lecture series that will be focusing on budgeting issues that concern local residents and municipalities. Financial management is one of the most important duties of local government's operations. We hope to improve the status of budgeting at the local government level across the nation through community involvement and participation. All lectures will be held in the Hayston Building on the Wurnster campus.

> Monday, February 1, 6:00 P.M., Room 401
Speaker: Tim Powell, Professor of Policy Analysis at Wurnster University
Strategic Planning—Learn how to develop budgets in order to monitor progress toward community goals and successful outcomes.

> Wednesday, February 3, 7:00 P.M., Room 305
Speaker: Melissa Simmons, Kennedy Institute for Policy Making
Focusing on Our Children—Studies show that building playgrounds and sports facilities for children helps make better communities.

> Monday, February 8, 6:00 P.M., Room 202
Speaker: Hank Ross, Michigan Municipal League
Managing Our County's Parks—Learn how to preserve our local parks as a valuable community resource.

> Wednesday, February 10, 5:30 P.M., Room 404
Speaker: Scott Watson, Executive Director, Local Government Academy
Economic Opportunities and Local Ecology—Economic opportunity is often accompanied by potential risks to the surrounding ecosystem, and balancing the two can be difficult.

Please contact Patricia Flores at pflores@wurnster.edu for additional information

---

To: Patricia Flores <pflores@wurnster.edu>
From: Jake Patterson <jpatterson@wurnster.edu>
Subject: Lecture Series
Date: January 24

Dear Ms. Flores,

I work for facilities management here at Wurnster University. It was recently brought to my attention that there is a scheduling conflict concerning one of your lecture dates. Room 305 has been reserved for every Wednesday this semester by the Wurnster Debate Club. Therefore, I'm sorry to inform you that you will need to move the location or the time of this talk. You can visit the facilities management website in order to check the availability of other room locations and reschedule the talk.

Jake Patterson

GO ON TO THE NEXT PAGE

176. For whom is the lecture series most likely intended?

(A) Community members
(B) Building superintendents
(C) University professors
(D) College students

177. In the brochure, the word "through" in paragraph 1, line 5, is closest in meaning to

(A) over
(B) via
(C) across
(D) until

178. What will most likely be discussed at the lecture on February 10?

(A) How to balance yearly budgets
(B) How to meet infrastructure needs
(C) How to avoid environmental damage
(D) How to stimulate economic development

179. According to Mr. Patterson, whose lecture must be rescheduled?

(A) Mr. Watson's
(B) Mr. Ross's
(C) Ms. Simmons's
(D) Mr. Powell's

180. What is Ms. Flores instructed to do on a website?

(A) Download a document
(B) Check room availability
(C) Update personal information
(D) Facilitate a forum

Questions 181-185 refer to the following email and list.

To: Sally Russell <srussell@ptmail.com>
From: Kelly Bennett <kbennett@msplanning.com>
Date: December 7
Subject: Wedding Services
Attachment: Packages

Dear Ms. Russell,

We received your email on Tuesday, December 4, inquiring about our wedding planning and event services. We specialize in all kinds of weddings (small- or large-scale, indoor or outdoor, and various kinds of decor tailored to your dream wedding). We are sure to have a solution just right for you.

You wrote that you want a wedding package that is less than $5,000 and will be held at a large venue close to a major highway because you expect many guests from all over the country. As I understand it, your other preferences are as follows:

- an outdoor venue
- a photographer and videographer available at all times for documentation
- decorations including colorful flowers and elegant tablecloths

I've attached a list of all our possible wedding packages that you might be interested in. They are all located within 15 minutes' drive of Highway 519. Please look through the provided information to decide which location fits your needs best. Once you have made a decision, please inform me via email when you would like the wedding to be held. This will help me secure a reservation for you.

Thanks,

Kelly Bennett
MS Planning

Package	Total Fee	Location	Notes
Diamond	$5,500	Hardy Theater	Everything from the Emerald package, plus a live string quartet
Emerald	$4,300	Zenith Park	Everything from the Ruby package, plus photo and video shoots
Ruby	$3,000	Country Springs Hotel	Everything from the Sapphire package, plus decorated tables and beautiful flowers
Sapphire	$1,750	Jubilee Garden	Buffet lunch and a variety of beverages

GO ON TO THE NEXT PAGE

181. What can be inferred about Ms. Russell?

(A) She is Ms. Bennett's co-worker.
(B) She is planning a honeymoon.
(C) She is currently engaged.
(D) She works for a catering company.

182. Which occupation does Ms. Bennett most likely have?

(A) A professional musician
(B) A wedding photographer
(C) An interior designer
(D) An event planner

183. What is suggested about all the locations on the list?

(A) They are close to a main road.
(B) They are indoor venues.
(C) They are located in the same city.
(D) They require a down payment.

184. What information is Ms. Russell asked to provide?

(A) A potential date
(B) A meal selection
(C) A list of guests
(D) A honeymoon location

185. What package would probably best suit Ms. Russell's needs?

(A) Diamond
(B) Emerald
(C) Ruby
(D) Sapphire

NEW **Questions 186-190** refer to the following emails.

To: <info@bountifulharvest.com>
From: Emily Hall <emilyhall@zipline.com>
Date: June 3
Subject: Food Delivery

To whom it may concern,

My name is Emily Hall, and I am the owner of a vegetarian restaurant located in downtown Huntsville. I am contacting you because I am interested in receiving regular shipments of fresh, organic vegetables to my restaurant weekly. My restaurant is just starting, so I do not need a large quantity of goods. After looking into different farms in the area, I chose to contact Bountiful Harvest because of your promise to deliver certified organic food. Therefore, I would like to receive a price estimate for the cost of having fresh vegetables delivered directly to our restaurant on a weekly basis.

Emily Hall

To: Emily Hall <emilyhall@zipline.com>
From: Bountiful Harvest <info@bountifulharvest.com>
Date: June 4
Subject: RE: Food Delivery

Dear Ms. Hall,

Thanks for contacting our farm. At Bountiful Harvest, we offer fresh organic produce that can be delivered directly to a customer's location on a regular basis. Our vegetables are harvested from the field and delivered immediately, which means that you are getting wholesome, nutritious, organic produce to serve at your restaurant. We also offer additional items such as fresh meat, cheese, and milk. Below is a table detailing the various pricing options we offer.

Package Option	Features	Weight	Delivery Frequency	Price Per Delivery
Personal	This package feeds approximately two to three people and contains fresh, seasonal vegetables.	5 lb.	Once a week	$15
Small	This package is ideal for small businesses and includes fresh, seasonal vegetables.	50 lb.	Once a week	$140
Medium	This package is for medium-sized businesses needing a constant supply of fresh vegetables and meats.	130 lb.	Twice a week	$500
Large	This package is our largest package and includes vegetables, meats, and dairy products.	250 lb.	Twice a week	$800

The prices listed above do not include the delivery price. Customers who do not pick up their packages in person will have to pay an extra $6 per package to be delivered. However, for customers who sign up for an entire year's worth of deliveries, we will deliver your package for free. The purchase of additional items will also affect the final price of your package. Additional options are available on our website. Payments can be made via cash, credit card, check, or money order on the day of delivery.

We know that our customers especially care about the quality of the food. Therefore, we offer a mini-package free of charge so you can assess our food. Please call Greg Lemons at 555-8141 to take advantage of this opportunity.

Indira Singh

GO ON TO THE NEXT PAGE

To: Bountiful Harvest <info@bountifulharvest.com>
From: Emily Hall <emilyhall@zipline.com>
Date: June 5
Subject: Harvest Schedule

Dear Ms. Singh,

Thank you for responding so promptly to my email. I appreciate the offer of the complimentary delivery, but I think I would like to just go ahead and set up regular deliveries. I may be interested in setting up a year's worth of deliveries, but I would first like to get a list of the range of produce that you will be offering through the different seasons. As I own a vegetarian restaurant, I will need to have an idea of the types of produce that will be delivered, so I can prepare my menus accordingly. Thank you so much for your consideration, and I look forward to working with Bountiful Harvest!

Kind regards,
Emily Hall

186. What is the purpose of the first email?

(A) To request cost information
(B) To inquire about a policy change
(C) To postpone an order
(D) To report an incorrect invoice

187. What package option most likely fits Ms. Hall's needs best?

(A) Personal
(B) Small
(C) Medium
(D) Large

188. What information is NOT needed for a final price?

(A) Length of contract
(B) Method of delivery
(C) Additional items
(D) Distance of shipping

189. What is indicated in Emily Hall's email?

(A) She wants to try it for a month.
(B) She wants the free gift.
(C) She is interested in a long term contract.
(D) She doesn't want winter produce.

190. Why does Emily Hall want to know about the vegetables that will be available throughout the year?

(A) She loves vegetables.
(B) She is thinking about adding meat.
(C) She might hire another employee.
(D) She wants to plan her future menus.

Questions 191-195 refer to the following notice and emails.

Important Notice

Dear Castelli customers,

Our quality assurance team has revealed that five hundred jars of Castelli's Classic Spaghetti Sauce do not meet our high standards of product quality.

The defect has been caused by an improper seal on the lid of the jar, and may have resulted in the contents spoiling due to contact with air. We are currently warning customers not to eat this product.

What you should do: If you have already purchased a jar of Castelli's Classic Spaghetti Sauce, please send an email to our Customer Service Department at cs@castellifood.com. One of our employees will provide you with a product replacement voucher. Please include your name, full address, phone number, and the product's serial number in the email. Customers will receive a $12 voucher for each jar purchased. Please do not try to get a refund for this product at a retailer.

Please remember that no other Castelli food products are affected. We encourage you to continue purchasing our products.

To: <cs@castellifood.com>
From: Tony Hester <tonyhester21@webzit.com>
Date: March 29
Subject: Replacement Voucher

To whom it may concern,

My name is Tony Hester, and I appreciate the precautionary step. Around two weeks ago I purchased two jars of Castelli's Classic Spaghetti Sauce from an Ace grocery store in Hermantown, Minnesota. A week later, I purchased one more jar of it at the same place.

I have attached the image file of both receipts to this email. I would like to receive a product replacement voucher for these defective products. My address is:

Tony Hester
27 Bloom Street
Hermantown, MN 55811

I look forward to receiving a reply soon.

Tony Hester

GO ON TO THE NEXT PAGE →

To: Tony Hester <tonyhester21@webzit.com>
From: <cs@castellifood.com>
Date: March 30
Subject: Voucher

Dear Mr. Hester,

Thank you very much for contacting Castelli Foods. We are committed to ensuring that our customers can continue to rely on the Castelli line of quality foods for all their dining needs. As such, we are happy to provide you with three vouchers for the cans of Classic Spaghetti Sauce you recently purchased. Please find the vouchers enclosed.

In addition to the vouchers for the Classic Spaghetti Sauce, we would like to offer you vouchers for our new line of linguini and spaghetti pasta, Pasta Prima. Please accept these as another way for us to say that we are sorry, and we hope that you continue to turn to us for delicious Italian flavors.

Sincerely,
Jan Olson, Customer Care Specialist

191. Where would the notice most likely be found?

(A) In a restaurant
(B) In a staff break room
(C) In a shipping agency
(D) In a grocery store

192. What is indicated about the jars?

(A) They were not closed tightly.
(B) They are currently out of stock.
(C) They were priced incorrectly.
(D) They were delivered to the wrong address.

193. According to the notice, what is NOT mentioned as advice for customers?

(A) Avoiding consuming the product
(B) Reporting on the product
(C) Returning the product to a store
(D) Purchasing other Castelli products

194. In the letter to Mr. Hester, what additional gift does Castelli offer?

(A) Pasta sauce
(B) A recipe book
(C) Vouchers for produce
(D) Vouchers for new products

195. Castelli is sending the vouchers for several reasons; which of the following is NOT one of them?

(A) To keep customers loyal
(B) To say that they were sorry
(C) To be fair to their customers
(D) To gain new customers

Questions 196-200 refer to the following form, email, and notice.

Auburn City Restaurant Inspection

Restaurant Name: Polito's Pizza **Location:** 43 Clark Street **Inspection Date:** January 22

A: Comply completely with safety and health requirements with no violations
B: Conform to most safety and health requirements with a few minor violations
C: Not meet some safety and health requirements with some violations
D: Not satisfy many safety and health requirements with serious violations that could result in harm or illness for a customer
(Fines will be imposed for any C or D level violations related to food preparation and storage.)

Item	Score
1. Personnel regularly wash hands and follow hygienic practices.	B
2. Raw meats and vegetables are refrigerated at proper temperatures.	A
3. All ingredients are properly stored and labeled.	C
4. Dishes and utensils are cleaned and sterilized.	A
5. Fire extinguishers are easily accessible.	B
6. Fire exits are clearly marked.	C
7. Floors are clean and dry.	B

To avoid additional penalties, restaurants are warned to correct violations before their next inspection.

Restaurant Owner: Greg Kluck
Inspector: Melissa Tenner

To: All Employees <employees@politospizza.com>
From: Greg Kluck <gregkluck@politospizza.com>
Subject: Inspection results
Date: January 25

Dear employees,

The results from our recent inspection on January 22 indicate that there are a few problems that we need to address.

First, it was brought to my attention that fire exit signs need to be installed again.

The most serious violation concerned the improper storage and labeling of food. All ingredients stored for later use must be labeled with an exact date and detailed contents. If we do not label containers properly, spoiled food could accidentally be served to customers.

We received relatively low grades for employee hygiene and the cleanliness of our facilities. All employees are required to wear their uniform and hairnet at all times and to wash their hands after every bathroom visit. We also need to mop floors more often and keep them dry.

In order to correct these poor situations, I will be posting a checklist that all employees will be required to complete every morning. It will include necessary preparations to ensure that we are not breaking any regulations. This measure will go into effect on January 29.

If you have any questions about these changes, please bring them up at the staff meeting tomorrow.

GO ON TO THE NEXT PAGE

NOTICE TO ALL EMPLOYEES

The checklist below must be signed by every employee every day that they have a shift at Polito's Pizza. Only sign the task once it has been completed or checked. Failure to fill out the checklist with the date, time, and signature will be treated as a violation of Polito's new health standards.

POLITO'S CHECKLIST

Polito's	Sun	Mon	Tue	Wed	Thu	Fri	Sat
Rotate Food	K.P.	K.P.	K.P.	K.P.			K.P.
Mop Floors	K.P.	K.P.	K.P.	K.P.			K.P.
Uniforms	K.P.	K.P.	K.P.	K.P.			K.P.
Wash hands	K.P.	K.P.	K.P.	K.P.			K.P.

196. Why was the inspection conducted?

(A) To monitor compliance with food industry regulations
(B) To rate the taste and quality of the cuisine
(C) To inspect the structural safety of the building
(D) To evaluate the effectiveness of new policies

197. Why has Polito's Pizza been charged a fine?

(A) Because fire extinguishers were not in place
(B) Because containers of food were not marked appropriately
(C) Because raw meats and vegetables were handled incorrectly
(D) Because the facilities were not cleaned according to standards

198. What does Mr. Kluck ask his employees to do?

(A) Apologize to customers
(B) Wear a name tag at all times
(C) File a complaint with Ms. Tenner
(D) Fill out a required form

199. What will happen if an employee fails to sign the work checklist?

(A) They will have a violation on their record.
(B) They will have to pay a fine.
(C) They will have to come in on the weekends.
(D) They will be fired.

200. Based on Polito's Checklist, what can we infer about K.P.?

(A) He works at night.
(B) He did not work on Thursday and Friday.
(C) He will be fired for violations.
(D) He is slow at work.

NO TEST MATERIAL ON THIS PAGE

Stop! This is the end of the test. If you finish before time is called, you may go back to Parts 5, 6, and 7 and check your work.

ACTUAL TEST 02

READING TEST

In the Reading test, you will read a variety of texts and answer several different types of reading comprehension questions. The entire Reading test will last 75 minutes. There are three parts, and directions are given for each part. You are encouraged to answer as many questions as possible within the time allowed.

You must mark your answers on the separate answer sheet. Do not write your answers in your test book.

PART 5

Directions: A word or phrase is missing in each of the sentences below. Four answer choices are given below each sentence. Select the best answer to complete the sentence. Then mark the letter (A), (B), (C), or (D) on your answer sheet.

101. With the help of one of the IT technicians, the missing accounting files have been -------.

(A) recover
(B) recovers
(C) recovering
(D) recovered

102. A private reception for gallery donors will be ------- on March 5, prior to the grand opening of the exhibit.

(A) held
(B) faced
(C) claimed
(D) made

103. Aurora Furnishings is finding it difficult to make a profit in its ------- competitive market.

(A) increases
(B) increased
(C) increasingly
(D) increase

104. A minor electrical malfunction was discovered by the pilot ------- before the plane took off.

(A) barely
(B) shortly
(C) absolutely
(D) exclusively

105. We will make a final decision about changing the landscaping of the property after reviewing the ------- costs.

(A) estimation
(B) estimate
(C) estimated
(D) estimating

106. MyHealth Co. has produced a wide range of vitamin supplements for ------- two decades.

(A) along
(B) during
(C) over
(D) when

107. The April edition of *Fishing and More* magazine looks ------- different from previous issues because of the new art editor.

(A) completed
(B) complete
(C) completely
(D) completing

108. The customer's order ------- will be sent by email within twenty-four hours.

(A) confirmation
(B) confirms
(C) confirmed
(D) confirm

109. The maintenance team's repair requests should be ------- in groups according to the urgency.

(A) organizing
(B) organize
(C) organized
(D) organizes

110. Following Ms. Rivera's ------- statement, the official awards ceremony for Plex Industries will commence.

(A) brief
(B) straight
(C) former
(D) steep

111. Due to the high volume of foot traffic, the shop must polish its floors more ------- than usual during the peak season.

(A) frequent
(B) frequented
(C) frequency
(D) frequently

112. The Master Gardeners Club had to ------- its monthly meeting because the community center's conference room was double-booked.

(A) prepare
(B) oppose
(C) postpone
(D) extend

113. Financial advisors report that older investors tend to be ------- than their younger counterparts.

(A) cautious
(B) cautioned
(C) more cautious
(D) caution

114. Mr. Albrecht's ------- in replying to the HR director's email demonstrated that he was highly interested in the position.

(A) promptness
(B) prompted
(C) prompt
(D) promptly

115. The soccer players usually practice on the main field at Waterbury Park, but they sometimes practice -------.

(A) everybody
(B) twice
(C) yet
(D) elsewhere

116. The accountants were unable to produce a full report by the deadline, but promised that ------- would give a summary of the important points.

(A) their
(B) themselves
(C) they
(D) theirs

GO ON TO THE NEXT PAGE →

117. Despite having some problems with the sound system during the performance, the concert was an ------- experience for everyone.

(A) enjoyable
(B) enjoyment
(C) enjoys
(D) enjoyably

118. ------- the building has an excellent location and a modern interior, it is popular among visitors.

(A) In view of
(B) Provided that
(C) Other than
(D) Seeing that

119. The Parks and Recreation Department offers ------- opportunities for volunteers to improve the community.

(A) reward
(B) rewards
(C) rewarded
(D) rewarding

120. The vacant rooms on the inn's second floor have ------- been cleaned.

(A) most
(B) every
(C) some
(D) all

121. The short story cannot be reprinted ------- explicit permission from the writer.

(A) without
(B) regarding
(C) among
(D) unlike

122. The restaurant has a ------- decorated room that is perfect for hosting children's parties.

(A) cheerful
(B) cheerfully
(C) cheerfulness
(D) cheer

123. A wildlife expert is scheduled to give a talk on the ------- that the factory has had on the surrounding forest.

(A) components
(B) degree
(C) requirements
(D) impact

124. The landlord raised the monthly rent for the first time in several years, and ------- so.

(A) reasonable
(B) reasonably
(C) reason
(D) reasons

125. As long as there are no further delays, the factory will be fully ------- by June 18.

(A) operational
(B) operate
(C) operates
(D) operation

126. Thanks to his experience, Mr. Warren is ------- capable of completing the job on his own.

(A) certainly
(B) certain
(C) certainty
(D) certify

127. Because of ------- fuel costs, some people are choosing to stay home for the summer vacation rather than drive to tourist sites.

(A) rising
(B) above
(C) dependable
(D) lengthy

128. The green light on the side of the water purifier lights up ------- the filter needs to be replaced.

(A) likewise
(B) whenever
(C) therefore
(D) whereas

129. Two items in Ms. Burke's order were out of stock, so her invoice was adjusted -------.

(A) continuously
(B) accordingly
(C) immeasurably
(D) recognizably

130. The notice indicated that a first aid training course will be provided free of charge to ------- next month.

(A) residents
(B) residence
(C) residential
(D) resides

GO ON TO THE NEXT PAGE

PART 6

Directions: Read the texts that follow. A word, phrase, or sentence is missing in parts of each text. Four answer choices for each question are given below the text. Select the best answer to complete the text. Then mark the letter (A), (B), (C), or (D) on your answer sheet.

Questions 131-134 refer to the following notice.

Employee Spring Training

Lawrence Paper is dedicated to helping all of its employees fulfill their potential. That is why we have once again organized two days of spring training. Human Resources has put together a wide range of topics for this year's workshops, ------- **131.** sales techniques, computer skills, communication strategies, and goal setting. We still have two workshop time slots available, so if there is something you've been dying to learn about, please let us know. It's quite possible we ------- **132.** it into this year's spring training. ------- **133.** Feel free to ------- **134.** any ideas you might have to Nancy Kensington in the Human Resources department.

131. (A) distributing
(B) locating
(C) including
(D) advancing

132. (A) were incorporating
(B) have incorporated
(C) are incorporating
(D) could incorporate

NEW

133. (A) If we get many suggestions, we could also hold a workshop on the following weekend, December 4th.
(B) We'll be finalizing our choices by the end of the week.
(C) A large amount of time and energy has gone into organizing this conference.
(D) Inviting friends and family to these events is always encouraged.

134. (A) create
(B) request
(C) submit
(D) transfer

Questions 135-138 refer to the following advertisement.

Vander Properties

Vander Properties has been serving Houston for over 29 years. It is through our commitment to providing the highest degree of expertise market knowledge and ------- (**135.**) service that we are recognized as an industry leader.

We specialize in ------- (**136.**) and corporate real estate here in the Denver area. ------- (**137.**) you are looking to buy a new home or start a new business, we are the people you should be talking with. With our office centrally located in downtown, we have our eyes on the whole city. Browse our site for available listings, or give us a call today. ------- (**138.**)

www.vanderproperties.com

Phone: (313) 782-9919

Address: 834 Walton St.

135. (A) personalize
(B) personalizes
(C) personalizing
(D) personalized

136. (A) productive
(B) promoted
(C) relevant
(D) residential

137. (A) Whether
(B) Even if
(C) Even though
(D) However

NEW

138. (A) Take a drive out of town and come see us today.
(B) We appreciate your assistance.
(C) Of course, drop-ins are always welcome.
(D) Our kitchen is open from eight to five daily.

GO ON TO THE NEXT PAGE

Questions 139-142 refer to the following notice.

Pizza Chef Wanted

Papa Gino's is hiring, and all ------- (139.) applicants will be considered. ------- (140.) Even If you have no experience, training will be provided if you meet our requirements. To meet our requirements you must have a ------- (141.) health card, have reliable transportation, and be able to work evenings and weekends. Please apply in person at Papa Gino's on State and Pine. ------- (142.) look forward to meeting you.

139. (A) qualify
(B) qualifying
(C) qualified
(D) to qualify

NEW

140. (A) We are looking for candidates that have some experience in Italian food.
(B) We are looking for candidates that can speak Italian.
(C) We are looking for people who like to eat pizza.
(D) We are looking for people who want to practice.

141. (A) valid
(B) working
(C) effective
(D) strong

142. (A) She
(B) They
(C) We
(D) He

Questions 143-146 refer to the following letter.

November 11th

John Adams

Tri-State, Apt. 408

New York, NY 10873

Dear Mr. Adams,

I am pleased to inform you that you ------- (143.) as one of the finalists for the position of sales director at Goldie Saks. Over 100 applicants applied for the ------- (144.) but we have narrowed down our list to eight candidates. You will be called in for an interview on November 15th from 1 P.M. to 6 P.M. ------- (145.) The location of the interview will be the company headquarters. Our assistant, Miss Lane, will meet you in the main lobby and take you to the interview room.

For the candidates that do well in these interviews, there will be a second interview. We will let you know as soon as possible whether you ------- (146.).

Please call us at 555-1234 if you have any further questions.

We hope to see you soon.

Sincerely,

Jennifer Law

Executive Manager

143. (A) were choosing
(B) had chosen
(C) have been chosen
(D) chose

144. (A) position
(B) location
(C) career
(D) appointment

NEW

145. (A) The building is easy to locate.
(B) We would like you to come in at 1 P.M.
(C) Our interviewers will ask you several questions.
(D) You will be given a specific schedule.

146. (A) enable
(B) approve
(C) refuse
(D) qualify

GO ON TO THE NEXT PAGE

PART 7

Directions: In this part you will read a selection of texts, such as magazine and newspaper articles, emails, and instant messages. Each text or set of texts is followed by several questions. Select the best answer for each question and mark the letter (A), (B), (C), or (D) on your answer sheet.

Questions 147-148 refer to the following advertisement.

This Amazing World Photography Competition

The monthly travel magazine *This Amazing World* is offering a discounted subscription rate for those who sign up during the month of November. *This Amazing World* has been in print for over 30 years and offers readers insider tips and expert know-how to help you plan the vacation of your dreams. The magazine includes vacation package advertisements, reviews from travelers, and insightful essays to introduce you to various cultures, cuisines, and travel destinations.

Submit your travel photos to our This Amazing World Photography Competition for a chance to win a fantastic vacation to Scotland! The winner of the top prize will receive round-trip tickets and a $2,000 travel voucher for a hotel stay for you and one other person.

147. What is mentioned about the magazine?

(A) It is a literary journal.
(B) It includes a recipe book as a supplement.
(C) It provides travel advice.
(D) It has an online version.

148. What is suggested about the competition?

(A) It is sponsored by professional photographers.
(B) It awards a complimentary vacation to the winner.
(C) It accepts digital photos only.
(D) It features photos of Scotland.

Questions 149-151 refer to the following text message chain.

Liz Bradley **8:14**
Sir, the arrangements have been made for your meeting with Mr. Johnson tomorrow afternoon. I've reserved a table for two at Sheraton Restaurant at 1 P.M.

Bernie Gibbs **8:17**
Thank you. And have you compiled the reports that I'll need at the meeting?

Liz Bradley **8:18**
Most of them, yes. I'm still waiting for Michael Steel's reports. He told me that he would have them ready for me sometime this morning.

Bernie Gibbs **8:20**
Well, they should have been completed last night. Can you contact him and see what's going on?

(Michael Steel was added to the conversation at 8:26)

Liz Bradley **8:27**
Michael, Mr. Gibbs wants to know where the reports are. Are you finished with them?

Michael Steele **8:28**
I apologize for the delay. Our intern accidentally deleted some files. I had to scour the database to locate the back-up material. It was a bit of a headache sorting through the files that I needed, but I think I have everything organized, and I'm printing them out now.

Liz Bradley **8:29**
Can you bring them to me as soon as you're done?

Michael Steel **8:30**
Of course. I'll be there in 10 minutes.

GO ON TO THE NEXT PAGE →

149. Who most likely is Liz Bradley?

(A) An intern
(B) An assistant
(C) A business partner
(D) An executive

150. Why was Michael Steel added to the conversation?

(A) To have him give an update about the missing reports
(B) To inform him about the upcoming meeting
(C) To let him know about the deadline
(D) To scold him for his lack of punctuality

NEW

151. What does Michael imply when he says, "I had to scour the database to locate the back-up material"?

(A) He took his time writing the report.
(B) He had to back up all the information first.
(C) He needed time to find the missing data.
(D) The computer was out of order.

Questions 152-153 refer to the following Web page.

www.turnerandco.com

Turner & Co.

158 Baskin Road, Redwood Bay, UK
Phone: 243-555-1541

HOME	ABOUT US	PRODUCTS	REPLACEMENT	CONTACT US

Turner & Co. has produced beautiful, energy-efficient windows that meet the taste and expectations of our customers since its founding in 1949. When you choose Turner & Co., you are buying more than just a window. You will be receiving the excellent services of our professionals who have been performing superb work for decades. We are passionate about helping you choose a quality window that exactly fits the specifications of your home. Additionally, we are fully committed to environmental protection and have recently been recognized for our sustainable business practices by the Environmental Protection Agency (EPA).

152. What is being advertised?

(A) An insurance company
(B) A window manufacturer
(C) A landscaping company
(D) A window cleaning service provider

153. What is indicated about Turner & Co.?

(A) It is a family-run business.
(B) Its branches are located nationwide.
(C) It is an eco-friendly company.
(D) It has recently hired experienced employees.

GO ON TO THE NEXT PAGE

Questions 154-155 refer to the following text message.

From: Sam Bell
To: Jane Brooks

Jane, please let me know Mr. Fraser's phone number. He has some data I need right now. I am a little behind schedule on the monthly financial report, and I need to dedicate all my time to it today.

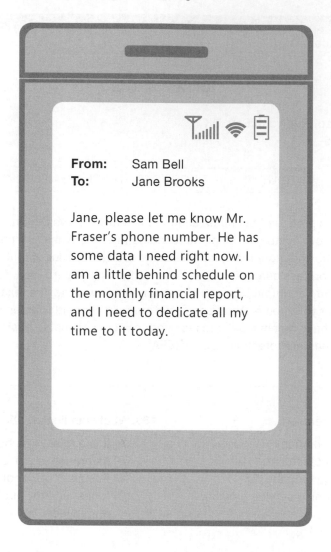

154. Why was the message sent?

(A) To ask for a favor
(B) To postpone a deadline
(C) To cancel a meeting
(D) To request a document

155. What is indicated about Mr. Bell?

(A) He is unable to attend a meeting.
(B) He expects profits to increase.
(C) He is trying to meet a deadline.
(D) He was recently hired.

Questions 156-158 refer to the following article.

SEOUL (July 19) – Breamin's Group opened the doors to its first B&G clothing shop on the famed Abgujeong Rodeo street in South Korea to long lines and frantic shoppers. – [1] – The frenzy was over the limited edition line designed by Marichio Bucci in partnership with B&G. Within just a couple of hours of opening the doors, most of the Bucci design items were sold out. Similar reports of chaos and empty shelves which once held items from the Bucci line were echoed in major cities around the world including New York, London, Tokyo, and Milan. – [2] – Although B&G has released limited edition collaborations with other famous designers, this is the first time that B&G shops have reported a complete depletion of items within hours of its release. The Bucci and B&G collaboration is the most successful to date, and talks are already in progress over future collaborations for more clothing lines. – [3] – Meanwhile in Seoul, shoppers who were unable to purchase from the Bucci line were disappointed but excited to have the popular retailer open in Korea. – [4] –

156. What is indicated about B&G?

(A) They have stores around the world.
(B) They only sell items designed by Bucci.
(C) The company has a few branches in Korea.
(D) Their products usually sell out within hours.

157. What is reported about the Bucci and B&G collaboration?

(A) It took years to put together.
(B) It was only sold in select stores.
(C) It's one of the most profitable collaborations for the company.
(D) It will only be a one-time event.

NEW

158. In which of the positions marked [1], [2], [3], and [4] does the following sentence best belong?

"This is a first for the company since all previous limited designer edition lines were simply a one-time partnership."

(A) [1]
(B) [2]
(C) [3]
(D) [4]

GO ON TO THE NEXT PAGE

Questions 159-161 refer to the following memo.

MEMO

To: All staff
From: Elizabeth Paine
Date: January 24
Subject: Sick leave

Attention employees,

We are going to make adjustments to our policies concerning sick leave here at Zimnet Corporation. We are considering reducing the number of paid vacation days and instead increasing the number of paid sick days available to employees. Before we make any changes, we would like to gather the opinions of employees on this matter. Please email Tony Nugent at tonynugent@zimnet.com. He will be collecting and analyzing your responses. Afterward, management will produce a corresponding policy proposal by February 24. Once the proposal has been made, a meeting will be called to discuss its implementation among all of our employees. I hope this process can be helpful to all of our employees. Please be active in your participation.

Sincerely,

Elizabeth Paine

159. What is the purpose of the memo?

(A) To suggest a budget proposal
(B) To solicit feedback
(C) To revise incorrect information
(D) To announce survey results

160. Which job is Mr. Nugent most likely to have?

(A) A sales representative
(B) A product developer
(C) An investment analyst
(D) A personnel employee

161. According to the memo, what will Ms. Paine probably do soon after February 24?

(A) Announce a merger
(B) Hire a medical specialist
(C) Participate in a tour
(D) Schedule a meeting

Questions 162-165 refer to the following text message chain.

Penny Jones **3:27**
I just got a call from Martin. His client, Mr. Patrick, would like to have his order two weeks earlier than originally planned. Essentially, by next week Monday. Do you think this is possible? I'd like your input.

Karen Norman **3:28**
There's no problem on our end. Most of the leather has already been cut. We've already sent many of the pieces to be sewn. The rest of the work should take a couple of hours.

Neil Park **3:29**
The handles are complete, and about half the bags are near completion. I'll get them to Lauren soon. I think we should be able to finish sewing the bags by tomorrow evening.

Penny Jones **3:30**
I'm glad to hear that most of the handbags are almost finished. Lauren, how long will it take to get the hardware attached or sewn in?

Lauren Nichols **3:31**
We're currently working on the Jenk and Cenk twins orders.

Penny Jones **3:32**
We have more than enough time to complete the twin's orders, so I can authorize your workers to put aside that project for now. How long will Mr. Patrick's order take?

Lauren Nichols **3:33**
The zippers need to be sewn in, but the studs will be glued, which makes the work easier. I think we need about a day.

Kevin Harding **3:34**
It'll only take us a couple of hours to have the order packaged safely to be shipped.

Penny Jones **3:35**
Thank you so much. I'll let our client know.

GO ON TO THE NEXT PAGE →

162. What kind of business does the client most likely own?

(A) A clothing shop
(B) A furniture company
(C) A shoe store
(D) A handbag business

163. According to the conversation, whose department must complete the work first?

(A) Karen Norman's
(B) Neil Park's
(C) Lauren Nichols's
(D) Kevin Harding's

NEW

164. At 3:31, why does Lauren Nichols say, "We're currently working on the Jenk and Cenk twins orders"?

(A) To inform everyone that they have their own clients
(B) To explain why they refuse to help
(C) To imply that they are busy with another project
(D) To make everyone speed up their work

165. What will Penny Jones most likely tell Mr. Patrick?

(A) That his order will be finished two weeks later
(B) That his request can be fulfilled
(C) That his order will cost him extra money
(D) That there may be a delay to his order

Questions 166-168 refer to the following notice.

Business Hours in Early March

Monday	Tuesday	Wednesday	Thursday	Friday	Saturday	Sunday
2:00 p.m. | 9:00 p.m.	2:00 p.m. | 8:00 p.m.	3:00 p.m. | 9:00 p.m.	4:00 p.m. | 9:00 p.m.	2:00 p.m. | 9:00 p.m.	2:00 p.m. | 10:00 p.m.	9:00 a.m. | 6:00 p.m.

Due to the current construction on Shilling Street, we have been forced to revise our business hours for the first week in March (see the chart above). During the morning hours, the construction makes it difficult for customers to reach our location by car. We will be extending our evening hours to accommodate this change. Additionally, due to the construction, our parking lot is also currently inaccessible. Therefore, during this period, customers are asked to utilize public parking spaces available on Patch Street. We apologize for this inconvenience and strive to be back to normal soon.

166. What is being announced?

(A) A renovation project
(B) A store expansion
(C) A change in operating hours
(D) A work schedule

167. When is the construction most likely NOT being performed?

(A) On Monday
(B) On Wednesday
(C) On Saturday
(D) On Sunday

168. Why are customers asked to go to Patch Street?

(A) To find a place to park
(B) To visit a new store location
(C) To take part in a promotional event
(D) To receive a sample

GO ON TO THE NEXT PAGE

Questions 169-171 refer to the following advertisement.

For Sale by Owner

Palmer Standard Cabin Yacht

Asking price: $45,000 or best offer

Basic Specifications:
This boat was built four years ago. It is 12 feet wide by 36 feet long. The hull is made of fiberglass, making it light yet strong. The boat includes two double bedrooms as well as a sleeper sofa, kitchen, and bathroom.

Features:
This boat is very stable and offers a spacious deck. It is perfect for large families and social gatherings. It includes an eight-speaker sound system with USB connectivity. It also has a lockable storage compartment where personal belongings can be kept.

Additional Information:
I have owned and operated this boat for three and a half years. The boat comes with a five-year warranty that still has one and a half years remaining. The warranty is transferable to the buyer upon purchase.

If you would like to see or test-ride the boat, contact Gary Thompson at (654) 555-8715.

169. What is indicated about the Palmer Standard Cabin Yacht?

(A) It is a fishing boat.
(B) Its original paint color has been changed.
(C) It can accommodate a group of people.
(D) It is currently being repaired.

170. What is NOT mentioned as a feature of the Palmer Standard Cabin Yacht?

(A) Capability to play music
(B) A lightweight construction material
(C) Ample sleeping accommodations
(D) A fuel-efficient engine

171. What is most likely true about Mr. Thompson?

(A) He will give a boat tour to a potential buyer.
(B) He has young children.
(C) He works at a shipyard.
(D) He wants to sell the warranty separately.

Questions 172-175 refer to the following letter.

Travel & Recreation

123 Gilmore Street
Orange County, CA 48857

November 15
Mr. Peter Kang
3820 Rivervalley Heights
Seattle, WA 19387

Dear Mr. Kang,

We at Travel & Recreation thank you for your subscription to our magazine. As you have been a long time subscriber, I am excited to inform you about our new subscription plan for our VIP members. – [1] – As a member, you will continue to receive monthly editions of our magazine and access to our new online e-magazine services. You can simply download a digital version of the print magazine to any mobile device at no extra cost. – [2] – Furthermore, you can access background information about our authors, journalists, and guest writers, as well as detailed information about the locations and places that are covered in the magazine. In addition, you can access the recipes to the most popular restaurants around the world, and most exciting of all, we will hold an exclusive competition for our VIP members with a chance to win a trip for two to Hawaii. – [3] – Our regular subscribers, as well as VIP members, will have a chance to win a dining experience at 5-star restaurant Bellisimo.

Again, we thank you for your continued support, and we hope you enjoy the many changes we have made to our services as we strive to entertain and educate our loyal subscribers. – [4] – Please fill out the application form that is attached to this letter. Please check which subscription plan you wish to join. If you send in a $100 fee, you will receive the regular subscription plan. If you send in a $200 fee, you will become a VIP member.

We appreciate your support and hope to hear from you soon.

Sincerely,
Victoria Adams

GO ON TO THE NEXT PAGE

172. Why was a letter sent to Mr. Kang?

(A) To remind him to send in his travel journals
(B) To explain about a new subscription plan
(C) To inquire about his travel plans
(D) To determine his qualifications for a position

173. What did Ms. Adams send with the letter?

(A) A travel itinerary
(B) A new contract
(C) An application form
(D) A revised schedule

174. In the middle of the first paragraph of the letter, the term "at no extra cost" is closest in meaning to

(A) for a small fee
(B) with a donation
(C) quite easily
(D) for free

175. In which of the positions [1], [2], [3], and [4] does the following sentence best belong?
"Your subscription expires next month, but we invite you to consider joining our VIP membership."

(A) [1]
(B) [2]
(C) [3]
(D) [4]

Questions 176-180 refer to the following invoice and email.

Taylor Fabrics
Invoice

Ordered by: Tammy Fleck
Order taken by: Craig Dell
Order date: August 11
Estimated delivery date: August 14–16
Delivery address: 628 Green Circle Drive, Austin, TX 78701
Email: tfleck@capnet.com
Mobile phone: (512) 555-9782

Quantity	Item	Description		Price
4 yards	Fabric 10	Solid white		$28.00
5 yards	Fabric 38	Floral pattern		$50.00
6 yards	Fabric 41	Checkered pattern		$48.00
2 yards	Fabric 48	Leopard pattern		$30.00
			Tax	$15.60
			Shipping	$12.00
			Total	$183.60

Payment method: Billed to credit card account ending in 4680
If you have questions about your order, please email us at customerservice@taylorfabrics.com. All of our packages sent within the United States are guaranteed to arrive within 10 days of order confirmation. If they don't arrive on time, we promise to reimburse you for 30% of your total purchase.

To: customerservice@taylorfabrics.com
From: Tammy Fleck <tfleck@capnet.com>
Date: August 25
Subject: Delivery Delay

Dear Customer Service,

I received my order from Taylor Fabrics yesterday that I placed two weeks ago. Not only was the package delivered later than promised, but one of my orders was incorrectly shipped. The invoice correctly reflects my wish to receive 5 yards of the floral pattern fabric, but only 2 yards of it were delivered. Because of this error, I won't be able to complete the dress I was making for my friend's birthday. I am very disappointed.

Once this issue has been resolved and the additional fabric has been sent, please send a text message to my mobile phone.

Thank you,

Tammy Fleck

GO ON TO THE NEXT PAGE

176. What job is Mr. Dell most likely to have?

(A) A designer
(B) A salesperson
(C) A customer
(D) A manufacturer

177. What is implied about Ms. Fleck?

(A) She is a long-term customer of Taylor Fabrics.
(B) She is a professional fashion designer.
(C) She is a former employee of Taylor Fabrics.
(D) She will be partially paid back for her purchase.

178. Why did Ms. Fleck send the email?

(A) Her credit card was incorrectly charged.
(B) She wants to return an item.
(C) She received the incorrect quantity of an item.
(D) One of her orders had the wrong pattern.

179. Which fabric will Ms. Fleck need more of to make a dress?

(A) Fabric 10
(B) Fabric 38
(C) Fabric 41
(D) Fabric 48

180. How should Taylor Fabrics customer service contact Ms. Fleck?

(A) By text message
(B) By voice mail
(C) By email
(D) By letter

Questions 181-185 refer to the following advertisement and email.

Next Month at the Belmont Historical Society

Documentary Film Night: *Exploring the Arctic*
May 5, Spruce Theater

Photo Exhibition: "America in the 20th Century"
Opening Night, May 9, Linda Cameron Art Gallery

Author Talk: Glen Campbell, "The Culture of Early America"
May 14, Chris Charlton Auditorium

Musical Performance: "American Folk Masters"
May 22, Spruce Theater

Children and seniors are allowed free entry to all events. Additionally, if you pay the registration fee and become a member of the Belmont Historical Society on our website, you can attend any event free of charge.

For questions about booking group visits, contact David Smith at dsmith@belmonthistoricalsociety.com. For more details regarding upcoming events and venue locations, or to rent one of our venues, visit us at www.belmonthistoricalsociety.com.

To: David Smith <dsmith@belmonthistoricalsociety.com>
From: Jared Tate <jtate@clarkuniversity.com>
Date: April 22
Subject: Group Visit

Dear Mr. Smith,

Hello, my name is Jared Tate, and I am a professor in the History Department at Clark University in downtown Maryville.

I am teaching an introductory history course for freshmen this semester, and I thought it would be helpful to attend the event featuring Mr. Campbell. His talk is very pertinent to the subjects we are currently covering in class.

I was also wondering if it would be possible to arrange a question-and-answer session between Mr. Campbell and my group of about 50 students. Please tell him that we are looking forward to seeing him.

I appreciate your reading my email, and I hope to hear back from you soon.

Jared Tate

History Department, Clark University

GO ON TO THE NEXT PAGE

181. What is indicated about the Belmont Historical Society?

(A) It does not allow children into some events.
(B) It is run by the city of Belmont.
(C) It was founded by Linda Cameron.
(D) It will hold its events at several places.

182. What is Mr. Tate most likely currently teaching?

(A) Environmental conditions of the Arctic
(B) Early American history
(C) American folk music
(D) Modern photography

183. What is NOT mentioned as being available on the Belmont Historical Society website?

(A) Information about scheduled events
(B) Member registration
(C) Rental details
(D) Descriptions of previous events

184. In the email, the word "introductory" in paragraph 2, line 1, is closest in meaning to

(A) basic
(B) required
(C) profound
(D) optional

185. What does Mr. Tate request?

(A) A signed copy of a book
(B) A detailed survey
(C) A chance to meet a speaker
(D) A group discount

Questions 186-190 refer to the following schedule and emails.

Newton Library

April Program and Events Schedule

Date and Time	Event	Location	Additional Notes
April 2 7 P.M.	A Trip to the Past: Silent Film Series	Decker Hall	Join us for a viewing of several films showcasing early American film history.
April 5 3 P.M.	Youth Creative Writing Workshop	Youth Wing, Room 304	Open to all students in high school who want to improve their writing skills.
April 10 11 A.M.	Beginner English Conversation Club	Education Center, Room 102	Join other adults who are learning to speak English. This class is free.
April 16 5 P.M.	Never Too Late to Learn	Media Lab, Room 202	Learning to use a computer is not just for young people. Join us as we explore the sea of information, using computers. (For senior citizens)
April 29 10 A.M.	Story Play	Youth Wing, Room 301	Play with toys and hear a story. (For ages 0-5)

We would like to thank all of you who made financial donations that allowed for the purchase of new laptops and the construction of the Media Lab.

To: Richard White <rwhite@newtonlibrary.edu>
From: Linda Carter <lcarter121@seprus.com>
Date: April 1
Subject: Beginner English Conversation Club

Hi Mr. White,

My name is Linda Carter, and I am the instructor for the Beginner English Conversation Club to be held on April 10. I noticed that the library recently built the Media Lab with funds raised by library patrons. I was hoping to change classrooms in order to use my new educational resources to integrate computers into my English conversation class. Could you please reschedule my class to be held in the same classroom as Never Too Late to Learn instead of the Education Center? I think my students will appreciate the practical English skills they can learn on computers. Also, could you please send an email to all of the students who have signed up for the class? They will need to be informed about the room change.

Thank you in advance for your assistance,

Linda Carter

GO ON TO THE NEXT PAGE

To: Linda Carter <lcarter121@seprus.com>
From: Richard White <rwhite@newtonlibrary.edu>
Date: April 2
Subject: Room Change

Dear Ms. Carter,

I would be happy to move your Beginners English Conversation course to the classroom with the updated media lab; for your reference, this is room 3A. Unfortunately, I do not have the emails for all of the students who signed up for your course. Many students only provided their names. I could post a sign at the entrance to the library advertising your course and noting the room change if that would be acceptable for you. Please let me know if you would like me to do this.

Thank you and all the best,

Richard White, Library Projects Coordinator

186. What is suggested about Newton Library?

(A) It recently renovated its facilities.
(B) It will hold a fundraising event soon.
(C) It offers educational activities for various ages.
(D) It is closed on Mondays.

187. What event is most suited for film students?

(A) Story Play
(B) Youth Creative Writing Workshop
(C) A Trip to the Past
(D) Never Too Late to Learn

188. In the first email, the word "held" in paragraph 1, line 2, is closest in meaning to

(A) carried
(B) attended
(C) delayed
(D) conducted

189. Why can't Richard White send Linda's students an email?

(A) He doesn't have their emails.
(B) It is not his job.
(C) He does not have the time.
(D) The library is not equipped with that kind of technology.

190. What is Richard White's solution to the problem of informing Linda's students about the room change?

(A) He can email them.
(B) He can direct them to the right room when they enter.
(C) He will post a sign.
(D) He will draw them a map with directions.

NEW **Questions 191-195** refer to the following email, article, and sign-up sheet.

To: Tony Walker <twalker@icmcorp.com>
From: Suzie Mason <smason@icmcorp.com>
Date: May 4
Subject: Summer Calendar
Attachment: budget.doc

Dear Mr. Walker,

I am finalizing the calendar of summer events for our company. Because we went over budget last year on employee appreciation events, I think it would be wise to find more affordable recreational activities. Attached is a breakdown of projected expenses for the summer events that I have planned.

July 6: Anchorage Flower Festival

July 22: Art in the Park at Lawrence Park

August 6: Bicycle Tours of the Anchorage Countryside

August 19: Horseback Riding at Sweet Meadow Ranch

I have scheduled fewer outdoor activities this year compared to last year. This year I would like to take advantage of a new outdoor recreational opportunity that I read about on the Anchorage Reporter website. You can read the article by clicking on this link: www.anchoragereporter.com/new_trails.

Please let me know your opinion.

Suzie Mason
Human Resources Manager

Anchorage Reporter

Bike Tours of the Anchorage Countryside to Start August 6

May 2—The Anchorage Bike Club will be hosting an annual bike riding event this summer, beginning on August 6 and running through August 7. The event will start at 10 A.M. on both days at the Anchorage Community Center. If you are driving a vehicle to the starting point, it would be better to use the parking lot behind the community center.

Anchorage Bike Club President Jean Frost stated, "The rides will range from 5 to 20 miles and will take bikers through scenic areas in Anchorage. Overall, the bike tours will go ahead at a leisurely pace so that bikers of all skill levels can participate. However, local bikers with ample experience might lead a faster-paced group."

Bikers participating in the tours will learn about riding techniques, bicycle maintenance, and proper nutrition half an hour before the event starts. All participants must have biking helmets on. They are also encouraged to bring their own water to prevent dehydration while biking.

GO ON TO THE NEXT PAGE

BICYCLE TOUR SIGN UP SHEET

If you intend to participate in the August 6 bicycle tour, please write down your name, department, and level of experience or fitness. If we have enough people sign up as advanced, we can coordinate two separate tours. If there are not enough for two tours, we would like to encourage all riders to stay together so that everyone can join in the team building exercises we have planned. Thank you for your participation, and we look forward to seeing everyone at the event!

Name	Department	Fitness/experience
Tom Cruz	Sales	Beginner
Vin Jones	Inventory	Beginner
Sally Jenkins	Inventory	Beginner
Barbara Blaster	Reception	Advanced
Hope Kinski	Sales	Beginner

191. What does Ms. Mason suggest doing?

(A) Keeping within a budget for recreational activities
(B) Appointing a new manager of human resources
(C) Increasing the number of temporary employees
(D) Scheduling more outdoor activities compared to last year

192. What date does Ms. Mason suggest for this year's new activity?

(A) July 6
(B) July 22
(C) August 6
(D) August 19

193. In what section of the website would the article most likely appear?

(A) Economy
(B) Leisure
(C) Entertainment
(D) Politics

194. Based upon the Bicycle Tour Sign Up Sheet, what can we infer about the upcoming bicycle tour?

(A) It will be canceled.
(B) There will be two groups, one for beginners, one for advanced.
(C) There will be only one group.
(D) They will stop along the way for a group meal and photo.

195. What will Barbara Blaster most likely do on the bicycle tour?

(A) She will become bored and quit the tour.
(B) She will complain that more people should sign up as advanced.
(C) She will join a faster paced group of more experienced bikers.
(D) She will stay with the group to participate in group activities.

GO ON TO THE NEXT PAGE

Questions 196-200 refer to the following form and emails.

Four Seasons Apparel Outlet

All returns must be sent back to Four Seasons Apparel Outlet within seven days of delivery. They can be exchanged for a different item or returned for a refund. If you choose a refund, we will credit the card used for purchase.

Individuals with official memberships can utilize our delivery tracking service and receive frequent shopper discounts.

Return shipment(s) to:
Four Seasons Apparel Outlet, 144 Fenton Rd., Denver, CO 80725 (303-555-4387)

Check the box that best describes your problem:

___ Product contained a defect or damage
✔ Wrong item was delivered
___ Product did not match expectations
___ Other: ______

Personal Information:

Name: Sally Nelson
Order Number: 2245
Phone: 432-555-6729
Address: 2154 Oak St., Denver, CO 80725
Email: snelson@clandon.net

✔ Exchange ___ Refund

I ordered a medium-sized Snowy Christmas Sweater from your online store on April 22, but I mistakenly received a small-sized one. I would like to exchange it for the correct one.

From: Debra Clarke <debraclarke@fourseasons.com>
To: Sally Nelson <snelson@clandon.net>
Date: April 30
Subject: Exchange

Dear Ms. Nelson,

We have received your request to exchange the sweater you purchased. We sincerely apologize for this mistake. We shipped the correct item immediately as per your request. Your shipment can be tracked on our website using the following tracking number: 447H57J.

Because this was our mistake, we have returned $7 to your credit card in order to reimburse you for the return shipping costs. Please check your balance to confirm this.

If you experience any future problems with this order, you may call me at 303-555-4387. I will help you solve any problem that may arise.

Debra Clarke

To: Debra Clarke <debraclarke@fourseasons.com>
From: Sally Nelson <snelson@clandon.net>
Date: May 4
Subject: Return Error

Dear Ms. Clarke,

I was glad to receive your email regarding my return and am thankful that Four Seasons was thoughtful enough to refund my shipping cost.

That being said, I checked my account and have received the promised refund. Additionally, the new sweater that was sent to me was the right size, but I had ordered the Snowy Christmas design. What I received was Winter Festival. They are both nice sweaters, but my husband really liked Snowy Christmas better. Could you please send the design that I originally ordered? I will send the Winter Festival sweater back after I receive the correct order and my shipping refund.

Thank you!

Sally Nelson

196. What problem with the original shipment does Ms. Nelson report?

(A) It was damaged.
(B) It does not fit.
(C) It arrived late.
(D) It has not reached its destination.

197. In the email from Debra Clarke, the phrase "as per" in paragraph 1, line 2, is closest in meaning to

(A) regardless of
(B) except for
(C) rather than
(D) according to

198. What is indicated about Ms. Nelson?

(A) She recently moved to Denver.
(B) She ordered a gift for a friend.
(C) She has a Four Seasons Apparel Outlet membership.
(D) She waited too long to request a refund.

199. What problem with the replacement shipment does Ms. Nelson report?

(A) The size was incorrect.
(B) The design was incorrect.
(C) The size and design were incorrect.
(D) Too much money was refunded to her from her original purchase.

200. When will Ms. Nelson return her Winter Festival sweater?

(A) When she receives her correct order and the shipping refund.
(B) When she has time.
(C) When her husband is happy with his sweater.
(D) When Four Seasons apologizes for her inconvenience.

Stop! This is the end of the test. If you finish before time is called, you may go back to Parts 5, 6, and 7 and check your work.

ACTUAL TEST 03

READING TEST

In the Reading test, you will read a variety of texts and answer several different types of reading comprehension questions. The entire Reading test will last 75 minutes. There are three parts, and directions are given for each part. You are encouraged to answer as many questions as possible within the time allowed.

You must mark your answers on the separate answer sheet. Do not write your answers in your test book.

PART 5

Directions: A word or phrase is missing in each of the sentences below. Four answer choices are given below each sentence. Select the best answer to complete the sentence. Then mark the letter (A), (B), (C), or (D) on your answer sheet.

101. Not far ------- the train station lies Starlight Park, which is a popular destination for tourists and locals alike.

(A) from
(B) with
(C) next
(D) until

102. The sales director will give a brief talk ------- the keynote speaker is introduced.

(A) before
(B) opposite
(C) about
(D) between

103. The charity's new reading program is ------- to increase literacy rates in developing countries over the next ten years.

(A) project
(B) projecting
(C) projected
(D) projects

104. Engaging in social -------, Ms. Mason quickly expanded her network after moving to a new city.

(A) active
(B) activities
(C) activates
(D) activated

105. Artists wanting to participate in the contest should submit their work by the ------- of June 30.

(A) admission
(B) possibility
(C) deadline
(D) output

106. Drake Pharmaceuticals is ------- to have world-renowned chemist Jonas Lund as its senior lab technician.

(A) absent
(B) fortunate
(C) approximate
(D) respective

107. The Zans Corporation ------- manufacturing all of its luxury wallets and footwear domestically next year.

(A) was starting
(B) started
(C) will start
(D) has started

108. Some voters have a clear ------- for candidates who have practiced law.

(A) selection
(B) reflection
(C) component
(D) preference

109. The clerk said that ------- fifteen customers had been waiting outside the store for it to open.

(A) rougher
(B) roughly
(C) rough
(D) roughness

110. The leaky faucet has been repaired, so visitors may ------- use the first-floor restroom.

(A) however
(B) once
(C) now
(D) quite

111. The ------- of the disease can be significantly slowed by taking the medicine developed by Dr. Toft's team.

(A) progressed
(B) progression
(C) progressive
(D) progressively

112. Unfortunately, when the hurricane hit the area, residents as well as public officials were ------- unprepared.

(A) subsequently
(B) totally
(C) beneficially
(D) currently

113. The company plans on ------- the salespeople for the expenses they incurred while attending the conference.

(A) reimbursement
(B) reimbursed
(C) reimburse
(D) reimbursing

114. Ms. Carlton felt comfortable crossing the road because there were no vehicles coming in her -------.

(A) directly
(B) direction
(C) direct
(D) directs

115. ------- the television coverage of the general election, a number of high-profile candidates were interviewed live on air.

(A) During
(B) About
(C) While
(D) Since

116. Mr. Hicks ------- seating near the stage in the concert hall for important clients.

(A) cooperated
(B) entertained
(C) loosened
(D) reserved

GO ON TO THE NEXT PAGE

117. Fritz Center, the venue ------- hosts the film industry's awards banquet, is undergoing an ambitious expansion project.

(A) that
(B) where
(C) what
(D) even

118. The monthly staff dinners give employees from different departments the chance to interact with ------- on a personal level.

(A) other
(B) neither
(C) every
(D) each other

119. Landlords are required to ------- with the regulations set by the Regional Department of Safe Housing.

(A) reinforce
(B) comply
(C) fulfill
(D) interfere

120. A sturdy support beam was added to the first story of the building for ------- reasons.

(A) structures
(B) structurally
(C) structure
(D) structural

121. Eco Unite is a non-profit organization ------- to educating the public about environmental issues.

(A) proposed
(B) deferred
(C) dedicated
(D) observed

122. It is essential that the logo for Prime Vitamins be integrated ------- all of its catalogs and mailings.

(A) into
(B) of
(C) as
(D) than

123. Despite receiving rejections from several major publishers, Ian Wright ------- to become a world-famous novelist.

(A) gave up
(B) figured out
(C) brought down
(D) went on

124. Mr. Burrows was praised for creating ------- user manuals which can be easily understood.

(A) inform
(B) informant
(C) informs
(D) informative

125. Even though Ms. Garcia had a small account at the financial institution, the employee treated her ------- she were a major investor.

(A) rather than
(B) in spite of
(C) as if
(D) provided that

126. When you return an item by mail, be sure the receipt is ------- to the request form to expedite processing.

(A) attachment
(B) attached
(C) attaching
(D) attach

127. The witness saw only a ------- figure standing near the lamppost shortly before the crime was committed.

(A) solitary
(B) spare
(C) previous
(D) random

128. Ben Sanders ------- designed the suitcase to fold up easily for compact storage.

(A) innovatively
(B) innovate
(C) innovative
(D) innovation

129. Because the weather was warmer than usual this summer, the crops ------- a few weeks early.

(A) have been harvesting
(B) will have harvested
(C) are harvesting
(D) will be harvested

130. ------- auditing the financial records of Rockford Consulting, the accountant will submit an official report.

(A) In addition
(B) Given
(C) For example
(D) Upon

GO ON TO THE NEXT PAGE

PART 6

Directions: Read the texts that follow. A word, phrase, or sentence is missing in parts of each text. Four answer choices for each question are given below the text. Select the best answer to complete the text. Then mark the letter (A), (B), (C), or (D) on your answer sheet.

Questions 131-134 refer to the following notice.

Urgent! Journeyman Plumber Needed

Ace Plumbing is looking for an experienced plumber to join our ------- **131.** business here in Columbia. ------- **132.** We have always been a family owned and run business, but with the ------- **133.** increase in Columbia's population over the last three years, we have an opportunity to welcome in a new journeyman plumber. The candidate should have experience with all ------- **134.** of plumbing, both commercial and residential. Please send your résumé to aceplumbing@gmail.com, and we will schedule an interview.

131. (A) expanding
(B) expecting
(C) contracting
(D) controlling

NEW

132. (A) Ace Plumbing has been servicing the Columbia area since 1954.
(B) We have little connection to the community.
(C) We have been struggling to pay our bills.
(D) Ace Plumbing is in financial trouble.

133. (A) monstrous
(B) dramatic
(C) impossible
(D) insane

134. (A) pieces
(B) flows
(C) constructions
(D) types

Questions 135-138 refer to the following web page.

Learn Social Media Marketing Tactics
Only at Genius Marketing's Power Conference

Are you ready to take your social media marketing to the next level? Then ------- (135.) Genius Marketing's Power Conference and learn cutting edge social media marketing tactics. ------- (136.) This could be the most educational two days of your year.

Genius Marketing will give you real-world tactics to boost your paid and organic social media marketing efforts. ------- (137.) you buy social media advertising or focus on organic social media engagement, Genius Marketing's Power Conference is the conference you need to attend this year. You'll be inspired by experts, meet others with your challenges, and get actionable tactics to drive traffic, increase sales, and ------- (138.) customer satisfaction.
To apply, just click the link below.

APPLICATION

135. (A) attend
(B) attends
(C) attended
(D) attending

NEW
136. (A) Guide people in the industry to greatness by joining today.
(B) The conference will be held in Houston on May 3rd and 4th.
(C) Registration for this two-week course will be on November 20.
(D) Classes will be held throughout the month of March.

137. (A) Either
(B) Whether
(C) Rather
(D) Not only

138. (A) divide
(B) gain
(C) devalue
(D) endure

GO ON TO THE NEXT PAGE

ACTUAL TEST 03

Questions 139-142 refer to the following email.

To: Nancy Craft

From: Omar Patel

Date: January 16

Subject: Pre-shipping Procedures

At the manufacturing team meeting, ------- **139.** was raised that inventory wasn't always being properly stored before being shipped. ------- **140.** to that concern, the team decided to review the written procedure to determine if additional steps should be added. ------- **141.** Please try to arrange the schedules of the team in the packaging and storage wing so a majority of the managers can attend this meeting.

I am confident that the packaging and storage team management ------- **142.** that the written procedure leaves no room for any inventory to accidently be improperly stored. Any suggestions made by the packaging and storage team will only lead to a superior checklist.

139. (A) understanding
(B) concern
(C) challenges
(D) patience

140. (A) However
(B) Due
(C) Regardless of
(D) Provided

NEW

141. (A) A meeting of the packaging and storage team has been set for Tuesday, January 23.
(B) All employees should be asked to review the procedure before starting work on Tuesday.
(C) The meeting will investigate the possibility of redundancies in the packaging process.
(D) Additional training sessions are planned to be added sometime at the end of December.

142. (A) is discovering
(B) have been discovered
(C) will discover
(D) has discovered

Questions 143-146 refer to the following letter.

June 3
Yui Minakuchi
143 Dean St. Apt. 3
Brooklyn, NY 10787

Dear Ms. Minakuchi,

It is my pleasure to inform you that Hannover Design would like ------- (**143.**) you to interview for our summer intern program. We are only interviewing fifteen candidates this year for the six positions we have available. You will be pleased to know that you were selected out of a group of over 200 people ------- (**144.**) applied for an interview.

We will be holding interviews on March 6th and 7th from 1 to 6 P.M. We would like for you to come on the 6th at 1:30 P.M. if you are able to. If not, we can ------- (**145.**) for you to come on the 7th. ------- (**146.**) If you have any questions, feel free to call our office (212-347-9919), and the human resources department will be able to assist you. We look forward to hearing from you soon.

Sincerely,

Max Wright
Office Manager
Hannover Design
212-326-1268
M.Wright@hannoverdesign.com

143. (A) to invite
(B) will invite
(C) has invited
(D) will be inviting

144. (A) whom
(B) that
(C) whose
(D) which

145. (A) order
(B) arrange
(C) oblige
(D) attend

NEW

146. (A) You will need to bring a completed application and some type of identification card.
(B) Please let us know as soon as possible if you will be able to attend.
(C) We wish we were able to accept your offer, but we must decline it.
(D) Please RSVP and indicate if you plan on bringing a guest.

GO ON TO THE NEXT PAGE

PART 7

Directions: In this part you will read a selection of texts, such as magazine and newspaper articles, emails, and instant messages. Each text or set of texts is followed by several questions. Select the best answer for each question and mark the letter (A), (B), (C), or (D) on your answer sheet.

Questions 147-148 refer to the following memo.

MEMO

To: All Employees
From: David Koch
Subject: Important information
Date: May 22

We will be holding our annual meeting for shareholders on June 3. I will be giving a short presentation during the opening ceremony, and I hope everyone can attend. Below is a basic schedule of the meeting.

Opening ceremony	1:00 P.M.
Annual report	2:00 P.M.
Discussion	4:00 P.M.
Dinner	6:00 P.M.

147. What is the purpose of the memo?

(A) To remind employees of a project deadline
(B) To suggest revisions to an annual report
(C) To provide a schedule for an event
(D) To report to shareholders on annual profits

148. At what time will David Koch speak?

(A) 1:00 P.M.
(B) 2:00 P.M.
(C) 4:00 P.M.
(D) 6:00 P.M.

Questions 149-150 refer to the following text message chain.

Judy Lynch **10:12**
Will we be able to charge this dinner gathering to the company credit card?

Nathan Lee **10:13**
Unfortunately, no. The company policy changed just last month. Only meetings conducted with clients during lunch or dinner can be covered as company expenses.

Judy Lynch **10:14**
That's too bad. I guess we'll just have to split the bill this time.

Nathan Lee **10:14**
Yes, but at least you can go to any restaurant you want.

Judy Lynch **10:15**
True. I'll let everyone know. Thanks!

149. Why does Judy contact Nathan?
(A) To get him to pay for the dinner
(B) To get information about company expenses
(C) To ask if he wanted to join the dinner
(D) To get recommendations for a good restaurant

150. At 10:14, what does Judy mean when she writes "we'll have to split the bill this time"?
(A) They will charge the company.
(B) They will ask the accounting department.
(C) They will have to choose who will pay.
(D) They will each have to pay a portion of the cost.

GO ON TO THE NEXT PAGE

Questions 151-152 refer to the following letter.

January 19

Dear Mr. Peterson,

The results have come back from the blood test you had done. Please call us at your earliest convenience to reserve a time to meet with Dr. Herman.

We would like to remind you that, due to changes in laws pertaining to health insurance, all patients are encouraged to make sure that their contact and insurance information is current and accurate. This can be done either by calling our customer service line at 555-6842 or stopping by the front desk on your next visit.

Sincerely,

Laura Pinkerton
Superior Health Clinic

151. What will Mr. Peterson most likely do in the near future?

(A) Renew an insurance policy
(B) Schedule a doctor's appointment
(C) Apply for a clerical position
(D) Run a blood test

152. What is Mr. Peterson asked to do?

(A) Submit an insurance form
(B) Reply to the letter
(C) Verify personal information
(D) Fill out a survey

Questions 153-154 refer to the following flyer.

Shopping Local

Seattle Business District Association

Did you know?

- **Shopping local puts twice as much revenue into the economy than using chain retailers.**
- **Shopping local supports the city of Seattle through local taxes.**
- **Shopping local helps the environment. It saves gas and causes less air pollution.**
- **Shopping local creates more jobs in Seattle and improves living standards in the community.**

We would like to encourage all residents of Seattle to support their local communities by shopping at traditional local stores and markets.

To find out more and learn about all the great shops and services available to local residents, visit the website of the Seattle Business District Association at www.sbda.org.

153. What is the purpose of the flyer?

(A) To promote sustainable living
(B) To notify shoppers about a sale
(C) To announce a new business opening
(D) To influence shopping patterns

154. What is NOT mentioned as a benefit of shopping local?

(A) It facilitates a job market.
(B) It is environmentally friendly.
(C) It supports the local economy.
(D) It encourages foreign investments.

GO ON TO THE NEXT PAGE →

Questions 155-157 refer to the following article.

Grandview Business News

The Burnelles launched their meal delivery service for busy families just six months ago, and the business is flourishing, exceeding expectations. – [1] – Their small shop, Farm-to-Table, located in Central Grandview Heights, has been forced to increase staff by 120% to keep up with demand.

The whole premise of the idea came up after Rachel and Robert Burnelle had their first child. Both working parents had constantly turned to fastfood for their meals and realized that many of their friends did as well. They wanted healthier options, which most fast-food franchises don't provide. – [2] –

The business is so popular that they have been getting orders from outside the city. "The response has been overwhelming," says Rachel. "Our customers especially appreciate the freshness and quality of our meals." Janet, a customer from the start, added, "Not only is the food healthy, it's not that much more expensive than fast-food meals, but it's much better for you." – [3] –

The Burnelles say they are planning to expand their delivery routes and open three Farm-to-Table grocery shops with ready-made meals around the city of Grandview within the next year. – [4] –

155. What is the article about?

(A) The changing role of fast-food companies
(B) The importance of healthy eating
(C) The expansion of farmland at Grandview
(D) The success and growth of a small business

156. What is the main selling point of Farm-to-Table meals according to the article?

(A) It is delivered very quickly.
(B) It is very inexpensive.
(C) It is healthy.
(D) It is delicious.

NEW

157. In which of the positions marked [1], [2], [3], and [4] does the following sentence belong?

"That is when the Burnelles decided to quit their office jobs and start their own healthy food delivery service for working people."

(A) [1]
(B) [2]
(C) [3]
(D) [4]

Questions 158-160 refer to the following notice.

Attention Shoppers

We regret to inform you that there has been a general recall on all Kent brand ladders manufactured between March 30 and July 30 this year.

- **The ladders do not comply with mandatory safety standards and could be unstable.**
- **The ladders could move while standing on them and could contribute to dangerous falls.**
- **Do not use the ladders for any reason. Contact the Kent Company to receive a refund or a replacement product. Customers will receive a full refund even without proof of purchase as long as they return the ladders.**

The Kent Company can be reached by calling 1-800-555-2493. Press 8 in order to be transferred to a representative who deals exclusively with product recalls. We sincerely apologize for this inconvenience.

158. Where could this notice most likely be found?

(A) At a real estate office
(B) At a hardware store
(C) At a recycling center
(D) At a grocery store

159. What are customers warned about?

(A) Using a defective product
(B) Renewing a warranty
(C) Submitting an order form
(D) Filing a complaint

160. According to the notice, how can more information be obtained?

(A) By filling out a form
(B) By consulting an instruction manual
(C) By contacting a company
(D) By watching a video tutorial

GO ON TO THE NEXT PAGE

Questions 161-164 refer to the following online chat discussion.

J&R International Group Discussion

9:15	**Patricia Noble (moderator)**	Good morning, everyone. I've posted some ideas for the upcoming Leadership Workshop in June.
9:16	**Patricia Noble (moderator)**	Please share some of your ideas. We would like some input.
9:20	**Jared Davis**	It looks very standard. Can we add some activities such as camping expeditions or something?
9:21	**Lawrence O'Donnell**	I don't know if I'll be able to attend this time. My group is finishing up a major project. Camping sounds great, though.
9:22	**Patricia Noble (moderator)**	Camping is a good idea, but it'll take more time to plan. We'll definitely keep this in mind for the next workshop.
9:24	**Jimmy Rhee**	I don't think videos are very effective. How about getting more speakers to present? I'd rather interact with someone.
9:27	**Monica Choi**	I'm looking forward to the camping idea. But for this workshop, I agree with Jimmy. Videos can be quite boring.
9:30	**Jared Davis**	I noticed that John Olive is not presenting this time. What happened? He was very popular. I'd like to attend his workshop.
9:41	**Patricia Noble (moderator)**	John hasn't confirmed with us yet because he may have conflicting schedules. He's trying to work around his schedule.
9:52	**Isabella Price**	I'd like to attend John's workshop as well. I noticed that there are still a couple of empty slots. Would anyone be interested in hearing Ge Xi? I'd love to get a different, cultural aspect.
9:58	**Jared Davis**	Great idea! Ge Xi has had a lot of experience as a supervisor in China, and she always has some interesting stories.
10:01	**Jimmy Rhee**	I second that. I would certainly like to hear what Ge Xi presents. And speaking of cultural perspectives, Adam has had experience managing employees in a number of countries. He'd be interesting, I think.
10:09	**Isabella Price**	Yes, let's get Adam to present in the workshop.
10:15	**Adam Cruz**	Wow, I'm flattered by your vote of confidence. I certainly wouldn't mind participating in the workshop. I'm free in the afternoons.
10:19	**Patricia Noble (moderator)**	Thank you, Adam. I'll put you down for the 3 to 4 P.M. slot if that's OK with you.
10:30	**Adam Cruz**	That sounds great. And could you send me a guideline if you have one?

161. Who is most likely participating in this group discussion?
(A) The general public
(B) All employees of the company
(C) Employees from different countries
(D) Managers and other group leaders of the company

162. What's being discussed?
(A) The best presentations from the meeting
(B) The best speakers at the company
(C) The schedule for the workshop
(D) International co-workers

163. At 10:15, what does Adam Cruz mean when he writes, "I'm flattered by your vote of confidence"?
(A) He's thankful that people want him to be manager.
(B) He's grateful that people see him as a good leader.
(C) He's happy that his favorite speaker has been invited.
(D) He's honored to have won the election.

164. What will Patricia Noble probably do next?
(A) Email some information to a co-worker
(B) Set up a meeting for employees
(C) Meet with international workers
(D) Call co-workers about the changes

GO ON TO THE NEXT PAGE

Questions 165-167 refer to the following email.

To	Samantha Russell <srussell@speednet.com>
From	Sam Berger <sberger@highlandshotel.com>
Subject	Reservation
Date	July 1
Attachment	receipt

Dear Ms. Russell,

Thank you for choosing Highlands Hotel as the location for your upcoming celebration. We are contacting you to confirm the details of your reservation for rooms on the nights of July 12 and 13. You have reserved all 12 rooms on the fourth floor of our hotel. Additionally, you will have unrestricted access to the main conference room for exclusive use on both of those days. You mentioned that family members from all around the country will be gathering for this event. We will provide you with any assistance you need during your stay.

Our hotel supplies free Wi-Fi as well as access to our Internet café, where guests can use our computers for free when they want to surf the Internet or send email. This café will be available from 5:00 A.M. to 12:00 P.M. Also, guests are encouraged to eat at our awarding-winning restaurant, which is open from 7:00 A.M. to 10:00 P.M. This email also contains a receipt for your $100 deposit paid by credit card on June 30. If you would like to view the layout and seating for our conference room, you can visit our website at www.highlandshotel.com.

Sincerely,

Sam Berger
Highlands Hotel

165. What kind of event is being held on July 12 and 13?

(A) A family reunion
(B) A business conference
(C) A shareholders' meeting
(D) A job fair

166. What is NOT mentioned as a benefit of the reservation?

(A) Exclusive use of an entire floor
(B) Complimentary meals
(C) Access to a conference room
(D) Free Internet access

167. According to the email, what can Ms. Russell find on the Highlands Hotel website?

(A) A reservation number
(B) A hotel restaurant menu
(C) A seating plan
(D) A discount coupon

Questions 168-171 refer to the following notice.

Attention Members of Super Fit Gym

One workout plan doesn't work for everyone. That is why here at Super Fit Gym we offer the largest variety of fitness programs in the area. You are sure to find something fun and exciting that helps you meet your fitness goals. Now we are excited to bring you a new dance fitness program. The class will run this summer from June 12 to August 23. Dance is an interesting and interactive way to exercise. It is also appropriate for those individuals who are not able to engage in strenuous physical activity.

Those who wish to sign up for this dance class are encouraged to sign up in pairs. If you don't have someone to sign up with, you will team up with another individual on the first day of class. Registration will be available from May 10 to June 1. You can register on our website by filling out a registration form. A class fee must be paid at the time of registration by credit card.

In accordance with our rules and regulations, those who wish to receive a class fee refund must withdraw from class a week or more before the scheduled start date. No refund will be given to those who withdraw from class after that deadline.

For more details concerning class content, schedules, and fees, contact our manager, Scott Peterson, at (231) 555-2523.

Sincerely,

Super Fit Gym Staff

168. What is the purpose of the notice?

(A) To postpone an opening ceremony
(B) To hire new instructors
(C) To explain payment options
(D) To announce a new class

169. What will most likely happen on June 12?

(A) Some instructors will be absent.
(B) Some members will be assigned partners.
(C) Some refunds will be given.
(D) Some certificates of completion will be issued.

170. According to the notice, what is the latest date that participants can receive a refund for the class?

(A) May 10
(B) June 5
(C) June 12
(D) August 23

171. What is mentioned as a reason to contact Mr. Peterson?

(A) To schedule an appointment
(B) To inquire about a class
(C) To update personal contact details
(D) To find a partner to dance with

GO ON TO THE NEXT PAGE

Questions 172-175 refer to the following memo.

MEMO

To: All employees
From: Veronica Jackman, Executive Manager
Date: October 10
Subject: staffing

– [1] – Sheila Roberts, our marketing director will be away on a business trip to Singapore from October 21st to November 5th. In her absence, Michael Lee will temporarily take over some of her responsibilities at Goldman's Department Store. However, for those of you who have projects near completion with Ms. Roberts, we ask that you make final arrangements with her before October 15th. – [2] – Some of the urgent projects have already been discussed with Michael. If your project can wait for Sheila's return, we ask that you inform both Sheila and Michael so that other projects can go forward.

– [3] – I realize this may seem like an inconvenience, especially so close to the holiday season, but I have great confidence that Michael will be able to handle the responsibilities in Sheila's absence. Michael has worked closely with Sheila and will deal with the newer projects handed to him. – [4] –

If you have further questions or concerns about this, please contact Sheila before October 20th or me at any time.

172. Where do the recipients of the memo work?

(A) At a marketing firm
(B) At a law office
(C) At a department store
(D) At a travel agency

173. What is indicated about Sheila Roberts?

(A) She is getting a new job.
(B) She has been promoted.
(C) She is going on vacation.
(D) She is going on a business trip.

174. When should employees with nearly completed projects contact Sheila by?

(A) October 15th
(B) October 20th
(C) October 21st
(D) November 5th

NEW

175. In which of the positions marked [1], [2], [3], and [4] does the following sentence belong?

"Michael will arrange separate meetings with different departments during Sheila's absence to ensure a smooth transition and communication during his temporary tenure."

(A) [1]
(B) [2]
(C) [3]
(D) [4]

Questions 176-180 refer to the following Web page and article.

http://www.instituteforruralservice.com

Rural Community Outreach Program

As part of its ongoing commitment to enhance the standard of living in rural communities across the state, the Institute for Rural Service provides annual grants for rural communities. The goal of this program is to support local efforts to sustain a convenient and satisfying life in the countryside. The grants available this year are as follows:

Business Development Grant: $250,000
Community Development Grant: $150,000
Communications Development Grant: $200,000
Educational Development Grant: $100,000

The institute will give priority to proposals that reflect a comprehensive approach to community development, promote community engagement, and make rural communities a better place to live and work. The grants will allow rural communities to take the first step toward a project or plan that can help improve the lives of rural community members. For the past decades, the grants have been used for a variety of purposes such as state-of-the-art farming equipment, road maintenance, communications infrastructure, educational facilities, and investments for young rural entrepreneurs.

Download this application to apply for a grant. The deadline for submission is February 28.

Village of Cranton Wins Funding

CRANTON, March 22—The Institute of Rural Service announced today that the village of Cranton is this year's recipient of the Educational Development Grant. The grant will be used to fund the construction of a large playground that will provide recreational activities for children under 12. Since the opening of the new electronics factory last year, the number of families in the area has risen dramatically. As a result, children have been left with less and less space to play in. The new playground will allow children to play and enjoy themselves when they are not at school.

Cranton is proud to be the recipient of this grant and plans to apply for more grants in the future to improve the living conditions of the town and attract more residents.

GO ON TO THE NEXT PAGE

176. What is the purpose of the Web page?

(A) To report that a project has been completed
(B) To encourage applications for a grant
(C) To announce a recipient of a grant
(D) To introduce local entrepreneurs

177. According to the Web page, what is NOT mentioned as a purpose of an Institute of Rural Service grant?

(A) Providing funds for local business people
(B) Building the basic systems for communications
(C) Organizing community health checkups
(D) Purchasing farming equipment

178. How much funding did Cranton receive?

(A) $100,000
(B) $150,000
(C) $200,000
(D) $250,000

179. According to the article, what will the grant enable Cranton to do?

(A) Improve local farming conditions
(B) Renovate an elementary school
(C) Hire more qualified teachers
(D) Provide a play area for children

180. What is indicated about Cranton?

(A) It has received grants in the past.
(B) It plans to open a new factory.
(C) Its population has increased.
(D) It will hold a community festival.

Questions 181-185 refer to the following email and form.

To: Charles Bell <charlesbell434@globalnet.com>
From: Carrie Cook <carriecook@freshfarmsgrocery.com>
Subject: Membership Card
Date: May 4

Dear Mr. Bell,

Your Silver Star Membership Card at Fresh Farms Grocery will expire on the 28th of this month. Your membership card entitles you to special sale prices as well as special points on most Fresh Farms Grocery purchases. Once you accumulate enough points, they can be redeemed for a discount on your next purchase. Without a valid Silver Star Membership Card, you will lose the ability to accumulate these frequent shopper points.

Please do not attempt to renew your membership over the phone. In order to do that, please stop by the customer service desk at one of our store locations. If you have any other questions, please call us at 204-555-2648.

Carrie Cook
Customer Service Representative
Fresh Farms Grocery

Fresh Farms Grocery

Membership Card Form

First Name: CHARLES
Last name: BELL
Membership Number: 14245FDA

☐ Create my membership card
☑ Renew my membership card
☐ Cancel my membership card

Membership card categories and fees:
Gold Star: Premium membership, $90 a year
Silver Star: Business membership, $70 a year
Bronze Star: Household membership, $50 a year
Shooting Star: Short-term membership, $10 a month

Please note:
Premium membership is reserved for those who hold shares in the Fresh Farms Grocery company.

Food vendors and restaurant owners are eligible to apply for the Silver Star Membership Card.

GO ON TO THE NEXT PAGE

181. What is the purpose of the email?

(A) To announce seasonal discounts
(B) To notify Mr. Bell of an outstanding fee
(C) To remind Mr. Bell to renew a membership
(D) To offer a free upgrade to Mr. Bell

182. What does the membership card allow Mr. Bell to do?

(A) Benefit from frequent shopping
(B) Park in designated spaces
(C) Receive expedited shipping
(D) Purchase new products in advance

183. What is Mr. Bell asked to do?

(A) Call the customer service desk
(B) Visit the store in person
(C) Write a customer review
(D) Attend a regular event

184. How much does Mr. Bell currently pay a year?

(A) $50
(B) $70
(C) $90
(D) $120

185. What is indicated about Mr. Bell?

(A) He is a celebrated chef.
(B) He runs a food-selling business.
(C) He is a shareholder of Fresh Farms Grocery.
(D) He applied for his membership this year.

Questions 186-190 refer to the following letter, brochure, and schedule.

May 12

Dear Mr. Gray,

You are a long-time member of the Georgian Society of Architects (GSA). We would like to inform you that we are adding some changes to the services provided to members this year. Specifically, we will be adding a new Gold Class level membership that will give privileged members access to more resources than ever before. We are excited to tell you that you meet all of the qualifications for this special membership offer and may sign up immediately. You should be receiving a brochure in the mail soon that will provide more information. We hope that you decide to join this amazing Gold Class membership.

As you know, the GSA's annual members' conference will be held on June 14 at the Stargate Conference Center in Atlanta, Georgia. We noticed you have already registered your attendance. We can't wait to see you there. If you need any further assistance making arrangements, don't hesitate to call our offices at (124) 555-5251.

Yours truly,

Joan Ross

Georgian Society of Architects

Georgian Society of Architects

GOLD CLASS MEMBERSHIP

In order to qualify for this special membership, applicants must have at least 20 years of experience in the field, in addition to holding a degree in architecture from an accredited university.

Benefits include: instantly expanding your contacts through access to our database of over 50,000 practicing colleagues, paying half the regular price when registering for conferences hosted by GSA, and receiving our monthly newsletter, which contains the latest market research and economic analysis to help your business.

Gold Class members will also be eligible to apply for professional liability insurance coverage offered exclusively to our Gold Class members.

To apply, simply fill out the form attached to this brochure and mail it to our headquarters. The $40.00 application fee can either be paid by check or credit card by calling our accountant at (124) 555-5253.

GO ON TO THE NEXT PAGE

STARGATE CONVENTION CENTER SCHEDULE OF EVENTS

JUNE 14th
GEORGIAN SOCIETY OF ARCHITECHTS

9:00 A.M.—9:45 A.M.	Sign in at the desk in the lobby
10 A.M.—11:45 A.M.	Guest Speaker Jerry Jenkins Jr. in Conference Room A
12:00 P.M.—1:30 P.M.	Lunch in the Diamond Room
2:00 P.M.—4:00 P.M.	Regional Presentations in Conference Room A
6:00 P.M.—9:00 P.M.	Dinner and cocktails in the Sapphire Lounge

Please remember to bring your Society ID to ensure a smooth registration for the day's events!

186. What is the purpose of the letter?

(A) To publicize a conference
(B) To advertise a new membership
(C) To confirm an appointment
(D) To attract a new member

187. What is Mr. Gray encouraged to do?

(A) Register for a conference
(B) Reschedule an appointment
(C) Upgrade his service
(D) Pay by credit card

188. What is indicated about Mr. Gray?

(A) He has worked as an architect for over two decades.
(B) He spoke at last year's GSA members' conference.
(C) He contributes to an architecture journal.
(D) He forgot to pay his membership fee in April.

189. What time should Mr. Gray sign in on the day of the conference?

(A) 8:45 A.M. to 10:00 A.M.
(B) 9:00 A.M. exactly
(C) Anytime
(D) 9:00 A.M. to 9:45 A.M.

190. How many meals are included in the event?

(A) Breakfast, lunch, and dinner
(B) Brunch and dinner
(C) Dinner and cocktails
(D) Lunch and dinner

Questions 191-195 refer to the following notice and emails.

Colonial Heights Nursing Home

Colonial Heights is proud to have served the elderly population of Houston, Texas for over 30 years. Our nursing home is equipped with state-of-the-art facilities. Our five-story building allows each floor to offer individualized levels of care for our residents. Our building houses a rehabilitation gym, and we also provide psychological counseling services for residents.

We currently have openings for several positions. We are looking to hire a nursing home administrator who has at least three years of experience and a valid license. There is also an opening for an admissions coordinator. Those applying for the admissions coordinator job must have a bachelor's degree and at least two years of related experience. We are also looking for hospice workers who can provide personal care to residents in a compassionate and caring manner. Previous experience is not necessary, so everyone interested is welcome to apply for this position.

You can see this job listing and submit an application online by visiting our website at www.chnh.com.

To: Tommy Jenkins <tommyjenkins7@zeusnet.com>
From: Greg Parker <g_parker@chnh.com>
Subject: Hiring procedure
Date: September 14

Dear Mr. Jenkins,

Congratulations! You have made it through the first round of the application process for the position of admissions coordinator. We require that all applicants visit Colonial Heights Nursing Home in order to attend an in-person interview. I would appreciate it if you let me know a convenient time for your interview on September 17.

I look forward to meeting you.

Sincerely,

Greg Parker
Human Resources Manager
Colonial Heights Nursing Home

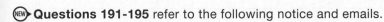

GO ON TO THE NEXT PAGE

To: Greg Parker <g_parker@chnh.com>
From: Tommy Jenkins <tommyjenkins7@zeusnet.com>
Date: September 15
Subject: RE: Hiring procedure

Dear Mr. Parker,

Thank you so much for giving me the opportunity to interview for the position of admissions coordinator. You requested that I inform you about my availability for September 17. I have another interview at 10 A.M., but I will be able to be at Colonial Heights Nursing Home by 1 P.M. I hope this is convenient for you. Shady Pines Nursing Home, as you know, is a competing facility located on the other side of town, and the hours they offer are very attractive. I would prefer to work in a modern facility such as Colonial Heights.
I look forward to interviewing with you and touring your facilities.

Sincerely,

Tommy Jenkins

191. What is mentioned about Colonial Heights Nursing Home?

(A) It has five locations in Texas.
(B) It has operated for over half a century.
(C) It provides art classes.
(D) It offers mental health services.

192. According to the notice, which position does not require experience?

(A) Nursing home administrator
(B) Hospice worker
(C) Admissions coordinator
(D) Front desk receptionist

193. What is indicated about Colonial Heights Nursing Home?

(A) It plans to expand its facilities.
(B) It accepts applications through its website.
(C) It offers the highest wages in the state.
(D) It recently renewed its operating certificate.

194. Why might Tommy Jenkins decide NOT to work for Colonial Heights Nursing Home?

(A) They do not have physical fitness centers.
(B) Their facilities are not modern.
(C) The job is too far away.
(D) Shady Pines Nursing Home can give him a better schedule.

195. When can Tommy Jenkins be at the interview at Colonial Heights?

(A) 10 A.M.
(B) before 1 P.M.
(C) after 1 P.M.
(D) after 4 P.M.

Questions 196-200 refer to the following emails.

To: Jake Baldwin <baldwinj@technet.com>
From: Dream Oasis Hotel <booking@dreamoasishotel.com>
Date: September 22
Subject: Your Reservation
Attachment: invoice.html

Dear Mr. Baldwin,

Thank you for reserving a room at the Dream Oasis Hotel. You have booked a room with a double bed for the nights of October 13 and 14. Your reservation number is 5259.

I am writing to inform you that you must pay your balance by September 29 in order to confirm your reservation. Your total room fee is $165.25 for both nights. Payment can be made via credit card by visiting our website at www.dreamoasishotel.com and entering your reservation number. You may also call us and complete your payment over the phone. If payment is not received by September 29, your reservation will be canceled automatically. Please see the attached invoice for related details.

When you arrive at the airport, the easiest way to travel to our hotel is by subway. We are located next to exit 3 at City Hall Station. If you have trouble finding us, please don't hesitate to call us at 555-2134. A staff member is available 24 hours a day to assist you.

Thank you again for choosing our hotel.

Amy Lee
Customer Services Manager
Dream Oasis Hotel

To: Dream Oasis Hotel <booking@dreamoasishotel.com>
From: Jake Baldwin <baldwinj@technet.com>
Date: September 23
Subject: RE: Your Reservation

Dear Ms. Lee,

I am writing in regard to my reservation at the Dream Oasis Hotel for October 13 and 14. I received your email about the payment for my upcoming stay at the hotel. However, I would like to inquire about extending my stay for an extra night. I recently heard that there will be a local food festival held on October 16 and I would like to attend it. Therefore, I would like to stay at your hotel through October 15. Please let me know a revised room fee so that I can make the correct payment as soon as possible.

Jake Baldwin

GO ON TO THE NEXT PAGE

To: Jake Baldwin <baldwinj@technet.com>
From: Amy Lee <alee@dreamoasishotel.com>
Date: September 24
Subject: The 15th

Dear Mr. Baldwin,

You are right to be excited about the food festival that will be held on the October 16th. Unfortunately, this event has become so popular that the city fills up for that weekend. I regret to inform you that there is no vacancy at the Dream Oasis Hotel for the night of the 15th. I went ahead and looked into some of our partner hotels in the area, but those properties are also at full occupancy. I do hope you are able to find someplace to stay in the city so you can enjoy the festival while you are in town; I just wish it could have been with us. You could try the Executive Inn, in Fairview. It is a large hotel, and they do have vacancies.

Sincere apologies,

Amy Lee
Customer Service Manager
Dream Oasis Hotel

196. What is the purpose of the first email?

(A) To explain a cancellation policy
(B) To request a payment
(C) To schedule a reservation
(D) To offer a special service

197. What is Mr. Baldwin asked to provide when making a payment online?

(A) His telephone number
(B) His email address
(C) His room number
(D) His reservation number

198. What information is NOT included in Ms. Lee's email?

(A) The cost of the stay
(B) The travel insurance
(C) The location of the hotel
(D) Staff contact information

199. Why can't Mr. Baldwin stay at the Dream Oasis Hotel on the night of the 15th?

(A) The hotel is full because of the food festival.
(B) The hotel is full because it is very popular.
(C) The hotel is full because there is a convention in town.
(D) The hotel is full because the food at the hotel is very good.

200. What does Amy Lee recommend?

(A) That Mr. Baldwin try another hotel in town
(B) That Mr. Baldwin try a hotel in Fairview
(C) That Mr. Baldwin try to attend the food festival next year
(D) That Mr. Baldwin ask again on the 14th, in case there is a cancellation

ACTUAL TEST 03

NO TEST MATERIAL ON THIS PAGE

Stop! This is the end of the test. If you finish before time is called, you may go back to Parts 5, 6, and 7 and check your work.

ACTUAL TEST 04

READING TEST

In the Reading test, you will read a variety of texts and answer several different types of reading comprehension questions. The entire Reading test will last 75 minutes. There are three parts, and directions are given for each part. You are encouraged to answer as many questions as possible within the time allowed.

You must mark your answers on the separate answer sheet. Do not write your answers in your test book.

PART 5

Directions: A word or phrase is missing in each of the sentences below. Four answer choices are given below each sentence. Select the best answer to complete the sentence. Then mark the letter (A), (B), (C), or (D) on your answer sheet.

101. All of the trees on the property were damaged by the storm ------- the one near the rear entrance.

(A) except
(B) considering
(C) still
(D) along

102. Mr. Hotei had to undergo several medical tests before receiving ------- diagnosis from the physician.

(A) he
(B) him
(C) himself
(D) his

103. Entrepreneur James Mosby is featured in the most ------- issue of the magazine.

(A) final
(B) former
(C) recent
(D) later

104. The judge's decision must be based ------- on the evidence presented.

(A) cooperatively
(B) strictly
(C) tensely
(D) remarkably

105. Due to his decades of experience, Mr. Finley was responsible for training the ------- for the new gym.

(A) instructors
(B) instructive
(C) instructively
(D) instructed

106. Customers at Blaze Restaurant may use the valet parking service or park their vehicles -------.

(A) their
(B) themselves
(C) they
(D) theirs

107. Last year, the young chemists contributed ------- to the development of a new adhesive.

(A) construction
(B) constructively
(C) constructive
(D) constructed

108. The experts at Prime Carpentry can restore any piece of wooden furniture ------- its original condition.

(A) to
(B) by
(C) at
(D) with

109. The library has requested funding for ------- doors for the convenience of patrons.

(A) underway
(B) automatic
(C) frequent
(D) energetic

110. After noticing the wardrobe's ------- condition, the owner of the antique shop lowered its price.

(A) deteriorates
(B) deteriorating
(C) deterioration
(D) deteriorate

111. For the past decade, Henley Vivian ------- to be a talented and motivated journalist.

(A) is proving
(B) proving
(C) prove
(D) has proven

112. ------- who suffers from sleep problems could benefit from drinking this herbal tea.

(A) Ourselves
(B) Whichever
(C) Anyone
(D) Others

113. An additional route was added to the rail line to reduce travel times in the southern -------.

(A) accent
(B) function
(C) distance
(D) region

114. During the holiday season, Schwartz Department Store will ------- special make-up gift sets.

(A) solve
(B) carry
(C) impress
(D) occupy

115. Buying a home for the first time can be complicated and even ------- without help from a licensed real estate agent.

(A) nervous
(B) risky
(C) decreased
(D) initial

116. The Brownsville Homeless Shelter has helped thousands of people since its ------- last year.

(A) creative
(B) created
(C) create
(D) creation

GO ON TO THE NEXT PAGE

117. The semifinalists of the community art contest will be ------- by a panel of judges tomorrow.

(A) selected
(B) ignored
(C) prevented
(D) complemented

118. The penalties for canceling the cell phone contract early are ------- stated in the agreement.

(A) express
(B) expression
(C) expressly
(D) expressed

119. ------- the researchers' report, eating fresh fruits and vegetables more often is a better health goal than avoiding fast food.

(A) Even though
(B) Rather than
(C) According to
(D) Because of

120. To make the tour accessible to Spanish speakers, the ------- plans to provide translation services.

(A) interpreted
(B) interpretation
(C) interpreting
(D) interpreter

121. Joggers are asked to keep to the right side of the path, as ------- cyclists need space to pass on the left.

(A) many
(B) each
(C) much
(D) either

122. Before potential buyers view a home, the real estate agent makes sure it is -------.

(A) presentation
(B) presenting
(C) presentable
(D) present

123. For the payment ------- last week, the necessary state and federal taxes must be paid by the recipient.

(A) was remitted
(B) remitted
(C) remitting
(D) to remit

124. Everyone is in favor of shortening working hours, but ------- the president approves the change, nothing will happen.

(A) after
(B) until
(C) yet
(D) because

125. The manufacturing company's recent ------- to reduce on-site accidents was appreciated by the staff.

(A) attempt
(B) industry
(C) value
(D) faculty

126. The dining room furniture was ------- left in the house because the new owner had bought it.

(A) intended
(B) intention
(C) intentional
(D) intentionally

127. The Garrison Theater will ------- allow student groups to view rehearsals during the day.

(A) vaguely
(B) substantially
(C) occasionally
(D) previously

128. *Pro Sports* magazine made a name for itself ------- the publication of a series of exclusive interviews with top athletes.

(A) like
(B) both
(C) so
(D) with

129. Only ------- delegates wearing their ID badges will be allowed into the conference venue.

(A) those
(B) who
(C) each
(D) that

130. ------- his announcement that he would run for office, the candidate met privately with his advisors.

(A) In advance of
(B) As long as
(C) On behalf of
(D) So as to

GO ON TO THE NEXT PAGE

PART 6

Directions: Read the texts that follow. A word, phrase, or sentence is missing in parts of each text. Four answer choices for each question are given below the text. Select the best answer to complete the text. Then mark the letter (A), (B), (C), or (D) on your answer sheet.

Questions 131-134 refer to the following notice.

Employee Workshop

T&R Group strives to help employees reach their potential by offering leadership retreats, employee training, and various workshops. This month, we ------- **131.** workshops for those interested in ------- **132.** their computer skills with several classes on how to use Professional Office, create a personal website, and run the messagecorp app. We have a couple of other slots that are currently ------- **133.** and will accept suggestions from employees. ------- **134.** Please email Jonas at jsmith@TRgroup.com if you are interested in attending any of the workshops. We hope you will all take advantage of the programs offered.

131. (A) offers
(B) were offering
(C) are offering
(D) have offered

132. (A) correcting
(B) diminishing
(C) elaborating
(D) improving

133. (A) dependent
(B) independent
(C) free
(D) obtainable

NEW

134. (A) Questions related to gaming and entertainment will not be answered.
(B) The most popular requests will be considered for the workshops.
(C) We ask all managers to make a suggestion.
(D) We hope the workshop is a success and wish you the very best.

Questions 135-138 refer to the following advertisement.

Citrusine Total Flu for Nighttime

Get ready for cold and flu season with Citrusine. Citrusine is a ------- (135.) medicated nighttime tea that can treat symptoms of the flu including fever, aches and pains, nasal congestion, cough, and sore throat. Wake up feeling ------- (136.) and ready to conquer another day. Citrusine should not be taken if you're planning to operate machinery or drive a vehicle. Keep out of reach of children. ------- (137.)

Citrusine is the number-one-selling medication ------- (138.) the flu and is guaranteed to provide relief if taken as directed. Visit our website for more information.

www.citrusine.com

135. (A) reassuring
(B) stimulating
(C) soothing
(D) consoling

136. (A) refreshing
(B) refreshed
(C) refreshes
(D) refresh

NEW

137. (A) This medication may cause serious side effects if not taken properly.
(B) Children should take Citrusine for Kids instead.
(C) The packets look like candy and may pose problems.
(D) And if symptoms persist for more than 10 days, consult a physician.

138. (A) for
(B) during
(C) with
(D) after

GO ON TO THE NEXT PAGE

Questions 139-142 refer to the following email.

To: Janet Don
From: Greenscape
Date: June 28
Subject: Inquiry

Dear Ms. Don,

We thank you for your inquiry. Greenscape has been the leading landscaper for businesses in the greater downtown area for over 10 years. ------- **139.** we specialize in gardens and Japanese-style landscape art, we also maintain lawns and fields. But to answer your question, yes, we even clear away thick shrubbery and trees. We can send a representative to ------- **140.** the amount of time it will take and the approximate costs. Furthermore, if you ------- **141.** to replace the dense shrubs with a lawn or garden, you can work with one of our designers to come up with a landscape you can be happy with.

------- **142.** We are more than happy to serve you.

139. (A) Although
(B) Because
(C) Therefore
(D) However

140. (A) conclude
(B) count
(C) estimate
(D) guess

141. (A) wishing
(B) wish
(C) wished
(D) wishes

NEW

142. (A) We welcome any opportunity to do business with you.
(B) Please don't cancel the order.
(C) Please call us at 555-1245 if you are interested in a consultation.
(D) Go to the park to see the city's landscape.

Questions 143-146 refer to the following advertisement.

Black Hill Beans

Black Hill Beans is a Louisianan coffee company and the pioneer of the Louisiana coffee fruit. We oversee a vertically ------- (**143.**) supply chain that starts with the highest quality coffee and coffee fruit from Black Hill, Louisiana. We ------- (**144.**) three award-winning beans: summer harvest, dark southern, and black earth. All can be shipped to you ------- (**145.**) 24 hours anywhere in the continental U.S. Black Hill Beans' coffee is also sold at every Launders Superstore in the U.S.

Whether you're looking for excellent coffee or a bit of southern comfort, Black Hill Beans is the right choice for your coffee. ------- (**146.**) It's nice to feel patriotic while you drink. Visit us online today to hear more of our story. www.blackhillbeans.com

143. (A) integrates
(B) to integrate
(C) integrated
(D) integration

144. (A) locate
(B) select
(C) evaluate
(D) maintain

145. (A) within
(B) by
(C) until
(D) at

NEW

146. (A) Try the best-selling frozen beverage around.
(B) It's American-made and organic.
(C) Let us help you find the right supplier.
(D) This discount is only available through October 1st.

GO ON TO THE NEXT PAGE

PART 7

Directions: In this part you will read a selection of texts, such as magazine and newspaper articles, emails, and instant messages. Each text or set of texts is followed by several questions. Select the best answer for each question and mark the letter (A), (B), (C), or (D) on your answer sheet.

Questions 147-148 refer to the following notice.

Notice

Crawford Apparel has refurbished dressing rooms where you can try on clothes before you make a purchase.

– Please take only an item or two at a time into a dressing room.

– You may leave your personal belongings, such as wallets and purses, with one of our clerks for safekeeping.

– Any personal items left behind in a dressing room will be kept in the lost and found room near the entrance.

147. For whom is this notice most likely intended?

(A) Storekeepers
(B) Customers
(C) Designers
(D) Clerks

148. According to the notice, where can missing items be found?

(A) At a police station
(B) At an information center
(C) In a storage area
(D) Behind a counter

Questions 149-150 refer to the following text message chain.

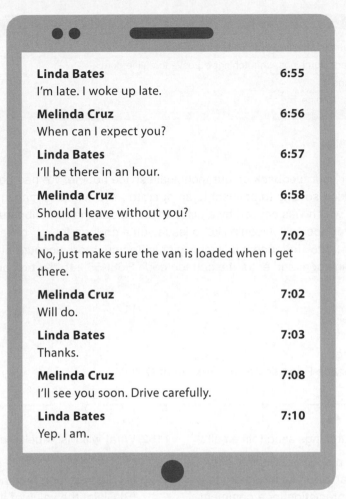

Linda Bates 6:55
I'm late. I woke up late.

Melinda Cruz 6:56
When can I expect you?

Linda Bates 6:57
I'll be there in an hour.

Melinda Cruz 6:58
Should I leave without you?

Linda Bates 7:02
No, just make sure the van is loaded when I get there.

Melinda Cruz 7:02
Will do.

Linda Bates 7:03
Thanks.

Melinda Cruz 7:08
I'll see you soon. Drive carefully.

Linda Bates 7:10
Yep. I am.

149. What is suggested about Ms. Bates?
(A) She works for Ms. Cruz.
(B) She is being held up in traffic.
(C) She is currently operating an automobile.
(D) She is frequently late.

150. At 7:02, what does Ms. Cruz mean when she writes, "Will do"?
(A) She will be waiting for Ms. Bates.
(B) She plans to load the vehicle.
(C) She is frustrated by Ms. Bates' tardiness.
(D) She has finished packing the van.

GO ON TO THE NEXT PAGE

Questions 151-152 refer to the following email.

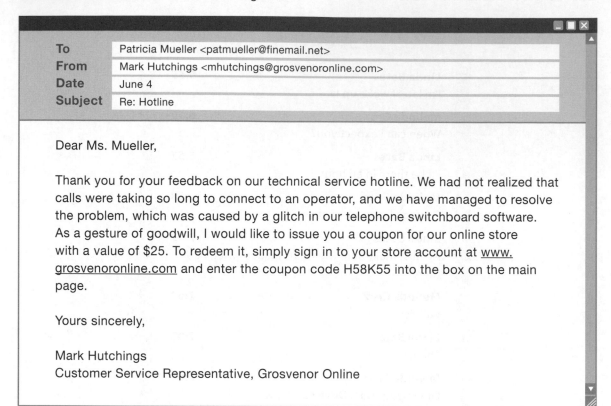

To	Patricia Mueller <patmueller@finemail.net>
From	Mark Hutchings <mhutchings@grosvenoronline.com>
Date	June 4
Subject	Re: Hotline

Dear Ms. Mueller,

Thank you for your feedback on our technical service hotline. We had not realized that calls were taking so long to connect to an operator, and we have managed to resolve the problem, which was caused by a glitch in our telephone switchboard software. As a gesture of goodwill, I would like to issue you a coupon for our online store with a value of $25. To redeem it, simply sign in to your store account at www.grosvenoronline.com and enter the coupon code H58K55 into the box on the main page.

Yours sincerely,

Mark Hutchings
Customer Service Representative, Grosvenor Online

151. Why did Mr. Hutchings send this email?

(A) To promote a special seasonal offer
(B) To confirm an address for an order
(C) To show appreciation for a comment
(D) To request further information about a problem

152. What will Ms. Mueller most likely do on her next visit to Grosvenor Online?

(A) Sign up for a membership program
(B) Claim the value of a coupon
(C) Use the customer feedback form
(D) Update her billing information

Questions 153-154 refer to the following web page.

http://www.jannisar.com

Home | Products | Contact | About Us | Account

Congratulations! Because of your high level of regular activity on our site, you have been selected to become a Premium Gold member. Please fill out the following form to complete the process:

First name	
Surname	
Shipping address	
Authorization code	
Email address	
Comments:	

Check the boxes for the merchandise categories that are of interest to you.
(You may check more than one.)

Electronics [ ] Music [ ] Books [ ] Furniture [ ] Computer Games [ ]

Please note that as a Premium Gold member you will receive email notifications four times a year on special offers for the categories selected. Your account details will be verified by email within 24 hours. An email confirmation will be sent to you. Follow the instructions in that email to confirm your membership.

153. Whom is this web page most likely aimed at?

(A) A new customer on an auction website
(B) An online marketing agency representative
(C) A supplier for a retail outlet
(D) A long-term customer of an online retailer

154. What is the reader asked to do?

(A) Indicate product preferences
(B) Supply payment details
(C) Print and sign the form
(D) Report shipping delays

GO ON TO THE NEXT PAGE

Questions 155-157 refer to the following article.

It's Raining Cats and Dogs

Brentwood City (May 2) — – [1] – Brentwood finally has its very own cat café called Catastrophe and dog café called Hotdogs, both opened by owners Kevin and Ginger Blake. Both cafés opened last month to fanfare and a great deal of press coverage. – [2] – "Business has been booming," says Kevin Blake. "We knew we'd be successful; we just didn't think we'd be this successful." Not only are customers enthusiastically flocking to both cafés to hang out with the animals while drinking coffee and tea; many of them are adopting the animals and giving them forever homes. – [3] – "We thought it would be a good idea to take in some of the animals because of the overcrowding in many of the shelters," explained Ginger Blake. "And customers have a chance to interact with the animals, which is the best form of advertisement for the shelters."

Since the cafés' opening, more than 10 dogs and 15 cats have been adopted. "I don't yet own a dog, but I've always wanted one," says Laurie Jordan, a regular customer. "I come here to play with them. Maybe one day I'll find a dog that I really want." – [4] –

Because of their success, the Blakes are considering expanding by purchasing the adjacent shops. "We need more space to fit all our customers and the animals," explained Kevin. "It can get very crowded at times." The Blakes are looking to renovate the dog café next month and the cat café during the fall.

155. What is indicated about the cafés?

(A) They serve an assortment of snacks.
(B) They sell puppies and kittens.
(C) They serve coffees and teas.
(D) They offer pet products.

156. What is reported about the cats and dogs?

(A) Several have been adopted.
(B) They are permanent residents of the cafés.
(C) They are friendly towards the customers.
(D) They are trained to entertain.

NEW

157. In which of the positions marked [1], [2], [3], and [4] does the following sentence belong?

"But the hype hasn't slowed down."

(A) [1]
(B) [2]
(C) [3]
(D) [4]

Questions 158-160 refer to the following advertisement.

Relax and Unwind at New Wave Spa!

Take a break from your hectic day with professional spa treatments from New Wave Spa, located at 458 Worley Avenue. Whether you stay for an hour or a full day, you'll leave feeling refreshed and energized. Check out our regular packages below.

Classic Getaway ($120)—Try this basic package that's perfect for those on the go.
30-minute back and neck massage / cucumber facial treatment / lilac body wrap

Rose Garden ($155)—Let the scent of roses revive your senses.
45-minute full-body massage / rosewater skin treatment / manicure

Ocean Experience ($180)—Take advantage of the ocean's healing powers in our most popular package.
60-minute full-body massage / head-to-toe sea salt scrub / hot stone treatment / seaweed facial treatment

Complete Rejuvenation ($210)—Indulge yourself in the luxury of a full day of treatments.
90-minute full-body massage / relaxation scalp massage / mud mask facial treatment / rosemary purifying scrub / manicure / pedicure

Book in advance to secure your spot by calling 555-2940. Groups of four or more people will receive a free lunch of sandwiches, steamed vegetables, and freshly squeezed juices. All patrons will be given a free New Wave lounging robe on their third visit to our facility.

158. What is the advertisement mainly about?

(A) The expansion of a health facility
(B) A discount on luxury services
(C) The relocation of a spa
(D) A business's standard options

159. Which package includes a heat treatment?

(A) Classic Getaway
(B) Rose Garden
(C) Ocean Experience
(D) Complete Rejuvenation

160. What will groups of four or more people be given?

(A) A free robe
(B) A reduced rate
(C) A complimentary meal
(D) A private room

GO ON TO THE NEXT PAGE

Questions 161-164 refer to the following online chat discussion.

Bill Flake (9:41)
Hello. I'd like to get an update on the progress of the drapes that the Manillo family ordered.

Lucy Mitt (9:41)
We're still waiting for the lace silks from Hand-Made Lace but we received most of the other fabrics yesterday. Our seamstresses will get to work on those today.

Bill Flake (9:42)
Then do you think the project will be completed by this Friday as the Manillos wanted?

Lucy Mitt (9:43)
I'm not sure. It'll depend on when the lace arrives. Our group can start sewing some of the pieces together, but we need the lace to complete the intricate designs.

Bill Flake (9:44)
Can you contact Hand-Made Lace and find out when the shipment will arrive?

Lucy Mitt (9:45)
Actually, Richard is taking care of that. Any word from them, Richard?

Richard Choi (9:45)
Yes, I just got off the phone with them. There was a bit of a delay because the lace artisans used the wrong silks. They had to rework the lace. We'll receive them this afternoon. They sent a rush delivery to us.

Bill Flake (9:46)
Excellent. Then can the drapes be finished by the end of this week?

Lucy Mitt (9:47)
No problem. We'll work around the clock to get them finished on time.

Bill Flake (9:48)
I'm glad to hear that. They are long-time customers and they need the drapes for their new condo this weekend.

161. What kind of business do the participants in this online chat probably work for?

(A) A clothing company
(B) A bridal shop
(C) A custom drapery shop
(D) A fabric warehouse

162. When will the shipment of lace arrive?

(A) In the morning
(B) In the afternoon
(C) The next day
(D) At the end of the week

163. At 9:47, what does Lucy Mitt mean when she says, "We'll work around the clock?"

(A) Her team will watch the time carefully.
(B) Her team will work as quickly as possible.
(C) Her team will take as much time as they need.
(D) Her team will work all day and night if they have to.

164. What will Bill Flake probably do next?

(A) Call the client
(B) Cancel the order
(C) Request a shipment of lace
(D) Organize a meeting

GO ON TO THE NEXT PAGE

Questions 165-167 refer to the following schedule.

Duluth City **5th Annual Summer Fun Festival** Sunday, July 23
10:00 A.M. to 6:00 P.M. ***Local Nature Art Competition*** Duluth artists will be displaying their paintings of local nature and wildlife in the Duluth Community Center. Visitors are asked to cast their vote for their favorite painting. The winner will be announced at the start of the singing competition.
11:00 A.M. to 12:00 P.M. ***Magic Show*** Please join us for an astonishing magic show. Magician Mick Turner is famous for his creative and entertaining magic tricks.
12:00 P.M. to 2:00 P.M. ***Live Jazz Concert*** Enjoy live jazz in the park performed by New York-based jazz band The Holloway Band. They will be playing a variety of jazz standards. They will also have their most recent record for sale.
10:00 A.M. to 7:00 P.M. ***Renewable Energy Expo*** Local company Sunshine Energy will be displaying some of its newest renewable energy projects, including solar panels and portable cell phone chargers.
7:00 P.M. to 9:00 P.M. ***Singing Competition*** Local residents are encouraged to take part in this year's singing competition. Those who would like to participate can register by visiting our website at www.duluthcitysff.com and filling out the necessary form.
For more information, please call us at 555-0157.

165. When will the winner of the art competition be announced?

(A) 2:00 P.M.
(B) 6:00 P.M.
(C) 7:00 P.M.
(D) 9:00 P.M.

166. According to the schedule, what will be available for purchase?

(A) A work of art
(B) A musical album
(C) A cell phone accessory
(D) A solar panel

167. How can participants sign up for the singing competition?

(A) By visiting an information booth
(B) By contacting the community center
(C) By visiting a website
(D) By sending an email

Questions 168-171 refer to the following flyer.

Movies in the Park

This fall, Glenwood Springs Park will host a weekly Movies in the Park night for residents of Glenwood Springs in cooperation with various local business sponsors including Paxton, Inc. and GS Mall. Family-friendly movies will be shown every Friday night at the center of the park. Tickets are not necessary for these events because they are free to the public.

Running from September through November, Movies in the Park promises a wonderful lineup of fun and touching movies for the whole family. You are encouraged to bring blankets and chairs as well as picnic snacks. Movie starting times depend on sunset times, so it is advised to come early to secure your spot beforehand. Please visit our website at www.glenwoodsprings.org/movies to see a schedule of upcoming films and a list of our local sponsors.

In the event of heavy rain, low temperatures, or strong winds, film screenings may be canceled. If this occurs, the announcement of the film cancellation will be made both on our website and on local radio. You can also ask about event cancellations by calling the Glenwood Springs Department of Parks and Recreation at 715-555-5358.

168. What is the purpose of the flyer?

(A) To announce park renovation plans
(B) To publicize a community event
(C) To solicit donations
(D) To promote a new film

169. Who will provide funding for Movies in the Park?

(A) A local radio station
(B) The residents of Glenwood Springs
(C) The Department of Parks and Recreation
(D) The businesses of Glenwood Springs

170. What is NOT mentioned as a recommendation for participants?

(A) Bringing food
(B) Purchasing tickets in advance
(C) Consulting a schedule
(D) Arriving early

171. According to the flyer, why would the phone number be used?

(A) To make a reservation
(B) To inquire about a schedule change
(C) To ask for driving directions
(D) To cancel an appointment

GO ON TO THE NEXT PAGE

Questions 172-175 refer to the following advertisement.

Wrightman Towers

1234 Broadway Street
New York, NY 49858

– [1] – Located in the financial district of the city, Wrightman Towers offers spectacular views of the skyline and office spaces that are ideal for any company that wishes to operate within the heart of New York. Just one block from the subway station and within walking distance of public buses and taxis, Wrightman Towers is conveniently located. – [2] – The first-floor lobby offers security as employees must scan their way through the gates to the elevators behind. At the same time, the spacious lobby is welcoming with its luxurious interior designs and friendly staff of attendants. – [3] –

The third and fourth floors are available for rent to businesses and corporations. High ceilings and tall glass windows offer open space and beautiful natural lighting. Hurry and send in your requests today. – [4] – Only serious inquiries will be taken and interviews must be conducted in person. Please visit our website at www.wrightmantowers.com/rent for more information. You can take a virtual tour of the premises, or you can call our offices at 555-1234.

172. What is indicated about the rental space?

(A) It is only for private residents.
(B) It is only for businesses.
(C) It is available to the public.
(D) It is very expensive.

173. What is indicated about the location of Wrightman Towers?

(A) It is near public transportation.
(B) There is heavy traffic around the building.
(C) There are no parking spaces.
(D) It is just outside the city.

174. What is featured on the website?

(A) A listing of all occupied spaces
(B) An exclusive discount promo code
(C) A virtual tour of the rental space
(D) A history of the building

NEW

175. In which of the positions marked [1], [2], [3], and [4] does the following sentence belong?

"These spaces are in high demand."

(A) [1]
(B) [2]
(C) [3]
(D) [4]

Questions 176-180 refer to the following announcement and email.

Kenneth Global Journalism Internship

The Kenneth Global Journalism Internship will provide you with the chance to train with the world's most renowned international multimedia news agency, work with professional reporters and editors, and gain valuable experience in fast-paced newsrooms in big cities such as London, Berlin, and Paris. It will offer talented college graduates an opportunity to learn and develop strong journalistic skills while acquiring first-hand knowledge.

This is a paid internship that offers free lodging as well as lunch and dinner. Interns will receive several weeks of formal training focused on writing skills, journalistic ethics, and basic workplace knowledge. They are also able to take advantage of other regularly scheduled training opportunities during the internship, free of charge. The internship will last four months, beginning on August 1.

Applications for the internship can be found on our website at www.kennethglobal.com and must be submitted by June 20. Applicants who advance past this stage will be asked to interview at our headquarters on June 27. Any questions can be directed to Ruby Hart at rubyhart@kennethglobal.com or asked in person at our headquarters in Austin.

From: Kyle Lane <kylelane12@mpnet.com>
To: Ruby Hart <rubyhart@kennethglobal.com>
Subject: Internship
Date: June 23

Dear Ms. Hart,

I am extremely grateful to have advanced past the first round of the Kenneth Global Journalism Internship's selection process. Applicants are supposed to interview in person on the specified date, but unfortunately I am scheduled to attend an important conference in Dallas with my professor. However, since I live just a few minutes from your headquarters, it would not be difficult to arrange an alternative time for an interview.

Thanks again for considering me for this position. I look forward to hearing back from you concerning a possible interview date. In the meantime, I will do my best to prepare myself.

Regards,

Kyle Lane

GO ON TO THE NEXT PAGE

176. What is indicated about internship applicants?

(A) They must have prior work experience.
(B) They must attend an upcoming conference.
(C) They must submit a letter of recommendation.
(D) They must hold a bachelor's degree.

177. What is true about the internship?

(A) It includes meals and accommodations.
(B) It is for professional journalists only.
(C) It will end in August.
(D) It is an unpaid position.

178. What other benefit is offered to interns?

(A) Health insurance
(B) Additional training
(C) Employee discounts
(D) Paid vacation

179. When is Mr. Lane supposed to attend an interview?

(A) On June 20
(B) On June 27
(C) On June 23
(D) On August 1

180. Where does Mr. Lane live?

(A) In Dallas
(B) In Austin
(C) In Berlin
(D) In London

Questions 181-185 refer to the following email and announcement.

To: Sam Berry <sberry@princetheater.com>
From: Bessie Wagner <bessiewagner@linsuniversity.edu>
Date: July 4
Subject: Openings

Dear Mr. Berry,

My name is Bessie Wagner and I am currently a student in the theater department at Lins University. I have almost finished my degree, and I am starting to look into possible career opportunities for the future. A professor of mine recommended that I contact you at the Prince Theater to ask about possible positions with your company.

At Lins University, I have specialized in the production elements of theater. Through both academic and practical experience, I have learned the skills necessary for stage management. As of September, I will be available to work either part-time or full-time and apply myself fully to whatever task is assigned to me.

I would really appreciate it if you would let me know if there are any available positions at the Prince Theater starting this fall. Thank you.

Bessie Wagner

Prince Theater

Job Openings

- **Artistic Intern**
Unpaid internship in the artistic department dealing with all aspects of administration and production. This person will perform assistant duties for the artistic director.

- **Assistant Technical Director**
Part-time position responsible for production management and stage machinery. Applicants should have related experience in stage management.

- **Director of Ticket Operations**
Full-time position responsible for overall management of ticket operations for all events taking place at the theater. Responsibilities include box office operations as well as planning and implementing all ticket sales processes, and supervision of the ticketing staff.

- **Marketing Director**
Full-time position responsible for marketing concerning all of the productions put on by the theater. Oversee the preparation of high-quality promotional materials to attract theatergoers to our plays, musicals, and concerts.

– All full-time employees of Prince Theater are eligible for complimentary access to all productions.
– All of the positions will be open starting this October.
– For more information or to apply, contact Sam Berry by email at sberry@princetheater.com.

GO ON TO THE NEXT PAGE

181. What is indicated about Ms. Wagner?

(A) She is a stage actress.
(B) She teaches classes in stage design.
(C) She will graduate soon.
(D) She is Mr. Berry's coworker.

182. Why did Ms. Wagner write to Mr. Berry?

(A) To seek a job opportunity
(B) To schedule an interview
(C) To express her gratitude
(D) To register for a training course

183. What is NOT suggested about the director of ticket operations?

(A) He or she has to manage various types of events.
(B) He or she must direct the work of other employees.
(C) He or she can watch any show free of charge.
(D) He or she must plan promotional events.

184. What do all of the advertised jobs have in common?

(A) They require musical talent.
(B) They will be available in the fourth quarter.
(C) They are part-time positions.
(D) They require a degree in theater arts.

185. Which job is most suitable for Ms. Wagner?

(A) Artistic intern
(B) Assistant technical director
(C) Director of ticket operations
(D) Marketing director

Questions 186-190 refer to the following article and letters.

April 5—Clearwater Hospital in downtown Scranton has launched a new pen pal letter-writing program between terminally ill hospital patients and adult volunteers. Hospital director Zack Chambers, who was recently presented with an Outstanding Leader Award from the National Health Care Alliance, started the program to create stronger connections between the hospital and the community. Mr. Chambers encourages adults of all types and occupations to apply even if they don't feel completely qualified. Simply visit the Clearwater Hospital website and become a member of the hospital free of charge.

"I hope through this program, volunteers can form close relationships with patients to help them get through these difficult times in their lives," said Mr. Chambers. He also hopes that the program will lead to more people visiting terminally ill patients in person.

Clearwater Hospital

May 4

Monica Greene
4100 Washington Road
Scranton, Wisconsin 54481

Dear Ms. Greene,

I was delighted to receive your letter. I am very excited to have been paired with you as a pen pal. I hope we can learn a lot from each other and build a lasting friendship.

As you know, I live in California, which is a long way from Wisconsin. I hope that in the coming months I can take some time off work and visit you. Please let me know when the most convenient time would be for me to meet you.

I look forward to hearing from you,

Jessica Wright

GO ON TO THE NEXT PAGE

Dear Jessica,

You don't know how much I appreciate your kind words. Although the staff at Clearwater is very kind, I feel the need to connect with people who are not part of the staff. My surviving family also lives a great distance away, in Florida, and so most of the time I am just communicating with the paid staff or the other patients. I would welcome a visit if you truly wanted to come, and the best time would be for our Thanksgiving party here at the center, I suppose. My own family might be here as well. If it is too much for you, or if you can't get the time off from work, don't worry about it too much. I do hope that we can continue to communicate through our letters.

All the best,

Monica Greene

186. What is the article about?

(A) A volunteer program
(B) A doctor's retirement
(C) A new hospital
(D) A writing competition

187. What is mentioned about Mr. Chambers?

(A) He is a patient at Clearwater Hospital.
(B) He teaches writing skills to adults.
(C) He is the head of a government organization.
(D) He was honored for his leadership.

188. What does Mr. Chambers invite people to do?

(A) Sign up for a newsletter
(B) Schedule regular health checkups
(C) Visit patients in critical condition
(D) Write a letter of recommendation

189. Who does Monica Greene spend most of her time with?

(A) Clearwater's staff
(B) Her family
(C) Jessica Wright
(D) Her friends

190. When does Monica want Jessica to visit?

(A) On Monica's birthday
(B) This Saturday
(C) The 7th of June
(D) Thanksgiving

NEW **Questions 191-195** refer to the following letter and emails.

Mr. John Morris
1423 Bernard Avenue
Millville, CA 90117

Dear Mr. Morris,

24/7 Fitness is the most successful workout facility in the United States. With over 3 million members nationwide, our franchise has become known as a reputable and trustworthy brand. Our success is a result of great relationships between us and our franchisees.

You are receiving this mailing because you expressed interest in partnering with 24/7 Fitness in order to open a new location in your town. According to our preliminary research, your town has a large population of young, single people working in professional fields. This is our target demographic, and means the business outlook for your 24/7 Fitness location positive. If you would like more information about the specific terms and regulations when partnering with 24/7 Fitness, please don't hesitate to call me at 347-555-3363. Additionally, if you would like to talk to another franchise owner, that information can be supplied by one of our associates.

Sincerely,

Lori Swanson
Chief Operating Officer

To: Zack Carter <zcarter@zenmail.com>
From: John Morris <jmorris@cbnet.com>
Subject: 24/7 Fitness
Date: March 6

Dear Mr. Carter,

My name is John Morris and I am a small business owner living in the Millville area. I am currently in negotiations with 24/7 Fitness to open my own location here in Millville. As someone who works with 24/7 Fitness, you would help me a lot by sharing your opinions.

I am interested in how you assess 24/7 Fitness as a franchiser. I have operated several franchises in the past, and I have always found that trust and honesty are the most important factors in a successful relationship. More importantly, I was also wondering what kind of support is provided by the parent company. Before opening your location, did you receive adequate training to allow you to smoothly begin operating your business? Any advice you can give me would be much appreciated.

Sincerely,

John Morris

GO ON TO THE NEXT PAGE

To: John Morris <jmorris@cbnet.com>
From: Zack Carter <zcarter@zenmail.com>
Subject: 24/7 Fitness
Date: March 7

Dear Mr. Morris,

I am happy to provide some insight into the operation of a 24/7 Fitness franchise. I have been working with 24/7 Fitness as a franchise owner for 10 years now. I actually run three different branches. I completely agree with you that trust and honesty are the two most important aspects of any business relationship. On that count, I believe the fact that I own three franchises is testament to my faith in the franchiser.

Let me put your mind at ease. First off, 24/7 Fitness has a very specific way that it wants its brand to develop, no matter who owns the branch. The parent company will not only provide training; it insists on controlling the actual layout of the facilities from the locker rooms to the free weights. The owners want any of their 3 million members to be able to walk into any one of their gyms and feel at home. Until you have been operating for one full year, you must make monthly reports to corporate headquarters detailing all aspects of sales, membership, and a flow chart describing the usage of the facilities. It really is hands-on until they have confidence that you can represent the brand. I hope all this helps you decide to join the 24/7 Fitness team!

All the Best,

Zack Carter

191. According to the letter, what is the key to 24/7 Fitness's success?

(A) Effective communication with regional owners
(B) Rapid nationwide expansion
(C) A team of experienced researchers
(D) Comprehensive training of employees

192. Where did Mr. Morris most likely get Mr. Carter's contact information?

(A) From a 24/7 Fitness representative
(B) From 24/7 Fitness's website
(C) From Mr. Carter's blog
(D) From Mr. Carter's employee

193. What concerns Mr. Morris most about 24/7 Fitness?

(A) Its reputation
(B) Its financial status
(C) The types of assistance it offers
(D) The regulations for its franchisees

194. What is the purpose of Zack Carter's email?

(A) To ask for information about a franchise
(B) To tell John Morris about 24/7 Fitness and the training it provides
(C) To persuade John Morris not to become the owner of a 24/7 Fitness franchise
(D) To remind 24/7 of its responsibility to its franchisees

195. In Zack Carter's email, what is indicated about 24/7 Fitness?

(A) It wants all of its fitness centers to be nearly identical.
(B) It would like its franchisees to personalize their locations.
(C) It would like to sell more supplements and memberships next year.
(D) It requires its franchisees to send quarterly reports about usage.

Questions 196-200 refer to the following emails.

To: Kevin Scott <kevinscott@starrealty.com>
From: Steven Mason <smason@turnerelectronics.com>
Date: February 2
Subject: A warehouse

Dear Mr. Scott,

My name is Steven Mason and I work for the consumer electronics company Turner Electronics. I am currently scouting for a warehouse in the Pittsburgh area. As you know, having an effective distribution strategy is critical for every company in today's fast-paced business world.

Therefore, I am looking for a warehouse located on the outskirts of Pittsburgh. The warehouse needs to be located close to the highway. We are shipping a high volume of products, so we would prefer a dedicated warehouse to be used exclusively for Turner Electronics' operations. A warehouse with a spacious loading bay for large trucks is necessary. Additionally, a warehouse that also has office space would be ideal. Because of the valuable nature of our products, we would like a warehouse that provides security against theft and damage.

I look forward to hearing your response as soon as possible.

Steven Mason
Turner Electronics

To: Steven Mason <smason@turnerelectronics.com>
From: Kevin Scott <kevinscott@starrealty.com>
Date: February 3
Subject: Re: A warehouse

Dear Mr. Mason,

It seems that as your company expands, you would like to improve the operations of your distribution network and deliver products to sellers more quickly. We have a variety of warehouse options, and I trust one of them will fit your company's needs. All locations have a state-of-the-art security system as well as experienced staff.

Location 1—$3,499 per month for a 10,000-square-foot warehouse space shared by multiple businesses. Because this location is a shared operations site, we offer it at a discounted price.
Location 2—$5,500 per month for an older warehouse located in downtown Pittsburgh. This warehouse is currently empty, and therefore can be used by your company exclusively. It also features a walk-in freezer.
Location 3—$6,500 per month for a very spacious warehouse located a few miles outside of Pittsburgh. Although currently used by two other businesses as a storage space, it can be converted into a warehouse only for your company.
Location 4—$2,600 per month for a medium-size warehouse. This warehouse is provided at a discounted price because it has no area for trucks to unload cargo conveniently. It is best for smaller-sized operations.

These are the locations currently available for use. If you have any questions or would like to visit a location in person, please contact me.

Kevin Scott

GO ON TO THE NEXT PAGE

To: Kevin Scott <kevinscott@starrealty.com>
From: Steven Mason <smason@turnerelectronics.com>
Date: February 3
Subject: Location 3

Dear Mr. Scott,

Thank you so much for responding to my inquiry so quickly. Although none of the warehouses is exactly what I was looking for, I think the best option for our business will be warehouse Location 3. This, of course, is contingent on the other two businesses moving their storage to another warehouse. Our operations, as I noted in my first email, are expanding, and I want to make sure that we have ample room to grow. I am delighted that there is security at your warehouses as well.

I have some time early next week if it would be possible to take a walk through Location 3. I think once I get a feel for the space I will be able to make a firm decision. Please contact me by phone at your convenience so we can set up a time.
You can reach me at (351) 546-9899.

All the best,

Steve Mason
Turner Electronics

196. What is the purpose of the first email?

(A) To look for a rental space
(B) To finalize a business proposal
(C) To ensure the arrival of a shipment
(D) To advertise a property for sale

197. Who most likely is Mr. Mason?

(A) A warehouse manager
(B) A truck driver
(C) A security guard
(D) A distribution manager

198. According to Mr. Scott, what does Turner Electronics intend to do?

(A) Hire more experienced truck drivers
(B) Enhance supply chain efficiency
(C) Improve overall product quality
(D) Expand into the Asian market

199. According to the third email, what has to happen for Turner Electronics to move into Location 3?

(A) The rent must be reduced.
(B) Two businesses must find other places to store their belongings.
(C) The space must be converted to include an office.
(D) A security system must be added to the building.

200. According to the third email, what is the most likely day that Mr. Mason will be available for a walk-through of Location 3?

(A) Monday
(B) Thursday
(C) Friday
(D) Saturday

NO TEST MATERIAL ON THIS PAGE

ACTUAL TEST 04

Stop! This is the end of the test. If you finish before time is called, you may go back to Parts 5, 6, and 7 and check your work.

ACTUAL TEST 05

READING TEST

In the Reading test, you will read a variety of texts and answer several different types of reading comprehension questions. The entire Reading test will last 75 minutes. There are three parts, and directions are given for each part. You are encouraged to answer as many questions as possible within the time allowed.

You must mark your answers on the separate answer sheet. Do not write your answers in your test book.

PART 5

Directions: A word or phrase is missing in each of the sentences below. Four answer choices are given below each sentence. Select the best answer to complete the sentence. Then mark the letter (A), (B), (C), or (D) on your answer sheet.

101. Should the customer feel that the proposed color scheme is not -------, the interior designer can make adjustments.

(A) attract
(B) attractive
(C) attracted
(D) attractively

102. For Friday's dinner reservation, please ------- the number of seats from eight to ten.

(A) increase
(B) reflect
(C) merge
(D) invite

103. Mr. Brandt asked for the banner to be hung ------- the exterior wall of the building.

(A) up
(B) next
(C) on
(D) with

104. In case you have problems with the device in the future, you should retain your newly ------- receipt.

(A) expressed
(B) predicted
(C) issued
(D) approached

105. If the patient's nasal problem does not show signs of improvement ------- two days, he should visit the clinic again.

(A) because of
(B) regarding
(C) apart from
(D) within

106. The people giving demonstrations at the department store ------- explained the product's features and benefits.

(A) enthusiasm
(B) enthusiast
(C) enthusiastically
(D) enthusiastic

107. Because its latest exhibit is highly valuable, the Gabe Gallery has taken more precautions than it ------- has in the past.

(A) ever
(B) yet
(C) such
(D) much

108. ------- making structural changes to a house must first apply for a building permit.

(A) Our
(B) Who
(C) Them
(D) Anyone

109. Employees who attend the workshop on improving communication skills will be given a certificate of ------- by the instructor.

(A) achieved
(B) achieving
(C) achieve
(D) achievement

110. ------- its distinguished science department faculty, the university has state-of-the-art laboratory facilities.

(A) In addition to
(B) Otherwise
(C) As well
(D) Hardly ever

111. The donations received at the fundraiser ------- among the charity's three locations equally.

(A) have divided
(B) is being divided
(C) are dividing
(D) will be divided

112. ------- the building's age, the ventilation system must be up-to-date with all safety codes.

(A) Instead of
(B) Toward
(C) Regardless of
(D) Since

113. The delays on the Trenton train line were caused by a ------- error at one of the stations.

(A) proceed
(B) proceeded
(C) procedural
(D) procedurally

114. As we expect to receive hundreds of applications for the position, please ------- your résumé to two pages.

(A) limit
(B) follow
(C) refrain
(D) unfold

115. The lecturer ------- on the country's struggle for independence when he gives his talk.

(A) has focused
(B) is focused
(C) will focus
(D) focusing

116. The welcome activity is an opportunity to improve communication ------- volunteers before the project begins.

(A) among
(B) like
(C) above
(D) under

GO ON TO THE NEXT PAGE

117. The balconies in the rooms at the Orwell Hotel provide a ------- view of the hotel's private beach.

(A) stunningly
(B) stuns
(C) stunning
(D) stunned

118. The travel agent's ------- of the ticket purchase was sent to the customer by email as soon as the payment had been made.

(A) extent
(B) confirmation
(C) awareness
(D) proposal

119. After examining the vehicle, the mechanic ------- identified the reason why the engine had lost power.

(A) corrections
(B) correctly
(C) correct
(D) corrects

120. Because of her hearing disability, Ms. Frasier will be ------- by a sign language expert so she can participate in the meeting.

(A) convinced
(B) anticipated
(C) accompanied
(D) cautioned

121. The project development team is partially responsible for the selection and ------- of potential building sites.

(A) appraisal
(B) appraises
(C) appraise
(D) appraised

122. The easy-to-prepare meal packets come with all the ingredients necessary for an individual dinner ------- boiling water.

(A) except
(B) despite
(C) elsewhere
(D) past

123. The education center provides training in key skills ------- that the unemployed can find jobs more easily.

(A) so
(B) ever
(C) only
(D) as

124. The terms of the licensing agreement are quite ------- and do not require a legal background to be understood.

(A) energetic
(B) frequent
(C) straightforward
(D) accomplished

125. The information sent to conference attendees ------- the presentation schedule and social events.

(A) expands
(B) solicits
(C) allows
(D) outlines

126. You may have the merchandise sent directly to your home or pick it up in person at the store, ------- you prefer.

(A) both
(B) whichever
(C) everybody
(D) another

127. ------- occurring substances are used in the vitamin supplement instead of chemicals.

(A) Naturally
(B) Natural
(C) Naturalize
(D) Nature

128. The bus driver used a side street rather than the main highway, ------- avoiding rush-hour traffic.

(A) such as
(B) than
(C) unless
(D) thereby

129. The crew members ------- the main section of the building by the time the waste removal trucks arrive at 3:30.

(A) demolish
(B) will have demolished
(C) demolished
(D) had demolished

130. Should you find any manufacturing ------- in your ultra-high-definition television, contact the place of purchase as soon as possible.

(A) premises
(B) defects
(C) impacts
(D) distractions

GO ON TO THE NEXT PAGE

PART 6

Directions: Read the texts that follow. A word, phrase, or sentence is missing in parts of each text. Four answer choices for each question are given below the text. Select the best answer to complete the text. Then mark the letter (A), (B), (C), or (D) on your answer sheet.

Questions 131-134 refer to the following advertisement.

> Come visit Wild Water Parks, the summer destination for families and friends of all ages. We have kiddie pools, we have outdoor pools, we have indoor pools, we have waves, and we have ------- **131.** water slides—including our Death Fall, the largest slide in the state. We have everything for everyone in ------- **132.** group. Don't forget our delicious snack stands and restaurants. We also have gift shops and playgrounds. ------- **133.** You can get tickets by calling 123-5555, or get a season pass for a ------- **134.** of the price. Call now and experience the fun!

131. (A) excite
(B) excited
(C) exciting
(D) excitement

132. (A) their
(B) his
(C) our
(D) your

NEW

133. (A) The pools are the best place to stay.
(B) We even have a dog park for that furry companion of yours.
(C) The chefs are top notch and the food is second to none.
(D) Hurry before the season is over and the promotion is finished.

134. (A) fraction
(B) section
(C) division
(D) total

Questions 135-138 refer to the following email.

From: Rhonda Cross

To: Mike Harris

Date: June 21

Subject: Re: Landscaping and Maintenance

Thank you for your ------- (135.) about our services. Arbor Care is a green lawn care and landscaping business. We only use environmentally friendly techniques and products when caring for the grounds of any business. We've been working in the Portland area for ------- (136.) 20 years. Currently, we are serving more than 150 businesses in the downtown area.

As for your specific request, yes, we can easily remove dead trees and replace them with something that fits the ------- (137.) landscaping. To give you an exact quote, we would need to stop by and assess the situation in person. To have one of our garden technicians stop by, please call us at (713) 678-9916. ------- (138.)

135. (A) submission
(B) placement
(C) review
(D) inquiry

136. (A) over
(B) less
(C) until
(D) through

137. (A) exist
(B) existed
(C) existing
(D) exists

NEW

138. (A) It is a pleasure doing business with you.
(B) We hope to hear from you soon.
(C) Please send us an email.
(D) Best wishes for your continued success.

GO ON TO THE NEXT PAGE

Questions 139-142 refer to the following notice.

Outbound Sales Lead Specialist/Telemarketer

Location: Atlanta, GA

Job Code: 3766

# of openings: 4

The sales lead specialist will place outbound calls to ------- (139.) customers seeking to purchase various services such as insurance, tax help, financial help, telecommunications, or transportation. They will also call on leads from our existing customer base. Cold calls are required.

You will work directly with customers via the telephone and email to describe products and services in order to persuade potential and current customers to purchase new products and services. The job will also require you to educate customers on product and service offerings. ------- (140.) There is also a minimum requirement for monthly sales that is set at $7,500 in net revenue. ------- (141.), all employees must regularly attend our product education course in order to better serve our customers.

To be eligible for the position you must have one or more years in telesales, strong customer service skills, and superior closing skills.

If you feel you ------- (142.) these requirements and are looking for an exciting, lucrative experience, please click below.

139. (A) substantial
(B) potential
(C) optimal
(D) logical

NEW

140. (A) The more you sell, the more opportunity you'll have for advancement.
(B) This managerial position will require an organized and highly motivated individual.
(C) If you could help find your replacement, it would be much appreciated.
(D) It will be crucial for you to place a minimum of 150 outbound calls each day.

141. (A) Actually
(B) However
(C) Additionally
(D) Therefore

142. (A) meet
(B) to meet
(C) meeting
(D) met

Questions 143-146 refer to the following notice.

From: James Jones, Executive Manager

To: Sales Agents

Date: July 15

Subject: policy change

Dear Sales Agents,

There has been a recent change to our reimbursement policy. In the past, you simply had to pay out of pocket first and then provide your receipts after renting vehicles, taking business trips, or ------- (**143.**) other business expenses. -------(**144.**), from now on you will be required to fill out an application form which must be approved by the accounting department first. ------- (**145.**) If you spend anything beyond the amount on the card, you will have to pay out of your own pocket and will not be reimbursed for that.

Please read the attachment for further details on what expenses can and cannot be ------- (**146.**) by the company.

143. (A) incur
(B) incurred
(C) incurring
(D) to incur

144. (A) However
(B) Therefore
(C) Furthermore
(D) Since

NEW

145. (A) They will not approve any card not authorized by a bank.
(B) You will have to spend with your own credit card.
(C) Then you will be provided with a company card which holds limited funds.
(D) They must decide whether our budget allows for our expenses.

146. (A) certain
(B) acknowledged
(C) established
(D) approved

ACTUAL TEST 05

GO ON TO THE NEXT PAGE

PART 7

Directions: In this part you will read a selection of texts, such as magazine and newspaper articles, emails, and instant messages. Each text or set of texts is followed by several questions. Select the best answer for each question and mark the letter (A), (B), (C), or (D) on your answer sheet.

Questions 147-148 refer to the following calendar.

Time	Monday	Tuesday	Wednesday	Thursday	Friday
9:00 A.M.–11:00 A.M.	Yoga Level 1: **Room 4**		Fitness Training: **Room 1**	Kickboxing Level 1: **Room 3**	
11:00 A.M.–2:00 P.M.		Weight Training: **Room 2**			Yoga Level 2: **Room 4**
2:00 P.M.–4:00 P.M.	Cycling: **Room 1**	Kickboxing Level 2: **Room 3**		Nutrition Advice: **Room 5** (book a personal appointment at reception)	
4:00 P.M.–6:00 P.M.	Yoga Level 3: **Room 4**		Fitness Training: **Room 1**		Marathon Training: **Room 2**

147. Where would this calendar most likely be seen?

(A) In the sports section of a newspaper
(B) In a travel itinerary
(C) On the wall in a gym facility
(D) In a program for a sports tournament

148. Which activities take place in the same room?

(A) Yoga and kickboxing
(B) Marathon training and cycling
(C) Yoga and nutrition advice
(D) Cycling and fitness training

Questions 149-150 refer to the following text message chain.

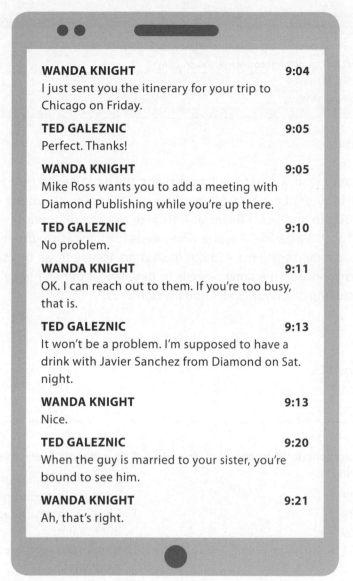

WANDA KNIGHT **9:04**
I just sent you the itinerary for your trip to Chicago on Friday.

TED GALEZNIC **9:05**
Perfect. Thanks!

WANDA KNIGHT **9:05**
Mike Ross wants you to add a meeting with Diamond Publishing while you're up there.

TED GALEZNIC **9:10**
No problem.

WANDA KNIGHT **9:11**
OK. I can reach out to them. If you're too busy, that is.

TED GALEZNIC **9:13**
It won't be a problem. I'm supposed to have a drink with Javier Sanchez from Diamond on Sat. night.

WANDA KNIGHT **9:13**
Nice.

TED GALEZNIC **9:20**
When the guy is married to your sister, you're bound to see him.

WANDA KNIGHT **9:21**
Ah, that's right.

149. What is suggested about Mr. Sanchez?

(A) He works for an accounting company.
(B) He is related to Wanda Knight.
(C) He was recently married.
(D) He will visit Chicago on Friday.

150. At 9:11, what does Ms. Knight mean when she writes, "I can reach out to them"?

(A) She can thank them.
(B) She can contact them.
(C) She can visit them.
(D) She can assist them.

ACTUAL TEST 05

GO ON TO THE NEXT PAGE

Questions 151-152 refer to the following email.

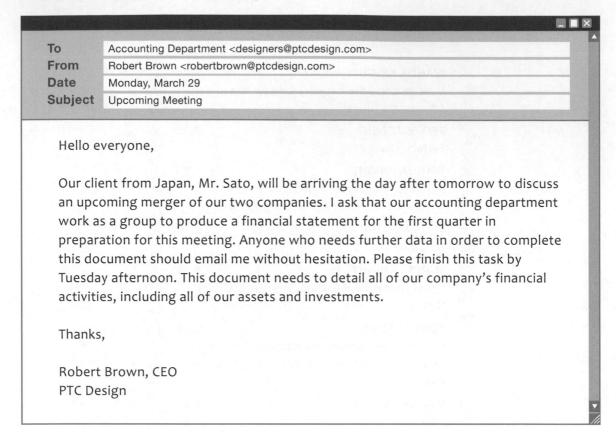

To	Accounting Department <designers@ptcdesign.com>
From	Robert Brown <robertbrown@ptcdesign.com>
Date	Monday, March 29
Subject	Upcoming Meeting

Hello everyone,

Our client from Japan, Mr. Sato, will be arriving the day after tomorrow to discuss an upcoming merger of our two companies. I ask that our accounting department work as a group to produce a financial statement for the first quarter in preparation for this meeting. Anyone who needs further data in order to complete this document should email me without hesitation. Please finish this task by Tuesday afternoon. This document needs to detail all of our company's financial activities, including all of our assets and investments.

Thanks,

Robert Brown, CEO
PTC Design

151. When is Mr. Sato scheduled to arrive at Mr. Brown's company?

(A) On March 28
(B) On March 29
(C) On March 30
(D) On March 31

152. Who will most likely contact Mr. Brown?

(A) Employees who want to transfer to the accounting department
(B) Employees who need additional information
(C) Employees who need a deadline extension
(D) Employees who disagree about a merger

Questions 153-154 refer to the following invitation.

American Architects Society Annual Awards

You are cordially invited to attend this year's event, to be held at the Merriton Hotel in Houston, Texas on Friday, July 24. As a member, you may bring up to two guests.

7:00 P.M.	**Reception**
7:30 P.M.	**Welcome speech and introduction by Barry Humphreys, President of the American Architects Society**
7:45 P.M.	**Dinner (Vegetarian options available; please specify when confirming attendance.)**
9:00 P.M.	**Awards ceremony—Best Design, Best Newcomer, Best Residential Building, Best Public Building—presented by comedian Alex Dashwood**
10:30 P.M.	**A special live performance by award-winning band The Pop Tones**

RSVP to event coordinator Janice Harton at janice.harton@amarchsoc.net no later than April 21.

153. Who most likely are the invitation recipients?

(A) Directors of building companies
(B) Members of an association
(C) Architects for the local government
(D) Award ceremony nominees

154. How can attendance be confirmed?

(A) By calling the Merriton Hotel
(B) By emailing Barry Humphreys
(C) By visiting Alex Dashwood
(D) By contacting a coordinator

ACTUAL TEST 05

GO ON TO THE NEXT PAGE

Questions 155-157 refer to the following article.

Northshore Financial News

June 29— A local mainstay of Northshore City may soon go national. - [1] - The Northshore Creamery first opened its doors in 1951 under owner Bill Bradley and has become an iconic landmark of the city with its huge rotating ice cream cone on the roof of the shop. Over the years it has remained a favorite local hangout for the residents of the city and captured the eyes of tourists driving through. - [2] - Bill Jr. took over the business 25 years ago and expanded the shop to keep up with the demand of locals and tourists. Northshore Creamery was even selected as a top ten shop to visit by *Travel & Tour Magazine*.

In 1988, Northshore Creamery was featured in the hit Hollywood movie *Future Then and Now*, which made it the top ice cream shop to visit by out-of-towners and tourists.

- [3] - Efforts have been made by various corporations to buy the business from the Bradley family, but Bill Jr. and his son William have insisted on keeping the business within the family, which pleases the residents of Northshore. - [4] - "We're keeping things small in scale and we're slowly expanding," explains William. "In order to maintain the quality and freshness of our ice cream and keep our recipes just the way my grandfather created them, we can't take any shortcuts. That's why we need time."

155. What is the article's purpose?

(A) To advertise the products of a shop
(B) To explain the details of a new business venture
(C) To discuss the history of a family business
(D) To explain the prices of some products

156. What is indicated about Northshore Creamery?

(A) It was purchased by a large corporation.
(B) It became famous in town because of a movie.
(C) It is the pride and joy of the locals.
(D) It doesn't have enough money to expand.

NEW

157. In which of the positions marked [1], [2], [3], and [4] does the following sentence belong?

"Now the family is ready to open two new franchises in neighboring cities, and within five years plans to open six new shops around the country."

(A) [1]
(B) [2]
(C) [3]
(D) [4]

Questions 158-160 refer to the following announcement.

Announcement from Acreton City Council

April 3

The Acreton City Council will be creating a new task force charged with reducing unnecessary spending over the next fiscal year. The team of 12 people will be comprised of local business leaders, union representatives, civil servants, and financial consultants. Group members are due to be selected by the 30th of this month and will begin working almost immediately, planning ways to reduce annual local government costs by 10 percent over the next year by eliminating waste.

Applications for positions on the task force are being accepted at this time. Please contact the city council at admin@acretoncc.gov for information on how to get yourself or your organization involved in this project.

158. What is the announcement mainly about?

(A) The formation of a new employees' union.
(B) The creation of a financial oversight committee
(C) The launch of a recruitment effort
(D) The start of a change in local legislation

159. When is the group due to begin work?

(A) At the beginning of May
(B) At the end of the year
(C) At the beginning of the summer
(D) At the end of April

160. What should interested parties do to get involved?

(A) Sign a petition
(B) Attend a meeting
(C) Send an email
(D) Fill out a form

GO ON TO THE NEXT PAGE

Questions 161-164 refer to the following online chat discussion.

Janet Logan	**[2:15]**	I just got off the phone and Mr. King informed me that he wanted his order a couple of weeks earlier than originally planned. Do you think this may be possible?
Margaret Lee	**[2:16]**	There's no problem on our end. We have all the fabrics ready and cut into their appropriate shapes and sizes. They are ready for the sewing machines.
Jason Brown	**[2:17]**	My team is currently working on the orders from Mr. Bartelli. We have over 1,000 units to sew and another order from Carla Bean after that.
Janet Logan	**[2:18]**	Mr. Bartelli doesn't need his order until the end of the month, and Ms. Bean's orders can wait until next week. I can authorize your team to begin this order first.
Jason Brown	**[2:19]**	What is being made and how many units are needed?
Janet Logan	**[2:20]**	Long-sleeved men's dress shirts. We need 100 units in small, 300 in medium, 300 in large, and 100 in extra large.
Jason Brown	**[2:21]**	OK, then. I think we can finish those in two days.
Peter Williams	**[2:22]**	We can get buttons on all 800 units within two to four hours.
Janet Logan	**[2:23]**	Thank you so much. I appreciate your help. I'm glad that we can accommodate one of our best clients this way.

161. At 2:16, what does Margaret Lee mean when she writes, "There's no problem on our end"?

(A) Her team can achieve the goal.
(B) Her team can help the other teams.
(C) Their project will take some time.
(D) The problems will be minimal.

162. For what type of company does Janet Logan work?

(A) A shoe shop
(B) A clothing manufacturer
(C) A fashion magazine
(D) A menswear boutique

163. According to the discussion, which department needs the most time?

(A) Ms. Lee's department
(B) Mr. Brown's department
(C) Mr. Williams' department
(D) Ms. Logan's department

164. What will Janet Logan most likely tell Mr. King?

(A) That his order will be delayed for a month
(B) That his order can be completed within two weeks
(C) That his request will be difficult to achieve
(D) That his order can be completed early

Questions 165-167 refer to the following memo.

Unsworthy Manufacturing

Date: Wednesday, October 17
Subject: Recycling

In response to pressure from local environmental groups, as of November 1 we will be separating all of our industrial waste for recycling. Collections will be made twice weekly on Tuesdays and Fridays from the regional recycling center, which will be supplying colored receptacles for different kinds of waste. All oils should be placed in the green container. All metals and glass belong in the red one. All paper waste should go into the blue one. Plastics will be collected for recycling as normal.

As this new policy also carries a financial benefit for the company, managers in all manufacturing bays are responsible for ensuring that the new protocols for waste disposal are followed, and failure to comply with the policy could result in disciplinary action.

Further information about our updated environmental practices will shortly be available on the website. Training sessions for managers will be held on Monday, October 22, but please contact me if you have any further questions in the meantime.

Regards,

Davis Jeeland
Operations Director, Unsworthy Manufacturing

165. What is the reason for the change?

(A) The company owners want to save money on labor.
(B) A new recycling center has opened near the business.
(C) The local government has changed its regulations.
(D) Environmentalists in the area have requested it.

166. What can be inferred about Unsworthy Manufacturing?

(A) It has good relations with local authorities.
(B) It already recycles its plastic industrial waste.
(C) It recently increased its workforce.
(D) It updates its environmental policy regularly.

167. What should supervisors do next week?

(A) Attend a workshop on the new procedures
(B) Update the company's website pages
(C) Make room for new waste receptacles
(D) Inform their teams of the changes

GO ON TO THE NEXT PAGE

Questions 168-171 refer to the following letter.

Normanville Farmers' Market

April 9

Dear Normanville Resident,

This year's first Normanville Farmers' Market will take place on Saturday, April 14 on Clark Street between Main Street and Park Street. The farmers' market will be open from 9 A.M. to 5 P.M. The mayor of Normanville, Tom Daley, will be present to deliver an address at the opening ceremony. A lot of local farmers, food vendors, and street performers will be at the venue.

"This vibrant market will give our local farmers a nice place to sell their fresh produce. Additionally, because we cut out some middle processes, our prices are lower than those of average grocery stores," said Suzy Hammer, executive director of the Normanville Farmers' Association.

Ms. Hammer also mentioned that currently there is not enough parking space to accommodate shoppers. The Normanville Farmers' Association plans to expand parking space over the coming months. In the meantime, she advises Normanville residents who will visit the market to use public transportation in order to avoid parking difficulties.

The Normanville Farmers' Market is different from grocery stores that supply mass-produced food products. The market will provide organic produce that is full of essential vitamins and minerals. As you know, the market will also help the local economy.

Please come this Saturday and see what the Normanville Farmers' Market has to offer!

Sincerely,

Normanville Farmers' Association

168. Why was the letter written?

(A) To describe a policy change
(B) To introduce a new grocery store
(C) To advertise a market opening
(D) To announce election results

169. What is indicated about Ms. Hammer?

(A) She is a vendor at the farmers' market.
(B) She represents other farmers.
(C) She owns a family-run farm.
(D) She is the mayor of Normanville.

170. What problem is mentioned?

(A) Inadequate parking spots
(B) Unfair product pricing
(C) Lack of quality control
(D) Inclement weather

171. What is NOT mentioned as a benefit of shopping at the venue?

(A) A boost for the local economy
(B) Competitive prices
(C) Healthy produce
(D) Longer opening hours

Questions 172-175 refer to the following notice.

Lost and Found

Parkway City is bracing for another holiday season and urging its citizens and tourists to keep track of their belongings. – [1] – Every year more than 2,000 items show up at the city lost and found located at Parkway City Hall. "But we get even more lost items during the holiday season," explains Jean King, the managing director of the lost and found. "From around November 25th to January 2nd we get a 25-percent increase in the number of items that are brought to us."

– [2] – Everything from keys, sunglasses, umbrellas, and jewelry to electronic devices, luggage, and shopping bags full of newly purchased items has been brought to the center over the years. "The strangest item we ever got was a suitcase full of period piece costumes," says Jean. "The intern working on a film at the time was happy to get it back."

– [3] – If the items are not claimed within 90 days, they are auctioned off at a public event to raise money for the community center. – [4] –

172. What is the purpose of the notice?

(A) To advertise an event for the holidays
(B) To warn citizens of increasing crime
(C) To inform people about lost and found items
(D) To give information about an auction

173. What is suggested about Jean King?

(A) She searches for lost items.
(B) She works for the city.
(C) She is an intern.
(D) She manages the community center.

174. What is suggested about the lost items?

(A) They are not kept at the center indefinitely.
(B) They are usually claimed by their owners.
(C) They are destroyed when unclaimed.
(D) They are generally new items.

NEW

175. In which of the positions marked [1], [2], [3], and [4] does the following sentence belong?

"Many people do come to claim their missing items, but the vast majority is still left unclaimed."

(A) [1]
(B) [2]
(C) [3]
(D) [4]

GO ON TO THE NEXT PAGE

Questions 176-180 refer to the following article and email.

Tech Life Hires New CEO

New York, April 12—Amid a crisis of low sales and disappointing performance, the technology company Tech Life has hired Steve Cross as its new chief executive officer. Previously, he was the chief financial officer at the technology investment firm Esta Resources in San Francisco, California. He assumed the position of CEO at the company—based in Dallas, Texas—just this Monday. Stockholders voted unanimously for the appointment, hoping the new CEO would bring renewed vitality and strength to the company.

"Mr. Cross has an impressive record as a business leader who makes smart decisions," commented Lynn Dyer, the director of human resources at Tech Life. "We have faith that he will lead us in a new direction that will help develop new markets and optimize our company operations in general."

Steve Cross graduated from Chester University in Harrisburg, Pennsylvania with a master's degree in business administration. He once served as head of the American League of Business Leaders and is a dedicated family man.

To: Steve Cross <scross@techlife.com>
From: Lynn Dyer <ldyer@techlife.com>
Subject: Welcome!
Date: April 15

Dear Mr. Cross,

It has been almost two years since we met. I am so glad to be collaborating with you again after we worked in the same department at Esta Resources. I felt we cooperated very well at that time, and I had been hoping to work with you again. You will find that we have very dedicated and hard-working teams here. If there is anything I can do to help you make the transition, please don't hesitate to ask.

Additionally, Tech Life has recently added five new managers to our company. If you have time, please visit them at 3:00 P.M. this afternoon, when they will all be attending a mandatory training session in Room 403.

Sincerely,

Lynn Dyer
Director of Human Resources

176. What problem is Tech Life facing?

(A) A shortage of employees
(B) An urgent audit
(C) A decline in profitability
(D) A potential competitor

177. What is mentioned about the shareholders?

(A) They are allowed to share financial information.
(B) They will hold a meeting next week.
(C) They are demanding more dividends.
(D) They agreed on the appointment of a new leader.

178. In the article, the word "optimize" in paragraph 2, line 6 is closest in meaning to

(A) merge
(B) improve
(C) analyze
(D) maintain

179. Where did Ms. Dyer work previously?

(A) In Harrisburg
(B) In Dallas
(C) In New York
(D) In San Francisco

180. What is Mr. Cross asked to do?

(A) Teach a training course
(B) Meet new employees
(C) Attend a stockholders' meeting
(D) Hire new managers

GO ON TO THE NEXT PAGE

Questions 181-185 refer to the following agenda and email.

The Association of Future and Culture (AFC)

Quarterly Conference

Homer Conference Center, January 10

2:00 P.M.	Kelly O'Neill, President, AFC; Principal, Mulligan Elementary School Welcoming speech
2:30 P.M.	Mark Kreskas, CEO, SEM Development Group Enhancing global awareness: leadership and diversity
3:30 P.M.	Lucy Hoover, Co-owner, Piedmont Adult Education Center Gender and fairness in leadership
4:30 P.M.	Jon Kimura, Store Manager, Kent Grocery Store The foundations of leadership in the workplace
5:30 P.M.	Kenneth Schneider, Professor, Brookstone University Ethics and morality in leadership
6:30 P.M.	Question-and-answer session

To: AFC Members <members@futureculture.org>
From: Kelly O'Neill <kellyoneill@futureculture.org>
Date: January 11
Attachment: free_talk.jpg
Subject: Quarterly Conference

Dear AFC Members,

This quarterly conference has been another monumental success. I thank all of you for participating and sharing your expertise with others. I hope you can take the skills learned during the conference and apply them in your local offices and workplaces. Additionally, I encourage all of you to consider giving a presentation at the next conference. If you are interested in doing so, contact Amy Garcia at amygarcia@futureculture.org.

I would also like to inform you of the invitation made by Kenneth Schneider, who will be giving a talk entitled "Gaining confidence through leadership" at his workplace next month. The talk will be free and open to the public. For more information, please see the attached file.

Finally, it has come to my attention that some members were not able to attend the conference due to scheduling conflicts. Therefore, all future conferences will be streamed simultaneously on our website so that distant members can watch and listen.

Sincerely,

Kelly O'Neill, President

181. What was the topic of the conference on January 10?

(A) How to start a small business
(B) How to manage finances
(C) How to lead other people
(D) How to expand business globally

182. When most likely will inquiries start being made?

(A) At 3:30 P.M.
(B) At 4:30 P.M.
(C) At 5:30 P.M.
(D) At 6:30 P.M.

183. Where will a talk be given at no charge?

(A) At Mulligan Elementary School
(B) At Brookstone University
(C) At Piedmont Adult Education Center
(D) At SEM Development Group

184. What does Ms. O'Neill invite AFC members to do?

(A) Attach a receipt
(B) Fill out a survey
(C) Prepare a presentation
(D) Evaluate speakers

185. What is mentioned about the next conference?

(A) It will be held at a new location.
(B) Its presentations will start later in the day.
(C) Its attendance fees will be increased.
(D) It will be broadcast online.

GO ON TO THE NEXT PAGE

Questions 186-190 refer to the following Web page and emails.

Stark Bank

Announcements	My Accounts	Transfer	Loans

Overdraft Fee

On the date of June 3, you withdrew $100.00 from an ATM in Jacksonville, Florida, exceeding the limit of your debit card account. Therefore, you will be charged an overdraft fee of $30.00. This may have resulted from an accumulation of account withdrawals that were in process at the time you withdrew money from the ATM. We regret having to charge this amount whenever a member's debit card transactions exceed his or her funds.

In the future, this mistake can be avoided by signing up for our Stark Bank mobile banking service. This service only costs two dollars a month. Using your smartphone, you can access your accounts no matter where you are. You can check the amount of money in your accounts, your history of deposits and withdrawals, and most importantly, pending transactions. To sign up, please email us at customerservice@starkbank.com or call us at 904-555-4514.

To: customerservice@starkbank.com
From: ssummers@zippynet.com
Subject: Overdraft Fee
Date: June 5

I am concerned that someone may have illegally accessed my account and made a withdrawal. I lost my debit card on June 2, and upon noticing the next day, I immediately froze all of my accounts. Considering these unfortunate circumstances, I politely ask that the bank refrain from charging a fee for this unforeseen overdraft.

I would like to sign up for the banking service you recommended. It sounds like a useful service that can help me manage my finances in a more efficient manner.

Thank you for your assistance.

Suzie Summers

To: Suzie Summers<ssummers@zippynet.com>
From: Customer Service<customerservice@starkbank.com>
Subject: Overdraft Review
Date: June 6

Dear Ms. Summers,

I am sorry to hear of your misfortunes. According to our account data, you did contact us and freeze your accounts, though it looks like it was too late to prevent the withdrawal and subsequent overdraft from your account. It is a little bit unusual that the transaction that caused the overdraft was at an ATM machine a day after you say that you lost your card. Have you given your access pin to anybody recently? I would be happy to pass your request for overdraft relief on to our fraud department, but you will need to file a police report and then send us the case number that the investigating officer gives you. Once we receive this number we can proceed with our review of your case.

Thank you and good day,

Laura Massey
Customer Service Specialist, Stark Bank

186. What is the purpose of the Web page information?

(A) To announce a new company policy
(B) To explain an upcoming relocation
(C) To inform a user about a charge
(D) To notify a user of phishing attempts

187. What is NOT mentioned as being able to be checked using the mobile banking service?

(A) Account balances
(B) Interest rates
(C) Unresolved transactions
(D) Account history

188. What request does Ms. Summers make?

(A) That her accounts be frozen
(B) That her contact information be updated
(C) That her overdraft fee be waived
(D) That her withdrawal limit be increased

189. In her customer service email to Suzie Summers, what does Laura Massey think is odd about Suzie's story?

(A) Suzie didn't have very much money in her account.
(B) Suzie didn't file a police report.
(C) Suzie lost her card on June 2 but her card was used at an ATM machine on June 3.
(D) Suzie does not live in Florida.

190. What does Laura Massey instruct Suzie Summers to do if she wants to get relief from the overdraft fee?

(A) Write the fraud department of Stark Bank
(B) File a police report and give the case number to Stark Bank
(C) File a claim against the criminal in a court and give the court number to Stark Bank
(D) File a case number with the fraud department of Stark Bank

GO ON TO THE NEXT PAGE

NEW **Questions 191-195** refer to the following emails.

From: customerservice@thomsonapp.com
To: dkerry@coolmail.com
Date: July 6
Subject: Malfunction

Dear Ms. Kerry,

We are very sorry to hear about the malfunction of your deluxe refrigerator model MK1213, purchased from Thomson Appliances. You indicated that the ice dispenser on the door of the fridge has stopped functioning. Actually, several other customers have reported the same problem. It turns out that the manufacturers made an error in the production process. Fortunately, this problem can easily be fixed by one of our technicians. Currently, our technicians are available next Monday, Wednesday, and Thursday. Please specify what day and what time work for you.

Additionally, if your refrigerator is under warranty, this repair will be absolutely free. Please let us know your warranty number so we can verify this before sending a technician to your house.

We apologize for this inconvenience. Thank you again for choosing Thomson Appliances.

Sincerely,

Greg Lewis
Customer Service

From: dkerry@coolmail.com
To: customerservice@thomsonapp.com
Date: July 7
Subject: Re: Malfunction

Dear Mr. Lewis,

Thank you for your prompt response. Actually, next week I will be away on a business trip in Arkansas and won't return until Saturday. However, I have a housekeeper who comes to clean on Monday and Friday. If your technician visits on either of those days, she can let him or her in.

My warranty number is A344F56J and is still valid. I will leave this document with my housekeeper in case you need to see it during your visit.

Dana Kerry

From: customerservice@thomsonapp.com
To: dkerry@coolmail.com
Date: July 7
Subject: repair time

Dear Ms. Kerry,

Our technician will be able to come by your house on Monday. You will need to be sure to leave the warranty documents so the technicians can scan them into our system. This is necessary for us to be reimbursed by the manufacturers. Our technicians will come by in the morning and try to be gone by lunch. Even though you have a housekeeper, they will try not to leave a mess. Safe travels and we appreciate your patience. Thank you for your loyalty to Thomson Appliances.

Sincerely,

Greg Lewis
Customer Service

191. What is one reason the first email was sent?

(A) To specify a warranty number
(B) To ask for a date for a visit
(C) To confirm an order
(D) To apologize for a shipping delay

192. According to the first email, what is true about the refrigerator?

(A) It is a newly released model.
(B) It is no longer covered by the warranty.
(C) It has a manufacturing defect.
(D) It is currently on sale.

193. What information does Mr. Lewis request from Ms. Kerry?

(A) Her current address
(B) Her warranty number
(C) Her refrigerator model
(D) Her contact information

194. Why do the technicians need to scan the warranty?

(A) To make sure it is still valid
(B) To make sure that the model is correct
(C) To make sure that there are enough spare parts to make the repairs
(D) To make sure that the manufacturer covers the repair costs

195. Why do you think the technicians will come on Monday?

(A) Because that is when they are available
(B) Because they are too busy on Friday
(C) Because the housekeeper will be there to let them in
(D) Because Ms. Kerry will be in Arkansas

GO ON TO THE NEXT PAGE

NEW **Questions 196-200** refer to the following emails.

To: Lillian Ross <lillianross@kingstonsportinggoods.com>
From: Eric West <ericwest@jmsolutions.com>
Date: November 4, 10:34 A.M.
Subject: Website Development
Attachment: Details

Dear Ms. Ross,

You contacted us last week to ask some of our computer programmers to help your company develop a website. JM Solutions would be happy to offer you our services.

As I said on the phone, we will help design and program a website that will attract more customers and offer an online sales platform. During this time, we will need to hold meetings with your marketing division in order to best capture your company's goals. Once the website has been completed in mid-February next year, we will hold a training seminar in order to train your employees in the skills necessary to maintain and update your website. The website development and training seminar will cost a total of $32,000. We request that a deposit of 10 percent be paid in advance. Please see the attached file for detailed costs and schedules.

We look forward to working with you in the near future. Our staff members will strive to meet all your needs. Just let me know when your marketing division is available to meet us in person and discuss some of the details of the project. Please contact me at your convenience.

Eric West

To: Lillian Ross <lillianross@kingstonsportinggoods.com>
From: Raymond Wells <raymondwells@kingstonsportinggoods.com>
Date: November 4, 10:37 A.M.
Subject: First Quarter Budget
Attachment: Q1_Budget

Dear Ms. Ross,

I have attached the current draft of the company's budget for the first quarter of next year. As you will notice, all of the profits made from this year's back-to-school sale are planned to be spent on billboard advertisements on major highways. I will call a design team later this afternoon and ask them to create eye-catching images for the advertisements.

At our last meeting, you mentioned that you would like to review the budget before it is finalized. I have already included employee raises in the first quarter's expenses, but if you can think of anything else, please let me know. I would like to have the budget finalized before next week's planning meeting.

Raymond Wells

To: Raymond Wells <raymondwells@kingstonsportinggoods.com>
From: Lillian Ross <lillianross@kingstonsportinggoods.com>
Date: November 4, 10:40 AM
Subject: Emergency Budget Addition

Dear Mr. Wells,

I am glad you forwarded me your proposed budget when you did. Just prior to receiving your email I received an estimate for our planned website development. It looks like it is going to be more expensive than I had anticipated. Although the final bill of $32,000 is not due immediately, we will have to find an extra $3,200 in next year's first quarter budget if we want to proceed with JM Solutions' proposal.

If you have any questions regarding this matter, please just come to my office and we can go over how to make the tough cuts needed to come up with this funding.

---

196. Why did Mr. West write the first email?

(A) To inquire about a service
(B) To schedule a meeting
(C) To report on a budget
(D) To apply for a position

197. What service does JM Solutions provide?

(A) Recruitment and employee training
(B) Graphic design
(C) Web programming
(D) Marketing strategy consultation

198. According to the second email, how will the profits from the back-to-school sale be spent?

(A) On repairing some roads
(B) On purchasing advertising space
(C) On paying for JM Solutions' service
(D) On hiring more employees

199. What is indicated by the third email?

(A) The budget for the first quarter of next year looks good.
(B) JM Solutions has a strong reputation.
(C) It will be easy for Kingston Sporting Goods to find money in its budget for web development.
(D) Some items in the budget may lose their funding in order to pay for web development.

200. Why does Kingston Sporting Goods need to allow for $3,200 for web development?

(A) They need the best website money can buy.
(B) They have to expand their business into other territories.
(C) They have to pay JM Solutions 10 percent of the overall cost as a deposit.
(D) They have to negotiate a better price after the deposit.

Stop! This is the end of the test. If you finish before time is called, you may go back to Parts 5, 6, and 7 and check your work.

ACTUAL TEST 06

READING TEST

In the Reading test, you will read a variety of texts and answer several different types of reading comprehension questions. The entire Reading test will last 75 minutes. There are three parts, and directions are given for each part. You are encouraged to answer as many questions as possible within the time allowed.

You must mark your answers on the separate answer sheet. Do not write your answers in your test book.

PART 5

Directions: A word or phrase is missing in each of the sentences below. Four answer choices are given below each sentence. Select the best answer to complete the sentence. Then mark the letter (A), (B), (C), or (D) on your answer sheet.

101. Pet owners are encouraged to register ------- the workshop on pet training and health offered by the community center.

(A) of
(B) from
(C) in
(D) for

102. The CEO held a press conference to ------- for the negative health effects caused by her company's products.

(A) apologized
(B) apologize
(C) apologizes
(D) apologizing

103. There is a ------- difference between the business's revenues during the peak season and during the off-peak season.

(A) prosperous
(B) rural
(C) significant
(D) preparatory

104. The path through Morrison Park was constructed not only for cyclists ------- for joggers.

(A) but also
(B) though
(C) in addition to
(D) neither

105. One of the supervisors questioned Ms. Marshall ------- her role in the misuse of the investment funds.

(A) unless
(B) among
(C) about
(D) into

106. The occupancy rate at Starburst Hotel has ------- by 24 percent due to increased competition.

(A) relied
(B) fallen
(C) expired
(D) coincided

107. A certificate of ------- was given to the participants in the public speaking skills course.

(A) accomplishment
(B) accomplish
(C) accomplished
(D) accomplishing

108. The chef ------- prepares the entrée for a restaurant critic often comes out to greet him or her in person.

(A) whose
(B) what
(C) either
(D) who

109. The negotiators made a few minor changes to the contract to make the terms ------- to both parties.

(A) agreeable
(B) agreement
(C) agree
(D) agreeing

110. The allocation of funds to local schools is ------- on the number of children living in the district.

(A) seen
(B) based
(C) placed
(D) taken

111. This palace was ------- used for public ceremonies and celebrations.

(A) traditionally
(B) traditional
(C) tradition
(D) traditions

112. The successful candidate will be contacted by an HR representative once the hiring committee has made its ------- decision.

(A) disposable
(B) numerous
(C) final
(D) portable

113. The chairperson ------- by an anonymous vote involving all members.

(A) has been selecting
(B) had to select
(C) is selecting
(D) will be selected

114. Providing low-interest loans to small businesses is a key ------- of the recovery plan.

(A) vacancy
(B) status
(C) component
(D) rate

115. The project would not have been a success without Mr. Ratcliffe's complete -------, which was demonstrated on several occasions.

(A) dedicated
(B) dedicate
(C) dedicates
(D) dedication

116. City politicians will debate this ------- issue at the town hall meeting so that voters can have a better understanding of it.

(A) competent
(B) observant
(C) complicated
(D) confused

GO ON TO THE NEXT PAGE →

117. ------- the hospital experiences a power outage, power generators will turn on automatically to supply the necessary electricity.

(A) If
(B) Until
(C) What
(D) So

118. After the tellers at Stewart Bank had undergone extensive training, they treated the customers -------.

(A) more courteously
(B) courteous
(C) most courteous
(D) courtesy

119. A gate agent at the airport announced a flight ------- caused by severe weather at the destination.

(A) canceling
(B) cancels
(C) cancellation
(D) cancel

120. ------- the outdated equipment is replaced with state-of-the-art machinery, productivity will be more than double.

(A) Whether
(B) Later
(C) When
(D) Momentarily

121. In order to be eligible for this position, you must have at least five years' experience in the insurance -------.

(A) preservation
(B) figure
(C) industry
(D) description

122. Through his extensive research into the acquisition of language skills, Dr. Harvey Ward has proven ------- to be a leader in the field.

(A) he
(B) his
(C) himself
(D) him

123. The seafood sold by Pacific Plus is ------- and therefore must be transported in a temperature-controlled vehicle.

(A) suitable
(B) widespread
(C) cautious
(D) perishable

124. The novelist said that his writing was ------- influenced by the late writer Edward Truitt.

(A) manually
(B) insecurely
(C) regretfully
(D) profoundly

125. As had been ------- by the researchers, the new environmentally friendly laundry detergent performed as well as its competitors.

(A) observing
(B) observed
(C) observation
(D) observe

126. The Green Society is dedicated to ------- public parks and other natural areas for future generations.

(A) preserving
(B) consulting
(C) escorting
(D) inquiring

127. The manufacturing plant that was damaged in the typhoon should ------- its operations later this month.

(A) resumed
(B) be resuming
(C) had resumed
(D) resuming

128. Because the team was already behind schedule, the manager did not ------- to Ms. Norton's vacation request.

(A) accept
(B) ensure
(C) consent
(D) finalize

129. The nasal spray allowed Bert to keep his seasonal allergies ------- control without having to get a prescription.

(A) against
(B) under
(C) around
(D) unto

130. Our sales ------- are unavailable to take your call at the moment, but will call you back as soon as possible.

(A) representation
(B) represents
(C) representatives
(D) representative

GO ON TO THE NEXT PAGE →

PART 6

Directions: Read the texts that follow. A word, phrase, or sentence is missing in parts of each text. Four answer choices for each question are given below the text. Select the best answer to complete the text. Then mark the letter (A), (B), (C), or (D) on your answer sheet.

Questions 131-134 refer to the following email.

To: Olivia Paulson

From: Jonathan Hicks

Date: July 19

Subject: Procedural Review

An issue was brought up at the executives' meeting last Thursday. Complaints about goods damaged after being shipped ------- **131.** dramatically in the last month. This may be a result of more fragile items' being added to the products we now ship. ------- **132.** We are reviewing our packaging procedures and looking to introduce additional steps to ------- **133.** that our products are packaged securely and delivered without damage.

Please inform all manufacturing managers to attend a(n) ------- **134.** meeting tonight at 7 P.M. We hope to address this problem and come up with a sound solution as quickly as possible so that normal business can resume.

131. (A) increasing
(B) have increased
(C) were increased
(D) increases

NEW
132. (A) We are thinking of dropping such items from our product list.
(B) We may need to increase shipping and handling costs.
(C) An added insurance cost for such items has been suggested.
(D) Because of this, we have temporarily suspended the shipping of accessories and other fragile items.

133. (A) secure
(B) affect
(C) ensure
(D) warrant

134. (A) emergency
(B) necessity
(C) decisive
(D) extensive

Questions 135-138 refer to the following advertisement.

Green Clean Services

Call us: 347-281-7834

------- (**135.**) 2005, Green Clean has been providing professional and environmentally friendly cleaning services of consistently high quality to all types of commercial and industrial facilities. ------- (**136.**) We understand the contribution a good employee makes toward our ------- (**137.**), and we are committed to selecting the best available people to work for you.

Green Clean's mission is to satisfy our customers' needs on a daily basis while providing the best possible combination of quality, price, and delivery. We accomplish this by continually improving our systems of ------- (**138.**). Our goal is to make your facility extremely clean in the greenest way possible. Visit us at www.greeenclean.com today.

135. (A) Until
(B) Around
(C) Since
(D) Through

NEW

136. (A) Drop in today to schedule a tour of one of our 20 facilities.
(B) We are the biggest manufacturer of environmentally friendly cleaning supplies in the Northwest.
(C) As a service company, we consider our employees to be our most important asset.
(D) Allow us to work for you by calling us today to take care of all of your accounting needs.

137. (A) success
(B) drive
(C) support
(D) determination

138. (A) to operate
(B) operates
(C) operated
(D) operation

GO ON TO THE NEXT PAGE

Questions 139-142 refer to the following notice.

Florist Wanted

Do you love making people smile? Does the idea of ------- (139.) your day being creative and working with nature appeal to you? If so, we would like to encourage you to apply to join our team at Wild Flowers Florists. ------- (140.) We are looking for someone who is customer- ------- (141.) first. Creativity is important, but it is secondary to the vision of the client. If you think ------- (142.) have what it takes to make people smile, please fill out the application form on our website, www.WildFlowersFlorists.com.

139. (A) spend
(B) to spend
(C) spending
(D) spent

NEW

140. (A) You must be good with animals.
(B) Our company is committed to providing the best floral arrangements for our clients, no matter what their needs.
(C) We use the best fabrics in our designs.
(D) Everyone loves our commitment to safety.

141. (A) oriented
(B) prime
(C) located
(D) sourced

142. (A) you
(B) I
(C) they
(D) we

Questions 143-146 refer to the following letter.

October 21

Larry Mills

226 Highland Rivers

Fairbank, WA 20037

Dear Mr. Mills,

I am writing in reply to your complaint about the noise coming from the businesses around your apartment complex. -------**143.**, a few people living in the west wing of the building -------**144.** concern over the noise levels. The building committee has held meetings on this issue and we have talked to the businesses involved. -------**145.** Because of this, we are also looking to fortify the complex's windows with noise proof glass in the west wing. Once we have agreed upon these proposals, we will post an announcement on our bulletin board and you may receive a call. Until then, we ask for your -------**146.** patience.

143. (A) As a result
(B) Moreover
(C) On the other hand
(D) Unfortunately

144. (A) is expressing
(B) have expressed
(C) expression
(D) be expressive

NEW

145. (A) However, some of the noises are inevitable due to the nature of those businesses.
(B) They will fully cooperate with our committee.
(C) They have responded to our concerns and will work to keep noise levels low.
(D) However, they are losing money over this matter.

146. (A) continue
(B) continues
(C) continued
(D) be continuing

GO ON TO THE NEXT PAGE

PART 7

Directions: In this part you will read a selection of texts, such as magazine and newspaper articles, emails, and instant messages. Each text or set of texts is followed by several questions. Select the best answer for each question and mark the letter (A), (B), (C), or (D) on your answer sheet.

Questions 147-148 refer to the following invoice.

Henderson, Inc.

1576 Stevens Road, Pleasantville, NY 10571
(231) 555-0786 www.hendersoninc.com

Order Number: 6694
Date: April 2
Customer: Susan Ward
709 Praise Street
Pleasantville, NY 10571
(203) 555-0167

Item	Model	Quantity	Price
Extra-large microwave	MW132	1	$150.00
Four-door refrigerator	RF4D	1	$2,399.99
Smart toaster	TR512	1	$45.50

Subtotal	$2,595.49
Tax	$230.18
Total due	$2,825.67

Local customers are eligible for free shipping on purchases over $1,000.

147. What does Henderson, Inc. sell?

(A) Home appliances
(B) Office furniture
(C) Computer equipment
(D) Construction materials

148. What is indicated about Ms. Ward?

(A) She must pick up her items in person.
(B) She is eligible for a special discount.
(C) She will receive her deliveries at no charge.
(D) She paid with a check.

Questions 149-150 refer to the following text message chain.

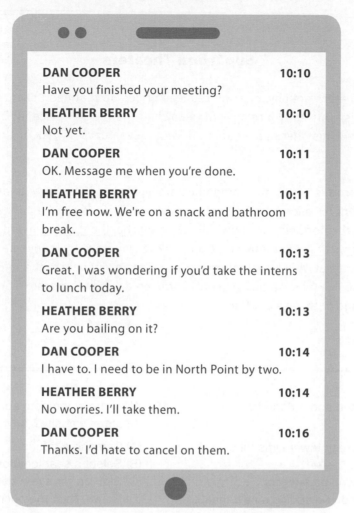

DAN COOPER **10:10**
Have you finished your meeting?

HEATHER BERRY **10:10**
Not yet.

DAN COOPER **10:11**
OK. Message me when you're done.

HEATHER BERRY **10:11**
I'm free now. We're on a snack and bathroom break.

DAN COOPER **10:13**
Great. I was wondering if you'd take the interns to lunch today.

HEATHER BERRY **10:13**
Are you bailing on it?

DAN COOPER **10:14**
I have to. I need to be in North Point by two.

HEATHER BERRY **10:14**
No worries. I'll take them.

DAN COOPER **10:16**
Thanks. I'd hate to cancel on them.

149. What is suggested about Ms. Berry?

(A) She is eating a snack.
(B) She will be promoted.
(C) She is in the middle of a meeting.
(D) She plans on cancelling a lunch appointment.

NEW

150. At 10:13, what does Ms. Berry mean when she writes, "Are you bailing on it?"

(A) She's asking if Mr. Cooper has finished his meeting.
(B) She's inquiring whether Mr. Cooper will be missing an appointment.
(C) She wants to know if Mr. Cooper will go to North Point.
(D) She would like Mr. Cooper to notify her when he leaves.

GO ON TO THE NEXT PAGE

Questions 151-152 refer to the following flyer.

Superbox Theaters

Superbox Theaters are now offering reduced prices on matinée tickets for December. Use this early bird special to pay half the regular price for our first matinée show. This offer applies to all movies, seven days a week, including new releases!

Group visits from schools and companies are welcome. If you have a large group, you might want to reserve your tickets in advance. Tickets can be purchased in person from theater staff, or online at www.superboxtheaters.com and www.abcticketworld.com. When buying tickets online, you have the convenience of choosing your seat. Additional information and reviews of current and upcoming films are also available on our website. Come on down to Superbox Theaters and take advantage of this great offer!

151. What is indicated about Superbox Theaters?

(A) They will screen fewer films this December.
(B) They are hiring part-timers.
(C) They will soon be adding a new theater location.
(D) They are offering reduced prices for certain screenings.

152. What are customers able to do on the theaters' website?

(A) Demand a refund
(B) Select a seat location
(C) Sign up for a newsletter
(D) Renew their membership

Questions 153-154 refer to the following email.

To	Aaron Sandler <asandler@milleradvertising.com>
From	Sam Miller <smiller@milleradvertising.com>
Subject	Tuesday's Meeting
Date	November 12

Dear Mr. Sandler,

This month's business review meeting is scheduled for Thursday, November 15. As you know, this meeting is a great opportunity for us to assess our operating plan and make any adjustments that might help us keep up with the constant changes in the marketplace. As an advertising agency, we must stay informed about the newest market trends. So I was very excited when I heard that Tsuyoshi Ito, manager of our Japanese branch, would be visiting this Friday. In order to take full advantage of Mr. Ito's expertise and knowledge, I would like to change the meeting date so that he can attend.

This will be Mr. Ito's first time in the country, so I would like you to pick him up from the airport. A company car will be provided to you for this purpose. I will email again once I have more details concerning Mr. Ito's arrival time.

Sincerely,

Sam Miller
President

153. What is the purpose of the email?

(A) To reschedule a meeting
(B) To request a monthly operating report
(C) To introduce a new employee
(D) To propose a new marketing strategy

154. What does the email indicate about Mr. Ito?

(A) He is changing positions.
(B) He often travels on business.
(C) He works in advertising.
(D) He is a client of Mr. Miller's.

GO ON TO THE NEXT PAGE

Questions 155-157 refer to the following email.

To	Bridget Lee
From	Victor Thomas
Subject	shipment
Date	June 25

Hello Bridget,

– [1] – Our shipment of beverages will arrive tomorrow morning around 10 A.M. Please keep inventory and make sure that all the shipments are accurate as they are unloaded. Also, some of the beverages will need to be refrigerated right away so please make sure that the issue is taken care of in a timely fashion. – [2] – The temperatures are expected to be high tomorrow, so we'll need to get all the shipments into storage as soon as possible. – [3] – We have two refrigerated trucks that we'll send with you and there will be a crew waiting for you at the warehouse. – [4] –

If there are any problems or if you need any help with issues that arise, please contact me by phone. I'll be in the office early tomorrow.

Thanks,

Victor

155. What is the purpose of the email?

(A) To inform suppliers of a mistake
(B) To give an employee instructions
(C) To order a shipment of beverages
(D) To keep inventory of products

156. Why is Victor concerned about the shipment?

(A) The products are fragile.
(B) It may arrive late.
(C) It is temperature-sensitive.
(D) It is for an important client.

NEW

157. In which of the places marked [1], [2], [3], and [4] does the following sentence belong?

"I'm worried about the weather."

(A) [1]
(B) [2]
(C) [3]
(D) [4]

Questions 158-160 refer to the following advertisement.

Marigold Bakery
451 Clark Street, Ellis Town
253-555-1298

Marigold Bakery is a family-run business that has been making delicious and irresistible sweet treats for over 30 years. Our store is located in historic downtown Ellis Town, and offers a warm decor and inviting atmosphere.

We offer:
- Made-to-order pastries for parties, weddings, and corporate events
- Gluten- and sugar-free refreshments and vegetarian sandwiches
- Custom cake designs

Hours:
Monday to Saturday, 9:00 A.M. to 5:00 P.M.
We will be closing this September in order to expand our store.

Sunday cooking class:
Marigold Bakery values positive interactions with the community. Therefore, we are currently holding a cooking class for local teenagers. Baking teaches the values of patience and hard work!

158. What is mentioned about Marigold Bakery?
(A) It is internationally known.
(B) It employs local students.
(C) It offers options for those with dietary restrictions.
(D) Its store space can be rented for various events.

159. According to the advertisement, what will happen in September?
(A) The store will shut down for renovations.
(B) A classroom will be constructed.
(C) The menu will be expanded.
(D) The shop will cater a community event.

160. What is indicated about the cooking class?
(A) It will be held at a community center this year.
(B) It has been going on for over 30 years.
(C) It is taught by an experienced baker.
(D) It is designed for young people in the community.

GO ON TO THE NEXT PAGE

Questions 161-164 refer to the following online chat discussion.

Peter Jones Lunch

Peter Jones	**[12:10]**	I'm heading to the new pizza parlor across the street for lunch. Does anyone want to join me?
Martin Lee	**[12:10]**	Count me in!
Laura Vans	**[12:11]**	Theo and I are working on our presentation for tomorrow so we can't.
Theo Gibbs	**[12:12]**	Can you bring back some pizza for us?
Peter Jones	**[12:13]**	Sure. What kind do you want?
Laura Vans	**[12:14]**	I'll take whatever their best-selling pizza is. One large slice will be enough for me.
Theo Gibbs	**[12:15]**	Pepperoni for me. One slice.
Peter Jones	**[12:15]**	No problem. I'll be back in one hour. Is your presentation about the new product line?
Laura Vans	**[12:16]**	Yes, we're almost finished, but we're working on making the visuals more impressive.
Martin Lee	**[12:17]**	If you'd like, I can help you with the visuals. I have a bit of a background in computer graphics.
Theo Gibbs	**[12:17]**	That would be great. Laura and I are good with basic computer programs, but neither of us is very good at making visuals.
Peter Jones	**[12:18]**	When Martin and I come back, we can help you finish your presentation.
Laura Vans	**[12:18]**	Thanks so much!
Theo Gibbs	**[12:19]**	Awesome!

161. Where most likely are the writers?

(A) At a restaurant
(B) At a pizza shop
(C) At a company
(D) In an electronics shop

NEW

162. At 12:10, what does Martin Lee mean when he says, "Count me in"?

(A) He's doing a presentation.
(B) He's in his office.
(C) He would like to go out for lunch.
(D) He's currently in a meeting.

163. What is indicated about the presentation?

(A) It will be presented after lunch.
(B) It is about new products.
(C) It is very long.
(D) It needs more information.

164. What will Martin Lee most likely help the presenters with?

(A) Their graphics
(B) Their information
(C) Their computer use
(D) Their presentation format

Questions 165-167 refer to the following email.

To: All Employees <staff@jointsystems.com>
From: Fred Hanes <fhanes@jointsystems.com>
Subject: Community Park Cleanup
Date: February 12

Joint Systems is a company that tries to take every opportunity to give back to our community. Therefore, I am urging all of our employees to take part in the upcoming community park cleanup sponsored by the city of Harrisburg. Without the dedication of volunteers, our parks and public spaces would not be free of litter. Donate some of your free time to keeping Harrisburg a beautiful and inviting city.

The community park cleanup will be held next Friday, February 18, from 1:00 to 5:00 P.M. Employees who wish to participate will leave work at lunchtime, yet will still be paid as if they had worked a full day. Volunteers are asked to bring supplies such as protective outerwear, tools, insect repellent, trash bags, and snacks.

A shuttle bus will depart from the company parking lot at 1:20 P.M. on Friday to take volunteers to the cleanup location. If you have a specific preference concerning the type of work you would like to do, please contact event organizer Don Lewis at 435-555-6768.

We appreciate everyone's enthusiasm and support.

Fred Hanes
Human Resources

165. What is the purpose of the email?

(A) To organize a business trip
(B) To request updated information
(C) To offer additional skills training
(D) To promote a community event

166. What would probably NOT be necessary for participants?

(A) A company uniform
(B) A can of mosquito spray
(C) A rake
(D) A sandwich

167. According to the email, what is Mr. Lewis responsible for?

(A) Raising awareness about food waste
(B) Analyzing customer feedback
(C) Assigning individuals tasks
(D) Cleaning a community center

GO ON TO THE NEXT PAGE

Questions 168-171 refer to the following Web page.

http://www.sanchezcardealership.com/about

Sanchez Motors

ABOUT	NEWS	MODELS	SERVICES	COMMUNITY

About Sanchez Motors

Carlos Sanchez dreamed of owning his own car dealership from the time he started working as an assistant at an auto repair shop. After saving his money for 10 years, he finally opened Sanchez Motors, and has been serving the community with integrity and pride ever since. Sanchez Motors carries all kinds of vehicles, from sports cars and vans to SUVs and trucks. Not sure what car fits your needs? Then come on down and try driving a variety of vehicles to see what's right for you.

Until the end of the year, Sanchez Motors is offering an amazing deal on our popular lines of Spitfire pickup trucks and Stark SUVs. If you make a down payment of just $3,000, you will be eligible for an extremely low interest rate on your monthly installments.

Sanchez Motors is located off Highway 5, just outside of the town of Stockton. We are open seven days a week, from 9:00 A.M. to 9:00 P.M. Don't hesitate; come pay us a visit!

168. What is indicated about Mr. Sanchez?

(A) He works at an auto repair shop.
(B) He started his own business.
(C) He is a race car driver.
(D) He designs a variety of vehicles.

169. The word "carries" in paragraph 1, line 4 is closest in meaning to

(A) moves
(B) manufactures
(C) sells
(D) develops

170. What is suggested about Sanchez Motors?

(A) It allows customers to test products.
(B) It operates a store in downtown Stockton.
(C) It offers vehicle customization.
(D) It closes on weekends.

171. What is available to customers until the end of the year?

(A) Discounts on sports cars and vans
(B) An extended warranty at no extra cost
(C) A special payment option
(D) A free oil change with any purchase

Questions 172-175 refer to the following article.

Clean and Green

The town of Korden has much to celebrate as the new hydrogen fuel car company, Newmark, plans to open a massive manufacturing plant here in the next few months. – [1] – Newmark already supplies some of the greenest cities around the world including Vancouver, Singapore, Honolulu, and Amsterdam with hydrogen-fueled public buses and taxis. – [2] –

The company is forecast to grow by 120% in the next five years. Furthermore, the opening of the plant in Korden is expected to bring in 300 new jobs. – [3] – The old Handai facilities will be the site of the new Newmark facilities. The mayor of Korden is also working to provide government subsidies for those who purchase hydrogen-fueled cars in the hope that gas-guzzling conventional cars will eventually become a thing of the past. – [4] –

172. What is the main topic of the article?

(A) Alternative energy sources
(B) Environmentally friendly cities
(C) The opening of a new factory
(D) The future of car companies

173. What will happen to the town's old car factories?

(A) They will be destroyed and rebuilt.
(B) They will be the new site of the hydrogen fuel car company.
(C) They will be turned into office buildings.
(D) They will house all the old conventional cars.

174. What is suggested about Korden?

(A) It will become one of the greenest cities.
(B) Its economy will stay stagnant.
(C) It will attract new car companies.
(D) It will grow economically.

NEW

175. In which of the places marked [1], [2], [3], and [4] does the following sentence belong?

"This is welcome news for a town that has suffered economically since the closure of its car manufacturing plants in the 1990s and its stagnant growth since then."

(A) [1]
(B) [2]
(C) [3]
(D) [4]

GO ON TO THE NEXT PAGE

Questions 176-180 refer to the following email and Web page.

To: Sam Brown <sbrown@zippy.com>
From: Kevin Draper <kdraper@fivestarbank.com>
Date: April 22
Subject: Home Loan

Dear Mr. Brown,

Thank you for choosing Five Star Financial Bank as the provider of your home loan. We strive to offer you the most competitive repayment plans as well as superb customer support. Below is a summary of the loan you have taken out with us.

Mortgage Type	Amount	Repayment Period
Home Opportunity Loan	$70,000.00	15 years

During the period of your loan, senior banker Martha King will be in charge of your repayment plan. Understanding the terms of your loan is crucial to successfully paying back the loan and avoiding penalties. We advise you to schedule a time to meet with Ms. King so she can further familiarize you with your home loan.

If you sign up for our online banking services, you will be able to quickly and conveniently check on your repayment progress.

Thanks again for trusting Five Star Financial Bank with your home loan.

Sincerely,

Kevin Draper
Loan Specialist
Five Star Financial Bank

Listed below are the various home loans available to customers of Five Star Financial Bank. Learning about different kinds of loans will help you make an informed decision. Review the loan choices below and decide which loan is right for your situation.

Fixed-Rate Mortgage Loan – This loan ensures that your interest rate and monthly principal repayment remain the same during the entire period of your loan. This loan protects you from rising interest rates and may be a good choice if you plan to live in your home for a long time.

Adjustable-Rate Mortgage Loan – Your interest rate remains fixed for the initial five years, and is then adjusted annually. Typically, this loan has a lower initial interest rate than a fixed-rate mortgage.

Interest-Only Mortgage Loan – During the initial five years of the loan, you are required to make payments on interest only. This option is suitable for those with fluctuating incomes. When your finances are tight you can make interest-only payments, and when your earnings increase you can make payments on the principal.

Home Opportunity Loan – This special loan is designed for first-time home buyers. You do not need a large down payment or a perfect credit rating in order to qualify for this loan.

176. What does Mr. Draper suggest that Mr. Brown do?

(A) Apply for a position
(B) Arrange a meeting
(C) Make a down payment in April
(D) Become a bank customer

177. How is Mr. Brown advised to keep track of his loan?

(A) By meeting with Mr. Draper
(B) By reading regular emails from the bank
(C) By using banking services on the Internet
(D) By calling a bank hotline

178. What information does the Web page provide?

(A) Bank account statements
(B) Quarterly interest rates
(C) Repayment options
(D) A roster of customers

179. Which plan is suitable for those with unstable earnings?

(A) Fixed-Rate Mortgage Loan
(B) Adjustable-Rate Mortgage Loan
(C) Interest-Only Mortgage Loan
(D) Home Opportunity Loan

180. What is indicated about Mr. Brown?

(A) He made a large down payment.
(B) He earns a steady salary.
(C) He recently bought his first home.
(D) He will retire in the near future.

GO ON TO THE NEXT PAGE

Questions 181-185 refer to the following article and email.

Madison Business Update

November 15—Sun Microchips is the country's largest producer of the integrated circuits that go into computers, smartphones, and other digital electronics. The company has recently built a new factory in Madison and will begin operations in January of next year. The chief executive officer of Sun Microchips, Melinda Piers, stated that "As the market for consumer electronics continues to become larger and larger globally, companies like Sun Microchips are expanding to meet its needs."

"We are looking to hire a variety of people such as factory workers, personnel employees, and accountants. We expect the opening of the factory to create over 200 jobs in Madison," said Ms. Piers. She noted that the company will try to hire local applicants first, but that those living outside of Madison are also encouraged to apply.

Applicants must submit their résumés by November 25 by emailing Tina Zimmerman at tzimmerman@sunmicrochips.com. Sun Microchips will be holding two separate sets of interviews next month. Those applying as general laborers for jobs on the assembly line should schedule an interview between December 3 and 8. Those interested in positions in personnel, accounting, and customer service are required to schedule an interview between December 9 and 11.

To: <tzimmerman@sunmicrochips.com>
From: <jakehenry@tnamail.com>
Date: November 21
Subject: Opening at Sun Microchips
Attachment: résumé.doc

Dear Ms. Zimmerman,

I recently read an article in the *Madison Business Update* about the openings at your new factory in Madison. As a former employee of Sun Microchips, I am excited by the prospect of joining your company again.

Please see the attached file. I would really appreciate it if you would schedule me for an interview. Anytime on December 10 will work for me. If you would like to learn more about my past work experience with Sun Microchips, you can contact my former supervisor, Todd Smith. He is still working there.

I look forward to meeting you.

Jake Henry

181. According to Ms. Piers, what is true about consumer electronics?
(A) The demand for them is constantly increasing.
(B) They are becoming more and more expensive.
(C) They will soon be produced in only a few countries.
(D) They can affect users' health.

182. What is Sun Microchips planning to do?
(A) Launch its latest model of smartphone
(B) Build a new factory overseas
(C) Give preference to local job candidates
(D) Hire a new chief executive officer

183. Who most likely is Ms. Zimmerman?
(A) A computer technician
(B) A human resources manager
(C) A factory worker
(D) An accountant

184. What is the purpose of the email?
(A) To quit a job
(B) To postpone an appointment
(C) To ask for an interview
(D) To accept a job offer

185. What can be inferred about Mr. Henry?
(A) He is a resident of Madison.
(B) He has a degree in computer science.
(C) He currently works at Sun Microchips.
(D) He wants an office position.

GO ON TO THE NEXT PAGE

Questions 186-190 refer to the following emails and advertisement.

From: Henry Choi <henrychoi@neatsolutions.com>
To: Jenny Davis <jennydavis@endlessacresgolfclub.com>
Date: August 8
Subject: Endless Acres Golf Club
Attachment: draft

Dear Ms. Davis,

Attached is the newest draft of the advertisement for Endless Acres Golf Club. I have incorporated the advertising slogan you sent me into my design. I've used a combination of eye-catching graphics to grab the attention of newspaper readers. I've also added some helpful information at the end of the advertisement. Please let me know if the design and new additions meet your expectations. Along with the concurrent television ad, I think this advertisement will help bring a lot of new customers to Endless Acres Golf Club.

Sincerely,

Henry Choi

Endless Acres Golf Club

1232 Hilly Meadows Drive, Mapleview, CO

Take a break from all the stress of life and play a round of relaxing golf at Endless Acres Golf Club. After your game, enjoy a meal at our restaurant in a sophisticated and welcoming environment.

We are currently offering the following promotion:
Reserve a tee time for a party of seven or more golfers and receive a 20-percent discount. Additionally, every member of your group will receive a coupon for $5 off any purchase from our golf shop.

We were recently praised by *The Rolling Meadows Daily* for the superb maintenance of our golf course and grounds. Come in and enjoy the best golf course in the state of Colorado. We are located off Exit 21 on Highway 5. Just look for our billboard. You can't miss it!

Reservations can now be made on our website at www.endlessacresgolf.com or by calling 555-4834.

From: Logan Mankins <lmankins@crushing.com>
To: <reservations@endlessacresgolfclub.com>
Date: July 6
Subject: Re: Tee time and dinner for 10

Hello,

I saw your ad in the newspaper and I have a couple of quick questions about your deals. First, we have a group of 10 golfers. Now, I know most courses generally limit a group to four players to keep up the pace of play, but I was really hoping you could make an exception for us and allow two groups of five. We will even rent golf carts to ensure that we don't cause a delay. As for the $5 gift cards for the pro shop, I was wondering if they could be pooled together for one large purchase. It is my son's birthday and I would like to buy him a new putter, but they are awfully expensive these days. Fifty bucks would go a long way toward giving him a great gift!

We would like to tee off at around 11:30 a.m. on Saturday, July 20th and then have dinner there at about 6 p.m. Please write back to confirm our tee time and answer my queries. Thank you for your time!

Have a great day,

Logan Mankins

GO ON TO THE NEXT PAGE

186. How does Logan Mankins propose to keep his two groups of five golfers from delaying the other golfers on the course?

(A) He guarantees they will play fast.
(B) He promises that they are very good at golf.
(C) He writes that he will buy a new putter for his son.
(D) He informs the club that the two groups will be driving golf carts.

187. Where would the advertisement most likely appear?

(A) On television
(B) In a magazine
(C) In a newspaper
(D) On a billboard

188. What has been added to the advertisement?

(A) Promotional details
(B) Driving directions
(C) Contact information
(D) Customer reviews

189. What does Logan Mankins want to do with the $5 credits the players get for the golf shop?

(A) He wants to buy his son a putter with his.
(B) He wants to use them to pay his green fees.
(C) He wants to combine them with the 20-percent group discount.
(D) He wants to combine them all and apply the amount to one purchase.

190. What did *The Rolling Meadows Daily* indicate about Endless Acres Golf Club?

(A) Its location is convenient.
(B) Its facilities are well kept.
(C) Its membership fees are affordable.
(D) Its restaurant updates its menu regularly.

NEW **Questions 191-195** refer to the following email, schedule, and online chat board.

To: Library Members <members@claytonlibrary.edu>
From: Holly Allen <hollyallen@claytonlibrary.edu>
Subject: Events This Month
Date: August 1
Attachment: August Events Calendar

Dear Members of the Clayton Library,

Thank you for your continued support of the Clayton Library. Your monthly membership fees help us to obtain new books, computers, journal subscriptions, and other resources that are useful to the entire community. We would like to inform you of some upcoming special events this month that you may be interested in attending.

First, famous children's book author and storyteller Ebert Butler will be visiting our library. He will be reading from his new book, *The Mysterious Cat*, and signing autographs. His book was recently nominated for the Children's Book of the Year Award. Kathy Butler, Mr. Butler's wife, will also be in attendance at this event. She has drawn the pictures for most of Mr. Butler's books, including *The Mysterious Cat*. This event costs $10, but is free for library members.

Later in the month, renowned wildlife photographer Nina Brooks will be holding an exhibition on the main floor of the library. Ms. Brooks recently returned from a trip to Kenya, where she photographed cheetahs, giraffes, elephants, and other animals. Her photographs capture the vividness of wildlife and the majesty of nature.

In addition to these two featured events, there will be a variety of workshops, games nights, and other events this month. Check the attached calendar for details. All events, including Movie Night, are free unless otherwise noted.

Sincerely,

Holly Allen
Library Events Coordinator

Clayton Library Events Calendar

August

Date/Time	Event Title	Notes
Saturday, Aug. 2, 5:00 P.M.	Creative Writers' Workshop	Led by Donna Ward
Friday, Aug. 8, 7:00 P.M.	Movie Night	Family-friendly event
Sunday, Aug. 17, 6:00 P.M.	*The Mysterious Cat* Reading	Entrance cost of $10
Wednesday, Aug. 20, 3:00 P.M.	Knitting Club	Complimentary refreshments
Saturday, Aug. 30, 2:00 P.M.	Photo Exhibition Opening	Entrance cost of $5

GO ON TO THE NEXT PAGE

Clayton Library Community Chat Board

August 1

> User ID: Jjohnson231
Subject: Creative Writers' Workshop, August 2

Hey, is anybody going to go to the writers' workshop tomorrow? I heard that Donna Ward is an outstanding teacher. I could really use some feedback on my latest short story, too. Post if you are going! ~Jim

---

> User ID: Storytimechuck
Subject: re: Creative Writers' Workshop, August 2

Hey Jjohnson231! I am going for sure. You are right; Donna is the best. Her knowledge of narrative and pacing have really helped me with my screenplay. Maybe I could read through your short story after the workshop and give you my feedback, too? The more eyes the better, I always say! I'll let you take a look through my screenplay, too, if you are interested. See you tomorrow! ~Chuck

191. What is the purpose of the email?

(A) To introduce new members
(B) To promote upcoming events
(C) To announce some schedule adjustments
(D) To solicit donations

192. What is indicated about Ebert Butler?

(A) His wife is an illustrator.
(B) He has recently published his first book.
(C) He has several cats.
(D) He will receive an award soon.

193. According to the chat board, what does Donna Ward excel at?

(A) Creating vivid photographs
(B) Writing successful screenplays
(C) Understanding the roles of timing and storyline
(D) Working with young poets

194. When can library users meet Kathy Butler?

(A) On Wednesday
(B) On Friday
(C) On Saturday
(D) On Sunday

195. What will likely happen after the creative writers' workshop on August 2?

(A) Everyone will know how to write better poetry.
(B) Chuck and Jim will trade their work to give each other feedback.
(C) Donna Ward will publish her novel.
(D) Chuck and Donna will work on Jim's short story.

Questions 196-200 refer to the following information, form, and letter.

Red Rock Leather Goods

Thank you for purchasing a leather product from Red Rock Leather Goods. We manufacture all of our products to meet the highest quality standards and pride ourselves on excellent customer service. All of our products are individually and meticulously made by skillful craftsmen. We offer a lifetime guarantee that covers all defects in craftsmanship except normal wear and tear. We will repair or replace any faulty piece for as long as you own your Red Rock product.

If your Red Rock product is not under warranty, we offer repairs at the following rates:

	Wallets	Handbags	Jackets
Missing button replacement	$10	$15	$20
Zipper repair or replacement	$20	$30	$45
Seam repair and stitching	$40	$50	$60

The warranty is non-transferable and covers only the original purchaser. Additionally, a sales receipt is required to validate your warranty and receive service. This warranty does not apply to products purchased from second-hand stores or unauthorized dealers.

Red Rock Leather Goods
Repair Request Form

Name: Melisa Perkins
Date: February 28
Address: 458 Center Circle Drive, Chicago, IL
Product: Coco TX Handbag

Description of repairs to be made:
I bought this item last year from a Red Rock Leather Goods store in Chicago, IL. However, after just six months, the zipper became jammed and no longer opens or closes. Because this is a manufacturing defect, I assume it will be covered by the warranty. I have been a regular customer of Red Rock Leather Goods for 12 years, and this is the first time I have had a problem.

I have read and agree to all the terms concerning returns and repairs. I certify that this product was purchased at an official Red Rock Leather Goods store and that I am the original purchaser of this product.
Signature: Melisa Perkins **Date:** February 28

Note: It may take some time for your product to be returned to you. If you have any questions, please call us at 812-555-8541.

GO ON TO THE NEXT PAGE

Dear Ms. Perkins,

Thank you for submitting your request for repairs to your Red Rock Leather Goods Coco TX Handbag. We have received and inspected your item and documents, and concluded that it falls within our warranty. It is scheduled to go in for repair this coming week. Once it has been returned to working order, we will express mail it to the address you provided on your repair request form. I would like to thank you on behalf of Red Rock Leather Goods for your 12 years of patronage and apologize for any inconvenience the failure of your Coco TX Handbag has caused you.

Sincerely,

Cheryl Timmins
Customer Service Specialist
Red Rock Leather Goods

196. What is indicated about Red Rock Leather Goods' products?

(A) They are sold nationwide.
(B) They are relatively expensive.
(C) They are made by hand.
(D) They come in a variety of colors.

197. Why did Ms. Perkins fill out a form?

(A) To receive a cash refund for a product
(B) To report a defective item
(C) To file a customer service complaint
(D) To extend a warranty period

198. How much would Ms. Perkins be charged if her item had been purchased at a second-hand store?

(A) $15
(B) $20
(C) $30
(D) $45

199. In the letter to Ms. Perkins, the word "patronage" in line 6 is closest in meaning to which of the following words?

(A) marketing
(B) business
(C) competition
(D) investment

200. What can you infer from the letter to Ms. Perkins approving her request for warranty coverage?

(A) Her handbag suffered normal wear and tear.
(B) Red Rock Leather Goods is a local brand.
(C) She included her receipt from an authorized Red Rock Leather Goods store.
(D) She included $30 for zipper repair to her Coco TX Handbag.

NO TEST MATERIAL ON THIS PAGE

Stop! This is the end of the test. If you finish before time is called, you may go back to Parts 5, 6, and 7 and check your work.

ACTUAL TEST 07

READING TEST

In the Reading test, you will read a variety of texts and answer several different types of reading comprehension questions. The entire Reading test will last 75 minutes. There are three parts, and directions are given for each part. You are encouraged to answer as many questions as possible within the time allowed.

You must mark your answers on the separate answer sheet. Do not write your answers in your test book.

PART 5

Directions: A word or phrase is missing in each of the sentences below. Four answer choices are given below each sentence. Select the best answer to complete the sentence. Then mark the letter (A), (B), (C), or (D) on your answer sheet.

101. Recyclable materials such as glass and plastic are collected ------- weekly on Mondays and Thursdays.

(A) twice
(B) much
(C) yet
(D) far

102. Due to congestion on the roads, an increasing number of manufacturers ------- transport their goods by train.

(A) either
(B) very
(C) now
(D) rather

103. Employees have been instructed ------- the supervisor on duty when a customer has a complaint.

(A) to inform
(B) to have informed
(C) to informing
(D) to be informed

104. Old furniture, vintage jewelry, and other ------- are available for purchase at this market.

(A) quantities
(B) antiques
(C) compartments
(D) statements

105. ------- the necessary safety precautions are not taken, there could be a higher risk of injury.

(A) Just
(B) If
(C) That
(D) From

106. Dissatisfied customers of Maple Housekeeping may terminate their contracts ------- three days of their first cleaning session.

(A) as
(B) by
(C) within
(D) unless

107. The free clinic on Warren Street is ------- by volunteer doctors and nurses.

(A) retained
(B) staffed
(C) founded
(D) produced

108. Ms. Fox extended the operating hours of the store because she agreed ------- Mr. Arbor that they were not long enough.

(A) for
(B) against
(C) to
(D) with

109. Investigators visited the site to ensure that it complied with the ------- industry regulations.

(A) applicability
(B) apply
(C) applies
(D) applicable

110. The majority of people ------- live in Regal Towers are upset about the ongoing problems with their air conditioning systems.

(A) what
(B) where
(C) they
(D) who

111. Mr. Hughes divided the staff into small discussion groups to improve ------- at meetings.

(A) participation
(B) participates
(C) participant
(D) participated

112. The exchange rate has increased by 3.2 percent since the ------- time last year.

(A) only
(B) same
(C) later
(D) true

113. Brenda Tipton is ------- to win the race for the mayor's office because she has the most experience of all the candidates.

(A) predictable
(B) predict
(C) predicts
(D) predicted

114. Those who attend the creative writing workshop will learn a variety of useful skills ------- the next two days.

(A) above
(B) at
(C) toward
(D) over

115. By ------- planning the relocation in advance, we can minimize unexpected expenses and maximize efficiency.

(A) carefully
(B) cares
(C) to care
(D) cared

116. According to company policy, ------- requests for reimbursement of business expenses must be accompanied by receipts.

(A) since
(B) every
(C) all
(D) much

GO ON TO THE NEXT PAGE

117. Safe-Co has ------- home security products since its founding in 2008.

(A) corresponded
(B) functioned
(C) manufactured
(D) enrolled

118. ------- of an error on the order form, some of the construction materials were never shipped.

(A) Because
(B) Even if
(C) In spite
(D) Instead

119. The new policies were implemented in an effort to inspire better ------- among the corporation's departments.

(A) communication
(B) communicative
(C) communicate
(D) communicator

120. Private tours of the old castle will be limited ------- ten people.

(A) to
(B) during
(C) than
(D) of

121. Please do not use metal utensils when cooking with the pan ------- its surface won't get scratched.

(A) since
(B) in order to
(C) while
(D) so that

122. To ------- the monthly mortgage payment, Mr. Tyler would need a substantial salary increase.

(A) admit
(B) suppose
(C) convene
(D) afford

123. Environmentalists were pleased with the community's ------- in increasing recycling in the area.

(A) indifference
(B) cooperation
(C) allocation
(D) separation

124. The National Health Organization reported on the ------- cases of the disease.

(A) confirmation
(B) confirms
(C) confirm
(D) confirmed

125. Due to a ------- in his political beliefs, the senator no longer supported the proposed law on immigration.

(A) shift
(B) compliment
(C) shortage
(D) description

126. ------- buildings in a neighborhood can lead to a net loss of property values for neighboring homeowners.

(A) Fertile
(B) Mandatory
(C) Vacant
(D) Compliant

127. Rather than decorate each conference room -------, the owner of Norris Hall bought furnishings in bulk and gave all the spaces the same appearance.

(A) differing
(B) difference
(C) differently
(D) differs

128. The director attributed the success of the film ------- to the experience and talent of the leading actor in the lead role.

(A) punctually
(B) attentively
(C) primarily
(D) importantly

129. The company's new online banking software is ------- with most smartphone models.

(A) tangible
(B) extensive
(C) mechanical
(D) compatible

130. Employees are allowed to use vacation time whenever they want ------- it does not disrupt their assignments.

(A) except for
(B) as well as
(C) depending on
(D) so long as

GO ON TO THE NEXT PAGE

PART 6

Directions: Read the texts that follow. A word, phrase, or sentence is missing in parts of each text. Four answer choices for each question are given below the text. Select the best answer to complete the text. Then mark the letter (A), (B), (C), or (D) on your answer sheet.

Questions 131-134 refer to the following email.

From: Vice President Donna Johnson

To: Helio Tech employees

Date: July 5th

Subject: Lobby Renovation

The federal grant money we received last month ------- **131.** us to invest in upgrading a few areas of our building. ------- **132.** We will be remodeling the lobby starting July 12th. It should take approximately two weeks. ------- **133.** that time, if you have a meeting with anyone from outside the company, please arrange to have it at the Rose Street Café on the corner. We have set up a special account that any employee can use for those two weeks. Please just sign and date your check and return it to your server. We are ------- **134.** that this is a bit of an inconvenience, and we thank you for your cooperation.

131. (A) did allow
(B) has allowed
(C) allows
(D) are allowing

NEW

132. (A) Construction will begin when the building permits are received.
(B) This celebration will last for most of the month of July.
(C) Considering the cost, the renovation might be postponed.
(D) The first area that will benefit from this is the lobby.

133. (A) Upon
(B) During
(C) Around
(D) Until

134. (A) aware
(B) disciplined
(C) reluctant
(D) content

Questions 135-138 refer to the following notice.

Part-Time Cook Needed

Paradise Café is looking ------- (135.) a part-time line cook. Applicants must be able to work in a fast-paced environment and be familiar with all standard breakfast fare. ------- (136.) This weekend schedule could change in the future. Ideally we are looking for an applicant that has ------- (137.) one year of experience working as a short-order cook. Paradise Café is located right next to the post office in downtown Millstown. Please apply in person with a résumé and be prepared to cook an egg dish to order. We ------- (138.) forward to welcoming you to our team!

135. (A) hiring
(B) hire
(C) to hire
(D) to hiring

NEW
136. (A) Applicants should know how to make scrambled eggs.
(B) People applying should know how to wash dishes.
(C) Anyone applying should be able to speak Spanish.
(D) Currently we can only offer weekday shifts, but the applicant must be willing to work weekends if required.

137. (A) at most
(B) below
(C) at least
(D) the least

138. (A) look
(B) looking
(C) looked
(D) looks

GO ON TO THE NEXT PAGE

Questions 139-142 refer to the following advertisement.

City Realty

City Realty is Washington's number-one real estate company, having served the state for over 50 years. We ------- (**139.**) recognized as the state's leading experts in the industry, and many of our agents have been awarded for their excellence in service by *Forbes Property* magazine. Our agents are ------- (**140.**) to bringing all of their knowledge and expertise to the table, and their knowledge of the housing market's dos and don'ts is second to none. Our agents specialize in different areas of the industry including corporate real estate, residential real estate, and rental properties. ------- (**141.**)

Our headquarters, where you can meet with one of our agents ------- (**142.**) a free consultation, is located in the central downtown area. You can also visit our website at www.cityrealty.com for property listings and further information.

139. (A) been
(B) had be
(C) are being
(D) have been

140. (A) attached
(B) faithful
(C) committed
(D) loyal

NEW

141. (A) You can be confident that they will serve your specific needs.
(B) You can choose from hundreds of properties in our listings.
(C) The corporate real estate agents make the most money.
(D) The residential agents are very busy due to the rising housing market.

142. (A) with
(B) for
(C) to
(D) from

Questions 143-146 refer to the following posting on a website.

Employee Message Board

Holiday Office Party

Success and Appreciation

Posted by Julie Norton

I want to thank everyone who ------- (143.) make this party a success. ------- (144.) We had some ups and downs when we started preparing for this, but the final result was extraordinary. In fact, the ------- (145.) consensus seems to be that this year's party was the best yet. We had the highest turnout ever and many seem to agree that this year's activities contributed to the party's success. It was a joy to see everyone get along so well and participate in all the events. We even ------- (146.) our children's charity fundraising goals by over $1,000. Once again, I would like to thank everyone.

143. (A) helps
(B) helped
(C) helping
(D) had help

NEW
144. (A) We should order more food and wine.
(B) I worked really hard to plan this event.
(C) Special thanks to Keith, Grant, Vanessa, and Melissa, who spent many hours outside of work to help plan everything.
(D) I'm glad to see that everyone dressed up for the event.

145. (A) regular
(B) familiar
(C) different
(D) general

146. (A) overstepped
(B) surrendered
(C) exceeded
(D) overwhelmed

GO ON TO THE NEXT PAGE

PART 7

Directions: In this part you will read a selection of texts, such as magazine and newspaper articles, emails, and instant messages. Each text or set of texts is followed by several questions. Select the best answer for each question and mark the letter (A), (B), (C), or (D) on your answer sheet.

Questions 147-148 refer to the following letter.

April 3

Larry Martin
Kansas Neat & Tidy
5448 Lakeside Drive
Arlington, Kansas 67514

Dear Mr. Martin,

We are interested in using your company's cleaning services for this year's Halley Valley Rock Festival. The festival will begin on Friday, June 14, and last the entire weekend, ending on the night of Sunday, June 16. However, unlike in previous years, this year we would like your company to clean the festival grounds intermittently throughout the festival. Therefore, we will be providing your company with a temporary office trailer where your workers can take breaks from the heat.

We look forward to working with your company again this year.

Sincerely,

Karen Johnson

Karen Johnson
Festival Coordinator, Halley Valley Foundation

147. Who most likely is Mr. Martin?

(A) A musical performer
(B) A truck driver
(C) A cleaning company's representative
(D) A festival coordinator

148. According to the letter, what will be provided?

(A) Food and water
(B) A sheltered area
(C) Musical equipment
(D) Cleaning supplies

Questions 149-150 refer to the following text message chain.

LAURA BURKE **5:09**
Are you back in the city on Monday?

ADVIK SHAN **5:15**
I might be.

LAURA BURKE **5:16**
So you're undecided?

ADVIK SHAN **5:17**
Yeah. This factory is running into all kinds of problems. Fix one thing and then something else comes up.

LAURA BURKE **5:17**
I heard. Well, at least it's nice not to be stuck in the office.

ADVIK SHAN **5:18**
That's true.

ADVIK SHAN **5:19**
What's happening on Monday?

LAURA BURKE **5:20**
Ms. Harris wants to have a meeting with you when you get back. Nothing urgent.

ADVIK SHAN **5:22**
OK. I'll let you know when I get my schedule set.

149. What is suggested about Mr. Shan?

(A) He has missed a meeting.
(B) He is considering a transfer.
(C) He has recently taken over the operations of a manufacturing facility.
(D) He doesn't know when he will be returning to his office.

NEW

150. At 5:18, what does Mr. Shan mean when he writes, "That's true"?

(A) He is worried about the conditions in the factory.
(B) He agrees that being out of the office is enjoyable.
(C) He has discovered an error.
(D) He is positive he will be back on Monday.

GO ON TO THE NEXT PAGE

Questions 151-152 refer to the following email.

To:	Pat Blackburn <pblackburn@fastweb.com>
From:	Go Natural Health Products <cs@gonatural.com>
Date:	February 4, 3:34 P.M.
Subject:	Product Order

We appreciate that you have chosen Go Natural Health Products for your vitamin and mineral supplements. All of our products are carefully inspected for quality and meet all government standards. Additionally, during the month of February, customers making purchases over $100.00 do not have to pay any shipping fees.

Order number: 4330XM21
Order date: February 4, 3:31 P.M.
Shipping address: Pat Blackburn, 2709 Michigan Ave., Clinton, WI
Details: six bottles of Green Source multivitamin pills
Total: $180.00, paid with credit card (XXXX XXXX XXXX 8766)

All our products come with a 100-percent customer satisfaction guarantee. If you are dissatisfied, please call our customer service center at 987-555-3427 for a full refund within a week of your order.

Go Natural Health Products

151. What is indicated about Ms. Blackburn's order?

(A) It has been insured against loss.
(B) It is out of stock.
(C) It was placed by her husband.
(D) It will be delivered free of charge.

152. Why might Ms. Blackburn call the customer service center by February 11?

(A) To revise her order
(B) To change payment options
(C) To get her payment back
(D) To apply for a membership

Questions 153-154 refer to the following article.

Midnight Moon, the new jazz album by guitarist Nick Stanton, will start being sold in stores this Thursday. *Midnight Moon* is Mr. Stanton's first album in five years and has received praise from numerous music critics. Mr. Stanton will be signing copies of his new album at Emerson Department Store, located at 4532 Main Street, this Saturday, March 12. An autograph is free with the purchase of the new album.

153. Who is Nick Stanton?

(A) A record producer
(B) A recording artist
(C) A music critic
(D) A music agent

154. According to the article, what will happen on March 12?

(A) A concert will be held.
(B) A book will be released.
(C) An autograph session will take place.
(D) Some tickets will go on sale.

GO ON TO THE NEXT PAGE

Questions 155-158 refer to the following memo.

MEMO

To: All employees
From: Betty Franklin, General Manager
Date: August 19
Subject: Receptionist

To all employees:

– [1] – Greta Jones, the receptionist at our studio, will be taking some time off to deal with a personal matter. She will be gone from August 21st to September 5th. – [2] – Ms. Blanche will take care of Ms. Jones' usual responsibilities including taking phone calls, handling appointments, organizing schedules, and dealing with clients. Please welcome Ms. Blanche to the studio and be available for her to ask questions if she has any.

Furthermore, if you have any long-time clients that you give special prices and discounts to, please let Ms. Blanche know ahead of time. – [3] – She will charge the fees that are programmed into the computer system.

If you have any urgent concerns you need to discuss with Ms. Jones, or if you need to purchase any special hair dyes, treatment shampoos, or other such items for customers, please do so today or tomorrow before Ms. Jones leaves. – [4] – You can contact me at any time if you have any further questions.

155. Where do the recipients of the memo most likely work?

(A) At a department store
(B) At a hair salon
(C) At a spa
(D) At a makeup studio

156. What is indicated about Greta Jones?

(A) She is retiring.
(B) She is going on vacation.
(C) She will take some time off from work.
(D) She will work only temporarily.

157. When should employees contact Ms. Jones with urgent business?

(A) Before she leaves
(B) After she leaves
(C) Anytime
(D) When she gets back

NEW

158. In which of the places marked [1], [2], [3], and [4] does the following sentence belong?

"For this period, we have hired a temporary replacement, Judith Blanche."

(A) [1]
(B) [2]
(C) [3]
(D) [4]

Questions 159-161 refer to the following web page.

Shoe Shine

Your number one source for sneakers

We see that you are currently registered as a basic member on our website. Click here to upgrade to our premium membership.

Once you become a premium member, you will enjoy the following benefits:
- Expedited shipping for $3 ($5 for a basic member)
- Exchanges on all items within 60 days of purchase at no extra charge (30 days for a basic member)
- Returns on all items within 30 days of purchase at no extra charge (seven days for a basic member)

Upgrading your service from basic to premium takes just one click. To welcome customers to our new online store, this month we are offering the upgrade to annual premium membership at a discounted rate of just $50.

159. What is the purpose of the web page?

(A) To advertise a new line of shoes
(B) To confirm an order
(C) To recommend a service upgrade
(D) To solicit donations

160. What is NOT mentioned as a benefit of premium membership?

(A) Discounts on new items
(B) Faster shipping at a reduced price
(C) A longer period for free returns
(D) A longer period for free exchanges

161. What is indicated about Shoe Shine?

(A) It has been in business for decades.
(B) It was founded by a local entrepreneur.
(C) Its merchandise is available through the Internet.
(D) It has three types of membership.

GO ON TO THE NEXT PAGE

Questions 162-165 refer to the following online chat discussion.

Lisa Hancock 9:39
I'm stopping by a coffee shop on my way to work. What does everyone want? It's on me.

Nick Morton 9:39
Wow! Thanks! I'll just have black coffee.

Lilly Smith 9:40
Thanks. I'd like a latte. Can you also bring some sugar?

Lisa Hancock 9:41
Sure. I'll bring a couple of sugar packets.

Richard Park 9:42
I can never turn down coffee. I'll also have a latte with some sugar.

Emily Jordan 9:42
I'd like an herbal tea if they have any. I don't drink anything caffeinated, so any tea without caffeine would be great. Thanks.

Lisa Hancock 9:43
All right, then. I'll be there in about 20 minutes with your drinks. See you soon. Oh, and before I forget, please make sure that our order from Cindy's Boutique gets set up in our showroom for our clients.

Richard Park 9:44
The boxes arrived this morning and our interns are unpacking them now. However, the order from Chantelle seems to have gone missing.

Lisa Hancock 9:45
What do you mean?

Nick Morton 9:45
We're trying to locate the package. We contacted Chantelle; they sent it to the wrong address.

Lisa Hancock 9:46
That's a disaster. Please try to find out where those dresses went.

Richard Park 9:47
Good news! I just got a message from the shipping company and they found the Chantelle order. They're redirecting the shipment to us.

Lisa Hancock 9:48
I almost had a panic attack. When will it get there?

Richard Park 9:48
This afternoon.

162. What type of business do the speakers probably work at?

(A) A fashion company
(B) A clothing shop
(C) A costume company
(D) A coffee shop

NEW

163. At 9:39, what does Lisa Hancock mean when she says, "It's on me"?

(A) She'll bring the coffee.
(B) She'll buy the drinks.
(C) She'll remember everyone's order.
(D) It's her turn to get drinks.

164. What is indicated about one of the speakers' shipments?

(A) It was incorrectly priced.
(B) It was returned to the boutique.
(C) It will arrive later in the day.
(D) It hasn't been located yet.

165. What kind of business is Chantelle?

(A) A fabric company
(B) A magazine company
(C) A shipping company
(D) A boutique

GO ON TO THE NEXT PAGE

Questions 166-168 refer to the following email.

To	All <csall@cherishedgoods.com>
From	Eric Nixon <enix@cherishedgoods.com>
Date	January 5, 10:00 A.M.
Subject	Shipping Error

Hello everyone,

Lilia Kent, the head of the shipping department, has informed me that yesterday our customer database experienced a system error and as a result many orders were sent to the wrong addresses. This morning our department has already received multiple calls from customers complaining that they received the wrong packages. Ms. Kent's department has been working hard to locate the cause of the mistake. Therefore, any customer that calls about a wrong delivery should be asked to return the package. Additionally, please inform the customers that they will be given a 10-percent discount on their next purchase.

Eric Nixon

166. Who most likely received this email?

(A) Employees in the shipping department
(B) Dissatisfied customers
(C) Customer service representatives
(D) Internet technology specialists

167. According to the email, what is Ms. Kent's staff trying to do?

(A) Create a customer database
(B) Fix a system malfunction
(C) Locate a lost package
(D) Take calls from customers

168. What are recipients of the email advised to do?

(A) Update their personal information
(B) Deliver packages in person
(C) Enter data into a customer database
(D) Offer a price reduction to some customers

Questions 169-171 refer to the following email.

To: carlhurst@nicknet.com
From: m_winters@tatecc.com
Date: June 1, 1:34 P.M.
Subject: Community Events

Dear Mr. Hurst,

As a loyal customer with a family membership at the Tate Community Center, you have sponsored us with your continued donations. We really appreciate your support.

The following table provides information on upcoming family events this month. We welcome your participation.

Crafts Day, June 7	Paul Simpson, June 15	Summer Picnic, June 22
A variety of craft supplies will be available for kids to make their own unique creations.	Come and listen to the beautiful music of local singer and songwriter Paul Simpson.	Everyone needs to bring a tasty dish to share with others. Free beverages will be provided.

For members, no purchase of tickets is necessary for participation in these events. We encourage you to attend these events and spend quality time with your family.

We look forward to seeing you.

Minnie Winters
Program Coordinator
Tate Community Center

169. What is suggested about Mr. Hurst?

(A) He is a local musician.
(B) He donates to an orphanage.
(C) He supports a public organization.
(D) He works at a community center.

170. Why was the email sent?

(A) To announce a community board meeting
(B) To apply for a family membership
(C) To publicize upcoming events
(D) To give information about a local election

171. What is indicated about the Tate Community Center?

(A) Its members gain free admission to events.
(B) It offers regular music classes.
(C) It takes reservations by phone.
(D) It serves beverages at all events.

GO ON TO THE NEXT PAGE

Questions 172-175 refer to the following letter.

J&P Industries
1462 Swinton Street
Cameron, NY 10288

March 29
Mr. Grant Lee
287 Silver Plains Road
Cameron, NY 18729

Dear Mr. Lee,

We thank you for your continued work and your dedication to your job at J&P Industries. We are sending all employees information about recent changes that have been made to your health insurance benefits with our company. You will continue to be covered by the same insurance company, but because of the new state regulations that have been put forth, all employees must now undergo a basic medical checkup at a local clinic or hospital. – [1] – This checkup will be covered by your health insurance, so you do not need to pay any extra fees and this will by no means affect your monthly insurance deductions. – [2] – Included in this envelope is detailed information about the new medical program for employees.

The medical checkup must include a blood test, urine test, eye test, height and weight measurements, hearing test, and chest X-rays. – [3] – Please make an appointment with a local clinic. You should have your results sent to Karen Leigh in human resources by December 30th at the latest. If you fail to get a medical exam, you may be subject to a fine of up to $2000. – [4] – We thank you for your cooperation and hope you will abide by the new changes.

If you have any further questions or concerns, please contact Karen at leighk@jpindustries.com.

Sincerely,

John Black

Executive Manager

J&P Industries

172. What is the purpose of the letter?

(A) To inform an employee about a mandatory exam
(B) To encourage employees to donate blood to a hospital
(C) To discuss the changes made to employees' health insurance coverage
(D) To advertise the services of a new clinic

173. What did Mr. Black send with the letter?

(A) An application form
(B) An insurance document
(C) A contract
(D) Extra information about the changes

174. The term "subject to" at the end of the second paragraph is closest in meaning to:

(A) dependent on
(B) responsible for
(C) withdrawn from
(D) added to

NEW

175. In which of places marked [1], [2], [3], and [4] does this sentence belong?

"The appointments should take no longer than 30 minutes."

(A) [1]
(B) [2]
(C) [3]
(D) [4]

GO ON TO THE NEXT PAGE

Questions 176-180 refer to the following advertisement and email.

Blooming Flower Yoga Studio

Summer Yoga Classes

This summer we will be offering a variety of yoga classes for all age groups and skill levels.

Summer Class Schedule and Prices (registration fee):

- Beginner class, twice a week for two months ($150)
- Intermediate and advanced class, twice a week for two months ($200)
- Yoga for senior citizens, once a week for two months ($100)
- Hot power yoga, three times a week for two months ($250)

All necessary supplies will be provided by the Blooming Flower Yoga Studio. Students should wear comfortable clothes that allow for free movement.

45 Clark Street
Indianapolis, IN 46202
715-555-5832
www.bloomingfloweryoga.com

To: Tammy Glenn <tammyglenn@mxmail.com>
From: Dwayne Moore <dwaynemoore@bloomingfloweryoga.com>
Date: May 23
Subject: New Student
Attachment: New member form

Dear Ms. Glenn,

I'm writing to let you know that you have one more student who has signed up for your class. Your new student is Jane Meyers and she will bring the $100 registration fee with her to the first class on Monday.

Also, on Monday, please give Ms. Meyers and any other new members the form they will need to fill out. I have attached the necessary paperwork to this email. All you have to do is print out copies and hand them out.

Your class now has nine students that will attend and is, therefore, almost at full capacity. In fact, all of the classes this summer have proven very popular, and I anticipate that they will all fill up by the end of the month. Thank you so much for your many years of hard work as a teacher here at Blooming Flower Yoga Studio. If you have any questions, let me know.

Dwayne Moore

176. What is stated about the summer classes?

(A) They started last week.
(B) They will be held outdoors.
(C) They are available to both children and adults.
(D) They are being offered at a discounted price.

177. What is suggested about Ms. Meyers?

(A) She has never studied yoga before.
(B) She is an elderly person.
(C) She wants to become a yoga instructor.
(D) She is a long-time student.

178. What is Ms. Glenn asked to do?

(A) Develop a new curriculum
(B) Attend a training seminar
(C) Sign a work contract
(D) Distribute some documents

179. In the email, the word "capacity" in paragraph 3, line 1, is closest in meaning to:

(A) volume
(B) ability
(C) vacancy
(D) role

180. What is indicated about Ms. Glenn?

(A) She works well with children.
(B) She is a long-time employee.
(C) She will be retiring soon.
(D) She will be receiving a pay raise.

GO ON TO THE NEXT PAGE

Questions 181-185 refer to the following website posts.

Mega Hobby Models Community Forum

Issue with the Blackbeard's Pirate Ship Model

August 3, 10:55 A.M.

Post by John Taylor

I recently purchased a model kit from the Mega Hobby online store. I bought the Blackbeard's Pirate Ship model to put together with my son, and I am having a problem. After carefully reading the instruction manual, I noticed that a few essential parts had been left out of the box. Specifically, some parts that make up the mast and sail seem to be absent from the kit. I have bought many Mega Hobby models over the years, and have always been happy with the products I've received.

Has anyone else had the same problem with this kit? My son and I were planning to submit our finished model to a local model-building contest at the end of the month, and we are very disappointed by this setback. If anyone else has experienced this problem and solved it, I would greatly appreciate your advice.

Mega Hobby Models Community Forum

RE: Issue with the Blackbeard's Pirate Ship Model

August 3, 4:24 P.M.

Post by Catherine Maxwell

Hi John,

I also recently purchased the Blackbeard's Pirate Ship model from the Mega Hobby online store for my son and had the same problem that you did. At first I thought I must have been mistaken, but after checking the list of all parts in the instruction manual, I determined that several parts must have been missing from the kit at the time of sale. I took the kit back to my local Mega Hobby store and a staff member confirmed my suspicion. The Mega Hobby employee was nice enough to exchange my model kit for one that had all of the parts. With the new kit, my son and I were able to put the model together exactly like the picture on the box. I suggest that you go to the Mega Hobby store closest to your home and ask to exchange your defective product. Be sure to make a note of the order number when you go there.

181. What is the subject of the first post?

(A) A defect with a purchased product
(B) Mistakes in an instruction manual
(C) A discrepancy with an advertised price
(D) Registration for a competition

182. What is suggested about Mr. Taylor?

(A) He knows Ms. Maxwell personally.
(B) He is a product designer at Mega Hobby.
(C) He owns a sailboat.
(D) He will enter a competition with his son.

183. How did both Mr. Taylor and Ms. Maxwell realize there was a problem?

(A) By talking with a customer service agent
(B) By watching an instructional video
(C) Be consulting a user manual
(D) By looking at a photograph

184. What is indicated about Ms. Maxwell?

(A) She is a regular customer of Mega Hobby.
(B) She works with Mr. Taylor at Mega Hobby.
(C) She successfully assembled the model.
(D) She received a full refund.

185. What does Ms. Maxwell recommend?

(A) Visiting a nearby store
(B) Canceling a membership
(C) Downloading a new instruction manual
(D) Purchasing replacement parts

GO ON TO THE NEXT PAGE

Questions 186-190 refer to the following advertisement, form, and meeting announcement.

Dreamspace Bed Emporium

Beds, Bedding, and Furniture
3600 Wilshire Road, Springfield, IL 62751
www.dreamspacebeds.com

Don't let yourself suffer tossing and turning, not getting a good night's sleep. Come down to Dreamspace Bed Emporium and treat yourself to a comfortable bed catered to your exact needs. Customers are welcome to lie on any bed in the store.

First Floor: Beds (single, double, queen, king, etc.)
Second Floor: Bedding (sheets, pillows, blankets, cushions, etc.)
Third Floor: Furniture (chairs, sofas, tables, etc.)

In response to customer suggestions, our store now stays open two hours later to accommodate those who may work irregular shifts.

Do you need express delivery of a bed? Simply ask one of our staff members at the checkout counter and it will be easily arranged.

If you have any comments or suggestions for our store, a comment box can be found inside the main entrance.

Comment and Suggestion Form

Dreamspace Bed Emporium

Customer name: Willy M. King
Date: August 9
Contact number: 456-555-6123

Comment: Last week, I came into your store to shop for a new pillow, sheet, and blanket set for my bed. However, when I went to that section, I couldn't find any available staff members to assist me. I waited for about half an hour, but no one came to me. I needed help determining what sheet and blanket set would fit the dimensions of my bed, but ended up just leaving the store frustrated. I hope you can provide better service to customers so something like this doesn't happen again in the future. I have been a loyal customer of yours for years. If you don't explain why no one helped me, I may have to start shopping at one of your competitors' stores.

Hello everybody. I have called this meeting to talk about some of the problems that our new store policy of staying open later has caused. At first, this seemed like a great idea to help customers who work all day. I know it can be hard to find time to do chores and shopping when you work from 9 to 5. Unfortunately, staying open later means that we have had to spread our staff too thin while we wait to hire and train more people.

As a result, we have been neglecting some of our customers lately. The photocopied comment and suggestion form I have passed out to you all from Willy King sums up our shortcomings better than I ever could. Please give it a read and think about ways we can be made to be aware of a customer in need in a store as large as ours. I understand that with our thin staff we have to cover more space than we used to, so this meeting isn't about punishment or blame; it's just about solutions. Please do some brainstorming on this and drop by my office if you think you have an idea. I have to go call Willy King.

186. What is NOT mentioned about the beds at Dreamspace Bed Emporium?

(A) They come in a variety of sizes.
(B) They can be tested by customers.
(C) They are displayed on the first floor.
(D) They come with a lifetime warranty.

187. According to the advertisement, what is true about Dreamspace Bed Emporium?

(A) It is located in a department store.
(B) It sells home appliances.
(C) It is hiring additional staff.
(D) It has extended its operating hours.

188. Where did Mr. King most likely search for the products he wanted?

(A) On the first floor
(B) On the second floor
(C) On the third floor
(D) Near the main entrance

189. Who do you believe is speaking at the meeting?

(A) The Dreamspace Bed Emporium manager
(B) Willy King
(C) A district manager from another city
(D) A checkout clerk

190. What is most likely true based upon the information from the meeting?

(A) Dreamspace Bed Emporium will change its hours back to what they used to be.
(B) Dreamspace Bed Emporium will extend its hours to serve more customers like Willy King.
(C) Dreamspace Bed Emporium will hire more employees so there are enough people to cover the whole store.
(D) Dreamspace Bed Emporium will hold a raffle event and invite Willy King.

GO ON TO THE NEXT PAGE

NEW **Questions 191-195** refer to the following web page, email, and schedule.

http://www.acestafftraining.com

Home	Contact Us	Location	About Ace

Ace Training is a company that offers developmental courses for the employees of your store or business. You can rely on our team of successful professionals to improve the quality of your staff and help your company achieve its goals. We provide effective and results-oriented programs. Below are the training courses available:

Leadership This program helps staff members develop strategic planning and management skills. It also enhances the supervisory skills of employees in leadership positions.	**Sales** We teach innovative strategies to increase sales and market share. This class is suitable for both in-store salespeople and employees who work over the phone.
Customer Service Never undervalue the importance of your customers' satisfaction. Your employees need the skills to be helpful and efficient when working directly with customers.	**Technologies** In rapidly changing work environments, staff members should keep up with new trends and developments in the technological field. Your staff members will learn how to research and master new technologies quickly and accurately.

To enroll staff members in a program, contact Joshua York at josh@acestafftraining.com.

From: Tiffany Tran <tifftran@zellengifts.com>
To: Joshua York <josh@acestafftraining.com>
Subject: Staff Training for Our Employees
Date: October 9

Dear Mr. York,

I'm contacting you about running a training program for some of our employees here at Zellen Gifts. We are planning on expanding our telemarketing department next month, but we don't have enough properly trained employees to fill the new positions. Therefore, we will be transferring some employees from the customer service department to the telemarketing department to solve this problem. As our products are mainly targeted towards children, we are hoping to increase our profits as much as possible during this Christmas season. Please let me know the maximum number of trainees that you can accommodate at one time.

Thank you,

Tiffany Tran
Zellen Gifts

PROPOSED ACE TRAINING SCHEDULE FOR ZELLEN GIFTS

November 1–5

Group Code and Trainee Numbers	**Monday** Sales Strategies	**Tuesday** Successful Negotiation	**Wednesday** Customers First!	**Thursday** Closing the Deal	**Friday** Start Polite, Stay Polite
Red Team 10 people	9–11	9–11:30	8–10:30	8–11	9–11
Blue Team 10 people	1–3	1–3	1–3	1–3	1–3
Green Team 10 people	3–5	3–5	3–5	3–5	3–5
White Team 10 people	5–7	5–7	5–7	5–7	5–7

Here is our proposed schedule for transitioning your customer service staff into successful telemarketers. You can see that we have an ambitious amount of material to cover, but I am confident that the program will be a success. We have tried to balance your need for a swift transition with your need to continue running Zellen Gifts while the training is in session. Therefore, we have divided your staff into groups and staggered them throughout the day. This will result in better trainee-to-trainer numbers for your staff, and should cause minimal disruption to your business. We look forward to a great week of training!

Joshua York,
Ace Training Coordinator

GO ON TO THE NEXT PAGE

191. Where does Mr. York work?

(A) At an accounting firm
(B) At a sports management agency
(C) At a skills development organization
(D) At an advertising agency

192. What is stated about the program on technologies?

(A) It is open to the public.
(B) It includes current web programming skills.
(C) It teaches environmental protection.
(D) It keeps employees up-to-date.

193. What program is Ms. Tran most likely interested?

(A) Leadership
(B) Sales
(C) Customer Service
(D) Technologies

194. What is indicated by the proposed training schedule and accompanying memo?

(A) It is an easy course to complete.
(B) There are five key topics that will be covered.
(C) Fifty employees will take part.
(D) Joshua York will be one of the trainers.

195. Based upon the proposed training schedule and accompanying memo, what can be inferred about Zellen Gifts?

(A) They are trying to become better at customer relations.
(B) They want to conduct business as usual during their training period.
(C) They have a small customer service staff.
(D) They want to finish their training before the end of October.

Questions 196-200 refer to the following Web page, email, and schedule.

Midcity Performing Arts Hall

Support the Midcity Performing Arts Hall in downtown Brenton by becoming a member. You can choose from the following membership plans:

General – For only $100 you can get a one-year membership and attend any two performances that have seats available in the D area of the theater.

Silver – For a fee of $200, you can attend any two performances that have seats available in the B area of the theater.

Gold – For a fee of $500, you will receive early alerts about popular programs, tickets to any two performances with seats in the B area, and a guaranteed front row seat at any show of your choice within a one-year period.

Diamond – For a fee of $1,000, you will have exclusive access to performers' autograph signings, invitations to two exclusive pre-showings of popular programs, and a guaranteed VIP seat at any show of your choice within a one-year period.

*Some restrictions do apply.

*Admission to orchestral performances excluded.

To: bates@midcityarthall.com
From: Alicia Norton
Date: January 16
Subject: membership

Thank you for your email about Midcity Performing Arts Hall memberships. I have paid a fee of $1,000. I was a general member last year, and I enjoyed a couple of the musicals that were performed. I have become a theater enthusiast thanks to that experience, and I look forward to the benefits of the new membership plan.

By the way, the arts hall has done a phenomenal job on its renovations. I'm excited to come back this year.

GO ON TO THE NEXT PAGE

Below is the tentative schedule for shows at the Midcity Performing Arts Hall in the coming months. Please have a look and call anytime if you wish to get seats.

Brenton Philharmonic Orchestra	January 28 to January 30
Dancing Princess	February 3 to February 23
Jazz that Dance	March 1 to March 26
Opera Ghost	April 3 to April 29

196. Which membership did Alicia Norton most likely purchase?

(A) General
(B) Silver
(C) Gold
(D) Diamond

197. What is suggested about the Midcity Performing Arts Hall?

(A) It hosts various sports programs.
(B) Some changes have been made to its building.
(C) It is a place popular among celebrities.
(D) It is an old museum.

198. When is a performance NOT free for members?

(A) January
(B) February
(C) March
(D) April

199. What is implied about the schedule?

(A) The shows have all sold out.
(B) More shows may be added.
(C) It is fixed.
(D) It may change.

200. What is meant by the expression "some restrictions do apply"?

(A) Only certain people will be considered for membership.
(B) The membership plans may change without notice.
(C) Not all performances are available to members.
(D) Non-members will not be admitted.

NO TEST MATERIAL ON THIS PAGE

Stop! This is the end of the test. If you finish before time is called, you may go back to Parts 5, 6, and 7 and check your work.

ACTUAL TEST 08

READING TEST

In the Reading test, you will read a variety of texts and answer several different types of reading comprehension questions. The entire Reading test will last 75 minutes. There are three parts, and directions are given for each part. You are encouraged to answer as many questions as possible within the time allowed.

You must mark your answers on the separate answer sheet. Do not write your answers in your test book.

PART 5

Directions: A word or phrase is missing in each of the sentences below. Four answer choices are given below each sentence. Select the best answer to complete the sentence. Then mark the letter (A), (B), (C), or (D) on your answer sheet.

101. Our spokesperson will explain an ------- opportunity for property investors.

(A) excitedly
(B) excitement
(C) excited
(D) exciting

102. Some of the leather used in this handbag must ------- from Italy.

(A) will import
(B) be imported
(C) to import
(D) have imported

103. Rockwell Bank's automated teller machines are ------- located in various sections of the city.

(A) abruptly
(B) conveniently
(C) fluently
(D) periodically

104. As soon as both sides reach ------- terms, the licensing contract will be signed.

(A) agreeable
(B) agree
(C) agreement
(D) agreed

105. Anyone who cannot ------- one of the safety training workshops before September 1 should inform his or her manager.

(A) impress
(B) employ
(C) attend
(D) reply

106. ------- for using the hotel's spa and dining services will appear on your final invoice.

(A) Charge
(B) Charges
(C) Charging
(D) Charged

107. Members of the security team have been instructed to report ------- unattended bag to the local police department.

(A) any
(B) much
(C) most
(D) all

108. The head chef has the restaurant manager ------- the order for ingredients every evening.

(A) authoritative
(B) authority
(C) authorities
(D) authorize

109. The automotive company ------- pursued technologies that would improve the efficiency of its engines.

(A) aggressive
(B) aggressiveness
(C) aggressively
(D) aggression

110. On the first day of the painting course, students should provide the teacher with proof of -------.

(A) registration
(B) proposal
(C) accumulation
(D) copyright

111. The furniture in this apartment is not -------, but belongs to the landlord and must be returned at the end of the lease.

(A) ours
(B) we
(C) our
(D) us

112. The driver ------- Mr. Dwight is expected to arrive at the conference venue 20 minutes prior to the finishing time.

(A) until
(B) in
(C) for
(D) among

113. Three of the new chemists, who ------- developed the material, will be recognized by the CEO at Saturday's ceremony.

(A) collaborating
(B) collaborate
(C) collaboratively
(D) collaborative

114. The goal of the program is to make health services readily available to those in both rural and urban -------.

(A) purposes
(B) settings
(C) monuments
(D) standards

115. Please send a check in the amount of £550 ------- the document that needs to be checked by our agency.

(A) despite
(B) while
(C) with
(D) through

116. Fingerprint systems are generally ------- as the primary form of security at laboratories in this country.

(A) to accept
(B) accept
(C) accepting
(D) accepted

GO ON TO THE NEXT PAGE

117. Living further from the city center will ------- your rental costs, but will also affect your commute.

(A) shorten
(B) misplace
(C) lower
(D) collapse

118. FryMate brand cookware can be purchased directly from the company's website or at a retailer ------- you.

(A) against
(B) to
(C) along
(D) near

119. Weekly ------- of the facility help to ensure that minor maintenance issues are discovered and resolved early.

(A) investigations
(B) investigated
(C) investigative
(D) investigates

120. Patients should call the emergency line immediately if they experience ------- changes in temperature.

(A) sudden
(B) contemporary
(C) ideal
(D) reasonable

121. Those who are taking part in the half-day historical tour should be at the meeting point ------- than 7:45 A.M.

(A) as for
(B) particularly
(C) whenever
(D) no later

122. The supervisor allowed Mr. Martin to take three additional vacation days because of his ------- achievement.

(A) unlimited
(B) noteworthy
(C) identical
(D) satisfied

123. Ms. Stevens ------- acknowledged that she had been unable to complete the task in the specified time frame.

(A) regretfully
(B) regret
(C) regrets
(D) regretful

124. The customer's steak was ------- undercooked, so he requested that it be sent back to the kitchen.

(A) rather
(B) such
(C) many
(D) rarely

125. The contact details provided on this survey are for in-house purposes and will not be ------- to any third party.

(A) suspended
(B) responded
(C) equipped
(D) released

126. Mr. Brannon can assemble the shelves for the booth ------- as long as he has a set of tools.

(A) his
(B) himself
(C) him
(D) his own

127. Ms. Stevenson contacted the real estate agent ------- name and phone number appeared in the advertisement.

(A) what
(B) which
(C) whose
(D) who

128. The home's sale becomes ------- when the official document is recorded at the county office.

(A) finally
(B) finalize
(C) finals
(D) final

129. The main activity at the workshop required team members to ------- with each other.

(A) cooperate
(B) oversee
(C) shrink
(D) encounter

130. According to the physician, Ms. Oliver's pain ------- within two hours of her taking the medication.

(A) alleviated
(B) will be alleviated
(C) is alleviating
(D) should be alleviated

GO ON TO THE NEXT PAGE

PART 6

Directions: Read the texts that follow. A word, phrase, or sentence is missing in parts of each text. Four answer choices for each question are given below the text. Select the best answer to complete the text. Then mark the letter (A), (B), (C), or (D) on your answer sheet.

Questions 131-134 refer to the following advertisement.

International Goods Fair

If you want ------- **131.** your packaged goods to an international audience, join the eighth annual International Goods Fair. The fair runs from March 5th to March 7th at the Galaxy Convention Center in downtown New York City. With over 200 companies from all over the world ------- **132.**, you can make business connections while promoting your own products to interested customers and businesses. The products should be mainly packaged foods ranging ------- **133.** desserts and snacks to canned meats and dried jerky. ------- **134.** Spots are limited and going fast.

131. (A) promotion
(B) promoting
(C) to promote
(D) have promoted

132. (A) represented
(B) expressed
(C) delivered
(D) revealed

133. (A) to
(B) for
(C) from
(D) with

NEW

134. (A) Ice creams will not be allowed on the premises.
(B) You can sample items as you browse.
(C) You'll have a chance to promote your food of choice.
(D) Apply for a booth now before they're all taken.

Questions 135-138 refer to the following notice.

From: Vice President, Jordan Smith

To: K Group Employees

Subject: Company Renovations

Date: February 26

To all employees,

This weekend the renovations to our second-floor offices -------. We ask that you take home
135.
all important documents and file away any loose materials on your desks. All electronic devices should be turned off and unplugged. -------, all cabinets and drawers should be
136.
locked.

The renovations will take approximately five days. ------- If you have any meetings scheduled
137.
with clients next week, please arrange to meet them outside the company premises due to the noise. We apologize for the inconvenience but we ask for your -------. Thank you.
138.

135. (A) has began
(B) will begin
(C) beginning
(D) begun

136. (A) Furthermore
(B) As a consequence
(C) Because
(D) Therefore

NEW

137. (A) If they need more space, we will notify you.
(B) All business will be suspended until the renovations end.
(C) During this time, your temporary workspace will be the first-floor conference room.
(D) Your office space will look new and improved after the renovations.

138. (A) service
(B) association
(C) connection
(D) cooperation

GO ON TO THE NEXT PAGE

Questions 139-142 refer to the following notice.

Attorney Opening

Johnson and Kindness PLC has an immediate opening for a contract attorney. The ideal candidate would have at least three years of experience ------- (139.) on complex business transactions. ------- (140.) The types of contract work that we ------- (141.) at Johnson and Kindness deal exclusively with business relationships between private companies and the government. If ------- (142.) feel that you are qualified to join our team, please email our HR manager at JK@law.com.

139. (A) working
(B) work
(C) to work
(D) worked

NEW

140. (A) Government experience would also be a plus.
(B) Working with children would help your résumé.
(C) Experience with animals is essential.
(D) Working with disabled people is a bonus.

141. (A) perform
(B) achieve
(C) allow
(D) transform

142. (A) you
(B) I
(C) we
(D) they

Questions 143-146 refer to the following email.

To: bobsaget@BobsJobs.com
From: HarrisonG@gmail.com
Date: September 20
Subject: business proposal

Dear Mr. Saget,

My name is Harrison Goodbody. I am ------- **143.** in response to the advertisement you placed in the *Times* for a new human resource manager. I have five years' ------- **144.** working in a fast-paced corporate environment. I understand that your firm employs upwards of 300 people and many of them speak Spanish. ------- **145.** I have attached my résumé and would be happy ------- **146.** provide excellent references should you request them. Thank you for your time.

Sincerely,

Harrison Goodbody

143. (A) message
(B) to write
(C) writing
(D) looking

144. (A) experience
(B) knowledge
(C) work
(D) internship

NEW

145. (A) I am a certified level five speaker of Spanish.
(B) Spanish people can be hard to work with.
(C) I don't know any Spanish, but I could study.
(D) Spanish speakers are good workers.

146. (A) in
(B) to
(C) for
(D) will

ACTUAL TEST 08

GO ON TO THE NEXT PAGE

PART 7

Directions: In this part you will read a selection of texts, such as magazine and newspaper articles, emails, and instant messages. Each text or set of texts is followed by several questions. Select the best answer for each question and mark the letter (A), (B), (C), or (D) on your answer sheet.

Questions 147-148 refer to the following information.

The new Sensonic curved television is now on sale at the shockingly low price of just $1,999. Enjoy your favorite television shows, movies, and games on a 55-inch screen that offers ultra-high-definition images! Best of all, you don't have to struggle with a complicated instruction manual. Just take the television home and install it, and it begins working with your preferences immediately without the need for annoying adjustments.

147. Where would this information most likely appear?

(A) In an instruction manual
(B) On a product receipt
(C) In a promotional flyer
(D) In a letter

148. What is mentioned as a convenient feature of the product?

(A) Its simple set-up procedure
(B) Its long warranty period
(C) Its compatibility with other devices
(D) Its detailed instructions

Questions 149-150 refer to the following text message chain.

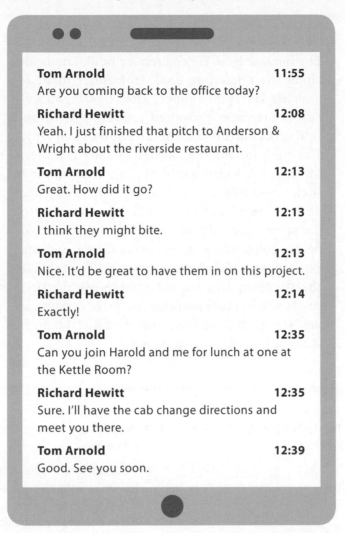

Tom Arnold **11:55**
Are you coming back to the office today?

Richard Hewitt **12:08**
Yeah. I just finished that pitch to Anderson & Wright about the riverside restaurant.

Tom Arnold **12:13**
Great. How did it go?

Richard Hewitt **12:13**
I think they might bite.

Tom Arnold **12:13**
Nice. It'd be great to have them in on this project.

Richard Hewitt **12:14**
Exactly!

Tom Arnold **12:35**
Can you join Harold and me for lunch at one at the Kettle Room?

Richard Hewitt **12:35**
Sure. I'll have the cab change directions and meet you there.

Tom Arnold **12:39**
Good. See you soon.

149. What is suggested about Mr. Hewitt?

(A) He is late for a lunch appointment.
(B) He has accepted a new position.
(C) He is in a taxi.
(D) He is on his way to a presentation.

NEW

150. At 12:14, what does Mr. Hewitt mean when he writes, "Exactly"?

(A) He would like to know where they're having lunch.
(B) He is looking forward to meeting Anderson & Wright.
(C) He is on his way back to the office.
(D) He would also like Anderson & Wright to join the project.

GO ON TO THE NEXT PAGE

Questions 151-152 refer to the following article.

The buzz at New York's premier book fair is all about the upcoming book from poet-turned-novelist Harry S. Tepper. *The Nightingales of Fall* is the eagerly awaited sequel to his best-selling debut novel, *The Swallows of Spring*. The book follows the journey of Sally Harknett through the weird world of Underfell, mixing social commentary with sharp wit and just a dash of magic and mystery. Tepper burst onto the scene over a decade ago with the acclaimed poetry collection *King Harmon's Castle*, and the expectation is that this latest novel will be another chart-topping success. Later this week the first copies will be made available in a prize drawing at the New York Book Fair, with the official launch at major bookstores next month.

151. How would Mr. Tepper's latest book most likely be classified?

(A) Romance
(B) Historical fiction
(C) Fantasy
(D) Poetry

152. Where will copies of the book be available this week?

(A) At all major bookstores
(B) On a website
(C) At a literary event
(D) In selected public libraries

Questions 153-154 refer to the following email.

To: All Subscribers
From: Customer Support <customersupport@stylefashionmz.com>
Date: June 5
Subject: New Edition

Dear loyal subscribers,

Style & Fashion Magazine is excited to announce the launch of the new digital edition of our monthly magazine this summer. Although the print and digital edition will be nearly identical, the digital edition will contain some longer articles and images that won't appear in the print edition.

Current subscribers to the print edition of our magazine will automatically receive a code that will allow access to the digital edition. Your code will be included with next month's print magazine when it is delivered to your house.

153. What is the purpose of the email?

(A) To offer a discounted subscription rate
(B) To advertise a new online shopping mall
(C) To introduce a digital publication
(D) To remind some subscribers to renew their subscriptions

154. What can subscribers find in the paper edition in July?

(A) A discount coupon
(B) A special supplement
(C) An exclusive interview
(D) An access code

GO ON TO THE NEXT PAGE

Questions 155-158 refer to the following article.

More Buses During the Holidays

November 28— – [1] – Although the holiday season signals a nice week-long vacation for many, bus drivers will work longer hours and straight through the holidays to accommodate the many tourists that are flooding the city at this time of year and the shoppers that are busy buying those last-minute gifts. – [2] – The city has announced new bus schedules for the next few weeks which include some routes on which buses will run all day and all night. While most buses stop running by 1 A.M., some parts of downtown will see buses running all night. The Bingham shopping district will see buses running until 3 A.M. "This is when we have the most tourists and out-of-town folks coming to visit," explained Mayor Bill Nate. "We felt it was important to provide the necessary services during this time." – [3] –

When the bus drivers' union leader, Nathan Reiner, was asked about the new schedules, he responded, "We worked out a payment plan that is agreeable on both sides and have enough drivers that can work in shifts so that there is no danger of overworking or exhaustion. Many of us will still get some time off during the holidays with our families." – [4] –

155. What is the purpose of the article?

(A) To report changes in public transportation
(B) To describe the city during the holidays
(C) To inform the public about traffic delays
(D) To advertise new shopping centers

156. What is suggested about Mr. Reiner?

(A) He is happy with the mayor.
(B) He may stage a protest.
(C) He is satisfied with the working conditions.
(D) He would like some time off for the holidays.

157. What is stated about the city during the holiday season?

(A) It closes down for the holidays.
(B) Many visitors come from out of town.
(C) Many taxi drivers lose business.
(D) The citizens travel to other cities.

NEW

158. In which of the places marked [1], [2], [3], and [4] does the following sentence belong?

"Overall, the city seems prepared for the influx of tourists and holiday shoppers as Christmas draws near."

(A) [1]
(B) [2]
(C) [3]
(D) [4]

Questions 159-161 refer to the following schedule.

Channel 19 Program Schedule

March 3

6:00 A.M. – 7:00 A.M.
Life in Alaska
Follow the life of Ken Ruskin, a fisherman living in the remote Alaskan tundra.

7:00 A.M. – 9:00 A.M.
Amazing Sights of Africa
Learn about the diverse animals and plants of the African savanna.

9:00 A.M. – 10:30 A.M.
Anatomy of a Dinosaur
In this episode, paleontologist Dr. Kerry Peterson tells you everything you want to know about the tyrannosaurus.

10:30 A.M. – 11:00 A.M.
Rocky
Host Dan Reed demonstrates how to survive the extreme conditions of the Canadian outdoors in winter.

11:00 A.M. – 1:00 P.M.
Natural Phenomenon
Host Julia Fromm investigates the most mysterious naturally occurring phenomena on Earth.

1:00 P.M. – 2:00 P.M.
Blue Ocean
Travel with us to the ocean waters around Australia, where diver Pat Russell finds dolphins, sharks, seals, and much more.

159. What is the focus of the channel?
(A) Plants
(B) Sports
(C) Nature
(D) Lifestyle

160. According to the schedule, who is a scientist?
(A) Pat Russell
(B) Dan Reed
(C) Kerry Peterson
(D) Ken Ruskin

161. Which program will teach viewers survival skills?
(A) *Anatomy of a Dinosaur*
(B) *Amazing Sights of Africa*
(C) *Blue Ocean*
(D) *Rocky*

GO ON TO THE NEXT PAGE

Questions 162-165 refer to the following online chat discussion.

J&R International Group Discussion

Sunny Rhee	**[5:37]**	Is anyone unable to make it to Friday's office party?
Kevin King	**[5:38]**	I can be there for the first hour, but I need to leave early for a family get-together.
Patrick Stone	**[5:39]**	I have a business trip to Hong Kong the next day so I'm going to take a pass this year.
Sunny Rhee	**[5:42]**	Is that everyone, then? I just want to make sure that we have enough snacks. Eva, have you contacted the caterers yet?
Eva Sanderson	**[5:43]**	I called a couple of different places, but only Four-Leaf Catering offers vegan options.
Sunny Rhee	**[5:44]**	Why don't we give them a try, then? I think a couple of people here are vegans.
Holly Johnson	**[5:45]**	I don't normally like to advertise my eating preferences, but I would love to have vegan options this time.
Eva Sanderson	**[5:46]**	I agree. I think it would make everything more interesting. I'm thinking of trying to go vegan myself and this would be a good first step for me.
Holly Johnson	**[5:47]**	Well, it's not easy, but I'll be there to support you.
Eva Sanderson	**[5:47]**	Thanks. I'll order our platters from the caterers, then.
Angelo Smith	**[5:48]**	But make sure there are some meat dishes for us meat-lovers.
Eva Sanderson	**[5:49]**	Of course. I've emailed everyone our tentative menu and most of you seem to like the choices.
Sunny Rhee	**[5:50]**	Don't forget to email the caterers about the security clearance they'll need to enter the building.
Eva Sanderson	**[5:51]**	I'll work on that now.

162. What is the discussion mainly about?

(A) Those who can't attend a party
(B) The best caterers
(C) Becoming a vegan
(D) Ordering food for a party

NEW

163. At 5:39, what does Patrick Stone mean by "I'm going to take a pass this year"?

(A) He'll stop by for a short time.
(B) He'll decline this time.
(C) He'll be late.
(D) He wants to get a free pass.

164. What is mentioned about Four-Leaf Catering?

(A) It offers vegan food.
(B) It has only vegan options.
(C) It has catered previous office parties.
(D) It specializes in special orders.

165. What will Eva Sanderson most likely do next?

(A) Work on the menu
(B) Contact the caterers
(C) Confirm a meeting
(D) Order some lunch

Questions 166-168 refer to the following contract.

Midas Touch Internet Provider

Contract Summary

Date: March 22

Customer: Ms. Tanya Sullivan
Address: 345 Oak Street, Parsons, WY 54055
Purchase Date: March 13

Services Purchased:

Item	Price
Midas Internet multimedia package – Download speed of 100 Mbps – 32 free movie channels – Video streaming services of the five latest movies every month	$40.00/month
Security Guard virus protection	$5.00/month
Modem and router rental service	$3.00/month
Subtotal	$48.00/month
Tax	$3.45/month
Total	$51.45/month

Just call us at 341-555-6487 and our technician will come to your house to take care of everything that you need to connect to the Internet via the modem and router.

166. What did Ms. Sullivan do on March 13?

(A) She purchased a home security system.
(B) She returned a product.
(C) She signed up for Internet service.
(D) She made an appointment.

167. What is suggested about Ms. Sullivan?

(A) She teaches a computer skills class.
(B) She had trouble installing some software.
(C) She will have access to movies.
(D) She has recently moved into her home.

168. What is indicated about Midas Touch Internet Provider?

(A) It dispatches its employees for installation work.
(B) It sells computer accessories.
(C) Its headquarters are located in Parsons.
(D) It offers website developing services.

GO ON TO THE NEXT PAGE

Questions 169-171 refer to the following article.

April 2—Repairs will begin next Friday on the historic Marion Hall in downtown Marion. In its heyday, Marion Hall was a popular downtown destination for residents to dance, enjoy live music, and watch movies. However, it has lost its popularity gradually since the multiplex building was completed on Henson Street four years ago.

After all of the necessary repairs have been made to Marion Hall, city officials will begin to invite various performers including famous theater companies, musicians, comedians, and speakers to the newly renovated theater. "We hope Marion Hall can serve as a new cultural center here in Marion," says Mayor Greg Fields.

The revitalization of Marion Hall is part of a larger project to enhance the public facilities in Marion. On April 29, the Marion Children's Park, which features a baseball field as well as several playgrounds, is scheduled to have its grand reopening.

169. What is suggested about Marion?

(A) It will restore an old building soon.
(B) It has closed a park for repairs.
(C) It is planning a music festival.
(D) Its population is decreasing.

170. What is the purpose of Marion Hall?

(A) To serve as a play center for children
(B) To hold city council meetings
(C) To offer public education classes
(D) To host cultural events

171. What will happen in April?

(A) A famous speaker will give a presentation.
(B) A new mayor will be elected.
(C) Some improved public facilities will open.
(D) A new play will be performed.

Questions 172-175 refer to the following article from a company newsletter.

As I'm sure you're aware, this week we must decide if we want to continue working with CC Wheel Delivery. As we learned at yesterday's meeting, they are being sued for the accident that happened last week. – [1] – We all agreed that the whole company shouldn't be held liable for the mistakes of a few careless workers, but that was a conversation we had before we had really thought about the ramifications of our decision. – [2] – Unfortunately, the situation is escalating and there is about to be a lot of bad press. – [3] – It's true that many of them are our friends, but we must protect our company. We can't handle anything that might affect our sales.

For the last four months we've been operating with a very thin margin for error. If our sales drop even slightly, it could be disastrous. So I'm suggesting that, as a means of protecting ourselves from any negative backlash, we cut our ties with CC Wheel Delivery. Maybe later, if they're able to rehabilitate their name, we'll work with them again. – [4] – I propose we vote one more time on whether or not to work with them.

172. What is true about CC Wheel Delivery?

(A) A contract of theirs has just been canceled.
(B) Legal action is being taking against them.
(C) Their president has just stepped down.
(D) Two of their trucks were in an accident.

173. What is indicated about the company that the writer works for?

(A) It is financially insecure.
(B) It has recently been created.
(C) It will be closing.
(D) It is a delivery company.

174. Why does the writer wish to stop working with CC Wheel Delivery?

(A) To protect his company from financial damage
(B) To cut production costs over the next four months
(C) To lower the price of an individual product
(D) To avoid legal trouble in the future

NEW

175. In which of the places marked [1], [2], [3], and [4] does this sentence belong?

"Yes, we've worked with them for a long time."

(A) [1]
(B) [2]
(C) [3]
(D) [4]

GO ON TO THE NEXT PAGE

Questions 176-180 refer to the following article and email.

September 21—What is the secret to delicious home-cooked meals? Kimberly Lee, host of the *My Home Cooking* television show and owner of her own restaurant chain, seems to know all the secrets. Her show has been on the air for over two years, and now she has a devoted group of followers around the country. When she sat down for an interview with us, she said that fresh vegetables and local produce are the key to cooking healthy and tasty food.

Ms. Lee is scheduled to publish her very first cookbook near the end of the month. The book is entitled *Kimberly Lee's My Home Cooking*, and it provides easy-to-follow recipes that can be made in less than 30 minutes. Over 40,000 copies have already been pre-ordered.

Ms. Lee says that the final page of the book will include a detachable fan club membership form. Those who fill the form out and send it in to the provided address will receive a monthly newsletter and exclusive recipes available only to those in the fan club. Fan club members will also receive a password that allows access to the *My Home Cooking* website.

To: Kimberly Lee <kimberlylee@kimberlylee.com>
From: Suzie Sanders <suziesanders@kimberlylee.com>
Date: October 12
Subject: Update

Dear Ms. Lee,

Great news! I'm happy to report that not only has your book been selling well, but the number of new members joining the fan club has been increasing drastically since it was published. I'm certain that the article in the newspaper helped generate considerable publicity for your book.

Also, we have received a lot of feedback from new members expressing a desire for more recipes for cakes, cookies, and candies to be featured in next month's newsletter. I think it would be a good idea to satisfy their requests this time.

Sincerely,

Suzie Sanders
Publicity Coordinator

176. What is the main purpose of the article?

(A) To publicize an upcoming book
(B) To provide advice for professional chefs
(C) To advertise a new restaurant
(D) To describe a television show

177. According to Ms. Lee, what is the secret to successful cooking?

(A) Following a recipe book
(B) Using quality ingredients
(C) Balancing all the flavors
(D) Choosing the correct spices

178. What is the thing one has to do in order to become a fan club member?

(A) Access a website
(B) Call a hotline
(C) Visit Ms. Lee's restaurant
(D) Purchase a book

179. In the email, what does Suzie Sanders say about the article?

(A) It was written by a famous journalist.
(B) It was featured on a popular cooking website.
(C) It helped increase fan club membership.
(D) It contained excerpts from Ms. Lee's book.

180. What is suggested about next month's newsletter?

(A) It will be mailed behind schedule.
(B) It will feature a column about healthy eating habits.
(C) It will contain an article on desserts.
(D) It will include a copy of Ms. Lee's book.

GO ON TO THE NEXT PAGE

Questions 181-185 refer to the following emails.

From: Stacey Watkins <staceywatkins@titus.com>
To: Ann Rose <annrose@putkincomp.com>
Subject: Conference of Bank Managers
Date: February 12

Dear Ms. Rose,

You recently contacted us about using our conference center again this year to host your annual conference of bank managers. This year we have updated our conference room with new projectors and more comfortable seating. We will be providing shuttle buses from the airport and a premium buffet in the dining hall as well as an Internet café where guests can use computers or print documents at no cost. For your convenience, we will also be providing useful supplies such as flip charts, 10-foot whiteboards, and projector screens.

Once you decide on a date, we ask that you please make a down payment of $1,000 as soon as we've confirmed that it is available. The remaining balance should be paid upon your arrival. We also ask that, as the organizer of the event, you arrive at the conference center one day before the conference begins. That way, any unforeseen issues can be taken care of beforehand.

We appreciate your doing business with the Titus Conference Center once again. We are looking forward to providing you with the best service possible.

Stacey Watkins, Director

From: Ann Rose <annrose@putkincomp.com>
To: Stacey Watkins <staceywatkins@titus.com>
Subject: RE: Conference of Bank Managers
Date: February 16

Dear Ms. Watkins,

I am also pleased to be working with you again this year. We would like to reserve your conference space for the weekend of August 15 to 16. The down payment will be handled by our financial department. I will have one of the employees contact you soon.

Also, there is one thing that I would like to ask of you. Last year, some of our attendees were disappointed because the dining hall didn't offer enough vegetarian options. I hope this issue can be dealt with in advance this year.

Thank you,

Ann Rose
Organizer, Annual Conference of Bank Managers

181. What is indicated about the Titus Conference Center?

(A) It recently improved its facilities.
(B) It demands full payment at the time of reservation.
(C) It is located next to an international airport.
(D) It currently has no vacancies for the month of August.

182. What is NOT mentioned as a benefit of using the Titus Conference Center?

(A) Convenient transportation
(B) Laptop rental services
(C) A printing service
(D) Presentation supplies

183. When will Ms. Rose most likely arrive at the Titus Conference Center?

(A) On August 7
(B) On August 14
(C) On August 15
(D) On August 16

184. What is the main purpose of the second email?

(A) To reserve tickets for an upcoming conference
(B) To request help in making a payment
(C) To confirm a reservation
(D) To inquire about payment options

185. What does Ms. Rose suggest about the Titus Conference Center?

(A) This will be her first time working with it.
(B) It will relocate in August.
(C) It has several locations across the country.
(D) It failed to satisfy some guests last year.

GO ON TO THE NEXT PAGE

Questions 186-190 refer to the following emails and memorandum.

To: John Masterson <jmasterson@masterstrokeindustries.com>
From: Carl Ennens <cennens@gmail.com>
Date: December 30
Subject: Internship

Dear Mr. Masterson,

My name is Carl Ennens and I am entering my final year at Evergreen State College. I am majoring in industrial engineering here, and my liquid dynamics professor, Dr. Alcobar, recommended Master Stroke Industries for a possible internship opportunity. Your company is recognized as a leader in flow research. If you would be willing to accept an intern for the coming spring semester, I could give you up to 15 hours per week of work, provided that you are able to write some performance evaluations that I can turn in to Dr. Alcobar for credit. Thank you for your consideration, and if you would like to see my transcript, I would be happy to forward it to you.

All the best,

Carl Ennens

To: Carl Ennens <cennens@gmail.com>
From: John Masterson <jmasterson@masterstrokeindustries.com>
Date: December 31
Subject: RE: Internship

Dear Carl,

I appreciate your interest in interning with us here at Master Stroke Industries. We have not accepted a lot of interns in the past, but I know Dr. Alcobar personally, and if he recommended that you contact us, he must have faith in your ability. I think we should set up an interview at our headquarters downtown on Holly Street. We can get to know each other a bit over some coffee and I will show you around our facilities. Don't worry about your transcripts; like I said, If Dr. Alcobar thinks you'd be a good fit, I'll trust his judgment. How about this coming Friday at 10 A.M.?

Looking forward to meeting you,

John Masterson

CEO, Master Stroke Industries

Memorandum To Master Stroke Industries Employees

This spring Master Stroke Industries will have an intern assisting us with everything from making coffee to solving complex equations. Carl Ennens is a student at the state college here and the University and has kindly offered his services in exchange for a piece of our operational knowledge. Please treat him with respect and don't be afraid to use him for an extra pair of hands or eyes or an opinion should you need it. And I do hear he makes a good cup of coffee!

186. What is indicated about Carl Ennens?

(A) He is a senior in high school.
(B) He will be a junior in college.
(C) He will graduate in two years.
(D) He will be a senior in college.

187. What is indicated about Dr. Alcobar?

(A) Nobody knows who he is.
(B) People do not appreciate his opinion.
(C) He is respected by John Masterson.
(D) He has done a lot of prominent research.

188. In the second email, the term "headquarters" in the fourth line is closest in meaning to:

(A) basement
(B) main office
(C) warehouse
(D) distribution center

189. According to the memorandum, what will Carl Ennens be expected to do?

(A) Research fluid dynamics
(B) Cook
(C) Help wherever he is needed
(D) Watch and learn

190. What position does John Masterson have in the company?

(A) Chief Executive Officer
(B) Chief Financial Officer
(C) Sales Executive
(D) Owner

GO ON TO THE NEXT PAGE

NEW Questions 191-195 refer to the following article, advertisement, and email.

Brand-X Coming to Town

March 9 – Popular Danish skin care company Brand-X is finally launching its best-selling line in America. The 88-year-old company is Denmark's leading skin-care brand and its top-selling cream, Xtreme 7, has been Europe's most popular facial cream for over 10 years. Though Americans may not have had access to these creams before, the brand is already generating much excitement.

Dermatologist Dr. Francis Keenan explains, "Tests have shown that Xtreme 7 dramatically reduces the fine lines around the eye area and laugh lines after only 30 days of use, but the price of the cream is only a fraction of what department store brands sell for. I'll definitely recommend this cream to my clients."

"People have been asking about Xtreme 7, but the product hasn't even arrived yet!" added Susan Chan, an employee at a beauty counter. "People are already calling in to pre-order."

A spokesperson for the company explained that Brand-X is making moves to expand into the North American and Asian markets. For now, only the company's best-selling line will be available outside of Europe (starting next month), but within a year more products will be available.

Brand-X Positions at American Headquarters in Westminster, California

Don't miss your chance to work in an exciting career in skin care and beauty with Brand-X. Eighty administrative and customer service positions are available with no experience necessary. Applicants must have strong communication and computer skills. Knowledge of both English and Spanish is preferred but not essential. Applicants with experience in cosmetics, dermatology, or marketing may qualify for management positions. Please visit our website at www.brandx.com/jobs for more information. Application forms must be sent in before March 20th. Interviews will take place at the Hillway Building at 143 Garden Road. Be sure to bring your résumé and reference letters.

To	Professor David Mills
From	Jacqueline O'Hare
Date	March 28
Subject	job

Dear Professor Mills,

Thank you so much for the reference letter you wrote for me. I was recently hired by Brand-X, and my orientation begins next Wednesday at 10 A.M. Unfortunately, we have our statistics test at that time. Is there any way that I can take a make-up test at a different time or hand in another assignment in place of the test? The orientation is mandatory, and I don't want to disappoint my new employers. The job should not have any impact on my school work otherwise. I appreciate your kind consideration in this matter.

Sincerely,

Jacqueline O'Hare

191. What does Dr. Keenan suggest about Xtreme 7?

(A) It is the most effective cream on the market.
(B) It is worth the high price.
(C) It is both effective and cheap.
(D) It is the only cream that a doctor would recommend.

192. What is suggested about Brand-X?

(A) Its products are currently only available in Europe.
(B) It is Europe's most popular brand.
(C) It is a luxury skin-care company.
(D) It was first launched 10 years ago.

193. According to the article, what does Brand-X plan to do?

(A) Sell more products in Europe
(B) Expand outside of Europe
(C) Develop a makeup line
(D) Build a factory in America

194. What is indicated in the advertisement?

(A) None of the positions requires previous work experience.
(B) Applicants must be bilingual.
(C) Experience in certain fields can lead to management positions.
(D) The available positions are only temporary.

195. For what position was Jacqueline most likely hired?

(A) Management
(B) Human Resource
(C) Marketing
(D) Customer Service

GO ON TO THE NEXT PAGE

NEW **Questions 196-200** refer to the following emails and schedule.

To: Bill Johnson<bj@action.net>
From: Laurie Wheeler<lwheeler@zipnet.com>
Date: October 11
Subject: Reservation info

Dear Mr. Johnson,

I am writing to you on behalf of the company I work for, Competitive Excellence. We specialize in productivity and efficiency training for corporations and small businesses. Lately our staff has been suffering from low morale, and while searching the Internet for solutions I came across your website www.action.net. I am interested in hearing more about the motivational speaking that you do. Specifically, could you tell me if your speeches are religious in nature? We have a diverse staff, and I am looking for something secular. Please write me back with an overview of what you do and what your presentation rates are.

Laurie Wheeler,

Managing Director, Competitive Excellence

To: Laurie Wheeler<lwheeler@zipnet.com>
From: Bill Johnson<bj@action.net>
Date: October 13
Subject: RE: Reservation info

Dear Ms. Wheeler,

Thank you so much for your interest in Action. I am happy to answer your questions and provide you with a full breakdown of what we can do for you, your team, and your company. To begin with, all of our talks are secular, though not necessarily free from the concept of spirituality. Our professional speakers seek to motivate people to look internally to find their own spirit and help it rise. Morale, after all, is an intangible but essential aspect of an effective team. Please refer to the topic list and pricing guide I have attached to this email. Once you have chosen a theme, speaker, and appropriate class size for your company, please send me a follow-up email to schedule your event.

Bill Johnson,
Action Coordinator

Action Course Topics and Price Guide

Theme	Location	Speaker	Class Size	Duration	Price
Stay in the Moment!	On-Site	Jim Grey	15-20	3 hours	$450
New You Every Day	Off-Site	Darlene Woodward	20-25	3 hours	$400
Stay Positive for the Team!	Off-Site	Jeff Boxer	15-30	3 hours	$400
Blessed Are We All	Off-Site	John Brown	20-30	4 hours	$500

196. How did Laurie Wheeler learn about Action?

(A) From a friend
(B) Through a client
(C) In a newspaper
(D) On the Internet

197. What is indicated about Action?

(A) They do not promote a religion.
(B) They are Christian.
(C) They are just building their brand.
(D) They are moving to a new location.

198. According to the graphic, what is NOT an option for customers?

(A) Off-site courses
(B) Classes for 10
(C) A four-hour course
(D) Courses to build positivity

199. What course will Laurie Wheeler likely sign her staff up for?

(A) Stay in the Moment!
(B) New You Every Day
(C) Stay Positive for the Team!
(D) Blessed are We All

200. What is indicated about Competitive Excellence?

(A) They are struggling financially.
(B) The mood in their office is not good.
(C) They are having a booming year of sales.
(D) They want to change their business focus.

Stop! This is the end of the test. If you finish before time is called, you may go back to Parts 5, 6, and 7 and check your work.

ACTUAL TEST 09

READING TEST

In the Reading test, you will read a variety of texts and answer several different types of reading comprehension questions. The entire Reading test will last 75 minutes. There are three parts, and directions are given for each part. You are encouraged to answer as many questions as possible within the time allowed.

You must mark your answers on the separate answer sheet. Do not write your answers in your test book.

PART 5

Directions: A word or phrase is missing in each of the sentences below. Four answer choices are given below each sentence. Select the best answer to complete the sentence. Then mark the letter (A), (B), (C), or (D) on your answer sheet.

101. The projector borrowed by Ms. Reid is ------- back at the IT department by five o'clock.

(A) due
(B) set
(C) paid
(D) prompt

102. Now that the annual conference is over, the planning committee will hold meetings ------- often.

(A) below
(B) less
(C) decreased
(D) lower

103. Before you distribute the report, ask Ms. Burns to make sure that ------- contains all the necessary information.

(A) them
(B) our
(C) her
(D) it

104. According to consumers, using the new website is no ------- than calling the help center directly.

(A) easily
(B) easy
(C) easiest
(D) easier

105. Anyone who participates ------- the city's annual baking competition will receive a coupon from Fresh Supermarket.

(A) to
(B) beside
(C) in
(D) among

106. City officials are still debating Irving Enterprises' request ------- the outdated building.

(A) demolishes
(B) have demolished
(C) to demolish
(D) demolished

107. Heron Glassworks ------- student groups of all ages for weekday tours of its warehouse and production floor.

(A) conveys
(B) preserves
(C) encloses
(D) welcomes

108. To combat mental illness, the clinic will take a more comprehensive ------- than it has in the past.

(A) approachably
(B) approached
(C) approach
(D) approachable

109. Brandy can withdraw money at any Salis Bank branch, but she usually visits the ------- one.

(A) closing
(B) closely
(C) closure
(D) closest

110. As a ------- for signing contracts with a lot of new clients, Mr. Skinner was given additional vacation days.

(A) reward
(B) progress
(C) solution
(D) routine

111. Please seat yourselves according to the ------- name cards that have been placed on each table.

(A) personalizes
(B) personalizing
(C) personalize
(D) personalized

112. The memo sent out by Mr. Lee addressed a few ------- that were discovered during the quarterly inspection.

(A) issuing
(B) issue
(C) issues
(D) issued

113. Many voters in this city are uninterested in the issues, and only about 15% of them are ------- active.

(A) politically
(B) political
(C) politics
(D) politician

114. This year's award winner, Cheryl Garner, taught basic first aid skills to students and adults ------- the region.

(A) between
(B) throughout
(C) during
(D) toward

115. -------, the cabin will be rented for the entire month, but the owner will agree to four weekly rentals instead.

(A) Reluctantly
(B) Absolutely
(C) Ideally
(D) Mutually

116. The non-profit organization released several documents to the press ------- its largest donors and how much they had contributed.

(A) detailed
(B) detail
(C) details
(D) detailing

GO ON TO THE NEXT PAGE

117. No passengers are allowed to board ------- the aircraft's door has been closed.

(A) that
(B) despite
(C) once
(D) rather

118. A government ------- will visit the site to speak with the protesters directly and seek a resolution.

(A) representative
(B) representation
(C) represent
(D) represented

119. An extensive ------- conducted by Ivanex Communications revealed that Internet speed was one of the most important factors for consumers.

(A) inventory
(B) strategy
(C) coverage
(D) survey

120. Mr. Denson wanted to purchase a special edition gold-plated watch from Utica Watches, but there were ------- left.

(A) none
(B) nothing
(C) something
(D) some

121. Ms. May reminded us that the agreement was only ------- as it had not been approved yet.

(A) perishable
(B) imperative
(C) accustomed
(D) tentative

122. Following the restoration project, the lobby of the historical Kirkwood Hotel looked ------- like it originally had.

(A) remarkably
(B) remarking
(C) remark
(D) remarked

123. ------- the right environmental conditions, this tree will yield fresh fruit for most of the year.

(A) With
(B) About
(C) On
(D) As

124. One of the interns ------- that the logo on the second page of the sales report was upside down.

(A) looked after
(B) accounted for
(C) pointed out
(D) came across

125. ------- the parking lot is closed, both employees and customers will have to park on the street.

(A) As if
(B) Until
(C) So that
(D) While

126. If the new athletic shoes do well in smaller test markets, their nationwide launch could be -------.

(A) convinced
(B) accelerated
(C) directed
(D) circulated

127. The city hosted an ------- fireworks display to celebrate the 100th anniversary of its founding.

(A) impressive
(B) impress
(C) impression
(D) impressively

128. After investing heavily in Internet marketing campaigns, Bailey Coffee increased its annual profits ------- 15 percent.

(A) by
(B) among
(C) between
(D) on

129. The receptionists ------- change the artwork in the clinic's waiting room and rearrange the layout of the furniture.

(A) periodically
(B) relatively
(C) tightly
(D) narrowly

130. The policy requiring businesses to provide medical insurance applies only to those ------- more than 25 people.

(A) employs
(B) employ
(C) employed
(D) employing

GO ON TO THE NEXT PAGE

PART 6

Directions: Read the texts that follow. A word, phrase, or sentence is missing in parts of each text. Four answer choices for each question are given below the text. Select the best answer to complete the text. Then mark the letter (A), (B), (C), or (D) on your answer sheet.

Questions 131-134 refer to the following notice.

Beverly Boutique: Sales Assistant Position

Our boutique is looking for enthusiastic candidates for a sales assistant position. ------- **131.** Previous experience in a similar position is preferred, but not necessary. Organizational skills are a must, as is some experience with computers. Most of all, we need someone who is personable, can make customers feel ------- **132.**, and is passionate about fashion. Duties will include serving customers, taking inventory, and minor jobs around the boutique such as sweeping the floor and locking the doors at closing time. Payment is by sales commission, which gives employees more ------- **133.** to provide our customers with the very best service they can. Hours will be flexible. For more information, please visit our website.

If you ------- **134.** in the position, please send your résumé to Rita at rlan@bboutique.com.

NEW

131. (A) Our boutique is a leader in trendy fashions.
(B) Hurry before the promotion ends.
(C) Candidates need to be friendly and able to communicate with customers in all kinds of situations.
(D) Come visit our store to see what our business is about.

132. (A) comfortable
(B) appropriate
(C) neglected
(D) convenient

133. (A) influence
(B) incentive
(C) insistence
(D) consideration

134. (A) be interesting
(B) were interesting
(C) interest
(D) are interested

Questions 135-138 refer to the following advertisement.

Handy Maids Home Service

Call us at 555-1244

Handy Maids Home Service ------- (135.) professional cleaning services for your business or home. We steam vacuum carpeted areas, polish hardwood flooring, wipe away all traces of dust and dirt in hard-to-reach areas, and clean out clutter. Our ------- (136.) service is second to none in the Tri-State Area. We provide one-day service after giving an estimate. ------- (137.), we provide weekly and monthly services for customers who request them.

The cleaning products we use are environmentally friendly and pet- and child-safe. ------- (138.) Please visit our website at www.handymaids.com or call us for more information.

135. (A) provide
(B) provides
(C) provided
(D) providing

136. (A) unusual
(B) peculiar
(C) best
(D) exceptional

137. (A) In addition
(B) Because
(C) On the other hand
(D) As a result

NEW

138. (A) We make sure that your pets and children don't go near the chemicals.
(B) In fact, we aim to make your home or business a safe and clean place without the use of harsh chemicals.
(C) Our all-natural cleaning agents may not be as effective as chemicals, but they are safe.
(D) Pets and children will be asked to leave the premises during cleaning.

GO ON TO THE NEXT PAGE →

Questions 139-142 refer to the following letter.

October 09

Bob Prosser

342 Winkler Ave

Fairbanks, AK 99705

Dear Mr. Prosser,

The information that you ------- (139.) about changes to the hunting permit scheme is enclosed. Please note that each permit you require must be applied for separately. When filling out your application(s), you must print all answers clearly in block letters with a black or blue pen. Please do not use cursive script, print only. Each application ------- (140.) enclosed in its own envelope and received before the applicable deadline. ------- (141.). Because of this, you must plan your submission(s) in a timely fashion to make sure that you receive your permit(s) while the applicable season is still open. I hope that the information ------- (142.) answers all of your questions. Take care and happy hunting.

Sincerely,

Shirley Horn, Executive Secretary

Department of Wildlife

Fairbanks, AK 99701

139. (A) provided
(B) provide
(C) request
(D) requested

140. (A) won't be
(B) can be
(C) must be
(D) couldn't be

NEW

141. (A) Once received, applications can take up to five weeks to process.
(B) Applications are never approved before the season is over.
(C) Sometimes applications get lost.
(D) Never make an application in person.

142. (A) enclose
(B) enclosing
(C) encloses
(D) enclosed

Questions 143-146 refer to the following notice.

Date: August 22

To: All Sales Team Members

From: Melinda Lackey, Sales Manager

Subject: Rental Policy

For some ------- (143.) now we have allowed sales reps to pay for their car rentals up front with their personal cards or cash, and then be reimbursed later. This is no longer our policy, and has not been our policy for over two months now. As of June 15th, all payments for rentals were supposed to have ------- (144.) with the company card that was assigned to you. Larry in accounting has informed me that he has received six separate reimbursement forms since then. I have gone ahead and allowed him to process those six forms. ------- (145.) I'm sorry for the ------- (146.) tone of this message, but everyone was asked to do this back in June. If you have any questions, please contact me directly.

143. (A) distances
(B) place
(C) event
(D) time

144. (A) making
(B) to be made
(C) makes
(D) been made

NEW

145. (A) Only Fonitna Rental should be used to book cars in the future.
(B) As of tomorrow, however, no one will be reimbursed for car rentals anymore.
(C) He will redesign the form by the beginning of next week.
(D) All sales reps are required to turn in their cards as soon as possible.

146. (A) overreaching
(B) gracious
(C) benevolent
(D) harsh

GO ON TO THE NEXT PAGE

PART 7

Directions: In this part you will read a selection of texts, such as magazine and newspaper articles, emails, and instant messages. Each text or set of texts is followed by several questions. Select the best answer for each question and mark the letter (A), (B), (C), or (D) on your answer sheet.

Questions 147-148 refer to the following flyer.

Jay Furniture

3105 Michigan Avenue, Chicago, IL 60611

Black Friday Weekend Sale
November 29 to December 1

Tables—20% off
Couches—30% off
Mattresses—20% to 50% off
Desks and Chairs—25% to 50% off

- During the sale, any customer who purchases over $500 worth of merchandise will receive a coupon for an extra 5% off any purchase during our Christmas sale. Coupons will be valid from December 9 to December 28.
- Mention the code BLKFRI for an additional $10 off any table or mattress during the sale.

Note: Jay Furniture will be closed the day before the weekend sale to prepare for it. Doors will open at 9:00 a.m. on November 29.

147. What is the purpose of the flyer?

(A) To announce the opening of a store
(B) To advertise a sale on furniture
(C) To introduce new products
(D) To inform customers of a business's relocation

148. When will the store be closed?

(A) On November 28
(B) On November 29
(C) On November 30
(D) On December 9

Questions 149-150 refer to the following text message chain.

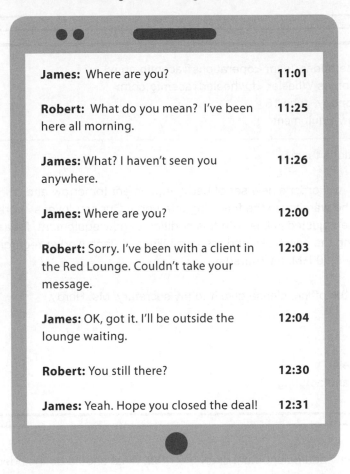

James: Where are you?	**11:01**
Robert: What do you mean? I've been here all morning.	**11:25**
James: What? I haven't seen you anywhere.	**11:26**
James: Where are you?	**12:00**
Robert: Sorry. I've been with a client in the Red Lounge. Couldn't take your message.	**12:03**
James: OK, got it. I'll be outside the lounge waiting.	**12:04**
Robert: You still there?	**12:30**
James: Yeah. Hope you closed the deal!	**12:31**

149. Why does James most likely say, "Hope you closed the deal!"?

(A) He thinks there will be a bonus.
(B) He has been waiting a long time.
(C) He loves the Red Lounge.
(D) There are too many deals open.

150. What can be inferred by the length of time between James's messages and Robert's responses?

(A) Robert isn't interested in James.
(B) Robert wants time to himself.
(C) Robert's phone has died.
(D) Robert cannot check his phone all the time.

GO ON TO THE NEXT PAGE

Questions 151-152 refer to the following email.

To: Operations Team <operations@acemfg.com>
From: Thomas Wheeler <t.wheeler@acemfg.com>
Date: Monday, June 16
Subject: New Equipment

To the operations team,

The company will order a new set of heavy equipment tomorrow and it will be delivered to the warehouse the following afternoon. Our employees' work schedules will have to be adjusted in line with this addition of new equipment. Please submit a report stating the new tasks and responsibilities of each worker regarding this equipment by 5:00 P.M. on Thursday.

If I am not in the office, please give it to my secretary, Ms. Hardy.

Thanks,

Thomas Wheeler
Director of Manufacturing

151. When will the new equipment most likely arrive at the warehouse?

(A) On Monday
(B) On Tuesday
(C) On Wednesday
(D) On Thursday

152. What should be included in the report?

(A) Workers' contact information
(B) Workers' assignments
(C) Workers' résumés
(D) Workers' suggestions

Questions 153-154 refer to the following memo.

To: R&D Department
From: Rick Campbell, Director of R&D
Subject: Change in Staff
Date: Tuesday, April 4, 3:40 P.M.

I am writing to share news with you regarding recent changes in the research and development office. Starting April 7, Bob Denkle will be our new project manager in the research and development department. He has just completed a month-long training session and will replace Benjamin Palmer by the end of the week.

Mike Garcia, the HR director, will post an announcement of several openings in different departments by next week. For those who wish to transfer into a different department within the company, now would be a good time to apply.

Please congratulate Benjamin Palmer, who will transition into a new position at Ion Industries, and welcome Bob Denkle as he joins our department.

153. What is expected to happen by next week?

(A) A new department will be formed.
(B) Job offers will be announced.
(C) An interview will be conducted.
(D) A training session will take place.

154. Who is leaving the company?

(A) Bob Denkle
(B) Mike Garcia
(C) Rick Campbell
(D) Benjamin Palmer

ACTUAL TEST 09

GO ON TO THE NEXT PAGE

Questions 155-157 refer to the following article.

Re-Fit Closing Stores

February 9 – Neway Group has announced that 80 Re-Fit stores will be closing down around the country in the next six months, with 100 more to follow within the year. – [1] – However, the past ten years have seen a steady decline in sales as consumers have turned to other clothing retailers such as Zanas and HRM. – [2] – "I don't know. I just found the clothing to be outdated," says a former customer. "They should have updated the styles and offered non-sporty options."

CEO Derrick Greenwich agrees. "We focused so much on particular styles of sportswear that we lost sight of the changing tastes of consumers. We're working on restructuring the company and offering consumers what they want. We'll come back bigger than ever." – [3] –

An internal review of the losses will continue to be conducted as nervous shareholders consider their next moves. – [4] – Neway is hoping that a good number of the Re-Fit stores will remain in operation as the company struggles to reinvent its brand.

155. What is indicated about the Re-Fit brand?

(A) Its popularity has dropped dramatically.
(B) It specializes in sports gear.
(C) The CEO is renaming the company.
(D) The brand has a 100-year history.

156. The phrase "lost sight of" in the second paragraph is closest in meaning to:

(A) restricted
(B) were not blinded by
(C) ignored
(D) selected

NEW

157. In which of the positions marked [1], [2], [3], and [4] does the following sentence belong?

"The clothing store, best known for its affordable but trendy sportswear, was very popular in the 1990s and early 2000s."

(A) [1]
(B) [2]
(C) [3]
(D) [4]

Questions 158-160 refer to the following table of contents from a booklet.

CONTENTS

9 *Easy Snacks* Donald Cohen offers recipes that are suitable for those who are always on the move.	26 *Wish You Were Here* Rebecca Barajas shares her pictures from her amazing trip to New Zealand.
14 *The Perfect Resort* Melissa Green discusses the features of the world's top 10 resorts.	30 *Delicious Diners* Barry Eason shares his tasty experiences on the road.
19 *Passport Guide* Henry Carroll shows you how to apply for a passport in five easy steps.	33 *On a Budget* Edward Boyd shares tips on how to save money on your next trip.
23 *Safety First* Tricia Oldham discusses basic first aid for first-time travelers.	35 *Light My Way* Reviews of the most popular guidebooks

158. What is the focus of the booklet?

(A) Food
(B) Transportation
(C) The environment
(D) Travel

159. Where in the booklet would pictures most likely be found?

(A) On page 9
(B) On page 19
(C) On page 26
(D) On page 30

160. According to the table of contents, who writes about spending less money?

(A) Ms. Green
(B) Mr. Carroll
(C) Mr. Eason
(D) Mr. Boyd

ACTUAL TEST 09

GO ON TO THE NEXT PAGE

Questions 161-164 refer to the following online chat discussion.

Ginger Lin	**[4:59]**	Just a reminder to everyone to please clear your desks and shut down all electronic devices before you leave today. The floors will be polished and cleaned over the weekend.
Dimitri Roberts	**[5:00]**	Should we lock all the cabinets and drawers as well?
Ginger Lin	**[5:01]**	Yes. Please make sure that when the furniture is moved around, nothing falls out.
Dimitri Roberts	**[5:02]**	I'll make sure that everything is secure and locked before I leave.
Janet Leigh	**[5:03]**	Ginger, I've finished our budget reports. I'll have copies emailed to you soon before I send them off.
Ginger Lin	**[5:04]**	Thank you. And Lance, you'll have to reschedule your meeting with your client tomorrow.
Lance Sibley	**[5:04]**	I've already rescheduled our meeting for a week from Monday. And just to be on the safe side in case our offices are not ready by then, we'll be meeting at a café nearby.
Ginger Lin	**[5:05]**	All right. It looks like most things are in order. Let me know if I've missed anything.
Janet Leigh	**[5:06]**	Actually, not everyone has sent me his or her overtime hours yet. I was still able to confirm through the sign-up sheets, but I need everyone to confirm by email before I send the payment forms to the finance department.
Dimitri Roberts	**[5:07]**	Oops! That's me. I'll send you an email right now.
Karen Walker	**[5:07]**	Me, too.
Janet Leigh	**[5:08]**	Great. I can send the forms once I get your emails.

161. What will take place on Saturday and Sunday?

(A) An office party
(B) A meeting with clients
(C) A renovation
(D) A cleaning services

162. Who most likely is Ginger Lin?

(A) A secretary
(B) A manager
(C) A technician
(D) A security guard

NEW

163. At 5:04, what does Lance Sibley mean by "just to be on the safe side?"

(A) The offices may not be safe.
(B) The client may need help.
(C) Just as a precaution.
(D) He's been given a warning.

164. What will Janet Leigh most likely do next?

(A) Check her email
(B) Contact the finance department
(C) Call some employees
(D) Print out some reports

Questions 165-167 refer to the following job advertisement.

Helping Hands

8732 Bakersfield Avenue, Santa Clara, California

Regional Manager—Employment Opportunity

Helping Hands is dedicated to providing quality affordable housing for low-income individuals and families. For over 25 years, we have been acquiring multifamily communities and improving these properties to maintain their availability for those earning less than 50 percent of the areas' average incomes. Our properties are currently located in cities throughout the state of Texas including Austin, Dallas and Houston, and our plans are to expand and make more homes available to more people.

We are looking for someone to fill the position of regional manager. The new manager will be stationed in Austin and will supervise and evaluate the performance of on-site management to ensure that all properties are well maintained. The candidate must have a bachelor's degree or higher in a business or management field, a minimum of three years of experience in supervising personnel, and certain certificates (more details are on the application page).

Applications can be submitted in person Monday through Friday from 9:00 A.M. to 5:00 P.M. or by mail or email. They will be accepted only if they are received before 5:00 P.M. on October 14.

165. What is mentioned about Helping Hands?
(A) It offers services for senior citizens.
(B) It is committed to nature conservation.
(C) It is sponsored by the government.
(D) It supplies homes to a disadvantaged group.

166. Where will the successful candidate be required to work?
(A) In Santa Clara
(B) In Austin
(C) In Dallas
(D) In Houston

167. What is NOT suggested about the position?
(A) It includes supervision of our local staff.
(B) It requires an academic degree.
(C) It requires official documents.
(D) It is limited to California residents.

GO ON TO THE NEXT PAGE

Questions 168-171 refer to the following email.

To	cmason@centersports.com
From	sdixon@instaprinting.com
Date	November 3
Subject	Your Inquiry

Dear Mr. Mason,

We are responding to the inquiry you made through our website yesterday. Insta Printing promises to provide faster, cheaper, and more reliable service than any of our competitors in the area. We also guarantee that we will beat any price offered by a competitor.

As per your request, our company would be happy to help design and print jerseys for your soccer team. In addition to casual wear, we have plenty of experience producing athletic wear for sports teams and clubs.

Customers can choose from a variety of materials and printing methods. Our materials include denim, cotton, flannel, nylon, and many more, and we use several printing methods including screen printing, heat press, and direct-to-garment printing.

Please feel free to contact me directly at 712-555-9804 to discuss further details about working with Insta Printing. We look forward to working with you and helping your organization achieve its goals.

Sincerely,

Stephen Dixon
Client Relations Representative, Insta Printing

168. Why did Mr. Dixon send the email?

(A) To give a quote for a project
(B) To explain a new policy
(C) To persuade a client to agree to a deal
(D) To confirm a reservation

169. What does Mr. Mason want to do?

(A) Purchase a set of shirts
(B) Apply for a position
(C) Devise a new printing technique
(D) Expand his business internationally

170. What is mentioned about Insta Printing?

(A) It opened a second branch yesterday.
(B) It offers various production options.
(C) It only produces athletic wear.
(D) It sponsors a local soccer team.

171. The word "further" in paragraph 4, line 1, is closest in meaning to:

(A) urgent
(B) official
(C) additional
(D) careful

Questions 172-175 refer to the following information.

(Man) – [1] – I remember when Sergio Hernandez first came to work here at Trout & Lee. He was a young man of 30 with a heart and mind filled with ambition and drive. – [2] – It is that ambition and drive, along with a lot of integrity and intelligence, that have made him one of the most valuable players in the garment business, and us one of its most successful companies.

– [3] – I can't help but remember how emotional I was when I left the company to pursue a life of leisure last year. – [4] – The speech Sergio gave then helped me during the difficult transition into living without an office to go to or colleagues to be continually inspired by, and I hope the few humble words I've strung together will remind him of how well respected he is and what an astounding life he has lived as he goes through the same process. Please put your hands together for Mr. Sergio Hernandez.

172. What is implied about Mr. Hernandez?

(A) He is the CEO of Trout & Lee.
(B) He is receiving a promotion.
(C) He is transferring to a new department.
(D) He is retiring from the company.

173. What is indicated about Trout & Lee?

(A) It is an international company.
(B) It is a real estate company.
(C) It has manufacturing plants in the U.S.
(D) It has existed for many decades.

174. What is NOT mentioned about Mr. Hernandez?

(A) When he started working for the company
(B) The type of employee he is
(C) The type of industry he works in
(D) His position in the company

NEW

175. In which of the places marked [1], [2], [3], and [4] does this sentence belong?

"I feel it a great honor to be asked to speak about him here today."

(A) [1]
(B) [2]
(C) [3]
(D) [4]

GO ON TO THE NEXT PAGE

Questions 176-180 refer to the following invoice and letter.

Order # 23710

Maple Outdoor
387 Maple Street, York, WA

Date: May 6

ITEM	BRAND	1 Unit	PRICE
Hiking Boots	Nordic Heights	$149.95	$149.59
Camping Stove	Avalanche	$58.79	$58.79
Fuel Canister	Avalanche	$9.98	$19.96
Socks	Northern Wool	$12.85	$00.00 (Comp.)*
		Total: $228.34	

* We've included a free pair of socks to keep you warm on your next camping trip.

Thank you for being a loyal patron of Maple Outdoor for more than a year!

As always, if there is anything we can assist you with, don't hesitate to ask. If you are contacting us about a specific order, remember to give us the order number and your name.

Call us: (601) 478-2129 Email us: MapleOutdoor@zmail.com

To: Customer Service, Maple Outdoor
From: Shana Sandberg
Date: May 9
Subject: Delivery Issues

I received my order yesterday, and it wasn't what I had expected. I ordered an Avalanche camping stove, but I received an MT Elite stove instead. I'd like to receive my Avalanche stove as soon as possible, as I'm going on a camping trip next weekend. Do you think you can get it to me in time, or should I just come in and exchange the MT stove at your store? Please get back to me soon. I'll be waiting.

Thank you,

Shana Sandberg

176. What does Maple Outdoor mention about Ms. Sandberg's order?

(A) It will be delayed for up to a month.
(B) They have expedited it for free.
(C) It may not be returned if it is damaged through misuse.
(D) They have included a complimentary item with it.

177. How much does an Avalanche fuel canister cost?

(A) $58.79
(B) $9.98
(C) $19.96
(D) $12.85

178. Why did Ms. Sandberg write the email?

(A) To praise the service she received
(B) To request a monthly newsletter
(C) To ask if she could return an item
(D) To complain about an incorrect item

179. What requested information did Ms. Sandberg forget to include?

(A) Her name
(B) Her mailing address
(C) Her order number
(D) Her credit card number

180. What is true about Ms. Sandberg?

(A) She has shopped at Maple Outdoor before.
(B) She frequently goes camping.
(C) She didn't receive her hiking boots.
(D) She will be visiting the Maple Outdoor store soon.

GO ON TO THE NEXT PAGE

Questions 181-185 refer to the following notice and email.

Attention Passengers

Clinton Bus Lines

In response to customer feedback, Clinton Bus Lines will be expanding its bus routes connecting Texas to other metropolitan centers in the Southwest. Starting on May 1, the new routes listed below will take effect. In order to promote these new bus lines, we will be offering tickets at half price during the first week of operation. Improving your satisfaction is our main priority. To get more detailed information such as departure and arrival times, please visit our website at www.clintonbuses.com.

- **From Dallas Bus Terminal to Phoenix, Arizona Bus Terminal**
- **From Austin Bus Terminal to Santa Fe, New Mexico Bus Terminal**
- **From Fort Worth Bus Terminal to Denver, Colorado Bus Terminal**

To: erichanson@prplanning.com
From: dangregory@trentonlogistics.com
Date: April 27
Subject: Upcoming Visit

Dear Mr. Hanson,

I am currently finalizing all the details of my visit to your company's headquarters in Santa Fe. Thank you for inviting me down to take part in these negotiations. Please let me know what time I should arrive. Will the meeting begin after lunch like it did last time?

You won't need to pick up me up, as I have arranged for a cab to pick me up at the Santa Fe bus terminal. Fortunately, a new bus line has been established between where I live and your offices. This has made transit in the region considerably more convenient. There are now routes to Denver and Phoenix as well. Best of all, thanks to a bit of good luck, I will be able to buy my ticket to Santa Fe at half the usual price.

I can't wait to see you and your coworkers again.

Dan Gregory

181. In the notice, what are Clinton Bus Lines' passengers encouraged to do on the company's website?

(A) Reserve tickets in advance
(B) Check bus schedules
(C) Apply for membership
(D) Request discount coupons

182. What is indicated about Mr. Gregory's previous meeting with Mr. Hanson?

(A) It took place in Texas.
(B) It lasted an entire week.
(C) It commenced in the afternoon.
(D) It was canceled due to bad weather.

183. In the email, the word "transit" in paragraph 2, line 3 is closest in meaning to:

(A) participation
(B) transportation
(C) investigation
(D) collaboration

184. Where does Mr. Gregory most likely live?

(A) In Santa Fe
(B) In Austin
(C) In Dallas
(D) In Denver

185. When is the meeting scheduled to take place?

(A) Before April 24
(B) Between April 24 and April 30
(C) Between May 1 and May 7
(D) After May 7

GO ON TO THE NEXT PAGE

NEW **Questions 186-190** refer to the following emails.

To: Brian Petersen <bpetersen@atasteofclass.com>
From: Jason Hostrum <jhostrum@jhfurnishing.com>
Date: November 20th
Subject: Office Christmas Party

Dear Mr. Petersen,

I am looking to engage the services of your catering company, A Taste of Class, for our Christmas party at the end of the year. Ideally, we would like to have our event on Saturday, December 20th. I just have a few questions about your services. First, do you provide decorations? I really want this year's party to be a hit; it is my first time being responsible for it and I really want to impress the boss. Second, do you offer a wide range of vegetarian dishes? We have 12 vegetarians on our staff of 35, so it will be important to provide them with a full meal, not just appetizers. If you could get back to me with the answers to my questions and your availability on the 20th, I would greatly appreciate it.

Sincerely,

Jason Hostrum
Junior Secretary, Johnson Home Furnishing

To: Jason Hostrum <jhostrum@jhfurnishing.com>
From: Brian Petersen <bpetersen@atasteofclass.com>
Date: November 21st
Subject: RE: Office Christmas Party

Dear Mr. Hostrum,

I am delighted that you have contacted A Taste of Class to help make your Christmas party one to remember. Let me answer all of your questions and put your mind at ease. To begin with, we have one team left that can cater you on the 20th of December, so you are in luck! As far as the decorations are concerned, we have several different themes to choose from, so please visit our website at www.atasteofclass.com to see pictures of some of our successful events from the past. They are labeled with themes, so you can just choose one that appeals to you.

Your final inquiry regarding vegetarian options will also require some decision-making on your part. We offer gourmet dining, and are happy to specially prepare 12 vegetarian meals, but that could be a little expensive. I don't know what your budget is, but might I suggest making the entire menu vegetarian? We have an outstanding vegetarian chef, Julia Monroe, who can prepare a full vegetarian buffet so delicious a lion would eat it! This option is also a lot more cost-effective than preparing two separate menus. After reviewing your options, please let me know what choices are best for you.

Sincerely,

Brian Petersen
Booking and Sales Manager
A Taste of Class

To: Brian Petersen <bpetersen@atasteofclass.com>
From: Jason Hostrum <jhostrum@jhfurnishing.com>
Date: November 22nd
Subject: RE: Office Christmas Party

Dear Mr. Petersen,

Thanks for your reply. I want to go ahead and book the event for Saturday the 20th of December. I want the decoration theme Winter Wonderland, and I have decided to take your advice and go with whatever menu your chef Julia Monroe can put together for us. I really appreciate all of your recommendations and I just know this will be a great event!

All the best,

Jason Hostrum
Junior Secretary, Johnson Home Furnishing

GO ON TO THE NEXT PAGE

186. Why is Jason Hostrum anxious about the party?

(A) His family will be there.
(B) It is the first time the boss will join in.
(C) This is the first party he has had to plan for the company.
(D) There is too much food for him to prepare.

187. In the third email, what is indicated about Jason Hostrum?

(A) He has visited atasteofclass.com.
(B) He has created his own theme.
(C) He wants to cancel the party.
(D) He wants to add more food and guests.

188. According to the emails, what kind of food will be served?

(A) Only meat
(B) A mixture of meat and vegetarian
(C) Only vegetarian
(D) Only appetizers

189. In the first email, what is a big concern about the food?

(A) The flavor
(B) The types of side dishes
(C) The dietary restrictions of some employees
(D) Where the buffet will be located

190. What is indicated about A Taste of Class?

(A) They are busy this holiday season.
(B) They have lots of free teams on the 20th.
(C) They would prefer to cater on another date.
(D) They are too busy to work Johnson Home Furnishing's party.

Questions 191-195 refer to the following emails and order form.

To: <cservice@starproducts.com>
From: Jose Ramos <jramos@zipnet.com>
Date: October 14
Subject: Defective Hose

Dear Ms. Jenkins,

Recently I purchased 5,000 yards of XP100 industrial hosing from your company, Star Products. The hosing was listed as being capable of handling up to 1,000 pounds of pressure per square inch (psi). My company, Advanced Dynamic Cleaning, refitted all of our pressure washers with your hosing, at a considerable cost of both money and time. Every single one of our pressure washers has since failed at some point along the hosing from the joint of the gun to the compressor. Our compressors only generate 500 psi, so I have to conclude that there is some defect in the design of your hose. I would like to get a refund for my purchase, or a replacement of my order with hosing that meets industry standards. I have included my purchase order and a copy of the invoice.

Sincerely,

Jose Ramos

To: Jose Ramos <jramos@zipnet.com>
From: Raquel Jenkins <cservice@starproducts.com>
Date: October 16
Subject: RE: Defective Hose

Dear Mr. Ramos,

We have received your report of defective hosing and reviewed the attached documents. We truly value your business, and are sorry that you went through such a waste of time and energy with our hosing. However, I am sorry to say that the mistake appears to be on your end. Your purchase order clearly shows that you ordered XP100 hosing x 5,000 yards. If you look at the specs for that hosing, you will see that it is only rated as appropriate for 100 psi. This could explain why all of your hosing failed. What I can offer you is an exchange of the remaining XP100 hosing in your inventory for a hosing more appropriate for your needs. We will do this at no charge, and pay for the shipping as a show of our appreciation for your business. Please fill out the purchase order that I have attached and include it with the XP100 hosing when you ship it back to us for exchange.

Thank you,

Raquel Jenkins

GO ON TO THE NEXT PAGE

Star Products Purchase Order Form

Product Name	PSI	Length required	Price per yard	Applicable discount
XP1000	1,000	2,500 yards	$.50	Total discount as per agreed-upon exchange with product XP100

191. Why did Jose Ramos write to Star Products?

(A) To inquire about a price
(B) To order new hosing
(C) To report a hosing malfunction
(D) To compliment them on their hosing

192. What is indicated about the hosing that Jose Ramos ordered?

(A) It did not have the right psi rating for his use.
(B) It was defective.
(C) It was installed incorrectly.
(D) It was delivered to the wrong address.

193. According to the purchase order form, how much XP100 hosing is Jose Ramos returning?

(A) 1,000 yards
(B) 2,000 yards
(C) 2,500 yards
(D) 5,000 yards

194. What is indicated in the letter from Star Products?

(A) Star Products does not value Jose Ramos's business.
(B) Star Products appreciates Jose Ramos's patronage.
(C) Star Products doesn't need any more business.
(D) Star Products wants to expand its business.

195. What job does Raquel Jenkins likely have?

(A) CEO
(B) CFO
(C) Customer service representative
(D) Sales representative

Questions 196-200 refer to the following emails and table.

To: Jason Roberts <jroberts@robertsparties.com>
From: Leroy Jenkins<ljenkins@smope.com>
Date: Sept. 24
Subject: Fall Party

Dear Mr. Roberts,

My name is Leroy Jenkins and I am planning a family reunion for the first weekend of October. I have heard from some friends that your parties are absolutely the best. I really want to make a good impression on my sister's new in-laws, as it will be the first time that they join our family for our annual reunion. I just have a few questions for you.

First, I need to know how much you would charge for a party for 25 people. I can afford $25 per person, not including alcohol. My family is also a little bit picky about food, so if it is possible for you to send a list of the foods that you offer and the cost per person, I would like to go through it and create my own menu.

The last question I have for you is about staffing. I really don't want to be cleaning up and doing dishes during the party. Do you provide staff, and if so how much do you charge for their service? Please write me back as soon as possible so we can get this party planned!

All the best,

Leroy Jenkins

GO ON TO THE NEXT PAGE

To: Leroy Jenkins<ljenkins@smope.com>
From: Jason Roberts <jroberts@robertsparties.com>
Date: Sept. 25
Subject: RE: Fall Party

Dear Mr. Jenkins,

So glad to hear that our parties have been such a success. We do have a catering menu for you to choose items from; and feel free to mix and match based on your own budget and tastes. I have included a menu as well as a staffing guide. I recommend hiring a banquet captain if you're nervous about the event. Our banquet captains are trained to engage and charm the guests at the parties we host; hence our strong reputation.

I look forward to making your party a success!

Jason Roberts

ROBERTS PARTIES CATERING LIST

Appetizer	Entrée	Salad	Dessert
Chips and dip 1.00	Steak 2.50*	Caesar 1.00	Cake .50*
Pastry bites 1.00	Chicken 1.50*	Cobb 2.00*	Pie .50*
Onion rings 1.00*	Pork 1.50	Wild Greens 2.00*	Ice Cream .50

ROBERTS PARTIES STAFFING PRICES

Chef	$5.00 per hour
Wait Staff	$2.50 per hour
Banquet Captain	$3.50 per hour

*recommended items

196. Who most likely is Jason Roberts?

(A) A chef
(B) A business owner
(C) A banquet captain
(D) A receptionist

197. Who is Leroy Jenkins worried about impressing?

(A) His boss
(B) His brother
(C) His sister's husband's family
(D) His parents

198. What does Jason Roberts recommend that Leroy Jenkins include for his event?

(A) An extra chef
(B) A banquet captain
(C) A vegetarian option
(D) Extra waiters

199. What is indicated about Leroy Jenkins' budget?

(A) He cannot afford Roberts Parties.
(B) He needs to choose a very small menu.
(C) He can afford everything that Roberts Parties recommends.
(D) He will have to cut out appetizers.

200. Who will be at Leroy Jenkins' reunion?

(A) His sister's in-laws
(B) 25 Jenkins family members
(C) Family members that live in town
(D) Every member of his family

Stop! This is the end of the test. If you finish before time is called, you may go back to Parts 5, 6, and 7 and check your work.

ACTUAL TEST 10

READING TEST

In the Reading test, you will read a variety of texts and answer several different types of reading comprehension questions. The entire Reading test will last 75 minutes. There are three parts, and directions are given for each part. You are encouraged to answer as many questions as possible within the time allowed.

You must mark your answers on the separate answer sheet. Do not write your answers in your test book.

PART 5

Directions: A word or phrase is missing in each of the sentences below. Four answer choices are given below each sentence. Select the best answer to complete the sentence. Then mark the letter (A), (B), (C), or (D) on your answer sheet.

101. ------- the difference between the two brands is minimal, most consumers purchase the cheaper one.

(A) Until
(B) Because
(C) Before
(D) So

102. Audience members were impressed that the questions asked of the candidate were answered -------.

(A) clearly
(B) clear
(C) cleared
(D) clearing

103. In an attempt ------- sustainable energy, city officials have had solar panels affixed to some public buildings.

(A) generates
(B) generated
(C) generating
(D) to generate

104. The slow ------- of the fire department resulted in severe damage to the building.

(A) duration
(B) response
(C) treatment
(D) maintenance

105. After hours of searching, the plumber ------- identified the source of the leak.

(A) routinely
(B) finally
(C) rarely
(D) strongly

106. Please tell ------- that the workshop has been moved to Conference Room 402.

(A) whatever
(B) themselves
(C) everyone
(D) something

107. Highway 16 was widened over the summer to ------- the increasing number of vehicles using it.

(A) duplicate
(B) extend
(C) accommodate
(D) propose

108. Meal vouchers were given to Beta Airways passengers ------- were not able to depart on time because of booking errors.

(A) when
(B) because
(C) recently
(D) who

109. The gallery's catalog contains an accurate ------- of each piece of artwork that is being offered for sale.

(A) described
(B) description
(C) descriptive
(D) describes

110. To ensure that old appliances are disposed of properly, the city will offer free removal of them ------- April 2 and April 5.

(A) into
(B) from
(C) until
(D) between

111. A buffet dinner is available for the guests, so they may eat ------- looks appetizing to them without having to place an order.

(A) anyway
(B) whatever
(C) wherever
(D) anything

112. During the music festival, goods will be sold only by ------- vendors who have registered with the organizers.

(A) controversial
(B) increased
(C) confident
(D) approved

113. The grocery store chain Refresh Foods has ------- in organic products since it opened in 2001.

(A) participated
(B) certified
(C) specialized
(D) admired

114. The malfunctioning of the printer was ------- a component that had been inserted incorrectly during the assembly process.

(A) due to
(B) whereas
(C) as though
(D) instead of

115. The proposed holiday schedule is ------- to most workers because they know it is fair.

(A) acceptably
(B) accept
(C) acceptable
(D) accepting

116. The test will ------- confirm whether or not the patient has the disease.

(A) like
(B) liking
(C) likable
(D) likely

GO ON TO THE NEXT PAGE

117. With over 200 unique stores, the Plainview Mall ------- millions of shoppers annually.

(A) attracts
(B) implements
(C) postpones
(D) contributes

118. The participants will be judged on ------- performance, and the winners will be announced later during the awards ceremony.

(A) athletically
(B) athletic
(C) athletes
(D) athlete

119. The York Foundation is an organization that has been supporting ------- in medical technology for the past decade.

(A) to advance
(B) advanced
(C) advances
(D) advancing

120. ------- the volleyball tournament is held indoors or outdoors depends primarily on the weather forecast for that day.

(A) Because
(B) Although
(C) Whether
(D) Whereas

121. The company came under investigation after several former employees made allegations of unfair -------.

(A) compositions
(B) assurances
(C) momentums
(D) practices

122. ------- joined Vince's Gym, Mr. Pinter could attend group classes and health counseling sessions for free.

(A) Being
(B) Having
(C) To have
(D) To be

123. The best way to improve the ------- of your home inexpensively is to give the exterior a fresh coat of paint.

(A) privacy
(B) appearance
(C) control
(D) location

124. Marketers believed that if the packaging were more ------- colored, consumers might pay more attention to the product.

(A) variously
(B) vary
(C) various
(D) variety

125. The police officer directed traffic ------- the detour ramp so that drivers could find the route easily.

(A) toward
(B) like
(C) of
(D) during

126. Every employee is asked to pair up with a ------- and find him or her at the predetermined meeting place during fire drills.

(A) reliance
(B) supervision
(C) colleague
(D) calculator

127. The car's owner submitted ------- evidence of the damage along with a mechanic's report to his insurance company.

(A) photographer
(B) photographically
(C) photographic
(D) photogenic

128. The restrooms on the second floor are ------- unavailable because one of the sinks is being replaced.

(A) temporarily
(B) previously
(C) respectively
(D) vitally

129. Because our sales representatives meet with high-level clients in the industry, ------- those with a professional manner will be considered for the position.

(A) only
(B) moreover
(C) except
(D) however

130. On next week's program, our host will interview Kristen Dabney about her time working as an ------- for a UN official.

(A) interpretation
(B) interpret
(C) interpreting
(D) interpreter

GO ON TO THE NEXT PAGE

PART 6

Directions: Read the texts that follow. A word, phrase, or sentence is missing in parts of each text. Four answer choices for each question are given below the text. Select the best answer to complete the text. Then mark the letter (A), (B), (C), or (D) on your answer sheet.

Questions 131-134 refer to the following notice.

To: All Staff

From: Michael Davis, Head Technician

Subject: Network Upgrade

We regret to inform everyone that from Monday the 13th of November until sometime midweek, the employee key card system will not be active. In order to get into and out of the building, you will need to buzz security. In order to lock or unlock any door, you will ------- **131.** assistance from the security team.

The old system was reviewed and many vulnerabilities were discovered. ------- **132.**, the company has decided to replace the old system. This process should take three to four days.

As part of the process, new key cards will be issued to all staff members. These key cards will be available for you to pick up starting Wednesday, the 15th of November, in the security office. Please feel free to stop by anytime ------- **133.** the day to collect yours. ------- **134.** We apologize for any inconvenience this may cause.

131. (A) is requesting
(B) has requested
(C) have to request
(D) had to request

132. (A) Unfortunately
(B) Therefore
(C) Regardless
(D) Finally

133. (A) upon
(B) during
(C) before
(D) at

NEW

134. (A) The switch from keys to keyless entry should make the facility more secure.
(B) We look forward to seeing you sometime next week.
(C) The security office is open 24 hours a day.
(D) This is for product security.

Questions 135-138 refer to the following notice.

Music Teacher Needed

Mike's Music School is ------- (135.) seeking a new piano instructor for weekend and evening classes. Mike's Music School has been operating in the Central district since 1992. ------- (136.) Because of this, we hope to hire a long-time resident of Central to join our team. Applicants should be well versed in ------- (137.) teaching techniques. If you are interested in ------- (138.) for the position, we will be holding interviews and auditions this Saturday at 12 noon at our main studio on Elm Street and Du Pont Avenue.

135. (A) active
(B) activation
(C) actively
(D) activated

NEW

136. (A) Our company tries to work with outside communities.
(B) Our commitment to the community is as important as our commitment to our students.
(C) Our company is unique and uses strange instruments.
(D) Our company is in a special location, next to an auto service center.

137. (A) contemporary
(B) unknown
(C) strange
(D) boring

138. (A) apply
(B) applied
(C) applying
(D) to apply

GO ON TO THE NEXT PAGE

Questions 139-142 refer to the following advertisement.

Saldesta

Rest Your Mind and Body

It's what you've been dreaming of. Peaceful sleep without a struggle is what you need. That's what Saldesta -------. Saldesta helps people fall asleep quickly, and stay asleep the entire
139.
night. It's the only nonnarcotic sleeping aid, and it's ------- for long-term use. ------- Talk to
140. **141.**
your doctor before using sleeping aids for extended periods. Tonight, just close your eyes and leave everything else to Saldesta.

Find out how to improve your sleep at www.saldesta.com, or call 1-800-SALDESTA.

Important Safety Information: Saldesta works quickly, and should be taken right -------
142.
bed. Be sure you have at least eight hours to devote to sleep before becoming active. Do not drink alcohol while taking Saldesta. Most sleep medications carry some risk of dependency.

139. (A) offers
(B) sustains
(C) mitigates
(D) maintains

140. (A) to approve
(B) approves
(C) approving
(D) approved

NEW

141. (A) So you can feel comfortable taking it night after night.
(B) Talk to your doctor today to see if it's right for you.
(C) This is the only stimulant approved for prolonged use by the FDA.
(D) Enter this code for a free sample and discounts.

142. (A) during
(B) around
(C) before
(D) after

Questions 143-146 refer to the following posting on a website.

Employee Message Board

Request for Feedback

Posted by James Frohm, Human Resources Director

Hello colleagues,

The holiday season is fast approaching and we need to ------- (**143.**) our office party! There have been several ------- (**144.**) for locations and themes made to me directly, but I wanted to invite everyone in the office to give me his or her feedback. All ideas are welcome, but I must remind everyone that our office ------- (**145.**). Our party can include all forms of secular celebration, but out of respect for everyone there can be no religious themes. Please respond to me directly by email at jamesfrohm@ccn.net, so I can get started making plans. ------- (**146.**)

Sincerely,

James

143. (A) make
(B) plan
(C) conceive
(D) deliver

144. (A) comments
(B) suggestions
(C) spots
(D) suggested

145. (A) is a safe space for all customs and cultures
(B) stays open late on Tuesday
(C) needs a new janitor
(D) will move next week

NEW

146. (A) I look forward to hearing your ideas!
(B) I don't want you to be late!
(C) I look forward to your undivided attention.
(D) I hope you reply before it's too late.

GO ON TO THE NEXT PAGE

PART 7

Directions: In this part you will read a selection of texts, such as magazine and newspaper articles, emails, and instant messages. Each text or set of texts is followed by several questions. Select the best answer for each question and mark the letter (A), (B), (C), or (D) on your answer sheet.

Questions 147-148 refer to the following flyer.

TriStar Sports Gear

5477 Fairmont Avenue
Bemidji, MN 56634
218-555-3412
www.tristarsportsgear.com

Summer Sale from July 1 to July 14

The school year has ended and summer has arrived. Stop by TriStar Sports Gear and take advantage of our huge annual summer sale beginning this Friday. Now is the time to get ready for summer fun. We will be selling jerseys featuring your favorite sports teams for 20 percent off our regular price. Also, if you buy two pairs of athletic shoes, you can get a third pair at half price. There is much more on sale, so please see our sale list on the back page.

* Bring this flyer to our store and you can get a 10-percent discount on all kinds of balls.

147. What is indicated about TriStar Sports Gear?

(A) It is a family business.
(B) It is located next to a school.
(C) It holds a sale every year.
(D) It mainly sells weight training equipment.

148. How can customers receive a discount on athletic shoes?

(A) By buying more than two pairs
(B) By visiting the store on July 1
(C) By placing an order online
(D) By presenting a flyer

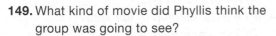

Questions 149-150 refer to the following text message chain.

Sylvia: What movie are we going to?	**19:01**
Jason: The one we agreed on last night!	**19:08**
Phyllis: Yeah. It looks sooooo good! I love horror movies!	**19:08**
Bern: !!! What do you mean?? I thought we decided on a comedy, that new one!	**19:20**
Sylvia: That's right! The comedy with Ruffle Yellowbeard, the famous mime!	**19:21**
Jason: Comedy? I was thinking horror too, but I do love Ruffle Yellowbeard. I'm in!	**19:25**
Phyllis: OK, comedy it is. Meet you outside the theater at 10 P.M. SHARP!	**19:35**

149. What kind of movie did Phyllis think the group was going to see?

(A) Horror
(B) Science fiction
(C) Comedy
(D) Romance

150. What does Jason mean when he texts, "I'm in"?

(A) He wants to see the horror movie they agreed on.
(B) He wants to be in a comedy movie.
(C) He wants to be included in the group.
(D) He wants to stay at home tonight.

GO ON TO THE NEXT PAGE

Questions 151-152 refer to the following article.

Brixton Science Journal

On March 3, famed archeologist Douglas Price will be presenting on the results of his year-long excavation of ancient burial sites in Egypt. The presentation will be held at the Brixton Public Library beginning at 6:00 P.M.

Attendees are encouraged to come early in order to view some ancient Egyptian tools and instruments that will be on display. These precious items were retrieved by Mr. Price during his expedition to Egypt, and they are truly one of a kind. They are believed to have been used for farming by ancient Egyptian people.

Those who want to attend can reserve seats by visiting www.brixtonlibrary.com. You can also find more information concerning Mr. Price's most recent research on the website.

151. What is mentioned about the event?

(A) It is sponsored by the Egyptian government.
(B) It will feature an artifact exhibition.
(C) It will be held in Egypt.
(D) It is already sold out.

152. What can be found on the library's website?

(A) An events calendar
(B) A detailed map of the area
(C) Facts about ancient Egypt
(D) A guide to Egyptian food

Questions 153-154 refer to the following invitation.

Spring Valley Center

Grand Opening on Birch Street

Monday, February 23

Spring Valley Center of Spring Valley, California
is happy to invite you to
tour our new office spaces available for rent!

All day Monday we will host an open house
and all are welcome to tour the premises.

Spring Valley Center is conveniently located off Highway 10.

153. What most likely is Spring Valley Center?

(A) A department store
(B) A conference center
(C) A logistics company
(D) A business park

154. Why is the event being held?

(A) To attract new employees to a company
(B) To schedule a sales conference
(C) To advertise commercial rental space
(D) To announce the opening of a shopping center

GO ON TO THE NEXT PAGE

Questions 155-157 refer to the following article.

Lockland Business News

September 8 — – [1] – This should come as a relief for residents on both sides of the Canadian-American border, as many shoppers from Lockland often make the one-and-a-half-hour drive into Canada to shop at the Cashco warehouse in Brentwood. – [2] – This usually results in long waits at the border and a very crowded Canadian Cashco with more than half its shoppers coming from across the border. Many Brentwood residents are resentful of the large crowds in their tiny town and Lockland residents have complained that the closest American Cashco is located almost five hours away. – [3] –

"I'm very excited," says Lockland resident Janice Burrows. "I heard it'll be huge. Maybe Canadians might start coming here to shop. But all kidding aside, we've been petitioning for a branch here for a long time." – [4] – The new Lockland Cashco is rumored to be one of the largest warehouses in America, with its own gas station, a pet center, a restaurant, cafeterias, a garden center, and a medical clinic.

155. What is the article about?

(A) Tension at the border
(B) Competition between neighboring residents
(C) Cross-border shopping expeditions
(D) The opening of a new Cashco branch in the near future

156. What is implied about Canadian residents?

(A) They want a Cashco branch.
(B) They dislike Americans' coming to shop.
(C) They don't like going to America.
(D) They have to travel far to get to a Cashco.

NEW

157. In which of the places marked [1], [2], [3], and [4] does the following sentence belong?

"A spokesperson for wholesale giant Cashco confirmed on Monday that a branch will finally open in Lockland next month."

(A) [1]
(B) [2]
(C) [3]
(D) [4]

Questions 158-160 refer to the following article.

Centerville County Shelter to Hold Marathon to Raise Money for the Homeless

A walking marathon will be held in Centerville County next Saturday. All proceeds from the event will be donated to the Centerville County Shelter. The shelter is a public institution that provides food, lodging, and support services for the homeless, the elderly, and anyone else in need.

This will be the second time the event has been held, and organizers expect more participants than they had last year. This event is open to children and adults of all ages. However, children must be accompanied by an adult family member at all times.

Centerville County Shelter was founded in 1981 with the mission of alleviating the hardships of homelessness, poverty, and hunger.

158. Why most likely would someone register for the event?

(A) To learn about staying fit
(B) To win a cash prize
(C) To apply for a job
(D) To contribute to the community

159. According to the article, who is NOT allowed to participate in the event?

(A) Senior citizens
(B) Students without student ID cards
(C) Unaccompanied children
(D) Foreign tourists

160. What is the main goal of the Centerville County Shelter?

(A) To build affordable housing
(B) To provide basic necessities
(C) To train professional athletes
(D) To educate community members

GO ON TO THE NEXT PAGE

Questions 161-164 refer to the following online chat discussion.

Molly	Who wants to go to the victory parade with me tomorrow?
Susan	I do! I've been following the team all season! Their games have been great, and their quarterback may be the best the school has ever had! It will also be a great opportunity to network and promote our new brand of beer, Winner's Ale!
Jeff	That might be fun. But I worry about our competition and their contracts with the university and the stadium's sponsors.
Molly	Ahhhhhhh. True; I didn't think of that . . . Well, we could do it "off the record." hahaha
Susan	Yeah, right. If corporate finds out, we will be fired for sure, or worse.
Jeff	True, true, but I still want to see the game and at least analyze our competitors' marketing strategies.
Susan	Good point, Jeff. We will go, but you'd better keep your mouth shut.
Jeff	Thanks, Susan. I will. So we'll all go and take notes, right?

161. What is indicated about Winner's Ale?

(A) It is an old variety of beer.
(B) People don't know about it yet.
(C) It is delicious.
(D) It is cheap.

162. What will the group most likely do next?

(A) Report to corporate about Jeff
(B) Go to the victory parade
(C) See a movie
(D) Go dancing and drink Winner's Ale

163. What does Molly mean when she says, "off the record"?

(A) An unreleased song
(B) A record of their activities is being kept.
(C) They won't go on official business
(D) Everything is being recorded and they want it to stop.

164. What is suggested about Jeff?

(A) He takes good notes.
(B) He likes to drink.
(C) He likes to talk.
(D) He loves parades.

Questions 165-167 refer to the following notice.

Lichtenberg Air

September 24

To our passengers:

Beginning October 1, Lichtenberg Air will ask passengers to pay an extra 20 percent in baggage fees. As you know, the reason for this increase is rising fuel costs. We regret that our baggage fees have to be increased.

However, passengers are still allowed to bring one carry-on bag free of charge. We would also like to emphasize that this is the first increase in baggage fees for Lichtenberg Air in 10 years.

As always, our goal is to provide safe and reliable transportation at a reasonable price. If the price of fuel lowers, we expect to reverse this fee increase.

We thank you for choosing Lichtenberg Air.

165. What is indicated about Lichtenberg Air?

(A) It is asking passengers to stay within a baggage limit.
(B) It is responding to customer complaints.
(C) It has not increased its baggage fees for a decade.
(D) It has added new destinations.

166. What is suggested about passengers?

(A) They are allowed to bring electronics on board.
(B) They can take one bag onto a plane at no charge.
(C) They must pay an increased ticket price from October 1.
(D) They can get a 20-percent discount next month.

167. According to the notice, what will happen when the price of fuel drops?

(A) The stock price for Lichtenberg Air will increase.
(B) Passengers will be offered gift certificates.
(C) More flight attendants will be employed.
(D) The extra charge will be eliminated.

GO ON TO THE NEXT PAGE

Questions 168-171 refer to the following letter.

April 4

Paula Lynch
344 Culler Boulevard
Ellie, MN 42195

Dear Ms. Lynch,

We are pleased that you have accepted our request to give a presentation at this year's Conference on Second Language Education. As you know, this conference will gather teachers of German, French, Chinese, and many other foreign languages in one place to share classroom techniques and approaches. Aside from attending workshops and seminars, attendees will have ample opportunity to converse and network at a variety of events. This is an opportunity not to be missed.

This year's conference will be held at the Wilson Convention Center in Salem, Oregon. It will begin on Thursday, July 12, and last through Sunday, July 15. If requested, laptops and other equipment can be loaned to speakers for use during the conference. Any borrowed supplies must be returned on the final day of the conference. In addition to your fee for speaking, all speakers are also allowed to attend any other workshops and seminars free of charge.

Please provide us with your detailed travel itinerary. One of our staff members will be at the airport to meet you and give you a ride to the venue. Please call our office at (456) 555-1345 to provide the requested information before April 10.

We are looking forward to seeing you at the conference.

Sincerely,

Dirk Klein

Conference Organizer

168. What can be inferred about Ms. Lynch?

(A) She lives in Salem, Oregon.
(B) She can speak a second language.
(C) She is a motivational speaker.
(D) She is a conference organizer.

169. What is the purpose of the conference?

(A) To attract foreign investment
(B) To share teaching methods
(C) To set curriculum standards
(D) To establish a charitable foundation

170. When must speakers return borrowed supplies?

(A) April 4
(B) April 10
(C) July 12
(D) July 15

171. What is Ms. Lynch asked to inform Mr. Klein about?

(A) When she will arrive
(B) What supplies she will need
(C) What room she will use
(D) Who will accompany her

Questions 172-175 refer to the following letter.

Bandit Pharmaceuticals

255 Highway Road
Boston, MA 48573

April 23
Mr. Timothy Jean
6844 Sylvia Place
Fresno, CA 97658

Dear Mr. Jean,

We at Bandit Pharmaceuticals are delighted you have accepted the position of research assistant. You will begin work on May 5th. The first day will be an orientation for all new hires with a workplace safety workshop, a seminar explaining your responsibilities on the job, and a tour of the facilities. – [1] –

Because you are coming in from out of town, we would like to make your move as smooth as possible. We understand that you will be arriving on April 29th and staying at the Boston Family Inn for a few days. The Inn is about a 10-minute taxi ride from the Bandit Pharmaceutical Headquarters. – [2] – You can go to the front desk in the main lobby and ask for Ms. Jenna Rhimes in human resources. She helps new out-of-town employees settle into the city and will answer any questions you may have. I have also attached the telephone numbers of some places and organizations that may be relevant to your move here. – [3] –

If you have any further questions or concerns, please feel free to call me at 555-1234 during my office hours, Monday to Friday from 9 A.M. to 7 P.M. – [4] – All the best with your move here and I will see you on May 5th.

Sincerely,

Joan Noonan
Human Resources

GO ON TO THE NEXT PAGE

172. Why did Ms. Noonan send a letter to Mr. Jean?

(A) To give him details about the time and place of a job interview
(B) To give him information about his first day of work
(C) To provide information about places for rent
(D) To confirm whether he would accept a job

173. What did Ms. Noonan send with the letter?

(A) Telephone numbers
(B) A copy of a contract
(C) Contact information of company employees
(D) A schedule

174. The phrase "settle into" in the second paragraph is closest in meaning to:

(A) look for
(B) explore
(C) become comfortable in
(D) navigate within

NEW

175. In which of the places marked [1], [2], [3], and [4] does the following sentence belong?

"Your laboratory manager will give you further details at the end of the first day."

(A) [1]
(B) [2]
(C) [3]
(D) [4]

Questions 176-180 refer to the following web page and email.

Blackrock Education Foundation

HOME	ABOUT US	NEWS	RESOURCES	CONTACT

February 10

Language Scholarship

The Blackrock Education Foundation would like to announce that we will begin taking applications for the 24th German Language Scholarship starting March 10 and ending on March 31. Applicants from diverse backgrounds are encouraged to apply. To qualify for the scholarship, applicants must:

- be currently enrolled in a master's program
- prove advanced proficiency in the German language
- submit a complete health check
- submit a recommendation from a previous language instructor

The German Language Scholarship is intended for students who already speak German at an advanced level. Therefore, this scholarship is for students who plan to use the German language to study in Germany in the near future.

Recipients of the scholarship must complete monthly progress reports, submit all monthly expenses to the foundation, and maintain a B+ grade average.

Applications can be downloaded under the RESOURCES tab on our website. Please submit all necessary materials to Mr. Hans Richter, Blackrock Education Foundation's director. The address is 459 Pearson Road, Chicago, IL 60616. The review and selection process will take approximately two weeks. Any application with incomplete or missing documents will be rejected without exception. Results will be announced on April 15.

To: Clint Porter <cporter@umc.com>
From: Hans Richter <richter@blackrockedu.com>
Date: April 15
Subject: Blackrock Scholarship
Attachment: scholarship_information

Dear Mr. Porter,

I would like to congratulate you on being chosen as a recipient of the 24th German Language Scholarship. As a recipient of the scholarship, you will be supplied with travel expenses to Germany, tuition fees, and living expenses for one year. Attached is a booklet containing information on scholarship regulations and requirements. Please make sure you read it carefully. If you have any questions or concerns, feel free to contact me. I will be emailing you within the next week with specific details on how to prepare for your upcoming studies.

Thanks,

Hans Richter

Director, Blackrock Education Foundation

GO ON TO THE NEXT PAGE

176. According to the web page, what must scholarship recipients do?

(A) Keep track of monthly expenses
(B) Write a research paper
(C) Submit an annual report
(D) Take an entrance examination

177. What is indicated about scholarship applications?

(A) They must be received by mid-April.
(B) They will be accepted only if requirements are met.
(C) They will be reviewed and selected by German professors.
(D) They must be submitted online.

178. On the web page, the word "proficiency" in paragraph 1, line 6 is closest in meaning to:

(A) system
(B) practice
(C) experience
(D) mastery

179. What is the purpose of the email?

(A) To confirm a departure date
(B) To schedule an interview
(C) To give some information to a scholarship winner
(D) To enroll in required courses at a university in Germany

180. What is suggested about Mr. Porter?

(A) He worked at the Blackrock Foundation.
(B) He is an entrepreneur working in Germany.
(C) He has a good command of German.
(D) He wants to be a language instructor.

Questions 181-185 refer to the following invoice and letter.

Sunny Day Cleaning

The only choice for your professional cleaning

Bill to: Randall Auto Body
957 Pacific Trail Rd.
Troutdale, Oregon 97055

Invoice #: 2348

Date: March 3

Date	Description of Service	Amount
February 5	Full office cleaning (Including: three rooms, two bathrooms, windows, carpet deep clean, furniture)	$95
February 19	Full office cleaning (Including: three rooms, two bathrooms, windows, carpet deep clean, furniture)	$95

Total: $190

*Payments received after April 1st will be subject to a $20 late charge.

Sunny Day Cleaning
283 Main St.
Troutdale, Oregon 97055

Questions or Additional Services: Please call 1-345-737-2209

ACTUAL TEST 10

GO ON TO THE NEXT PAGE

March 8

Dear Sunny Day Cleaning,

I have received your invoice for the services we received in February, which I have to say were excellent. I see we were charged 95 dollars for each time you cleaned our offices. This is what we had initially agreed upon and have been paying for your services since last year at this time. However, Rod Sanford told me we'd be receiving a five-dollar discount each time you visited us because we have arranged for you to clean our other location just off of Highway 26. He said that this new price would go into effect starting in February. I have included a copy of the email he sent me. Could you please adjust the price to reflect our new agreement and send us a new bill? I'd appreciate it. We look forward to seeing you again.

Thank you for your assistance,

Patricia Collins

Patricia Collins

Manager
Randall Auto Body

181. According to the invoice, what amount is due by April 1?

(A) $20
(B) $90
(C) $95
(D) $190

182. What service was NOT provided to Randall Auto Body?

(A) Window cleaning
(B) Floor cleaning
(C) Furniture cleaning
(D) Carpet cleaning

183. Why did Ms. Collins write a letter?

(A) The cleaning service missed an appointment.
(B) She was overcharged for a service.
(C) The cleaning service added an extra fee to her bill.
(D) She would like to renew her contract.

184. What is implied about Sunny Day Cleaning?

(A) They provide decent service.
(B) They are often late for appointments.
(C) They frequently overcharge their clients.
(D) They offer late payment options.

185. What did Ms. Collins send besides her letter?

(A) A coupon for auto repairs
(B) A copy of an email
(C) A signed contract
(D) A check for the amount due

NEW **Questions 186-190** refer to the following article, web page, and certificate.

Respite for Commuters

A new ride-sharing app is gaining in popularity as bus and taxi fees continue to rise and commuters continue to look for more efficient routes. Jordan Mills, a small business owner who commutes into the city from his home in Brentwood, had to change buses twice and then take the subway to get to his workplace. Not only did he find the commute quite costly and uncomfortable with the rush-hour crowds; he also found it time-consuming. But with the availability of the new Freewheel app, he found that he could save time and money with a quick ride available within five minutes from any location he was at. "This is definitely the future of transportation," says Jordan. "I wouldn't go to work and back any other way now."

Jordan Mills isn't the only commuter who feels this way. An estimated 2,000 commuters in the city of Sherwood alone are expected to use the ride-sharing app within the next year and almost 500 drivers have signed up for the program.

Freewheel is available for download on the Freewheel website and on Miniapp.com and Amacom.com.

www.freewheel.com/history

The idea for Freewheel began when Michael Owens and his coworkers started a carpooling program at the company they worked at. Owens had to change subways three times and buses twice to get to work and although he could drive, parking was limited. He managed the carpooling group by assigning drivers and mapping out a route to each coworker's home. He then created an app that everyone could connect and communicate through so that the designated drivers and passengers could easily find each other. Five years later, Freewheel is a major company with tens of thousands of users, both drivers and commuters, around the country.

Freewheel is dedicated to keeping the cost of commuting down and the efficiency up. In time, it hopes to offer its services to people around the world.

GO ON TO THE NEXT PAGE

Technology Initiatives
is proud to present the
New Innovation Award to:
Michael Owens, CEO of Freewheel

This award recognizes the innovation and creativity of new talent in the technology industry. It also acknowledges efforts to help consumers through the use of technology with novel ideas that have transformed the nature of transportation.

Susan Vaneer

Executive Manager, Technology Initiatives

186. How are Jordan Mills and Michael Owens similar?

(A) Both started technology companies.
(B) Both wanted an efficient way to commute.
(C) Both were employed in public transportation.
(D) Both won awards for their achievements.

187. What is indicated about Freewheel?

(A) It started out small.
(B) It is an international company.
(C) It employs bus drivers.
(D) It is good for the environment.

188. What is most likely true about Michael Owens?

(A) He dislikes driving.
(B) He owns a taxi company.
(C) He wants to expand his business.
(D) He has met Jordan Mills.

189. The word "Respite" in the title of the article is closest in meaning to:

(A) employment
(B) immunity
(C) a refund
(D) a break

190. What is the certificate rewarding?

(A) The best driver
(B) Environmental efforts
(C) A good idea
(D) The highest-earning company

Questions 191-195 refer to the following emails.

To: Ken Alberts <kalberts@emergentsolutions.com>
From: Clarissa Pierce <cpierce@actionservices.com>
Date: June 13
Subject: shipping contracts

Hello Mr. Alberts,

I am writing on behalf of my company, Action Services. Our company specializes in creating personalized flower arrangements, gift baskets, and novelty gifts. Recently we have been going over our books and have realized we have been paying too much to our current shipping company. We would be interested in offering you the opportunity to take over our account if you could offer us more competitive rates. I have included a recent invoice of shipping cost from our current carrier, Express Corp. If you feel that you could beat their prices, we would like to try working with you. Please let me know what you think.

Sincerely,

Clarissa Pierce
Account Manager, Action Services

To: Clarissa Pierce <cpierce@actionservices.com>
From: Ken Alberts <kalberts@emergentsolutions.com>
Date: June 14
Subject: shipping contracts

Dear Ms. Pierce,

Thank you for contacting us at Emergent Solutions. I have taken a look at your invoice from your last bill from Express Corp. and I believe that we can beat their prices. I would be happy to send over my account director to try to tailor a delivery package that is perfect for your needs. Since most of the shipping that you do is within the state, and composed of relatively small items, I believe our express courier service would be perfect. We use fuel-efficient hybrid vehicles to run our small deliveries and are able to pass the savings on to our customers. As account director, I look forward to working with Action Services in the future.

Sincerely,

Ken Alberts

GO ON TO THE NEXT PAGE

To: Ken Alberts <kalberts@emergentsolutions.com>
From: Clarissa Pierce <cpierce@actionservices.com>
Date: June 16
Subject: shipping contracts

Dear Mr. Alberts,

This sounds amazing! You have no idea how much it means to our company that you are using environmentally responsible transportation. Action Services was originally formed by a group of environmental studies majors at City College here. Everything we sell is ethically sourced and recyclable. We can't wait to meet with your team.

Best,

Clarissa Pierce
Account Manager, Action Services

191. What job does Mr. Alberts have?

(A) President
(B) HR manager
(C) CEO
(D) Account director

192. What is indicated about Action Services?

(A) They care about art.
(B) They are concerned about the environment.
(C) They need to sell more packages.
(D) Their old delivery service delivered packages to the wrong addresses.

193. From the emails, what can you infer?

(A) Emergent Solutions offers lower shipping costs than Express Corp.
(B) Emergent Solutions will not be efficient.
(C) Emergent Solutions' business ethics are at odds with those of Action Services.
(D) Action Services is in debt.

194. Why did Action Services contact Emergent Solutions?

(A) They needed new customers.
(B) They were spending too much on shipping.
(C) They wanted to expand their operation.
(D) They wanted to ship internationally.

195. What kind of business is Action Services?

(A) Technology consultants
(B) Leadership experts
(C) Hotel and resort specialists
(D) Florists and novelty suppliers

Questions 196-200 refer to the following emails and table.

To: Aaron Donald <adonald@acemail.com>
From: James Holt <holtrain@zipnet.net>
Date: Jan. 12
Subject: First Quarter Performance Review

Dear Aaron,

I just wanted to give you a heads-up that the performance evaluations will be going forward as discussed. I know this was an area of stress for you in the fourth quarter of last year, so I wanted to give you plenty of advance warning. You will need to bring your numbers up significantly if you want to pass the review. As you know, we have been struggling to meet our sales goals over the past several years, and I am afraid Mr. Jones is determined to trim the staff if things don't change. I have far exceeded my target numbers, so I have included an attachment with some possible leads for sales; give them a shot.

Good Luck,

James

To: James Holt <holtrain@zipnet.net>
From: Aaron Donald <adonald@acemail.com>
Date: Jan. 12
Subject: RE: First Quarter Performance Review

James,

Thank you so much for the leads. I will get on them right away. I don't know why my sales in the technology division are slumping so much lately. It seems like every sales technique I learned in school isn't working anymore. I am thinking about changing industries if I don't pass our review when it comes out in March. My sister is opening a beauty parlor and she's been asking me to become a barber. Imagine that! Anyway, thank you again for the notice about the possible layoffs coming up. I will try to get my numbers up to standard, but I think that Mr. Jones may have already decided to let me go.

All the best,

Aaron

GO ON TO THE NEXT PAGE

Possible Sales Leads for January

Name	Division	Account Potential	Rating
Sally Jones	technologies	$35,000-$50,000	Silver
Bob Knuddle	technologies	$100,000 and up	Gold
Marquise Lee	technologies	$12,000-$20,000	Bronze/Silver

196. What is most likely true about James and Aaron?

(A) They are competitors.
(B) They are related.
(C) They are married.
(D) They are friends.

197. What is indicated about Aaron?

(A) He is not very good at his job these days.
(B) The owner loves him.
(C) He has problems with all of his coworkers.
(D) He will keep his job after the evaluations are reviewed.

198. According to the information provided, what is true about James?

(A) He has done very well at work.
(B) He needs more sales.
(C) He wants to work with Aaron.
(D) He will become a barber.

199. What is the problem with the sales leads James gave to Aaron?

(A) They are rated too highly.
(B) They aren't worth very much money.
(C) Aaron doesn't know the contacts.
(D) They are in a field Aaron is struggling in.

200. What job does Mr. Jones most likely have?

(A) Human resources agent
(B) Sales executive
(C) Owner
(D) Associate secretary

Stop! This is the end of the test. If you finish before time is called, you may go back to Parts 5, 6, and 7 and check your work.

TRANSLATION

ACTUAL TEST ①

PART 5 P.18–21

◎ **Part 5 解答請見 P.457**

101. 填寫訂購單時，請清楚**寫上**您的地址以避免延誤。

102. 摩根女士招募了公司接下來三個月**將聘用**的人員。

103. 在本地報紙刊登廣告後，承包商的生意**成長**了百分之十五。

104. 這間免費診所是由一群醫生設立的，為各種疾病提供**治療**。

105. 參加徒步行程的人應該在星期六上午**於**貝茲街 533 號集合。

106. 藝術家將**他**最棒的作品送到藝廊讓老闆品評。

107. 財務報表所附的數據應該與支出項目**有關**。

108. 業主三個月前**才**買下這棟大樓，但她已經花了一大筆錢裝潢了。

109. 我們打算在下次的員工會議上開誠**布公**地討論這個問題。

110. 店經理打算**趕快**展示新產品以宣傳秋季系列時裝。

111. 在旺季時，僱用更多員工來輪週末的班是**必要的**。

112. **既然**已經換成了隔熱材料，這棟大樓就更節能了。

113. 西蒙斯先生需要一部更**可靠**的車以往返郊區的住家和市中心的辦公室。

114. 為了比其他競爭對手銷售更多產品並吸引更多顧客，這家公司**策略性地**降低售價。

115. **在**威廉斯先生對聽眾演講**前**，他播放了一部短片，是關於他所設計的引擎。

116. 為了在道路駕駛時的安全起見，避免**阻擋**後車窗與左右後視鏡的視線。

117. 整棟大樓有良好的通風，對保護員工健康和福祉來說是**必要**的。

118. 垃圾食物銷售量持續下滑的**事實**顯示出消費者已經更有健康概念了。

119. 草地灑水系統的灑水器是由**機械**控制的。

120. 圖書館員張貼公告，**通知**讀者因裝修即將閉館的消息。

121. 幫大廳內部重新粉刷**的**羅斯先生，是由大樓經理的朋友推薦的。

122. 月刊的撰寫體例會**定期地**修改，以因應不斷變化的讀者。

123. **儘管**腳踝受傷，那位棒球員還是參加了該季的最後一場比賽。

124. 政府部門以前會提供財務協助，但現在只提供**法律**服務。

125. 應房客**要求**，多送了一組毛巾與免費香皂到客房。

126. 高檔精品店珍的衣櫥以銷售最時髦的**飾品**給年輕專業人士著名。

127. 公司開始體認到有責任地運用資源這件事日益增加的**重要性**。

128. **在**重組公司內部幾個部門**後**，大多數溝通不良的問題都消失了。

129. 新藥物研發中最危險的**階段**就是人體實驗。

130. 應徵圖萊里設計公司**的人都**必須繳交作品集。

PART 6 P.22–25

131–134 電子郵件

收件者：samsmith@digitalIT.com
寄件者：sharronb@bmail.com
日期：9 月 24 日
主旨：商業合約

親愛的史密斯先生：

我是雪倫．畢格斯，我是畢格斯平面設計公司的創辦人兼執行長。最近看到您的廣告，是為貴公司的一些專案尋求配合的平面設計公司。畢格斯設計有豐富的經驗，與各種小型企業與公司合作過設計廣告活動、商標與網站。我已附上本公司之前的設計案，以說明我們的專項。本公司的網站 www.biggs-graphics.com 上也有相關資訊。

我對與貴公司合作進行您的專案相當感興趣，希望彼此能夠建立有利的合作關係。期待收到您的回覆。

畢格斯平面設計執行長

雪倫．畢格斯 敬上

131. A 尋求
B 以尋求
C 尋求
D 正在尋求

132. **A 大量的**
B 受限制的
C 慷慨的
D 無限的

133. A 我會很感激有機會與您合作。
B 我聽聞數位 IT 是一間很棒的公司。
C 事實上，我們的設計常被其他公司抄襲。
D 我已附上本公司之前的設計案，以說明我們的專項。

134. A 在
B 對
C 和
D 來自

135–138 公告

感謝您惠顧勞森瓷器店。我們的產品以時尚又獨特的花紋、色彩搭配以及耐用與堅固著名。可使用於洗碗機與微波爐，而且我們有信心您絕對可以用上好幾年。但是，請注意，反覆摔落或粗魯使用將終造成毀損。我們建議您小心存放，在清潔時避免使用刺激性化學藥劑、鋼製海綿或激烈擦洗。有關使用與照料上的資訊，請上本店網站 www.larsonchina.com。若有任何疑慮，也可來電 555-1234。

135. A 耐用的
B 耐用性
C 耐用
D 持續時間

136. A 勞森的器皿與銀器很適合搭配餐具。
B 我們最受歡迎的春花瓷器系列，在大多數的門市都銷售一空。
C 到我們店裡看看其他美麗的產品。
D 可使用於洗碗機與微波爐，而且我們有信心您絕對可以用上好幾年。

137. **A 造成**
B 想到
C 終止於
D 停止

138. A 有野心的
B 好戰的
C 激烈的
D 滿足的

139–142 告示

初級職位：高登暨史賴會計事務所

我們正在徵求充滿熱忱、具財務或會計教育背景的應徵者。所有應徵者需有一定的電腦操作經驗。無工作經驗可，但具工作經驗者尤佳。具雙語能力者將優先考慮。職務包括：會計、統計與總務處助理。意者請上本公司網站 www.

G&Saccountingfirm.com/employment 了解更多資訊。可將求職信與履歷寄給凱倫．希爾，電子郵件是 khill@G&S.com。我們將於 11 月 5 日星期一開始進行面試，該職位從次月到職上班。

139. Ⓐ 帳戶
Ⓑ 會計師
Ⓒ 會計
Ⓓ 説明

140. Ⓐ 基本的
Ⓑ 決定的
Ⓒ 額外的
Ⓓ 必要的

141. Ⓐ 正在
Ⓑ 將會
Ⓒ 已經
Ⓓ 之前在

142. Ⓐ 我們衷心地感謝您的好意。
Ⓑ 該職位從次月到職上班。
Ⓒ 請來電洽詢更多資訊。
Ⓓ 我們為所造成的不便致歉。

143–146 電子郵件

收件者：廚房人員、辦公室員工
寄件者：賴瑞．派克經理
日期：3 月 23 日
主旨：整修

給廚房人員及漢默全體員工：

自 3 月 23 日星期日起至 3 月 27 日星期四止，員工自助餐廳因廚房汰換老舊器具，進駐新廚具設備而進行整修工程。為此，將無法提供熱食給顧客。但這段時間便利商店將為員工們準備更多的三明治、便當及點心。

這個整修工程將增加水槽、烤箱和爐子的數量，這樣在午餐與晚餐的巔峰時段就能提供大量餐點。我們為所造成的不便致歉，但我們也希望這些變革可以改善餐廳的服務。

143. Ⓐ 正帶來
Ⓑ 已經帶來
Ⓒ 帶來
Ⓓ 被帶來

144. Ⓐ 這要花上很多功夫。
Ⓑ 因此，便利商店要關門了。
Ⓒ 為此，將無法提供熱食給顧客。
Ⓓ 因此會出現噪音與混亂。

145. Ⓐ 在……之前
Ⓑ 在……之後
Ⓒ 在……期間
Ⓓ 在……之外

146. Ⓐ 發展
Ⓑ 改善
Ⓒ 矯正
Ⓓ 恢復

PART 7 P.26–47

147–148 電子郵件

收件者：employees@simnetsolutions.com
寄件者：management@simnetsolutions.com
主旨：研討會機會
日期：2 月 5 日

親愛的女性同仁：

距離女性領導力研討會報名截止日期還有一週的時間，這個研討會將免費提供給我們新網顧問公司的所有女性同仁。為了配合女性同仁們忙碌的工作時間表，將分別於 2 月 21 日和 2 月 23 日兩天，舉辦一樣的研討會。

欲報名這場特別安排的研討會，請於 2 月 12 日下午五點前以電子郵件方式告知人力資源部的詹姆斯．泰勒。這場研討會將教導女性同仁如何在職場上以自信與值得信賴的方式表達想法。

新網顧問公司管理團隊 敬上

147. 下列何者和研討會有關？

A 它的特色是主講人詹姆斯．泰勒
B 它每年都會舉行
C 它的費用比前一場還貴
D 為女性而設計

148. 免費報名何時截止？

A 2 月 5 日
B 2 月 12 日
C 2 月 21 日
D 2 月 23 日

149–150 訊息串

凱爾	**2:42**
南西，是我，凱爾。我在 B 會議室為五點的會議做準備。投影機不能用，你可以到用品儲藏室拿另一台來嗎？	
南西	**2:45**
嘿，沒問題。我現在就過去。	
凱爾	**2:46**
謝啦。真的很感激。	
南西	**2:57**
凱爾，這裡沒有投影機。我已經打給資訊科技部，問他們有沒有備用機。等我收到回覆再跟你說。	
凱爾	**3:00**
再次感謝你。喔，你可以找一下有沒有多的麥克風嗎？	
南西	**3:08**
這裡有兩個，我會把兩個都帶上。同時，資訊科技部說，他們沒有多的投影機。不過他們現在就派人過去看看出了什麼問題。他們說，昨天簡報時還是好的。	
凱爾	**3:09**
太好了！待會見。	

149. 南西最有可能在哪裡？

A 會議室
B 資訊科技部門
C 用品儲藏室
D 她的辦公室

150. 南西說：「我現在就過去」是什麼意思？

A 她要過去那個地方
B 她會帶領簡報
C 她知道那個房間在哪裡
D 她要直接過去找他

151–152 票券

購票者：提姆．貝利

泰特劇院
凱莉．庫柏演唱會

時間：晚上七點
日期：5 月 20 日，星期五
區域：搖滾區
排：F
座位：26

- 搖滾區來賓請於演唱會開始前至少 30 分鐘入場
- 自行開車者，可上網站 www.tatetheater.com 查詢劇院位置
- 票券售出，概不退款

151. 貝利先生被建議做什麼事？

A 聯絡劇院要求退款
B 在網站上挑選喜歡的座位
C 提早入場
D 稍後發表評論

152. 根據票券，劇院的網站上可以看到什麼？

A 以前的表演清單
B 行車路線
C 演唱會評論
D 劇院照片

153–154 資訊

基墨尚好買
訂單確認

姓名：珍妮．柯林斯
顧客編號：F833J
地址：10025 紐約州紐約市哥倫布大道 808 號
訂購日期：8 月 22 日

品項	價格
彈簧圓模烤盤（單價5元5入）	25元
可可油四盎司	10.99元
糖衣（單價5.9元3入）*	17.70元
杯子蛋糕烤盤（單價4元2入）	8.00元
商品金額	61.69元
運費	8.99元
合計	70.68元
付款方式： 信用卡 xxxx xxxx xxxx 4026	

*備註：為防融化或毀損，將加速送達

153. 這些物品最有可能給哪種行業使用？

(A) 購物中心
(B) 麵包店
(C) 電器行
(D) 便利商店

154. 下列何者與訂單有關？

(A) 將使用分期付款
(B) 商品將分開遞送
(C) 已經打折了
(D) 將免費運送

155–157 文章

社區大獲全勝

在歷經長達數月的抗爭，力阻在河谷法院大樓的前院址興建開發新購物商場後，當地居民與民間團體皆歡欣鼓舞，因為最後裁決將完整無缺地保住這棟150年的建築。原本計劃興建購物中心的開發公司布蘭福德建設，現在正打算在河谷社區之外另蓋商場。「我們很失望。」布蘭福德建設執行長補充說道，「我們認為這地區可因此受益成長。但顯然地，居民們想保存他們的歷史，而我尊重他們的決定。」

他們正在努力修復廢棄的舊法院大樓，讓它恢復昔日榮景。「整個社區為此凝聚在一起，我們正在募款整修這棟大樓。」當地居民陳依尼表示：「我們希望把這棟大樓改建成公立圖書館或學校。」

「從我有記憶以來，它就在這裡了。事實上，我的祖父就在這裡當過職員。」當地商家老闆凱文．蘭伯說：「它是我們社區的一個象徵標誌，我們不希望它被破壞。」透過線上連署，該社區已經募集了十萬多元，而捐款仍然持續注入。該社區希望大樓的修復工程能在未來的幾個月內展開。

155. 文中提到舊法院大樓的什麼？

(A) 布蘭福德建設想修復這棟大樓
(B) 居民想把這棟大樓改成購物中心
(C) 它可能會變成公立圖書館或學校
(D) 它可能被破壞

156. 下列句子最適合出現在 [1]、[2]、[3]、[4] 的哪個位置？「原本計劃興建購物中心的開發公司布蘭福德建設，現在正打算在河谷社區之外另蓋商場。」

(A) [1]
(B) [2]
(C) [3]
(D) [4]

157. 下列何者與募款一事有關？

(A) 社區從土地上賺了很多錢
(B) 在網路上進行
(C) 市政府提供協助
(D) 他們還沒募到足夠的錢

158–160 電子郵件

收件者：史黛西．強生
<sjohnson@toplineelec.com>
寄件者：喬許．佛列克
<jfleck@toplineelec.com>
日期：10月22日
主旨：戰略規劃

親愛的強生女士：

泰菱電子區域管理部要通知您一個可能會影響您店面的新發展，另一家同您競爭消費者的電器行將於11月12日在克雷維爾區開幕。

為了確保泰菱電子的生意不會因為這家新店而失去生意，區域管理部建議您針對新型超高畫質曲面液晶電視推出特別優惠活動。這些電視有最先進的功能，卻有平實的價格。只要讓顧客知道泰菱電子會提供本地區中最實惠的價格，您就能維持顧客的忠誠度。我們將於下週內將新電視機配送到您的店裡。建議您在店內安排一塊顯眼的區域做展示，特別介紹它們。您也應更新網頁來宣傳這個促銷活動。

保持您與我們之間的溝通管道暢通對有效經營非常重要。如果您對新電視機或一般的行銷活動有任何問題，請不要猶豫，隨時歡迎與區域管理部聯絡。

泰菱電子 區域經理
喬許．佛列克 敬上

158. 強生女士最有可能是誰？

A 店經理
B 顧客
C 產品開發人員
D 行銷專家

159. 下列何者與泰菱電子有關？

A 它最近新開了一家門市
B 它將搬到克雷維爾區
C 它對市場競爭感到憂心
D 它在一項年度大獎中被提名

160. 強生女士未被指示做哪件事？

A 在網站上增加新資訊
B 多僱用員工
C 如有需要聯絡管理部
D 安排一個銷售展示區

161–164 網路討論區

哈利．尼克森 10:10
批發商那裡有任何關於書桌和辦公椅的消息嗎？我們週二就應該要就收到了。

強尼．喬登 10:11
莫妮卡正在等他們的消息。上回我聽到的是，因為生產線的問題而造成了一些延誤。看樣子，是有條傳輸帶故障了。

哈利．尼克森 10:12
你有把這件事告訴我們在 P&R 企業的客戶嗎？

強尼．喬登 10:13
沒有。我想在轉達任何延誤相關訊息前，先得到製造商的明確說法。嗨，莫妮卡，你收到回覆了嗎？

莫妮卡．史丹 10:14
是的，我剛跟他們談過。好消息，看來我們可以照原先計劃在週五完工。桌椅會在星期四時直接從生產線送達 P&R 企業。

哈利．尼克森 10:15
這消息真是太棒了，請通知克萊先生這件事。一旦家具送達，我們就可以開始進行五樓辦公室的工程，從那裡繼續往下做。

莫妮卡．史丹 10:15
我馬上處理。

強尼．喬登 10:16
好，我會召集一大群工作人員去那裡，這樣就能照計劃在週五時完工。

哈利．尼克森 10:17
好的，請確認不但是要有效率地完工，還要做得完善。他們還有幾間別的大樓，可能也會需要我們的服務。

強尼．喬登 10:18
我會牢記在心的。

161. 這幾位線上交談者從事何種行業？

A 法律事務所
B 辦公家具公司
C 家具店
D 搬家公司

162. 工作人員何時開工？

A 週二
B 週三
C 週四
D 週五

163. 強尼．喬登接下來可能會做什麼？

A 聯絡批發商
B 籌備會議
C 召集工作人員
D 打電話給客戶

164. 莫妮卡．史丹說的「我馬上處理」是什麼意思？

A 她會安排搬遷事宜
B 她會等到有更多資訊
C 她會拜訪製造商
D 她會聯絡客戶

165–167 企業介紹

富頓不鏽鋼製品

富頓不鏽鋼製品是一家大規模的製造商，在德國與法國的工廠生產不鏽鋼工業廚房用具。世界各地的廚師與烘焙師都相信本公司的產品耐用、持久，而且品質極佳。本公司生產廚房爐具、烤箱、微波爐、冰箱、食物調理機、電水壺、咖啡機以及其他產品。

本公司在上個月的交易中收購「微舍家庭用品公司」後，與去年財政年度相比，整體利潤可望提高 20%。因此，為了滿足增加的需求量，本公司將在六個廠區中增聘 300 多位全職員工，並提供優渥薪資以及絕佳的福利津貼。本公司視全體員工為富頓家族的寶貴成員。除此之外，本公司也將繼續研發新產品以滿足顧客需求，並與其他公司展開競爭。

165. 誰最有可能是富頓不鏽鋼製品的客戶？

A 汽車製造商
B 餐廳
C 房地產經紀公司
D 服飾店

166. 富頓不鏽鋼製品上個月做了什麼？

A 舉辦記者會
B 開設一家新工廠
C 取得一家公司
D 解聘一些工人

167. 文中提到有關富頓不鏽鋼製品的什麼？

A 它最近提供額外經費用於研發
B 它已公布明年的預算計劃
C 它為兼職員工提供了福利津貼
D 它打算僱用更多員工在工廠工作

168–171 公司通訊

員工榮獲全國比賽優勝

我們艾羅設計研究室的同仁珍妮佛．霍爾特，在網頁設計師協會（AWD）所舉辦的網頁設計比賽中榮獲第一名。參賽作品的評比準則是依據概念表達清晰度、製作品質以及美學。爾特女士從 300 多位參賽者獲選。我們為她的成就鼓掌，也很榮幸她是艾羅設計研究室的一員。

網頁設計師協會成立於 2002 年，旨在強調網頁設計的重要性及保護網頁設計師的權益。AWD 的會員來自世界各地，並持續增加新會員。為了推廣網頁設計至專業領域，AWD 舉辦各種比賽。AWD 相信好的設計可以改善人們生活，建立更好的社群。

身為網頁設計大賽的第一名得主，霍爾特女士將獲頒獎金，以及免費加入網頁設計師協會的會員資格。除此之外，她也受邀在下個月於加州洛杉磯舉辦的網頁設計師年度大會上發表演說。AWD 未來將舉辦更多比賽，意者可至官網 www.awd.com/contests 了解更多資訊。

168. 撰寫這篇文章最有可能的原因為何？

A 介紹新員工
B 報導一名獲獎者
C 宣布年度競賽
D 說明公司規定的改變

169. 第二段第一行的「founded」與下列哪個字意思最接近？

Ⓐ 發現
Ⓑ 學習
Ⓒ 建立
Ⓓ 裝備

170. 文中指出何者與網頁設計師協會有關？

Ⓐ 每年舉辦一場會議
Ⓑ 總部在洛杉磯
Ⓒ 目前提供免費加入會員
Ⓓ 捐錢給社區計劃

171. 根據這篇文章，網站上可以看到什麼？

Ⓐ 演講全文
Ⓑ 職缺的應徵函
Ⓒ 即將舉辦的比賽細節
Ⓓ 霍爾特女士的成就列表

172–175 文章

7 月 16 日新城——健康小屋位於新城市中心，是健身愛好者和公司員工們最熱門的新去處。老闆吉兒和貝瑞．貝克夫婦上個月開了這家店，受到熱烈的好評與大排長龍的人潮。生意好的時候，想在健康小屋等到位子得花上半小時之久，不管是什麼時段，那裡永遠擠滿人潮。健康小屋的菜單上只提供六種餐點：各式乳清蛋白暢銷飲品，有蘋果派、花生醬巧克力杯和什錦水果。儘管菜單的餐點種類有限，顧客們對於其美味又健康的乳清蛋白飲品讚不絕口。

「我們被大家的反應嚇到了，」吉兒．貝克說：「事實上，這一切都靠口耳相傳，所以我們甚至連廣告都不需要。」健身教練朱利安．邁爾斯說：「我喜歡來這裡吃頓不會破壞健身目標的簡單午餐，我甚至把這裡推薦給我所有的客戶。」「我和同事在短暫的午休時間來這裡吃頓健康但令人滿足的餐點」，商業人士提姆．漢默補充說道：「沒有健康小屋，我們就要吃垃圾食物了。」健康小屋的營業時間是每週一至週五的早上七點到晚上八點，週六上午九點至晚上七點，週日休息。老闆希望接下來幾個月內，在菜單上增加新餐點。

172. 文中暗示關於這家店的哪件事情？

Ⓐ 它很成功
Ⓑ 它只提供外帶服務
Ⓒ 它已經營業很久了
Ⓓ 只有健身達人光顧這家店

173. 下列何者與健康小屋的產品有關？

Ⓐ 它們很美味
Ⓑ 它們很健康
Ⓒ 它們很便宜
Ⓓ 它們很容易取得

174. 為什麼老闆不需要廣告宣傳？

Ⓐ 他們沒有足夠的錢
Ⓑ 他們太忙了
Ⓒ 他們的顧客向別人推薦了這家店
Ⓓ 他們不想

175. 下列句子最適合出現在 [1]、[2]、[3]、[4] 的哪個位置？「儘管菜單餐點種類有限，顧客們對於美味又健康的乳清蛋白飲品讚不絕口。」

Ⓐ [1]
Ⓑ [2]
Ⓒ [3]
Ⓓ [4]

176–180 簡章和電子郵件

夏季講座系列

由溫斯特大學城市規劃系主辦

城市規劃系很開心宣布一系列夏季講座，重點關注與本地居民和市政當局有關的預算議題。財務管理是地方政府營運最重要的職責之一。我們希望透過社區參與，來改善全國地方政府層級的預算編列的情況。所有的演講都將於溫斯特大學校區內的海頓斯大樓舉行。

2 月 1 日，星期一，下午 6 點，401 教室
演講者：提姆．鮑爾，溫斯特大學政策分析教授
策略規劃——學習如何編列預算以監督社區目標與成效的達成進度。

2 月 3 日，星期三，晚上 7 點，305 教室
演講者：瑪麗莎・西蒙斯，康乃迪政策制定中心
將重點放在孩童——研究顯示為孩童建造遊樂場與運動設施，有助於營造更好的社區環境。

2 月 8 日，星期一，下午 6 點，202 教室
演講者：漢克・羅斯，密西根市聯會縣立公園地管理——學習如何以寶貴的社區資源來維護地方公園區域。

2 月 10 日，星期三，下午 5 點 30 分，404 教室
演講者：史考特・華生，地方政府研究院常務董事
經濟機會與地方生態——經濟機會經常伴隨著潛在危險，對週遭生態系統造成威脅，在兩者間取得平衡並非易事。

欲知更多資訊，請洽派翠西亞・弗洛勒斯 pflores@wurnster.edu。

收件者：派翠西亞・弗洛勒斯
<pflores@wurnster.edu>
寄件者：傑克・彼得森
<jpatterson@wurnster.edu>
主旨：講座系列
日期：1 月 24 日

親愛的弗洛勒斯女士：

本人任職於溫斯頓大學的設備管理處，我最近發現您的講座日期出現了排程上的衝突。溫斯頓辯論社本學期每週三已經預約了 305 教室，因此，很遺憾地通知您，您需要更動這場演講的地點或時間。您可以上設備管理處的網站確認其他教室可使用的時間，並重新安排演講。

傑克・派得森

176. 這場講座系列最有可能是為誰安排的？

A 社區成員
B 大樓管理員
C 大學教授
D 大學生

177. 在簡章中，第一段第五行的「through」與下列哪個字意思最接近？

A 在……上面
B 透過
C 越過
D 直到

178. 2 月 10 日最有可能在講座中討論什麼？

A 如何平衡年度預算
B 如何符合公共建設的需求
C 如何避免環境傷害
D 如何刺激經濟發展

179. 根據派得森先生所言，誰的演講必須改期？

A 華生先生的
B 羅斯先生的
C 西蒙斯女士的
D 鮑爾先生的

180. 弗洛勒斯女士被指示要在網站上做什麼？

A 下載檔案
B 查看空教室
C 更新個人資料
D 推行論壇

181–185 電子郵件和清單

收件者：莎莉・羅素
<srussell@ptmail.com>
寄件者：凱莉・班尼特
<kbennett@msplanning.com>
日期：12 月 7 日
主旨：婚禮服務
附件：套裝專案

親愛的羅素小姐：

我們在 12 月 4 日星期二收到了您的電子郵件，詢問我們的婚禮策劃與活動服務。本公司專長各式婚禮（大小型，室內外，以及為您夢幻婚禮量身打造的各類場地布置），我們絕對有適合您的最佳方案。

您寫道，您想要一場低於五千元的婚禮套裝方案，並且要在一個接近主要公路的大型場地舉辦婚禮，因為您預計將有許多來自全國各地的賓客。據我了解，您其他的要求如下：

- 戶外場地
- 拍照攝影師與錄影師全程記錄
- 場地布置，包括各色花卉與高雅桌巾

我已隨信附上本公司所有您可能感興趣的套裝婚禮專案表，它們全位於距 519 號公路 15 分鐘的車程內。請您瀏覽所提供的資訊，決定哪個地點最符合您的需求。請您決定後，透過電子郵件告知您預計舉行婚禮的時間。這能幫助我為您確保預約。

感謝。

MS 婚禮策畫
凱莉．班尼特 敬上

套裝專案	全額費用	地點	備註
鑽石專案	5,500 元	哈帝劇院	綠寶石專案內容，加上現場弦樂四重奏
綠寶石專案	4,300 元	真立時公園	紅寶石專案內容，加上拍照及錄影服務
紅寶石專案	3,000 元	鄉間溫泉旅館	藍寶石專案內容，加上餐桌布置及美麗花卉
藍寶石專案	1,750 元	銀禧花園	自助式午餐及各式飲料

181. 文中可判斷出羅素小姐的什麼事情？

(A) 她是班尼特女士的同事
(B) 她正在規劃蜜月旅行
(C) 她現在已經訂婚了
(D) 她在外燴公司上班

182. 班尼特女士最有可能從事哪一行？

(A) 職業樂手
(B) 婚禮攝影師
(C) 室內設計師
(D) 活動策劃員

183. 下列何者與表單中的所有地點有關？

(A) 它們都接近主要道路
(B) 它們都是室內場地
(C) 它們都位在同一城市
(D) 它們都要求預付訂金

184. 羅素小姐被要求提供什麼資訊？

(A) 可能的日期
(B) 餐點選擇
(C) 賓客名單
(D) 蜜月地點

185. 哪一個套裝專案可能最符合羅素小姐的需求？

(A) 鑽石專案
(B) 綠寶石專案
(C) 紅寶石專案
(D) 藍寶石專案

186–190 電子郵件

收件者：<info@bountifulharvest.com>
寄件者：艾蜜莉．霍爾
<emilyhall@zipline.com>
日期：6 月 3 日
主旨：食物配送

敬啟者：

我叫艾蜜莉．霍爾，是亨茨維爾市中心一家素食餐廳的老闆。會與您連絡，是因為我對每週定期配送新鮮有機蔬菜到本餐廳的服務感興趣。我的餐廳才剛開幕，所以不需要大量貨品。在研究過本地不同的農場後，我選擇聯絡大豐收農場，就是因為你們保證配送有機認證的食物。因此，我想索取一份每週直送新鮮蔬菜到本餐廳的費用估價單。

艾蜜莉．霍爾

收件者：艾蜜莉．霍爾
<emilyhall@zipline.com>
寄件者：大豐收農場
<info@bountifulharvest.com>
日期：6 月 4 日
主旨：回覆：食物配送

親愛的霍爾女士：

感謝您與本農場聯絡。在大豐收農場，我們提供新鮮有機農產品，可定期直送給客戶。我們的蔬菜從田地採收後會立刻配送，這表示您可以收到有益健康、營養、有機的農產品，以供貴餐廳使用。我們也提供其他的商品，像是新鮮的肉類、起士和牛奶。以下是詳列我們各式商品的價目表。

方案選擇	特點	重量	配送頻率	單次配送價格
個人	這個套裝供大約二到三人食用，內含新鮮當季蔬菜。	5 磅	一週一次	15 元
小型	這個套裝適合小型商家，內含新鮮當季蔬菜。	50 磅	一週一次	140 元
中型	這個套裝適合需要長期供應新鮮蔬菜與肉類的中型商家。	130 磅	一週兩次	500 元
大型	這是我們最大的套裝，內含蔬菜、肉類和乳製品。	250 磅	一週兩次	800 元

以上所列的價格未含運費。無法自取的顧客，則需要多付六元的運費。但是對於簽訂整年度配送合約的顧客，則免運費。若購買其他商品，也會影響該方案的最終價格。其他可選購的商品請參考本農場網站。款項可於出貨日以現金、信用卡、支票或匯票方式給付。

我們知道顧客特別在意食物的品質。因此我們提供了免費的迷你包，方便您先行評估我們的食物。請來電 555-8141 與格雷格．雷蒙斯聯絡並索取。

英迪拉．辛格

收件者：大豐收農場
<info@bountifulharvest.com>
寄件者：艾蜜莉．霍爾
<emilyhall@zipline.com>
日期：6 月 5 日
主旨：收成時間表

親愛的辛格女士：

感謝您如此迅速地回覆我的電子郵件。我很感謝你們提供免費試用品，但我想我乾脆就直接安排定期配送。我對安排整年度的配送很感興趣，但我想先取得不同季節時你們會提供的農產品項目清單。由於我經營的是素食餐廳，我需要對所配送的農產品種類有個概念，這樣我才能依此準備菜單。非常感謝您的體諒，很期待與大豐收農場合作！

祝好

艾蜜莉．霍爾

186. 第一封電子郵件的目的是什麼？

A 要求費用資料
B 詢問規定更動
C 延後訂單
D 通報錯誤的發票

187. 哪一個選擇方案可能最符合霍爾女士的需求？

A 個人
B 小型
C 中型
D 大型

188. 最終價格裡不需要哪一項資訊？

A 合約期限
B 配送方式
C 加購物品
D 運送距離

189. 艾蜜莉．霍爾的電子郵件中提到了什麼？

A 她想要試一個月看看
B 她想要免費贈品
C 她對長期合約有興趣
D 她不想要冬季農產品

190. 艾蜜莉．霍爾為什麼想知道整年度會收到的蔬菜種類？

A 她喜愛蔬菜
B 她正在考慮增加肉類
C 她可能會多僱用一位員工
D 她想規劃未來的菜單

191–195 告示和電子郵件

重要公告

親愛的卡斯泰利顧客：

本公司品保團隊表示，有五百罐卡斯泰利經典義大利麵醬未符合本公司產品品質的高標準。

這個瑕疵是由罐蓋的密封不當所造成的，且因為接觸到空氣，可能已經造成內容物的腐壞。目前我們正警告顧客不得食用該產品。

您該怎麼做：如果您已經購買了卡斯泰利經典義大利麵醬，請寄電子郵件至本公司客服部 cs@castellifood.com，本公司同仁將提供您商品兌換券。請在電子郵件中註明您的姓名、完整地址、電話號碼以及產品序號，顧客所購買的每一罐商品都會收到一張 12 元的折價券。請勿於零售店辦理退貨。

請記得卡斯泰利食品的其他產品都未受影響。我們鼓勵您繼續購買本公司的產品。

收件者：<cs@castellifood.com>
寄件者：湯尼．赫斯特
<tonyhester21@webzit.com>
日期：3 月 29 日
主旨：兌換券

敬啟者：

我叫湯尼．赫斯特，很感謝這個防範措施。大約在兩週前，我在明尼蘇達州赫曼鎮的艾斯雜貨店，買了兩罐卡斯泰利經典義大利麵醬。一週後，我又在同一家店買了另一罐。

我已隨電子郵件附上兩張收據的圖片檔，希望能收到這些不良品的商品兌換券。我的地址是：

湯尼．赫斯特
55811 明尼蘇達州赫曼鎮布魯街 27 號
期待儘快收到回覆。

湯尼．赫斯特

收件者：湯尼．赫斯特
<tonyhester21@webzit.com>
寄件者：<cs@castellifood.com>
日期：3 月 30 日
主旨：折價券

親愛的赫斯特先生：

非常感謝您與卡斯泰利食品聯繫。我們承諾確保顧客可以繼續信賴卡斯泰利的高品質食品，以滿足其所有用餐需求。為此，我們很樂意為您最近所購買的卡斯泰利經典義大利麵醬，提供您三張兌換券。請查看所附上的兌換券。

除了經典義大利麵醬的兌換券外，我們也提供您本公司新系列細扁麵、義大利麵與通心粉的折價券，請接受這些做為我們表達歉意的另一種方式。我們希望您繼續惠顧本公司美味的義大利食品。

客服專員
珍．奧森 敬上

191. 這張公告最有可能在哪裡看到？

A 餐廳
B 員工休息室
C 航運公司
D 雜貨店

192. 下列何者與罐子有關？

A 沒有關緊
B 目前缺貨
C 標價錯誤
D 送到錯的地址

193. 根據這張公告，何者不是給顧客的建議？

A 不要食用該產品
B 通報該產品
C 將產品退回商店
D 購買卡斯泰利其他產品

194. 在給赫斯特先生的電子郵件中，卡斯泰利公司額外提供了什麼贈品？

Ⓐ 通心粉醬
Ⓑ 食譜
Ⓒ 農產品折價券
Ⓓ 新產品折價券

195. 下列何者不是卡斯泰利公司送出折價券的理由？

Ⓐ 保住客戶忠誠度
Ⓑ 表達歉意
Ⓒ 對顧客公平
Ⓓ 獲得新顧客

196–200 表格、電子郵件和告示

奧本市餐廳查驗

餐廳名稱：波利多比薩
地址：克拉克街 43 號
抽查日期：1 月 22 日

A：無違規，完全符合安全與健康法規。

B：輕微違規，符合大多數安全與健康法規。

C：部分違規，未符合部分安全與健康法規。

D：未符合安全與健康法規，出現可能對顧客造成傷害或致病的嚴重違規。

（食物準備與存放方面出現 C、D 等級違規行為，將處以罰款）

項目	分數
1. 人員定期洗手並遵守衛生規定	B
2. 生肉與蔬菜以適當溫度冷藏	A
3. 所有的食材都適當存放與標示	C
4. 碗盤與用具經清潔與消毒	A
5. 滅火器可方便取用	B
6. 火災逃生口標示清楚	C
7. 地面乾淨並保持乾燥	B

為避免更多罰款，餐廳應於下次查驗前改善違規情況。

餐廳所有人：葛瑞格・克魯克
檢驗員：瑪莉莎・坦嚀

收件者：全體員工
<employees@politospizza.com>
寄件者：葛瑞格・克魯克
<gregkluck@politospizza.com>
主旨：檢驗結果
日期：1 月 25 日

親愛的同仁：

最近在 1 月 22 日的檢驗報告指出了一些我們需要注意的問題。

首先，我注意到的就是必須重新裝設火災逃生出口標示。最嚴重的違規是有關食物的不當存放與標示。所有之後會用到的食材都必須標示確切日期與詳細內容，如果沒有將容器標示清楚，可能會不小心把腐壞的食物提供給顧客。我們在員工衛生與設備的清潔度上拿到了相對低的分數，全體員工隨時都要穿著制服，戴上髮網，並在每次使用洗手間之後洗手。我們也需要更常拖地，並保持乾燥。

為了改正這些不良狀況，我會貼一張確認表，全體同仁每天早上都必須完成，裡面包括了必要的準備工作，以確保我們沒有違反任何規定。這個措施將於 1 月 29 日實施。如果您對

這些變革有任何疑問，請在明天的員工會議上提出。

全體同仁注意

每位波利多比薩的同仁在每天輪值時，都必須簽寫以下確認表。只有在工作完成或檢查後才能簽名。未在確認表上填寫日期、時間與簽名者，將視同違反波利多比薩新的健康標準規定。

波利多確認表

波利多	星期日	星期一	星期二	星期三	星期四	星期五	星期六
輪換食物	K.P.	K.P.	K.P.	K.P.			K.P.
拖地	K.P.	K.P.	K.P.	K.P.			K.P.
制服	K.P.	K.P.	K.P.	K.P.			K.P.
洗手	K.P.	K.P.	K.P.	K.P.			K.P.

196. 為什麼要進行檢驗？

A 監督食品業法規的符合狀況
B 評價美食的口味與品質
C 檢查大樓的結構安全
D 評估新政策的效率

197. 波利多比薩為什麼被罰款？

A 因為滅火器沒有在場
B 因為食物容器沒有適當標示
C 因為不當處置生肉與蔬菜
D 因為設備沒有依標準清理

198. 克魯克先生要求員工做什麼？

A 向顧客道歉
B 隨時配戴名牌
C 投訴坦孽女士
D 填寫必要的表格

199. 如果員工沒有簽寫工作確認表，會發生什麼事？

A 他們的紀錄上會有違規紀錄
B 他們必須付罰款
C 他們必須在週末上班
D 他們會被開除

200. 根據波利多確認表，我們可以推論出有關 K.P. 的什麼事？

A 他上晚班
B 他週四週五休假
C 他因違規被開除
D 他做事動作很慢

ACTUAL TEST ②

PART 5 P.48–51

◎ Part 5 解答請見 P.457

101. 有了資訊科技人員的協助，遺失的會計文件已經被**救回來**了。

102. 一場專為藝廊贊助者舉辦的私人招待會將於 3 月 5 日**舉行**，就在展覽盛大開幕會之前。

103. 歐若拉家具發現，要在**日益**競爭的市場中獲利很困難。

104. 機師在飛機起飛前**不久**，發現電機出了一點小問題。

105. 在檢視**估算**成本後，我們將對這棟房子的造景變動做出最終決定。

106. 我的健康公司已經生產**超過** 20 年的各種維他命保養品。

107. 由於新進的美編，四月號的《不僅是釣魚》雜誌看起來與之前的期數**完全**不同。

108. 客戶的訂單**確認函**將於 24 小時內以電子郵件寄出。

109. 維修團隊的修繕申請必須根據緊急程度分組**安排**。

110. 在李維拉女士的**簡短**聲明後，普列士企業的正式頒獎典禮隨即展開。

111. 由於大量人潮往來，商店在旺季時必須比平時更**常**擦地板。

112. 由於社區活動中心的會議室被重複預訂了，大師園藝社的月會必須**延後**。

113. 財務顧問報告說，較年長的投資者往往比年輕人**更謹慎**。

114. 阿爾布雷希特先生**迅速**回了人資主管的電子郵件，這證明他對這個職務有高度興趣。

115. 足球員們通常在沃特伯里公園的主運動場練習，但他們偶爾也會在**其他地方**練習。

116. 會計師們無法在截止日期前提出完整報告，但**他們**保證會給一份重點摘要。

117. 儘管表演中音響系統出了問題，但對每個人來說，這場音樂會仍然是個**愉快的**經驗。

118. **由於**這棟建築有極佳的位置和現代化的內部裝潢，很受遊客的歡迎。

119. 公園與遊憩部門為志工們提供了改善社區的**寶貴**機會。

120. 旅社二樓的空房已經**全部**打掃過了。

121. 這個短篇故事在**沒有**得到作者明確同意的狀況下無法再行印製。

122. 餐廳裡有一間裝潢**活潑**的包廂，非常適合舉辦兒童派對。

123. 一位野生動物專家預定發表一場演講，有關工廠對週遭森林所產生的**影響**。

124. 房東第一次調漲幾年來沒變的每月房租，這樣做是**合理**的。

125. 只要別再出現延誤，工廠就可以在 6 月 18 日前全面**運作**。

126. 多虧他的個人經驗，華倫先生**一定**可以獨力完成這份工作。

127. 由於燃料成本**上漲**，有些人選擇暑假時待在家裡，而非開車到觀光勝地。

128. **每當**需要更換濾心**時**，濾水器側邊的綠燈就會亮起。

129. 伯克女士的訂單中有兩項物品缺貨，所以她的發票也**跟著**修改。

130. 公告指出，有一場急救訓練課程將於下個月免費提供給**居民**參加。

131–134 告示

春季員工培訓

勞倫斯報致力協助全體員工發揮他們的潛能，這就是為什麼我們再度安排了兩天的春季培訓課程。人資部已經為今年的培訓準備了廣泛的主題，包括銷售技巧、電腦技能、溝通策略以及目標設定。培訓還有兩個空的時段，所以如果大家有任何非常渴望學習的事物，請告訴我們，我們或許可以將它納入今年的春季培訓當中。我們將於本週末前確定最終的選擇。如果您有任何想法，歡迎向人力資源部的南西・肯辛頓提出。

131. A 分發
B 設置
C 包括
D 促進

132. A 當時正納入
B 已經納入
C 現在納入
D 可納入

133. A 如果我們收到很多建議，我們也可以在下週週末 12 月 4 日舉辦培訓。
B 我們將於本週末前確定最終的選擇。
C 我們投入大量的時間和精力籌備這場會議。
D 我們一向鼓勵大家邀請親友來參加這些活動。

134. A 創造
B 要求
C 提出
D 轉調

135–138 廣告

萬達房地產

萬達房地產已經在休士頓地區服務超過 29 年。我們保證提供最高等級的市場專業知識及客製化服務，因此被公認是業界的領導者。

本公司專營丹佛地區自用與企業房地產。不管您想買新家，還是開展新事業，您都應該與我們洽談。由於本公司就位於市中心，我們關注整個城市的動向。請參考本公司網站上的物件清單，或今天就來電。當然，我們永遠歡迎您隨時大駕光臨。

www.vanderproperties.com
電話：(313) 782-9919
地址：沃頓街 834 號

135. A 客製
B 客製
C 客製中
D 客製化的

136. A 有成效的
B 獲得升遷
C 有關聯的
D 住宅的

137. **A 不論**
B 即使
C 儘管
D 不管怎樣

138. A 今天就開車出城來看看我們吧。
B 我們感謝您的協助。
C 當然，我們永遠歡迎您隨時大駕光臨。
D 我們的餐廳每天從八點營業到五點。

139–142 告示

> **誠徵比薩廚師**
>
> 吉諾老爹正在徵才，所有符合資格的應徵者都將列入考量中。我們正在找具有料理義式餐點經驗的人。即使您沒有經驗，只要符合資格條件，我們將提供訓練。為了符合條件，您必須具備有效的保健卡、可靠的交通工具，還要能夠在晚上與週末時上班。請親自至州街與松街的吉諾老爹應徵。期待見到您。

139. A 使合格
B 合格的
C 合格的
D 使合格

140. **A 我們正在找具有料理義式餐點經驗的人。**
B 我們正在找會說義大利文的人。
C 我們正在找喜歡吃比薩的人。
D 我們正在找想練習的人。

141. **A 有效的**
B 工作的
C 生效的
D 強壯的

142. A 她
B 他們
C 我們
D 他

143–146 信件

> 11 月 11 日
> 約翰・亞當斯
> 10873 紐約州紐約市三州區 408 公寓
>
> 親愛的亞當斯先生：
>
> 很高興通知您，您已經獲選為高第薩克斯公司銷售經理一職的最終人選。在該職位的一百多位應徵者中，我們已經將名單減縮至八位。我們邀請您來參加 11 月 15 日下午一點到六點的面試，我們希望您能在下午一點時抵達，地點就在公司總部。助理藍恩小姐將於大廳與您碰面，帶您到面試室。
>
> 對於面談表現良好的應徵者，我們將進行第二次面試。我們將儘快通知您合格與否。
>
> 若有任何疑問，請打 555-1234 與我們聯絡。
>
> 希望很快就可以見到您。
>
> 行政經理
> 珍妮佛・羅 敬上

143. A 正在選擇
B 已經選擇
C 已經被選擇
D 選擇

144. **A 職位**
B 地點
C 職業
D 預約

145. A 那棟大樓很容易找。
B 我們希望您能在下午一點時抵達。
C 我們的面試官將問您一些問題。
D 您將拿到一份明確的時程表。

146. A 使能夠
B 批准
C 拒絕
D 合格

PART 7 P.56–79

147–148 廣告

> **驚奇世界攝影比賽**
>
> 旅遊月刊《驚奇世界》現正為 11 月註冊的人士提供訂閱優惠。《驚奇世界》已經發行 30 餘年，提供讀者行家情報及專業知識，幫助您規劃夢想之旅。本雜誌包含了度假套裝行程廣告、遊客評論以及具有深度見解的短文，介紹您認識各種不同的文化、美食和旅遊勝地。

將您的旅遊照片寄來參加驚奇世界攝影比賽，就有機會贏得一趟蘇格蘭美妙之旅。首獎優勝者將獲贈兩人來回機票，以及價值 2,000 元的旅遊住宿券。

147. 文中提到有關雜誌的什麼？

Ⓐ 這是一本文學雜誌
Ⓑ 內含一本食譜副刊
Ⓒ 提供旅遊建議
Ⓓ 有線上版

148. 下列何者與比賽有關？

Ⓐ 由專業攝影師所贊助
Ⓑ 獲勝者將獲得一趟免費旅程
Ⓒ 只接受數位照片
Ⓓ 以英格蘭的照片為主軸

149–151 訊息串

麗滋・布雷德利 **8:14**
長官，您與強生先生明天下午的會議都已安排妥當，我已在喜來登餐廳訂了下午一點兩人的座位。

伯尼・吉布斯 **8:17**
謝謝你，會議所需的報告都彙整好了嗎？

麗滋・布雷德利 **8:18**
大部分都好了。我還在等麥可・斯蒂爾的報告。他告訴我，他今天早上會準備好給我。

伯尼・吉布斯 **8:20**
好。這應該要在昨天晚上就弄好，你可以聯絡他看看到底是怎麼一回事？

（麥可・斯蒂爾於 8:26 加入對話）

麗滋・布雷德利 **8:27**
麥可，吉布斯先生想知道報告在哪裡。你做完了沒？

麥可・斯蒂爾 **8:28**
很抱歉耽誤了。我們的實習生不小心刪除了一些檔案，我必須搜尋整個資料庫才能找到備份資料。要查看所有我需要的文件並加以分類有點棘手，但我想我已經處理好了，現在要列印出來了。

麗滋・布雷德利 **8:29**
你可以一印好就拿來給我嗎？

麥可・斯蒂爾 **8:30**
當然，十分鐘後到。

149. 麗滋・布雷德利最有可能是誰？

Ⓐ 實習生
Ⓑ 助理
Ⓒ 生意夥伴
Ⓓ 行政主管

150. 麥可・斯蒂爾為什麼加入對話？

Ⓐ 要他提供缺失報告的最新狀況
Ⓑ 通知他即將到來的會議
Ⓒ 讓他知道截止日期
Ⓓ 責備他不守時

151. 麥可說：「我必須搜尋整個資料庫才能找到備份資料」是什麼意思？

Ⓐ 他從容不迫地寫報告
Ⓑ 他必須先將所有資料備份
Ⓒ 他需要時間找遺失的資料
Ⓓ 電腦故障了

152–153 網頁

透納公司

英國紅木灣巴金絲路 158 號
電話：243-555-1541

首頁	關於我們	產品	配件	聯絡我們

透納公司自 1949 年成立以來，一直製造美麗且節能的窗戶，以滿足顧客的品味與期望。當您選擇透納公司，您所購買的不只是一扇窗戶，您將獲得我們專業人員數十年來一向表現卓越的絕佳服務。我們熱情地協助您挑選完全符合您住家規格的高品質窗戶，除此之外，我們全心致力於環保，而且我們的永續企業經營最近還通過了環境保護局（EPA）的認可。

152. 這篇文章在廣告什麼？

Ⓐ 保險公司
Ⓑ 窗戶製造商
Ⓒ 庭園造景公司
Ⓓ 窗戶清潔服務公司

153. 下列何者與透納公司有關？

Ⓐ 它是家族企業
Ⓑ 它的分公司遍及全國
Ⓒ 它是間注重環保的公司
Ⓓ 它最近聘用了經驗豐富的員工

154–155 簡訊

傳送者：山姆・貝爾
接收者：珍・布魯斯

珍，請告訴我佛雷澤先生的電話號碼。他那裡有一些我現在就要的資料。我的財務月報表進度已經有點落後，我今天需要把所有時間都花在這上面。

154. 為什麼要傳這則訊息？

Ⓐ 請求協助
Ⓑ 延後期限
Ⓒ 取消會議
Ⓓ 索取文件資料

155. 下列何者與貝爾先生有關？

Ⓐ 他無法出席會議
Ⓑ 他希望利潤提高
Ⓒ 他試著趕上截止日期
Ⓓ 他最近得到新工作

156–158 文章

首爾（7 月 19 日）——布里明集團在南韓著名的狎鷗亭洞羅德奧街上開設了第一家 B&G 服飾店，開幕便大排長龍，吸引許多狂熱買家。造成瘋狂的是馬利奇歐・布奇和 B&G 合作設計的限量版商品。就在營業後的幾個小時內，大部分由布奇所設計的商品已銷售一空。類似的騷動及被掃蕩一空的布奇商品架的報導，在世界各大城市像是紐約、倫敦、東京和米蘭也曾發生過。雖然 B&G 也曾和其他著名設計師合作發行限量商品，但這是第一次 B&G 門市回報有商品在推出幾小時後就銷售一空的現象。布奇和 B&G 的合作是目前為止最成功的案例，並已開始著手洽談日後更多服飾系列的合作案。這是該公司的創舉，因為之前的限量設計商品都只是一次性的合作關係。同時，在首爾買不到布奇系列的顧客雖然感到失望，但對於高人氣店家能在進駐韓國也感到興奮。

156. 下列何者與 B&G 有關？

Ⓐ 全世界都有分店
Ⓑ 他們只賣由布奇設計的商品
Ⓒ 在韓國有幾家分店
Ⓓ 商品通常在幾小時內銷售一空

157. 文中報導什麼關於布奇和 B&G 的合作案？

Ⓐ 花好幾年才談妥
Ⓑ 只在特定商店才有販售
Ⓒ 對該公司而言是最賺錢的合作案之一
Ⓓ 這將只是一次性的活動

158. 下列句子最適合出現在 [1]、[2]、[3]、[4] 的哪個位置？「這是該公司的創舉，因為之前的限量設計商品都只是一次性的合作關係。」

Ⓐ [1]
Ⓑ [2]
Ⓒ [3]
Ⓓ [4]

159–161 備忘錄

備忘錄

收文者：全體職員
發文者：伊莉莎白・潘恩
日期：1 月 24 日
主旨：病假

全體同仁，請注意：

本公司星網企業將針對病假規定做出調整。我們正在考慮減少帶薪休假的天數，增加員工們可申請的帶薪病假的天數。在我們做出任何異動前，我們想收集同仁們對這件事的意見。請寄電子郵件給湯尼．納金特 tonynugent@zimnet.com，他會彙集並分析各位的回覆。之後，管理部將於 2 月 24 日前做出相對應的政策提案。一旦完成提案，將召開會議以討論全體員工的實行事宜。希望這個做法對全體同仁有所助益，請大家踴躍參與。

伊莉莎白．潘恩 敬上

159. 這份備忘錄的目的是什麼？

Ⓐ 建議預算企劃
Ⓑ 徵求回饋意見
Ⓒ 修正錯誤資訊
Ⓓ 宣布調查結果

160. 納金特先生最有可能擔任什麼職務？

Ⓐ 業務
Ⓑ 產品開發人員
Ⓒ 投資分析師
Ⓓ 人事部職員

161. 根據這份備忘錄，潘恩女士可能會在 2 月 24 日後就做什麼？

Ⓐ 宣布合併
Ⓑ 聘用專科醫師
Ⓒ 參加旅遊
Ⓓ 安排會議

162–165 訊息串

潘妮．瓊斯 3:27
我剛接到馬丁的電話，他的客戶派翠克先生希望他的訂單能比原定計劃提早兩週完成。基本上，就是下週一前。你們認為有可能嗎？我想知道大家的看法。

凱倫．諾曼 3:28
我們這邊沒問題。大多數的皮革都已經裁切好了，我們已經把很多皮革送去縫接了。剩下的工作應該只要幾個小時。

尼爾．帕克 3:29
把手已經做好了，大約一半的包包都接近完工，我可以儘快送到羅倫那裡。我想我們應該可以在明天傍晚前縫好那些包包。

潘妮．瓊斯 3:30
很高興聽到大部分的手提包都快完工了。羅倫，把那些金屬貼上去或縫上去要多久時間？

勞倫．尼可斯 3:31
我們現在正在做詹克和堅克雙胞胎的訂單。

潘妮．瓊斯 3:32
我們有非常充裕的時間來完成那對雙胞胎的訂單，所以我批准你的工作人員先把那邊的工作擱置一旁。那派翠克先生的訂單要花多久時間？

勞倫．尼可斯 3:33
拉鍊需要用縫的，但飾釘可以用黏的，這樣會簡單一點。我想我們需要大約一天的時間。

凱文．哈汀 3:34
妥善包裝以安全出貨只需要幾小時。

潘妮．瓊斯 3:35
太感謝各位了。我會告訴客戶的。

162. 這個客戶最有可能經營哪種生意？

Ⓐ 服飾店
Ⓑ 家具公司
Ⓒ 鞋店
Ⓓ 手提包業

163. 根據對話內容，誰的部門必須先完工？

Ⓐ 凱倫．諾曼的
Ⓑ 尼爾．帕克的
Ⓒ 勞倫．尼可斯的
Ⓓ 凱文．哈汀的

164. 在 3:31 時，勞倫．尼可斯為什麼會說：「我們現在正在做詹克和堅克雙胞胎的訂單。」

Ⓐ 為了告訴大家他們現在有自己的客戶了
Ⓑ 為了解釋他們為什麼拒絕幫忙
Ⓒ 為了暗示他們正忙著其他的工作
Ⓓ 為了讓大家加快速度完成工作

165. 潘妮・瓊斯最有可能跟派翠克先生說什麼？

A 他的訂單兩週後才會完成
B 他的要求可以達成
C 他的訂單要額外加錢
D 他的訂單可能會延誤

166–168 告示

三月初的營業時間

星期一	星期二	星期三
下午 2:00－晚上 9:00	下午 2:00－晚上 8:00	下午 3:00－晚上 9:00
星期四	**星期五**	**星期六**
下午 4:00－晚上 9:00	下午 2:00－晚上 9:00	下午 2:00－晚上 10:00
星期日		
早上 9:00－下午 6:00		

由於仙令街目前正在進行工程，我們必須不更動三月第一週的營業時間（請參考上列表格）。早上時間，工程的進行讓顧客很難開車到我們門市，為了順應這個變化，我們將延長夜間營業時間。另外，由於工程的關係，目前我們的停車場也無法使用。因此，在這段期間，請顧客利用沛奇街上的公共停車場。我們為此不便深感抱歉，也會努力儘快恢復正常。

166. 這篇文章公告了什麼？

A 整修計劃
B 展店
C 營業時間異動
D 工作時程表

167. 何時最不可能施工？

A 星期一
B 星期三
C 星期六
D 星期日

168. 顧客為什麼被要求到沛奇街？

A 找地方停車
B 造訪一家新門市
C 參加促銷活動
D 拿樣品

169–171 廣告

船主求售
帕默爾標準艙遊艇

要價：45,000 元或最佳出價

基本規格：
這艘船建於四年前，寬 12 呎，長 36 呎。船身由纖維玻璃打造而成，使得整艘船輕盈但堅固。這艘船內有兩間雙人房、一張沙發床、廚房和浴室。

特點：
這艘船非常平穩並有寬敞的甲板，適合大家族與社交聚會。船上有套八揚聲器的音響系統，可連接 USB，還有一個可存放私人物品的上鎖式儲藏隔間。

其他資訊：
我已經擁有並使用這艘船三年半。這艘船有五年的保固期，所以現在還剩一年半的時間。一經購買後，保固可移轉給買家。

如果您想看看這艘船或試乘，請來電 (654) 555-8715 找格瑞・湯普森。

169. 下列何者和帕默爾標準艙遊艇有關？

A 它是一艘漁船
B 它原始的油漆顏色已經換了
C 它可容納一群人
D 它目前正在維修中

170. 下列何者不是帕默爾標準艙遊艇的特點？

A 播放音樂的功能
B 輕量建材
C 寬敞的睡眠空間
D 省油引擎

171. 關於湯普森先生，下列何者最有可能為真？

A 他會為潛在買家提供一趟遊艇之旅
B 他有年幼的小孩
C 他在造船廠工作
D 他想要另外賣保證書

172–175 信件

旅遊與休閒
48857 加州橘郡吉爾摩街 123 號

11 月 15 日
彼得・康先生
19387 華盛頓州西雅圖市河谷高地 3820 號

親愛的康先生：

《旅遊與休閒》雜誌感謝您的訂閱。由於您是我們的長期訂戶，我很高興通知您一個針對我們 VIP 會員的新訂閱方案。您的訂閱方案將於下個月到期，但我們邀請您考慮加入 VIP 會員。以會員來說，您可以繼續收到本雜誌的月刊號，也可以使用我們新的線上電子雜誌服務。您不需額外付費，就可以將紙本雜誌的數位版本下載至任何行動裝置中。而且，您還可以取得本雜誌的作者、記者與特約撰稿人的背景資料，以及雜誌提及之場所與地點的詳細資訊。此外，您還可以得到全世界最受歡迎餐廳的食譜。最棒的是，我們為 VIP 會員舉辦了一場可贏得夏威夷雙人遊的獨家比賽。一般訂戶和 VIP 會員，將有機會贏得在貝利西默五星級餐廳用餐的體驗。

再次感謝您持續的支持，希望您喜歡我們在服務上做的異動，我們努力娛樂並教育忠實訂戶。請填寫本函所附上的申請表，確認您欲參加的訂閱方案。如果您付 100 元的費用，將得到一般訂戶的訂閱方案。如果您付 200 元的費用，即可成為 VIP 會員。

感謝您的支持，希望很快收到您的回音。

維多莉雅・亞當斯 敬上

172. 為什麼要寄信給康先生？

A 提醒他提交旅遊日誌
B 說明新的訂閱方案
C 詢問他的旅遊計劃
D 確定他合乎某個職位的資格

173. 亞當斯女士隨信附上了什麼？

A 旅遊行程表
B 新合約
C 申請表
D 修改過的時程表

174. 在信件中，第一段中間的「at no extra cost」意思最接近？

A 很少的費用
B 捐款
C 相當簡單
D 免費

175. 下列句子最適合出現在 [1]、[2]、[3]、[4] 的哪個位置？「您的訂閱方案將於下個月到期，但我們邀請您考慮加入 VIP 會員。」

A [1]
B [2]
C [3]
D [4]

176–180 發票和電子郵件

泰勒織品
發票

訂購者：譚米・弗列克
經手人：克雷格・戴爾
訂購日期：8 月 11 日
預計送達日：8 月 14 日到 16 日
運送地址：78701 德州奧斯汀綠圓道 628 號
電子信箱：tfleck@capnet.com
行動電話：(512) 555-9782

數量	品項	說明	價格
4 碼	10 號布料	純白色	28.00 元
5 碼	38 號布料	印花	50.00 元
6 碼	41 號布料	方格	48.00 元
2 碼	48 號布料	豹紋	30.00 元

TEST 2
PART 7

	稅 15.60 元
	運費 12.00 元
	總計 183.60 元

付款方式：
以末四碼為 4680 的信用卡支付帳單
如果您對訂單有任何疑問，請寄電子郵件至 customerservice@taylorfabrics.com。所有美國境內的包裹保證於訂單確認後十天內送達。若未於時間內送達，我們保證退還 30% 的全額購物金。

收件者：
customerservice@taylorfabrics.com
寄件者：譚米・弗列克
<tfleck@capnet.com>
日期：8 月 25 日
主旨：運送延誤

客服部您好：

我昨天才收到兩週前在泰勒織品所訂購的東西。包裹不僅比原先承諾的時間要晚到，其中一項物品還寄錯了。發票上正確地載明了我要的是五碼的印花布，但是送來的只有兩碼。因為這個失誤，我無法完成原本要為朋友生日所做的洋裝。我深感失望。

等這個問題一處理好，補寄的織布也寄出後，請傳簡訊到我的行動電話。

謝謝

譚米・弗列克

176. 戴爾先生的工作最有可能是什麼？

Ⓐ 設計師
Ⓑ 銷售員
Ⓒ 顧客
Ⓓ 製造商

177. 下列何者與弗列克女士有關？

Ⓐ 她是泰勒織品的長期客戶
Ⓑ 她是專業的時尚設計師
Ⓒ 她是泰勒織品的前員工
Ⓓ 她將拿回部分的購物金

178. 弗列克女士為什麼寄這封電子郵件？

Ⓐ 她的信用卡被錯誤扣款
Ⓑ 她想退還一項物品
Ⓒ 她收到某項數量錯誤的商品
Ⓓ 她訂的某項商品的樣式是錯的

179. 弗列克女士還需要哪一款布來做洋裝？

Ⓐ 10 號布料
Ⓑ 38 號布料
Ⓒ 41 號布料
Ⓓ 48 號布料

180. 泰勒織品的客服要如何聯絡弗列克女士？

Ⓐ 透過簡訊
Ⓑ 透過語音信箱
Ⓒ 透過電子郵件
Ⓓ 透過郵件

181–185 廣告和電子郵件

下個月在貝爾蒙特市歷史協會舉行

紀錄片之夜：《探索北極》
5 月 5 日，雲杉劇院

攝影展：「二十世紀的美國」
5 月 9 日開幕夜，琳達・卡麥隆藝廊

作家演講：葛倫・坎貝爾「早期美國文化」
5 月 14 日，克里斯 ・ 查爾頓禮堂

音樂表演：「美國民謠大師」
5 月 22 日，雲杉劇院

兒童與年長者可免費參加所有活動。此外，如果您在網站上支付了報名費，並成為貝爾蒙特市歷史協會的會員，也可免費參加任何活動。

有關團體參觀登記問題，聯絡大衛・史密斯 dsmith@belmonthistoricalsociety.com。有關接下來的活動與場地地點或租借場地的細節，請上本協會網站 www.belmonthistoricalsociety.com。

收件者：大衛・史密斯
<dsmith@belmonthistoricalsociety.com>
寄件者：傑瑞德・泰特
<jtate@clarkuniversity.com>
日期：4 月 22 日
主旨：團體參觀

親愛的史密斯先生：

您好，我叫傑瑞德・泰特，是馬里維爾市中心克拉克大學歷史系的教授。

我這學期教授大一的歷史導論，我認為參加坎貝爾先生主講的活動會對我的課程有益，他的演講與我們現在課堂上正在討論的主題相關。

我也在想，有沒有可能安排一場坎貝爾先生與我班上約 50 名學生之間的問答座談。請告訴他，我們很期待見到他。

感謝您撥冗讀我的電子郵件，希望儘快收到您的回覆。

克拉克大學歷史系
傑瑞德・泰特

181. 下列何者與貝爾蒙特市歷史協會有關？

A 它不允許兒童參加某些活動
B 它由貝爾蒙特市所經營
C 它是由琳達 ・ 卡麥隆所創辦的
D 它將在幾個不同的地方舉辦活動

182. 泰特先生目前的授課內容最有可能是什麼？

A 北極的環境狀況
B 美國早期歷史
C 美國民俗音樂
D 現代攝影

183. 下列何者無法在貝爾蒙特市歷史協會的網站上找到？

A 已排定活動的資訊
B 會員註冊
C 租借細節
D 之前活動的記敘

184. 在電子郵件中，第二段第一行的「introductory」意思最接近？

A 基本的
B 必要的
C 深度的
D 非必要的

185. 泰特先生要求什麼？

A 一本簽了名的書
B 一份詳細的調查
C 和主講者見面的機會
D 團體優惠

186–190 行程表和電子郵件

紐頓圖書館
四月節目與活動時間表

日期與時間	活動	地點	其他備註
4 月 2 日晚上 7 點	昔日之旅：默片系列	德克廳	和我們一起觀賞幾部呈現美國早期電影史的影片。
4 月 5 日下午 3 點	青年創意寫作坊	青年部 304 室	開放給所有想增進寫作技巧的高中生。
4 月 10 日上午 11 點	初級英語會話社	教育中心 102 室	加入其他想學英語會話的成人。此課程免費。
4 月 16 日下午五點	活到老學到老	媒體教室 202 室	學會使用電腦不只是年輕人獨享的權利。加入我們，一起利用電腦探索資訊汪洋。（適合年長者）
4 月 29 日上午 10 點	故事劇	青年部 301 室	邊玩玩具邊聽故事。（給 0 到 5 歲的孩童）

感謝所有捐款讓我們得以購買新筆記型電腦與設立媒體教室的人士。

收件者：李察・懷特
<rwhite@newtonlibrary.com>
寄件者：琳達・卡特
<lcarter121@seprus.com>
日期：4 月 1 日
主旨：初級英語會話社

懷特先生您好：

我叫琳達・卡特，我是即將於 4 月 10 日舉辦的初級英語會話社的指導老師。我注意到圖書館最近用向讀者募集的捐款設立了媒體教室，我希望能更換教室，以便我使用新的教學資源，將電腦融入我的英語會話課程中。您可以將我的班改到和「活到老學到老」同一間教室，而非教育中心嗎？我想我的學生會很喜歡他們從電腦上學到的實用英語技巧。同時，可以請您寄電子郵件給所有已經報名本課程的學生嗎？他們需要被告知教室異動一事。

先感謝您的協助。

琳達・卡特

收件者：琳達・卡特
<lcarter121@seprus.com>
寄件者：李察・懷特
<rwhite@newtonlibrary.com>
日期：4 月 2 日
主旨：教室異動

親愛的卡特女士：

我很樂意將您的初級英語會話課挪至擁有最新媒體設備的教室，請知悉，那是 3A 教室。很遺憾的是，我沒有報名該課程所有學生的電子郵件信箱。很多學生只提供了他們的姓名。如果您可以接受的話，我可以在圖書館入口處貼上告示，公告您的課程，並註明教室異動。請告訴我，您是否要我這樣做。

感謝您，並祝安好

圖書館活動籌劃員
李察・懷特

186. 下列何者與紐頓圖書館有關？

A 它最近裝修了設施
B 它不久後將舉辦募款活動
C 它提供各種年齡層的教育活動
D 它週一休館

187. 哪一項活動最適合電影系學生？

A 故事劇
B 青年創意寫作坊
C 昔日之旅
D 活到老學到老

188. 在第一封電子郵件中，第一段第二行的「held」意思最接近？

A 搬運
B 參加
C 延誤
D 進行

189. 李察・懷特為什麼無法發電子郵件給琳達・卡特的學生？

A 他沒有他們的電子郵件信箱
B 那不是他的工作
C 他沒有時間
D 圖書館內沒有那種科技

190. 對於無法通知琳達的學生教室異動的問題，李察・懷特提出了什麼解決方法？

A 他可以寄電子郵件給他們
B 他可以在他們進來時引導他們至正確的教室
C 他會張貼告示
D 他會畫一張上頭有路線指引的地圖給他們

191–195 電子郵件、文章和報名表

收件者：湯尼・沃克
<twalker@icmcorp.com >
寄件者：蘇西・梅森
<smason@icmcorp.com>
日期：5 月 4 日
主旨：夏季行事曆
附件：預算 .doc

親愛的沃克先生：

我正要確定公司的夏季活動行事曆。由於我們去年在員工的感恩活動上超出預算，所以我想比較明智的做法應該是找更實惠的休閒活動。附件是我為已規劃的夏季活動所做的費用預估分析明細。

7 月 6 日：安克拉治花卉節

7 月 22 日：勞倫斯公園的公園藝術

8 月 6 日：安克拉治鄉間自行車之旅

8 月 19 日：甜心牧場騎馬

相較於去年，今年我安排了較少的戶外活動。今年我想利用一個新的戶外休閒活動機會，是我在安克拉治記者網上看到的。您可以點擊這個連結，閱讀這篇文章：www.anchoragereporter.com/new_trails

請告訴我您的看法。

人力資源部經理
蘇西．梅森

安克拉治記者
自 8 月 6 日起安克拉治鄉間自行車之旅

5 月 2 日——安克拉治自行車社今年夏天將舉辦年度騎自行車活動，自 8 月 6 日起至 8 月 7 日止。這個活動將於那兩天的上午 10 點，在安克拉治社區活動中心揭開序幕。如果您欲開車前往起點，最好利用社區活動中心後面的停車場。

安克拉治自行車社社長琴．佛洛斯特表示：「騎車的路程從 5 英里到 20 英里不等，將帶領自行車騎士們穿過安克拉治風景秀麗的地區。整體來說，這些自行車之旅將以一種悠閒的步調進行，所以各種程度的自行車騎士皆可參加。不過，本地經驗豐富的騎士將帶領一組步調較快的隊伍。」

於活動開始前半個小時，參加自行車之旅的騎士們將學到騎車技巧、自行車保養，以及適當的營養補給方式。所有參加者都必須戴上安全帽，也鼓勵他們自行攜帶飲水，以防騎車時脫水。

自行車之旅報名表

如果您有意參加 8 月 6 日的自行車之旅，請寫下您的姓名、所屬部門，以及經驗或體能程度。如果進階組報名人數夠多，我們就可以協調成兩組獨立的行程。如果人數不夠分成兩組，那我們鼓勵所有騎士待在一起，這樣每個人都可以參與到我們所規劃的團體運動。感謝您的參與，希望能在活動上見到各位！

姓名	部門	體能／經驗
湯姆．克魯茲	業務	初級
維恩．瓊斯	倉管	初級
莎莉．杰金斯	倉管	初級
芭芭拉．布雷斯特	接待	進階
哈潑．金斯基	業務	初級

191. 梅森女士提議做什麼？

Ⓐ 休閒活動的支出要限制在預算內
Ⓑ 派任新的人力資源部經理
Ⓒ 增加臨時僱員的數量
Ⓓ 比去年安排更多戶外活動

192. 梅森女士建議今年的新活動要安排在哪一天？

Ⓐ 7 月 6 日
Ⓑ 7 月 22 日
Ⓒ 8 月 6 日
Ⓓ 8 月 19 日

193. 這篇文章最有可能出現在網站的哪一個版面？

Ⓐ 經濟
Ⓑ 休閒
Ⓒ 娛樂
Ⓓ 政治

194. 根據自行車之旅報名表，我們可推知下列何者與即將舉辦的自行車之旅有關？

Ⓐ 活動將被取消
Ⓑ 將會有兩個隊伍，初級組與進階組
Ⓒ 將只有一個隊伍
Ⓓ 他們將會半路停下來用餐並合照

195. 芭芭拉・布雷斯特最有可能在自行車之旅中做什麼？

Ⓐ 她會很無聊，然後放棄行程
Ⓑ 她會抱怨進階組應該要有更多人報名
Ⓒ 她會加入經驗豐富騎士的快步調隊伍
Ⓓ 她會留在隊伍參加團體活動

196–200 表格和電子郵件

四季服飾暢貨中心

所有退換貨必須在送達七天內寄回四季服飾暢貨中心，退還的商品可以更換成其他商品或要求退款。如果您選擇退款，我們會將款項退還至購買時所使用的信用卡帳戶中。

具正式會員資格者可利用我們的宅配查詢服務並收到常客優惠。

退換貨請寄至：
80725 科羅拉多州丹佛市芬頓街 144 號（303-555-4387），四季服飾暢貨中心

請勾選最符合您的問題的描述：
___ 商品有瑕疵或毀損
___ 商品不符預期
_V_ 送錯商品
___ 其他：________________

個人資料：
姓名：莎莉・尼爾森
訂單號碼：2245
電話：432-555-6729
地址：80725 科羅拉多州丹佛市橡樹街 2154 號
電子郵件：snelson@clandon.net

_V_ 更換　___ 退款

我於 4 月 22 日在貴公司的網路商店訂購了一件中號的白雪聖誕毛衣，但我卻收到小號的。我想要更換成正確尺寸的毛衣。

寄件者：黛博拉・克拉克
<debraclarke@fourseasons.com>
收件者：莎莉・尼爾森
<snelson@clandon.net>
日期：4 月 30 日
主旨：更換

親愛的尼爾森女士：

我們已經收到您想更換所購買的毛衣的要求，我們誠心地為此錯誤道歉。我們會立即依照您的要求將正確的商品宅配給您。貨物配送狀況可利用以下貨物追蹤查詢號碼，於本公司網站查詢：447H57J。

由於這是本公司的失誤，我們已經將七元退回您的信用卡帳戶內，以補償您退換貨的運費。請核對餘額進行確認。

如果您對本訂單還有任何問題，歡迎來電 303-555-4387，我將協助您處理所有問題。

黛博拉・克拉克

收件者：黛博拉・克拉克
<debraclarke@fourseasons.com>
寄件者：莎莉・尼爾森
< snelson@clandon.net >
日期：5 月 4 日
主旨：退換錯誤

親愛的克拉克女士：

很高興收到您的電子郵件，內容事關於我退換貨一事，也很感謝四季如此貼心地退還我的運費。

話雖如此，我確認過帳戶，也收到了所說的款項。此外，寄來的新毛衣也是正確的尺寸。但是我訂的是白雪聖誕款，收到的卻是冬季慶典款。這兩款都是很棒的毛衣，但是我先生就是比較喜歡白雪聖誕款。您可以將我原本訂的款式寄給我嗎？待我收到正確貨品與運費退款後，我會將冬季慶典毛衣寄回。

謝謝您！

莎莉・尼爾森

196. 尼爾森女士呈報說原本宅配的商品有什麼問題？

Ⓐ 有受損
Ⓑ 尺寸不合
Ⓒ 延遲收到
Ⓓ 未抵達目的地

197. 在黛博拉・克拉克寄出的電子郵件中，第一段第二行的「as per」哪個意思最接近？

Ⓐ 不論
Ⓑ 除了……之外
Ⓒ 而不是
Ⓓ 根據

198. 下列何者與尼爾森女士有關？

Ⓐ 她最近才搬到丹佛市
Ⓑ 她訂了禮物要給朋友
Ⓒ 她有四季服飾暢貨中心的會員資格
Ⓓ 她太晚要求退款

199. 尼爾森女士呈報說更換的宅配商品有什麼問題？

Ⓐ 尺寸錯誤
Ⓑ 款式錯誤
Ⓒ 尺寸跟款式都錯了
Ⓓ 原本購買商品的退款金額溢給

200. 尼爾森女士將於何時退還冬季慶典毛衣？

Ⓐ 當她收到正確的貨品與運費退款時
Ⓑ 當她有空時
Ⓒ 當她的老公喜歡他的毛衣時
Ⓓ 當四季為她的不便道歉時

ACTUAL TEST ③

PART 5 P.80-83

◎ **Part 5 解答請見 P.457**

101. **離**火車站不遠**處**就是星光公園，是個遊客或在地人都喜歡的景點。

102. **在**介紹主講人之**之前**，銷售主任會先簡短致詞。

103. 慈善團體的新閱讀計劃**預計**在未來十年內提升發展中國家的識字率。

104. 搬到新的城市後，梅森女士以參與社交**活動**來快速地擴展她的人際網絡。

105. 欲參賽的藝術家應於**截止日期** 6 月 30 日之前繳交作品。

106. 德瑞克藥廠很**幸運的**聘請到世界知名的化學家喬納斯・倫德成為其實驗室資深技術員。

107. 扎恩公司明年**將開始**在國內製造生產所有高檔皮夾與鞋子。

108. 有些投票者明顯**偏好**那些從事法律工作的候選人。

109. 店員說**大約**有 15 位客人已經在店門外等著店家開門。

110. 漏水的水龍頭已經修好，所以訪客**現在**可以使用一樓的洗手間。

111. 藉由服用托夫特醫生團隊所研發出來的藥，可以明顯地延緩病**程**。

112. 不幸地，當颶風襲擊該地時，居民和官員**完全**措手不及。

113. 公司計劃**補助**業務員出席會議時所產生的開銷。

114. 卡爾頓女士很自在地過馬路，因為沒有車輛朝她的**方向**開來。

115. **在**電視新聞報導大選**期間**，很多備受矚目的候選人接受了現場採訪。

116. 希克斯先生在音樂廳替重要的客戶**保留**靠近舞台的位子。

117. 舉辦電影產業頒獎盛會**的**費里茲中心正在進行浩大的擴建工程。

118. 每月一次的員工晚餐，讓來自不同部門的員工有機會以個人層面**彼此**互動。

119. 房東必須**遵守**由住宅安全區域部門所訂定的法規。

120. 由於**結構**因素，在大樓的一樓加上堅固的支撐橫樑。

121. 生態聯盟是個非營利的組織，**致力於**教育大眾環保相關議題。

122. 將所有目錄與郵件加**入**維他命公司的商標是很重要的。

123. 儘管遭到數大出版商拒絕，伊恩・萊特仍**繼續努力**，後來成為世界知名的小說家。

124. 布洛斯先生因撰寫出**資訊豐富**且簡單易懂的使用手冊而受到讚揚。

125. 雖然賈西亞女士在該金融機構中的資金不多，但其員工仍視她**如**重要投資者。

126. 當您郵寄退貨時，請確保收據已**附**在申請表上以便加速作業。

127. 案發不久前，目擊者看到只有**單**人身影站在路燈旁。

128. 班・山德斯**創新地**設計了一款容易收合，可精巧收納的行李箱。

129. 因為今年夏天氣候較往年溫暖，農作物**將**可提早幾週**收成**。

130. **在一**查完羅克福德顧問公司的財務記錄**後**，會計師即呈交一份正式報告。

131–134 公告

緊急！誠徵熟手水管工

王牌配管工程公司位於哥倫比亞，現正擴大徵求熟手的水管工。自 1954 年起，王牌配管工程就開始在哥倫比亞地區服務。我們一直以來都是家族企業，但是隨著過去三年哥倫比亞人口急遽增長，讓我們有機會歡迎熟練的水管工加入我們。應徵者應具安裝商用與住宅的各型水管之經驗。請將履歷表寄至 aceplumbing@gmail.com，我們將安排面試。

131. **Ⓐ 擴展**
 Ⓑ 期待
 Ⓒ 承包
 Ⓓ 控制

132. **Ⓐ 自 1954 年起，王牌配管工程就開始在哥倫比亞地區服務。**
 Ⓑ 我們與社區的連結較少。
 Ⓒ 我們一直難以支付帳單。
 Ⓓ 王牌配管工程有財務困難。

133. Ⓐ 怪異的
 Ⓑ 急遽性的
 Ⓒ 不可能的
 Ⓓ 荒唐的

134. Ⓐ 片段
 Ⓑ 流量
 Ⓒ 工程
 Ⓓ 種類

135–138 網頁

學習到社群媒體行銷策略
就在天才行銷力研討會

準備好要讓您的社群媒體行銷進入下個階段了嗎？那麼就參加天才行銷力研討會，並學習最前衛的社群行銷策略。研討會將於 5 月 3 日及 4 日在休士頓舉辦。這可能是您一年中最富教育意義的兩天。

天才行銷將傳授您現實世界的策略，來提高您的付費與自然社群媒體的行銷成效。不論您是購買社群媒體廣告，或是把重點放在社群媒體的自然曝光上，天才行銷力研討會都是您今年必須參加的一場研討會。您將獲得專家啟發、與他人交流您面臨的挑戰、取得可行的策略來驅動流量，提高銷售量並增加客戶滿意度。

欲申請者，只需點擊以下連結。

申請

135. **Ⓐ 參加**
 Ⓑ 參加
 Ⓒ 參加了
 Ⓓ 正參加

136. Ⓐ 今日就加入，並將業界的人帶往偉大之境。
 Ⓑ 研討會將於 5 月 3 日至 4 日於休士頓舉辦。
 Ⓒ 將於 11 月 20 日開放兩週課程的報名登記。
 Ⓓ 整個三月都有提供課程。

137. Ⓐ 兩者之一
 Ⓑ 不論
 Ⓒ 寧願
 Ⓓ 不只

138. Ⓐ 劃分
 Ⓑ 增加
 Ⓒ 貶值
 Ⓓ 忍受

139–142 電子郵件

收件者：南西・克拉夫
寄件者：歐瑪・帕托
日期：1 月 16 日
主旨：宅配前流程

在產製團隊會議中，存貨在出貨前並未全部都有妥善的儲放這點令人疑慮。由於這點疑慮，團隊決定要檢視書面流程來確認是否需要多增加步驟。包裝與倉儲團隊的會議已經安排在 1 月 23 日星期二舉行。請安排時間表，讓包裝與倉儲團隊中大多數的主管都能出席這個會議。

我有信心包裝與倉儲團隊的管理部將會發現，書面流程不會讓儲放不良的這種問題有機會發生。包裝與倉儲團隊所提出的任何建議，只會修改出更完善的檢核表。

139. Ⓐ 理解
Ⓑ 疑慮
Ⓒ 挑戰
Ⓓ 耐心

140. Ⓐ 然而
Ⓑ 由於
Ⓒ 不管
Ⓓ 假如

141. **Ⓐ 包裝與倉儲團隊的會議已經安排在 1 月 23 日星期二舉行。**
Ⓑ 在星期二上班前，所有員工都被要求要檢視流程。
Ⓒ 會議將會調查包裝過程中冗餘步驟的可能性。
Ⓓ 計劃在 12 月底時加入額外的訓練課程。

142. Ⓐ 正發現
Ⓑ 已經被發現
Ⓒ 將發現
Ⓓ 已經發現

143–146 信件

6 月 3 日
水口結衣
10787 紐約州布魯克林狄恩街
143 號 3 號公寓

水口女士您好：

很高興通知您，漢諾威設計公司想要邀請您參加夏季實習專案的面試。在本公司今年的六個職缺中，我們只面試 15 名應徵者。您會很開心知道您在 200 多位應徵者中脫穎而出。

面試將安排在三月六日和七日下午一至六點。若時間允許，我們希望您能於六日下午 1 點 30 分前來。若時間上不允許，也可安排在七日。請盡快告知我們您是否可以出席。若有任何問題，請撥打辦公室電話（212-347-9919），人力資源部將協助您。期待盡快收到您的回覆。

漢諾威設計公司行政主管
麥克斯．萊特 敬上
212-326-1268
M.Wright@hannoverdesign.com

143. **Ⓐ 邀請**
Ⓑ 將邀請
Ⓒ 已經邀請
Ⓓ 將被邀請

144. Ⓐ ……的人
Ⓑ ……的那個
Ⓒ ……人的
Ⓓ ……的那個

145. Ⓐ 訂購
Ⓑ 安排
Ⓒ 迫使
Ⓓ 參加

146. Ⓐ 您需要帶一份已填好的應徵函與某種身分證件。
Ⓑ 請盡快告知我們您是否可以出席。
Ⓒ 我們真希望能接受您的提議，但是我們必須回絕您。
Ⓓ 請回覆，若攜伴也請一併告知。

PART 7 P.88–109

147–148 備忘錄

備忘錄

收文者：全體員工
發文者：大衛．科霍
主旨：重要訊息
日期：5 月 22 日

我們將於 6 月 3 日召開股東年會。在開幕式時，我將發表簡短的演說，希望各位都可以出席。以下是會議的初步時程表。

開幕式	下午一點
年度報告	下午兩點
討論	下午四點
晚宴	下午六點

147. 這份備忘錄的目的是什麼？

- Ⓐ 提醒員工專案截止日期
- Ⓑ 建議修改年度報告
- **Ⓒ 提供活動時程表**
- Ⓓ 向股東報告年度獲利

148. 大衛．科霍將於幾點發表演說？

- **Ⓐ 下午一點**
- Ⓑ 下午二點
- Ⓒ 下午四點
- Ⓓ 下午六點

149–150 訊息串

茱蒂．林區 **10:12**
我們可以用公司信用卡刷這次的晚餐費用嗎？

奈森．李 **10:13**
很遺憾地，不行。公司政策上個月才修改過。只有在午餐或晚餐時與客戶開會的餐費才能報公帳。

茱蒂．林區 **10:14**
太可惜了，我猜我們這次要平均分攤了。

奈森．李 **10:14**
是的，但至少你可以去任何你想去的餐廳用餐。

茱蒂．林區 **10:15**
沒錯。我會告訴大家的。謝謝！

149. 茱蒂為什麼要聯絡奈森？

- Ⓐ 要他付晚餐費用
- **Ⓑ 詢問公司開銷的資訊**
- Ⓒ 詢問他是否要一起用晚餐
- Ⓓ 請他推薦好的餐廳

150. 在 10:14 時，茱蒂寫：「我們這次要平均分攤了」是什麼意思？

- Ⓐ 他們將請公司付款
- Ⓑ 他們將詢問會計部
- Ⓒ 他們將決定誰要付款
- **Ⓓ 他們每個人必須支付部分帳單**

151–152 信件

1 月 19 日

親愛的彼德森先生：

您所做的血液檢測結果已經出爐了。請盡快來電預約可以和赫門醫生會面的時間。

我們要提醒您，由於健康保險法規的變更，所有病患都被鼓勵要確認聯絡方式與保險資訊是最新且準確的，您可以撥打客戶服務專線 555-6842，或下次來診所時在櫃台完成確認。

尊榮健康診所
蘿拉．林克頓 敬上

151. 彼得森先生在不久的未來是可能做什麼？

- Ⓐ 更新保單
- **Ⓑ 安排與醫生的預約**
- Ⓒ 應徵辦事員一職
- Ⓓ 做血液檢測

152. 彼得森先生被要求做什麼？

- Ⓐ 繳交保險表格
- Ⓑ 回信
- **Ⓒ 確認個人資訊**
- Ⓓ 填寫問卷

153–154 傳單

在地購物
西雅圖商業區協會

您知道嗎？

- 比起向連鎖零售商購買，在本地店家購物能為經濟帶來兩倍的收益。
- 在本地店家購物，可以透過地方稅收來支持西雅圖市。

- 在本地店家購物有益於環保，節省汽油並減少空氣污染。
- 在本地購物可以在西雅圖創造更多工作機會，改善社區的生活水準。

我們想要鼓勵所有西雅圖的居民，藉由在當地傳統商店和市場購物來支持在地社區。

想要更了解或知悉所有在地居民可利用的優質商店與服務，請上西雅圖商業區協會的網站 www.sbda.org 查詢。

153. 這份宣傳單的目的是什麼？

Ⓐ 推廣永續生活
Ⓑ 通知特價訊息
Ⓒ 宣布新店開幕
Ⓓ 影響消費模式

154. 下列何者不是文中所提到在當地店家消費的好處？

Ⓐ 促進就業市場
Ⓑ 對環境友善
Ⓒ 支持當地經濟
Ⓓ 鼓勵外商投資

155–157 文章

格蘭德維尤商業新聞

柏奈爾餐廳在六個月前開始為忙碌的家庭提供外送服務，其業績之卓越，超乎預期。他們的小店「農場上桌」位於格蘭德維尤中央高地，被迫增加 1.2 倍的人力，才能趕上需求。

當瑞秋和羅伯·柏奈爾夫婦有了第一個孩子之後，整間餐廳的概念發想就出現了。兩位職業父母不斷地以速食當餐點，並發現身邊有許多朋友也是如此。他們需要更健康的選擇，而這正是大多數速食店無法提供的健康選擇。於是柏奈爾夫婦決定在那時辭掉辦公室的工作，開始創業，為上班人士提供健康餐點的外送服務。

他們的生意大受歡迎，一直接到來自外縣市的訂單。「顧客的反應令人覺得吃驚。」瑞秋説，「顧客特別喜愛餐點的新鮮與品質。」一位在外送服務創始時就訂購的顧客珍娜補充説：「不只是食物健康，價格沒比速食餐點更貴，但卻是更好的選擇。」

柏奈爾餐廳説他們計劃在下年度內擴大外送路線，並且在格蘭德維尤市各地開設三間「農場上桌」販賣熟食餐點。

155. 這篇文章是有關什麼？

Ⓐ 速食公司的角色變化
Ⓑ 健康飲食的重要性
Ⓒ 格蘭德維尤農地的擴展
Ⓓ 小型店家的成功與成長

156. 根據這篇文章，農場上桌餐點的主要賣點是什麼？

Ⓐ 運送速度非常快
Ⓑ 價格很便宜
Ⓒ 健康
Ⓓ 美味

157. 下列句子最適合出現在 [1]、[2]、[3]、[4] 的哪個位置？「於是柏奈爾夫婦決定在那時辭掉辦公室的工作，開始創業，為上班人士提供健康餐點的外送服務。」

Ⓐ [1]
Ⓑ [2]
Ⓒ [3]
Ⓓ [4]

158–160 告示

顧客請注意

很遺憾要通知大家，我們要全面回收肯特牌今年 3 月 30 日至 7 月 30 日間所生產的各類型梯子。

- 梯子不符合強制性安全標準，可能不穩。
- 站在上面時梯子會移動，可能導致危險性摔傷。
- 任何情況下都不要使用梯子，請與肯特公司聯絡進行退換貨。只要將梯子退還，即使沒有購買證明，顧客仍可拿到全額退款。

請撥打 1-800-555-2493 與肯特公司聯絡。按 8 即可轉接專門負責處理產品回收的客服人員。造成您的不便，我們深感抱歉。

158. 這個公告最有可能會在哪裡看到？

(A) 房地產辦公室
(B) 五金行
(C) 回收站
(D) 雜貨店

159. 公告裡告誡顧客不要做什麼事？

(A) 使用有瑕疵的產品
(B) 更新保固
(C) 繳交訂單
(D) 提出客訴

160. 根據公告，要如何獲得更多資訊？

(A) 填寫表格
(B) 查看使用手冊
(C) 與公司聯絡
(D) 看教學影片

161–164 網路聊天室

J&R 國際公司的小組討論區

9:15	派翠西亞・諾貝爾（管理人）	大家早。關於即將於六月舉辦的領袖研討會，我已經張貼了一些構想。
9:16	派翠西亞・諾貝爾（管理人）	請分享你的想法，我們需要大家提供意見。
9:20	傑瑞・戴維斯	看起來非常制式化。可以加入一些像是露營遠征之類的活動嗎？
9:21	羅倫斯・歐丹尼爾	我不知道這次是否可以參加，我的團隊正在為一個重要的企劃案收尾。不過露營聽起來很棒。
9:22	派翠西亞・諾貝爾（管理人）	露營是個好主意，但是需要更多時間規劃。下次研討會絕對會將它納入考慮。
9:24	傑米・李	我不認為影片會很有效。若是找更多演講者來發表演說呢？我比較希望能與他人互動。
9:27	莫妮卡・崔	我很期待那個露營的點子，但是這次的研討會，我同意傑米的看法。影片會很無聊。
9:30	傑瑞・戴維斯	我發現約翰・奧利維這次沒有要發表演說。發生了什麼事嗎？他很受歡迎，我想參加他的研討會。
9:41	派翠西亞・諾貝爾（管理人）	約翰還沒有跟我們確認，因為他行程上可能有衝突。他正努力調整行程。
9:52	伊莎貝拉・普瑞斯	我也想要參加約翰的研討會。我注意到還有幾個空的時段。有人有興趣聽耿欣演講嗎？我想要聽聽不同的文化觀點。
9:58	傑瑞・戴維斯	好主意！耿欣在中國擔任主管經驗豐富，她總是有一些有趣的故事。
10:01	傑米・李	我附議，我真的很想聽聽耿欣的演講。而說到文化觀點，亞當也有在多國管理員工的經驗。我想他應該也會很有趣。
10:09	伊莎貝拉・普瑞斯	好，邀請亞當來研討會演講吧。
10:15	亞當・克魯茲	哇，我很高興你們對我的信任。我很樂意參與研討會，我下午都有空。
10:19	派翠西亞・諾貝爾（管理人）	謝謝你，亞當。如果可以的話，我會把你安排在下午三至四點的時段。
10:30	亞當・克魯茲	聽起來很棒。如果有的話，可以寄一份準則給我嗎？

161. 誰最有可能參加這個小組討論？

Ⓐ 一般大眾
Ⓑ 公司全體員工
Ⓒ 來自不同國家的員工
Ⓓ 公司經理及其他主管

162. 文中討論了什麼？

Ⓐ 會議中最佳的演說
Ⓑ 公司裡最佳的講者
Ⓒ 工作坊的時程表
Ⓓ 國際同事

163. 在 10:15 時，亞當．克魯斯說：「我很高興你們對我的信任」是什麼意思？

Ⓐ 他感謝大家要他擔任經理
Ⓑ 他感謝大家認為他是一位好主管
Ⓒ 他很高興他最喜歡的演講者受到邀請
Ⓓ 他為贏得選舉而感到榮幸

164. 派翠西亞．諾貝爾接下來可能會做什麼？

Ⓐ 以電子郵件寄一些資料給同事
Ⓑ 敲定員工會議
Ⓒ 與全球同仁見面
Ⓓ 打電話給同事說明異動

165–167 電子郵件

收件者：莎曼珊．羅素
<srussell@speednet.com>
寄件者：山姆．柏格
<sberer@highlandshotel.com>
主旨：預約
日期：7 月 1 日
附件：收據

親愛的羅素女士：

感謝您選擇高地飯店作為您即將舉行慶祝活動的場地。與您聯絡是為了確認您 7 月 12 日與 13 日兩晚房間的預約細節。您預定了本飯店四樓整層的 12 間房。除此之外，在那兩天，主會議室將專屬於您，供您無限制使用。您提到家族成員將從全國各地前來出席這個活動。在住宿期間，本飯店將提供任何您所需要的協助。

本飯店提供免費無線網路，也提供免費網路咖啡廳，讓顧客想上網或寄送電子郵件時可免費使用我們的電腦。咖啡廳開放時間為上午 5 點至中午 12 點。另外，也歡迎貴賓至我們獲獎的餐廳用餐，服務時間為上午 7 點至晚上 10 點。

這封電子郵件還附上您的收據，是您在 6 月 30 日以信用卡所支付的訂金 100 元。若您想看看會議室的格局與座椅安排，可至本飯店網站 www.highlandshotel.com 瀏覽。

高地飯店
山姆．柏格 敬上

165. 7 月 12 日和 13 日將舉辦什麼活動？

Ⓐ 家族聚會
Ⓑ 商務會議
Ⓒ 股東會議
Ⓓ 就業博覽會

166. 下列何者不是此次訂房的好處？

Ⓐ 單獨使用一整層樓
Ⓑ 免費餐點
Ⓒ 使用會議室
Ⓓ 免費上網

167. 根據電子郵件，羅素女士可以在高地飯店網站上查詢到什麼？

Ⓐ 訂房編號
Ⓑ 飯店餐廳的菜單
Ⓒ 座位規劃
Ⓓ 折價券

168–171 公告

超強健身房會員請注意

一種健身計劃無法適用於每個人，這就是為什麼超強健身房提供本地區最多元的健身課程，保證您能找到有趣又刺激的課程，幫助您達到健身目標。現在我們很興奮地要介紹您一個新的舞蹈體適能課程。上課時間是今年夏季的 6 月 12 日至 8 月 23 日。

舞蹈是種既有趣又能互動的運動方式，也適合那些無法進行高強度健身活動的人。

我們鼓勵想要報名這堂舞蹈課的人，以兩人為一組來登記。如果您沒有其他人可以一起報名，那第一堂課時將與其他人一起配對。報名時間為 5 月 10 日至 6 月 1 日。您可以在網站上填寫報名表。課程費用必須於報名時以信用卡支付。

依照我們的規定，學員必須在課程開始至少前一週取消報名才能退費。在截止日期後取消報名者將不予退費。

欲知更多課程內容、課表及費用的相關資訊，請來電 (231) 555-2523 找經理史考特．彼得森。

168. 這個公告的目的是什麼？

Ⓐ 延後開幕典禮
Ⓑ 聘用新教練
Ⓒ 解釋付款方式
Ⓓ 宣布新的課程

169. 6 月 12 日最有可能發生什麼事？

Ⓐ 有些教練將會缺席
Ⓑ 有些會員將會被分配搭檔
Ⓒ 會退費
Ⓓ 會核發結業證明

170. 根據公告，報名者能得到退費的最後日期是哪一天？

Ⓐ 5 月 10 日
Ⓑ 6 月 5 日
Ⓒ 6 月 12 日
Ⓓ 8 月 23 日

171. 文中提到與彼得森先生聯絡的原因是什麼？

Ⓐ 安排預約
Ⓑ 詢問課程
Ⓒ 更新個人聯絡資料
Ⓓ 找舞伴

172–175 備忘錄

備忘錄

收文者：全體員工
發文者：維蘿妮卡．傑克曼執行經理
日期：10 月 10 日
主旨：人員配置

我們的行銷主管席拉．羅伯絲將於 10 月 21 日至 11 月 5 日前往新加坡出差。在她出差期間，麥可．李將暫時代理她在高曼百貨公司的部分職務。但是，對於那些和羅伯絲女士一起執行企劃案且接近完成的人，公司要求你們在 10 月 15 日前與她敲定最後的工作安排。部分緊急的企劃案已經和麥可討論過了。如果你的企劃案可以等席拉出差回來，公司要求你們告知席拉和麥可，好讓其他的企劃案可以先進行。

我知道這可能造成工作不便，特別是如此接近過節的時候，但我相信在席拉出差期間，麥可能夠擔負起這些職責。麥可一直與席拉合作密切，他將會處理交到他手上的新企劃案。在席拉出差期間，麥可將安排與不同部門單獨開會，以確保在他暫代期間能順利交接與溝通。

若有其他問題或疑慮，請在 10 月 20 日前與席拉聯絡，或隨時來找我。

172. 備忘錄的收文者在哪裡工作？

Ⓐ 在行銷公司
Ⓑ 在法律事務所
Ⓒ 在百貨公司
Ⓓ 在旅行社

173. 下列何者與席拉．羅伯絲有關？

Ⓐ 她得到一份新工作
Ⓑ 她升官了
Ⓒ 她要去度假
Ⓓ 她要出差

174. 專案即將完成的員工要在何時前與席拉聯絡？

A 10 月 15 日
B 10 月 20 日
C 10 月 21 日
D 11 月 5 日

175. 下列句子最適合出現在 [1]、[2]、[3]、[4] 的哪個位置？「在席拉出差期間，麥可將安排與不同部門單獨開會，以確保在他暫代期間能順利交接與溝通。」

A [1]
B [2]
C [3]
D [4]

176–180 網站和文章

鄉村地區擴展計畫

為了持續致力於改善本州各地鄉村社區的生活水準，鄉村服務協會提供鄉村社區年度補助金。這個計劃的目的是要資助當地為維持鄉村生活的便利性及滿意度的人，慰勞他們在地所付出的努力。今年提供的補助金如下：

商業發展補助金：250,000 元
社區發展補助金：150,000 元
交流發展補助金：200,000 元
教育發展補助金：100,000 元

協會將優先補助的提案是那些反映整體社區多元發展，提升社區參與，以及讓鄉村社區成為一個更適合安居樂業的地區。補助金可以讓鄉村社區邁出第一步，利用提案或規劃幫助改善社區居民的生活。在過去數十年中，補助款被用在各種不同用途上，如最先進的耕種器具、道路維護、通訊基礎設備、教育設施以及投資鄉村青年企業家。

下載申請表來申請補助金吧。送件截止日期是 2 月 28 日。

克拉頓村贏得資金補助

克拉頓，3 月 22 日——鄉村服務協會今天宣布克拉頓村是今年教育發展補助金的得主。補助金將用於興建大型遊樂場的工程上，為 12 歲以下兒童提供休閒娛樂用。自從去年新的電子工廠開業以來，該地區的家庭數量急遽上升。因此，留給兒童玩耍的空間變得越來越少。新的遊樂場將可讓兒童在放學時玩樂。

克拉頓很榮幸能獲得這筆補助金，計劃未來要申請更多的補助金，以改善該村的生活條件，吸引更多居民。

176. 網頁的目的是什麼？

A 報告企劃案已完成
B 鼓勵申請補助金
C 宣布補助金的得主
D 介紹當地企業家

177. 根據網頁，下列何者不是鄉村服務協會補助金的目的？

A 提供資金給當地商業人士
B 建設通訊基礎設備
C 安排社區健康檢查
D 購買農耕器具

178. 克拉頓村獲得多少補助？

A 100,000 元
B 150,000 元
C 200,000 元
D 250,000 元

179. 根據這篇文章，補助金讓克拉頓村可以做什麼？

A 改善當地農耕條件
B 整修小學
C 聘用更多合格教師
D 提供兒童遊樂場所

180. 下列何者與克拉頓村有關？

A 以前也曾獲得補助
B 計劃開設新的工廠
C 人口數增加
D 將舉辦社區慶祝活動

181–185 電子郵件和表格

收件者：查理斯．貝爾
<charlesbell434@globalnet.com>
寄件者：凱莉．庫克
<carriecook@freshfarmsgrocery.com>
主旨：會員卡
日期：5 月 4 日

親愛的貝爾先生：

您在新鮮農產商場的銀星會員卡將於本月 28 日到期，您的會員卡讓您享有特價以及購買大多數產品的特別積點權益。一旦您累積到足夠的點數，就可以於下次購物時享有折扣。若無有效的銀星會員卡，您將無法累積這些常客點數。

請勿以電話續延您的會員資格。若欲續延會員資格，請至各分店的客戶服務櫃台辦理。若有任何疑問，請來電 204-555-2648。

新鮮農產商場 客戶服務專員
凱莉．庫克

新鮮農產商場
會員卡申請表

名：查理斯
姓：貝爾
會員編號：14245FDA

☐ 建立我的會員卡
☑ 續延我的會員卡
☐ 取消我的會員卡

會員卡種類與費用：

金星：頂級會員，每年 90 元
銀星：商業會員，每年 70 元
銅星：家庭會員，每年 50 元
流星：短期會員，每月 10 元

請注意：

頂級會員僅限新鮮農產商場股東申請。食品賣家和餐廳老闆有資格申請銀星會員。

181. 這封電子郵件的目的是什麼？

(A) 宣布季節性折扣
(B) 通知貝爾先生未付款項
(C) 提醒貝爾先生續延會員資格
(D) 提供貝爾先生免費升等

182. 會員卡讓貝爾先生可以做什麼？

(A) 受惠於經常性的消費
(B) 在指定的區域停車
(C) 獲得快速配送
(D) 預先購買新產品

183. 貝爾先生被要求做什麼？

(A) 打電話給客戶服務櫃台
(B) 親自到店
(C) 填寫客戶評價
(D) 參加定期活動

184. 貝爾先生目前一年要付多少會費？

(A) 50 元
(B) 70 元
(C) 90 元
(D) 120 元

185. 下列何者與貝爾先生有關？

(A) 他是個著名的廚師
(B) 他經營食品販賣的商店
(C) 他是新鮮農產商場的股東
(D) 他今年才申請加入會員

186–190 信件、小手冊和時間表

5 月 12 日

親愛的葛瑞先生：

您是喬治亞建築師協會（GSA）的長期會員。我們要通知您協會今年為所提供的會員服務增加一些變化。具體而言，我們新增了金級會員，讓有特殊權限的會員能獲得比以往更多的資源。很開心通知您符合這個特殊會員的所有資格條件，現在就可立即註冊。您很快就會收到一份郵寄的手冊，裡面有更多資訊。我們希望您決定加入這個令人驚奇的金級會員。

如您所知，GSA 年度會員大會將於 6 月 14 日在喬治亞洲亞特蘭大市的星門會議中心舉行。我們注意到您已經報名了，我們等不及在那與您相會。如您需要任何安排上的協助，歡迎來電本會，電話是 (124) 555-5251。

喬治亞建築師協會
喬安．蘿絲 敬上

喬治亞建築師協會
金級會員

為符合這特別會員的資格，申請者在該領域須有 20 年以上的工作經驗，並擁有認可大學的建築學位。

福利包含：透過登入擁有超過 50,000 筆執業同業的資料庫，立即擴展您的聯絡網、只需繳交一半的報名費即可報名由 GSA 所舉辦的研討會、收到每月會訊，內容包含最新的市場研究及經濟分析，有助您的事業發展。

金級會員同時也符合申請該級會員專屬的專業責任保險資格。

如欲申請，只需填寫手冊所附的表格，寄至總部。40 元的申請費可以支票給付，或來電 (124) 555-5253 洽會計人員，以信用卡支付。

星門會議中心活動時程表

6 月 14 日
喬治亞建築師協會

上午 9:00 – 上午 9:45	大廳櫃台報到
上午 10:00 – 上午 11:45	演講貴賓傑瑞．詹金斯二世於 A 會議室
中午 12:00 – 下午 1:30	鑽石廳午宴
下午 2:00 – 下午 4:00	地區簡報於 A 會議室
晚上 6:00 – 晚上 9:00	藍寶石宴客廳晚宴與雞尾酒會
為確保當天活動報到順利，請記得攜帶您的協會會員證！	

186. 這封信的目的是什麼？

(A) 宣傳會議
(B) 推銷新的會員身分
(C) 確認預約
(D) 吸引新會員

187. 葛瑞先生被鼓勵做什麼？

(A) 報名參加會議
(B) 重新安排預約
(C) 升級他的服務
(D) 以信用卡付款

188. 下列何者與葛瑞先生有關？

(A) 他當建築師已經超過 20 年了
(B) 他在去年 GSA 會員大會上發表演說
(C) 他投稿至建築期刊
(D) 他在四月時忘記繳交會費

189. 葛瑞先生在會議當天應該要幾點報到？

(A) 上午 8:45 到上午 10:00
(B) 上午 9:00 整
(C) 任何時間
(D) 上午 9: 00 到上午 9:45

190. 活動中包含幾餐？

(A) 早餐、午餐和晚餐
(B) 早午餐和晚餐
(C) 晚餐和雞尾酒會
(D) 午餐和晚餐

191–195 告示和電子郵件

科洛尼爾高地安養院

科洛尼爾高地很自豪已經在德州休士頓服務長者超過 30 年了。本安養院擁有最先進的設備，本院的五樓大樓讓每一層樓都可提供住戶個人化的照護。大樓裡設有復健用健身房，另外也提供住戶心理諮詢服務。

本院現正有數個職缺。我們希望聘用一名安養院行政人員，至少具三年的經驗及有效執照。另外，徵求一位住院協調員，應徵者需具備大學學歷及至少兩年的相關工作經歷。我們還招募臨終照護工作人員，需要能以富同情心與關懷的方式來提供住戶個人化照護，無須相關經驗，所以歡迎任何有興趣的人來應徵。

您可到本安養院網站查詢職缺，並上傳求職表，網站是 www.chnh.com。

收件者：湯米・詹金斯
<tommyjenkins7@zeusnet.com>
寄件者：貴格・帕克
<g_parker@chnh.com>
主旨：聘用程序
日期：9 月 14 日

親愛的詹金斯先生：

恭喜您！您已經通過住院協調員的第一輪應徵程序。我們要求所有應徵者親自前來科洛尼爾高地安養院參加面試。請您告知在 9 月 17 日方便前來面試的時間。

期盼與您見面。

科洛尼爾高地安養院 人力資源部主管
貴格・帕克 敬上

收件者：貴格・帕克
<g_parker@chnh.com>
寄件者：湯米・詹金斯
<tommyjenkins7@zeusnet.com>
日期：9 月 15 日
主旨：回覆：聘用程序

親愛的帕克先生：

感謝您給我住院協調員一職的面試機會。您要求我告知 9 月 17 日有空的時間。我在上午 10 點有另一場面試，但下午 1 點就可以到科洛尼爾高地安養院，希望您那個時間方便。如您所知，位於市區另一頭的松蔭安養院是另一家與您競爭的安養機構，而他們所提出的時數非常誘人。但我更想在像科洛尼爾高地安養院這樣有現代化設備的場所工作。期盼這次與您的面談，並參觀貴院設施。

湯米・詹金斯 敬上

191. 文中提到與科洛尼爾高地安養院有關的什麼事？

(A) 在德州有五個據點
(B) 已經營運超過半世紀
(C) 提供藝術課程
(D) 提供心理健康服務

192. 根據公告，哪個職位不需要經驗？

(A) 安養院行政人員
(B) 臨終照護人員
(C) 住院協調員
(D) 櫃台接待員

193. 下列何者與科洛尼爾高地安養院有關？

(A) 計劃要擴大設施
(B) 接受網站上遞出求職表
(C) 提供該州最高的薪水
(D) 最近更新了營業執照

194. 下列何者可能是湯米・詹金斯決定不去科洛尼爾高地安養院工作的原因？

(A) 他們沒有健身中心
(B) 他們的設備不先進
(C) 工作地點太遠
(D) 松蔭安養院可以提供他更好的時間表

195. 湯米・詹金斯幾點可以到科洛尼爾高地安養院？

(A) 上午 10 點
(B) 下午 1 點以前
(C) 下午 1 點以後
(D) 下午 4 點以後

196–200 電子郵件

收件者：傑克・包德溫
<baldwinj@technet.com>
寄件者：夢幻綠洲飯店
<booking@dreamoasishotel.com>
日期：9 月 22 日
主旨：您的訂房紀錄
附件：請款單 .html

親愛的包德溫先生：

感謝您在夢幻綠洲飯店訂房。您預約了 10 月 13 日和 14 日兩晚一間一張雙人床的房間。您的訂房編號是 5259。

僅以此信通知您，您必須於 9 月 29 日前支付尾款以便確認訂房。兩晚的費用總額為 165.25 元。您可以在飯店網站上以信用卡支付帳款，網址為 www.dreamoasishotel.com，支付時需輸入訂房編號。您也可以來電以電話完成支付手續。若未於 9 月 29 日前收到款項，將自動取消您的預約。有關詳細資訊，請參考附件的請款單。

當您抵達機場時，前往本飯店最簡單的方式就是搭乘地鐵。本飯店位於市政廳站三號出口旁。若找不到飯店，請隨時來電 555-2134。我們 24 小時皆有人員提供協助。

再次感謝您選擇本飯店。

夢幻綠洲飯店 客戶服務部經理
艾咪・李

收件者：夢幻綠洲飯店
<booking@dreamoasishotel.com>
寄件者：傑克・包德溫
<baldwinj@technet.com>
日期：9 月 23 日
主旨：回覆：您的訂房紀錄

親愛的李小姐：

這封信是有關我在夢幻綠洲飯店 10 月 13 日和 14 日這兩天的訂房。您在電子郵件中提到我即將入住貴飯店的款項問題。但是，我想要詢問住宿時間是否能延長一晚。我最近聽說 10 月 16 日將舉辦在地美食節，我想要參加。因此，我打算在貴飯店住到 10 月 15 日。請告知我修改後的費用，這樣我就能盡快支付正確的款項。

傑克・包德溫

收件者：傑克・包德溫
<baldwinj@technet.com>
寄件者：艾咪・李
<alee@dreamoasishotel.com>
日期：9 月 24 日
主旨：15 號

親愛的包德溫先生：

將於 10 月 16 日舉辦的美食節的確值得讓您感到興奮。遺憾的是，這個活動太熱門了，所以該週末整個市區都已經客滿了。很遺憾要通知您，夢幻綠洲飯店在 10 月 15 日已經沒有空房。我逕自查了附近合作的飯店，但是也都沒有空房。我真的希望您能在市區找到住宿的地方，這樣就能在此享受這個節慶，我多麼希望您能和我們一同歡度。您可以試試位於費爾維尤的高檔旅舍，那是一間大型飯店，他們還有空房。

誠摯地深感抱歉。

夢幻綠洲飯店 客戶服務部經理
艾咪・李

196. 第一封電子郵件的目的是什麼？

- Ⓐ 解釋取消的規定
- **Ⓑ 要求付款**
- Ⓒ 安排預約
- Ⓓ 提供特殊服務

197. 當包德溫先生線上付款時，會被要求提供什麼？

- Ⓐ 他的電話號碼
- Ⓑ 他的電子郵件信箱
- Ⓒ 他的房間號碼
- **Ⓓ 他的訂房編號**

198. 李小姐的電子郵件中不包含以下哪一項資訊？

- Ⓐ 住宿的費用
- **Ⓑ 旅遊保險**
- Ⓒ 飯店位置
- Ⓓ 員工聯絡方式

199. 包德溫先生 15 號那晚為什麼無法住在夢幻綠洲飯店？

A 飯店因為美食節而客滿了
B 飯店因為太熱門而客滿了
C 因為市區要舉辦會議，所以客滿了
D 因為飯店餐點太好吃，所以客滿了

200. 艾咪．李提供了什麼建議？

A 要包德溫先生試試市區另一間飯店
B 要包德溫先生試試位於費爾維尤的飯店
C 要包德溫先生明年再來參加美食節
D 要包德溫 14 號再來問看看是否有人取消訂房

ACTUAL TEST ④

PART 5 P.110–113

◎ **Part 5 解答請見 P.457**

101. **除了**靠近後門的那棵樹外，這塊地上所有的樹木都在暴風雨中受損了。

102. 在內科醫生為**他**確診前，賀帝先生必須先進行幾項醫療檢查。

103. 企業家詹姆斯．莫斯比是**最近**一期雜誌的專題人物。

104. 法官的判決必須**嚴格地**依據所提供的證據。

105. 基於他數十年的經驗，芬利先生負責訓練新健身房的**指導員**。

106. 火焰餐廳的顧客可使用代客泊車服務，也可**自行**停車。

107. 去年，那些年輕的化學家**積極地**投入新黏著劑的研發。

108. 第一木業的專家可以將任何木頭家具修復**到**其原始的狀況。

109. 圖書館為了讀者的方便，要求資助裝設**自動**門。

110. 在注意到衣櫃**耗損的**狀況後，骨董店的老闆降低了價格。

111. 過去的十年來，亨利．維維安**證明**是位有才華又有上進心的記者。

112. **任何**患有睡眠問題**的人**在喝了這種花草茶後能獲得改善。

113. 為了減少南部**地區**的交通時間，在原有的鐵路線外又新增了一條。

114. 在節日期間，施瓦茨百貨公司將**推出**特別的化妝品禮盒組。

115. 沒有合格房地產經紀人的協助，首次購屋會是複雜甚至**有風險的**事情。

116. 布朗斯維爾的遊民之家自去年**創立**以來，已經幫助了數千人。

117. 明天評審小組將**評選出**社區美術大賽的準決賽參賽者。

118. 手機提早解約的罰金**明確地**記載在合約書中。

119. **根據**研究者報告，更常食用新鮮蔬果比避免吃速食是更好的健康終極目標。

120. 為了讓西班牙文母語者也能參加導覽，**口譯者**打算提供翻譯服務。

121. 慢跑者被要求靠道路右側跑，因為**很多**自行車騎士需要利用左邊的空間通行。

122. 在潛在買家看屋前，房地產經紀人要確定那房子是**美輪美奐的**。

123. 至於上週的**匯**款，必繳的州稅與聯邦稅須由領款者支付。

124. 每個人都支持縮短工時，但是**直到**總裁批准之前，一切都將依照原樣。

125. 該製造公司最近在減少工地意外事件上的**努力**受到了全體員工的讚賞。

126. 飯廳的家具**故意**留在屋內，因為新屋主已經買下它們。

127. 葛瑞森劇院**偶爾**會讓學生團體在白天時觀看彩排。

128. 《專業運動》雜誌**以**出版一系列頂尖運動員的獨家專訪而出名。

129. 只有**那些**配戴識別證的代表人員，才能進入會議場地。

130. **在**候選人正式宣布參加競選**前**，他私下與顧問群會面。

131–134 告示

員工工作坊

T&R 集團以提供領導能力進修、員工訓練及各種工作坊等方式，盡力幫助員工發揮潛能。這個月，我們為那些有意加強電腦技能的員工提供了工作坊，包括如何操作專業文書套件軟體、架設個人網站和操作通訊應用軟體等數種課程。我們目前還有幾個空檔時段，歡迎同仁提供建議，最受歡迎的提案將會考慮列入工作坊。如果您有意參加任何一個工作坊，請寄電子郵件給瓊納斯 jsmith@TRgroup.com。我們希望大家都能善用所提供的課程。

131. A 提供
B 當時正提供
C 現正提供
D 已提供

132. A 改正
B 減少
C 詳述
D 改善

133. A 依賴的
B 獨立的
C 閒置的
D 能得到的

134. A 有關賭博與娛樂的問題恕不回答。
B 最受歡迎的提案將會考慮列入工作坊。
C 我們要求所有主管提出建議。
D 我們希望這個工作坊成功，並祝您一切順利。

135–138 廣告

西卓辛：夜間型流感全效

以西卓辛做好迎接感冒與流感季節。西卓辛是一種含藥物成分的舒緩夜飲，可治療流感症狀，包括發燒、全身疼痛、鼻塞、咳嗽和喉嚨痛。讓您醒來感到精神充沛，準備好戰勝新的一天。如果您打算操作機械或開車，請勿服用西卓辛。請置於孩童不易接觸之處。如果症狀持續十天以上，請向醫生諮詢。

西卓辛是銷售第一的流感治療藥物，請依指示服用，保證有效。欲知詳情請上網站 www.citrusine.com。

135. A 使人放心的
B 增強活力的
C 舒緩的
D 安慰的

136. A 提神的
B 恢復精神的
C 恢復活力
D 恢復活力

137. A 若不當服用，可能造成嚴重副作用。
B 兒童應該服用兒童用西卓辛。
C 小包裝看起來像糖果，可能會引起問題。
D 如果症狀持續十天以上，請向醫生諮詢。

138. **A 為了**
B 在……期間
C 和……一起
D 在……之後

139–142 電子郵件

收件者：珍娜・唐
寄件者：綠景
日期：6 月 28 日
主旨：詢問

唐女士您好：

感謝您的提問。十多年來，綠景向來是郊區商家愛用的主要庭園設計公司。雖然本公司專長園藝與日式庭園造景，但我們也保養草坪與運動場。至於您的提問，是的，我們也清除茂密的灌木叢和樹木。我們可以派專人前去估算所需的時間與大概的費用。此外，如果您希望將稠密的樹叢改成草地或花園，您可與我們的設計師合作，一起發想您喜歡的造景設計。

若您有意洽詢，請來電 555-1245。我們很樂意為您服務。

139. **A 雖然**
B 因為
C 因此
D 然而

140. A 斷定
B 計算
C 估算
D 猜測

141. A 正希望
B 希望
C 過去希望
D 希望

142. A 我們歡迎任何與您合作的機會。
B 請勿取消訂單。
C 如果您有意洽詢，請來電 555-1245。
D 去公園看看本市的景色。

143–146 廣告

黑山豆

黑山豆是路易西安納的一間咖啡公司，也是路易西安納咖啡豆的先驅。本公司監管一條垂直整合供應鏈，以來自路易西安納州黑山最高品質的咖啡豆為始。本公司嚴選了三種獲獎咖啡豆：夏收、烏南與黑地。所有產品都可在 24 小時內配送至全美各地。黑山豆的咖啡也在全美所有隆德超商中販售。

不論您要的是優質咖啡，還是想來點南方風情的安逸。黑山豆都會是您正確的咖啡選擇，全部都是美國生產製造且有機。當您飲用的同時，還可以感受到愛國情操。今天就上本公司網站 www.blackhillbeans.com 聽聽我們更多的故事吧！

143. A 結合
B 結合
C 整合的
D 整合

144. A 位於
B 挑選
C 評估
D 維持

145. **A 在……範圍內**
B 在……之前
C 直到
D 在

146. A 試試這附近最暢銷的凍飲。
B 全部都是美國生產製造且有機。
C 讓我們幫您找到適合的供應商。
D 這個優惠只在 10 月 1 日前有效。

147–148 公告

公告

克勞佛服飾已整修試衣間，讓您可以在購買前試穿衣服。

- 一次請拿一到兩件衣物進試衣間。
- 您可以將個人物品，像是皮夾或皮包交由店員保管。
- 任何留在試衣間的個人物品．將存放在入口旁的失物招領處。

147. 這張公告最有可能是給誰看的？

A 店長
B 顧客
C 設計師
D 店員

148. 根據這張公告，在哪裡可以找到遺失物品？

A 警察局
B 服務中心
C 存放處
D 櫃台後方

149–150 訊息串

琳達．貝茲 **6:55**
我遲到了。我睡太晚了。

梅琳達．克魯茲 **6:56**
那你幾點會到？

琳達．貝茲 **6:57**
我一個小時內可以到。

梅琳達．克魯茲 **6:58**
我要先走嗎？

琳達．貝茲 **7:02**
不用，只要確定我到時，貨物都裝上車就行了。

梅琳達．克魯茲 **7:02**
好的。

琳達．貝茲 **7:03**
謝了。

梅琳達．克魯茲 **7:08**
等會見，小心開車。

琳達．貝茲 **7:10**
好，我會的。

149. 下列何者與貝茲女士有關？

A 她為克魯茲女士工作
B 她被困在車陣中
C 她目前正在開車
D 她常遲到

150. 在 7:02 時，克魯茲女士寫：「好的。」是什麼意思？

A 她會等貝茲女士
B 她打算把貨裝到貨車上
C 她對貝茲女士的遲到很不滿
D 她已經裝滿貨車了

151–152 電子郵件

收件者：派翠西亞．穆勒
<patmueller@finemail.net>
寄件者：馬克．哈欽斯
<mhutchings@grosvenoronline.com>
日期：6 月 4 日
主旨：回覆：熱線

親愛的穆勒女士：

感謝您對我們技術服務熱線的指教，我們並不知道電話轉到總機要花這麼久的時間。我們已經設法解決了這個因電話總機軟體的小故障而引發的問題。作為善意的表示，謹在此提供您一張本公司網路商店價值 25 元的折價券。只要在 www.grosvenoronline.com 登入您的帳戶，在主頁欄位中輸入折價券序號 H58K55，即可兑換。

格羅夫納網路公司 客服專員
馬克．哈欽斯 敬上

151. 馬克．哈欽斯為什麼會寄這封電子郵件？

Ⓐ 為了促銷當季特別優惠
Ⓑ 為了確認訂單地址
Ⓒ 為了對一份意見表達感謝
Ⓓ 為了對某個問題要求更多資訊

152. 穆勒女士下次登上格羅夫納網路公司時，最有可能會做什麼？

Ⓐ 報名加入會員
Ⓑ 兌換優惠券
Ⓒ 使用顧客意見表
Ⓓ 更新帳單資料

153–154 網頁

http://www.jannisar.com

首頁	產品	聯絡我們	關於我們	帳戶

恭喜！因為您經常造訪本站，已經獲選成為白金會員。請填寫下列表格，以完成整個程序：

名	
姓	
郵寄地址	
授權碼	
電子郵件信箱	
意見：	

勾選您有興趣購買的商品類別（可複選）

電子用品〔 〕 音樂〔 〕 書籍〔 〕
家具〔 〕 電腦遊戲〔 〕

請注意，身為白金會員，您將於一年內收到四次電子郵件，通知您所勾選類別之商品優惠。您的帳戶資料將於 24 小時內以電子郵件查核。我們會寄給您一封電子郵件確認函，請遵照郵件中指示，確認您的會員資格。

153. 這個網頁針對的對象是誰？

Ⓐ 拍賣網站上的新客戶
Ⓑ 網路行銷公司專員
Ⓒ 零售商店的供應商
Ⓓ 網路零售店的長期客戶

154. 該網頁的讀者被要求做什麼？

Ⓐ 說明喜歡的商品
Ⓑ 提供付款資料
Ⓒ 列印表格並簽名
Ⓓ 報告配送延誤

155–157 文章

貓狗風潮

布蘭特伍德市（5 月 2 日）——布蘭特伍德市終於有了自己的貓咪咖啡廳，叫做喵喵浩劫，還有一家叫做熱狗的小狗咖啡店。這兩家店是凱文和金潔．布萊克夫婦所開設的。這兩家咖啡廳於上月熱烈開幕，並受到大篇幅的媒體報導，但這股熱潮並未消退。「生意很興隆，」凱文．布萊克說，「我們知道我們會很成功，只是沒想到會這麼成功。」客人不僅熱情蜂擁到這兩家咖啡廳，和動物們一同消磨喝茶或咖啡的時光，還有很多人認養了這些動物，給牠們永遠的家。「我們認為能為一些動物提供住處是很棒的，因為許多收容所都已經過度擁擠。」金潔．布萊克解釋，「同時客人也有機會和動物們互動，這對收容所而言是最好的宣傳方式。」

自咖啡廳開幕以來，已經有超過 10 隻狗和 15 隻貓被認養。「我還沒養狗，但我一直想養一隻。」一位常客蘿莉．喬登說，「我來這裡和牠們玩，或許有一天我會找到一隻自己真正想要的小狗。」

由於他們的成功，布萊克夫婦正考慮買下鄰近的店面來拓展商機。「我們需要更多空間以容納所有客人和動物們，」凱文解釋道，「有時候真的很擠。」布萊克夫婦正計劃於下個月整修小狗咖啡店，並於秋天時整修貓咪咖啡廳。

155. 下列何者與咖啡廳有關？

Ⓐ 它們供應各種點心
Ⓑ 它們販賣小狗和小貓
Ⓒ 它們提供咖啡和茶
Ⓓ 它們提供寵物用品

156. 文中報導了什麼有關貓和狗的敘述？

A 有好幾隻已經被認養
B 牠們會永遠住在咖啡廳裡
C 牠們對客人都很友善
D 牠們被訓練來娛樂大家

157. 下列句子最適合出現在 [1]、[2]、[3]、[4] 的哪個位置？「但這股熱潮並未消退。」

A [1]
B [2]
C [3]
D [4]

158–160 廣告

來新浪潮水療中心休息放鬆！

從忙亂的一天中，享受新浪潮水療中心的專業水療服務來好好休息一下吧。我們位於沃利大道 458 號。不管您只待上一小時或是一整天，在您離開時都將感到神清氣爽並充滿活力。請參考我們以下的一般療程：

經典假期（120 元）——試試這個最適合忙碌人士的基本療程
30 分鐘背部與肩頸按摩／小黃瓜臉部護理／紫丁香全身裹敷

玫瑰花園（155 元）——讓玫瑰的香氣喚醒您的所有感官
45 分鐘全身按摩／玫瑰水護膚療程／手部美甲

海洋體驗（180 元）——來體驗我們最受歡迎的療程，海洋療癒之力
60 分鐘全身按摩／全身海鹽去角質／熱石療程／海草臉部護理

完美活化（210 元）——讓自己沉浸在一整天的豪華療程中
90 分鐘全身按摩／頭皮放鬆按摩／火山泥臉部護理／迷迭香純淨去角質／手部美甲／足部護理

請事先來電 555-2940 預約，以免向隅。四人以上同行，可享免費三明治、清蒸蔬食與鮮榨果汁午餐組。所有貴賓在第三次光臨時將免費獲贈新浪潮浴袍。

158. 這則廣告主要和什麼有關？

A 保健機構的擴展
B 奢華服務的優惠
C 水療中心的搬遷
D 店家的標準方案

159. 哪一項療程包含了熱氣護理？

A 經典假期
B 玫瑰花園
C 海洋體驗
D 完美活化

160. 四人以上的團體可獲贈什麼？

A 免費浴袍
B 減價優惠
C 免費餐點
D 私人包廂

161–164 網路討論區

比爾・佛萊克 **9:41**
你好，我想知道米蘭諾家窗簾訂單的最新進度。

露西・米特 **9:41**
我們還在等手工蕾絲的花邊絲綢，不過我們昨天收到大部分的布料，我們的裁縫師今天就會進行處理。

比爾・佛萊克 **9:42**
那你認為這些工作可以如米蘭諾家要求的在本週五完成嗎？

露西・米特 **9:43**
我不確定。這要看那些花邊何時到。我們的小組可以開始接縫其中一部分，但我們需要那些花邊來完成複雜的圖樣。

比爾・佛萊克 **9:44**
你可以聯絡手工蕾絲，了解一下貨運幾時到嗎？

露西・米特 **9:45**
事實上，理查正在處理。理查，他們那裡有消息嗎？

理查・崔 **9:45**
是，我剛和他們通完電話。出貨有些延誤，因為他們的花邊師傅用錯絲綢，他們必須重做花邊。我們可以在今天下午收到，他們會用急件送來。

比爾・佛萊克 **9:46**
太好了。這週末就可以把這些窗簾做好嗎？

露西・米特 **9:47**
沒問題。我們會日夜趕工讓它們準時完工。

比爾・佛萊克 **9:48**
很高興聽到你這樣說。他們是長期老客戶了，他們的新公寓這週末需要用到這些窗簾。

161. 在線上聊天的這些人可能從事何種行業？
Ⓐ 服飾公司
Ⓑ 婚紗店
Ⓒ 窗簾客製店
Ⓓ 布料批發行

162. 花邊的貨運何時會到？
Ⓐ 早上
Ⓑ 下午
Ⓒ 隔天
Ⓓ 週末

163. 在 9:47 時，露西・米特說：「我們會日以繼夜地工作」是什麼意思？
Ⓐ 她的團隊將仔細注意時間
Ⓑ 她的團隊會盡快工作
Ⓒ 她的團隊完全不用趕時間
Ⓓ 如果有必要，她的團隊將日夜趕工

164. 比爾・佛萊克接下來可能會做什麼？
Ⓐ 打電話給客戶
Ⓑ 取消訂單
Ⓒ 要求花邊配送
Ⓓ 安排會議

165–167 時間表

杜魯斯市
第五屆夏季歡樂慶
7 月 23 日 星期日

早上 10 點到下午 6 點《鄉土自然美術大賽》
杜魯斯的藝術家們將於杜魯斯社區活動中心展出畫作，作品描繪本地大自然與野生動物。來賓可票選自己最喜愛的畫作，優勝者名單將於歌唱比賽開始時宣布。

早上 11 點到中午 12 點《魔術秀》
請和我們一起來欣賞令人驚奇的魔術表演吧。魔術師米克・透納以他頗富創意與娛樂效果的魔術花招著名。

中午 12 點到下午 2 點《現場爵士音樂會》
在公園享受現場爵士樂，由來自紐約的爵士樂團哈洛威樂團所演奏。他們將演奏各種經典爵士樂曲，也將販售他們最新發行的唱片。

早上 10 點到晚上 7 點《可再生能源博覽會》
本地的陽光能源公司將展示最新的可再生能源專案，包括太陽能面板與手機行動電源。

晚上 7 點到晚上 9 點《歌唱大賽》
歡迎當地居民參加今年的歌唱大賽。有意參賽者可上網站報名並填寫必要表格 www.duluthcitysff.com。

欲知更多資訊，請來電 555-0157。

165. 畫畫比賽的優勝者將於何時宣布？
Ⓐ 下午 2 點
Ⓑ 下午 6 點
Ⓒ 晚上 7 點
Ⓓ 晚上 9 點

166. 根據時程表，有什麼可供購買？
Ⓐ 藝術品
Ⓑ 音樂專輯
Ⓒ 手機配件
Ⓓ 太陽能面板

167. 參賽者要如何報名歌唱大賽？

A 前往詢問處
B 聯絡社區活動中心
C 上網站
D 寄電子郵件

168–171 傳單

公園露天電影

今年秋天，格倫伍德溫泉公園將為格倫伍德溫泉居民每週舉辦名為「公園露天電影夜」的活動，並與帕克斯頓企業、GS 購物商場等的本地商家合作。將於每週五晚上在公園中心播放適合闔家觀賞的電影。這些活動不需門票，因為它們是免費開放給大眾的。

自 9 月到 11 月，公園露天電影夜保證為全家帶來一系列有趣又感人的電影，鼓勵您帶著毛毯、椅子和野餐點心前來。電影開演時間依日落時間而定，因此建議您提早到場以優先選定位置。請上我們的網站 www.glenwoodsprings.org/movies 查看即將播放的電影時刻表及本地贊助商的名單。

如果遇上大雨、低溫或強風，將有可能取消電影播放。如果發生這種狀況，將於網站與本地電台公告電影取消事宜。您也可以來電 715-555-5358 格倫伍德溫泉的公園與休憩部，詢問活動取消的相關訊息。

168. 這個傳單的目的是什麼？

A 宣布公園整修計劃
B 宣傳社區活動
C 請求捐款
D 宣傳新電影

169. 誰會提供公園露天電影的資金？

A 當地廣播電台
B 格倫伍德溫泉的居民
C 公園與休憩部門
D 格倫伍德溫泉的商家

170. 下列何者不是給參加者的建議？

A 帶食物
B 事先買票
C 參考時間表
D 提早到場

171. 根據這張傳單，為什麼會用到這個電話號碼？

A 做預約
B 詢問時間表的異動
C 詢問交通路線
D 取消預約

172–175 廣告

賴特曼塔

49858 紐約州紐約市百老匯街 1234 號

位於本市金融區，賴特曼塔提供了壯麗的市景，更提供了辦公空間，適合任何有意在紐約市中心營運的企業。離地鐵站僅一個街區，步行即可抵達公車與計程車站，賴特曼塔的位置相當便利。一樓大廳提供保全措施，所有職員都需經過安檢門的掃瞄檢查才能到達後方的電梯。同時，寬敞的大廳以豪華的室內裝潢與親切的服務員迎賓。

三樓與四樓可出租給公司企業使用。高挑的樓板與高聳的玻璃窗提供了開放空間與完美的自然採光。今天就盡快提出申請吧。市場上對這些場地的需求極高。必須親自面談，非誠者勿試。更多資訊請上網站 www.wrightmantowers.com/rent，您可以在網路上參觀或來電 555-1234 洽詢本公司。

172. 下列何者與出租的場所有關？

A 只提供給私人住戶
B 只提供給企業
C 提供給大眾
D 非常昂貴

173. 下列何者與賴特曼塔的地點有關？

A 靠近大眾運輸
B 大樓周遭交通繁忙
C 沒有停車場
D 在市郊

174. 網站有什麼特色？

A 列出所有使用中的場所
B 獨家優惠促銷代碼
C 出租場所的虛擬導覽
D 大樓的歷史

175. 下列句子最適合出現在 [1]、[2]、[3]、[4] 的哪個位置？「市場上對這些場所的需求極高。」

A [1]
B [2]
C [3]
D [4]

176–180 公告和電子郵件

肯尼斯環球新聞實習

肯尼斯環球新聞實習職將提供您大好機會，可以在世界最知名的國際多媒體新聞通訊社接受培訓，與專業的記者及編輯一起工作，並且在各大都市（如倫敦、柏林和巴黎）中步調快速的新聞編輯室獲得寶貴經驗。這將為才華橫溢的大學畢業生提供一個機會，學習並培養新聞工作的專業技能並習得第一手知識。

這是一份帶薪的實習職，提供免費住宿與午晚餐。實習生將接受數週的正式培訓，著重於寫作技巧、新聞倫理和職場基本知識等方面的訓練。實習生也可在實習期間免費利用其他固定安排的培訓機會。這個實習將自 8 月 1 日起，歷時四個月。

實習申請表可於網站 www.kennethglobal.com 取得，必須在 6 月 20 前繳交。通過此階段的應徵者必須於 6 月 27 日到總部進行面談。任何問題都可寫信至 rubyhart@kennethglobal.com 向露比．哈特提出，或親至我們位於奧斯汀的總部詢問。

寄件者：凱爾．蘭恩 <kylelane12@mpnet.com>
收件者：露比．哈特 <rubyhart@kennethglobal.com>
主旨：實習
日期：6 月 23 日

親愛的哈特女士：

我相當高興能夠通過肯尼斯環球新聞實習職的第一階段甄選。應徵者應該要在指定日期親自參加面試，但是很遺憾地，我預計要和教授一起參加一場在達拉斯舉辦的重要會議。但因為我就住在離貴公司總部只有幾分鐘路程的地方，安排另一場面談時間應該不是難事。

再次感謝貴公司將我列入該職務的考量人選。期待收到您有關面談日期的回覆。同時，我也會盡全力做好準備。

凱爾．蘭恩 敬上

176. 下列何者與實習應徵者有關？

A 他們必須先有工作經驗
B 他們必須參加即將舉辦的會議
C 他們必須交一封推薦信
D 他們必須有學士學位

177. 關於實習職，下列何者為真？

A 含餐點與住宿
B 只提供給專業新聞工作者
C 將於八月結束
D 是無薪職務

178. 實習生還可享有什麼好處？

A 健康保險
B 額外的培訓
C 員工優惠
D 帶薪假

179. 蘭恩先生應該在何時參加面談？

A 6 月 20 日
B 6 月 27 日
C 6 月 23 日
D 8 月 1 日

180. 蘭恩先生住在哪裡？

Ⓐ 達拉斯
Ⓑ 奧斯汀
Ⓒ 柏林
Ⓓ 倫敦

181–185 電子郵件和宣布

收件者：山姆．貝瑞
<sberry@princetheater.com>
寄件者：貝思．華格納
<bessiewagner@linsuniveristy.edu>
日期：7 月 4 日
主旨：職缺

親愛的貝瑞先生：

我叫貝思．華格納，目前是林斯大學戲劇系的學生。我即將完成學業，正開始探詢未來可能的就業機會。有位教授推薦我可與在王子劇院服務的您聯絡，詢問貴公司可能開缺的職缺。

在林斯大學就讀時，我專攻戲劇製作。透過學術與實務經驗，我學到舞台管理的必要技能。從九月開始，我就可以從事兼職或全職的工作，並全力投入所有指派給我的工作中。

若王子劇院於今年秋季開始有任何職缺的話，煩請您不吝告知，我將感激不盡。

貝思．華格納

王子劇院
工作職缺

- **美術實習**
在美術部門的無償實習，處理各層面行政與製作職務。此人須執行美術主管的助理職務。

- **技術副總監**
兼職職務，負責演出管理與舞台機械設備。應徵者須具備舞台管理相關經驗。

- **票務管理主管**
全職職務，負責劇院所有活動的整體票務管理工作。職責包括管理售票處，規劃並執行售票流程，以及督導售票員工。

- **行銷主管**
全職職務，負責行銷劇院推出的所有演出活動。監督高品質宣傳資料的準備工作，以吸引戲迷來看我們的戲劇、音樂劇與音樂會。

■ 所有王子劇院的全職員工皆能免費觀賞所有演出。

■ 所有職務皆自今年十月起出缺。

■ 欲知更多資訊或有意應徵，請以電子郵件聯絡山姆．貝瑞 sberry@princetheater.com。

181. 下列何者與華格納女士有關？

Ⓐ 她是舞台演員
Ⓑ 她教舞台設計
Ⓒ 她即將畢業
Ⓓ 她是貝瑞先生的同事

182. 華格納女士為什麼寫信給貝瑞先生？

Ⓐ 要尋求工作機會
Ⓑ 要安排面試
Ⓒ 要表達感謝之意
Ⓓ 要報名訓練課程

183. 下列何者與票務管理主管無關？

Ⓐ 他／她必須管理各種活動
Ⓑ 他／她必須指導其他員工的工作
Ⓒ 他／她可以免費看所有表演
Ⓓ 他／她必須規劃宣傳活動

184. 這些刊登的職務有什麼共同點？

Ⓐ 都需要音樂才華
Ⓑ 都將在第四季開缺
Ⓒ 都是兼職工作
Ⓓ 都需要戲劇學位

185. 哪一個工作最適合華格納女士？

Ⓐ 美術實習生
Ⓑ 技術副總監
Ⓒ 票務管理主管
Ⓓ 行銷主管

186–190 文章和信件

4 月 5 日——斯克蘭頓市中心的清水醫院發起了一項筆友計劃，讓絕症患者和成人志工相互通信。這項計劃由院長查克·錢伯斯發起，他最近才剛獲得全國健康護理聯盟所頒發的傑出領導獎。這計劃將使醫院與社區間有更穩固的關係。錢伯斯先生鼓勵各行各業的成人提出申請，即使他們可能覺得自己不完全合乎資格。只要上清水醫院網站，就可免費成為醫院會員。

錢伯斯先生說：「我希望透過這個計劃，讓志工可以和病人形成緊密的關係，幫助他們度過生命中這些艱難的時刻。」他也希望這個計劃能引起更多人親自探訪這些絕症患者。

清水醫院

5 月 4 日

莫妮卡·格尼
54481 威斯康辛州斯克蘭頓市華盛頓路 4100 號

親愛的格尼女士：

很高興收到您的來信。我非常興奮能和您配對成為筆友。希望我們可以從彼此身上學到很多東西，建立起永恆的友誼。

正如您所知，我住在加州，離威斯康辛州很遠。希望接下來的幾個月中我能休假去探望您。請告訴我最適合去探訪您的時間。

期待收到您的回音。

潔西卡·萊特

親愛的潔西卡：

您不知道您那親切的話語讓我有多感激。雖然清水醫院的工作人員非常和善，我仍然有種渴望，想與醫護人員以外的人交流。我其他的家人也住在遙遠的地方，在佛羅里達州，因此大多數的時候，我只能和工作人員或其他病友說話。如果您真的想來的話，我非常歡迎，我想最適合的時間應該就是中心的感恩節派對了。我自己的家人也可能會來這裡。如果您覺得這樣太勉強，或您無法休假，也別太掛心。我真的希望我們可以透過信件繼續交流。

祝安好。

莫妮卡·格尼

186. 這篇文章是有關什麼？

Ⓐ 志工計劃
Ⓑ 醫生退休
Ⓒ 新醫院
Ⓓ 寫作比賽

187. 下列何者和錢伯斯先生有關？

Ⓐ 他是清水醫院的病人
Ⓑ 他教授成人寫作技巧
Ⓒ 他是政府機構的首長
Ⓓ 他因領導長才受到表揚

188. 錢伯斯先生邀請人們做什麼事？

Ⓐ 訂閱商務通訊
Ⓑ 安排定期健康檢查
Ⓒ 探視病情嚴重的病人
Ⓓ 寫推薦信

189. 潔西卡·格尼大部分的時間都和誰一起度過？

Ⓐ 清水醫院員工
Ⓑ 她的家人
Ⓒ 莫妮卡·萊特
Ⓓ 她的朋友

190. 莫妮卡要潔西卡何時去探訪？

Ⓐ 在莫妮卡的生日
Ⓑ 這週六
Ⓒ 6 月 7 日
Ⓓ 感恩節

191–195 信件和電子郵件

約翰・莫里斯先生
90117 加州米爾維爾伯納爾大道 1423 號

親愛的莫里斯先生：

24/7 健身中心是全美最成功的健身中心。我們全國有超過三百萬名會員，我們加盟企業已被公認為聲譽良好且值得信賴的品牌。我們的成功來自於我們與各分店的良好關係。

您之所以收到此函，是因為您表達了有意加盟 24/7 健身中心，要在您的鎮上開設新據點。根據我們初步的研究，您所居住的城鎮有大量在專業領域服務的年輕單身人口。這是我們的目標客群，表示此 24/7 健身中心據點的生意前景頗被看好。如果您想要有更多加盟 24/7 健身中心的具體條款和規則等相關資料，請來電 347-555-3363 與我聯絡。此外，如果您想與其他分店店長聯絡，我們的同事也能提供相關資訊給您。

營運總長
洛麗斯・旺森 敬上

收件者：查克・卡特
<zcarter@zenmail.com>
寄件者：約翰・莫里斯
<jmorris@cbnet.com>
主旨：24/7 健身中心
日期：3 月 6 日

親愛的卡特先生：

我叫約翰・莫里斯，是住在米爾維爾地區的小型企業主。目前我正和 24/7 健身中心協商在米爾維爾這裡開設我自己的據點。作為 24/7 健身中心的加盟業者，您或許可以藉由分享您的看法來助我一臂之力。

我想了解您作為加盟業者，對 24/7 健身中心的評價如何。我以前曾經營過數家加盟店，一直認為信任與誠實是一段成功關係中最重要的因素。更重要的是，我也在想知道母公司提供了何種的協助。在開設您的據點前，您是否得到了充足的訓練，讓您得以順利地經營業務？非常感謝您所提供的任何建議。

約翰・莫里斯 敬上

收件者：約翰・莫里斯
<jmorris@cbnet.com>
寄件者：查克・卡特
<zcarter@zenmail.com>
主旨：24/7 健身中心
日期：3 月 7 日

親愛的莫里斯先生：

我很樂意提供對 24/7 健身中心加盟管理的一些看法。截至目前為止，我已經和 24/7 健身中心以加盟身分合作十年了。事實上，我目前經營三家分店。我完全同意您所說的話，信任與誠實是商業關係中最重要的兩個部分。在這方面，我相信擁有三家加盟店的事實，就是我對這加盟總部的信心證明。

我來讓您更放心。首先，不管分店店長是誰，24/7 健身中心對於品牌發展有很明確的方向。母公司不但提供了訓練，他們還堅持掌控設施的實際配置，從更衣間到自由重量訓練區皆是。母公司要自己的 300 萬名會員能夠走進任何一間分店，並且感到自在。在您經營滿一年之前，您每個月都必須向總部詳細報告業績、會員績效，和設備使用的流量表。他們將事必躬親，直到他們有信心您能代表這個品牌。我希望這能有助於您決定加入 24/7 健身中心這個團隊！

祝一切安好。

查克・卡特

191. 根據信件內容，24/7 健身中心的成功關鍵是什麼？

Ⓐ 與分店長有效率的溝通
Ⓑ 快速的全國展店
Ⓒ 有經驗的研究團隊
Ⓓ 員工全面性的訓練

192. 莫里斯先生最有可能從哪裡得到卡特先生的聯絡資料？

Ⓐ 從 24/7 健身中心的專員
Ⓑ 從 24/7 健身中心的網站
Ⓒ 從卡特先生的部落格
Ⓓ 從卡特先生的員工

193. 莫里斯先生最在意 24/7 健身中心的什麼？

Ⓐ 品牌名聲
Ⓑ 財務狀況
Ⓒ 提供協助方式
Ⓓ 加盟店規定

194. 查克・卡特寫這封電子郵件的目的是什麼？

Ⓐ 要求有關加盟的資訊
Ⓑ 告訴約翰・莫里斯有關 24/7 健身中心的事宜與提供的訓練
Ⓒ 說服約翰・莫里斯不要加盟 24/7 健身中心
Ⓓ 提醒 24/7 健身中心他們對加盟店的責任

195. 在查克・卡特的電子郵件中，下列何者與 24/7 健身中心有關？

Ⓐ 他們要所有的健身中心幾乎都一樣
Ⓑ 他們要加盟商將分店個人化
Ⓒ 他們明年想賣出更多補給品與會籍
Ⓓ 他們要求加盟商繳交使用的季報

196–200 電子郵件

收件者：凱文・史考特
<kevinscott@starrealty.com>
寄件者：史蒂文・梅森
<smason@turnerelectronics.com>
日期：2 月 2 日
主旨：倉庫

親愛的史考特先生：

我叫史蒂文・梅森，在消費性電子產品公司透納電器服務。我現在正在找位於匹茲堡地區的倉庫，正如您所知，在現今步調快速的商業世界中，擁有高效率的配送策略對每家公司來說都很重要。

因此，我正在尋找位於匹茲堡近郊的倉庫。倉庫需要靠近高速公路。本公司配送大量商品，所以我們想要一個專屬透納電器使用的倉庫。倉庫需備有可供大型卡車使用的寬敞裝卸區。此外，若倉庫也具辦公空間會更理想。由於本公司產品的貴重性質，我們希望倉庫能有預防竊盜與損害的保全設施。

期待儘快收到您的回覆。

透納電器
史蒂文・梅森

收件者：史蒂文・梅森
<smason@turnerelectronics.com>
寄件者：凱文・史考特
<kevinscott@starrealty.com>
日期：2 月 3 日
主旨：回覆：倉庫

親愛的梅森先生：

聽起來貴公司因為拓展業務，所以想要加強配送網絡的營運，以更快速將商品送到賣家手上。我們有各式的倉庫可供選擇，我相信其中一定有符合貴公司需求的倉庫。所有場地都有最先進的保全系統及經驗豐富的職員。

地點一——月租 3,499 元，10,000 平方英尺，倉庫由不同企業共用。由於該場所屬於共用地，因此我們提供優惠價。

地點二——月租 5,500 元，舊型倉庫，位於匹茲堡市中心。這個倉庫目前閒置中，因此可專屬貴公司使用。特點是還有一個人可進入的冷凍間。

地點三——月租 6,500 元，位於匹茲堡市郊數英哩處非常寬敞的倉庫。雖然目前有其他兩家公司做為儲藏室使用，但可改成讓貴公司專用的倉庫。

地點四——月組 2,600 元，中型倉庫。這個倉庫因為沒有方便卡車卸貨的空間，因此以優惠價提供。最適合小型企業。

以上這些是目前可供使用的場地，如果您有任何疑問或想親自參觀，請與我聯絡。

凱文・史考特

收件者：凱文．史考特
<kevinscott@startrealty.com>
寄件者：史蒂文．梅森
<smason@turnerelectronics.com>
日期：2 月 3 日
主旨：地點三

親愛的史考特先生：

非常感謝您如此快速地回覆我的詢問。雖然所有的倉庫沒有一間完全符合我正在找的，但我想對本公司最好的選擇應該是地點三的倉庫。當然，這前提是另外兩家公司能將他們所存放的貨物搬到其他倉庫。正如我在第一封電子郵件中提到的，本公司的營運正在擴展中，我要確定我們有大量空間可供成長。我也很樂見倉庫有保全措施。

下週初我有時間，如果有可能的話可以去地點三走走。我想如果我能親自造訪那個地方，才能做出果斷的決定。您方便時，請來電與我聯絡，這樣我們就可以安排時間。您可以打 (351) 546-9899 找我。

祝好。

透納電器
史蒂文．梅森

196. 第一封電子郵件的目的是什麼？

A 找出租的場所
B 敲定營運計劃
C 確定宅配送達
D 宣傳要出售的房地產

197. 梅森先生最有可能是誰？

A 倉庫管理人
B 卡車司機
C 保全警衛
D 配送部主管

198. 根據史考特先生所說，透納電器想做什麼？

A 僱用更多有經驗的卡車司機
B 提升供應鏈效率
C 改善產品整體品質
D 拓展到亞洲市場

199. 根據第三封電子郵件，要怎麼樣透納電器才會搬進地點三？

A 租金要減少
B 兩家公司必須找到其他地點儲藏它們的東西
C 場地必須改建以容納辦公室
D 大樓必須再增加一名警衛

200. 在第三封郵件中，梅森先生最有可能在哪一天去地點三參觀？

A 星期一
B 星期四
C 星期五
D 星期六

ACTUAL TEST ⑤

PART 5 P.140-143

◎ **Part 5 解答請見 P.457**

101. 如果客戶認為所提出的色系不夠**吸引人**，室內設計師是可以調整的。

102. 星期五晚餐的訂位，請將賓客人數由八名**增加**為十名。

103. 白朗特先生要求將橫幅懸掛在大樓的外牆**上**。

104. 為了以免日後設備有問題，你應該保留最近**開立**的收據。

105. 如果病患鼻子的症狀**在**兩天**內**沒有改善的跡象，那他就應該再去診所。

106. 百貨公司裡的展示員**熱情地**解說產品的功能與優點。

107. 因為最近的展品相當珍貴，加貝藝廊比以往**任何時候**採取了更多的防護措施。

108. **任何**要改變房屋結構的**人**必須先申請建物准可。

109. 出席改善溝通技巧工作坊的員工將得到一張由講師頒發的**結業**證書。

110. **除了**科學系優秀的教職員外，該大學也擁有最先進的實驗設備。

111. 募款者募得的捐款**將**平均**分配**給該慈善機構的三個據點。

112. **不論**建築物的年份，通風系統必須符合最新的安全法規。

113. 造成特頓線火車延誤的原因是其中一個車站發生了**程序上的**錯誤。

114. 由於我們預期會收到數百封求職申請書，所以您的履歷表以兩頁**為限**。

115. 講者在演講時，**將把焦點放在**國家爭取獨立的奮鬥上。

116. 在專案開始之前，歡迎活動是個增進志工**之間**交流的好機會。

117. 歐威飯店房間的陽台提供了該飯店**令人驚艷的**私人海灘景色。

118. 一付款後，旅行社人員就以電子郵件將購票**確認函**寄給顧客。

119. 在檢查車子之後，技師已經**正確地**找出引擎失去動力的原因。

120. 由於費雪女士的聽障問題，她將有一位手語專家**陪同**，好讓她可以參加會議。

121. 專案開發小組對挑選**鑑定**可能的大樓位址負有部分責任。

122. 方便烹調的料理包**除了**熱水外，附有一人份晚餐所需要的所有食材。

123. 教育中心提供關鍵技能的訓練，**好讓**失業者更容易找到工作。

124. 授權同意書的條款非常**簡單易懂**，不需要有法律背景即可了解。

125. 寄給研討會與會者的說明資料**羅列**了演講時間表和聯誼活動。

126. 你可以**依**你喜好，讓商品直接送到家或親自前往店家取貨。

127. 維他命補充劑上使用的是**天然**物質，而非化學物質。

128. 巴士司機利用小路而非主要快速道路，**從而**避開尖峰時刻的交通。

129. 當搬運廢棄物的卡車在 3:30 抵達時，組員**將已拆除**大樓的主體部分。

130. 如果您發現超高畫質電視有任何製造**瑕疵**，請盡快與原購買經銷商聯絡。

PART 6 P.144–147

131–134 廣告

來參觀狂野親水公園，它是個夏季好去處，適合和各年齡層的家人及朋友一起前往。我們有兒童泳池、戶外泳池、室內泳池、海浪以及刺激的滑水道，包括我們的「死亡墜落」，是本州最大型的滑水道。園內能滿足所有人的所有需求。別忘了我們美味的零食攤和餐廳，我們也有禮品店與遊樂園。我們甚至為您的毛小孩提供小狗公園。您可以撥打電話 123-5555 購買門票，或用優惠價格買季票。現在就來電，體驗樂趣吧！

131. A 使興奮
B 興奮的
C 刺激的
D 刺激

132. A 他們的
B 他的
C 我們的
D 您的

133. A 泳池是最棒的遊玩所在。
B 我們甚至為您的毛小孩提供小狗公園。
C 廚師是最頂級的，而餐點也是首屈一指的。
D 在本季與促銷結束前快來玩吧。

134. **A 部分**
B 部分
C 部分
D 全部

135–138 電子郵件

寄件者：朗達・克羅斯
收件者：麥可・哈利斯
日期：6 月 21 日
主旨：回覆：庭園造景與維護

感謝您詢問本公司的服務內容。「植樹管理」是一間草皮維護與庭園造景公司。在照料所有客戶的草皮時，我們只使用對環境無害的技術和產品。我們已經在波特蘭營業超過 20 年了。目前，我們在市中心服務逾 150 家企業。

至於您所提出的特定需求，是的，我們可以毫不費力地移除枯木，改種適合目前造景的植物。為了給您正確的報價，我們需要到場親自查看狀況。若要安排本公司的園藝技工前往，請來電 (713) 678-9916。希望能盡快得到您的回覆。

135. A 提交
B 替換
C 審閱
D 詢問

136. **A 超過**
B 少於
C 直到
D 在……整個期間

137. A 存在
B 存在的
C 現存的
D 存在

138. A 很高興能與您交易。
B 希望能盡快得到您的回覆。
C 請寄電子郵件給我們。
D 祝福您持續邁向成功。

139–142 告示

電銷線索專員／電銷人員

地點：喬治亞州亞特蘭大市
工作代碼：3766
職缺人數：4

銷售線索專員要撥打電話給有意購買各種服務的潛在客戶，像是保險、稅務協助、財務協助、電信或運輸等。他們也要從現有客戶群中拜訪潛在客戶。必須進行電話行銷。

為說服潛在與現有客戶購買新產品與服務，你需透過電話與電子郵件直接向客戶說明產品及服務項目。這份工作也要你教導客戶產品與服務的內容。**最重要的是，你每天至少要打 150 通電話。**每月銷售額最低的要求是淨利 7,500 元。除此之外，全體員工必須定期參加我們的產品教育課程，以提供顧客更好的服務。

為了符合職務要求，你必須擁有至少一年以上的電話銷售經驗、優秀的客服技巧，以及高超的成交技巧。

若您自認符合這些條件，並正在尋求刺激且高薪的經驗，請點擊以下的連結。

139. A 實質的
B 潛在的
C 最理想的
D 合理的

140. A 賣的越多，升遷的機會就越多。
B 管理職位需要的是一位有組織能力且幹勁十足的人。
C 如果你可以幫忙找到替代你的人選，那就太感謝了。
D 最重要的是，你每天至少要打 150 通電話。

141. A 實際上
B 然而
C 除此之外
D 因此

142. **A 符合**
B 去符合
C 符合
D 符合了

143–146 告示

寄件者：行政經理詹姆斯．瓊斯
收件者：銷售人員
日期：7 月 15 日
主旨：政策變動

親愛的銷售人員：

公司最近修改了核銷規定。過去，你只要先自費付款，然後再提供租車、出差或其他的業務花費收據來核銷即可。但是，從現在開始你必須填寫申請表，要先通過會計部門的審核。**然後你會領到內含有限金額的公司卡。**若是支出超過卡片中的金額，你就必須自費，而且無法核銷。

請詳讀附件，以更了解公司接受與拒絕何種支出項目。

143. A 產生
B 已產生的
C 產生
D 會產生

144. **A 但是**
B 因此
C 此外
D 自從

145. A 他們不會核准任何非經銀行授權的卡。
B 你必須以你個人信用卡支付。
C 然後你會領到內含有限金額的公司卡。
D 他們必須決定我們的預算是否能支付開銷。

146. A 確定的
B 公認的
C 建立的
D 批准的

PART 7 P.148–167

147–148 行事曆

時間	星期一	星期二	星期三	星期四	星期五
上午 9 點 ｜ 上午 11 點	瑜伽 1 級： **4 號教室**		健身訓練： **1 號教室**	踢拳擊 1 級： **3 號教室**	
上午 11 點 ｜ 下午 2 點		重量訓練： **2 號教室**			瑜伽 2 級： **4 號教室**

下午 2 點 | 下午 4 點	飛輪： **1 號教室**	踢拳擊 2 級： **3 號教室**		營養建議： **5 號教室** （在櫃檯預約個人諮詢）	
下午 4 點 | 下午 6 點	瑜伽 3 級： **4 號教室**		健身訓練： **1 號教室**		馬拉松訓練： **2 號教室**

147. 最有可能在哪裡看到這份行事曆？

A 報紙上的運動版
B 在旅遊行程表上
C 在健身房的牆上
D 在運動錦標賽的節目手冊上

148. 哪些活動在同一個教室上課？

A 瑜伽與踢拳擊
B 馬拉松訓練和飛輪
C 瑜伽和營養建議
D 飛輪和健身訓練

149–150 訊息串

汪達・奈特 **9:04**
我剛剛把你週五要去芝加哥的行程表寄給你了。

泰德・格列茲尼克 **9:05**
太棒了，謝謝！

汪達・奈特 **9:05**
麥克・羅斯希望趁你在那裡時，能增加一場和鑽石出版社的會議。

泰德・格列茲尼克 **9:10**
沒問題。

汪達・奈特 **9:11**
好。我可以和他們連絡，假如你太忙的話，就這樣。

泰德・格列茲尼克 **9:13**
沒問題的。我星期六晚上應該會和鑽石出版社的傑維爾・山伽茲小酌。

汪達・奈特 **9:13**
真好。

泰德・格列茲尼克 **9:20**
當那傢伙娶了你妹時，見到他是必然的。

汪達・奈特 **9:21**
啊，那倒是。

149. 下列何者與山伽茲先生有關？

A 他在會計公司上班
B 他和汪達・奈特有親戚關係
C 他最近結婚了
D 他星期五會到芝加哥

150. 在 9:11 時，奈特女士寫：「我可以和他們連絡」是什麼意思？

A 她可以向他們致謝
B 她可以和他們聯繫
C 她可以去拜訪他們
D 她可以協助他們

151–152 電子郵件

收件者：會計部
<designers@ptcdesign.com>
寄件者：羅伯特・布朗
<robertbrown@ptcdesign.com>
日期：3 月 29 日星期一
主旨：即將舉辦的會議

大家好：

本公司來自日本的客戶佐藤先生將於後天抵達，討論我們兩家公司即將進行的合併事宜。為了準備這個會議，我要求會計部同心協力做出第一季的財務報告。任何需要更多資料來完成這份文件的人，歡迎寄電子郵件給我。請於週二下午前完成這項任務。這份文件需要詳細說明本公司的所有財務活動，包含本公司全部的資產與投資。

謝謝。

PTC 設計 執行長
羅伯特・布朗

151. 佐藤先生預計何時抵達布朗先生的公司？

Ⓐ 在 3 月 28 日
Ⓑ 在 3 月 29 日
Ⓒ 在 3 月 30 日
Ⓓ 在 3 月 31 日

152. 誰最有可能和布朗先生聯絡？

Ⓐ 想要調職到會計部門的員工
Ⓑ 需要額外資訊的員工
Ⓒ 需要延長期限的員工
Ⓓ 不同意合併的員工

153–154 邀請函

美國建築師協會年度大獎

誠摯地邀請您出席今年於 7 月 24 日星期五，在德州休士頓梅立頓飯店舉辦的盛事。會員可以攜帶兩位貴賓同行。

晚上 7:00	歡迎會
晚上 7:30	歡迎致詞與介紹（由美國建築師協會會長貝里．韓福瑞主持）
晚上 7:45	晚宴（提供素食，請於確認出席時提出）
晚上 9:00	頒獎典禮（最佳設計、最佳新人、最佳住宅建築、最佳公共建築），頒獎人為喜劇演員艾力克斯．達斯伍
晚上 10:30	由得獎樂團流行調調現場特別演出

請於 4 月 21 日前回覆出席意願給活動承辦人珍妮絲．哈頓 janice.harton@amarchsoc.net。

153. 誰最有可能是收到邀請函的人？

Ⓐ 建築公司的主管
Ⓑ 協會會員
Ⓒ 當地政府的建築師
Ⓓ 頒獎典禮的提名者

154. 要如何確認出席？

Ⓐ 打電話到梅立頓飯店
Ⓑ 寄電子郵件給貝里．韓福瑞
Ⓒ 拜訪艾力克斯．達斯伍
Ⓓ 與承辦人連絡

155–157 文章

北岸財經新聞

6 月 29 日——北岸市的在地支柱即將向全國發展。北岸乳品廠於 1951 年由老闆比爾．布得利創立，以商店屋頂上的大型旋轉冰淇淋甜筒成為北岸市的地標。多年來，它仍舊是當地居民最喜歡的聚會場所，也吸引了許多開車經過遊客的目光。比爾二世於 25 年前接手事業後，為了滿足當地居民與觀光客的需求擴展了商店。北岸乳品廠甚至被《旅遊雜誌》評選為十大商店之一。

1988 年，北岸乳品廠還出現在當紅好萊塢電影《未來、現在與過去》中，此舉讓它成為外地居民與觀光客造訪的首選冰淇淋店。

雖然有很多企業努力想從布得利家族手中買下這事業，但是比爾二世和兒子威廉堅持以家族方式來經營，這點讓北岸市的市民感到滿意。現在，這個家族準備要在鄰近城市開設兩家新分店，而且預計五年內，在全國開設六間新分店。「我們將維持小規模的經營模式，慢慢擴展。」威廉解釋，「為了維持冰淇淋的新鮮品質，並讓產品與我爺爺所創的食譜一樣，我們不想投機取巧，這也就是為什麼我們需要時間的原因。」

155. 這篇文章的目的是什麼？

Ⓐ 宣傳商店產品
Ⓑ 解釋新創業型態的細節
Ⓒ 討論一間家族企業的歷史
Ⓓ 解釋某些商品的價格

156. 下列何者與北岸乳品廠有關？

A 被一家大型企業收購
B 因為一部電影而在全市出名
C 是當地居民的驕傲與快樂
D 沒有足夠的經費可以擴展

157. 下列句子最適合出現在 [1]、[2]、[3]、[4] 的哪個位置？「現在，這個家族準備要在鄰近城市開設兩家新分店，而且預計五年內，在全國開設六間新分店。」

A [1]
B [2]
C [3]
D [4]

158–160 公告

阿克頓市議會公告

4 月 3 日

阿克頓市議會局將成立一個新的特別小組，負責在下個會計年度裡減少不必要的支出。這個 12 人小組將由當地企業負責人、工會代表、公務員及財經顧問所組成，小組成員訂於本月 30 號選出，接著立即開始運作，規劃以消除浪費的方式以減少 10% 明年當地政府的支出。

即日起接受小組成員的申請。有關以個人或單位名義參與這個計劃的資訊，請洽市議會 admin@acretoncc.gov。

158. 這份公告主要是有關什麼？

A 成立新的職業工會
B 成立財務監督小組
C 開始招募工作
D 當地法令變革開始

159. 小組訂於何時開始運作？

A 五月初
B 年底
C 夏季初
D 四月底

160. 有興趣的各方要如何參與？

A 簽署請願書
B 出席會議
C 寄送電子郵件
D 填寫表格

161–164 網路討論區

珍娜·羅根	[2:15]	我剛講完電話，金先生跟我說，他想要比預定時間提早幾個禮拜拿到訂貨。你們覺得可行嗎？
瑪格麗特·李	[2:16]	我們這邊沒問題。所有的布料都準備就緒，也裁切成適當的形狀與大小，已經準備給裁縫機作業了。
傑森·布朗	[2:17]	我的小組正在處理巴特利先生的訂單。有 1,000 多件要縫，之後還得處理卡拉·賓恩的訂單。
珍娜·羅根	[2:18]	巴特利先生月底才需要取貨，而賓恩女士的訂單可以等到下週再處理。我可以授權你的小組先著手處理這筆訂單。
傑森·布朗	[2:19]	正在處理什麼？需要多少件？
珍娜·羅根	[2:20]	長袖的男子襯衫。需要 S 號 100 件，M 號 300 件，L 號 300 件，XL 號 100 件。
傑森·布朗	[2:21]	好，我覺得兩天可以完工。
彼得·威廉斯	[2:22]	我們可以在兩至四小時內縫好 800 件的鈕釦。
珍娜·羅根	[2:23]	謝謝你們，感謝各位的協助。很開心我們可以這樣配合本公司最好的顧客。

161. 在 2:16 時，瑪格麗特·李寫：「我們這邊沒問題」是什麼意思？

A 她的小組可以達成目標
B 她的小組可以協助其他小組
C 他們的計劃需要一點時間
D 問題會很小

162. 珍娜・羅根在何種公司上班？

Ⓐ 鞋店
Ⓑ 服飾工廠
Ⓒ 時尚雜誌
Ⓓ 男裝精品店

163. 根據這段討論，哪個部門需要最多的時間？

Ⓐ 李女士的部門
Ⓑ 布朗先生的部門
Ⓒ 威廉先生的部門
Ⓓ 羅根女士的部門

164. 珍娜・羅根最有可能告訴金先生什麼？

Ⓐ 他的訂單將延遲一個月交貨
Ⓑ 可以在兩週內完成他的訂單
Ⓒ 他的要求不容易達成
Ⓓ 他的訂單可以提早完成

165–167 備忘錄

安斯渥西製造公司

日期：10 月 17 日星期三
主旨：回收

為了因應來自當地環保團體的施壓，自 11 月 1 日起，我們將所有的工業廢棄物分類以便回收。資源回收將一週收兩次，地區的回收中心將於每週二和五進行回收，他們會提供彩色的容器來分裝不同種類的廢棄物。所有的油類必須裝在綠色容器裡，所有的金屬和玻璃要裝進紅色容器中，紙類則放進藍色容器裡，塑膠類就依照一般的方式回收。

由於這個新政策也會為公司帶來財務上的獲益，所有製造區的主管要負責確保遵循新的廢棄物處理程序，若是未遵守規定，將受到懲戒處分。

更多有關最新環保措施的資訊，很快就會公告在網站上。主管的培訓講習將於 10 月 22 日星期一舉行。在此期間，若有任何進一步的問題，請與我聯絡。

安斯渥西製造公司 營運主管
大衛・基蘭 敬上

165. 異動的原因是什麼？

Ⓐ 公司老闆想要省下工錢
Ⓑ 公司附近開了一間新的回收中心
Ⓒ 當地政府更改了法規
Ⓓ 當地環保人士提出要求

166. 可推論出何者與安斯渥西製造公司有關？

Ⓐ 與當地權威人士關係良好
Ⓑ 已進行塑膠工業廢棄物的回收
Ⓒ 最近增加了人力
Ⓓ 定期更新環保政策

167. 公司主管下週應該要做什麼？

Ⓐ 參加新程序的工作坊
Ⓑ 更新公司網頁
Ⓒ 挪出空間來放新的廢棄物容器
Ⓓ 通知他們的團隊同仁有異動

168–171 信件

諾門維爾農夫市集

4 月 9 日

親愛的諾門維爾居民們：

今年第一次的諾門維爾農夫市集將於 4 月 14 日星期六開幕，地點是大街和帕克街之間的克拉克街上。農夫市集的開放時間是上午九點至下午五點。諾門維爾市長湯姆・戴倫將於開幕式上致詞。許多當地農夫、食品攤販與街頭藝人都將出席。

諾門維爾農夫協會的執行理事蘇西・漢默說：「朝氣蓬勃的市集將提供在地農夫一個銷售新鮮農產品的好場所。除此之外，因為我們省去一些中間程序，所以價格也會比一般雜貨店便宜。」

漢默女士也提到目前並沒有足夠的停車空間可以容納購物者。諾門維爾農夫協會計劃在未來幾個月內擴大停車空間。在此期間，她建議會來參觀的諾門維爾居民搭乘大眾運輸以避開停車難題。

諾門維爾農夫市集不同於其他食品量販店，市集將提供富含重要維他命和礦物質的有機產品。如大家所知，市集也將有益在地經濟。

本週六請來看看諾門維爾市集賣了那些東西吧！

諾門維爾農夫協會 敬上

168. 這封信的目的是什麼？

Ⓐ 描述政策改變
Ⓑ 介紹新的雜貨店
Ⓒ 宣傳市集的開幕
Ⓓ 宣布競選結果

169. 下列何者與漢默女士有關？

Ⓐ 她是農夫市集的攤販
Ⓑ 她代表其他農夫
Ⓒ 她擁有一座家族經營的農場
Ⓓ 她是諾門維爾市市長

170. 文中提到了什麼樣的問題？

Ⓐ 停車空間不足
Ⓑ 產品價格不公
Ⓒ 缺少品質管控
Ⓓ 天氣險惡

171. 下列何者不是文中提到在市集採買的優點？

Ⓐ 促進當地經濟
Ⓑ 具有競爭力的價格
Ⓒ 健康的農產品
Ⓓ 較長的營業時間

172–175 告示

失物招領

帕克威市正為了即將到來的節慶季做好準備，並強烈要求市民及遊客看顧好個人物品。每一年都會有超過 2, 000 件的遺失物品，被送至位於帕克威市政廳的失物招領處。「但節慶季期間我們會收到更多的遺失物品。」失物招領處的管理主任珍・金恩表示，「從 11 月 25 日左右至 1 月 2 日，被送過來的遺失物大約增加了 25%。」

這幾年送來中心的遺失物品五花八門，從鑰匙、太陽眼鏡、雨傘、珠寶，到電子產品、行李箱、和裝滿新添購戰利品的購物袋。「我們收過最奇特的物品是裝滿了古裝戲服的行李箱。」珍說，「當時一位在拍片的實習生很高興能尋回失物。」

許多人會來認領他們的遺失物，但是絕大部分的遺失物都無人認領。如果物品在 90 天內沒有人來認領，那些物品就會在公開活動中被拍賣，為社區活動中心募款。

172. 這篇告示的目的是什麼？

Ⓐ 宣傳一項節慶活動
Ⓑ 警告市民犯罪案的增加
Ⓒ 告知民眾失物招領的物品
Ⓓ 提供關於拍賣的訊息

173. 下列何者與珍・金恩有關？

Ⓐ 她在尋找遺失物
Ⓑ 她在市政府上班
Ⓒ 她是個實習生
Ⓓ 她管理社區活動中心

174. 下列何者與遺失物品有關？

Ⓐ 不會被永久存放在中心
Ⓑ 通常會被失主領回
Ⓒ 無人領取的時候會被銷毀
Ⓓ 通常都是新的物品

175. 下列句子最適合出現在 [1]、[2]、[3]、[4] 的哪個位置？「許多人會來認領他們的遺失物，但是絕大部分的遺失物都無人認領。」

Ⓐ [1]
Ⓑ [2]
Ⓒ [3]
Ⓓ [4]

176–180 文章和電子郵件

科技生活聘僱新執行長

紐約，4 月 12 日——深陷銷售量低迷和表現令人失望的危機當中，「科技生活」科技公司聘用了史帝夫・克羅斯擔任新的執行長。在此之前，他曾擔任過在加州舊金山的科技投信公司艾斯塔資源的財務長。就在本週一，他接下了該公司的執行長一職，此公司位於德州達拉斯。股東們一致投票通過這項任命，期盼新執行長可以重新為公司燃起活力與力量。

「克羅斯先生是一位決策睿智的企業主管，擁有令人驚豔的記錄。」科技生活人力資源部主任琳恩．代爾表示。「我們有信心，他將帶領我們走向新方向，協助開發新市場，使公司整體運作更加完善。」

史帝夫．克羅斯畢業於賓州哈里斯堡的徹斯特大學，擁有企業管理碩士學位。他曾經擔任美國商業聯盟會長，也是位盡責的居家好男人。

收件者：史帝夫．克羅斯
<scross@techlife.com>
寄件者：琳恩．代爾
<ldyer@techlife.com>
主旨：歡迎！
日期：4 月 15 日

克羅斯先生您好：

上次見面已是將近兩年前的事了。很開心在艾斯塔資源跟您在同部門共事後，還能再次與您合作。我覺得我們那時合作無間，很期待能再和您一起共事。您會發現我們有非常盡責且認真工作的團隊。過渡時期若有任何我能幫得上忙的，歡迎隨時提出。

此外，科技生活最近新增了五位公司主管。若果您有空，請於下午三點來見見他們，他們將出席在 403 室舉行的強制培訓課程。

科技生活 人力資源部主任
琳恩．代爾 敬上

176. 科技生活面臨了什麼問題？

(A) 員工短缺
(B) 緊急查帳
(C) 獲利減少
(D) 潛在的競爭對手

177. 下列何者與股東有關？

(A) 他們可以獲取財務資訊
(B) 他們下週將開會
(C) 他們要求更多股息
(D) 他們同意新主管的任命

178. 文章中第二段第六行的「optimize」意思最接近？

(A) 合併
(B) 改善
(C) 分析
(D) 維持

179. 代爾女士先前在哪裡工作？

(A) 在哈里斯堡
(B) 在達拉斯
(C) 在紐約
(D) 在舊金山

180. 克羅斯先生被要求做什麼？

(A) 教授訓練課程
(B) 和新員工見面
(C) 出席股東會議
(D) 聘用新主管

181–185 議程表和電子郵件

未來與文化協會（AFC）
季度研討會
荷馬會議中心，1 月 10 日

下午 2:00	凱莉．歐尼爾（AFC 會長，慕里根小學校長），歡迎致詞
下午 2:30	馬克．貴斯克斯（SEM 開發集團執行長），強化全球意識：領導力與多樣化
下午 3:30	露西．胡佛（皮埃蒙特成人教育中心合夥人），領導階層的性別與公平性
下午 4:30	瓊恩．木村（肯特商場經理），工作場域中領導階層的基礎
下午 5:30	肯尼斯．施耐德（布魯克史東大學教授），領導階層的倫理與道德
下午 6:30	問答時間

收件者：AFC 會員
<menbers@futureculture.org>
寄件者：凱莉・歐尼爾
<kellyoneill@futureculture.org>
日期：1 月 11 日
附件：free_talk.jpg
主旨：季度研討會

親愛的 AFC 會員：

這場季度研討會已經成為另一項值得紀念的成功。感謝大家的參與及專業分享，希望大家可以將在研討會中所學到的技能運用在辦公室和工作場合裡。除此之外，我也要鼓勵大家在下一次的研討會中考慮發表演說。若您有意參加，請與艾咪・賈西亞聯絡，電子郵件為 amygarcia@futureculture.org。

我也要通知各位肯尼斯・施耐德的邀請，他將於下個月於其工作地點發表一場演說，主題是〈從領導得來的自信〉。這是場免費的演講，並開放給一般民眾參加。若需更多資訊，請參考附件。

最後，我注意到有些會員因為行程衝突而無法出席研討會。因此，從現在開始，未來所有的研討會將同步在網站上播出，這樣遠距的會員也可以收看收聽了。

會長
凱莉・歐尼爾 敬上

181. 1 月 10 日的研討會主題是什麼？

(A) 如何創立小型企業
(B) 如何管理財務
(C) 如何領導他人
(D) 如何將企業擴展至全球

182. 提問最有可能從幾點開始？

(A) 下午 3:30
(B) 下午 4:30
(C) 下午 5:30
(D) 下午 6:30

183. 免費的演講地點在哪裡？

(A) 慕里根小學
(B) 布魯克史東大學
(C) 皮埃蒙特成人教育中心
(D) SEM 開發集團

184. 歐尼爾女士邀請 AFC 的會員們做什麼？

(A) 附上收據
(B) 填寫問卷
(C) 準備演說
(D) 評估演講者

185. 文中提到什麼與之後舉辦的研討會有關？

(A) 將在新的地點舉辦
(B) 演說將晚點開始
(C) 將提高出席費用
(D) 將在網路上播放

186–190 網站和電子郵件

史塔克銀行

公告	我的帳戶	轉帳	貸款

透支費用

6 月 3 日當天，您於佛羅里達州傑克遜威爾市的提款機提領了 100 元，已超過您簽帳金融卡的額度限制，因此，您將被收取一筆 30 元的透支費。這可能是由於您從提款機提款之時，正在進行提款金額的累積所致。只要客戶金融卡交易金額超過其存款金額時，本行很遺憾必須收取這筆款項。

未來，藉由加入史塔克銀行的網銀服務，就能避免這項失誤。這個服務每個月只需 2 元的費用。利用您的智慧型手機，無論您身在何處都能登入帳號。您可以查看帳戶金額，存取款的歷史記錄，最重要的是還能辦理延後交易。欲加入，請寄電子郵件到 customerservice@starkbank.com 或撥打本行電話 904-555-4514。

收件者：customerservice@starkbank.com
寄件者：ssummers@zippynet.com
主旨：透支費用
日期：6 月 5 日

我擔心可能有人非法從我的帳戶提款。我在 6 月 2 日遺失了簽帳金融卡，隔天一發現後，我就立即凍結了所有帳戶。考慮到這些不幸的情況，懇請貴行能免收因這個意外而產生的透支費用。

我想要加入您所建議的銀行服務。這服務聽起來很不錯，可以幫我用更有效率的方式管理我的財務。

感謝您的協助。

蘇西・桑莫斯

收件者：蘇西・桑莫斯
<ssummers@zippynet.com>
寄件者：客戶服務部
<customerservice@starbank.com>
主旨：檢視透支
日期：6 月 6 日

親愛的桑莫斯女士：

本行對於您不幸的遭遇深感遺憾。根據我們所看到的帳戶資料，雖然看來已來不及防止盜領與隨後發生的帳戶透支，但您確實與我們聯繫要求凍結帳戶。在您報告遺失金融卡的隔天後，才發生以提款機交易而產生透支的情況有點不尋常。您最近是否有告訴他人您的密碼呢？我很樂意將您取消透支費的要求轉交給本行負責處理詐騙的部門，但您必須向警方報案，然後將偵查員給您的報案編號傳給我們。等我們一收到那個編號，就可以開始複審您的案件了。

謝謝您，祝您有美好的一天。

史塔克銀行 客戶服務專員
蘿拉・梅西

186. 網頁資訊的目的是什麼？

(A) 宣布公司的新規定
(B) 說明即將進行的搬遷
(C) 告知使用者需支付的費用
(D) 告知使用者網路釣魚的手法

187. 下列何者不是網銀的查詢項目？

(A) 帳戶結餘
(B) 利率
(C) 待處理的交易
(D) 帳戶歷史記錄

188. 桑莫斯女士要求銀行做什麼事？

(A) 凍結帳戶
(B) 更新聯絡資料
(C) 免除透支費用
(D) 提高提款上限

189. 在客戶服務部寄給桑莫斯女士的電子郵件中，蘿拉・梅西認為蘇西的事件有何奇怪之處？

(A) 蘇西帳戶裡沒有很多錢
(B) 蘇西沒有去警局報案
(C) 蘇西在 6 月 2 日遺失金融卡，但是金融卡卻在 6 月 3 日被拿去提款機提款
(D) 蘇西不住在佛羅里達

190. 如果蘇西・桑莫斯想要免除透支的費用，蘿拉・梅西教她該怎麼做？

(A) 寫信給史塔克銀行負責處理詐騙的部門
(B) 去警察局報案，然後提供報案編號給史塔克銀行
(C) 去法院向罪犯提告，將法案編號給史塔克銀行
(D) 向史塔克銀行負責詐騙的部門立案

191–195 電子郵件

寄件者：customerservice@thomsonapp.com
收件者：dkerry@coolmail.com
日期：7 月 6 日
主旨：故障

親愛的凱莉女士：

您在湯森家電行買的豪華冰箱型號 MK1213 發生故障，本公司對此感到非常抱歉。您說冰箱門上的製冰機停止運作，事實上，有幾位顧客也回報了相同的問題。結果是製造商在產品製造過程中產生失誤。所幸，我們的技師可以輕易地解決這個問題。目前技師下週一、三和四都有空。請明確告知您哪天與幾點方便。

此外，如果您的冰箱仍在保固期中，維修完全免費。請告知您的保固編號，以便在技師到訪前，讓我們先行確認。

我們十分抱歉造成不便。再次感謝您光臨湯森家電行。

客戶服務部
貴格．路易斯 敬上

寄件者：dkerry@coolmail.com
收件者：customerservice@thomsonapp.com
日期：7 月 7 日
主旨：回覆：故障

親愛的路易斯先生：

感謝您迅速的回覆。事實上，下週我將到阿肯色州出差，星期六才會回來。但是，星期一和五會有管家來打掃。若您的技師可以在這其中一天過來，那她就可以讓他或她進來。

我的保固編號是 A344F56J，目前仍在保固有效期間內。我會將這個文件留給管家，以備你們來的時候需要查看。

堂娜．凱瑞

寄件者：customerservice@thomsonapp.com
收件者：dkerry@coolmail.com
日期：7 月 7 日
主旨：維修時間

親愛的凱瑞女士：

技師可以在星期一到府維修。請務必留下保固文件，如此一來技師才能將它掃描至系統內，以利我們向製造商報帳。技師將於上午前往，盡量在中午以前修好。雖然您有管家，但他們會盡量維持整潔。祝您旅途平安，感謝您的耐心等候。感謝您對湯森家電行的忠誠惠顧。

客戶服務部
貴格．路易斯　敬上

191. 第一封電子郵件寄出的原因是什麼？

(A) 說明保固編號
(B) 詢問到訪日期
(C) 確認訂單
(D) 為運送延遲致歉

192. 根據第一封電子郵件，有關冰箱的敘述，下列何者為真？

(A) 是最新推出的款式
(B) 已超過保固期限
(C) 有製造上的缺陷
(D) 最近特價中

193. 路易斯先生要求凱瑞女士提供什麼資料？

(A) 目前的地址
(B) 保固編號
(C) 冰箱型號
(D) 聯絡資料

194. 技師為什麼要掃描保固文件？

(A) 確定仍在保固期內
(B) 確定型號正確
(C) 確定有足夠的備用零件可以進行維修
(D) 確定製造商會支付維修費用

195. 技師星期一可以到訪的原因是什麼？

(A) 因為那時候技師才會有空
(B) 因為技師星期五太忙了
(C) 因為管家那時候會讓他進門
(D) 因為凱莉女士會在阿肯色州

196–200 電子郵件

收件者：莉莉安．羅斯
<lillianross@kingstonsportinggoods.com>
寄件者：艾瑞克．衛斯特
<ericwest@jmsolutions.com>
日期：11 月 4 日上午 10 點 34 分
主旨：網站開發
附件：明細

親愛的羅斯女士：

您上週與本公司聯絡，詢問要本公司的電腦程式工程師協助貴公司開發網站。JM 科技很樂意為您提供服務。

正如在電話中所説的，我們將會協助設計並開發一個可以吸引更多顧客的網站，並提供線上銷售平台。在這期間，我們需要和貴公司的行銷部門開會，以完整掌握貴公司的銷售目標。明年二月中網站一完成後，我們將舉辦訓練課程，教導貴公司員工維護與更新網站所需的技巧。網站開發與訓練課程的總金額是 32,000 元。依規定貴公司需先支付 10% 的金額作為訂金。詳細的費用與時間表請參考附檔。

本公司期待在不久的未來能跟貴公司合作。本公司全體職員將努力滿足您的需求。因此，請告知貴公司行銷部門何時可以親自與我們會面，討論此案的一些細節。請在方便時與我聯絡。

艾瑞克・衛斯特

收件者：莉莉安・羅斯
<lillianross@kingstonsportinggoods.com>
寄件者：雷蒙・威爾斯
<raymondwells@kingstonsportinggoods.com>
日期：11 月 4 日上午 10 點 37 分
主旨：第一季預算
附檔：Q1_ 預算

親愛的羅斯女士：

我已隨信附上明年第一季公司的預算草案附上。如您將注意到的，今年開學特賣的所有獲利，將用在主要公路上的廣告看板上。今天下午晚點我會打電話給設計組，請他們為廣告設計吸睛的圖案。

在我們上次的會議中，您提到希望在定案前再檢視一次預算。我已經將員工調薪加入第一季的支出中，但若您想到其他的部分，請告訴我。我打算在下週的籌劃會議前將預算定案。

雷蒙・威爾斯

收件者：雷蒙・威爾斯
<raymondwells@kingstonsportinggoods.com>
寄件者：莉莉安・羅斯
<lillianross@kingstonsportinggoods.com>
日期：11 月 4 日上午 10 點 40 分
主旨：緊急追加預算

親愛的威爾斯：

很開心收到你做好的預算表。就在收到你的電子郵件前，我收到規劃中的網站建置估價單，看起來比我預期的還貴。雖然不需立即支付總額 32,000 元的帳單，但若要與 JM 科技公司合作進行企劃案的話，明年第一季的預算表需要另外撥出 3,200 元來。

如果你對這件事有任何的問題，請到我辦公室來，我們可以看看哪邊還可以再緊縮一些以支付這筆費用。

196. 衛斯特先生為什麼會寫第一封電子郵件？

Ⓐ 詢問服務
Ⓑ 安排會議
Ⓒ 報告預算
Ⓓ 求職

197. JM 科技公司提供什麼服務？

Ⓐ 徵才與員工訓練
Ⓑ 平面設計
Ⓒ 網路程式設計
Ⓓ 行銷策略諮詢

198. 根據第二封電子郵件，開學特賣的獲利將用在哪裡？

Ⓐ 道路維修
Ⓑ 購買廣告空間
Ⓒ 支付 JM 科技公司的服務費用
Ⓓ 聘請更多員工

199. 下列何者與第三封電子郵件有關？

Ⓐ 明年第一季的預算看起來沒有問題

Ⓑ JM 科技公司的名聲很好

Ⓒ 對於金斯頓運動用品公司來說，要從預算裡找到經費來支付網站建構是很容易的

Ⓓ 為了要支付網站建構費用，一些項目可能會失去資金

200. 金斯頓運動用品公司為什麼要花 3,200 元在網站建構上？

Ⓐ 他們需要能購買到最好的網站

Ⓑ 他們須將生意擴展到其他領域

Ⓒ 他們須支付 JM 科技公司總金額的 10% 作為訂金

Ⓓ 在付訂金後，他們需要協商一個更好的價格

ACTUAL TEST ⑥

PART 5 P.168–171

◎ Part 5 解答請見 P.457

101. 寵物主人被鼓勵**報名**由社區活動中心所提供的寵物訓練與健康工作坊。

102. 執行長舉行了記者會，為該公司產品造成的不良健康影響**道歉**。

103. 旺季與淡季期間的營業收入有**明顯的**差異。

104. 貫穿莫里森公園的步道不僅是為了自行車騎士，**也是**為了慢跑者而建。

105. 其中一位主管質疑馬歇爾女士**有關**她在濫用投資基金中所扮演的角色。

106. 由於競爭增加，星霸飯店的住房率已經**下滑**了 24%。

107. **結業**證書已經發給公開演說技巧課程的參加者。

108. 為餐廳評論家準備主菜**的**主廚，通常會親自出來打招呼。

109. 協商者對合約做了些微更動，讓雙方都能**接受**那些條款。

110. 給當地學校的資金是**根據**住在該地區的孩童數量來分配。

111. 這座宮殿**傳統上**是作為公開典禮與慶祝活動之用。

112. 一旦招聘委員會做出**最終**決定，人力資源部代表將聯絡獲選的應徵者。

113. 主席**將由**所有會員匿名投票**選出**。

114. 提供低利貸款給小型企業是經濟復甦計劃的關鍵**要件**。

115. 這個計劃若沒有拉特克里夫先生的全力**付出**就不會成功，這從幾個時機點上得到證明。

116. 本市政治人物將於市政廳上辯論這個**複雜的**議題，讓投票者更加了解。

117. **如果**醫院遭逢斷電，發電機將自動運轉以供應所需電力。

118. 在史都華銀行的行員接受大量的訓練後，他們對待客戶**更有禮貌**了。

119. 登機門的地勤人員宣布航班**取消**，是由於目的地的天氣狀況惡劣所導致。

120. **當**老舊的設備被汰換成最先進的機械，產量將超過兩倍。

121. 要符合這個職位的資格，你必須要有至少五年的保險**業界**經驗。

122. 透過他對語言技巧習得上的廣泛研究，哈維．沃德博士已經證明**自己**是這個領域的領導者。

123. 太平洋食品公司所販售的海鮮容易**腐敗**，因此必須以溫控車輛運送。

124. 那位小說家說他的寫作，**深遠地**受到已故作家愛德華．特魯伊特的影響。

125. 正如研究者**所觀察**到的那樣，這新環保洗衣精和它的競爭對手一樣表現出色。

126. 綠化社致力為未來世代**維護**公立公園及其他自然區域。

127. 在颱風中受損的製造工廠將於本月稍後**重新恢復**運作。

128. 由於整個團隊的進度已經落後，經理沒有**同意**諾頓女士的休假申請。

129. 那個鼻塞噴劑讓伯特得以控制**好**他的季節性過敏，不必索取醫師處方。

130. 我們的業務**代表**目前無法接聽您的電話，但將盡快回電給您。

PART 6 P.172–175

131–134 電子郵件

收件者：奧莉維亞．鮑爾森
寄件者：強納生．希克斯
日期：7 月 19 日
主旨：流程檢視

上週四在主管會議上提出了一項議題，針對上個月商品在出貨後的毀損客訴急遽增加，原因可能是因為我們現在配送易碎品的量增加。因此，我們已經暫停配送飾品與其他易碎物品。我們正在檢視產品的包裝流程，並打算增加更多步驟來確保產品有妥善包裝，並在毫無毀損的狀況下送達。

請通知所有產製主管參加今晚七點的緊急會議。我們希望提出這個問題，並盡快想出一個妥善的解決方案以恢復正常營運。

131. (A) 增加中
(B) 已增加
(C) 被增加
(D) 增加

132. (A) 我們正考慮將這類商品從產品清單上除名。
(B) 我們可能需要增加運費與處理費。
(C) 已經建議增加這類商品的保險費。
(D) 因此，我們已經暫停配送飾品與其他易碎物品。

133. (A) 使安全
(B) 影響
(C) 確保
(D) 授權

134. **(A) 緊急情況**
(B) 必需
(C) 決定的
(D) 廣泛的

135–138 廣告

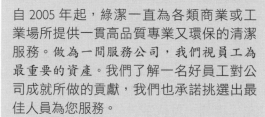

綠潔服務公司
請來電：347-281-7834

自 2005 年起，綠潔一直為各類商業或工業場所提供一貫高品質專業又環保的清潔服務。做為一間服務公司，我們視員工為最重要的資產。我們了解一名好員工對公司成就所做的貢獻，我們也承諾挑選出最佳人員為您服務。

綠潔的使命就是滿足客人的每日需求，同時提供最佳品質、價格與服務，我們藉由不斷改善營運制度以達成此任務。我們的目標就是盡可能以最環保的方式讓您的處所極整潔。今天就上我們的網站看看 www.greenclean.com。

135. (A) 直到
(B) 大約
(C) 自從
(D) 在……期間

136. (A) 今天就來安排參觀我們 20 家分店的其中一家吧。
(B) 我們是西北部最大的環保清潔用品製造商。
(C) 做為一間服務公司，我們視員工為最重要的資產。
(D) 今天就來電讓我們為您處理所有的會計需求。

137. **(A) 成就**
(B) 驅使
(C) 支持
(D) 決心

138. (A) 操作
(B) 操作
(C) 操作
(D) 營運

139–142 公告

誠徵花藝師

您喜歡讓人們微笑嗎？過著充滿創造力的一天並和大自然緊密工作的想法吸引您嗎？若是如此，我們想鼓勵您加入我們野花花藝團隊。本公司致力於為客戶提供最棒的花藝設計，無論他們的需求為何。我們尋求以客戶為優先導向的人士。創意很重要，但與客戶的想像力相較之下卻是其次。如果您認為自己有具備讓人們微笑的才能，請填寫本公司網站 www.WildFlowersFlorists.com 的線上求職表。

139. (A) 度過
(B) 度過
(C) 度過
(D) 已度過

140. (A) 你必須善於和動物相處。
(B) 本公司致力於為客戶提供最棒的花藝設計，無論他們的需求為何。
(C) 我們在設計中使用了最好的布料。
(D) 所有人都喜愛我們對安全性的承諾。

141. **(A) 以……為導向**
(B) 主要的
(C) 位於
(D) 獲得

142. **(A) 您**
(B) 我
(C) 他們
(D) 我們

143–146 信件

10 月 21 日
賴瑞．米爾斯
20037 華盛頓州費爾班克斯高地河區 226 號

親愛的米爾斯先生：

我來信是為了回覆您投訴公寓大樓週遭商家所發出的噪音。很遺憾，一些住在大樓西翼的住戶已經表達過對這些噪音的關切。大樓委員會已經針對這個問題開過會議，我們也跟那些商家說過了。不過，由於那些商業場所的性質，有些噪音是無可避免的。為此，我們也正打算幫住在西翼的住戶加強窗戶的隔音效果。一旦這些提案核准後，就會在公布欄上張貼公告，您也可能會接到電話通知。在那之前，只好請您繼續耐心等待。

143. (A) 因此
(B) 此外
(C) 另一方面
(D) 遺憾地

144. (A) 正在表達
(B) 已經表達
(C) 表達
(D) 表情豐富的

145. **(A) 不過，由於該那些商業場所的性質，有些噪音是無可避免的。**
(B) 他們將完全配合我們委員會。
(C) 他們已經回應了我們的關切，將努力減低噪音。
(D) 但是，他們正因此事而賠錢。

146. (A) 繼續
(B) 繼續
(C) 繼續的
(D) 連續的

PART 7 P.176–197

147–148 請款單

韓德森企業

10571 紐約歡樂谷史蒂文斯路 1576 號
(231) 555-0786 www.hendersoninc.com

訂單編號：6694
日期：4 月 2 日
客戶：蘇珊．沃德
10571 紐約歡樂谷讚美街 709 號
(203) 555-0167

品項	型號	數量	價格
加大微波爐	MW132	1	150.00 元
四門冰箱	RF4D	1	2,399.99 元
智慧型烤麵包機	TR512	1	45.50 元
小計：2,595.49 元 稅：230.18 元 總計：2,825.67 元			

本地顧客消費滿一千元以上，可獲免運資格。

147. 韓德森企業販售什麼？

A 家用電器
B 辦公家具
C 電腦設備
D 建築材料

148. 下列何者和沃德女士有關？

A 她必須親自提貨
B 她合乎特別優惠的資格
C 她可獲得免費宅配
D 她以支票付款

149–150 對話串

丹・庫柏 **10:10**
你開完會了嗎？

海瑟・貝瑞 **10:10**
還沒。

丹・庫柏 **10:11**
好，結束後傳訊給我。

海瑟・貝瑞 **10:11**
我現在有空。現在是吃點心和上洗手間的休息時間。

丹・庫柏 **10:13**
太好了，我在想你今天可不可以帶實習生去吃午餐？

海瑟・貝瑞 **10:13**
你要拋下我嗎？

丹・庫柏 **10:14**
沒辦法，我兩點得到北角。

海瑟・貝瑞 **10:14**
別擔心。我會帶他們去。

丹・庫柏 **10:16**
謝啦。我真的很不想取消跟他們的約會。

149. 文中提到什麼和貝瑞女士有關？

A 她正在吃點心
B 她將獲得升遷
C 她開會開到一半
D 她打算取消午餐約會

150. 在 10:13 時，貝瑞女士寫道：「你要拋下我嗎？」是什麼意思？

A 她在問庫伯先生是否已經開完會了。
B 她在問庫伯先生是否無法赴約。
C 她想知道庫伯先生是否會去北角。
D 她要庫伯先生在離開時通知她。

151–152 傳單

超級包廂戲院

超級包廂戲院在今年 12 月提供日場票券的減價優惠。利用這個早鳥特別優惠，日場第一場電影只要半價。這個優惠適用於所有電影，每週七天，還包括最新院線片。

歡迎學校及公司團體觀賞。如果您的團體人數較多，可預先訂票，可親自向戲院職員購票或上網 www.superboxtheaters.com 和 www.abcticketworld.com 購買。您在網路購票時還可以順便選位。也可在網站上看到現正上映以及即將上映的影片資訊與評論。來超級包廂戲院，享受這個超棒的優惠吧。

151. 下列何者和超級包廂戲院有關？

A 今年 12 月播放的電影較少
B 正在招聘兼職人員
C 不久將新開一家戲院
D 對特定場次提供折價優惠

152. 顧客可以在戲院的網站上做什麼？

Ⓐ 要求退款
Ⓑ 選座位
Ⓒ 訂閱商業通訊
Ⓓ 續延會員資格

153–154 電子郵件

收件者：亞倫・山德勒
<asandler@milleradvertising.com>
寄件者：山姆・米勒
<smiller@milleradvertising.com>
主旨：週二會議
日期：11 月 12 日

親愛的山德勒先生：

本月的業務審查會議定於 11 月 15 日週四召開。正如您所知，這個會議是個評估營運計劃的好機會，並做出調整讓我們跟上持續不斷的市場變化。做為廣告公司，了解最新市場趨勢是必要的。因此，當我聽到日本分公司的經理伊藤剛將於本週五來訪時，我非常興奮。為了善用他的專長與知識，我想更改會議日期，好讓伊藤先生也可與會。

這是伊藤先生第一次到本國，所以我希望您可以到機場接他。為此，將提供公司車供您使用。一旦我得到更多有關伊藤先生抵達的時間資訊，我會再寄電子郵件給您。

總裁山姆・米勒

153. 這封電子郵件的目的是什麼？

Ⓐ 重新安排會議
Ⓑ 要求月營運報告
Ⓒ 介紹新員工
Ⓓ 提出新的行銷策略

154. 這封電子郵件提到了什麼有關伊藤先生的事？

Ⓐ 他的職務變動
Ⓑ 他常出差
Ⓒ 他在廣告業工作
Ⓓ 他是米勒先生的客戶

155–157 電子郵件

收件者：布麗奇特・李
寄件者：維多・湯瑪斯
主旨：宅配
日期：6 月 25 日

布麗奇特你好：

我們飲料的貨運將於明天早上大約 10 點左右送達。請做好庫存紀錄，並於卸貨時確認所有配送的貨物正確無誤。同時，部分飲料需要即刻冷藏，因此請確保這部分能及時處理。我很擔心天氣的狀況。明天的氣溫預計將會頗高，所以我們需要盡快將所有配送的貨物存放妥當。我們會派兩台冷藏貨車給你，也會有職員在倉庫等你。

如你有任何問題，或你有任何突發狀況需要協助，請打電話給我。我明天一早就會進辦公室。

維多

155. 這封電子郵件的目的是什麼？

Ⓐ 通知供應商有失誤
Ⓑ 給員工指令
Ⓒ 訂購一批飲料
Ⓓ 記錄商品庫存

156. 維多為什麼擔心配送的事？

Ⓐ 產品易碎
Ⓑ 可能會晚到
Ⓒ 對溫度變化很敏感
Ⓓ 要配送給重要客戶

157. 下列句子最適合出現在 [1]、[2]、[3]、[4] 的哪個位置？「我很擔心天氣的狀況。」

Ⓐ [1]
Ⓑ [2]
Ⓒ [3]
Ⓓ [4]

158–160 廣告

金盞花麵包店
艾利斯鎮克拉克街 451 號
253-555-1298

金盞花麵包店是個家族企業，製作美味又誘人的甜點已有三十年多的時間。我們的門市就位在歷史悠久的艾利斯鎮市中心，提供溫馨的裝潢與迷人的氛圍。

我們提供：

- 派對、婚禮與公司活動所需的訂製點心
- 無麩質且無糖的茶點與蔬食三明治
- 客製蛋糕

營業時間：

週一至週六，早上九點至下午五點。
今年九月將因擴展店面而暫停營業。

週日烹飪課程：

金盞花麵包店重視與社區的正面互動關係。因此，我們現正為社區青少年舉辦烹飪課程，烘焙可教我們領悟耐心與努力的價值觀。

158. 文中提到下列何者與金盞花麵包店有關？

(A) 是國際知名的店
(B) 僱用當地學生
(C) 為有飲食限制的人提供各種選擇
(D) 店面空間可出租給各種活動使用

159. 根據這則廣告，九月會發生什麼事？

(A) 這家店因整修而歇業
(B) 將興建教室
(C) 將增加菜單內容
(D) 店家將為社區活動提供外燴服務

160. 下列何者與烹飪課程有關？

(A) 今年將於社區活動中心舉辦
(B) 已經進行三十多年了
(C) 由經驗豐富的烘焙師教授
(D) 為社區裡的青少年所設計

161–164 網路討論區

彼得・瓊斯	[12:10]	我要去對街新開的比薩店吃午餐。有人要一起來嗎？
馬丁・李	[12:10]	算我一份！
蘿拉・文斯	[12:11]	西奧和我要做明天的簡報，所以我們不能去。
西奧・吉伯斯	[12:12]	你可以幫我們外帶些比薩嗎？
彼得・瓊斯	[12:13]	當然可以。你們要哪一種？
蘿拉・文斯	[12:14]	我要他們賣得最好的那種，我吃一片大的就夠了。
西奧・吉伯斯	[12:15]	我要義大利臘腸口味，一片。
彼得・瓊斯	[12:15]	沒問題。我一個小時後回來。你們的報告和新產品系列有關嗎？
蘿拉・文斯	[12:16]	是啊，我們快做好了，但是我們正努力讓視覺圖像更吸睛。
馬丁・李	[12:17]	如果你們願意的話，我可以幫你們做視覺圖像。我在電腦繪圖上有點底子。
西奧・吉伯斯	[12:17]	那太好了。蘿拉和我對基本電腦程式還可以，但我們兩個都不擅長視覺圖像的製作。
彼得・瓊斯	[12:18]	等馬丁和我回來後，我們可以幫你們完成簡報。
蘿拉・文斯	[12:18]	太感謝了！
西奧・吉伯斯	[12:19]	太好了！

161. 對話者有可能在哪裡？

(A) 餐廳
(B) 比薩店
(C) 公司
(D) 電器行

162. 在 12:10 時，馬丁寫下：「算我一份」是什麼意思？

Ⓐ 他正在做簡報
Ⓑ 他在他的辦公室
Ⓒ 他想外出吃午餐
Ⓓ 他正在開會

163. 下列何者和簡報有關？

Ⓐ 將在午餐後報告
Ⓑ 與新產品有關
Ⓒ 很長
Ⓓ 需要更多資料

164. 馬丁・李最有可能幫報告者做什麼？

Ⓐ 他們的圖表
Ⓑ 他們的資料
Ⓒ 他們使用電腦的方式
Ⓓ 他們的簡報格式

165–167 電子郵件

收件者：全體職員
<staff@jointsystems.com>
寄件者：佛瑞德・哈奈斯
<fhanes@jointsystems.com>
主旨：清掃社區公園
日期：2 月 12 日

聯合系統是一家努力把握每個機會回饋社區的公司。因此，我鼓勵所有同仁參加由哈里斯堡市所贊助的社區公園清掃活動。沒有志工們的努力，我們的公園和公共空間將充滿垃圾。貢獻一點休閒時間讓哈里斯堡成為一個美麗又迷人的城市吧。

社區公園的清掃活動將於下週五 2 月 18 日下午一點至五點舉行。有意參加的同仁可以在午餐時間下班，但將仍以全薪計薪。志工須攜帶用具，像是防護性外衣、打掃用具、驅蚊劑、垃圾袋和點心。

接駁車將於週五下午 1:20 從公司停車場出發，載志工到清潔地點。如果您對想做的工作有特定的偏好，請來電 435-555-6768 與活動籌辦人唐・路易斯聯絡。

我們感謝所有人的熱心支持。

佛瑞德・哈奈斯
人力資源部

165. 這封電子郵件的目的是什麼？

Ⓐ 安排出差
Ⓑ 索取最新資料
Ⓒ 提供額外的技能訓練
Ⓓ 宣傳社區活動

166. 何者對參加者來說不是必要的？

Ⓐ 公司制服
Ⓑ 一罐防蚊劑
Ⓒ 耙子
Ⓓ 三明治

167. 根據電子郵件，路易斯先生負責什麼？

Ⓐ 引起對浪費食物的關注
Ⓑ 分析顧客意見
Ⓒ 分派個人任務
Ⓓ 打掃社區活動中心

168–171 網頁

http://www.sanchezcardealership.com/about

桑切斯汽車

認識我們	最新消息	車款	服務	相關社群

有關桑切斯汽車

卡洛斯・桑切斯從開始在汽車修理廠當助理以來，就一直有開設個人汽車代理商行的夢想。在儲蓄十年之後，他終於開設了桑切斯汽車公司，而且從那時起，就一直誠信且自豪為鄉里服務。桑切斯汽車提供各式車輛，從跑車、廂型車、休旅車到卡車皆有。不確定什麼車可以滿足您的需求嗎？那麼就來試駕各種車輛，看看哪款最適合您吧。

到年底為止，桑切斯汽車將提供優惠價給最受歡迎的噴火皮卡車及史塔克休旅車兩款。只要支付 3,000 元的頭期款，您就享有每月超低利率的分期車貸。

桑切斯汽車位於五號公路下，就在史塔克頓鎮外。我們一週營業七天，上午九點至晚上九點。別遲疑，現在就來找我們！

168. 下列何者與桑切斯先生有關？

(A) 他在汽車修理廠工作
(B) 他開創了自己的事業
(C) 他是跑車駕駛
(D) 他設計各種車輛

169. 第一段第四行的「carries」意思最接近？

(A) 移動
(B) 製造
(C) 販售
(D) 開發

170. 文中提到何者與桑切斯汽車有關？

(A) 可讓顧客測試產品
(B) 在史塔克頓市中心開店
(C) 提供客製化汽車
(D) 週末不營業

171. 到年底為止，顧客可以得到什麼？

(A) 跑車與廂型車的優惠
(B) 不加價的延長保固
(C) 特別的付款方式
(D) 購買商品後免費更換一次機油

172–175 文章

乾淨又環保

科登鎮有連連好事要慶祝，因為新的氫動力汽車公司紐馬克企業，打算在接下來的幾個月內設立一家大型製造廠。紐馬克企業已經為全球最環保的幾個都市提供氫動力公共汽車與計程車，包括溫哥華、新加坡、檀香山和阿姆斯特丹。

該公司預測未來五年內的業績將成長百分之 120%。同時，柯登廠的啟用也預計帶來 300 個新的工作機會。該鎮自當地汽車製造廠在 1990 年代關閉後，經濟就一蹶不振，故這對他們而言是個可喜的消息。松山舊廠區將是紐馬克企業的新廠址。科登鎮市長也努力提供政府津貼給那些購買氫動力汽車的人，期盼那些耗油的傳統汽車最終能走入歷史。

172. 這篇文章的主題是甚麼？

(A) 替代能源
(B) 環保城市
(C) 新工廠的啟用
(D) 汽車公司的未來

173. 舊汽車工廠會發生什麼事？

(A) 它們會被摧毀再重建
(B) 它們會成為氫動力汽車公司的新廠址
(C) 它們會變成辦公大樓
(D) 它們將收藏所有傳統舊車

174. 下列何者與科登有關？

(A) 將成為最環保的城市之一
(B) 它的經濟將持續蕭條不振
(C) 它將吸引新的汽車公司
(D) 它在經濟上會有所成長

175. 下列句子最適合出現在 [1]、[2]、[3]、[4] 的哪個位置？「該鎮自當地汽車製造廠在 1990 年代關閉後，經濟就一蹶不振，故這對他們而言是個可喜的消息」？

(A) [1]
(B) [2]
(C) [3]
(D) [4]

176–180 電子郵件和網頁

收件者：山姆．布朗
<sbrown@zippy.com>
寄件者：凱文．德雷伯
<kdraper@fivestarbank.com>
日期：4 月 22 日
主旨：房屋貸款

親愛的布朗先生：

感謝您選擇五星金融銀行為您提供房屋貸款。我們竭力提供您最具競爭力的還款計劃及超優的客戶支助。以下是您向本行申請的貸款摘要：

抵押貸款種類	金額	償還期間
購屋佳機貸款	70,000.00 元	15 年

在您貸款期間，資深行員瑪莎·金將負責您的還款計劃。了解您的貸款條款至關重要，能讓您成功償還貸款並避免罰款。我們建議您安排個時間和金女士會面，這樣她才能協助您進一步了解您的房屋貸款內容。

如果您註冊本行網路銀行服務，您就能快速便利地查詢您的還款進度。

再次感謝您將房屋貸款託付給五星金融銀行。

凱文·德雷伯 敬上
貸款專員

五星金融銀行

以下是提供給五星金融銀行會員的各種房屋貸款。了解不同種類的貸款可幫助您做出明智的決定。檢閱以下的貸款選擇，決定哪一種貸款最適合您的狀況。

固定利率抵押貸款——這項貸款保證在整個貸款期間您的利率與每個月還款的本金維持不變。這項貸款保護您免受利息調升的影響。如果您打算長期居住，這會是一個不錯的選擇。

浮動利率抵押貸款——您的利率在前五年維持固定不變。接下來每年調整。通常，這項貸款一開始的利率都會低於固定利率抵押貸款。

無本金抵押貸款——在貸款最初的五年期間，您只需支付利息。這個選擇適合那些收入不穩定者。當您的財務吃緊時，可以只支付利息。當您的收入增加，就可以支付本金。

購屋佳機貸款——這個特別的貸款是專為首次購屋者所設計的。您不需要一大筆頭期款和良好的信用評等就有資格申請這項貸款。

176. 德雷伯先生建議布朗先生做什麼？

A 應徵職位
B 安排會面
C 在四月付頭期款
D 成為銀行會員

177. 布朗先生被建議如何追蹤貸款？

A 和德雷伯先生會面
B 閱讀銀行發的定期電子郵件
C 利用網路上的銀行服務
D 撥打銀行熱線

178. 網頁提供了什麼資訊？

A 銀行帳戶明細
B 季利率
C 還款選擇
D 會員名冊

179. 哪一項計畫適合那些沒有穩定收入的人？

A 固定利率抵押貸款
B 浮動利率抵押貸款
C 無本金抵押貸款
D 購屋佳機貸款

180. 下列何者與布朗先生有關？

A 他付了一大筆頭期款
B 他有穩定收入
C 他最近買了第一間房子
D 他不久將退休

181–185 文章和電子郵件

《麥迪森商業快報》

11 月 15 日——太陽微晶片是國內積體電路規模最大的製造商，其產品用於電腦、智慧型手機和其他數位電子用品內。這家公司最近在麥迪森設立了新廠房，即將於明年一月開始運作。太陽微晶片的執行長梅琳達·皮爾斯解釋：「隨著消費性電子產品的市場在全球持續成長，像太陽微晶片這樣的公司也要擴大營運來滿足需求。」

「我們正在尋聘各類人員，像是工廠員工、人事部僱員和會計。我們預估開設這個工廠將能為麥迪森地區創造 200 多個工作機會。」皮爾斯女士說。她提到公司將優先聘僱當地居民，但非麥迪森的居民也歡迎應徵。

應徵者必須在 11 月 25 日前將履歷以電子郵件方式寄給蒂娜·齊默爾曼 tzimmerman@sunmicrochips.com。太陽微晶片將於下個月分別舉辦兩場面試。應徵裝配線的一般員工應於 12 月 3 日至 8 日間舉辦面試，至於那些對人事、會計與客服等職務有興趣者，將於 12 月 9 日至 11 日間安排面試。

收件者：
<tzimmerman@sunmicrochips.com>
寄件者：<jakehenry@tnamail.com>
日期：11 月 21 日
主旨：太陽微晶片公司的職缺
附件：履歷表

親愛的齊默爾曼女士：

我最近在《麥迪森商業快報》上看到貴公司新工廠的職缺。身為太陽微晶片的前職員，我對於再次加入貴公司的前景感到很興奮。

請參看附件檔案。如果您能給我面試機會，我將感激不盡。12 月 10 日的任何時段我都可以。如果您想多了解我之前在太陽微晶片的工作經歷，您可以和我的前主管塔德．史密斯聯絡。他仍在公司服務。

期待與您見面。

傑克．亨利

181. 根據皮爾斯女士所言，關於消費性電子產品，下列何者為真？

A 它們的需求持續增加
B 它們變得愈來愈昂貴
C 它們很快地只會在一些國家製造
D 它們會影響使用者的健康

182. 太陽微晶片公司打算做什麼？

A 推出最新款的智慧型手機
B 在海外建新廠房
C 優先聘僱當地應徵者
D 聘僱新的執行長

183. 齊默爾曼女士最有可能是誰？

A 電腦技師
B 人力資源部經理
C 工廠員工
D 會計師

184. 這封電子郵件的目的是什麼？

A 辭職
B 延後約定會面
C 要求面試
D 接受工作邀約

185. 下列何者與亨利先生有關？

A 他是麥迪森的居民
B 他有電腦科學的學位
C 他目前在太陽微晶片公司工作
D 他想要辦公職務

186–190 電子郵件和廣告

寄件者：亨利．崔
<henrychoi@neatsolutions.com>
收件者：珍妮．戴維斯
<jennydavis@endlessacresgolfclub.com>
日期：8 月 8 日
主旨：無盡大地高爾夫球俱樂部
附件：草稿

親愛的戴維斯女士：

附件是「無盡大地高爾夫球俱樂部」廣告的最新草稿。我已經將您寄給我的廣告標語加入設計中。我結合了各種吸睛圖像來吸引報紙讀者的注意，我也在廣告結尾加上了實用的資訊，請告訴我這個設計與新添加的部分是否符合您的期望。配合目前的電視廣告，我想這個廣告將為無盡大地高爾夫球俱樂部帶來許多新顧客。

亨利．崔 敬上

無盡大地高爾夫球俱樂部
科羅拉多州美寶市山丘草原大道 1232 號

暫離生活中的所有壓力，來無盡大地高爾夫球俱樂部打一輪輕鬆的高爾夫球吧。在打完球後，來俱樂部餐廳精緻舒適的用餐環境中享用餐點。

我們目前提供了以下的優惠活動：

預約七人以上組團比賽可享八折優惠。除此之外，每位成員都將得到五元折價券，可於本俱樂部的專賣店消費時折抵。

我們最近才受到《滾動草原日報》讚揚我們優質的場地維護，請來享受科羅拉多州最棒的高爾夫球場吧。我們位於五號公路 21 號出口附近，只要找一下我們的看板，您絕對不會錯過！

現在可於本俱樂部的網站 www.endlessacresgolf.com 線上預約，或來電 555-4834。

寄件者：羅根．曼金斯
<lmankins@crushing.com>
收件者：
<reservations@endlessacresgolfclub.com >
日期：7 月 6 日
主旨：回覆：十人開球與晚餐

您好：

我在報上看到你們的廣告，對於你們的優惠有幾個簡短的問題。第一，我們有十位球員。我知道大多的場地一般都會限制最多四人下場比賽，是為了加速賽程，但我們真的很希望您能為我們破例，一次讓兩隊各五人下場。我們甚至願意租用高爾夫球車來確保不會造成延遲。至於高爾夫球專賣店的五元禮券。我不知道是否可以合起來購買價位較高的物品。這是我兒子的生日。我想送他一支新球桿，但球桿現在真的很貴，50 塊錢應該可以買給他一份很棒的禮物！

我們想在 7 月 20 日星期六早上 11:30 時開打，然後大約在傍晚 6 點時用餐。煩請回信確認開球時間，並回覆我的提問。感謝您撥冗讀信！

祝您有個美好的一天
羅根．曼金斯

186. 羅根．曼金斯建議要如何讓兩組五人的隊伍不會耽誤到場上其他球員？

A 他保證他們會打得很快
B 他保證他們都很擅長打高爾夫球
C 他寫說他會買新的球桿給他兒子
D 他告訴俱樂部那兩隊都會開高爾夫球車

187. 這則廣告最有可能在哪裡出現？

A 電視上
B 雜誌裡
C 報紙上
D 看板上

188. 廣告上加了什麼？

A 促銷細節
B 交通資訊
C 聯絡資料
D 顧客評論

189. 羅根．曼金斯想怎麼利用會員在專賣品店可用的五元折價券？

A 他想用他的折價券買一支球桿給兒子
B 他想用它們來支付果嶺費
C 他想和八折的團體優惠合用
D 他想集合所有折價券來買一樣商品

190. 《滾動草原日報》提到了無盡大地高爾夫球俱樂部的什麼？

A 地點便利
B 場地維護良好
C 會費合理
D 餐廳定期更新菜單

191–195 電子郵件、行事曆和網路討論區

寄件者：圖書館會員
<members@claytonlibrary.edu>
收件者：荷莉．艾倫
<hollyallen@claytonlibrary.edu>
主旨：本月活動
日期：8 月 1 日
附件：8 月活動行事曆

親愛的克萊頓圖書館會員：

感謝您對克萊頓圖書館持續的支持。您所繳的月費幫助我們購買新書、電腦、訂閱期刊還有添購其他對整個社區有益的資源。我們想知會您一些本月即將舉辦的特別活動，您或許會有興趣參加。

首先，著名的童書作家與說書人艾伯特．巴特勒將來訪本圖書館。他將選讀他的新書《神秘貓》，並親筆簽名。他的書最近被提名入選年度最佳童書獎。他的妻子凱西・巴特勒也將出席這場活動，她為巴特勒先生大部分的書籍繪製插圖，也包括《神秘貓》。這場活動費為 10 元，但圖書館會員免費。

本月底，著名的野生動物攝影師妮娜・布魯克斯將於圖書館一樓舉辦展覽。布魯克斯女士最近剛從肯亞旅行回來，在那裡她拍攝了獵豹、長頸鹿、大象和其他動物。她的照片捕捉了野生動物的生動樣貌與大自然的雄偉。

除了這兩項主打活動，本月還有各種工作坊、遊戲之夜與其他活動。細節請參考附上的行事曆。除非另有註記，所有的活動，包括電影之夜會都可免費入場。

圖書館活動籌辦者
荷莉・艾倫 敬上

克萊頓圖書館活動行事曆
八月

日期／時間	活動名稱	附註
8 月 2 日 星期六 下午五點	創意作家工作坊	由多娜・沃德主持
8 月 8 日 星期五 晚上七點	電影之夜	闔家活動
8 月 17 日 星期日 下午六點	《神秘貓》讀書會	入場費 10 元
8 月 20 日 星期三 下午三點	針織社	免費茶點
8 月 30 日 星期六 下午兩點	攝影展開幕	入場費 5 元

克萊頓圖書館社群聊天室

8 月 1 日

■**使用者身分：Jjohnson231**

主旨：8 月 2 日創意作家工作坊

嘿，有人要參加明天的作家工作坊嗎？我聽說多娜・沃德是位優秀的老師。我最新的短篇故事很需要一些意見。如果要去的人請喊個聲吧！～吉姆

■**使用者身分：Storytimechuck**

主旨：回覆：8 月 2 日創意作家工作坊

嗨，Jjohnson231！我一定會去。你說的沒錯，多娜超棒的。她對敘事與節奏的知識真的對我的電影劇本助益很大。或許我也可以在工作坊結束後讀你的短篇故事，提供我的意見。就像我一直在說的，愈多人看愈好！如果你有興趣的話，我也可以讓你看一下我的劇本。明天見！～恰克

191. 這封電子郵件的目的是什麼？
- A 介紹新成員
- **B 宣傳即將舉辦的活動**
- C 公告時間表的調整
- D 請求捐款

192. 下列何者與艾伯特・巴特勒有關？
- **A 他的妻子是插畫家**
- B 他最近出版了第一本書
- C 他有好幾隻貓
- D 他即將得獎

193. 根據聊天室，多娜・沃德擅長什麼？
- A 拍攝生動的照片
- B 編寫成功的電影劇本
- **C 了解步調與故事情節的作用**
- D 和年輕詩人合作

194. 圖書館讀者何時可以見到凱西・巴特勒？
- A 星期三
- B 星期五
- C 星期六
- **D 星期日**

195. 8 月 2 日創意作家工作坊結束後可能會發生什麼事？
- A 每個人都知道如何把詩寫得更好
- **B 恰克和吉姆將交換作品提供彼此的意見**
- C 多娜・沃德將出版她的小說
- D 恰克與多娜將一起寫吉姆的短篇故事

196–200 資訊、表格和信件

紅岩皮件

感謝您購買紅岩皮件的商品。我們製造的商品都符合最高品質標準，並以優質的客服為豪。我們所有的商品都是由技術純熟的工匠一絲不苟地逐一製作，我們提供終生保固，除了正常磨損以外，所有做工上的瑕疵皆適用。只要在您使用紅岩產品期間，我們將維修或更換任何瑕疵部分。

如果您的紅岩商品不在保固期間，則維修費如下：

	皮夾	手提包	外套
更換遺失鈕扣	10 元	15 元	20 元
拉鍊維修或更換	20 元	30 元	45 元
縫線修補及縫合	40 元	50 元	50 元

保固不可轉讓，且僅限原始購買人使用。此外，必須要有銷售收據以確認保固並使用服務。這個保固不適用於購自二手商店或未獲授權代理商之商品。

紅岩皮件
維修申請表

姓名：梅莉莎．波金斯
日期：2 月 28 日
地址：伊利諾伊州芝加哥中圓大道 458 號
商品：可可 TX 手提包

維修說明：
我去年在伊利諾伊州芝加哥的紅岩皮件店買了這件商品，但才不到在六個月，拉鍊就卡住了，無法開合。由於這是製作上的瑕疵，我想這應該在保固範圍內。12 年來我一直是紅岩皮件的忠實常客，這是我第一次碰到問題。

本人已經閱讀並同意所有退貨與維修的相關條款。本人保證這個商品是在紅岩皮件的官方商店購得，而且本人是這項商品的原始購買人。

簽名：梅莉莎．波金斯
日期：2 月 28 日

備註：您的商品可能需要一段時間才能取回。若您有任何問題，請來電 812-555-8541。

親愛的梅莉莎．波金斯：

感謝您提出了紅岩皮件可可 TX 手提包的維修申請。我們已經收到並檢查了您的商品與文件，確定這的確是在我們的保固範圍內，並安排於下週進行維修。一旦恢復正常，我們將以快遞寄到您在維修申請表中所提供的地址。僅代表紅岩皮件感謝您 12 年來的惠顧，也為這個可可 TX 手提包的瑕疵對您造成的不便感到抱歉。

紅岩皮件客戶服務專員
雪若．蒂明斯 敬上

196. 下列何者與紅岩皮件的商品有關？

(A) 它們在全國都有販售
(B) 它們相當昂貴
(C) 它們是手工製
(D) 它們有各種顏色

197. 波金斯女士為什麼填寫申請表？

(A) 要得到商品的退款
(B) 要告知商品有瑕疵
(C) 向客服投訴
(D) 延長保固期限

198. 如果波金斯女士的商品是從二手商店買來的，她會被收多少錢？

(A) 15 元
(B) 20 元
(C) 30 元
(D) 45 元

199. 在給波金斯女士的信中，第六行的「patronage」意思最接近？

(A) 行銷
(B) 惠顧
(C) 競爭
(D) 投資

200. 從核准波金斯女士所提出的保固一信中，可推論出什麼？

Ⓐ 她的手提包有正常的磨損
Ⓑ 紅岩皮件是當地的品牌
Ⓒ 她附上了紅岩皮件專賣店的銷售收據
Ⓓ 她為她的可可 TX 手提包附上 30 元的拉鍊維修費

ACTUAL TEST ⑦

PART 5 P.198–201

◎ **Part 5 解答請見 P.457**

101. 每週於星期一與星期四收**兩次**可回收物品，如玻璃及塑膠。

102. 因為道路交通壅塞，愈來愈多的製造商**現在**會利用火車來運送商品。

103. 員工被指示當顧客抱怨時，要**通知**值班的主管。

104. 老舊傢俱、復古珠寶和其他的**古董**都可在這個市集裡買到。

105. **如果**沒有做好必要的安全預防措施，受傷的風險可能會更高。

106. 不滿意楓葉家庭清潔服務的顧客，可以在首期清潔作業的三天**內**終止契約。

107. 華倫街上免費診所裡的**員工都是**由志工醫師和護士**組成**。

108. 福克斯女士延長店家營業時間，因為她認同亞柏先生**所說的**營業時間不夠長。

109. 偵查員查看了這個地方，確保該地符合**適用的**業界規範。

110. 大部分住在利嘉塔**的**居民，對於冷氣系統不斷出現的問題感到苦惱。

111. 休斯先生將員工分成小型討論小組以加強會議的**參與度**。

112. 自去年**同**期以來，匯率已經上漲了 3.2 個百分比。

113. 布蘭達．提頓被**預測**將贏得市長競選，因為她是所有候選人中資歷最豐富的。

114. 那些參加創意寫作工作坊的人，在未來兩天**中**將學到各種有用的技巧。

115. 藉由事先**仔細**規劃搬遷事宜，我們可以將意外的支出降至最低，並盡量提高效率。

116. 根據公司規定，**所有**出差費用的申請必須附上收據才能核銷。

117. 安全公司自 2008 年創立以來就一直**生產**居家安全產品。

118. **因為**訂單上的一個錯誤，部分建築材料從沒寄送出去。

119. 實施新政策是為了加強公司各部門之間的**溝通**。

120. 古堡的私人旅行團人數將限制**在**十人內。

121. 使用平底鍋烹煮時，請勿使用金屬用具，**這樣**表面才不會被刮花。

122. 為了**負擔**每個月的房貸，泰勒先生需要大幅度的加薪。

123. 環保人士對於社區**配合**提升當地的資源回收再利用感到滿意。

124. 國家健康組織報告了該疾病的**確診**案例。

125. 由於政治傾向的**改變**，參議員不再支持提出的移民法案。

126. 對附近的屋主來說，鄰里裡的**空**屋會造成房產淨值的損失。

127. 諾里斯大樓的屋主大量購進家具，讓每個會議室看起來都一模一樣，而非讓每間有**不同的**裝潢。

128. 導演將影片的成功**主要**歸功於男主角的經驗與才華。

129. 公司新的網路銀行軟體與大多數型號的智慧型手機**相容**。

130. **只要**不中斷工作，員工可隨時休假。

PART 6 P.202–205

131–134 電子郵件

寄件者：副總裁堂娜．強森
收件者：赫力奧科技公司員工
日期：7 月 5 日
主旨：大廳翻新

上個月收到的聯邦政府補助款已可讓我們改善大樓的幾個區域，第一個從中獲益的地方就是大廳，我們將自 7 月 12 日起開始改建大廳。大概需要兩個禮拜的時間。在那段期間內，如需與公司以外的人開會，請安排到轉角的羅斯街咖啡店。我們已經設定了一個特別帳目，這兩個禮拜內公司的人都可以使用。請在帳單上簽名並寫上日期，然後將帳單交還給服務生。我們知道這樣會有點不方便，感謝大家的配合。

131. A 之前允許
B 已允許
C 允許
D 正允許

132. A 當收到建物准許通知後就會開始動工。
B 這個慶祝活動將持續大半個七月。
C 考量到花費，改建將延後進行。
D 第一個從中獲益的地方就是大廳。

133. A 一……就
B 在……期間
C 大約
D 直到

134. **A 知道**
B 受過訓練的
C 不情願的
D 滿意的

135–138 告示

誠徵兼職廚師

天堂咖啡廳正在找一位兼職廚師。應徵者必須能在步調快速的環境裡工作，且熟悉所有的制式早餐餐點。我們目前只提供平日班，但若有必要，應徵者必須願意在週末上班。週末的時間表日後將有異動。理想上，我們希望應徵者最好有至少一年以上快餐廚師的工作經驗。天堂咖啡廳位於磨坊鎮市區的郵局旁。請親自繳交履歷表，並準備烹煮一份可供點餐的蛋類餐點。我們期盼並歡迎您加入本團隊！

135. A 聘用
B 聘用
C 聘用
D 聘用

136. A 應徵者必須知道如何炒蛋。
B 來應徵的人必須知道怎麼洗碗。
C 應徵者需要能說西班牙文。
D 我們目前只提供平日班，但若有必要，應徵者必須願意在週末上班。

137. A 最多
B 低於
C 至少
D 最少

138. **A 期盼**
B 期盼
C 期盼
D 期盼

139–142 廣告

城市不動產

城市不動產是華盛頓州首屈一指的不動產公司，在本州服務超過 50 年。我們被公認為是本州業界的權威專家，我們的許多仲介人員也因他們傑出的服務而獲得《富比士地產》雜誌頒發的獎項。本公司仲介人員竭盡心力將他們最棒的知識與專業端上檯面，而且他們對於房地產市場的準則也是數一數二的。本公司仲介人員專精房地產業的各個區塊，包含企業不動產、住家不動產及租賃不動產。您可以確信的是他們絕對能滿足您的特定需求。

本公司總部位於市中心，您可以與我們的仲介人員在此會面並做免費諮詢。您也可以上本公司網站 www.cityrealty.com 查看不動產物件列表及更多資訊。

139. Ⓐ 是
Ⓑ 曾是
Ⓒ 正是
Ⓓ 已經是

140. Ⓐ 附屬的
Ⓑ 忠誠的
Ⓒ 盡心盡責的
Ⓓ 忠心的

141. **Ⓐ 您可以確信的是他們絕對能滿足您的特定需求。**
Ⓑ 本公司有上百筆的房產清單供您選擇。
Ⓒ 企業不動產的房仲賺最多錢。
Ⓓ 由於住房市場日漸上漲，住家不動產的房仲很忙。

142. Ⓐ 和
Ⓑ 為了
Ⓒ 到
Ⓓ 來自

143–146 網站貼文

員工留言板

辦公室節慶派對
成就與感恩

發表人：朱利・諾頓

我要感謝每一位曾經提供協助而讓這場派對成功的人。特別要感謝凱斯、格蘭特、凡妮莎和瑪莉莎，他們在工作之餘還花了許多時間協助規劃這一切。在開始準備的時候，我們經歷了一些起落，但是最終結果卻是非凡的。事實上，全體一致認為今年的派對是有史以來最棒的。這次參加的人數破了紀錄，而且很多人都覺得今年的活動是派對成功的主因。很開心看到大家都相處融洽，還參與了所有活動。兒童慈善募款甚至超越目標 1,000 多元。再一次地，我要感謝大家。

143. Ⓐ 協助
Ⓑ 曾協助
Ⓒ 正協助
Ⓓ 已協助

144. Ⓐ 我應該再多點些食物和酒。
Ⓑ 我很認真地規劃了這次的活動。
Ⓒ 特別要感謝凱斯、格蘭特、凡妮莎和瑪莉莎，他們在工作之餘還花了許多時間協助規劃這一切
Ⓓ 今天很開心看到各位為此活動盛裝出席。

145. Ⓐ 一般的
Ⓑ 熟悉的
Ⓒ 不同的
Ⓓ 全體的

146. Ⓐ 踰越
Ⓑ 投降
Ⓒ 超過
Ⓓ 征服

PART 7 P.206–229

147–148 信件

4 月 3 日

賴瑞・馬汀
堪薩斯整齊清潔公司
67514 堪薩斯州阿靈頓湖邊路 5448 號

親愛的馬汀先生：

今年我們哈雷谷搖滾嘉年華有意僱用貴公司的清潔服務。嘉年華將於 6 月 14 日星期五開始，持續一整個週末，到 6 月 16 日星期天晚上結束。但是，和前幾年不同，今年我們希望貴公司能在嘉年華期間不定時地清潔環境。因此，我們將提供貴公司一輛拖車作為臨時辦公室，讓員工可以避暑休息。

期盼今年再次與貴公司合作。

哈雷谷基金會嘉年華籌劃人
凱倫．強森 敬上

147. 馬汀先生最有可能是誰？

(A) 音樂表演者
(B) 卡車司機
(C) 清潔公司的專員
(D) 嘉年華籌劃人

148. 根據這封信，將提供什麼？

(A) 食物與水
(B) 休息區
(C) 音樂器材
(D) 清潔用品

149–150 訊息串

蘿拉．伯克 **5:09**
你星期一會回市區嗎？

阿德溫．尚恩 **5:15**
可能會。

蘿拉．伯克 **5:16**
所以，你還沒決定嗎？

阿德溫．尚恩 **5:17**
是啊，工廠正面臨各種問題。處理好一件，另一件又出現。

蘿拉．伯克 **5:17**
我聽說了。嗯，至少不用被綁在辦公室裡。

阿德溫．尚恩 **5:18**
這倒是真的。

阿德溫．尚恩 **5:19**
星期一有什麼事嗎？

蘿拉．伯克 **5:20**
你回來之後，哈里斯女士想要和你開個會。沒什麼要緊的事。

阿德溫．尚恩 **5:22**
好，等我確定好行程之後再告訴你。

149. 下列何者與尚恩先生有關？

(A) 他錯過了一場會議
(B) 他考慮轉調
(C) 他最近接管了工廠的經營
(D) 他不知道他什麼時候會回辦公室

150. 在 5:18 時，尚恩先生寫下：「這倒是真的。」是什麼意思？

(A) 他擔心工廠的狀況
(B) 他同意不在辦公室還蠻愉快的
(C) 他發現一個錯誤
(D) 他確信星期一會回來

151–152 電子郵件

收件者：派特．布萊克本
<pblackburn@fastweb.com>
寄件者：自然而然健康產品
<cs@gonatural.com>
日期：2 月 4 日，下午 3 點 34 分
主旨：產品訂購

感謝您選擇自然而然健康產品做為您維他命及礦物質的補充品。本公司所有的產品品質都經過仔細的品質檢驗，符合政府所有法規。此外，在二月期間，顧客消費滿 100 元將不需支付任何運費。

訂單編號：4330XM21
訂購日期：2 月 4 日，下午 3 點 31 分
寄件地址：威斯康辛州克林頓密西根大道 2709 號，派特．布萊克本收
明細：六瓶綠源綜合維他命
總價：180 元，以信用卡支付（XXXX XXXX XXXX 8766）

本公司所有產品都有顧客百分百的滿意保證。若您有任何不滿，請撥打客戶服務中心電話 987-555-3427，訂單成立一週內皆可全額退費。

自然而然健康產品

151. 下列何者與布萊克本女士的訂單有關？

(A) 已保遺失險
(B) 缺貨中
(C) 她先生下的訂單
(D) 將不用支付運費

152. 布萊克本女士為什麼有可能在 2 月 11 日前打電話給客戶服務中心？

(A) 為了修改訂單
(B) 為了更改付款方式
(C) 為了退款
(D) 為了申請會員資格

153–154 文章

本週四，吉他手尼克．史丹頓的新爵士專輯《午夜之月》將開始在店面販售。《午夜之月》是史丹頓先生這五年來的第一張專輯，已經獲得許多音樂評論家的讚賞。史丹頓先生將於 3 月 12 日本週六，在位於主街 4532 號的艾默生百貨公司舉辦簽名會。購買新專輯就能免費獲得親筆簽名。

153. 尼克．史丹頓是誰？

(A) 唱片製作人
(B) 唱片藝人
(C) 音樂評論家
(D) 音樂經紀人

154. 根據文章內容，3 月 12 日會發生什麼事？

(A) 將舉辦演唱會
(B) 新書發表
(C) 將舉辦簽名會
(D) 將販售部分門票

155–158 備忘錄

備忘錄

收件者：全體員工
寄件者：總經理貝蒂．富蘭克林
日期：8 月 19 日

主旨：接待員

致全體員工：

我們工作室的接待員葛瑞塔．瓊斯將請假一段時間去處理私事，請假時間是從 8 月 21 日至 9 月 5 日。在這段期間，我們聘請了一位臨時代理人，朱蒂絲．布蘭琪。布蘭琪女士將處理瓊斯女士的平常業務，包括接聽電話、處理預約、安排時間及接待顧客。請歡迎布蘭琪女士的加入工作室，當她有任何問題時，也請協助她。

此外，若各位有提供優惠及折扣給長期客戶，也請提早告訴布蘭琪女士，否則她將依照電腦系統裡設定的價格收費。

若有需要和瓊斯女士討論的緊急狀況，或需要購買特殊染髮劑、調理洗髮精及客戶要的其他品項，請在今天與明天瓊斯女士離開前處理完畢。如果還有其他問題，隨時都可以和我聯絡。

155. 備忘錄裡的接待員最有可能在哪裡工作？

(A) 百貨公司
(B) 美髮沙龍
(C) 水療按摩沙龍
(D) 造型工作室

156. 下列何者與葛瑞塔．瓊斯有關？

(A) 她要退休了
(B) 她要去度假
(C) 她要請假一段時間
(D) 她是臨時工

157. 員工應該在什麼時候和瓊斯女士聯絡緊急業務？

(A) 在她離開前
(B) 在她離開後
(C) 隨時
(D) 等她回來後

158. 下列句子最適合出現在 [1]、[2]、[3]、[4] 的哪個位置？「在這段期間，我們聘請了一位臨時代理人，朱蒂絲・布蘭琪。」

Ⓐ [1]
Ⓑ [2]
Ⓒ [3]
Ⓓ [4]

159–161 網頁

閃亮鞋店
您運動鞋的最佳首選

我們看到您目前在本公司網站登記為基本會員。

請點選這裡升級為優質會員。

一旦成為優質會員，您將享有以下福利：

- 快遞只要 3 元（基本會員為 5 元）
- 購買 60 天以內可免費更換所有商品（基本會員為 30 天）
- 購買 30 天內可免費退還所有商品（基本會員為 7 天）

只需要點擊一下就能享有從基本會員升級至優質會員的服務。為了歡迎顧客到我們新的網路商店，本月提供優惠價，只要 50 元就能升級成一年期的優質會員。

159. 這個網頁的目的是什麼？

Ⓐ 宣傳新系列鞋款
Ⓑ 確認訂單
Ⓒ 推薦服務升級
Ⓓ 募集捐款

160. 下列何者不是優質會員的福利？

Ⓐ 新產品折扣
Ⓑ 減價快遞費
Ⓒ 免費退貨期限較長
Ⓓ 免費換貨期限較長

161. 下列何者與閃亮鞋店有關？

Ⓐ 已經在業界好幾十年了
Ⓑ 由當地的企業家所創立
Ⓒ 可在網路上購買商品
Ⓓ 有三種會員模式

162–165 網路聊天室

麗莎・漢考克 **9:39**
我在上班途中會去咖啡店一下。大家想喝什麼？我請客。

尼克・莫頓 **9:39**
哇，謝謝妳！我只要黑咖啡就好。

莉莉・史密斯 **9:40**
謝謝。我要拿鐵。你可以順便拿一些糖嗎？

麗莎・漢考克 **9:41**
好。我會拿幾個糖包。

理查・帕克 **9:42**
我永遠沒辦法向咖啡說不。我也要拿鐵加糖。

愛蜜莉・喬丹 **9:42**
如果有的話，我想要花草茶。我不喝含咖啡因的飲料，所以任何沒有咖啡因的茶類都可以。謝謝。

麗莎・漢考克 **9:43**
好，20 分鐘後我會帶著你們的飲料到。等會見。喔，在我忘記之前，請確認我們從欣蒂精品店訂購的物品，已經在展示間準備給客戶看了。

理查・帕克 **9:44**
箱子早上送到了，實習生正在把東西從箱子裡拿出來。但是從仙黛爾訂的東西似乎不見了。

麗莎・漢考克 **9:45**
什麼意思？

尼克・莫頓 **9:45**
我們正努力確定包裹的下落。我們聯絡過仙黛爾，他們把東西送錯地址了。

麗莎・漢考克 **9:46**
真是太糟糕了，請盡量查出那些洋裝到哪去了。

理查·帕克 **9:47**
好消息。我剛從貨運公司接到消息，他們找到仙黛爾的貨了，正重新送過來。

麗莎·漢考克 **9:48**
我差點恐慌症發作。什麼時候會送到？

理查·帕克 **9:48**
今天下午。

162. 說話者們可能在哪種公司上班？

A 時裝公司
B 服飾店
C 戲服公司
D 咖啡廳

163. 在9:39分，麗莎·漢考克寫下:「我請客」是什麼意思？

A 她會帶咖啡來
B 她會買飲料
C 她會記得每個人訂的東西
D 輪到她去買飲料了

164. 下列何者與他們其中一件配送的貨物有關？

A 定價錯誤
B 被送回精品店
C 當天晚點會到
D 還沒找到貨物

165. 仙黛爾是何種公司？

A 布料公司
B 雜誌公司
C 宅配公司
D 精品店

166–168 電子郵件

收件者：全體人員
<csall@cherishedgoods.com>
寄件者：艾瑞克·尼克森
<enix@cherishedgoods.com>
日期：1月5日，上午10點
主旨：寄送錯誤

大家好：

配送部門主管莉莉亞·肯特告訴我，昨天公司的客戶資料庫發生了系統錯誤，導致許多訂單送錯地址。今天早上我們部門已經接到了許多顧客的抱怨電話，說他們收到錯的包裹。肯特女士的部門已經很努力地在確認錯誤源頭，因此，任何來電說運送錯誤的顧客，都要請他們退回包裹。除此之外，請告知顧客，他們下次購物時可享有九折的優惠。

艾瑞克·尼克森

166. 誰最有可能收到這封電子郵件？

A 配送部門員工
B 不滿的顧客
C 客戶服務代表人員
D 網路技術專員

167. 根據這封電子郵件，肯特女士的員工正在努力做什麼？

A 建立客戶資料庫
B 修理系統故障
C 尋找一個遺失的包裹
D 接聽客戶電話

168. 電子郵件的收件者被告知要做什麼？

A 更新個人資料
B 親自運送包裹
C 將資料輸入客戶資料庫中
D 提供減價優惠給某些客戶

169–171 電子郵件

收件者：carlhurst@nicknet.com
寄件者：m_winters@tatecc.com
日期：6 月 1 日，下午 1 點 34 分
主旨：社區活動

親愛的赫斯特先生：

作為泰特社區活動中心家庭會員的忠實顧客，您以持續性捐款的方式資助我們。我們真的很感謝您的支持。

下列表格提供了本月即將舉辦的家庭活動資訊，我們歡迎您的參與。

手工日 6 月 7 日	保羅．辛普森 6 月 15 日	夏季野餐 6 月 22 日
提供孩子各種手工材料，讓他們可以創作個人獨特的作品。	來聆聽本地歌手暨詞曲創作者保羅．辛普森美妙的音樂。	每個人都要帶一道美味的餐點來與大家分享。將免費提供飲料。

對於會員而言，參加這些活動不需買票。我們鼓勵大家來參與這些活動，與家人共享優質時光。

期待見到您。

泰特社區活動中心活動籌劃者
米妮．華特斯

169. 下列何者與赫斯特先生有關？

Ⓐ 他是當地音樂家
Ⓑ 他捐款給孤兒院
Ⓒ 他支持公共組織
Ⓓ 他在社區活動中心工作

170. 寄這封電子郵件的目的是什麼？

Ⓐ 宣布社區理事會會議
Ⓑ 申請家庭會員資格
Ⓒ 宣傳將舉辦的活動
Ⓓ 提供當地選舉資訊

171. 下列何者與泰特社區活動中心有關？

Ⓐ 會員可以免費參加活動
Ⓑ 提供定期的音樂課程
Ⓒ 接受電話預約
Ⓓ 所有活動都將提供飲料

172–175 信件

J&P 企業
10288 紐約州卡麥隆史雲頓街 1462 號

3 月 29 日
格蘭特．李先生
18729 紐約州卡麥隆銀原路 287 號

親愛的李先生：

感謝您在 J&P 企業多年來的服務與工作上的貢獻。我們正將公司健康保險福利近來的異動資訊寄給全體員工。您的保險將由同一間保險公司承保，但是由於新實施的州立規定，現在全體員工都必須在當地的診所或醫院接受基本健康檢查。檢查費用將由健康保險支付，所以您不需支付任何額外費用，而且絕不影響每個月的保費扣減。信封內含供員工參考的新醫療計劃詳細資訊。

健康檢查必須包括血液檢查、尿液檢查、眼睛檢查、身高與體重測量、聽力檢查、以及胸部 X 光檢查，不需 30 分鐘即可檢查完畢，請至當地診所預約。請最晚在 12 月 30 日以前將檢查結果交給人力資源部的凱倫．李，如果沒有做健康檢查，將被處以高達 2,000 元的罰鍰。感謝您的配合且希望您能遵守這個新的異動。

若有任何問題或疑慮，請洽凱倫 leighk@jpindustries.com。

J&P 企業 執行經理
約翰．布雷克 敬上

172. 這封信的目的是什麼？

Ⓐ 通知員工一項強制性的檢查
Ⓑ 鼓勵員工去醫院捐血
Ⓒ 討論員工健康保險給付範圍的異動
Ⓓ 宣傳新診所的服務項目

173. 布雷克先生隨信寄了什麼？

Ⓐ 申請表
Ⓑ 保險資料
Ⓒ 合約
Ⓓ 有關異動的更多資料

174. 在第二段結尾的「subject to」與下列哪個字意思最接近？

Ⓐ 取決於
Ⓑ 對……負責
Ⓒ 退出
Ⓓ 增加

175. 下列句子最適合出現在 [1]、[2]、[3]、[4] 的哪個位置？「不需 30 分鐘即可檢查完畢。」

Ⓐ [1]
Ⓑ [2]
Ⓒ [3]
Ⓓ [4]

176–180 廣告和電子郵件

花兒朵朵開瑜伽工作室

夏季瑜伽課程

今年夏天，我們將為各年齡層與程度的人開設各式瑜伽課程。

夏季課程時間表及價格（註冊費）：

- 初級班，每週兩次，共兩個月（150 元）
- 中級班及進階班，每週兩次，共兩個月（200 元）
- 銀髮族瑜伽，每週一次，共兩個月（100 元）
- 熱力瑜伽，每週三次，共兩個月（250 元）

花兒朵朵開瑜伽工作室將提供所有必需器材。

會員須穿著可活動自如的舒適服裝。

46202 印地安納州印地安納波里克拉克街 45 號
715-555-5832
www.bloomingfloweryoga.com

收件者：潭美・格倫 <tammyglenn@mxmail.com>
寄件者：德威恩・摩爾 <dwaynemoore@bloomingfloweryoga.com>
日期：5 月 23 日
主旨：新學員
附件：新會員表

親愛的格倫女士：

我寫信是為了通知您，您班上多了一位報名課程的學員。新學員是珍・梅爾斯，她星期一上第一堂課時會帶 100 元的註冊費來。

另外，星期一時請給梅爾斯小姐和其他新學員需要填寫的表格。我已在這封電子郵件中附上所需文件，您只要印出紙本交給她們即可。

目前您的課程有九位學員報名，所以幾乎額滿。實際上，今年夏季的所有課程都證明相當受歡迎，我預估在月底時將全部額滿。感謝您多年來在花兒朵朵開瑜伽工作室辛勤的教學。若您有任何問題，請告訴我。

德威恩・摩爾

176. 下列何者與夏季課程有關？

Ⓐ 上禮拜開始上課
Ⓑ 將在戶外上課
Ⓒ 小孩大人都可以上
Ⓓ 課程費用有折扣

177. 下列何者與梅爾斯女士有關？

Ⓐ 她從沒學過瑜伽
Ⓑ 她是位銀髮族
Ⓒ 她想要成為瑜伽老師
Ⓓ 她是位長期會員

178. 格倫女士被要求做什麼？

Ⓐ 開發新課程
Ⓑ 參加訓練
Ⓒ 簽署工作合約
Ⓓ 發送一些文件

179. 在電子郵件中，第三段第一行的「capacity」意思最接近？

A 量
B 能力
C 空間
D 角色

180. 下列何者與格倫女士有關？

A 她和小孩相處得很好
B 她是位長期員工
C 她即將退休
D 她將被加薪

181–185 網站貼文

超級模型愛好社群論壇

黑鬍子海盜模型船有問題

8 月 3 日，上午 10 點 55 分

由約翰・泰勒發布

我最近從超級愛好網路商店買了一組模型。我買了黑鬍子海盜模型船和兒子一起組裝，但是碰到了一個問題。在仔細閱讀使用說明書後，我注意到一些必要的零件不在盒子裡。具體來說，組成桅桿和風帆的零件不在套組裡。幾年來，我已經在超級模型愛好買了許多組模型，也一直對收到的產品感到滿意。

還有其他人在這個套組上碰到一樣的問題嗎？我兒子和我打算在月底將完成的模型送去參加本地的模型組裝比賽，我們對這個狀況都感到很失望。如果有碰過這個問題並且已經解決的人提供建議，我會十分感激。

超級模型愛好社群論壇

回覆：黑鬍子海盜模型船有問題

8 月 3 日，下午 4 點 24 分

由凱瑟琳・麥斯威爾發布

嗨，約翰：

我最近也從超級愛好網路商店買了黑鬍子海盜模型船給我兒子，而且也碰上和你一樣的問題。起初我以為一定是我搞錯了，但在確認使用說明書上所有零件清單後，我確定套組裡幾個零件一定是在販售時就已經不見了。我把套組帶回去本地的超級愛好門市，店員證實了我的懷疑，超級愛好的員工很好心地換給我一組零件完整的套組。有了新套組，我兒子和我就能將模型組裝成和盒子上的圖片一模一樣。我建議你到離家最近的超級愛好門市，要求他們更換瑕疵品。記得去的時候，要寫下訂單號碼。

181. 第一則貼文的主旨是什麼？

A 購買的產品有瑕疵
B 使用說明書的錯誤
C 售價與廣告不符
D 報名一項比賽

182. 下列何者與泰勒先生有關？

A 他認識麥斯威爾女士這個人
B 他是超級愛好的產品設計師
C 他有一艘帆船
D 他將和兒子一起參加比賽

183. 泰勒先生和麥斯威爾女士如何得知套組有問題？

A 透過和客服人員談話
B 透過觀賞教學影片
C 透過參考使用手冊
D 透過查看照片

184. 下列何者與麥斯威爾女士有關？

A 她是超級愛好的常客
B 她和泰勒先生都在超級愛好上班
C 她成功地組裝模型套組
D 她收到全額退費

185. 麥斯威爾女士提供了什麼建議？

Ⓐ 到附近的門市去
Ⓑ 取消會員資格
Ⓒ 下載新的使用手冊
Ⓓ 購買替代零件

186–190 廣告、表格和會議公告

夢想空間床鋪商場

床鋪、寢具和家具
62751 伊利諾州春田市威爾夏路 3600 號
www.dreamspacebeds.com

別讓自己飽受翻來覆去之苦，不得一夜安眠。來一趟夢想空間床鋪商場，找一張完全符合需求的舒適床鋪來款待自己。歡迎顧客來試躺店裡的任何一張床。

一樓：床鋪（單人床、雙人床、加大床、超級加大床等）
二樓：寢具（床單、枕頭、毯子、靠墊等）
三樓：家具（椅子、沙發、桌子等）

因應顧客的建議，為了那些上班時間不固定的顧客，本商場現在延長營業兩小時。

需要快遞床鋪嗎？只要在結帳時詢問店員就能輕鬆安排妥當。

如果您對本商場有任何意見或建議，請利用大門內側的意見箱。

意見與建議表
夢想空間床鋪商場

顧客姓名：威利・M・金
日期：8 月 9 日
聯絡電話：456-555-6123

意見：上禮拜，我到你們的商場去買我床要用的新枕頭、床單和毛毯組。但是，當我走到那一區時，卻找不到任何員工可以幫我。我等了大概半個小時，也沒有人來。我需要幫忙確認哪種床單和毛毯組能符合我床的尺寸，但最後卻只能洩氣地離開。希望你們可以為顧客提供更好的服務，不讓類似的狀況再度發生。身為貴店多年的忠實顧客，若你們無法說明為什麼沒人可以協助我，我也許得開始光顧貴店競爭對手的商場。

大家好，本人召開這個會議，是想討論延長營業時間這個新政策所帶來的一些問題。首先，這似乎是個好構想，可以幫助全天候上班的顧客。我知道要朝九晚五地上班，很難找空檔處理家務及購物。但遺憾的是，延長營業時間也表示我們人手過於分身乏術，而我們只能等待日後聘用並訓練更多人力。

結果，我們最近忽略了一些顧客。剛傳給大家看的是威利・金所寫的意見與建議表影本，他比我更清楚地歸納出缺失。請看一下，然後想想有什麼方法讓我們在這樣大型的商場裡注意到有需求的顧客。我了解以我們微薄的人力卻得負責比以往更大的空間，所以這個會議並不是要處罰或責怪，而是要想出解決方法。請腦力激盪一下，如果有任何構想，請送到我辦公室來。我必須打電話給威利・金。

186. 下列何者與夢想空間床鋪商場的床無關？

Ⓐ 有各種不同的尺寸
Ⓑ 顧客可以試躺
Ⓒ 陳列在一樓
Ⓓ 提供終身保固

187. 根據廣告的內容，關於夢想空間床鋪商場，下列何者為真？

Ⓐ 它位於百貨公司內
Ⓑ 它銷售居家用品
Ⓒ 它正在在聘用更多員工
Ⓓ 它已延長營業時間

188. 金先生最有可能在哪裡找到想買的產品？

Ⓐ 一樓
Ⓑ 二樓
Ⓒ 三樓
Ⓓ 大門入口附近

189. 您認為會議中講話的人是誰？

Ⓐ 夢想空間床鋪商場的主管
Ⓑ 威利・金
Ⓒ 其他城市的地區經理
Ⓓ 結帳櫃台職員

190. 根據會議中的資訊，下列何者為真？

(A) 夢想空間床鋪商場將把營業時間改回來。

(B) 夢想空間床鋪商場將延長營業時間來服務更多像威利．金這類的顧客。

(C) 夢想空間床鋪商場將聘用更多員工，才有足夠人力來負責整個商場。

(D) 夢想空間床鋪商場將舉辦抽獎活動並邀請威利．金參加。

191–195 網頁、電子郵件和時間表

www.acestafftraining.com

首頁	與我們聯絡	門市據點	關於我們

王牌教育訓練是一間為商店或企業員工提供開發課程的公司。您可以倚賴我們成功專業人士所組成的團隊來改善員工素質，並幫助公司達成目標。我們提供有效並以結果為導向的課程。以下是現有的訓練課程：

領導力 這個課程幫助員工培養策略規劃與管理技能，同時也改善領導階層的員工管理技巧。	**銷售** 我們傳授創新策略來提高銷售量與市場佔有率。這個課程適合門市銷售員和電話行銷人員。
顧客服務 絕對不要低估顧客滿意度的重要性。當直接面對顧客時，您的員工需要有幫助有效果的技能。	**科技** 在變化快速的工作環境中，員工需要跟上科技領域的新潮流與發展。您的員工將學到如何快速且精準地搜尋並掌控新科技。

為員工報名課程，請洽約書亞．約克
josh@acestafftraining.com

寄件者：蒂芬妮．陳
<tifftran@zellengifts.com>
收件者：約書亞．約克
<josh@acestafftraining.com>
主旨：本公司員工訓練課程
日期：10 月 9 日

親愛的約克先生：

會與您聯絡是因本公司澤聯禮品想為一些員工開設訓練課程。我們打算下個月擴大電話行銷部門，但是我們訓練有素的員工人數不足以填補這些新職缺。因此，我們將從客服部門轉調部分員工到電話行銷部門，以解決這個問題。由於本公司的產品主要針對兒童，我們希望盡可能地能在今年的聖誕季增加獲利。請告訴我一次課程能容納的最多人數是多少。

感謝您。

澤聯禮品
蒂芬妮．陳

澤聯禮品的王牌教育訓練課程企劃
11 月 1 日至 5 日

小組代號與學員人數	**星期一** 行銷策略	**星期二** 成功談判	**星期三** 顧客第一！	**星期四** 完成交易	**星期五** 以禮開始，以禮相待
紅色小組 10 人	9–11	9–11:30	8–10:30	8–11	9–11
藍色小組 10 人	1–3	1–3	1–3	1–3	1–3
綠色小組 10 人	3–5	3–5	3–5	3–5	3–5
白色小組 10 人	5–7	5–7	5–7	5–7	5–7

這是我們的課程表企劃，能幫忙貴公司將客服員工轉換為成功的電話行銷人員。您可以看到，這課程雄心壯志地涵蓋大量的資料，但我有信心這是一場勝戰。我們試著在課程進行時，取得順利轉換與保持澤聯禮品公司持續營運這兩個需求之間的平衡。因此，

我們將貴公司員工分成小組，交錯安排在一整天的課程中。這對您的員工來說會有比較好的師生人數比，而且對貴公司業務造成的影響最小。我們很期待這優質教育訓練的一週！

王牌教育訓練籌劃員
約書亞．約克

191. 約克先生在哪裡上班？

Ⓐ 會計事務所
Ⓑ 運動管理經紀公司
Ⓒ 技能發展機構
Ⓓ 廣告公司

192. 下列何者與課程中的科技內容有關？

Ⓐ 開放給社會大眾
Ⓑ 包括當前的網頁程式設計技巧
Ⓒ 教導環境保護
Ⓓ 讓員工跟上潮流

193. 陳女士最有可能對哪一個課程感興趣？

Ⓐ 領導力
Ⓑ 銷售
Ⓒ 客戶服務
Ⓓ 科技

194. 下列何者與訓練課程的提案及其後的備註有關？

Ⓐ 是個能完成的簡單課程
Ⓑ 將涵蓋五個重要的主題
Ⓒ 將有 50 名員工參與
Ⓓ 約書亞．約克將是其中一名訓練師

195. 根據訓練課程的提案及其後的備註，我們可以推論出澤聯禮品公司的什麼？

Ⓐ 他們試著改善客戶關係
Ⓑ 他們希望在訓練期間能正常營運
Ⓒ 客服員工人數不多
Ⓓ 他們想要在十月底前完成訓練

196–200 網頁、電子郵件和時間表

中城藝術表演廳

藉著加入會員來支持位於布倫頓市區的中城藝術表演廳，您可以從以下的會員方案裡選擇：

普級 – 只要 100 元，即可獲得整年度的會員資格，可以觀賞任兩場座位在 D 區的藝術表演。

銀級 – 200 元的費用，您可以觀賞任兩場座位在 B 區的藝術表演。

金級 – 500 元的費用，您可以收到熱門表演的預先通知、任兩場座位在 B 區的藝術表演票，並保證在一年內選到任何表演的前排座位。

鑽石級 – 1,000 元的費用，可以獨家取得表演者的親筆簽名，受邀參加兩場熱門演出的獨家試映會，並保證在一年內選到任何表演的貴賓 VIP 座位。

■ 適用部分限制規定
■ 不含管弦樂表演門票

收件者：bates@midcityarthall.com
寄件者：愛利希亞．諾頓
日期：1 月 16 日
主旨：會員

感謝您寄給我關於中城藝術表演廳的會員資訊，我已經繳交上 1,000 元的費用。去年我是普級會員，很喜歡幾場音樂劇。自從體驗過後，我就變成劇場狂熱者了，期待新的會員方案所帶來的福利。

順便一提，整修工程為表演廳增色不少。很期待今年回去看表演。

以下是未來幾個月中城藝術表演廳暫訂的節目表。請閱讀，如欲訂位，歡迎隨時來電洽詢。

《布倫頓愛樂管弦樂團》
1月28日至1月30日
《舞動的公主》
2月3日至2月23日
《舞吧爵士》
3月1日至3月26日
《歌劇之魂》
4月3日至4月29日

196. 愛利希雅．諾頓最可能購買的是何種會員？

(A) 普級
(B) 銀級
(C) 金級
(D) 鑽石級

197. 下列何者與中城表演藝術廳有關？

(A) 它舉辦過各種運動競賽
(B) 建築物有些改變
(C) 它是個受到名人喜愛的地方
(D) 它是個老舊的博物館

198. 對會員來說，何時的表演不是免費的？

(A) 一月
(B) 二月
(C) 三月
(D) 四月

199. 下列何者與時間表有關？

(A) 表演門票都已銷售一空
(B) 會增加更多的演出
(C) 時間表是固定
(D) 有可能會更改

200. 文中「適用部分限制規定」是什麼意思？

(A) 只有特定人士才能成為會員
(B) 會員方案可能在未告知狀況下異動
(C) 不是所有的演出都開放給會員
(D) 非會員者不可入場

ACTUAL TEST ⑧

PART 5 P.230–233

◎ **Part 5 解答請見 P.457**

101. 我們的講者將為房地產投資人說明一個**令人振奮的**良機。

102. 這個手提包所使用的部分皮革必須是自義大利**進口**的。

103. 洛克威爾銀行的自動櫃員機**便利地**設置於這個城市的不同區域。

104. 待雙方達成**一致的**協議，就立即簽訂這個授權合約。

105. 任何無法在 9 月 1 日之前**參加**安全訓練研習的人必須告知主管。

106. 使用飯店水療中心與用餐服務的**費用**，將列在最終發票上。

107. 保全小組的成員已被囑咐要將**任何**無人看管的包包呈報當地警局。

108. 主廚每天晚上都請餐廳經理**批准**食材的訂單。

109. 這家汽車公司**積極地**追求能夠改善引擎效能的科技。

110. 在繪畫課程的第一天，學生們應該把**報名**證明給老師看。

111. 這間公寓的家具並不是**我們的**而是房東的，必須在租約到期時歸還。

112. 德懷特先生**的**司機預計在結束前 20 分鐘抵達會議地點。

113. **合作**研發新材料的三位新進的化學家，將於週六的典禮上接受執行長的表揚。

114. 這個計劃的目的是要讓住在鄉間與都市**地區**的人，都馬上能得到醫療服務。

115. 請將金額 550 英鎊的支票**及**需要本公司檢核的文件**一併**寄上。

116. 在這國家的實驗室，指紋辨認系統普遍**被接受**當作保全措施的主要方法。

117. 住在遠離市中心的地方將**減少**租屋開銷，但卻會影響你通勤。

118. 煎友的廚具可以直接從該公司的網站購得，也可以在您**附近的**零售點購買。

119. 每週的設備**檢查**有助於確保及早發現及處理細微的維修問題。

120. 病人如果察覺到**突然的**體溫變化，應立即撥打緊急專線。

121. 參加歷史導覽半日遊的人，必須**最晚在**早上 7:45 **前**必須到集合地點。

122. 由於他的**重大**成就，主管允許馬丁先生多休三天假。

123. 史蒂文斯女士**懊悔地**承認她無法在特定的期間內完成這個任務。

124. 這個客人的牛排煎的火侯**有些**不足，所以要求將餐點送回廚房。

125. 這個問卷調查所提供的聯絡資料僅供公司內部使用，不會**透露**給第三方。

126. 只要有一套工具，布蘭諾先生就可以**自己**組裝攤位的隔板。

127. 史蒂文森女士聯絡了**那個**名字和電話出現在廣告上的房地產仲介。

128. 當正式文件被登錄在郡辦公室時，房屋的出售就已**定案**。

129. 工作坊中進行的主要活動需要團隊成員相互**合作**。

130. 根據內科醫師表示，奧利佛女士的疼痛**將**在吃完藥的兩個小時內**緩解**。

131–134 廣告

國際商品展

如果您想把自己的包裝商品推廣到國際，就來參加第八屆年度國際商品展吧。這個商展將從3月5日到3月7日，在紐約市中心的銀河會議中心舉行。來自世界各地兩百多家公司代表參展，在您推銷自家產品給有興趣的顧客和商家之時，您也可以建立商業網絡。產品以包裝商品為主，範圍從甜點、零食到罐頭肉品與肉乾。快趁所有攤位被登記一空前申請，攤位有限，而且很快就沒了。

131. A 推銷
B 正在推銷
C 欲推銷
D 已推銷

132. **A 代理**
B 表達
C 遞送
D 顯露

133. A 到
B 為了
C 從
D 和……一起

134. A 會場禁止冰淇淋。
B 您可以在參觀時試吃商品。
C 您有機會推廣食品。
D 快趁所有攤位被登記一空前申請。

135–138 告示

寄件者：副總裁喬登・史密斯
收件者：K集團員工
主旨：公司整修
日期：2月26日

致全體同仁：

本週末我們二樓辦公室的整修工程即將開工，我們要求各位將所有重要文件帶回家，並且把桌上零散的資料歸檔。所有的電子產品都要關閉，並將插頭拔掉。此外，所有的櫃子與抽屜也要上鎖。

這個整修工程大約需要五天的時間。在這段期間，各位的臨時辦公處就在一樓的會議室。由於噪音干擾，如果您預定下週與客戶會面，請安排至公司以外的其他地點。我們為所有的不便深感抱歉，但也懇請各位配合。感謝大家。

135. A 已經開始
B 即將開始
C 開始
D 開始

136. **A 此外**
B 因此
C 因為
D 因此

137. A 如果需要更多空間，我們會通知大家。
B 所有的業務都將暫停，直到整修完成。
C 在這段期間，各位的臨時辦公處就在一樓的會議室。
D 整修後，各位的辦公場所會看起來嶄新且變得更好。

138. A 服務
B 聯合
C 連結
D 合作

139–142 告示

律師職缺

強生暨慈愛公共有限公司目前有一個合同律師的職缺。理想的應徵者需具備至少三年處理複雜商業交易的經驗，有公家單位服務經驗者尤佳。我們在強生暨慈愛公司處理的合約型態，僅限於私人企業與政府之間的業務關係。如果您認為自己合乎加入本團隊的資格，請寄電子郵件給本公司人資部經理 JK@law.com。

139. **A 工作**
B 工作
C 工作
D 工作

140. **A 有公家單位服務經驗者尤佳。**
B 和孩子互動可以替你的履歷增色。
C 必須具備應付動物的經驗。
D 有與身障人士共事過的經驗會加分。

141. **A 執行**
B 達成
C 允許
D 改變

142. **A 您**
B 我
C 我們
D 他們

143–146 電子郵件

收件者：bobsaget@BobsJobs.com
寄件者：HarrisonG@gmail.com
日期：9 月 20 日
主旨：業務企劃

親愛的薩格先生：

我叫哈里遜．谷巴蒂。我寫這封信是要回應您刊登在《泰晤士報》上新人事經理一職的廣告。我有五年在步調快速企業環境中工作的經驗。我知道貴公司僱用了 300 多名員工，其中有許多是講西班牙文的，我有取得西班牙文口語的五級證照，已隨信附上履歷表，如果您有需求，我也很樂意提供推薦函。感謝您撥冗閱讀。

哈里遜．谷巴蒂 敬上

143. A 發訊息
B 寫
C 寫
D 看

144. **A 經驗**
B 知識
C 工作
D 實習

145. **A 我有取得西班牙文口語的五級證照。**
B 西班牙人有時很難合作。
C 我不懂任何西班牙文，但我可以學。
D 講西班牙文的人都是好員工。

146. A 在……之內
B 為了給
C 為了
D 將會

147–148 資訊

新款的聖桑尼克曲面電視現正以驚人的超低價 1,999 元出售。用 55 吋超高畫質的螢幕享受您最喜歡的電視節目、電影和比賽吧！最棒的是，您不必費力搞懂複雜的操作手冊。只要把電視機帶回家並安裝好，不需任何惱人的調整就可以立即依照您的喜好播放節目。

147. 這則資訊最可能在哪裡出現？

A 操作手冊
B 商品收據
C 宣傳單
D 信件

148. 文中提到產品有什麼便利之處？

A 簡單的設置程序
B 長期保固
C 與其他器材的相容性
D 詳細的操作說明

149–150 訊息串

湯姆．阿諾 **11:55**
你今天會回辦公室嗎？

理查．休伊特 **12:08**
會。我剛向安德森和萊特做完有關河濱餐廳的提案報告。

湯姆．阿諾 **12:13**
很好。進行得如何？

理查．休伊特 **12:13**
我想他們可能有意願。

湯姆．阿諾 **12:13**
好。有他們加入這個計劃就太棒了。

理查．休伊特 **12:14**
沒錯！

湯姆．阿諾 **12:35**
你可以和哈羅德跟我在一點時去釜室吃午餐嗎？

理查．休伊特 **12:35**
沒問題。我請計程車掉頭，跟你們在那裡碰面。

湯姆．阿諾 **12:39**
好。待會見。

149. 下列何者與休伊特先生有關？

A 他的午餐約遲到了
B 他接受了一個新職位
C 他在計程車上
D 他正在去做簡報的路上

150. 在 12:14 時，休伊特先生寫下：「沒錯」是什麼意思？

A 他想知道他們在哪裡吃午餐
B 他期待和安德森與萊特會面
C 他正在回辦公室的路上
D 他也希望安德森與萊特能加入計劃

151–152 文章

紐約書展開幕會的熱門話題，全圍繞在詩人轉小說家哈利．S．泰伯的新書上。書迷殷切期盼的《秋之夜鶯》，是他最暢銷的小說處女作《春之燕》的續集。這本書跟著莎莉．哈奈特一起展開奇幻的「地伏世界」之旅，並結合了尖銳機智的社論，及些許魔幻與神秘。十年多前，泰伯以備受好評的詩集《哈蒙王的城堡》嶄露頭角，而這本最新的小說也被預期將登上週暢銷排行榜。本週稍晚，本書首刷將成為紐約書展抽獎的獎品，下個月即將於各大書店正式發行。

151. 泰伯先生最新的作品將如何被歸類？

A 浪漫愛情
B 歷史小說
C 奇幻小說
D 詩集

152. 本週在哪裡可看到書？

A 各大書店
B 網站
C 文學活動
D 選定的公立圖書館

153–154 電子郵件

收件者：所有訂戶
寄件者：客服部
<customersupport@stylefashionmz.com>
日期：6月5日
主旨：新版

親愛的忠實訂戶：

《風格與時尚雜誌》很開心地宣布，本月刊的新數位版本即將於今年夏季發行。雖然紙本與數位版幾近相同，但數位版將包含了一些紙本未刊登的長篇文章及圖片。

本雜誌目前的紙本訂戶將自動收到一組代碼，可直接獲得數位版本。您的代碼將附於下個月寄達的雜誌中。

153. 這封電子郵件的目的是什麼？

(A) 提供訂閱優惠價
(B) 宣傳新開的網路購物商場
(C) 介紹數位出版品
(D) 提醒訂戶續訂

154. 訂戶可以在七月號的紙本雜誌中找到什麼？

(A) 優惠折價券
(B) 特刊
(C) 獨家專訪
(D) 代碼

155–158 文章

節日公車增班

11月28日——雖然對很多人而言，節慶季代表了一整週的美好長假，但公車司機將在整個假期裡延長工作時間，以因應每年這個時節湧入市區的大批遊客，以及忙著在最後一刻採買禮物的購物者。市府已經宣布接下來幾週的新公車時刻表，其中包括將全天候營運的部分公車路線。雖然大部分的公車將行駛至凌晨一點收班，市中心的部分地區將有公車運行，整夜不收班，賓漢購物區的公車將延駛至凌晨三點收班。「這是我們有最多遊客與外地人到訪的時節，」市長比爾．奈特說，「我們認為在這段時間中提供必要的服務是很重要的。」

當公車司機工會會長納森．雷納被問到對新時刻表的看法時，他回道，「我們已經制定出雙方都同意的薪資，也有足夠的司機可以排班，所以不會有過度工作或過勞的危險。我們很多人還是有例假，可以和家人共度佳節。」整體而言，隨著聖誕節的接近，這個城市似乎已經準備好迎接遊客與節慶購物入潮了。

155. 這篇文章的目的是什麼？

(A) 報導公共交通運輸的異動
(B) 描述節日中的城市狀況
(C) 告知大眾交通延遲
(D) 為新的購物中心打廣告

156. 下列何者與雷納先生有關？

(A) 他對市長很滿意
(B) 他可能會發動抗議
(C) 他對工作條件感到滿意
(D) 他想要在節日中休假

157. 文中提到這個城市在節慶季中是怎樣的？

(A) 在節日期間關閉
(B) 很多遊客自外地來
(C) 更多計程車司機業績下滑
(D) 市民要到其他城市去旅行

158. 下列句子最適合出現在 [1]、[2]、[3]、[4] 的哪個位置？「整體而言，隨著聖誕節的接近，這個城市似乎已經準備好迎接遊客與節慶購物的人潮了。」

(A) [1]
(B) [2]
(C) [3]
(D) [4]

159–161 時間表

19 台節目時間表

三月三日

上午 6:00 – 上午 7:00
《阿拉斯加的生活》

關注住在阿拉斯加偏遠凍原的漁夫肯．拉斯金的生活。

上午 7:00 – 上午 9:00
《非洲奇景》

了解非洲大草原上的各類動植物。

上午 9:00 – 上午 10:30
《恐龍解剖學》

在這一集中，古生物學家凱瑞．彼得森博士將告訴您有關暴龍的一切。

上午 10:30 – 上午 11:00
《洛基》

主持人丹．里德將説明如何在加拿大戶外寒冬的極端條件下生存。

上午 11:00 – 下午 1:00
《自然現象》

主持人茱莉亞．富朗研究了發生在地球上最神秘的自然現象。

下午 1:00– 下午 2:00
《湛藍海洋》

與我們一起遨遊澳洲海域吧，與潛水員派特．羅素一起探索海豚、鯊魚、海豹，還有許多生物。

159. 這個頻道的重點是什麼？

A 植物
B 運動
C 大自然
D 生活

160. 根據這個時間表，哪一位是科學家？

A 派特．羅素
B 丹．里德
C 凱瑞．彼得森
D 肯．拉斯金

161. 哪個節目將教導觀眾求生技巧？

A 《恐龍解剖學》
B 《非洲奇景》
C 《湛藍海洋》
D 《洛基》

162–165 網路討論區

J&R 國際小組討論區

桑妮．李	[5:37]	有人不能參加週五的辦公室派對嗎？
凱文．金	[5:38]	我第一個小時可以參加，但我得提早離席去參加家庭聚會。
派翠克．史東	[5:39]	我隔天要到香港出差，所以我今年就免了。
桑妮．李	[5:42]	那還有其他人嗎？我只是要確定我們有足夠的點心。伊娃，你聯絡外燴公司了嗎？
伊娃．山德森	[5:43]	我打電話給好幾家，但只有四葉外燴提供素食。
桑妮．李	[5:44]	那我們就試試那家吧，我想我們有些人是吃素的。
荷莉．強生	[5:45]	我通常不太表明自己對食物的偏好，不過這次我希望有素食的選擇。
伊娃．山德森	[5:46]	我同意，我想這應該會讓這一切變得更有意思。我自己也想嘗試吃素，這對我來説會是個很好的開始。
荷莉．強生	[5:47]	嗯，這並不容易，不過我會到場支持你。
伊娃．山德森	[5:47]	謝啦，那我就跟外燴業者訂餐了。
安傑羅．史密斯	[5:48]	但要確保有肉食給我們這些無肉不歡的人喔。

伊娃・山德森	[5:49]	沒問題。我已經把暫定的菜單以電子郵件寄給大家了，大多數的人好像還蠻喜歡的。
桑妮・李	[5:50]	別忘了寄電子郵件通知外燴業者，他們進入大樓時需要通過安全檢查。
伊娃・山德森	[5:51]	我現在就去處理。

162. 這段討論主要是關於什麼？

Ⓐ 那些無法參加派對的人
Ⓑ 最佳外燴業者
Ⓒ 成為素食者
Ⓓ 為派對訂餐

163. 在 5:39 分時，派翠克・史東寫下：「我今年就免了」是什麼意思？

Ⓐ 他會到場一下
Ⓑ 他這次婉拒參加
Ⓒ 他會遲到
Ⓓ 他想要免費通行證

164. 文中提到什麼和四葉外燴有關？

Ⓐ 它提供素食
Ⓑ 它只有素食
Ⓒ 它曾為辦公室派對提供過外燴
Ⓓ 它擅長處理特殊訂單

165. 伊娃・山德森接下來最有可能會做什麼？

Ⓐ 處理菜單
Ⓑ 聯絡外燴業者
Ⓒ 確認會議
Ⓓ 訂午餐

166–168 合約

點石成金網路服務供應商
契約摘要

日期：3 月 22 日
顧客：譚雅・蘇利文小姐
地址：54055 懷俄明州帕森市橡樹街 345 號
購買日期：3 月 13 日

購買服務：

項目	價格
點石成金網路多媒體套組	40.00 元／月
■ 下載速度 100MB	
■ 32 個免費電影頻道	
■ 每月五部最新電影的串流服務	
防毒軟體	5.00 元／月
數據機與路由器租借服務	3.00 元／月
小計	48.00 元／月
稅	3.45 元／月
總計	51.45 元／月

只要撥打 341-555-6487，我們的技術人員就會到府處理任何經由數據機與路由器連接上網的問題。

166. 蘇利文女士在 3 月 13 日做了什麼？

Ⓐ 她購買居家保全系統
Ⓑ 她退還商品
Ⓒ 她簽訂網路服務合約
Ⓓ 她預約服務

167. 下列何者與蘇利文女士有關？

Ⓐ 她教授電腦技能課程
Ⓑ 她在安裝部分軟體上碰到麻煩
Ⓒ 她將可以看電影
Ⓓ 她最近剛搬家

168. 下列何者與點石成金網路服務供應商有關？

Ⓐ 它會派人員進行安裝工作
Ⓑ 它販售電腦配件
Ⓒ 它的總部就在帕森市
Ⓓ 它提供了網站架設服務

169–171 文章

4 月 2 日——馬里安市中心頗具歷史意義的馬里安會堂即將於下週五展開修復工程。在它的全盛時期，馬里安會堂是市中心頗受居民歡迎的場所，他們在那裡跳舞、欣賞現場音樂跟看電影。但是，自從四年前亨森街上的複合式大樓完工後，它就逐漸失去人氣了。

在馬里安會堂完成所有必要的整修工程後，市府官員將開始邀請不同的表演者（包括知名劇團、音樂家、喜劇演員和演講者）前來新整修的劇院。「我們希望馬里安會堂能夠成為馬里安市的新文化中心。」馬里安市長格雷葛．菲爾斯說。

重振馬里安會堂是改善馬里安市公共設施大型計劃中的一部分。4 月 29 日那天，以棒球場和數個遊樂場為特色的馬里安兒童樂園，預定將重新盛大開放。

169. 何者與馬里安市有關？

A 即將修復一棟舊建築
B 已關閉一座公園好進行修復
C 正在規劃音樂節
D 人口正在下降

170. 馬里安會堂的用途是什麼？

A 作為兒童遊樂中心
B 舉辦市議會會議
C 提供公共教育課程
D 舉辦文化活動

171. 四月將發生什麼事？

A 知名的演說家將發表演說
B 要選新市長
C 一些改善後的公共設施將開放使用
D 將上演一齣新戲

172–175 企業會報中的文章

我相信你已經知道，我們必須在本週決定是否繼續和 CC 貨運公司合作。正如我們在昨天的會議上所了解的，他們將為上週所發生的事故被起訴。我們都同意整個公司不應該為幾個粗心的員工所犯的過錯負責，但是這個想法是出現在我們討論過這個決定的後果之前。不幸地是，現在情況惡化了，而且也出現許多負面報導。沒錯，我們已經跟他們合作很久了，他們之中有許多人確實也是我們的朋友。但是，我們必須保護自己的公司。我們無法承受任何可能影響銷售量的事情。

這四個月來，我們幾乎沒有犯錯的餘地，即便銷售量只掉了一點點，後果可能不堪設想。所以我建議，作為保護本公司不受任何負面反應傷害的方法，我們應該與 CC 貨運公司劃清界限。也許日後如果他們能夠恢復名聲，我們再和他們合作。我提議針對要不要和他們合作一事再投一次票。

172. 關於 CC 貨運公司，下列何者為真？

A 他們其中一個合約剛被取消
B 有人對他們提起法律行動
C 他們的總裁退位了
D 他們有兩部卡車發生意外

173. 下列何者與撰文者服務的公司有關？

A 有財務危機
B 最近才被創立
C 將停止營業
D 是一家貨運公司

174. 撰文者為什麼希望停止和 CC 貨運公司合作？

A 保護他的公司免於財務損害
B 減少接下來四個月的生產成本
C 降低個別產品的價格
D 避免未來法律糾紛

175. 下列句子最適合出現在 [1]、[2]、[3]、[4] 的哪個位置？「沒錯，我們已經跟他們合作很久了。」

A [1]
B [2]
C [3]
D [4]

176–180 文章和電子郵件

9 月 21 日——美味自製餐點的秘密到底是什麼？電視節目主持人暨連鎖餐廳老闆金柏莉・李，似乎知道所有的秘密。她的節目已經開播兩年多，現在擁有一群來自全國各地的死忠追隨者。當她坐下來接受我們的專訪時，她表示新鮮蔬菜和在地農產品就是烹煮健康美味食物的關鍵。

李女士預計於月底出版她的第一本烹飪書。這本書的書名就叫《金柏莉・李的家常菜》，書中提供了可以在 30 分鐘內完成的簡易食譜。到目前為止，預購數量已經超過 40,000 本。

李女士表示，書的末頁有一張可撕下的粉絲俱樂部會員申請表。填寫申請表並寄到指定地址的人，將收到一份月訊與粉絲俱樂部會員專屬的獨家食譜。粉絲俱樂部的會員也將收到「我的家常菜」網站的登入密碼。

收件者：金柏莉・李
<kimberlylee@kimberlylee.com>
寄件者：蘇西・桑德斯
<suziesanders@kimberlylee.com>
日期：10 月 12 日

主旨：最新狀況

親愛的李女士：

好消息！很開心地向您報告，您的書不僅熱賣，自從書出版後加入粉絲俱樂部的新會員人數也急遽增加。我相信報上的文章為您的書增加了相當的曝光率。

同時，我們也收到了許多新會員的回饋意見，表達希望下個月的會訊能刊出更多蛋糕、餅乾和糖果的食譜。我想，滿足他們這次的需求會是個好主意。

公關協調員
蘇西・桑德斯 敬上

176. 這篇文章的主要目的是什麼？

A 宣傳即將出版的書
B 為專業廚師提供意見
C 為新餐廳打廣告
D 描述電視節目

177. 根據李女士所說，成功烹飪的秘密是什麼？

A 仿效食譜
B 使用優質的食材
C 調衡所有的味道
D 選擇正確的香料

178. 若要成為粉絲俱樂部會員必須怎麼做？

A 登入網站
B 撥打熱線電話
C 造訪李女士的餐廳
D 買書

179. 在電子郵件中，蘇西・桑德斯說了什麼有關那篇文章的事？

A 那是由知名記者所寫的
B 它被刊登在一個熱門的烹飪網站上
C 它對增加粉絲俱樂部的會員有所助益
D 它節錄了李女士書中內容

180. 文中提到什麼與下個月會訊有關的事？

A 將會比預定時間晚寄
B 將有一個關於健康飲食習慣的專欄
C 將包含一篇有關甜點的文章
D 將附上一本李女士的書

181–185 電子郵件

寄件者：史黛西．沃金斯
<staceywatkins@titus.com>
收件者：安．羅斯
<annrose@putkincomp.com>
主旨：銀行主管會議
日期：2 月 12 日

親愛的羅斯女士：

您最近聯絡我們，提到今年想再次使用我們的會議中心來舉辦銀行主管年會。今年我們已經為會議室換新的投影機和更舒適的座椅。我們還將提供機場的接駁公車服務、高級餐廳自助餐，以及網咖讓來賓可以免費使用電腦或列印文件。為了您的方便，我們還提供實用的設備，像是掛紙白板、10 英尺的白板以及投影屏幕。

一旦您決定好日期，在我們確認能配合後，將請您先付 1,000 元的訂金，您來的時候再支付餘額。同時我們也要求身為活動籌辦人的您，在會議開始前一天到會議中心，以事先處理任何意外狀況。

感謝您再次與鐵達時會議中心合作，我們期盼提供您最好的服務。

史黛西．沃金斯主任

寄件者：安．羅斯
<annrose@putkincomp.com>
收件者：史黛西．沃金斯
<staceywatkins@titus.com>
主旨：回覆：銀行主管會議
日期：2 月 16 日

親愛的沃金斯女士：

我也很高興今年能再度與您合作。我們想預約 8 月 15 和 16 日這個週末的會議中心。訂金是由我們的財務部門負責處理，我會請本公司同仁盡快跟您聯絡。

同時，有件事想請您幫忙。去年因為餐廳沒有提供足夠的素食選擇，讓我們部分的與會者頗為失望。我希望今年可以提前處理這個問題。

感謝您。

銀行主管年會　籌辦人
安．羅斯

181. 下列何者與鐵達時會議中心有關？

(A) 最近改善了設備
(B) 預約時需支付全額款項
(C) 位於國際機場旁
(D) 目前八月全滿

182. 下列何者不是使用鐵達時會議中心的優點？

(A) 便利的交通
(B) 筆記型電腦租借服務
(C) 列印服務
(D) 簡報設備

183. 羅斯女士最有可能何時抵達鐵達時會議中心？

(A) 8 月 7 日
(B) 8 月 14 日
(C) 8 月 15 日
(D) 8 月 16 日

184. 第二封電子郵件的目的是什麼？

(A) 為即將到來的研討會預約門票
(B) 請求協助付款
(C) 確認預約
(D) 詢問付款方式

185. 羅斯女士提到什麼有關鐵達時會議中心的事？

(A) 她第一次在這裡辦活動
(B) 將於八月遷移
(C) 在全國有數個據點
(D) 去年無法讓一些賓客滿意

186–190 電子郵件和備忘錄

收件者：約翰．馬斯特森
<jmasterson@masterstrokeindustries.com>
寄件者：卡爾．艾尼斯
<cennens@gmail.com>
日期：12 月 30 日
主旨：實習

親愛的馬斯特森先生：

我叫卡爾．艾尼斯，即將升上長春州立大學四年級。我在這裡主修工業工程學，而我的流體動力學教授艾可赫巴博士向我推薦神技企業，認為貴公司是個適合實習的單位。貴公司被公認為流體研究的翹楚，如果您願意在接下來的春季學期接受實習生，並能夠寫表現評估報告讓我交給艾可赫巴博士抵學分的話，我可以一週工作多達 15 個小時。感謝您給予考慮。如果您想要看成績單的話，我很樂意轉寄給您。

祝安好。

卡爾．艾尼斯

收件者：卡爾．艾尼斯
<cennens@gmail.com>
寄件者：約翰．馬斯特森
<jmasterson@masterstrokeindustries.com>
日期：12 月 31 日
主旨：回覆：實習

親愛的卡爾：

感謝你對本公司神技企業的實習工作感興趣。我們以往不太收實習生，不過我認識艾可赫巴博士本人，如果他推薦你跟我們聯絡，那他一定對你的能力非常有信心。我想我們應該在本公司位於市中心合利街的總部安排面試，我們可以邊喝咖啡邊認識彼此，我也會帶你看看我們公司。別擔心成績單的事，就像我說的，如果艾可赫巴博士認為你適合的話，我相信他的判斷。這週五早上十點方便嗎？

期待見到你。

神技企業執行長
約翰．馬斯特森

給神技企業全體員工的備忘錄

今年春季神技企業將有一位實習生協助我們處理大小事，包括從煮咖啡到解出複雜的方程式。卡爾．艾尼斯是本地州立大學的學生，他願意提供服務來交換我們的實務知識。請對他以禮相待，如果有需要，別怕請他幫忙提供見解或意見。而且我聽說他泡得一手好咖啡喔！

186. 下列何者與卡爾．艾尼斯有關？

Ⓐ 他是高三生
Ⓑ 他將成為大三生
Ⓒ 他再兩年就畢業了
Ⓓ 他將成為大四生

187. 下列何者與艾可赫巴博士有關？

Ⓐ 沒人知道他是誰
Ⓑ 人們不喜歡他的意見
Ⓒ 他受到約翰．馬斯特森的尊敬
Ⓓ 他已經做了很多重要的研究

188. 在第二封電子郵件中，第四行的「headquarters」意思最接近？

Ⓐ 地下室
Ⓑ 總公司
Ⓒ 倉庫
Ⓓ 物流中心

189. 根據備忘錄的內容，卡爾．艾尼斯被期待要做哪些事？

Ⓐ 研究流體力學
Ⓑ 烹飪
Ⓒ 有需要他幫忙的地方就幫忙
Ⓓ 觀察學習

190. 約翰．馬斯特森在公司擔任什麼職務？

Ⓐ 執行長
Ⓑ 財務長
Ⓒ 業務主管
Ⓓ 老闆

191–195 文章、廣告和電子郵件

Brand-X 進駐

3 月 9 日——頗具人氣的丹麥護膚公司 Brand-X 終於在美國推出他們最暢銷的系列產品。這家有 88 年歷史的公司是丹麥的護膚領導品牌，十多年來他們最熱賣的乳霜 Xtreme 7 一直是歐洲最受歡迎的面霜。儘管美國人以前可能沒機會接觸這些乳霜，但這個品牌已經引起相當熱潮。

皮膚科醫師法蘭西斯．基南解釋：「測試結果顯示，在只使用 Xtreme 7 30 天後，眼週的細紋和笑紋明顯地減少了，但乳霜的價格卻只是百貨公司品牌的一小部分。我當然推薦這款乳霜給我的客人。」

「產品都還沒到貨，大家就已經在詢問 Xtreme 7 了，」一位美容專櫃的櫃員蘇珊．陳說，「人們已經來電預購了。」

公司發言人解釋，Brand-X 正進軍北美與亞洲市場。目前只有公司最暢銷的系列產品會在歐洲以外的地方上市（自下個月起），但在一年後將可以買到更多商品。

Brand-X 在美國加州西敏市總部的職缺

不要錯過在刺激的護膚美容行業 Brand-X 的工作機會，有 80 個行政與客服職缺等著您，且不限經驗，應徵者需要有良好的溝通技巧，懂電腦操作。具英文與西班牙雙語能力尤佳，但非必要。若有化妝品、皮膚科或行銷經驗的應徵者，可有資格從事主管職。更多資訊，請參考本公司網站 www.brandx.com/jobs。申請表需於 3 月 20 日前送交。面試將於花園路 143 號的希爾威大樓舉行，請記得攜帶履歷與推薦函。

收件者：大衛．米爾斯教授
寄件者：賈桂琳．歐海爾
日期：3 月 28 日
主旨：工作

親愛的米爾斯教授：

非常感謝您幫我寫推薦信。我最近被 Brand-X 錄取，下週三上午 10 點就要開始新進員工訓練。但是很不巧地，那個時間我們剛好有統計學考試。是不是有方法可以讓我在其他時間補考，或是用交作業的方式來代替考試？新進員工訓練是強制參加的，而我不想讓新老闆失望。除此之外，這份工作應該不會對我的學校課業有任何影響。我衷心地感謝您能考慮這件事。

賈桂琳．歐海爾 敬上

191. 基南醫師提到了有關 Xtreme 7 的什麼事？

(A) 它是市面上最有效的面霜
(B) 它值得高價
(C) 它有效又便宜
(D) 它是醫生唯一會推薦的乳霜

192. 文中提到下列何者與 Brand-X 有關？

(A) 商品目前只能在歐洲買到
(B) 它是歐洲最受歡迎的品牌
(C) 它是高檔護膚公司
(D) 它十年前首次上市

193. 根據文章內容，Brand-X 打算做什麼？

(A) 在歐洲販售更多商品
(B) 拓展到歐洲以外
(C) 開發彩妝系列商品
(D) 在美國建廠

194. 下列何者與廣告有關？

(A) 所有的職務都不需經驗
(B) 應徵者必須是雙語人士
(C) 在特定領域有經驗的人可以得到管理職
(D) 可應徵的職務都是暫時性的

195. 賈桂琳最有可能被錄取了什麼職務？

Ⓐ 管理
Ⓑ 人資
Ⓒ 行銷
Ⓓ 客服

196–200 電子郵件和時間表

收件者：比爾．強生 <bj@action.net>
寄件者：羅莉．惠勒
<lwheeler@zipnet.com>
日期：10 月 11 日
主旨：預約資訊

親愛的強生先生：

本人謹代表所服務的公司競爭優勢公司寫信給您。我們專為公司與小型企業進行生產力與效率訓練。最近，我們的員工士氣低落。在網路上搜尋解決辦法時，我看到了貴公司的網站 www.action.net。我很想多了解你們激勵人心的演講。特別是想請您告訴我，你們的演講是否屬於宗教性質？我們有各類員工，我需要的是非宗教性質的演講。請回信告訴我你們的服務內容概要以及演講費用。

競爭優勢常務董事
羅莉．惠勒

收件者：羅莉．惠勒
<lwheeler@zipnet.com>
寄件者：比爾．強生 <bj@action.net>
日期：10 月 13 日
主旨：回覆：預約資訊

親愛的惠勒女士：

非常感謝您對行動公司的興趣。我很樂意回答您的疑問，並為您、您的團隊以及貴公司提供一份完整的服務內容分析。首先，我們所有的演講雖然無法撇開心靈的概念，但卻是屬於非宗教性的內容。我們的專業講師試圖激勵人們觀看內在，找到自己的心性，並協助其提升。畢竟士氣實屬無形，卻也是有效率的團隊不可或缺的部分。請參考我隨電子郵件附上的課程主題表以及價目表。一旦您選好主題、講者和適合貴公司的課程規模，請發後續電郵給我以便安排您的活動。

行動公司專員
比爾．強生

行動公司課程主題及價目表

主題	地點	演講者	人數	演講時間	價格
把握當下！	現場	吉姆．葛雷	15–20	三小時	450 元
每天都是全新的自己	非現場	達琳．伍德沃德	20–25	三小時	400 元
為團隊而積極！	非現場	傑夫．巴舍	15–30	三小時	400 元
我們都幸福	非現場	約翰．布朗	20–30	四小時	500 元

196. 羅莉．惠勒是怎麼知道行動公司的？

Ⓐ 從朋友那
Ⓑ 透過客戶
Ⓒ 在報紙上
Ⓓ 在網路上

197. 下列何者與行動公司有關？

Ⓐ 他們不推廣宗教
Ⓑ 他們是基督徒
Ⓒ 他們正在建立自己的品牌
Ⓓ 他們正搬到新址

198. 根據圖表，哪一個不是客戶有的選項？

Ⓐ 非現場課程
Ⓑ 十人課程
Ⓒ 四個小時的課程
Ⓓ 建立積極性的課程

199. 羅莉．惠勒可能會報名何種課程？

Ⓐ 把握當下！
Ⓑ 每天都是全新的自己
Ⓒ 為團隊而積極！
Ⓓ 我們都幸福

200. 下列何者與競爭優勢有關？

Ⓐ 他們財務困窘
Ⓑ 辦公室的氣氛不好
Ⓒ 他們今年業績大好
Ⓓ 他們想要改變業務重心

TEST 8
PART 7

ACTUAL TEST ⑨

PART 5 P.258–261

◎ Part 5 解答請見 P.457

101. 李德女士借的投影機**要在**五點前歸還給資訊科技部門。

102. 既然年會結束了，籌備委員會也就**不會那麼常**開會了。

103. 在你分發報告前，問一下伯恩斯女士以確認**報告**有全部所需的資料。

104. 據消費者表示，使用新網頁並不**比**直接打電話給服務中心**簡單**。

105. 參加**了**本市年度烘焙競賽者，將獲得新鮮超市折價券一張。

106. 市府官員們仍然就厄文企業要求**拆除**老舊大樓一事爭論著。

107. 蒼鷺玻璃廠**歡迎**各年齡層的學生團體，參加倉庫與生產區的平日導覽。

108. 為了對抗精神疾病，這診所將採取比過去更全面性的**策略**。

109. 布蘭蒂可以從沙利斯銀行的任何分行提款，但她通常是去離她**最近的**那間。

110. 做為他與許多新客戶簽約的**獎勵**，史金納先生得到了額外的假期。

111. 請依已放置在桌上的**個人**專屬名牌就坐。

112. 李先生所寄的備忘錄中提出了一些在季檢中發現的**問題**。

113. 這城市有很多對這些議題不感興趣的選民，其中大約只有 15% 的人**在政治上**很活躍。

114. 今年的得獎者雪若．迦納教導**整個**地區的學生與成人基本急救技巧。

115. **理想的狀況是**，這棟小木屋可以出租一整個月，但屋主只同意分成四週各別出租。

116. 這個非營利組織向新聞界發佈幾份文件，**詳細**說明大筆款項的捐贈者以及他們捐款的金額。

117. **一旦**機艙門已經關閉，乘客都不得再登機。

118. 一名政府**代表**將來到現場與抗議者直接對話並尋求解決方案。

119. 由伊旺尼可斯通訊所進行的大規模**民調**顯示，網路速度對消費者來說是最重要的影響因素。

120. 丹森先生想要從尤蒂卡錶店買一支特別版的鍍金手錶，但是卻**沒**貨了。

121. 梅女士提醒我們那份協議只是**暫定的**，因為它還沒有被核准。

122. 依照整修計劃，頗具歷史的柯克伍德飯店大廳看起來與它原始的模樣**神**似。

123. **在**適當的環境條件下，這棵樹一年當中大多可以結出新鮮的果實。

124. 有位實習生**指出**銷售報告第二頁上的商標顛倒了。

125. **當**停車場關閉時，員工和顧客將必須利用路邊停車。

126. 如果新款運動鞋在小型試售市場上表現良好，就可以**加速**在全國上市。

127. 這城市舉辦了**令人驚豔的**煙火表演來慶祝建城一百週年。

128. 在大量投資網路行銷活動後，貝利咖啡的年獲利成長**了** 15%。

129. 接待員**定期地**更換診所候診室的藝術品，並重新布置家具的擺放位置。

130. 要求企業提供醫療保險的規定，只適用於那些**聘僱** 25 人以上的公司。

PART 6 P.262–265

131–134 告示

貝芙莉精品服飾：誠徵銷售助理

本精品服飾店現正徵求充滿熱忱的銷售助理人員。應徵者必須親切，能夠在各種情況下與顧客交流。有相似工作經驗佳，無經驗可，須具組織能力及電腦使用經驗。最重要的是，我們需要品貌兼優、可讓顧客感到自在，並對時尚充滿熱情的人。工作職責包括服務顧客，記錄庫存以及店內零碎雜務，像是打掃和下班時鎖門。薪資將按銷售佣金計酬，能更激勵員工盡力提供顧客最棒的服務。工作時間彈性，若需要更多資訊，請參考本店網站。如果您對這職位有興趣，請將履歷寄到 rlan@bboutique.com 給瑞塔。

131. Ⓐ 本精品服飾是流行時尚的領導者。
Ⓑ 在促銷結束前，動作要快。
Ⓒ 應徵者必須親切，能夠在各種情況下與顧客交流。
Ⓓ 來參觀門市，看看我們的業務內容。

132. **Ⓐ 自在的**
Ⓑ 適當的
Ⓒ 忽視的
Ⓓ 方便的

133. Ⓐ 影響
Ⓑ 激勵
Ⓒ 堅持
Ⓓ 考量

134. Ⓐ 有趣的
Ⓑ 以前有趣的
Ⓒ 興趣
Ⓓ 感興趣

135–138 廣告

巧傭居家服務

請來電 555-1244

巧傭居家服務為您的公司或住家提供專業的清潔服務。我們以蒸汽吸塵器清理地毯區域、擦亮硬木地板、擦拭所有死角的灰塵與髒汙，並處理雜物。我們的優質服務在三州地區是首屈一指的。在估價後，我們會提供單日服務。此外，我們也為提出要求的顧客提供包週及包月的服務。

我們所使用的清潔用品都是環保的，對寵物和兒童都無害。事實上，我們致力讓住家或公司在不使用刺激性化學藥劑的情況下，成為安全又乾淨的地方。欲知更多資訊，請來電或上本公司網站 www.handymaids.com。

135. Ⓐ 提供
Ⓑ 提供
Ⓒ 提供過
Ⓓ 正提供

136. Ⓐ 不尋常
Ⓑ 特別的
Ⓒ 應最好的
Ⓓ 優秀的

137. **Ⓐ 此外**
Ⓑ 因為
Ⓒ 另一方面
Ⓓ 因此

138. Ⓐ 我們確保您的寵物與小孩不會接近化學藥劑。
Ⓑ 事實上，我們致力讓住家或公司在不使用刺激性化學的情況下，成為安全又乾淨的地方。
Ⓒ 我們的全天然清潔劑也許不如化學藥劑有效，但它們是安全的。
Ⓓ 在清潔時，孩童與寵物將被要求離開該地。

139–142 信件

10 月 9 日
鮑伯・普羅瑟

99705 阿拉斯加州費爾班克斯溫克勒大道 342 號

親愛的普羅瑟先生：

您要求變更狩獵許可計劃的相關資料已經隨函附上。請注意，每一張許可證都必須分開申請。填寫申請書時，請用黑筆或藍筆以大寫清楚地填寫，請勿使用書寫字體，只能以正楷字體書寫。每張申請書需放入個別的信封中，於申請截止日前收件。受理申請後，可能需要長達五週的時間處理。因此，您必須規劃適當的繳交時間，以確保您在收到許可證之時，仍然開放狩獵。希望附上的這些資料能答覆您所有的疑問。祝安好並狩獵愉快。

99701 阿拉斯加費爾班克斯野生動物部
執行秘書 雪莉・宏恩 敬上

139. Ⓐ 提供
Ⓑ 供應
Ⓒ 要求
Ⓓ 要求

140. Ⓐ 將不會
Ⓑ 可以是
Ⓒ 一定是
Ⓓ 不可能是

141. **Ⓐ 受理申請後，可能需要長達五週的時間處理。**
Ⓑ 在狩獵季結束前，決不會核准申請。
Ⓒ 申請書有時候會遺失。
Ⓓ 請勿親自申請。

142. Ⓐ 附上
Ⓑ 正附上
Ⓒ 附上
Ⓓ 被附上

143–146 告示

日期：8 月 22 日
收件者：業務團隊全體成員

寄件者：業務經理梅琳達・雷基

主旨：租賃規定

好一段時間裡，公司讓業務代表先用個人信用卡或現金支付他們租車的費用，之後再報帳核銷。這已非本公司的規定了，早在兩個月前就沒有此規定，至今已經取消兩個多月。自 6 月 15 日起，所有租車的費用要由分配給各位的公司信用卡支付。會計部的賴瑞通知我，自那之後，他還是收到了六筆核銷申請表。我已經先核准，讓賴瑞處理那六份申請表。但是從明天起，大家都不能再將租車的費用報帳了。很遺憾這封通知要用如此嚴厲的語氣，但我們在六月時就已經要求大家這麼做了。如果您還有任何問題，請直接和我聯絡。

143. Ⓐ 距離
Ⓑ 地方
Ⓒ 事件
Ⓓ 時間

144. Ⓐ 做出
Ⓑ 被做出
Ⓒ 做出
Ⓓ 已被做出

145. Ⓐ 以後只能跟方提那租車公司預約租車。
Ⓑ 但是從明天起，大家都不能再將租車的費用報帳了。
Ⓒ 他在下週初會重新設計表格。
Ⓓ 所有業務代表都必須盡快繳交自己的名片。

146. Ⓐ 誇大的
Ⓑ 親切的
Ⓒ 仁慈的
Ⓓ 嚴厲的

147–148 傳單

潔家具

60611 伊利諾州芝加哥密西根大道 3105 號

黑色星期五週末特賣
11 月 29 日至 12 月 1 日

桌子——八折
沙發——七折
床墊——五折至八折
書桌和椅子——五折至七五折

■ 特賣期間，消費滿 500 元的顧客，皆可獲得聖誕特賣會的 95 折折價券，其有效期限為 12 月 9 日至 12 月 28 日。

■ 特賣期間出示代碼 BLKFRI，就可多獲得桌子和床墊的 10 元抵扣優惠。

備註： 潔家具將在週末特賣會前一天暫停營業以做準備。11 月 29 日上午九點開門營業。

147. 這張傳單的目的是什麼？

(A) 宣布店家開幕
(B) 宣傳家具特賣
(C) 介紹新產品
(D) 通知顧客店家搬遷

148. 店家何時暫停營業？

(A) 11 月 28 日
(B) 11 月 29 日
(C) 11 月 30 日
(D) 12 月 9 日

149–150 訊息串

詹姆士 **11:01**
你在哪裡？

羅伯特 **11:25**
什麼意思？我整個早上都在這裡啊。

詹姆士 **11:26**
什麼？我到處都找不到你。

詹姆士 **12:00**
你在哪裡？

羅伯特 **12:03**
抱歉，我一直都和客戶在紅室。
無法收到你的訊息。

詹姆士 **12:04**
好，了解。我會在外面等。

羅伯特 **12:30**
你還在那裡嗎？

詹姆士 **12:31**
是啊，希望你已經成交了。

149. 詹姆士為什麼寫下：「希望你已經成交了」？

(A) 他覺得會有分紅獎金
(B) 他已經等很久了
(C) 他喜歡紅室
(D) 有太多交易未成交

150. 從詹姆士的訊息和羅伯特的回覆中間相隔的時間可推論出什麼？

(A) 羅伯特對詹姆士毫無興趣
(B) 羅伯特想要有自己的時間
(C) 羅伯特的電話壞了
(D) 羅伯特無法一直查看電話

151–152 電子郵件

收件者：營運小組
<operations@acemfg.com>
寄件者：湯瑪士．惠勒
<t.wheeler@acemfg.com>
日期：6 月 16 日星期一
主旨：新設備

致營運小組：

公司將於明天訂購一套新的重型設備，並於隔天下午送達倉庫。員工工作時間表將配合我們設備的新增有所調整。請在週四下午五點前送交一份報告，說明每位同仁與這套設備相關的新工作與職責。

如果我不在辦公室，請交給我的秘書哈蒂女士。

製造部 主管
湯瑪士．惠勒

151. 新設備最有可能何時抵達倉庫？

(A) 星期一
(B) 星期二
(C) 星期三
(D) 星期四

152. 報告裡應該包括了什麼？

(A) 員工的聯絡資料
(B) 員工的指派任務
(C) 員工的履歷表
(D) 員工的建議

153–154 備忘錄

收文者：研發部
發文者：研發部主管瑞克．坎貝爾
主旨：員工異動
日期：4 月 4 日星期二，下午 3:40

我寫這篇訊息是為了跟各位分享有關研發部門最近的異動消息。從 4 月 7 日起，鮑伯．丹坷將成為研發部的新專案經理。他剛完成了一個月的訓練講習，將於週末前頂替班傑明．帕瑪。

人力資源部主管麥克．賈西亞將於下週前公布不同部門的人事空缺。對那些有意轉調公司其他部門的人來說，現在正是申請的好時機。

請大家恭喜班傑明．帕瑪將轉任「離子企業」的新職，同時也歡迎鮑伯．丹坷加入本部門。

153 下週前預計會發生什麼事？

(A) 將成立新部門
(B) 將宣布職缺
(C) 將進行面試
(D) 將舉辦訓練講習

154. 誰將離開公司？

(A) 鮑伯．丹坷
(B) 麥克．賈西亞
(C) 瑞克．坎貝爾
(D) 班傑明．帕瑪

155–157 文章

Re-Fit 關閉店面

2 月 9 日——紐章集團剛宣布接下來六個月內即將關閉全國 80 家 Re-Fit 門市，今年內還有 100 家也會跟著結束營業。這家服飾店以價格合理但款式時髦的運動服飾出名，在 1990 年代和 2000 年代初期非常受歡迎。不過，在過去十年它們的業績下滑，因為顧客轉向其他服飾零售店像是扎納斯和 HRM 消費。「我不知道，我只是覺得那些衣服過時了。」一名以前的顧客說，「他們應該要更新款式，提供非運動風的選擇。」

執行長戴瑞克．格林威治同意說：「我們太過單獨專注在特定的運動風格上，以致於忽略了顧客喜好的改變。我們正努力重組公司，提供顧客想要的商品。我們會再次盛大回歸。」

針對虧損的內部檢討將持續進行，而不安的股東們也在考慮他們的下一步。紐章希望在公司致力於重新改造品牌之際，大部分的 Re-Fit 門市仍能維持營運。

155. 下列何者與 Re-Fit 這品牌有關？

A 它受歡迎的程度已經急遽下滑

B 專攻運動器材

C 執行長要為公司重新命名

D 這品牌有百年歷史

156. 在第二段的「lost sight of」意思最接近？

A 限制

B 沒被蒙蔽

C 忽略

D 挑選

157. 下列句子最適合出現在 [1]、[2]、[3]、[4] 的哪個位置？「這家服飾店以價格合理但款式時髦的運動服飾出名，在 1990 年代和 2000 年代初期非常受歡迎。」

A [1]

B [2]

C [3]

D [4]

158–160 小手冊目錄

目錄

9 簡單做點心」 唐諾．柯恩為總是忙碌的人們提供了適合的食譜。	**26 希望你也在** 瑞貝卡．巴拉哈斯分享她到紐西蘭絕妙旅程的照片。
14 完美渡假勝地 梅麗莎．格林討論了全球十大著名渡假勝地的特色。	**30 美味餐館** 貝瑞．伊森分享了旅程中的美食經驗。
19 護照指南 亨利．卡羅爾告訴你如何以五個簡單的步驟申請護照。	**33 預算有限** 愛德華．鮑伊分享秘訣，讓你在下次的旅遊中省錢。
23 安全第一 翠西亞．奧德蘭姆為旅遊新手說明基本急救法。	**35 照亮前路** 評論最受歡迎的旅遊指南。

158. 這本手冊的重點是什麼？

A 食物

B 交通

C 環境

D 旅遊

159. 可以在手冊中的何處找到照片？

A 第 9 頁

B 第 19 頁

C 第 26 頁

D 第 30 頁

160. 根據目錄的內容，誰寫了節省花費的議題？

A 格林女士

B 卡羅爾先生

C 伊森先生

D 鮑伊先生

161–164 網路討論區

金潔．林	[4:59]	只是想提醒大家在今天下班前清空桌子並關閉所有電子設備，整個地板要在這個週末清理打磨。
迪米崔．羅伯茲	[5:00]	我們也要將所有櫃子跟抽屜上鎖嗎？
金潔．林	[5:01]	是的，麻煩了。請確定家具搬動時，不會有東西掉出來。
迪米崔．羅伯茲	[5:02]	我會在離開前確定所有東西都已放妥且上鎖。
珍娜．李	[5:03]	金潔，我已經做好預算報告了。在我送出前，我會以電子郵件寄一份給妳。
金潔．林	[5:04]	謝謝。對了藍斯，你必須重新安排你明天和客戶的會議。
藍斯．西伯利	[5:04]	我已經把會議重新安排到下週一了。為了慎重起見，以防辦公室屆時還沒弄好，我們將在附近的咖啡廳會面。
金潔．林	[5:05]	好。看起來大部分的事情都已就緒。如果我遺漏了什麼，請告訴我。

珍娜・李	[5:06]	事實上，還有人沒有給我加班時數。我是可以透過簽到表確認，但是在我將薪資表送到財務部前，我需要大家利用電子郵件確認。
迪米崔・羅伯茲	[5:07]	喔！就是我。我現在就寄電子郵件給你。
凱倫・沃克	[5:07]	我也是。
珍娜・麗	[5:08]	好。我一收到你們的電子郵件，就可以把表單送出去。

161. 星期六和星期日會發生什麼事？

A 辦公室派對
B 與客戶會面
C 整修
D 清潔服務

162. 金潔・林最有可能是誰？

A 秘書
B 經理
C 技術人員
D 保全警衛

163. 在 5:04 時，藍斯・西伯利寫下：「為了慎重起見」是什麼意思？

A 辦公室可能不安全
B 客戶可能需要協助
C 只是個預防措施
D 他被警告

164. 珍娜・李接下來最有可能做什麼？

A 查看電子郵件
B 聯絡財務部門
C 打電話給一些員工
D 列印一些報告

165–167 徵才廣告

援助之手

加州聖塔克拉貝克斯斐爾德大道 8732 號

就業機會——區域經理

援助之手一直致力為低收入的個人及家庭提供優質且價格合理的住屋。25 多年來，我們一直購進集合住宅式社區，改善住宅並維持供需量以供給那些所得低於地區平均收入一半的人。我們的住宅目前分布在全德州各都市，包括奧斯汀、達拉斯和休士頓，我們的計劃是擴大服務以提供更多的房子給更多人。

我們正在尋找能擔任區域經理的人才。新經理將派駐奧斯汀，負責監督並評估當地管理部門的績效，並確保房產受到良好的維護。求職者需具商業或管理領域學士以上學位、至少三年的人事監督經驗，並具備特定證照（徵才網頁上有更多詳細資訊）。

申請書可於週一至週五上午九點至下午五點間親送，或以郵寄或以電子郵件寄送。於 10 月 14 日下午五點前收件方可受理，逾時不候。

165. 文中提到什麼和援助之手有關？

A 它為年長者提供服務
B 它致力於自然保育
C 它受到政府贊助
D 它為弱勢族群提供住屋

166. 成功的應徵者必須到哪裡工作？

A 聖塔克拉拉
B 奧斯汀
C 達拉斯
D 休士頓

167. 下列何者與該職務無關？

A 包括監督當地員工
B 需要學位
C 需要正式文件
D 僅限加州居民

168–171 電子郵件

收件者：cmason@centersports.com
寄件者：sdixon@instaprinting.com
日期：11 月 3 日
主旨：您的提問

親愛的梅森先生：

這封信是要回覆您昨天在本公司網站上所提出的疑問。即刻印刷承諾提供比同區競爭對手更快速、更便宜且更可靠的服務。本公司也保證能在價錢方面擊敗競爭對手。

至於您的要求，本公司很樂意協助您的足球隊設計及印製運動服。除了休閒服裝之外，本公司也在製作體育隊服和俱樂部運動服上也經驗豐富。

顧客可以選用各種不同的布料與印製方式，我們的布料包括丹寧、棉布、法蘭絨、尼龍等其他布料，而印製方式則有網版印刷、熱印刷和衣物直印法。

歡迎直接來電 712-555-9804 與本人聯絡，以便洽詢更多細節。本公司期盼與您合作，幫助您的單位達成目標。

即刻印刷 客服代表
史帝芬・狄克森

168. 狄克森先生為什麼會寄這封電子郵件？
- (A) 為專案報價
- (B) 說明新規定
- **(C) 說服客戶達成交易**
- (D) 確認預約

169. 梅森先生想做什麼？
- **(A) 購買一組上衣**
- (B) 應徵職務
- (C) 發明新印刷技術
- (D) 拓展國際業務

170. 下列何者與即刻印刷有關？
- (A) 昨天第二家分店開張
- **(B) 提供各種印製方式**
- (C) 只生產運動服
- (D) 贊助在地足球隊

171. 第四段、第一行的「further」意思最接近？
- (A) 緊急地
- (B) 正式地
- **(C) 額外地**
- (D) 謹慎地

172–175 資訊

（男子）我還記得塞爾吉奧・赫南德茲剛到「趙特暨李」公司上班的模樣。他是個 30 歲的小伙子，充滿了雄心壯志和幹勁。就是那股雄心壯志和幹勁，加上滿懷正直與智慧，讓他成為服裝業界最有價值的一員，也讓本公司成為最成功的企業之一。

今天受邀在此訴說他的事蹟讓我備感榮幸，讓我不由自主地想起去年當我離開公司去追求清閒生活時，心裡有多傷感。塞爾吉奧的那段話幫助我度過難熬的過渡期，過著沒公司可去，也沒有同事激勵的日子，而我希望我這番不足為道的話語能在他經歷同樣的歷程時，讓他記得自己有多麼受人敬重，還有他過了多麼令人敬佩的生活。請大家以熱烈掌聲來歡迎塞爾吉奧・赫南德茲先生。

172. 文中提到了什麼有關赫南德茲先生的事？
- (A) 他是趙特暨李公司的執行長
- (B) 他被升職
- (C) 他要轉調到新部門
- **(D) 他將從公司退休**

173. 下列何者與趙特暨李公司有關？
- (A) 它是國際性企業
- (B) 它是房地產公司
- (C) 它在美國有製造廠
- **(D) 它已經成立好幾十年了**

174. 關於赫南德茲先生，下列何者未在文中提到？
- (A) 他從何時開始在公司工作
- (B) 他是哪一類型的員工
- (C) 他所服務的產業類型
- **(D) 他在公司的職務**

175. 下列句子最適合出現在 [1]、[2]、[3]、[4] 的哪個位置？「今天受邀在此訴說他的事蹟讓我備感榮幸。」

A [1]
B [2]
C [3]
D [4]

176–180 請款單和信件

訂單號碼：23710

楓林戶外用品

華盛頓州約克楓林街 387 號
日期：5 月 6 日

品項	品牌	單價	總價
登山靴	北歐高地	149.95 元	149.95 元
野營爐	阿凡藍奇	58.79 元	58.79 元
燃油罐	阿凡藍奇	9.98 元	19.96 元
襪子	北國羊毛	12.85 元	0 元（贈品）*
			總計：228.34 元

* 我們免費附贈一雙襪子，讓您在下次露營時可以保暖。

感謝您在楓林戶外用品一年多來的惠顧。和往常一樣，若有任何我們可協助之處，歡迎洽詢。如果您詢問的是訂單相關事宜，請記得給我們您的訂單號碼與大名。

電話：(601) 478-2129
電子郵件信箱：MapleOutdoor@zmail.com

收件者：楓林戶外用品客服
寄件者：莎娜．桑德柏格
日期：5 月 9 日
主旨：宅配問題

我昨天收到了訂購的東西，但那並不是我預期會收到的商品。我訂購的是阿凡藍奇野營爐，但我收到的卻是 MT 菁英爐。我希望能盡快收到阿凡藍奇野營爐，因為下個週末我就要參加露營之旅了。你們來得及寄給我嗎？還是我直接到門市更換即可？請盡快與我聯絡。我會等您的回音。

謝謝。
莎娜．桑德柏格

176. 楓林戶外用品提到了什麼有關桑德柏格女士的訂單？

A 將延誤長達一個月的時間
B 他們已經免費快遞
C 如果因使用不當而毀損將無法退貨
D 他們隨件附送一份贈品

177. 阿凡藍奇燃油罐價值多少錢？

A 58.79 元
B 9.98 元
C 19.96 元
D 12.85 元

178. 桑德柏格女士為什麼要寫這封電子郵件？

A 稱讚她所得到的服務
B 要求一份通訊月刊
C 詢問可否退還商品
D 投訴送錯商品

179. 桑德柏格女士忘記附上什麼資料？

A 她的姓名
B 她的郵寄地址
C 她的訂單號碼
D 她的信用卡號碼

180. 下列有關桑德柏格女士，何者為真？

A 她以前在楓林戶外用品買過東西
B 她常去露營
C 她沒有收到登山靴
D 她即將前往楓林戶外用品門市

181–185 告示和電子郵件

各位乘客，請注意

克林頓客運

為回應乘客的反應，克林頓客運將拓展連接德州與西南部其他大都會中心的巴士路線。以下所列的新路線將自 5 月 1 日起運行。為了推廣這些新巴士路線，我們將於營運的第一週提供票券半價優惠。增進大家的滿意程度是我們的首要之務，更多詳細資訊（像是發車與抵達時間），請參考本公司網站 www.clintonbuses.com。

■ 自達拉斯公車總站，至亞歷桑納州鳳凰城公車總站
■ 自奧斯汀公車總站，至新墨西哥州聖塔菲公車總站
■ 自沃斯堡公車總站，至科羅拉多州丹佛公車總站

收件者：erichanson@prplanning.com
寄件者：dangregory@trentonlogistics.com
日期：4 月 27 日
主旨：即將到訪

親愛的漢森先生：

我現在正為前往貴公司於聖塔菲的總部拜訪一事確認細節。感謝您邀請我前去參加業務協商。請告訴我應該抵達的時間，會議是否和上次一樣在午餐後開始呢？

您不需要來接我，我已經安排了計程車在聖塔菲巴士總站接我。很幸運地，我住的地方到您的公司有一條新巴士路線，這讓地區間的交通變得更加便利，現在也有到丹佛和鳳凰城的巴士了。最棒的是，我幸運地可以用半價買到到聖塔菲的車票。

等不及再次見到您與您的同事了。

丹．格雷戈里

181. 根據公告內容，克林頓客運的乘客被鼓勵在網站上做什麼？

A 預先訂票
B 查詢公車時刻表
C 申請會員資格
D 索取優惠券

182. 下列何者與格雷戈里先生和漢森先生之前的會面有關？

A 在德州舉行
B 持續了一整週
C 在下午開始
D 因天候惡劣取消

183. 在電子郵件中，第二段第三行的「transit」意思最接近？

A 參與
B 交通
C 調查
D 合作

184. 格雷戈里先生最有可能住在哪裡？

A 聖塔菲
B 奧斯汀
C 達拉斯
D 丹佛

185. 會議預計何時舉行？

A 在 4 月 24 日前
B 在 4 月 24 日與 4 月 30 日間
C 在 5 月 1 日與 5 月 7 日間
D 在 5 月 7 日後

TEST 9
PART 7

186–190 電子郵件

收件者：布萊恩．彼得森
<bpetersen@atasteofclass.com>
寄件者：傑森．郝士楚
<jhostrum@jhfurnishing.com>
日期：11 月 20 日
主旨：辦公室聖誕派對

親愛的彼得森先生：

我希望於本公司年底舉辦的聖誕派對上，使用貴公司優味的外燴服務。理想上，我們最希望能在 12 月 20 日星期六舉辦活動。我對貴公司提供的服務項目有些問題想請教。第一，你們提供會場布置服務嗎？我真的很希望今年的派對能大成功，這是我第一次負責這個活動，我真的希望能給上司留下好印象。第二，您們素食餐點的種類多嗎？本公司 35 名職員中有 12 位素食者，所以能為他們供應全素食餐點是很重要的，不要只有開胃菜是素食。如果您能回覆這些問題，並告知 20 號當天是否有空，我會非常感激的。

傑森．郝士楚 敬上
強森家飾 初級秘書

收件者：傑森．郝士楚
<jhostrum@jhfurnishing.com>
寄件者：布萊恩．彼得森
<bpetersen@atasteofclass.com>
日期：11 月 21 日
主旨：回覆：辦公室聖誕派對

親愛的郝士楚先生：

很高興您與優味公司聯繫，讓我們協助您讓聖誕派對成為難以忘懷的一場盛會。就讓我來回答您所有的問題，使您寬心。首先，我們還有一組人員可以承辦您在12 月 20 日舉辦的派對，所以您很幸運！至於會場布置一事，我們有好幾種不同的主題可供選擇，請上我們的網站 www.atasteofclass.com 參考我們過去圓滿舉辦的活動照片。上面都已標示主題，所以您只要選出吸引您的就可以了。

您最後關於素食餐點的問題，這需要由您來決定。本公司提供美味佳餚，也很樂意特別準備 12 份素食餐點，但這價格會偏高。我不知道您的預算如何，但我會建議考慮將整份菜單換成素食。我們有非常優秀的素食主廚，茱莉亞．摩爾能準備全素食的自助餐，而且好吃到連獅子都願意吃！這個方案也會比準備兩種不同的餐點要來的划算。在衡量過您可選擇的方案後，請告訴我什麼樣的方案最適合您。

優味 預約暨業務經理
布萊恩．彼得森 敬上

收件者：布萊恩．彼得森
<bpetersen@atasteofclass.com>
寄件者：傑森．郝士楚
<jhostrum@jhfurnishing.com>
日期：11 月 22 日
主旨：回覆：辦公室聖誕派對

親愛的彼得森先生：

感謝您的回覆。我決定將活動訂在 12 月 20 日星期六。我想要的布置主題是冬季仙境。我也決定接受您的建議，採用主廚茱莉亞．摩爾為我們搭配的餐點。很感謝您所有的建議。我知道這將是一場很棒的盛會！

強森家飾 初級秘書
傑森．郝士楚 敬上

186. 傑森．郝士楚為什麼擔心那場派對？

Ⓐ 他的家人會到場
Ⓑ 這是老闆第一次一起參加
Ⓒ 這是他為公司規劃的第一場派對
Ⓓ 食物太多，他無法準備

187. 在第三封電子郵件中，何者與傑森．郝士楚有關？

Ⓐ 他已看過 atasteofclass.com 網站
Ⓑ 他已自創主題
Ⓒ 他要取消派對
Ⓓ 他要增加更多食物與賓客

188. 根據電子郵件，哪一種食物會供應？

Ⓐ 只有肉類
Ⓑ 肉類與素食混搭
Ⓒ 只有素食
Ⓓ 只有開胃菜

189. 在第一封電子郵件中，和食物有關的大問題是什麼？

Ⓐ 口味
Ⓑ 副食種類
Ⓒ 部分員工的飲食限制
Ⓓ 自助餐擺設的位置

190. 下列何者與優味有關？

Ⓐ 今年節慶季很忙
Ⓑ 還有很多小組在 20 日有空
Ⓒ 他們寧可在其他日期承辦派對
Ⓓ 他們太忙無法承辦強森家飾的派對

191–195 電子郵件和訂購表格

收件者：<cservice@starproducts.com>
寄件者：荷西．拉莫斯
<jramos@zipnet.com>
日期：10 月 14 日
主旨：瑕疵水管

親愛的潔金斯女士：

我最近向貴公司星辰製業購買了 5,000 碼的 XP100 工業用水管。那水管標示可應付每平方英寸 1,000 磅的壓力。我們「先進動力清潔公司」為了配合你們的水管，花了可觀的成本改裝壓力清洗裝置。但每一個壓力清洗裝置，從噴槍到壓縮機間的水管某處都出現故障。我們的壓縮機只能產生 500 磅的壓力，因此我只能推論貴公司的水管在設計上有瑕疵。我想要退款，或是將訂購的產品換成符合工業標準的水管。我已經附上訂購單及請款單影本。

荷西．拉莫斯 敬上

收件者：荷西．拉莫斯
<jramos@zipnet.com>
寄件者：拉蔻兒．潔金斯
<cservice@starproducts.com>
日期：10 月 16 日
主旨：回覆：瑕疵水管

親愛的拉莫斯先生：

我們已經收到您提出的瑕疵水管報告，也審閱過所附上的資料。我們真的很重視貴公司的惠顧，也很遺憾您花如此多時間和力氣來處理我們的水管。但是，我恐怕要告訴您，這個問題可能出在貴公司。您的訂單明確顯示您訂購了 5,000 碼的 XP100 水管。如果您仔細研究過那組水管的規格，就會發現它被列在適用於約 100 磅壓力的等級，這可以解釋為什麼您的所有管線會故障。我可以提供給您的是讓貴公司目前庫存的 XP100 水管更換成更符合您需求的管線。我們將免費處理，並支付運費，以感謝您的惠顧。請填寫隨信附上的請購單，並於寄回 XP100 水管時一併附上，以便換貨。

感謝您。

拉蔻兒．潔金斯

星辰製業請購單

品名	磅力	需要長度	每碼單價	適用折扣
XP1000	1,000	2,500 碼	0.5 元	總折扣依更換 XP100 時所商定

191. 荷西．拉莫斯為什麼寫信給星辰製造業？
- (A) 要詢問價格
- (B) 要訂購新水管
- **(C) 要提出水管的瑕疵**
- (D) 要稱讚他們的水管

192. 下列何者與荷西．拉莫斯訂購的水管有關？
- **(A) 不在他適用的磅力範圍中**
- (B) 有瑕疵
- (C) 安裝不當
- (D) 送錯地址

193. 根據請購單，荷西．拉莫斯退還了多少 XP100 的水管？
- (A) 1,000 碼
- (B) 2,000 碼
- **(C) 2,500 碼**
- (D) 5,000 碼

194. 下列何者與星辰製造業所發出的信件有關？
- (A) 星辰製造業並不重視荷西．拉莫斯的生意
- **(B) 星辰製造業很感謝荷西．拉莫斯的惠顧**
- (C) 星辰製造業不需要更多的業務
- (D) 星辰製造業想拓展業務

195. 拉蔻兒・潔金斯最有可能做什麼工作？

Ⓐ 執行長
Ⓑ 財務長
Ⓒ 客服
Ⓓ 銷售

196–200 電子郵件和表格

收件者：傑森・羅伯茲
<jroberts@robertsparties.com>
寄件者：萊羅伊・杰金斯
<ljenkins@smope.com>
日期：9 月 24 日
主旨：秋季派對

親愛的羅伯茲先生：

我叫萊羅伊・杰金斯。我正在規劃十月第一個週末的家庭聚會，我聽幾位朋友說貴公司辦的派對絕對是最棒的。我真的想讓我姊姊的新夫家留下一個好印象，這是他們第一次參加我們的家族年度聚會。我有幾個問題想請教您。

第一，我想知道 25 人的團體收費是多少。不含酒類的話，我可以負擔每人 25 元的預算。我家人對食物有點挑剔，所以是否可以請您將所提供的食物清單與每人費用寄給我，我想先看過後，再設計自己的菜單。

最後要請教的問題就是服務人員。我真的不想在派對時還要打掃、洗碗盤。貴公司可提供人員嗎？如果有，服務的收費又是如何計算？請盡快回覆給我，好讓我們可以著手規劃這場派對！

祝好。

萊羅伊・杰金斯

收件者：萊羅伊・杰金斯
<ljenkins@smope.com>
寄件者：傑森・羅伯茲
<jroberts@robertsparties.com>
日期：9 月 25 日
主旨：回覆：秋季派對

親愛的杰金斯先生：

很高興聽您說本公司的派對一向都很成功。我們的確有外繪菜單供您選擇，歡迎您根據您的預算與口味喜好混合搭配。我已經附上菜單和服務人員配置簡介，如果您很擔心活動的進行，那我建議您雇用宴會總召。本公司的宴會總召皆受過培訓，專門在我們所主辦的派對上負責接待賓客，使他們開心；也因此我們有良好的聲譽。

期待讓您的派對大成功！

傑森・羅伯茲

羅伯茲派對外燴菜單

開胃菜	主菜	沙拉	甜點
玉米片加沾醬 1 元	牛排 2.50 元 *	凱薩 1 元	蛋糕 0.5 元 *
一口酥 1 元	雞肉 1.50 元 *	柯布 2 元 *	派 0.5 元 *
洋蔥圈 1 元 *	豬肉 1.50 元	蔬菜 2 元 *	冰淇淋 0.5 元

羅伯茲派對服務人員價目表

主廚	時薪 5 元
侍者	時薪 2.5 元
宴會總召	時薪 3.5 元

* 推薦品項

196. 傑森・羅伯茲最有可能是誰？

Ⓐ 主廚
Ⓑ 老闆
Ⓒ 宴會總召
Ⓓ 接待員

197. 萊羅伊．杰金斯在擔心要給誰留下好印象？

A 他的老闆
B 他的兄弟
C 他姊夫的家人
D 他的父母

198. 傑森．羅伯茲建議萊羅伊．杰金斯將什麼列入他的活動中？

A 多一名主廚
B 宴會總召
C 素食餐點
D 更多服務生

199. 下列何者與萊羅伊．杰金斯的預算有關？

A 他無法負擔羅伯茲派對的價格
B 他需要選一份便宜的菜單
C 他可以負擔羅伯茲派對所有的建議
D 他必須捨棄開胃菜

200. 誰會出席萊羅伊．杰金斯的聚會？

A 他姊夫家的人
B 25 名杰金斯家族成員
C 住在鎮上的家族成員
D 家族中的每位成員

ACTUAL TEST ⑩

PART 5 P.288-291

◎ **Part 5 解答請見 P.457**

101. **由於**兩個品牌間的差異性很小，大多數的消費者會購買較便宜的那個。

102. 觀眾們對候選人能**清楚地**回答被問到的問題都感到印象深刻。

103. 為了**生產**永續能源，市府官員已經在部分公共建築上加裝了太陽能板。

104. 消防局遲緩的**應變**造成該大樓的嚴重毀損。

105. 在幾個小時的搜尋後，水管工人**終於**找到漏水的源頭。

106. 請告訴**大家**，研討會已經被移至 402 會議室了。

107. 16 號公路於夏季時進行道路拓寬，以**容納**日益增加的交通流量。

108. 餐券發給了那些因訂位錯誤而無法準時起飛**的**貝塔航空旅客。

109. 藝廊的目錄裡包含了每件待售的藝術作品的精確**說明**。

110. 為了確保老舊家電得到妥善處理，本市將於 4 月 2 日至 4 月 5 日**間**免費清除。

111. 賓客們可享用自助式晚餐，所以他們不須點餐就可以吃到**任何**他們想吃的美食。

112. 音樂季期間，只有向籌辦單位登記且**獲得許可的**攤販可以販售商品。

113. 自 2001 年開業以來，快活食品連鎖量販店**專門**販售有機產品。

114. 列表機故障是**因為**組裝過程中有個零件嵌入不當。

115. 大多數的員工能**接受**被提議的假日時間表，因為他們知道它是公平的。

116. 這個檢測**可望**證實病人是否得到該疾病。

117. 擁有兩百多家的獨特店面，普萊恩維爾商場每年**吸引了**上百萬的購物人潮。

118. 參賽者將以**運動**表現接受評比，之後將於頒獎典禮上宣布優勝者。

119. 約克基金會是一個在過去十年來，一直支持醫療科技**發展**的組織。

120. **是否**在室內或室外舉行排球錦標賽，主要取決於當天的天氣預報。

121. 在幾位前職員指控該公司的不當**交易**後，該公司就被調查。

122. 加入文斯健身房**後**，品特先生可免費參加團體課程及健康諮詢。

123. 要以小資改善房屋**外觀**的最好的方式，就是在外牆塗上新漆。

124. 市場營銷員相信，如果包裝的顏色更**繽紛**，消費者可能更容易注意到商品。

125. 警察指揮交通車輛**前往**繞道匝道，好讓駕駛人可以輕易地找到路線。

126. 所有員工被要求與**同事**兩人一組，並在在消防演習中與對方到預定地點集合。

127. 那個車主繳交了車輛的毀損**照片**證據及技師的報告給保險公司。

128. 二樓的洗手間**暫時**無法使用，因為有個水槽正在被更換中。

129. 因為我們的業務代表需要與業界的高層客戶會面，**只有**具專業態度的人才會被列入這個職位人選的考量。

130 在下週的廣播節目中，我們的主持人將訪問克莉絲汀．達布尼，談談她擔任聯合國官員**口譯員**的時光。

131–134 告示

收件者：全體員工
寄件者：首席技師麥克・戴維斯
主旨：網路升級

我們很遺憾要通知大家，自 11 月 13 日下週一起至下週中的某天，員工鑰匙卡系統將無法使用。要進出大樓，各位需要按電鈴通知警衛。要開門或鎖門，各位也必須請求保全小組的幫忙。

舊系統經檢視後發現有很多漏洞。因此，公司決定更換舊系統。這個過程應該會花上三至四天的時間。

其中一個流程是發新的鑰匙卡給每位員工。鑰匙卡將於 11 月 15 日星期三起在警衛室供您領取。請在當天任何時間內領取，警衛室一天 24 小時全天候開放。若造成您的不便，我們深感抱歉。

131. A 正請求
B 已經請求
C 必須請求
D 過去必須請求

132. A 不幸地
B 因此
C 不管怎樣
D 終於

133. A 一……就
B 在……期間
C 在……之前
D 在

134. A 出入從鑰匙轉成無鑰匙，應該可以讓場所更安全。
B 我們期待在下週見到您。
C 警衛室一天 24 小時全天候開放。
D 這是為了產品安全。

135–138 告示

誠徵音樂老師

麥可音樂學校正積極徵求週末及晚間課程的新鋼琴老師。麥可音樂學校自 1992 年起，就在中央區營運至今。我們對社區的責任感，就和我們對學生的責任感一樣重要。為此，我們希望能聘用中央地區的長期住戶加入本團隊。應徵者必須精通現代教學技巧。如果您有意應徵該職，我們將於本週六中午 12 點在榆樹街與杜邦大道的大錄音室舉行面試及甄選。

135. A 積極的
B 活化的
C 積極地
D 活性化的

136. A 本公司試著與外面的社區合作。
B 我們對社區的責任感就和我們對學生的責任感一樣重要。
C 本公司非常獨特，使用奇特的樂器。
D 本公司地點特殊，就在汽車修理廠旁邊。

137. **A 現代的**
B 不知名的
C 奇怪的
D 無聊的

138. A 申請
B 申請
C 申請
D 申請

139–142 廣告

薩爾達斯塔

放鬆您的身心

這就是您一直夢寐以求的。不須翻來覆去即可一夜安眠正是您所需要的，這也是薩爾達斯塔所提供的。薩爾達斯塔幫助人們快速入睡，整夜好眠。這是唯一非麻醉性的安眠藥，經驗證能長期使用，*因此您可以安心每夜服用*。長期服用安眠藥前請先與醫師討論。今晚，只要閉上您的眼睛，把一切都交給薩爾達斯塔。

請參考網站 www.saldesta.com 或撥打 1-800-SALDESTA 看看如何改善您的睡眠。

重要安全資訊：薩爾達斯塔藥效發揮快速，請在睡前服用。甦醒活動前，請確保您至少有八小時的睡眠時間。服用薩爾達斯塔時，請勿飲酒。大部分的安眠藥都有一定的風險，會產生依賴性。

139. **A 提供**
B 支撐
C 緩和
D 維持

140. A 核准
B 核准
C 贊成的
D 經過檢驗的

141. **A 因此您可以安心每夜服用。**
B 今天就和醫生討論，看是否適合您。
C 這是唯一經食品藥物管理局核准可長期使用的興奮劑。
D 輸入這個代碼就可獲得免費樣品與折扣優惠。

142. A 在……期間
B 在……附近
C 在……前
D 在……後

143–146 網頁文章

員工留言板

請求回應

人力資源部主管，詹姆斯．弗羅姆發布

同仁們大家好：

節慶季很快就到來了，我們需要規劃一下我們的辦公室派對！已經有好幾個地點和主題的提案直接送到我這來了，但我想邀請辦公室的各位給我一點回應。所有的構想都很歡迎，但我必須提醒各位本辦公室接納各種習俗與文化。我們的派對可涵蓋各種世俗的慶祝活動，但出於對所有人的尊重，不能有與宗教相關的主題。請直接以電子郵件回覆到 jamesfrohm@ccn.net 給我，這樣我就可以開始規劃了。*期待收到各位的點子！*

詹姆斯 敬上

143. A 製作
B 計劃
C 設想
D 遞送

144. A 評論
B 建議
C 地點
D 建議的

145. **A 接納各種習俗與文化**
B 週二會營業到很晚
C 需要新的清潔工
D 下週要搬家

146. **A 期待收到各位的點子！**
B 我可不希望你們遲到！
C 期待各位的全神留意。
D 希望各位來得及回覆。

147–148 傳單

三星運動器材行

56634 明尼蘇達州伯米吉費爾蒙大道 5477 號
218-555-3412
www.tristarsportsgear.com

7 月 1 日至 7 月 14 日夏季特賣

學年已經結束，夏天也已經到了。來三星運動器材行，好好地利用本週五開始的年度盛大夏季拍賣會吧。現在正是準備好迎接夏季樂活的時候。我們將以原價八折的優惠販售您最喜愛的運動隊伍的球衣。此外，如果您購買兩雙運動鞋，就可以用半價購買第三雙。還有更多特價商品，請參考背頁的特賣清單。

■ 持本傳單到本店，即可以九折的優惠購買各種球類。

147. 下列何者與三星運動器材行有關？
- (A) 是家族企業
- (B) 位於學校旁邊
- **(C) 每年舉辦特賣會**
- (D) 主要販售重量訓練器材

148. 顧客要如何獲得運動鞋的優惠？
- **(A) 購買兩雙以上的運動鞋**
- (B) 7 月 1 日到店
- (C) 網路訂購
- (D) 出示傳單

149–150 訊息串

希薇亞 19:01
我們要去看什麼電影？

傑森 19:08
我們昨晚説好的那部啊！

菲利斯 19:08
對啊，看起來超好看！我愛恐怖片！

伯恩 19:20
！！！你是什麼意思？我以為我們決定的是喜劇片，新的那部！

希薇亞 19:21
沒錯！那部有知名諧星黃亂翳的喜劇片。

傑森 19:25
喜劇片？我也以為是恐怖片，不過我喜歡黃亂翳。算我一份！

菲利斯 19:35
好，那就是喜劇片了。晚上 10 點整在戲院外頭見。

149. 菲利斯以為大夥兒要去看哪一類的電影？
- **(A) 恐怖片**
- (B) 科幻片
- (C) 喜劇片
- (D) 浪漫愛情片

150. 傑森的簡訊寫：「算我一份！」是什麼意思？
- (A) 他想看大家同意的恐怖片
- (B) 他想演喜劇片
- **(C) 他想加入大家**
- (D) 他今晚想待在家

151-152 文章

布里克斯頓科學期刊

3 月 3 日，知名考古學家道格拉斯．普瑞斯將介紹他長年挖掘埃及古墓遺址的成果。這場演講將於布里克頓公立圖書館舉行，晚間六點開始。

希望與會者能提早到場，以參觀一些展示的古埃及用具和器械。這些寶貴的展品是普瑞斯先生在他遠征埃及時所取得，真的是獨一無二。它們被認為是古埃及人用來耕作的器具。

有意參加者，可上網 www.brixtonlibrary.com 預約席位。您也可以在網頁上找到更多有關普瑞斯先生最近的研究資料。

151. 文中提到有關這個活動的什麼？
- (A) 由埃及政府贊助
- **(B) 將特別介紹工藝品展**
- (C) 將於埃及舉行
- (D) 票券已經全數售完

152. 在圖書館的網站上可以找到什麼？

Ⓐ 活動行事曆
Ⓑ 該地區的詳細地圖
Ⓒ 有關古埃及的事
Ⓓ 埃及食物指南

153–154 邀請函

> **春谷中心**
>
> **在樺木街盛大開幕**
>
> 2 月 23 日，星期一
>
> 加州春谷的春谷中心誠摯地邀請您
>
> 參觀我們可供出租的新辦公場所！
>
> 週一整天我們將舉辦開放參觀日
>
> 歡迎所有人到場參觀
>
> 春谷中心交通便利，就在 10 號公路下。

153. 春谷中心最有可能是什麼場所？

Ⓐ 百貨公司
Ⓑ 會議中心
Ⓒ 物流公司
Ⓓ 辦公園區

154. 為什麼要舉辦活動？

Ⓐ 吸引新員工到公司
Ⓑ 安排銷售會議
Ⓒ 宣傳商業出租場所
Ⓓ 宣布購物中心的開幕

155–157 文章

> **羅克蘭商業新聞**
>
> 9 月 8 日——批發商巨擘卡旭可大賣場的發言人星期一證實，下個月終於要羅克蘭開新分店。這消息讓加拿大和美國邊境雙邊的居民都備感安慰，因為許多從羅克蘭來的購物者通常得花上一個半小時，開車進加拿大到布倫特伍德的卡旭可大賣場買東西。這通常造成邊境大排長龍，而且擠滿加拿大卡旭可大賣場的購物者半數以上都是來自邊境。許多住在布倫特伍德的加拿大居民對於大批民眾擠進他們的小城鎮感到憤怒，而羅克蘭的居民也抱怨美國境內最近的卡旭可大賣場居然相距將近五小時車程之遙。
>
> 「我覺得很興奮，」羅克蘭居民珍妮絲．布洛斯說，「聽說賣場很大。或許加拿大人也會開始來這裡買東西。但正經地說，我們要求在這裡開設分店已經很長一段時間了。」有傳聞說新的羅克蘭卡旭可大賣場將成為美國最大的賣場之一，擁有自己的加油站、寵物中心、餐廳、自助餐廳、園藝中心與醫療診所。

155. 這篇文章是有關什麼？

Ⓐ 邊境的緊張情勢
Ⓑ 鄰近居民間的競爭
Ⓒ 跨境遠征購物
Ⓓ 近期即將開幕的卡旭可新分店

156. 下列何者與加拿大居民有關？

Ⓐ 他們想要一間卡旭可分店
Ⓑ 他們不喜歡美國人過來購物
Ⓒ 他們不喜歡去美國
Ⓓ 他們要走很遠才能到一家卡旭可賣場

157. 下列句子最適合出現在 [1]、[2]、[3]、[4] 的哪個位置？「批發商巨擘卡旭可大賣場的發言人星期一證實，下個月終於要在羅克蘭開新分店。」

Ⓐ [1]
Ⓑ [2]
Ⓒ [3]
Ⓓ [4]

158-160 文章

> **森特維爾郡立收容所舉辦馬拉松比賽為街友募款**
>
> 下週六將於森特維爾郡舉辦一場馬拉松競走比賽。活動的所有收入都將捐給森特維爾郡立收容所。這個公立機構為街友、年長者或任何有需要的人提供食物、住宿與協助服務。
>
> 這活動將是第二次舉辦，籌辦單位期盼能有比去年更多的參與者。這個活動開放給

各年齡層的孩童與成人參加。但是孩童必須全程由成年家人陪伴。

森特維爾郡立收容所成立於 1981 年，其宗旨為減輕無家可歸、貧困及飢餓者的苦難。

158. 最有可能報名這個活動的原因是什麼？
- A 學習保持身材的方法
- B 贏得現金獎項
- C 應徵工作
- **D 對社區做出貢獻**

159. 根據本篇文章，誰不可以參加這個活動？
- A 該郡的老年民眾
- B 沒有學生證的學生
- **C 無人陪伴的孩童**
- D 外國遊客

160. 森特維爾郡立收容所的主要目標是什麼？
- A 建造價格便宜的房屋
- **B 提供基本需求**
- C 培訓專業運動員
- D 教育社區成員

161–164 網路討論區

茱莉	有誰明天要和我一起去勝利遊行的嗎？
蘇珊	我要！我整個球季都有在關注這個球隊。他們的球賽都很好看，而他們的四分衛可能是該校有史以來最厲害的！這也將是個好機會，可以建立關係同時宣傳我們新款的贏家啤酒！
傑夫	可能會很好玩吧。但是我擔心的是我們的競爭對手，以及他們與大學和球場的贊助合約。
茱莉	啊。沒錯，我沒想到那些……嗯，我們可以「私底下」進行……哈哈。
蘇珊	是啊，如果被公司發現，我們一定會被開除……或者更慘。
傑夫	沒錯，但我還是想去看比賽，至少分析我們競爭對手的行銷策略。
蘇珊	說的好，傑夫。我們去吧，但是你最好閉上你的嘴。
傑夫	謝啦，蘇珊，我會的。所以我們都會去，還要做筆記，對吧？

161. 下列何者與贏家啤酒有關？
- A 是老牌子啤酒
- **B 人們還不知道這個牌子**
- C 很好喝
- D 價格便宜

162. 這群人接下來最有可能會做什麼？
- A 向公司報告傑夫的事
- **B 去參加勝利遊行**
- C 看電影
- D 去跳舞並喝贏家啤酒

163. 茱莉寫：「私底下」是什麼意思？
- A 是一條尚未發表的歌
- B 是記載他們活動的紀錄
- **C 他們不會進行公務**
- D 所有事情都被紀錄，而他們不想再被記錄

164. 下列何者與傑夫有關？
- A 他的筆記做得很好
- B 他喜歡喝酒
- **C 他喜歡講話**
- D 他熱愛遊行

165–167 告示

利希滕貝格航空

9 月 24 日

致旅客：

自 10 月 1 日開始，利希滕貝格航空將要求旅客額外支付 20% 的行李托運費用。如各位所知，調漲的原因是因為燃油價格上揚。本公司很遺憾地必須調漲行李托運費用。

然而，旅客仍可免費攜帶一件隨身行李。本公司也要強調，這是利希滕貝格航空 10 年來第一次調漲行李托運費用。

一如既往，本公司的目標就是以合理的價格來提供既安全又可靠的交通運輸。當燃油價格調降時，本公司亦期盼能調回原先的價格。

感謝您選擇搭乘利希滕貝格航空。

165. 下列何者與利希滕貝格航空有關？

A 要求乘客遵守行李限制
B 回應顧客的抱怨
C 已經 10 年未曾調漲行李託運費用
D 已經新增目的地

166. 下列何者與乘客有關？

A 允許攜帶電子產品上飛機
B 可免費攜帶一件行李上飛機
C 從 10 月 1 日起必須支付調漲的機票錢
D 下個月可以獲得 20% 的優惠折扣

167. 根據公告所示，當燃油價格調降時，將發生什麼事？

A 利希滕貝格航空的股價會上漲
B 將提供乘客禮券
C 將聘僱更多空服員
D 將取消額外收取的費用

168–171 信件

4 月 4 日

寶拉．林區

42195 明尼蘇達州埃利市庫勒大道 344 號

親愛的林區女士：

很高興您接受我們的邀請，於今年的第二語言教育研討會上發表演說。如您所知，研討會將有德語、法語、中文與其他許多外國語言的老師，齊聚一堂分享教學技巧與方法。除了參加工作坊與研討會外，與會者也有許多機會在各種活動裡交談以及建立關係。這是個不容錯過的機會。

今年的研討會將於奧勒岡州撒冷市的威爾森會議中心舉行，時間是 7 月 12 日星期四至 7 月 15 日星期日。如果提出申請的話，演講嘉賓可租借筆電與其他器材於研討會期間使用，所有出借的器材必須於研討會最後一天歸還。除了演講費之外，所有的演講嘉賓亦可免費參加所有其他工作坊與研討會。

煩請告知您的詳細行程。我們會請工作人員開車至機場接機，並將您送至會場。請於 4 月 10 日前撥打辦公室電話 (456) 555-1345 以提供資訊。

期待在研討會上與您見面。

研討會籌辦人
德克 ・ 克萊 敬上

168. 下列何者與林區女士有關？

A 她住在奧勒岡州撒冷市
B 她會說第二種語言
C 她是位能激發人的講者
D 她是研討會的籌辦人

169. 研討會的目的是什麼？

A 吸引國外投資客
B 分享教學方法
C 設定課程標準
D 建立慈善基金會

170. 講者必須在何時歸還借用的器材？

Ⓐ 4 月 4 日
Ⓑ 4 月 10 日
Ⓒ 7 月 12 日
Ⓓ 7 月 15 日

171. 林區女士被要求告知克萊先生什麼事？

Ⓐ 她何時抵達
Ⓑ 她需要何種器材
Ⓒ 她要用哪種會議室
Ⓓ 誰會陪她一起來

172–175 信件

班迪特製藥廠
48573 麻薩諸塞州波士頓高速道路 255 號

4 月 23 日
提摩西．簡恩先生
97658 加州佛雷斯諾希微亞區 6844 號

親愛的簡恩先生：

班迪特製藥廠很開心您接受了研究助理一職。您的到職日為 5 月 5 日。第一天是安排給全體新進員工的任職培訓會，內容包括職場安全工作坊、工作職責說明會及設施導覽。您的實驗室主管將在第一天尾聲給您更詳細的說明。

因為您來自外地，公司想讓您的搬遷過程能順利進行。公司知道您將於 4 月 29 日抵達，並在波士頓家庭旅社住幾天。該旅社距離班迪特製藥廠總公司大約 10 分鐘的計程車車程。您可以到大廳櫃台找人力資源部的珍娜．萊姆絲女士。她會協助非本地新進員工適應本地環境，並回答您可能有的疑慮。我也附上與您搬遷相關的場所和機構的電話號碼。

若您有其他問題或疑慮，請於星期一至五上午 9 點至晚上 7 點上班時間來電 555-1234 與我聯絡。祝您搬遷順利，5 月 5 日見。

人力資源部
瓊安．諾南 敬上

172. 諾南女士為什麼寄信給簡恩先生？

Ⓐ 提供工作面試的時間與地點細節
Ⓑ 提供第一天上班的資訊
Ⓒ 提供租屋資訊
Ⓓ 確認他是否接受這份工作

173. 諾南女士隨信寄了什麼？

Ⓐ 電話號碼
Ⓑ 一份合約
Ⓒ 公司員工的聯絡資料
Ⓓ 時間表

174. 第二段的「settle into」意思最接近？

Ⓐ 尋找
Ⓑ 探索
Ⓒ 變得自在
Ⓓ 引導

175. 下列句子最適合出現在 [1]、[2]、[3]、[4] 的哪個位置？「您的實驗室主管將在第一天尾聲給您更詳細的說明。」

Ⓐ [1]
Ⓑ [2]
Ⓒ [3]
Ⓓ [4]

176–180 網站和電子郵件

黑石教育基金會

首頁	關於我們	最新消息	資源連結	與我們聯絡

2 月 10 日

語言獎學金

黑石教育基金會宣布，我們即將開始受理第 24 屆德語獎學金的申請，時間自 3 月 10 日起至 3 月 31 日為止，鼓勵不同專業背景的人士前來申請。為符合獎學金的申請資格，申請者必須：

- 現為碩士生
- 證明具進階德語能力
- 繳交一份完整的健康檢查報告
- 繳交一份以前的語言教師的推薦信

德語獎學金的對象為具德語口說進階程度的學生。因此，這份獎學金將提供給打算近期以德語到德國求學的學生。

獎學金得主必須完成每月的進度報告，繳交完整的每月支出明細給基金會，並維持平均 B+ 的成績。

申請者可於網站的「資源連結」下載申請表。請將所有必要文件繳交給黑石教育基金會的主任漢斯．里希特先生，地址是 60616 伊利諾州芝加哥市皮爾森路 459 號。審查與選拔程序大約需兩週的時間，不完整或缺件的申請案件一律退件。結果將於 4 月 15 日公布。

收件者：克林特．波特
<cporter@umc.com>
寄件者：漢斯．里希特
<richter@blackrockedu.com>
日期：4 月 15 日
主旨：黑石獎學金
附件：獎學金 _ 資料

親愛的波特先生：

我要恭喜您獲得第 24 屆德語獎學金。身為獎學金得主，您將獲得基金會提供您到德國的旅費、學費以及一整年的生活費。隨信附上簡章一本，內含獎學金規定與條件等相關資料，請務必仔細閱讀。若有任何問題或疑慮，歡迎與我聯絡。下週之內我會把如何準備未來求學的詳細資料以電子郵件寄給您。

謝謝。

漢斯．里希特
黑石教育基金會主任

176. 根據網頁，獎學金得主必須做什麼？

A 記錄每月支出
B 寫研究報告
C 繳交年度報告
D 參加入學考試

177. 下列何者與獎學金申請有關？

A 必須在四月中旬前收到
B 只有符合條件才能申請
C 將由德國教授來審查和選拔
D 必須線上繳交

178. 在網頁上，第一段第六行的「proficiency」意思最接近？

A 系統
B 練習
C 經驗
D 精通

179. 這封電子郵件的目的是什麼？

A 確認出發日期
B 安排面試
C 提供獎學金得主一些資料
D 報名德國大學必修課程

180. 以下何者與波特先生有關？

A 他在黑石基金會上班
B 他是在德國工作的企業家
C 他精通德語
D 他想要成為語言教師

181–185 請款單和信件

晴天清潔公司
專業清潔的唯一選擇

付款人：藍道車體公司（97055 奧勒岡州勞特代爾太平洋道 957 號）
請款編號：2348
日期： 3 月 3 日

日期	服務說明	總額
2 月 5 日	辦公室全套清潔（含：辦公室三間、浴室兩間、窗戶、地毯深層清潔、家具）	95 元
2 月 19 日	辦公室全套清潔（含：辦公室三間，浴室兩間、窗戶、地毯深層清潔、家具）	95 元
		總計：190 元

*4 月 1 日後付款需支付滯延金 20 元晴天

清潔公司

97055 奧勒岡州勞特代爾主街 283 號

若有疑問或需額外服務，請撥 1-345-737-2209

3 月 8 日

親愛的晴天清潔公司：

我已收到貴公司二月份清潔服務的請款單，我必須說服務品質很棒。我看到每次清潔辦公室的費用是 95 元。這是我們最初達成協議的價格，並且從去年此時就開始支付這樣的價碼。但是，羅德．山福告訴我，因為我們請貴公司去清掃本公司在 26 號高速道路旁的另一間辦公室，因此接下來貴公司的每次清潔服務都將提供五元的優惠折扣。他說新價碼將自二月份開始生效，我附上了羅德．山福寄給我的電子郵件影本。能否請您依照新的協議調整價格，並再寄一份新帳單過來？感謝您。期待再次見到您們。

感謝您的協助！

藍道車體公司經理

派翠西亞．柯林斯

181. 根據請款單，4 月 1 日前須支付的金額是多少？

A 20 元
B 90 元
C 95 元
D 190 元

182. 下列何者未在提供給藍道車體公司的服務中？

A 窗戶清潔
B 地板清潔
C 家具清潔
D 地毯清潔

183. 柯林斯女士為什麼寫這封信？

A 清潔公司少打掃一次
B 她被多收錢
C 清潔公司在帳單裡增加了額外的費用
D 她想要續約

184. 下列何者與晴天清潔公司有關？

A 提供不錯的服務
B 通常比預定時間晚到
C 經常向客戶多收錢
D 提供延後付款的選擇

185. 除了信之外，柯林斯女士還寄了什麼？

A 汽車維修的折價卷
B 一封電子郵件的影本
C 已簽名的合約
D 應付金額的支票

186–190 文章、網頁和獎狀

給通勤者的緩解方法

由於公車及計程車費用不斷上漲，加上通勤者不斷地尋求更有效率的交通路線，一個新的共乘應用程式正大受歡迎。小企業老闆喬丹．密爾斯，從布倫特伍德的家必須轉兩趟公車再搭乘地鐵，才能到市中心的公司上班。他發現不只通勤的費用頗高，尖峰時段擁擠的人群令人不適外，他也發現太過耗費時間。但是使用新的應用程式飛輪後，他發現不管身在何處，五分鐘之內就有車可搭，節省了時間和金錢。「這絕對是交通運輸的未來樣貌。」喬丹說，「我無法再以其他的方式通勤上下班了。」

喬丹．密爾斯不是唯一有這種感覺的通勤者。估計光在西華市就約有 2,000 名的通勤者將在明年內使用這個共乘應用程式，且將近 500 位駕駛已登記加入了這個計劃。

飛輪應用程式可於飛輪網站以及 Miniapp.com 和 Amacom.com 下載。

www.freewheel.com/history

當麥可．歐文斯和他同事在他們工作的公司首次發起汽車共乘計劃時，飛輪的構想便萌芽了。歐文斯必須轉三次地鐵和兩次公車才能到辦公室，雖然他可以開車，但停車位有限。他管理共乘群組的方式，是透過指派不同的駕駛及劃出每位同事家的路線圖。然後，他設計了一個應用程式，讓大家都可以透過它相互連結交流，如此一來，被指派的駕駛與乘客便能輕鬆的找到對方。五年後，飛輪已經是間大公司，在全國擁有數以萬計的使用者包含駕駛和乘客。

飛輪致力於壓低通勤費用並提高效率。希望有天能將這個服務提供給全世界的人使用。

創新科技

很驕傲地將新創獎頒發給飛輪公司的執行長麥可．歐文斯！

這個獎項表彰了科技產業中新人才的革新與創造力，同時也表揚他努力透過科技的運用及創新的構想，來改革運輸業的本質。

創新科技總經理
蘇珊．凡尼爾

186. 喬丹．密爾斯和麥可．歐文斯有什麼相似之處？

- A 都創立了科技公司
- **B 都想要一個有效率的通勤方式**
- C 都在公共運輸業上班
- D 都因其成就而獲獎

187. 下列何者與飛輪公司有關？

- **A 以小型企業起家**
- B 是間國際化的公司
- C 聘用公車司機
- D 對環境有益

188. 有關麥可．歐文斯的敘述，下列何者為真？

- A 他不喜歡開車
- B 他擁有一間計程車公司
- **C 他想要擴展事業版圖**
- D 他見過喬丹．密爾斯

189. 文章標題「Respite」意思最接近？

- A 就業
- B 免疫力
- C 退款
- **D 改變**

190. 獎狀是在獎勵什麼？

- A 最佳駕駛人
- B 對環保的努力
- **C 好的構想**
- D 獲利最高的公司

191–195 電子郵件

收件者：肯恩．亞伯斯
<kalberts@emergentsolutions.com>
寄件者：克拉麗莎．皮爾斯
<cpierce@actionservices.com>
日期：6月13日
主旨：運送合約

親愛的亞伯斯先生：

僅代表本公司行動服務寫信給您。本公司專長創作客製化花卉擺設、禮物籃及新穎禮品。最近我們檢視帳冊後，發現我們支付太多運費給目前合作的貨運公司。若貴公司能提供更具競爭力的價格，我們有意讓貴公司接手這項業務。我已附上目前配合的貨運公司快捷公司最近所開立的運費請款單。若貴公司認為您能提供更優惠的價格，本公司願意嘗試與貴公司合作。請告知貴公司的想法。

行動服務 客戶經理
克拉麗莎．皮爾斯 敬上

收件者：克拉麗莎．皮爾斯
<cpierce@actionservices.com>
寄件者：肯恩．亞伯斯
<kalberts@emergentsolutions.com>
日期：6月14日
主旨：運送合約

親愛的皮爾斯女士：

感謝您與本公司緊急物流聯絡。我已看過快捷公司最新一期的單據，我相信本公司能在價格上取勝。我很樂意派本公司的客戶主管制定出一份最符合貴公司需求的運送方案。既然貴公司大部分的運送地點都在本州內，而且運送的是小型物品，我相信我們的快遞服務會很適合。我們使用省油的油電混合車來運送小型物品，將省下的金額回饋給顧客。身為客戶總監，我期盼未來能與行動服務合作。

肯恩．亞伯斯 敬上

收件者：肯恩・亞伯斯
<kalberts@emergentsolutions.com>
寄件者：克拉麗莎・皮爾斯
<cpierce@actionservices.com>
日期：6 月 16 日
主旨：運送合約

亞伯斯先生：

這聽起來很棒！您不知道貴公司使用節能交通工具這點對本公司有多重要。行動服務最初就是由一群城市大學環境研究的學生所組成的，我們賣的所有產品都透過道德貿易而來並且是可回收的。我們迫不及待與貴公司團隊會面了。

行動服務 客戶經理
克拉麗莎・皮爾斯 敬上

191. 亞伯斯先生的工作是什麼？

- (A) 總裁
- (B) 人資主管
- (C) 執行長
- **(D) 客戶總監**

192. 下列何者與行動服務有關？

- (A) 他們關心藝術
- **(B) 他們關懷環境**
- (C) 他們需要販售更多包裹
- (D) 他們舊的貨運公司將包裹送錯地方

193. 根據電子郵件內容，可推論出什麼？

- **(A) 緊急物流提供比快捷公司便宜的收費**
- (B) 緊急物流的效率不高
- (C) 緊急物流的企業倫理與行動服務不合
- (D) 行動服務目前負債中

194. 行動服務為什麼要與緊急物流聯絡？

- (A) 他們需要新客戶
- **(B) 他們在運費上花太多錢**
- (C) 他們想要擴展業務
- (D) 他們想要運貨到國外

195. 行動服務是何種企業？

- (A) 科技顧問
- (B) 領導專家
- (C) 飯店與度假村專家
- **(D) 花卉與新奇小物供應商**

196–200 電子郵件和表格

收件者：亞倫・唐諾
<adonald@acemail.com>
寄件者：詹姆斯・浩特
<holtrain@zipnet.net>
日期：1 月 12 日
主旨：第一季績效評估

親愛的亞倫：

我想要先提醒您績效評估將如同先前討論的要開始進行了。我知道你在去年第四季承受了些壓力，所以我想要先給你一些預警。如果你想要通過評估，就必須讓數字顯著上升。正如你所知道的，我們過去幾年一直很努力要達到銷售目標，我很擔心要是業績毫無起色，瓊斯先生會決定裁員。我的業績數字已經遠遠超過我的目標值，所以我附上一份文件，裡面有一些可能的銷售對象，試看看吧。

祝好運！

詹姆斯

收件者：詹姆斯・浩特
<holtrain@zipnet.net>
寄件者：亞倫・唐諾
<adonald@acemail.com>
日期：1 月 12 日
主旨：回覆：第一季績效評估

詹姆斯：

非常感謝你的客戶名單，我會立刻聯絡他們的。我不知道為什麼最近自己在科技部門的業績會衰退這麼多，在學校學的銷售技巧好像都不管用了。如果我沒通過三月公布的評估，我打算換個跑道。我妹妹要開一間美容院，她要我去當理髮師。想像那畫面吧！不管怎樣，再次感謝你提醒未來可能裁員一事。我會努力將業績提升到公司標準，但我覺得瓊斯先生可能已經決定要叫我走路了。

祝一切順利。

亞倫

一月份可能的銷售客戶名單

姓名	類別	可能進帳	等級
沙莉・瓊斯	科技類	35,000 元 – 50,000 元	銀級
鮑伯・納德	科技類	100,000 元以上	金級
馬基斯・李	科技類	12,000 元 – 20,000 元	銅級／銀級

196. 下列關於詹姆斯和亞倫的敘述，何者正確？

Ⓐ 他們是競爭對手
Ⓑ 他們有親戚關係
Ⓒ 他們結婚了
Ⓓ 他們是朋友

197. 下列何者與亞倫有關？

Ⓐ 他最近在工作上表現不好
Ⓑ 老闆喜歡他
Ⓒ 跟所有同事間有些問題
Ⓓ 評估結果出爐後他還能保住工作

198. 根據所提供的資訊，下列與詹姆斯有關的敘述，何者為真？

Ⓐ 他工作上的表現非常好
Ⓑ 他需要更多業績
Ⓒ 他想要和亞倫一起工作
Ⓓ 他將成為一名理髮師

199. 詹姆斯給亞倫的銷售名單有什麼問題？

Ⓐ 等級太高
Ⓑ 值不了多少錢
Ⓒ 亞倫不認識這些人
Ⓓ 正是他處境艱難的領域

200. 下列何者最有可能是瓊斯先生的工作？

Ⓐ 人力資源仲介
Ⓑ 銷售經理
Ⓒ 老闆
Ⓓ 助理秘書

ANSWER KEY

Actual Test 01

101 (B)	126 (D)	151 (C)	176 (A)
102 (A)	127 (C)	152 (B)	177 (B)
103 (B)	128 (A)	153 (B)	178 (C)
104 (A)	129 (D)	154 (B)	179 (C)
105 (B)	130 (A)	155 (C)	180 (B)
106 (C)	131 (C)	156 (A)	181 (C)
107 (D)	132 (A)	157 (B)	182 (D)
108 (B)	133 (D)	158 (A)	183 (A)
109 (C)	134 (B)	159 (C)	184 (A)
110 (A)	135 (B)	160 (B)	185 (B)
111 (C)	136 (D)	161 (B)	186 (A)
112 (A)	137 (A)	162 (C)	187 (B)
113 (B)	138 (C)	163 (C)	188 (D)
114 (B)	139 (C)	164 (D)	189 (C)
115 (C)	140 (D)	165 (B)	190 (D)
116 (D)	141 (B)	166 (C)	191 (D)
117 (C)	142 (B)	167 (D)	192 (A)
118 (B)	143 (D)	168 (B)	193 (C)
119 (A)	144 (C)	169 (C)	194 (D)
120 (A)	145 (C)	170 (A)	195 (D)
121 (C)	146 (B)	171 (C)	196 (A)
122 (C)	147 (D)	172 (A)	197 (B)
123 (A)	148 (B)	173 (B)	198 (D)
124 (A)	149 (C)	174 (C)	199 (A)
125 (C)	150 (A)	175 (B)	200 (B)

Actual Test 02

101 (D)	126 (A)	151 (C)	176 (B)
102 (A)	127 (A)	152 (B)	177 (D)
103 (C)	128 (B)	153 (C)	178 (C)
104 (B)	129 (B)	154 (A)	179 (B)
105 (C)	130 (A)	155 (C)	180 (A)
106 (C)	131 (C)	156 (A)	181 (D)
107 (C)	132 (D)	157 (C)	182 (B)
108 (A)	133 (B)	158 (C)	183 (D)
109 (C)	134 (C)	159 (B)	184 (A)
110 (A)	135 (D)	160 (D)	185 (C)
111 (D)	136 (D)	161 (D)	186 (C)
112 (C)	137 (A)	162 (D)	187 (C)
113 (C)	138 (C)	163 (A)	188 (D)
114 (A)	139 (C)	164 (C)	189 (A)
115 (D)	140 (A)	165 (B)	190 (C)
116 (C)	141 (A)	166 (C)	191 (A)
117 (A)	142 (C)	167 (D)	192 (C)
118 (D)	143 (C)	168 (A)	193 (B)
119 (D)	144 (A)	169 (C)	194 (C)
120 (D)	145 (B)	170 (D)	195 (D)
121 (A)	146 (D)	171 (A)	196 (B)
122 (B)	147 (C)	172 (B)	197 (D)
123 (D)	148 (B)	173 (C)	198 (C)
124 (B)	149 (B)	174 (D)	199 (B)
125 (A)	150 (A)	175 (A)	200 (A)

Actual Test 03

101 (A)	126 (B)	151 (B)	176 (B)
102 (A)	127 (A)	152 (C)	177 (C)
103 (C)	128 (A)	153 (D)	178 (A)
104 (B)	129 (D)	154 (D)	179 (D)
105 (C)	130 (D)	155 (D)	180 (C)
106 (B)	131 (A)	156 (C)	181 (C)
107 (C)	132 (A)	157 (B)	182 (A)
108 (D)	133 (B)	158 (B)	183 (B)
109 (B)	134 (D)	159 (A)	184 (B)
110 (C)	135 (A)	160 (C)	185 (B)
111 (B)	136 (B)	161 (D)	186 (B)
112 (B)	137 (B)	162 (C)	187 (C)
113 (D)	138 (B)	163 (B)	188 (A)
114 (B)	139 (B)	164 (A)	189 (D)
115 (A)	140 (B)	165 (A)	190 (D)
116 (D)	141 (A)	166 (B)	191 (D)
117 (A)	142 (C)	167 (C)	192 (B)
118 (D)	143 (A)	168 (D)	193 (B)
119 (B)	144 (B)	169 (B)	194 (D)
120 (D)	145 (B)	170 (B)	195 (B)
121 (C)	146 (B)	171 (B)	196 (B)
122 (A)	147 (C)	172 (C)	197 (D)
123 (D)	148 (A)	173 (D)	198 (B)
124 (D)	149 (B)	174 (A)	199 (A)
125 (C)	150 (D)	175 (D)	200 (B)

Actual Test 04

101 (A)	126 (D)	151 (C)	176 (D)
102 (D)	127 (C)	152 (B)	177 (A)
103 (C)	128 (D)	153 (D)	178 (B)
104 (B)	129 (A)	154 (A)	179 (B)
105 (A)	130 (A)	155 (C)	180 (B)
106 (B)	131 (C)	156 (A)	181 (C)
107 (B)	132 (D)	157 (B)	182 (A)
108 (A)	133 (C)	158 (D)	183 (D)
109 (B)	134 (B)	159 (C)	184 (B)
110 (B)	135 (C)	160 (C)	185 (B)
111 (D)	136 (B)	161 (C)	186 (A)
112 (C)	137 (D)	162 (B)	187 (D)
113 (D)	138 (A)	163 (D)	188 (C)
114 (B)	139 (A)	164 (A)	189 (A)
115 (B)	140 (C)	165 (C)	190 (D)
116 (D)	141 (B)	166 (B)	191 (A)
117 (A)	142 (C)	167 (C)	192 (A)
118 (C)	143 (C)	168 (B)	193 (C)
119 (C)	144 (B)	169 (D)	194 (B)
120 (D)	145 (A)	170 (B)	195 (A)
121 (A)	146 (B)	171 (B)	196 (A)
122 (C)	147 (B)	172 (B)	197 (D)
123 (B)	148 (C)	173 (A)	198 (B)
124 (B)	149 (C)	174 (C)	199 (B)
125 (A)	150 (B)	175 (D)	200 (A)

Actual Test 05

101 (B)	126 (B)	151 (D)	176 (C)
102 (A)	127 (A)	152 (B)	177 (D)
103 (C)	128 (D)	153 (B)	178 (B)
104 (C)	129 (B)	154 (D)	179 (D)
105 (D)	130 (B)	155 (C)	180 (B)
106 (C)	131 (C)	156 (C)	181 (C)
107 (A)	132 (D)	157 (D)	182 (D)
108 (D)	133 (B)	158 (B)	183 (B)
109 (D)	134 (A)	159 (A)	184 (C)
110 (A)	135 (D)	160 (C)	185 (D)
111 (D)	136 (A)	161 (A)	186 (C)
112 (C)	137 (C)	162 (B)	187 (B)
113 (C)	138 (B)	163 (B)	188 (C)
114 (A)	139 (B)	164 (D)	189 (C)
115 (C)	140 (D)	165 (D)	190 (B)
116 (A)	141 (C)	166 (B)	191 (B)
117 (C)	142 (A)	167 (A)	192 (C)
118 (B)	143 (C)	168 (C)	193 (B)
119 (B)	144 (A)	169 (B)	194 (D)
120 (C)	145 (C)	170 (A)	195 (C)
121 (A)	146 (D)	171 (D)	196 (B)
122 (A)	147 (C)	172 (C)	197 (C)
123 (A)	148 (D)	173 (B)	198 (B)
124 (C)	149 (B)	174 (A)	199 (D)
125 (D)	150 (B)	175 (C)	200 (C)

Actual Test 06

101 (D)	126 (A)	151 (D)	176 (B)
102 (B)	127 (B)	152 (B)	177 (C)
103 (C)	128 (C)	153 (A)	178 (C)
104 (A)	129 (B)	154 (C)	179 (C)
105 (C)	130 (C)	155 (B)	180 (C)
106 (B)	131 (B)	156 (C)	181 (A)
107 (A)	132 (D)	157 (B)	182 (C)
108 (D)	133 (C)	158 (C)	183 (B)
109 (A)	134 (A)	159 (A)	184 (C)
110 (B)	135 (C)	160 (D)	185 (D)
111 (A)	136 (C)	161 (C)	186 (D)
112 (C)	137 (A)	162 (C)	187 (C)
113 (D)	138 (D)	163 (B)	188 (C)
114 (C)	139 (C)	164 (A)	189 (D)
115 (D)	140 (B)	165 (D)	190 (B)
116 (C)	141 (A)	166 (A)	191 (B)
117 (A)	142 (A)	167 (C)	192 (A)
118 (A)	143 (D)	168 (B)	193 (C)
119 (C)	144 (B)	169 (C)	194 (D)
120 (C)	145 (A)	170 (A)	195 (B)
121 (C)	146 (C)	171 (C)	196 (C)
122 (C)	147 (A)	172 (C)	197 (B)
123 (D)	148 (C)	173 (B)	198 (C)
124 (D)	149 (C)	174 (D)	199 (B)
125 (B)	150 (B)	175 (C)	200 (C)

Actual Test 07

101 (A)	126 (C)	151 (D)	176 (C)
102 (C)	127 (C)	152 (C)	177 (B)
103 (A)	128 (C)	153 (B)	178 (D)
104 (B)	129 (D)	154 (C)	179 (A)
105 (B)	130 (D)	155 (B)	180 (B)
106 (C)	131 (B)	156 (C)	181 (A)
107 (B)	132 (D)	157 (A)	182 (D)
108 (D)	133 (B)	158 (B)	183 (C)
109 (D)	134 (A)	159 (C)	184 (C)
110 (D)	135 (C)	160 (A)	185 (A)
111 (A)	136 (D)	161 (C)	186 (D)
112 (B)	137 (C)	162 (A)	187 (D)
113 (D)	138 (A)	163 (B)	188 (B)
114 (D)	139 (D)	164 (C)	189 (A)
115 (A)	140 (C)	165 (D)	190 (C)
116 (C)	141 (A)	166 (C)	191 (C)
117 (C)	142 (B)	167 (B)	192 (D)
118 (A)	143 (B)	168 (D)	193 (B)
119 (A)	144 (C)	169 (C)	194 (B)
120 (A)	145 (D)	170 (C)	195 (B)
121 (D)	146 (C)	171 (A)	196 (D)
122 (D)	147 (C)	172 (A)	197 (B)
123 (B)	148 (B)	173 (D)	198 (A)
124 (D)	149 (D)	174 (B)	199 (D)
125 (A)	150 (B)	175 (C)	200 (C)

Actual Test 08

101 (D)	126 (B)	151 (C)	176 (A)
102 (B)	127 (C)	152 (C)	177 (B)
103 (B)	128 (D)	153 (C)	178 (D)
104 (A)	129 (A)	154 (D)	179 (C)
105 (C)	130 (B)	155 (A)	180 (C)
106 (B)	131 (C)	156 (C)	181 (A)
107 (A)	132 (A)	157 (B)	182 (B)
108 (D)	133 (C)	158 (D)	183 (B)
109 (C)	134 (D)	159 (C)	184 (C)
110 (A)	135 (B)	160 (C)	185 (D)
111 (A)	136 (A)	161 (D)	186 (D)
112 (C)	137 (C)	162 (D)	187 (C)
113 (C)	138 (D)	163 (B)	188 (B)
114 (B)	139 (A)	164 (A)	189 (C)
115 (C)	140 (A)	165 (B)	190 (A)
116 (D)	141 (A)	166 (C)	191 (C)
117 (C)	142 (A)	167 (C)	192 (A)
118 (D)	143 (C)	168 (A)	193 (B)
119 (A)	144 (A)	169 (A)	194 (C)
120 (A)	145 (A)	170 (D)	195 (D)
121 (D)	146 (B)	171 (C)	196 (D)
122 (B)	147 (C)	172 (B)	197 (A)
123 (A)	148 (A)	173 (A)	198 (B)
124 (A)	149 (C)	174 (A)	199 (C)
125 (D)	150 (D)	175 (C)	200 (B)

Actual Test 09

101 (A)	126 (B)	151 (C)	176 (D)
102 (B)	127 (A)	152 (B)	177 (B)
103 (D)	128 (A)	153 (B)	178 (D)
104 (D)	129 (A)	154 (D)	179 (C)
105 (C)	130 (D)	155 (A)	180 (A)
106 (C)	131 (C)	156 (C)	181 (B)
107 (D)	132 (A)	157 (A)	182 (C)
108 (C)	133 (B)	158 (D)	183 (B)
109 (D)	134 (D)	159 (C)	184 (B)
110 (A)	135 (B)	160 (D)	185 (C)
111 (D)	136 (D)	161 (D)	186 (C)
112 (C)	137 (A)	162 (B)	187 (A)
113 (A)	138 (B)	163 (C)	188 (C)
114 (B)	139 (D)	164 (A)	189 (C)
115 (C)	140 (C)	165 (D)	190 (A)
116 (D)	141 (A)	166 (B)	191 (C)
117 (C)	142 (D)	167 (D)	192 (A)
118 (A)	143 (D)	168 (C)	193 (C)
119 (D)	144 (D)	169 (A)	194 (B)
120 (A)	145 (B)	170 (B)	195 (C)
121 (D)	146 (D)	171 (C)	196 (B)
122 (A)	147 (B)	172 (D)	197 (C)
123 (A)	148 (A)	173 (D)	198 (B)
124 (C)	149 (B)	174 (D)	199 (C)
125 (D)	150 (D)	175 (C)	200 (A)

Actual Test 10

101 (B)	126 (C)	151 (B)	176 (A)
102 (A)	127 (C)	152 (C)	177 (B)
103 (D)	128 (A)	153 (D)	178 (D)
104 (B)	129 (A)	154 (C)	179 (C)
105 (B)	130 (D)	155 (D)	180 (C)
106 (C)	131 (C)	156 (B)	181 (D)
107 (C)	132 (B)	157 (A)	182 (B)
108 (D)	133 (B)	158 (D)	183 (B)
109 (B)	134 (C)	159 (C)	184 (A)
110 (D)	135 (C)	160 (B)	185 (B)
111 (B)	136 (B)	161 (B)	186 (B)
112 (D)	137 (A)	162 (B)	187 (A)
113 (C)	138 (C)	163 (C)	188 (C)
114 (A)	139 (A)	164 (C)	189 (D)
115 (C)	140 (D)	165 (C)	190 (C)
116 (D)	141 (A)	166 (B)	191 (D)
117 (A)	142 (C)	167 (D)	192 (B)
118 (B)	143 (B)	168 (B)	193 (A)
119 (C)	144 (B)	169 (B)	194 (B)
120 (C)	145 (A)	170 (D)	195 (D)
121 (D)	146 (A)	171 (A)	196 (D)
122 (B)	147 (C)	172 (B)	197 (A)
123 (B)	148 (A)	173 (A)	198 (A)
124 (A)	149 (A)	174 (C)	199 (D)
125 (A)	150 (C)	175 (A)	200 (C)

答案紙

ACTUAL TEST 01

READING SECTION

101	Ⓐ Ⓑ Ⓒ Ⓓ	111	Ⓐ Ⓑ Ⓒ Ⓓ	121	Ⓐ Ⓑ Ⓒ Ⓓ	131	Ⓐ Ⓑ Ⓒ Ⓓ	141	Ⓐ Ⓑ Ⓒ Ⓓ	151	Ⓐ Ⓑ Ⓒ Ⓓ	161	Ⓐ Ⓑ Ⓒ Ⓓ	171	Ⓐ Ⓑ Ⓒ Ⓓ	181	Ⓐ Ⓑ Ⓒ Ⓓ	191	Ⓐ Ⓑ Ⓒ Ⓓ
102	Ⓐ Ⓑ Ⓒ Ⓓ	112	Ⓐ Ⓑ Ⓒ Ⓓ	122	Ⓐ Ⓑ Ⓒ Ⓓ	132	Ⓐ Ⓑ Ⓒ Ⓓ	142	Ⓐ Ⓑ Ⓒ Ⓓ	152	Ⓐ Ⓑ Ⓒ Ⓓ	162	Ⓐ Ⓑ Ⓒ Ⓓ	172	Ⓐ Ⓑ Ⓒ Ⓓ	182	Ⓐ Ⓑ Ⓒ Ⓓ	192	Ⓐ Ⓑ Ⓒ Ⓓ
103	Ⓐ Ⓑ Ⓒ Ⓓ	113	Ⓐ Ⓑ Ⓒ Ⓓ	123	Ⓐ Ⓑ Ⓒ Ⓓ	133	Ⓐ Ⓑ Ⓒ Ⓓ	143	Ⓐ Ⓑ Ⓒ Ⓓ	153	Ⓐ Ⓑ Ⓒ Ⓓ	163	Ⓐ Ⓑ Ⓒ Ⓓ	173	Ⓐ Ⓑ Ⓒ Ⓓ	183	Ⓐ Ⓑ Ⓒ Ⓓ	193	Ⓐ Ⓑ Ⓒ Ⓓ
104	Ⓐ Ⓑ Ⓒ Ⓓ	114	Ⓐ Ⓑ Ⓒ Ⓓ	124	Ⓐ Ⓑ Ⓒ Ⓓ	134	Ⓐ Ⓑ Ⓒ Ⓓ	144	Ⓐ Ⓑ Ⓒ Ⓓ	154	Ⓐ Ⓑ Ⓒ Ⓓ	164	Ⓐ Ⓑ Ⓒ Ⓓ	174	Ⓐ Ⓑ Ⓒ Ⓓ	184	Ⓐ Ⓑ Ⓒ Ⓓ	194	Ⓐ Ⓑ Ⓒ Ⓓ
105	Ⓐ Ⓑ Ⓒ Ⓓ	115	Ⓐ Ⓑ Ⓒ Ⓓ	125	Ⓐ Ⓑ Ⓒ Ⓓ	135	Ⓐ Ⓑ Ⓒ Ⓓ	145	Ⓐ Ⓑ Ⓒ Ⓓ	155	Ⓐ Ⓑ Ⓒ Ⓓ	165	Ⓐ Ⓑ Ⓒ Ⓓ	175	Ⓐ Ⓑ Ⓒ Ⓓ	185	Ⓐ Ⓑ Ⓒ Ⓓ	195	Ⓐ Ⓑ Ⓒ Ⓓ
106	Ⓐ Ⓑ Ⓒ Ⓓ	116	Ⓐ Ⓑ Ⓒ Ⓓ	126	Ⓐ Ⓑ Ⓒ Ⓓ	136	Ⓐ Ⓑ Ⓒ Ⓓ	146	Ⓐ Ⓑ Ⓒ Ⓓ	156	Ⓐ Ⓑ Ⓒ Ⓓ	166	Ⓐ Ⓑ Ⓒ Ⓓ	176	Ⓐ Ⓑ Ⓒ Ⓓ	186	Ⓐ Ⓑ Ⓒ Ⓓ	196	Ⓐ Ⓑ Ⓒ Ⓓ
107	Ⓐ Ⓑ Ⓒ Ⓓ	117	Ⓐ Ⓑ Ⓒ Ⓓ	127	Ⓐ Ⓑ Ⓒ Ⓓ	137	Ⓐ Ⓑ Ⓒ Ⓓ	147	Ⓐ Ⓑ Ⓒ Ⓓ	157	Ⓐ Ⓑ Ⓒ Ⓓ	167	Ⓐ Ⓑ Ⓒ Ⓓ	177	Ⓐ Ⓑ Ⓒ Ⓓ	187	Ⓐ Ⓑ Ⓒ Ⓓ	197	Ⓐ Ⓑ Ⓒ Ⓓ
108	Ⓐ Ⓑ Ⓒ Ⓓ	118	Ⓐ Ⓑ Ⓒ Ⓓ	128	Ⓐ Ⓑ Ⓒ Ⓓ	138	Ⓐ Ⓑ Ⓒ Ⓓ	148	Ⓐ Ⓑ Ⓒ Ⓓ	158	Ⓐ Ⓑ Ⓒ Ⓓ	168	Ⓐ Ⓑ Ⓒ Ⓓ	178	Ⓐ Ⓑ Ⓒ Ⓓ	188	Ⓐ Ⓑ Ⓒ Ⓓ	198	Ⓐ Ⓑ Ⓒ Ⓓ
109	Ⓐ Ⓑ Ⓒ Ⓓ	119	Ⓐ Ⓑ Ⓒ Ⓓ	129	Ⓐ Ⓑ Ⓒ Ⓓ	139	Ⓐ Ⓑ Ⓒ Ⓓ	149	Ⓐ Ⓑ Ⓒ Ⓓ	159	Ⓐ Ⓑ Ⓒ Ⓓ	169	Ⓐ Ⓑ Ⓒ Ⓓ	179	Ⓐ Ⓑ Ⓒ Ⓓ	189	Ⓐ Ⓑ Ⓒ Ⓓ	199	Ⓐ Ⓑ Ⓒ Ⓓ
110	Ⓐ Ⓑ Ⓒ Ⓓ	120	Ⓐ Ⓑ Ⓒ Ⓓ	130	Ⓐ Ⓑ Ⓒ Ⓓ	140	Ⓐ Ⓑ Ⓒ Ⓓ	150	Ⓐ Ⓑ Ⓒ Ⓓ	160	Ⓐ Ⓑ Ⓒ Ⓓ	170	Ⓐ Ⓑ Ⓒ Ⓓ	180	Ⓐ Ⓑ Ⓒ Ⓓ	190	Ⓐ Ⓑ Ⓒ Ⓓ	200	Ⓐ Ⓑ Ⓒ Ⓓ

ACTUAL TEST 02

READING SECTION

101	Ⓐ Ⓑ Ⓒ Ⓓ	111	Ⓐ Ⓑ Ⓒ Ⓓ	121	Ⓐ Ⓑ Ⓒ Ⓓ	131	Ⓐ Ⓑ Ⓒ Ⓓ	141	Ⓐ Ⓑ Ⓒ Ⓓ	151	Ⓐ Ⓑ Ⓒ Ⓓ	161	Ⓐ Ⓑ Ⓒ Ⓓ	171	Ⓐ Ⓑ Ⓒ Ⓓ	181	Ⓐ Ⓑ Ⓒ Ⓓ	191	Ⓐ Ⓑ Ⓒ Ⓓ
102	Ⓐ Ⓑ Ⓒ Ⓓ	112	Ⓐ Ⓑ Ⓒ Ⓓ	122	Ⓐ Ⓑ Ⓒ Ⓓ	132	Ⓐ Ⓑ Ⓒ Ⓓ	142	Ⓐ Ⓑ Ⓒ Ⓓ	152	Ⓐ Ⓑ Ⓒ Ⓓ	162	Ⓐ Ⓑ Ⓒ Ⓓ	172	Ⓐ Ⓑ Ⓒ Ⓓ	182	Ⓐ Ⓑ Ⓒ Ⓓ	192	Ⓐ Ⓑ Ⓒ Ⓓ
103	Ⓐ Ⓑ Ⓒ Ⓓ	113	Ⓐ Ⓑ Ⓒ Ⓓ	123	Ⓐ Ⓑ Ⓒ Ⓓ	133	Ⓐ Ⓑ Ⓒ Ⓓ	143	Ⓐ Ⓑ Ⓒ Ⓓ	153	Ⓐ Ⓑ Ⓒ Ⓓ	163	Ⓐ Ⓑ Ⓒ Ⓓ	173	Ⓐ Ⓑ Ⓒ Ⓓ	183	Ⓐ Ⓑ Ⓒ Ⓓ	193	Ⓐ Ⓑ Ⓒ Ⓓ
104	Ⓐ Ⓑ Ⓒ Ⓓ	114	Ⓐ Ⓑ Ⓒ Ⓓ	124	Ⓐ Ⓑ Ⓒ Ⓓ	134	Ⓐ Ⓑ Ⓒ Ⓓ	144	Ⓐ Ⓑ Ⓒ Ⓓ	154	Ⓐ Ⓑ Ⓒ Ⓓ	164	Ⓐ Ⓑ Ⓒ Ⓓ	174	Ⓐ Ⓑ Ⓒ Ⓓ	184	Ⓐ Ⓑ Ⓒ Ⓓ	194	Ⓐ Ⓑ Ⓒ Ⓓ
105	Ⓐ Ⓑ Ⓒ Ⓓ	115	Ⓐ Ⓑ Ⓒ Ⓓ	125	Ⓐ Ⓑ Ⓒ Ⓓ	135	Ⓐ Ⓑ Ⓒ Ⓓ	145	Ⓐ Ⓑ Ⓒ Ⓓ	155	Ⓐ Ⓑ Ⓒ Ⓓ	165	Ⓐ Ⓑ Ⓒ Ⓓ	175	Ⓐ Ⓑ Ⓒ Ⓓ	185	Ⓐ Ⓑ Ⓒ Ⓓ	195	Ⓐ Ⓑ Ⓒ Ⓓ
106	Ⓐ Ⓑ Ⓒ Ⓓ	116	Ⓐ Ⓑ Ⓒ Ⓓ	126	Ⓐ Ⓑ Ⓒ Ⓓ	136	Ⓐ Ⓑ Ⓒ Ⓓ	146	Ⓐ Ⓑ Ⓒ Ⓓ	156	Ⓐ Ⓑ Ⓒ Ⓓ	166	Ⓐ Ⓑ Ⓒ Ⓓ	176	Ⓐ Ⓑ Ⓒ Ⓓ	186	Ⓐ Ⓑ Ⓒ Ⓓ	196	Ⓐ Ⓑ Ⓒ Ⓓ
107	Ⓐ Ⓑ Ⓒ Ⓓ	117	Ⓐ Ⓑ Ⓒ Ⓓ	127	Ⓐ Ⓑ Ⓒ Ⓓ	137	Ⓐ Ⓑ Ⓒ Ⓓ	147	Ⓐ Ⓑ Ⓒ Ⓓ	157	Ⓐ Ⓑ Ⓒ Ⓓ	167	Ⓐ Ⓑ Ⓒ Ⓓ	177	Ⓐ Ⓑ Ⓒ Ⓓ	187	Ⓐ Ⓑ Ⓒ Ⓓ	197	Ⓐ Ⓑ Ⓒ Ⓓ
108	Ⓐ Ⓑ Ⓒ Ⓓ	118	Ⓐ Ⓑ Ⓒ Ⓓ	128	Ⓐ Ⓑ Ⓒ Ⓓ	138	Ⓐ Ⓑ Ⓒ Ⓓ	148	Ⓐ Ⓑ Ⓒ Ⓓ	158	Ⓐ Ⓑ Ⓒ Ⓓ	168	Ⓐ Ⓑ Ⓒ Ⓓ	178	Ⓐ Ⓑ Ⓒ Ⓓ	188	Ⓐ Ⓑ Ⓒ Ⓓ	198	Ⓐ Ⓑ Ⓒ Ⓓ
109	Ⓐ Ⓑ Ⓒ Ⓓ	119	Ⓐ Ⓑ Ⓒ Ⓓ	129	Ⓐ Ⓑ Ⓒ Ⓓ	139	Ⓐ Ⓑ Ⓒ Ⓓ	149	Ⓐ Ⓑ Ⓒ Ⓓ	159	Ⓐ Ⓑ Ⓒ Ⓓ	169	Ⓐ Ⓑ Ⓒ Ⓓ	179	Ⓐ Ⓑ Ⓒ Ⓓ	189	Ⓐ Ⓑ Ⓒ Ⓓ	199	Ⓐ Ⓑ Ⓒ Ⓓ
110	Ⓐ Ⓑ Ⓒ Ⓓ	120	Ⓐ Ⓑ Ⓒ Ⓓ	130	Ⓐ Ⓑ Ⓒ Ⓓ	140	Ⓐ Ⓑ Ⓒ Ⓓ	150	Ⓐ Ⓑ Ⓒ Ⓓ	160	Ⓐ Ⓑ Ⓒ Ⓓ	170	Ⓐ Ⓑ Ⓒ Ⓓ	180	Ⓐ Ⓑ Ⓒ Ⓓ	190	Ⓐ Ⓑ Ⓒ Ⓓ	200	Ⓐ Ⓑ Ⓒ Ⓓ

答案紙

ACTUAL TEST 03

READING SECTION	101	Ⓐ Ⓑ Ⓒ Ⓓ	111	Ⓐ Ⓑ Ⓒ Ⓓ	121	Ⓐ Ⓑ Ⓒ Ⓓ	131	Ⓐ Ⓑ Ⓒ Ⓓ	141	Ⓐ Ⓑ Ⓒ Ⓓ	151	Ⓐ Ⓑ Ⓒ Ⓓ	161	Ⓐ Ⓑ Ⓒ Ⓓ	171	Ⓐ Ⓑ Ⓒ Ⓓ	181	Ⓐ Ⓑ Ⓒ Ⓓ	191	Ⓐ Ⓑ Ⓒ Ⓓ
	102	Ⓐ Ⓑ Ⓒ Ⓓ	112	Ⓐ Ⓑ Ⓒ Ⓓ	122	Ⓐ Ⓑ Ⓒ Ⓓ	132	Ⓐ Ⓑ Ⓒ Ⓓ	142	Ⓐ Ⓑ Ⓒ Ⓓ	152	Ⓐ Ⓑ Ⓒ Ⓓ	162	Ⓐ Ⓑ Ⓒ Ⓓ	172	Ⓐ Ⓑ Ⓒ Ⓓ	182	Ⓐ Ⓑ Ⓒ Ⓓ	192	Ⓐ Ⓑ Ⓒ Ⓓ
	103	Ⓐ Ⓑ Ⓒ Ⓓ	113	Ⓐ Ⓑ Ⓒ Ⓓ	123	Ⓐ Ⓑ Ⓒ Ⓓ	133	Ⓐ Ⓑ Ⓒ Ⓓ	143	Ⓐ Ⓑ Ⓒ Ⓓ	153	Ⓐ Ⓑ Ⓒ Ⓓ	163	Ⓐ Ⓑ Ⓒ Ⓓ	173	Ⓐ Ⓑ Ⓒ Ⓓ	183	Ⓐ Ⓑ Ⓒ Ⓓ	193	Ⓐ Ⓑ Ⓒ Ⓓ
	104	Ⓐ Ⓑ Ⓒ Ⓓ	114	Ⓐ Ⓑ Ⓒ Ⓓ	124	Ⓐ Ⓑ Ⓒ Ⓓ	134	Ⓐ Ⓑ Ⓒ Ⓓ	144	Ⓐ Ⓑ Ⓒ Ⓓ	154	Ⓐ Ⓑ Ⓒ Ⓓ	164	Ⓐ Ⓑ Ⓒ Ⓓ	174	Ⓐ Ⓑ Ⓒ Ⓓ	184	Ⓐ Ⓑ Ⓒ Ⓓ	194	Ⓐ Ⓑ Ⓒ Ⓓ
	105	Ⓐ Ⓑ Ⓒ Ⓓ	115	Ⓐ Ⓑ Ⓒ Ⓓ	125	Ⓐ Ⓑ Ⓒ Ⓓ	135	Ⓐ Ⓑ Ⓒ Ⓓ	145	Ⓐ Ⓑ Ⓒ Ⓓ	155	Ⓐ Ⓑ Ⓒ Ⓓ	165	Ⓐ Ⓑ Ⓒ Ⓓ	175	Ⓐ Ⓑ Ⓒ Ⓓ	185	Ⓐ Ⓑ Ⓒ Ⓓ	195	Ⓐ Ⓑ Ⓒ Ⓓ
	106	Ⓐ Ⓑ Ⓒ Ⓓ	116	Ⓐ Ⓑ Ⓒ Ⓓ	126	Ⓐ Ⓑ Ⓒ Ⓓ	136	Ⓐ Ⓑ Ⓒ Ⓓ	146	Ⓐ Ⓑ Ⓒ Ⓓ	156	Ⓐ Ⓑ Ⓒ Ⓓ	166	Ⓐ Ⓑ Ⓒ Ⓓ	176	Ⓐ Ⓑ Ⓒ Ⓓ	186	Ⓐ Ⓑ Ⓒ Ⓓ	196	Ⓐ Ⓑ Ⓒ Ⓓ
	107	Ⓐ Ⓑ Ⓒ Ⓓ	117	Ⓐ Ⓑ Ⓒ Ⓓ	127	Ⓐ Ⓑ Ⓒ Ⓓ	137	Ⓐ Ⓑ Ⓒ Ⓓ	147	Ⓐ Ⓑ Ⓒ Ⓓ	157	Ⓐ Ⓑ Ⓒ Ⓓ	167	Ⓐ Ⓑ Ⓒ Ⓓ	177	Ⓐ Ⓑ Ⓒ Ⓓ	187	Ⓐ Ⓑ Ⓒ Ⓓ	197	Ⓐ Ⓑ Ⓒ Ⓓ
	108	Ⓐ Ⓑ Ⓒ Ⓓ	118	Ⓐ Ⓑ Ⓒ Ⓓ	128	Ⓐ Ⓑ Ⓒ Ⓓ	138	Ⓐ Ⓑ Ⓒ Ⓓ	148	Ⓐ Ⓑ Ⓒ Ⓓ	158	Ⓐ Ⓑ Ⓒ Ⓓ	168	Ⓐ Ⓑ Ⓒ Ⓓ	178	Ⓐ Ⓑ Ⓒ Ⓓ	188	Ⓐ Ⓑ Ⓒ Ⓓ	198	Ⓐ Ⓑ Ⓒ Ⓓ
	109	Ⓐ Ⓑ Ⓒ Ⓓ	119	Ⓐ Ⓑ Ⓒ Ⓓ	129	Ⓐ Ⓑ Ⓒ Ⓓ	139	Ⓐ Ⓑ Ⓒ Ⓓ	149	Ⓐ Ⓑ Ⓒ Ⓓ	159	Ⓐ Ⓑ Ⓒ Ⓓ	169	Ⓐ Ⓑ Ⓒ Ⓓ	179	Ⓐ Ⓑ Ⓒ Ⓓ	189	Ⓐ Ⓑ Ⓒ Ⓓ	199	Ⓐ Ⓑ Ⓒ Ⓓ
	110	Ⓐ Ⓑ Ⓒ Ⓓ	120	Ⓐ Ⓑ Ⓒ Ⓓ	130	Ⓐ Ⓑ Ⓒ Ⓓ	140	Ⓐ Ⓑ Ⓒ Ⓓ	150	Ⓐ Ⓑ Ⓒ Ⓓ	160	Ⓐ Ⓑ Ⓒ Ⓓ	170	Ⓐ Ⓑ Ⓒ Ⓓ	180	Ⓐ Ⓑ Ⓒ Ⓓ	190	Ⓐ Ⓑ Ⓒ Ⓓ	200	Ⓐ Ⓑ Ⓒ Ⓓ

ACTUAL TEST 04

READING SECTION	101	Ⓐ Ⓑ Ⓒ Ⓓ	111	Ⓐ Ⓑ Ⓒ Ⓓ	121	Ⓐ Ⓑ Ⓒ Ⓓ	131	Ⓐ Ⓑ Ⓒ Ⓓ	141	Ⓐ Ⓑ Ⓒ Ⓓ	151	Ⓐ Ⓑ Ⓒ Ⓓ	161	Ⓐ Ⓑ Ⓒ Ⓓ	171	Ⓐ Ⓑ Ⓒ Ⓓ	181	Ⓐ Ⓑ Ⓒ Ⓓ	191	Ⓐ Ⓑ Ⓒ Ⓓ
	102	Ⓐ Ⓑ Ⓒ Ⓓ	112	Ⓐ Ⓑ Ⓒ Ⓓ	122	Ⓐ Ⓑ Ⓒ Ⓓ	132	Ⓐ Ⓑ Ⓒ Ⓓ	142	Ⓐ Ⓑ Ⓒ Ⓓ	152	Ⓐ Ⓑ Ⓒ Ⓓ	162	Ⓐ Ⓑ Ⓒ Ⓓ	172	Ⓐ Ⓑ Ⓒ Ⓓ	182	Ⓐ Ⓑ Ⓒ Ⓓ	192	Ⓐ Ⓑ Ⓒ Ⓓ
	103	Ⓐ Ⓑ Ⓒ Ⓓ	113	Ⓐ Ⓑ Ⓒ Ⓓ	123	Ⓐ Ⓑ Ⓒ Ⓓ	133	Ⓐ Ⓑ Ⓒ Ⓓ	143	Ⓐ Ⓑ Ⓒ Ⓓ	153	Ⓐ Ⓑ Ⓒ Ⓓ	163	Ⓐ Ⓑ Ⓒ Ⓓ	173	Ⓐ Ⓑ Ⓒ Ⓓ	183	Ⓐ Ⓑ Ⓒ Ⓓ	193	Ⓐ Ⓑ Ⓒ Ⓓ
	104	Ⓐ Ⓑ Ⓒ Ⓓ	114	Ⓐ Ⓑ Ⓒ Ⓓ	124	Ⓐ Ⓑ Ⓒ Ⓓ	134	Ⓐ Ⓑ Ⓒ Ⓓ	144	Ⓐ Ⓑ Ⓒ Ⓓ	154	Ⓐ Ⓑ Ⓒ Ⓓ	164	Ⓐ Ⓑ Ⓒ Ⓓ	174	Ⓐ Ⓑ Ⓒ Ⓓ	184	Ⓐ Ⓑ Ⓒ Ⓓ	194	Ⓐ Ⓑ Ⓒ Ⓓ
	105	Ⓐ Ⓑ Ⓒ Ⓓ	115	Ⓐ Ⓑ Ⓒ Ⓓ	125	Ⓐ Ⓑ Ⓒ Ⓓ	135	Ⓐ Ⓑ Ⓒ Ⓓ	145	Ⓐ Ⓑ Ⓒ Ⓓ	155	Ⓐ Ⓑ Ⓒ Ⓓ	165	Ⓐ Ⓑ Ⓒ Ⓓ	175	Ⓐ Ⓑ Ⓒ Ⓓ	185	Ⓐ Ⓑ Ⓒ Ⓓ	195	Ⓐ Ⓑ Ⓒ Ⓓ
	106	Ⓐ Ⓑ Ⓒ Ⓓ	116	Ⓐ Ⓑ Ⓒ Ⓓ	126	Ⓐ Ⓑ Ⓒ Ⓓ	136	Ⓐ Ⓑ Ⓒ Ⓓ	146	Ⓐ Ⓑ Ⓒ Ⓓ	156	Ⓐ Ⓑ Ⓒ Ⓓ	166	Ⓐ Ⓑ Ⓒ Ⓓ	176	Ⓐ Ⓑ Ⓒ Ⓓ	186	Ⓐ Ⓑ Ⓒ Ⓓ	196	Ⓐ Ⓑ Ⓒ Ⓓ
	107	Ⓐ Ⓑ Ⓒ Ⓓ	117	Ⓐ Ⓑ Ⓒ Ⓓ	127	Ⓐ Ⓑ Ⓒ Ⓓ	137	Ⓐ Ⓑ Ⓒ Ⓓ	147	Ⓐ Ⓑ Ⓒ Ⓓ	157	Ⓐ Ⓑ Ⓒ Ⓓ	167	Ⓐ Ⓑ Ⓒ Ⓓ	177	Ⓐ Ⓑ Ⓒ Ⓓ	187	Ⓐ Ⓑ Ⓒ Ⓓ	197	Ⓐ Ⓑ Ⓒ Ⓓ
	108	Ⓐ Ⓑ Ⓒ Ⓓ	118	Ⓐ Ⓑ Ⓒ Ⓓ	128	Ⓐ Ⓑ Ⓒ Ⓓ	138	Ⓐ Ⓑ Ⓒ Ⓓ	148	Ⓐ Ⓑ Ⓒ Ⓓ	158	Ⓐ Ⓑ Ⓒ Ⓓ	168	Ⓐ Ⓑ Ⓒ Ⓓ	178	Ⓐ Ⓑ Ⓒ Ⓓ	188	Ⓐ Ⓑ Ⓒ Ⓓ	198	Ⓐ Ⓑ Ⓒ Ⓓ
	109	Ⓐ Ⓑ Ⓒ Ⓓ	119	Ⓐ Ⓑ Ⓒ Ⓓ	129	Ⓐ Ⓑ Ⓒ Ⓓ	139	Ⓐ Ⓑ Ⓒ Ⓓ	149	Ⓐ Ⓑ Ⓒ Ⓓ	159	Ⓐ Ⓑ Ⓒ Ⓓ	169	Ⓐ Ⓑ Ⓒ Ⓓ	179	Ⓐ Ⓑ Ⓒ Ⓓ	189	Ⓐ Ⓑ Ⓒ Ⓓ	199	Ⓐ Ⓑ Ⓒ Ⓓ
	110	Ⓐ Ⓑ Ⓒ Ⓓ	120	Ⓐ Ⓑ Ⓒ Ⓓ	130	Ⓐ Ⓑ Ⓒ Ⓓ	140	Ⓐ Ⓑ Ⓒ Ⓓ	150	Ⓐ Ⓑ Ⓒ Ⓓ	160	Ⓐ Ⓑ Ⓒ Ⓓ	170	Ⓐ Ⓑ Ⓒ Ⓓ	180	Ⓐ Ⓑ Ⓒ Ⓓ	190	Ⓐ Ⓑ Ⓒ Ⓓ	200	Ⓐ Ⓑ Ⓒ Ⓓ

答案紙

ACTUAL TEST 05

READING SECTION																				
	101	Ⓐ Ⓑ Ⓒ Ⓓ	111	Ⓐ Ⓑ Ⓒ Ⓓ	121	Ⓐ Ⓑ Ⓒ Ⓓ	131	Ⓐ Ⓑ Ⓒ Ⓓ	141	Ⓐ Ⓑ Ⓒ Ⓓ	151	Ⓐ Ⓑ Ⓒ Ⓓ	161	Ⓐ Ⓑ Ⓒ Ⓓ	171	Ⓐ Ⓑ Ⓒ Ⓓ	181	Ⓐ Ⓑ Ⓒ Ⓓ	191	Ⓐ Ⓑ Ⓒ Ⓓ
	102	Ⓐ Ⓑ Ⓒ Ⓓ	112	Ⓐ Ⓑ Ⓒ Ⓓ	122	Ⓐ Ⓑ Ⓒ Ⓓ	132	Ⓐ Ⓑ Ⓒ Ⓓ	142	Ⓐ Ⓑ Ⓒ Ⓓ	152	Ⓐ Ⓑ Ⓒ Ⓓ	162	Ⓐ Ⓑ Ⓒ Ⓓ	172	Ⓐ Ⓑ Ⓒ Ⓓ	182	Ⓐ Ⓑ Ⓒ Ⓓ	192	Ⓐ Ⓑ Ⓒ Ⓓ
	103	Ⓐ Ⓑ Ⓒ Ⓓ	113	Ⓐ Ⓑ Ⓒ Ⓓ	123	Ⓐ Ⓑ Ⓒ Ⓓ	133	Ⓐ Ⓑ Ⓒ Ⓓ	143	Ⓐ Ⓑ Ⓒ Ⓓ	153	Ⓐ Ⓑ Ⓒ Ⓓ	163	Ⓐ Ⓑ Ⓒ Ⓓ	173	Ⓐ Ⓑ Ⓒ Ⓓ	183	Ⓐ Ⓑ Ⓒ Ⓓ	193	Ⓐ Ⓑ Ⓒ Ⓓ
	104	Ⓐ Ⓑ Ⓒ Ⓓ	114	Ⓐ Ⓑ Ⓒ Ⓓ	124	Ⓐ Ⓑ Ⓒ Ⓓ	134	Ⓐ Ⓑ Ⓒ Ⓓ	144	Ⓐ Ⓑ Ⓒ Ⓓ	154	Ⓐ Ⓑ Ⓒ Ⓓ	164	Ⓐ Ⓑ Ⓒ Ⓓ	174	Ⓐ Ⓑ Ⓒ Ⓓ	184	Ⓐ Ⓑ Ⓒ Ⓓ	194	Ⓐ Ⓑ Ⓒ Ⓓ
	105	Ⓐ Ⓑ Ⓒ Ⓓ	115	Ⓐ Ⓑ Ⓒ Ⓓ	125	Ⓐ Ⓑ Ⓒ Ⓓ	135	Ⓐ Ⓑ Ⓒ Ⓓ	145	Ⓐ Ⓑ Ⓒ Ⓓ	155	Ⓐ Ⓑ Ⓒ Ⓓ	165	Ⓐ Ⓑ Ⓒ Ⓓ	175	Ⓐ Ⓑ Ⓒ Ⓓ	185	Ⓐ Ⓑ Ⓒ Ⓓ	195	Ⓐ Ⓑ Ⓒ Ⓓ
	106	Ⓐ Ⓑ Ⓒ Ⓓ	116	Ⓐ Ⓑ Ⓒ Ⓓ	126	Ⓐ Ⓑ Ⓒ Ⓓ	136	Ⓐ Ⓑ Ⓒ Ⓓ	146	Ⓐ Ⓑ Ⓒ Ⓓ	156	Ⓐ Ⓑ Ⓒ Ⓓ	166	Ⓐ Ⓑ Ⓒ Ⓓ	176	Ⓐ Ⓑ Ⓒ Ⓓ	186	Ⓐ Ⓑ Ⓒ Ⓓ	196	Ⓐ Ⓑ Ⓒ Ⓓ
	107	Ⓐ Ⓑ Ⓒ Ⓓ	117	Ⓐ Ⓑ Ⓒ Ⓓ	127	Ⓐ Ⓑ Ⓒ Ⓓ	137	Ⓐ Ⓑ Ⓒ Ⓓ	147	Ⓐ Ⓑ Ⓒ Ⓓ	157	Ⓐ Ⓑ Ⓒ Ⓓ	167	Ⓐ Ⓑ Ⓒ Ⓓ	177	Ⓐ Ⓑ Ⓒ Ⓓ	187	Ⓐ Ⓑ Ⓒ Ⓓ	197	Ⓐ Ⓑ Ⓒ Ⓓ
	108	Ⓐ Ⓑ Ⓒ Ⓓ	118	Ⓐ Ⓑ Ⓒ Ⓓ	128	Ⓐ Ⓑ Ⓒ Ⓓ	138	Ⓐ Ⓑ Ⓒ Ⓓ	148	Ⓐ Ⓑ Ⓒ Ⓓ	158	Ⓐ Ⓑ Ⓒ Ⓓ	168	Ⓐ Ⓑ Ⓒ Ⓓ	178	Ⓐ Ⓑ Ⓒ Ⓓ	188	Ⓐ Ⓑ Ⓒ Ⓓ	198	Ⓐ Ⓑ Ⓒ Ⓓ
	109	Ⓐ Ⓑ Ⓒ Ⓓ	119	Ⓐ Ⓑ Ⓒ Ⓓ	129	Ⓐ Ⓑ Ⓒ Ⓓ	139	Ⓐ Ⓑ Ⓒ Ⓓ	149	Ⓐ Ⓑ Ⓒ Ⓓ	159	Ⓐ Ⓑ Ⓒ Ⓓ	169	Ⓐ Ⓑ Ⓒ Ⓓ	179	Ⓐ Ⓑ Ⓒ Ⓓ	189	Ⓐ Ⓑ Ⓒ Ⓓ	199	Ⓐ Ⓑ Ⓒ Ⓓ
	110	Ⓐ Ⓑ Ⓒ Ⓓ	120	Ⓐ Ⓑ Ⓒ Ⓓ	130	Ⓐ Ⓑ Ⓒ Ⓓ	140	Ⓐ Ⓑ Ⓒ Ⓓ	150	Ⓐ Ⓑ Ⓒ Ⓓ	160	Ⓐ Ⓑ Ⓒ Ⓓ	170	Ⓐ Ⓑ Ⓒ Ⓓ	180	Ⓐ Ⓑ Ⓒ Ⓓ	190	Ⓐ Ⓑ Ⓒ Ⓓ	200	Ⓐ Ⓑ Ⓒ Ⓓ

ACTUAL TEST 06

READING SECTION																				
	101	Ⓐ Ⓑ Ⓒ Ⓓ	111	Ⓐ Ⓑ Ⓒ Ⓓ	121	Ⓐ Ⓑ Ⓒ Ⓓ	131	Ⓐ Ⓑ Ⓒ Ⓓ	141	Ⓐ Ⓑ Ⓒ Ⓓ	151	Ⓐ Ⓑ Ⓒ Ⓓ	161	Ⓐ Ⓑ Ⓒ Ⓓ	171	Ⓐ Ⓑ Ⓒ Ⓓ	181	Ⓐ Ⓑ Ⓒ Ⓓ	191	Ⓐ Ⓑ Ⓒ Ⓓ
	102	Ⓐ Ⓑ Ⓒ Ⓓ	112	Ⓐ Ⓑ Ⓒ Ⓓ	122	Ⓐ Ⓑ Ⓒ Ⓓ	132	Ⓐ Ⓑ Ⓒ Ⓓ	142	Ⓐ Ⓑ Ⓒ Ⓓ	152	Ⓐ Ⓑ Ⓒ Ⓓ	162	Ⓐ Ⓑ Ⓒ Ⓓ	172	Ⓐ Ⓑ Ⓒ Ⓓ	182	Ⓐ Ⓑ Ⓒ Ⓓ	192	Ⓐ Ⓑ Ⓒ Ⓓ
	103	Ⓐ Ⓑ Ⓒ Ⓓ	113	Ⓐ Ⓑ Ⓒ Ⓓ	123	Ⓐ Ⓑ Ⓒ Ⓓ	133	Ⓐ Ⓑ Ⓒ Ⓓ	143	Ⓐ Ⓑ Ⓒ Ⓓ	153	Ⓐ Ⓑ Ⓒ Ⓓ	163	Ⓐ Ⓑ Ⓒ Ⓓ	173	Ⓐ Ⓑ Ⓒ Ⓓ	183	Ⓐ Ⓑ Ⓒ Ⓓ	193	Ⓐ Ⓑ Ⓒ Ⓓ
	104	Ⓐ Ⓑ Ⓒ Ⓓ	114	Ⓐ Ⓑ Ⓒ Ⓓ	124	Ⓐ Ⓑ Ⓒ Ⓓ	134	Ⓐ Ⓑ Ⓒ Ⓓ	144	Ⓐ Ⓑ Ⓒ Ⓓ	154	Ⓐ Ⓑ Ⓒ Ⓓ	164	Ⓐ Ⓑ Ⓒ Ⓓ	174	Ⓐ Ⓑ Ⓒ Ⓓ	184	Ⓐ Ⓑ Ⓒ Ⓓ	194	Ⓐ Ⓑ Ⓒ Ⓓ
	105	Ⓐ Ⓑ Ⓒ Ⓓ	115	Ⓐ Ⓑ Ⓒ Ⓓ	125	Ⓐ Ⓑ Ⓒ Ⓓ	135	Ⓐ Ⓑ Ⓒ Ⓓ	145	Ⓐ Ⓑ Ⓒ Ⓓ	155	Ⓐ Ⓑ Ⓒ Ⓓ	165	Ⓐ Ⓑ Ⓒ Ⓓ	175	Ⓐ Ⓑ Ⓒ Ⓓ	185	Ⓐ Ⓑ Ⓒ Ⓓ	195	Ⓐ Ⓑ Ⓒ Ⓓ
	106	Ⓐ Ⓑ Ⓒ Ⓓ	116	Ⓐ Ⓑ Ⓒ Ⓓ	126	Ⓐ Ⓑ Ⓒ Ⓓ	136	Ⓐ Ⓑ Ⓒ Ⓓ	146	Ⓐ Ⓑ Ⓒ Ⓓ	156	Ⓐ Ⓑ Ⓒ Ⓓ	166	Ⓐ Ⓑ Ⓒ Ⓓ	176	Ⓐ Ⓑ Ⓒ Ⓓ	186	Ⓐ Ⓑ Ⓒ Ⓓ	196	Ⓐ Ⓑ Ⓒ Ⓓ
	107	Ⓐ Ⓑ Ⓒ Ⓓ	117	Ⓐ Ⓑ Ⓒ Ⓓ	127	Ⓐ Ⓑ Ⓒ Ⓓ	137	Ⓐ Ⓑ Ⓒ Ⓓ	147	Ⓐ Ⓑ Ⓒ Ⓓ	157	Ⓐ Ⓑ Ⓒ Ⓓ	167	Ⓐ Ⓑ Ⓒ Ⓓ	177	Ⓐ Ⓑ Ⓒ Ⓓ	187	Ⓐ Ⓑ Ⓒ Ⓓ	197	Ⓐ Ⓑ Ⓒ Ⓓ
	108	Ⓐ Ⓑ Ⓒ Ⓓ	118	Ⓐ Ⓑ Ⓒ Ⓓ	128	Ⓐ Ⓑ Ⓒ Ⓓ	138	Ⓐ Ⓑ Ⓒ Ⓓ	148	Ⓐ Ⓑ Ⓒ Ⓓ	158	Ⓐ Ⓑ Ⓒ Ⓓ	168	Ⓐ Ⓑ Ⓒ Ⓓ	178	Ⓐ Ⓑ Ⓒ Ⓓ	188	Ⓐ Ⓑ Ⓒ Ⓓ	198	Ⓐ Ⓑ Ⓒ Ⓓ
	109	Ⓐ Ⓑ Ⓒ Ⓓ	119	Ⓐ Ⓑ Ⓒ Ⓓ	129	Ⓐ Ⓑ Ⓒ Ⓓ	139	Ⓐ Ⓑ Ⓒ Ⓓ	149	Ⓐ Ⓑ Ⓒ Ⓓ	159	Ⓐ Ⓑ Ⓒ Ⓓ	169	Ⓐ Ⓑ Ⓒ Ⓓ	179	Ⓐ Ⓑ Ⓒ Ⓓ	189	Ⓐ Ⓑ Ⓒ Ⓓ	199	Ⓐ Ⓑ Ⓒ Ⓓ
	110	Ⓐ Ⓑ Ⓒ Ⓓ	120	Ⓐ Ⓑ Ⓒ Ⓓ	130	Ⓐ Ⓑ Ⓒ Ⓓ	140	Ⓐ Ⓑ Ⓒ Ⓓ	150	Ⓐ Ⓑ Ⓒ Ⓓ	160	Ⓐ Ⓑ Ⓒ Ⓓ	170	Ⓐ Ⓑ Ⓒ Ⓓ	180	Ⓐ Ⓑ Ⓒ Ⓓ	190	Ⓐ Ⓑ Ⓒ Ⓓ	200	Ⓐ Ⓑ Ⓒ Ⓓ

答案紙

ACTUAL TEST 07

READING SECTION																			
101	Ⓐ Ⓑ Ⓒ Ⓓ	111	Ⓐ Ⓑ Ⓒ Ⓓ	121	Ⓐ Ⓑ Ⓒ Ⓓ	131	Ⓐ Ⓑ Ⓒ Ⓓ	141	Ⓐ Ⓑ Ⓒ Ⓓ	151	Ⓐ Ⓑ Ⓒ Ⓓ	161	Ⓐ Ⓑ Ⓒ Ⓓ	171	Ⓐ Ⓑ Ⓒ Ⓓ	181	Ⓐ Ⓑ Ⓒ Ⓓ	191	Ⓐ Ⓑ Ⓒ Ⓓ
102	Ⓐ Ⓑ Ⓒ Ⓓ	112	Ⓐ Ⓑ Ⓒ Ⓓ	122	Ⓐ Ⓑ Ⓒ Ⓓ	132	Ⓐ Ⓑ Ⓒ Ⓓ	142	Ⓐ Ⓑ Ⓒ Ⓓ	152	Ⓐ Ⓑ Ⓒ Ⓓ	162	Ⓐ Ⓑ Ⓒ Ⓓ	172	Ⓐ Ⓑ Ⓒ Ⓓ	182	Ⓐ Ⓑ Ⓒ Ⓓ	192	Ⓐ Ⓑ Ⓒ Ⓓ
103	Ⓐ Ⓑ Ⓒ Ⓓ	113	Ⓐ Ⓑ Ⓒ Ⓓ	123	Ⓐ Ⓑ Ⓒ Ⓓ	133	Ⓐ Ⓑ Ⓒ Ⓓ	143	Ⓐ Ⓑ Ⓒ Ⓓ	153	Ⓐ Ⓑ Ⓒ Ⓓ	163	Ⓐ Ⓑ Ⓒ Ⓓ	173	Ⓐ Ⓑ Ⓒ Ⓓ	183	Ⓐ Ⓑ Ⓒ Ⓓ	193	Ⓐ Ⓑ Ⓒ Ⓓ
104	Ⓐ Ⓑ Ⓒ Ⓓ	114	Ⓐ Ⓑ Ⓒ Ⓓ	124	Ⓐ Ⓑ Ⓒ Ⓓ	134	Ⓐ Ⓑ Ⓒ Ⓓ	144	Ⓐ Ⓑ Ⓒ Ⓓ	154	Ⓐ Ⓑ Ⓒ Ⓓ	164	Ⓐ Ⓑ Ⓒ Ⓓ	174	Ⓐ Ⓑ Ⓒ Ⓓ	184	Ⓐ Ⓑ Ⓒ Ⓓ	194	Ⓐ Ⓑ Ⓒ Ⓓ
105	Ⓐ Ⓑ Ⓒ Ⓓ	115	Ⓐ Ⓑ Ⓒ Ⓓ	125	Ⓐ Ⓑ Ⓒ Ⓓ	135	Ⓐ Ⓑ Ⓒ Ⓓ	145	Ⓐ Ⓑ Ⓒ Ⓓ	155	Ⓐ Ⓑ Ⓒ Ⓓ	165	Ⓐ Ⓑ Ⓒ Ⓓ	175	Ⓐ Ⓑ Ⓒ Ⓓ	185	Ⓐ Ⓑ Ⓒ Ⓓ	195	Ⓐ Ⓑ Ⓒ Ⓓ
106	Ⓐ Ⓑ Ⓒ Ⓓ	116	Ⓐ Ⓑ Ⓒ Ⓓ	126	Ⓐ Ⓑ Ⓒ Ⓓ	136	Ⓐ Ⓑ Ⓒ Ⓓ	146	Ⓐ Ⓑ Ⓒ Ⓓ	156	Ⓐ Ⓑ Ⓒ Ⓓ	166	Ⓐ Ⓑ Ⓒ Ⓓ	176	Ⓐ Ⓑ Ⓒ Ⓓ	186	Ⓐ Ⓑ Ⓒ Ⓓ	196	Ⓐ Ⓑ Ⓒ Ⓓ
107	Ⓐ Ⓑ Ⓒ Ⓓ	117	Ⓐ Ⓑ Ⓒ Ⓓ	127	Ⓐ Ⓑ Ⓒ Ⓓ	137	Ⓐ Ⓑ Ⓒ Ⓓ	147	Ⓐ Ⓑ Ⓒ Ⓓ	157	Ⓐ Ⓑ Ⓒ Ⓓ	167	Ⓐ Ⓑ Ⓒ Ⓓ	177	Ⓐ Ⓑ Ⓒ Ⓓ	187	Ⓐ Ⓑ Ⓒ Ⓓ	197	Ⓐ Ⓑ Ⓒ Ⓓ
108	Ⓐ Ⓑ Ⓒ Ⓓ	118	Ⓐ Ⓑ Ⓒ Ⓓ	128	Ⓐ Ⓑ Ⓒ Ⓓ	138	Ⓐ Ⓑ Ⓒ Ⓓ	148	Ⓐ Ⓑ Ⓒ Ⓓ	158	Ⓐ Ⓑ Ⓒ Ⓓ	168	Ⓐ Ⓑ Ⓒ Ⓓ	178	Ⓐ Ⓑ Ⓒ Ⓓ	188	Ⓐ Ⓑ Ⓒ Ⓓ	198	Ⓐ Ⓑ Ⓒ Ⓓ
109	Ⓐ Ⓑ Ⓒ Ⓓ	119	Ⓐ Ⓑ Ⓒ Ⓓ	129	Ⓐ Ⓑ Ⓒ Ⓓ	139	Ⓐ Ⓑ Ⓒ Ⓓ	149	Ⓐ Ⓑ Ⓒ Ⓓ	159	Ⓐ Ⓑ Ⓒ Ⓓ	169	Ⓐ Ⓑ Ⓒ Ⓓ	179	Ⓐ Ⓑ Ⓒ Ⓓ	189	Ⓐ Ⓑ Ⓒ Ⓓ	199	Ⓐ Ⓑ Ⓒ Ⓓ
110	Ⓐ Ⓑ Ⓒ Ⓓ	120	Ⓐ Ⓑ Ⓒ Ⓓ	130	Ⓐ Ⓑ Ⓒ Ⓓ	140	Ⓐ Ⓑ Ⓒ Ⓓ	150	Ⓐ Ⓑ Ⓒ Ⓓ	160	Ⓐ Ⓑ Ⓒ Ⓓ	170	Ⓐ Ⓑ Ⓒ Ⓓ	180	Ⓐ Ⓑ Ⓒ Ⓓ	190	Ⓐ Ⓑ Ⓒ Ⓓ	200	Ⓐ Ⓑ Ⓒ Ⓓ

ACTUAL TEST 08

READING SECTION																			
101	Ⓐ Ⓑ Ⓒ Ⓓ	111	Ⓐ Ⓑ Ⓒ Ⓓ	121	Ⓐ Ⓑ Ⓒ Ⓓ	131	Ⓐ Ⓑ Ⓒ Ⓓ	141	Ⓐ Ⓑ Ⓒ Ⓓ	151	Ⓐ Ⓑ Ⓒ Ⓓ	161	Ⓐ Ⓑ Ⓒ Ⓓ	171	Ⓐ Ⓑ Ⓒ Ⓓ	181	Ⓐ Ⓑ Ⓒ Ⓓ	191	Ⓐ Ⓑ Ⓒ Ⓓ
102	Ⓐ Ⓑ Ⓒ Ⓓ	112	Ⓐ Ⓑ Ⓒ Ⓓ	122	Ⓐ Ⓑ Ⓒ Ⓓ	132	Ⓐ Ⓑ Ⓒ Ⓓ	142	Ⓐ Ⓑ Ⓒ Ⓓ	152	Ⓐ Ⓑ Ⓒ Ⓓ	162	Ⓐ Ⓑ Ⓒ Ⓓ	172	Ⓐ Ⓑ Ⓒ Ⓓ	182	Ⓐ Ⓑ Ⓒ Ⓓ	192	Ⓐ Ⓑ Ⓒ Ⓓ
103	Ⓐ Ⓑ Ⓒ Ⓓ	113	Ⓐ Ⓑ Ⓒ Ⓓ	123	Ⓐ Ⓑ Ⓒ Ⓓ	133	Ⓐ Ⓑ Ⓒ Ⓓ	143	Ⓐ Ⓑ Ⓒ Ⓓ	153	Ⓐ Ⓑ Ⓒ Ⓓ	163	Ⓐ Ⓑ Ⓒ Ⓓ	173	Ⓐ Ⓑ Ⓒ Ⓓ	183	Ⓐ Ⓑ Ⓒ Ⓓ	193	Ⓐ Ⓑ Ⓒ Ⓓ
104	Ⓐ Ⓑ Ⓒ Ⓓ	114	Ⓐ Ⓑ Ⓒ Ⓓ	124	Ⓐ Ⓑ Ⓒ Ⓓ	134	Ⓐ Ⓑ Ⓒ Ⓓ	144	Ⓐ Ⓑ Ⓒ Ⓓ	154	Ⓐ Ⓑ Ⓒ Ⓓ	164	Ⓐ Ⓑ Ⓒ Ⓓ	174	Ⓐ Ⓑ Ⓒ Ⓓ	184	Ⓐ Ⓑ Ⓒ Ⓓ	194	Ⓐ Ⓑ Ⓒ Ⓓ
105	Ⓐ Ⓑ Ⓒ Ⓓ	115	Ⓐ Ⓑ Ⓒ Ⓓ	125	Ⓐ Ⓑ Ⓒ Ⓓ	135	Ⓐ Ⓑ Ⓒ Ⓓ	145	Ⓐ Ⓑ Ⓒ Ⓓ	155	Ⓐ Ⓑ Ⓒ Ⓓ	165	Ⓐ Ⓑ Ⓒ Ⓓ	175	Ⓐ Ⓑ Ⓒ Ⓓ	185	Ⓐ Ⓑ Ⓒ Ⓓ	195	Ⓐ Ⓑ Ⓒ Ⓓ
106	Ⓐ Ⓑ Ⓒ Ⓓ	116	Ⓐ Ⓑ Ⓒ Ⓓ	126	Ⓐ Ⓑ Ⓒ Ⓓ	136	Ⓐ Ⓑ Ⓒ Ⓓ	146	Ⓐ Ⓑ Ⓒ Ⓓ	156	Ⓐ Ⓑ Ⓒ Ⓓ	166	Ⓐ Ⓑ Ⓒ Ⓓ	176	Ⓐ Ⓑ Ⓒ Ⓓ	186	Ⓐ Ⓑ Ⓒ Ⓓ	196	Ⓐ Ⓑ Ⓒ Ⓓ
107	Ⓐ Ⓑ Ⓒ Ⓓ	117	Ⓐ Ⓑ Ⓒ Ⓓ	127	Ⓐ Ⓑ Ⓒ Ⓓ	137	Ⓐ Ⓑ Ⓒ Ⓓ	147	Ⓐ Ⓑ Ⓒ Ⓓ	157	Ⓐ Ⓑ Ⓒ Ⓓ	167	Ⓐ Ⓑ Ⓒ Ⓓ	177	Ⓐ Ⓑ Ⓒ Ⓓ	187	Ⓐ Ⓑ Ⓒ Ⓓ	197	Ⓐ Ⓑ Ⓒ Ⓓ
108	Ⓐ Ⓑ Ⓒ Ⓓ	118	Ⓐ Ⓑ Ⓒ Ⓓ	128	Ⓐ Ⓑ Ⓒ Ⓓ	138	Ⓐ Ⓑ Ⓒ Ⓓ	148	Ⓐ Ⓑ Ⓒ Ⓓ	158	Ⓐ Ⓑ Ⓒ Ⓓ	168	Ⓐ Ⓑ Ⓒ Ⓓ	178	Ⓐ Ⓑ Ⓒ Ⓓ	188	Ⓐ Ⓑ Ⓒ Ⓓ	198	Ⓐ Ⓑ Ⓒ Ⓓ
109	Ⓐ Ⓑ Ⓒ Ⓓ	119	Ⓐ Ⓑ Ⓒ Ⓓ	129	Ⓐ Ⓑ Ⓒ Ⓓ	139	Ⓐ Ⓑ Ⓒ Ⓓ	149	Ⓐ Ⓑ Ⓒ Ⓓ	159	Ⓐ Ⓑ Ⓒ Ⓓ	169	Ⓐ Ⓑ Ⓒ Ⓓ	179	Ⓐ Ⓑ Ⓒ Ⓓ	189	Ⓐ Ⓑ Ⓒ Ⓓ	199	Ⓐ Ⓑ Ⓒ Ⓓ
110	Ⓐ Ⓑ Ⓒ Ⓓ	120	Ⓐ Ⓑ Ⓒ Ⓓ	130	Ⓐ Ⓑ Ⓒ Ⓓ	140	Ⓐ Ⓑ Ⓒ Ⓓ	150	Ⓐ Ⓑ Ⓒ Ⓓ	160	Ⓐ Ⓑ Ⓒ Ⓓ	170	Ⓐ Ⓑ Ⓒ Ⓓ	180	Ⓐ Ⓑ Ⓒ Ⓓ	190	Ⓐ Ⓑ Ⓒ Ⓓ	200	Ⓐ Ⓑ Ⓒ Ⓓ

答案紙

ACTUAL TEST 09

READING SECTION	101	Ⓐ Ⓑ Ⓒ Ⓓ	111	Ⓐ Ⓑ Ⓒ Ⓓ	121	Ⓐ Ⓑ Ⓒ Ⓓ	131	Ⓐ Ⓑ Ⓒ Ⓓ	141	Ⓐ Ⓑ Ⓒ Ⓓ	151	Ⓐ Ⓑ Ⓒ Ⓓ	161	Ⓐ Ⓑ Ⓒ Ⓓ	171	Ⓐ Ⓑ Ⓒ Ⓓ	181	Ⓐ Ⓑ Ⓒ Ⓓ	191	Ⓐ Ⓑ Ⓒ Ⓓ
	102	Ⓐ Ⓑ Ⓒ Ⓓ	112	Ⓐ Ⓑ Ⓒ Ⓓ	122	Ⓐ Ⓑ Ⓒ Ⓓ	132	Ⓐ Ⓑ Ⓒ Ⓓ	142	Ⓐ Ⓑ Ⓒ Ⓓ	152	Ⓐ Ⓑ Ⓒ Ⓓ	162	Ⓐ Ⓑ Ⓒ Ⓓ	172	Ⓐ Ⓑ Ⓒ Ⓓ	182	Ⓐ Ⓑ Ⓒ Ⓓ	192	Ⓐ Ⓑ Ⓒ Ⓓ
	103	Ⓐ Ⓑ Ⓒ Ⓓ	113	Ⓐ Ⓑ Ⓒ Ⓓ	123	Ⓐ Ⓑ Ⓒ Ⓓ	133	Ⓐ Ⓑ Ⓒ Ⓓ	143	Ⓐ Ⓑ Ⓒ Ⓓ	153	Ⓐ Ⓑ Ⓒ Ⓓ	163	Ⓐ Ⓑ Ⓒ Ⓓ	173	Ⓐ Ⓑ Ⓒ Ⓓ	183	Ⓐ Ⓑ Ⓒ Ⓓ	193	Ⓐ Ⓑ Ⓒ Ⓓ
	104	Ⓐ Ⓑ Ⓒ Ⓓ	114	Ⓐ Ⓑ Ⓒ Ⓓ	124	Ⓐ Ⓑ Ⓒ Ⓓ	134	Ⓐ Ⓑ Ⓒ Ⓓ	144	Ⓐ Ⓑ Ⓒ Ⓓ	154	Ⓐ Ⓑ Ⓒ Ⓓ	164	Ⓐ Ⓑ Ⓒ Ⓓ	174	Ⓐ Ⓑ Ⓒ Ⓓ	184	Ⓐ Ⓑ Ⓒ Ⓓ	194	Ⓐ Ⓑ Ⓒ Ⓓ
	105	Ⓐ Ⓑ Ⓒ Ⓓ	115	Ⓐ Ⓑ Ⓒ Ⓓ	125	Ⓐ Ⓑ Ⓒ Ⓓ	135	Ⓐ Ⓑ Ⓒ Ⓓ	145	Ⓐ Ⓑ Ⓒ Ⓓ	155	Ⓐ Ⓑ Ⓒ Ⓓ	165	Ⓐ Ⓑ Ⓒ Ⓓ	175	Ⓐ Ⓑ Ⓒ Ⓓ	185	Ⓐ Ⓑ Ⓒ Ⓓ	195	Ⓐ Ⓑ Ⓒ Ⓓ
	106	Ⓐ Ⓑ Ⓒ Ⓓ	116	Ⓐ Ⓑ Ⓒ Ⓓ	126	Ⓐ Ⓑ Ⓒ Ⓓ	136	Ⓐ Ⓑ Ⓒ Ⓓ	146	Ⓐ Ⓑ Ⓒ Ⓓ	156	Ⓐ Ⓑ Ⓒ Ⓓ	166	Ⓐ Ⓑ Ⓒ Ⓓ	176	Ⓐ Ⓑ Ⓒ Ⓓ	186	Ⓐ Ⓑ Ⓒ Ⓓ	196	Ⓐ Ⓑ Ⓒ Ⓓ
	107	Ⓐ Ⓑ Ⓒ Ⓓ	117	Ⓐ Ⓑ Ⓒ Ⓓ	127	Ⓐ Ⓑ Ⓒ Ⓓ	137	Ⓐ Ⓑ Ⓒ Ⓓ	147	Ⓐ Ⓑ Ⓒ Ⓓ	157	Ⓐ Ⓑ Ⓒ Ⓓ	167	Ⓐ Ⓑ Ⓒ Ⓓ	177	Ⓐ Ⓑ Ⓒ Ⓓ	187	Ⓐ Ⓑ Ⓒ Ⓓ	197	Ⓐ Ⓑ Ⓒ Ⓓ
	108	Ⓐ Ⓑ Ⓒ Ⓓ	118	Ⓐ Ⓑ Ⓒ Ⓓ	128	Ⓐ Ⓑ Ⓒ Ⓓ	138	Ⓐ Ⓑ Ⓒ Ⓓ	148	Ⓐ Ⓑ Ⓒ Ⓓ	158	Ⓐ Ⓑ Ⓒ Ⓓ	168	Ⓐ Ⓑ Ⓒ Ⓓ	178	Ⓐ Ⓑ Ⓒ Ⓓ	188	Ⓐ Ⓑ Ⓒ Ⓓ	198	Ⓐ Ⓑ Ⓒ Ⓓ
	109	Ⓐ Ⓑ Ⓒ Ⓓ	119	Ⓐ Ⓑ Ⓒ Ⓓ	129	Ⓐ Ⓑ Ⓒ Ⓓ	139	Ⓐ Ⓑ Ⓒ Ⓓ	149	Ⓐ Ⓑ Ⓒ Ⓓ	159	Ⓐ Ⓑ Ⓒ Ⓓ	169	Ⓐ Ⓑ Ⓒ Ⓓ	179	Ⓐ Ⓑ Ⓒ Ⓓ	189	Ⓐ Ⓑ Ⓒ Ⓓ	199	Ⓐ Ⓑ Ⓒ Ⓓ
	110	Ⓐ Ⓑ Ⓒ Ⓓ	120	Ⓐ Ⓑ Ⓒ Ⓓ	130	Ⓐ Ⓑ Ⓒ Ⓓ	140	Ⓐ Ⓑ Ⓒ Ⓓ	150	Ⓐ Ⓑ Ⓒ Ⓓ	160	Ⓐ Ⓑ Ⓒ Ⓓ	170	Ⓐ Ⓑ Ⓒ Ⓓ	180	Ⓐ Ⓑ Ⓒ Ⓓ	190	Ⓐ Ⓑ Ⓒ Ⓓ	200	Ⓐ Ⓑ Ⓒ Ⓓ

ACTUAL TEST 10

READING SECTION	101	Ⓐ Ⓑ Ⓒ Ⓓ	111	Ⓐ Ⓑ Ⓒ Ⓓ	121	Ⓐ Ⓑ Ⓒ Ⓓ	131	Ⓐ Ⓑ Ⓒ Ⓓ	141	Ⓐ Ⓑ Ⓒ Ⓓ	151	Ⓐ Ⓑ Ⓒ Ⓓ	161	Ⓐ Ⓑ Ⓒ Ⓓ	171	Ⓐ Ⓑ Ⓒ Ⓓ	181	Ⓐ Ⓑ Ⓒ Ⓓ	191	Ⓐ Ⓑ Ⓒ Ⓓ
	102	Ⓐ Ⓑ Ⓒ Ⓓ	112	Ⓐ Ⓑ Ⓒ Ⓓ	122	Ⓐ Ⓑ Ⓒ Ⓓ	132	Ⓐ Ⓑ Ⓒ Ⓓ	142	Ⓐ Ⓑ Ⓒ Ⓓ	152	Ⓐ Ⓑ Ⓒ Ⓓ	162	Ⓐ Ⓑ Ⓒ Ⓓ	172	Ⓐ Ⓑ Ⓒ Ⓓ	182	Ⓐ Ⓑ Ⓒ Ⓓ	192	Ⓐ Ⓑ Ⓒ Ⓓ
	103	Ⓐ Ⓑ Ⓒ Ⓓ	113	Ⓐ Ⓑ Ⓒ Ⓓ	123	Ⓐ Ⓑ Ⓒ Ⓓ	133	Ⓐ Ⓑ Ⓒ Ⓓ	143	Ⓐ Ⓑ Ⓒ Ⓓ	153	Ⓐ Ⓑ Ⓒ Ⓓ	163	Ⓐ Ⓑ Ⓒ Ⓓ	173	Ⓐ Ⓑ Ⓒ Ⓓ	183	Ⓐ Ⓑ Ⓒ Ⓓ	193	Ⓐ Ⓑ Ⓒ Ⓓ
	104	Ⓐ Ⓑ Ⓒ Ⓓ	114	Ⓐ Ⓑ Ⓒ Ⓓ	124	Ⓐ Ⓑ Ⓒ Ⓓ	134	Ⓐ Ⓑ Ⓒ Ⓓ	144	Ⓐ Ⓑ Ⓒ Ⓓ	154	Ⓐ Ⓑ Ⓒ Ⓓ	164	Ⓐ Ⓑ Ⓒ Ⓓ	174	Ⓐ Ⓑ Ⓒ Ⓓ	184	Ⓐ Ⓑ Ⓒ Ⓓ	194	Ⓐ Ⓑ Ⓒ Ⓓ
	105	Ⓐ Ⓑ Ⓒ Ⓓ	115	Ⓐ Ⓑ Ⓒ Ⓓ	125	Ⓐ Ⓑ Ⓒ Ⓓ	135	Ⓐ Ⓑ Ⓒ Ⓓ	145	Ⓐ Ⓑ Ⓒ Ⓓ	155	Ⓐ Ⓑ Ⓒ Ⓓ	165	Ⓐ Ⓑ Ⓒ Ⓓ	175	Ⓐ Ⓑ Ⓒ Ⓓ	185	Ⓐ Ⓑ Ⓒ Ⓓ	195	Ⓐ Ⓑ Ⓒ Ⓓ
	106	Ⓐ Ⓑ Ⓒ Ⓓ	116	Ⓐ Ⓑ Ⓒ Ⓓ	126	Ⓐ Ⓑ Ⓒ Ⓓ	136	Ⓐ Ⓑ Ⓒ Ⓓ	146	Ⓐ Ⓑ Ⓒ Ⓓ	156	Ⓐ Ⓑ Ⓒ Ⓓ	166	Ⓐ Ⓑ Ⓒ Ⓓ	176	Ⓐ Ⓑ Ⓒ Ⓓ	186	Ⓐ Ⓑ Ⓒ Ⓓ	196	Ⓐ Ⓑ Ⓒ Ⓓ
	107	Ⓐ Ⓑ Ⓒ Ⓓ	117	Ⓐ Ⓑ Ⓒ Ⓓ	127	Ⓐ Ⓑ Ⓒ Ⓓ	137	Ⓐ Ⓑ Ⓒ Ⓓ	147	Ⓐ Ⓑ Ⓒ Ⓓ	157	Ⓐ Ⓑ Ⓒ Ⓓ	167	Ⓐ Ⓑ Ⓒ Ⓓ	177	Ⓐ Ⓑ Ⓒ Ⓓ	187	Ⓐ Ⓑ Ⓒ Ⓓ	197	Ⓐ Ⓑ Ⓒ Ⓓ
	108	Ⓐ Ⓑ Ⓒ Ⓓ	118	Ⓐ Ⓑ Ⓒ Ⓓ	128	Ⓐ Ⓑ Ⓒ Ⓓ	138	Ⓐ Ⓑ Ⓒ Ⓓ	148	Ⓐ Ⓑ Ⓒ Ⓓ	158	Ⓐ Ⓑ Ⓒ Ⓓ	168	Ⓐ Ⓑ Ⓒ Ⓓ	178	Ⓐ Ⓑ Ⓒ Ⓓ	188	Ⓐ Ⓑ Ⓒ Ⓓ	198	Ⓐ Ⓑ Ⓒ Ⓓ
	109	Ⓐ Ⓑ Ⓒ Ⓓ	119	Ⓐ Ⓑ Ⓒ Ⓓ	129	Ⓐ Ⓑ Ⓒ Ⓓ	139	Ⓐ Ⓑ Ⓒ Ⓓ	149	Ⓐ Ⓑ Ⓒ Ⓓ	159	Ⓐ Ⓑ Ⓒ Ⓓ	169	Ⓐ Ⓑ Ⓒ Ⓓ	179	Ⓐ Ⓑ Ⓒ Ⓓ	189	Ⓐ Ⓑ Ⓒ Ⓓ	199	Ⓐ Ⓑ Ⓒ Ⓓ
	110	Ⓐ Ⓑ Ⓒ Ⓓ	120	Ⓐ Ⓑ Ⓒ Ⓓ	130	Ⓐ Ⓑ Ⓒ Ⓓ	140	Ⓐ Ⓑ Ⓒ Ⓓ	150	Ⓐ Ⓑ Ⓒ Ⓓ	160	Ⓐ Ⓑ Ⓒ Ⓓ	170	Ⓐ Ⓑ Ⓒ Ⓓ	180	Ⓐ Ⓑ Ⓒ Ⓓ	190	Ⓐ Ⓑ Ⓒ Ⓓ	200	Ⓐ Ⓑ Ⓒ Ⓓ

新制 New TOEIC 聽力閱讀超高分

最新多益改版黃金試題 2000 題【聽力＋閱讀雙書裝】

作　　者	Ki Taek Lee
譯　　者	林育珊
編　　輯	Gina Wang
審　　訂	Maddie Smith (Tests 1-3), Richard Luhrs (Tests 4-10)
校　　對	黃詩韻
內文排版	林書玉
封面設計	林書玉
製程管理	洪巧玲
出 版 者	寂天文化事業股份有限公司
發 行 人	黃朝萍
電　　話	+886-(0)2-2365-9739
傳　　真	+886-(0)2-2365-9835
網　　址	www.icosmos.com.tw
讀者服務	onlineservice@icosmos.com.tw
出版日期	2024 年 8 月 初版再刷 (寂天雲隨身聽 APP 版) (0106)

郵撥帳號 1998620-0 寂天文化事業股份有限公司
訂書金額未滿 1000 元，請外加運費 100 元。
〔若有破損，請寄回更換，謝謝〕

國家圖書館出版品預行編目 (CIP) 資料

新制 New TOEIC 聽力閱讀超高分：最新多益改版黃金試題 2000 題 (聽力 + 閱讀雙書版)(寂天雲隨身聽 APP 版) / Ki Taek Lee, The Mozilge Language Research Institute 著 ; 王傳明 , 林育珊譯 .
-- 初版 . -- [臺北市] : 寂天文化 , 2022.05
面 ;　公分

ISBN 978-626-300-126-8 (16K 平裝)
1. 多益測驗
805.1895　　111005748